A READER'S GUIDE and BOOKMARK

for the INNER SANCTUM Edition of

WAR AND PEACE

by Leo Tolstóy

CONTAINING:

NOTE: *For the reader's convenience, this can be used as a bookmark, making this map and lists of characters and dates available on any page where the particular information is needed. For reference purposes, the material is also printed in the body of the book. at the end of the text, so as to be available in permanent form. See "A Note About the Inner Sanctum Edition" [on page v at the beginning of this volume] for a summary of the new and distinctive features of this presentation of War and Peace.*

SIMON AND SCHUSTER · PUBLISHERS · NEW YORK

THE PRINCIPAL CHARACTERS
ARRANGED IN FAMILY GROUPS

THE BEZÚKHOVS

Count Cyril Bezúkhov, *a wealthy nobleman of Catherine the Great's time*
Pierre, *his son, who, legitimized after his father's death, becomes* Count
 Bezúkhov—*the central character of the novel.*
Princess Catiche, *Pierre's cousin*

THE ROSTÓVS

Count Ilyá Rostóv, *a wealthy nobleman*
Countess Nataly Rostóva, *his wife*
Count Nicholas Rostóv, *their elder son, who goes into the army as a cadet*
Count Peter (Pétya) Rostóv, *their younger son*
Countess Véra Rostóva, *their elder daughter*
Countess Nataly (Natásha) Rostóva, *their younger daughter, the central
 female character*
Sónya, *a poor niece of the Rostóvs*
Lieutenant Alphonse Kárlovich Berg, *an officer who marries Véra*

THE BOLKÓNSKIS

Prince Nicholas Andréevich Bolkónski, *a retired general*
Prince Andrew Bolkónski, *his son, a member of Kutúzov's staff*
Princess Mary Bolkónskaya, *his daughter*
Princess Elisabeth (Lise) Bolkónskaya, *Prince Andrew's wife, "the most
 fascinating woman in Petersburg"*
Prince Nicholas (Koko) Andréevich Bolkónski, *Prince Andrew's son*

THE KURÁGINS

Prince Vasíli Kurágin, *an elderly nobleman*
Prince Hippolyte Kurágin, *his weak-minded elder son*
Prince Anatole Kurágin, *his profligate younger son*
Princess Hélène Kurágina, *his daughter, "the beautiful Hélène"*

THE DRUBETSKÓYS

Princess Anna Mikháylovna Drubetskáya, *an impoverished noblewoman*
Prince Borís (Bóry) Drubetskóy, *her son, who enters the army*
Julie Karágina, *an heiress, who later marries Borís*

DATES OF PRINCIPAL HISTORICAL EVENTS

OLD STYLE	NEW STYLE	1805
Oct. 11	Oct. 23	Kutúzov inspects regiment near Braunau. *Le malheureux Mack* arrives.
Oct. 23	Nov. 4	The Russian army crosses the Enns.
Oct. 24	Nov. 5	Fight at Amstetten.
Oct. 28	Nov. 9	The Russian army crosses the Danube.
Oct. 30	Nov. 11	Defeats Mortier at Dürrenstein.
Nov. 4	Nov. 16	Napoleon writes to Murat from Schönbrunn.
Nov. 4	Nov. 16	Battle of Schön Grabern.
Nov. 19	Dec. 1	The Council of War at Ostralitz.
Nov. 20	Dec. 2	Battle of Austerlitz.

1807

Jan. 27	Feb. 8	Battle of Preussisch-Eylau.
June 2	June 14	Battle of Friedland.
June 13	June 25	The Emperors meet at Tilsit.

1812

May 17	May 29	Napoleon leaves Dresden.
June 12	June 24	Napoleon crosses the Niemen and enters Russia.
June 14	June 26	Alexander sends Balashëv to Napoleon.
July 13	July 25	The Pávlograd hussars in action at Ostróvna.
Aug. 4	Aug. 16	Alpátych at Smolénsk hears distant firing.
Aug. 5	Aug. 17	Bombardment of Smolénsk.
Aug. 7	Aug. 19	Prince Nicholas Bolkónski leaves Bald Hills for Boguchárovo.
Aug. 8	Aug. 20	Kutúzov appointed Commander in Chief.
Aug. 10	Aug. 22	Prince Andrew's column abreast of Bald Hills.
Aug. 17	Aug. 29	Kutúzov reaches Tsárevo-Zaymíshche and takes command of the army.
Aug. 17	Aug. 29	Nicholas Rostóv rides to Boguchárovo.
Aug. 24	Sept. 5	Battle of the Shevárdino Redoubt.
Aug. 26	Sept. 7	Battle of Borodinó.
Sept. 1	Sept. 13	Kutúzov orders retreat through Moscow.
Oct. 6	Oct. 18	Battle of Tarútino.
Oct. 6, 7, and 8	Oct. 18, 19, and 20	The French leave Moscow.
Oct. 12	Oct. 24	Battle of Málo-Yaroslávets.
Oct. 21	Nov. 2	Cossacks harry the French at Vyázma.
Oct. 28-Nov. 2	Nov. 9-Nov. 14	The French at Smolénsk.
Nov. 4-8	Nov. 16-20	Battles at Krásnoe.
Nov. 9	Nov. 21	Ney, with rearguard, reaches Orshá.
Nov. 14-16	Nov. 26-28	Crossing of the Berëzina.
Nov. 23	Dec. 5	Napoleon abandons the army at Smorgóni.
Dec. 6	Dec. 18	He reaches Paris.

NAPOLEON
IN RUSSIA ~ 1812

NAPOLEON'S ADVANCE ——————
NAPOLEON'S RETREAT ----------

Scale of Miles
0 50 100 150

STEINBERG

HÓV
ÓVNO

Volga River

DMÍTROV

MOSCOW MYTISHCHI

RÚZA

MOZHÁYSK
BORODINÓ PODÓLSK
GZHATSK TARÚTINO RYAZÁN
DRÍSSA SÉRPUKHOV
BOGUCHÁROVO MEDÝN
VÍTEBSK VYÁZMA MALO-YAROSLÁVETS
DOROGOBÚZH KALÚGA
Bald Hills YUKHNÓV TÚLA
ORSHÁ SMOLÉNSK
KRÁSNOE

Berëzina

NI River

MOGHILËV

BRYÁNSK

Oká River

ORËL

To Sokólniki

Sadóvaya

Sadóvaya
Súkharev
Water
Tower

Patriarch's
Ponds
Bazdéev
House

Neglinaya River

Lubyánka

Kudrino

Tverskáya

Myasnitskaya

Povarskáya

Nikítskaya

Pokróvka

Moskvá River

Rostóv
House

Vozdvízhenka
Tróitsa
Gate

Nikólski
Bazar
Red Square
Ilyínka

Moroséyka

Arbát

Mokhaváya

Senate
Square
Kremlin
Palace

Varvárka

Orphanage

Yaúza River

Dorogomílov
Bridge

Moskvá
Bridge

Yaúza
Bridge

To Nízhni-
Nóvgorod

Virgin's
Field

Stone
(Kámmeni)
Bridge

Zúbovski
Rampart

Bolótnoe
Place

Ryazán Road

Khamóvniki

Crimean
Bridge

Great Ordýnka

To Sparrow
Hills

Moskvá River

Kalúga Road

Túla Road

MOSCOW ~ 1812

0 ½ 1 1½ Miles

CHARACTERS IN WAR AND PEACE

Arranged in Order of Their Appearance

A NOTE ON RUSSIAN NAMES

The suffixes "ovich," "evich," "ich," and "ych" at the end of a Russian name mean "son of"; the suffixes "ovna," and "evna" mean "daughter of." Thus, Tolstóy's full name in Russian is Count Lev Nikolaievich Tolstóy. Nikolaievich is Tolstóy's patronymic. This indicates that Lev (or Leo) is the son of Nikolai (or Nicholas) Tolstóy.

Frequently a character is referred to by his own first name, followed by his patronymic; sometimes by the patronymic alone.

The Russians also add suffixes to first names to express endearment—as when they refer to Natásha as Natáshenka.

BOOK ONE

Introduced at Anna Schérer's soiree (St. Petersburg), Chapter 1

Anna Pávlovna Schérer, *Maid of Honor to the Dowager Empress Márya Fëdorovna*

*Prince Vasíli Kurágin, *an elderly nobleman*

*Princess Hélène Kurágina, *his daughter, "the beautiful Hélène"*

Princess Elisabeth (Lise) Bolkónskaya, *Prince Andrew's wife, "the most fascinating woman in Petersburg"*

Prince Hippolyte Kurágin, *Prince Vasíli's weak-minded elder son*

*Pierre, *Count Cyril Bezúkhov's son, who, when legitimized after his father's death, becomes the fantastically wealthy Count Bezúkhov*

*Prince Andrew Bolkónski, *Prince Nicholas Bolkónski's son, one of the major characters in the novel. He is scion of a wealthy landowning family noted for its military achievements*

[NOTE: *Pierre and Andrew are the two central male figures of* War and Peace *and are believed to embody some of the characteristics of Leo Tolstóy himself and his own kinsmen. The author of* War and·Peace *made great use of historical and military records and family archives.*]

Princess Anna Mikháylovna Drubetskáya, *an elderly lady of a good but impoverished family*

* *An asterisk before the names indicates the most important characters.*

CHARACTERS IN WAR AND PEACE

Introduced at the party at Anatole's house (St. Petersburg), Chapter 3

- *Prince Anatole Kurágin, *Prince Vasíli's profligate younger son*
- Dólokhov, *an officer of the Semënov Regiment who lives with Anatole (supposedly a combination of Count Theodore Tolstóy, a famous traveler, and R. I. Dórokhov, a reckless daredevil of the period of* War and Peace)

Introduced at the Rostóvs' name-day party (Moscow), Chapters 4-5

- Countess Nataly Rostóva, *Count Ilyá Rostóv's wife*
- *Count Ilyá Rostóv, *a wealthy nobleman of the upper aristocracy † with large estates in city and country (supposedly patterned after Tolstóy's grandfather, Count Ilyá A. Tolstóy)*
- Julie Karágina, *an heiress*
- *Countess Nataly (Natásha) Rostóva, *the Rostóvs' younger daughter, the major female character (supposedly patterned after Tolstóy's youngest sister-in-law, Tatiána Behrs)*
- *Prince Borís (Bóry) Drubetskóy, *Anna Mikháylovna's son †*
- *Count Nicholas Rostóv, *the Rostóvs' elder son, one of the central characters (supposedly patterned after Tolstóy's father, Count Nicholas Tolstóy)*
- *Sónya, *a poor niece of the Rostóvs (supposedly patterned after Tolstóy's aunt who supervised his education)*
- *Count Peter (Pétya) Rostóv, *the Rostóvs' younger son*
- Countess Véra Rostóva, *the Rostóvs' elder daughter (supposedly patterned after Liza Behrs, the older of Tolstóy's two sisters-in-law)*

Introduced in the house where Count Bezúkhov lies dying (Moscow), Chapter 6

- Princess Catiche (Catherine Semënovna), *Pierre's cousin*

Introduced at the Rostóvs' dinner party (Moscow), Chapters 8-10

- Dmítri Vasílevich, *Count Ilyá Rostóv's estate manager*
- Peter Nikoláevich Shinshín, *Countess Rostóva's cousin*
- Alphonse Kárlovich Berg, *an officer of the Guards, engaged to Véra Rostóva*
- Márya Dmítrievna Akhrosímova, "le terrible dragon"

† [NOTE ON TITLES OF RUSSIAN ARISTOCRATIC RANK] *In Imperial Russia, as elsewhere in Europe, a prince ranked above a count, but by the beginning of the nineteenth century certain princely families had become impoverished, so that a man's place in the hierarchy of aristocracy was not necessarily consistent with his wealth and power.*

CHARACTERS IN WAR AND PEACE

CHARACTERS IN WAR AND PEACE

Introduced at the army review at Olmütz, sixty-seven miles north-east of Brünn, Chapter 7

*Alexander I, Tsar of Russia

Introduced at Olmütz, Chapter 8

Prince Yúri Dolgorúkov, *an adjutant general*

Introduced at battle of Austerlitz, fifteen miles east of Brünn, Chapter 13

*Napoleon Bonaparte, *Emperor of the French*

BOOK FOUR

Introduced at the English Club dinner (Moscow), Chapter 3

Count F. V. Rostopchín, *governor general of Moscow*
Alexander Dmítrievich Balashëv, *an adjutant general*

Chapter 9

*Prince Nicholas (Koko) Andréevich Bolkónski, *Prince Andrew's son*

BOOK FIVE

Chapter 1

Joseph Alexéevich Bazdéev, *a leading Freemason*

BOOK SIX

Introduced at Count Kochubéy's (St. Petersburg), Chapter 2

Alexey Andréevich Arakchéev, *Minister of War*, "Síla Andréevich"
Michael Mikháylovich Speránski, *Secretary of State*

BOOK SEVEN

Introduced at the hunt on the Rostóvs' country estate at Otrádnoe, Chapters 3-6

Daniel, *the Rostóvs' head huntsman*
Michael Nikanórovich, "Uncle," *a distant relative of the Rostóvs'*
Nastásya Ivánovna, *the Rostóvs' buffoon*
Ilyágin, *the Rostóvs' neighbor*

Chapter 11

Pelagéya Danílovna Melyukóva, *the Rostóvs' neighbor*

CHARACTERS IN WAR AND PEACE
BOOK NINE

Introduced in Nicholas Rostóv's regiment, Chapters 12-13

Ilyín, *Nicholas Rostóv's protégé*
Mary Hendríkhovna, *wife of the regimental doctor*

BOOK TEN

Chapter 4

Ferapóntov, *an innkeeper at Smolénsk*

Introduced at Boguchárovo, between Bald Hills and Moscow, Chapters 9-14

Dron, *the village elder of Boguchárovo*
Karp, *a villager of Boguchárovo*

BOOK ELEVEN

Introduced at Bazdéev's house (Moscow), Chapters 9-14

Makár Alexéevich Bazdéev, *Joseph Bazdéev's half-insane brother*
Captain Ramballe, *a French officer*
Morel, *Ramballe's orderly*

BOOK TWELVE

Introduced in the prison with Pierre (Moscow), Chapter 3

*Platón Karatáev, *a captured Russian peasant soldier*

BOOK FOURTEEN

Introduced with Denísov's guerrillas near Mikúlino, on the road to Smolénsk, Chapter 2

Esaul Michael Feoklítych, *a Cossack guerrilla*
Tíkhon Shcherbáty, *a peasant guerrilla*

FIRST EPILOGUE

Introduced at Bolkónski's, now Mary Rostóva's, Bald Hills estate, Chapter 2

Count Andrew Rostóv, *Nicholas Rostóv's son*
Countess Natásha Rostóva, *Nicholas Rostóv's daughter*

IN PRAISE OF WAR AND PEACE

JOHN GALSWORTHY: *This is the greatest novel ever written.*

WILLIAM LYON PHELPS: War and Peace *is a dictionary of life, where one may look up any passion, any ambition, and find its meaning.*

V. SACKVILLE-WEST: *I think myself that Tolstóy stands among novelists as Shakespeare stands among poets—head and shoulders above the rest of them.*

WALTER DURANTY: *Tolstóy's masterpiece,* War and Peace, *is truer to-day* [1941], *far truer, than when it was written, in 1864, and gives you a vision seen and depicted by an artist of something which happened a hundred and thirty years ago and is being repeated, miraculously.*

TURGENEV: *There are things in* War and Peace *that are unbearable, and things that are wonderful; and the wonderful things (they predominate) are so magnificently good that we have never had anything better written by anybody, and it is doubtful whether anything as good has been written.*

COMPTON MACKENZIE: *The younger generation which has attempted to discover what war is from books about the Great War will learn more about it from* War and Peace *than from anything I have read about the Great War. A knowledge of this novel is essential to the intelligent equipment of any young man or young woman who pretends to a view of life.*

J. B. PRIESTLEY: *If one has read* War and Peace *for a page, great chords begin to sound; they come from the immense area of Russia, over which episodes and characters have been scattered, which accumulate grandeur and sonority after we have passed them. Many novelists have the feeling of time; very few have the sense of space also, and the possession of it ranks high in Tolstóy's divine equipment.*

E. M. FORSTER: *Here is the greatest novel ever written. It has been called "life itself." Everything is in it. And it's also as free as life. Its private joys and sorrows seem to continue when one has closed the pages. . . . I am going to reread it. There are several good reasons for doing this. It is not about the present situation; but it throws light on the present situation, which is what I want. It is the kind of novel which one can take up and lay down without losing the thread. A masterpiece*

like War and Peace *helps to restore the balance and to recall our vision of humanity.* [1939]

FRANCIS HACKETT: *Persons who tell you that* War and Peace *has for its subject-matter the fate of Russia in the wars a hundred years ago are sticking to an important fact. But there is more in it than their honest reports can tell you. There is a great testimony to life generously and deeply experienced; to mankind's emotions in peace or strife; to the vast variety of human nature that this one man has embraced and transmuted. There is in this miraculous imaginative organism, as in any other organism, life and the impulse of life. There is something that belongs only to life itself. There is a beauty and a reality indefinable.* [1916]

VIRGINIA WOOLF: *If you think of the novels which seem to you great novels—*War and Peace, Vanity Fair, Tristram Shandy, Madame Bovary, Pride and Prejudice, The Mayor of Casterbridge, Villette—*if you think of these books, you do at once think of some character who has seemed to you so real (I do not by that mean so lifelike) that it has the power to make you think not merely of it itself, but of all sorts of things through its eyes—of religion, of love, of war, of peace, of family life, of balls in county towns, of sunsets, moonrises, the immortality of the soul. There is hardly any subject of human experience that is left out of* War and Peace.

WILLIAM DEAN HOWELLS: War and Peace *is not only as a drama incomparably vaster than has filled the imagination before, but as a homily, comprehensive, and penetrating beyond any direct sermoning, that it moves and stirs the heart. It is one of Tolstóy's earliest books, but already his ethics were realized if not formulated. . . . We behold a multitudinous movement of human beings, each of whom is a strongly defined character in himself and is a type of innumerable like characters. Every passion is portrayed, every affection, every propensity, not because the author wished to include all in his scheme, but because the scheme was so vast that they could not be excluded.* [1908]

HUGH WALPOLE: *The greatest novel of all literature, I think, using the modern term, is Tolstóy's* War and Peace. *This magnificent work has taught me more about life than any other novel in any language.* War and Peace *contains everything. Its final effect is as concrete and symbolic as a sonnet by Keats; its theme is as simple and singlehearted as the theme of a story by Chekhov: and yet the vast canvas is covered by hundreds of figures, every one alive and distinct, and some of the leading characters, like Natásha and Prince Andrew, are companions for one during the rest of one's life. . . . In this vast book every human being is created with the same power and authenticity. The beautiful happy freshness of Natásha, the stumbling honesty of Pierre, the suffering questioning of Prince Andrew, the contented worldliness of Véra and Berg, the habits, weaknesses of generals and soldiers, even (although here there*

is less certainty) *the conceit, arrogance, and humanity of Napoleon. . . . It is in this union of all the worlds, material and spiritual—a union won without preaching or any falsification of human nature—that* War and Peace *achieves its final greatness.*

MARK VAN DOREN: War and Peace *is generally considered the greatest novel of all novels. . . . It has everything, and has it in baffling abundance. It is as credible as Defoe and yet immeasurably more important; it is as finely organized as a tale of minor proportions would be, and yet it never loses its grasp of a single vast subject. This is Napoleon's invasion of Russia and the retreat from Moscow as witnessed by a host of individuals whom Tolstóy creates with lavish and painstaking ease. These individuals come from all classes and have all degrees of virtue or vice, of strength or weakness, of ugliness or beauty, just as the action embraces every imaginable experience. I read it always with the greatest absorption. . . . Tolstóy couldn't state the theme of* War and Peace, *short of writing 1400 pages. That is my way of saying that it is a really successful novel. It is about much more than Tolstóy realized. It is about everything that he knew, believed, felt, saw. . . . For Tolstóy—not as a man, not as a thinker, but as a novelist—anything that human beings do has its glory. Humanity is equally glorious in its wars, its peace, its quarrels, its love affairs. I think he can be said to have hated nothing that ever happened.* [1941]

J. DONALD ADAMS: *Reading* War and Peace *for the first time is one of the greatest literary experiences; reading it again and again is to realize the immeasurable gulf that is fixed between a merely good book and a great one.*

By a very close approach to common consent War and Peace *may be regarded as the greatest novel that has been written, the supreme fictional achievement in the literature of the world.*

Here is a novel that is worth whatever time one gives to it. There is more of life between its covers than in any other existent fictional narrative. All the normal human emotions find play in this novel; practically every facet of human experience is there. Its characters become as real to us as people whom we have known all our lives; we see them develop and change with the years and the development and change is something that proceeds from within them; Tolstóy does not tell us that the change takes place—we observe it for ourselves. It is a novel of which one cannot accurately state the theme. One can say that it is a broadly inclusive picture of Russian life during the Napoleonic period, but that is merely the accident of its setting and time. In its universal value it is simply human life, greatly grasped and extraordinarily presented over a period of something less than a generation. No intelligent person can read it without a deep enrichment of experience. And having once read it, he is certain to turn to it again, to be amazed once more by its veracity, its tremendous vitality, its epic scope. [1941]

WAR AND PEACE

The Inner Sanctum Edition

WAR AND

PEACE

by LEO TOLSTOY

Translated by Louise and Aylmer Maude
with a Foreword by Clifton Fadiman

SIMON AND SCHUSTER, NEW YORK, 1942

This authorized translation by Louise and Aylmer Maude is published by special arrangement with the Oxford University Press, London and New York.

A NOTE ABOUT

The Inner Sanctum Edition of

WAR AND PEACE

The publishers believe there is need now for a new edition of War and Peace. In this foreword they summarize the editorial and typographic features which are embodied in this presentation:

Tolstóy's acknowledged masterpiece, hailed by outstanding novelists and critics generally as the "greatest novel ever written," is presented here unabridged and complete, the text absolutely inviolate.

The translation is that of Louise and Aylmer Maude, ranked by most critics as the best rendition in English, and is here published in its authorized form by special arrangement with the Oxford University Press.

Both of Tolstóy's own epilogues and his own supplementary section, headed "Some Words About War and Peace," are also added to the text.

In addition to the translator's preface, which includes a brief biography of Tolstóy, Clifton Fadiman has written for this Inner Sanctum Edition an entirely new introduction. In this he presents a critical interpretation of the novel, as well as an analysis of the present-day historical and military significance of War and Peace. This is particularly timely now, in view of the striking parallel between Napoleon's invasion of Russia in 1812, the main theme of the novel, and Hitler's invasion in 1941–42.

New maps showing the principal battles and places mentioned in the text, including a Plan of Moscow, are available in the body of the book and on the end papers. The maps on pages 116, 216, 376, 666, and 760 have been reproduced, by permission of The Limited Editions Club, from that club's six-volume edition of War and Peace, for which Louise and Aylmer Maude revised their translation and Barnett Freedman made hundreds of lithographs in color as illustrations; these maps were executed by cartographers associated with The British Museum in London.

v

In each copy of the Inner Sanctum Edition of War and Peace there is inserted a supplemental leaflet, entitled:

A READER'S GUIDE AND BOOKMARK

This enclosure is a twelve-page folder containing a full list of the characters in order of their appearance, with detailed identifications, and a note on Russian names, idioms, and titles, together with the characters also arranged in family groups, and a chronological table of principal historical events from 1805 to 1812.

For the reader's convenience, this leaflet can be used as a bookmark, making the map and lists of characters and dates available on any page where the particular information is needed. Should the "Reader's Guide and Bookmark" enclosed in each copy of the book be lost, a duplicate can be obtained from the bookseller from whom the book was bought, or by writing directly to the publishers. For reference purposes, the material is also printed in the body of the book, at the end of the text, so as to be available in permanent form. The structural divisions of Tolstóy's novel have been clearly indicated by the rearrangement of the author's own descriptive headings for each section and each chapter, both in the Table of Contents and at the opening of each part. Tables of dates of the principal historical dates are given for the main divisions.

In addition to the basic notes prepared by Aylmer Maude (indicated by the initials A. M.), new and supplementary notes have been added where necessary to explain obscure passages, vital historical or biographical background, and difficult phrases. For the reader's convenience, all notes have been placed on the same page as the text to which they refer. An introductory section, "In Praise of War and Peace," gives a summary of both contemporary and later tributes to this masterpiece.

M. LINCOLN SCHUSTER

MARCH 12, 1942

CONTENTS

BOOK THREE

BOOK SIX

BOOK SEVEN

BOOK EIGHT

BOOK NINE

BOOK TEN

CONTENTS

BOOK ELEVEN

BOOK FOURTEEN

BOOK FIFTEEN

FIRST EPILOGUE

SECOND EPILOGUE

LIST OF MAPS

This sketch plan of Borodinó was made by Tolstóy in the summer of 1867, when he spent two days in the locality to study the ground before writing his description of the battle. He depended partly on Russian and French maps, plans, and historical accounts, partly on his own military experience, and partly on the Memoirs of Radozhítski, who viewed the position from some rising ground and noticed its weak places some time before the fight occurred, and who like Pierre was present at the battle itself. The four decades that passed from Napoleon's time to the beginning of Tolstóy's army service had not much changed the muskets and smooth-bore, muzzle-loading cannon used in the Russian army, nor had the general conditions of warfare much altered.—A.M.

CONTENTS

LIST OF MAPS

This sketch plan of Borodino was made by Tolstoy in the summer of
1867, when he spent two days in the locality, studied the ground be-
fore attempting his description of the battle. He depended partly on Rus-
sian and French maps, plans, and historical accounts, partly on his
own military experience, and partly on the Memoirs of Radozhitski,
who viewed the position from some strong standpoint and noticed its
weak places some time before the fight occurred, and who like those
who fought at the battle itself. The four decades that passed from
Napoleon's time to the beginning of Tolstoy's army service had not
much changed the muskets and smooth-bore, but the loading cannon
used in the Russian army had not and the general conditions of warfare
much altered. — A.M.

FOREWORD

This foreword falls into two sections. The first, immediately following, is an attempt at a discussion of some of the literary qualities of War and Peace. The second, beginning on page xxxix, draws a few obvious analogies between Napoleon's Russian campaign, as described by Tolstóy, and Hitler's Russian campaign, as it seemed to a nonmilitary observer toward the middle of February, 1942. The reason for the second section will be apparent to any contemporary reader of War and Peace. Great as it is, the book gains an added interest through its uncanny prefiguring of some of the events of our time. In a certain sense it may be said that the finest account of Hitler's Russian adventure (so far) was written by Leo Tolstóy.

Section One may be read without reference to Section Two, and vice versa.

1

War and Peace hardly calls for comment. It is translucent. It seems to have been composed in the sunlight. Yet so fascinating is it that almost all critics who are interested in the novel as such have at one time or another had their say concerning it. I do not claim to add anything to their words. I hope merely to set Tolstóy's masterpiece before the reader in such a way that he will not be dismayed by its labyrinthine length or put off by its seeming remoteness from our own concerns.

War and Peace has been called the greatest novel ever written. These very words have been used, to my knowledge, by E. M. Forster, Hugh Walpole, John Galsworthy, and Compton Mackenzie; and a similar judgment has been made by many others. Note that it is particularly novelists themselves who hold this opinion. Is not this the book all novelists would like to write? Is it not to the novelist what Hamlet is to the playwright?

That War and Peace is one of the greatest novels ever written is beyond question. But I do not know what is meant by calling it "the greatest." No calipers exist to measure the relative greatness of great novels. It

is more useful, rather, to repeat the judgment of J. Donald Adams: "Reading it again and again is to realize the immeasurable gulf that is fixed between a merely good book and a great one." Let us not fret therefore over whether War and Peace is the greatest novel ever written. Let us rather try to discover together why it is a great novel.

The first thing to do is to read it. A supreme book usually argues its own supremacy quite efficiently, and War and Peace is no exception. Still, we may be convinced of its magnitude and remain puzzled by certain of its aspects—for no first-rate book is completely explicit, either.

On finishing War and Peace what questions do we tend to ask ourselves? Here is a very simple one: What is it about? The title tells us it is about war and peace. True. But it deals also with other pairs of gigantic opposites —life and death, youth and age, good and evil, wealth and poverty, men and women, strength and weakness, love and hate, growth and decay. Smaller novels deal with one of these pairs of opposites or one aspect of one of these pairs. Here all are present.

"But," you reply, "these abstractions are too vague to be called the subject of this novel or any novel. They do not really tell us what the book is about." Very well. Shall we say, then, that War and Peace is concerned with the Napoleonic Era and its aftermath and with the varying fortunes of a large group of Russians, and of some French and Germans during the period? Or shall we say that War and Peace is a family novel tracing the careers of the Bolkónskis, the Rostóvs, the Kurágins, and the Bezúkhovs over a span of some fifteen years? Or shall we speak of it as a social novel painting a broad picture of Russian society from the Tsar down to the lowliest peasant? Or shall we alter our emphasis again and, with Tolstóy himself, say that in essence the book deals with the vast movement of men first from west to east and then from east to west—a movement that changes the lives of all those caught up in it? Or shall we see in War and Peace a philosophical novel whose purpose is to dramatize a particular view of history? Or, finally, shall we say, as does Percy Lubbock in The Craft of Fiction, that at least part of it is concerned simply with the spectacle of youth becoming age and of age giving way to youth: that is, with the procession of the generations?

But War and Peace is all these things. In fact, we are forced in the end to make the apparently vapid judgment that the subject of War and Peace is Life itself. Not life seen from a special angle, or given a special interpretation, but just Life. It is hard to name another novel of which the same statement can be made with equal justice.

We do not know what Tolstóy had in mind as the main subject of War and Peace, for he stated its theme differently at different periods of his

career. Looking back on it, as a fairly old man, he said that his only aim had been to amuse his readers. There is a quirk in genius, a kind of last gasp of egotism in reverse, that makes it sometimes demean its own masterpieces. In the case of Tolstóy, of course, it is possible to explain this perverse judgment in terms of his religious conversion, after which he viewed such books as War and Peace and Anna Karénina as trivial and worldly. (No saint has ever been a good literary critic. Also vice versa.) More seriously, Tolstóy at times spoke of War and Peace as a picture of the wanderings of a people.

But whatever he thought its subject was, he transcended it. In one sense he put into this book everything that interested him, and everything interested him. That he managed to make it more than a collection of characters and incidents is equivalent to saying that in addition to being a man with a consuming interest in life he was also an artist who was not content until he had shaped that interest into harmonious forms.

Now, there are some who would demur, who feel that it is precisely in this quality of form that War and Peace is defective. Percy Lubbock, for example, finds it unsatisfactory because for him it is really two books. One book, he thinks, deals with youth and age, with the procession of the generations, with the private lives of the Bolkónskis, the Rostóvs, and all the others. The second book, inserted layerlike into the first, is really the story of war and peace—of the movements of Napoleon's and Kutúzov's armies, of Austerlitz and Borodinó, and of the laws of history which, in Tolstóy's view, underlie these movements. Lubbock thinks that these two themes never quite coalesce and that therefore, great as the book is, it is deficient in the quality of form, deficient in unity of subject matter.

Many readers would agree. Some would go even further, arguing, on the ground that they are both extraneous and indigestible, that Tolstóy would have done better to omit his historical disquisitions and particularly the two epilogues.

Suppose we admit at once that there is no classic unity of subject matter as there is, for instance, in the Iliad. Homer tells the story of Hector and Achilles at the same time that he tells the story of the Trojan War in general. But we feel that he is telling one story, not two. This simple unity Tolstóy does not have. But a profounder unity I think he does have. When we have come to feel this unity, the philosophical and historical disquisitions cease to seem long-winded and become both interesting in themselves and an integral part of the Tolstóyan scheme. We are no longer disturbed as we should be if such digressions appeared in a work of narrower compass. We accept the fact that mountains are never perfect pyramids. Let us see whether we can get this clear. In the course of one of his

digressions Tolstóy writes, "Only by taking an infinitesimally small unit for observation (the differential of history, i.e., the individual tendencies of men) and attaining to the art of integrating them (i.e., finding the sum of these infinitesimals) can we hope to arrive at the laws of history." This rather obscure statement, if closely analyzed, gives us at least a partial solution to the problem that worried Lubbock. For in this sentence, perhaps, is concealed the theme of the book: the movement of history which Tolstóy must examine by observing "the individual tendencies of men," on the one hand, and by attempting to "integrate them," on the other. Putting it in another way, we may say that it is not enough for Tolstóy to examine the individual lives of his characters as if they were separate atoms. He must also sweep up all these atoms into one larger experience. Now, this larger experience is the Napoleonic campaign. But the campaign itself, which fuses or enlarges or focuses the lives of Andrew and Natásha and Pierre and the rest, must itself be studied, not merely as a background—that is how an ordinary historical novelist would study it— but as thoughtfully as Tolstóy studies each individual life. In order fully to understand this focusing experience he is forced to elaborate a theory of history to explain it. And so he is forced to understand the major historical characters, such as Napoleon, Kutúzov, and the others, who are the dramatic symbols of the experience.

The result of this integration may not please everyone, but the integration is there. When one reflects upon the task, one is driven to concede, I think, that Tolstóy, in his attempt to understand history through human beings and human beings through history, is undertaking the greatest task conceivable to the creative novelist of the nineteenth century, just as Milton, attempting to justify the ways of God to man, undertook the greatest poetical theme possible to a man of his century.

The titanic dimensions of the theme compel Tolstóy to ignore the usual canons of form. War and Peace, for instance, is a novel without a hero. Those who think of Pierre as the hero neglect the fact that Andrew, despite the circumstance that his death occurs long before the end of the book, is no less the hero—and no more. Indeed, we may say that if there is a hero in the antique sense it is Russia herself, rather than any single human being. Yet the herolessness of War and Peace, instead of decreasing the interest of the novel, merely gives it a more natural and lifelike quality. For in the eye of nature there are neither heroes nor villains, but merely striving human beings.

War and Peace is so vast that each reader may pick out for himself its literary qualities he most admires. Let us select three. They have doubt-

less been generally noted. These three are its inclusiveness, its naturalness, and its timelessness.

The first thing to strike the reader is the range of Tolstóy's interest and knowledge. His touch is equally sure and penetrating whether he depicts the shelling of Smolénsk, or the progress of a hunt; a Freemasonry initiation, or a deathbed scene; Napoleon surveying Moscow from the Poklónny Hill, or a full-fig soiree; the bourgeois atmosphere of the household of Pierre and Natásha, or the sullen rebellion of a group of peasants; a party at Berg's, or a public hanging; Natásha in love with Andrew, or Natásha in love with Anatole Kurágin; a field hospital, or a dinner at a men's club; a woman's confinement or a drunken orgy.

He works, as J. B. Priestley says, like "a happy God, with a whole world to play with." There seems no limit to the characters at his disposal. The more life he touches with his pen, the easier it seems for him to create still more life. The more crowded his canvas, the more fluent his brush. Yet this fecundity does not seem mere facility, as it does occasionally with Jules Romains, and it is more than a natural overflow of fancy as it often is with Dickens.

At first glance this inclusiveness seems so overpowering that one inclines to agree with Hugh Walpole when he says that War and Peace "contains everything," or with E. M. Forster who is no less sure that "everything is in it." Naturally, these statements cannot be literally true. But it is true to say that when we have finished War and Peace we do not feel the lack of anything. It is only when one stops short and makes a list of the things Tolstóy leaves out that one realizes he is a novelist and not a god. We get very little awareness, for example, of the Russian middle class which was just beginning to emerge at the opening of the nineteenth century. Also, while Tolstóy does describe many peasants for us, the emphasis is thrown disproportionately on the aristocratic class with which he was most familiar. Another thing: obeying the literary conventions of his period, Tolstóy touches upon the sex relations of his men and women with great caution—and yet, so true and various is his presentation of love that we hardly seem to notice his omissions. That, after all, is the point: we do not notice the omissions, and we are overwhelmed by the inclusiveness.

But inclusiveness in itself is no virtue unless informed by understanding. Anthony Adverse and Gone With the Wind also have an enormous range of scene and character. Still, they are merely skillful fictions because the insight that the author has put into these scenes and characters is of only ordinary dimensions. It is Tolstóy's attitude toward his own tremendous knowledge that makes him great rather than merely encyclopedic.

What is this attitude? We say that Tolstóy had great understanding, but the secret of this understanding does not lie only in his intellect, which is hardly among the first-order intellects of Europe. The secret lies elsewhere. Looking back on his work many years afterward, Tolstóy said, "To write a good work, one must love its basic, fundamental idea. In War and Peace I loved the people's emotions arising from the War of 1812. . . . I strove to write a history of the people."

The key word here is "love." One of the most penetrating comments ever made about War and Peace is Mark Van Doren's, "I think he can be said to have hated nothing that ever happened." This exaggeration contains a profound truth. Tolstóy's love for his characters in War and Peace is very different from the mystic and, some would say, morbid sentimentality of his later years. It is more like the enthusiasm of a young man for everything he sees about him during the period of his greatest vigor. It is not Christian tolerance or loftiness of soul. Indeed, it does not seem ethically based at all but is rather a product of that large animal serenity which at this epoch of his life formed the base of Tolstóy's character. He knows a great deal but it is his enormous capacity to love what he knows that makes his knowledge live for us.

At his best Tolstóy seems to write as if Nature herself were guiding his pen.

In Opinions of Oliver Allston Van Wyck Brooks (another of those who believe War and Peace the greatest of all novels) says, "It is true that to make the obvious not commonplace one has to be a Tolstóy." There is no formula to explain how Tolstóy does this. All we know is that he does it. Tolstóy is like Homer: he does not fear banalities because he is not aware that they are banalities. A small example: Captain Túshin, on the eve of battle, reflecting on immortality. Now, it is a fact that the simple soldier does think about life after death on the eve of battle, but most writers would never mention it for fear of being accused of sentimentality or rhetoric. Fearing neither, Tolstóy avoids both.

The constant impression of naturalness one gets from reading Tolstóy comes partly from his lack of obsessions. He does not specialize in a particular emotion, as Balzac, say, specializes in the emotions deriving from the desire for money. Perhaps we may say that if Tolstóy has an obsession, it is a passion for showing people merely living. It is the quantity and quality of life in any particular scene or any particular person that interests him. In a sense all his characters are of equal value. He does not grade them in some fancied order of moral importance.

It is because his eye is always on the central current of life that his per-

ceptions seem so inevitable. Indeed, they are inevitable rather than searching, for there are writers—Dostoevsky, for example—who penetrate to levels barred to Tolstóy.

We could adduce a thousand examples of these Tolstóyan touches of nature. We think perhaps of the hospital scene toward the end of Book 5 in which the wounded men cast "envious, jealous" eyes at the healthy visitors. Sometimes it is a tiny touch of character: Prince Vasíli "who, like a wound-up clock, by force of habit, said things he did not even wish to be believed." Or it will be an insight, such as the one he gives us as he describes Pierre's taking leave of the young Borís after a pleasant conversation. "As often happens in early youth, especially to one who leads a lonely life, he felt an unaccountable tenderness for this young man and made up his mind that they would be friends." Nor is he afraid of giving us a man's character in a single, simple sentence: "Berg, with his joyful, pleasant smile, as if it were obvious to him that his success must always be the chief desire of everyone else."

Tolstóy's natural sympathy overleaps the boundary of sex; his women are as convincing as his men. Indeed, he has a special talent for the presentation of women at their most female. Who can forget his description of the pregnancy of Princess Lise?

For me, one of the supreme illustrations of Tolstóy's naturalness is the forty-odd words in which he describes the Countess Rostóva and her friend Anna weeping in each other's arms after the Countess has given Anna some money with which to outfit the latter's son Borís as he prepares to enter the army. "They wept because they were friends, and because they were kindhearted, and because they—friends from childhood—had to think about such a base thing as money, and because their youth was over. . . . But those tears were pleasant to them both." This is the touch of Shakespeare translated into prose.

We think of certain Tolstóyan scenes as other men would do them and then we realize the quality of his supremacy. Where coterie writers would use complex techniques, he uses the simplest. One can imagine what one of our smart young men would do with a scene like Andrew's delirium, cramming it full of Daliesque imagery and muddied streams of consciousness. Or take that great passage in which the daredevil Dólokhov balances himself on the window sill and drinks a bottle of rum on a bet. Imagine one of our more sophisticated novelists handling this scene. What subtle emotions that aren't really there he would put into it, what unnecessary underwriting, what overtones! But Tolstóy gives us only the scene itself, simply and vividly, yet with every desired effect obtained. Or take the death of Count Bezúkhov. Think of how Arnold Bennett would

manipulate it, piling up the detail, smothering it with atmosphere. Tolstóy describes the death scene so that it becomes one of the most living scenes in the book. It is free of morbidity, false pathos, and extraneous sentimentality, but it is moving and passionate.

It is normal. Tolstóy is the epic poet of the conscious and the normal, just as Dostoevsky, complementing him, is the dramatic poet of the subconscious and the abnormal. His instinct is always to identify the unnatural with the unpleasant. "But the smile did not enhance Véra's beauty as smiles generally do; on the contrary, it gave her an unnatural and therefore unpleasant expression." This genius for the normal operates with notable effect when Tolstóy is describing situations that, it might seem to another and lesser observer, should produce abnormal reactions. Young Rostóv, for example, wounded, watching the enemy French approach him, cries, "Can they be coming at me? And why? To kill me? Me—of whom everyone is so fond?" At first this strikes us as absurd. But when we consider his youth, his sheltered childhood, his naïveté, his lovableness, and all the other characteristics that Tolstóy has shown in him previously, we perceive with a start of admiration that this is precisely the reaction Rostóv would have in the face of approaching death.

This almost abnormal normality in Tolstóy makes him able to do what would seem a very easy thing but is really very hard: describe people engaged in nothing but being happy. Some of the most moving scenes in War and Peace have little to do with profound emotions or great battles or lofty thoughts or critical conflicts. They are merely pictures of people doing things that seem pleasant to them. We think at once of the famous hunt scene in Book 7, the one that is followed by the Rostóvs' visit to "Uncle's" home. Here all is simple gaiety, charm, happiness. The ability to describe this sort of incident has died out in our time, perhaps because the simple glow of happiness itself seems at the moment so much less common than it did in the nineteenth century.

The inclusiveness of War and Peace. Its naturalness. Finally, its timelessness, the quality that makes it possible for this new edition to appear some seventy years after the book's first publication.

Here we have a story that deals largely, though not exclusively, with the members of a class long ago liquidated by war and revolution. The feudal nobility of which Tolstóy wrote is as dead as the feudal nobility of the tenth century. How is it, then, that these people still interest us so intensely? It is because Tolstóy does not describe them in terms of their class position only, but as whole men and women. And even when his characters seem almost pure representatives of their class, they still

have a permanent value as symbols. For example, the dissipated exquisite, Dólokhov, exhibits that desperate courage his class has always had and always will have, though it may change its locale and its name. One finds Dólokhovs today in the R.A.F.

Here is a book, too, that seems to deal with people caught in a particular cleft of history. As that limited epoch recedes, we might suppose the people should dim accordingly. Yet this is not the case. It is impossible to say just how Tolstóy manages to give the impression both of particularity and universality. Anna Schérer remains permanently the type of the fashionable hostess and yet she is herself and no other person. No one but Tolstóy could have created Pierre Bezúkhov, and yet, though he is not Hamlet, he calls out like a kinsman to the Hamlet hidden in all of us. Hélène is an individual and at the same time the personification of that radiant, completely self-assured imbecility which is the special quality of merely beautiful women. One could go on noting the same double character in all the other personages of the vast scene: Berg, the eternal arriviste; Borís, the fortune hunter; the wonderful Prince Andrew with his temperament at once so complex and so clear; the cynical Prince Vasíli Kurágin. As for the young Rostóvs, they are themselves and yet they are youth itself. There are other characters in other novels who at the moment of reading are much more vivid than any of these. But they have the vividness of glowing coals that fade like ashes in the memory, whereas Tolstóy's characters live with a steady light long after you have closed the book that seems to contain them.

War and Peace may not have a classic form. But it does have a classic content. It is full of scenes and situations which, in slightly altered forms, have recurred again and again, and will continue to recur, in the history of civilized man.

Not long ago I happened to observe a mother lifting her eight-year-old boy in her arms. As she did so she laughed and said, "You're getting so big you'll be lifting me soon." It was the simplest of statements. Yet I felt something transiently touching about the scene merely because millions upon millions of mothers reaching back into the dawn of history must have said the same thing to their children at some time and because other millions will say it in the remote future long after this mother and child are dead. Here is a minor example of a recurrent human situation.

You will find hundreds of these recurrent situations—small and large—in the pages of War and Peace, and indeed in the pages of any great novel or play. It is as if the human race, despite its apparent complexity, were capable of but a limited set of gestures. To this set of gestures great artists have the key. You may recollect Aristotle's comment upon the dramatic

value of the "recognition scene" in Greek tragedy. One of the great climaxes of War and Peace is just such a recognition scene, after Natásha is told that the wounded officer who has been traveling with her family is Andrew. The scene is not only great in itself but it gathers up something of the greatness of all the other supreme recognition scenes in literature.

A great many of the moments in the story most charged with emotion have this quality of permanence: Andrew on the battlefield looking up at the sky and comparing its vastness with the littleness of Napoleon, Pierre listening to the peasant wisdom of Karatáev, Natásha at the ball, Mary receiving her mystical, fey peasants. These are timeless moments; they help to make a timeless book—as we May-fly mortals measure time.

Also the very looseness of the book's form, the fact that it has neither beginning nor end, helps to convey the sense of enduring life. As we read the first page we seem to encounter people who have been living for many years, and as we turn the last page, little Nicholas is merely carrying on the life that has been streaming through this vast story and these nineteen years of time.

We open the book at random and read a chance sentence. We are at the Rostóvs'. "In the drawing room the conversation was still going on." And it still is.

Has War and Peace, then, no defects? It has many. It is far from being a technically perfect novel, like Madame Bovary. It is filled with minor weaknesses of characterization. To take just one example: Pierre's complete unconsciousness of the fact that it is only his fortune that wins him both the regard of the world and the marmoreal breasts of Hélène. Despite his glasses, it is hard to think of Pierre as being quite so nearsighted as all that. There are also many places in the narrative where the pace lags. Certain characters in the crowded canvas tend to get lost in the shuffle and never become entirely clear. For example, I have a blind spot for Denísov— he never emerges quite plainly in my mind's eye. At times, so complex is the panorama that the reader has difficulty following the story, just as we have difficulty in following everything happening in a three-ring circus. Some of these defects seem to disappear on a second or third or fourth reading. Some are permanent. But none of them is so great nor are all of them taken together so great as to shake War and Peace from the pinnacle it occupies. Flaubert cannot afford to make mistakes. Tolstóy can.

This is not to say that War and Peace contains all the qualities of greatness. Tolstóy can project only what is in himself. And he is one man, limited, fallible, confined. We feel his limitations not when we are reading his novels, but when we read his novels and then, immediately there-

after, read the masterpieces of other writers dissimilar to him in temperament. If, for example, you follow War and Peace with The Brothers Karamázov you begin to perceive that Tolstóy's vision, far-ranging and humane as it is, is unaware of those murky depths to which the vision of Dostoevsky could pierce. Tolstóy is vast. Dostoevsky is vast too. But his vastness is vertical, Tolstóy's horizontal. Epic writing is generally of this horizontal character whereas dramatic writing—and Dostoevsky is more akin to Shakespeare than he is to most novelists—is vertical. The insights in Tolstóy are at their best enormously moving and exactly true. But they rarely give us that uneasy sense of psychic discovery peculiar to Dostoevsky. This is not to disparage Tolstóy or to exalt Dostoevsky. It is merely a simple way of realizing the absurdity of the notion that Tolstóy "has everything."

So far in these comments I have emphasized those qualities—inclusiveness, naturalness, timelessness—that make War and Peace universal rather than Russian. But part of its appeal for us, I think, derives from the fact that though there is nothing in the book that is incomprehensible to the American or the Western European, everything in it, owing to its Russian character, seems to us just a trifle off-center. This gives the novel a piquancy, even a strangeness at times, that it may not possess for the Russians. No doubt the Russians get the same feeling from Huckleberry Finn.

There are certain central motives in War and Peace that are particularly (though not uniquely) Russian. The motive of moral conversion is a case in point. At some time in the story nearly all the major characters undergo this conversion experience—Pierre, Andrew particularly, Natásha, and even Mary, although perhaps we should say of her that, as the book progresses, her piety merely deepens. Note that the changes in the souls of Pierre and Andrew issue in both cases from suffering and pain. The sense of human freedom, it seems to Tolstóy, is given only to those who have suffered. In his later works we are to find this doctrine emphasized more dogmatically and more unconvincingly. In War and Peace it is presented with passion and power.

It is this longing for regeneration, present even in the rake Dólokhov, that makes Tolstóy's people at one or another point in their lives stop suddenly and ask themselves, as Pierre does, "What is life and what is death?"

Slavic characters do not ask themselves small questions. In Rebecca West's masterly book about Yugoslavia, Black Lamb and Grey Falcon, the narrator encounters an old woman somewhere in Montenegro, I think. An old peasant woman, trudging the roads, absorbed in thought. Miss

West and her husband greet her and ask her, as I remember, where she is bound. In three or four sentences she outlines for them, without any preliminaries, the curve of her life—a broken and tragic curve—and then says, quite simply, that she is now walking the roads and asking herself what her life means. Now, for Miss West, this is a character one could meet only in a Slavic country, and I think she is right. Most of the characters in War and Peace are like this old woman. They ask themselves questions that would be impossible in, let us say, Steinbeck or Hemingway. Perhaps this is what marks our current American literature off from the greater tradition of such men as Dostoevsky and Tolstóy. The characters in Steinbeck and Hemingway have no interest in themselves as wholes. They have no analytical curiosity about themselves. They are studied by the author; they do not study themselves.

In War and Peace, with varying degrees of success, the characters study themselves. All their critical experiences but lead them to further self-examination. Even the volatile and certainly not profound Natásha, after her sad experience with Anatole Kurágin, begins to explore whatever depths she possesses and emerges from these depths a woman ready for her reconciliation with Andrew and later on for her marriage to Pierre. She also emerges a much duller woman—evidence of Tolstóy's inability to sentimentalize.

This regeneration impulse, this desire for conversion, sometimes takes forms that may seem absurd to us and may even have seemed absurd to Tolstóy. But that does not deter him from describing these forms if they seem to him to represent the truth. Recall Pierre's Freemasonry. He is taken in, we say, by a combination of windy idealism and fraternity-house mumbo-jumbo. Yet, silly as the experience may seem to our eyes, it is a necessary one for Pierre. Without it he would perhaps be unable, at a later time, to absorb the far deeper spiritual message of the peasant Karatáev.

The purpose, if we may use so precise a word, of the regeneration experience is to enable the characters to attain to Pierre's state: "By loving people without cause, he discovered indubitable causes for loving them." In this sentence, it seems to me, lies the essence, the center, the inner flame, of the prerevolutionary Russian novel. It is only after one has pondered its meaning that one can understand what lies back of the sudden changes in Tolstóy's and Dostoevsky's characters.

It is interesting to speculate on why the Russians, and particularly the aristocratic class described in War and Peace and Anna Karénina, should have this thirst for salvation. One reason may be the circumstance that

deep within the heart of the Russian aristocrat lay certain agonizing con-
flicts which could be resolved only by the grace of God, i.e., by regen-
eration.

One of these conflicts lay in the fact that culturally he was a mixture
of barbarian, medieval Christian, and Western European. The attempt to
reconcile these discordant elements produced those agonies of conscience
that we find expressed in different forms in characters such as Andrew and
Pierre. That there was a barbarian underlay in these apparently highly
sophisticated people seems obvious to the Western European reader.
Even such a minor survival as Nastásya Ivánovna, the epicene buffoon of
the Rostóv household, points backward to the Middle Ages and to even
earlier times. The savage irritability of the old Prince Nicholas Bolkónski
as well as the neurotic piety of Princess Mary are both examples of bar-
barian excess. They are the gestures of unstable souls. Only on the assump-
tion that many of the habits of Tolstóy's aristocrats are derived from a more
primitive culture can we understand certain actions. When, for example,
Sónya, Natásha's best friend and a well-brought-up girl, does not for a
moment hesitate to read a love letter addressed to Natásha, we find this
somewhat startling. But even more startling is the fact that Natásha hardly
seems at all indignant about it and indeed is even glad that it happened,
as it gives her an opportunity to talk with Sónya about her love affair. Such
behavior is not the behavior we should expect in aristocratic circles in the
France or the England of the period.

These Russians must have been unconsciously aware of this barbarian
underlay, for otherwise they would not have been so anxious to speak
French rather than their native tongue. An impulse on the part of the
upper class of any nation away from its own vernacular is generally an indi-
cation of lack of self-confidence.

There is a witty and not entirely cogent paragraph in Book 9 of War
and Peace in which Tolstóy compares the self-assurance of various nations:

> Pfuel was one of those hopelessly and immutably self-confident
> men, self-confident to the point of martyrdom as only Germans are,
> because only Germans are self-confident on the basis of an abstract
> notion—science, that is, the supposed knowledge of absolute truth.
> A Frenchman is self-assured because he regards himself personally
> both in mind and body as irresistibly attractive to men and women.
> An Englishman is self-assured as being a citizen of the best-organized
> state in the world and therefore, as an Englishman, always knows what
> he should do and knows that all he does as an Englishman is un-
> doubtedly correct. An Italian is self-assured because he is excitable

and easily forgets himself and other people. A Russian is self-assured just because he knows nothing and does not want to know anything, since he does not believe that anything can be known.

There is a certain truth in all of these generalizations, even in the one about the Russian. But I think the reader will admit that the self-assurance based on the kind of negativism Tolstóy mentions is very insecurely based.

The conflict in the soul of the Russian aristocrat derived not only from the conflict of cultures within him but from the moral falsity of his social position. Although Tolstóy—and this is one of his omissions—does not lay great stress on it, the Russian upper class in varying degrees suffered from a guilt complex arising from the institution of serfdom. While that serfdom was in many respects benevolent, it was nevertheless a basic moral evil. Why? Because there is beneath all our cruelty and lethargy something in us (most of us) which says that we must not enslave others or be enslaved by them, even when such a system seems to offer immediate advantages to both master and serf. Note that the form Prince Andrew's higher moral impulses takes is his successful endeavor to improve the lives of the serfs on his estate.

Much of the soul-searching in War and Peace, though it would seem to pivot only on each individual's personal problems, is in part a result of this vague pervasive guilt-feeling. Perhaps, indeed, a large part of the genius of the prerevolutionary Russian novel comes from the conflict engendered by this sense of guilt. It is even arguable that one of the reasons for the flatness and mediocrity of the postrevolutionary Russian novel is due to the absence of that guilt—which is no argument, of course, for Tsarism.

Finally, the Russian sought spiritual regeneration because he found no outlet for his idealistic energies in the state itself. On this point Tolstóy is clear and definite. He shows us an inefficient, slothful, uncertain Russian state, weakened by internal jealousies and rigid with hierarchy. The Russian upper class had at this time not developed the sense of national responsibility which the better element of the British ruling class, despite its brutalities and stupidities, has always had. Tolstóy's Russians are frustrated in their attempt to improve the character of their government— witness, toward the end of the book, Pierre's half-impressive, half-ludicrous political reformism. Because they cannot efficiently discharge, within the framework of politics, their impulses toward good, they are driven to discharge them in the form of personal spiritual crises and regeneration experiences.

I have made these perhaps hackneyed comments in order to show that

Tolstóy is a Russian novelist first and a universal novelist only by accident of genius. He did not know that he was writing for the world. He did not even know that he was writing for all of Russia because in his time the Russian reading class was limited pretty much to the (rather numerous) aristocracy. He wrote as a Russian about Russian people—indeed about his own family, for many of the characters in War and Peace are transcripts from reality. But he wrote about them not only as Russians but as people. And therein lies part of the secret of his greatness.

There remains for us at least one more aspect of War and Peace to consider—that is, Tolstóy's view of men, war, and history and their interrelationships. At the outset let me say that the truly conscientious reader should not be dismayed by the historical essays scattered throughout the book. He will find, if he reads them carefully, that he has been amply repaid for the effort. As I have tried to point out, they are not as extraneous as they seem. For those who prefer digests, however, I hesitantly submit herewith a brief account of Tolstóy's central thought on history.

Tolstóy's theory of history is that there is no theory of history. Or, to put it more cautiously, if there are grand laws determining the movement and flow of historical events, we can, in the present state of our knowledge, only guess at them. Until our vision and our knowledge are so extended that they reveal these underlying laws, the most intelligent thing for us to do is at least to deny validity to all superficial explanations of historical experience.

Since War and Peace was first conceived, there have been numerous theories of history, such as the materialist theory, the cyclical theory of Spengler, Pareto's theory of the elite, etc. Tolstóy would doubtless have vigorously opposed each of these in turn on the ground that they were too simplified. In War and Peace he attacks those theories which were popular in his own time.

Of these, the most appealing was the notion that great events come about through the operation of chance and genius combined. It is part of the purpose of War and Peace to prove that there is no such thing as chance and no such thing as genius.

There is no such thing as chance, Tolstóy thinks, because each event, small or large, is linked by a thousand subtle chains to all other events. We, who cannot see the linkage, cry Chance. Thus to the fallible eye of man Luck rather than Destiny seems at moments to operate.

But the notion of mere chance as the only governing factor in human affairs is unsatisfactory to human egotism. To satisfy that egotism we project the idea of the hero, the grand homme, the military genius, through

whom we vicariously secure the satisfaction which comes of feeling that in part at least the governance of human affairs is in human hands.

This great-man theory, of course, is most picturesquely developed by the vulgarian Carlyle. (It is the theory of history to which vulgar intellects are almost always drawn.) It is Tolstóy's particular bugaboo and abomination.

His method of exposing its falsity is threefold. First, he presents the typical grand homme, Napoleon. Second, he gives us a complementary presentation of Kutúzov. Third, he presents the battles themselves with intent to show their unmanageable waywardness and complexity.

Though Tolstóy has been dead now for more than thirty years, one can almost hear the scorn vibrating in his voice as he speaks of "that genius, Napoleon." For him Napoleon was pre-eminently the fake grand homme, "that most insignificant tool of history who never anywhere, even in exile, showed human dignity." To understand this seemingly iconoclastic judgment it is necessary to remember that in Tolstóy's view evil and cruelty can never have dignity. Only the good man or he who strives for the good can have dignity. It follows then that no conqueror can have dignity. Someday the human race will learn this, and it will despise conquerors as it despises necrophiles or eaters of offal.

Not only, however, is the fatuity of Napoleon depicted—his ill-temper, his peccadillos of conduct—but Tolstóy attacks him at his central point—his faith in himself. For Tolstóy, Napoleon, precisely because he is a "leader," is so limited in his freedom of action that only that capacity for self-deception which is the special characteristic of the conqueror type can give him the illusion that he is commanding events rather than surrendering to them. "Such is the inevitable fate of men of action, and the higher they stand in the social hierarchy, the less are they free."

To Napoleon, the pseudo-grand homme, Tolstóy opposes the Russian Kutúzov. Kutúzov is not, in the heroic sense, a great man. He is lethargic, old, slightly doddering, pietistic. He is incapable of "grand strategy," gives few orders, hardly listens to the reports of his subordinates. Yet just because Kutúzov is not a hero, he is able to understand or merely to sense the historical undercurrents that will in the end defeat Napoleon and leave the Russians in possession of their own country. He is one of "those rare and always solitary individuals who, discerning the will of Providence, submit their personal will to it." This is not mere mystical verbiage. Kutúzov alone among all the Russian generals understands that Borodinó is not a French victory but a French defeat. He knows also that the abandonment of Moscow means the salvation of Russia. From Tolstóy's point of view, Kutúzov does not come to these conclusions through

the exercise of the rational faculty but by a kind of intuitive identity with the ordinary Russian soldier. Kutúzov governs best because he governs least.

Finally, with Tolstóy's conceptions of Napoleon and Kutúzov is associated his general contempt for the art of warfare. For Tolstóy each battle is an affair of contingencies so numerous and so complexly related that no one mind or group of minds can foresee them. Therefore, military experts are to him a parcel of fools. The best expression of his contempt for the military profession he puts into the mind of Prince Andrew as the Prince listens, in Book 9, Chapter 11, to the council of war:

Prince Andrew, listening to this polyglot talk and to these surmises, plans, refutations, and shouts, felt nothing but amazement at what they were saying. A thought that had long since and often occurred to him during his military activities—the idea that there is not, and cannot be, any science of war, and that therefore there can be no such thing as a military genius—now appeared to him an obvious truth. "What theory and science is possible about a matter the conditions and circumstances of which are unknown and cannot be defined, especially when the strength of the acting forces cannot be ascertained? No one was or is able to foresee in what condition our or the enemy's armies will be in a day's time, and no one can gauge the force of this or that detachment. Sometimes— when there is not a coward at the front to shout, 'We are cut off' and start running, but a brave and jolly lad who shouts 'Hurrah!'—a detachment of five thousand is worth thirty thousand, as at Schön Grabern, while at times fifty thousand run from eight thousand as at Austerlitz. What science can there be in a matter in which, as in all practical matters, nothing can be defined, and everything depends on innumerable conditions the significance of which is determined at a particular moment which arrives no one knows when? Armfelt says our army is cut in half, and Paulucci says we have got the French army between two fires, Michaud says that the worthlessness of the Drissa camp lies in having the river behind it, and Pfuel says that is what constitutes its strength, Toll proposes one plan, Armfelt another, and they are all good and all bad, and the advantages of any suggestion can only be seen at the moment of trial. And why do they all speak of a 'military genius'? Is a man a genius who can order bread to be brought up at the right time and say who is to go to the right and who to the left? It is only because military men are invested with pomp and power, and crowds of sycophants flatter power, attributing to it qualities of genius it does not possess. The best generals I have known were, on the contrary, stupid or absent-minded men. Bagratión was the best, Napoleon himself admitted that. And Bona-

parte himself! I remember his limited, self-satisfied face on the field
of Austerlitz. Not only does a good army commander not need any
special qualities, on the contrary he needs the absence of the highest
and best human attributes—love, poetry, tenderness, and philo-
sophic inquiring doubt. He should be limited, firmly convinced that
what he is doing is very important (otherwise he will not have suffi-
cient patience), and only then will he be a brave leader. God forbid
that he should be humane, should love, or pity, or think of what is
just and unjust. It is understandable that a theory of their 'genius'
was invented for them long ago because they have power! The suc-
cess of a military action depends not on them, but on the man
in the ranks who shouts 'We are lost!' or who shouts 'Hurrah!' And
only in the ranks can one serve with assurance of being useful."

For Tolstóy the fate of battles therefore is decided less by prefabricated
strategies than by the absence or presence of what he calls "moral hesi-
tation," or what we would call morale.

This theory he carries to what may seem absurd lengths. The military
men he most admires are passive generals like Kutúzov, or subordinates
like the officer Dokhtúrov who has no plans and no theories but is always
on the spot when needed and who therefore succeeds while the strategists
merely become "heroes." For Tolstóy, indeed, the victor in a historical
crisis is usually he who does the opposite of what the textbooks lay down.
A good example is his comment on the conduct of the citizens during
their abandonment of Moscow: "Those who went about their business as
Moscow was evacuated helped to save the city. Those who performed
heroic labors hindered things."

It is essential to realize that Tolstóy's conception of war as something
both too complicated to be foreseen and too complicated to be explained
after the event is a conception based on his observation of the wars of his
period. (He served for several years in the Russian army and was a soldier
at the siege of Sevastopol.) In other words, his observations are of rela-
tively unmechanized warfare—warfare in which the unit is still the indi-
vidual soldier fighting on foot or on a horse, and able to communicate
only with difficulty with his fellow soldiers and his superiors.

Were Tolstóy alive today would he moderate his views because the char-
acter of warfare has changed so radically in the interim? Have mechaniza-
tion and two-way radio communication abolished the individual soldier?
Have they made possible a foresight and a planning impossible to Na-
poleon? Have they also changed the quality of the emotions within the
hearts of those engaged in war? It is Tolstóy's great good fortune as a
novelist that he is describing warfare in which, because the action is non-

mechanized, the soldier himself is nonmechanized. Thus, he can show us the young Rostóv who, during his baptism of fire, feels "perfectly happy" and who, within a short time, is overtaken by an equally intense fear of death. Does the regimented Nazi soldier have similar or different reactions?

Tolstóy, I think, would reply that any change is only apparent and only temporary. He would say that human nature is a constant, that it will rise to the surface despite all the deformation, the drill, the conditioning, the dehumanizing to which it may be subjected. But this leads us to a consideration of warfare in Napoleon's time as compared with warfare in our own. The best way to examine the problem is by means of detailed instances.

<div align="center">2</div>

Not long ago, as this is written, the London Sunday Graphic printed a cartoon showing Hitler and Göring saluting an army of men and a swarm of planes all moving eastward. Hitler is saying, "Do you ever get that feeling that it has all happened before, Hermann?" Behind the pair rises the ghost of Napoleon.

It is impossible to reread War and Peace in this Year of Death 1942 without being constantly reminded of the fact that history can at times be sensationally repetitious. If Hitler, as the cartoon suggests, is filled with that odd sense we all have had of déjà vu, the reader of War and Peace is similarly filled with a sense of encore vu.

I happen to be writing these words in February, 1942. It is understood, therefore, that the obvious parallels any amateur can draw between the Napoleonic campaigns of 1805 and 1812 as described by Tolstóy and the Nazi campaign of 1941-42 are good only as of today. I have no competence as a military theorist nor any ability to pierce the future, preferring to leave this profession to Nostradamus and the radio commentators. It is interesting, however, to indicate as of this date the curious, the almost thrilling similarities between the history of Hitler and the history of Napoleon, the link being furnished by what seems to be a constant in European history—the character and geographical setting of the Russian people.

At this writing, the titanic battle of Russia, a part of the general battle for the soul of man, is far from a decision. Hitler's retreat, while obviously not strategic in the sense he planned, is, on the other hand, far from being the rout that some wishful thinkers would make it out. But it represents

a physical and moral defeat, the proportions of which probably no one knows except the German General Staff. Certainly the back of Fascism does not appear to be broken, as Napoleon's back was broken after Moscow. Napoleon's dream died with his dying legions in the snow. Hitler's dream—the same vision, dreamed by a people instead of a single tyrant—is by no means dead. We do not yet know (unless faith is knowledge) whether Hitler will retrace completely the mighty Napoleonic parabola or whether he will succeed temporarily in his nightmare design of covering our planet with an Egyptian night. If he should fail, a new Tolstóy may arise fifty years hence to chronicle the vast drama of his rise and fall. If he should succeed, that new Tolstóy will not arise. For there will be no novelists and no poets. The humane and philosophic view of life from which supreme works of art spring will have been blotted out.

If we glance first at the general situation obtaining just before the start of the two invasions, we find Napoleon in 1812 military master of Europe, as Hitler is today. We see Napoleon endeavoring to express that military mastery in a politico-economic pattern—the Continental System. We see Hitler endeavoring to do the same: he calls it the New Order. Napoleon's Continental System is a semifailure; Hitler's New Order is a semifailure. In both cases Russia refuses to fit into the system. This refusal is one of the factors impelling the two conquerors eastward. It is apparent to both Napoleon and Hitler that effective (rather than nominal) domination of the Continent is impossible as long as one other great power, Russia, exists as a standing threat.

We note, however, that Hitler's invasion starts only after he has made the same three moves tried by Napoleon.

The first of these is the attempted invasion of England. Napoleon goes no farther than the preparation of a navy of flatboats at Boulogne. Hitler not only readies his barge fleet at the Channel ports but actually achieves the first part of his plan through the use of bombers. But no true invasion is effected in either case. (There are curious minor echoes and parallels. Almost a century and a half ago the British erected against the threat of Napoleon a system of seacoast fortresses known as Martello towers. Today these towers are being repaired against the threat of a renewed attempt at invasion by Hitler.)

Before invading Russia, Hitler and Napoleon both make another move. In 1807 Napoleon and Tsar Alexander I meet on a raft at Tilsit in the Niemen River and in effect divide up Europe. It takes five years for that agreement to sour. The analogy with the Nazi-Soviet pact is clear. But in

our time events move faster. Hitler does not take five years to realize that he must advance toward the east.

There is still a third move. Before invading Russia Napoleon tries to persuade Alexander to join him in an alliance against England. He fails. Hitler duplicates this move but with what may be called reverse English —that is, Hess (if we are to believe the most credible of the explanations) tries to persuade certain people—by courtesy called Englishmen—to join Hitler in an alliance against Russia. He fails. In both cases Russia and England, despite their radical difference in political outlook, ally themselves against a common enemy.

But Napoleon and Hitler have their allies too. Napoleon, ever anxious to conserve the blood of Frenchmen, manipulates Austria and Prussia. Today Hitler too has his puppets—Finland, Rumania, Italy, others. But both Napoleon and Hitler have allies more important than these. Today such allies are called appeasement groups. War and Peace offers an excellent picture of the 1805 appeasement group (analogous to the men of Munich) in St. Petersburg. This consists mainly of spiritually diseased nobles and cowards of all stripes, including a few romantic intellectuals— for a while Pierre Bezúkhov himself is one of them—who are taken in by the "glory" of Napoleon. In 1812 the same group is headed by the Tsarévich. At this writing there seems to be no appeasement group in Russia, but the reader of Tolstóy cannot help thinking of the Cliveden set and of the French upper classes who succeeded in betraying their country. Nor are Nazappeasers lacking in our own nation.

In War and Peace the representative of the superficially hard-boiled but basically sentimental Napoleon-worship is the diplomat Bilíbin with his admiration for the tricky intelligence of the French. His is the aristocratic form defeatism takes. His unconscious desire to be a traitor disguises itself as worldly cynicism. Today the same unconscious desire manifests itself as admiration for Nazi technical efficiency, as "realism," as advance agenting for the wave of the future.

Pierre is not a traitor, but even he is taken in early in the book by the Napoleon myth. "The English will come off badly, you know, if Napoleon gets across the Channel. I think the expedition is quite feasible." Anna Schérer, the salon gossiper, says, "Prussia has always declared that Bonaparte is invincible and that all Europe is powerless before him." We too (before Pearl Harbor and, if the truth were known, after Pearl Harbor, too) have our Pierres and our Anna Schérers, our café-table and boardroom cynics, who take a special pleasure in their conviction that Hitler is invincible. If heroism is a permanent in human history, so are baseness and degeneracy.

Before Napoleon starts his campaign, he is warned against it by Caulaincourt, formerly his Ambassador to Russia. Caulaincourt is pessimistic over Napoleon's chances but Napoleon, by this time an obsessed man, does not heed him. Not only does Napoleon pay no attention to Caulaincourt but he goes further. He prophesies, "In less than two months' time Russia will be suing for peace." Similarly, it is now the general belief that a certain group of Nazi generals, possibly including Göring, warned Hitler against the Russian campaign. Napoleon tweaked Caulaincourt's ear with good-natured contempt. Hitler, no ear-tweaker, purged and perhaps murdered his Cassandras. Hitler's self-confidence is equal to Napoleon's. This excess of self-confidence seems to mark both men at exactly the same point in their careers. The ancient Greeks called it hubris. We know it as the sin of pride. By it Satan fell.

There we have the general situation just before the campaigns begin. The analogy so far has been easy, perhaps too easy, to make. Does it break down as we continue the story? Let us see.

As Napoleon starts his eastward march, he of course disguises his rapacity and lust for power under the cloak of idealistic slogans, maxims that have caused many good people really to believe that Napoleon is in the European tradition. Thus the invasion of Russia becomes not a war but a crusade against Asiatic barbarism. Similarly Hitler's invasion of Russia is not a war of aggression but a "crusade" against Bolshevism. Hitler's crusade may still succeed, but the world will never accept his moral evaluation of it any more than it accepted Napoleon's evaluation of his own reasons for invading Russia.

On June 23, 1812, Napoleon crosses the Niemen into Russian territory. On June 22, 1941, following Napoleon's timetable almost to the day, Hitler strikes at Russia. Napoleon's initial successes are great, as are Hitler's. During the opening stages of the campaigns the names that crop up in War and Peace reoccur in our morning newspaper: Vílna, Riga, Smolénsk, Vítebsk, the Berëzina, the Dnieper. There is nothing noteworthy about this. Only one road leads to Moscow. Geography is immutable.

Now, we know that Napoleon, on the way to Moscow, fought the Russians at Borodinó, and achieved what the French histories call a Napoleonic victory. It opened the gates to Moscow, he entered the city, it was burnt, he remained there for a few weeks—and retreated.

Napoleon failed. The reasons for that failure and the drama that attended it have never been more effectively presented anywhere than in the pages of War and Peace. Tolstóy seizes on its essentials. He knows, for example,

that Borodinó, technically a French victory inasmuch as the French army is left in possession of the field, was really a Russian victory because the Russian army, though undergoing severe losses, retreated in good order. After Borodinó Napoleon's army, as Tolstóy describes it in a magnificent image, was like a wounded beast—still capable of sporadic vicious efforts but inevitably fated to bleed to death. Its morale was disrupted because it had not achieved its object, for the whole purpose of the campaign was not to invest Moscow, which Napoleon succeeded in doing, but to annihilate the Russian army, which he did not succeed in doing.

Hitler did not invest Moscow but he got within ten miles of it before being repulsed. That repulse was not his Borodinó, for it was but part of a general defeat. His Borodinó was no single battle but rather a series of bloody encounters along a two-thousand-mile front. This battle he has lost, despite initial victories, despite the fact that he still holds thousands of square miles of Russian territory. Part of his object (which was Napoleon's) has certainly not been gained—the destruction of the Russian armies. Another part of his object he probably has gained—the reduction of Russian industrial capacity. But the effort has, unless all signs are meaningless, been too much for him, as it was for Napoleon. His Eastern forces must be reorganized, possibly for a new Russian offensive in the spring of '42, possibly for an invasion of Spain and North Africa, possibly for an assault on the Caucasus through Turkey. But the first battle of Russia has been lost. Napoleon lost his, and could never attempt a second. We have yet to see whether Hitler's second try, which is inevitable, will be successful.

Analogies drawn from a detailed study of tactics and strategy have but a limited value. What is more important are certain more general considerations that occur to us as we read War and Peace. Tolstóy, with his somewhat mystical and determinist view of history, does not ascribe Napoleon's failure to his ineptitude any more than he ascribes his previous successes to his so-called genius. In fact, he does not try to explain Napoleon's collapse as due to any one factor or even any combination of factors. Among other things, however, he points out one element as present in our own time as it was in the day of Napoleon—the character of the Russian people, once it is convinced that it is defending its homeland rather than engaging in a purely military war.

The military tradition of the Russian peoples is based on the character of their land. That character—the same is true of China—makes it possible to use slow retreat as a weapon. This weapon is particularly suitable to countries with a preponderantly peasant population and which are

industrially backward, with few fatally important nerve centers. The de-
fenders take advantage of a combination of time and space—a combination
which can be utilized only in countries that are really continents. Along
with the technique of slow retreat goes the technique of guerrilla war-
fare. Guerrilla warfare plus slow retreat helped to beat Napoleon who
apparently did not understand the immense force the proper use of these
techniques can generate.

It is probable, to go on with our analogy, that Hitler, who must have
studied Napoleon's campaigns carefully, understands the Russian char-
acter better than did his predecessor. Yet it would seem that he has already
been harassed by the same kind of withdrawal and guerrilla fighting that
harassed Napoleon; and that today the harassment has gone so far that
the Russians can afford to take the offensive.

But, as Tolstóy points out, the Russians have an even more deeply
based weapon. This is what military theorists unimaginatively call morale.
Essentially it is the soul of a people, the peculiar and unique national
spirit which underlies all training and all conditioning and which rises
to the surface only in the most extreme of emergencies. In the case of
the Russians in 1812 this national spirit meant a kind of near-mystical
attachment to "Mother Russia," a blind, passionate, and, if necessary,
suicidal devotion to the land which Napoleon's army, with all its talk of
gloire, lacked. This national spirit is crescent today. It underlies the thin
veneer of Communist doctrine and lives a life apart from it. It helped
to defeat Napoleon. It will probably yet defeat Hitler.

Essentially nonmilitary, it takes certain forms both in 1812 and in 1942
which are incomprehensible to the strictly military mind. Recently the
Germans, with characteristic lack of humor, objected to what they called
the "unsportsmanlike" tactics of the Russians. That is to say, the Nazis
were enraged because the Russians refused to die in the manner prescribed
for them by the protocols of their would-be conquerors. Compare this
Nazi reaction with a passage from the first chapter of Book 14 of
War and Peace:

> It is well for a people who do not—as the French did in 1813—
> salute according to all the rules of art, and presenting the hilt of their
> rapier gracefully and politely hand it to their magnanimous con-
> queror, but at the moment of trial, without asking what rules others
> have adopted in similar cases, simply and easily pick up the first
> cudgel that comes to hand, and strike with it till the feeling of resent-
> ment and revenge in their soul yields to a feeling of contempt and
> compassion.

Beneath this national spirit there is something even deeper, a force very hard to describe and whose value in offense it is almost impossible to determine. That force may be called the messianic spirit in the Russian people—the same spirit which Hitler, realizing its value, tries to graft on to the soul of his own folk. In other words, the Russian in 1812 felt not only that he was defending his own country, which he was, but defending Europe, which is questionable. Whether what he felt was true or not, however, he felt it, and it gave to his determination an extra dimension and strength. Scratch a Russian and you find a martyr. Remember Anna Schérer's outburst in War and Peace: "Russia alone must save Europe." This sense of being the bringers of salvation seems to be the deepest thing in the Russian character. All the Soviet leaders have tried to do is to divert its force in a particular revolutionary direction. Tolstóy is aware of that force and he feels that it is in part the reason for the destruction of Napoleon. It is something Napoleon—with his cheap notions of la gloire, his essentially vulgarian and nonreligious conception of power—cannot be expected to understand or properly evaluate, and it may be that Hitler will make the same grand psychological error. For it is a special talent of the German mind to make no errors except the very biggest. Ribbentrop's complete miscomprehension of England as well as the Nazis' general miscomprehension of America are examples of this supreme lack of psychological sensitivity.

I am aware that military historians make light of phrases like national spirit and messianic conscience. They are much more inclined to lay Napoleon's defeat to factors that can be mathematically demonstrated. The two factors most commonly adduced are, as Walter Millis, in an excellent analysis, reminds us, "the failure of Napoleon's supply system to stand up under the terrific strain imposed upon it, and the successes of the Russians in avoiding encirclement and maintaining their armies 'in being.' " So far, Hitler's supply system—far vaster and more complex than Napoleon's— has stood up under the strain, though at this writing it is beginning to crack. It cracks much more slowly than did Napoleon's, for the Russian "scorched earth" policy of 1941 could not in the nature of things be as successful as the same policy was in 1812.

As for the second factor—the success of the Russians in avoiding encirclement—it is at this writing impossible to make any final prognosis. So far the Russians seem not only to have avoided encirclement but to have partially encircled the Nazis. But, even if a new German offensive should be started, the Russians could withdraw to the Urals where no doubt fresh armies are being held in reserve. In this case Hitler would have

to face the problem of a ten or twenty years' war—or abandon the idea of conquering Russia. There is still a third military factor that operated against Napoleon in 1812 and which is operating against Hitler in 1942—and that is pressure on the rear. In 1812 the rear was Spain: Napoleon's retreat was in part necessitated by his desire to protect himself in the Peninsula. Today the geography has changed slightly but the force is the same. Again it is the English who are pressing on Hitler's rear, only they are now the fighters and bombers of the R.A.F., and Spain is changed to the Ruhr Valley, the Channel ports, and (though at this moment the issue is doubtful) Libya. If Italy should be knocked out of the war and become a real handicap to Hitler, the analogy will be even more forcible.

It is necessary to remind the reader at this point that the one factor which did not defeat the French was General Winter. It is true that on their retreat Napoleon's armies suffered untold horrors because of the cold. But it is Tolstóy's point, and it seems to me a valid one, that the French army was lost long before it started its retreat in October, that it was lost even before it entered Moscow, that it was lost at Borodinó, and, Tolstóy might even add, that it was lost from the moment it crossed the Niemen. No, winter did not defeat Napoleon. Caulaincourt tells us, as a matter of fact, that the cold weather did not begin till November 5, 1812. Remember, however, that the French were already withdrawn from Moscow on October 16. Caulaincourt had warned Napoleon in advance about the weather: "Winter will come like a bombshell." But it was a bombshell that exploded too late to do more than intensify already irreparable damage.

To continue with our analogy, it is probable that though winter has hindered the operations of Hitler's Panzer divisions and regular infantry, it will not be the determining factor in his defeat that some wishful thinkers imagine.

Is there any way by which Napoleon could have won? Tolstóy thinks that had Napoleon turned southwestward into the Ukraine, he might have wintered there successfully and reattacked in the spring. Instead, he made the error of retreating, and so lost Europe. But to Tolstóy the question of whether Napoleon might have done otherwise than he did is meaningless. He did what he did because—given his character, the character of the Russian people, the character of the war, and the whole sweep of events of the time—he could have done only what he did.

Some authorities think that Hitler committed the same error. He concentrated on Moscow and Leningrad whereas many of his generals wanted the main effort to be directed against the Ukraine. Hitler's defeat at

Rostóv may have been the turning point of the campaign, with Timo-shenko occupying a position similar to that of Kutúzov in 1812.

Other authorities think that Hitler could have succeeded had he pushed on eastward directly after the vanquishing of Poland, at a time when Russia was psychologically and militarily unprepared. He withdrew his armies, as Napoleon did, and so lost his grand chance. This makes a very neat parallel but is based, of course, on a supposition.

One of the causes of the defeat of Napoleon was Napoleon. Note, however, that Tolstóy does not exaggerate the importance of Napo-leon's character either in victory or defeat. One of the chief purposes of his book, as we have seen elsewhere in this discussion, is to show us how relatively helpless the "great man" is in the hands of the historical forces that control him, even though the uniqueness of his position and the egotism of his temperament combine to make him believe that he controls them. When you read Tolstóy, so overpowering is his imagina-tion that you are convinced of the truth of his view of history and begin to look upon Napoleon very much as Tolstóy does, with a kind of tolerant interest punctuated by spasms of revulsion.

When one begins to apply the anti-great-man theory of Tolstóy to the world of today, one is at first bewildered. Superficially, the horizon seems to be filled with a few overpowering figures leading a great mass of anonymous human beings. We say Hitler, Churchill, Roosevelt, Chiang Kai-shek, Stalin, thinking that we are naming men of power and wisdom, whether for good or evil. Tolstóy would tell us that we are not naming men in that sense at all, but that each of these personalities is himself riding a mount he cannot control. In the midst of events this may not seem clear. But fifty years later it may seem somewhat clearer, as it did to Tolstóy when he sat down to write the first part of War and Peace.

The simplest of the ways by which Tolstóy makes us feel the littleness, the mere humanity of Napoleon, is by presenting him as a fallible man and not as the demigod of the French tradition. Perhaps Tolstóy may be considered the first of the debunkers. Yet there is nothing cheap or malicious about his portrait. One feels it to be true—unless one is a worshiper of the values Napoleon himself worshiped.

The similarities between the character of Napoleon as Tolstóy limns him and the character of Hitler as it has been portrayed for us by Rauschning, Strasser, and a dozen other formerly intimate friends of the Führer are so striking that they lead to the question: Is it possible that the desire to enslave the world and the seeming capacity to do so reappear century after century in only one type of man?

The base of Napoleon's character in 1812, its motive power, is a kind of low vengefulness, a pervasive resentment manifesting itself in strange outbursts of fury, savage threats, loss of temper. One recollects the interview that Tolstóy describes between Tsar Alexander's envoy Balashëv and Napoleon: "Balashëv continually made the gesture of a man wishing to say something, but Napoleon always interrupted him." . . . "But Napoleon did not let him speak. He evidently wanted to do all the talking himself and continued to talk with the sort of eloquence and unrestrained irritability to which spoilt people are so prone." . . . "The more he talked the less he could control his words."

Is this not an amazingly exact picture of the way in which Hitler is reported to have talked to Henderson, Schuschnigg, Chamberlain, and others? We cannot explain this by saying that it is the natural impatience of a great man with men who are inferior to him. Washington did not talk thus, nor Lincoln. Rather must we ask ourselves whether this frenzied irritability, this refusal to allow others to speak, is not the mark always of a certain type of dictatorial temperament, a temperament totally immured in its own egotism.

It is hard to understand the mental processes of men like Hitler and Napoleon who are at times so incomparably shrewder and more perceptive than their fellow men and at times so incomparably purblind. The true explanation is doubtless inordinately complex, but part of it, I think, is contained in a trenchant comment that Tolstóy makes about Napoleon, again in connection with Balashëv's interview. "It was plain that Balashëv's personality did not interest him at all. Evidently only what took place within his own mind interested him. Nothing outside himself had any significance for him, because everything in the world, it seemed, depended entirely on his will." This is the psychological trap that God sets for tyrants. It is the trap into which Hitler will yet fall.

In Rebecca West's Black Lamb and Grey Falcon there is a long conversation between Miss West and her husband concerning the character of one of their companions—whom they do not like—in their travels through Yugoslavia. Gerda is a German woman married to a Serb. Though politically no Nazi, she is one spiritually. I should like to quote briefly from the long analysis Miss West's husband makes of the character of Gerda because I think it throws light on the character of Hitler and of the Nazi type generally, and re-enforces the analysis Tolstóy makes of the character of Napoleon.

"Gerda has no sense of process. That is what is the matter with Gerda. She wants the result without doing any of the work that goes to make it.

. . . She is angry because we have some money. She feels that it might just as well belong to her. . . . For her, the money might as easily have been attached to her as to us by a movement as simple as that which pastes a label on a trunk. . . . As she has no sense of what goes to bring people love, or friendship, or distinction, or wealth, it seems to her that the whole world is enjoying undeserved benefits; and in a universe where all is arbitrary, it might just as well happen that the injustice was pushed a little further and that all these benefits were taken from other people, leaving them nothing, and transferred to her, giving her everything. Given the premise that the universe is purely arbitrary, that there is no causality at work anywhere, there is nothing absurd in that proposal. This is the conqueror's point of view. . . . Let us admit it, for a little while the whole of our world may belong to Gerda. She will snatch it out of hands too well bred and compassionate and astonished to defend it. What we must remember is that she will not be able to keep it. For her contempt for the process makes her unable to conduct any process. . . . To go up in an aeroplane and drop bombs is a simple use of an elaborate process that has already been developed. But you cannot administer a country on this principle. . . . Gerda's empire . . . will be an object of fear and nothing else. For this reason, I believe that Gerda's empire cannot last long. But while it lasts it will be terrible. And what it leaves when it passes will also be terrible. For we cannot hope for anything but a succession of struggles for leadership among men whose minds will have been unfitted for leadership by the existence of tyranny and the rupture of European tradition, until, slowly and painfully, the nations re-emerge, civilization re-emerges."

Now Tolstóy's depiction of Napoleon is the depiction of a man who has lost his "sense of process." Though he speaks of himself as a Man of Destiny, he does not believe in destiny, does not believe that human history is continuous. He believes, instead, that he can arrest its course or divert its direction because he wishes to do so.

Tolstóy himself, on the other hand, wrote War and Peace in part to express his sense of the thick continuity of human events, the multitudinous linkages which even a Napoleon cannot break. It is those characters who have an awareness of this continuity, like Prince Andrew, that he admires. It is those characters who have no such awareness that he scorns. The Tolstóyan viewpoint is evidenced even in the creation of such minor personages as the fatuous Berg who, simply because he is himself, is convinced that everything he does is right. A more significant example is the aristocratic waster, Anatole Kurágin, "who regarded his whole life as a continual round of amusement which someone for some reason had to provide for him." It is this inability to conceive reality which is to

ruin the class Anatole represents. It is this lack of a sense of process on the part of an insulated class which is to lead straight to 1917 in Russia. Someday it may be shown that it led also to Pearl Harbor.

Now, from time to time, as Miss West reminds us, a group of powerful people deficient in a sense of process arises and for a time dominates the world or a part of it. They are able to effect such domination because this lack of a sense of process is a great strength. The Nazi is automatically insulated from the doubts, hesitations, and fears of those of us who possess such a sense. And, if the world were so simple that fanatical courage and superhuman energy could control it, Hitler, the man with no sense of process, would succeed permanently.

But, as Tolstóy reminds us, the world is not so simple. History is far more complicated than even the most wide-visioned conqueror—and Hitler's perspectives, one must admit, are enormous—can understand. In the end the Hitler-type is defeated by his inability to judge his own limitations.

Is there not something supremely childlike about both Napoleon and Hitler? Just as the child in the dawn of his life cannot make a distinction between an object and himself, so the conqueror cannot understand why there should be any disjunction between himself and what he wants. When a disjunction appears, both the child and the conqueror express their frustration by fits of temper. Such fits are described by Tolstóy as characteristic of Napoleon and are described by contemporaries as characteristic of Hitler.

There are a large number of minor parallels that might be drawn between the characters of Hitler and Napoleon, unimportant but interesting parallels. It is odd, for example, that just as Napoleon, so Tolstóy tells us, resorted with apparent gullibility to soothsayers, so Hitler, according to report, consults an astrologer.

It is notable that in periods of enormous stress and strain, the irrational, the savage, hidden deep in man, raises its stone-age head and asks again its mumbling questions of the dark gods it has itself invented. Pierre becomes interested in the mystic numbers of the Revelation of Saint John. He and many others like him feverishly manipulate the symbols so that they may foretell the end of Napoleon. Freemasonry makes its occult appeal to him. The Napoleonic period was one of omens and prophecies and dark stirrings in the minds of men.

Today, too, in our own country, there are ample evidences of this curious ferment. It is no accident that the medicine-man cults which have long flourished on our West Coast should be enjoying greater popularity today than ever before. It is no accident that the gibberings of Nostrada-

mus should be republished and become something like a minor best seller, and even reach the screen. A conqueror like Hitler not only forces the weaker among us to lose faith in everything we have believed in. He forces some of us to seek faith in things that our savage forefathers believed in. It is ironical that Hitler, who proclaims himself the apostle of science, control, order, and rationality, should cause such an excess of frenzy, superstition, and irrationality.

The prime example of this irrationality is the tyrant's own conception of himself as God. The mania may clothe itself in varying forms. Tolstóy shows us the confused Pierre, who in 1805 is a Napoleon-worshiper, reflecting that "The execution of the Duc d'Enghien was a political necessity and it seems to me that Napoleon showed greatness of soul by not fearing to take on himself the whole responsibility of that deed." To take on himself the whole responsibility of that deed. And just as Napoleon had his Duc d'Enghien and horrified the world with the murder, so Hitler had his Röhm and announced, "For twenty-four hours I was the Supreme Court of Germany."

So much for the parallels, which could be extended much further at the risk of trying the reader's patience. Now for the differences, which at first glance seem to be far more striking than the similarities.

In the days of Kutúzov and Napoleon there was no Blitzkrieg, there were no planes, tanks, railroads, radio communications, land mines—one could extend the list easily. In 1812 oil was not a war weapon. Today it is the war weapon without which Hitler cannot win and possessing which he may win—for a time. Strategically the situations present enormous differences. Napoleon attacked on one narrow front whereas Hitler is attacking (or retreating) on what amounts to a line drawn along the breadth of a continent. From the angle of international relations too the line-up is different. Napoleon had no ally like Japan to rely on nor any adversary like the United States to fear.

There was much dissatisfaction in Napoleon's conquered territory as he marched into Russia. But it is entirely out of relation to the giant wave of disaffection and rebellion now rising and which may yet engulf Hitler's New Order.

Furthermore, readers will object, does not the whole analogy begin to seem a little strained when we focus our attention upon the difference in scale between the two wars? For Tolstóy the movement back and forth of Napoleon's army is a vast process. Its battles are vast. Its consequences are vast. And when we keep our eyes riveted only upon the pages of War and Peace we catch completely the Tolstóyan sense of the size of the

forces involved. But when we raise our eyes from the page and compare these forces with those that are now shaking the world we are at once affrighted by the enormous increase in their intensity since the time of Napoleon.

For it is true that Napoleon's war was a Continental one. Hitler's is planetary. Napoleon's war was largely an affair of foot soldiers, cavalry, and simple artillery. Hitler's war, while utilizing all these elements of battle, is conceived in three dimensions and in terms, if necessary, of total destruction—which was not Napoleon's aim at all. This disparity in scale is so overpowering and so manifest that it may be that the analogies we have drawn will seem of but minor interest.

Yet, though the bombing plane is new and the radio transmitter is new, the man in the plane and the man behind the transmitter are not much different from the men of the time of Napoleon. Just as there are constants in geography that cannot change, so, too, there are constants in human nature. For a time, these constants in human nature may seemingly be clouded over by the force of such men as Napoleon and Hitler and the great historical waves they ride. But in the end these constants will rise above the surface and re-establish themselves as the determining motives of history.

CLIFTON FADIMAN

TRANSLATOR'S PREFACE

Leo Tolstóy, the greatest of Russian prose writers, was born in 1828 on the ancestral estate he inherited about a hundred miles south of Moscow. After a very happy childhood and a couple of years at Kazán University, he went in 1851 to the Caucasus, where he entered the army as a cadet, not obtaining his commission as an officer in the artillery till 1854, the year the Crimean War broke out. He then applied to be transferred to that front, and from November, 1854, to September, 1855, when the town was abandoned, he served in the defense of Sevastopol while it was besieged by the French and English. When the war was over he retired from the army, and in 1862 he married, having by then written his Nine Stories and Tales of Army Life, to which he referred as "trials of the pen." He had also devoted himself ardently to the education of the peasant children on his estate and in the neighborhood.

When the family property was divided among his three brothers, his sister, and himself, his means were small, and in consequence of losses at cards he found himself in straitened circumstances. It was natural enough therefore that, when he married, his wife should insist on his abandoning the educational work to which he was devoted but which instead of bringing in an income cost him money. After his marriage he accordingly set himself the task of repairing his fortune by improving his estate, which he did very successfully, becoming so absorbed in estate management that, as he himself expressed it, he almost forgot that he was an author and for months at a time did not "soil his hand with ink or his soul with thought." A year after his marriage, however, he began his great novel War and Peace, the first part of which was published in February, 1865, and the final part in November, 1869.

Of War and Peace it may be said that it stands at the crucial point where the modern novel begins. Its predecessors (and many of its successors) seem to belong almost to a prehistoric stage of the novel. If there can be said to be a dividing line between the old and the modern novel Tolstóy marks it—unless indeed we take the earlier Richardson as doing so. Tolstóy's immediate predecessors in the development of the modern novel

were the great French analytical novelists of the late eighteenth and early nineteenth centuries, Rousseau and Stendhal. Tolstóy always mentions these two when speaking of those who influenced him. He himself heralds a change in the texture of the narrative from the old dramatic method (which was still Dostoévsky's) to a new one, "the point of view" method. The dramatic method consists of giving the actions and words of the characters without an explanation. Tolstóy in his earlier period never does this. With him the psychological explanation is the important thing. What is important is not what his people do, it is why they do it that matters. But this applies only to the early Tolstóy.

His work falls into two distinct parts—before and after what has been called his "conversion." This was not only a religious and moral conversion, it was also a literary one, involving a complete change of literary method. The latter period, however, falls outside the scope of our present subject. The first period, covering the years 1852-77, again falls into two parts: a preparatory period and a period of fulfillment. The first is the period before War and Peace; the second is the period of War and Peace and Anna Karénina.

In the first period Tolstóy was only preparing himself for his great works. His first object in his writings then was the formation of a certain technique of analysis by which he could lay his finger on the mechanism of the psychological preparation of human action. It is amusing to note how he reveled in the classification of various types of character, especially in his Caucasian and Sevastopol stories. He was gradually perfecting an instrument of analysis which allowed him to go far deeper than anyone before him into the lower layers of consciousness. This gives him the specious appearance of a man who was particularly near to unreasoning life—which is a very easy but very bad fallacy.

In War and Peace this instrument of analysis is fully perfected and is only a means to an end, not an end in itself. Tolstóy placed his novel in an historical setting. This is one of the vital points of War and Peace. There have been many disputes as to the correctness of his view of Napoleon's character and actions, but besides his practical experience of war in the Russian army, he unquestionably had what is very important in dealing with history—an acute sense of the uninterrupted stream of happenings, of time! It is this placing of the family novel, based on a thoroughgoing explanatory analysis of action, in this stream of time, that gives War and Peace its peculiar place in the history of the novel. Tolstóy created something that may be said to be no longer a novel—it is the open form of the novel as opposed to the closed form. Flaubert in Madame Bovary was bringing the closed form to perfection. It had a beginning, a middle, and

an end, a single jet, ending in a definite solution of the conflicts inside the novel. Tolstóy in War and Peace transcends the limit of the novel and does what had previously been done by the epic. Thus War and Peace has to be put in a group not with Madame Bovary, Vanity Fair, or The Mill on the Floss, but with the Iliad, in the sense that when the novel is finished nothing is finished—the stream of life flows on, and with the appearance of Prince Andrew's son the novel ends on the beginning of a new life. All the time there are openings out of the story into the world beyond. This is a thing that had never been attempted by historical novelists before Tolstóy.

As for the open form, it has often been attempted, but never so successfully. In a very different way the open form was achieved by James Joyce in Ulysses. As Tolstóy is compared with the Iliad and the Odyssey, so critics say that Joyce's novel is of a mythological nature. John Galsworthy's Forsyte Saga and Arnold Bennett's The Old Wives' Tale may also claim to belong to the category of "open" novels.

No novel has received more enthusiastic praise both in Russia and England than War and Peace.

John Galsworthy spoke of it as "the greatest novel ever written," and those fine critics Percy Lubbock and E. M. Forster have been no less emphatic. In The Craft of Fiction Lubbock says that War and Peace is: "a picture of life that has never been surpassed for its grandeur and its beauty. . . . The business of the novelist is to create life, and here is life created indeed! In the whole of fiction no scene is so continually washed by the common air, free to us all, as the scene of Tolstóy, the supreme genius among novelists.

"Pierre and Andrew and Natásha and the rest of them are the children of yesterday and today and tomorrow; there is nothing in any of them that is not of all time. To an English reader of today it is curious—and more, it is strangely moving—to note how faithfully the creations of Tolstóy, the nineteenth-century Russian, copy the young people of the twentieth century and of England: it is all one, life in Moscow then, life in London now, provided only that it is young enough."

E. M. Forster in Aspects of the Novel says: "No English novelist is as great as Tolstóy, that is to say, has given so complete a picture of man's life, both on its domestic and heroic side.

"Cranford, The Heart of Midlothian, Jane Eyre, Richard Feverel—all four are little mansions not mighty edifices, and we shall see and respect them for what they are if we stand them for an instant in the colonnades of War and Peace. . . .

"Why is War and Peace not depressing? Probably because it has ex-

panded over space as well as time, and the sense of space, until it terrifies us, is exhilarating and leaves behind it an effect like music. After one has read War and Peace for a bit, great chords begin to sound . . . they come from the immense area of Russia, over which episodes and characters have been scattered, from the sum total of bridges, frozen rivers, forests, roads, gardens, fields, which accumulate grandeur and sonority after we have passed them. Many novelists have the feeling of time . . . very few have the sense of space, and the possession of it ranks high in Tolstóy's divine equipment. Space is the lord of War and Peace, not time. As we read it do not great chords begin to sound behind us, and when we have finished does not every item—even the catalogue of strategies—lead a larger existence than was possible at the time?"

De Vogüé, the greatest French authority on Russian literature, in Le Roman russe, remarks that: "It is easy to predict the impression that readers of War and Peace and Anna Karénina will receive. I have noticed that sequence among all those who have tasted of these books. At first, and for a fairly long time, their minds are confused, not knowing where they are being led, and they experience fatigue or—to put it bluntly—ennui. But little by little they are carried away and captivated by the complex play of all those interests, they secure a footing among all these people, find friends, become passionately interested in the secrets of their destinies, and on closing the book feel real regret, like that of parting from a family that has adopted them and with whom they have lived for years. It is a faithful picture of life: the experience of a traveler thrown among a society new to him—constraint and boredom at first, then curiosity and at last a firm attachment.

"I admit sotto voce that I know nothing superior to it in any literature."

What de Vogüé there says of the difficulty readers encounter when starting on the book is certainly sometimes true, and this is so partly because many people have forgotten the incidents of Napoleon's early career which were discussed at Anna Schérer's soiree—besides which, the number of Russian names mentioned proves perplexing. In the present edition, however, both these difficulties are mitigated, for the editor's notes supply the information necessary to enable the reader to understand the reference to the Duc d'Enghien's murder and to the other events alluded to, while the bookmarker which gives the names of the principal characters arranged in order of appearance should render it easier for readers to remember who is who.

Tolstóy's skill in driving his teams—the domestic and the historic—without letting them get entangled is very remarkable. He originally intended to tell the story of the Decembrist movement which culminated in

the émeute of 1825, and which was the disastrous forerunner of the "back to the people" movement of the seventies, and the revolutionary movements which eventually culminated in the downfall of the tsardom and the Revolution of 1917. But while studying the Decembrist conspiracy Tolstóy's thoughts went back to the period during which it had ripened—to the French invasion in 1812—and further back still to the Russian reverses which preceded that.

When dealing with the revolutionary spirit, and the secret Masonic movement in which it was germinating, he had to reckon with the censor, who had mutilated his first story, The Raid, as well as his Sevastopol sketches. This consideration had a hampering effect on the latter portion of the novel which extends from 1805, the year of Austerlitz, to the days when the influence of the Decembrist movement was already being felt.

The reader may wonder why Tolstóy was so interested in the Masonic movement and what connection it has with the main thread of the novel. In reality he was profoundly sensitive to the fundamental wrongness and consequent rottenness of the system under which everything depended on the wish and whim of an autocrat, and he felt a keen interest in the group which—though often rashly and with mixed motives—aimed at overthrowing the established order and replacing it by a better one. That this is not clearly expressed in the novel was, no doubt, due to the censor.

I feel almost ashamed, however, to allude to such a minor flaw in so great a story, and prefer to conclude this preface by quoting a remark made by a Chicago heiress, Miss Mary Landon Baker, who said: "I should like to live my life over again, in order to have once again the pleasure of reading War and Peace for the first time!"

The notes form an important feature of this edition, particularly—though not exclusively—for readers interested in the historical events mentioned. A number of political affairs are alluded to in the opening pages of the story and for that reason the first notes immediately follow this preface.

As readers often find the Russian names of the numerous characters in the book a difficulty, the stress accent has been marked on them throughout, though not on Polish names which always have it on the penultimate syllable. Readers should bear in mind that the letter ë is pronounced yo.

AYLMER MAUDE

NOTES TO THE OPENING CHAPTERS

Books One, Two, and Three of War and Peace deal with the campaign waged by Russia against the French in Austria, which ended with the battle of Austerlitz.

After the coup d'état of 18 Brumaire (November 9, 1799) Napoleon from a general in the service of the Revolutionary Directorate had become chief ruler of France under the title of First Consul. Three years later he became chief ruler for life, and two years after that (in December, 1804) was proclaimed Emperor of the French. Having already in his first Italian campaign in 1796-7 made himself, by the treaty of Campo Formio, master of northern Italy and the left bank of the Rhine, he strengthened and increased that position by the second Italian war in 1800. At first he encountered little serious opposition. Prussia and Austria, the neighbors most nearly concerned in his seizures, having already been repeatedly defeated, were afraid of him, and by the partition of Poland found compensation for the territories he seized.

Only two important opponents faced Napoleon—England and Russia. The young Tsar, Alexander I, realized the danger to Europe of Napoleon's ambitions but was hampered by the inertia of Prussia and Austria and at first proceeded cautiously, so that Napoleon first prepared to attack England. He seized Hanover, a possession of the British Crown, and in 1803 formed a great fortified camp at Boulogne where he could concentrate an army. In alliance with Spain he prepared a large fleet to cover the "Boulogne expedition" and make an invasion of England possible. The efforts of Admiral Villeneuve who was to have brought a fleet into the channel were, however, unsuccessful, and his fleet was destroyed by Nelson at Trafalgar in 1805. In 1804 an event had occurred which produced a great impression on the European courts and inclined them to action against Napoleon. Investigation of the Cadoudal-Pichegru conspiracy against Napoleon disclosed a connection with the Bourbons and, as was wrongly supposed, with their heir, L. A. M. de Bourbon Condé, Duc d'Enghien. Napoleon had the Duke seized on Baden territory by French mounted gendarmes, who crossed the Rhine secretly and brought him to the castle

of Vincennes near Paris, where he was shot after an irregular trial by a commission of French colonels acting under pressure.

In all the courts of Europe talk of "the martyrdom of the just one" was rife, but Alexander I was the only ruler who took action. The Russian ambassador left Paris, and the French ambassador left Petersburg. The conversations in June, 1805, in Anna Schérer's salon, with which War and Peace begins, are full of indignation against Napoleon on account of this execution. He is spoken of as a murderer, as Antichrist, and a usurper; no one speaks of him as Emperor, though he had assumed the throne half a year previously. They did not even speak of him as Napoleon, but merely as Bonaparte, or even Buonaparte, with ironic reference to his not being French but Corsican, by birth.

In June, 1805, this "villain" had added to the villainies which revolted Europe. First, in March, he had formed a Kingdom of Italy and had himself crowned King of Italy at Milan, and a little later he annexed the Republic of Genoa to France and formed the principality of Lucca, which he gave to his sister Elisa and her husband. This is referred to as fresh news in the first sentence of the book.

Anna Schérer wants Prince Vasíli to say that there will be war with France. Her anticipation was correct. The negotiations Alexander I had begun with the other European powers were drawing to a head. In March a treaty, negotiated by Novosíltsev, had been concluded with England which aimed at compelling Napoleon to withdraw his armies from Hanover and Italy and to acknowledge the independence of Holland and Switzerland. In May, General Wintzingerode had been sent to Austria with a plan of action by a fresh alliance of England, Russia, Sweden, Austria, and Naples. Prussia, which hesitated, was to be drawn in almost by force. The details of this plan are given in Book One, Chapter 15, where old Bolkónski and Prince Andrew discuss it.

Napoleon, having learned of the preparations against him and wishing to destroy the coalition, unexpectedly proposed peace to England. England asked Alexander to act as intermediary and the latter sent Novosíltsev to Paris to act as his representative. But on reaching Berlin in June Novosíltsev heard of the seizure of Genoa and did not proceed to Paris. War was now inevitable, and it soon broke out, though Prussia (whose ministers, Haugwitz and Hardenburg, are referred to) still avoided it.

In the first draft of the novel Tolstóy mentions the Abbé Piatoli by his real name, but afterwards changed it to Abbé Morio, assigning him a more important part. Piatoli had been at one time tutor to Adam Czartoryski, a friend and adviser of Alexander I and in close touch with him at that pe-

riod. Piatoli's project of perpetual peace, in which a prominent position was allotted to Russia, interested Petersburg for a while. It had some influence on Alexander's later plan of a Holy Alliance and should be counted among the many projects and suggestions that gradually led up to the League of Nations.

The old Prince Bolkónski, described in a later chapter, was drawn from Tolstóy's grandfather, Prince N. S. Volkónski, a general of Catherine the Great's time. Tolstóy's father married his only daughter. Volkónski had no son, and Prince Andrew of the novel is a type created by Tolstóy, to which he attributed some aspects of himself as well as some characteristics of his elder brother, Sergius Tolstóy. Another side of Tolstóy is allotted in the novel to Pierre.

AYLMER MAUDE

DATES OF PRINCIPAL HISTORICAL EVENTS

OLD STYLE	NEW STYLE	1805
Oct. 11	Oct. 23	Kutúzov inspects regiment near Braunau. *Le malheureux Mack* arrives.
Oct. 23	Nov. 4	The Russian army crosses the Enns.
Oct. 24	Nov. 5	Fight at Amstetten.
Oct. 28	Nov. 9	The Russian army crosses the Danube.
Oct. 30	Nov. 11	Defeats Mortier at Dürrenstein.
Nov. 4	Nov. 16	Napoleon writes to Murat from Schönbrunn.
Nov. 4	Nov. 16	Battle of Schön Grabern.
Nov. 19	Dec. 1	The Council of War at Ostralitz.
Nov. 20	Dec. 2	Battle of Austerlitz.

		1807
Jan. 27	Feb. 8	Battle of Preussisch-Eylau.
June 2	June 14	Battle of Friedland.
June 13	June 25	The Emperors meet at Tilsit.

		1812
May 17	May 29	Napoleon leaves Dresden.
June 12	June 24	Napoleon crosses the Niemen and enters Russia.
June 14	June 26	Alexander sends Balashëv to Napoleon.
July 13	July 25	The Pávlograd hussars in action at Ostróvna.
Aug. 4	Aug. 16	Alpátych at Smolénsk hears distant firing.
Aug. 5	Aug. 17	Bombardment of Smolénsk.
Aug. 7	Aug. 19	Prince Nicholas Bolkónski leaves Bald Hills for Boguchárovo.
Aug. 8	Aug. 20	Kutúzov appointed Commander in Chief.
Aug. 10	Aug. 22	Prince Andrew's column abreast of Bald Hills.
Aug. 17	Aug. 29	Kutúzov reaches Tsárevo-Zaymíshche and takes command of the army.
Aug. 17	Aug. 29	Nicholas Rostóv rides to Boguchárovo.
Aug. 24	Sept. 5	Battle of the Shevárdino Redoubt.
Aug. 26	Sept. 7	Battle of Borodinó.
Sept. 1	Sept. 13	Kutúzov orders retreat through Moscow.
Oct. 6	Oct. 18	Battle of Tarútino.
Oct. 6, 7, and 8	Oct. 18, 19, and 20	The French leave Moscow.
Oct. 12	Oct. 24	Battle of Málo-Yaroslávets.
Oct. 21	Nov. 2	Cossacks harry the French at Vyázma.
Oct. 28- Nov. 2	Nov. 9- Nov. 14	The French at Smolénsk.
Nov. 4-8	Nov. 16-20	Battles at Krásnoe.
Nov. 9	Nov. 21	Ney, with rearguard, reaches Orshá.
Nov. 14-16	Nov. 26-28	Crossing of the Berëzina.
Nov. 23	Dec. 5	Napoleon abandons the army at Smorgóni.
Dec. 6	Dec. 18	He reaches Paris.

WAR and PEACE

PEACE

LEO TOLSTOY

BOOK ONE

1805

BOOK ONE

1. Anna Schérer's soiree

WELL, PRINCE, so Genoa and Lucca are now just family estates of the Buonapartes. But I warn you, if you don't tell me that this means war, if you still try to defend the infamies and horrors perpetrated by that Antichrist—I really believe he is Antichrist—I will have nothing more to do with you and you are no longer my friend, no longer my 'faithful slave,' as you call yourself! But how do you do? I see I have frightened you—sit down and tell me all the news."

It was in July, 1805, and the speaker was the well-known Anna Pávlovna Schérer, maid of honor and favorite of the Empress Márya Fëdorovna. With these words she greeted Prince Vasíli Kurágin, a man of high rank and importance, who was the first to arrive at her reception. Anna Pávlovna had had a cough for some days. She was, as she said, suffering from la grippe; grippe being then a new word in St. Petersburg,* used only by the elite.

All her invitations without exception, written in French, and delivered by a scarlet-liveried footman that morning, ran as follows:

"If you have nothing better to do, Count [or Prince], and if the prospect of spending an evening with a poor invalid is not too terrible, I shall be very charmed to see you tonight between 7 and 10—Annette Schérer."

"Heavens! what a virulent attack!" replied the prince, not in the least disconcerted by this reception. He had just entered, wearing an embroidered court uniform, knee breeches, and shoes, and had stars on his breast and a serene expression on his flat face. He spoke in that refined French in which our grandfathers not only spoke but thought, and with the gentle, patronizing intonation natural to a man of importance who had grown old in society and at court. He went up to Anna Pávlovna, kissed her hand, presenting to her his bald, scented, and shining head, and complacently seated himself on the sofa.

* Now Leningrad.

3

"First of all, dear friend, tell me how you are. Set your friend's mind at rest," said he without altering his tone, beneath the politeness and affected sympathy of which indifference and even irony could be discerned.

"Can one be well while suffering morally? Can one be calm in times like these if one has any feeling?" said Anna Pávlovna. "You are staying the whole evening, I hope?"

"And the fete at the English ambassador's? Today is Wednesday. I must put in an appearance there," said the prince. "My daughter is coming for me to take me there."

"I thought today's fete had been canceled. I confess all these festivities and fireworks are becoming wearisome."

"If they had known that you wished it, the entertainment would have been put off," said the prince, who, like a wound-up clock, by force of habit said things he did not even wish to be believed.

"Don't tease! Well, and what has been decided about Novosíltsev's dispatch? You know everything."

"What can one say about it?" replied the prince in a cold, listless tone. "What has been decided? They have decided that Buonaparte has burnt his boats, and I believe that we are ready to burn ours."

Prince Vasíli always spoke languidly, like an actor repeating a stale part. Anna Pávlovna Schérer on the contrary, despite her forty years, overflowed with animation and impulsiveness. To be an enthusiast had become her social vocation and, sometimes even when she did not feel like it, she became enthusiastic in order not to disappoint the expectations of those who knew her. The subdued smile which, though it did not suit her faded features, always played round her lips expressed, as in a spoiled child, a continual consciousness of her charming defect, which she neither wished, nor could, nor considered it necessary, to correct.

In the midst of a conversation on political matters Anna Pávlovna burst out:

"Oh, don't speak to me of Austria. Perhaps I don't understand things, but Austria never has wished, and does not wish, for war. She is betraying us! Russia alone must save Europe. Our gracious sovereign recognizes his high vocation and will be true to it. That is the one thing I have faith in! Our good and wonderful sovereign has to perform the noblest role on earth, and he is so virtuous and noble that God will not forsake him. He will fulfill his vocation and crush the hydra of revolution, which has become more terrible than ever in the person of this murderer and villain! We alone must avenge the blood of the just one. . . . Whom, I ask you, can we rely on? . . . England with her commercial spirit will not and cannot understand the Emperor Alexander's loftiness of soul. She has

refused to evacuate Malta. She wanted to find, and still seeks, some secret motive in our actions. What answer did Novosíltsev get? None. The English have not understood and cannot understand the self-abnegation of our Emperor who wants nothing for himself, but only desires the good of mankind. And what have they promised? Nothing! And what little they have promised they will not perform! Prussia has always declared that Buonaparte is invincible and that all Europe is powerless before him. . . . And I don't believe a word that Hardenburg says, or Haugwitz either. This famous Prussian neutrality is just a trap. I have faith only in God and the lofty destiny of our adored monarch. He will save Europe!"

She suddenly paused, smiling at her own impetuosity.

"I think," said the prince with a smile, "that if you had been sent instead of our dear Wintzingerode you would have captured the King of Prussia's consent by assault. You are so eloquent. Will you give me a cup of tea?"

"In a moment. À propos," she added, becoming calm again, "I am expecting two very interesting men tonight, le Vicomte de Mortemart, who is connected with the Montmorencys through the Rohans, one of the best French families. He is one of the genuine émigrés, the good ones. And also the Abbé Morio. Do you know that profound thinker? He has been received by the Emperor. Had you heard?"

"I shall be delighted to meet them," said the prince. "But tell me," he added with studied carelessness as if it had only just occurred to him, though the question he was about to ask was the chief motive of his visit, "is it true that the Dowager Empress wants Baron Funke to be appointed first secretary at Vienna? The baron by all accounts is a poor creature."

Prince Vasíli wished to obtain this post for his son, but others were trying through the Dowager Empress Márya Fëdorovna to secure it for the baron.

Anna Pávlovna almost closed her eyes to indicate that neither she nor anyone else had a right to criticize what the Empress desired or was pleased with.

"Baron Funke has been recommended to the Dowager Empress by her sister," was all she said, in a dry and mournful tone.

As she named the Empress, Anna Pávlovna's face suddenly assumed an expression of profound and sincere devotion and respect mingled with sadness, and this occurred every time she mentioned her illustrious patroness. She added that Her Majesty had deigned to show Baron Funke beaucoup d'estime, and again her face clouded over with sadness.

The prince was silent and looked indifferent. But, with the womanly and courtierlike quickness and tact habitual to her, Anna Pávlovna wished

both to rebuke him (for daring to speak as he had done of a man recommended to the Empress) and at the same time to console him, so she said:

"Now about your family. Do you know that since your daughter came out everyone has been enraptured by her? They say she is amazingly beautiful."

The prince bowed to signify his respect and gratitude.

"I often think," she continued after a short pause, drawing nearer to the prince and smiling amiably at him as if to show that political and social topics were ended and the time had come for intimate conversation—"I often think how unfairly sometimes the joys of life are distributed. Why has fate given you two such splendid children? I don't speak of Anatole, your youngest. I don't like him," she added in a tone admitting of no rejoinder and raising her eyebrows. "Two such charming children. And really you appreciate them less than anyone, and so you don't deserve to have them."

And she smiled her ecstatic smile.

"I can't help it," said the prince. "Lavater * would have said I lack the bump of paternity."

"Don't joke; I mean to have a serious talk with you. Do you know I am dissatisfied with your younger son? Between ourselves" (and her face assumed its melancholy expression), "he was mentioned at Her Majesty's and you were pitied. . . ."

The prince answered nothing, but she looked at him significantly, awaiting a reply. He frowned.

"What would you have me do?" he said at last. "You know I did all a father could for their education, and they have both turned out fools. Hippolyte is at least a quiet fool, but Anatole is an active one. That is the only difference between them." He said this smiling in a way more natural and animated than usual, so that the wrinkles round his mouth very clearly revealed something unexpectedly coarse and unpleasant.

"And why are children born to such men as you? If you were not a father there would be nothing I could reproach you with," said Anna Pávlovna, looking up pensively.

"I am your faithful slave and to you alone I can confess that my children are the bane of my life. It is the cross I have to bear. That is how I explain it to myself. It can't be helped!"

He said no more, but expressed his resignation to cruel fate by a gesture. Anna Pávlovna meditated.

"Have you never thought of marrying your prodigal son Anatole?" she

* Johann Kaspar Lavater (1741-1801) was a Swiss clergyman and physician who related physiognomy to mental attributes.

asked. "They say old maids have a mania for matchmaking, and though I
don't feel that weakness in myself as yet, I know a little person who is very
unhappy with her father. She is a relation of yours, Princess Mary Bol-
kónskaya."

Prince Vasíli did not reply though, with the quickness of memory and
perception befitting a man of the world, he indicated by a movement of
the head that he was considering this information.

"Do you know," he said at last, evidently unable to check the sad cur-
rent of his thoughts, "that Anatole is costing me forty thousand rubles a
year? And," he went on after a pause, "what will it be in five years, if he
goes on like this?" Presently he added: "That's what we fathers have to
put up with. . . . Is this princess of yours rich?"

"Her father is very rich and stingy. He lives in the country. He is the
well-known Prince Bolkónski who had to retire from the army under the
late Emperor, and was nicknamed 'the King of Prussia.' He is very clever
but eccentric, and a bore. The poor girl is very unhappy. She has a brother;
I think you know him, he married Lise Meinen lately. He is an aide-de-
camp of Kutúzov's and will be here tonight."

"Listen, dear Annette," said the prince, suddenly taking Anna Pávlov-
na's hand and for some reason drawing it downwards. "Arrange that affair
for me and I shall always be your most devoted slave—*slafe* with an f, as a
village elder of mine writes in his reports. She is rich and of good family
and that's all I want."

And with the familiarity and easy grace peculiar to him, he raised the
maid of honor's hand to his lips, kissed it, and swung it to and fro as he
lay back in his armchair, looking in another direction.

"*Attendez*," said Anna Pávlovna, reflecting, "I'll speak to Lise, young
Bolkónski's wife, this very evening, and perhaps the thing can be arranged.
It shall be on your family's behalf that I'll start my apprenticeship as old
maid."

ANNA PÁVLOVNA's drawing room was gradually filling. The highest Peters-
burg society was assembled there: people differing widely in age and char-
acter but alike in the social circle to which they belonged. Prince Vasíli's
daughter, the beautiful Hélène, came to take her father to the ambassa-
dor's entertainment; she wore a ball dress and her badge as maid of honor.
The youthful little Princess Bolkónskaya,* known as *la femme la plus
séduisante de Pétersbourg* [the most fascinating woman in Petersburg],
was also there. She had been married during the previous winter, and be-
ing pregnant did not go to any large gatherings, but only to small recep-

* *Sister-in-law of the Princess Mary Bolkónskaya just mentioned.*

tions. Prince Vasíli's son, Hippolyte, had come with Mortemart, whom he introduced. The Abbé Morio and many others had also come.

To each new arrival Anna Pávlovna said, "You have not yet seen my aunt," or "You do not know my aunt?" and very gravely conducted him or her to a little old lady, wearing large bows of ribbon in her cap, who had come sailing in from another room as soon as the guests began to arrive; and slowly turning her eyes from the visitor to her aunt, Anna Pávlovna mentioned each one's name and then left them.

Each visitor performed the ceremony of greeting this old aunt whom not one of them knew, not one of them wanted to know, and not one of them cared about; Anna Pávlovna observed these greetings with mournful and solemn interest and silent approval. The aunt spoke to each of them in the same words, about their health and her own, and the health of Her Majesty, "who, thank God, was better today." And each visitor, though politeness prevented his showing impatience, left the old woman with a sense of relief at having performed a vexatious duty and did not return to her the whole evening.

The young Princess Bolkónskaya had brought some work in a gold-embroidered velvet bag. Her pretty little upper lip, on which a delicate dark down was just perceptible, was too short for her teeth, but it lifted all the more sweetly, and was especially charming when she occasionally drew it down to meet the lower lip. As is always the case with a thoroughly attractive woman, her defect—the shortness of her upper lip and her half-open mouth—seemed to be her own special and peculiar form of beauty. Everyone brightened at the sight of this pretty young woman, so soon to become a mother, so full of life and health, and carrying her burden so lightly. Old men and dull dispirited young ones who looked at her, after being in her company and talking to her a little while, felt as if they too were becoming, like her, full of life and health. All who talked to her, and at each word saw her bright smile and the constant gleam of her white teeth, thought that they were in a specially amiable mood that day.

The little princess went round the table with quick, short, swaying steps, her workbag on her arm, and gaily spreading out her dress sat down on a sofa near the silver samovar, as if all she was doing was a pleasure to herself and to all around her. "I have brought my work," said she in French, displaying her bag and addressing all present. "Mind, Annette, I hope you have not played a wicked trick on me," she added, turning to her hostess. "You wrote that it was to be quite a small reception, and just see how badly I am dressed." And she spread out her arms to show her short-waisted, lace-trimmed, dainty gray dress, girdled with a broad ribbon just below the breast.

"*Soyez tranquille, Lise,* you will always be prettier than anyone else," replied Anna Pávlovna.

"You know," said the princess in the same tone of voice and still in French, turning to a general, "my husband is deserting me? He is going to get himself killed. Tell me what this wretched war is for?" she added, addressing Prince Vasíli, and without waiting for an answer she turned to speak to his daughter, the beautiful Hélène.

"What a delightful woman this little princess is!" said Prince Vasíli to Anna Pávlovna.

One of the next arrivals was a stout, heavily built young man with close-cropped hair, spectacles, the light-colored breeches fashionable at that time, a very high ruffle, and a brown dress coat. This stout young man was an illegitimate son of Count Bezúkhov, a well-known grandee of Catherine's time who now lay dying in Moscow. The young man had not yet entered either the military or civil service, as he had only just returned from abroad where he had been educated, and this was his first appearance in society. Anna Pávlovna greeted him with the nod she accorded to the lowest hierarchy in her drawing room. But in spite of this lowest-grade greeting, a look of anxiety and fear, as at the sight of something too large and unsuited to the place, came over her face when she saw Pierre * enter. Though he was certainly rather bigger than the other men in the room, her anxiety could only have reference to the clever though shy, but observant and natural, expression which distinguished him from everyone else in that drawing room.

"It is very good of you, Monsieur Pierre, to come and visit a poor invalid," said Anna Pávlovna, exchanging an alarmed glance with her aunt as she conducted him to her.

Pierre murmured something unintelligible, and continued to look round as if in search of something. On his way to the aunt he bowed to the little princess with a pleased smile, as to an intimate acquaintance.

Anna Pávlovna's alarm was justified, for Pierre turned away from the aunt without waiting to hear her speech about Her Majesty's health. Anna Pávlovna in dismay detained him with the words: "Do you know the Abbé Morio? He is a most interesting man."

"Yes, I have heard of his scheme for perpetual peace, and it is very interesting but hardly feasible."

"You think so?" rejoined Anna Pávlovna in order to say something and get away to attend to her duties as hostess. But Pierre now committed a reverse act of impoliteness. First he had left a lady before she had finished

* *Count Pierre Bezúkhov is one of the two main characters in* War and Peace.

speaking to him, and now he continued to speak to another who wished to get away. With his head bent, and his big feet spread apart, he began explaining his reasons for thinking the abbé's plan chimerical.

"We will talk of it later," said Anna Pávlovna with a smile.

And having got rid of this young man who did not know how to behave, she resumed her duties as hostess and continued to listen and watch, ready to help at any point where the conversation might happen to flag. As the foreman of a spinning mill, when he has set the hands to work, goes round and notices here a spindle that has stopped or there one that creaks or makes more noise than it should, and hastens to check the machine or set it in proper motion, so Anna Pávlovna moved about her drawing room, approaching now a silent, now a too-noisy group, and by a word or slight rearrangement kept the conversational machine in steady, proper, and regular motion. But amid these cares her anxiety about Pierre was evident. She kept an anxious watch on him when he approached the group round Mortemart to listen to what was being said there, and again when he passed to another group whose center was the abbé.

Pierre had been educated abroad, and this reception at Anna Pávlovna's was the first he had attended in Russia. He knew that all the intellectual lights of Petersburg were gathered there and, like a child in a toyshop, did not know which way to look, afraid of missing any clever conversation that was to be heard. Seeing the self-confident and refined expression on the faces of those present he was always expecting to hear something very profound. At last he came up to Morio. Here the conversation seemed interesting and he stood waiting for an opportunity to express his own views, as young people are fond of doing.

Anna Pávlovna's reception was in full swing. The spindles hummed steadily and ceaselessly on all sides. With the exception of the aunt, beside whom sat only one elderly lady, who with her thin careworn face was rather out of place in this brilliant society, the whole company had settled into three groups. One, chiefly masculine, had formed round the abbé. Another, of young people, was grouped round the beautiful Princess Hélène, Prince Vasíli's daughter, and the little Princess Bolkónskaya, very pretty and rosy, though rather too plump for her age. The third group was gathered round Mortemart and Anna Pávlovna.

The vicomte was a nice-looking young man with soft features and polished manners, who evidently considered himself a celebrity but out of politeness modestly placed himself at the disposal of the circle in which he found himself. Anna Pávlovna was obviously serving him up as a treat to her guests. As a clever maître d'hôtel serves up as a specially choice

delicacy a piece of meat that no one who had seen it in the kitchen would have cared to eat, so Anna Pávlovna served up to her guests, first the vicomte and then the abbé, as peculiarly choice morsels. The group about Mortemart immediately began discussing the murder of the Duc d'Enghien.* The vicomte said that the Duc d'Enghien had perished by his own magnanimity, and that there were particular reasons for Buonaparte's hatred of him.

"Ah, yes! Do tell us all about it, Vicomte," said Anna Pávlovna, with a pleasant feeling that there was something à la Louis XV in the sound of that sentence: "Contez nous çela, Vicomte."

The vicomte bowed and smiled courteously in token of his willingness to comply. Anna Pávlovna arranged a group round him, inviting everyone to listen to his tale.

"The vicomte knew the duc personally," whispered Anna Pávlovna to one of the guests. "The vicomte is a wonderful raconteur," said she to another. "How evidently he belongs to the best society," said she to a third; and the vicomte was served up to the company in the choicest and most advantageous style, like a well-garnished joint of roast beef on a hot dish.

The vicomte wished to begin his story and gave a subtle smile.

"Come over here, Hélène, dear," said Anna Pávlovna to the beautiful young princess who was sitting some way off, the center of another group.

The princess smiled. She rose with the same unchanging smile with which she had first entered the room—the smile of a perfectly beautiful woman. With a slight rustle of her white dress trimmed with moss and ivy, with a gleam of white shoulders, glossy hair, and sparkling diamonds, she passed between the men who made way for her, not looking at any of them but smiling on all, as if graciously allowing each the privilege of admiring her beautiful figure and shapely shoulders, back, and bosom—which in the fashion of those days were very much exposed—and she seemed to bring the glamour of a ballroom with her as she moved toward Anna Pávlovna. Hélène was so lovely that not only did she not show any trace of coquetry, but on the contrary she even appeared shy of her unquestionable and all too victorious beauty. She seemed to wish, but to be unable, to diminish its effect.

"How lovely!" said everyone who saw her; and the vicomte lifted his shoulders and dropped his eyes as if startled by something extraordinary when she took her seat opposite and beamed upon him also with her unchanging smile.

* The Duc d'Enghien had been charged with conspiracy to assassinate Napoleon, had been found guilty, and had been executed at Vincennes on March 21, 1804.

"Madame, I doubt my ability before such an audience," said he, smilingly inclining his head.

The princess rested her bare round arm on a little table and considered a reply unnecessary. She smilingly waited. All the time the story was being told she sat upright, glancing now at her beautiful round arm, altered in shape by its pressure on the table, now at her still more beautiful bosom, on which she readjusted a diamond necklace. From time to time she smoothed the folds of her dress, and whenever the story produced an effect she glanced at Anna Pávlovna, at once adopted just the expression she saw on the maid of honor's face, and again relapsed into her radiant smile.

The little princess had also left the tea table and followed Hélène.

"Wait a moment, I'll get my work. . . . Now then, what are you thinking of?" she went on, turning to Prince Hippolyte. "Fetch me my workbag."

There was a general movement as the princess, smiling and talking merrily to everyone at once, sat down and gaily arranged herself in her seat.

"Now I am all right," she said, and asking the vicomte to begin, she took up her work.

Prince Hippolyte, having brought the workbag, joined the circle and moving a chair close to hers seated himself beside her.

Le charmant Hippolyte was surprising by his extraordinary resemblance to his beautiful sister, but yet more by the fact that in spite of this resemblance he was exceedingly ugly. His features were like his sister's, but while in her case everything was lit up by a joyous, self-satisfied, youthful, and constant smile of animation, and by the wonderful classic beauty of her figure, his face on the contrary was dulled by imbecility and a constant expression of sullen self-confidence, while his body was thin and weak. His eyes, nose, and mouth all seemed puckered into a vacant, wearied grimace, and his arms and legs always fell into unnatural positions.

"It's not going to be a ghost story?" said he, sitting down beside the princess and hastily adjusting his lorgnette, as if without this instrument he could not begin to speak.

"Why no, my dear fellow," said the astonished narrator, shrugging his shoulders.

"Because I hate ghost stories," said Prince Hippolyte in a tone which showed that he only understood the meaning of his words after he had uttered them.

He spoke with such self-confidence that his hearers could not be sure whether what he said was very witty or very stupid. He was dressed in a dark-green dress coat, knee breeches of the color of cuisse de nymphe effrayée, as he called it, shoes, and silk stockings.

The vicomte told his tale very neatly. It was an anecdote, then current, to the effect that the Duc d'Enghien had gone secretly to Paris to visit Mademoiselle George; * that at her house he came upon Bonaparte, who also enjoyed the famous actress' favors, and that in his presence Napoleon happened to fall into one of the fainting fits to which he was subject, and was thus at the duc's mercy. The latter spared him, and this magnanimity Bonaparte subsequently repaid by death.

The story was very pretty and interesting, especially at the point where the rivals suddenly recognized one another; and the ladies looked agitated.

"Charming!" said Anna Pávlovna with an inquiring glance at the little princess.

"Charming!" whispered the little princess, sticking the needle into her work as if to testify that the interest and fascination of the story prevented her from going on with it.

The vicomte appreciated this silent praise and smiling gratefully prepared to continue, but just then Anna Pávlovna, who had kept a watchful eye on the young man who so alarmed her, noticed that he was talking too loudly and vehemently with the abbé, so she hurried to the rescue. Pierre had managed to start a conversation with the abbé about the balance of power, and the latter, evidently interested by the young man's simple-minded eagerness, was explaining his pet theory. Both were talking and listening too eagerly and too naturally, which was why Anna Pávlovna disapproved.

"The means are . . . the balance of power in Europe and the rights of the people," the abbé was saying. "It is only necessary for one powerful nation like Russia—barbaric as she is said to be—to place herself disinterestedly at the head of an alliance having for its object the maintenance of the balance of power in Europe, and it would save the world!"

"But how are you to get that balance?" Pierre was beginning.

At that moment Anna Pávlovna came up and, looking severely at Pierre, asked the Italian how he stood the Russian climate. The Italian's face instantly changed and assumed an offensively affected, sugary expression, evidently habitual to him when conversing with women.

"I am so enchanted by the brilliancy of the wit and culture of the society, more especially of the feminine society, in which I have had the honor of being received, that I have not yet had time to think of the climate," said he.

* *Mademoiselle George appears in person later on in the novel. She was a great tragic actress, who was for some years Napoleon's mistress. In 1808 she went to Petersburg where she had much success, and it was then that Natásha heard her declaim in Hélène's salon, as described later.*—A.M.

Not letting the abbé and Pierre escape, Anna Pávlovna, the more conveniently to keep them under observation, brought them into the larger circle.

JUST THEN another visitor entered the drawing room: Prince Andrew Bolkónski, the little princess' husband. He was a very handsome young man, of medium height, with firm, clear-cut features. Everything about him, from his weary, bored expression to his quiet, measured step, offered a most striking contrast to his lively little wife. It was evident that he not only knew everyone in the drawing room, but had found them to be so tiresome that it wearied him to look at or listen to them. And among all these faces that he found so tedious, none seemed to bore him so much as that of his pretty wife. He turned away from her with a grimace that distorted his handsome face, kissed Anna Pávlovna's hand, and screwing up his eyes scanned the whole company.

"You are off to the war, Prince?" said Anna Pávlovna.

"General Kutúzov," said Bolkónski, speaking French and stressing the last syllable of the general's name like a Frenchman, "has been pleased to take me as an aide-de-camp. . . ."

"And Lise, your wife?"

"She will go to the country."

"Are you not ashamed to deprive us of your charming wife?"

"André," said his wife, addressing her husband in the same coquettish manner in which she spoke to other men, "the vicomte has been telling us such a tale about Mademoiselle George and Buonaparte!"

Prince Andrew screwed up his eyes and turned away. Pierre, who from the moment Prince Andrew entered the room had watched him with glad, affectionate eyes, now came up and took his arm. Before he looked round Prince Andrew frowned again, expressing his annoyance with whoever was touching his arm, but when he saw Pierre's beaming face he gave him an unexpectedly kind and pleasant smile.

"There now! . . . So you, too, are in the great world?" said he to Pierre.

"I knew you would be here," replied Pierre. "I will come to supper with you. May I?" he added in a low voice so as not to disturb the vicomte who was continuing his story.

"No, impossible!" said Prince Andrew, laughing and pressing Pierre's hand to show that there was no need to ask the question. He wished to say something more, but at that moment Prince Vasíli and his daughter got up to go and the two young men rose to let them pass.

"You must excuse me, dear Vicomte," said Prince Vasíli to the Frenchman, holding him down by the sleeve in a friendly way to prevent his ris-

ing. "This unfortunate fete at the ambassador's deprives me of a pleasure, and obliges me to interrupt you. I am very sorry to leave your enchanting party," said he, turning to Anna Pávlovna.

His daughter, Princess Hélène, passed between the chairs, lightly holding up the folds of her dress, and the smile shone still more radiantly on her beautiful face. Pierre gazed at her with rapturous, almost frightened, eyes as she passed him.

"Very lovely," said Prince Andrew.

"Very," said Pierre.

In passing, Prince Vasíli seized Pierre's hand and said to Anna Pávlovna: "Educate this bear for me! He has been staying with me a whole month and this is the first time I have seen him in society. Nothing is so necessary for a young man as the society of clever women."

ANNA PÁVLOVNA smiled and promised to take Pierre in hand. She knew his father to be a connection of Prince Vasíli's. The elderly lady who had been sitting with the old aunt rose hurriedly and overtook Prince Vasíli in the anteroom. All the affectation of interest she had assumed had left her kindly and tear-worn face and it now expressed only anxiety and fear.

"How about my son Borís, Prince?" said she, hurrying after him into the anteroom. "I can't remain any longer in Petersburg. Tell me what news I may take back to my poor boy."

Although Prince Vasíli listened reluctantly and not very politely to the elderly lady, even betraying some impatience, she gave him an ingratiating and appealing smile, and took his hand that he might not go away.

"What would it cost you to say a word to the Emperor, and then he would be transferred to the Guards at once?" said she.

"Believe me, Princess, I am ready to do all I can," answered Prince Vasíli, "but it is difficult for me to ask the Emperor. I should advise you to appeal to Rumyántsev through Prince Golítsyn. That would be the best way."

The elderly lady was a Princess Drubetskáya, belonging to one of the best families in Russia, but she was poor, and having long been out of society had lost her former influential connections. She had now come to Petersburg to procure an appointment in the Guards for her only son. It was, in fact, solely to meet Prince Vasíli that she had obtained an invitation to Anna Pávlovna's reception and had sat listening to the vicomte's story. Prince Vasíli's words frightened her, an embittered look clouded her once handsome face, but only for a moment; then she smiled again and clutched Prince Vasíli's arm more tightly.

"Listen to me, Prince," said she. "I have never yet asked you for anything and I never will again, nor have I ever reminded you of my father's

friendship for you; but now I entreat you for God's sake to do this for my son—and I shall always regard you as a benefactor," she added hurriedly. "No, don't be angry, but promise! I have asked Golítsyn and he has refused. Be the kindhearted man you always were," she said, trying to smile though tears were in her eyes.

"Papa, we shall be late," said Princess Hélène, turning her beautiful head and looking over her classically molded shoulder as she stood waiting by the door.

Influence in society, however, is capital which has to be economized if it is to last. Prince Vasíli knew this, and having once realized that if he asked on behalf of all who begged of him, he would soon be unable to ask for himself, he became chary of using his influence. But in Princess Drubetskáya's case he felt, after her second appeal, something like qualms of conscience. She had reminded him of what was quite true; he had been indebted to her father for the first steps in his career. Moreover, he could see by her manners that she was one of those women—mostly mothers—who, having once made up their minds, will not rest until they have gained their end, and are prepared if necessary to go on insisting day after day and hour after hour, and even to make scenes. This last consideration moved him.

"My dear Anna Mikháylovna," said he with his usual familiarity and weariness of tone, "it is almost impossible for me to do what you ask; but to prove my devotion to you and how I respect your father's memory, I will do the impossible—your son shall be transferred to the Guards. Here is my hand on it. Are you satisfied?"

"My dear benefactor! This is what I expected from you—I knew your kindness!" He turned to go.

"Wait—just a word! When he has been transferred to the Guards . . ." she faltered. "You are on good terms with Michael Ilariónovich Kutúzov * . . . recommend Borís to him as adjutant! Then I shall be at rest, and then . . ."

Prince Vasíli smiled.

"No, I won't promise that. You don't know how Kutúzov is pestered since his appointment as Commander in Chief. He told me himself that all the

* In 1805 M. I. Kutúzov (1745-1813) *already enjoyed a great military reputation. He had taken part in the Turkish wars in Catherine's reign and together with Suvórov had captured the fortresses of Ochákov and Ismail, but was seriously wounded and lost an eye. Having displeased Alexander in the post of Governor General of Petersburg, he had been living for three years in disfavor in the country, but was now recalled to lead an army of 50,000 men to the aid of Austria.*—A.M.

Moscow ladies have conspired to give him all their sons as adjutants."

"No, but do promise! I won't let you go! My dear benefactor . . ."

"Papa," said his beautiful daughter in the same tone as before, "we shall be late."

"Well, au revoir! Good-by! You hear her?"

"Then tomorrow you will speak to the Emperor?"

"Certainly; but about Kutúzov, I don't promise."

"Do promise, do promise, Vasíli!" cried Anna Mikháylovna as he went, with the smile of a coquettish girl, which at one time probably came naturally to her, but was now very ill-suited to her careworn face.

Apparently she had forgotten her age and by force of habit employed all the old feminine arts. But as soon as the prince had gone her face resumed its former cold, artificial expression. She returned to the group where the vicomte was still talking, and again pretended to listen, while waiting till it would be time to leave. Her task was accomplished.

"And what do you think of this latest comedy, the coronation at Milan?" * asked Anna Pávlovna, "and of the comedy of the people of Genoa and Lucca laying their petitions before Monsieur Buonaparte, and Monsieur Buonaparte sitting on a throne and granting the petitions of the nations? Adorable! It is enough to make one's head whirl! It is as if the whole world had gone crazy."

Prince Andrew looked Anna Pávlovna straight in the face with a sarcastic smile.

" 'Dieu me la donne, gare à qui la touche!' [God has given it to me, let him who touches it beware!] [Bonaparte's words at his coronation.] They say he was very fine when he said that," he remarked, repeating the words in Italian: " 'Dio mi l'ha dato. Guai a chi la tocchi!' "

"I hope this will prove the last drop that will make the glass run over," Anna Pávlovna continued. "The sovereigns will not be able to endure this man who is a menace to everything."

"The sovereigns? I do not speak of Russia," said the vicomte, polite but hopeless: "The sovereigns, madame . . . What have they done for Louis XVII, for the Queen, or for Madame Elizabeth? ² Nothing!" and he

* Napoleon had crowned himself King of Italy at Milan on May 26, 1805.

² The Vicomte de Mortemart refers to the fact that the sovereigns of Europe had saved neither the son, the wife, nor the sister of Louis XVI from execution or death in prison. An obvious mistake in the Russian text, as well as in previous translations, obscures this meaning by mentioning Louis XVIII (who was still alive, and reigned in France for ten years from 1815 onwards) in place of Louis XVII—the son of Louis XVI—who is said to have died in prison.—A.M.

became more animated. "And believe me, they are reaping the reward of their betrayal of the Bourbon cause. The sovereigns! Why, they are sending ambassadors to compliment the usurper."

And sighing disdainfully, he again changed his position.

Prince Hippolyte, who had been gazing at the vicomte for some time through his lorgnette, suddenly turned completely round toward the little princess, and having asked for a needle began tracing the Condé coat of arms on the table. He explained this to her with as much gravity as if she had asked him to do it.

"*Bâton de gueules, engrêlé de gueules d' azur—maison Condé,*" * said he.

The princess listened, smiling.

"If Buonaparte remains on the throne of France a year longer," the vicomte continued, with the air of a man who, in a matter with which he is better acquainted than anyone else, does not listen to others but follows the current of his own thoughts, "things will have gone too far. By intrigues, violence, exile, and executions, French society—I mean good French society—will have been forever destroyed, and then . . ."

He shrugged his shoulders and spread out his hands. Pierre wished to make a remark, for the conversation interested him, but Anna Pávlovna, who had him under observation, interrupted:

"The Emperor Alexander," said she, with the melancholy which always accompanied any reference of hers to the Imperial family, "has declared that he will leave it to the French people themselves to choose their own form of government; and I believe that once free from the usurper, the whole nation will certainly throw itself into the arms of its rightful king," she concluded, trying to be amiable to the royalist emigrant.

"That is doubtful," said Prince Andrew. "Monsieur le Vicomte quite rightly supposes that matters have already gone too far. I think it will be difficult to return to the old regime."

"From what I have heard," said Pierre, blushing and breaking into the conversation, "almost all the aristocracy has already gone over to Bonaparte's side."

"It is the Buonapartists who say that," replied the vicomte without looking at Pierre. "At the present time it is difficult to know the real state of French public opinion."

"Bonaparte has said so," remarked Prince Andrew with a sarcastic smile.

It was evident that he did not like the vicomte and was aiming his remarks at him, though without looking at him.

* *Hippolyte's heraldry, like the rest of his conversation and conduct, is that of an utter fool. The arms of Condé are D'or à la fasce de gueules, or a fess gules. What Hippolyte says they are is untranslatable nonsense.—A.M.*

" 'I showed them the path to glory, but they did not follow it,' " Prince Andrew continued after a short silence, again quoting Napoleon's words. " 'I opened my antechambers and they crowded in.' I do not know how far he was justified in saying so."

"Not in the least," replied the vicomte. "After the murder of the duc even the most partial ceased to regard him as a hero. If to some people," he went on, turning to Anna Pávlovna, "he ever was a hero, after the murder of the duc there was one martyr more in heaven and one hero less on earth."

Before Anna Pávlovna and the others had time to smile their appreciation of the vicomte's epigram, Pierre again broke into the conversation, and though Anna Pávlovna felt sure he would say something inappropriate, she was unable to stop him.

"The execution of the Duc d'Enghien," declared Monsieur Pierre, "was a political necessity, and it seems to me that Napoleon showed greatness of soul by not fearing to take on himself the whole responsibility of that deed."

"*Dieu! Mon Dieu!*" muttered Anna Pávlovna in a terrified whisper.

"What, Monsieur Pierre . . . Do you consider that assassination shows greatness of soul?" said the little princess, smiling and drawing her work nearer to her.

"Oh! Oh!" exclaimed several voices.

"Capital!" said Prince Hippolyte in English, and began slapping his knee with the palm of his hand.

The vicomte merely shrugged his shoulders. Pierre looked solemnly at his audience over his spectacles and continued.

"I say so," he continued desperately, "because the Bourbons fled from the Revolution leaving the people to anarchy, and Napoleon alone understood the Revolution and quelled it, and so for the general good, he could not stop short for the sake of one man's life."

"Won't you come over to the other table?" suggested Anna Pávlovna.

But Pierre continued his speech without heeding her.

"No," cried he, becoming more and more eager, "Napoleon is great because he rose superior to the Revolution, suppressed its abuses, preserved all that was good in it—equality of citizenship and freedom of speech and of the press—and only for that reason did he obtain power."

"Yes, if having obtained power, without availing himself of it to commit murder he had restored it to the rightful king, I should have called him a great man," remarked the vicomte.

"He could not do that. The people only gave him power that he might rid them of the Bourbons and because they saw that he was a great man.

The Revolution was a grand thing!" continued Monsieur Pierre, betraying by this desperate and provocative proposition his extreme youth and his wish to express all that was in his mind.

"What? Revolution and regicide a grand thing? . . . Well, after that . . . But won't you come to this other table?" repeated Anna Pávlovna.

"Rousseau's *Contrat social*," said the vicomte with a tolerant smile.

"I am not speaking of regicide, I am speaking about ideas."

"Yes: ideas of robbery, murder, and regicide," again interjected an ironical voice.

"Those were extremes, no doubt, but they are not what is most important. What is important are the rights of man, emancipation from prejudices, and equality of citizenship, and all these ideas Napoleon has retained in full force."

"Liberty and equality," said the vicomte contemptuously, as if at last deciding seriously to prove to this youth how foolish his words were, "high-sounding words which have long been discredited. Who does not love liberty and equality? Even our Saviour preached liberty and equality. Have people since the Revolution become happier? On the contrary. We wanted liberty, but Buonaparte has destroyed it."

Prince Andrew kept looking with an amused smile from Pierre to the vicomte and from the vicomte to their hostess. In the first moment of Pierre's outburst Anna Pávlovna, despite her social experience, was horror-struck. But when she saw that Pierre's sacrilegious words had not exasperated the vicomte, and had convinced herself that it was impossible to stop him, she rallied her forces and joined the vicomte in a vigorous attack on the orator.

"But, my dear Monsieur Pierre," said she, "how do you explain the fact of a great man executing a duc—or even an ordinary man—who is innocent and untried?"

"I should like," said the vicomte, "to ask how monsieur explains the 18th Brumaire; * was not that an imposture? It was a swindle, and not at all like the conduct of a great man!"

"And the prisoners he killed in Africa? [2] That was horrible!" said the little princess, shrugging her shoulders.

"He's a low fellow, say what you will," remarked Prince Hippolyte.

Pierre, not knowing whom to answer, looked at them all and smiled.

* *The ninth of November (according to the French Revolutionary calendar)—the day on which Napoleon overthrew the existing French Revolutionary Government by a coup d'état which led to his becoming First Consul.*

[2] *This refers to the cruelties committed at the time of Napoleon's suppression of a rising against him in Egypt.*—A.M.

His smile was unlike the half-smile of other people. When he smiled, his grave, even rather gloomy, look was instantaneously replaced by another— a childlike, kindly, even rather silly look, which seemed to ask forgiveness.

The vicomte who was meeting him for the first time saw clearly that this young Jacobin was not so terrible as his words suggested. All were silent.

"How do you expect him to answer you all at once?" said Prince Andrew. "Besides, in the actions of a statesman one has to distinguish between his acts as a private person, as a general, and as an emperor. So it seems to me."

"Yes, yes, of course!" Pierre chimed in, pleased at the arrival of this reinforcement.

"One must admit," continued Prince Andrew, "that Napoleon as a man was great on the bridge of Arcola,* and in the hospital at Jaffa where he gave his hand to the plague-stricken; but . . . but there are other acts which it is difficult to justify."

Prince Andrew, who had evidently wished to tone down the awkwardness of Pierre's remarks, rose and made a sign to his wife that it was time to go.

Suddenly Prince Hippolyte started up making signs to everyone to attend, and asking them all to be seated began:

"I was told a charming Moscow story today and must treat you to it. Excuse me, Vicomte—I must tell it in Russian or the point will be lost. . . ." And Prince Hippolyte began to tell his story in such Russian as a Frenchman would speak after spending about a year in Russia. Everyone waited, so emphatically and eagerly did he demand their attention to his story.

"There is in Moscow a lady, une dame, and she is very stingy. She must have two footmen behind her carriage, and very big ones. That was her taste. And she had a lady's maid, also big. She said . . ."

Here Prince Hippolyte paused, evidently collecting his ideas with difficulty.

"She said . . . Oh yes! She said, 'Girl,' to the maid, 'put on a livery, get up behind the carriage, and come with me while I make some calls.'"

Here Prince Hippolyte spluttered and burst out laughing long before his audience, which produced an effect unfavorable to the narrator. Sev-

* Napoleon, with standard in hand, had faced the Austrian fire and captured the bridge at Arcola near Verona, Italy, November 15-17, 1796. He had taken Jaffa, a seaport in Palestine, on March 7, 1799, where he visited the hospital referred to in text.

eral persons, among them the elderly lady and Anna Pávlovna, did however smile.

"She went. Suddenly there was a great wind. The girl lost her hat and her long hair came down. . . ." Here he could contain himself no longer and went on, between gasps of laughter: "And the whole world knew. . . ."

And so the anecdote ended. Though it was unintelligible why he had told it, or why it had to be told in Russian, still Anna Pávlovna and the others appreciated Prince Hippolyte's social tact in so agreeably ending Pierre's unpleasant and unamiable outburst. After the anecdote the conversation broke up into insignificant small talk about the last and next balls, about theatricals, and who would meet whom, and when and where.

2. Pierre at Prince Andrew's

HAVING THANKED Anna Pávlovna for her charming soiree, the guests began to take their leave.

Pierre was ungainly. Stout, about the average height, broad, with huge red hands; he did not know, as the saying is, how to enter a drawing room and still less how to leave one; that is, how to say something particularly agreeable before going away. Besides this he was absent-minded. When he rose to go, he took up instead of his own, the general's three-cornered hat, and held it, pulling at the plume, till the general asked him to restore it. All his absent-mindedness and inability to enter a room and converse in it was, however, redeemed by his kindly, simple, and modest expression. Anna Pávlovna turned toward him and, with a Christian mildness that expressed forgiveness of his indiscretion, nodded and said: "I hope to see you again, but I also hope you will change your opinions, my dear Monsieur Pierre."

When she said this, he did not reply and only bowed, but again everybody saw his smile, which said nothing, unless perhaps, "Opinions are opinions, but you see what a capital, good-natured fellow I am." And everyone, including Anna Pávlovna, felt this.

Prince Andrew had gone out into the hall, and, turning his shoulders to the footman who was helping him on with his cloak, listened indifferently to his wife's chatter with Prince Hippolyte who had also come into the hall. Prince Hippolyte stood close to the pretty, pregnant princess, and stared fixedly at her through his eyeglass.

"Go in, Annette, or you will catch cold," said the little princess, taking leave of Anna Pávlovna. "It is settled," she added in a low voice.

Anna Pávlovna had already managed to speak to Lise about the match she contemplated between Anatole and the little princess' sister-in-law.

"I rely on you, my dear," said Anna Pávlovna, also in a low tone. "Write to her and let me know how her father looks at the matter. *Au revoir!*"— and she left the hall.

Prince Hippolyte approached the little princess and, bending his face close to her, began to whisper something.

Two footmen, the princess' and his own, stood holding a shawl and a cloak, waiting for the conversation to finish. They listened to the French sentences which to them were meaningless, with an air of understanding but not wishing to appear to do so. The princess as usual spoke smilingly and listened with a laugh.

"I am very glad I did not go to the ambassador's," said Prince Hippolyte "—so dull—. It has been a delightful evening, has it not? Delightful!"

"They say the ball will be very good," replied the princess, drawing up her downy little lip. "All the pretty women in society will be there."

"Not all, for you will not be there; not all," said Prince Hippolyte smiling joyfully; and snatching the shawl from the footman, whom he even pushed aside, he began wrapping it round the princess. Either from awkwardness or intentionally (no one could have said which) after the shawl had been adjusted he kept his arm around her for a long time, as though embracing her.

Still smiling, she gracefully moved away, turning and glancing at her husband. Prince Andrew's eyes were closed, so weary and sleepy did he seem.

"Are you ready?" he asked his wife, looking past her.

Prince Hippolyte hurriedly put on his cloak, which in the latest fashion reached to his very heels, and, stumbling in it, ran out into the porch following the princess, whom a footman was helping into the carriage.

"*Princesse, au revoir,*" cried he, stumbling with his tongue as well as with his feet.

The princess, picking up her dress, was taking her seat in the dark carriage, her husband was adjusting his saber; Prince Hippolyte, under pretense of helping, was in everyone's way.

"Allow me, sir," said Prince Andrew in Russian in a cold, disagreeable tone to Prince Hippolyte who was blocking his path.

"I am expecting you, Pierre," said the same voice, but gently and affectionately.

The postilion started, the carriage wheels rattled. Prince Hippolyte laughed spasmodically as he stood in the porch waiting for the vicomte whom he had promised to take home.

"Well, *mon cher,*" said the vicomte, having seated himself beside Hippolyte in the carriage, "your little princess is very nice, very nice indeed, quite French," and he kissed the tips of his fingers. Hippolyte burst out laughing.

"Do you know, you are a terrible chap for all your innocent airs," continued the vicomte. "I pity the poor husband, that little officer who gives himself the airs of a monarch."

Hippolyte spluttered again, and amid his laughter said, "And you were saying that the Russian ladies are not equal to the French? One has to know how to deal with them."

Pierre reaching the house first went into Prince Andrew's study like one quite at home, and from habit immediately lay down on the sofa, took from the shelf the first book that came to his hand (it was Caesar's *Commentaries*), and resting on his elbow, began reading it in the middle.

"What have you done to Mlle Schérer? She will be quite ill now," said Prince Andrew, as he entered the study, rubbing his small white hands.

Pierre turned his whole body, making the sofa creak. He lifted his eager face to Prince Andrew, smiled, and waved his hand.

"That abbé is very interesting but he does not see the thing in the right light. . . . In my opinion perpetual peace is possible but—I do not know how to express it . . . not by a balance of political power. . . ."

It was evident that Prince Andrew was not interested in such abstract conversation.

"One can't everywhere say all one thinks, *mon cher.* Well, have you at last decided on anything? Are you going to be a guardsman or a diplomatist?" asked Prince Andrew after a momentary silence.

Pierre sat up on the sofa, with his legs tucked under him.

"Really, I don't yet know. I don't like either the one or the other."

"But you must decide on something! Your father expects it."

Pierre at the age of ten had been sent abroad with an abbé as tutor, and had remained away till he was twenty. When he returned to Moscow his father dismissed the abbé and said to the young man, "Now go to Petersburg, look round, and choose your profession. I will agree to anything. Here is a letter to Prince Vasíli, and here is money. Write to me all about it, and I will help you in everything." Pierre had already been choosing a career for three months, and had not decided on anything. It was about this choice that Prince Andrew was speaking. Pierre rubbed his forehead.

"But he must be a Freemason," said he, referring to the abbé whom he had met that evening.

"That is all nonsense," Prince Andrew again interrupted him, "let us talk business. Have you been to the Horse Guards?"

"No, I have not; but this is what I have been thinking and wanted to tell you. There is a war now against Napoleon. If it were a war for freedom I could understand it and should be the first to enter the army; but to help England and Austria against the greatest man in the world is not right."

Prince Andrew only shrugged his shoulders at Pierre's childish words. He put on the air of one who finds it impossible to reply to such nonsense, but it would in fact have been difficult to give any other answer than the one Prince Andrew gave to this naïve question.

"If no one fought except on his own conviction, there would be no wars," he said.

"And that would be splendid," said Pierre.

Prince Andrew smiled ironically.

"Very likely it would be splendid, but it will never come about. . . ."

"Well, why are you going to the war?" asked Pierre.

"What for? I don't know. I must. Besides that I am going . . ." He paused. "I am going because the life I am leading here does not suit me!"

THE RUSTLE of a woman's dress was heard in the next room. Prince Andrew shook himself as if waking up, and his face assumed the look it had had in Anna Pávlovna's drawing room. Pierre removed his feet from the sofa. The princess came in. She had changed her gown for a house dress as fresh and elegant as the other. Prince Andrew rose and politely placed a chair for her.

"How is it," she began, as usual in French, settling down briskly and fussily in the easy chair, "how is it Annette never got married? How stupid you men all are not to have married her! Excuse me for saying so, but you have no sense about women. What an argumentative fellow you are, Monsieur Pierre!"

"And I am still arguing with your husband. I can't understand why he wants to go to the war," replied Pierre, addressing the princess with none of the embarrassment so commonly shown by young men in their intercourse with young women.

The princess started. Evidently Pierre's words touched her to the quick.

"Ah, that is just what I tell him!" said she. "I don't understand it; I don't in the least understand why men can't live without wars. How is it that we women don't want anything of the kind, don't need it? Now you shall judge between us. I always tell him: here he is Uncle's aide-de-camp, a most brilliant position. He is so well known, so much appreciated by

everyone. The other day at the Apráksins' I heard a lady asking, 'Is that the famous Prince Andrew?' I did indeed." She laughed. "He is so well received everywhere. He might easily become aide-de-camp to the Emperor. You know the Emperor spoke to him most graciously. Annette and I were speaking of how to arrange it. What do you think?"

Pierre looked at his friend and, noticing that he did not like the conversation, gave no reply.

"When are you starting?" he asked.

"Oh, don't speak of his going, don't! I won't hear it spoken of," said the princess in the same petulantly playful tone in which she had spoken to Hippolyte in the drawing room and which was so plainly ill-suited to the family circle of which Pierre was almost a member. "Today when I remembered that all these delightful associations must be broken off . . . and then you know, André . . ." (she looked significantly at her husband) "I'm afraid, I'm afraid!" she whispered, and a shudder ran down her back.

Her husband looked at her as if surprised to notice that someone besides Pierre and himself was in the room, and addressed her in a tone of frigid politeness.

"What is it you are afraid of, Lise? I don't understand," said he.

"There, what egotists men all are: all, all egotists! Just for a whim of his own, goodness only knows why, he leaves me and locks me up alone in the country."

"With my father and sister, remember," said Prince Andrew gently.

"Alone all the same, without my friends. . . . And he expects me not to be afraid."

Her tone was now querulous and her lip drawn up, giving her not a joyful, but an animal, squirrel-like expression. She paused as if she felt it indecorous to speak of her pregnancy before Pierre, though the gist of the matter lay in that.

"I still can't understand what you are afraid of," said Prince Andrew slowly, not taking his eyes off his wife.

The princess blushed, and raised her arms with a gesture of despair.

"No, Andrew, I must say you have changed. Oh, how you have . . ."

"Your doctor tells you to go to bed earlier," said Prince Andrew. "You had better go."

The princess said nothing, but suddenly her short downy lip quivered. Prince Andrew rose, shrugged his shoulders, and walked about the room.

Pierre looked over his spectacles with naïve surprise, now at him and now at her, moved as if about to rise too, but changed his mind.

"Why should I mind Monsieur Pierre being here?" exclaimed the little princess suddenly, her pretty face all at once distorted by a tearful grimace.

"I have long wanted to ask you, Andrew, why you have changed so to me? What have I done to you? You are going to the war and have no pity for me. Why is it?"

"Lise!" was all Prince Andrew said. But that one word expressed an entreaty, a threat, and above all conviction that she would herself regret her words. But she went hurriedly:

"You treat me like an invalid or a child. I see it all! Did you behave like that six months ago?"

"Lise, I beg you to desist," said Prince Andrew still more emphatically.

Pierre, who had been growing more and more agitated as he listened to all this, rose and approached the princess. He seemed unable to bear the sight of tears and was ready to cry himself.

"Calm yourself, Princess! It seems so to you because . . . I assure you I myself have experienced . . . and so . . . because . . . No, excuse me! An outsider is out of place here . . . No, don't distress yourself . . . Good-by!"

Prince Andrew caught him by the hand.

"No, wait, Pierre! The princess is too kind to wish to deprive me of the pleasure of spending the evening with you."

"No, he thinks only of himself," muttered the princess without restraining her angry tears.

"Lise!" said Prince Andrew dryly, raising his voice to the pitch which indicates that patience is exhausted.

Suddenly the angry, squirrel-like expression of the princess' pretty face changed into a winning and piteous look of fear. Her beautiful eyes glanced askance at her husband's face, and her own assumed the timid, deprecating expression of a dog when it rapidly but feebly wags its drooping tail.

"*Mon Dieu, mon Dieu!*" she muttered, and lifting her dress with one hand she went up to her husband and kissed him on the forehead.

"Good night, Lise," said he, rising and courteously kissing her hand as he would have done to a stranger.

THE FRIENDS were silent. Neither cared to begin talking. Pierre continually glanced at Prince Andrew; Prince Andrew rubbed his forehead with his small hand.

"Let us go and have supper," he said with a sigh, going to the door.

They entered the elegant, newly decorated, and luxurious dining room. Everything from the table napkins to the silver, china, and glass bore that imprint of newness found in the households of the newly married. Halfway through supper Prince Andrew leaned his elbows on the table and,

with a look of nervous agitation such as Pierre had never before seen on his face, began to talk—as one who has long had something on his mind and suddenly determines to speak out.

"Never, never marry, my dear fellow! That's my advice: never marry till you can say to yourself that you have done all you are capable of, and until you have ceased to love the woman of your choice and have seen her plainly as she is, or else you will make a cruel and irrevocable mistake. Marry when you are old and good for nothing—or all that is good and noble in you will be lost. It will all be wasted on trifles. Yes! Yes! Yes! Don't look at me with such surprise. If you marry expecting anything from yourself in the future, you will feel at every step that for you all is ended, all is closed except the drawing room, where you will be ranged side by side with a court lackey and an idiot! . . . But what's the good? . . ." and he waved his arm.

Pierre took off his spectacles, which made his face seem different and the good-natured expression still more apparent, and gazed at his friend in amazement.

"My wife," continued Prince Andrew, "is an excellent woman, one of those rare women with whom a man's honor is safe; but, O God, what would I not give now to be unmarried! You are the first and only one to whom I mention this, because I like you."

As he said this Prince Andrew was less than ever like that Bolkónski who had lolled in Anna Pávlovna's easy chairs and with half-closed eyes had uttered French phrases between his teeth. Every muscle of his thin face was now quivering with nervous excitement; his eyes, in which the fire of life had seemed extinguished, now flashed with brilliant light. It was evident that the more lifeless he seemed at ordinary times, the more impassioned he became in these moments of almost morbid irritation.

"You don't understand why I say this," he continued, "but it is the whole story of life. You talk of Bonaparte and his career," said he (though Pierre had not mentioned Bonaparte), "but Bonaparte when he worked went step by step toward his goal. He was free, he had nothing but his aim to consider, and he reached it. But tie yourself up with a woman and, like a chained convict, you lose all freedom! And all you have of hope and strength merely weighs you down and torments you with regret. Drawing rooms, gossip, balls, vanity, and triviality—these are the enchanted circle I cannot escape from. I am now going to the war, the greatest war there ever was, and I know nothing and am fit for nothing. I am very amiable and have a caustic wit," continued Prince Andrew, "and at Anna Pávlovna's they listen to me. And that stupid set without whom my wife cannot exist, and those women . . . If you only knew what those society women are,

and women in general! My father is right. Selfish, vain, stupid, trivial in everything—that's what women are when you see them in their true colors! When you meet them in society it seems as if there were something in them, but there's nothing, nothing, nothing! No, don't marry, my dear fellow; don't marry!" concluded Prince Andrew.

"It seems funny to me," said Pierre, "that you, you should consider yourself incapable and your life a spoiled life. You have everything before you, everything. And you . . ."

He did not finish his sentence, but his tone showed how highly he thought of his friend and how much he expected of him in the future.

"How can he talk like that?" thought Pierre. He considered his friend a model of perfection because Prince Andrew possessed in the highest degree just the very qualities Pierre lacked, and which might be best described as strength of will. Pierre was always astonished at Prince Andrew's calm manner of treating everybody, his extraordinary memory, his extensive reading (he had read everything, knew everything, and had an opinion about everything), but above all at his capacity for work and study. And if Pierre was often struck by Andrew's lack of capacity for philosophical meditation (to which he himself was particularly addicted), he regarded even this not as a defect but as a sign of strength.

Even in the best, most friendly and simplest relations of life, praise and commendation are essential, just as grease is necessary to wheels that they may run smoothly.

"My part is played out," said Prince Andrew. "What's the use of talking about me? Let us talk about you," he added after a silence, smiling at his reassuring thoughts.

That smile was immediately reflected on Pierre's face.

"But what is there to say about me?" said Pierre, his face relaxing into a careless, merry smile. "What am I? An illegitimate son!" He suddenly blushed crimson, and it was plain that he had made a great effort to say this. "Without a name and without means . . . And it really . . ." But he did not say what "it really" was. "For the present I am free and am all right. Only I haven't the least idea what I am to do; I wanted to consult you seriously."

Prince Andrew looked kindly at him, yet his glance—friendly and affectionate as it was—expressed a sense of his own superiority.

"I am fond of you, especially as you are the one live man among our whole set. Yes, you're all right! Choose what you will; it's all the same. You'll be all right anywhere. But look here: give up visiting those Kurágins and leading that sort of life. It suits you so badly—all this debauchery, dissipation, and the rest of it!"

"What would you have, my dear fellow?" answered Pierre, shrugging his shoulders. "Women, my dear fellow; women!"

"I don't understand it," replied Prince Andrew. "Women who are comme il faut, that's a different matter; but the Kurágins' set of women, 'women and wine,' I don't understand!"

Pierre was staying at Prince Vasíli Kurágin's and sharing the dissipated life of his son Anatole, the son whom they were planning to reform by marrying him to Prince Andrew's sister.

"Do you know?" said Pierre, as if suddenly struck by a happy thought, "seriously, I have long been thinking of it. . . . Leading such a life I can't decide or think properly about anything. One's head aches, and one spends all one's money. He asked me for tonight, but I won't go."

"You give me your word of honor not to go?"

"On my honor!"

3. Pierre at Anatole Kurágin's. Dólokhov's bet

I T WAS past one o'clock when Pierre left his friend. It was a cloudless, northern, summer night. Pierre took an open cab intending to drive straight home. But the nearer he drew to the house the more he felt the impossibility of going to sleep on such a night. It was light enough to see a long way in the deserted street and it seemed more like morning or evening than night. On the way Pierre remembered that Anatole Kurágin was expecting the usual set for cards that evening, after which there was generally a drinking bout, finishing with visits of a kind Pierre was very fond of.

"I should like to go to Kurágin's," thought he.

But he immediately recalled his promise to Prince Andrew not to go there. Then, as happens to people of weak character, he desired so passionately once more to enjoy that dissipation he was so accustomed to that he decided to go. The thought immediately occurred to him that his promise to Prince Andrew was of no account, because before he gave it he had already promised Prince Anatole to come to his gathering; "besides," thought he, "all such 'words of honor' are conventional things with no definite meaning, especially if one considers that by tomorrow one may be dead, or something so extraordinary may happen to one that honor and dishonor will be all the same!" Pierre often indulged in reflections of this sort, nullifying all his decisions and intentions. He went to Kurágin's.

Reaching the large house near the Horse Guards' barracks, in which Anatole lived, Pierre entered the lighted porch, ascended the stairs, and went in at the open door. There was no one in the anteroom; empty

bottles, cloaks, and overshoes were lying about; there was a smell of alcohol, and sounds of voices and shouting in the distance.

Cards and supper were over, but the visitors had not yet dispersed. Pierre threw off his cloak and entered the first room, in which were the remains of supper. A footman, thinking no one saw him, was drinking on the sly what was left in the glasses. From the third room came sounds of laughter, the shouting of familiar voices, the growling of a bear, and general commotion. Some eight or nine young men were crowding anxiously round an open window. Three others were romping with a young bear, one pulling him by the chain and trying to set him at the others.

"I bet a hundred on Stevens!" shouted one.

"Mind, no holding on!" cried another.

"I bet on Dólokhov!" cried a third. "Kurágin, you part our hands." *

"There, leave Bruin alone; here's a bet on."

"At one draught, or he loses!" shouted a fourth.

"Jacob, bring a bottle!" shouted the host, a tall, handsome fellow who stood in the midst of the group, without a coat, and with his fine linen shirt unfastened in front. "Wait a bit, you fellows. . . . Here is Pétya! Good man!" cried he, addressing Pierre.

Another voice, from a man of medium height with clear blue eyes, particularly striking among all these drunken voices by its sober ring, cried from the window: "Come here; part the bets!" This was Dólokhov, an officer of the Seménov regiment, a notorious gambler and duelist, who was living with Anatole. Pierre smiled, looking about him merrily.

"I don't understand. What's it all about?"

"Wait a bit, he is not drunk yet! A bottle here," said Anatole, and taking a glass from the table he went up to Pierre.

"First of all you must drink!" ·

Pierre drank one glass after another, looking from under his brows at the tipsy guests who were again crowding round the window, and listening to their chatter. Anatole kept on refilling Pierre's glass while explaining that Dólokhov was betting with Stevens, an English naval officer, that he would drink a bottle of rum sitting on the outer ledge of the third-floor window with his legs hanging out.

"Go on, you must drink it all," said Anatole, giving Pierre the last glass, "or I won't let you go!"

"No, I won't," said Pierre, pushing Anatole aside, and he went up to the window.

Dólokhov was holding the Englishman's hand and clearly and distinctly

* The Russian custom was to shake hands on a bet and for some third person, acting as a witness, to separate the hands.—A.M.

repeating the terms of the bet, addressing himself particularly to Anatole and Pierre.

Dólokhov was of medium height, with curly hair and light-blue eyes. He was about twenty-five. Like all infantry officers he wore no mustache, so that his mouth, the most striking feature of his face, was clearly seen. The lines of that mouth were remarkably finely curved. The middle of the upper lip formed a sharp wedge and closed firmly on the firm lower one, and something like two distinct smiles played continually round the two corners of the mouth; this, together with the resolute, insolent intelligence of his eyes, produced an effect which made it impossible not to notice his face. Dólokhov was a man of small means and no connections. Yet, though Anatole spent tens of thousands of rubles, Dólokhov lived with him and had placed himself on such a footing that all who knew them, including Anatole himself, respected him more than they did Anatole. Dólokhov could play all games and nearly always won. However much he drank, he never lost his clearheadedness. Both Kurágin and Dólokhov were at that time notorious among the rakes and scapegraces of Petersburg.

The bottle of rum was brought. The window frame which prevented anyone from sitting on the outer sill was being forced out by two footmen, who were evidently flurried and intimidated by the directions and shouts of the gentlemen around.

Anatole with his swaggering air strode up to the window. He wanted to smash something. Pushing away the footmen he tugged at the frame, but could not move it. He smashed a pane.

"You have a try, Hercules," said he, turning to Pierre.

Pierre seized the crossbeam, tugged, and wrenched the oak frame out with a crash.

"Take it right out, or they'll think I'm holding on," said Dólokhov.

"Is the Englishman bragging? . . . Eh? Is it all right?" said Anatole.

"First-rate," said Pierre, looking at Dólokhov, who with a bottle of rum in his hand was approaching the window, from which the light of the sky, the dawn merging with the afterglow of sunset, was visible.

Dólokhov, the bottle of rum still in his hand, jumped onto the window sill. "Listen!" cried he, standing there and addressing those in the room. All were silent.

"I bet fifty imperials" *—he spoke French that the Englishman might understand him, but he did not speak it very well—"I bet fifty imperials

* About $380. The imperial was 10 rubles. The value of the ruble at par was at that time about 76 cents. The purchasing power of money in Russia was then very much higher than it has been in our generation.—A.M.

. . . or do you wish to make it a hundred?" added he, addressing the Englishman.

"No, fifty," replied the latter.

"All right. Fifty imperials . . . that I will drink a whole bottle of rum without taking it from my mouth, sitting outside the window on this spot" (he stooped and pointed to the sloping ledge outside the window) "and without holding on to anything. Is that right?"

"Quite right," said the Englishman.

Anatole turned to the Englishman and taking him by one of the buttons of his coat and looking down at him—the Englishman was short—began repeating the terms of the wager to him in English.

"Wait!" cried Dólokhov, hammering with the bottle on the window sill to attract attention. "Wait a bit, Kurágin. Listen! If anyone else does the same, I will pay him a hundred imperials. Do you understand?"

The Englishman nodded, but gave no indication whether he intended to accept this challenge or not. Anatole did not release him, and though he kept nodding to show that he understood, Anatole went on translating Dólokhov's words into English. A thin young lad, an hussar of the Life Guards, who had been losing that evening, climbed on the window sill, leaned over, and looked down.

"Oh! Oh! Oh!" he muttered, looking down from the window at the stones of the pavement.

"Shut up!" cried Dólokhov, pushing him away from the window. The lad jumped awkwardly back into the room, tripping over his spurs.

Placing the bottle on the window sill where he could reach it easily, Dólokhov climbed carefully and slowly through the window and lowered his legs. Pressing against both sides of the window, he adjusted himself on his seat, lowered his hands, moved a little to the right and then to the left, and took up the bottle. Anatole brought two candles and placed them on the window sill, though it was already quite light. Dólokhov's back in his white shirt, and his curly head, were lit up from both sides. Everyone crowded to the window, the Englishman in front. Pierre stood smiling but silent. One man, older than the others present, suddenly pushed forward with a scared and angry look and wanted to seize hold of Dólokhov's shirt.

"I say, this is folly! He'll be killed," said this more sensible man.

Anatole stopped him.

"Don't touch him! You'll startle him and then he'll be killed. Eh? . . . What then? . . . Eh?"

Dólokhov turned round and, again holding on with both hands, arranged himself on his seat.

"If anyone comes meddling again," said he, emitting the words sepa-

rately through his thin compressed lips, "I will throw him down there. Now then!"

Saying this he again turned round, dropped his hands, took the bottle and lifted it to his lips, threw back his head, and raised his free hand to balance himself. One of the footmen who had stooped to pick up some broken glass remained in that position without taking his eyes from the window and from Dólokhov's back. Anatole stood erect with staring eyes. The Englishman looked on sideways, pursing up his lips. The man who had wished to stop the affair ran to a corner of the room and threw himself on a sofa with his face to the wall. Pierre hid his face, from which a faint smile forgot to fade though his features now expressed horror and fear. All were still. Pierre took his hand from his eyes. Dólokhov still sat in the same position, only his head was thrown further back till his curly hair touched his shirt collar, and the hand holding the bottle was lifted higher and higher and trembled with the effort. The bottle was emptying perceptibly and rising still higher and his head tilting yet further back. "Why is it so long?" thought Pierre. It seemed to him that more than half an hour had elapsed. Suddenly Dólokhov made a backward movement with his spine, and his arm trembled nervously; this was sufficient to cause his whole body to slip as he sat on the sloping ledge. As he began slipping down, his head and arm wavered still more with the strain. One hand moved as if to clutch the window sill, but refrained from touching it. Pierre again covered his eyes and thought he would never open them again. Suddenly he was aware of a stir all around. He looked up: Dólokhov was standing on the window sill, with a pale but radiant face.

"It's empty!"

He threw the bottle to the Englishman, who caught it neatly. Dólokhov jumped down. He smelt strongly of rum.

"Well done! . . . Fine fellow! . . . There's a bet for you! . . . Devil take you!" came from different sides.

The Englishman took out his purse and began counting out the money. Dólokhov stood frowning and did not speak. Pierre jumped upon the window sill.

"Gentlemen, who wishes to bet with me? I'll do the same thing!" he suddenly cried. "Even without a bet, there! Tell them to bring me a bottle. I'll do it. . . . Bring a bottle!"

"Let him do it, let him do it," said Dólokhov, smiling.

"What next? Have you gone mad? . . . No one would let you! . . . Why, you go giddy even on a staircase," exclaimed several voices.

"I'll drink it! Let's have a bottle of rum!" shouted Pierre, banging the

table with a determined and drunken gesture and preparing to climb out of the window.

They seized him by his arms; but he was so strong that everyone who touched him was sent flying.

"No, you'll never manage him that way," said Anatole. "Wait a bit and I'll get round him. . . . Listen! I'll take your bet tomorrow, but now we are all going to —'s."

"Come on then," cried Pierre. "Come on! . . . And we'll take Bruin with us."

And he caught the bear, took it in his arms, lifted it from the ground, and began dancing round the room with it.

4. A name day at the Rostóvs'

Prince Vasíli kept the promise he had given to Princess Drubetskáya who had spoken to him on behalf of her only son Borís on the evening of Anna Pávlovna's soiree. The matter was mentioned to the Emperor, an exception made, and Borís transferred into the regiment of Semënov Guards with the rank of cornet.* He received, however, no appointment to Kutúzov's staff despite all Anna Mikháylovna's endeavors and entreaties. Soon after Anna Pávlovna's reception Anna Mikháylovna returned to Moscow and went straight to her rich relations, the Rostóvs, with whom she stayed when in the town and where her darling Bóry [Borís], who had only just entered a regiment of the line and was being at once transferred to the Guards as a cornet, had been educated from childhood and lived for years at a time. The Guards had already left Petersburg on the tenth of August, and her son, who had remained in Moscow for his equipment, was to join them on the march to Radzivílov.[2]

It was St. Natalia's day and the name day of two of the Rostóvs—the mother and the youngest daughter—both named Nataly. Ever since the morning, carriages with six horses had been coming and going continually, bringing visitors to the Countess Rostóva's big house on the Povarskáya, so well known to all Moscow. The countess herself and her handsome eldest daughter were in the drawing room with the visitors who came to congratulate, and who constantly succeeded one another in relays.

The countess was a woman of about forty-five, with a thin Oriental type

* A rank corresponding to the fifth commissioned officer in a troop of cavalry in the British army.

[2] A frontier town where the Russian army, going to the assistance of Austria, was to cross into Galicia.—A.M.

of face, evidently worn out with childbearing—she had had twelve. A languor of motion and speech, resulting from weakness, gave her a distinguished air which inspired respect. Princess Anna Mikháylovna Drubetskáya, who as a member of the household was also seated in the drawing room, helped to receive and entertain the visitors. The young people were in one of the inner rooms, not considering it necessary to take part in receiving the visitors. The count * met the guests and saw them off, inviting them all to dinner.

"I am very, very grateful to you, mon cher," or "ma chère"—he called everyone without exception and without the slightest variation in his tone, "my dear," whether they were above or below him in rank—"I thank you for myself and for our two dear ones whose name day we are keeping. But mind you come to dinner or I shall be offended, ma chère! On behalf of the whole family I beg you to come, mon cher!" These words he repeated to everyone without exception or variation, and with the same expression on his full, cheerful, clean-shaven face, the same firm pressure of the hand and the same quick, repeated bows. As soon as he had seen a visitor off he returned to one of those who were still in the drawing room, drew a chair toward him or her, and jauntily spreading out his legs and putting his hands on his knees with the air of a man who enjoys life and knows how to live, he swayed to and fro with dignity, offered surmises about the weather, or touched on questions of health, sometimes in Russian and sometimes in very bad but self-confident French; then again, like a man weary but unflinching in the fulfillment of duty, he rose to see some visitors off and, stroking his scanty gray hairs over his bald patch, also asked them to dinner. Sometimes on his way back from the anteroom he would pass through the conservatory and pantry into the large marble dining hall, where tables were being set out for eighty people; and looking at the footmen, who were bringing in silver and china, moving tables, and unfolding damask table linen, he would call Dmítri Vasílevich, a man of good family and the manager of all his affairs, and while looking with pleasure at the enormous table would say: "Well, Dmítri, you'll see that things are all as they should be? That's right! The great thing is the serving, that's it." And with a complacent sigh he would return to the drawing room.

"Márya Lvóvna Karágina and her daughter!" announced the countess' gigantic footman in his bass voice, entering the drawing room. The countess reflected a moment and took a pinch from a gold snuffbox with her husband's portrait on it.

* Count Ilyá Rostóv is a close copy of Tolstóy's grandfather, Count Ilyá Andréevich Tolstóy, and his wife has much in common with the author's grandmother, Countess P. N. Tolstóy.—A.M.

"I'm quite worn out by these callers. However, I'll see her and no more. She is so affected. Ask her in," she said to the footman in a sad voice, as if saying: "Very well, finish me off."

A tall, stout, and proud-looking woman, with a round-faced smiling daughter, entered the drawing room, their dresses rustling.

"Dear Countess, what an age . . . She has been laid up, poor child . . . at the Razumóvski's ball . . . and Countess Apráksina . . . I was so delighted . . ." came the sounds of animated feminine voices, interrupting one another and mingling with the rustling of dresses and the scraping of chairs. Then one of those conversations began which last out until, at the first pause, the guests rise with a rustle of dresses and say, "I am so delighted . . . Mamma's health . . . and Countess Apráksina . . ." and then, again rustling, pass into the anteroom, put on cloaks or mantles, and drive away. The conversation was on the chief topic of the day: the illness of the wealthy and celebrated beau of Catherine's day, Count Bezúkhov, and about his illegitimate son Pierre, the one who had behaved so improperly at Anna Pávlovna's reception.

"I am so sorry for the poor count," said the visitor. "He is in such bad health, and now this vexation about his son is enough to kill him!"

"What is that?" asked the countess as if she did not know what the visitor alluded to, though she had already heard about the cause of Count Bezúkhov's distress some fifteen times.

"That's what comes of a modern education," exclaimed the visitor. "It seems that while he was abroad this young man was allowed to do as he liked, and now in Petersburg I hear he has been doing such terrible things that he has been expelled by the police."

"You don't say so!" replied the countess.

"He chose his friends badly," interposed Anna Mikháylovna. "Prince Vasíli's son, he, and a certain Dólokhov have, it is said, been up to heaven only knows what! And they have had to suffer for it. Dólokhov has been degraded to the ranks and Bezúkhov's son sent back to Moscow. Anatole Kurágin's father managed somehow to get his son's affair hushed up, but even he was ordered out of Petersburg."

"But what have they been up to?" asked the countess.

"They are regular brigands, especially Dólokhov," replied the visitor. "He is a son of Márya Ivánovna Dólokhova, such a worthy woman, but there, just fancy! Those three got hold of a bear somewhere, put it in a carriage, and set off with it to visit some actresses! The police tried to interfere, and what did the young men do? They tied a policeman and the bear back to back and put the bear into the Moyka Canal. And there was the bear swimming about with the policeman on his back!"

"What a nice figure the policeman must have cut, my dear!" shouted the count, dying with laughter.

"Oh, how dreadful! How can you laugh at it, Count?"

Yet the ladies themselves could not help laughing.

"It was all they could do to rescue the poor man," continued the visitor. "And to think it is Cyril Vladímirovich Bezúkhov's son who amuses himself in this sensible manner! And he was said to be so well educated and clever. This is all that his foreign education has done for him! I hope that here in Moscow no one will receive him, in spite of his money. They wanted to introduce him to me, but I quite declined: I have my daughters to consider."

"Why do you say this young man is so rich?" asked the countess, turning away from the girls, who at once assumed an air of inattention. "His children are all illegitimate. I think Pierre also is illegitimate."

The visitor made a gesture with her hand.

"I should think he has a score of them."

Princess Anna Mikháylovna intervened in the conversation, evidently wishing to show her connections and knowledge of what went on in society.

"The fact of the matter is," said she significantly, and also in a half whisper, "everyone knows Count Cyril's reputation. . . . He has lost count of his children, but this Pierre was his favorite."

"How handsome the old man still was only a year ago!" remarked the countess. "I have never seen a handsomer man."

"He is very much altered now," said Anna Mikháylovna. "Well, as I was saying, Prince Vasíli is the next heir through his wife, but the count is very fond of Pierre, looked after his education, and wrote to the Emperor about him; so that in the case of his death—and he is so ill that he may die at any moment, and Dr. Lorrain has come from Petersburg—no one knows who will inherit his immense fortune, Pierre or Prince Vasíli. Forty thousand serfs and millions of rubles! I know it all very well for Prince Vasíli told me himself. Besides, Cyril Vladímirovich is my mother's second cousin. He's also my Bóry's godfather," she added, as if she attached no importance at all to the fact.

"Prince Vasíli arrived in Moscow yesterday. I hear he has come on some inspection business," remarked the visitor.

"Yes, but between ourselves," said the princess, "that is a pretext. The fact is he has come to see Count Cyril Vladímirovich, hearing how ill he is."

"But do you know, my dear, that was a capital joke," said the count; and

seeing that the elder visitor was not listening, he turned to the young ladies. "I can just imagine what a funny figure that policeman cut!"

And as he waved his arms to impersonate the policeman, his portly form again shook with a deep ringing laugh, the laugh of one who always eats well and, in particular, drinks well. "So do come and dine with us!" he said.

5. Natásha and Borís

SILENCE ENSUED. The countess looked at her callers, smiling affably, but not concealing the fact that she would not be distressed if they now rose and took their leave. The visitor's daughter was already smoothing down her dress with an inquiring look at her mother, when suddenly from the next room were heard the footsteps of boys and girls running to the door and the noise of a chair falling over, and a girl of thirteen, hiding something in the folds of her short muslin frock, darted in and stopped short in the middle of the room. It was evident that she had not intended her flight to bring her so far. Behind her in the doorway appeared a student with a crimson coat collar, an officer of the Guards, a girl of fifteen, and a plump rosy-faced boy in a short jacket.

The count jumped up and, swaying from side to side, spread his arms wide and threw them round the little girl who had run in.

"Ah, here she is!" he exclaimed laughing. "My pet, whose name day it is. My dear pet!"

"Ma chère, there is a time for everything," said the countess with feigned severity. "You spoil her, Ilyá," she added, turning to her husband.

"How do you do, my dear? I wish you many happy returns of your name day," said the visitor. "What a charming child," she added, addressing the mother.

This black-eyed, wide-mouthed girl, not pretty but full of life—with childish bare shoulders which after her run heaved and shook her bodice, with black curls tossed backward, thin bare arms, little legs in lace-frilled drawers, and feet in low slippers—was just at that charming age when a girl is no longer a child, though the child is not yet a young woman. Escaping from her father she ran to hide her flushed face in the lace of her mother's mantilla—not paying the least attention to her severe remark—and began to laugh. She laughed, and in fragmentary sentences tried to explain about a doll which she produced from the folds of her frock.

"Do you see? . . . My doll . . . Mimi . . . You see . . ." was all Natásha [Nataly] * managed to utter (to her everything seemed funny).

* *Natásha Rostóva, the most important female character in War and Peace.*

She leaned against her mother and burst into such a loud, ringing fit of laughter that even the prim visitor could not help joining in.

"Now then, go away and take your monstrosity with you," said the mother, pushing away her daughter with pretended sternness, and turning to the visitor she added: "She is my youngest girl."

Natásha, raising her face for a moment from her mother's mantilla, glanced up at her through tears of laughter, and again hid her face.

The visitor, compelled to look on at this family scene, thought it necessary to take some part in it.

"Tell me, my dear," said she to Natásha, "is Mimi a relation of yours? A daughter, I suppose?"

Natásha did not like the visitor's tone of condescension to childish things. She did not reply, but looked at her seriously.

Meanwhile the younger generation: Borís, the officer, Anna Mikháylovna's son; Nicholas, the undergraduate, the count's eldest son; Sónya, the count's fifteen-year-old niece, and little Pétya,* his youngest boy, had all settled down in the drawing room and were obviously trying to restrain within the bounds of decorum the excitement and mirth that shone in all their faces. Evidently in the back rooms, from which they had dashed out so impetuously, the conversation had been more amusing than the drawing-room talk of society scandals, the weather, and Countess Apráksina. Now and then they glanced at one another, hardly able to suppress their laughter.[2]

The two young men, the student and the officer, friends from childhood, were of the same age and both handsome fellows, though not alike. Borís was tall and fair, and his calm and handsome face had regular, delicate features. Nicholas was short with curly hair and an open expression. Dark hairs were already showing on his upper lip, and his whole face expressed impetuosity and enthusiasm. Nicholas blushed when he entered

* Diminutive of Peter.—A.M.

[2] In describing the young Rostóvs, Tolstóy made much use of his family traditions and his impressions of his wife's family, the Behrs. To Nicholas Rostóv he has given many of his (Tolstóy's) father's features, and has even retained his name (Nicholas Ilých). Sónya is drawn from "Auntie" Tatiána Alexándrovna Érgolski, Tolstóy's favorite aunt—as family tradition depicted her as having been in her youth. Her relations to Nicholas in the novel are just those of Tatiána Alexándrovna to Tolstóy's father in real life. Véra is taken from his elder sister-in-law, Lisa Behrs, and Natásha from his younger sister-in-law, Tatiána Behrs, with some admixture of his own wife. The atmosphere of the Rostóv family reproduces much that was characteristic of the Behrs' family circle.—A.M.

the drawing room. He evidently tried to find something to say, but failed. Borís on the contrary at once found his footing, and related quietly and humorously how he had known that doll Mimi when she was still quite a young lady, before her nose was broken; how she had aged during the five years he had known her, and how her head had cracked right across the skull. Having said this he glanced at Natásha. She turned away from him and glanced at her younger brother, who was screwing up his eyes and shaking with suppressed laughter, and unable to control herself any longer, she jumped up and rushed from the room as fast as her nimble little feet would carry her. Borís did not laugh.

"You were meaning to go out, weren't you, Mamma? Do you want the carriage?" he asked his mother with a smile.

"Yes, yes, go and tell them to get it ready," she answered, returning his smile.

Borís quietly left the room and went in search of Natásha. The plump boy ran after them angrily, as if vexed that their program had been disturbed.

THE ONLY young people remaining in the drawing room, not counting the young lady visitor and the countess' eldest daughter (who was four years older than her sister and behaved already like a grown-up person), were Nicholas and Sónya, the niece. Sónya was a slender little brunette with a tender look in her eyes which were veiled by long lashes, thick black plaits coiling twice round her head, and a tawny tint in her complexion and especially in the color of her slender but graceful and muscular arms and neck. By the grace of her movements, by the softness and flexibility of her small limbs, and by a certain coyness and reserve of manner, she reminded one of a pretty, half-grown kitten which promises to become a beautiful little cat. She evidently considered it proper to show an interest in the general conversation by smiling, but in spite of herself her eyes under their thick long lashes watched her cousin who was going to join the army, with such passionate girlish adoration that her smile could not for a single instant impose upon anyone, and it was clear that the kitten had settled down only to spring up with more energy and again play with her cousin as soon as they too could, like Natásha and Borís, escape from the drawing room.

"Ah yes, my dear," said the count, addressing the visitor and pointing to Nicholas, "his friend Borís has become an officer, and so for friendship's sake he is leaving the university and me, his old father, and entering the military service, my dear. And there was a place and everything waiting for him in the Archives Department! Isn't that friendship?" remarked the count in an inquiring tone.

"But they say that war has been declared," replied the visitor.

"They've been saying so a long while," said the count, "and they'll say so again and again, and that will be the end of it. My dear, there's friendship for you," he repeated. "He's joining the hussars."

The visitor, not knowing what to say, shook her head.

"It's not at all from friendship," declared Nicholas, flaring up and turning away as if from a shameful aspersion. "It is not from friendship at all; I simply feel that the army is my vocation."

He glanced at his cousin and the young lady visitor; and they were both regarding him with a smile of approbation.

"Schubert, the colonel of the Pávlograd Hussars, is dining with us today. He has been here on leave and is taking Nicholas back with him. It can't be helped!" said the count, shrugging his shoulders and speaking playfully of a matter that evidently distressed him.

"I have already told you, Papa," said his son, "that if you don't wish to let me go, I'll stay. But I know I am no use anywhere except in the army; I am not a diplomat or a government clerk.—I don't know how to hide what I feel." As he spoke he kept glancing with the flirtatiousness of a handsome youth at Sónya and the young lady visitor.

The little kitten, feasting her eyes on him, seemed ready at any moment to start her gambols again and display her kittenish nature.

"All right, all right!" said the old count. "He always flares up! This Buonaparte has turned all their heads; they all think of how he rose from an ensign and became Emperor. Well, well, God grant it," he added, not noticing his visitor's sarcastic smile.

The elders began talking about Bonaparte. Julie Karágina turned to young Rostóv.

"What a pity you weren't at the Arkhárovs' on Thursday. It was so dull without you," said she, giving him a tender smile.

The young man, flattered, sat down nearer to her with a coquettish smile, and engaged the smiling Julie in a confidential conversation without at all noticing that his involuntary smile had stabbed the heart of Sónya, who blushed and smiled unnaturally. In the midst of his talk he glanced round at her. She gave him a passionately angry glance, and hardly able to restrain her tears and maintain the artificial smile on her lips, she got up and left the room. All Nicholas' animation vanished. He waited for the first pause in the conversation, and then with a distressed face left the room to find Sónya.

"How plainly all these young people wear their hearts on their sleeves!" said Anna Mikháylovna, pointing to Nicholas as he went out. "*Cousinage*

—*dangereux voisinage* [Cousinhood is a dangerous neighborhood]," she added.

"Yes," said the countess when the brightness these young people had brought into the room had vanished; and as if answering a question no one had put but which was always in her mind, "and how much suffering, how much anxiety one has had to go through that we might rejoice in them now! And yet really the anxiety is greater now than the joy. One is always, always anxious! Especially just at this age, so dangerous both for girls and boys."

"It all depends on the bringing up," remarked the visitor.

"Yes, you're quite right," continued the countess. "Till now I have always, thank God, been my children's friend and had their full confidence," said she, repeating the mistake of so many parents who imagine that their children have no secrets from them. "I know I shall always be my daughters' first confidante, and that if Nicholas, with his impulsive nature, does get into mischief (a boy can't help it), he will all the same never be like those Petersburg young men."

"Yes, they are splendid, splendid youngsters," chimed in the count, who always solved questions that seemed to him perplexing by deciding that everything was splendid. "Just fancy: wants to be an hussar. What's one to do, my dear?"

"What a charming creature your younger girl is," said the visitor; "a little volcano!"

"Yes, a regular volcano," said the count. "Takes after me! And what a voice she has; though she's my daughter, I tell the truth when I say she'll be a singer, a second Salomoni! * We have engaged an Italian to give her lessons."

"Isn't she too young? I have heard that it harms the voice to train it at that age."

"Oh no, not at all too young!" replied the count. "Why, our mothers used to be married at twelve or thirteen."

"And she's in love with Borís already. Just fancy!" said the countess with a gentle smile, looking at Borís' mother, and went on, evidently concerned with a thought that always occupied her: "Now you see if I were to be severe with her and to forbid it . . . goodness knows what they might be up to on the sly" (she meant that they would be kissing), "but as it is, I know every word she utters. She will come running to me of her own

* *In 1805 Salomoni was leading singer and actress in the German troupe in Moscow. "She was born in Russia and only her voice was Italian; she spoke Russian like a native, was admirably educated, played the violin and piano, and danced enchantingly."*—A.M.

accord in the evening and tell me everything. Perhaps I spoil her, but really that seems the best plan. With her elder sister I was stricter."

"Yes, I was brought up quite differently," remarked the handsome elder daughter, Countess Véra, with a smile.

But the smile did not enhance Véra's beauty as smiles generally do; on the contrary it gave her an unnatural, and therefore unpleasant, expression. Véra was good-looking, not at all stupid, quick at learning, was well brought up, and had a pleasant voice; what she said was true and appropriate, yet, strange to say, everyone—the visitors and countess alike—turned to look at her as if wondering why she had said it, and they all felt awkward.

"People are always too clever with their eldest children and try to make something exceptional of them," said the visitor.

"What's the good of denying it, my dear? Our dear countess was too clever with Véra," said the count. "Well, what of that? She's turned out splendidly all the same," he added, winking at Véra.

The guests got up and took their leave, promising to return to dinner.

"What manners! I thought they would never go," said the countess, when she had seen her guests out.

WHEN Natásha ran out of the drawing room she only went as far as the conservatory. There she paused and stood listening to the conversation in the drawing room, waiting for Borís to come out. She was already growing impatient, and stamped her foot, ready to cry at his not coming at once, when she heard the young man's discreet steps approaching neither quickly nor slowly. At this Natásha dashed swiftly among the flower tubs and hid there.

Borís paused in the middle of the room, looked round, brushed a little dust from the sleeve of his uniform, and going up to a mirror examined his handsome face. Natásha, very still, peered out from her ambush, waiting to see what he would do. He stood a little while before the glass, smiled, and walked toward the other door. Natásha was about to call him but changed her mind. "Let him look for me," thought she. Hardly had Borís gone than Sónya, flushed, in tears, and muttering angrily, came in at the other door. Natásha checked her first impulse to run out to her, and remained in her hiding place, watching—as under an invisible cap—to see what went on in the world. She was experiencing a new and peculiar pleasure. Sónya, muttering to herself, kept looking round toward the drawing-room door. It opened and Nicholas came in.

"Sónya, what is the matter with you? How can you?" said he, running up to her.

"It's nothing, nothing; leave me alone!" sobbed Sónya.

"Ah, I know what it is."

"Well, if you do, so much the better, and you can go back to her!"

"Só-o-onya! Look here! How can you torture me and yourself like that, for a mere fancy?" said Nicholas taking her hand.

Sónya did not pull it away, and left off crying. Natásha, not stirring and scarcely breathing, watched from her ambush with sparkling eyes. "What will happen now?" thought she.

"Sónya! What is anyone in the world to me? You alone are everything!" said Nicholas. "And I will prove it to you."

"I don't like you to talk like that."

"Well, then, I won't; only forgive me, Sónya!" He drew her to him and kissed her.

"Oh, how nice," thought Natásha; and when Sónya and Nicholas had gone out of the conservatory she followed and called Borís to her.

"Borís, come here," said she with a sly and significant look. "I have something to tell you. Here, here!" and she led him into the conservatory to the place among the tubs where she had been hiding.

Borís followed her, smiling.

"What is the *something*?" asked he.

She grew confused, glanced round, and, seeing the doll she had thrown down on one of the tubs, picked it up.

"Kiss the doll," said she.

Borís looked attentively and kindly at her eager face, but did not reply.

"Don't you want to? Well, then, come here," said she, and went further in among the plants and threw down the doll. "Closer, closer!" she whispered.

She caught the young officer by his cuffs, and a look of solemnity and fear appeared on her flushed face.

"And me? Would you like to kiss me?" she whispered almost inaudibly, glancing up at him from under her brows, smiling, and almost crying from excitement.

Borís blushed.

"How funny you are!" he said, bending down to her and blushing still more, but he waited and did nothing.

Suddenly she jumped up onto a tub to be higher than he, embraced him so that both her slender bare arms clasped him above his neck, and, tossing back her hair, kissed him full on the lips.

Then she slipped down among the flowerpots on the other side of the tubs and stood, hanging her head.

"Natásha," he said, "you know that I love you, but . . ."

"You are in love with me?" Natásha broke in.

"Yes, I am, but please don't let us do like that. . . . In another four years . . . then I will ask for your hand."

Natásha considered.

"Thirteen, fourteen, fifteen, sixteen," she counted on her slender little fingers. "All right! Then it's settled?"

A smile of joy and satisfaction lit up her eager face.

"Settled!" replied Borís.

"Forever?" said the little girl. "Till death itself?"

She took his arm and with a happy face went with him into the adjoining sitting room.

AFTER RECEIVING her visitors, the countess was so tired that she gave orders to admit no more, but the porter was told to be sure to invite to dinner all who came "to congratulate." * The countess wished to have a tête-à-tête talk with the friend of her childhood, Princess Anna Mikháylovna, whom she had not seen properly since she returned from Petersburg. Anna Mikháylovna, with her tear-worn but pleasant face, drew her chair nearer to that of the countess.

"With you I will be quite frank," said Anna Mikháylovna. "There are not many left of us old friends! That's why I so value your friendship."

Anna Mikháylovna looked at Véra and paused. The countess pressed her friend's hand.

"Véra," she said to her eldest daughter who was evidently not a favorite, "how is it you have so little tact? Don't you see you are not wanted here? Go to the other girls, or . . ."

The handsome Véra smiled contemptuously but did not seem at all hurt.

"If you had told me sooner, Mamma, I would have gone," she replied as she rose to go to her own room.

But as she passed the sitting room she noticed two couples sitting, one pair at each window. She stopped and smiled scornfully. Sónya was sitting close to Nicholas who was copying out some verses for her, the first he had ever written. Borís and Natásha were at the other window and ceased talking when Véra entered. Sónya and Natásha looked at Véra with guilty, happy faces.

It was pleasant and touching to see these little girls in love; but apparently the sight of them roused no pleasant feeling in Véra.

* It is a Russian custom formally to congratulate people not only on births, engagements, marriages, and other auspicious occasions, but also on holidays, saints' days (or name days), birthdays, and so on.—A.M.

"How often have I asked you not to take my things?" she said. "You have a room of your own," and she took the inkstand from Nicholas.

"In a minute, in a minute," he said, dipping his pen.

"You always manage to do things at the wrong time," continued Véra. "You came rushing into the drawing room so that everyone felt ashamed of you."

Though what she said was quite just, perhaps for that very reason no one replied, and the four simply looked at one another. She lingered in the room with the inkstand in her hand.

"And at your age what secrets can there be between Natásha and Borís, or between you two? It's all nonsense!"

"Now, Véra, what does it matter to you?" said Natásha in defense, speaking very gently.

She seemed that day to be more than ever kind and affectionate to everyone.

"Very silly," said Véra. "I am ashamed of you. Secrets indeed!"

"All have secrets of their own," answered Natásha, getting warmer. "We don't interfere with you and Berg."

"I should think not," said Véra, "because there can never be anything wrong in my behavior. But I'll just tell Mamma how you are behaving with Borís."

"Natálya Ilyníchna behaves very well to me," remarked Borís. "I have nothing to complain of."

"Don't, Borís! You are such a diplomat that it is really tiresome," said Natásha in a mortified voice that trembled slightly. (She used the word "diplomat," which was just then much in vogue among the children, in the special sense they attached to it.) "Why does she bother me?" And she added, turning to Véra, "You'll never understand it, because you've never loved anyone. You have no heart! You are a Madame de Genlis * and nothing more" (this nickname, bestowed on Véra by Nicholas, was considered very stinging), "and your greatest pleasure is to be unpleasant to people! Go and flirt with Berg as much as you please," she finished quickly.

"I shall at any rate not run after a young man before visitors . . ."

"Well, now you've done what you wanted," put in Nicholas—"said

* A *French writer of that period, authoress of educational works and novels. Later on, Kutúzov is described as reading a novel of hers on the eve of Borodinó. They were stories of good society, refined and correct, but the young Rostóvs evidently found them dull, and aptly enough nicknamed Véra "Madame de Genlis" when annoyed by her insistence on the proprieties.—*A.M.

unpleasant things to everyone and upset them. Let's go to the nursery."

All four, like a flock of scared birds, got up and left the room.

"The unpleasant things were said to me," remarked Véra, "I said none to anyone."

"Madame de Genlis! Madame de Genlis!" shouted laughing voices through the door.

The handsome Véra, who produced such an irritating and unpleasant effect on everyone, smiled and, evidently unmoved by what had been said to her, went to the looking glass and arranged her hair and scarf. Looking at her own handsome face she seemed to become still colder and calmer.

In the drawing room the conversation was still going on.

"Ah, my dear," said the countess, "my life is not all roses either. Don't I know that at the rate we are living our means won't last long? It's all the Club and his easygoing nature. Even in the country do we get any rest? Theatricals, hunting, and heaven knows what besides! But don't let's talk about me; tell me how you managed everything. I often wonder at you, Annette—how at your age you can rush off alone in a carriage to Moscow, to Petersburg, to those ministers and great people, and know how to deal with them all! It's quite astonishing. How did you get things settled? I couldn't possibly do it."

"Ah, my love," answered Anna Mikháylovna, "God grant you never know what it is to be left a widow without means and with a son you love to distraction! One learns many things then," she added with a certain pride. "That lawsuit taught me much. When I want to see one of those big people I write a note: 'Princess So-and-So desires an interview with So-and-So,' and then I take a cab and go myself two, three, or four times—till I get what I want. I don't mind what they think of me."

"Well, and to whom did you apply about Bóry?" asked the countess. "You see yours is already an officer in the Guards, while my Nicholas is going as a cadet.* There's no one to interest himself for him. To whom did you apply?"

"To Prince Vasíli. He was so kind. He at once agreed to everything, and put the matter before the Emperor," said Princess Anna Mikháylovna enthusiastically, quite forgetting all the humiliation she had endured to gain her end.

* A cadet was a volunteer, usually of good family, who had not yet received a commission, but whose place in the army was with the officers and not in the ranks.—A.M.

"Has Prince Vasíli aged much?" asked the countess. "I have not seen him since we acted together at the Rumyántsovs' theatricals. I expect he has forgotten me. He paid me attentions in those days," said the countess, with a smile.

"He is just the same as ever," replied Anna Mikháylovna, "overflowing with amiability. His position has not turned his head at all. He said to me, 'I am sorry I can do so little for you, dear Princess. I am at your command.' Yes, he is a fine fellow and a very kind relation. But, Nataly, you know my love for my son: I would do anything for his happiness! And my affairs are in such a bad way that my position is now a terrible one," continued Anna Mikháylovna, sadly, dropping her voice. "My wretched lawsuit takes all I have and makes no progress. Would you believe it, I have literally not a penny and don't know how to equip Borís." She took out her handkerchief and began to cry. "I need five hundred rubles, and have only one twenty-five-ruble note. I am in such a state. . . . My only hope now is in Count Cyril Vladímirovich Bezúkhov. If he will not assist his godson—you know he is Bóry's godfather—and allow him something for his maintenance, all my trouble will have been thrown away. . . . I shall not be able to equip him."

The countess' eyes filled with tears and she pondered in silence.

"I often think, though, perhaps it's a sin," said the princess, "that here lives Count Cyril Vladímirovich Bezúkhov so rich, all alone . . . that tremendous fortune . . . and what is his life worth? It's a burden to him, and Bóry's life is only just beginning. . . ."

"Surely he will leave something to Borís," said the countess.

"Heaven only knows, my dear! These rich grandees are so selfish. Still, I will take Borís and go to see him at once, and I shall speak to him straight out. Let people think what they will of me, it's really all the same to me when my son's fate is at stake." The princess rose. "It's now two o'clock and you dine at four. There will just be time."

And like a practical Petersburg lady who knows how to make the most of time, Anna Mikháylovna sent someone to call her son, and went into the anteroom with him.

"Good-by, my dear," said she to the countess who saw her to the door, and added in a whisper so that her son should not hear, "Wish me good luck."

"Are you going to Count Cyril Vladímirovich, my dear?" said the count coming out from the dining hall into the anteroom, and he added: "If he is better, ask Pierre to dine with us. He has been to the house, you know, and danced with the children. Be sure to invite him, my dear. We will see

how Tarás distinguishes himself today. He says Count Orlóv never gave such a dinner as ours will be!" *

6. Anna Mikháylovna and Borís go to the dying Count Bezúkhov's

"MY DEAR BORÍS," said Princess Anna Mikháylovna to her son as Countess Rostóva's carriage in which they were seated drove over the straw-covered street and turned into the wide courtyard of Count Cyril Vladímirovich Bezúkhov's house. "My dear Borís," said the mother, drawing her hand from beneath her old mantle and laying it timidly and tenderly on her son's arm, "be affectionate and attentive to him. Count Cyril Vladímirovich is your godfather after all, and your future depends on him. Remember that, my dear, and be nice to him, as you so well know how to be."

"If only I knew that anything besides humiliation would come of it . . ." answered her son coldly. "But I have promised and will do it for your sake."

Although the hall porter saw someone's carriage standing at the entrance, after scrutinizing the mother and son (who without asking to be announced had passed straight through the glass porch between the rows of statues in niches) and looking significantly at the lady's old cloak, he asked whether they wanted the count or the princesses, and, hearing that they wished to see the count, said his excellency was worse today, and that his excellency was not receiving anyone.

"We may as well go back," said the son in French.

"My dear!" exclaimed his mother imploringly, again laying her hand on his arm as if that touch might soothe or rouse him.

Borís said no more, but looked inquiringly at his mother without taking off his cloak.

"My friend," said Anna Mikháylovna in gentle tones, addressing the hall porter, "I know Count Cyril Vladímirovich is very ill . . . that's why I have come . . . I am a relation. I shall not disturb him, my friend . . .

* This was Count Alexéy Orlóv. He and his brother Gregory played leading roles in the palace revolution of 1762, which led to the death of Peter III and to Catherine's securing the throne. After distinguishing himself in the Turkish war of 1774, Alexéy Orlóv retired and lived in his Neskúchni palace near Moscow, giving luxurious balls and dinners, and amazing everybody by his open-handed hospitality. In the early years of the nineteenth century he was the most popular man in Moscow.—A.M.

I only need see Prince Vasíli Sergéevich: he is staying here, is he not? Please announce me."

The hall porter sullenly pulled a bell that rang upstairs, and turned away.

"Princess Drubetskáya to see Prince Vasíli Sergéevich," he called to a footman dressed in knee breeches, shoes, and a swallow-tail coat, who ran downstairs and looked over from the halfway landing.

The mother smoothed the folds of her dyed silk dress before a large Venetian mirror in the wall, and in her trodden-down shoes briskly ascended the carpeted stairs.

"My dear," she said to her son, once more stimulating him by a touch, "you promised me!"

The son, lowering his eyes, followed her quietly.

They entered the large hall, from which one of the doors led to the apartments assigned to Prince Vasíli.

Just as the mother and son, having reached the middle of the hall, were about to ask their way of an elderly footman who had sprung up as they entered, the bronze handle of one of the doors turned and Prince Vasíli came out—wearing a velvet coat with a single star on his breast, as was his custom when at home—taking leave of a good-looking, dark-haired man. This was the celebrated Petersburg doctor, Lorrain.

"Then it is certain?" said the prince.

"Prince, *humanum est errare* [to err is human], but . . ." replied the doctor, swallowing his r's, and pronouncing the Latin words with a French accent.

"Very well, very well . . ."

Seeing Anna Mikháylovna and her son, Prince Vasíli dismissed the doctor with a bow and approached them silently and with a look of inquiry. The son noticed that an expression of profound sorrow suddenly clouded his mother's face, and he smiled slightly.

"Ah, Prince! In what sad circumstances we meet again! And how is our dear invalid?" said she, as though unaware of the cold offensive look fixed on her.

Prince Vasíli stared at her and at Borís questioningly and perplexed. Borís bowed politely. Prince Vasíli without acknowledging the bow turned to Anna Mikháylovna, answering her query by a movement of the head and lips indicating very little hope for the patient.

"Is it possible?" exclaimed Anna Mikháylovna. "Oh, how awful! It is terrible to think. . . . This is my son," she added, indicating Borís. "He wanted to thank you himself."

Borís bowed again politely.

"Believe me, Prince, a mother's heart will never forget what you have done for us."

"I am glad I was able to do you a service, my dear Anna Mikháylovna," said Prince Vasíli, arranging his lace frill, and in tone and manner, here in Moscow to Anna Mikháylovna whom he had placed under an obligation, assuming an air of much greater importance than he had done in Petersburg at Anna Schérer's reception.

"Try to serve well and show yourself worthy," added he, addressing Borís with severity. "I am glad. . . . Are you here on leave?" he went on in his usual tone of indifference.

"I am awaiting orders to join my new regiment, your excellency," replied Borís, betraying neither annoyance at the prince's brusque manner nor a desire to enter into conversation, but speaking so quietly and respectfully that the prince gave him a searching glance.

"Are you living with your mother?"

"I am living at Countess Rostóva's," replied Borís, again adding, "your excellency."

"That is, with Ilyá Rostóv who married Nataly Shinshiná," said Anna Mikháylovna.

"I know, I know," answered Prince Vasíli in his monotonous voice. "I never could understand how Nataly made up her mind to marry that unlicked bear! A perfectly absurd and stupid fellow, and a gambler too, I am told."

"But a very kind man, Prince," said Anna Mikháylovna with a pathetic smile, as though she too knew that Count Rostóv deserved this censure, but asked him not to be too hard on the poor old man. "What do the doctors say?" asked the princess after a pause, her worn face again expressing deep sorrow.

"They give little hope," replied the prince.

"And I should so like to thank Uncle once for all his kindness to me and Borís. He is his godson," she added, her tone suggesting that this fact ought to give Prince Vasíli much satisfaction.

Prince Vasíli became thoughtful and frowned. Anna Mikháylovna saw that he was afraid of finding in her a rival for Count Bezúkhov's fortune, and hastened to reassure him.

"If it were not for my sincere affection and devotion to Uncle," said she, uttering the word with peculiar assurance and unconcern, "I know his character: noble, upright . . . but you see he has no one with him except the young princesses. . . . They are still young. . . ." She bent her

head and continued in a whisper: "Has he performed his final duty,* Prince? How priceless are those last moments! It can make things no worse, and it is absolutely necessary to prepare him if he is so ill. We women, Prince," and she smiled tenderly, "always know how to say these things. I absolutely must see him, however painful it may be for me. I am used to suffering."

Evidently the prince understood her, and also understood, as he had done at Anna Pávlovna's, that it would be difficult to get rid of Anna Mikháylovna.

"Would not such a meeting be too trying for him, dear Anna Mikháylovna?" said he. "Let us wait until evening. The doctors are expecting a crisis."

"But one cannot delay, Prince, at such a moment! Consider that the welfare of his soul is at stake. Ah, it is awful: the duties of a Christian . . ."

A door of one of the inner rooms opened and one of the princesses, the count's niece, entered with a cold, stern face. The length of her body was strikingly out of proportion to her short legs. Prince Vasíli turned to her.

"Well, how is he?"

"Still the same; but what can you expect, this noise . . ." said the princess, looking at Anna Mikháylovna as at a stranger.

"Ah, my dear, I hardly knew you," said Anna Mikháylovna with a happy smile, ambling lightly up to the count's niece. "I have come, and am at your service to help you nurse my uncle. I imagine what you have gone through," and she sympathetically turned up her eyes.

The princess gave no reply and did not even smile, but left the room at once. Anna Mikháylovna took off her gloves and, occupying the position she had conquered, settled down in an armchair, inviting Prince Vasíli to take a seat beside her.

"Borís," she said to her son with a smile, "I shall go in to see the count, my uncle; but you, my dear, had better go to Pierre meanwhile and don't forget to give him the Rostóvs' invitation. They ask him to dinner. I suppose he won't go?" she continued, turning to the prince.

"On the contrary," replied the prince, who had plainly become depressed, "I shall be only too glad if you relieve me of that young man. . . . Here he is, and the count has not once asked for him."

He shrugged his shoulders. A footman conducted Borís down one flight of stairs and up another, to Pierre's rooms.

* *The duty being to receive unction.*—A.M.

7. Pierre at his father's house; talks with Borís

PIERRE, after all, had not managed to choose a career for himself in Petersburg, and had been expelled from there for riotous conduct and sent to Moscow. The story told about him at Count Rostóv's was true. Pierre had taken part in tying a policeman to a bear. He had now been for some days in Moscow and was staying as usual at his father's house. Though he expected that the story of his escapade would be already known in Moscow and that the ladies about his father—who were never favorably disposed toward him—would have used it to turn the count against him, he nevertheless on the day of his arrival went to his father's part of the house. Entering the drawing room, where the princesses spent most of their time, he greeted the ladies, two of whom were sitting at embroidery frames while a third read aloud. It was the eldest who was reading—the one who had met Anna Mikháylovna. The two younger ones were embroidering: both were rosy and pretty and they differed only in that one had a little mole on her lip which made her much prettier. Pierre was received as if he were a corpse or a leper. The eldest princess paused in her reading and silently stared at him with frightened eyes: the second assumed precisely the same expression: while the youngest, the one with the mole, who was of a cheerful and lively disposition, bent over her frame to hide a smile probably evoked by the amusing scene she foresaw. She drew her wool down through the canvas and, scarcely able to refrain from laughing, stooped as if trying to make out the pattern.

"How do you do, cousin?" said Pierre. "You don't recognize me?"

"I recognize you only too well, too well."

"How is the count? Can I see him?" asked Pierre, awkwardly as usual, but unabashed.

"The count is suffering physically and mentally, and apparently you have done your best to increase his mental sufferings."

"Can I see the count?" Pierre again asked.

"Hm. . . . If you wish to kill him, to kill him outright, you can see him . . . Olga, go and see whether Uncle's beef tea is ready—it is almost time," she added, giving Pierre to understand that they were busy, and busy making his father comfortable, while evidently he, Pierre, was only busy causing him annoyance.

Olga went out. Pierre stood looking at the sisters; then he bowed and said: "Then I will go to my rooms. You will let me know when I can see him."

And he left the room, followed by the low but ringing laughter of the sister with the mole.

Next day Prince Vasíli had arrived and settled in the count's house. He sent for Pierre and said to him: "My dear fellow, if you are going to behave here as you did in Petersburg, you will end very badly; that is all I have to say to you. The count is very, very ill, and you must not see him at all."

Since then Pierre had not been disturbed and had spent the whole time in his rooms upstairs.

When Borís appeared at his door Pierre was pacing up and down his room, stopping occasionally at a corner to make menacing gestures at the wall, as if running a sword through an invisible foe, and glaring savagely over his spectacles, and then again resuming his walk, muttering indistinct words, shrugging his shoulders and gesticulating.

"England is done for," said he, scowling and pointing his finger at someone unseen. "Mr. Pitt, as a traitor to the nation and to the rights of man, is sentenced to . . ." But before Pierre—who at that moment imagined himself to be Napoleon in person and to have just effected the dangerous crossing of the Straits of Dover and captured London—could pronounce Pitt's sentence, he saw a well-built and handsome young officer entering his room. Pierre paused. He had left Moscow when Borís was a boy of fourteen, and had quite forgotten him, but in his usual impulsive and hearty way he took Borís by the hand with a friendly smile.

"Do you remember me?" asked Borís quietly with a pleasant smile. "I have come with my mother to see the count, but it seems he is not well."

"Yes, it seems he is ill. People are always disturbing him," answered Pierre, trying to remember who this young man was.

Borís felt that Pierre did not recognize him but did not consider it necessary to introduce himself, and without experiencing the least embarrassment looked Pierre straight in the face.

"Count Rostóv asks you to come to dinner today," said he, after a considerable pause which made Pierre feel uncomfortable.

"Ah, Count Rostóv!" exclaimed Pierre joyfully. "Then you are his son, Ilyá? Only fancy, I didn't know you at first. Do you remember how we went to the Sparrow Hills with Madame Jacquot? . . . It's such an age . . ."

"You are mistaken," said Borís deliberately, with a bold and slightly sarcastic smile. "I am Borís, son of Princess Anna Mikháylovna Drubetskáya. Rostóv, the father, is Ilyá, and his son is Nicholas. I never knew any Madame Jacquot."

Pierre shook his head and arms as if attacked by mosquitoes or bees.

"Oh dear, what am I thinking about? I've mixed everything up. One has so many relatives in Moscow! So you are Borís? Of course. Well, now we know where we are. And what do you think of the Boulogne expedition? The English will come off badly, you know, if Napoleon gets across the Channel. I think the expedition is quite feasible. If only Villeneuve doesn't make a mess of things!"

Borís knew nothing about the Boulogne expedition; he did not read the papers and it was the first time he had heard Villeneuve's name.

"We here in Moscow are more occupied with dinner parties and scandal than with politics," said he in his quiet ironical tone. "I know nothing about it and have not thought about it. Moscow is chiefly busy with gossip," he continued. "Just now they are talking about you and your father."

Pierre smiled in his good-natured way as if afraid for his companion's sake that the latter might say something he would afterwards regret. But Borís spoke distinctly, clearly, and dryly, looking straight into Pierre's eyes.

"Moscow has nothing else to do but gossip," Borís went on. "Everybody is wondering to whom the count will leave his fortune, though he may perhaps outlive us all, as I sincerely hope he will . . ."

"Yes, it is all very horrid," interrupted Pierre, "very horrid."

Pierre was still afraid that this officer might inadvertently say something disconcerting to himself.

"And it must seem to you," said Borís flushing slightly, but not changing his tone or attitude, "it must seem to you that everyone is trying to get something out of the rich man?"

"So it does," thought Pierre.

"But I just wish to say, to avoid misunderstandings, that you are quite mistaken if you reckon me or my mother among such people. We are very poor, but for my own part at any rate, for the very reason that your father is rich, I don't regard myself as a relation of his, and neither I nor my mother would ever ask or take anything from him."

For a long time Pierre could not understand, but when he did, he jumped up from the sofa, seized Borís under the elbow in his quick, clumsy way, and, blushing far more than Borís, began to speak with a feeling of mingled shame and vexation.

"Well, this is strange! Do you suppose I . . . who could think? . . . I know very well . . ."

But Borís again interrupted him.

"I am glad I have spoken out fully. Perhaps you did not like it? You must excuse me," said he, putting Pierre at ease instead of being put at ease by him, "but I hope I have not offended you. I always make it a rule to speak

out. . . . Well, what answer am I to take? Will you come to dinner at
the Rostóvs'?"

And Borís, having apparently relieved himself of an onerous duty and
extricated himself from an awkward situation and placed another in it,
became quite pleasant again.

"No, but I say," said Pierre, calming down, "you are a wonderful fel-
low! What you have just said is good, very good. Of course you don't
know me. We have not met for such a long time . . . not since we were
children. You might think that I . . . I understand, quite understand.
I could not have done it myself, I should not have had the courage, but
it's splendid. I am very glad to have made your acquaintance. It's queer,"
he added after a pause, "that you should have suspected me!" He began
to laugh. "Well, what of it! I hope we'll get better acquainted," and he
pressed Borís' hand. "Do you know, I have not once been in to see the
count. He has not sent for me. . . . I am sorry for him as a man, but
what can one do?"

"And so you think Napoleon will manage to get an army across?" asked
Borís with a smile.

Pierre saw that Borís wished to change the subject, and being of the
same mind he began explaining the advantages and disadvantages of the
Boulogne expedition.

A footman came in to summon Borís—the princess was going. Pierre,
in order to make Borís' better acquaintance, promised to come to dinner,
and warmly pressing his hand looked affectionately over his spectacles
into Borís' eyes. After he had gone Pierre continued pacing up and down
the room for a long time, no longer piercing an imaginary foe with his
imaginary sword, but smiling at the remembrance of that pleasant, intel-
ligent, and resolute young man.

As often happens in early youth, especially to one who leads a lonely
life, he felt an unaccountable tenderness for this young man and made
up his mind that they would be friends.

Prince Vasíli saw the princess off. She held a handkerchief to her eyes
and her face was tearful.

"It is dreadful, dreadful!" she was saying, "but cost me what it may I
shall do my duty. I will come and spend the night. He must not be left
like this. Every moment is precious. I can't think why his nieces put it
off. Perhaps God will help me to find a way to prepare him! . . . Adieu,
Prince! May God support you . . ."

"Adieu, ma bonne," answered Prince Vasíli turning away from her.

"Oh, he is in a dreadful state," said the mother to her son when they
were in the carriage. "He hardly recognizes anybody."

"I don't understand, Mamma—what is his attitude to Pierre?" asked the son.

"The will will show that, my dear; our fate also depends on it."

"But why do you expect that he will leave us anything?"

"Ah, my dear! He is so rich, and we are so poor!"

"Well, that is hardly a sufficient reason, Mamma . . ."

"Oh, Heaven! How ill he is!" exclaimed the mother.

8. Countess Rostóva and Anna Mikháylovna

AFTER ANNA MIKHÁYLOVNA had driven off with her son to visit Count Cyril Vladímirovich Bezúkhov, Countess Rostóva sat for a long time all alone applying her handkerchief to her eyes. At last she rang.

"What is the matter with you, my dear?" she said crossly to the maid who kept her waiting some minutes. "Don't you wish to serve me? Then I'll find you another place."

The countess was upset by her friend's sorrow and humiliating poverty, and was therefore out of sorts, a state of mind which with her always found expression in calling her maid "my dear" and speaking to her with exaggerated politeness.

"I am very sorry, ma'am," answered the maid.

"Ask the count to come to me."

The count came waddling in to see his wife with a rather guilty look as usual.

"Well, little countess? What a sauté of game au madère we are to have, my dear! I tasted it. The thousand rubles I paid for Tarás were not ill-spent. He is worth it!" *

He sat down by his wife, his elbows on his knees and his hands ruffling his gray hair.

"What are your commands, little countess?"

"You see, my dear . . . What's that mess?" she said, pointing to his waistcoat. "It's the sauté, most likely," she added with a smile. "Well, you see, Count, I want some money."

Her face became sad.

* Tarás was evidently a serf. Serfs were usually only sold with the estates to which they belonged, but trained domestics were sometimes sold separately. Tarás had probably learned to be a cook under a foreign chef at the English Club. A thousand rubles would at that time have purchased eight or ten ordinary serfs.—A.M.

"Oh, little countess!" . . . and the count began bustling to get out his pocketbook.

"I want a great deal, Count! I want five hundred rubles," and taking out her cambric handkerchief she began wiping her husband's waistcoat.

"Yes, immediately, immediately! Hey, who's there?" he called out in a tone only used by persons who are certain that those they call will rush to obey the summons. "Send Dmítri to me!"

Dmítri, a man of good family who had been brought up in the count's house and now managed all his affairs, stepped softly into the room.

"This is what I want, my dear fellow," said the count to the deferential young man who had entered. "Bring me . . ." he reflected a moment, "yes, bring me seven hundred rubles, yes! But mind, don't bring me such tattered and dirty notes as last time, but nice clean ones for the countess."

"Yes, Dmítri, clean ones, please," said the countess, sighing deeply.

"When would you like them, your excellency?" asked Dmítri. "Allow me to inform you . . . But, don't be uneasy," he added, noticing that the count was beginning to breathe heavily and quickly which was always a sign of approaching anger. "I was forgetting . . . Do you wish it brought at once?"

"Yes, yes; just so! Bring it. Give it to the countess."

"What a treasure that Dmítri is," added the count with a smile when the young man had departed. "There is never any 'impossible' with him. That's a thing I hate! Everything is possible."

"Ah, money, Count, money! How much sorrow it causes in the world," said the countess. "But I am in great need of this sum."

"You, my little countess, are a notorious spendthrift," said the count, and having kissed his wife's hand he went back to his study.

When Anna Mikháylovna returned from Count Bezúkhov's the money, all in clean notes, was lying ready under a handkerchief on the countess' little table, and Anna Mikháylovna noticed that something was agitating her.

"Well, my dear?" asked the countess.

"Oh, what a terrible state he is in! One would not know him, he is so ill! I was only there a few moments and hardly said a word . . ."

"Annette, for heaven's sake don't refuse me," the countess began, with a blush that looked very strange on her thin, dignified, elderly face, and she took the money from under the handkerchief.

Anna Mikháylovna instantly guessed her intention and stooped to be ready to embrace the countess at the appropriate moment.

"This is for Borís from me, for his outfit."

Anna Mikháylovna was already embracing her and weeping. The countess wept too. They wept because they were friends, and because they were kindhearted, and because they—friends from childhood—had to think about such a base thing as money, and because their youth was over. . . . But those tears were pleasant to them both.

9. Dinner at the Rostóvs'. Márya Dmítrievna

COUNTESS ROSTÓVA, with her daughters and a large number of guests, was already seated in the drawing room. The count took the gentlemen into his study and showed them his choice collection of Turkish pipes. From time to time he went out to ask: "Hasn't she come yet?" They were expecting Márya Dmítrievna Akhrosímova, known in society as le terrible dragon, a lady distinguished not for wealth or rank, but for common sense and frank plainness of speech. Márya Dmítrievna was known to the Imperial family as well as to all Moscow and Petersburg, and both cities wondered at her, laughed privately at her rudenesses, and told good stories about her, while none the less all without exception respected and feared her.*

In the count's room, which was full of tobacco smoke, they talked of the war that had been announced in a manifesto, and about the recruiting. None of them had yet seen the manifesto, but they all knew it had appeared. The count sat on the sofa between two guests who were smoking and talking. He neither smoked nor talked, but bending his head first to one side and then to the other watched the smokers with evident pleasure and listened to the conversation of his two neighbors, whom he egged on against each other.

One of them was a sallow, clean-shaven civilian with a thin and wrinkled face, already growing old, though he was dressed like a most fashionable young man. He sat with his legs up on the sofa as if quite at home and, having stuck an amber mouthpiece far into his mouth, was inhaling the smoke spasmodically and screwing up his eyes. This was an old bachelor, Shinshín, a cousin of the countess', a man with "a sharp tongue" as they said in Moscow society. He seemed to be condescending to his companion. The latter, a fresh, rosy officer of the Guards, irreproachably washed, brushed, and buttoned, held his pipe in the middle of his mouth and with

* Márya Dmítrievna Akhrosímova was a real person, well known in Moscow. Tolstóy while keeping her other names has changed her Christian name from Natálya to Márya. He is not the only Russian writer who has made use of her in fiction.—A.M.

red lips gently inhaled the smoke, letting it escape from his handsome mouth in rings. This was Lieutenant Berg, an officer in the Seménov regiment with whom Borís was to travel to join the army, and about whom Natásha had teased her elder sister Véra, speaking of Berg as her "intended." The count sat between them and listened attentively. His favorite occupation when not playing boston, a card game he was very fond of, was that of listener, especially when he succeeded in setting two loquacious talkers at one another.

"Well, then, old chap, *mon très honorable* Alphonse Kárlovich," said Shinshín, laughing ironically and mixing the most ordinary Russian expressions with the choicest French phrases—which was a peculiarity of his speech. "*Vous comptez vous faire des rentes sur l'état* [You expect to make an income out of the government]; you want to make something out of your company?"

"No, Peter Nikoláevich; I only want to show that in the cavalry the advantages are far less than in the infantry. Just consider my own position now, Peter Nikoláevich . . ."

Berg always spoke quietly, politely, and with great precision. His conversation always related entirely to himself; he would remain calm and silent when the talk related to any topic that had no direct bearing on himself. He could remain silent for hours without being at all put out of countenance himself or making others uncomfortable, but as soon as the conversation concerned himself he would begin to talk circumstantially and with evident satisfaction.

"Consider my position, Peter Nikoláevich. Were I in the cavalry I should get not more than two hundred rubles every four months, even with the rank of lieutenant; but as it is I receive two hundred and thirty," said he, looking at Shinshín and the count with a joyful, pleasant smile, as if it were obvious to him that his success must always be the chief desire of everyone else.

"Besides that, Peter Nikoláevich, by exchanging into the Guards I shall be in a more prominent position," continued Berg, "and vacancies occur much more frequently in the Foot Guards. Then just think what can be done with two hundred and thirty rubles! I even manage to put a little aside and to send something to my father," he went on, emitting a smoke ring.

"*La balance y est* [So that squares matters]. . . . A German knows how to skin a flint, as the proverb says," remarked Shinshín, moving his pipe to the other side of his mouth and winking at the count.

The count burst out laughing. The other guests seeing that Shinshín

was talking came up to listen. Berg, oblivious of irony or indifference, continued to explain how by exchanging into the Guards he had already gained a step on his old comrades of the Cadet Corps; how in wartime the company commander might get killed and he, as senior in the company, might easily succeed to the post; how popular he was with everyone in the regiment, and how satisfied his father was with him. Berg evidently enjoyed narrating all this, and did not seem to suspect that others, too, might have their own interests. But all he said was so prettily sedate, and the naïveté of his youthful egotism was so obvious, that he disarmed his hearers.

"Well, my boy, you'll get along wherever you go—foot or horse—that I'll warrant," said Shinshín, patting him on the shoulder and taking his feet off the sofa.

Berg smiled joyously. The count, followed by his guests, went into the drawing room.

It was just the moment before a big dinner when the assembled guests, expecting the summons to zakúska,* avoid engaging in any long conversation but think it necessary to move about and talk, in order to show that they are not at all impatient for their food. The host and hostess look toward the door, and now and then glance at one another, and the visitors try to guess from these glances who, or what, they are waiting for—some important relation who has not yet arrived, or a dish that is not yet ready.

Pierre had come just at dinnertime and was sitting awkwardly in the middle of the drawing room on the first chair he had come across, blocking the way for everyone. The countess tried to make him talk, but he went on naïvely looking around through his spectacles as if in search of somebody and answered all her questions in monosyllables. He was in the way and was the only one who did not notice the fact. Most of the guests, knowing of the affair with the bear, looked with curiosity at this big, stout, quiet man, wondering how such a clumsy, modest fellow could have played such a prank on a policeman.

"You have only lately arrived?" the countess asked him.

"Oui, madame," replied he, looking around him.

"You have not yet seen my husband?"

"Non, madame." He smiled quite inappropriately.

* The zakúska, "little bite," is the hors d'oeuvre, consisting according to circumstances of a more or less varied choice of snacks: caviar, salt fish, cheese, radishes, or whatnot, with small glasses of vodka and other spirits. It is usually laid on a small table and serves to whet the appetite.—A.M.

"You have been in Paris recently, I believe? I suppose it's very interesting."

"Very interesting."

The countess exchanged glances with Anna Mikháylovna. The latter understood that she was being asked to entertain this young man, and sitting down beside him she began to speak about his father; but he answered her, as he had the countess, only in monosyllables. The other guests were all conversing with one another. "The Razumóvskis . . . It was charming . . . You are very kind . . . Countess Apráksina . . ." was heard on all sides. The countess rose and went into the ballroom.

"Márya Dmítrievna?" came her voice from there.

"Herself," came the answer in a rough voice, and Márya Dmítrievna entered the room.

All the unmarried ladies and even the married ones except the very oldest rose. Márya Dmítrievna paused at the door. Tall and stout, holding high her fifty-year-old head with its gray curls, she stood surveying the guests, and leisurely arranged her wide sleeves as if rolling them up. Márya Dmítrievna always spoke in Russian.

"Health and happiness to her whose name day we are keeping and to her children," she said, in her loud, full-toned voice which drowned all others. "Well, you old sinner," she went on, turning to the count who was kissing her hand, "you're feeling dull in Moscow, I daresay? Nowhere to hunt with your dogs? But what is to be done, old man? Just see how these nestlings are growing up," and she pointed to the girls. "You must look for husbands for them whether you like it or not. . . .

"Well," said she, "how's my Cossack?" (Márya Dmítrievna always called Natásha a Cossack) and she stroked the child's arm as she came up fearless and gay to kiss her hand. "I know she's a scamp of a girl, but I like her."

She took a pair of pear-shaped ruby earrings from her huge reticule and, having given them to the rosy Natásha, who beamed with the pleasure of her saint's-day fete,* turned away at once and addressed herself to Pierre.

"Eh, eh, friend! Come here a bit," said she, assuming a soft high tone of voice. "Come here, my friend . . ." and she ominously tucked up her sleeves still higher. Pierre approached, looking at her in a childlike way through his spectacles.

"Come nearer, come nearer, friend! I used to be the only one to tell

* *Every Russian received the name of one of the saints in the Church calendar, and that saint's day was his or her name day and was kept much as a birthday is kept in England and the United States.*—A.M.

your father the truth when he was in favor, and in your case it's my evident duty."

She paused. All were silent, expectant of what was to follow, for this was clearly only a prelude.

"A fine lad! My word! A fine lad! . . , His father lies on his deathbed and he amuses himself setting a policeman astride a bear! For shame, sir, for shame! It would be better if you went to the war."

She turned away and gave her hand to the count, who could hardly keep from laughing.

"Well, I suppose it is time we were at table?" said Márya Dmítrievna.

The count went in first with Márya Dmítrievna, the countess followed on the arm of a colonel of hussars, a man of importance to them because Nicholas was to go with him to the regiment; then came Anna Mikháylovna with Shinshín. Berg gave his arm to Véra. The smiling Julie Karágina went in with Nicholas. After them other couples followed, filling the whole dining hall, and last of all the children, tutors, and governesses followed singly. The footmen began moving about, chairs scraped, the band struck up in the gallery, and the guests settled down in their places. Then the strains of the count's household band were replaced by the clatter of knives and forks, the voices of visitors, and the soft steps of the footmen. At one end of the table sat the countess with Márya Dmítrievna on her right and Anna Mikháylovna on her left, the other lady visitors were farther down. At the other end sat the count, with the hussar colonel on his left and Shinshín and the other male visitors on his right. Midway down the long table on one side sat the grown-up young people: Véra beside Berg, and Pierre beside Borís; and on the other side the children, tutors, and governesses. From behind the crystal decanters and fruit vases the count kept glancing at his wife and her tall cap with its light-blue ribbons, and busily filled his neighbors' glasses, not neglecting his own. The countess in turn, without omitting her duties as hostess, threw significant glances from behind the pineapples at her husband whose face and bald head seemed by their redness to contrast more than usual with his gray hair. At the ladies' end an even chatter of voices was heard all the time, at the men's end the voices sounded louder and louder, especially that of the colonel of hussars who, growing more and more flushed, ate and drank so much that the count held him up as a pattern to the other guests. Berg with tender smiles was saying to Véra that love is not an earthly but a heavenly feeling. Borís was telling his new friend Pierre who the guests were and exchanging glances with Natásha, who was sitting opposite. Pierre spoke little but examined the new faces, and ate a great deal. Of the two soups he chose turtle with savory patties and went

on to the game without omitting a single dish or one of the wines. These latter the butler thrust mysteriously forward, wrapped in a napkin, from behind the next man's shoulders and whispered: "Dry Madeira" . . . "Hungarian" . . . or "Rhine wine" as the case might be. Of the four crystal glasses engraved with the count's monogram that stood before his plate, Pierre held out one at random and drank with enjoyment, gazing with ever-increasing amiability at the other guests. Natásha, who sat opposite, was looking at Borís as girls of thirteen look at the boy they are in love with and have just kissed for the first time. Sometimes that same look fell on Pierre, and that funny lively little girl's look made him inclined to laugh without knowing why.

Nicholas sat at some distance from Sónya, beside Julie Karágina, to whom he was again talking with the same involuntary smile. Sónya wore a company smile but was evidently tormented by jealousy; now she turned pale, now blushed and strained every nerve to overhear what Nicholas and Julie were saying to one another. The governess kept looking round uneasily as if preparing to resent any slight that might be put upon the children. The German tutor was trying to remember all the dishes, wines, and kinds of dessert, in order to send a full description of the dinner to his people in Germany; and he felt greatly offended when the butler with a bottle wrapped in a napkin passed him by. He frowned, trying to appear as if he did not want any of that wine, but was mortified because no one would understand that it was not to quench his thirst or from greediness that he wanted it, but simply from a conscientious desire for knowledge.

AT THE MEN's end of the table the talk grew more and more animated. The colonel told them that the declaration of war had already appeared in Petersburg and that a copy, which he had himself seen, had that day been forwarded by courier to the commander in chief.

"And why the deuce are we going to fight Bonaparte?" remarked Shinshín. "He has stopped Austria's cackle and I fear it will be our turn next."

The colonel was a stout, tall, plethoric German, evidently devoted to the service and patriotically Russian. He resented Shinshín's remark.

"It is for the reasson, my goot sir," said he, speaking with a German accent, "for the reasson zat ze Emperor knows zat. He declares in ze manifessto zat he cannot fiew wiz indifference ze danger vreatening Russia and zat ze safety and dignity of ze Empire as vell as ze sanctity of its alliances . . ." he spoke this last word with particular emphasis as if in it lay the gist of the matter.

Then with the unerring official memory that characterized him he repeated from the opening words of the manifesto:

. . . *and the wish, which constitutes the Emperor's sole and absolute aim—to establish peace in Europe on firm foundations—has now decided him to despatch part of the army abroad and to create a new condition for the attainment of that purpose.*

"Zat, my dear sir, is vy . . ." he concluded, drinking a tumbler of wine with dignity and looking to the count for approval.

"*Connaissez-vous le proverbe* [Do you know the proverb]: 'Jerome, Jerome, do not roam, but turn spindles at home!' ?" said Shinshín, puckering his brows and smiling. "*Cela nous convient à merveille* [That suits us down to the ground]. Suvórov now—he knew what he was about; yet they beat him *à plate couture* [hollow], and where are we to find Suvórovs now? * *Je vous demande un peu* [I just ask you that]," said he, continually changing from French to Russian.

"Ve must vight to the last tr-r-op of our plood!" said the colonel, thumping the table; "and ve must tie for our Emperor, and zen all vill pe vell. And ve must discuss it as little as po-o-ossible" . . . he dwelt particularly on the word *possible* . . . "as po-o-ossible," he ended, again turning to the count. "Zat is how ve old hussars look at it, and zere's an end of it! And how do you, a young man and a young hussar, how do you judge of it?" he added, addressing Nicholas, who when he heard that the war was being discussed had turned from his partner with eyes and ears intent on the colonel.

"I am quite of your opinion," replied Nicholas, flaming up, turning his plate round and moving his wineglasses about with as much decision and desperation as though he were at that moment facing some great danger. "I am convinced that we Russians must die or conquer," he concluded, conscious—as were others—after the words were uttered that his remarks were too enthusiastic and emphatic for the occasion and were therefore awkward.

"What you said just now was splendid!" said his partner Julie.

Sónya trembled all over and blushed to her ears and behind them and down to her neck and shoulders while Nicholas was speaking.

Pierre listened to the colonel's speech and nodded approvingly.

"That's fine," said he.

* *Shinshín exaggerates grossly. Suvórov* (1729-1800) *after winning victories at Cassano, Trebbia, and Novi, and almost clearing the French out of Italy was, it is true, by the failure of the Austrians to co-operate with him, reduced to great straits while forcing his way through Switzerland. History, however, gives no instance of his having been "beaten hollow."*—A.M.

"The young man's a real hussar!" shouted the colonel, again thumping the table.

"What are you making such a noise about over there?" Màrya Dmítrievna's deep voice suddenly inquired from the other end of the table. "What are you thumping the table for?" she demanded of the hussar, "and why are you exciting yourself? Do you think the French are here?"

"I am speaking ze truce," replied the hussar with a smile.

"It's all about the war," the count shouted down the table. "You know my son's going, Márya Dmítrievna? My son is going."

"I have four sons in the army but still I don't fret. It is all in God's hands. You may die in your bed or God may spare you in a battle," replied Márya Dmítrievna's deep voice, which easily carried the whole length of the table.

"That's true!"

Once more the conversations concentrated, the ladies' at the one end and the men's at the other.

"You won't ask," Natásha's little brother was saying; "I know you won't ask!"

"I will," replied Natásha.

Her face suddenly flushed with reckless and joyous resolution. She half rose, by a glance inviting Pierre, who sat opposite, to listen to what was coming, and turning to her mother:

"Mamma!" rang out the clear contralto notes of her childish voice, audible the whole length of the table.

"What is it?" asked the countess, startled; but seeing by her daughter's face that it was only mischief, she shook a finger at her sternly with a threatening and forbidding movement of her head.

The conversation was hushed.

"Mamma! What sweets are we going to have?" and Natásha's voice sounded still more firm and resolute.

The countess tried to frown, but could not. Márya Dmítrievna shook her fat finger.

"Cossack!" she said threateningly.

Most of the guests, uncertain how to regard this sally, looked at the elders.

"You had better take care!" said the countess.

"Mamma! What sweets are we going to have?" Natásha again cried boldly, with saucy gaiety, confident that her prank would be taken in good part.

Sónya and fat little Pétya doubled up with laughter.

"You see! I *have* asked," whispered Natásha to her little brother and to Pierre, glancing at him again.

"Ice pudding, but you won't get any," said Márya Dmítrievna.

Natásha saw there was nothing to be afraid of and so she braved even Márya Dmítrievna.

"Márya Dmítrievna! What kind of ice pudding? I don't like ice cream."

"Carrot ices."

"No! What kind, Márya Dmítrievna? What kind?" she almost screamed; "I want to know!"

Márya Dmítrievna and the countess burst out laughing, and all the guests joined in. Everyone laughed, not at Márya Dmítrievna's answer but at the incredible boldness and smartness of this little girl who had dared to treat Márya Dmítrievna in this fashion.

Natásha only desisted when she had been told that there would be pineapple ice. Before the ices, champagne was served round. The band again struck up, the count and countess kissed, and the guests, leaving their seats, went up to "congratulate" the countess, and reached across the table to clink glasses with the count, with the children, and with one another. Again the footmen rushed about, chairs scraped, and in the same order in which they had entered but with redder faces, the guests returned to the drawing room and to the count's study.

10. *Sónya and Natásha. Nicholas sings. The Daniel Cooper*

THE CARD TABLES were drawn out, sets made up for boston, and the count's visitors settled themselves, some in the two drawing rooms, some in the sitting room, some in the library.

The count, holding his cards fanwise, kept himself with difficulty from dropping into his usual after-dinner nap, and laughed at everything. The young people, at the countess' instigation, gathered round the clavichord and harp. Julie by general request played first. After she had played a little air with variations on the harp, she joined the other young ladies in begging Natásha and Nicholas, who were noted for their musical talent, to sing something. Natásha, who was treated as though she were grown up, was evidently very proud of this but at the same time felt shy.

"What shall we sing?" she said.

" 'The Brook,' " suggested Nicholas.

"Well, then, let's be quick. Borís, come here," said Natásha. "But where is Sónya?"

She looked round and seeing that her friend was not in the room ran to look for her.

Running into Sónya's room and not finding her there, Natásha ran to the nursery, but Sónya was not there either. Natásha concluded that she must be on the chest in the passage. The chest in the passage was the place of mourning for the younger female generation in the Rostóv household. And there in fact was Sónya lying face downward on Nurse's dirty feather bed on the top of the chest, crumpling her gauzy pink dress under her, hiding her face with her slender fingers, and sobbing so convulsively that her bare little shoulders shook. Natásha's face, which had been so radiantly happy all that saint's day, suddenly changed: her eyes became fixed, and then a shiver passed down her broad neck and the corners of her mouth drooped.

"Sónya! What is it? What is the matter? . . . Oo . . . Oo . . . Oo . . . !" And Natásha's large mouth widened, making her look quite ugly, and she began to wail like a baby without knowing why, except that Sónya was crying. Sónya tried to lift her head to answer but could not, and hid her face still deeper in the bed. Natásha wept, sitting on the blue-striped feather bed and hugging her friend. With an effort Sónya sat up and began wiping her eyes and explaining.

"Nicholas is going away in a week's time, his . . . papers . . . have come . . . he told me himself . . . but still I should not cry," and she showed a paper she held in her hand—with the verses Nicholas had written, "still, I should not cry, but you can't . . . no one can understand . . . what a soul he has!"

And she began to cry again because he had such a noble soul.

"It's all very well for you . . . I am not envious . . . I love you and Borís also," she went on, gaining a little strength; "he is nice . . . there are no difficulties in your way. . . . But Nicholas is my cousin . . . one would have to . . . the Metropolitan himself * . . . and even then it can't be done. And besides, if she tells Mamma" (Sónya looked upon the countess as her mother and called her so) "that I am spoiling Nicholas' career and am heartless and ungrateful, while truly . . . God is my witness," and she made the sign of the cross, "I love her so much, and all of you, only Véra . . . And what for? What have I done to her? I am so grateful to you that I would willingly sacrifice everything, only I have nothing. . . ."

Sónya could not continue, and again hid her face in her hands and in

* In the Russian Church cousins came within the prohibited degrees of affinity and a special permission had to be obtained for their marriage.—A.M.

the feather bed. Natásha began consoling her, but her face showed that she understood all the gravity of her friend's trouble.

"Sónya," she suddenly exclaimed, as if she had guessed the true reason of her friend's sorrow, "I'm sure Véra has said something to you since dinner? Hasn't she?"

"Yes, these verses Nicholas wrote himself and I copied some others, and she found them on my table and said she'd show them to Mamma, and that I was ungrateful, and that Mamma would never allow him to marry me, but that he'll marry Julie. You see how he's been with her all day . . . Natásha, what have I done to deserve it? . . ."

And again she began to sob, more bitterly than before. Natásha lifted her up, hugged her, and, smiling through her tears, began comforting her.

"Sónya, don't believe her, darling! Don't believe her! Do you remember how we and Nicholas, all three of us, talked in the sitting room after supper? Why, we settled how everything was to be. I don't quite remember how, but don't you remember that it could all be arranged and how nice it all was? There's Uncle Shinshín's brother has married his first cousin. And we are only second cousins, you know. And Borís says it is quite possible. You know I have told him all about it. And he is so clever and so good!" said Natásha. "Don't you cry, Sónya, dear love, darling Sónya!" and she kissed her and laughed. "Véra's spiteful; never mind her! And all will come right and she won't say anything to Mamma. Nicholas will tell her himself, and he doesn't care at all for Julie."

Natásha kissed her on the hair.

Sónya sat up. The little kitten brightened, its eyes shone, and it seemed ready to lift its tail, jump down on its soft paws, and begin playing with the ball of worsted as a kitten should.

"Do you think so? . . . Really? Truly?" she said, quickly smoothing her frock and hair.

"Really, truly!" answered Natásha, pushing in a crisp lock that had strayed from under her friend's plaits.

Both laughed.

"Well, let's go and sing 'The Brook.'"

"Come along!"

"Do you know, that fat Pierre who sat opposite me is so funny!" said Natásha, stopping suddenly. "I feel so happy!"

And she set off at a run along the passage.

Sónya, shaking off some down which clung to her and tucking away the verses in the bosom of her dress close to her bony little chest, ran after Natásha down the passage into the sitting room with flushed face and light, joyous steps. At the visitors' request the young people sang

the quartette, 'The Brook,' with which everyone was delighted. Then Nicholas sang a song he had just learned:

> At nighttime in the moon's fair glow
> How sweet, as fancies wander free,
> To feel that in this world there's one
> Who still is thinking but of thee!

> That while her fingers touch the harp
> Wafting sweet music o'er the lea,
> It is for thee thus swells her heart,
> Sighing its message out to thee. . . .

> A day or two, then bliss unspoilt,
> But oh! till then I cannot live! . . .

He had not finished the last verse before the young people began to get ready to dance in the large hall, and the sound of the feet and the coughing of the musicians were heard from the gallery.

Pierre was sitting in the drawing room where Shinshín had engaged him, as a man recently returned from abroad, in a political conversation in which several others joined but which bored Pierre. When the music began Natásha came in and walking straight up to Pierre said, laughing and blushing:

"Mamma told me to ask you to join the dancers."

"I am afraid of mixing the figures," Pierre replied; "but if you will be my teacher . . ." And lowering his big arm he offered it to the slender little girl.

While the couples were arranging themselves and the musicians tuning up, Pierre sat down with his little partner. Natásha was perfectly happy; she was dancing with a grown-up man, who had been abroad. She was sitting in a conspicuous place and talking to him like a grown-up lady. She had a fan in her hand that one of the ladies had given her to hold. Assuming quite the pose of a society woman (heaven knows when and where she had learned it) she talked with her partner, fanning herself and smiling over the fan.

"Dear, dear! Just look at her!" exclaimed the countess as she crossed the ballroom, pointing to Natásha.

Natásha blushed and laughed.

"Well, really, Mamma! Why should you? What is there to be surprised at?"

In the midst of the third écossaise there was a clatter of chairs being pushed back in the sitting room where the count and Márya Dmítrievna

had been playing cards with the majority of the more distinguished and older visitors. They now, stretching themselves after sitting so long, and replacing their purses and pocketbooks, entered the ballroom. First came Márya Dmítrievna and the count, both with merry countenances. The count, with playful ceremony somewhat in ballet style, offered his bent arm to Márya Dmítrievna. He drew himself up, a smile of debonair gallantry lit up his face, and as soon as the last figure of the écossaise was ended, he clapped his hands to the musicians and shouted up to their gallery, addressing the first violin:

"Semën! Do you know the *Daniel Cooper?*"

This was the count's favorite dance, which he had danced in his youth. (Strictly speaking, *Daniel Cooper* was one figure of the *anglaise.**)

"Look at Papa!" shouted Natásha to the whole company, and quite forgetting that she was dancing with a grown-up partner she bent her curly head to her knees and made the whole room ring with her laughter.

And indeed everybody in the room looked with a smile of pleasure at the jovial old gentleman, who standing beside his tall and stout partner, Márya Dmítrievna, curved his arms, beat time, straightened his shoulders, turned out his toes, tapped gently with his foot, and, by a smile that broadened his round face more and more, prepared the onlookers for what was to follow. As soon as the provocatively gay strains of *Daniel Cooper* (somewhat resembling those of a merry peasant dance) began to sound, all the doorways of the ballroom were suddenly filled by the domestic serfs—the men on one side and the women on the other—who with beaming faces had come to see their master making merry.

"Just look at the master! A regular eagle he is!" loudly remarked the nurse, as she stood in one of the doorways.

The count danced well and knew it. But his partner could not and did not want to dance well. Her enormous figure stood erect, her powerful arms hanging down (she had handed her reticule to the countess), and only her stern but handsome face really joined in the dance. What was expressed by the whole of the count's plump figure, in Márya Dmítrievna found expression only in her more and more beaming face and quivering nose. But if the count, getting more and more into the swing of it, charmed the spectators by the unexpectedness of his adroit maneuvers and the agility with which he capered about on his light feet, Márya Dmítrievna produced no less impression by slight exertions—the least effort to move her shoulders or bend her arms when turning, or stamp

* *The* anglaise *was a contredanse with many figures to which arbitrary and fantastic names were given. Tolstóy obtained his knowledge of it from family tradition.—*A.M.

her foot—which everyone appreciated in view of her size and habitual severity. The dance grew livelier and livelier. The other couples could not attract a moment's attention to their own evolutions and did not even try to do so. All were watching the count and Márya Dmítrievna. Natásha kept pulling everyone by sleeve or dress, urging them to "look at Papa!" though as it was they never took their eyes off the couple. In the intervals of the dance the count, breathing deeply, waved and shouted to the musicians to play faster. Faster, faster, and faster; lightly, more lightly, and yet more lightly whirled the count, flying round Márya Dmítrievna, now on his toes, now on his heels; until, turning his partner round to her seat, he executed the final *pas*, raising his soft foot backwards, bowing his perspiring head, smiling and making a wide sweep with his arm, amid a thunder of applause and laughter led by Natásha. Both partners stood still, breathing heavily and wiping their faces with their cambric handkerchiefs.

"That's how we used to dance in our time, *ma chère*," said the count.

"That was a *Daniel Cooper*!" exclaimed Márya Dmítrievna, tucking up her sleeves and puffing heavily.

11. At Count Bezúkhov's. Prince Vasíli and Catiche

WHILE in the Rostóvs' ballroom the sixth *anglaise* was being danced, to a tune in which the weary musicians blundered, and while tired footmen and cooks were getting the supper, Count Bezúkhov had a sixth stroke. The doctors pronounced recovery impossible. After a mute confession, communion was administered to the dying man, preparations made for the sacrament of unction, and in his house there was the bustle and thrill of suspense usual at such moments. Outside the house, beyond the gates, a group of undertakers, who hid whenever a carriage drove up, waited in expectation of an important order for an expensive funeral. The Military Governor of Moscow, who had been assiduous in sending aides-de-camp to inquire after the count's health, came himself that evening to bid a last farewell to the celebrated grandee of Catherine's court, Count Bezúkhov.

The magnificent reception room was crowded. Everyone stood up respectfully when the Military Governor, having stayed about half an hour alone with the dying man, passed out, slightly acknowledging their bows and trying to escape as quickly as possible from the glances fixed on him by the doctors, clergy, and relatives of the family. Prince Vasíli, who had

grown thinner and paler during the last few days, escorted him to the door, repeating something to him several times in low tones.

When the Military Governor had gone, Prince Vasíli sat down all alone on a chair in the ballroom, crossing one leg high over the other, leaning his elbow on his knee and covering his face with his hand. After sitting so for a while he rose, and, looking about him with frightened eyes, went with unusually hurried steps down the long corridor leading to the back of the house, to the room of the eldest princess.

Those who were in the dimly lit reception room spoke in nervous whispers, and, whenever anyone went into or came from the dying man's room, grew silent and gazed with eyes full of curiosity or expectancy at his door, which creaked slightly when opened.

"The limits of human life . . . are fixed and may not be o'erpassed," said an old priest to a lady who had taken a seat beside him and was listening naïvely to his words.

"I wonder, is it not too late to administer unction?" asked the lady, adding the priest's clerical title, as if she had no opinion of her own on the subject.

"Ah, madam, it is a great sacrament," replied the priest, passing his hand over the thin grizzled strands of hair combed back across his bald head.

"Who was that? The Military Governor himself?" was being asked at the other side of the room. "How young-looking he is!"

"Yes, and he is over sixty. I hear the count no longer recognizes anyone. They wished to administer the sacrament of unction."

"I knew someone who received that sacrament seven times."

The second princess had just come from the sickroom with her eyes red from weeping and sat down beside Dr. Lorrain, who was sitting in a graceful pose under a portrait of Catherine, leaning his elbow on a table.

"Beautiful," said the doctor in answer to a remark about the weather. "The weather is beautiful, Princess; and besides, in Moscow one feels as if one were in the country."

"Yes, indeed," replied the princess with a sigh. "So he may have something to drink?"

Lorrain considered.

"Has he taken his medicine?"

"Yes."

The doctor glanced at his watch.

"Take a glass of boiled water and put a pinch of cream of tartar," and he indicated with his delicate fingers what he meant by a pinch.

"Dere has neffer been a gase," a German doctor was saying to an aide-de-camp, "dat one liffs after de sird sdroke."

"And what a well-preserved man he was!" remarked the aide-de-camp. "And who will inherit his wealth?" he added in a whisper.

"It von't go begging," replied the German with a smile.

Everyone again looked toward the door, which creaked as the second princess went in with the drink she had prepared according to Lorrain's instructions. The German doctor went up to Lorrain.

"Do you think he can last till morning?" asked the German, addressing Lorrain in French which he pronounced badly.

Lorrain, pursing up his lips, waved a severely negative finger before his nose.

"Tonight, not later," said he in a low voice, and he moved away with a decorous smile of self-satisfaction at being able clearly to understand and state the patient's condition.

Meanwhile Prince Vasíli had opened the door into the princess' room.

In this room it was almost dark; only two tiny lamps were burning before the icons and there was a pleasant scent of flowers and burnt pastilles. The room was crowded with small pieces of furniture, whatnots, cupboards, and little tables. The quilt of a high, white feather bed was just visible behind a screen. A small dog began to bark.

"Ah, is it you, cousin?"

She rose and smoothed her hair, which was as usual so extremely smooth that it seemed to be made of one piece with her head and covered with varnish.

"Has anything happened?" she asked. "I am so terrified."

"No, there is no change. I only came to have a talk about business, Catiche [Catherine]," muttered the prince, seating himself wearily on the chair she had just vacated. "You have made the place warm, I must say," he remarked. "Well, sit down: let's have a talk."

"I thought perhaps something had happened," she said with her unchanging stonily severe expression; and, sitting down opposite the prince, she prepared to listen.

"I wished to get a nap, *mon cousin,* but I can't."

"Well, my dear?" said Prince Vasíli, taking her hand and bending it downwards as was his habit.

It was plain that this "well?" referred to much that they both understood without naming.

The princess, who had a straight, rigid body, abnormally long for her legs, looked directly at Prince Vasíli with no sign of emotion in her

prominent gray eyes. Then she shook her head and glanced up at the icons with a sigh. This might have been taken as an expression of sorrow and devotion, or of weariness and hope of resting before long. Prince Vasíli understood it as an expression of weariness.

"And I?" he said; "do you think it is easier for me? I am as worn out as a post horse, but still I must have a talk with you, Catiche, a very serious talk."

Prince Vasíli said no more and his cheeks began to twitch nervously, now on one side, now on the other, giving his face an unpleasant expression which was never to be seen on it in a drawing room. His eyes too seemed strange; at one moment they looked impudently sly and at the next glanced round in alarm.

The princess, holding her little dog on her lap with her thin bony hands, looked attentively into Prince Vasíli's eyes evidently resolved not to be the first to break silence, if she had to wait till morning.

"Well, you see, my dear princess and cousin, Catherine Semënovna," continued Prince Vasíli, returning to his theme, apparently not without an inner struggle; "at such a moment as this one must think of everything. One must think of the future, of all of you . . . I love you all, like children of my own, as you know."

The princess continued to look at him without moving, and with the same dull expression.

"And then of course my family has also to be considered," Prince Vasíli went on, testily pushing away a little table without looking at her. "You know, Catiche, that we—you three sisters, Mámontov, and my wife —are the count's only direct heirs. I know, I know how hard it is for you to talk or think of such matters. It is no easier for me; but, my dear, I am getting on for sixty and must be prepared for anything. Do you know I have sent for Pierre? The count," pointing to his portrait, "definitely demanded that he should be called."

Prince Vasíli looked questioningly at the princess, but could not make out whether she was considering what he had just said or whether she was simply looking at him.

"There is one thing I constantly pray God to grant, mon cousin," she replied, "and it is that He would be merciful to him and would allow his noble soul peacefully to leave this . . ."

"Yes, yes, of course," interrupted Prince Vasíli impatiently, rubbing his bald head and angrily pulling back toward him the little table that he had pushed away. "But . . . in short, the fact is . . . you know yourself that last winter the count made a will by which he left all his property, not to us his direct heirs, but to Pierre."

"He has made wills enough!" quietly remarked the princess. "But he cannot leave the estate to Pierre. Pierre is illegitimate."

"But, my dear," said Prince Vasíli suddenly, clutching the little table and becoming more animated and talking more rapidly: "what if a letter has been written to the Emperor in which the count asks for Pierre's legitimation? Do you understand that in consideration of the count's services, his request would be granted? . . ."

The princess smiled as people do who think they know more about the subject under discussion than those they are talking with.

"I can tell you more," continued Prince Vasíli, seizing her hand, "that letter was written, though it was not sent, and the Emperor knew of it. The only question is, has it been destroyed or not? If not, then as soon as *all is over*," and Prince Vasíli sighed to intimate what he meant by the words *all is over*, "and the count's papers are opened, the will and letter will be delivered to the Emperor, and the petition will certainly be granted. Pierre will get everything as the legitimate son."

"And our share?" asked the princess smiling ironically, as if anything might happen, only not that.

"But, my poor Catiche, it is as clear as daylight! He will then be the legal heir to everything and you won't get anything. You must know, my dear, whether the will and letter were written, and whether they have been destroyed or not. And if they have somehow been overlooked, you ought to know where they are, and must find them, because . . ."

"What next?" the princess interrupted, smiling sardonically and not changing the expression of her eyes. "I am a woman, and you think we are all stupid; but I know this: an illegitimate son cannot inherit . . . *un bâtard* [a bastard]!" she added, as if supposing that this translation of the word would effectively prove to Prince Vasíli the invalidity of his contention.

"Well, really, Catiche! Can't you understand! You are so intelligent, how is it you don't see that if the count has written a letter to the Emperor begging him to recognize Pierre as legitimate, it follows that Pierre will not be Pierre but will become Count Bezúkhov, and will then inherit everything under the will? And if the will and letter are not destroyed, then you will have nothing but the consolation of having been dutiful *et tout ce qui s'ensuit* [and all that follows therefrom]! That's certain."

"I know the will was made, but I also know that it is invalid; and you, *mon cousin*, seem to consider me a perfect fool," said the princess with the expression women assume when they suppose they are saying something witty and stinging.

"My dear Princess Catherine Semënovna," began Prince Vasíli im-

patiently, "I came here not to wrangle with you, but to talk about your interests as with a kinswoman, a good, kind, true relation. And I tell you for the tenth time that if the letter to the Emperor and the will in Pierre's favor are among the count's papers, then, my dear girl, you and your sisters are not heiresses! If you don't believe me, then believe an expert. I have just been talking to Dmítri Onúfrich" (the family solicitor) "and he says the same."

At this a sudden change evidently took place in the princess' ideas; her thin lips grew white, though her eyes did not change, and her voice when she began to speak passed through such transitions as she herself evidently did not expect.

"That would be a fine thing!" said she. "I never wanted anything and I don't now."

She pushed the little dog off her lap and smoothed her dress.

"And this is gratitude—this is recognition for those who have sacrificed everything for his sake!" she cried. "It's splendid! Fine! I don't want anything, Prince."

"Yes, but you are not the only one. There are your sisters . . ." replied Prince Vasíli.

But the princess did not listen to him.

"Yes, I knew it long ago but had forgotten. I knew that I could expect nothing but meanness, deceit, envy, intrigue, and ingratitude—the blackest ingratitude—in this house . . ."

"Do you or do you not know where that will is?" insisted Prince Vasíli, his cheeks twitching more than ever.

"Yes, I was a fool! I still believed in people, loved them, and sacrificed myself. But only the base, the vile succeed! I know who has been intriguing!"

The princess wished to rise, but the prince held her by the hand. She had the air of one who has suddenly lost faith in the whole human race. She gave her companion an angry glance.

"There is still time, my dear. You must remember, Catiche, that it was all done casually in a moment of anger, of illness, and was afterwards forgotten. Our duty, my dear, is to rectify his mistake, to ease his last moments by not letting him commit this injustice, and not to let him die feeling that he is rendering unhappy those who . . ."

"Who sacrificed everything for him," chimed in the princess, who would again have risen had not the prince still held her fast, "though he never could appreciate it. No, mon cousin," she added with a sigh, "I shall always remember that in this world one must expect no reward, that in

this world there is neither honor nor justice. In this world one has to be cunning and cruel."

"Now come, come! Be reasonable. I know your excellent heart."

"No, I have a wicked heart."

"I know your heart," repeated the prince. "I value your friendship and wish you to have as good an opinion of me. Don't upset yourself, and let us talk sensibly while there is still time, be it a day or be it but an hour. . . . Tell me all you know about the will, and above all where it is. You must know. We will take it at once and show it to the count. He has, no doubt, forgotten it and will wish to destroy it. You understand that my sole desire is conscientiously to carry out his wishes; that is my only reason for being here. I came simply to help him and you."

"Now I see it all! I know who has been intriguing—I know!" cried the princess.

"That's not the point, my dear."

"It's that protégé of yours, that sweet Princess Drubetskáya, that Anna Mikháylovna whom I would not take for a housemaid . . . the infamous, vile woman!"

"Do not let us lose any time . . ."

"Ah, don't talk to me! Last winter she wheedled herself in here and told the count such vile, disgraceful things about us, especially about Sophie—I can't repeat them—that it made the count quite ill and he would not see us for a whole fortnight. I know it was then he wrote this vile, infamous paper, but I thought the thing was invalid."

"We've got to it at last—why did you not tell me about it sooner?"

"It's in the inlaid portfolio that he keeps under his pillow," said the princess, ignoring his question. "Now I know! Yes; if I have a sin, a great sin, it is hatred of that vile woman!" almost shrieked the princess, now quite changed. "And what does she come worming herself in here for? But I will give her a piece of my mind. The time will come!"

12. Anna Mikháylovna and Pierre at Count Bezúkhov's

WHILE these conversations were going on in the reception room and the princess' room, a carriage containing Pierre (who had been sent for) and Anna Mikháylovna (who found it necessary to accompany him) was driving into the court of Count Bezúkhov's house. As the wheels rolled softly over the straw beneath the windows, Anna Mikháylovna, having turned with words of comfort to her companion, realized that he was asleep in his corner and woke him up. Rousing himself, Pierre fol-

lowed Anna Mikháylovna out of the carriage, and only then began to think of the interview with his dying father which awaited him. He noticed that they had not come to the front entrance but to the back door. While he was getting down from the carriage steps two men, who looked like tradespeople, ran hurriedly from the entrance and hid in the shadow of the wall. Pausing for a moment, Pierre noticed several other men of the same kind hiding in the shadow of the house on both sides. But neither Anna Mikháylovna nor the footman nor the coachman, who could not help seeing these people, took any notice of them. "It seems to be all right," Pierre concluded, and followed Anna Mikháylovna. She hurriedly ascended the narrow dimly lit stone staircase, calling to Pierre, who was lagging behind, to follow. Though he did not see why it was necessary for him to go to the count at all, still less why he had to go by the back stairs, yet judging by Anna Mikháylovna's air of assurance and haste, Pierre concluded that it was all absolutely necessary. Halfway up the stairs they were almost knocked over by some men who, carrying pails, came running downstairs, their boots clattering. These men pressed close to the wall to let Pierre and Anna Mikháylovna pass and did not evince the least surprise at seeing them there.

"Is this the way to the princesses' apartments?" asked Anna Mikháylovna of one of them.

"Yes," replied a footman in a bold loud voice, as if anything were now permissible; "the door to the left, ma'am."

"Perhaps the count did not ask for me," said Pierre when he reached the landing. "I'd better go to my own room."

Anna Mikháylovna paused and waited for him to come up.

"Ah, my friend!" she said, touching his arm as she had done her son's when speaking to him that afternoon, "believe me I suffer no less than you do, but be a man!"

"But really, hadn't I better go away?" he asked, looking kindly at her over his spectacles.

"Ah, my dear friend! Forget the wrongs that may have been done you. Think that he is your father . . . perhaps in the agony of death." She sighed. "I have loved you like a son from the first. Trust yourself to me, Pierre. I shall not forget your interests."

Pierre did not understand a word, but the conviction that all this had to be grew stronger, and he meekly followed Anna Mikháylovna who was already opening a door.

This door led into a back anteroom. An old man, a servant of the princesses, sat in a corner knitting a stocking. Pierre had never been in this part of the house and did not even know of the existence of these

rooms. Anna Mikháylovna, addressing a maid who was hurrying past
with a decanter on a tray as "my dear" and "my sweet," asked about
the princesses' health and then led Pierre along a stone passage. The first
door on the left led into the princesses' apartments. The maid with the
decanter in her haste had not closed the door (everything in the house
was done in haste at that time), and Pierre and Anna Mikháylovna
in passing instinctively glanced into the room, where Prince Vasíli and
the eldest princess were sitting close together talking. Seeing them pass,
Prince Vasíli drew back with obvious impatience, while the princess
jumped up and with a gesture of desperation slammed the door with all
her might.

This action was so unlike her usual composure and the fear depicted
on Prince Vasíli's face so out of keeping with his dignity that Pierre
stopped and glanced inquiringly over his spectacles at his guide. Anna
Mikháylovna evinced no surprise, she only smiled faintly and sighed, as
if to say that this was no more than she had expected.

"Be a man, my friend. I will look after your interests," said she in reply
to his look, and went still faster along the passage.

Pierre could not make out what it was all about, and still less what
"watching over his interests" meant, but he decided that all these things
had to be. From the passage they went into a large, dimly lit room
adjoining the count's reception room. It was one of those sumptuous
but cold apartments known to Pierre only from the front approach, but
even in this room there now stood an empty bath, and water had been
spilled on the carpet. They were met by a deacon with a censer and by
a servant who passed out on tiptoe without heeding them. They went
into the reception room familiar to Pierre, with two Italian windows open-
ing into the conservatory, with its large bust and full-length portrait of
Catherine the Great. The same people were still sitting here on almost
the same positions as before, whispering to one another. All became silent
and turned to look at the pale tear-worn Anna Mikháylovna as she en-
tered, and at the big stout figure of Pierre who, hanging his head, meekly
followed her.

Anna Mikháylovna's face expressed a consciousness that the decisive
moment had arrived. With the air of a practical Petersburg lady she now,
keeping Pierre close beside her, entered the room even more boldly than
that afternoon. She felt that as she brought with her the person the dying
man wished to see, her own admission was assured. Casting a rapid glance
at all those in the room and noticing the count's confessor there, she
glided up to him with a sort of amble, not exactly bowing, yet seeming

to grow suddenly smaller, and respectfully received the blessing first of one and then of another priest.

"God be thanked that you are in time," said she to one of the priests; "all we relatives have been in such anxiety. This young man is the count's son," she added more softly. "What a terrible moment!"

Having said this she went up to the doctor.

"Dear doctor," said she, "this young man is the count's son. Is there any hope?"

The doctor cast a rapid glance upwards and silently shrugged his shoulders. Anna Mikháylovna with just the same movement raised her shoulders and eyes, almost closing the latter, sighed, and moved away from the doctor to Pierre. To him, in a particularly respectful and tenderly sad voice, she said:

"Trust in His mercy!" and pointing out a small sofa for him to sit and wait for her, she went silently toward the door that everyone was watching and it creaked very slightly as she disappeared behind it.

Pierre, having made up his mind to obey his monitress implicitly, moved toward the sofa she had indicated. As soon as Anna Mikháylovna had disappeared he noticed that the eyes of all in the room turned to him with something more than curiosity and sympathy. He noticed that they whispered to one another, casting significant looks at him with a kind of awe and even servility. A deference such as he had never before received was shown him. A strange lady, the one who had been talking to the priests, rose and offered him her seat; an aide-de-camp picked up and returned a glove Pierre had dropped; the doctors became respectfully silent as he passed by, and moved to make way for him. At first Pierre wished to take another seat so as not to trouble the lady, and also to pick up the glove himself and to pass round the doctors who were not even in his way; but all at once he felt that this would not do, and that tonight he was a person obliged to perform some sort of awful rite which everyone expected of him, and that he was therefore bound to accept their services. He took the glove in silence from the aide-de-camp, and sat down in the lady's chair, placing his huge hands symmetrically on his knees in the naïve attitude of an Egyptian statue, and decided in his own mind that all was as it should be, and that in order not to lose his head and do foolish things he must not act on his own ideas tonight, but must yield himself up entirely to the will of those who were guiding him.

Not two minutes had passed before Prince Vasíli with head erect majestically entered the room. He was wearing his long coat with three stars on his breast. He seemed to have grown thinner since the morning; his eyes seemed larger than usual when he glanced round and noticed

Pierre. He went up to him, took his hand (a thing he never used to do), and drew it downwards as if wishing to ascertain whether it was firmly fixed on.

"Courage, courage, my friend! He has asked to see you. That is well!" and he turned to go.

But Pierre thought it necessary to ask: "How is . . ." and hesitated, not knowing whether it would be proper to call the dying man "the count," yet ashamed to call him "father."

"He had another stroke about half an hour ago. Courage, my friend . . ."

Pierre's mind was in such a confused state that the word "stroke" suggested to him a blow from something. He looked at Prince Vasíli in perplexity, and only later grasped that a stroke was an attack of illness. Prince Vasíli said something to Lorrain in passing and went through the door on tiptoe. He could not walk well on tiptoe and his whole body jerked at each step. The eldest princess followed him, and the priests and deacons and some servants also went in at the door. Through that door was heard a noise of things being moved about, and at last Anna Mikháylovna, still with the same expression, pale but resolute in the discharge of duty, ran out and touching Pierre lightly on the arm said:

"The divine mercy is inexhaustible! Unction is about to be administered. Come."

Pierre went in at the door, stepping on the soft carpet, and noticed that the strange lady, the aide-de-camp, and some of the servants, all followed him in, as if there were now no further need for permission to enter that room.

PIERRE well knew this large room divided by columns and an arch, its walls hung round with Persian carpets. The part of the room behind the columns, with a high silk-curtained mahogany bedstead on one side and on the other an immense case containing icons, was brightly illuminated with red light like a Russian church during evening service. Under the gleaming icons stood a long invalid chair, and in that chair on snowy-white smooth pillows, evidently freshly changed, Pierre saw—covered to the waist by a bright green quilt—the familiar, majestic figure of his father, Count Bezúkhov, with that gray mane of hair above his broad forehead which reminded one of a lion, and the deep characteristically noble wrinkles of his handsome, ruddy face. He lay just under the icons; his large thick hands outside the quilt. Into the right hand, which was lying palm downwards, a wax taper had been thrust between forefinger and thumb, and an old servant, bending over from behind the chair, held it in position. By the chair stood the priests, their long hair falling over

their magnificent glittering vestments, with lighted tapers in their hands, slowly and solemnly conducting the service. A little behind them stood the two younger princesses holding handkerchiefs to their eyes, and just in front of them their eldest sister, Catiche, with a vicious and determined look steadily fixed on the icons, as though declaring to all that she could not answer for herself should she glance round. Anna Mikháylovna, with a meek, sorrowful, and all-forgiving expression on her face, stood by the door near the strange lady. Prince Vasíli in front of the door, near the invalid chair, a wax taper in his left hand, was leaning his left arm on the carved back of a velvet chair he had turned round for the purpose, and was crossing himself with his right hand, turning his eyes upward each time he touched his forehead. His face wore a calm look of piety and resignation to the will of God. "If you do not understand these sentiments," he seemed to be saying, "so much the worse for you!"

Behind him stood the aide-de-camp, the doctors, and the menservants; the men and women had separated as in church. All were silently crossing themselves, and the reading of the church service, the subdued chanting of deep bass voices, and in the intervals sighs and the shuffling of feet were the only sounds that could be heard. Anna Mikháylovna, with an air of importance that showed that she felt she quite knew what she was about, went across the room to where Pierre was standing and gave him a taper. He lit it and, distracted by observing those around him, began crossing himself with the hand that held the taper.

Sophie, the rosy, laughter-loving, youngest princess with the mole, watched him. She smiled, hid her face in her handkerchief, and remained with it hidden for a while; then looking up and seeing Pierre she again began to laugh. She evidently felt unable to look at him without laughing, but could not resist looking at him: so to be out of temptation she slipped quietly behind one of the columns. In the midst of the service the voices of the priests suddenly ceased, they whispered to one another, and the old servant who was holding the count's hand got up and said something to the ladies. Anna Mikháylovna stepped forward and, stooping over the dying man, beckoned to Lorrain from behind her back. The French doctor held no taper; he was leaning against one of the columns in a respectful attitude implying that he, a foreigner, in spite of all differences of faith, understood the full importance of the rite now being performed and even approved of it. He now approached the sick man with the noiseless step of one in full vigor of life, with his delicate white fingers raised from the green quilt the hand that was free, and turning sideways felt the pulse and reflected a moment. The sick man was

given something to drink, there was a stir around him, then the people resumed their places and the service continued. During this interval Pierre noticed that Prince Vasíli left the chair on which he had been leaning, and—with an air which intimated that he knew what he was about and if others did not understand him it was so much the worse for them—did not go up to the dying man, but passed by him, joined the eldest princess, and moved with her to the side of the room where stood the high bedstead with its silken hangings. On leaving the bed both Prince Vasíli and the princess passed out by a back door, but returned to their places one after the other before the service was concluded. Pierre paid no more attention to this occurrence than to the rest of what went on, having made up his mind once for all that what he saw happening around him that evening was in some way essential.

The chanting of the service ceased, and the voice of the priest was heard respectfully congratulating the dying man on having received the sacrament. The dying man lay as lifeless and immovable as before. Around him everyone began to stir: steps were audible and whispers, among which Anna Mikháylovna's was the most distinct.

Pierre heard her say:

"Certainly he must be moved onto the bed; here it will be impossible . . ."

The sick man was so surrounded by doctors, princesses, and servants that Pierre could no longer see the reddish-yellow face with its gray mane —which, though he saw other faces as well, he had not lost sight of for a single moment during the whole service. He judged by the cautious movements of those who crowded round the invalid chair that they had lifted the dying man and were moving him.

"Catch hold of my arm or you'll drop him!" he heard one of the servants say in a frightened whisper. "Catch hold from underneath. Here!" exclaimed different voices; and the heavy breathing of the bearers and the shuffling of their feet grew more hurried, as if the weight they were carrying were too much for them.

As the bearers, among whom was Anna Mikháylovna, passed the young man he caught a momentary glimpse between their heads and backs of the dying man's high, stout, uncovered chest and powerful shoulders, raised by those who were holding him under the armpits, and of his gray, curly, leonine head. This head, with its remarkably broad brow and cheekbones, its handsome, sensual mouth, and its cold, majestic expression, was not disfigured by the approach of death. It was the same as Pierre remembered it three months before, when the count had sent him to Petersburg.

But now this head was swaying helplessly with the uneven movements of the bearers, and the cold listless gaze fixed itself upon nothing.

After a few minutes' bustle beside the high bedstead, those who had carried the sick man dispersed. Anna Mikháylovna touched Pierre's hand and said, "Come." Pierre went with her to the bed on which the sick man had been laid in a stately pose in keeping with the ceremony just completed. He lay with his head propped high on the pillows. His hands were symmetrically placed on the green silk quilt, the palms downward. When Pierre came up the count was gazing straight at him, but with a look the significance of which could not be understood by mortal man. Either this look meant nothing but that as long as one has eyes they must look somewhere, or it meant too much. Pierre hesitated, not knowing what to do, and glanced inquiringly at his guide. Anna Mikháylovna made a hurried sign with her eyes, glancing at the sick man's hand and moving her lips as if to send it a kiss. Pierre, carefully stretching his neck so as not to touch the quilt, followed her suggestion and pressed his lips to the large-boned, fleshy hand. Neither the hand nor a single muscle of the count's face stirred. Once more Pierre looked questioningly at Anna Mikháylovna to see what he was to do next. Anna Mikháylovna with her eyes indicated a chair that stood beside the bed. Pierre obediently sat down, his eyes asking if he were doing right. Anna Mikháylovna nodded approvingly. Again Pierre fell into the naïvely symmetrical pose of an Egyptian statue, evidently distressed that his stout and clumsy body took up so much room and doing his utmost to look as small as possible. He looked at the count, who still gazed at the spot where Pierre's face had been before he sat down. Anna Mikháylovna indicated by her attitude her consciousness of the pathetic importance of these last moments of meeting between the father and son. This lasted about two minutes, which to Pierre seemed an hour. Suddenly the broad muscles and lines of the count's face began to twitch. The twitching increased, the handsome mouth was drawn to one side (only now did Pierre realize how near death his father was), and from that distorted mouth issued an indistinct, hoarse sound. Anna Mikháylovna looked attentively at the sick man's eyes, trying to guess what he wanted; she pointed first to Pierre, then to some drink, then named Prince Vasíli in an inquiring whisper, then pointed to the quilt. The eyes and face of the sick man showed impatience. He made an effort to look at the servant who stood constantly at the head of the bed.

"Wants to turn on the other side," whispered the servant, and got up to turn the count's heavy body toward the wall.

Pierre rose to help him.

While the count was being turned over, one of his arms fell back helplessly and he made a fruitless effort to pull it forward. Whether he noticed the look of terror with which Pierre regarded that lifeless arm, or whether some other thought flitted across his dying brain, at any rate he glanced at the refractory arm, at Pierre's terror-stricken face, and again at the arm, and on his face a feeble, piteous smile appeared, quite out of keeping with his features, that seemed to deride his own helplessness. At sight of this smile Pierre felt an unexpected quivering in his breast and a tickling in his nose, and tears dimmed his eyes. The sick man was turned onto his side with his face to the wall. He sighed.

"He is dozing," said Anna Mikháylovna, observing that one of the princesses was coming to take her turn at watching. "Let us go."

Pierre went out.

13. Anna Mikháylovna and Catiche struggle for the inlaid portfolio

THERE WAS now no one in the reception room except Prince Vasíli and the eldest princess, who were sitting under the portrait of Catherine the Great and talking eagerly. As soon as they saw Pierre and his companion they became silent, and Pierre thought he saw the princess hide something as she whispered:

"I can't bear the sight of that woman."

"Catiche has had tea served in the small drawing room," said Prince Vasíli to Anna Mikháylovna. "Go and take something, my poor Anna Mikháylovna, or you will not hold out."

To Pierre he said nothing, merely giving his arm a sympathetic squeeze below the shoulder. Pierre went with Anna Mikháylovna into the small drawing room.

"There is nothing so refreshing after a sleepless night as a cup of this delicious Russian tea," Lorrain was saying with an air of restrained animation as he stood sipping tea from a delicate Chinese handleless cup before a table on which tea and a cold supper were laid in the small circular room. Around the table all who were at Count Bezúkhov's house that night had gathered to fortify themselves. Pierre well remembered this small circular drawing room with its mirrors and little tables. During balls given at the house, Pierre, who did not know how to dance, had liked sitting in this room to watch the ladies who, as they passed through in their ball dresses with diamonds and pearls on their bare shoulders, looked at themselves in the brilliantly lighted mirrors which repeated

their reflections several times. Now this same room was dimly lighted by two candles. On one small table tea things and supper dishes stood in disorder, and in the middle of the night a motley throng of people sat there, not merrymaking, but somberly whispering, and betraying by every word and movement that they none of them forgot what was happening and what was about to happen in the bedroom. Pierre did not eat anything though he would very much have liked to. He looked inquiringly at his monitress and saw that she was again going on tiptoe to the reception room where they had left Prince Vasíli and the eldest princess. Pierre concluded that this also was essential, and after a short interval followed her. Anna Mikháylovna was standing beside the princess, and they were both speaking in excited whispers.

"Permit me, Princess, to know what is necessary and what is not necessary," said the younger of the two speakers, evidently in the same state of excitement as when she had slammed the door of her room.

"But, my dear princess," answered Anna Mikháylovna blandly but impressively, blocking the way to the bedroom and preventing the other from passing, "won't this be too much for poor Uncle at a moment when he needs repose? Worldly conversation at a moment when his soul is already prepared . . ."

Prince Vasíli was seated in an easy chair in his familiar attitude, with one leg crossed high above the other. His cheeks, which were so flabby that they looked heavier below, were twitching violently; but he wore the air of a man little concerned in what the two ladies were saying.

"Come, my dear Anna Mikháylovna, let Catiche do as she pleases. You know how fond the count is of her."

"I don't even know what is in this paper," said the younger of the two ladies, addressing Prince Vasíli and pointing to an inlaid portfolio she held in her hand. "All I know is that his real will is in his writing table, and this is a paper he has forgotten. . . ."

She tried to pass Anna Mikháylovna, but the latter sprang so as to bar her path.

"I know, my dear, kind princess," said Anna Mikháylovna, seizing the portfolio so firmly that it was plain she would not let go easily. "Dear princess, I beg and implore you, have some pity on him! Je vous en conjure . . ."

The princess did not reply. Their efforts in the struggle for the portfolio were the only sounds audible, but it was evident that if the princess did speak, her words would not be flattering to Anna Mikháylovna. Though the latter held on tenaciously, her voice lost none of its honeyed firmness and softness.

"Pierre, my dear, come here. I think he will not be out of place in a family consultation; is it not so, Prince?"

"Why don't you speak, cousin?" suddenly shrieked the princess so loud that those in the drawing room heard her and were startled. "Why do you remain silent when heaven knows who permits herself to interfere, making a scene on the very threshold of a dying man's room? Intriguer!" she hissed viciously, and tugged with all her might at the portfolio.

But Anna Mikháylovna went forward a step or two to keep her hold on the portfolio, and changed her grip.

Prince Vasíli rose. "Oh!" said he with reproach and surprise, "this is absurd! Come, let go I tell you."

The princess let go.

"And you too!"

But Anna Mikháylovna did not obey him.

"Let go, I tell you! I will take the responsibility. I myself will go and ask him, I! . . . does that satisfy you?"

"But, Prince," said Anna Mikháylovna, "after such a solemn sacrament, allow him a moment's peace! Here, Pierre, tell them your opinion," said she, turning to the young man who, having come quite close, was gazing with astonishment at the angry face of the princess which had lost all dignity, and at the twitching cheeks of Prince Vasíli.

"Remember that you will answer for the consequences," said Prince Vasíli severely. "You don't know what you are doing."

"Vile woman!" shouted the princess, darting unexpectedly at Anna Mikháylovna and snatching the portfolio from her.

Prince Vasíli bent his head and spread out his hands.

At this moment that terrible door, which Pierre had watched so long and which had always opened so quietly, burst noisily open and banged against the wall, and the second of the three sisters rushed out wringing her hands.

"What are you doing!" she cried vehemently. "He is dying and you leave me alone with him!"

Her sister dropped the portfolio. Anna Mikháylovna, stooping, quickly caught up the object of contention and ran into the bedroom. The eldest princess and Prince Vasíli, recovering themselves, followed her. A few minutes later the eldest sister came out with a pale hard face, again biting her underlip. At sight of Pierre her expression showed an irrepressible hatred.

"Yes, now you may be glad!" said she; "this is what you have been waiting for." And bursting into tears she hid her face in her handkerchief and rushed from the room.

Prince Vasíli came next. He staggered to the sofa on which Pierre was sitting and dropped onto it, covering his face with his hand. Pierre noticed that he was pale and that his jaw quivered and shook as if in an ague.

"Ah, my friend!" said he, taking Pierre by the elbow; and there was in his voice a sincerity and weakness Pierre had never observed in it before. "How often we sin, how much we deceive, and all for what? I am near sixty, dear friend . . . I too . . . All will end in death, all! Death is awful . . ." and he burst into tears.

Anna Mikháylovna came out last. She approached Pierre with slow, quiet steps.

"Pierre!" she said.

Pierre gave her an inquiring look. She kissed the young man on his forehead, wetting him with her tears. Then after a pause she said:

"He is no more. . . ."

Pierre looked at her over his spectacles.

"Come, I will go with you. Try to weep, nothing gives such relief as tears."

She led him into the dark drawing room and Pierre was glad no one could see his face. Anna Mikháylovna left him, and when she returned he was fast asleep with his head on his arm.

In the morning Anna Mikháylovna said to Pierre:

"Yes, my dear, this is a great loss for us all, not to speak of you. But God will support you: you are young, and are now, I hope, in command of an immense fortune. The will has not yet been opened. I know you well enough to be sure that this will not turn your head, but it imposes duties on you, and you must be a man."

Pierre was silent.

"Perhaps later on I may tell you, my dear boy, that if I had not been there, God only knows what would have happened! You know, Uncle promised me only the day before yesterday not to forget Borís. But he had no time. I hope, my dear friend, you will carry out your father's wish?"

Pierre understood nothing of all this and coloring shyly looked in silence at Princess Anna Mikháylovna. After her talk with Pierre, Anna Mikháylovna returned to the Rostóvs' and went to bed. On waking in the morning she told the Rostóvs and all her acquaintances the details of Count Bezúkhov's death. She said the count had died as she would herself wish to die, that his end was not only touching but edifying. As to the last meeting between father and son, it was so touching that she could not think of it without tears, and did not know which had behaved better during those awful moments—the father who so remembered

everything and everybody at the last and had spoken such pathetic words to the son, or Pierre, whom it had been pitiful to see, so stricken was he with grief, though he tried hard to hide it in order not to sadden his dying father. "It is painful, but it does one good. It uplifts the soul to see such men as the old count and his worthy son," said she. Of the behavior of the eldest princess and Prince Vasíli she spoke disapprovingly, but in whispers and as a great secret.

14. Bald Hills. Prince N. A. Bolkónski. Princess Mary's correspondence with Julie Karágina

AT BALD HILLS, Prince Nicholas Andréevich Bolkónski's estate, the arrival of young Prince Andrew and his wife was daily expected, but this expectation did not upset the regular routine of life in the old prince's household. General in Chief * Prince Nicholas Andréevich (nicknamed in society, "the King of Prussia") ever since the Emperor Paul had exiled him to his country estate had lived there continuously with his daughter, Princess Mary, and her companion, Mademoiselle Bourienne. Though in the new reign he was free to return to the capitals, he still continued to live in the country, remarking that anyone who wanted to see him could come the hundred miles from Moscow to Bald Hills, while he himself needed no one and nothing. He used to say that there are only two sources of human vice—idleness and superstition, and only two virtues—activity and intelligence. He himself undertook his daughter's education, and to develop these two cardinal virtues in her gave her lessons in algebra and geometry till she was twenty, and arranged her life so that her whole time was occupied. He was himself always occupied: writing his memoirs, solving problems in higher mathematics, turning snuffboxes on a lathe, working in the garden, or superintending the building that was always going on at his estate. As regularity is a prime condition facilitating activity, regularity in his household was carried to the highest point of exactitude. He always came to table under precisely the same conditions, and not only at the same hour but at the same minute. With those about him, from his daughter to his serfs, the prince was sharp and invariably exacting, so that without being a hardhearted man he inspired such fear and respect as few hardhearted men would have aroused. Although he was in retirement and had now no influence in political affairs, every high official

* This title was originally applied only to field marshals, but by Catherine's time it was used of all generals who reached the third and highest grade of generalship.—A.M.

appointed to the province in which the prince's estate lay considered it his duty to visit him and waited in the lofty antechamber just as the architect, gardener, or Princess Mary did, till the prince appeared punctually to the appointed hour. Everyone sitting in this antechamber experienced the same feeling of respect and even fear when the enormously high study door opened and showed the figure of a rather small old man, with powdered wig, small withered hands, and bushy gray eyebrows which, when he frowned, sometimes hid the gleam of his shrewd, youthfully glittering eyes.

On the morning of the day that the young couple were to arrive, Princess Mary entered the antechamber as usual at the time appointed for the morning greeting, crossing herself with trepidation and repeating a silent prayer. Every morning she came in like that, and every morning she prayed that the daily interview might pass off well.

An old powdered manservant who was sitting in the antechamber rose quietly and said in a whisper: "Please walk in."

Through the door came the regular hum of a lathe. The princess timidly opened the door which moved noiselessly and easily. She paused at the entrance. The prince was working at the lathe and after glancing round continued his work.

The enormous study was full of things evidently in constant use. The large table covered with books and plans, the tall glass-fronted bookcases with keys in the locks, the high desk for writing while standing up, on which lay an open exercise book, and the lathe with tools laid ready to hand and shavings scattered around—all indicated continuous, varied, and orderly activity. The motion of the small foot shod in a Tartar boot embroidered with silver, and the firm pressure of the lean sinewy hand, showed that the prince still possessed the tenacious endurance and vigor of hardy old age. After a few more turns of the lathe he removed his foot from the pedal, wiped his chisel, dropped it into a leather pouch attached to the lathe, and, approaching the table, summoned his daughter. He never gave his children a blessing, so he simply held out his bristly cheek (as yet unshaven) and, regarding her tenderly and attentively, said severely:

"Quite well? All right then, sit down." He took the exercise book containing lessons in geometry written by himself and drew up a chair with his foot.

"For tomorrow!" said he, quickly finding the page and making a scratch from one paragraph to another with his hard nail.

The princess bent over the exercise book on the table.

"Wait a bit, here's a letter for you," said the old man suddenly, taking

a letter addressed in a woman's hand from a bag hanging above the table, onto which he threw it.

At the sight of the letter red patches showed themselves on the princess' face. She took it quickly and bent her head over it.

"From Héloïse?" asked the prince with a cold smile that showed his still sound, yellowish teeth.*

"Yes, it's from Julie," replied the princess with a timid glance and a timid smile.

"I'll let two more letters pass, but the third I'll read," said the prince sternly; "I'm afraid you write much nonsense. I'll read the third!"

"Read this if you like, Father," said the princess, blushing still more and holding out the letter.

"The third, I said the third!" cried the prince abruptly, pushing the letter away, and leaning his elbows on the table he drew toward him the exercise book containing geometrical figures.

"Well, madam," he began, stooping over the book close to his daughter and placing an arm on the back of the chair on which she sat, so that she felt herself surrounded on all sides by the acrid scent of old age and tobacco, which she had known so long. "Now, madam, these triangles are equal; please note that the angle ABC . . ."

The princess looked in a scared way at her father's eyes glittering close to her; the red patches on her face came and went, and it was plain that she understood nothing and was so frightened that her fear would prevent her understanding any of her father's further explanations, however clear they might be. Whether it was the teacher's fault or the pupil's, this same thing happened every day: the princess' eyes grew dim, she could not see and could not hear anything, but was only conscious of her stern father's withered face close to her, of his breath and the smell of him, and could think only of how to get away quickly to her own room to make out the problem in peace. The old man was beside himself: moved the chair on which he was sitting noisily backward and forward, made efforts to control himself and not become vehement, but almost always did become vehement, scolded, and sometimes flung the exercise book away.

The princess gave a wrong answer.

"Well now, isn't she a fool!" shouted the prince, pushing the book aside and turning sharply away; but rising immediately, he paced up and down, lightly touched his daughter's hair and sat down again.

He drew up his chair and continued to explain.

* The prince is ironical. He knows the letter is from Julie, but alludes to Rousseau's novel, Julie, ou la nouvelle Héloïse, which he, an admirer of Voltaire and of cold reason, heartily despised.—A.M.

"This won't do, Princess; it won't do," said he, when Princess Mary, having taken and closed the exercise book with the next day's lesson, was about to leave: "Mathematics are most important, madam! I don't want to have you like our silly ladies. Get used to it and you'll like it," and he patted her cheek. "It will drive all the nonsense out of your head."

She turned to go, but he stopped her with a gesture and took an uncut book from the high desk.

"Here is some sort of *Key to the Mysteries* that your Héloïse has sent you.* Religious! I don't interfere with anyone's belief . . . I have looked at it. Take it. Well, now go. Go."

He patted her on the shoulder and himself closed the door after her.

Princess Mary went back to her room with the sad, scared expression that rarely left her and which made her plain, sickly face yet plainer. She sat down at her writing table, on which stood miniature portraits and which was littered with books and papers. The princess was as untidy as her father was tidy. She put down the geometry book and eagerly broke the seal of her letter. It was from her most intimate friend from childhood; that same Julie Karágina who had been at the Rostóvs' name-day party.

Julie wrote in French:

"Dear and precious Friend, How terrible and frightful a thing is separation! Though I tell myself that half my life and half my happiness are wrapped up in you, and that in spite of the distance separating us our hearts are united by indissoluble bonds, my heart rebels against fate and in spite of the pleasures and distractions around me I cannot overcome a certain secret sorrow that has been in my heart ever since we parted. Why are we not together as we were last summer, in your big study, on the blue sofa, the confidential sofa? Why cannot I now, as three months ago, draw fresh moral strength from your look, so gentle, calm, and penetrating, a look I loved so well and seem to see before me as I write?"

Having read thus far, Princess Mary sighed and glanced into the mirror which stood on her right. It reflected a weak, ungraceful figure and thin face. Her eyes, always sad, now looked with particular hopelessness at her reflection in the glass. "She flatters me," thought the princess, turning away and continuing to read. But Julie did not flatter her friend; the princess' eyes—large, deep and luminous (it seemed as if at times there radiated from them shafts of warm light)—were so beautiful that

* *The book in question was a mystical one by Eckartshausen (1752-1803)* —*A Key to the Mysteries of Nature. In 1805 it had recently been translated into Russian and was being eagerly read, especially among the Freemasons.*— A.M.

very often in spite of the plainness of her face they gave her an attraction more powerful than that of beauty. But the princess never saw the beautiful expression of her own eyes—the look they had when she was not thinking of herself. As with everyone, her face assumed a forced unnatural expression as soon as she looked in a glass. She went on reading:

"All Moscow talks of nothing but war. One of my two brothers is already abroad, the other is with the Guards, who are starting on their march to the frontier. Our dear Emperor has left Petersburg and it is thought intends to expose his precious person to the chances of war. God grant that the Corsican monster who is destroying the peace of Europe may be overthrown by the angel whom it has pleased the Almighty, in His goodness, to give us as sovereign! To say nothing of my brothers, this war has deprived me of one of the associations nearest my heart. I mean young Nicholas Rostóv, who with his enthusiasm could not bear to remain inactive and has left the university to join the army. I will confess to you, dear Mary, that in spite of his extreme youth his departure for the army was a great grief to me. This young man, of whom I spoke to you last summer, is so noble-minded and full of that real youthfulness which one seldom finds nowadays among our old men of twenty and, particularly, he is so frank and has so much heart. He is so pure and poetic that my relations with him, transient as they were, have been one of the sweetest comforts to my poor heart, which has already suffered so much. Someday I will tell you about our parting and all that was said then. That is still too fresh. Ah, dear friend, you are happy not to know these poignant joys and sorrows. You are fortunate, for the latter are generally the stronger! I know very well that Count Nicholas is too young ever to be more to me than a friend, but this sweet friendship, this poetic and pure intimacy, were what my heart needed. But enough of this! The chief news, about which all Moscow gossips, is the death of old Count Bezúkhov, and his inheritance. Fancy! The three princesses have received very little, Prince Vasíli nothing, and it is Monsieur Pierre who has inherited all the property and has besides been recognized as legitimate; so that he is now Count Bezúkhov and possessor of the finest fortune in Russia. It is rumored that Prince Vasíli played a very despicable part in this affair and that he returned to Petersburg quite crestfallen.

"I confess I understand very little about all these matters of wills and inheritance; but I do know that since this young man, whom we all used to know as plain Monsieur Pierre, has become Count Bezúkhov and the owner of one of the largest fortunes in Russia, I am much amused to watch the change in the tone and manners of the mammas burdened by marriageable daughters, and of the young ladies themselves, toward him,

though, between you and me, he always seemed to me a poor sort of fellow. As for the past two years people have amused themselves by finding husbands for me (most of whom I don't even know), the matchmaking chronicles of Moscow now speak of me as the future Countess Bezúkhova. But you will understand that I have no desire for the post. À propos of marriages: do you know that a while ago that *universal auntie* Anna Mikháylovna told me, under the seal of strict secrecy, of a plan of marriage for you. It is neither more nor less than with Prince Vasíli's son Anatole, whom they wish to reform by marrying him to someone rich and *distinguée*, and it is on you that his relations' choice has fallen. I don't know what you will think of it, but I consider it my duty to let you know of it. He is said to be very handsome and a terrible scapegrace. That is all I have been able to find out about him.

"But enough of gossip. I am at the end of my second sheet of paper, and Mamma has sent for me to go and dine at the Apráksins'. Read the mystical book I am sending you; it has an enormous success here. Though there are things in it difficult for the feeble human mind to grasp, it is an admirable book which calms and elevates the soul. Adieu! Give my respects to monsieur your father and my compliments to Mademoiselle Bourienne. I embrace you as I love you. JULIE

"P.S. Let me have news of your brother and his charming little wife."

The princess pondered awhile with a thoughtful smile and her luminous eyes lit up so that her face was entirely transformed. Then she suddenly rose and with her heavy tread went up to the table. She took a sheet of paper and her hand moved rapidly over it. This is the reply she wrote, also in French:

"Dear and precious Friend, Your letter of the 13th has given me great delight. So you still love me, my romantic Julie? Separation, of which you say so much that is bad, does not seem to have had its usual effect on you. You complain of our separation. What then should I say, if I *dared* complain, I who am deprived of all who are dear to me? Ah, if we had not religion to console us life would be very sad. Why do you suppose that I should look severely on your affection for that young man? On such matters I am only severe with myself. I understand such feelings in others, and if never having felt them I cannot approve of them, neither do I condemn them. Only it seems to me that Christian love, love of one's neighbor, love of one's enemy, is worthier, sweeter, and better than the feelings which the beautiful eyes of a young man can inspire in a romantic and loving young girl like yourself.

"The news of Count Bezúkhov's death reached us before your letter and my father was much affected by it. He says the count was the last

representative but one of the great century, and that it is his own turn now, but that he will do all he can to let his turn come as late as possible. God preserve us from that terrible misfortune!

"I cannot agree with you about Pierre, whom I knew as a child. He always seemed to me to have an excellent heart, and that is the quality I value most in people. As to his inheritance and the part played by Prince Vasíli, it is very sad for both. Ah, my dear friend, our divine Saviour's words, that it is easier for a camel to go through the eye of a needle than for a rich man to enter the Kingdom of God, are terribly true. I pity Prince Vasíli but am still more sorry for Pierre. So young, and burdened with such riches—to what temptations he will be exposed! If I were asked what I desire most on earth, it would be to be poorer than the poorest beggar. A thousand thanks, dear friend, for the volume you have sent me and which has such success in Moscow. Yet since you tell me that among some good things it contains others which our weak human understanding cannot grasp, it seems to me rather useless to spend time in reading what is unintelligible and can therefore bear no fruit. I never could understand the fondness some people have for confusing their minds by dwelling on mystical books that merely awaken their doubts and excite their imagination, giving them a bent for exaggeration quite contrary to Christian simplicity. Let us rather read the Epistles and Gospels. Let us not seek to penetrate what mysteries they contain; for how can we, miserable sinners that we are, know the terrible and holy secrets of Providence while we remain in this flesh which forms an impenetrable veil between us and the Eternal? Let us rather confine ourselves to studying those sublime rules which our divine Saviour has left for our guidance here below. Let us try to conform to them and follow them, and let us be persuaded that the less we let our feeble human minds roam, the better we shall please God, who rejects all knowledge that does not come from Him; and the less we seek to fathom what He has been pleased to conceal from us, the sooner will He vouchsafe its revelation to us through His divine Spirit.

"My father has not spoken to me of a suitor, but has only told me that he has received a letter and is expecting a visit from Prince Vasíli. In regard to this project of marriage for me, I will tell you, dear sweet friend, that I look on marriage as a divine institution to which we must conform. However painful it may be to me, should the Almighty ever lay the duties of wife and mother upon me I shall try to perform them as faithfully as I can, without disquieting myself by examining my feelings toward him whom He may give me for husband.

"I have had a letter from my brother, who announces his speedy arrival at Bald Hills with his wife. This pleasure will be but a brief one, however,

for he will leave us again to take part in this unhappy war into which we have been drawn, God knows how or why. Not only where you are—at the heart of affairs and of the world—is the talk all of war, even here amid fieldwork and the calm of nature—which townsfolk consider characteristic of the country—rumors of war are heard and painfully felt. My father talks of nothing but marches and countermarches, things of which I understand nothing; and the day before yesterday during my daily walk through the village I witnessed a heartrending scene. . . . It was a convoy of conscripts enrolled from our people and starting to join the army. You should have seen the state of the mothers, wives, and children of the men who were going and should have heard the sobs. It seems as though mankind has forgotten the laws of its divine Saviour, Who preached love and forgiveness of injuries—and that men attribute the greatest merit to skill in killing one another.

"Adieu, dear and kind friend; may our divine Saviour and His most Holy Mother keep you in their holy and all-powerful care!

MARY"

"Ah, you are sending off a letter, Princess? I have already dispatched mine. I have written to my poor mother," said the smiling Mademoiselle Bourienne rapidly, in her pleasant mellow tones and with guttural r's. She brought into Princess Mary's strenuous, mournful, and gloomy world a quite different atmosphere, careless, lighthearted, and self-satisfied.

"Princess, I must warn you," she added, lowering her voice and evidently listening to herself with pleasure, and speaking with exaggerated *grasseyement,** "the prince has been scolding Michael Ivánovich. He is in a very bad humor, very morose. Be prepared."

"Ah, dear friend," replied Princess Mary, "I have asked you never to warn me of the humor my father is in. I do not allow myself to judge him and would not have others do so."

The princess glanced at her watch and, seeing that she was five minutes late in starting her practice on the clavichord, went into the sitting room with a look of alarm. Between twelve and two o'clock, as the day was mapped out, the prince rested and the princess played the clavichord.

* *The guttural pronunciation of the letter* r, *chiefly affected by Parisians.*
—A.M.

15. *Prince Andrew at Bald Hills*

THE GRAY-HAIRED valet was sitting drowsily listening to the snoring of the prince, who was in his large study. From the far side of the house through the closed doors came the sound of difficult passages—twenty times repeated—of a sonata by Dussek.*

Just then a closed carriage and another with a hood drove up to the porch. Prince Andrew got out of the carriage, helped his little wife to alight, and let her pass into the house before him. Old Tíkhon, wearing a wig, put his head out of the door of the antechamber, reported in a whisper that the prince was sleeping, and hastily closed the door. Tíkhon knew that neither the son's arrival nor any other unusual event must be allowed to disturb the appointed order of the day. Prince Andrew apparently knew this as well as Tíkhon; he looked at his watch as if to ascertain whether father's habits had changed since he was at home last, and, having assured himself that they had not, he turned to his wife.

"He will get up in twenty minutes. Let us go across to Mary's room," he said.

The little princess had grown stouter during this time, but her eyes and her short, downy, smiling lip lifted when she began to speak just as merrily and prettily as ever.

"Why, this is a palace!" she said to her husband, looking around with the expression with which people compliment their host at a ball. "Let's come, quick, quick!" And with a glance round, she smiled at Tíkhon, at her husband, and at the footman who accompanied them.

"Is that Mary practicing? Let's go quietly and take her by surprise."

Prince Andrew followed her with a courteous but sad expression.

"You've grown older, Tíkhon," he said in passing to the old man, who kissed his hand.

Before they reached the room from which the sounds of the clavichord came, the pretty, fair-haired Frenchwoman, Mademoiselle Bourienne, rushed out apparently beside herself with delight.

"Ah! what joy for the princess!" exclaimed she: "At last! I must let her know."

"No, no, please not . . . You are Mademoiselle Bourienne," said the little princess, kissing her. "I know you already through my sister-in-law's friendship for you. She was not expecting us?"

They went up to the door of the sitting room from which came the

* *Jan Ladislav Dussek (1760-1812), composer of fifty-three now nearly forgotten piano sonatas.*

sound of the oft-repeated passage of the sonata. Prince Andrew stopped and made a grimace, as if expecting something unpleasant.

The little princess entered the room. The passage broke off in the middle, a cry was heard, then Princess Mary's heavy tread and the sound of kissing. When Prince Andrew went in the two princesses, who had only met once before for a short time at his wedding, were in each other's arms warmly pressing their lips to whatever place they happened to touch. Mademoiselle Bourienne stood near them pressing her hand to her heart, with a beatific smile and obviously equally ready to cry or to laugh. Prince Andrew shrugged his shoulders and frowned, as lovers of music do when they hear a false note. The two women let go of one another, and then, as if afraid of being too late, seized each other's hands, kissing them and pulling them away, and again began kissing each other on the face, and then to Prince Andrew's surprise both began to cry and kissed again. Mademoiselle Bourienne also began to cry. Prince Andrew evidently felt ill at ease, but to the two women it seemed quite natural that they should cry, and apparently it never entered their heads that it could have been otherwise at this meeting.

"Ah! my dear! . . . Ah! Mary! . . ." they suddenly exclaimed, and then laughed. "I dreamed last night . . ."—"You were not expecting us? . . ."—"Ah! Mary, you have got thinner! . . ." "And you have grown stouter! . . ."

"I knew the princess at once," put in Mademoiselle Bourienne.

"And I had no idea! . . ." exclaimed Princess Mary. "Ah, Andrew, I did not see you."

Prince Andrew and his sister, hand in hand, kissed one another, and he told her she was still the same crybaby as ever. Princess Mary had turned toward her brother, and through her tears the loving, warm, gentle look of her large luminous eyes, very beautiful at that moment, rested on Prince Andrew's face.

The little princess talked incessantly, her short, downy upper lip continually and rapidly touching her rosy nether lip when necessary and drawing up again next moment when her face broke into a smile of glittering teeth and sparkling eyes. She told of an accident they had had on the Spásski Hill which might have been serious for her in her condition, and immediately after that informed them that she had left all her clothes in Petersburg and that heaven knew what she would have to dress in here; and that Andrew had quite changed, and that Kitty Odýntsova had married an old man, and that there was a suitor for Mary, a real one, but that they would talk of that later. Princess Mary was still looking silently at her brother and her beautiful eyes were full of love and sadness. It was

plain that she was following a train of thought independent of her sister-in-law's words. In the midst of a description of the last Petersburg fete she addressed her brother:

"So you are really going to the war, Andrew?" she said sighing.

Lise sighed too.

"Yes, and even tomorrow," replied her brother.

"He is leaving me here; God knows why, when he might have had promotion . . ."

Princess Mary did not listen to the end, but continuing her train of thought turned to her sister-in-law with a tender glance at her figure.

"Is it certain?" she said.

The face of the little princess changed. She sighed and said: "Yes, quite certain. Ah! it is very dreadful . . ."

Her lip descended. She brought her face close to her sister-in-law's and unexpectedly again began to cry.

"She needs rest," said Prince Andrew with a frown. "Don't you, Lise? Take her to your room and I'll go to Father. How is he? Just the same?"

"Yes, just the same. Though I don't know what your opinion will be," answered the princess joyfully.

"And are the hours the same? And the walks in the avenues? And the lathe?" asked Prince Andrew with a scarcely perceptible smile which showed that, in spite of all his love and respect for his father, he was aware of his weaknesses.

"The hours are the same, and the lathe, and also the mathematics and my geometry lessons," said Princess Mary gleefully, as if her lessons in geometry were among the greatest delights of her life.

When the twenty minutes had elapsed and the time had come for the old prince to get up, Tíkhon came to call the young prince to his father. The old man made a departure from his usual routine in honor of his son's arrival: he gave orders to admit him to his apartments while he dressed for dinner. The old prince always dressed in old-fashioned style, wearing an antique coat and powdered hair; and when Prince Andrew entered his father's dressing room (not with the contemptuous look and manner he wore in drawing rooms, but with the animated face with which he talked to Pierre), the old man was sitting on a large leather-covered chair, wrapped in a powdering mantle, entrusting his head to Tíkhon.

"Ah! here's the warrior! Wants to vanquish Buonaparte?" said the old man, shaking his powdered head as much as the tail, which Tíkhon was holding fast to plait, would allow.

"You at least must tackle him properly, or else if he goes on like this

he'll soon have us, too, for his subjects! How are you?" And he held out his cheek.

The old man was in a good temper after his nap before dinner. (He used to say that a nap "after dinner was silver—before dinner, golden.") He cast happy, sidelong glances at his son from under his thick, bushy eyebrows. Prince Andrew went up and kissed his father on the spot indicated to him. He made no reply on his father's favorite topic—making fun of the military men of the day, and more particularly of Bonaparte.

"Yes, Father, I have come to you and brought my wife who is pregnant," said Prince Andrew, following every movement of his father's face with an eager and respectful look. "How is your health?"

"Only fools and rakes fall ill, my boy. You know me: I am busy from morning till night and abstemious, so of course I am well."

"Thank God," said his son smiling.

"God has nothing to do with it! Well, go on," he continued, returning to his hobby; "tell me how the Germans have taught you to fight Buonaparte by this new science you call 'strategy.'"

Prince Andrew smiled.

"Give me time to collect my wits, Father," said he, with a smile that showed that his father's foibles did not prevent his son from loving and honoring him. "Why, I have not yet had time to settle down!"

"Nonsense, nonsense!" cried the old man, shaking his pigtail to see whether it was firmly plaited, and grasping his son by the hand. "The house for your wife is ready. Princess Mary will take her there and show her over, and they'll talk nineteen to the dozen. That's their woman's way! I am glad to have her. Sit down and talk. About Mikhelson's army I understand—Tolstóy's too . . . a simultaneous expedition. . . . But what's the southern army to do? Prussia is neutral . . . I know that. What about Austria?" said he, rising from his chair and pacing up and down the room followed by Tíkhon, who ran after him, handing him different articles of clothing. "What of Sweden? How will they cross Pomerania?" *

* Old Bolkónski's inquiries about the war relate to the plan Wintzingerode had taken to Vienna for final settlement. It arranged for attacks on the French from three sides. The Swedes, British, and Russians (one corps of the latter under a Count Tolstóy) were to attack from the north through Pomerania and Hanover; the central European blow was to be dealt by Austrians and Russians —for this Russia was to furnish two more armies, one in Poland under Mikhelson and Bennigsen to draw Prussia into the war, and another in Galicia under Kutúzov and Buxhöwden, which was to advance and operate along the Danube; the Austrians were to provide two armies—one in Bavaria to act with

Prince Andrew, seeing that his father insisted, began—at first reluctantly, but gradually with more and more animation, and from habit changing unconsciously from Russian to French as he went on—to explain the plan of operation for the coming campaign. He explained how an army, ninety thousand strong, was to threaten Prussia so as to bring her out of her neutrality and draw her into the war; how part of that army was to join some Swedish forces at Stralsund; how two hundred and twenty thousand Austrians, with a hundred thousand Russians, were to operate in Italy and on the Rhine; how fifty thousand Russians and as many English were to land at Naples, and how a total force of five hundred thousand men was to attack the French from different sides. The old prince did not evince the least interest during this explanation, but as if he were not listening to it continued to dress while walking about, and three times unexpectedly interrupted. Once he stopped it by shouting: "The white one, the white one!"

This meant that Tíkhon was not handing him the waistcoat he wanted. Another time he interrupted, saying:

"And will she soon be confined?" and shaking his head reproachfully said: "That's bad! Go on, go on."

The third interruption came when Prince Andrew was finishing his description. The old man began to sing, in the cracked voice of old age: "*Malbrook s'en va-t-en guerre. Dieu sait quand reviendra.*" [Marlborough is going to the wars; God knows when he'll return.*]

His son only smiled.

"I don't say it's a plan I approve of," said the son; "I am only telling you what it is. Napoleon has also formed his plan by now, not worse than this one."

"Well, you've told me nothing new," and the old man repeated, meditatively and rapidly:

"*Dieu sait quand reviendra.* Go to the dining room."

AT THE appointed hour the prince, powdered and shaven, entered the dining room where his daughter-in-law, Princess Mary, and Mademoiselle Bourienne were already awaiting him together with his architect, who by a strange caprice of his employer's was admitted to table though the position of that insignificant individual was such as could certainly

the Russians, and one in Italy to operate in Lombardy. The third attack was to be made through central Italy, by Russians from Corfu and by the British from Malta and the Kingdom of Naples.—A.M.

* A very well-known French song.—A.M.

not have caused him to expect that honor. The prince, who generally kept very strictly to social distinctions and rarely admitted even important government officials to his table, had unexpectedly selected Michael Ivánovich (who always went into a corner to blow his nose on his checked handkerchief) to illustrate the theory that all men are equals, and had more than once impressed on his daughter that Michael Ivánovich was "not a whit worse than you or I." At dinner the prince usually spoke to the taciturn Michael Ivánovich more often than to anyone else.

In the dining room, which like all the rooms in the house was exceedingly lofty, the members of the household and the footmen—one behind each chair—stood waiting for the prince to enter. The head butler, napkin on arm, was scanning the setting of the table, making signs to the footmen, and anxiously glancing from the clock to the door by which the prince was to enter. Prince Andrew was looking at a large gilt frame, new to him, containing the genealogical tree of the Princes Bolkónski, opposite which hung another such frame with a badly painted portrait (evidently by the hand of the artist belonging to the estate) * of a ruling prince, in a crown—an alleged descendant of Rúrik and ancestor of the Bolkónskis. Prince Andrew, looking again at that genealogical tree, shook his head, laughing as a man laughs who looks at a portrait so characteristic of the original as to be amusing.

"How thoroughly like him that is!" he said to Princess Mary, who had come up to him.

Princess Mary looked at her brother in surprise. She did not understand what he was laughing at. Everything her father did inspired her with reverence and was beyond question.

"Everyone has his Achilles' heel," continued Prince Andrew. "Fancy, with *his* powerful mind, indulging in such nonsense!"

Princess Mary could not understand the boldness of her brother's criticism and was about to reply, when the expected footsteps were heard coming from the study. The prince walked in quickly and jauntily as was his wont, as if intentionally contrasting the briskness of his manners with the strict formality of his house. At that moment the great clock struck two and another with a shrill tone joined in from the drawing room. The prince stood still; his lively glittering eyes from under their thick, bushy eyebrows sternly scanned all present and rested on the little princess. She felt, as courtiers do when the Tsar enters, the sensation of fear and respect which the old man inspired in all around him. He stroked her hair and then patted her awkwardly on the back of her neck.

* It was not unusual on large estates for a proprietor to have painters, musicians, etc., from among his own serfs.—A.M.

"I'm glad, glad, to see you," he said, looking attentively into her eyes, and then quickly went to his place and sat down. "Sit down, sit down! Sit down, Michael Ivánovich!"

He indicated a place beside him to his daughter-in-law. A footman moved the chair for her.

"Ho, ho!" said the old man, casting his eyes on her rounded figure. "You've been in a hurry. That's bad!"

He laughed in his usual dry, cold, unpleasant way, with his lips only and not with his eyes.

"You must walk, walk as much as possible, as much as possible," he said.

The little princess did not, or did not wish to, hear his words. She was silent and seemed confused. The prince asked her about her father, and she began to smile and talk. He asked about mutual acquaintances, and she became still more animated and chattered away giving him greetings from various people and retailing the town gossip.

"Countess Apráksina, poor thing, has lost her husband and she has cried her eyes out," she said, growing more and more lively.

As she became animated the prince looked at her more and more sternly, and suddenly, as if he had studied her sufficiently and had formed a definite idea of her, he turned away and addressed Michael Ivánovich.

"Well, Michael Ivánovich, our Buonaparte will be having a bad time of it. Prince Andrew" (he always spoke thus of his son) "has been telling me what forces are being collected against him! While you and I never thought much of him."

Michael Ivánovich did not at all know when "you and I" had said such things about Bonaparte, but understanding that he was wanted as a peg on which to hang the prince's favorite topic, he looked inquiringly at the young prince, wondering what would follow.

"He is a great tactician!" said the prince to his son, pointing to the architect.

And the conversation again turned on the war, on Bonaparte, and the generals and statesmen of the day. The old prince seemed convinced not only that all the men of the day were mere babies who did not know the A B C of war or of politics, and that Bonaparte was an insignificant little Frenchy, successful only because there were no longer any Potëmkins * or Suvórovs left to oppose him; but he was also convinced that there were no political difficulties in Europe and no real war, but only a sort of

* *Grigori Alexandrovich Potëmkin (1739-91), Russian Field Marshal during the reign of Catherine the Great, who helped extend the southern boundaries of Russia.*

puppet show at which the men of the day were playing, pretending to do something real. Prince Andrew gaily bore with his father's ridicule of the new men, and drew him on and listened to him with evident pleasure.

"The past always seems good," said he, "but did not Suvórov himself fall into a trap Moreau set him, and from which he did not know how to escape?"

"Who told you that? Who?" cried the prince. "Suvórov!" And he jerked away his plate, which Tíkhon briskly caught. "Suvórov! . . . Consider, Prince Andrew. Two . . . Frederick and Suvórov; Moreau! . . . Moreau would have been a prisoner if Suvórov had had a free hand; but he had the Hofs-kriegs-wurst-schnapps-Rath * on his hands. It would have puzzled the devil himself! When you get there you'll find out what those Hofs-kriegs-wurst-Raths are! Suvórov couldn't manage them so what chance has Michael Kutúzov? No, my dear boy," he continued, "you and your generals won't get on against Buonaparte; you'll have to call in the French, so that birds of a feather may fight together. The German, Pahlen,[2] has been sent to New York in America, to fetch the Frenchman, Moreau," [3] he said, alluding to the invitation made that year to Moreau to enter the Russian service. . . . "Wonderful! . . . Were the Potëmkins, Suvórovs, and Orlóvs Germans? No, lad, either you fellows have all lost your wits, or I have outlived mine. May God help you, but we'll see what will happen. Buonaparte has become a great commander among them! Hm! . . ."

"I don't at all say that all the plans are good," said Prince Andrew, "I am only surprised at your opinion of Bonaparte. You may laugh as much as you like, but all the same Bonaparte is a great general!"

"Michael Ivánovich!" cried the old prince to the architect who, busy with his roast meat, hoped he had been forgotten: "Didn't I tell you Buonaparte was a great tactician? Here, he says the same thing."

"To be sure, your excellency," replied the architect.

The prince again laughed his frigid laugh.

"Buonaparte was born with a silver spoon in his mouth. He has got splendid soldiers. Besides he began by attacking Germans. And only idlers have failed to beat the Germans. Since the world began everybody

* "Court-war-sausage-schnapps-Council," Prince Bolkónski's contemptuous name for the Austrian Council of War.—A.M.

[2] An ironical reference to P. A. Pahlen, who had been Governor General of Petersburg under Paul in whose assassination he took part.—A.M.

[3] Jean Victor Marie Moreau (1763-1813), French General who was living in retirement in Morrisville, New Jersey.

has beaten the Germans. They beat no one—except one another. He made his reputation fighting them."

And the prince began explaining all the blunders which, according to him, Bonaparte had made in his campaigns and even in politics. His son made no rejoinder, but it was evident that whatever arguments were presented he was as little able as his father to change his opinion. He listened, refraining from a reply, and involuntarily wondered how this old man, living alone in the country for so many years, could know and discuss so minutely and acutely all the recent European military and political events.

"You think I'm an old man and don't understand the present state of affairs?" concluded his father. "But it troubles me. I don't sleep at night. Come now, where has this great commander of yours shown his skill?" he concluded.

"That would take too long to tell," answered the son.

"Well, then go off to your Buonaparte! Mademoiselle Bourienne, here's another admirer of that powder-monkey emperor of yours," he exclaimed in excellent French.

"You know, Prince, I am not a Bonapartist!"

"*Dieu sait quand reviendra*" . . . hummed the prince out of tune and, with a laugh still more so, he quitted the table.

The little princess during the whole discussion and the rest of the dinner sat silent, glancing with a frightened look now at her father-in-law and now at Princess Mary. When they left the table she took her sister-in-law's arm and drew her into another room.

"What a clever man your father is," said she; "perhaps that is why I am afraid of him."

"Oh, he is so kind!" answered Princess Mary.

16. Prince Andrew leaves to join the army. Princess Mary gives him an icon

PRINCE ANDREW was to leave next evening. The old prince, not altering his routine, retired as usual after dinner. The little princess was in her sister-in-law's room. Prince Andrew in a traveling coat without epaulettes had been packing with his valet in the rooms assigned to him. After inspecting the carriage himself and seeing the trunks put in, he ordered the horses to be harnessed. Only those things he always kept with him remained in his room; a small box, a large canteen fitted with silver plate, two Turkish pistols and a saber—a present from his father who had brought it from the siege of Ochákov. All these traveling effects of Prince

Andrew's were in very good order: new, clean, and in cloth covers carefully tied with tapes.

When starting on a journey or changing their mode of life, men capable of reflection are generally in a serious frame of mind. At such moments one reviews the past and plans for the future. Prince Andrew's face looked very thoughtful and tender. With his hands behind him he paced briskly from corner to corner of the room, looking straight before him and thoughtfully shaking his head. Did he fear going to the war, or was he sad at leaving his wife?—perhaps both, but evidently he did not wish to be seen in that mood, for hearing footsteps in the passage he hurriedly unclasped his hands, stopped at a table as if tying the cover of the small box, and assumed his usual tranquil and impenetrable expression. It was the heavy tread of Princess Mary that he heard.

"I hear you have given orders to harness," she cried, panting (she had apparently been running), "and I did so wish to have another talk with you alone! God knows how long we may again be parted. You are not angry with me for coming? You have changed so, Andrúsha," she added, as if to explain such a question.

She smiled as she uttered his pet name, "Andrúsha." It was obviously strange to her to think that this stern handsome man should be Andrúsha—the slender mischievous boy who had been her playfellow in childhood.

"And where is Lise?" he asked, answering her question only by a smile.

"She was so tired that she has fallen asleep on the sofa in my room. Oh, Andrew! What a treasure of a wife you have," said she, sitting down on the sofa, facing her brother. "She is quite a child: such a dear, merry child. I have grown so fond of her."

Prince Andrew was silent, but the princess noticed the ironical and contemptuous look that showed itself on his face.

"One must be indulgent to little weaknesses; who is free from them, Andrew? Don't forget that she has grown up and been educated in society, and so her position now is not a rosy one. We should enter into everyone's situation. *Tout comprendre, c'est tout pardonner* [To understand all is to forgive all]. Think what it must be for her, poor thing, after what she has been used to, to be parted from her husband and be left alone in the country, in her condition! It's very hard."

Prince Andrew smiled as he looked at his sister, as we smile at those we think we thoroughly understand.

"You live in the country and don't think the life terrible," he replied.

"I . . . that's different. Why speak of me? I don't want any other life, and can't, for I know no other. But think, Andrew: for a young society woman to be buried in the country during the best years of her life, all

alone—for Papa is always busy, and I . . . well, you know what poor resources I have for entertaining a woman used to the best society. There is only Mademoiselle Bourienne. . . ."

"I don't like your Mademoiselle Bourienne at all," said Prince Andrew.

"No? She is very nice and kind and, above all, she's much to be pitied. She has no one, no one. To tell the truth, I don't need her, and she's even in my way. You know I always was a savage, and now am even more so. I like being alone. . . . Father likes her very much. She and Michael Ivánovich are the two people to whom he is always gentle and kind, because he has been a benefactor to them both. As Sterne says: 'We don't love people so much for the good they have done us, as for the good we have done them.' Father took her when she was homeless after losing her own father. She is very good-natured, and my father likes her way of reading. She reads to him in the evenings and reads splendidly."

"To be quite frank, Mary, I expect Father's character sometimes makes things trying for you, doesn't it?" Prince Andrew asked suddenly.

Princess Mary was first surprised and then aghast at this question.

"For me? For me? . . . Trying for me! . . ." said she.

"He always was rather harsh; and now I should think he's getting very trying," said Prince Andrew, apparently speaking lightly of their father in order to puzzle or test his sister.

"You are good in every way, Andrew, but you have a kind of intellectual pride," said the princess, following the train of her own thoughts rather than the trend of the conversation—"and that's a great sin. How can one judge Father? But even if one might, what feeling except veneration could such a man as my father evoke? And I am so contented and happy with him. I only wish you were all as happy as I am."

Her brother shook his head incredulously.

"The only thing that is hard for me . . . I will tell you the truth, Andrew . . . is Father's way of treating religious subjects. I don't understand how a man of his immense intellect can fail to see what is as clear as day, and can go so far astray. That is the only thing that makes me unhappy. But even in this I can see lately a shade of improvement. His satire has been less bitter of late, and there was a monk he received and had a long talk with."

"Ah! my dear, I am afraid you and your monk are wasting your powder," said Prince Andrew banteringly yet tenderly.

"Ah! mon ami, I only pray, and hope that God will hear me. Andrew . . ." she said timidly after a moment's silence, "I have a great favor to ask of you."

"What is it, dear?"

"No—promise that you will not refuse! It will give you no trouble and is

nothing unworthy of you, but it will comfort me. Promise, Andrúsha! . . ." said she, putting her hand in her reticule but not yet taking out what she was holding inside it, as if what she held were the subject of her request and must not be shown before the request was granted.

She looked timidly at her brother.

"Even if it were a great deal of trouble . . ." answered Prince Andrew, as if guessing what it was about.

"Think what you please! I know you are just like Father. Think as you please, but do this for my sake! Please do! Father's father, our grandfather, wore it in all his wars." (She still did not take out what she was holding in her reticule.) "So you promise?"

"Of course. What is it?"

"Andrew, I bless you with this icon and you must promise me you will never take it off. Do you promise?"

"If it does not weigh a hundredweight and won't break my neck . . . To please you . . ." said Prince Andrew. But immediately, noticing the pained expression his joke had brought to his sister's face, he repented and added: "I am glad; really, dear, I am very glad."

"Against your will He will save and have mercy on you and bring you to Himself, for in Him alone is truth and peace," said she in a voice trembling with emotion, solemnly holding up in both hands before her brother a small, oval, antique, dark-faced icon of the Saviour in a gold setting, on a finely wrought silver chain.

She crossed herself, kissed the icon, and handed it to Andrew.

"Please, Andrew, for my sake! . . ."

Rays of gentle light shone from her large, timid eyes. Those eyes lit up the whole of her thin, sickly face and made it beautiful. Her brother would have taken the icon, but she stopped him. Andrew understood, crossed himself and kissed the icon. There was a look of tenderness, for he was touched, but also a gleam of irony on his face.

"Thank you, my dear." She kissed him on the forehead and sat down again on the sofa. They were silent for a while.

"As I was saying to you, Andrew, be kind and generous as you always used to be. Don't judge Lise harshly," she began. "She is so sweet, so good-natured, and her position now is a very hard one."

"I do not think I have complained of my wife to you, Másha,* or blamed her. Why do you say all this to me?"

Red patches appeared on Princess Mary's face and she was silent as if she felt guilty.

* The diminutive of Mary.—A.M.

"I have said nothing to you, but you have already been talked to. And I am sorry for that," he went on.

The patches grew deeper on her forehead, neck, and cheeks. She tried to say something but could not. Her brother had guessed right: the little princess had been crying after dinner and had spoken of her forebodings about her confinement, and of how she dreaded it, and had complained of her fate, her father-in-law, and her husband. After crying she had fallen asleep. Prince Andrew felt sorry for his sister.

"Know this, Másha: I can't reproach, have not reproached, and never shall reproach my wife with anything, and I cannot reproach myself with anything in regard to her; and that always will be so in whatever circumstances I may be placed. But if you want to know the truth . . . if you want to know whether I am happy? No! Is she happy? No! But why this is so I don't know . . ."

As he said this he rose, went to his sister, and, stooping, kissed her forehead. His fine eyes lit up with a thoughtful, kindly, and unaccustomed brightness, but he was looking not at his sister but over her head toward the darkness of the open doorway.

"Let us go to her, I must say good-by. Or—go and wake her, and I'll come in a moment. Petrúshka!" he called to his valet: "Come here, take these away. Put this on the seat and this to the right."

Princess Mary rose and moved to the door, then stopped and said: "Andrew, if you had faith you would have turned to God and asked him to give you the love you do not feel, and your prayer would have been answered."

"Well, may be!" said Prince Andrew. "Go, Másha; I'll come immediately."

On the way to his sister's room, in the passage which connected one wing with the other, Prince Andrew met Mademoiselle Bourienne smiling sweetly. It was the third time that day that, with an ecstatic and artless smile, she had met him in secluded passages.

"Oh! I thought you were in your room," she said, for some reason blushing and dropping her eyes.

Prince Andrew looked sternly at her and an expression of anger suddenly came over his face. He said nothing to her but looked at her forehead and hair, without looking at her eyes, with such contempt that the Frenchwoman blushed and went away without a word. When he reached his sister's room his wife was already awake and her merry voice, hurrying one word after another, came through the open door. She was speaking as usual in French, and as if after long self-restraint she wished to make up for lost time.

"No, but imagine the old Countess Zúbova,* with false curls and her mouth full of false teeth, as if she were trying to cheat old age. . . . Ha, ha, ha! Mary!"

This very sentence about Countess Zúbova and this same laugh Prince Andrew had already heard from his wife in the presence of others some five times. He entered the room softly. The little princess, plump and rosy, was sitting in an easy chair with her work in her hands, talking incessantly, repeating Petersburg reminiscences and even phrases. Prince Andrew came up, stroked her hair, and asked if she felt rested after their journey. She answered him and continued her chatter.

The coach with six horses was waiting at the porch. It was an autumn night, so dark that the coachman could not see the carriage pole. Servants with lanterns were bustling about in the porch. The immense house was brilliant with lights shining through its lofty windows. The domestic serfs were crowding in the hall, waiting to bid good-by to the young prince. The members of the household were all gathered in the reception hall: Michael Ivánovich, Mademoiselle Bourienne, Princess Mary, and the little princess. Prince Andrew had been called to his father's study as the latter wished to say good-by to him alone. All were waiting for them to come out.

When Prince Andrew entered the study the old man in his old-age spectacles and white dressing gown, in which he received no one but his son, sat at the table writing. He glanced round.

"Going?" And he went on writing.

"I've come to say good-by."

"Kiss me here," and he touched his cheek: "Thanks, thanks!"

"What do you thank me for?"

"For not dilly-dallying and not hanging to a woman's apron strings. The Service before everything. Thanks, thanks!" And he went on writing, so that his quill spluttered and squeaked. "If you have anything to say, say it. These two things can be done together," he added.

"About my wife . . . I am ashamed as it is to leave her on your hands. . . ."

"Why talk nonsense? Say what you want."

"When her confinement is due, send to Moscow for an *accoucheur.* . . . Let him be here. . . ."

The old prince stopped writing and, as if not understanding, fixed his stern eyes on his son.

"I know that no one can help if nature does not do her work," said Prince Andrew, evidently confused. "I know that out of a million cases only one goes wrong, but it is her fancy and mine. They have been telling her things. She has had a dream and is frightened."

* *The word* zub *means tooth, and a pun on this is intended.*—A.M.

"Hm . . . Hm . . ." muttered the old prince to himself, finishing what he was writing. "I'll do it."

He signed with a flourish and suddenly turning to his son began to laugh.

"It's a bad business, eh?"

"What is bad, Father?"

"The wife!" said the old prince, briefly and significantly.

"I don't understand!" said Prince Andrew.

"No, it can't be helped, lad," said the prince. "They're all like that; one can't unmarry. Don't be afraid; I won't tell anyone, but you know it yourself."

He seized his son by the hand with small bony fingers, shook it, looked straight into his son's face with keen eyes which seemed to see through him, and again laughed his frigid laugh.

The son sighed, thus admitting that his father had understood him. The old man continued to fold and seal his letter, snatching up and throwing down the wax, the seal, and the paper, with his accustomed rapidity.

"What's to be done? She's pretty! I will do everything. Make your mind easy," said he in abrupt sentences while sealing his letter.

Andrew did not speak; he was both pleased and displeased that his father understood him. The old man got up and gave the letter to his son.

"Listen!" said he; "don't worry about your wife: what can be done shall be. Now listen! Give this letter to Michael Ilariónovich.* I have written that he should make use of you in proper places and not keep you long as an adjutant: a bad position! Tell him I remember and like him. Write and tell me how he receives you. If he is all right—serve him. Nicholas Bolkón-ski's son need not serve under anyone if he is in disfavor. Now come here."

He spoke so rapidly that he did not finish half his words, but his son was accustomed to understand him. He led him to the desk, raised the lid, drew out a drawer, and took out an exercise book filled with his bold, tall, close handwriting.

"I shall probably die before you. So remember, these are my memoirs; hand them to the Emperor after my death. Now here is a Lombard bond [2] and a letter; it is a premium for the man who writes a history of Suvórov's wars. Send it to the Academy. Here are some jottings for you to read when I am gone. You will find them useful."

Andrew did not tell his father that he would no doubt live a long time yet. He felt that he must not say it.

"I will do it all, Father," he said.

* Kutúzov.—A.M.

[2] The Lombards, or pawnshops, were state institutions at that time and issued interest-bearing securities—"Lombard bonds."—A.M.

"Well, now, good-by!" He gave his son his hand to kiss, and embraced him. "Remember this, Prince Andrew, if they kill you it will hurt me, your old father . . ." he paused unexpectedly, and then in a querulous voice suddenly shrieked: "but if I hear that you have not behaved like a son of Nicholas Bolkónski, I shall be ashamed!"

"You need not have said that to me, Father," said the son with a smile.

The old man was silent.

"I also wanted to ask you," continued Prince Andrew, "if I'm killed and if I have a son, do not let him be taken away from you—as I said yesterday . . . let him grow up with you. . . . Please."

"Not let the wife have him?" said the old man, and laughed.

They stood silent, facing one another. The old man's sharp eyes were fixed straight on his son's. Something twitched in the lower part of the old prince's face.

"We've said good-by. Go!" he suddenly shouted in a loud, angry voice, opening his door.

"What is it? What?" asked both princesses when they saw for a moment at the door Prince Andrew and the figure of the old man in a white dressing gown, spectacled and wigless, shouting in an angry voice.

Prince Andrew sighed and made no reply.

"Well!" he said, turning to his wife.

And this "Well!" sounded coldly ironic, as if he were saying: "Now go through your performance."

"Andrew, already!" said the little princess, turning pale and looking with dismay at her husband.

He embraced her. She screamed and fell unconscious on his shoulder.

He cautiously released the shoulder she leaned on, looked into her face, and carefully placed her in an easy chair.

"Adieu, Mary," said he gently to his sister, taking her by the hand and kissing her, and then he left the room with rapid steps.

The little princess lay in the armchair, Mademoiselle Bourienne chafing her temples. Princess Mary, supporting her sister-in-law, still looked with her beautiful eyes full of tears at the door through which Prince Andrew had gone and made the sign of the cross in his direction. From the study, like pistol shots, came the frequent sound of the old man angrily blowing his nose. Hardly had Prince Andrew gone when the study door opened quickly and the stern figure of the old man in the white dressing gown looked out.

"Gone? That's all right!" said he; and looking angrily at the unconscious little princess, he shook his head reprovingly and slammed the door.

BOOK TWO

DATES OF PRINCIPAL HISTORICAL EVENTS
1805

OLD STYLE	NEW STYLE	
Oct. 11	Oct. 23	Kutúzov inspects regiment near Braunau. *Le malheureux Mack* arrives.
Oct. 23	Nov. 4	The Russian army crosses the Enns.
Oct. 24	Nov. 5	Fight at Amstetten.
Oct. 28	Nov. 9	The Russian army crosses the Danube.
Oct. 30	Nov. 11	Defeats Mortier at Dürrenstein.
Nov. 4	Nov. 16	Napoleon writes to Murat from Schönbrunn.
Nov. 4	Nov. 16	Battle of Schön Grabern.

THE CAMPAIGN
OF 1805
Scale of Miles

0 10 20 30 40 50

Olmütz

M O R A V I A

Wischau

Austerlitz

Schlappanitz

Brünn

R. Morava (March)

Znaim

Guntersdorf

Schön Grabern

Hollabrünn

VIENNA

Schönbrunn

Krems

R. Danube

Dürrenstein

A U S T R I A

Melk

Ips

Amstetten

Linz

Enns

R. Ips

R. Danube

R. Traun

R. Enns

N

Lambach

R. Inn

Ulm
140 miles

Braunau

1805

BOOK TWO

1. *Review near Braunau. Zherkóv and Dólokhov*

IN OCTOBER, 1805, a Russian army was occupying the villages and towns of the Archduchy of Austria, and yet other regiments freshly arriving from Russia were settling near the fortress of Braunau and burdening the inhabitants on whom they were quartered. Braunau was the headquarters of the commander in chief, Kutúzov.

On October 11, 1805, one of the infantry regiments that had just reached Braunau had halted half a mile from the town, waiting to be inspected by the commander in chief. Despite the un-Russian appearance of the locality and surroundings—fruit gardens, stone fences, tiled roofs, and hills in the distance—and despite the fact that the inhabitants (who gazed with curiosity at the soldiers) were not Russians, the regiment had just the appearance of any Russian regiment preparing for an inspection anywhere in the heart of Russia.

On the evening of the last day's march an order had been received that the commander in chief would inspect the regiment on the march. Though the words of the order were not clear to the regimental commander, and the question arose whether the troops were to be in marching order or not, it was decided at a consultation between the battalion commanders to present the regiment in parade order, on the principle that it is always better to "bow too low than not bow low enough." So the soldiers, after a twenty-mile march, were kept mending and cleaning all night long without closing their eyes, while the adjutants and company commanders calculated and reckoned, and by morning the regiment—instead of the straggling, disorderly crowd it had been on its last march the day before—presented a well-ordered array of two thousand men each of whom knew his place and his duty, had every button and every strap in place, and shone with cleanliness. And not only externally was all in order, but had it pleased the commander in chief to look under the uniforms he would have found on every man a clean shirt, and in every knapsack the appointed number

117

of articles, "awl, soap, and all," as the soldiers say. There was only one cir-
cumstance concerning which no one could be at ease. It was the state of
the soldiers' boots. More than half the men's boots were in holes. But this
defect was not due to any fault of the regimental commander, for in spite
of repeated demands boots had not been issued by the Austrian commis-
sariat, and the regiment had marched some seven hundred miles.

The commander of the regiment was an elderly, choleric, stout, and
thick-set general with grizzled eyebrows and whiskers, and wider from
chest to back than across the shoulders. He had on a brand-new uniform
showing the creases where it had been folded and thick gold epaulettes
which seemed to stand rather than lie down on his massive shoulders. He
had the air of a man happily performing one of the most solemn duties of
his life. He walked about in front of the line and at every step pulled him-
self up, slightly arching his back. It was plain that the commander admired
his regiment, rejoiced in it, and that his whole mind was engrossed by it,
yet his strut seemed to indicate that, besides military matters, social inter-
ests and the fair sex occupied no small part of his thoughts.

"Well, Michael Mítrich, sir?" he said, addressing one of the battalion
commanders who smilingly pressed forward (it was plain that they both
felt happy). "We had our hands full last night. However, I think the regi-
ment is not a bad one, eh?"

The battalion commander perceived the jovial irony and laughed.

"It would not be turned off the field even on the Tsarítsin Meadow." *

"What?" asked the commander.

At that moment, on the road from the town on which signalers had been
posted, two men appeared on horseback. They were an aide-de-camp fol-
lowed by a Cossack.

The aide-de-camp was sent to confirm the order which had not been
clearly worded the day before, namely, that the commander in chief
wished to see the regiment just in the state in which it had been on the
march: in their greatcoats, and packs, and without any preparation what-
ever.

A member of the Hofkriegsrath from Vienna had come to Kutúzov the
day before with proposals and demands for him to join up with the army
of the Archduke Ferdinand and Mack, and Kutúzov, not considering this
junction advisable, meant, among other arguments in support of his view,
to show the Austrian general the wretched state in which the troops ar-
rived from Russia. With this object he intended to meet the regiment; so

* The "Tsarítsin Meadow" was in Petersburg, on the bank of the Néva.
Later on it was called "the Field of Mars." It was used for parades and reviews.
—A.M.

the worse the condition it was in, the better pleased the commander in chief would be. Though the aide-de-camp did not know these circumstances, he nevertheless delivered the definite order that the men should be in their greatcoats and in marching order, and that the commander in chief would otherwise be dissatisfied. On hearing this the regimental commander hung his head, silently shrugged his shoulders, and spread out his arms with a choleric gesture.

"A fine mess we've made of it!" he remarked.

"There now! Didn't I tell you, Michael Mítrich, that if it was said 'on the march' it meant in greatcoats?" said he reproachfully to the battalion commander. "Oh, my God!" he added, stepping resolutely forward. "Company commanders!" he shouted in a voice accustomed to command. "Sergeants major! . . . How soon will he be here?" he asked the aide-de-camp with a respectful politeness evidently relating to the personage he was referring to.

"In an hour's time, I should say."

"Shall we have time to change clothes?"

"I don't know, General. . . ."

The regimental commander, going up to the line himself, ordered the soldiers to change into their greatcoats. The company commanders ran off to their companies, the sergeants major began bustling (the greatcoats were not in very good condition), and instantly the squares that had up to then been in regular order and silent began to sway and stretch and hum with voices. On all sides soldiers were running to and fro, throwing up their knapsacks with a jerk of their shoulders and pulling the straps over their heads, unstrapping their overcoats and drawing the sleeves on with upraised arms.

In half an hour all was again in order, only the squares had become gray instead of black. The regimental commander walked with his jerky steps to the front of the regiment and examined it from a distance.

"Whatever is this? This!" he shouted and stood still. "Commander of the third company!"

"Commander of the third company wanted by the general! . . . commander to the general . . . third company to the commander." The words passed along the lines and an adjutant ran to look for the missing officer.

When the eager but misrepeated words had reached their destination in a cry of: "The general to the third company," the missing officer appeared from behind his company and, though he was a middle-aged man and not in the habit of running, trotted awkwardly stumbling on his toes toward the general. The captain's face showed the uneasiness of a schoolboy who is told to repeat a lesson he has not learned. Spots appeared on

his nose, the redness of which was evidently due to intemperance, and his mouth twitched nervously. The general looked the captain up and down as he came up panting, slackening his pace as he approached.

"You will soon be dressing your men in petticoats! What is this?" shouted the regimental commander, thrusting forward his jaw and pointing at a soldier in the ranks of the third company in a greatcoat of bluish cloth, which contrasted with the others. "What have you been after? The commander in chief is expected and you leave your place? Eh? I'll teach you to dress the men in fancy coats for a parade. . . . Eh . . . ?"

The commander of the company, with his eyes fixed on his superior, pressed two fingers more and more rigidly to his cap, as if in this pressure lay his only hope of salvation.

"Well, why don't you speak? Whom have you got there dressed up as a Hungarian?" said the commander with an austere gibe.

"Your excellency . . ."

"Well, your excellency, what? Your excellency! But what about your excellency? . . . nobody knows."

"Your excellency, it's the officer Dólokhov, who has been reduced to the ranks," said the captain softly.

"Well? Has he been degraded into a field marshal, or into a soldier? If a soldier, he should be dressed in regulation uniform like the others."

"Your excellency, you gave him leave yourself, on the march."

"Gave him leave? Leave? That's just like you young men," said the regimental commander cooling down a little. "Leave indeed. . . . One says a word to you and you . . . What?" he added with renewed irritation, "I beg you to dress your men decently."

And the commander, turning to look at the adjutant, directed his jerky steps down the line. He was evidently pleased at his own display of anger and walking up to the regiment wished to find a further excuse for wrath. Having snapped at an officer for an unpolished badge, at another because his line was not straight, he reached the third company.

"H-o-o-w are you standing? Where's your leg? Your leg?" shouted the commander with a tone of suffering in his voice, while there were still five men between him and Dólokhov with his bluish-gray uniform.

Dólokhov slowly straightened his bent knee, looking straight with his clear, insolent eyes in the general's face.

"Why a blue coat? Off with it . . . Sergeant major! Change his coat . . . the ras . . ." he did not finish.

"General, I must obey orders, but I am not bound to endure . . ." Dólokhov hurriedly interrupted.

"No talking in the ranks! . . . No talking, no talking!"

"Not bound to endure insults," Dólokhov concluded in loud, ringing tones.

The eyes of the general and the soldier met. The general became silent, angrily pulling down his tight scarf.

"I request you to have the goodness to change your coat," he said as he turned away.

"He's coming!" shouted the signaler at that moment.

The regimental commander, flushing, ran to his horse, seized the stirrup with trembling hands, threw his body across the saddle, righted himself, drew his saber, and with a happy and resolute countenance, opening his mouth awry, prepared to shout. The regiment fluttered like a bird preening its plumage and became motionless.

"Att-ention!" shouted the regimental commander in a soul-shaking voice which expressed joy for himself, severity for the regiment, and welcome for the approaching chief.

Along the broad country road, edged on both sides by trees, came a high, light-blue Viennese calèche,* slightly creaking on its springs and drawn by six horses at a smart trot. Behind the calèche galloped the suite and a convoy of Croats. Beside Kutúzov sat an Austrian general, in a white uniform that looked strange among the Russian black ones. The calèche stopped in front of the regiment. Kutúzov and the Austrian general were talking in low voices and Kutúzov smiled slightly as treading heavily he stepped down from the carriage just as if those two thousand men breathlessly gazing at him and the regimental commander did not exist.

The word of command rang out, and again the regiment quivered, as with a jingling sound it presented arms. Then amidst a dead silence the feeble voice of the commander in chief was heard. The regiment roared, "Health to your ex . . . len . . . len . . . lency!" and again all became silent. At first Kutúzov stood still while the regiment moved; then he and the general in white, accompanied by the suite, walked between the ranks.

From the way the regimental commander saluted the commander in chief and devoured him with his eyes, drawing himself up obsequiously, and from the way he walked through the ranks behind the generals, bending forward and hardly able to restrain his jerky movements, and from the way he darted forward at every word or gesture of the commander in chief, it was evident that he performed his duty as a subordinate with even greater zeal than his duty as a commander. Thanks to the strictness and assiduity of its commander the regiment, in comparison with others that had reached Braunau at the same time, was in splendid condition. There

* A *light four-wheeled carriage with a folding hood.*

were only 217 sick and stragglers. Everything was in good order except the boots.

Kutúzov walked through the ranks, sometimes stopping to say a few friendly words to officers he had known in the Turkish war, sometimes also to the soldiers. Looking at their boots he several times shook his head sadly, pointing them out to the Austrian general with an expression which seemed to say that he was not blaming anyone, but could not help noticing what a bad state of things it was. The regimental commander ran forward on each such occasion, fearing to miss a single word of the commander in chief's regarding the regiment. Behind Kutúzov, at a distance that allowed every softly spoken word to be heard, followed some twenty men of his suite. These gentlemen talked among themselves and sometimes laughed. Nearest of all to the commander in chief walked a handsome adjutant. This was Prince Bolkónski. Beside him was his comrade Nesvítski, a tall staff officer, extremely stout, with a kindly, smiling, handsome face and moist eyes. Nesvítski could hardly keep from laughter provoked by a swarthy hussar officer who walked beside him. This hussar, with a grave face and without a smile or a change in the expression of his fixed eyes, watched the regimental commander's back and mimicked his every movement. Each time the commander started and bent forward, the hussar started and bent forward in exactly the same manner. Nesvítski laughed and nudged the others to make them look at the wag.

Kutúzov walked slowly and languidly past thousands of eyes which were starting from their sockets to watch their chief. On reaching the third company he suddenly stopped. His suite, not having expected this, involuntarily came closer to him.

"Ah, Timókhin!" said he, recognizing the red-nosed captain who had been reprimanded on account of the blue greatcoat.

One would have thought it impossible for a man to stretch himself more than Timókhin had done when he was reprimanded by the regimental commander, but now that the commander in chief addressed him he drew himself up to such an extent that it seemed he could not have sustained it had the commander in chief continued to look at him, and so Kutúzov, who evidently understood his case and wished him nothing but good, quickly turned away, a scarcely perceptible smile flitting over his scarred and puffy face.

"Another Ismail * comrade," said he. "A brave officer! Are you satisfied with him?" he asked the regimental commander.

And the latter—unconscious that he was being reflected in the hussar

* *In Bessarabia, called Tuchkov in Russian.*

officer as in a looking glass—started, moved forward, and answered: "Highly satisfied, your excellency!"

"We all have our weaknesses," said Kutúzov smiling and walking away from him. "He used to have a predilection for Bacchus."

The regimental commander was afraid he might be blamed for this and did not answer. The hussar at that moment noticed the face of the red-nosed captain and his drawn-in stomach, and mimicked his expression and pose with such exactitude that Nesvítski could not help laughing. Kutúzov turned round. The officer evidently had complete control of his face, and while Kutúzov was turning managed to make a grimace and then assume a most serious, deferential, and innocent expression.

The third company was the last, and Kutúzov pondered, apparently trying to recollect something. Prince Andrew stepped forward from among the suite and said softly in French:

"You told me to remind you of the officer Dólokhov, reduced to the ranks in this regiment."

"Where is Dólokhov?" asked Kutúzov.

Dólokhov, who had already changed into a soldier's gray greatcoat, did not wait to be called. The shapely figure of the fair-haired soldier, with his clear blue eyes, stepped forward from the ranks, went up to the commander in chief, and presented arms.

"Have you a complaint to make?" Kutúzov asked with a slight frown.

"This is Dólokhov," said Prince Andrew.

"Ah!" said Kutúzov. "I hope this will be a lesson to you. Do your duty. The Emperor is gracious, and I shan't forget you if you deserve well."

The clear blue eyes looked at the commander in chief just as boldly as they had looked at the regimental commander, seeming by their expression to tear open the veil of convention that separates a commander in chief so widely from a private.

"One thing I ask of your excellency," Dólokhov said in his firm, ringing, deliberate voice. "I ask an opportunity to atone for my fault and prove my devotion to His Majesty the Emperor and to Russia!"

Kutúzov turned away. The same smile of the eyes with which he had turned from Captain Timókhin again flitted over his face. He turned away with a grimace as if to say that everything Dólokhov had said to him and everything he could say had long been known to him, that he was weary of it and it was not at all what he wanted. He turned away and went to the carriage.

The regiment broke up into companies, which went to their appointed quarters near Braunau, where they hoped to receive boots and clothes and to rest after their hard marches.

"You won't bear me a grudge, Prokhór Ignátych?" said the regimental commander, overtaking the third company on its way to its quarters and riding up to Captain Timókhin who was walking in front. (The regimental commander's face now that the inspection was happily over beamed with irrepressible delight.) "It's in the Emperor's service . . . it can't be helped . . . one is sometimes a bit hasty on parade . . . I am the first to apologize, you know me! . . . He was very pleased!" And he held out his hand to the captain.

"Don't mention it, General, as if I'd be so bold!" replied the captain, his nose growing redder as he gave a smile which showed where two front teeth were missing that had been knocked out by the butt end of a gun at Ismail.

"And tell Mr. Dólokhov that I won't forget him—he may be quite easy. And tell me, please—I've been meaning to ask—how is he behaving himself, and in general . . ."

"As far as the service goes he is quite punctilious, your excellency; but his character . . ." said Timókhin.

"And what about his character?" asked the regimental commander.

"It's different on different days," answered the captain. "One day he is sensible, well educated, and good-natured, and the next he's a wild beast. . . . In Poland, if you please, he nearly killed a Jew."

"Oh, well, well!" remarked the regimental commander. "Still, one must have pity on a young man in misfortune. You know he has important connections . . . Well, then, you just . . ."

"I will, your excellency," said Timókhin, showing by his smile that he understood his commander's wish.

"Well, of course, of course!"

The regimental commander sought out Dólokhov in the ranks and, reining in his horse, said to him:

"After the next affair . . . epaulettes."

Dólokhov looked round but did not say anything, nor did the mocking smile on his lips change.

"Well, that's all right," continued the regimental commander. "A cup of vodka for the men from me," he added so that the soldiers could hear. "I thank you all! God be praised!" and he rode past that company and overtook the next one.

"Well, he's really a good fellow, one can serve under him," said Timókhin to the subaltern beside him.

"In a word, a hearty one . . ." said the subaltern, laughing (the regimental commander was nicknamed *King of Hearts*).

The cheerful mood of their officers after the inspection infected the sol-

diers. The company marched on gaily. The soldiers' voices could be heard on every side.

"And they said Kutúzov was blind of one eye?"

"And so he is! Quite blind!"

"No, friend, he is sharper-eyed than you are. Boots and leg bands * . . . he noticed everything . . ."

"When he looked at my feet, friend . . . well, thinks I . . ."

"And that other one with him, the Austrian, looked as if he were smeared with chalk—as white as flour! I suppose they polish him up as they do the guns."

"I say, Fédeshon! . . . Did he say when the battles are to begin? You were near him. Everybody said that Buonaparte himself was at Braunau."

"Buonaparte himself! . . . Just listen to the fool, what he doesn't know! The Prussians are up in arms now. The Austrians, you see, are putting them down. When they've been put down, the war with Buonaparte will begin. And he says Buonaparte is in Braunau! Shows you're a fool. You'd better listen more carefully!"

"What devils these quartermasters are! See, the fifth company is turning into the village already . . . they will have their buckwheat cooked before we reach our quarters."

"Give me a biscuit, you devil!"

"And did you give me tobacco yesterday? That's just it, friend! Ah, well, never mind, here you are."

"They might call a halt here or we'll have to do another four miles without eating."

"Wasn't it fine when those Germans gave us lifts! You just sit still and are drawn along." [2]

"And here, friend, the people are quite beggarly. There they all seemed to be Poles—all under the Russian crown—but here they're all regular Germans."

"Singers to the front!" came the captain's order.

* *Russian soldiers wore long strips of linen round their feet and legs, instead of stockings.*—A.M.

[2] *The Russian army had started from Radzivílov on August 13, O.S., and it had taken them two months to get near the seat of war. The Austrians had also been very slow. Believing Napoleon and his army to be at Boulogne preparing for an invasion of England, the Austrians were taken by surprise in September to learn that he had reached the Rhine. Kutúzov was then still so far off that his corps was quickly supplied with carts, which traveled over thirty miles a day instead of the fourteen to twenty the soldiers had been doing on foot.*—A.M.

And from the different ranks some twenty men ran to the front. A drummer, their leader, turned round facing the singers, and flourishing his arm, began a long-drawn-out soldiers' song, commencing with the words: "*Morning dawned, the sun was rising,*" and concluding: "*On then, brothers, on to glory, led by Father Kámenski.*" This song had been composed in the Turkish campaign and was now being sung in Austria, the only change being that the words "Father Kámenski" were replaced by "Father Kutúzov."

Having jerked out these last words as soldiers do and waved his arms as if flinging something to the ground, the drummer—a lean, handsome soldier of forty—looked sternly at the singers and screwed up his eyes. Then having satisfied himself that all eyes were fixed on him, he raised both arms as if carefully lifting some invisible but precious object above his head and, holding it there for some seconds, suddenly flung it down and began:

"*Oh, my bower, oh, my bower . . . !*"

"*Oh, my bower new . . . !*" chimed in twenty voices, and the castanet player, in spite of the burden of his equipment, rushed out to the front and, walking backwards before the company, jerked his shoulders and flourished his castanets as if threatening someone. The soldiers, swinging their arms and keeping time spontaneously, marched with long steps. Behind the company the sound of wheels, the creaking of springs, and the tramp of horses' hoofs were heard. Kutúzov and his suite were returning to the town. The commander in chief made a sign that the men should continue to march at ease, and he and all his suite showed pleasure at the sound of the singing and the sight of the dancing soldier and the gay and smartly marching men. In the second file from the right flank, beside which the carriage passed the company, a blue-eyed soldier involuntarily attracted notice. It was Dólokhov marching with particular grace and boldness in time to the song and looking at those driving past as if he pitied all who were not at that moment marching with the company. The hussar cornet of Kutúzov's suite who had mimicked the regimental commander, fell back from the carriage and rode up to Dólokhov.

Hussar cornet Zherkóv had at one time, in Petersburg, belonged to the wild set led by Dólokhov. Zherkóv had met Dólokhov abroad as a private and had not seen fit to recognize him. But now that Kutúzov had spoken to the gentleman ranker, he addressed him with the cordiality of an old friend.

"My dear fellow, how are you?" said he through the singing, making his horse keep pace with the company.

"How am I?" Dólokhov answered coldly. "I am as you see."

The lively song gave a special flavor to the tone of free and easy gaiety

with which Zherkóv spoke, and to the intentional coldness of Dólokhov's reply.

"And how do you get on with the officers?" inquired Zherkóv.

"All right. They are good fellows. And how have you wriggled onto the staff?"

"I was attached; I'm on duty."

Both were silent.

"*She let the hawk fly upward from her wide right sleeve*," went the song, arousing an involuntary sensation of courage and cheerfulness. Their conversation would probably have been different but for the effect of that song.

"Is it true that Austrians have been beaten?" asked Dólokhov.

"The devil only knows! They say so."

"I'm glad," answered Dólokhov briefly and clearly, as the song demanded.

"I say, come round some evening and we'll have a game of faro!" said Zherkóv.

"Why, have you too much money?"

"Do come."

"I can't. I've sworn not to. I won't drink and won't play till I get reinstated."

"Well, that's only till the first engagement."

"We shall see."

They were again silent.

"Come if you need anything. One can at least be of use on the staff . . ."

Dólokhov smiled. "Don't trouble. If I want anything, I won't beg—I'll take it!"

"Well, never mind; I only . . ."

"And I only . . ."

"Good-by."

"Good health . . ."

> "*It's a long, long way*
> *To my native land . . .*"

Zherkóv touched his horse with the spurs; it pranced excitedly from foot to foot uncertain with which to start, then settled down, galloped past the company, and overtook the carriage, still keeping time to the song.

2. *Kutúzov and an Austrian general. Le malheureux Mack.* Zherkóv's foolery

O N RETURNING from the review, Kutúzov took the Austrian general into his private room and, calling his adjutant, asked for some papers relating to the condition of the troops on their arrival, and the letters that had come from the Archduke Ferdinand, who was in command of the advanced army. Prince Andrew Bolkónski came into the room with the required papers. Kutúzov and the Austrian member of the Hofkriegsrath were sitting at the table on which a plan was spread out.

"Ah! . . ." said Kutúzov glancing at Bolkónski as if by this exclamation he was asking the adjutant to wait, and he went on with the conversation in French.

"All I can say, General," said he with a pleasant elegance of expression and intonation that obliged one to listen to each deliberately spoken word. It was evident that Kutúzov himself listened with pleasure to his own voice. "All I can say, General, is that if the matter depended on my personal wishes, the will of His Majesty the Emperor Francis would have been fulfilled long ago. I should long ago have joined the archduke. And believe me on my honor that to me personally it would be a pleasure to hand over the supreme command of the army into the hands of a better informed and more skillful general—of whom Austria has so many—and to lay down all this heavy responsibility. But circumstances are sometimes too strong for us, General."

And Kutúzov smiled in a way that seemed to say, "You are quite at liberty not to believe me and I don't even care whether you do or not, but you have no grounds for telling me so. And that is the whole point."

The Austrian general looked dissatisfied, but had no option but to reply in the same tone.

"On the contrary," he said, in a querulous and angry tone that contrasted with his flattering words, "on the contrary, your excellency's participation in the common action is highly valued by His Majesty; but we think the present delay is depriving the splendid Russian troops and their commander of the laurels they have been accustomed to win in their battles," he concluded his evidently prearranged sentence.

Kutúzov bowed with the same smile.

"But that is my conviction, and judging by the last letter with which His Highness the Archduke Ferdinand has honored me,* I imagine that

* *Tolstóy has taken the middle part of an actual letter, quoted in the works of the Russian military historian, Mikháylovski-Danílevski. Throughout the*

the Austrian troops, under the direction of so skillful a leader as General Mack, have by now already gained a decisive victory and no longer need our aid," said Kutúzov.

The general frowned. Though there was no definite news of an Austrian defeat, there were many circumstances confirming the unfavorable rumors that were afloat, and so Kutúzov's suggestion of an Austrian victory sounded much like irony. But Kutúzov went on blandly smiling with the same expression, which seemed to say that he had a right to suppose so. And, in fact, the last letter he had received from Mack's army informed him of a victory and stated that strategetically the position of the army was very favorable.

"Give me that letter," said Kutúzov turning to Prince Andrew. "Please have a look at it"—and Kutúzov with an ironical smile about the corners of his mouth read to the Austrian general the following passage, in German, from the Archduke Ferdinand's letter:

"We have fully concentrated forces of nearly seventy thousand men with which to attack and defeat the enemy should he cross the Lech. Also, as we are masters of Ulm, we cannot be deprived of the advantage of commanding both sides of the Danube, so that should the enemy not cross the Lech, we can cross the Danube, throw ourselves on his line of communications, recross the river lower down, and frustrate his intention should he try to direct his whole force against our faithful ally. We shall therefore confidently await the moment when the Imperial Russian army will be fully equipped, and shall then, in conjunction with it, easily find a way to prepare for the enemy the fate he deserves."

Kutúzov sighed deeply on finishing this paragraph and looked at the member of the Hofkriegsrath mildly and attentively.

"But you know the wise maxim, your excellency, advising one to expect the worst," said the Austrian general, evidently wishing to have done with jests and to come to business. He involuntarily looked round at the aide-de-camp.

"Excuse me, General," interrupted Kutúzov, also turning to Prince Andrew. "Look here, my dear fellow, get from Kozlóvski all the reports from our scouts. Here are two letters from Count Nostitz and here is one

novel Tolstóy is very careful to keep closely to the historical facts. He made much use of Danílevski's works on the Russian side and Thiers' on the French, besides consulting many other authorities and private letters and memoirs of members of his own and other families that had been engaged in the war. These private sources sometimes enabled him to correct mistakes the historians had made.—A.M.

from His Highness the Archduke Ferdinand and here are these," he said,
handing him several papers, "make a neat memorandum in French out of
all this, showing all the news we have had of the movements of the Aus-
trian army, and then give it to his excellency."

Prince Andrew bowed his head in token of having understood from the
first not only what had been said but also what Kutúzov would have liked
to tell him. He gathered up the papers and, with a bow to both, stepped
softly over the carpet and went out into the waiting room.

Though not much time had passed since Prince Andrew had left Russia,
he had changed greatly during that period. In the expression of his face,
in his movements, in his walk, scarcely a trace was left of his former af-
fected languor and indolence. He now looked like a man who has no time
to think of the impression he makes on others, but is occupied with agree-
able and interesting work. His face expressed more satisfaction with him-
self and those around him, his smile and glance were brighter and more
attractive.

Kutúzov, whom he had overtaken in Poland, had received him very
kindly, promised not to forget him, distinguished him above the other
adjutants, and had taken him to Vienna and given him the more serious
commissions. From Vienna Kutúzov wrote to his old comrade, Prince
Andrew's father:

"Your son bids fair to become an officer distinguished by his industry,
firmness, and expedition. I consider myself fortunate to have such a sub-
ordinate by me."

On Kutúzov's staff, among his fellow officers and in the army generally,
Prince Andrew had, as he had had in Petersburg society, two quite oppo-
site reputations. Some, a minority, acknowledged him to be different from
themselves and from everyone else, expected great things of him, listened
to him, admired, and imitated him, and with them Prince Andrew was
natural and pleasant. Others, the majority, disliked him and considered
him conceited, cold, and disagreeable. But among these people Prince An-
drew knew how to take his stand so that they respected and even feared
him.

Coming out of Kutúzov's room into the waiting room with the papers
in his hand Prince Andrew came up to his comrade, the aide-de-camp on
duty, Kozlóvski, who was sitting at the window with a book.

"Well, Prince?" asked Kozlóvski.

"I am ordered to write a memorandum explaining why we are not ad-
vancing."

"And why is it?"

Prince Andrew shrugged his shoulders.

"Any news from Mack?"

"No."

"If it were true that he has been beaten, news would have come."

"Probably," said Prince Andrew moving toward the outer door.

But at that instant a tall Austrian general in a greatcoat, with the order of Maria Theresa on his neck and a black bandage round his head, who had evidently just arrived, entered quickly, slamming the door. Prince Andrew stopped short.

"Commander in Chief Kutúzov?" said the newly arrived general speaking quickly with a harsh German accent, looking to both sides and advancing straight toward the inner door.

"The commander in chief is engaged," said Kozlóvski, going hurriedly up to the unknown general and blocking his way to the door. "Whom shall I announce?"

The unknown general looked disdainfully down at Kozlóvski, who was rather short, as if surprised that anyone should not know him.

"The commander in chief is engaged," repeated Kozlóvski calmly.

The general's face clouded, his lips quivered and trembled. He took out a notebook, hurriedly scribbled something in pencil, tore out the leaf, gave it to Kozlóvski, stepped quickly to the window, and threw himself into a chair, gazing at those in the room as if asking, "Why do they look at me?" Then he lifted his head, stretched his neck as if he intended to say something, but immediately, with affected indifference, began to hum to himself, producing a queer sound which immediately broke off. The door of the private room opened and Kutúzov appeared in the doorway. The general with the bandaged head bent forward as though running away from some danger, and, making long, quick strides with his thin legs, went up to Kutúzov.

"Vous voyez le malheureux Mack," * he uttered in a broken voice.

Kutúzov's face as he stood in the open doorway remained perfectly immobile for a few moments. Then wrinkles ran over his face like a wave and his forehead became smooth again, he bowed his head respectfully, closed his eyes, silently let Mack enter his room before him, and closed the door himself behind him.

The report which had been circulated that the Austrians had been beaten and that the whole army had surrendered at Ulm proved to be correct. Within half an hour adjutants had been sent in various directions with orders which showed that the Russian troops, who had hitherto been inactive, would also soon have to meet the enemy.

* *Baron Karl Mack von Leiberich (1752-1828), in command of the Austrian army at Ulm.*

Prince Andrew was one of those rare staff officers whose chief interest lay in the general progress of the war. When he saw Mack and heard the details of his disaster he understood that half the campaign was lost, understood all the difficulties of the Russian army's position, and vividly imagined what awaited it and the part he would have to play. Involuntarily he felt a joyful agitation at the thought of the humiliation of arrogant Austria and that in a week's time he might, perhaps, see and take part in the first Russian encounter with the French since Suvórov met them. He feared that Bonaparte's genius might outweigh all the courage of the Russian troops, and at the same time could not admit the idea of his hero being disgraced.

Excited and irritated by these thoughts Prince Andrew went toward his room to write to his father, to whom he wrote every day. In the corridor he met Nesvítski, with whom he shared a room, and the wag Zherkóv; they were as usual laughing.

"Why are you so glum?" asked Nesvítski noticing Prince Andrew's pale face and glittering eyes.

"There's nothing to be gay about," answered Bolkónski.

Just as Prince Andrew met Nesvítski and Zherkóv, there came toward them from the other end of the corridor, Strauch, an Austrian general who was on Kutúzov's staff in charge of the provisioning of the Russian army, and the member of the Hofkriegsrath who had arrived the previous evening. There was room enough in the wide corridor for the generals to pass the three officers quite easily, but Zherkóv, pushing Nesvítski aside with his arm, said in a breathless voice,

"They're coming! . . . they're coming! . . . Stand aside, make way, please make way!"

The generals were passing by, looking as if they wished to avoid embarrassing attentions. On the face of the wag Zherkóv there suddenly appeared a stupid smile of glee which he seemed unable to suppress.

"Your excellency," said he in German, stepping forward and addressing the Austrian general, "I have the honor to congratulate you."

He bowed his head and scraped first with one foot and then with the other, awkwardly, like a child at a dancing lesson.

The member of the Hofkriegsrath looked at him severely but, seeing the seriousness of his stupid smile, could not but give him a moment's attention. He screwed up his eyes showing that he was listening.

"I have the honor to congratulate you. General Mack has arrived, quite well, only a little bruised just here," he added, pointing with a beaming smile to his head.

The general frowned, turned away, and went on.

"*Gott, wie naiv* [Good God, what simplicity]!" said he angrily, after he had gone a few steps.

Nesvítski with a laugh threw his arms round Prince Andrew, but Bolkónski, turning still paler, pushed him away with an angry look and turned to Zherkóv. The nervous irritation aroused by the appearance of Mack, the news of his defeat, and the thought of what lay before the Russian army found vent in anger at Zherkóv's untimely jest.

"If you, sir, choose to make a *buffoon* of yourself," he said sharply, with a slight trembling of the lower jaw, "I can't prevent your doing so; but I warn you that if you dare to play the fool in my presence, I will teach you to behave yourself."

Nesvítski and Zherkóv were so surprised by this outburst that they gazed at Bolkónski silently with wide-open eyes.

"What's the matter? I only congratulated them," said Zherkóv.

"I am not jesting with you; please be silent!" cried Bolkónski, and taking Nesvítski's arm he left Zherkóv, who did not know what to say.

"Come, what's the matter, old fellow?" said Nesvítski trying to soothe him.

"What's the matter?" exclaimed Prince Andrew standing still in his excitement. "Don't you understand that either we are officers serving our Tsar and our country, rejoicing in the successes and grieving at the misfortunes of our common cause, or we are merely lackeys who care nothing for their master's business. *Quarante mille hommes massacrés et l'armée de nos alliés détruite, et vous trouvez là le mot pour rire* [Forty thousand men massacred and the army of our allies destroyed, and you find that a cause for jesting]," he said, as if strengthening his views by this French sentence. "*C'est bien pour un garçon de rien comme cet individu dont vous avez fait un ami, mais pas pour vous, pas pour vous* [It is all very well for that good-for-nothing fellow of whom you have made a friend, but not for you, not for you]. Only a *hobbledehoy* could amuse himself in this way," he added in Russian—but pronouncing the word with a French accent—having noticed that Zherkóv could still hear him.

He waited a moment to see whether the cornet would answer, but he turned and went out of the corridor.

3. Nicholas and Denísov. Telyánin and the missing purse

THE PAVLOGRAD HUSSARS were stationed two miles from Braunau. The squadron in which Nicholas Rostóv served as a cadet was quartered in the German village of Salzeneck. The best quarters in the village were

assigned to cavalry-captain Denísov, the squadron commander, known throughout the whole cavalry division as Váska Denísov. Cadet Rostóv, ever since he had overtaken the regiment in Poland, had lived with the squadron commander.

On October 11, the day when all was astir at headquarters over the news of Mack's defeat, the camp life of the officers of this squadron was proceeding as usual. Denísov, who had been losing at cards all night, had not yet come home when Rostóv rode back early in the morning from a foraging expedition. Rostóv in his cadet uniform, with a jerk to his horse, rode up to the porch, swung his leg over the saddle with a supple youthful movement, stood for a moment in the stirrup as if loath to part from his horse, and at last sprang down and called to his orderly.

"Ah, Bondarénko, dear friend!" said he to the hussar who rushed up headlong to the horse. "Walk him up and down, my dear fellow," he continued, with that gay brotherly cordiality which goodhearted young people show to everyone when they are happy.

"Yes, your excellency," answered the Ukrainian gaily, tossing his head.

"Mind, walk him up and down well!"

Another hussar also rushed toward the horse, but Bondarénko had already thrown the reins of the snaffle bridle over the horse's head. It was evident that the cadet was liberal with his tips and that it paid to serve him. Rostóv patted the horse's neck and then his flank, and lingered for a moment.

"Splendid! What a horse he will be!" he thought with a smile, and holding up his saber, his spurs jingling, he ran up the steps of the porch. His landlord, who in a waistcoat and a pointed cap, pitchfork in hand, was clearing manure from the cowhouse, looked out, and his face immediately brightened on seeing Rostóv. "Schön gut Morgen! Schön gut Morgen! [A very good morning! A very good morning!]" he said winking with a merry smile, evidently pleased to greet the young man.

"Schon fleissig [Busy already]?" said Rostóv with the same gay brotherly smile which did not leave his eager face. "Hoch Oestreicher! Hoch Russen! Kaiser Alexander hoch! [Hurrah for the Austrians! Hurrah for the Russians! Hurrah for the Emperor Alexander!]" said he, quoting words often repeated by the German landlord.

The German laughed, came out of the cowshed, pulled off his cap, and waving it above his head cried:

"Und die ganze Welt hoch [And hurrah for the whole world]!"

Rostóv waved his cap above his head like the German and cried laughing, "Und vivat die ganze Welt!" Though neither the German cleaning his cowshed nor Rostóv back with his platoon from foraging for hay

had any reason for rejoicing, they looked at each other with joyful delight and brotherly love, wagged their heads in token of their mutual affection, and parted smiling, the German returning to his cowshed and Rostóv going to the cottage he occupied with Denísov.

"What about your master?" he asked Lavrúshka, Denísov's orderly, whom all the regiment knew for a rogue.

"Hasn't been in since the evening. Must have been losing," answered Lavrúshka. "I know by now, if he wins he comes back early to brag about it, but if he stays out till morning it means he's lost and will come back in a rage. Will you have coffee?"

"Yes, bring some."

Ten minutes later Lavrúshka brought the coffee. "He's coming!" said he. "Now for trouble!" Rostóv looked out of the window and saw Denísov coming home. Denísov was a small man with a red face, sparkling black eyes, and black tousled mustache and hair. He wore an unfastened cloak, wide breeches hanging down in creases, and a crumpled shako on the back of his head. He came up to the porch gloomily, hanging his head.

"Lavwúska!" he shouted loudly and angrily, "take it off, blockhead!"

"Well, I am taking it off," replied Lavrúshka's voice.

"Ah, you're up already," said Denísov, entering the room.

"Long ago," answered Rostóv, "I have already been for the hay, and have seen Fräulein Mathilde."

"Weally! And I've been losing, bwother. I lost yesterday like a damned fool!" cried Denísov, not pronouncing his r's. "Such ill luck! Such ill luck. As soon as you left, it began and went on. Hullo there! Tea!"

Puckering up his face as though smiling, and showing his short strong teeth, he began with the stubby fingers of both hands to ruffle up his thick tangled black hair.

"And what devil made me go to that wat?" (an officer nicknamed "the rat") he said, rubbing his forehead and whole face with both hands. "Just fancy, he didn't let me win a single cahd, not one cahd."

He took the lighted pipe that was offered to him, gripped it in his fist, and tapped it on the floor, making the sparks fly, while he continued to shout.

"He lets one win the singles and collahs it as soon as one doubles it; gives the singles and snatches the doubles!"

He scattered the burning tobacco, smashed the pipe, and threw it away. Then he remained silent for a while, and all at once looked cheerfully with his glittering, black eyes at Rostóv.

"If at least we had some women here; but there's nothing foh one to do but dwink. If we could only get to fighting soon. Hullo, who's there?"

he said, turning to the door as he heard a tread of heavy boots and the clinking of spurs that came to a stop, and a respectful cough.

"The squadron quartermaster!" said Lavrúshka.

Denísov's face puckered still more.

"Wetched!" he muttered, throwing down a purse with some gold in it. "Wostóv, deah fellow, just see how much there is left and shove the purse undah the pillow," he said, and went out to the quartermaster.

Rostóv took the money and, mechanically arranging the old and new coins in separate piles, began counting them.

"Ah! Telyánin! How d'ye do? They plucked me last night," came Denísov's voice from the next room.

"Where? At Bykov's, at the rat's . . . I knew it," replied a piping voice, and Lieutenant Telyánin, a small officer of the same squadron, entered the room.

Rostóv thrust the purse under the pillow and shook the damp little hand which was offered him. Telyánin for some reason had been transferred from the Guards just before this campaign. He behaved very well in the regiment but was not liked; Rostóv especially detested him and was unable to overcome or conceal his groundless antipathy to the man.

"Well, young cavalryman, how is my Rook behaving?" he asked. (Rook was a young horse Telyánin had sold to Rostóv.)

The lieutenant never looked the man he was speaking to straight in the face; his eyes continually wandered from one object to another.

"I saw you riding this morning . . ." he added.

"Oh, he's all right, a good horse," answered Rostóv, though the horse for which he had paid seven hundred rubles was not worth half that sum. "He's begun to go a little lame on the left foreleg," he added.

"The hoof's cracked! That's nothing. I'll teach you what to do and show you what kind of rivet to use."

"Yes, please do," said Rostóv.

"I'll show you, I'll show you! It's not a secret. And it's a horse you'll thank me for."

"Then I'll have it brought round," said Rostóv wishing to avoid Telyánin, and he went out to give the order.

In the passage Denísov, with a pipe, was squatting on the threshold facing the quartermaster who was reporting to him. On seeing Rostóv, Denísov screwed up his face and pointing over his shoulder with his thumb to the room where Telyánin was sitting, he frowned and gave a shudder of disgust.

"Ugh! I don't like that fellow," he said, regardless of the quartermaster's presence.

Rostóv shrugged his shoulders as much as to say: "Nor do I, but what's one to do?" and, having given his order, he returned to Telyánin.

Telyánin was sitting in the same indolent pose in which Rostóv had left him, rubbing his small white hands.

"Well there certainly are disgusting people," thought Rostóv as he entered.

"Have you told them to bring the horse?" asked Telyánin, getting up and looking carelessly about him.

"I have."

"Let us go ourselves. I only came round to ask Denísov about yesterday's order. Have you got it, Denísov?"

"Not yet. But where are you off to?"

"I want to teach this young man how to shoe a horse," said Telyánin.

They went through the porch and into the stable. The lieutenant explained how to rivet the hoof and went away to his own quarters.

When Rostóv went back there was a bottle of vodka and a sausage on the table. Denísov was sitting there scratching with his pen on a sheet of paper. He looked gloomily in Rostóv's face and said: "I am witing to her."

He leaned his elbows on the table with his pen in his hand and, evidently glad of a chance to say quicker in words what he wanted to write, told Rostóv the contents of his letter.

"You see, my fwiend," he said, "we sleep when we don't love. We are childwen of the dust . . . but one falls in love and one is a God, one is pua' as on the fihst day of cweation . . . Who's that now? Send him to the devil, I'm busy!" he shouted to Lavrúshka, who went up to him not in the least abashed.

"Who should it be? You yourself told him to come. It's the quartermaster for the money."

Denísov frowned and was about to shout some reply but stopped.

"Wetched business," he muttered to himself. "How much is left in the puhse?" he asked, turning to Rostóv.

"Seven new and three old imperials."

"Oh, it's wetched! Well, what are you standing there for, you sca'-cwow? Call the quahtehmasteh," he shouted to Lavrúshka.

"Please, Denísov, let me lend you some: I have some, you know," said Rostóv, blushing.

"Don't like bowwowing from my own fellows, I don't," growled Denísov.

"But if you won't accept money from me like a comrade, you will offend me. Really I have some," Rostóv repeated.

"No, I tell you."

And Denísov went to the bed to get the purse from under the pillow. "Where have you put it, Wostóv?"

"Under the lower pillow."

"It's not there."

Denísov threw both pillows on the floor. The purse was not there.

"That's a miwacle."

"Wait, haven't you dropped it?" said Rostóv, picking up the pillows one at a time and shaking them.

He pulled off the quilt and shook it. The purse was not there.

"Dear me, can I have forgotten? No, I remember thinking that you kept it under your head like a treasure," said Rostóv. "I put it just here. Where is it?" he asked, turning to Lavrúshka.

"I haven't been in the room. It must be where you put it."

"But it isn't? . . ."

"You're always like that; you thwow a thing down anywhere and forget it. Feel in your pockets."

"No, if I hadn't thought of it being a treasure," said Rostóv, "but I remember putting it there."

Lavrúshka turned all the bedding over, looked under the bed and under the table, searched everywhere, and stood still in the middle of the room. Denísov silently watched Lavrúshka's movements, and when the latter threw up his arms in surprise saying it was nowhere to be found Denísov glanced at Rostóv.

"Wostóv, you've not been playing schoolboy twicks. . . ."

Rostóv felt Denísov's gaze fixed on him, raised his eyes, and instantly dropped them again. All the blood which had seemed congested somewhere below his throat rushed to his face and eyes. He could not draw breath.

"And there hasn't been anyone in the room except the lieutenant and yourselves. It must be here somewhere," said Lavrúshka.

"Now then, you devil's puppet, look alive and hunt for it!" shouted Denísov, suddenly, turning purple and rushing at the man with a threatening gesture. "If the purse isn't found I'll flog you, I'll flog you all."

Rostóv, his eyes avoiding Denísov, began buttoning his coat, buckled on his saber, and put on his cap.

"I must have that purse, I tell you," shouted Denísov, shaking his orderly by the shoulders and knocking him against the wall.

"Denísov, let him alone, I know who has taken it," said Rostóv, going toward the door without raising his eyes.

Denísov paused, thought a moment, and, evidently understanding what Rostóv hinted at, seized his arm.

"Nonsense!" he cried, and the veins on his forehead and neck stood out like cords. "You are mad, I tell you. I won't allow it. The purse is here! I'll flay this scoundwel alive, and it will be found."

"I know who has taken it," repeated Rostóv in an unsteady voice, and went to the door.

"And I tell you, don't you dahe to do it!" shouted Denísov, rushing at the cadet to restrain him.

But Rostóv pulled away his arm and, with as much anger as though Denísov were his worst enemy, firmly fixed his eyes directly on his face.

"Do you understand what you're saying?" he said in a trembling voice. "There was no one else in the room except myself. So that if it is not so, then . . ."

He could not finish, and ran out of the room.

"Ah, may the devil take you and evewybody," were the last words Rostóv heard.

Rostóv went to Telyánin's quarters.

"The master is not in, he's gone to headquarters," said Telyánin's orderly. "Has something happened?" he added, surprised at the cadet's troubled face.

"No, nothing."

"You've only just missed him," said the orderly.

The headquarters were situated two miles away from Salzeneck, and Rostóv, without returning home, took a horse and rode there. There was an inn in the village which the officers frequented. Rostóv rode up to it and saw Telyánin's horse at the porch.

In the second room of the inn the lieutenant was sitting over a dish of sausages and a bottle of wine.

"Ah, you've come here too, young man!" he said, smiling and raising his eyebrows.

"Yes," said Rostóv as if it cost him a great deal to utter the word; and he sat down at the nearest table.

Both were silent. There were two Germans and a Russian officer in the room. No one spoke and the only sounds heard were the clatter of knives and the munching of the lieutenant.

When Telyánin had finished his lunch he took out of his pocket a double purse and, drawing its rings aside with his small, white, turned-up fingers, drew out a gold imperial, and lifting his eyebrows gave it to the waiter.

"Please be quick," he said.

The coin was a new one. Rostóv rose and went up to Telyánin.

"Allow me to look at your purse," he said in a low, almost inaudible, voice.

With shifting eyes but eyebrows still raised, Telyánin handed him the purse.

"Yes, it's a nice purse. Yes, yes," he said, growing suddenly pale, and added, "Look at it, young man."

Rostóv took the purse in his hand, examined it and the money in it, and looked at Telyánin. The lieutenant was looking about in his usual way and suddenly seemed to grow very merry.

"If we get to Vienna I'll get rid of it there but in these wretched little towns there's nowhere to spend it," said he. "Well, let me have it, young man, I'm going."

Rostóv did not speak.

"And you? Are you going to have lunch too? They feed you quite decently here," continued Telyánin. "Now then, let me have it."

He stretched out his hand to take hold of the purse. Rostóv let go of it. Telyánin took the purse and began carelessly slipping it into the pocket of his riding breeches, with his eyebrows lifted and his mouth slightly open, as if to say, "Yes, yes, I am putting my purse in my pocket and that's quite simple and is no one else's business."

"Well, young man?" he said with a sigh, and from under his lifted brows he glanced into Rostóv's eyes.

Some flash as of an electric spark shot from Telyánin's eyes to Rostóv's and back, and back again and again in an instant.

"Come here," said Rostóv, catching hold of Telyánin's arm and almost dragging him to the window. "That money is Denísov's; you took it . . ." he whispered just above Telyánin's ear.

"What? What? How dare you? What?" said Telyánin.

But these words came like a piteous, despairing cry and an entreaty for pardon. As soon as Rostóv heard them, an enormous load of doubt fell from him. He was glad, and at the same instant began to pity the miserable man who stood before him, but the task he had begun had to be completed.

"Heaven only knows what the people here may imagine," muttered Telyánin, taking up his cap and moving toward a small empty room. "We must have an explanation . . ."

"I know it and shall prove it," said Rostóv.

"I . . ."

Every muscle of Telyánin's pale, terrified face began to quiver, his eyes

still shifted from side to side but with a downward look not rising to Rostóv's face, and his sobs were audible.

"Count! . . . Don't ruin a young fellow . . . here is this wretched money, take it . . ." He threw it on the table. "I have an old father and mother! . . ."

Rostóv took the money, avoiding Telyánin's eyes, and went out of the room without a word. But at the door he stopped and then retraced his steps. "O God," he said with tears in his eyes, "how could you do it?"

"Count . . ." said Telyánin drawing nearer to him.

"Don't touch me," said Rostóv, drawing back. "If you need it, take the money," and he threw the purse to him and ran out of the inn.

4. Nicholas in trouble with his fellow officers

THAT SAME EVENING there was an animated discussion among the squadron's officers in Denísov's quarters.

"And I tell you, Rostóv, that you must apologize to the colonel!" said a tall, grizzly-haired staff captain, with enormous mustaches and many wrinkles on his large features, to Rostóv who was crimson with excitement.

The staff captain, Kírsten, had twice been reduced to the ranks for affairs of honor and had twice regained his commission.

"I will allow no one to call me a liar!" cried Rostóv. "He told me I lied, and I told him he lied. And there it rests. He may keep me on duty every day, or may place me under arrest, but no one can make me apologize, because if he, as commander of this regiment, thinks it beneath his dignity to give me satisfaction, then . . ."

"You just wait a moment, my dear fellow, and listen," interrupted the staff captain in his deep bass, calmly stroking his long mustache. "You tell the colonel in the presence of other officers that an officer has stolen . . ."

"I'm not to blame that the conversation began in the presence of other officers. Perhaps I ought not to have spoken before them, but I am not a diplomatist. That's why I joined the hussars, thinking that here one would not need finesse; and he tells me that I am lying—so let him give me satisfaction . . ."

"That's all right. No one thinks you a coward, but that's not the point. Ask Denísov whether it is not out of the question for a cadet to demand satisfaction of his regimental commander?"

Denísov sat gloomily biting his mustache and listening to the conver-

sation, evidently with no wish to take part in it. He answered the staff captain's question by a disapproving shake of his head.

"You speak to the colonel about this nasty business before other officers," continued the staff captain, "and Bogdánich" (the colonel was called Bogdánich) "shuts you up."

"He did not shut me up, he said I was telling an untruth."

"Well, have it so, and you talked a lot of nonsense to him and must apologize."

"Not on any account!" exclaimed Rostóv.

"I did not expect this of you," said the staff captain seriously and severely. "You don't wish to apologize, but, man, it's not only to him but to the whole regiment—all of us—you're to blame all round. The case is this: you ought to have thought the matter over and taken advice; but no, you go and blurt it all straight out before the officers. Now what was the colonel to do? Have the officer tried and disgrace the whole regiment? Disgrace the whole regiment because of one scoundrel? Is that how you look at it? We don't see it like that. And Bogdánich was a brick: he told you you were saying what was not true. It's not pleasant, but what's to be done, my dear fellow? You landed yourself in it. And now, when one wants to smooth the thing over, some conceit prevents your apologizing, and you wish to make the whole affair public. You are offended at being put on duty a bit, but why not apologize to an old and honorable officer? Whatever Bogdánich may be, anyway he is an honorable and brave old colonel! You're quick at taking offense, but you don't mind disgracing the whole regiment!" The staff captain's voice began to tremble. "You have been in the regiment next to no time, my lad, you're here today and tomorrow you'll be appointed adjutant somewhere and can snap your fingers when it is said 'There are thieves among the Pávlograd officers!' But it's not all the same to us! Am I not right, Denísov? It's not the same!"

Denísov remained silent and did not move, but occasionally looked with his glittering black eyes at Rostóv.

"You value your own pride and don't wish to apologize," continued the staff captain, "but we old fellows, who have grown up in and, God willing, are going to die in the regiment, we prize the honor of the regiment, and Bogdánich knows it. Oh, we do prize it, old fellow! And all this is not right, it's not right! You may take offense or not but I always stick to mother truth. It's not right!"

And the staff captain rose and turned away from Rostóv.

"That's twue, devil take it!" shouted Denísov, jumping up. "Now then, Wostóv, now then!"

Rostóv, growing red and pale alternately, looked first at one officer and then at the other.

"No, gentlemen, no . . . you mustn't think . . . I quite understand. You're wrong to think that of me . . . I . . . for me . . . for the honor of the regiment I'd . . . Ah well, I'll show that in action, and for me the honor of the flag . . . Well, never mind, it's true I'm to blame, to blame all round. Well, what else do you want? . . ."

"Come, that's right, Count!" cried the staff captain, turning round and clapping Rostóv on the shoulder with his big hand.

"I tell you," shouted Denísov, "he's a fine fellow."

"That's better, Count," said the staff captain, beginning to address Rostóv by his title, as if in recognition of his confession. Go and apologize, your excellency. Yes, go!"

"Gentlemen, I'll do anything. No one shall hear a word from me," said Rostóv in an imploring voice, "but I can't apologize, by God I can't, do what you will! How can I go and apologize like a little boy asking forgiveness?"

Denísov began to laugh.

"It'll be worse for you. Bogdánich is vindictive and you'll pay for your obstinacy," said Kírsten.

"No, on my word it's not obstinacy! I can't describe the feeling. I can't . . ."

"Well, it's as you like," said the staff captain. "And what has become of that scoundrel?" he asked Denísov.

"He has weported himself sick, he's to be stwuck off the list tomowwwow," muttered Denísov.

"It is an illness, there's no other way of explaining it," said the staff captain.

"Illness or not, he'd better not cwoss my path. I'd kill him!" shouted Denísov in a bloodthirsty tone.

Just then Zherkóv entered the room.

"What brings you here?" cried the officers turning to the newcomer.

"We're to go into action, gentlemen! Mack has surrendered with his whole army."

"It's not true!"

"I've seen him myself!"

"What? Saw the real Mack? With hands and feet?"

"Into action! Into action! Bring him a bottle for such news! But how did you come here?"

"I've been sent back to the regiment all on account of that devil, Mack. An Austrian general complained of me. I congratulated him on

Mack's arrival . . . What's the matter, Rostóv? You look as if you'd just come out of a hot bath."

"Oh, my dear fellow, we're in such a stew here these last two days."

The regimental adjutant came in and confirmed the news brought by Zherkóv. They were under orders to advance next day.

"We're going into action, gentlemen!"

"Well, thank God! We've been sitting here too long!"

5. Crossing the Enns. Burning the bridge. Rostóv's baptism of fire

Kutúzov FELL BACK toward Vienna, destroying behind him the bridges over the rivers Inn (at Braunau) and Traun (near Linz). On October 23 the Russian troops were crossing the river Enns. At midday the Russian baggage train, the artillery, and columns of troops were defiling through the town of Enns on both sides of the bridge.*

* The military position dealt with in Chapter 5 was this. After Mack's surrender, Kutúzov began to retreat toward Vienna, beating back as he went the attacks of the French advanced guard under Murat. On October 23, O.S., he crossed the rapid river Enns. Murat was pressing all day on the troops under Bagratión, trying to intercept him and cut him off from the crossing. Failing to do this, he reached the river almost simultaneously with Bagratión and tried to seize the bridge. As described in the novel, the Pávlograd hussars managed to fire it after the Russian troops had crossed.

Murat, who is repeatedly mentioned in the novel, was the son of an inn-keeper and had risen from the ranks. He helped Napoleon to suppress a royalist rising on 13 Vendémiaire 1795, and through him received rapid promotion. After highly distinguishing himself in the Italian campaigns, he accompanied Napoleon to Egypt and proved to be a brilliant cavalry leader. Returning to France with Napoleon he led the sixty grenadiers whose appearance broke up the Council of Five Hundred on 18 Brumaire 1799; which event led to Napoleon becoming Consul. In 1800 Murat married Napoleon's sister Caroline. As governor of Paris in 1804 he appointed the commission by which the Duc d'Enghien was tried and shot. He distinguished himself afresh in the German campaign of 1805. In 1808 Napoleon made him King of Naples, where he set up a sumptuous court and was upbraided by the Emperor for his "monkey tricks." He commanded Napoleon's cavalry in the invasion of Russia in 1812, but threw up his command in December and returned to Naples. In 1813 he withdrew his support from Napoleon and tried to obtain Austrian help for the continuance of his kingship. In 1814 he was deposed, and escaped into hiding

It was a warm, rainy, autumnal day. The wide expanse that opened out before the heights on which the Russian batteries stood guarding the bridge was at times veiled by a diaphanous curtain of slanting rain, and then, suddenly spread out in the sunlight, far-distant objects could be clearly seen glittering as though freshly varnished. Down below, the little town could be seen with its white, red-roofed houses, its cathedral, and its bridge, on both sides of which streamed jostling masses of Russian troops. At the bend of the Danube, vessels, an island, and a castle with a park surrounded by the waters of the confluence of the Enns and the Danube became visible, and the rocky left bank of the Danube covered with pine forests, with a mystic background of green treetops and bluish gorges. The turrets of a convent stood out beyond a wild virgin pine forest, and far away on the other side of the Enns the enemy's horse patrols could be discerned.

Among the field guns on the brow of the hill the general in command of the rearguard stood with a staff officer, scanning the country through his fieldglass. A little behind them Nesvítski, who had been sent to the rearguard by the commander in chief, was sitting on the trail of a gun carriage. A Cossack who accompanied him had handed him a knapsack and a flask, and Nesvítski was treating some officers to pies and real *doppelkümmel*. The officers gladly gathered round him, some on their knees, some squatting Turkish fashion on the wet grass.

"Yes, the Austrian prince who built that castle was no fool. It's a fine place! Why are you not eating anything, gentlemen?" Nesvítski was saying.

"Thank you very much, Prince," answered one of the officers, pleased to be talking to a staff officer of such importance. "It's a lovely place! We passed close to the park and saw two deer . . . and what a splendid house!"

"Look, Prince," said another, who would have dearly liked to take another pie but felt shy, and therefore pretended to be examining the countryside—"See, our infantrymen have already got there. Look there in the meadow behind the village, three of them are dragging something. They'll ransack that castle," he remarked with evident approval.

"So they will," said Nesvítski. "No, but what I should like," added he,

near Toulon, a price being set on his head. He then, after Waterloo, attempted to recover his kingdom, but was captured, court-martialed, and shot. Despite his agility and reckless courage, he was a man of limited intelligence whose head was turned by success. Tolstóy repeatedly alludes to his limitations, love of ostentation, showy clothes, and comical swagger.—A.M.

munching a pie in his moist-lipped handsome mouth, "would be to slip in over there."

He pointed with a smile to a turreted nunnery, and his eyes narrowed and gleamed.

"That would be fine, gentlemen!"

The officers laughed.

"Just to flutter the nuns a bit. They say there are Italian girls among them. On my word I'd give five years of my life for it!"

"They must be feeling dull, too," said one of the bolder officers, laughing.

Meanwhile the staff officer standing in front pointed out something to the general, who looked through his field glass.

"Yes, so it is, so it is," said the general angrily, lowering the field glass and shrugging his shoulders, "so it is! They'll be fired on at the crossing And why are they dawdling there?"

On the opposite side the enemy could be seen by the naked eye, and from their battery a milk-white cloud arose. Then came the distant report of a shot, and our troops could be seen hurrying to the crossing.

Nesvítski rose, puffing, and went up to the general, smiling.

"Would not your excellency like a little refreshment?" he said.

"It's a bad business," said the general without answering him, "our men have been wasting time."

"Hadn't I better ride over, your excellency?" asked Nesvítski.

"Yes, please do," answered the general, and he repeated the order that had already once been given in detail: "and tell the hussars that they are to cross last and to fire the bridge as I ordered; and the inflammable material on the bridge must be reinspected."

"Very good," answered Nesvítski.

He called the Cossack with his horse, told him to put away the knapsack and flask, and swung his heavy person easily into the saddle.

"I'll really call in on the nuns," he said to the officers who watched him smilingly, and he rode off by the winding path down the hill.

"Now then, let's see how far it will carry, Captain. Just try!" said the general, turning to an artillery officer. "Have a little fun to pass the time."

"Crew, to your guns!" commanded the officer.

In a moment the men came running gaily from their campfires and began loading.

"One!" came the command.

Number one jumped briskly aside. The gun rang out with a deafening metallic roar, and a whistling grenade flew above the heads of our

troops below the hill and fell far short of the enemy, a little smoke showing the spot where it burst.

The faces of officers and men brightened up at the sound. Everyone got up and began watching the movements of our troops below, as plainly visible as if but a stone's throw away, and the movements of the approaching enemy farther off. At the same instant the sun came fully out from behind the clouds, and the clear sound of the solitary shot and the brilliance of the bright sunshine merged in a single joyous and spirited impression.

Two of the enemy's shots had already flown across the bridge, where there was a crush. Halfway across stood Prince Nesvítski, who had alighted from his horse and whose big body was jammed against the railings. He looked back laughing to the Cossack who stood a few steps behind him holding two horses by their bridles. Each time Prince Nesvítski tried to move on, soldiers and carts pushed him back again and pressed him against the railings, and all he could do was to smile.

"What a fellow you are, friend!" said the Cossack to a convoy soldier with a wagon, who was pressing onto the infantrymen who were crowded together close to his wheels and his horses. "What a fellow! You can't wait a moment! Don't you see the general wants to pass?"

But the convoyman took no notice of the word "general" and shouted at the soldiers who were blocking his way. "Hi there, boys! Keep to the left! Wait a bit." But the soldiers, crowded together shoulder to shoulder, their bayonets interlocking, moved over the bridge in a dense mass. Looking down over the rails Prince Nesvítski saw the rapid, noisy little waves of the Enns, which rippling and eddying round the piles of the bridge chased each other along. Looking on the bridge he saw equally uniform living waves of soldiers, shoulder straps, covered shakos, knapsacks, bayonets, long muskets, and, under the shakos, faces with broad cheekbones, sunken cheeks, and listless tired expressions, and feet that moved through the sticky mud that covered the planks of the bridge. Sometimes through the monotonous waves of men, like a fleck of white foam on the waves of the Enns, an officer, in a cloak and with a type of face different from that of the men, squeezed his way along; sometimes like a chip of wood whirling in the river, an hussar on foot, an orderly, or a townsman was carried through the waves of infantry; and sometimes like a log floating down the river, an officers' or company's baggage wagon, piled high, leather-covered, and hemmed in on all sides, moved across the bridge.

"It's as if a dam had burst," said the Cossack hopelessly. "Are there many more of you to come?"

"A million all but one!" replied a waggish soldier in a torn coat, with a wink, and passed on followed by another, an old man.

"If he" (he meant the enemy) "begins popping at the bridge now," said the old soldier dismally to a comrade, "you'll forget to scratch yourself."

That soldier passed on, and after him came another sitting on a cart.

"Where the devil have the leg bands been shoved to?" said an orderly, running behind the cart and fumbling in the back of it.

And he also passed on with the wagon. Then came some merry soldiers who had evidently been drinking.

"And then, old fellow, he gives him one in the teeth with the butt end of his gun . . ." a soldier whose greatcoat was well tucked up said gaily, with a wide swing of his arm.

"Yes, the ham was just delicious . . ." answered another with a loud laugh. And they, too, passed on, so that Nesvítski did not learn who had been struck on the teeth, or what the ham had to do with it.

"Bah! How they scurry. He just sends a ball and they think they'll all be killed," a sergeant was saying angrily and reproachfully.

"As it flies past me, Daddy, the ball I mean," said a young soldier with an enormous mouth, hardly refraining from laughing, "I felt like dying of fright. I did, 'pon my word, I got that frightened!" said he, as if bragging of having been frightened.

That one also passed. Then followed a cart unlike any that had gone before. It was a German cart with a pair of horses led by a German, and seemed loaded with a whole houseful of effects. A fine brindled cow with a large udder was attached to the cart behind. A woman with an unweaned baby, an old woman, and a healthy German girl with bright red cheeks were sitting on some feather beds. Evidently these fugitives were allowed to pass by special permission. The eyes of all the soldiers turned toward the women, and while the vehicle was passing at foot pace all the soldiers' remarks related to the two young ones. Every face bore almost the same smile, expressing unseemly thoughts about the women.

"Just see, the German sausage is making tracks, too!"

"Sell me the missis," said another soldier, addressing the German, who, angry and frightened, strode energetically along with downcast eyes.

"See how smart she's made herself! Oh, the devils!"

"There, Fedótov, you should be quartered on them!"

"I have seen as much before now, mate!"

"Where are you going?" asked an infantry officer who was eating an apple, also half smiling as he looked at the handsome girl.

The German closed his eyes, signifying that he did not understand.

"Take it if you like," said the officer, giving the girl an apple.

The girl smiled and took it. Nesvítski like the rest of the men on the bridge did not take his eyes off the women till they had passed. When they had gone by, the same stream of soldiers followed, with the same kind of talk, and at last all stopped. As often happens, the horses of a convoy wagon became restive at the end of the bridge, and the whole crowd had to wait.

"And why are they stopping? There's no proper order!" said the soldiers. "Where are you shoving to? Devil take you! Can't you wait? It'll be worse if he fires the bridge. See, here's an officer jammed in too" —different voices were saying in the crowd, as the men looked at one another, and all pressed toward the exit from the bridge.

Looking down at the waters of the Enns under the bridge, Nesvítski suddenly heard a sound new to him, of something swiftly approaching . . . something big, that splashed into the water.

"Just see where it carries to!" a soldier near by said sternly, looking round at the sound.

"Encouraging us to get along quicker," said another uneasily.

The crowd moved on again. Nesvítski realized that it was a cannon ball.

"Hey, Cossack, my horse!" he said. "Now, then, you there! get out of the way! Make way!"

With great difficulty he managed to get to his horse, and shouting continually he moved on. The soldiers squeezed themselves to make way for him, but again pressed on him so that they jammed his leg, and those nearest him were not to blame for they were themselves pressed still harder from behind.

"Nesvítski, Nesvítski! you numskull!" came a hoarse voice from behind him.

Nesvítski looked round and saw, some fifteen paces away but separated by the living mass of moving infantry, Váska Denísov, red and shaggy, with his cap on the back of his black head and a cloak hanging jauntily over his shoulder.

"Tell these devils, these fiends, to let me pass!" shouted Denísov evidently in a fit of rage, his coal-black eyes with their bloodshot whites glittering and rolling as he waved his sheathed saber in a small bare hand as red as his face.

"Ah, Váska!" joyfully replied Nesvítski. "What's up with you?"

"The squadwon can't pass," shouted Váska Denísov, showing his white

teeth fiercely and spurring his black thoroughbred Arab, which twitched its ears as the bayonets touched it, and snorted, spurting white foam from his bit, tramping the planks of the bridge with his hoofs, and apparently ready to jump over the railings had his rider let him. "What is this? They're like sheep! Just like sheep! Out of the way! . . . Let us pass! . . . Stop there, you devil with the cart! I'll hack you with my saber!" he shouted, actually drawing his saber from its scabbard and flourishing it.

The soldiers crowded against one another with terrified faces, and Denísov joined Nesvítski.

"How's it you're not drunk today?" said Nesvítski when the other had ridden up to him.

"They don't even give one time to dwink!" answered Váska Denísov. "They keep dwagging the wegiment to and fwo all day. If they mean to fight, let's fight. But the devil knows what this is."

"What a dandy you are today!" said Nesvítski, looking at Denísov's new cloak and saddlecloth.

Denísov smiled, took out of his sabretache a handkerchief that diffused a smell of perfume, and put it to Nesvítski's nose.

"Of course. I'm going into action! I've shaved, bwushed my teeth, and scented myself."

The imposing figure of Nesvítski followed by his Cossack, and the determination of Denísov who flourished his sword and shouted frantically, had such an effect that they managed to squeeze through to the farther side of the bridge and stopped the infantry. Beside the bridge Nesvítski found the colonel to whom he had to deliver the order, and having done this he rode back.

Having cleared the way Denísov stopped at the end of the bridge. Carelessly holding in his stallion that was neighing and pawing the ground, eager to rejoin its fellows, he watched his squadron draw nearer. Then the clang of hoofs, as of several horses galloping, resounded on the planks of the bridge, and the squadron, officers in front and men four abreast, spread across the bridge and began to emerge on his side of it.

The infantry who had been stopped crowded near the bridge in the trampled mud and gazed with that particular feeling of ill-will, estrangement, and ridicule with which troops of different arms usually encounter one another at the clean, smart hussars who moved past them in regular order.

"Smart lads! Only fit for a fair!" said one.

"What good are they? They're led about just for show!" remarked another.

"Don't kick up the dust, you infantry!" jested an hussar whose prancing horse had splashed mud over some foot soldiers.

"I'd like to put you on a two days' march with a knapsack! Your fine cords would soon get a bit rubbed," said an infantryman, wiping the mud off his face with his sleeve. "Perched up there, you're more like a bird than a man."

"There now, Zíkin, they ought to put you on a horse. You'd look fine," said a corporal, chaffing a thin little soldier who bent under the weight of his knapsack.

"Take a stick between your legs, that'll suit you for a horse!" the hussar shouted back.

THE LAST of the infantry hurriedly crossed the bridge, squeezing together as they approached it as if passing through a funnel. At last the baggage wagons had all crossed, the crush was less, and the last battalion came onto the bridge. Only Denísov's squadron of hussars remained on the farther side of the bridge facing the enemy, who could be seen from the hill on the opposite bank but was not yet visible from the bridge, for the horizon as seen from the valley through which the river flowed was formed by the rising ground only half a mile away. At the foot of the hill lay wasteland over which a few groups of our Cossack scouts were moving. Suddenly on the road at the top of the high ground, artillery and troops in blue uniform were seen. These were the French. A group of Cossack scouts retired down the hill at a trot. All the officers and men of Denísov's squadron, though they tried to talk of other things and to look in other directions, thought only of what was there on the hilltop, and kept constantly looking at the patches appearing on the skyline, which they knew to be the enemy's troops. The weather had cleared again since noon and the sun was descending brightly upon the Danube and the dark hills around it. It was calm, and at intervals the bugle calls and the shouts of the enemy could be heard from the hill. There was no one now between the squadron and the enemy except a few scattered skirmishers. An empty space of some seven hundred yards was all that separated them. The enemy ceased firing, and that stern, threatening, inaccessible, and intangible line which separates two hostile armies was all the more clearly felt.

"One step beyond that boundary line which resembles the line dividing the living from the dead lies uncertainty, suffering, and death. And what is there? Who is there?—there beyond that field, that tree, that roof lit up by the sun? No one knows, but one wants to know. You fear and yet long to cross that line, and know that sooner or later it must be crossed and you will have to find out what is there, just as you will inevitably

have to learn what lies the other side of death. But you are strong, healthy, cheerful, and excited, and are surrounded by other such excitedly ani- mated and healthy men." So thinks, or at any rate feels, anyone who comes in sight of the enemy, and that feeling gives a particular glamour and glad keenness of impression to everything that takes place at such moments.

On the high ground where the enemy was, the smoke of a cannon rose, and a ball flew whistling over the heads of the hussar squadron. The officers who had been standing together rode off to their places. The hussars began carefully aligning their horses. Silence fell on the whole squadron. All were looking at the enemy in front and at the squadron commander, awaiting the word of command. A second and a third cannon ball flew past. Evidently they were firing at the hussars, but the balls with rapid rhythmic whistle flew over the heads of the horsemen and fell somewhere beyond them. The hussars did not look round, but at the sound of each shot, as at the word of command, the whole squadron with its rows of faces so alike yet so different, holding its breath while the ball flew past, rose in the stirrups and sank back again. The soldiers without turning their heads glanced at one another, curious to see their comrades' impression. Every face, from Denísov's to that of the bugler, showed one common expression of conflict, irritation, and excitement, around chin and mouth. The quartermaster frowned, looking at the soldiers as if threatening to punish them. Cadet Mirónov ducked every time a ball flew past. Rostóv on the left flank, mounted on his Rook—a handsome horse despite its game leg—had the happy air of a schoolboy called up before a large audience for an examination in which he feels sure he will distinguish himself. He was glancing at everyone with a clear, bright expression, as if asking them to notice how calmly he sat under fire. But despite himself, on his face too that same indication of some- thing new and stern showed round the mouth.

"Who's that curtseying there? Cadet Miwónov! That's not wight! Look at me," cried Denísov who, unable to keep still on one spot, kept turning his horse in front of the squadron.

The black, hairy, snub-nosed face of Váska Denísov, and his whole short sturdy figure with the sinewy hairy hand and stumpy fingers in which he held the hilt of his naked saber, looked just as it usually did, especially toward evening when he had emptied his second bottle; he was only redder than usual. With his shaggy head thrown back like birds when they drink, pressing his spurs mercilessly into the sides of his good horse, Bedouin, and sitting as though falling backwards in the saddle, he galloped to the other flank of the squadron and shouted in a hoarse voice

to the men to look to their pistols. He rode up to Kírsten. The staff captain on his broad-backed, steady mare came at a walk to meet him. His face with its long mustache was serious as always, only his eyes were brighter than usual.

"Well, what about it?" said he to Denísov. "It won't come to a fight. You'll see—we shall retire."

"The devil only knows what they've about!" muttered Denísov. "Ah, Wostóv," he cried noticing the cadet's bright face, "you've got it at last."

And he smiled approvingly, evidently pleased with the cadet. Rostóv felt perfectly happy. Just then the commander appeared on the bridge. Denísov galloped up to him.

"Your excellency! Let us attack them! I'll dwive them off."

"Attack indeed!" said the colonel in a bored voice, puckering up his face as if driving off a troublesome fly. "And why are you stopping here? Don't you see the skirmishers are retreating? Lead the squadron back."

The squadron crossed the bridge and drew out of range of fire without having lost a single man. The second squadron that had been in the front line followed them across and the last Cossacks quitted the farther side of the river.

The two Pávlograd squadrons, having crossed the bridge, retired up the hill one after the other. Their colonel, Karl Bogdánich Schubert,* came up to Denísov's squadron and rode at a footpace not far from Rostóv, without taking any notice of him although they were now meeting for the first time since their encounter concerning Telyánin. Rostóv, feeling that he was at the front and in the power of a man toward whom he now admitted that he had been to blame, did not lift his eyes from the colonel's athletic back, his nape covered with light hair, and his red neck. It seemed to Rostóv that Bogdánich was only pretending not to notice him, and that his whole aim now was to test the cadet's courage, so he drew himself up and looked around him merrily; then it seemed to him that Bogdánich rode so near in order to show him his courage. Next he thought that his enemy would send the squadron on a desperate attack just to punish him—Rostóv. Then he imagined how, after the attack, Bogdánich would come up to him as he lay wounded and would magnanimously extend the hand of reconciliation.

The high-shouldered figure of Zherkóv, familiar to the Pávlograds as he had but recently left their regiment, rode up to the colonel. After his dismissal from headquarters Zherkóv had not remained in the regiment, saying he was not such a fool as to slave at the front when he could get

* A Russo-German, one of many such in the Russian service. Tolstóy represents him as speaking very poor Russian.—A.M.

more rewards by doing nothing on the staff, and had succeeded in attaching himself as an orderly officer to Prince Bagratión. He now came to his former chief with an order from the commander of the reatguard.

"Colonel," he said, addressing Rostóv's enemy with an air of gloomy gravity and glancing round at his comrades, "there is an order to stop and fire the bridge."

"An order to who?" asked the colonel morosely.

"I don't myself know 'to who,' " replied the cornet in a serious tone, "but the prince told me to 'go and tell the colonel that the hussars must return quickly and fire the bridge.' "

Zherkóv was followed by an officer of the suite who rode up to the colonel of hussars with the same order. After him the stout Nesvítski came galloping up on a Cossack horse that could scarcely carry his weight.

"How's this, Colonel?" he shouted as he approached. "I told you to fire the bridge, and now someone has gone and blundered; they are all beside themselves over there and one can't make anything out."

The colonel deliberately stopped the regiment and turned to Nesvítski.

"You spoke to me of inflammable material," said he, "but you said nothing about firing it."

"But, my dear sir," said Nesvítski as he drew up, taking off his cap and smoothing his hair wet with perspiration with his plump hand, "wasn't I telling you to fire the bridge, when inflammable material had been put in position?"

"I am not your 'dear sir,' Mr. Staff Officer, and you did not tell me to burn the bridge! I know the service, and it is my habit orders strictly to obey. You said the bridge would be burned, but who would it burn, I could not know by the holy spirit!"

"Ah, that's always the way!" said Nesvítski with a wave of the hand. "How did you get here?" said he, turning to Zherkóv.

"On the same business. But you are damp! Let me wring you out!"

"You were saying, Mr. Staff Officer . . ." continued the colonel in an offended tone.

"Colonel," interrupted the officer of the suite, "you must be quick or the enemy will bring up his guns to use grapeshot."

The colonel looked silently at the officer of the suite, at the stout staff officer, and at Zherkóv, and he frowned.

"I will the bridge fire," he said in a solemn tone as if to announce that in spite of all the unpleasantness he had to endure he would still do the right thing.

Striking his horse with his long muscular legs as if it were to blame for everything, the colonel moved forward and ordered the second squadron,

that in which Rostóv was serving under Denísov, to return to the bridge.

"There, it's just as I thought," said Rostóv to himself. "He wishes to test me!" His heart contracted and the blood rushed to his face. "Let him see whether I am a coward!" he thought.

Again on all the bright faces of the squadron the serious expression appeared that they had worn when under fire. Rostóv watched his enemy, the colonel, closely—to find in his face confirmation of his own conjecture, but the colonel did not once glance at Rostóv, and looked as he always did when at the front, solemn and stern. Then came the word of command.

"Look sharp! Look sharp!" several voices repeated around him.

Their sabers catching in the bridles and their spurs jingling, the hussars hastily dismounted, not knowing what they were to do. The men were crossing themselves. Rostóv no longer looked at the colonel, he had no time. He was afraid of falling behind the hussars, so much afraid that his heart stood still. His hand trembled as he gave his horse into an orderly's charge, and he felt the blood rush to his heart with a thud. Denísov rode past him, leaning back and shouting something. Rostóv saw nothing but the hussars running all around him, their spurs catching and their sabers clattering.

"Stretchers!" shouted someone behind him.

Rostóv did not think what this call for stretchers meant; he ran on, trying only to be ahead of the others; but just at the bridge, not looking at the ground, he came on some sticky, trodden mud, stumbled, and fell on his hands. The others outstripped him.

"At boss zides, Captain," he heard the voice of the colonel, who, having ridden ahead, had pulled up his horse near the bridge, with a triumphant, cheerful face.

Rostóv wiping his muddy hands on his breeches looked at his enemy and was about to run on, thinking that the farther he went to the front the better. But Bogdánich, without looking at or recognizing Rostóv, shouted to him:

"Who's that running on the middle of the bridge? To the right! Come back, Cadet!" he cried angrily; and turning to Denísov, who, showing off his courage, had ridden on to the planks of the bridge:

"Why run risks, Captain? You should dismount," he said.

"Oh, every bullet has its billet," answered Váska Denísov, turning in his saddle.

Meanwhile Nesvítski, Zherkóv, and the officer of the suite were standing together out of range of the shots, watching, now the small group of

men with yellow shakos, dark-green jackets braided with cord, and blue riding breeches, who were swarming near the bridge, and then at what was approaching in the distance from the opposite side—the blue uniforms and groups with horses, easily recognizable as artillery.

"Will they burn the bridge or not? Who'll get there first? Will they get there and fire the bridge or will the French get within grapeshot range and wipe them out?" These were the questions each man of the troops on the high ground above the bridge involuntarily asked himself with a sinking heart—watching the bridge and the hussars in the bright evening light and the blue tunics advancing from the other side with their bayonets and guns.

"Ugh. The hussars will get it hot!" said Nesvítski; "they are within grapeshot range now."

"He shouldn't have taken so many men," said the officer of the suite.

"True enough," answered Nesvítski; "two smart fellows could have done the job just as well."

"Ah, your excellency," put in Zherkóv, his eyes fixed on the hussars, but still with that naïve air that made it impossible to know whether he was speaking in jest or in earnest. "Ah, your excellency! How you look at things! Send two men? And who then would give us the Vladímir medal and ribbon? But now, even if they do get peppered, the squadron may be recommended for honors and he may get a ribbon. Our Bogdánich knows how things are done."

"There now!" said the officer of the suite, "that's grapeshot."

He pointed to the French guns, the limbers of which were being detached and hurriedly removed.

On the French side, amid the groups with cannon, a cloud of smoke appeared, then a second and a third almost simultaneously, and at the moment when the first report was heard a fourth was seen. Then two reports one after another, and a third.

"Oh! Oh!" groaned Nesvítski as if in fierce pain, seizing the officer of the suite by the arm. "Look! A man has fallen! Fallen, fallen!"

"Two, I think."

"If I were Tsar I would never go to war," said Nesvítski, turning away.

The French guns were hastily reloaded. The infantry in their blue uniforms advanced toward the bridge at a run. Smoke appeared again but at irregular intervals, and grapeshot cracked and rattled onto the bridge. But this time Nesvítski could not see what was happening there, as a dense cloud of smoke arose from it. The hussars had succeeded in setting it on fire and the French batteries were now firing at them, no longer

to hinder them but because the guns were trained and there was someone to fire at.

The French had time to fire three rounds of grapeshot before the hussars got back to their horses. Two were misdirected and the shot went too high, but the last round fell in the midst of a group of hussars and knocked three of them over.

Rostóv, absorbed by his relations with Bogdánich, had paused on the bridge not knowing what to do. There was no one to hew down (as he had always imagined battles to himself), nor could he help to fire the bridge because he had not brought any burning straw with him like the other soldiers. He stood looking about him, when suddenly he heard a rattle on the bridge as if nuts were being spilt, and the hussar nearest to him fell against the rails with a groan. Rostóv ran up to him with the others. Again someone shouted, "Stretchers!" Four men seized the hussar and began lifting him.

"Oooh! For Christ's sake let me alone!" cried the wounded man, but still he was lifted and laid on the stretcher.

Nicholas Rostóv turned away and, as if searching for something, gazed into the distance, at the waters of the Danube, at the sky, and at the sun. How beautiful the sky looked; how blue, how calm, and how deep! How bright and glorious was the setting sun! With what soft glitter the waters of the distant Danube shone. And fairer still were the faraway blue mountains beyond the river, the nunnery, the mysterious gorges, and the pine forests veiled in mist to their summits . . . There was peace and happiness . . . "I should wish for nothing else, nothing, if only I were there," thought Rostóv. "In myself alone and in that sunshine there is so much happiness; but here . . . groans, suffering, fear, and this uncertainty and hurry . . . There—they are shouting again, and again are all running back somewhere, and I shall run with them, and it, death, is here above me and around . . . Another instant and I shall never again see the sun, this water, that gorge! . . ."

At that instant the sun began to hide behind the clouds, and other stretchers came into view before Rostóv. And the fear of death and of the stretchers, and love of the sun and of life, all merged into one feeling of sickening agitation.

"O Lord God! Thou who art in that heaven, save, forgive, and protect me!" Rostóv whispered.

The hussars ran back to the men who held their horses; their voices sounded louder and calmer, the stretchers disappeared from sight.

"Well, fwiend? So you've smelt powdah!" shouted Váska Denísov just above his ear.

"It's all over; but I am a coward—yes, a coward!" thought Rostóv, and sighing deeply he took Rook, his horse, which stood resting one foot, from the orderly and began to mount.

"Was that grapeshot?" he asked Denísov.

"Yes and no mistake!" cried Denísov. "You worked like wegular bwicks and it's nasty work! An attack's pleasant work! Hacking away at the dogs! But this sort of thing is the very devil, with them shooting at you like a target."

And Denísov rode up to a group that had stopped near Rostóv, composed of the colonel, Nesvítski, Zherkóv, and the officer from the suite.

"Well, it seems that no one has noticed," thought Rostóv. And this was true. No one had taken any notice, for everyone knew the sensation which the cadet under fire for the first time had experienced.

"Here's something for you to report," said Zherkóv. "See if I don't get promoted to a sublieutenancy."

"Inform the prince that I the bridge fired!" said the colonel triumphantly and gaily.

"And if he asks about the losses?"

"A trifle," said the colonel in his bass voice: "two hussars wounded, and one knocked out," he added, unable to restrain a happy smile, and pronouncing the phrase "knocked out" with ringing distinctness.

6. Prince Andrew sent with dispatches to the Austrian court. The Minister of War

Pursued by the French army of a hundred thousand men under the command of Bonaparte, encountering a population that was unfriendly to it, losing confidence in its allies, suffering from shortness of supplies, and compelled to act under conditions of war unlike anything that had been foreseen, the Russian army of thirty-five thousand men commanded by Kutúzov was hurriedly retreating along the Danube, stopping where overtaken by the enemy and fighting rearguard actions only as far as necessary to enable it to retreat without losing its heavy equipment. There had been actions at Lambach, Amstetten, and Melk; but despite the courage and endurance—acknowledged even by the enemy—with which the Russians fought, the only consequence of these actions was a yet more rapid retreat. Austrian troops that had escaped capture at Ulm and had joined Kutúzov at Braunau now separated from the Russian army, and Kutúzov was left with only his own weak and exhausted forces. The defense of Vienna was no longer to be thought of. Instead of an

offensive, the plan of which, carefully prepared in accord with the modern science of strategics, had been handed to Kutúzov when he was in Vienna by the Austrian Hofkriegsrath, the sole and almost unattainable aim remaining for him was to effect a junction with the forces that were advancing from Russia, without losing his army as Mack had done at Ulm.

On the twenty-eighth of October Kutúzov with his army crossed to the left bank of the Danube and took up a position for the first time with the river between himself and the main body of the French. On the thirtieth he attacked Mortier's division, which was on the left bank, and broke it up. In this action for the first time trophies were taken: banners, cannon, and two enemy generals. For the first time, after a fortnight's retreat, the Russian troops had halted and after a fight had not only held the field but had repulsed the French. Though the troops were ill-clad, exhausted, and had lost a third of their number in killed, wounded, sick, and stragglers; though a number of sick and wounded had been abandoned on the other side of the Danube with a letter in which Kutúzov entrusted them to the humanity of the enemy; and though the big hospitals and the houses in Krems converted into military hospitals could no longer accommodate all the sick and wounded, yet the stand made at Krems and the victory over Mortier raised the spirits of the army considerably. Throughout the whole army and at headquarters most joyful though erroneous rumors were rife of the imaginary approach of columns from Russia, of some victory gained by the Austrians, and of the retreat of the frightened Bonaparte.

Prince Andrew during the battle had been in attendance on the Austrian General Schmidt, who was killed in the action. His horse had been wounded under him and his own arm slightly grazed by a bullet. As a mark of the commander in chief's special favor he was sent with the news of this victory to the Austrian court, now no longer at Vienna (which was threatened by the French) but at Brünn.* Despite his apparently delicate build Prince Andrew could endure physical fatigue far better than many very muscular men, and on the night of the battle, having arrived at Krems excited but not weary, with dispatches from Dokhtúrov² to Kutúzov, he was sent immediately with a special dispatch to Brünn. To be so sent meant not only a reward but an important step toward promotion.

The night was dark but starry, the road showed black in the snow that had fallen the previous day—the day of the battle. Reviewing his impressions of the recent battle, picturing pleasantly to himself the impression

* As part of Czechoslovakia, called Brno.

² One of the Russian generals.—A.M.

his news of a victory would create, or recalling the sendoff given him by the commander in chief and his fellow officers, Prince Andrew was galloping along in a post chaise enjoying the feelings of a man who has at length begun to attain a long-desired happiness. As soon as he closed his eyes his ears seemed filled with the rattle of the wheels and the sensation of victory. Then he began to imagine that the Russians were running away and that he himself was killed, but he quickly roused himself with a feeling of joy, as if learning afresh that this was not so but that on the contrary the French had run away. He again recalled all the details of the victory and his own calm courage during the battle, and feeling reassured he dozed off. . . . The dark starry night was followed by a bright cheerful morning. The snow was thawing in the sunshine, the horses galloped quickly, and on both sides of the road were forests of different kinds, fields, and villages.

At one of the post stations he overtook a convoy of Russian wounded. The Russian officer in charge of the transport lolled back in the front cart, shouting and scolding a soldier with coarse abuse. In each of the long German carts six or more pale, dirty, bandaged men were being jolted over the stony road. Some of them were talking (he heard Russian words), others were eating bread; the more severely wounded looked silently, with the languid interest of sick children, at the envoy hurrying past them.

Prince Andrew told his driver to stop, and asked a soldier in what action they had been wounded. "Day before yesterday, on the Danube," answered the soldier. Prince Andrew took out his purse and gave the soldier three gold pieces.

"That's for them all," he said to the officer who came up. "Get well soon, lads!" he continued, turning to the soldiers. "There's plenty to do still."

"What news, sir?" asked the officer, evidently anxious to start a conversation.

"Good news! . . . Go on!" he shouted to the driver, and they galloped on.

It was already quite dark when Prince Andrew rattled over the paved streets of Brünn and found himself surrounded by high buildings, the lights of shops, houses, and street lamps, fine carriages, and all that atmosphere of a large and active town which is always so attractive to a soldier after camp life. Despite his rapid journey and sleepless night, Prince Andrew when he drove up to the palace felt even more vigorous and alert than he had done the day before. Only his eyes gleamed feverishly and his thoughts followed one another with extraordinary clearness

and rapidity. He again vividly recalled the details of the battle, no longer dim, but definite and in the concise form in which he imagined himself stating them to the Emperor Francis. He vividly imagined the casual questions that might be put to him and the answers he would give. He expected to be at once presented to the Emperor. At the chief entrance to the palace, however, an official came running out to meet him, and learning that he was a special messenger led him to another entrance.

"To the right from the corridor, *Euer Hochgeboren!* There you will find the adjutant on duty," said the official. "He will conduct you to the Minister of War."

The adjutant on duty, meeting Prince Andrew, asked him to wait, and went in to the Minister of War. Five minutes later he returned and bowing with particular courtesy ushered Prince Andrew before him along a corridor to the cabinet where the Minister of War was at work. The adjutant by his elaborate courtesy appeared to wish to ward off any attempt at familiarity on the part of the Russian messenger.

Prince Andrew's joyous feeling was considerably weakened as he approached the door of the minister's room. He felt offended, and without his noticing it the feeling of offense immediately turned into one of disdain which was quite uncalled for. His fertile mind instantly suggested to him a point of view which gave him a right to despise the adjutant and the minister. "Away from the smell of powder, they probably think it easy to gain victories!" he thought. His eyes narrowed disdainfully, he entered the room of the Minister of War with peculiarly deliberate steps. This feeling of disdain was heightened when he saw the minister seated at a large table reading some papers and making pencil notes on them, and for the first two or three minutes taking no notice of his arrival. A wax candle stood at each side of the minister's bent bald head with its gray temples. He went on reading to the end, without raising his eyes at the opening of the door and the sound of footsteps.

"Take this and deliver it," said he to his adjutant, handing him the papers and still taking no notice of the special messenger.

Prince Andrew felt that either the actions of Kutúzov's army interested the Minister of War less than any of the other matters he was concerned with, or he wanted to give the Russian special messenger that impression. "But that is a matter of perfect indifference to me," he thought. The minister drew the remaining papers together, arranged them evenly, and then raised his head. He had an intellectual and distinctive head, but the instant he turned to Prince Andrew the firm, intelligent expression on his face changed in a way evidently deliberate and habitual to him. His face took on the stupid artificial smile (which does not even attempt to hide

its artificiality) of a man who is continually receiving many petitioners one after another.

"From General Field Marshal Kutúzov?" he asked. "I hope it is good news? There has been an encounter with Mortier? A victory? It was high time!"

He took the dispatch which was addressed to him and began to read it with a mournful expression.

"Oh, my God! My God! Schmidt!" he exclaimed in German. "What a calamity! What a calamity!"

Having glanced through the dispatch he laid it on the table and looked at Prince Andrew, evidently considering something.

"Ah, what a calamity! You say the affair was decisive? But Mortier is not captured." Again he pondered. "I am very glad you have brought good news, though Schmidt's death is a heavy price to pay for the victory. His Majesty will no doubt wish to see you, but not today. I thank you! You must have a rest. Be at the levee tomorrow after the parade. However, I will let you know."

The stupid smile, which had left his face while he was speaking, reappeared.

"Au revoir! Thank you very much. His Majesty will probably desire to see you," he added, bowing his head.

When Prince Andrew left the palace he felt that all the interest and happiness the victory had afforded him had been now left in the indifferent hands of the Minister of War and the polite adjutant. The whole tenor of his thoughts instantaneously changed; the battle seemed the memory of a remote event long past.

7. Prince Andrew and Bilíbin

Prince Andrew stayed at Brünn with Bilíbin,* a Russian acquaintance of his in the diplomatic service.

"Ah, my dear prince! I could not have a more welcome visitor," said Bilíbin as he came out to meet Prince Andrew. "Franz, put the prince's things in my bedroom," said he to the servant who was ushering Bol-

* There is reason to suppose that Bilíbin is drawn partly from Prince A. M. Gorchakóv, who directed Russian foreign policy for many years from 1856 onwards. He was said to be "in love with his inkpot," and to show more ability in the concoction of epigrams than in the conduct of political affairs.— A.M.

kónski in. "So you're a messenger of victory, eh? Splendid! And I am sitting here ill, as you see."

After washing and dressing, Prince Andrew came into the diplomat's luxurious study and sat down to the dinner prepared for him. Bilíbin settled down comfortably beside the fire.

After his journey and the campaign during which he had been deprived of all the comforts of cleanliness and all the refinements of life, Prince Andrew felt a pleasant sense of repose among luxurious surroundings such as he had been accustomed to from childhood. Besides it was pleasant, after his reception by the Austrians, to speak if not in Russian (for they were speaking French) at least with a Russian who would, he supposed, share the general Russian antipathy to the Austrians which was then particularly strong.

Bilíbin was a man of thirty-five, a bachelor, and of the same circle as Prince Andrew. They had known each other previously in Petersburg, but had become more intimate when Prince Andrew was in Vienna with Kutúzov. Just as Prince Andrew was a young man who gave promise of rising high in the military profession, so to an even greater extent Bilíbin gave promise of rising in his diplomatic career. He was still a young man but no longer a young diplomat, as he had entered the service at the age of sixteen, had been in Paris and Copenhagen, and now held a rather important post in Vienna. Both the foreign minister and our ambassador in Vienna knew him and valued him. He was not one of those many diplomats who are esteemed because they have certain negative qualities, avoid doing certain things, and speak French. He was one of those, who, liking work, knew how to do it, and despite his indolence would sometimes spend a whole night at his writing table. He worked equally well whatever the import of his work. It was not the question "What for?" but the question "How?" that interested him. What the diplomatic matter might be he did not care, but it gave him great pleasure to prepare a circular, memorandum, or report, skillfully, pointedly, and elegantly. Bilíbin's services were valued not only for what he wrote, but also for his skill in dealing and conversing with those in the highest spheres.

Bilíbin liked conversation as he liked work, only when it could be made elegantly witty. In society he always awaited an opportunity to say something striking and took part in a conversation only when that was possible. His conversation was always sprinkled with wittily original, finished phrases of general interest. These sayings were prepared in the inner laboratory of his mind in a portable form as if intentionally, so that insignificant society people might carry them from drawing room to drawing room. And, in fact, Bilíbin's witticisms were hawked about in the Vien-

nese drawing rooms and often had an influence on matters considered important.

His thin, worn, sallow face was covered with deep wrinkles, which always looked as clean and well washed as the tips of one's fingers after a Russian bath. The movement of these wrinkles formed the principal play of expression on his face. Now his forehead would pucker into deep folds and his eyebrows were lifted, then his eyebrows would descend and deep wrinkles would crease his cheeks. His small, deep-set eyes always twinkled and looked out straight.

"Well, now tell me about your exploits," said he.

Bolkónski, very modestly without once mentioning himself, described the engagement and his reception by the Minister of War.

"They received me and my news as one receives a dog in a game of skittles," * said he in conclusion.

Bilíbin smiled and the wrinkles on his face disappeared.

"*Cependant, mon cher* [But, my dear fellow]," he remarked, examining his nails from a distance and puckering the skin above his left eye, "*malgré la haute estime que je professe pour* [with all my respects for] the Orthodox Russian army, *j'avoue que votre victoire n'est pas des plus victorieuses* [I must say that your victory was not particularly victorious]."

He went on talking in this way in French, uttering only those words in Russian on which he wished to put a contemptuous emphasis.

"Come now! You with all your forces fall on the unfortunate Mortier and his one division, and even then Mortier slips through your fingers! Where's the victory?"

"But seriously," said Prince Andrew, "we can at any rate say without boasting that it was a little better than at Ulm . . ."

"Why didn't you capture one, just one, marshal for us?"

"Because not everything happens as one expects or with the smoothness of a parade. We had expected, as I told you, to get at their rear by seven in the morning but had not reached it by five in the afternoon."

"And why didn't you do it at seven in the morning? You ought to have been there at seven in the morning," returned Bilíbin with a smile. "You ought to have been there at seven in the morning."

"Why did you not succeed in impressing on Bonaparte by diplomatic methods that he had better leave Genoa alone?" retorted Prince Andrew in the same tone.

"I know," interrupted Bilíbin, "you're thinking it's very easy to take marshals, sitting on a sofa by the fire! That is true, but still why didn't you capture him? So don't be surprised if not only the Minister of War

* *A French proverb.*—A.M.

but also his Most August Majesty the Emperor and King Francis is not much delighted by your victory. Even I, a poor secretary of the Russian Embassy, do not feel any need in token of my joy to give my Franz a thaler, or let him go with his *Liebchen* to the Prater.* . . . True, we have no Prater here . . ."

He looked straight at Prince Andrew and suddenly unwrinkled his forehead.

"It is now my turn to ask you 'why?' *mon cher*," said Bolkónski. "I confess I do not understand: perhaps there are diplomatic subtleties here beyond my feeble intelligence, but I can't make it out. Mack loses a whole army, the Archduke Ferdinand and the Archduke Karl give no signs of life and make blunder after blunder. Kutúzov alone at last gains a real victory, destroying the spell of the invincibility of the French, and the Minister of War does not even care to hear the details."

"That's just it, my dear fellow. You see it's *hurrah* for the Tsar, for Russia, for the Orthodox Greek faith! All that is beautiful, but what do we, I mean the Austrian court, care for your victories? Bring us nice news of a victory by the Archduke Karl or Ferdinand (one archduke's as good as another, as you know) and even if it is only over a fire brigade of Bonaparte's, that will be another story and we'll fire off some cannon! But this sort of thing seems done on purpose to vex us. The Archduke Karl does nothing, the Archduke Ferdinand disgraces himself. You abandon Vienna, give up its defense—as much as to say: 'Heaven is with us, but heaven help you and your capital!' The one general whom we all loved, Schmidt, you expose to a bullet, and then you congratulate us on the victory! Admit that more irritating news than yours could not have been conceived. It's as if it had been done on purpose, on purpose. Besides, suppose you did gain a brilliant victory, if even the Archduke Karl gained a victory, what effect would that have on the general course of events? It's too late now when Vienna is occupied by the French army!"

"What? Occupied? Vienna occupied?"

"Not only occupied, but Bonaparte is at Schönbrunn,[2] and the count, our dear Count Vrbna, goes to him for orders."

After the fatigues and impressions of the journey, his reception, and especially after having dined, Bolkónski felt that he could not take in the full significance of the words he heard.

"Count Lichtenfels was here this morning," Bilíbin continued, "and showed me a letter in which the parade of the French in Vienna was

* *A beautiful park in Vienna, bordered by the Danube.*

[2] *Schönbrunn—the Austrian Emperor's summer palace at Vienna.*—A.M.

fully described: Prince Murat et tout le tremblement . . .* You see that your victory is not a matter for great rejoicing and that you can't be received as a savior."

"Really I don't care about that, I don't care at all," said Prince Andrew, beginning to understand that his news of the battle before Krems was really of small importance in view of such events as the fall of Austria's capital. "How is it Vienna was taken? What of the bridge and its celebrated bridgehead and Prince Auersperg? We heard reports that Prince Auersperg was defending Vienna?" he said.

"Prince Auersperg is on this, on our side of the river, and is defending us—doing it very badly, I think, but still he is defending us. But Vienna is on the other side. No, the bridge has not yet been taken and I hope it will not be, for it is mined and orders have been given to blow it up. Otherwise we should long ago have been in the mountains of Bohemia, and you and your army would have spent a bad quarter of an hour between two fires."

"But still this does not mean that the campaign is over," said Prince Andrew.

"Well, I think it is. The bigwigs here think so too, but they daren't say so. It will be as I said at the beginning of the campaign, it won't be your skirmishing at Dürrenstein,[2] or gunpowder at all, that will decide the matter, but those who devised it," said Bilíbin quoting one of his own mots, releasing the wrinkles on his forehead, and pausing. "The only question is what will come of the meeting between the Emperor Alexander and the King of Prussia in Berlin? If Prussia joins the Allies, Austria's hand will be forced and there will be war. If not it is merely a question of settling where the preliminaries of the new Campo Formio are to be drawn up." [3]

"What an extraordinary genius!" Prince Andrew suddenly exclaimed, clenching his small hand and striking the table with it, "and what luck the man has!"

* In the Tolstóy family le tremblement had long been ironically used to denote the bustle usually accompanying official celebrations and rejoicings. Many years after War and Peace was written, one encounters in Tolstóy's letters such phrases as: "The arrival of the Governor et tout le tremblement."

[2] The victory over Mortier mentioned in Chapter 6 and in this chapter a couple of pages back.—A.M.

[3] The Berlin Conference between Alexander and the King of Prussia took place at Potsdam a few days before Bilíblin's conversation with Prince Andrew. The monarchs knelt at the grave of Frederick the Great and swore friendship with one another, but Prussia still avoided taking part in the war.—A.M.

"Buonaparte?" said Bilíbin inquiringly, puckering up his forehead to indicate that he was about to say something witty. "Buonaparte?" he repeated, accentuating the *u*: "I think, however, now that he lays down laws for Austria at Schönbrunn, *il faut lui faire grâce de l'u!* [we must let him off the *u!*] I shall certainly adopt an innovation and call him simply Bonaparte!"

"But joking apart," said Prince Andrew, "do you really think the campaign is over?"

"This is what I think. Austria has been made a fool of, and she is not used to it. She will retaliate. And she has been fooled in the first place because her provinces have been pillaged—they say the Holy Russian army loots terribly—her army is destroyed, her capital taken, and all this for the *beaux yeux* [fine eyes] of His Sardinian Majesty.* And therefore —this is between ourselves—I instinctively feel that we are being deceived, my instinct tells me of negotiations with France and projects for peace, a secret peace concluded separately." [2]

"Impossible!" cried Prince Andrew. "That would be too base."

"If we live we shall see," replied Bilíbin, his face again becoming smooth as a sign that the conversation was at an end.

When Prince Andrew reached the room prepared for him and lay down in a clean shirt on the feather bed with its warmed and fragrant pillows, he felt that the battle of which he had brought tidings was far, far away from him. The alliance with Prussia, Austria's treachery, Bonaparte's new triumph, tomorrow's levee and parade, and the audience with the Emperor Francis occupied his thoughts.

He closed his eyes, and immediately a sound of cannonading, of musketry and the rattling of carriage wheels seemed to fill his ears, and now again drawn out in a thin line the musketeers were descending the hill, the French were firing, and he felt his heart palpitating as he rode forward beside Schmidt with the bullets merrily whistling all around, and

* At the Potsdam Conference Prussia insisted that an ultimatum should be sent to Napoleon which, among other demands, stipulated that he should compensate the King of Sardinia. Napoleon rejected all the demands, but Prussia was so frightened by his defeat of the Austrians that it remained passive.—A.M.

[2] The Emperor Francis was at that time actually asking Napoleon for a truce, but in reply only received from him insulting demands: the withdrawal of the Russian army, an immediate cession of Venice and the Tirol, and to furnish securities; "then we can talk about peace." Even Francis did not accede to these terms.—A.M.

he experienced tenfold the joy of living, as he had not done since child-
hood.

He woke up . . .

"Yes, that all happened!" he said, and, smiling happily to himself like a
child, he fell into a deep, youthful slumber.

8. *Hippolyte Kurágin and* les nôtres

NEXT DAY he woke late. Recalling his recent impressions, the first
thought that came into his mind was that today he had to be pre-
sented to the Emperor Francis; he remembered the Minister of War, the
polite Austrian adjutant, Bilíbin, and last night's conversation. Having
dressed for his attendance at court in full parade uniform, which he had
not worn for a long time, he went into Bilíbin's study fresh, animated,
and handsome, with his hand bandaged. In the study were four gentle-
men of the diplomatic corps. With Prince Hippolyte Kurágin, who was a
secretary to the embassy, Bolkónski was already acquainted. Bilíbin intro-
duced him to the others.

The gentlemen assembled at Bilíbin's were young, wealthy, gay society
men, who here, as in Vienna, formed a special set which Bilíbin, their
leader, called les nôtres [ours]. This set, consisting almost exclusively of
diplomats, evidently had its own interests which had nothing to do with
war or politics but related to high society, to certain women, and to the
official side of the service. These gentlemen received Prince Andrew as
one of themselves, an honor they did not extend to many. From polite-
ness and to start conversation, they asked him a few questions about the
army and the battle, and then the talk went off into merry jests and
gossip.

"But the best of it was," said one, telling of the misfortune of a fellow
diplomat, "that the Chancellor told him flatly that his appointment to
London was a promotion and that he was so to regard it. Can you fancy
the figure he cut? . . ."

"But the worst of it, gentlemen—I am giving Kurágin away to you—is
that that man suffers, and this Don Juan, wicked fellow, is taking advan-
tage of it!"

Prince Hippolyte was lolling in a lounge chair with his legs over its
arm. He began to laugh.

"Tell me about that!" he said.

"Oh, you Don Juan! You serpent!" cried several voices.

"You, Bolkónski, don't know," said Bilíbin turning to Prince Andrew,

"that all the atrocities of the French army (I nearly said of the Russian army) are nothing compared to what this man has been doing among the women!"

"La femme est la compagne de l'homme [Woman is man's companion]," announced Prince Hippolyte, and began looking through a lorgnette at his elevated legs.

Bilíbin and the rest of "ours" burst out laughing in Hippolyte's face, and Prince Andrew saw that Hippolyte, of whom—he had to admit—he had almost been jealous on his wife's account, was the butt of this set.

"Oh, I must give you a treat," Bilíbin whispered to Bolkónski. "Kurágin is exquisite when he discusses politics—you should see his gravity!"

He sat down beside Hippolyte and wrinkling his forehead began talking to him about politics. Prince Andrew and the others gathered round these two.

"The Berlin cabinet cannot express a feeling of alliance," began Hippolyte gazing round with importance at the others, "without expressing . . . as in its last note . . . you understand . . . Besides, unless His Majesty the Emperor derogates from the principle of our alliance . . .

"Wait, I have not finished . . ." he said to Prince Andrew, seizing him by the arm, "I believe that intervention will be stronger than non-intervention. And . . ." he paused. "Finally one cannot impute the nonreceipt of our dispatch of November 18. That is how it will end." And he released Bolkónski's arm to indicate that he had now quite finished.

"Demosthenes, I know thee by the pebble thou secretest in thy golden mouth!" said Bilíbin, and the mop of hair on his head moved with satisfaction.

Everybody laughed, and Hippolyte louder than anyone. He was evidently distressed, and breathed painfully, but could not restrain the wild laughter that convulsed his usually impassive features.

"Well now, gentlemen," said Bilíbin, "Bolkónski is my guest in this house and in Brünn itself. I want to entertain him as far as I can, with all the pleasures of life here. If we were in Vienna it would be easy, but here, in this wretched Moravian hole, it is more difficult, and I beg you all to help me. Brünn's attractions must be shown him. You can undertake the theater, I society, and you, Hippolyte, of course the women."

"We must let him see Amelie, she's exquisite!" said one of "ours," kissing his finger tips.

"In general we must turn this bloodthirsty soldier to more humane interests," said Bilíbin.

"I shall scarcely be able to avail myself of your hospitality, gentlemen,

it is already time for me to go," replied Prince Andrew looking at his watch.

"Where to?"

"To the Emperor."

"Oh! Oh! Oh!"

"Well, au revoir, Bolkónski! Au revoir, Prince! Come back early to dinner," cried several voices. "We'll take you in hand."

"When speaking to the Emperor, try as far as you can to praise the way that provisions are supplied and the routes indicated," said Bilíbin, accompanying him to the hall.

"I should like to speak well of them, but as far as I know the facts, I can't," replied Bolkónski, smiling.

"Well, talk as much as you can, anyway. He has a passion for giving audiences, but he does not like talking himself and can't do it, as you will see."

9. Prince Andrew received by the Emperor Francis. Bilíbin's story of the Thabor Bridge

At the levee Prince Andrew stood among the Austrian officers as he had been told to, and the Emperor Francis merely looked fixedly into his face and just nodded to him with his long head. But after it was over, the adjutant he had seen the previous day ceremoniously informed Bolkónski that the Emperor desired to give him an audience. The Emperor Francis received him standing in the middle of the room. Before the conversation began Prince Andrew was struck by the fact that the Emperor seemed confused and blushed as if not knowing what to say.

"Tell me, when did the battle begin?" he asked hurriedly.

Prince Andrew replied. Then followed other questions just as simple: "Was Kutúzov well? When had he left Krems?" and so on. The Emperor spoke as if his sole aim were to put a given number of questions—the answers to these questions, as was only too evident, did not interest him.

"At what o'clock did the battle begin?" asked the Emperor.

"I cannot inform Your Majesty at what o'clock the battle began at the front, but at Dürrenstein, where I was, our attack began after five in the afternoon," replied Bolkónski growing more animated and expecting that he would have a chance to give a reliable account, which he had ready in his mind, of all he knew and had seen. But the Emperor smiled and interrupted him.

"How many miles?"

"From where to where, Your Majesty?"

"From Dürrenstein to Krems."

"Three and a half miles, Your Majesty."

"The French have abandoned the left bank?"

"According to the scouts the last of them crossed on rafts during the night."

"Is there sufficient forage in Krems?"

"Forage has not been supplied to the extent . . ."

The Emperor interrupted him.

"At what o'clock was General Schmidt killed?"

"At seven o'clock, I believe."

"At seven o'clock? It's very sad, very sad!"

The Emperor thanked Prince Andrew and bowed. Prince Andrew withdrew and was immediately surrounded by courtiers on all sides. Everywhere he saw friendly looks and heard friendly words. Yesterday's adjutant reproached him for not having stayed at the palace, and offered him his own house. The Minister of War came up and congratulated him on the Maria Theresa Order of the third grade, which the Emperor was conferring on him. The Empress' chamberlain invited him to see Her Majesty. The archduchess also wished to see him. He did not know whom to answer, and for a few seconds collected his thoughts. Then the Russian ambassador took him by the shoulder, led him to the window, and began to talk to him.

Contrary to Bilíbin's forecast the news he had brought was joyfully received. A thanksgiving service was arranged, Kutúzov was awarded the Grand Cross of Maria Theresa, and the whole army received rewards. Bolkónski was invited everywhere, and had to spend the whole morning calling on the principal Austrian dignitaries. Between four and five in the afternoon, having made all his calls, he was returning to Bilíbin's house thinking out a letter to his father about the battle and his visit to Brünn. At the door he found a vehicle half full of luggage. Franz, Bilíbin's man, was dragging a portmanteau with some difficulty out of the front door.

Before returning to Bilíbin's Prince Andrew had gone to a bookshop to provide himself with some books for the campaign, and had spent some time in the shop.

"What is it?" he asked.

"Oh, your excellency!" said Franz, with difficulty rolling the portmanteau into the vehicle, "we are to move on still farther. The scoundrel is again at our heels!"

"Eh? What?" asked Prince Andrew.

Bilíbin came out to meet him. His usually calm face showed excitement.

"There now! Confess that this is delightful," said he. "This affair of the Thabor Bridge, at Vienna. . . . They have crossed without striking a blow!"

Prince Andrew could not understand.

"But where do you come from not to know what every coachman in the town knows?"

"I come from the archduchess'. I heard nothing there."

"And you didn't see that everybody is packing up?"

"I did not . . . What is it all about?" inquired Prince Andrew impatiently.

"What's it all about? Why, the French have crossed the bridge that Auersperg was defending, and the bridge was not blown up: so Murat is now rushing along the road to Brünn and will be here in a day or two."

"What? Here? But why did they not blow up the bridge, if it was mined?"

"That is what I ask you. No one, not even Bonaparte, knows why."

Bolkónski shrugged his shoulders.

"But if the bridge is crossed it means that the army too is lost? It will be cut off," said he.

"That's just it," answered Bilíbin. "Listen! The French entered Vienna as I told you. Very well. Next day, which was yesterday, those gentlemen, *messieurs les maréchaux* [the marshals], Murat, Lannes, and Belliard, mount and ride to the bridge. (Observe that all three are Gascons.) 'Gentlemen,' says one of them, 'you know the Thabor Bridge is mined and doubly mined and that there are menacing fortifications at its head and an army of fifteen thousand men has been ordered to blow up the bridge and not let us cross? But it will please our sovereign the Emperor Napoleon if we take this bridge, so let us three go and take it!' 'Yes, let's!' say the others. And off they go and take the bridge, cross it, and now with their whole army are on this side of the Danube, marching on us, you, and your lines of communication."

"Stop jesting," said Prince Andrew sadly and seriously. This news grieved him and yet he was pleased.

As soon as he learned that the Russian army was in such a hopeless situation it occurred to him that it was he who was destined to lead it out of this position; that here was the Toulon * that would lift him from the ranks of obscure officers and offer him the first step to fame! Listening to

* *It was at Toulon, when the Republicans besieged it in 1793, that Napoleon first greatly distinguished himself.*—A.M.

Bilíbin he was already imagining how on reaching the army he would give an opinion at the war council which would be the only one that could save the army, and how he alone would be entrusted with the executing of the plan.

"Stop this jesting," he said.

"I am not jesting," Bilíbin went on. "Nothing is truer or sadder. These gentlemen ride onto the bridge alone and wave white handkerchiefs; they assure the officer on duty that they, the marshals, are on their way to negotiate with Prince Auersperg. He lets them enter the *tête-de-pont* [bridgehead]. They spin him a thousand gasconades, saying that the war is over, that the Emperor Francis is arranging a meeting with Bonaparte, that they desire to see Prince Auersperg, and so on. The officer sends for Auersperg; these gentlemen embrace the officers, crack jokes, sit on the cannon, and meanwhile a French battalion gets to the bridge unobserved, flings the bags of incendiary material into the water, and approaches the *tête-de-pont*. At length appears the lieutenant general, our dear Prince Auersperg von Mautern himself. 'Dearest foe! Flower of the Austrian army, hero of the Turkish wars! Hostilities are ended, we can shake one another's hand. . . . The Emperor Napoleon burns with impatience to make Prince Auersperg's acquaintance.' In a word, those gentlemen, Gascons indeed, so bewildered him with fine words, and he is so flattered by his rapidly established intimacy with the French marshals, and so dazzled by the sight of Murat's mantle and ostrich plumes, *qu'il n'y voit que du feu, et oublie celui qu'il devait faire faire sur l'ennemi* [that their fire gets into his eyes and he forgets that he ought to be firing at the enemy]!" In spite of the animation of his speech, Bilíbin did not forget to pause after this *mot* to give time for its due appreciation. "The French battalion rushes to the bridgehead, spikes the guns, and the bridge is taken! But what is best of all," he went on, his excitement subsiding under the delightful interest of his own story, "is that the sergeant in charge of the cannon which was to give the signal to fire the mines and blow up the bridge, this sergeant, seeing that the French troops were running onto the bridge, was about to fire, but Lannes stayed his hand. The sergeant, who was evidently wiser than his general, goes up to Auersperg and says: 'Prince, you are being deceived, here are the French!' Murat, seeing that all is lost if the sergeant is allowed to speak, turns to Auersperg with feigned astonishment (he is a true Gascon) and says: 'I don't recognize the world-famous Austrian discipline, if you allow a subordinate to address you like that!' It was a stroke of genius. Prince Auersperg feels his dignity at stake and orders the sergeant to be arrested. Come, you must

own that this affair of the Thabor Bridge is delightful! It is not exactly stupidity, nor rascality. . . ."

"It may be treachery," said Prince Andrew, vividly imagining the gray overcoats, wounds, the smoke of gunpowder, the sounds of firing, and the glory that awaited him.

"Not that either. That puts the court in too bad a light," replied Bilí-bin. "It's not treachery nor rascality nor stupidity: it is just as at Ulm . . . it is . . ."—he seemed to be trying to find the right expression. "C'est . . . c'est du Mack. Nous sommes mackés [It is . . . it is a bit of Mack. We are Macked]," he concluded, feeling that he had produced a good epigram, a fresh one that would be repeated. His hitherto puck-ered brow became smooth as a sign of pleasure, and with a slight smile he began to examine his nails.

"Where are you off to?" he said suddenly to Prince Andrew who had risen and was going toward his room.

"I am going away."

"Where to?"

"To the army."

"But you meant to stay another two days?"

"But now I am off at once."

And Prince Andrew after giving directions about his departure went to his room.

"Do you know, mon cher," said Bilíbin following him, "I have been thinking about you. Why are you going?"

And in proof of the conclusiveness of his opinion all the wrinkles van-ished from his face.

Prince Andrew looked inquiringly at him and gave no reply.

"Why are you going? I know you think it your duty to gallop back to the army now that it is in danger. I understand that. Mon cher, it is heroism!"

"Not at all," said Prince Andrew.

"But as you are a philosopher, be a consistent one, look at the other side of the question and you will see that your duty, on the contrary, is to take care of yourself. Leave it to those who are no longer fit for any-thing else. . . . You have not been ordered to return and have not been dismissed from here; therefore, you can stay and go with us wherever our ill-luck takes us. They say we are going to Olmütz,* and Olmütz is a very decent town. You and I will travel comfortably in my calèche."

"Do stop joking, Bilíbin," cried Bolkónski.

"I am speaking sincerely as a friend! Consider! Where and why are

* As part of Czechoslovakia, called Olomouc.

you going, when you might remain here? You are faced by one of two things," and the skin over his left temple puckered, "either you will not reach your regiment before peace is concluded, or you will share defeat and disgrace with Kutúzov's whole army."

And Bilíbin unwrinkled his temple, feeling that the dilemma was insoluble.

"I cannot argue about it," replied Prince Andrew coldly, but he thought: "I am going to save the army."

"My dear fellow, you are a hero!" said Bilíbin.

10. *Prince Andrew returns to Kutúzov. Bagratión sent to Hollabrünn. Napoleon's letter to Murat*

THAT SAME NIGHT, having taken leave of the Minister of War, Bolkónski set off to rejoin the army, not knowing where he would find it and fearing to be captured by the French on the way to Krems.

In Brünn everybody attached to the court was packing up, and the heavy baggage was already being dispatched to Olmütz. Near Hetzelsdorf Prince Andrew struck the highroad along which the Russian army was moving with great haste and in the greatest disorder. The road was so obstructed with carts that it was impossible to get by in a carriage. Prince Andrew took a horse and a Cossack from a Cossack commander, and hungry and weary, making his way past the baggage wagons, rode in search of the commander in chief and of his own luggage. Very sinister reports of the position of the army reached him as he went along, and the appearance of the troops in their disorderly flight confirmed these rumors.

"*Cette armée russe que l'or de l'Angleterre a transportée des extrémités de l'univers, nous allons lui faire éprouver le même sort—(le sort de l'armée d'Ulm).*" [That Russian army which has been brought from the ends of the earth by English gold, we shall cause to share the same fate—(the fate of the army at Ulm).] He remembered these words in Bonaparte's address to his army at the beginning of the campaign, and they awoke in him astonishment at the genius of his hero, a feeling of wounded pride, and a hope of glory. "And should there be nothing left but to die?" he thought. "Well, if need be, I shall do it no worse than others."

He looked with disdain at the endless confused mass of detachments, carts, guns, artillery, and again baggage wagons and vehicles of all kinds overtaking one another and blocking the muddy road, three and sometimes four abreast. From all sides, behind and before, as far as ear could

reach, there were the rattle of wheels, the creaking of carts and gun car-
riages, the tramp of horses, the crack of whips, shouts, the urging of horses,
and the swearing of soldiers, orderlies, and officers. All along the sides of
the road fallen horses were to be seen, some flayed, some not, and broken-
down carts beside which solitary soldiers sat waiting for something, and
again soldiers straggling from their companies, crowds of whom set off to
the neighboring villages, or returned from them dragging sheep, fowls,
hay, and bulging sacks. At each ascent or descent of the road the crowds
were yet denser and the din of shouting more incessant. Soldiers flounder-
ing knee-deep in mud pushed the guns and wagons themselves. Whips
cracked, hoofs slipped, traces broke, and lungs were strained with shout-
ing. The officers directing the march rode backward and forward between
the carts. Their voices were but feebly heard amid the uproar and one saw
by their faces that they despaired of the possibility of checking this dis-
order.

"Here is our dear Orthodox Russian army," thought Bolkónski, recall-
ing Bilíbin's words.

Wishing to find out where the commander in chief was, he rode up to
a convoy. Directly opposite to him came a strange one-horse vehicle, evi-
dently rigged up by soldiers out of any available materials and looking like
something between a cart, a cabriolet, and a calèche. A soldier was driving,
and a woman enveloped in shawls sat behind the apron under the leather
hood of the vehicle. Prince Andrew rode up and was just putting his ques-
tion to a soldier when his attention was diverted by the desperate shrieks
of the woman in the vehicle. An officer in charge of transport was beating
the soldier who was driving the woman's vehicle for trying to get ahead of
others, and the strokes of his whip fell on the apron of the equipage. The
woman screamed piercingly. Seeing Prince Andrew she leaned out from
behind the apron and, waving her thin arms from under the woolen shawl,
cried:

"Mr. Aide-de-camp! Mr. Aide-de-camp! . . . For heaven's sake . . .
Protect me! What will become of us? I am the wife of the doctor of the
Seventh Chasseurs. . . . They won't let us pass, we are left behind and
have lost our people . . ."

"I'll flatten you into a pancake!" shouted the angry officer to the soldier.
"Turn back with your slut!"

"Mr. Aide-de-camp! Help me! . . . What does it all mean?" screamed
the doctor's wife.

"Kindly let this cart pass. Don't you see it's a woman?" said Prince
Andrew riding up to the officer.

The officer glanced at him, and without replying turned again to the soldier. "I'll teach you to push on! . . . Back!"

"Let them pass, I tell you!" repeated Prince Andrew, compressing his lips.

"And who are you?" cried the officer, turning on him with tipsy rage, "who are you? Are you in command here? Eh? I am commander here, not you! Go back or I'll flatten you into a pancake," repeated he. This expression evidently pleased him.

"That was a nice snub for the little aide-de-camp," came a voice from behind.

Prince Andrew saw that the officer was in that state of senseless, tipsy rage when a man does not know what he is saying. He saw that his championship of the doctor's wife in her queer trap might expose him to what he dreaded more than anything in the world—to ridicule; but his instinct urged him on. Before the officer finished his sentence Prince Andrew, his face distorted with fury, rode up to him and raised his riding whip.

"Kind . . . ly let—them—pass!"

The officer flourished his arm and hastily rode away.

"It's all the fault of these fellows on the staff that there's this disorder," he muttered. "Do as you like."

Prince Andrew without lifting his eyes rode hastily away from the doctor's wife, who was calling him her deliverer, and recalling with a sense of disgust the minutest details of this humiliating scene he galloped on to the village where he was told that the commander in chief was.

On reaching the village he dismounted and went to the nearest house, intending to rest if but for a moment, eat something, and try to sort out the stinging and tormenting thoughts that confused his mind. "This is a mob of scoundrels and not an army," he was thinking as he went up to the window of the first house, when a familiar voice called him by name.

He turned round. Nesvítski's handsome face looked out of the little window. Nesvítski, moving his moist lips as he chewed something, and flourishing his arm, called him to enter.

"Bolkónski! Bolkónski! . . . Don't you hear? Eh? Come quick . . ." he shouted.

Entering the house, Prince Andrew saw Nesvítski and another adjutant having something to eat. They hastily turned round to him asking if he had any news. On their familiar faces he read agitation and alarm. This was particularly noticeable on Nesvítski's usually laughing countenance.

"Where is the commander in chief?" asked Bolkónski.

"Here, in that house," answered the adjutant.

"Well, is it true that it's peace and capitulation?" asked Nesvítski.

"I was going to ask you. I know nothing except that it was all I could do to get here."

"And we, my dear boy! It's terrible! I was wrong to laugh at Mack, we're getting it still worse," said Nesvítski. "But sit down and have something to eat."

"You won't be able to find either your baggage or anything else now, Prince. And God only knows where your man Peter is," said the other adjutant.

"Where are headquarters?"

"We are to spend the night in Znaim." *

"Well, I have got all I need into packs for two horses," said Nesvítski. "They've made up splendid packs for me—fit to cross the Bohemian mountains with. It's a bad lookout, old fellow! But what's the matter with you? You must be ill to shiver like that," he added, noticing that Prince Andrew winced as at an electric shock.

"It's nothing," replied Prince Andrew.

He had just remembered his recent encounter with the doctor's wife and the convoy officer.

"What is the commander in chief doing here?" he asked.

"I can't make out at all," said Nesvítski.

"Well, all I can make out is that everything is abominable, abominable, quite abominable!" said Prince Andrew, and he went off to the house where the commander in chief was.

Passing by Kutúzov's carriage and the exhausted saddle horses of his suite, with their Cossacks who were talking loudly together, Prince Andrew entered the passage. Kutúzov himself, he was told, was in the house with Prince Bagratión and Weyrother. Weyrother was the Austrian general who had succeeded Schmidt. In the passage little Kozlóvski was squatting on his heels in front of a clerk. The clerk, with cuffs turned up, was hastily writing at a tub turned bottom upwards. Kozlóvski's face looked worn—he too had evidently not slept all night. He glanced at Prince Andrew and did not even nod to him.

"Second line . . . have you written it?" he continued dictating to the clerk. "The Kiev Grenadiers, Podolian . . ."

"One can't write so fast, your honor," said the clerk, glancing angrily and disrespectfully at Kozlóvski.

Through the door came the sounds of Kutúzov's voice, excited and dissatisfied, interrupted by another, an unfamiliar voice. From the sound of these voices, the inattentive way Kozlóvski looked at him, the disre-

* Later, as part of Czechoslovakia, called Znojmo.

spectful manner of the exhausted clerk, the fact that the clerk and Koz-lóvski were squatting on the floor by a tub so near to the commander in chief, and from the noisy laughter of the Cossacks holding the horses near the window, Prince Andrew felt that something important and disastrous was about to happen.

He turned to Kozlóvski with urgent questions.

"Immediately, Prince," said Kozlóvski. "Dispositions for Bagratión."

"What about capitulation?"

"Nothing of the sort. Orders are issued for a battle."

Prince Andrew moved toward the door from whence voices were heard. Just as he was going to open it the sounds ceased, the door opened, and Kutúzov with his eagle nose and puffy face appeared in the doorway. Prince Andrew stood right in front of Kutúzov but the expression of the commander in chief's one sound eye showed him to be so preoccupied with thoughts and anxieties as to be oblivious of his presence. He looked straight at his adjutant's face without recognizing him.

"Well, have you finished?" said he to Kozlóvski.

"One moment, your excellency."

Bagratión, a gaunt middle-aged man of medium height with a firm, impassive face of Oriental type, came out after the commander in chief.

"I have the honor to present myself," repeated Prince Andrew rather loudly, handing Kutúzov an envelope.

"Ah, from Vienna? Very good. Later, later!"

Kutúzov went out into the porch with Bagratión.

"Well, good-by, Prince," said he to Bagratión. "My blessing, and may Christ be with you in your great endeavor!"

His face suddenly softened and tears came into his eyes. With his left hand he drew Bagratión toward him, and with his right, on which he wore a ring, he made the sign of the cross over him with a gesture evidently habitual, offering his puffy cheek, but Bagratión kissed him on the neck instead.

"Christ be with you!" Kutúzov repeated and went toward his carriage. "Get in with me," said he to Bolkónski.

"Your excellency, I should like to be of use here. Allow me to remain with Prince Bagratión's detachment."

"Get in," said Kutúzov, and noticing that Bolkónski still delayed, he added: "I need good officers myself, need them myself!"

They got into the carriage and drove for a few minutes in silence.

"There is still much, much before us," he said, as if with an old man's penetration he understood all that was passing in Bolkónski's mind. "If a

tenth part of his detachment returns I shall thank God," he added as if speaking to himself.

Prince Andrew glanced at Kutúzov's face only a foot distant from him and involuntarily noticed the carefully washed seams of the scar near his temple, where an Ismail bullet had pierced his skull, and the empty eye socket. "Yes, he has a right to speak so calmly of those men's death," thought Bolkónski.

"That is why I beg to be sent to that detachment," he said.

Kutúzov did not reply. He seemed to have forgotten what he had been saying, and sat plunged in thought. Five minutes later, gently swaying on the soft springs of the carriage, he turned to Prince Andrew. There was not a trace of agitation on his face. With delicate irony he questioned Prince Andrew about the details of his interview with the Emperor, about the remarks he had heard at court concerning the Krems affair, and about some ladies they both knew.

On November 1 Kutúzov had received, through a spy, news that the army he commanded was in an almost hopeless position. The spy reported that the French, after crossing the bridge at Vienna, were advancing in immense force upon Kutúzov's line of communication with the troops that were arriving from Russia. If Kutúzov decided to remain at Krems, Napoleon's army of one hundred and fifty thousand men would cut him off completely and surround his exhausted army of forty thousand, and he would find himself in the position of Mack at Ulm. If Kutúzov decided to abandon the road connecting him with the troops arriving from Russia, he would have to march with no road into unknown parts of the Bohemian mountains, defending himself against superior forces of the enemy and abandoning all hope of a junction with Buxhöwden. If Kutúzov decided to retreat along the road from Krems to Olmütz, to unite with the troops arriving from Russia, he risked being forestalled on that road by the French who had crossed the Vienna bridge, and encumbered by his baggage and transport, having to accept battle on the march against an enemy three times as strong, who would hem him in from two sides.

Kutúzov chose this latter course.

The French, the spy reported, having crossed the Vienna bridge, were advancing by forced marches toward Znaim, which lay sixty-six miles off on the line of Kutúzov's retreat. If he reached Znaim before the French, there would be great hope of saving the army; to let the French forestall him at Znaim meant the exposure of his whole army to a disgrace such as that of Ulm, or to utter destruction. But to forestall the French with his whole army was impossible. The road for the French from Vienna to

Znaim was shorter and better than the road for the Russians from Krems to Znaim.*

The night he received the news, Kutúzov sent Bagratión's vanguard, four thousand strong, to the right across the hills from the Krems-Znaim to the Vienna-Znaim road. Bagratión was to make this march without resting, and to halt facing Vienna with Znaim to his rear, and if he succeeded in forestalling the French he was to delay them as long as possible. Kutúzov himself with all his transport took the road to Znaim.

Marching thirty miles that stormy night across roadless hills, with his hungry, ill-shod soldiers, and losing a third of his men as stragglers by the way, Bagratión came out on the Vienna-Znaim road at Hollabrünn a few hours ahead of the French who were approaching Hollabrünn from Vienna. Kutúzov with his transport had still to march for some days before he could reach Znaim. Hence Bagratión with his four thousand hungry, exhausted men would have to detain for days the whole enemy army that came upon him at Hollabrünn, which was clearly impossible. But a freak of fate made the impossible possible. The success of the trick that had placed the Vienna bridge in the hands of the French without a fight led Murat to try to deceive Kutúzov in a similar way. Meeting Bagratión's weak detachment on the Znaim road he supposed it to be Kutúzov's whole army. To be able to crush it absolutely he awaited the arrival of the rest of the troops who were on their way from Vienna, and with this object offered a three days' truce on condition that both armies should remain in position without moving. Murat declared that negotiations for peace were already proceeding, and that he therefore offered this truce to avoid unnecessary bloodshed. Count Nostitz, the Austrian general occupying the advanced posts, believed Murat's emissary and retired, leaving Bagratión's division exposed. Another emissary rode to the Russian line to announce the peace negotiations and to offer the Russian army the three days' truce. Bagratión replied that he was not authorized either to accept or refuse a truce and sent his adjutant to Kutúzov to report the offer he had received.

A truce was Kutúzov's sole chance of gaining time, giving Bagratión's

* *The road from Vienna to Znaim by which Murat was advancing ran parallel, and to the east, of the road from Krems by which Kutúzov was retiring. These roads approached each other at an angle. From the Krems road one could cross to the Vienna road at two places; either at Hollabrünn (where Bagratión was sent) or farther on by a more convenient road which came out at the village of Grunth. When Bagratión succeeded in reaching Hollabrünn before Murat, Kutúzov crossed to Grunth to join him, letting his baggage go straight on to Znaim. At Schön Grabern the battle took place which is described in the following chapters.—A.M.*

exhausted troops some rest, and letting the transport and heavy convoys (whose movements were concealed from the French) advance if but one stage nearer Znaim. The offer of a truce gave the only, and a quite unexpected, chance of saving the army. On receiving the news he immediately dispatched Adjutant General Wintzingerode, who was in attendance on him, to the enemy camp. Wintzingerode was not merely to agree to the truce but also to offer terms of capitulation, and meanwhile Kutúzov sent his adjutants back to hasten to the utmost the movements of the baggage trains of the entire army along the Krems-Znaim road. Bagratión's exhausted and hungry detachment, which alone covered this movement of the transport and of the whole army, had to remain stationary in face of an enemy eight times as strong as itself.

Kutúzov's expectations that the proposals of capitulation (which were in no way binding) might give time for part of the transport to pass, and also that Murat's mistake would very soon be discovered, proved correct. As soon as Bonaparte (who was at Schönbrunn, sixteen miles from Hollabrünn) received Murat's dispatch with the proposal of a truce and a capitulation, he detected a ruse and wrote the following letter to Murat:

> Schönbrunn, 25th Brumaire, 1805,
> at eight o'clock in the morning

To Prince Murat,

I cannot find words to express to you my displeasure. You command only my advance guard, and have no right to arrange an armistice without my order. You are causing me to lose the fruits of a campaign. Break the armistice immediately and march on the enemy. Inform him that the general who signed that capitulation had no right to do so, and that no one but the Emperor of Russia has that right.

If, however, the Emperor of Russia ratifies that convention, I will ratify it; but it is only a trick. March on, destroy the Russian army. . . . You are in a position to seize its baggage and artillery.

The Russian Emperor's aide-de-camp is an impostor. Officers are nothing when they have no powers; this one had none. . . . The Austrians let themselves be tricked at the crossing of the Vienna bridge, you are letting yourself be tricked by an aide-de-camp of the Emperor.

NAPOLEON *

Bonaparte's adjutant rode full gallop with this menacing letter to Murat. Bonaparte himself, not trusting to his generals, moved with all the Guards

* *Napoleon's letter to Murat is taken from Thiers'* Histoire du Consulat et de l'Empire.—A.M.

to the field of battle, afraid of letting a ready victim escape, and Bagratión's four thousand men merrily lighted campfires, dried and warmed themselves, cooked their porridge for the first time for three days, and not one of them knew or imagined what was in store for him.

11. Prince Andrew reports to Bagratión. Captain Túshin. Soldiers at the front. Dólokhov talks to a French grenadier

BETWEEN three and four o'clock in the afternoon Prince Andrew, who had persisted in his request to Kutúzov, arrived at Grunth and reported himself to Bagratión. Bonaparte's adjutant had not yet reached Murat's detachment and the battle had not yet begun. In Bagratión's detachment no one knew anything of the general position of affairs. They talked of peace but did not believe in its possibility; others talked of a battle but also disbelieved in the nearness of an engagement. Bagratión, knowing Bolkónski to be a favorite and trusted adjutant, received him with distinction and special marks of favor, explaining to him that there would probably be an engagement that day or the next, and giving him full liberty to remain with him during the battle or to join the rearguard and have an eye on the order of retreat, "which is also very important."

"However, there will hardly be an engagement today," said Bagratión as if to reassure Prince Andrew.

"If he is one of the ordinary little staff dandies sent to earn a medal he can get his reward just as well in the rearguard, but if he wishes to stay with me, let him . . . he'll be of use here if he's a brave officer," thought Bagratión. Prince Andrew, without replying, asked the prince's permission to ride round the position to see the disposition of the forces, so as to know his bearings should he be sent to execute an order. The officer on duty, a handsome, elegantly dressed man with a diamond ring on his forefinger, who was fond of speaking French though he spoke it badly, offered to conduct Prince Andrew.

On all sides they saw rain-soaked officers with dejected faces who seemed to be seeking something, and soldiers dragging doors, benches, and fencing from the village.

"There now, Prince! We can't stop those fellows," said the staff officer pointing to the soldiers. "The officers don't keep them in hand. And there," he pointed to a sutler's tent, "they crowd in and sit. This morning I turned them all out and now look, it's full again. I must go there, Prince, and scare them a bit. It won't take a moment."

"Yes, let's go in and I will get myself a roll and some cheese," said Prince Andrew who had not yet had time to eat anything.

"Why didn't you mention it, Prince? I would have offered you something."

They dismounted and entered the tent. Several officers, with flushed and weary faces, were sitting at the table eating and drinking.

"Now what does this mean, gentlemen?" said the staff officer, in the reproachful tone of a man who has repeated the same thing more than once. "You know it won't do to leave your posts like this. The prince gave orders that no one should leave his post. Now you, Captain," and he turned to a thin, dirty little artillery officer who without his boots (he had given them to the canteen keeper to dry), in only his stockings, rose when they entered, smiling not altogether comfortably.

"Well, aren't you ashamed of yourself, Captain Túshin?" he continued. "One would think that as an artillery officer you would set a good example, yet here you are without your boots! The alarm will be sounded and you'll be in a pretty position without your boots!" (The staff officer smiled.) "Kindly return to your posts, gentlemen, all of you, all!" he added in a tone of command.

Prince Andrew smiled involuntarily as he looked at the artillery officer Túshin, who silent and smiling, shifting from one stockinged foot to the other, glanced inquiringly with his large, intelligent, kindly eyes from Prince Andrew to the staff officer.

"The soldiers say it feels easier without boots," said Captain Túshin smiling shyly in his uncomfortable position, evidently wishing to adopt a jocular tone. But before he had finished he felt that his jest was unacceptable and had not come off. He grew confused.

"Kindly return to your posts," said the staff officer trying to preserve his gravity.

Prince Andrew glanced again at the artillery officer's small figure. There was something peculiar about it, quite unsoldierly, rather comic, but extremely attractive.

The staff officer and Prince Andrew mounted their horses and rode on.

Having ridden beyond the village, continually meeting and overtaking soldiers and officers of various regiments, they saw on their left some entrenchments being thrown up, the freshly dug clay of which showed up red. Several battalions of soldiers, in their shirt sleeves despite the cold wind, swarmed in these earthworks like a host of white ants; spadefuls of red clay were continually being thrown up from behind the bank by unseen hands. Prince Andrew and the officer rode up, looked at the entrenchment, and went on again. Just behind it they came upon some dozens of

soldiers, continually replaced by others, who ran from the entrenchment. They had to hold their noses and put their horses to a trot to escape from the poisoned atmosphere of these latrines.

"Voilà l'agrément des camps, monsieur le prince [This is a pleasure one gets in camp, Prince]," said the staff officer.

They rode up the opposite hill. From there the French could already be seen. Prince Andrew stopped and began examining the position.

"That's our battery," said the staff officer indicating the highest point. "It's in charge of the queer fellow we saw without his boots. You can see everything from there; let's go there, Prince."

"Thank you very much, I will go on alone," said Prince Andrew, wishing to rid himself of this staff officer's company, "please don't trouble yourself further."

The staff officer remained behind and Prince Andrew rode on alone.

The farther forward and nearer the enemy he went, the more orderly and cheerful were the troops. The greatest disorder and depression had been in the baggage train he had passed that morning on the Znaim road seven miles away from the French. At Grunth also some apprehension and alarm could be felt, but the nearer Prince Andrew came to the French lines the more confident was the appearance of our troops. The soldiers in their greatcoats were ranged in lines, the sergeants major and company officers were counting the men, poking the last man in each section in the ribs and telling him to hold his hand up. Soldiers scattered over the whole place were dragging logs and brushwood and were building shelters with merry chatter and laughter; around the fires sat others, dressed and undressed, drying their shirts and leg bands or mending boots or overcoats and crowding round the boilers and porridge cookers. In one company dinner was ready, and the soldiers were gazing eagerly at the steaming boiler, waiting till the sample, which a quartermaster sergeant was carrying in a wooden bowl to an officer who sat on a log before his shelter, had been tasted.

Another company, a lucky one for not all the companies had vodka, crowded round a pockmarked, broad-shouldered sergeant major who, tilting a keg, filled one after another the canteen lids held out to him. The soldiers lifted the canteen lids to their lips with reverential faces, emptied them, rolling the vodka in their mouths, and walked away from the sergeant major with brightened expressions, licking their lips and wiping them on the sleeves of their greatcoats. All their faces were as serene as if all this were happening at home awaiting peaceful encampment, and not within sight of the enemy before an action in which at least half of them

would be left on the field. After passing a chasseur regiment and in the lines of the Kiev grenadiers—fine fellows busy with similar peaceful affairs —near the shelter of the regimental commander, higher than and different from the others, Prince Andrew came out in front of a platoon of grenadiers before whom lay a naked man. Two soldiers held him while two others were flourishing their switches and striking him regularly on his bare back. The man shrieked unnaturally. A stout major was pacing up and down the line, and regardless of the screams kept repeating:

"It's a shame for a soldier to steal; a soldier must be honest, honorable, and brave, but if he robs his fellows there is no honor in him, he's a scoundrel. Go on! Go on!"

So the swishing sound of the strokes, and the desperate but unnatural screams, continued.

"Go on, go on!" said the major.

A young officer with a bewildered and pained expression on his face stepped away from the man and looked round inquiringly at the adjutant as he rode by.

Prince Andrew, having reached the front line, rode along it. Our front line and that of the enemy were far apart on the right and left flanks, but in the center where the men with a flag of truce had passed that morning, the lines were so near together that the men could see one another's faces and speak to one another. Besides the soldiers who formed the picket line on either side, there were many curious onlookers who, jesting and laughing, stared at their strange foreign enemies.

Since early morning—despite an injunction not to approach the picket line—the officers had been unable to keep sight-seers away. The soldiers forming the picket line, like showmen exhibiting a curiosity, no longer looked at the French but paid attention to the sight-seers and grew weary waiting to be relieved. Prince Andrew halted to have a look at the French.

"Look! Look there!" one soldier was saying to another, pointing to a Russian musketeer who had gone up to the picket line with an officer and was rapidly and excitedly talking to a French grenadier. "Hark to him jabbering! Fine, isn't it? It's all the Frenchy can do to keep up with him. There now, Sídorov!"

"Wait a bit and listen. It's fine!" answered Sídorov, who was considered an adept at French.

The soldier to whom the laughers referred was Dólokhov. Prince Andrew recognized him and stopped to listen to what he was saying. Dólokhov had come from the left flank where their regiment was stationed, with his captain.

"Now then, go on, go on!" incited the officer, bending forward and trying not to lose a word of the speech which was incomprehensible to him. "More, please: more! What's he saying?"

Dólokhov did not answer the captain; he had been drawn into a hot dispute with the French grenadier. They were naturally talking about the campaign. The Frenchman, confusing the Austrians with the Russians, was trying to prove that the Russians had surrendered and had fled all the way from Ulm, while Dólokhov maintained that the Russians had not surrendered but had beaten the French.

"We have orders to drive you off here, and we shall drive you off," said Dólokhov.

"Only take care you and your Cossacks are not all captured!" said the French grenadier.

The French onlookers and listeners laughed.

"We'll make you dance as we did under Suvórov . . . [*on vous fera danser*]," said Dólokhov.

"*Qu'est-ce qu'il chante?* [What's he singing about?]" asked a Frenchman.

"It's ancient history," said another, guessing that it referred to a former war. "The Emperor will teach your Suvara as he has taught the others . . ."

"Bonaparte . . ." began Dólokhov, but the Frenchman interrupted him.

"Not Bonaparte. He is the Emperor! *Sacré nom . . . !*" cried he angrily.

"The devil skin your Emperor."

And Dólokhov swore at him in coarse soldier's Russian and shouldering his musket walked away.

"Let us go, Iván Lukích," he said to the captain.

"Ah, that's the way to talk French," said the picket soldiers. "Now, Sídorov, you have a try!"

Sídorov, turning to the French, winked, and began to jabber meaningless sounds very fast: "*Kari, mala, tafa, safi, muter, Kaská*," he said, trying to give an expressive intonation to his voice.

"Ho! ho! ho! Ha! ha! ha! ha! Ouh! ouh!" came peals of such healthy and good-humored laughter from the soldiers that it infected the French involuntarily, so much so that the only thing left to do seemed to be to unload the muskets, explode the ammunition, and all return home as quickly as possible.

But the guns remained loaded, the loopholes in blockhouses and entrenchments looked out just as menacingly, and the unlimbered cannon confronted one another as before.

12. *Prince Andrew surveys the position. The first shot*

HAVING RIDDEN round the whole line from right flank to left, Prince Andrew made his way up to the battery from which the staff officer had told him the whole field could be seen. Here he dismounted, and stopped beside the farthest of the four unlimbered cannon. Before the guns an artillery sentry was pacing up and down; he stood at attention when the officer arrived, but at a sign resumed his measured, monotonous pacing. Behind the guns were their limbers and still farther back picket ropes and artillerymen's bonfires. To the left, not far from the farthest cannon, was a small, newly constructed wattle shed from which came the sound of officers' voices in eager conversation.

It was true that a view over nearly the whole Russian position and the greater part of the enemy's opened out from this battery. Just facing it, on the crest of the opposite hill, the village of Schön Grabern could be seen, and in three places to left and right the French troops amid the smoke of their campfires, the greater part of whom were evidently in the village itself and behind the hill. To the left from that village, amid the smoke, was something resembling a battery, but it was impossible to see it clearly with the naked eye. Our right flank was posted on a rather steep incline which dominated the French position. Our infantry were stationed there, and at the farthest point the dragoons. In the center, where Túshin's battery stood and from which Prince Andrew was surveying the position, was the easiest and most direct descent and ascent to the brook separating us from Schön Grabern. On the left our troops were close to a copse, in which smoked the bonfires of our infantry who were felling wood. The French line was wider than ours, and it was plain that they could easily outflank us on both sides. Behind our position was a steep and deep dip, making it difficult for artillery and cavalry to retire. Prince Andrew took out his notebook and, leaning on the cannon, sketched a plan of the position. He made some notes on two points, intending to mention them to Bagratión. His idea was, first, to concentrate all the artillery in the center, and secondly, to withdraw the cavalry to the other side of the dip. Prince Andrew, being always near the commander in chief, closely following the mass movements and general orders, and constantly studying historical accounts of battles, involuntarily pictured to himself the course of events in the forthcoming action in broad outline. He imagined only important possibilities: "If the enemy attacks the right flank," he said to himself, "the Kiev grenadiers and the Podólsk chasseurs must hold their position till reserves from the center come up. In that case the dragoons could suc-

cessfully make a flank counterattack. If they attack our center we, having the center battery on this high ground, shall withdraw the left flank under its cover, and retreat to the dip by echelons." So he reasoned.. . . . All the time he had been beside the gun, he had heard the voices of the officers distinctly, but as often happens had not understood a word of what they were saying. Suddenly, however, he was struck by a voice coming from the shed, and its tone was so sincere that he could not but listen.

"No, friend," said a pleasant and, as it seemed to Prince Andrew, a familiar voice, "what I say is that if it were possible to know what is beyond death, none of us would be afraid of it. That's so, friend."

Another, a younger voice, interrupted him: "Afraid or not, you can't escape it anyhow."

"All the same, one is afraid! Oh, you clever people," said a third manly voice interrupting them both. "Of course you artillery men are very wise, because you can take everything along with you—vodka and snacks."

And the owner of the manly voice, evidently an infantry officer, laughed.

"Yes, one is afraid," continued the first speaker, he of the familiar voice. "One is afraid of the unknown, that's what it is. Whatever we may say about the soul going to the sky . . . we know there is no sky but only an atmosphere."

The manly voice again interrupted the artillery officer.

"Well, stand us some of your herb vodka, Túshin," it said.

"Why," thought Prince Andrew, "that's the captain who stood up in the sutler's hut without his boots." He recognized the agreeable, philosophizing voice with pleasure.

"Some herb vodka? Certainly!" said Túshin. "But still, to conceive a future life . . ."

He did not finish. Just then there was a whistle in the air; nearer and nearer, faster and louder, louder and faster, a cannon ball, as if it had not finished saying what was necessary, thudded into the ground near the shed with superhuman force, throwing up a mass of earth. The ground seemed to groan at the terrible impact.

And immediately Túshin, with a short pipe in the corner of his mouth and his kind, intelligent face rather pale, rushed out of the shed followed by the owner of the manly voice, a dashing infantry officer who hurried off to his company, buttoning up his coat as he ran.

13. Bagratión in action. Túshin's battery. Setting Schön Grabern on fire

MOUNTING HIS HORSE again Prince Andrew lingered with the battery, looking at the puff from the gun that had sent the ball. His eyes ran rapidly over the wide space, but he only saw that the hitherto motionless masses of the French now swayed and that there really was a battery to their left. The smoke above it had not yet dispersed. Two mounted Frenchmen, probably adjutants, were galloping up the hill. A small but distinctly visible enemy column was moving down the hill, probably to strengthen the front line. The smoke of the first shot had not yet dispersed before another puff appeared, followed by a report. The battle had begun! Prince Andrew turned his horse and galloped back to Grunth to find Prince Bagratión. He heard the cannonade behind him growing louder and more frequent. Evidently our guns had begun to reply. From the bottom of the slope, where the parleys had taken place, came the report of musketry.

Lemarrois had just arrived at a gallop with Bonaparte's stern letter, and Murat, humiliated and anxious to expiate his fault, had at once moved his forces to attack the center and outflank both the Russian wings, hoping before evening and before the arrival of the Emperor to crush the contemptible detachment that stood before him.

"It has begun. Here it is!" thought Prince Andrew, feeling the blood rush to his heart. "But where and how will my Toulon present itself?"

Passing between the companies that had been eating porridge and drinking vodka a quarter of an hour before, he saw everywhere the same rapid movement of soldiers forming ranks and getting their muskets ready, and on all their faces he recognized the same eagerness that filled his heart. "It has begun! Here it is, dreadful but enjoyable!" was what the face of each soldier and each officer seemed to say.

Before he had reached the embankments that were being thrown up, he saw, in the light of the dull autumn evening, mounted men coming toward him. The foremost, wearing a Cossack cloak and lambskin cap and riding a white horse, was Prince Bagratión. Prince Andrew stopped, waiting for him to come up; Prince Bagratión reined in his horse and recognizing Prince Andrew nodded to him. He still looked ahead while Prince Andrew told him what he had seen.

The feeling, "It has begun! Here it is!" was seen even on Prince Bagratión's hard brown face with its half-closed, dull, sleepy eyes. Prince Andrew gazed with anxious curiosity at that impassive face and wished he could tell

what, if anything, this man was thinking and feeling at that moment. "Is there anything at all behind that impassive face?" Prince Andrew asked himself as he looked. Prince Bagratión bent his head in sign of agreement with what Prince Andrew told him, and said, "Very good!" in a tone that seemed to imply that everything that took place and was reported to him was exactly what he had foreseen. Prince Andrew, out of breath with his rapid ride, spoke quickly. Prince Bagratión, uttering his words with an Oriental accent, spoke particularly slowly, as if to impress the fact that there was no need to hurry. However, he put his horse to a trot in the direction of Túshin's battery. Prince Andrew followed with the suite. Behind Prince Bagratión rode an officer of the suite, the prince's personal adjutant, Zherkóv, an orderly officer, the staff officer on duty, riding a fine bobtailed horse, and a civilian—an accountant who had asked permission to be present at the battle out of curiosity. The accountant, a stout, full-faced man, looked around him with a naïve smile of satisfaction and presented a strange appearance among the hussars, Cossacks, and adjutants, in his camlet coat, as he jolted on his horse with a convoy officer's saddle.

"He wants to see a battle," said Zherkóv to Bolkónski, pointing to the accountant, "but he feels a pain in the pit of his stomach already."

"Oh, leave off!" said the accountant with a beaming but rather cunning smile, as if flattered at being made the subject of Zherkóv's joke, and purposely trying to appear stupider than he really was.

"It is very strange, mon Monsieur Prince," said the staff officer. (He remembered that in French there is some peculiar way of addressing a prince, but could not get it quite right.)

By this time they were all approaching Túshin's battery, and a ball struck the ground in front of them.

"What's that that has fallen?" asked the accountant with a naïve smile.

"A French pancake," answered Zherkóv.

"So that's what they hit with?" asked the accountant. "How awful!"

He seemed to swell with satisfaction. He had hardly finished speaking when they again heard an unexpectedly violent whistling which suddenly ended with a thud into something soft . . . f-f-flop! and a Cossack, riding a little to their right and behind the accountant, crashed to earth with his horse. Zherkóv and the staff officer bent over their saddles and turned their horses away. The accountant stopped, facing the Cossack, and examined him with attentive curiosity. The Cossack was dead, but the horse still struggled.

Prince Bagratión screwed up his eyes, looked round, and, seeing the cause of the confusion, turned away with indifference, as if to say, "Is it

worth while noticing trifles?" He reined in his horse with the ease of a skillful rider and, slightly bending over, disengaged his saber which had caught in his cloak. It was an old-fashioned saber of a kind no longer in general use. Prince Andrew remembered the story of Suvórov giving his saber to Bagratión in Italy, and the recollection was particularly pleasant at that moment. They had reached the battery at which Prince Andrew had been when he examined the battlefield.

"Whose company?" asked Prince Bagratión of an artilleryman standing by the ammunition wagon.

He asked, "Whose company?" but he really meant, "Are you frightened here?" and the artilleryman understood him.

"Captain Túshin's, your excellency!" shouted the red-haired, freckled gunner in a merry voice, standing to attention.

"Yes, yes," muttered Bagratión as if considering something, and he rode past the limbers to the farthest cannon.

As he approached, a ringing shot issued from it deafening him and his suite, and in the smoke that suddenly surrounded the gun they could see the gunners who had seized it straining to roll it quickly back to its former position. A huge, broad-shouldered gunner, Number One, holding a mop, his legs far apart, sprang to the wheel; while Number Two with a trembling hand placed a charge in the cannon's mouth. The short, round-shouldered Captain Túshin, stumbling over the tail of the gun carriage, moved forward and, not noticing the general, looked out shading his eyes with his small hand.

"Lift it two lines more and it will be just right," cried he in a feeble voice to which he tried to impart a dashing note, ill suited to his weak figure. "Number Two!" he squeaked. "Fire, Medvédev!"

Bagratión called to him, and Túshin, raising three fingers to his cap with a bashful and awkward gesture not at all like a military salute but like a priest's benediction, approached the general. Though Túshin's guns had been intended to cannonade the valley, he was firing incendiary balls at the village of Schön Grabern visible just opposite, in front of which large masses of French were advancing.

No one had given Túshin orders where and at what to fire, but after consulting his sergeant major, Zakharchénko, for whom he had great respect, he had decided that it would be a good thing to set fire to the village. "Very good!" said Bagratión in reply to the officer's report, and began deliberately to examine the whole battlefield extended before him. The French had advanced nearest on our right. Below the height on which the Kiev regiment was stationed, in the hollow where the rivulet flowed, the

soul-stirring rolling and crackling of musketry was heard, and much farther to the right beyond the dragoons, the officer of the suite pointed out to Bagratión a French column that was outflanking us. To the left the horizon was bounded by the adjacent wood. Prince Bagratión ordered two battalions from the center to be sent to reinforce the right flank. The officer of the suite ventured to remark to the prince that if these battalions went away, the guns would remain without support. Prince Bagratión turned to the officer and with his dull eyes looked at him in silence. It seemed to Prince Andrew that the officer's remark was just and that really no answer could be made to it. But at that moment an adjutant galloped up with a message from the commander of the regiment in the hollow and news that immense masses of the French were coming down upon them and that his regiment was in disorder and was retreating upon the Kiev grenadiers. Prince Bagratión bowed his head in sign of assent and approval. He rode off at a walk to the right and sent an adjutant to the dragoons with orders to attack the French. But this adjutant returned half an hour later with the news that the commander of the dragoons had already retreated beyond the dip in the ground, as a heavy fire had been opened on him and he was losing men uselessly, and so had hastened to throw some sharpshooters into the wood.

"Very good!" said Bagratión.

As he was leaving the battery, firing was heard on the left also, and as it was too far to the left flank for him to have time to go there himself, Prince Bagratión sent Zherkóv to tell the general in command (the one who had paraded his regiment before Kutúzov at Braunau) that he must retreat as quickly as possible behind the hollow in the rear, as the right flank would probably not be able to withstand the enemy's attack very long. About Túshin and the battalion that had been in support of his battery all was forgotten. Prince Andrew listened attentively to Bagratión's colloquies with the commanding officers and the orders he gave them and, to his surprise, found that no orders were really given, but that Prince Bagratión tried to make it appear that everything done by necessity, by accident, or by the will of subordinate commanders was done, if not by his direct command, at least in accord with his intentions. Prince Andrew noticed, however, that though what happened was due to chance and was independent of the commander's will, owing to the tact Bagratión showed, his presence was very valuable. Officers who approached him with disturbed countenances became calm; soldiers and officers greeted him gaily, grew more cheerful in his presence, and were evidently anxious to display their courage before him.

14. Battle scenes. Quarrelsome commanders.
Nicholas injured

PRINCE BAGRATIÓN, having reached the highest point of our right flank,
began riding downhill to where the roll of musketry was heard but
where on account of the smoke nothing could be seen. The nearer they
got to the hollow the less they could see but the more they felt the nearness
of the actual battlefield. They began to meet wounded men. One with a
bleeding head and no cap was being dragged along by two soldiers who
supported him under the arms. There was a gurgle in his throat and he was
spitting blood. A bullet had evidently hit him in the throat or mouth. An-
other was walking sturdily by himself but without his musket, groaning
aloud and swinging his arm which had just been hurt, while blood from it
was streaming over his greatcoat as from a bottle. He had that moment
been wounded and his face showed fear rather than suffering. Crossing a
road they descended a steep incline and saw several men lying on the
ground; they also met a crowd of soldiers some of whom were unwounded.
The soldiers were ascending the hill breathing heavily, and despite the
general's presence were talking loudly and gesticulating. In front of them
rows of gray cloaks were already visible through the smoke, and an officer
catching sight of Bagratión rushed shouting after the crowd of retreating
soldiers, ordering them back. Bagratión rode up to the ranks along which
shots crackled now here and now there, drowning the sound of voices and
the shouts of command. The whole air reeked with smoke.* The excited
faces of the soldiers were blackened with it. Some were using their ram-
rods, others putting powder on the touchpans or taking charges from their
pouches, while others were firing, though who they were firing at could
not be seen for the smoke which there was no wind to carry away. A pleas-
ant humming and whistling of bullets were often heard. "What is this?"
thought Prince Andrew approaching the crowd of soldiers. "It can't be an
attack, for they are not moving; it can't be a square—for they are not drawn
up for that."

The commander of the regiment, a thin, feeble-looking old man with a
pleasant smile—his eyelids drooping more than half over his old eyes, giv-
ing him a mild expression, rode up to Bagratión and welcomed him as a

* The passage gives a picture of musketry fire in those days. The powder and
bullet were inserted through the muzzle and rammed in. When the trigger was
drawn the hammer fell and steel struck the flint, sparks lit the gunpowder on
the pan around the touch hole, and the musket went off if it did not miss fire.
—A.M.

host welcomes an honored guest. He reported that his regiment had been attacked by French cavalry and that, though the attack had been repulsed, he had lost more than half his men. He said the attack had been repulsed, employing this military term to describe what had occurred to his regiment, but in reality he did not himself know what had happened during that half-hour to the troops entrusted to him, and could not say with certainty whether the attack had been repulsed or his regiment had been broken up. All he knew was that at the commencement of the action balls and shells began flying all over his regiment and hitting men and that afterwards someone had shouted "Cavalry!" and our men had begun firing. They were still firing, not at the cavalry which had disappeared, but at French infantry who had come into the hollow and were firing at our men. Prince Bagratión bowed his head as a sign that this was exactly what he had desired and expected. Turning to his adjutant he ordered him to bring down the two battalions of the Sixth Chasseurs whom they had just passed. Prince Andrew was struck by the changed expression on Prince Bagratión's face at this moment. It expressed the concentrated and happy resolution you see on the face of a man who on a hot day takes a final run before plunging into the water. The dull, sleepy expression was no longer there, nor the affectation of profound thought. The round, steady, hawk's eyes looked before him eagerly and rather disdainfully, not resting on anything although his movements were still slow and measured.

The commander of the regiment turned to Prince Bagratión, entreating him to go back as it was too dangerous to remain where they were. "Please, your excellency, for God's sake!" he kept saying, glancing for support at an officer of the suite who turned away from him. "There, you see!" and he drew attention to the bullets whistling, singing, and hissing continually around them. He spoke in the tone of entreaty and reproach that a carpenter uses to a gentleman who has picked up an ax: "We are used to it, but you, sir, will blister your hands." He spoke as if those bullets could not kill him, and his half-closed eyes gave still more persuasiveness to his words. The staff officer joined in the colonel's appeals, but Bagratión did not reply; he only gave an order to cease firing and re-form, so as to give room for the two approaching battalions. While he was speaking, the curtain of smoke that had concealed the hollow, driven by a rising wind, began to move from right to left as if drawn by an invisible hand, and the hill opposite, with the French moving about on it, opened out before them. All eyes fastened involuntarily on this French column advancing against them and winding down over the uneven ground. One could already see the soldiers' shaggy caps, distinguish the officers from the men, and see the standard flapping against its staff.

"They march splendidly," remarked someone in Bagratión's suite.

The head of the column had already descended into the hollow. The clash would take place on this side of it. . . .

The remains of our regiment which had been in action rapidly formed up and moved to the right; from behind it, dispersing the laggards, came two battalions of the Sixth Chasseurs in fine order. Before they had reached Bagratión, the weighty tread of the mass of men marching in step could be heard. On their left flank, nearest to Bagratión, marched a company commander, a fine round-faced man, with a stupid and happy expression—the same man who had rushed out of the wattle shed. At that moment he was clearly thinking of nothing but how dashing a fellow he would appear as he passed the commander.

With the self-satisfaction of a man on parade, he stepped lightly with his muscular legs as if sailing along, stretching himself to his full height without the smallest effort, his ease contrasting with the heavy tread of the soldiers who were keeping step with him. He carried close to his leg a narrow unsheathed sword (small, curved, and not like a real weapon) and looked now at the superior officers and now back at the men without losing step, his whole powerful body turning flexibly. It was as if all the powers of his soul were concentrated on passing the commander in the best possible manner, and feeling that he was doing it well he was happy. "Left . . . left . . . left . . ." he seemed to repeat to himself at each alternate step; and in time to this, with stern but varied faces, the wall of soldiers burdened with knapsacks and muskets marched in step, and each one of these hundreds of soldiers seemed to be repeating to himself at each alternate step, "Left . . . left . . . left . . ." A fat major skirted a bush, puffing and falling out of step; a soldier who had fallen behind, his face showing alarm at his defection, ran at a trot, panting to catch up with his company. A cannon ball, cleaving the air, flew over the heads of Bagratión and his suite, and fell into the column to the measure of "Left . . . left!" "Close up!" came the company commander's voice in jaunty tones. The soldiers passed in a semicircle round something where the ball had fallen, and an old trooper on the flank, a noncommissioned officer who had stopped beside the dead men, ran to catch up his line and, falling into step with a hop, looked back angrily, and through the ominous silence and the regular tramp of feet beating the ground in unison, one seemed to hear left . . . left . . . left.

"Well done, lads!" said Prince Bagratión.

"Glad to do our best, your ex'len-lency!" came a confused shout from the ranks. A morose soldier marching on the left turned his eyes on Bagratión as he shouted, with an expression that seemed to say: "We know that

ourselves!" Another, without looking round, as though fearing to relax, shouted with his mouth wide open and passed on.

The order was given to halt and down knapsacks.

Bagratión rode round the ranks that had marched past him and dismounted. He gave the reins to a Cossack, took off and handed over his felt coat, stretched his legs, and set his cap straight. The head of the French column, with its officers leading, appeared from below the hill.

"Forward, with God!" said Bagratión, in a resolute, sonorous voice, turning for a moment to the front line, and slightly swinging his arms, he went forward uneasily over the rough field with the awkward gait of a cavalryman. Prince Andrew felt that an invisible power was leading him forward, and experienced great happiness.

The French were already near. Prince Andrew, walking beside Bagratión, could clearly distinguish their bandoliers, red epaulets, and even their faces. (He distinctly saw an old French officer who, with gaitered legs and turned-out toes, climbed the hill with difficulty.) Prince Bagratión gave no further orders and silently continued to walk on in front of the ranks. Suddenly one shot after another rang out from the French, smoke appeared all along their uneven ranks, and musket shots sounded. Several of our men fell, among them the round-faced officer who had marched so gaily and complacently. But at the moment the first report was heard, Bagratión looked round and shouted, "Hurrah!"

"Hurrah—ah!—ah!" rang a long-drawn shout from our ranks, and passing Bagratión and racing one another they rushed in an irregular but joyous and eager crowd down the hill at their disordered foe.*

The attack of the Sixth Chasseurs secured the retreat of our right flank. In the center Túshin's forgotten battery, which had managed to set fire to the Schön Grabern village, delayed the French advance. The French were putting out the fire which the wind was spreading, and thus gave us time to retreat. The retirement of the center to the other side of the dip in the ground at the rear was hurried and noisy, but the different companies did not get mixed. But our left—which consisted of the Azóv and Podólsk infantry and the Pávlograd hussars—was simultaneously attacked and outflanked by superior French forces under Lannes and was thrown into con-

* This was the attack of which Thiers says: "The Russians behaved courageously and, what seldom happens in war, two bodies of infantry were seen marching resolutely against one another without either of them giving way before meeting." And Napoleon at St. Helena said: "Some Russian battalions showed entire fearlessness."—A.M.

fusion. Bagratión had sent Zherkóv to the general commanding that left flank with orders to retreat immediately.

Zherkóv, not removing his hand from his cap, turned his horse about and galloped off. But no sooner had he left Bagratión than his courage failed him. He was seized by panic and could not go where it was dangerous.

Having reached the left flank, instead of going to the front where the firing was, he began to look for the general and his staff where they could not possibly be, and so did not deliver the order.

The command of the left flank belonged by seniority to the commander of the regiment Kutúzov had reviewed at Braunau and in which Dólokhov was serving as a private. But the command of the extreme left flank had been assigned to the commander of the Pávlograd regiment in which Rostóv was serving, and a misunderstanding arose. The two commanders were much exasperated with one another and long after the action had begun on the right flank and the French were already advancing were engaged in discussion with the sole object of offending one another. But the regiments, both cavalry and infantry, were by no means ready for the impending action. From privates to general they were not expecting a battle and were engaged in peaceful occupations, the cavalry feeding the horses and the infantry collecting wood.

"He higher iss dan I in rank," said the German colonel of the hussars, flushing and addressing an adjutant who had ridden up, "so let him do vhat he vill, but I cannot sacrifice my hussars . . . Bugler, sount ze retreat!"

But haste was becoming imperative. Cannon and musketry, mingling together, thundered on the right and in the center, while the capotes of Lannes' sharpshooters were already seen crossing the milldam and forming up within twice the range of a musket shot. The general in command of the infantry went toward his horse with jerky steps, and having mounted drew himself up very straight and tall and rode to the Pávlograd commander. The commanders met with polite bows but with secret malevolence in their hearts.

"Once again, Colonel," said the general, "I can't leave half my men in the wood. I beg of you, I beg of you," he repeated, "to occupy the position and prepare for an attack."

"I peg of you yourself not to mix in vot is not your pusiness!" suddenly replied the irate colonel. "If you vere in the cavalry . . ."

"I am not in the cavalry, Colonel, but I am a Russian general and if you are not aware of the fact . . ."

"Quite avare, your excellency," suddenly shouted the colonel, touching

his horse and turning purple in the face. "Vill you be so goot to come to ze front and see dat zis position iss no goot? I don't vish to desstroy my men for your pleasure!"

"You forget yourself, Colonel. I am not considering my own pleasure and I won't allow it to be said!"

Taking the colonel's outburst as a challenge to his courage, the general expanded his chest and rode, frowning, beside him to the front line, as if their differences would be settled there amongst the bullets. They reached the front, several bullets sped over them, and they halted in silence. There was nothing fresh to be seen from the line, for from where they had been before it had been evident that it was impossible for cavalry to act among the bushes and broken ground, as well as that the French were outflanking our left. The general and colonel looked sternly and significantly at one another like two fighting cocks preparing for battle, each vainly trying to detect signs of cowardice in the other. Both passed the examination successfully. As there was nothing to be said, and neither wished to give occasion for it to be alleged that he had been the first to leave the range of fire, they would have remained there for a long time testing each other's courage had it not been that just then they heard the rattle of musketry and a muffled shout almost behind them in the wood. The French had attacked the men collecting wood in the copse. It was no longer possible for the hussars to retreat with the infantry. They were cut off from the line of retreat on the left by the French. However inconvenient the position, it was now necessary to attack in order to cut a way through for themselves.

The squadron in which Rostóv was serving had scarcely time to mount before it was halted facing the enemy. Again, as at the Enns bridge, there was nothing between the squadron and the enemy, and again that terrible dividing line of uncertainty and fear—resembling the line separating the living from the dead—lay between them. All were conscious of this unseen line, and the question whether they would cross it or not, and how they would cross it, agitated them all.

The colonel rode to the front, angrily gave some reply to questions put to him by the officers, and, like a man desperately insisting on having his own way, gave an order. No one said anything definite, but the rumor of an attack spread through the squadron. The command to form up rang out and the sabers whizzed as they were drawn from their scabbards. Still no one moved. The troops of the left flank, infantry and hussars alike, felt that the commander did not himself know what to do, and this irresolution communicated itself to the men.

"If only they would be quick!" thought Rostóv, feeling that at last the

time had come to experience the joy of an attack of which he had so often heard from his fellow hussars.

"Fo'ward, with God, lads!" rang out Denísov's voice. "At a twot fo'-ward!"

The horses' croups began to sway in the front line. Rook pulled at the reins and started of his own accord.

Before him, on the right, Rostóv saw the front lines of his hussars and still farther ahead a dark line which he could not see distinctly but took to be the enemy. Shots could be heard, but some way off.

"Faster!" came the word of command, and Rostóv felt Rook's flanks drooping as he broke into a gallop.

Rostóv anticipated his horse's movements and became more and more elated. He had noticed a solitary tree ahead of him. This tree had been in the middle of the line that had seemed so terrible—and now he had crossed that line and not only was there nothing terrible, but everything was becoming more and more happy and animated. "Oh, how I will slash at him!" thought Rostóv, gripping the hilt of his saber.

"Hur-a-a-a-ah!" came a roar of voices. "Let anyone come my way now," thought Rostóv driving his spurs into Rook and letting him go at a full gallop so that he outstripped the others. Ahead, the enemy was already visible. Suddenly something like a birch broom seemed to sweep over the squadron. Rostóv raised his saber, ready to strike, but at that instant the trooper Nikítenko, who was galloping ahead, shot away from him, and Rostóv felt as in a dream that he continued to be carried forward with unnatural speed but yet stayed on the same spot. From behind him Bondarchúk, an hussar he knew, jolted against him and looked angrily at him. Bondarchúk's horse swerved and galloped past.

"How is it I am not moving? I have fallen, I am killed!" Rostóv asked and answered at the same instant. He was alone in the middle of a field. Instead of the moving horses and hussars' backs, he saw nothing before him but the motionless earth and the stubble around him. There was warm blood under his arm. "No, I am wounded and the horse is killed." Rook tried to rise on his forelegs but fell back, pinning his rider's leg. Blood was flowing from his head; he struggled but could not rise. Rostóv also tried to rise but fell back, his sabretache having become entangled in the saddle. Where our men were, and where the French, he did not know. There was no one near.

Having disentangled his leg, he rose. "Where, on which side, was now the line that had so sharply divided the two armies?" he asked himself and could not answer. "Can something bad have happened to me?" he

wondered as he got up: and at that moment he felt that something super-
fluous was hanging on his benumbed left arm. The wrist felt as if it were
not his. He examined his hand carefully, vainly trying to find blood on it.
"Ah, here are people coming," he thought joyfully, seeing some men run-
ning toward him. "They will help me!" In front came a man wearing a
strange shako and a blue cloak, swarthy, sunburned, and with a hooked
nose. Then came two more, and many more running behind. One of them
said something strange, not in Russian. In among the hindmost of these
men wearing similar shakos was a Russian hussar. He was being held by
the arms and his horse was being led behind him.

"It must be one of ours, a prisoner. Yes. Can it be that they will take
me too? Who are these men?" thought Rostóv, scarcely believing his eyes.
"Can they be French?" He looked at the approaching Frenchmen, and
though but a moment before he had been galloping to get at them and
hack them to pieces, their proximity now seemed so awful that he could
not believe his eyes. "Who are they? Why are they running? Can they
be coming at me? And why? To kill me? Me whom everyone is so fond
of?" He remembered his mother's love for him, and his family's, and his
friends', and the enemy's intention to kill him seemed impossible. "But
perhaps they may do it!" For more than ten seconds he stood not moving
from the spot or realizing the situation. The foremost Frenchman, the
one with the hooked nose, was already so close that the expression of his
face could be seen. And the excited, alien face of that man, his bayonet
hanging down, holding his breath, and running so lightly, frightened
Rostóv. He seized his pistol and, instead of firing it, flung it at the French-
man and ran with all his might toward the bushes. He did not now run
with the feeling of doubt and conflict with which he had trodden the
Enns bridge, but with the feeling of a hare fleeing from the hounds.
One single sentiment, that of fear for his young and happy life, pos-
sessed his whole being. Rapidly leaping the furrows, he fled across the
field with the impetuosity he used to show at catchplay, now and then
turning his good-natured, pale, young face to look back. A shudder of
terror went through him: "No, better not look," he thought, but having
reached the bushes he glanced round once more. The French had fallen
behind, and just as he looked round the first man changed his run to a
walk and, turning, shouted something loudly to a comrade farther back.
Rostóv paused. "No, there's some mistake," thought he. "They can't
have wanted to kill me." But at the same time, his left arm felt as heavy
as if a seventy-pound weight were tied to it. He could run no more. The
Frenchman also stopped and took aim. Rostóv closed his eyes and stooped

down. One bullet and then another whistled past him. He mustered his last remaining strength, took hold of his left hand with his right, and reached the bushes. Behind these were some Russian sharpshooters.

15. Panic. Timókhin's counterattack. Dólokhov's insistence. Túshin's battery. Prince Andrew sent to order him to retreat

THE INFANTRY regiments that had been caught unawares in the outskirts of the wood ran out of it, the different companies getting mixed, and retreated as a disorderly crowd. One soldier, in his fear, uttered the senseless cry, "Cut off!" that is so terrible in battle, and that word infected the whole crowd with a feeling of panic.

"Surrounded! Cut off! We're lost!" shouted the fugitives.

The moment he heard the firing and the cry from behind, the general realized that something dreadful had happened to his regiment, and the thought that he, an exemplary officer of many years' service who had never been to blame, might be held responsible at headquarters for negligence or inefficiency so staggered him that, forgetting the recalcitrant cavalry colonel, his own dignity as a general, and above all quite forgetting the danger and all regard for self-preservation, he clutched the crupper of his saddle and, spurring his horse, galloped to the regiment under a hail of bullets which fell around, but fortunately missed him. His one desire was to know what was happening and at any cost correct, or remedy, the mistake if he had made one, so that he, an exemplary officer of twenty-two years' service, who had never been censured, should not be held to blame.

Having galloped safely through the French, he reached a field behind the copse across which our men, regardless of orders, were running and descending the valley. That moment of moral hesitation which decides the fate of battles had arrived. Would this disorderly crowd of soldiers attend to the voice of their commander, or would they, disregarding him, continue their flight? Despite his desperate shouts that used to seem so terrible to the soldiers, despite his furious purple countenance distorted out of all likeness to his former self, and the flourishing of his saber, the soldiers all continued to run, talking, firing into the air, and disobeying orders. The moral hesitation which decided the fate of battles was evidently culminating in a panic.

The general had a fit of coughing as a result of shouting and of the powder smoke and stopped in despair. Everything seemed lost. But at that moment the French who were attacking, suddenly and without any ap-

parent reason, ran back and disappeared from the outskirts, and Russian sharpshooters showed themselves in the copse. It was Timókhin's company, which alone had maintained its order in the wood and, having lain in ambush in a ditch, now attacked the French unexpectedly. Timókhin, armed only with a sword, had rushed at the enemy with such a desperate cry and such mad, drunken determination that, taken by surprise, the French had thrown down their muskets and run. Dólokhov, running beside Timókhin, killed a Frenchman at close quarters and was the first to seize the surrendering French officer by his collar. Our fugitives returned, the battalions re-formed, and the French who had nearly cut our left flank in half were for the moment repulsed. Our reserve units were able to join up, and the fight was at an end. The regimental commander and Major Ekonómov had stopped beside a bridge, letting the retreating companies pass by them, when a soldier came up and took hold of the commander's stirrup, almost leaning against him. The man was wearing a bluish coat of broadcloth, he had no knapsack or cap, his head was bandaged, and over his shoulder a French munition pouch was slung. He had an officer's sword in his hand. The soldier was pale, his blue eyes looked impudently into the commander's face, and his lips were smiling. Though the commander was occupied in giving instructions to Major Ekonómov, he could not help taking notice of the soldier.

"Your excellency, here are two trophies," said Dólokhov, pointing to the French sword and pouch. "I have taken an officer prisoner. I stopped the company." Dólokhov breathed heavily from weariness and spoke in abrupt sentences. "The whole company can bear witness. I beg you will remember this, your excellency!"

"All right, all right," replied the commander, and turned to Major Ekonómov.

But Dólokhov did not go away; he untied the handkerchief around his head, pulled it off, and showed the blood congealed on his hair.

"A bayonet wound. I remained at the front. Remember, your excellency!"

Túshin's battery had been forgotten and only at the very end of the action did Prince Bagratión, still hearing the cannonade in the center, send his orderly staff officer, and later Prince Andrew also, to order the battery to retire as quickly as possible. When the supports attached to Túshin's battery had been moved away in the middle of the action by someone's order, the battery had continued firing and was only not captured by the French because the enemy could not surmise that anyone could have the effrontery to continue firing from four quite undefended

guns. On the contrary, the energetic action of that battery led the French to suppose that here—in the center—the main Russian forces were concentrated. Twice they had attempted to attack this point, but on each occasion had been driven back by grapeshot from the four isolated guns on the hillock.

Soon after Prince Bagratión had left him, Túshin had succeeded in setting fire to Schön Grabern.

"Look at them scurrying! It's burning! Just see the smoke! Fine! Grand! Look at the smoke, the smoke!" exclaimed the artillerymen, brightening up.

All the guns, without waiting for orders, were being fired in the direction of the conflagration. As if urging each other on, the soldiers cried at each shot: "Fine! That's good! Look at it . . . Grand!" The fire, fanned by the breeze, was rapidly spreading. The French columns that had advanced beyond the village went back; but as though in revenge for this failure, the enemy placed ten guns to the right of the village and began firing them at Túshin's battery.

In their childlike glee, aroused by the fire and their luck in successfully cannonading the French, our artillerymen only noticed this battery when two balls, and then four more, fell among our guns, one knocking over two horses and another tearing off a munition-wagon driver's leg. Their spirits once roused were, however, not diminished, but only changed character. The horses were replaced by others from a reserve gun carriage, the wounded were carried away, and the four guns were turned against the ten-gun battery. Túshin's companion officer had been killed at the beginning of the engagement and within an hour seventeen of the forty men of the guns' crews had been disabled, but the artillerymen were still as merry and lively as ever. Twice they noticed the French appearing below them, and then they fired grapeshot at them.

Little Túshin, moving feebly and awkwardly, kept telling his orderly to "refill my pipe for that one!" and then, scattering sparks from it, ran forward shading his eyes with his small hand to look at the French.

"Smack at 'em, lads!" he kept saying, seizing the guns by the wheels and working the screws himself.

Amid the smoke, deafened by the incessant reports which always made him jump, Túshin not taking his pipe from his mouth ran from gun to gun, now aiming, now counting the charges, now giving orders about replacing dead or wounded horses and harnessing fresh ones, and shouting in his feeble voice, so high-pitched and irresolute. His face grew more and more animated. Only when a man was killed or wounded did he frown and turn away from the sight, shouting angrily at the men who,

as is always the case, hesitated about lifting the injured or dead. The soldiers, for the most part handsome fellows and, as is always the case in an artillery company, a head and shoulders taller and twice as broad as their officer—all looked at their commander like children in an embarrassing situation, and the expression on his face was invariably reflected on theirs.

Owing to the terrible uproar and the necessity for concentration and activity, Túshin did not experience the slightest unpleasant sense of fear, and the thought that he might be killed or badly wounded never occurred to him. On the contrary, he became more and more elated. It seemed to him that it was a very long time ago, almost a day, since he had first seen the enemy and fired the first shot, and that the corner of the field he stood on was well-known and familiar ground. Though he thought of everything, considered everything, and did everything the best of officers could do in his position, he was in a state akin to feverish delirium or drunkenness.

From the deafening sounds of his own guns around him, the whistle and thud of the enemy's cannon balls, from the flushed and perspiring faces of the crew bustling round the guns, from the sight of the blood of men and horses, from the little puffs of smoke on the enemy's side (always followed by a ball flying past and striking the earth, a man, a gun, a horse), from the sight of all these things a fantastic world of his own had taken possession of his brain and at that moment afforded him pleasure. The enemy's guns were in his fancy not guns but pipes from which occasional puffs were blown by an invisible smoker.

"There . . . he's puffing again," muttered Túshin to himself, as a small cloud rose from the hill and was borne in a streak to the left by the wind.

"Now look out for the ball . . . we'll throw it back."

"What do you want, your honor?" asked an artilleryman, standing close by, who heard him muttering.

"Nothing . . . only a shell . . ." he answered.

"Come along, our Matvévna!" he said to himself. "Matvévna" [daughter of Matthew] was the name his fancy gave to the farthest gun of the battery, which was large and of an old pattern. The French swarming round their guns seemed to him like ants. In that world, the handsome drunkard Number One of the second gun's crew was "uncle"; Túshin looked at him more often than at anyone else and took delight in his every movement. The sound of musketry at the foot of the hill, now diminishing, now increasing, seemed like someone's breathing. He listened intently to the ebb and flow of these sounds.

"Ah! Breathing again, breathing!" he muttered to himself.

He imagined himself as an enormously tall, powerful man who was throwing cannon balls at the French with both hands.

"Now then, Matvévna, dear old lady, don't let me down!" he was saying as he moved from the gun, when a strange, unfamiliar voice called above his head: "Captain Túshin! Captain!"

Túshin turned round in dismay. It was the staff officer who had turned him out of the booth at Grunth. He was shouting in a gasping voice:

"Are you mad? You have twice been ordered to retreat, and you . . ."

"Why are they down on me?" thought Túshin, looking in alarm at his superior.

"I . . . don't . . ." he muttered, holding up two fingers to his cap. "I . . ."

But the staff officer did not finish what he wanted to say. A cannon ball, flying close to him, caused him to duck and bend over his horse. He paused, and just as he was about to say something more, another ball stopped him. He turned his horse and galloped off.

"Retire! All to retire!" he shouted from a distance.

The soldiers laughed. A moment later, an adjutant arrived with the same order.

It was Prince Andrew. The first thing he saw on riding up to the space where Túshin's guns were stationed was an unharnessed horse with a broken leg, that lay screaming piteously beside the harnessed horses. Blood was gushing from its leg as from a spring. Among the limbers lay several dead men. One ball after another passed over as he approached and he felt a nervous shudder run down his spine. But the mere thought of being afraid roused him again. "I cannot be afraid," thought he, and dismounted slowly among the guns. He delivered the order and did not leave the battery. He decided to have the guns removed from their positions and withdrawn in his presence. Together with Túshin, stepping across the bodies and under a terrible fire from the French, he attended to the removal of the guns.

"A staff officer was here a minute ago, but skipped off," said an artilleryman to Prince Andrew. "Not like your honor!"

Prince Andrew said nothing to Túshin. They were both so busy as to seem not to notice one another. When having limbered up the only two cannon that remained uninjured out of the four, they began moving down the hill (one shattered gun and one unicorn * were left behind), Prince Andrew rode up to Túshin.

* The "unicorn," like all other guns of the period, was a smooth-bore muzzle-loader, but was peculiar in the way it narrowed toward the muzzle.— A.M.

"Well, till we meet again . . ." he said, holding out his hand to Túshin.
"Good-by, my dear fellow," said Túshin. "Dear soul! Good-by, my
dear fellow!" and for some unknown reason tears suddenly filled his eyes.

16. *Withdrawal of the forces. Nicholas rides on a gun*
carriage. Túshin called to account by Bagratión.
Prince Andrew defends him. Nicholas'
depression

THE WIND had fallen and black clouds, merging with the powder
smoke, hung low over the field of battle on the horizon. It was
growing dark and the glow of two conflagrations was the more conspicu-
ous. The cannonade was dying down, but the rattle of musketry behind
and on the right sounded oftener and nearer. As soon as Túshin with his
guns, continually driving round or coming upon wounded men, was out
of range of fire and had descended into the dip, he was met by some of
the staff, among them the staff officer and Zherkóv, who had been twice
sent to Túshin's battery but had never reached it. Interrupting one
another, they all gave, and transmitted, orders as to how to proceed,
reprimanding and reproaching him. Túshin gave no orders, and silently
—fearing to speak because at every word he felt ready to weep without
knowing why—rode behind on his artillery nag. Though the orders were
to abandon the wounded, many of them dragged themselves after the
troops and begged for seats on the gun carriages. The jaunty infantry
officer who just before the battle had rushed out of Túshin's wattle shed
was laid, with a bullet in his stomach, on "Matvévna's" carriage. At the
foot of the hill, a pale hussar cadet, supporting one hand with the other,
came up to Túshin and asked for a seat.

"Captain, for God's sake! I've hurt my arm," he said timidly. "For
God's sake . . . I can't walk. For God's sake!"

It was plain that this cadet had already repeatedly asked for a lift and
been refused. He asked in a hesitating, piteous voice.

"Tell them to give me a seat, for God's sake!"

"Give him a seat," said Túshin. "Lay a cloak for him to sit on, lad,"
he said, addressing his favorite soldier. "And where is the wounded officer?"

"He has been set down. He died," replied someone.

"Help him up. Sit down, dear fellow, sit down! Spread out the cloak,
Antónov."

The cadet was Rostóv. With one hand he supported the other; he was
pale and his jaw trembled, shivering feverishly. He was placed on "Mat-

vévna," the gun from which they had removed the dead officer. The cloak they spread under him was wet with blood which stained his breeches and arm.

"What, are you wounded, my lad?" said Túshin, approaching the gun on which Rostóv sat.

"No, it's a sprain."

"Then what is this blood on the gun carriage?" inquired Túshin.

"It was the officer, your honor, stained it," answered the artilleryman, wiping away the blood with his coat sleeve, as if apologizing for the state of his gun.

It was all that they could do to get the guns up the rise aided by the infantry, and having reached the village of Gruntersdorf they halted. It had grown so dark that one could not distinguish the uniforms ten paces off, and the firing had begun to subside. Suddenly, near by on the right, shouting and firing were again heard. Flashes of shot gleamed in the darkness. This was the last French attack and was met by soldiers who had sheltered in the village houses. They all rushed out of the village again, but Túshin's guns could not move, and the artillerymen, Túshin, and the cadet exchanged silent glances as they awaited their fate. The firing died down and soldiers, talking eagerly, streamed out of a side street.

"Not hurt, Petróv?" asked one.

"We've given it 'em hot, mate! They won't make another push now," said another.

"You couldn't see a thing. How they shot at their own fellows! Nothing could be seen. Pitch-dark, brother! Isn't there something to drink?"

The French had been repulsed for the last time. And again and again in the complete darkness Túshin's guns moved forward, surrounded by the humming infantry as by a frame.

In the darkness, it seemed as though a gloomy unseen river was flowing always in one direction, humming with whispers and talk and the sound of hoofs and wheels. Amid the general rumble, the groans and voices of the wounded were more distinctly heard than any other sound in the darkness of the night. The gloom that enveloped the army was filled with their groans, which seemed to melt into one with the darkness of the night. After a while the moving mass became agitated, someone rode past on a white horse followed by his suite, and said something in passing: "What did he say? Where to, now? Halt, is it? Did he thank us?" came eager questions from all sides. The whole moving mass began pressing closer together and a report spread that they were ordered to halt: evidently those in front had halted. All remained where they were in the middle of the muddy road.

Fires were lighted and the talk became more audible. Captain Túshin, having given orders to his company, sent a soldier to find a dressing station or a doctor for the cadet, and sat down by a bonfire the soldiers had kindled on the road. Rostóv, too, dragged himself to the fire. From pain, cold, and damp, a feverish shivering shook his whole body. Drowsiness was irresistibly mastering him, but he was kept awake by an excruciating pain in his arm, for which he could find no satisfactory position. He kept closing his eyes and then again looking at the fire, which seemed to him dazzlingly red, and at the feeble, round-shouldered figure of Túshin who was sitting cross-legged like a Turk beside him. Túshin's large, kind, intelligent eyes were fixed with sympathy and commiseration on Rostóv, who saw that Túshin with his whole heart wished to help him but could not.

From all sides were heard the footsteps and talk of the infantry, who were walking, driving past, and settling down all around. The sound of voices, the tramping feet, the horses' hoofs moving in mud, the crackling of wood fires near and afar, merged into one tremulous rumble.

It was no longer, as before, a dark, unseen river flowing through the gloom, but a dark sea swelling and gradually subsiding after a storm. Rostóv looked at and listened listlessly to what passed before and around him. An infantryman came to the fire, squatted on his heels, held his hands to the blaze, and turned away his face.

"You don't mind, your honor?" he asked Túshin. "I've lost my company, your honor. I don't know where . . . such bad luck!"

With the soldier, an infantry officer with a bandaged cheek came up to the bonfire, and addressing Túshin asked him to have the guns moved a trifle to let a wagon go past. After he had gone, two soldiers rushed to the campfire. They were quarreling and fighting desperately, each trying to snatch from the other a boot they were both holding on to.

"You picked it up? . . . I dare say! You're very smart!" one of them shouted hoarsely.

Then a thin, pale soldier, his neck bandaged with a bloodstained leg band, came up and in angry tones asked the artillerymen for water.

"Must one die like a dog?" said he.

Túshin told them to give the man some water. Then a cheerful soldier ran up, begging a little fire for the infantry.

"A nice little hot torch for the infantry! Good luck to you, fellow countrymen. Thanks for the fire—we'll return it with interest," said he, carrying away into the darkness a glowing stick.

Next came four soldiers, carrying something heavy on a cloak, and passed by the fire. One of them stumbled.

"Who the devil has put the logs on the road?" snarled he.

"He's dead—why carry him?" said another.

"Shut up!"

And they disappeared into the darkness with their load.

"Still aching?" Túshin asked Rostóv in a whisper.

"Yes."

"Your honor, you're wanted by the general. He is in the hut here," said a gunner, coming up to Túshin.

"Coming, friend."

Túshin rose and, buttoning his greatcoat and pulling it straight, walked away from the fire.

Not far from the artillery campfire, in a hut that had been prepared for him, Prince Bagratión sat at dinner, talking with some commanding officers who had gathered at his quarters. The little old man with the half-closed eyes was there greedily gnawing a mutton bone, and the general who had served blamelessly for twenty-two years, flushed by a glass of vodka and the dinner; and the staff officer with the signet ring, and Zherkóv, uneasily glancing at them all, and Prince Andrew, pale, with compressed lips and feverishly glittering eyes.

In a corner of the hut stood a standard captured from the French, and the accountant with the naïve face was feeling its texture, shaking his head in perplexity—perhaps because the banner really interested him, perhaps because it was hard for him, hungry as he was, to look on at a dinner where there was no place for him. In the next hut there was a French colonel who had been taken prisoner by our dragoons. Our officers were flocking in to look at him. Prince Bagratión was thanking the individual commanders and inquiring into details of the action and our losses. The general whose regiment had been inspected at Braunau was informing the prince that as soon as the action began he had withdrawn from the wood, mustered the men who were woodcutting, and, allowing the French to pass him, had made a bayonet charge with two battalions and had broken up the French troops.

"When I saw, your excellency, that their first battalion was disorganized, I stopped in the road and thought: 'I'll let them come on and will meet them with the fire of the whole battalion'—and that's what I did."

The general had so wished to do this and was so sorry he had not managed to do it that it seemed to him as if it had really happened. Perhaps it might really have been so? Could one possibly make out amid all that confusion what did or did not happen?

"By the way, your excellency, I should inform you," he continued—remembering Dólokhov's conversation with Kutúzov and his last interview with the gentleman-ranker—"that Private Dólokhov, who was re-

duced to the ranks, took a French officer prisoner in my presence and particularly distinguished himself."

"I saw the Pávlograd hussars attack there, your excellency," chimed in Zherkóv, looking uneasily around. He had not seen the hussars all that day, but had heard about them from an infantry officer. "They broke up two squares, your excellency."

Several of those present smiled at Zherkóv's words, expecting one of his usual jokes, but noticing that what he was saying redounded to the glory of our arms and of the day's work, they assumed a serious expression, though many of them knew that what he was saying was a lie devoid of any foundation. Prince Bagratión turned to the old colonel:

"Gentlemen, I thank you all; all arms have behaved heroically: infantry, cavalry, and artillery. How was it that two guns were abandoned in the center?" he inquired, searching with his eyes for someone. (Prince Bagratión did not ask about the guns on the left flank; he knew that all the guns there had been abandoned at the very beginning of the action.) "I think I sent you?" he added, turning to the staff officer on duty.

"One was damaged," answered the staff officer, "and the other I can't understand. I was there all the time giving orders and had only just left. . . . It is true that it was hot there," he added, modestly.

Someone mentioned that Captain Túshin was bivouacking close to the village and had already been sent for.

"Oh, but you were there?" said Prince Bagratión, addressing Prince Andrew.

"Of course, we only just missed one another," said the staff officer, with a smile to Bolkónski.

"I had not the pleasure of seeing you," said Prince Andrew, coldly and abruptly.

All were silent. Túshin appeared at the threshold and made his way timidly from behind the backs of the generals. As he stepped past the generals in the crowded hut, feeling embarrassed as he always was by the sight of his superiors, he did not notice the staff of the banner and stumbled over it. Several of those present laughed.

"How was it a gun was abandoned?" asked Bagratión, frowning, not so much at the captain as at those who were laughing, among whom Zherkóv laughed loudest.

Only now, when he was confronted by the stern authorities, did his guilt and the disgrace of having lost two guns and yet remaining alive present themselves to Túshin in all their horror. He had been so excited that he had not thought about it until that moment. The officers' laughter confused him still more. He stood before Bagratión with his lower jaw

trembling and was hardly able to mutter: "I don't know . . . your excellency . . . I had no men . . . your excellency."

"You might have taken some from the covering troops."

Túshin did not say that there were no covering troops, though that was perfectly true. He was afraid of getting some other officer into trouble, and silently fixed his eyes on Bagratión as a schoolboy who has blundered looks at an examiner.

The silence lasted some time. Prince Bagratión, apparently not wishing to be severe, found nothing to say; the others did not venture to intervene. Prince Andrew looked at Túshin from under his brows and his fingers twitched nervously.

"Your excellency!" Prince Andrew broke the silence with his abrupt voice, "you were pleased to send me to Captain Túshin's battery. I went there and found two thirds of the men and horses knocked out, two guns smashed, and no supports at all."

Prince Bagratión and Túshin looked with equal intentness at Bolkónski, who spoke with suppressed agitation.

"And, if your excellency will allow me to express my opinion," he continued, "we owe today's success chiefly to the action of that battery and the heroic endurance of Captain Túshin and his company," and without awaiting a reply, Prince Andrew rose and left the table.

Prince Bagratión looked at Túshin, evidently reluctant to show distrust in Bolkónski's emphatic opinion yet not feeling able fully to credit it, bent his head, and told Túshin that he could go. Prince Andrew went out with him.

"Thank you; you saved me, my dear fellow!" said Túshin.

Prince Andrew gave him a look, but said nothing and went away. He felt sad and depressed. It was all so strange, so unlike what he had hoped.

"Who are they? Why are they here? What do they want? And when will all this end?" thought Rostóv, looking at the changing shadows before him. The pain in his arm became more and more intense. Irresistible drowsiness overpowered him, red rings danced before his eyes, and the impression of those voices and faces and a sense of loneliness merged with the physical pain. It was they, these soldiers—wounded and unwounded— it was they who were crushing, weighing down, and twisting the sinews and scorching the flesh of his sprained arm and shoulder. To rid himself of them, he closed his eyes.

For a moment he dozed, but in that short interval innumerable things appeared to him in a dream: his mother and her large white hand, Sónya's thin little shoulders, Natásha's eyes and laughter, Denísov with his voice

and mustache, and Telyánin and all that affair with Telyánin and Bog-dánich. That affair was the same thing as this soldier with the harsh voice, and it was that affair and this soldier that were so agonizingly, incessantly pulling and pressing his arm and always dragging it in one direction. He tried to get away from them, but they would not for an instant let his shoulder move a hair's breadth. It would not ache—it would be well—if only they did not pull it, but it was impossible to get rid of them.

He opened his eyes and looked up. The black canopy of night hung less than a yard above the glow of the charcoal. Flakes of falling snow were fluttering in that light. Túshin had not returned, the doctor had not come. He was alone now, except for a soldier who was sitting naked at the other side of the fire, warming his thin yellow body.

"Nobody wants me!" thought Rostóv. "There is no one to help me or pity me. Yet I was once at home, strong, happy, and loved." He sighed and, doing so, groaned involuntarily.

"Eh, is anything hurting you?" asked the soldier, shaking his shirt out over the fire, and not waiting for an answer he gave a grunt and added: "What a lot of men have been crippled today—frightful!"

Rostóv did not listen to the soldier. He looked at the snowflakes fluttering above the fire and remembered a Russian winter at his warm, bright home, his fluffy fur coat, his quickly gliding sleigh, his healthy body, and all the affection and care of his family. "And why did I come here?" he wondered.

Next day the French army did not renew their attack, and the remnant of Bagratión's detachment was reunited to Kutúzov's army.

BOOK THREE

DATES OF PRINCIPAL HISTORICAL EVENTS

1805

OLD STYLE	NEW STYLE	
Nov. 19	Dec. 1	The Council of War at Ostralitz.
Nov. 20	Dec. 2	Battle of Austerlitz.

1805

1. Prince Vasíli and Pierre. A soiree at Anna Pávlovna's. Hélène's name day. Pierre's marriage

PRINCE VASÍLI was not a man who deliberately thought out his plans. Still less did he think of injuring anyone for his own advantage. He was merely a man of the world who had got on and to whom getting on had become a habit. Schemes and devices for which he never rightly accounted to himself, but which formed the whole interest of his life, were constantly shaping themselves in his mind, arising from the circumstances and persons he met. Of these plans he had not merely one or two in his head but dozens, some only beginning to form themselves, some approaching achievement, and some in course of disintegration. He did not, for instance, say to himself: "This man now has influence, I must gain his confidence and friendship and through him obtain a special grant." Nor did he say to himself: "Pierre is a rich man, I must entice him to marry my daughter and lend me the forty thousand rubles I need." But when he came across a man of position his instinct immediately told him that this man could be useful, and without any premeditation Prince Vasíli took the first opportunity to gain his confidence, flatter him, become intimate with him, and finally make his request.

He had Pierre at hand in Moscow and procured for him an appointment as Gentleman of the Bedchamber, which at that time conferred the status of Councilor of State,* and insisted on the young man accompanying him to Petersburg and staying at his house. With apparent absentmindedness, yet with unhesitating assurance that he was doing the right thing, Prince Vasíli did everything to get Pierre to marry his daughter. Had he thought out his plans beforehand he could not have been so natural and shown such unaffected familiarity in intercourse with every-

* A less important functionary than the title in English suggests. It was the fifth of the eleven classes in which all officials, civil or military, were ranged.— A.M.

body both above and below him in social standing. Something always drew him toward those richer and more powerful than himself and he had rare skill in seizing the most opportune moment for making use of people.

Pierre, on unexpectedly becoming Count Bezúkhov and a rich man, felt himself after his recent loneliness and freedom from cares so beset and preoccupied that only in bed was he able to be by himself. He had to sign papers, to present himself at government offices, the purpose of which was not clear to him, to question his chief steward, to visit his estate near Moscow, and to receive many people who formerly did not even wish to know of his existence but would now have been offended and grieved had he chosen not to see them. These different people—businessmen, relations, and acquaintances alike—were all disposed to treat the young heir in the most friendly and flattering manner: they were all evidently firmly convinced of Pierre's noble qualities. He was always hearing such words as: "With your remarkable kindness," or, "With your excellent heart," "You are yourself so honorable, Count," or, "Were he as clever as you," and so on, till he began sincerely to believe in his own exceptional kindness and extraordinary intelligence, the more so as in the depth of his heart it had always seemed to him that he really was very kind and intelligent. Even people who had formerly been spiteful toward him and evidently unfriendly now became gentle and affectionate. The angry eldest princess, with the long waist and hair plastered down like a doll's, had come into Pierre's room after the funeral. With drooping eyes and frequent blushes she told him she was very sorry about their past misunderstandings and did not now feel she had a right to ask him for anything, except only for permission, after the blow she had received, to remain for a few weeks longer in the house she so loved and where she had sacrificed so much. She could not refrain from weeping at these words. Touched that this statuesque princess could so change, Pierre took her hand and begged her forgiveness, without knowing what for. From that day the eldest princess quite changed toward Pierre and began knitting a striped scarf for him.

"Do this for my sake, mon cher; after all, she had to put up with a great deal from the deceased," said Prince Vasíli to him, handing him a deed to sign for the princess' benefit.

Prince Vasíli had come to the conclusion that it was necessary to throw this bone—a bill for thirty thousand rubles—to the poor princess that it might not occur to her to speak of his share in the affair of the inlaid portfolio. Pierre signed the deed and after that the princess grew still kinder. The younger sisters also became affectionate to him, especially

the youngest, the pretty one with the mole, who often made him feel confused by her smiles and her own confusion when meeting him.

It seemed so natural to Pierre that everyone should like him, and it would have seemed so unnatural had anyone disliked him, that he could not but believe in the sincerity of those around him. Besides, he had no time to ask himself whether these people were sincere or not. He was always busy and always felt in a state of mild and cheerful intoxication. He felt as though he were the center of some important and general movement; that something was constantly expected of him, that if he did not do it he would grieve and disappoint many people, but if he did this and that, all would be well; and he did what was demanded of him, but still that happy result always remained in the future.

More than anyone else, Prince Vasíli took possession of Pierre's affairs and of Pierre himself in those early days. From the death of Count Bezúkhov he did not let go his hold of the lad. He had the air of a man oppressed by business, weary and suffering, who yet would not, for pity's sake, leave this helpless youth who, after all, was the son of his old friend and the possessor of such enormous wealth, to the caprice of fate and the designs of rogues. During the few days he spent in Moscow after the death of Count Bezúkhov, he would call Pierre, or go to him himself, and tell him what ought to be done in a tone of weariness and assurance, as if he were adding every time: "You know I am overwhelmed with business and it is purely out of charity that I trouble myself about you, and you also know quite well that what I propose is the only thing possible."

"Well, my dear fellow, tomorrow we are off at last," said Prince Vasíli one day, closing his eyes and fingering Pierre's elbow, speaking as if he were saying something which had long since been agreed upon and could not now be altered. "We start tomorrow and I'm giving you a place in my carriage. I am very glad. All our important business here is now settled, and I ought to have been off long ago. Here is something I have received from the chancellor. I asked him for you, and you have been entered in the diplomatic corps and made a Gentleman of the Bedchamber. The diplomatic career now lies open before you."

Notwithstanding the tone of wearied assurance with which these words were pronounced, Pierre, who had so long been considering his career, wished to make some suggestion. But Prince Vasíli interrupted him in the special deep cooing tone, precluding the possibility of interrupting his speech, which he used in extreme cases when special persuasion was needed.

"Mais, mon cher, I did this for my own sake, to satisfy my conscience, and there is nothing to thank me for. No one has ever complained yet of

being too much loved; and besides, you are free, you could throw it up tomorrow. But you will see everything for yourself when you get to Petersburg. It is high time for you to get away from these terrible recollections." Prince Vasíli sighed. "Yes, yes, my boy. And my valet can go in your carriage. Ah! I was nearly forgetting," he added. "You know, mon cher, your father and I had some accounts to settle, so I have received what was due from the Ryazán estate and will keep it; you won't require it. We'll go into the accounts later."

By "what was due from the Ryazán estate" Prince Vasíli meant several thousand rubles quitrent received from Pierre's peasants, which the prince had retained for himself.

In Petersburg, as in Moscow, Pierre found the same atmosphere of gentleness and affection. He could not refuse the post, or rather the rank (for he did nothing), that Prince Vasíli had procured for him, and acquaintances, invitations, and social occupations were so numerous that, even more than in Moscow, he felt a sense of bewilderment, bustle, and continual expectation of some good, always in front of him but never attained.

Of his former bachelor acquaintances many were no longer in Petersburg. The Guards had gone to the front; Dólokhov had been reduced to the ranks; Anatole was in the army somewhere in the provinces; Prince Andrew was abroad; so Pierre had not the opportunity to spend his nights as he used to like to spend them, or to open his mind by intimate talks with a friend older than himself and whom he respected. His whole time was taken up with dinners and balls and was spent chiefly at Prince Vasíli's house in the company of the stout princess, his wife, and his beautiful daughter Hélène.

Like the others, Anna Pávlovna Schérer showed Pierre the change of attitude toward him that had taken place in society.

Formerly in Anna Pávlovna's presence, Pierre had always felt that what he was saying was out of place, tactless and unsuitable, that remarks which seemed to him clever while they formed in his mind became foolish as soon as he uttered them, while on the contrary Hippolyte's stupidest remarks came out clever and apt. Now everything Pierre said was charmant. Even if Anna Pávlovna did not say so, he could see that she wished to and only refrained out of regard for his modesty.

In the beginning of the winter of 1805-6 Pierre received one of Anna Pávlovna's usual pink notes with an invitation to which was added: "You will find the beautiful Hélène here, whom it is always delightful to see."

When he read that sentence, Pierre felt for the first time that some link which other people recognized had grown up between himself and

Hélène, and that thought both alarmed him, as if some obligation were being imposed on him which he could not fulfill, and pleased him as an entertaining supposition.

Anna Pávlovna's "At Home" was like the former one, only the novelty she offered her guests this time was not Mortemart, but a diplomatist fresh from Berlin with the very latest details of the Emperor Alexander's visit to Potsdam, and of how the two august friends had pledged themselves in an indissoluble alliance to uphold the cause of justice against the enemy of the human race.* Anna Pávlovna received Pierre with a shade of melancholy, evidently relating to the young man's recent loss by the death of Count Bezúkhov (everyone constantly considered it a duty to assure Pierre that he was greatly afflicted by the death of the father he had hardly known), and her melancholy was just like the august melancholy she showed at the mention of her most august Majesty the Empress Márya Fëdorovna. Pierre felt flattered by this. Anna Pávlovna arranged the different groups in her drawing room with her habitual skill. The large group, in which were Prince Vasíli and the generals, had the benefit of the diplomat. Another group was at the tea table. Pierre wished to join the former, but Anna Pávlovna—who was in the excited condition of a commander on a battlefield to whom thousands of new and brilliant ideas occur which there is hardly time to put in action—seeing Pierre, touched his sleeve with her finger, saying:

"Wait a bit, I have something in view for you this evening." (She glanced at Hélène and smiled at her.) "My dear Hélène, be charitable to my poor aunt who adores you. Go and keep her company for ten minutes. And that it will not be too dull, here is the dear count who will not refuse to accompany you."

The beauty went to the aunt, but Anna Pávlovna detained Pierre, looking as if she had to give some final necessary instructions.

"Isn't she exquisite?" she said to Pierre, pointing to the stately beauty as she glided away. "And how she carries herself! For so young a girl, such tact, such masterly perfection of manner! It comes from her heart. Happy the man who wins her! With her the least worldly of men would occupy a most brilliant position in society. Don't you think so? I only wanted to know your opinion," and Anna Pávlovna let Pierre go.

Pierre, in reply, sincerely agreed with her as to Hélène's perfection of manner. If he ever thought of Hélène, it was just of her beauty and her remarkable skill in appearing silently dignified in society.

* *This was one of the strangest scenes in history. The German and Russian Emperors took an oath of eternal mutual fealty before the tomb of Frederick the Great.*

The old aunt received the two young people in her corner, but seemed desirous of hiding her adoration for Hélène and inclined rather to show her fear of Anna Pávlovna. She looked at her niece, as if inquiring what she was to do with these people. On leaving them, Anna Pávlovna again touched Pierre's sleeve, saying: "I hope you won't say that it is dull in my house again," and she glanced at Hélène.

Hélène smiled, with a look implying that she did not admit the possibility of anyone seeing her without being enchanted. The aunt coughed, swallowed, and said in French that she was very pleased to see Hélène, then she turned to Pierre with the same words of welcome and the same look. In the middle of a dull and halting conversation, Hélène turned to Pierre with the beautiful bright smile that she gave to everyone. Pierre was so used to that smile, and it had so little meaning for him, that he paid no attention to it. The aunt was just speaking of a collection of snuff-boxes that had belonged to Pierre's father, Count Bezúkhov, and showed them her own box. Princess Hélène asked to see the portrait of the aunt's husband on the box lid.

"That is probably the work of Vinesse," said Pierre, mentioning a celebrated miniaturist, and he leaned over the table to take the snuffbox while trying to hear what was being said at the other table.

He half rose, meaning to go round, but the aunt handed him the snuffbox, passing it across Hélène's back. Hélène stooped forward to make room, and looked round with a smile. She was, as always at evening parties, wearing a dress such as was then fashionable, cut very low at front and back. Her bust, which had always seemed like marble to Pierre, was so close to him that his shortsighted eyes could not but perceive the living charm of her neck and shoulders, so near to his lips that he need only have bent his head a little to have touched them. He was conscious of the warmth of her body, the scent of perfume, and the creaking of her corset as she moved. He did not see her marble beauty forming a complete whole with her dress, but all the charm of her body only covered by her garments. And having once seen this he could not help being aware of it, just as we cannot renew an illusion we have once seen through.

"So you have never noticed before how beautiful I am?" Hélène seemed to say. "You had not noticed that I am a woman? Yes, I am a woman who may belong to anyone—to you too," said her glance. And at that moment Pierre felt that Hélène not only could, but must, be his wife, and that it could not be otherwise.

He knew this at that moment as surely as if he had been standing at the altar with her. How and when this would be he did not know, he did

not even know if it would be a good thing (he even felt, he knew not why, that it would be a bad thing), but he knew it would happen.

Pierre dropped his eyes, lifted them again, and wished once more to see her as a distant beauty far removed from him, as he had seen her every day until then, but he could no longer do it. He could not, any more than a man who has been looking at a tuft of steppe grass through the mist and taking it for a tree can again take it for a tree after he has once recognized it to be a tuft of grass. She was terribly close to him. She already had power over him, and between them there was no longer any barrier except the barrier of his own will.

"Well, I will leave you in your little corner," came Anna Pávlovna's voice, "I see you are all right there."

And Pierre, anxiously trying to remember whether he had done anything reprehensible, looked round with a blush. It seemed to him that everyone knew what had happened to him as he knew it himself.

A little later when he went up to the large circle, Anna Pávlovna said to him: "I hear you are refitting your Petersburg house?"

This was true. The architect had told him that it was necessary, and Pierre, without knowing why, was having his enormous Petersburg house done up.

"That's a good thing, but don't move from Prince Vasíli's. It is good to have a friend like the prince," she said, smiling at Prince Vasíli. "I know something about that. Don't I? And you are still so young. You need advice. Don't be angry with me for exercising an old woman's privilege." She paused, as women always do, expecting something after they have mentioned their age. "If you marry it will be a different thing," she continued, uniting them both in one glance. Pierre did not look at Hélène nor she at him. But she was just as terribly close to him. He muttered something and colored.

When he got home he could not sleep for a long time for thinking of what had happened. What had happened? Nothing. He had merely understood that the woman he had known as a child, of whom when her beauty was mentioned he had said absent-mindedly: "Yes, she's good-looking," he had understood that this woman might belong to him.

"But she's stupid. I have myself said she is stupid," he thought. "There is something nasty, something wrong, in the feeling she excites in me. I have been told that her brother Anatole was in love with her and she with him, that there was quite a scandal and that that's why he was sent away. Hippolyte is her brother . . . Prince Vasíli is her father . . . It's bad. . . ." he reflected, but while he was thinking this (the reflection was still incomplete), he caught himself smiling and was conscious that

another line of thought had sprung up, and while thinking of her worthlessness he was also dreaming of how she would be his wife, how she would love him and become quite different, and how all he had thought and heard of her might be false. And he again saw her not as the daughter of Prince Vasíli, but visualized her whole body only veiled by its gray dress. "But no! Why did this thought never occur to me before?" and again he told himself that it was impossible, that there would be something unnatural, and as it seemed to him dishonorable, in this marriage. He recalled her former words and looks and the words and looks of those who had seen them together. He recalled Anna Pávlovna's words and looks when she spoke to him about his house, recalled thousands of such hints from Prince Vasíli and others, and was seized by terror lest he had already, in some way, bound himself to do something that was evidently wrong and that he ought not to do. But at the very time he was expressing this conviction to himself, in another part of his mind her image rose in all its womanly beauty.

In November, 1805, Prince Vasíli had to go on a tour of inspection in four different provinces. He had arranged this for himself so as to visit his neglected estates at the same time and pick up his son Anatole where his regiment was stationed, and take him to visit Prince Nicholas Bolkónski in order to arrange a match for him with the daughter of that rich old man. But before leaving home and undertaking these new affairs, Prince Vasíli had to settle matters with Pierre, who, it is true, had latterly spent whole days at home, that is, in Prince Vasíli's house where he was staying, and had been absurd, excited, and foolish in Hélène's presence (as a lover should be), but had not yet proposed to her.

"This is all very fine, but things must be settled," said Prince Vasíli to himself, with a sorrowful sigh, one morning, feeling that Pierre who was under such obligations to him ("But never mind that") was not behaving very well in this matter. "Youth, frivolity . . . well, God be with him," thought he, relishing his own goodness of heart, "but it must be brought to a head. The day after tomorrow will be Lëlya's * name day. I will invite two or three people, and if he does not understand what he ought to do then it will be my affair—yes, my affair. I am her father."

Six weeks after Anna Pávlovna's "At Home" and after the sleepless night when he had decided that to marry Hélène would be a calamity and that he ought to avoid her and go away, Pierre, despite that decision, had not left Prince Vasíli's and felt with terror that in people's eyes he was every day more and more connected with her, that it was impossible

* Lëlya, a pet name for Hélène.—A.M.

for him to return to his former conception of her, that he could not break away from her, and that though it would be a terrible thing he would have to unite his fate with hers. He might perhaps have been able to free himself but that Prince Vasíli (who had rarely before given receptions) now hardly let a day go by without having an evening party at which Pierre had to be present unless he wished to spoil the general pleasure and disappoint everyone's expectation. Prince Vasíli, in the rare moments when he was at home, would take Pierre's hand in passing and draw it downwards, or absent-mindedly hold out his wrinkled, clean-shaven cheek for Pierre to kiss and would say: "Till tomorrow," or, "Be in to dinner or I shall not see you," or, "I am staying in for your sake," and so on. And though Prince Vasíli, when he stayed in (as he said) for Pierre's sake, hardly exchanged a couple of words with him, Pierre felt unable to disappoint him. Every day he said to himself one and the same thing: "It is time I understood her and made up my mind what she really is. Was I mistaken before, or am I mistaken now? No, she is not stupid, she is an excellent girl," he sometimes said to himself, "she never makes a mistake, never says anything stupid. She says little, but what she does say is always clear and simple, so she is not stupid. She never was abashed and is not abashed now, so she cannot be a bad woman!" He had often begun to make reflections or think aloud in her company, and she had always answered him either by a brief but appropriate remark—showing that it did not interest her—or by a silent look and smile which more palpably than anything else showed Pierre her superiority. She was right in regarding all arguments as nonsense in comparison with that smile.

She always addressed him with a radiantly confiding smile meant for him alone, in which there was something more significant than in the general smile that usually brightened her face. Pierre knew that everyone was waiting for him to say a word and cross a certain line, and he knew that sooner or later he would step across it, but an incomprehensible terror seized him at the thought of that dreadful step. A thousand times during that month and a half while he felt himself drawn nearer and nearer to that dreadful abyss, Pierre said to himself: "What am I doing? I need resolution. Can it be that I have none?"

He wished to take a decision, but felt with dismay that in this matter he lacked that strength of will which he had known in himself and really possessed. Pierre was one of those who are only strong when they feel themselves quite innocent, and since that day when he was overpowered by a feeling of desire while stooping over the snuffbox at Anna Pávlovna's, an unacknowledged sense of the guilt of that desire paralyzed his will.

On Hélène's name day, a small party of just their own people—as his

wife said—met for supper at Prince Vasíli's. All these friends and relations had been given to understand that the fate of the young girl would be decided that evening. The visitors were seated at supper. Princess Kurágina, a portly imposing woman who had once been handsome, was sitting at the head of the table. On either side of her sat the more important guests— an old general and his wife, and Anna Pávlovna Schérer. At the other end sat the younger and less important guests, and there too sat the members of the family, and Pierre and Hélène, side by side. Prince Vasíli was not having any supper: he went round the table in a merry mood, sitting down now by one, now by another, of the guests. To each of them he made some careless and agreeable remark except to Pierre and Hélène, whose presence he seemed not to notice. He enlivened the whole party. The wax candles burned brightly, the silver and crystal gleamed, so did the ladies' toilets and the gold and silver of the men's epaulets; servants in scarlet liveries moved round the table, and the clatter of plates, knives, and glasses mingled with the animated hum of several conversations. At one end of the table, the old chamberlain was heard assuring an old baroness that he loved her passionately, at which she laughed; at the other could be heard the story of the misfortunes of some Mary Víkto-rovna or other. At the center of the table, Prince Vasíli attracted every-body's attention. With a facetious smile on his face, he was telling the ladies about last Wednesday's meeting of the Imperial Council, at which Sergéy Kuzmích Vyazmítinov, the new military governor general of Petersburg, had received and read the then famous rescript of the Emperor Alexander from the army to Sergéy Kuzmích, in which the Em-peror said that he was receiving from all sides declarations of the people's loyalty, that the declaration from Petersburg gave him particular pleasure, and that he was proud to be at the head of such a nation and would endeavor to be worthy of it. This rescript began with the words: "Sergéy Kuzmích, From all sides reports reach me," etc.

"Well, and so he never got farther than: 'Sergéy Kuzmích'?" asked one of the ladies.

"Exactly, not a hair's breadth farther," answered Prince Vasíli, laugh-ing, " 'Sergéy Kuzmích . . . From all sides . . . From all sides . . . Ser-géy Kuzmích . . .' Poor Vyazmítinov could not get any farther. He began the rescript again and again, but as soon as he uttered 'Sergéy' he sobbed, 'Kuz-mí-ch,' tears, and 'From all sides' was smothered in sobs and he could get no farther. And again his handkerchief, and again: 'Sergéy Kuzmích, From all sides,' . . . and tears, till at last somebody else was asked to read it."

"Kuzmích . . . From all sides . . . and then tears," someone repeated laughing.

"Don't be unkind," cried Anna Pávlovna from her end of the table holding up a threatening finger. "He is such a worthy and excellent man, our dear Vyazmítinov. . . ."

Everybody laughed a great deal. At the head of the table, where the honored guests sat, everyone seemed to be in high spirits and under the influence of a variety of exciting sensations. Only Pierre and Hélène sat silently side by side almost at the bottom of the table, a suppressed smile brightening both their faces, a smile that had nothing to do with Sergéy Kuzmích—a smile of bashfulness at their own feelings. But much as all the rest laughed, talked, and joked, much as they enjoyed their Rhine wine, sauté, and ices, and however they avoided looking at the young couple, and heedless and unobservant as they seemed of them, one could feel by the occasional glances they gave that the story about Sergéy Kuzmích, the laughter and the food, were all a pretense, and that the whole attention of that company was directed to—Pierre and Hélène. Prince Vasíli mimicked the sobbing of Sergéy Kuzmích and at the same time his eyes glanced toward his daughter, and while he laughed the expression on his face clearly said: "Yes . . . it's getting on, it will all be settled today." Anna Pávlovna threatened him on behalf of "our dear Vyazmítinov," and in her eyes, which, for an instant, glanced at Pierre, Prince Vasíli read a congratulation on his future son-in-law and on his daughter's happiness. The old princess sighed sadly as she offered some wine to the old lady next to her and glanced angrily at her daughter, and her sigh seemed to say: "Yes, there's nothing left for you and me but to sip sweet wine, my dear, now that the time has come for these young ones to be thus boldly, provocatively happy." "And what nonsense all this is that I am saying!" thought a diplomatist, glancing at the happy faces of the lovers. "That's happiness?"

Into the insignificant, trifling, and artificial interests uniting that society had entered the simple feeling of the attraction of a healthy and handsome young man and woman for one another. And this human feeling dominated everything else and soared above all their affected chatter. Jests fell flat, news was not interesting, and the animation was evidently forced. Not only the guests but even the footmen waiting at table seemed to feel this, and they forgot their duties as they looked at the beautiful Hélène with her radiant face and at the red, broad, and happy though uneasy face of Pierre. It seemed as if the very light of the candles was focused on those two happy faces alone.

Pierre felt that he was the center of it all, and this both pleased and

embarrassed him. He was like a man entirely absorbed in some occupation. He did not see, hear, or understand anything clearly. Only now and then detached ideas and impressions from the world of reality shot unexpectedly through his mind.

"So it is all finished!" he thought. "And how has it all happened? How quickly! Now I know that not because of her alone, nor of myself alone, but because of everyone, *it* must inevitably come about. They are all expecting *it*, they are so sure that it will happen that I cannot, I cannot, disappoint them. But how will it be? I do not know, but it will certainly happen!" thought Pierre, glancing at those dazzling shoulders close to his eyes.

Or he would suddenly feel ashamed of he knew not what. He felt it awkward to attract everyone's attention and to be considered a lucky man and, with his plain face, to be looked on as a sort of Paris possessed of a Helen. "But no doubt it always is and must be so!" he consoled himself. "And besides, what have I done to bring it about? How did it begin? I traveled from Moscow with Prince Vasíli. Then there was nothing. So why should I not stay at his house? Then I played cards with her and picked up her reticule and drove out with her. How did it begin, when did it all come about?" And here he was sitting by her side as her betrothed, seeing, hearing, feeling her nearness, her breathing, her movements, her beauty. Then it would suddenly seem to him that it was not she but he who was so unusually beautiful, and that that was why they all looked so at him, and flattered by this general admiration he would expand his chest, raise his head, and rejoice at his good fortune. Suddenly he heard a familiar voice repeating something to him a second time. But Pierre was so absorbed that he did not understand what was said.

"I am asking you when you last heard from Bolkónski," repeated Prince Vasíli a third time. "How absent-minded you are, my dear fellow."

Prince Vasíli smiled, and Pierre noticed that everyone was smiling at him and Hélène. "Well, what of it, if you all know it?" thought Pierre. "What of it? It's the truth!" and he himself smiled his gentle childlike smile, and Hélène smiled too.

"When did you get the letter? Was it from Olmütz?" repeated Prince Vasíli, who pretended to want to know this in order to settle a dispute.

"How can one talk or think of such trifles?" thought Pierre.

"Yes, from Olmütz," he answered, with a sigh.

After supper Pierre with his partner followed the others into the drawing room. The guests began to disperse, some without taking leave of Hélène. Some, as if unwilling to distract her from an important occupation, came up to her for a moment and made haste to go away, refusing

to let her see them off. The diplomatist preserved a mournful silence as he left the drawing room. He pictured the vanity of his diplomatic career in comparison with Pierre's happiness. The old general grumbled at his wife when she asked how his leg was. "Oh, the old fool," he thought. "That Princess Hélène will be beautiful still when she's fifty."

"I think I may congratulate you," whispered Anna Pávlovna to the old princess, kissing her soundly. "If I hadn't this headache I'd have stayed longer."

The old princess did not reply, she was tormented by jealousy of her daughter's happiness.

While the guests were taking their leave, Pierre remained for a long time alone with Hélène in the little drawing room where they were sitting. He had often before, during the last six weeks, remained alone with her, but had never spoken to her of love. Now he felt that it was inevitable, but he could not make up his mind to take the final step. He felt ashamed; he felt that he was occupying someone else's place here beside Hélène. "This happiness is not for you," some inner voice whispered to him. "This happiness is for those who have not in them what there is in you."

But, as he had to say something, he began by asking her whether she was satisfied with the party. She replied in her usual simple manner that this name day of hers had been one of the pleasantest she had ever had.

Some of the nearest relatives had not yet left. They were sitting in the large drawing room. Prince Vasíli came up to Pierre with languid footsteps. Pierre rose and said it was getting late. Prince Vasíli gave him a look of stern inquiry, as though what Pierre had just said was so strange that one could not take it in. But then the expression of severity changed, and he drew Pierre's hand downwards, made him sit down, and smiled affectionately.

"Well, Lëlya?" he asked, turning instantly to his daughter and addressing her with the careless tone of habitual tenderness natural to parents who have petted their children from babyhood, but which Prince Vasíli had only acquired by imitating other parents.

And he again turned to Pierre.

"Sergéy Kuzmích—From all sides—" he said, unbuttoning the top button of his waistcoat.

Pierre smiled, but his smile showed that he knew it was not the story about Sergéy Kuzmích that interested Prince Vasíli just then, and Prince Vasíli saw that Pierre knew this. He suddenly muttered something and went away. It seemed to Pierre that even the prince was disconcerted. The sight of the discomposure of that old man of the world touched

Pierre: he looked at Hélène and she too seemed disconcerted, and her look seemed to say: "Well, it is your own fault."

"The step must be taken but I cannot, I cannot!" thought Pierre, and he again began speaking about indifferent matters, about Sergéy Kuzmích, asking what the point of the story was as he had not heard it properly. Hélène answered with a smile that she too had missed it.

When Prince Vasíli returned to the drawing room, the princess, his wife, was talking in low tones to the elderly lady about Pierre.

"Of course, it is a very brilliant match, but happiness, my dear . . ."

"Marriages are made in heaven," replied the elderly lady.

Prince Vasíli passed by, seeming not to hear the ladies, and sat down on a sofa in a far corner of the room. He closed his eyes and seemed to be dozing. His head sank forward and then he roused himself.

"Aline," he said to his wife, "go and see what they are about."

The princess went up to the door, passed by it with a dignified and indifferent air, and glanced into the little drawing room. Pierre and Hélène still sat talking just as before.

"Still the same," she said to her husband.

Prince Vasíli frowned, twisting his mouth, his cheeks quivered and his face assumed the coarse, unpleasant expression peculiar to him. Shaking himself, he rose, threw back his head, and with resolute steps went past the ladies into the little drawing room. With quick steps he went joyfully up to Pierre. His face was so unusually triumphant that Pierre rose in alarm on seeing it.

"Thank God!" said Prince Vasíli. "My wife has told me everything!" —(He put one arm around Pierre and the other around his daughter.)— "My dear boy . . . Lëlya . . . I am very pleased." (His voice trembled.) "I loved your father . . . and she will make you a good wife . . . God bless you! . . ."

He embraced his daughter, and then again Pierre, and kissed him with his malodorous mouth. Tears actually moistened his cheeks.

"Princess, come here!" he shouted.

The old princess came in and also wept. The elderly lady was using her handkerchief too. Pierre was kissed, and he kissed the beautiful Hélène's hand several times. After a while they were left alone again.

"All this had to be and could not be otherwise," thought Pierre, "so it is useless to ask whether it is good or bad. It is good because it's definite and one is rid of the old tormenting doubt." Pierre held the hand of his betrothed in silence, looking at her beautiful bosom as it rose and fell.

"Hélène!" he said aloud and paused.

"Something special is always said in such cases," he thought, but

could not remember what it was that people say. He looked at her face. She drew nearer to him. Her face flushed.

"Oh, take those off . . . those . . ." she said, pointing to his spectacles.

Pierre took them off, and his eyes, besides the strange look eyes have from which spectacles have just been removed, had also a frightened and inquiring look. He was about to stoop over her hand and kiss it, but with a rapid, almost brutal movement of her head, she intercepted his lips and met them with her own. Her face struck Pierre, by its altered, unpleasantly excited expression.

"It is too late now, it's done; besides I love her," thought Pierre.

"Je vous aime!" he said, remembering what has to be said at such moments: but his words sounded so weak that he felt ashamed of himself.

Six weeks later he was married, and settled in Count Bezúkhov's large, newly furnished Petersburg house, the happy possessor, as people said, of a wife who was a celebrated beauty and of millions of money.

2. *Prince Vasíli and Anatole visit Prince N. A. Bolkónski. Princess Mary's appearance*

OLD PRINCE NICHOLAS BOLKÓNSKI received a letter from Prince Vasíli in November, 1805, announcing that he and his son would be paying him a visit. "I am starting on a journey of inspection, and of course I shall think nothing of an extra seventy miles to come and see you at the same time, my honored benefactor," wrote Prince Vasíli. "My son Anatole is accompanying me on his way to the army, so I hope you will allow him personally to express the deep respect that, emulating his father, he feels for you."

"It seems that there will be no need to bring Mary out, suitors are coming to us of their own accord," incautiously remarked the little princess on hearing the news.

Prince Nicholas frowned, but said nothing.

A fortnight after the letter Prince Vasíli's servants came one evening in advance of him, and he and his son arrived next day.

Old Bolkónski had always had a poor opinion of Prince Vasíli's character, but more so recently, since in the new reigns of Paul and Alexander Prince Vasíli had risen to high position and honors. And now, from the hints contained in his letter and given by the little princess, he saw which way the wind was blowing, and his low opinion changed into a feeling of contemptuous ill will. He snorted whenever he mentioned him. On the

day of Prince Vasíli's arrival, Prince Bolkónski was particularly discontented and out of temper. Whether he was in a bad temper because Prince Vasíli was coming, or whether his being in a bad temper made him specially annoyed at Prince Vasíli's visit, he was in a bad temper, and in the morning Tíkhon had already advised the architect not to go to the prince with his report.

"Do you hear how he's walking?" said Tíkhon, drawing the architect's attention to the sound of the prince's footsteps. "Stepping flat on his heels—we know what that means. . . ."

However, at nine o'clock the prince, in his velvet coat with a sable collar and cap, went out for his usual walk. It had snowed the day before and the path to the hothouse, along which the prince was in the habit of walking, had been swept: the marks of the broom were still visible in the snow and a shovel had been left sticking in one of the soft snowbanks that bordered both sides of the path. The prince went through the conservatories, the serfs' quarters, and the outbuildings, frowning and silent.

"Can a sleigh pass?" he asked his overseer, a venerable man, resembling his master in manners and looks, who was accompanying him back to the house.

"The snow is deep. I am having the avenue swept, your honor."

The prince bowed his head and went up to the porch. "God be thanked," thought the overseer, "the storm has blown over!"

"It would have been hard to drive up, your honor," he added. "I heard, your honor, that a minister is coming to visit your honor."

The prince turned round to the overseer and fixed his eyes on him, frowning.

"What? A minister? What minister? Who gave orders?" he said in his shrill, harsh voice. "The road is not swept for the princess my daughter, but for a minister! For me, there are no ministers!"

"Your honor, I thought . . ."

"You thought!" shouted the prince, his words coming more and more rapidly and indistinctly. "You thought! . . . Rascals! Blackguards! . . . I'll teach you to think!" and lifting his stick he swung it and would have hit Alpátych, the overseer, had not the latter instinctively avoided the blow. "Thought . . . Blackguards . . ." shouted the prince rapidly.

But although Alpátych, frightened at his own temerity in avoiding the stroke, came up to the prince, bowing his bald head resignedly before him, or perhaps for that very reason, the prince, though he continued to shout: "Blackguards! . . . Throw the snow back on the road!" did not lift his stick again but hurried into the house.

Before dinner, Princess Mary and Mademoiselle Bourienne, who knew

that the prince was in a bad humor, stood awaiting him; Mademoiselle Bourienne with a radiant face that said: "I know nothing, I am the same as usual," and Princess Mary, pale, frightened, and with downcast eyes. What she found hardest to bear was to know that on such occasions she ought to behave like Mademoiselle Bourienne, but could not. She thought: "If I seem not to notice he will think that I do not sympathize with him; if I seem sad and out of spirits myself, he will say (as he has done before) that I'm in the dumps."

The prince looked at his daughter's frightened face and snorted.

"Fool . . . or dummy!" he muttered.

. "And the other one is not here. They've been telling tales," he thought —referring to the little princess who was not in the dining room.

"Where is the princess?" he asked. "Hiding?"

"She is not very well," answered Mademoiselle Bourienne with a bright smile, "so she won't come down. It is natural in her state."

"Hm! Hm!" muttered the prince, sitting down.

His plate seemed to him not quite clean, and pointing to a spot he flung it away. Tíkhon caught it and handed it to a footman. The little princess was not unwell, but had such an overpowering fear of the prince that, hearing he was in a bad humor, she had decided not to appear.

"I am afraid for the baby," she said to Mademoiselle Bourienne: "Heaven knows what a fright might do."

In general at Bald Hills the little princess lived in constant fear, and with a sense of antipathy to the old prince which she did not realize because the fear was so much the stronger feeling. The prince reciprocated this antipathy, but it was overpowered by his contempt for her. When the little princess had grown accustomed to life at Bald Hills, she took a special fancy to Mademoiselle Bourienne, spent whole days with her, asked her to sleep in her room, and often talked with her about the old prince and criticized him.

"So we are to have visitors, mon prince?" remarked Mademoiselle Bourienne, unfolding her white napkin with her rosy fingers. "His Excellency Prince Vasíli Kurágin and his son, I understand?" she said inquiringly.

"Hm!—his excellency is a puppy. . . . I got him his appointment in the service," said the prince disdainfully. "Why his son is coming I don't understand. Perhaps Princess Elizabeth and Princess Mary know. I don't want him." (He looked at his blushing daughter.) "Are you unwell today? Eh? Afraid of the 'minister' as that idiot Alpátych called him this morning?"

"No, mon père."

Though Mademoiselle Bourienne had been so unsuccessful in her choice of a subject, she did not stop talking, but chattered about the conservatories and the beauty of a flower that had just opened, and after the soup the prince became more genial.

After dinner, he went to see his daughter-in-law. The little princess was sitting at a small table, chattering with Másha, her maid. She grew pale on seeing her father-in-law.

She was much altered. She was now plain rather than pretty. Her cheeks had sunk, her lip was drawn up, and her eyes drawn down.

"Yes, I feel a kind of oppression," she said in reply to the prince's question as to how she felt.

"Do you want anything?"

"No, merci, mon père."

"Well, all right, all right."

He left the room and went to the waiting room where Alpátych stood with bowed head.

"Has the snow been shoveled back?"

"Yes, your excellency. Forgive me for heaven's sake . . . It was only my stupidity."

"All right, all right," interrupted the prince, and laughing in his unnatural way, he stretched out his hand for Alpátych to kiss, and then proceeded to his study.

Prince Vasíli arrived that evening. He was met in the avenue by coachmen and footmen, who, with loud shouts, dragged his sleighs up to one of the lodges over the road purposely laden with snow.

Prince Vasíli and Anatole had separate rooms assigned to them.

Anatole, having taken off his overcoat, sat with arms akimbo before a table on a corner of which he smilingly and absent-mindedly fixed his large and handsome eyes. He regarded his whole life as a continual round of amusement which someone for some reason had to provide for him. And he looked on this visit to a churlish old man and a rich and ugly heiress in the same way. All this might, he thought, turn out very well and amusingly. "And why not marry her if she really has so much money? That never does any harm," thought Anatole.

He shaved and scented himself with the care and elegance which had become habitual to him and, his handsome head held high, entered his father's room with the good-humored and victorious air natural to him. Prince Vasíli's two valets were busy dressing him, and he looked round with much animation and cheerfully nodded to his son as the latter entered, as if to say: "Yes, that's how I want you to look."

"I say, Father, joking apart, is she very hideous?" Anatole asked, as if

continuing a conversation the subject of which had often been mentioned during the journey.

"Enough! What nonsense! Above all, try to be respectful and cautious with the old prince."

"If he starts a row I'll go away," said Prince Anatole. "I can't bear those old men! Eh?"

"Remember, for you everything depends on this."

In the meantime, not only was it known in the maidservants' rooms that the minister and his son had arrived, but the appearance of both had been minutely described. Princess Mary was sitting alone in her room, vainly trying to master her agitation.

"Why did they write, why did Lise tell me about it? It can never happen!" she said, looking at herself in the glass. "How shall I enter the drawing room? Even if I like him I can't now be myself with him." The mere thought of her father's look filled her with terror. The little princess and Mademoiselle Bourienne had already received from Másha, the lady's maid, the necessary report of how handsome the minister's son was, with his rosy cheeks and dark eyebrows, and with what difficulty the father had dragged his legs upstairs while the son had followed him like an eagle, three steps at a time. Having received this information, the little princess and Mademoiselle Bourienne, whose chattering voices had reached her from the corridor, went into Princess Mary's room.

"You know they've come, Marie?" said the little princess, waddling in, and sinking heavily into an armchair.

She was no longer in the loose gown she generally wore in the morning, but had on one of her best dresses. Her hair was carefully done and her face was animated, which, however, did not conceal its sunken and faded outlines. Dressed as she used to be in Petersburg society, it was still more noticeable how much plainer she had become. Some unobtrusive touch had been added to Mademoiselle Bourienne's toilet which rendered her fresh and pretty face yet more attractive.

"What! Are you going to remain as you are, dear princess?" she began. "They'll be announcing that the gentlemen are in the drawing room and we shall have to go down, and you have not smartened yourself up at all!"

The little princess got up, rang for the maid, and hurriedly and merrily began to devise and carry out a plan of how Princess Mary should be dressed. Princess Mary's self-esteem was wounded by the fact that the arrival of a suitor agitated her, and still more so by both her companions' not having the least conception that it could be otherwise. To tell them that she felt ashamed for herself and for them would be to betray her agitation, while to decline their offers to dress her would prolong their

banter and insistence. She flushed, her beautiful eyes grew dim, red blotches came on her face, and it took on the unattractive martyrlike expression it so often wore, as she submitted herself to Mademoiselle Bourienne and Lise. Both these women *quite sincerely* tried to make her look pretty. She was so plain that neither of them could think of her as a rival, so they began dressing her with perfect sincerity, and with the naïve and firm conviction women have that dress can make a face pretty.

"No really, my dear, this dress is not pretty," said Lise, looking sideways at Princess Mary from a little distance. "You have a maroon dress, have it fetched. Really! You know the fate of your whole life may be at stake. But this one is too light, it's not becoming!"

It was not the dress, but the face and whole figure of Princess Mary that was not pretty, but neither Mademoiselle Bourienne nor the little princess felt this; they still thought that if a blue ribbon were placed in the hair, the hair combed up, and the blue scarf arranged lower on the best maroon dress, and so on, all would be well. They forgot that the frightened face and the figure could not be altered, and that however they might change the setting and adornment of that face, it would still remain piteous and plain. After two or three changes to which Princess Mary meekly submitted, just as her hair had been arranged on the top of her head (a style that quite altered and spoiled her looks) and she had put on a maroon dress with a pale-blue scarf, the little princess walked twice round her, now adjusting a fold of the dress with her little hand, now arranging the scarf and looking at her with her head bent first on one side and then on the other.

"No, it will not do," she said decidedly, clasping her hands. "No, Mary, really this dress does not suit you. I prefer you in your little gray everyday dress. Now please, do it for my sake. Katie," she said to the maid, "bring the princess her gray dress, and you'll see, Mademoiselle Bourienne, how I shall arrange it," she added, smiling with a foretaste of artistic pleasure.

But when Katie brought the required dress, Princess Mary remained sitting motionless before the glass, looking at her face, and saw in the mirror her eyes full of tears and her mouth quivering, ready to burst into sobs.

"Come, dear princess," said Mademoiselle Bourienne, "just one more little effort."

The little princess, taking the dress from the maid, came up to Princess Mary.

"Well, now we'll arrange something quite simple and becoming," she said.

The three voices, hers, Mademoiselle Bourienne's, and Katie's, who

was laughing at something, mingled in a merry sound, like the chirping of birds.

"No, leave me alone," said Princess Mary.

Her voice sounded so serious and so sad that the chirping of the birds was silenced at once. They looked at the beautiful, large, thoughtful eyes full of tears and of thoughts, gazing shiningly and imploringly at them, and understood that it was useless and even cruel to insist.

"At least, change your coiffure," said the little princess. "Didn't I tell you," she went on, turning reproachfully to Mademoiselle Bourienne, "Mary's is a face which such a coiffure does not suit in the least. Not in the least! Please change it."

"Leave me alone, please leave me alone! It is all quite the same to me," answered a voice struggling with tears.

Mademoiselle Bourienne and the little princess had to own to themselves that Princess Mary in this guise looked very plain, worse than usual, but it was too late. She was looking at them with an expression they both knew, an expression thoughtful and sad. This expression in Princess Mary did not frighten them (she never inspired fear in anyone), but they knew that when it appeared on her face, she became mute and was not to be shaken in her determination.

"You will change it, won't you?" said Lise. And as Princess Mary gave no answer, she left the room.

Princess Mary was left alone. She did not comply with Lise's request, she not only left her hair as it was, but did not even look in her glass. Letting her arms fall helplessly, she sat with downcast eyes and pondered. A husband, a man, a strong dominant and strangely attractive being rose in her imagination, and carried her into a totally different happy world of his own. She fancied a child, her own—such as she had seen the day before in the arms of her nurse's daughter—at her own breast, the husband standing by and gazing tenderly at her and the child. "But no, it is impossible, I am too ugly," she thought.

"Please come to tea. The prince will be out in a moment," came the maid's voice at the door.

She roused herself, and felt appalled at what she had been thinking, and before going down she went into the room where the icons hung and, her eyes fixed on the dark face of a large icon of the Saviour lit by a lamp, she stood before it with folded hands for a few moments. A painful doubt filled her soul. Could the joy of love, of earthly love for a man, be for her? In her thoughts of marriage Princess Mary dreamed of happiness and of children, but her strongest, most deeply hidden longing was for earthly love. The more she tried to hide this feeling from others and even from

herself, the stronger it grew. "O God," she said, "how am I to stifle in my heart these temptations of the devil? How am I to renounce forever these vile fancies, so as peacefully to fulfill Thy will?" And scarcely had she put that question than God gave her the answer in her own heart. "Desire nothing for thyself, seek nothing, be not anxious or envious. Man's future and thy own fate must remain hidden from thee, but live so that thou mayest be ready for anything. If it be God's will to prove thee in the duties of marriage, be ready to fulfill His will." With this consoling thought (but yet with a hope for the fulfillment of her forbidden earthly longing) Princess Mary sighed, and having crossed herself went down, thinking neither of her gown and coiffure nor of how she would go in nor of what she would say. What could all that matter in comparison with the will of God, without Whose care not a hair of man's head can fall?

3. Lise, Mademoiselle Bourienne, Mary, Anatole, and old Bolkónski

WHEN PRINCESS MARY came down, Prince Vasíli and his son were already in the drawing room, talking to the little princess and Mademoiselle Bourienne. When she entered with her heavy step, treading on her heels, the gentlemen and Mademoiselle Bourienne rose and the little princess, indicating her to the gentlemen, said: "Voilà Marie!" Princess Mary saw them all and saw them in detail. She saw Prince Vasíli's face, serious for an instant at the sight of her, but immediately smiling again, and the little princess curiously noting the impression "Marie" produced on the visitors. And she saw Mademoiselle Bourienne, with her ribbon and pretty face, and her unusually animated look which was fixed on him, but him she could not see, she only saw something large, brilliant, and handsome moving toward her as she entered the room. Prince Vasíli approached first, and she kissed the bald forehead that bent over her hand and answered his question by saying that, on the contrary, she remembered him quite well. Then Anatole came up to her. She still could not see him. She only felt a soft hand taking hers firmly, and she touched with her lips a white forehead, over which was beautiful light-brown hair smelling of pomade. When she looked up at him she was struck by his beauty. Anatole stood with his right thumb under a button of his uniform, his chest expanded and his back drawn in, slightly swinging one foot, and, with his head a little bent, looked with beaming face at the princess without speaking and evidently not thinking about her at all. Anatole was not quick-witted, nor ready or eloquent in conversation, but

he had the faculty, so invaluable in society, of composure and imperturbable self-possession. If a man lacking in self-confidence remains dumb on a first introduction and betrays a consciousness of the impropriety of such silence and an anxiety to find something to say, the effect is bad. But Anatole was dumb, swung his foot, and smilingly examined the princess' hair. It was evident that he could be silent in this way for a very long time. "If anyone finds this silence inconvenient, let him talk, but I don't want to," he seemed to say. Besides this, in his behavior to women Anatole had a manner which particularly inspires in them curiosity, awe, and even love—a supercilious consciousness of his own superiority. It was as if he said to them: "I know you, I know you, but why should I bother about you? You'd be only too glad, of course." Perhaps he did not really think this when he met women—even probably he did not, for in general he thought very little—but his looks and manner gave that impression. The princess felt this, and as if wishing to show him that she did not even dare expect to interest him, she turned to his father. The conversation was general and animated, thanks to Princess Lise's voice and little downy lip that lifted over her white teeth. She met Prince Vasíli with that playful manner often employed by lively chatty people, and consisting in the assumption that between the person they so address and themselves there are some semiprivate, long-established jokes and amusing reminiscences, though no such reminiscences really exist—just as none existed in this case. Prince Vasíli readily adopted her tone and the little princess also drew Anatole, whom she hardly knew, into these amusing recollections of things that had never occurred. Mademoiselle Bourienne also shared them and even Princess Mary felt herself pleasantly made to share in these merry reminiscences.

"Here at least we shall have the benefit of your company all to ourselves, dear prince," said the little princess (of course, in French) to Prince Vasíli. "It's not as at Annette's [Anna Pávlovna] receptions where you always ran away; you remember *cette chère Annette!*"

"Ah, but you won't talk politics to me like Annette!"

"And our little tea table?"

"Oh, yes!"

"Why is it you were never at Annette's?" the little princess asked Anatole. "Ah, I know, I know," she said with a sly glance, "your brother Hippolyte told me about your goings on. Oh!" and she shook her finger at him, "I have even heard of your doings in Paris!"

"And didn't Hippolyte tell you?" asked Prince Vasíli, turning to his son and seizing the little princess' arm as if she would have run away and he had just managed to catch her, "didn't he tell you how he himself

was pining for the dear princess, and how she showed him the door? Oh, she is a pearl among women, Princess," he added, turning to Princess Mary.

When Paris was mentioned, Mademoiselle Bourienne for her part seized the opportunity of joining in the general current of recollections.

She took the liberty of inquiring whether it was long since Anatole had left Paris and how he had liked that city. Anatole answered the Frenchwoman very readily and, looking at her with a smile, talked to her about her native land. When he saw the pretty little Bourienne, Anatole came to the conclusion that he would not find Bald Hills dull either. "Not at all bad!" he thought, examining her, "not at all bad, that little companion! I hope she will bring her along with her when we're married, *la petite est gentille* [the little one is charming]."

The old prince dressed leisurely in his study, frowning and considering what he was to do. The coming of these visitors annoyed him. "What are Prince Vasíli and that son of his to me? Prince Vasíli is a shallow braggart and his son, no doubt, is a fine specimen," he grumbled to himself. What angered him was that the coming of these visitors revived in his mind an unsettled question he always tried to stifle, one about which he always deceived himself. The question was whether he could ever bring himself to part from his daughter and give her to a husband. The prince never directly asked himself that question, knowing beforehand that he would have to answer it justly, and justice clashed not only with his feelings but with the very possibility of life. Life without Princess Mary, little as he seemed to value her, was unthinkable to him. "And why should she marry?" he thought. "To be unhappy for certain. There's Lise, married to Andrew—a better husband one would think could hardly be found nowadays—but is she contented with her lot? And who would marry Marie for love? Plain and awkward! They'll take her for her connections and wealth. Are there no women living unmarried, and even the happier for it?" So thought Prince Bolkónski while dressing, and yet the question he was always putting off demanded an immediate answer. Prince Vasíli had brought his son with the evident intention of proposing, and today or tomorrow he would probably ask for an answer. His birth and position in society were not bad. "Well, I've nothing against it," the prince said to himself, "but he must be worthy of her. And that is what we shall see."

"That is what we shall see! That is what we shall see!" he added aloud.

He entered the drawing room with his usual alert step, glancing rapidly round the company. He noticed the change in the little princess' dress, Mademoiselle Bourienne's ribbon, Princess Mary's unbecoming coiffure,

Mademoiselle Bourienne's and Anatole's smiles, and the loneliness of his daughter amid the general conversation. "Got herself up like a fool!" he thought, looking irritably at her. "She is shameless, and he ignores her!"

He went straight up to Prince Vasíli.

"Well! How d'ye do? How d'ye do? Glad to see you!"

"Friendship laughs at distance," began Prince Vasíli in his usual rapid, self-confident, familiar tone. "Here is my second son; please love and befriend him."

Prince Bolkónski surveyed Anatole.

"Fine young fellow! Fine young fellow!" he said. "Well, come and kiss me," and he offered his cheek.

Anatole kissed the old man, and looked at him with curiosity and perfect composure, waiting for a display of the eccentricities his father had told him to expect.

Prince Bolkónski sat down in his usual place in the corner of the sofa and, drawing up an armchair for Prince Vasíli, pointed to it and began questioning him about political affairs and news. He seemed to listen attentively to what Prince Vasíli said, but kept glancing at Princess Mary.

"And so they are writing from Potsdam already?" he said, repeating Prince Vasíli's last words. Then rising, he suddenly went up to his daughter.

"Is it for visitors you've got yourself up like that, eh?" said he. "Fine, very fine! You have done up your hair in this new way for the visitors, and before the visitors I tell you that in future you are never to dare to change your way of dress without my consent."

"It was my fault, mon père," interceded the little princess, with a blush.

"You must do as you please," said Prince Bolkónski, bowing to his daughter-in-law, "but she need not make a fool of herself, she's plain enough as it is."

And he sat down again, paying no more attention to his daughter, who was reduced to tears.

"On the contrary, that coiffure suits the princess very well," said Prince Vasíli.

"Now you, young prince, what's your name?" said Prince Bolkónski, turning to Anatole, "come here, let us talk and get acquainted."

"Now the fun begins," thought Anatole, sitting down with a smile beside the old prince.

"Well, my dear boy, I hear you've been educated abroad, not taught to read and write by the deacon, like your father and me. Now tell me, my dear boy, are you serving in the Horse Guards?" asked the old man, scrutinizing Anatole closely and intently.

"No, I have been transferred to the line," said Anatole, hardly able to restrain his laughter.

"Ah! That's a good thing. So, my dear boy, you wish to serve the Tsar and the country? It is wartime. Such a fine fellow must serve. Well, are you off to the front?"

"No, Prince, our regiment has gone to the front, but I am attached . . . what is it I am attached to, Papa?" said Anatole, turning to his father with a laugh.

"A splendid soldier, splendid! 'What am I attached to!' Ha, ha, ha!" laughed Prince Bolkónski, and Anatole laughed still louder. Suddenly Prince Bolkónski frowned.

"You may go," he said to Anatole.

Anatole returned smiling to the ladies.

"And so you've had him educated abroad, Prince Vasíli, haven't you?" said the old prince to Prince Vasíli.

"I have done my best for him, and I can assure you the education there is much better than ours."

"Yes, everything is different nowadays, everything is changed. The lad's a fine fellow, a fine fellow! Well, come with me now." He took Prince Vasíli's arm and led him to his study. As soon as they were alone together, Prince Vasíli announced his hopes and wishes to the old prince.

"Well, do you think I shall prevent her, that I can't part from her?" said the old prince angrily. "What an idea! I'm ready for it tomorrow! Only let me tell you, I want to know my son-in-law better. You know my principles—everything aboveboard! I will ask her tomorrow in your presence; if she is willing, then he can stay on. He can stay and I'll see." The old prince snorted. "Let her marry, it's all the same to me!" he screamed in the same piercing tone as when parting from his son.

"I will tell you frankly," said Prince Vasíli in the tone of a crafty man convinced of the futility of being cunning with so keen-sighted a companion. "You know, you see right through people. Anatole is no genius, but he is an honest, goodhearted lad; an excellent son or kinsman."

"All right, all right, we'll see!"

As always happens when women lead lonely lives for any length of time without male society, on Anatole's appearance all the three women of Prince Bolkónski's household felt that their life had not been real till then. Their powers of reasoning, feeling, and observing immediately increased tenfold, and their life, which seemed to have been passed in darkness, was suddenly lit up by a new brightness, full of significance.

Princess Mary grew quite unconscious of her face and coiffure. The handsome open face of the man who might perhaps be her husband ab-

sorbed all her attention. He seemed to her kind, brave, determined, manly, and magnanimous. She felt convinced of that. Thousands of dreams of a future family life continually rose in her imagination. She drove them away and tried to conceal them.

"But am I not too cold with him?" thought the princess. "I try to be reserved because in the depth of my soul I feel too near to him already, but then he cannot know what I think of him and may imagine that I do not like him."

And Princess Mary tried, but could not manage, to be cordial to her new guest. "Poor girl, she's devilish ugly!" thought Anatole.

Mademoiselle Bourienne, also roused to great excitement by Anatole's arrival, thought in another way. Of course, she, a handsome young woman without any definite position, without relations or even a country, did not intend to devote her life to serving Prince Bolkónski, to reading aloud to him and being friends with Princess Mary. Mademoiselle Bourienne had long been waiting for a Russian prince who, able to appreciate at a glance her superiority to the plain, badly dressed, ungainly Russian princesses, would fall in love with her and carry her off; and here at last was a Russian prince. Mademoiselle Bourienne knew a story, heard from her aunt but finished in her own way, which she liked to repeat to herself. It was the story of a girl who had been seduced, and to whom her poor mother (sa pauvre mère) appeared, and reproached her for yielding to a man without being married. Mademoiselle Bourienne was often touched to tears as in imagination she told this story to him, her seducer. And now he, a real Russian prince, had appeared. He would carry her away and then sa pauvre mère would appear and he would marry her. So her future shaped itself in Mademoiselle Bourienne's head at the very time she was talking to Anatole about Paris. It was not calculation that guided her (she did not even for a moment consider what she should do), but all this had long been familiar to her, and now that Anatole had appeared it just grouped itself around him and she wished and tried to please him as much as possible.

The little princess, like an old war horse that hears the trumpet, unconsciously and quite forgetting her condition, prepared for the familiar gallop of coquetry, without any ulterior motive or any struggle, but with naïve and lighthearted gaiety.

Although in female society Anatole usually assumed the role of a man tired of being run after by women, his vanity was flattered by the spectacle of his power over these three women. Besides that, he was beginning to feel for the pretty and provocative Mademoiselle Bourienne that

passionate animal feeling which was apt to master him with great sudden-
ness and prompt him to the coarsest and most reckless actions.

After tea, the company went into the sitting room and Princess Mary
was asked to play on the clavichord. Anatole, laughing and in high spirits,
came and leaned on his elbows, facing her and beside Mademoiselle
Bourienne. Princess Mary felt his look with a painfully joyous emotion.
Her favorite sonata bore her into a most intimately poetic world and the
look she felt upon her made that world still more poetic. But Anatole's
expression, though his eyes were fixed on her, referred not to her but to
the movements of Mademoiselle Bourienne's little foot, which he was
then touching with his own under the clavichord. Mademoiselle Bouri-
enne was also looking at Princess Mary, and in her lovely eyes there was
a look of fearful joy and hope that was also new to the princess.

"How she loves me!" thought Princess Mary. "How happy I am now,
and how happy I may be with such a friend and such a husband! Hus-
band? Can it be possible?" she thought, not daring to look at his face, but
still feeling his eyes gazing at her.

In the evening, after supper, when all were about to retire, Anatole
kissed Princess Mary's hand. She did not know how she found the cour-
age, but she looked straight into his handsome face as it came near to her
shortsighted eyes. Turning from Princess Mary he went up and kissed
Mademoiselle Bourienne's hand. (This was not etiquette, but then he
did everything so simply and with such assurance!) Mademoiselle Bouri-
enne flushed, and gave the princess a frightened look.

"What delicacy!" thought the princess. "Is it possible that Amélie"
(Mademoiselle Bourienne) "thinks I could be jealous of her, and not
value her pure affection and devotion to me?" She went up to her and
kissed her warmly. Anatole went up to kiss the little princess' hand.

"No! No! No! When your father writes to tell me that you are behaving
well I will give you my hand to kiss. Not till then!" she said. And smil-
ingly raising a finger at him, she left the room.

4. Her father's opposition to Mary's marrying. She finds Mademoiselle Bourienne and Anatole in the conservatory; declines marriage

THEY ALL SEPARATED, but, except Anatole who fell asleep as soon as
he got into bed, all kept awake a long time that night.

"Is he really to be my husband, this stranger who is so kind—yes, kind,
that is the chief thing," thought Princess Mary; and fear, which she had

seldom experienced, came upon her. She feared to look round, it seemed to her that someone was there standing behind the screen in the dark corner. And this someone was *he*—the devil—and *he* was also this man with the white forehead, black eyebrows, and red lips.

She rang for her maid and asked her to sleep in her room.

Mademoiselle Bourienne walked up and down the conservatory for a long time that evening, vainly expecting someone, now smiling at someone, now working herself up to tears with the imaginary words of her *pauvre mère* rebuking her for her fall.

The little princess grumbled to her maid that her bed was badly made. She could not lie either on her face or on her side. Every position was awkward and uncomfortable, and her burden oppressed her now more than ever because Anatole's presence had vividly recalled to her the time when she was not like that and when everything was light and gay. She sat in an armchair in her dressing jacket and nightcap and Katie, sleepy and disheveled, beat and turned the heavy feather bed for the third time, muttering to herself.

"I told you it was all lumps and holes!" the little princess repeated. "I should be glad enough to fall asleep, so it's not my fault!" and her voice quivered like that of a child about to cry.

The old prince did not sleep either. Tíkhon, half asleep, heard him pacing angrily about and snorting. The old prince felt as though he had been insulted through his daughter. The insult was the more pointed because it concerned not himself but another, his daughter, whom he loved more than himself. He kept telling himself that he would consider the whole matter and decide what was right and how he should act, but instead of that he only excited himself more and more.

"The first man that turns up—she forgets her father and everything else, runs upstairs and does up her hair and wags her tail and is unlike herself! Glad to throw her father over! And she knew I should notice it. Fr . . . fr . . . fr . . . ! And don't I see that that idiot had eyes only for Bourienne—I shall have to get rid of her. And how is it she has not pride enough to see it? If she has no pride for herself she might at least have some for my sake! She must be shown that the blockhead thinks nothing of her and looks only at Bourienne. No, she has no pride . . . but I'll let her see. . . ."

The old prince knew that if he told his daughter she was making a mistake and that Anatole meant to flirt with Mademoiselle Bourienne, Princess Mary's self-esteem would be wounded and his point (not to be parted from her) would be gained, so pacifying himself with this thought, he called Tíkhon and began to undress.

"What devil brought them here?" thought he, while Tíkhon was putting the nightshirt over his dried-up old body and gray-haired chest. "I never invited them. They came to disturb my life—and there is not much of it left."

"Devil take 'em!" he muttered, while his head was still covered by the shirt.

Tíkhon knew his master's habit of sometimes thinking aloud, and therefore met with unaltered looks the angrily inquisitive expression of the face that emerged from the shirt.

"Gone to bed?" asked the prince.

Tíkhon, like all good valets, instinctively knew the direction of his master's thoughts. He guessed that the question referred to Prince Vasíli and his son.

"They have gone to bed and put out their lights, your excellency."

"No good . . . no good . . ." said the prince rapidly, and thrusting his feet into his slippers and his arms into the sleeves of his dressing gown, he went to the couch on which he slept.

Though no words had passed between Anatole and Mademoiselle Bourienne, they quite understood one another as to the first part of their romance, up to the appearance of the *pauvre mère*; they understood that they had much to say to one another in private and so they had been seeking an opportunity since morning to meet one another alone. When Princess Mary went to her father's room at the usual hour, Mademoiselle Bourienne and Anatole met in the conservatory.

Princess Mary went to the door of the study with special trepidation. It seemed to her that not only did everybody know that her fate would be decided that day, but that they also knew what she thought about it. She read this in Tíkhon's face and in that of Prince Vasíli's valet, who made her a low bow when she met him in the corridor carrying hot water.

The old prince was very affectionate and careful in his treatment of his daughter that morning. Princess Mary well knew this painstaking expression of her father's. His face wore that expression when his dry hands clenched with vexation at her not understanding a sum in arithmetic, when rising from his chair he would walk away from her, repeating in a low voice the same words several times over.

He came to the point at once, treating her ceremoniously.

"I have had a proposition made me concerning you," he said with an unnatural smile. "I expect you have guessed that Prince Vasíli has not come and brought his pupil with him" (for some reason Prince Bolkónski referred to Anatole as a "pupil") "for the sake of my beautiful eyes. Last

night a proposition was made me on your account and, as you know my principles, I refer it to you."

"How am I to understand you, mon père?" said the princess, growing pale and then blushing.

"How understand me!" cried her father angrily. "Prince Vasíli finds you to his taste as a daughter-in-law and makes a proposal to you on his pupil's behalf. That's how it's to be understood! 'How understand it'! . . . And I ask you!"

"I do not know what you think, Father," whispered the princess.

"I? I? What of me? Leave me out of the question. I'm not going to get married. What about you? That's what I want to know."

The princess saw that her father regarded the matter with disapproval, but at that moment the thought occurred to her that her fate would be decided now or never. She lowered her eyes so as not to see the gaze under which she felt that she could not think, but would only be able to submit from habit, and she said: "I wish only to do your will, but if I had to express my own desire . . ." She had no time to finish. The old prince interrupted her.

"That's admirable!" he shouted. "He will take you with your dowry and take Mademoiselle Bourienne into the bargain. She'll be the wife, while you . . ."

The prince stopped. He saw the effect these words had produced on his daughter. She lowered her head and was ready to burst into tears.

"Now then, now then, I'm only joking!" he said. "Remember this, Princess, I hold to the principle that a maiden has a full right to choose. I give you freedom. Only remember that your life's happiness depends on your decision. Never mind me!"

"But I do not know, Father!"

"There's no need to talk! He receives his orders and will marry you or anybody; but you are free to choose. . . . Go to your room, think it over, and come back in an hour and tell me in his presence: yes or no. I know you will pray over it. Well, pray if you like, but you had better think it over. Go! Yes or no, yes or no, yes or no!" he still shouted when the princess, as if lost in a fog, had already staggered out of the study.

Her fate was decided and happily decided. But what her father had said about Mademoiselle Bourienne was dreadful. It was untrue to be sure, but still it was terrible, and she could not help thinking of it. She was going straight on through the conservatory, neither seeing nor hearing anything, when suddenly the well-known whispering of Mademoiselle Bourienne aroused her. She raised her eyes, and two steps away saw Anatole embracing the Frenchwoman and whispering something to her.

With a horrified expression on his handsome face, Anatole looked at Princess Mary, but did not at once take his arm from the waist of Mademoiselle Bourienne who had not yet seen her.

"Who's that? Why? Wait a moment!" Anatole's face seemed to say. Princess Mary looked at them in silence. She could not understand it. At last Mademoiselle Bourienne gave a scream and ran away. Anatole bowed to Princess Mary with a gay smile, as if inviting her to join in a laugh at this strange incident, and then shrugging his shoulders went to the door that led to his own apartments.

An hour later, Tíkhon came to call Princess Mary to the old prince; he added that Prince Vasíli was also there. When Tíkhon came to her Princess Mary was sitting on the sofa in her room, holding the weeping Mademoiselle Bourienne in her arms and gently stroking her hair. The princess' beautiful eyes with all their former calm radiance were looking with tender affection and pity at Mademoiselle Bourienne's pretty face.

"No, Princess, I have lost your affection forever!" said Mademoiselle Bourienne.

"Why? I love you more than ever," said Princess Mary, "and I will try to do all I can for your happiness."

"But you despise me. You who are so pure can never understand being so carried away by passion. Oh, only my poor mother . . ."

"I quite understand," answered Princess Mary, with a sad smile. "Calm yourself, my dear. I will go to my father," she said, and went out.

Prince Vasíli, with one leg thrown high over the other and a snuffbox in his hand, was sitting there with a smile of deep emotion on his face, as if stirred to his heart's core and himself regretting and laughing at his own sensibility, when Princess Mary entered. He hurriedly took a pinch of snuff.

"Ah, my dear, my dear!" he began, rising and taking her by both hands. Then, sighing, he added: "My son's fate is in your hands. Decide, my dear, good, gentle Marie, whom I have always loved as a daughter!"

He drew back and a real tear appeared in his eye.

"Fr . . . fr . . ." snorted Prince Bolkónski. "The prince is making a proposition to you in his pupil's—I mean, his son's—name. Do you wish or not to be Prince Anatole Kurágin's wife? Reply: yes or no," he shouted, "and then I shall reserve the right to state my opinion also. Yes, my opinion, and only my opinion," added Prince Bolkónski, turning to Prince Vasíli and answering his imploring look. "Yes, or no?"

"My desire is never to leave you, Father, never to separate my life from yours. I don't wish to marry," she answered positively, glancing at Prince Vasíli and at her father with her beautiful eyes.

"Humbug! Nonsense! Humbug, humbug, humbug!" cried Prince Bol-kónski, frowning and taking his daughter's hand; he did not kiss her, but only bending his forehead to hers just touched it, and pressed her hand so that she winced and uttered a cry.

Prince Vasíli rose.

"My dear, I must tell you that this is a moment I shall never, never forget. But, my dear, will you not give us a little hope of touching this heart, so kind and generous? Say 'perhaps' . . . The future is so long. Say 'perhaps.' "

"Prince, what I have said is all there is in my heart. I thank you for the honor, but I shall never be your son's wife."

"Well, so that's finished, my dear fellow! I am very glad to have seen you. Very glad! Go back to your rooms, Princess. Go!" said the old prince. "Very, very glad to have seen you," repeated he, embracing Prince Vasíli.

"My vocation is a different one," thought Princess Mary. "My voca-tion is to be happy with another kind of happiness, the happiness of love and self-sacrifice. And cost what it may, I will arrange poor Amélie's hap-piness, she loves him so passionately, and so passionately repents. I will do all I can to arrange the match between them. If he is not rich I will give her the means; I will ask my father and Andrew. I shall be so happy when she is his wife. She is so unfortunate, a stranger, alone, helpless! And, oh God, how passionately she must love him if she could so far forget herself! Perhaps I might have done the same! . . ." thought Prin-cess Mary.

5. A letter from Nicholas. Sónya and Natásha

IT WAS long since the Rostóvs had news of Nicholas. Not till midwinter was the count at last handed a letter addressed in his son's handwriting. On receiving it, he ran on tiptoe to his study in alarm and haste, trying to escape notice, closed the door, and began to read the letter.

Anna Mikháylovna, who always knew everything that passed in the house, on hearing of the arrival of the letter went softly into the room and found the count with it in his hand, sobbing and laughing at the same time.

Anna Mikháylovna, though her circumstances had improved, was still living with the Rostóvs.

"My dear friend?" said she, in a tone of pathetic inquiry, prepared to sympathize in any way.

The count sobbed yet more.

"Nikólenka * . . . a letter . . . wa . . . a . . . s . . . wounded . . . my darling boy . . . the countess . . . promoted to be an officer . . . thank God . . . How tell the little countess!"

Anna Mikháylovna sat down beside him, with her own handkerchief wiped the tears from his eyes and from the letter, then having dried her own eyes she comforted the count, and decided that at dinner and till tea-time she would prepare the countess, and after tea, with God's help, would inform her.

At dinner Anna Mikháylovna talked the whole time about the war news and about Nikólenka, twice asked when the last letter had been received from him, though she knew that already, and remarked that they might very likely be getting a letter from him that day. Each time that these hints began to make the countess anxious and she glanced un-easily at the count and at Anna Mikháylovna, the latter very adroitly turned the conversation to insignificant matters. Natásha, who, of the whole family, was the most gifted with a capacity to feel any shades of intonation, look, and expression, pricked up her ears from the beginning of the meal and was certain that there was some secret between her father and Anna Mikháylovna, that it had something to do with her brother, and that Anna Mikháylovna was preparing them for it. Bold as she was, Natásha, who knew how sensitive her mother was to anything relating to Nikólenka, did not venture to ask any questions at dinner, but she was too excited to eat anything and kept wriggling about on her chair regard-less of her governess' remarks. After dinner, she rushed headlong after Anna Mikháylovna and, dashing at her, flung herself on her neck as soon as she overtook her in the sitting room.

"Auntie, darling, do tell me what it is!"

"Nothing, my dear."

"No, dearest, sweet one, honey, I won't give up—I know you know something."

Anna Mikháylovna shook her head.

"You are a little slyboots," she said.

"A letter from Nikólenka! I'm sure of it!" exclaimed Natásha, reading confirmation in Anna Mikháylovna's face.

"But for God's sake, be careful, you know how it may affect your mamma."

"I will, I will, only tell me! You won't? Then I will go and tell at once."

Anna Mikháylovna, in a few words, told her the contents of the letter, on condition that she should tell no one.

* Nikólenka—an affectionate diminutive of Nicholas.—A.M.

"No, on my true word of honor," said Natásha, crossing herself, "I won't tell anyone!" and she ran off at once to Sónya.

"Nikólenka . . . wounded . . . a letter," she announced in gleeful triumph.

"Nicholas!" was all Sónya said, instantly turning white.

Natásha, seeing the impression the news of her brother's wound produced on Sónya, felt for the first time the sorrowful side of the news.

She rushed to Sónya, hugged her, and began to cry.

"A little wound, but he has been made an officer; he is well now, he wrote himself," said she through her tears.

"There now! It's true that all you women are crybabies," remarked Pétya, pacing the room with large, resolute strides. "Now I'm very glad, very glad indeed, that my brother has distinguished himself so. You are all blubberers and understand nothing."

Natásha smiled through her tears.

"You haven't read the letter?" asked Sónya.

"No, but she said that it was all over and that he's now an officer."

"Thank God!" said Sónya, crossing herself. "But perhaps she deceived you. Let us go to Mamma."

Pétya paced the room in silence for a time.

"If I'd been in Nikólenka's place I would have killed even more of those Frenchmen," he said. "What nasty brutes they are! I'd have killed so many that there'd have been a heap of them."

"Hold your tongue, Pétya, what a goose you are!"

"I'm not a goose, but they are who cry about trifles," said Pétya.

"Do you remember him?" Natásha suddenly asked, after a moment's silence.

Sónya smiled.

"Do I remember Nicholas?"

"No, Sónya, but do you remember so that you remember him perfectly, remember everything?" said Natásha, with an expressive gesture, evidently wishing to give her words a very definite meaning. "I remember Nikólenka too, I remember him well," she said. "But I don't remember Borís. I don't remember him a bit."

"What! You don't remember Borís?" asked Sónya in surprise.

"It's not that I don't remember—I know what he is like, but not as I remember Nikólenka. Him—I just shut my eyes and remember, but Borís . . . No!" (She shut her eyes.) "No! there's nothing at all."

"Oh, Natásha!" said Sónya, looking ecstatically and earnestly at her friend as if she did not consider her worthy to hear what she meant to

say and as if she were saying it to someone else, with whom joking was out of the question, "I am in love with your brother once for all and, whatever may happen to him or to me, shall never cease to love him as long as I live."

Natásha looked at Sónya with wondering and inquisitive eyes, and said nothing. She felt that Sónya was speaking the truth, that there was such love as Sónya was speaking of. But Natásha had not yet felt anything like it. She believed it could be, but did not understand it.

"Shall you write to him?" she asked.

Sónya became thoughtful. The question of how to write to Nicholas, and whether she ought to write, tormented her. Now that he was already an officer and a wounded hero, would it be right to remind him of herself and, as it might seem, of the obligations to her he had taken on himself?

"I don't know. I think if he writes, I will write too," she said, blushing.

"And you won't feel ashamed to write to him?"

Sónya smiled.

"No."

"And I should be ashamed to write to Borís. I'm not going to."

"Why should you be ashamed?"

"Well, I don't know. It's awkward and would make me ashamed."

"And I know why she'd be ashamed," said Pétya, offended by Natásha's previous remark. "It's because she was in love with that fat one in spectacles" (that was how Pétya described his namesake, the new Count Bezúkhov) "and now she's in love with that singer" (he meant Natásha's Italian singing master), "that's why she's ashamed!"

"Pétya, you're a stupid!" said Natásha.

"Not more stupid than you, madam," said the nine-year-old Pétya, with the air of an old brigadier.

The countess had been prepared by Anna Mikháylovna's hints at dinner. On retiring to her own room, she sat in an armchair, her eyes fixed on a miniature portrait of her son on the lid of a snuffbox, while the tears kept coming into her eyes. Anna Mikháylovna, with the letter, came on tiptoe to the countess' door and paused.

"Don't come in," she said to the old count who was following her. "Come later." And she went in, closing the door behind her.

The count put his ear to the keyhole and listened.

At first he heard the sound of indifferent voices, then Anna Mikháylovna's voice alone in a long speech, then a cry, then silence, then both voices together with glad intonations, and then footsteps. Anna Mikháylovna opened the door. Her face wore the proud expression of a surgeon

who has just performed a difficult operation and admits the public to appreciate his skill.

"It is done!" she said to the count, pointing triumphantly to the countess, who sat holding in one hand the snuffbox with its portrait and in the other the letter, and pressing them alternately to her lips.

When she saw the count, she stretched out her arms to him, embraced his bald head, over which she again looked at the letter and the portrait, and in order to press them again to her lips, she slightly pushed away the bald head. Véra, Natásha, Sónya, and Pétya now entered the room, and the reading of the letter began. After a brief description of the campaign and the two battles in which he had taken part, and his promotion, Nicholas said that he kissed his father's and mother's hands asking for their blessing, and that he kissed Véra, Natásha, and Pétya. Besides that, he sent greetings to Monsieur Schelling, Madame Schoss, and his old nurse, and asked them to kiss for him "dear Sónya, whom he loved and thought of just the same as ever." When she heard this Sónya blushed so that tears came into her eyes and, unable to bear the looks turned upon her, ran away into the dancing hall, whirled round it at full speed with her dress puffed out like a balloon, and, flushed and smiling, plumped down on the floor. The countess was crying.

"Why are you crying, Mamma?" asked Véra. "From all he says one should be glad and not cry."

This was quite true, but the count, the countess, and Natásha looked at her reproachfully. "And who is it she takes after?" thought the countess.

Nicholas' letter was read over hundreds of times, and those who were considered worthy to hear it had to come to the countess, for she did not let it out of her hands. The tutors came, and the nurses, and Dmítri, and several acquaintances, and the countess reread the letter each time with fresh pleasure and each time discovered in it fresh proofs of Nikólenka's virtues. How strange, how extraordinary, how joyful it seemed, that her son, the scarcely perceptible motion of whose tiny limbs she had felt twenty years ago within her, that son about whom she used to have quarrels with the too-indulgent count, that son who had first learned to say "pear" and then "granny," that this son should now be away in a foreign land amid strange surroundings, a manly warrior doing some kind of man's work of his own, without help or guidance. The universal experience of ages, showing that children do grow imperceptibly from the cradle to manhood, did not exist for the countess. Her son's growth toward manhood, at each of its stages, had seemed as extraordinary to her as if there had never existed the millions of human beings who grew up in the same way. As twenty years before, it seemed impossible that the little

creature who lived somewhere under her heart would ever cry, suck her breast, and begin to speak, so now she could not believe that that little creature could be this strong, brave man, this model son and officer that, judging by this letter, he now was.

"What a *style!* How charmingly he describes!" said she, reading the descriptive part of the letter. "And what a soul! Not a word about himself. . . . Not a word! About some Denísov or other, though he himself, I dare say, is braver than any of them. He says nothing about his sufferings. What a heart! How like him it is! And how he has remembered everybody! Not forgetting anyone. I always said when he was only so high—I always said . . ."

For more than a week preparations were being made, rough drafts of letters to Nicholas from all the household were written and copied out, while under the supervision of the countess and the solicitude of the count, money and all things necessary for the uniform and equipment of the newly commissioned officer were collected. Anna Mikháylovna, practical woman that she was, had even managed by favor with army authorities to secure advantageous means of communication for herself and her son. She had opportunities of sending her letters to the Grand Duke Constantine Pávlovich, who commanded the Guards. The Rostóvs supposed that *The Russian Guards, Abroad,* was quite a definite address, and that if a letter reached the Grand Duke in command of the Guards there was no reason why it should not reach the Pávlograd regiment, which was presumably somewhere in the same neighborhood. And so it was decided to send the letters and money by the Grand Duke's courier to Borís and Borís was to forward them to Nicholas. The letters were from the old count, the countess, Pétya, Véra, Natásha, and Sónya, and finally there were six thousand rubles for his outfit and various other things the old count sent to his son.

6. Nicholas visits Borís and Berg in camp. Nicholas tells of Schön Grabern. His encounter with Prince Andrew

ON THE twelfth of November, Kutúzov's active army, in camp before Olmütz, was preparing to be reviewed next day by the two Emperors —the Russian and the Austrian. The Guards, just arrived from Russia, spent the night ten miles from Olmütz and next morning were to come straight to the review, reaching the field at Olmütz by ten o'clock.

That day Nicholas Rostóv received a letter from Borís, telling him that

the Ismáylov regiment * was quartered for the night ten miles from Olmütz and that he wanted to see him as he had a letter and money for him. Rostóv was particularly in need of money now that the troops, after their active service, were stationed near Olmütz and the camp swarmed with well-provisioned sutlers and Austrian Jews offering all sorts of tempting wares. The Pávlograds held feast after feast, celebrating awards they had received for the campaign, and made expeditions to Olmütz to visit a certain Caroline the Hungarian, who had recently opened a restaurant there with girls as waitresses. Rostóv, who had just celebrated his promotion to a cornetcy and bought Denísov's horse, Bedouin, was in debt all round, to his comrades and the sutlers. On receiving Borís' letter he rode with a fellow officer to Olmütz, dined there, drank a bottle of wine, and then set off alone to the Guards' camp to find his old playmate. Rostóv had not yet had time to get his uniform. He had on a shabby cadet jacket, decorated with a soldier's cross, equally shabby cadet's riding breeches lined with worn leather, and an officer's saber with a sword knot. The Don horse he was riding was one he had bought from a Cossack during the campaign, and he wore a crumpled hussar cap stuck jauntily back on one side of his head. As he rode up to the camp he thought how he would impress Borís and all his comrades of the Guards by his appearance—that of a fighting hussar who had been under fire.

The Guards had made their whole march as if on a pleasure trip, parading their cleanliness and discipline. They had come by easy stages, their knapsacks conveyed on carts, and the Austrian authorities had provided excellent dinners for the officers at every halting place. The regiments had entered and left the town with their bands playing, and by the Grand Duke's orders the men had marched all the way in step (a practice on which the Guards prided themselves), the officers on foot and at their proper posts. Borís had been quartered, and had marched all the way, with Berg who was already in command of a company. Berg, who had obtained his captaincy during the campaign, had gained the confidence of his superiors by his promptitude and accuracy and had arranged his money matters very satisfactorily. Borís, during the campaign, had made the acquaintance of many persons who might prove useful to him, and by a letter of recommendation he had brought from Pierre had become acquainted with Prince Andrew Bolkónski, through whom he hoped to obtain a post on the commander in chief's staff. Berg and Borís, having rested after yesterday's march, were sitting, clean and neatly dressed, at a round table in the

* Tolstóy has made very few slips in this long novel, but here there seems to be one, for in Chapter 4 of Book One, we were told that Borís had been transferred to the Semënov Guards.—A.M.

clean quarters allotted to them, playing chess. Berg held a smoking pipe
between his knees. Borís, in the accurate way characteristic of him, was
building a little pyramid of chessmen with his delicate white fingers while
awaiting Berg's move, and watched his opponent's face, evidently think-
ing about the game as he always thought only of whatever he was en-
gaged on.

"Well, how are you going to get out of that?" he remarked.

"We'll try to," replied Berg, touching a pawn and then removing his
hand.

At that moment the door opened.

"Here he is at last!" shouted Rostóv. "And Berg too! Oh, you *petisen-
fans, allay cushay dórmir!*" * he exclaimed, imitating his Russian nurse's
French, at which he and Borís used to laugh long ago.

"Dear me, how you have changed!"

Borís rose to meet Rostóv, but in doing so did not omit to steady and
replace some chessmen that were falling. He was about to embrace his
friend, but Nicholas avoided him. With that peculiar feeling of youth,
that dread of beaten tracks, and wish to express itself in a manner different
from that of its elders which is often insincere, Nicholas wished to do
something special on meeting his friend. He wanted to pinch him, push
him, do anything but kiss him—a thing everybody did. But notwithstand-
ing this, Borís embraced him in a quiet, friendly way and kissed him three
times.

They had not met for nearly half a year and, being at the age when
young men take their first steps on life's road, each saw immense changes
in the other, quite a new reflection of the society in which they had taken
those first steps. Both had changed greatly since they last met and both
were in a hurry to show the changes that had taken place in them.

"Oh, you damned dandies! Clean and fresh as if you'd been to a fete, not
like us sinners of the line," cried Rostóv, with martial swagger and with
baritone notes in his voice, new to Borís, pointing to his own mud-
bespattered breeches. The German landlady, hearing Rostóv's loud voice,
popped her head in at the door.

"Eh, is she pretty?" he asked with a wink.

"Why do you shout so? You'll frighten them!" said Borís. "I did not
expect you today," he added. "I only sent you the note yesterday by Bol-
kónski—an adjutant of Kutúzov's, who's a friend of mine. I did not think
he would get it to you so quickly. . . . Well, how are you? Been under
fire already?" asked Borís.

* A *Russian nurse's attempt to say in French: "Little children, go to bed and
sleep.*"—A.M.

Without answering, Rostóv shook the soldier's Cross of St. George fastened to the cording of his uniform and, indicating a bandaged arm, glanced at Berg with a smile.

"As you see," he said.

"Indeed? Yes, yes!" said Boris, with a smile. "And we too have had a splendid march. You know, of course, that His Imperial Highness rode with our regiment all the time, so that we had every comfort and every advantage. What receptions we had in Poland! What dinners and balls! I can't tell you. And the Tsarévich was very gracious to all our officers "

And the two friends told each other of their doings, the one of his hussar revels and life in the fighting line, the other of the pleasures and advantages of service under members of the Imperial family.

"Oh, you Guards!" said Rostóv. "I say, send for some wine."

Borís made a grimace.

"If you really want it," said he.

He went to his bed, drew a purse from under the clean pillow, and sent for wine.

"Yes, and I have some money and a letter to give you," he added.

Rostóv took the letter and, throwing the money on the sofa, put both arms on the table and began to read. After reading a few lines, he glanced angrily at Berg, then, meeting his eyes, hid his face behind the letter.

"Well, they've sent you a tidy sum," said Berg, eying the heavy purse that sank into the sofa. "As for us, Count, we get along on our pay. I can tell you for myself . . ."

"I say, Berg, my dear fellow," said Rostóv, "when you get a letter from home and meet one of your own people whom you want to talk everything over with, and I happen to be there, I'll go at once, to be out of your way! Do go somewhere, anywhere . . . to the devil!" he exclaimed, and immediately seizing him by the shoulder and looking amiably into his face, evidently wishing to soften the rudeness of his words, he added, "Don't be hurt, my dear fellow; you know I speak from my heart as to an old acquaintance."

"Oh, don't mention it, Count! I quite understand," said Berg, getting up and speaking in a muffled and guttural voice.

"Go across to our hosts: they invited you," added Borís.

Berg put on the cleanest of coats, without a spot or speck of dust, stood before a looking glass and brushed the hair on his temples upwards, in the way affected by the Emperor Alexander, and, having assured himself from the way Rostóv looked at it that his coat had been noticed, left the room with a pleasant smile.

"Oh dear, what a beast I am!" muttered Rostóv, as he read the letter.

"Why?"

"Oh, what a pig I am, not to have written and to have given them such a fright! Oh, what a pig I am!" he repeated, flushing suddenly. "Well, have you sent Gabriel for some wine? All right let's have some!"

In the letter from his parents was enclosed a letter of recommendation to Bagratión which the old countess at Anna Mikháylovna's advice had obtained through an acquaintance and sent to her son, asking him to take it to its destination and make use of it.

"What nonsense! Much I need it!" said Rostóv, throwing the letter under the table.

"Why have you thrown that away?" asked Borís.

"It is some letter of recommendation . . . what the devil do I want it for!"

"Why 'What the devil'?" said Borís, picking it up and reading the address. "This letter would be of great use to you."

"I want nothing, and I won't be anyone's adjutant."

"Why not?" inquired Borís.

"It's a lackey's job!"

"You are still the same dreamer, I see," remarked Borís, shaking his head.

"And you're still the same diplomatist! But that's not the point. . . . Come, how are you?" asked Rostóv.

"Well, as you see. So far everything's all right, but I confess I should much like to be an adjutant and not remain at the front."

"Why?"

"Because when once a man starts on military service, he should try to make as successful a career of it as possible."

"Oh, that's it!" said Rostóv, evidently thinking of something else.

He looked intently and inquiringly into his friend's eyes, evidently trying in vain to find the answer to some question.

Old Gabriel brought in the wine.

"Shouldn't we now send for Berg?" asked Borís. "He would drink with you. I can't."

"Well, send for him . . . and how do you get on with that German?" asked Rostóv, with a contemptuous smile.

"He is a very, very nice, honest, and pleasant fellow," answered Borís.

Again Rostóv looked intently into Borís' eyes and sighed. Berg returned, and over the bottle of wine conversation between the three officers became animated. The Guardsmen told Rostóv of their march and how they had been made much of in Russia, Poland, and abroad. They spoke of the sayings and doings of their commander, the Grand Duke, and told stories of

his kindness and irascibility. Berg, as usual, kept silent when the subject did not relate to himself, but in connection with the stories of the Grand Duke's quick temper he related with gusto how in Galicia he had managed to deal with the Grand Duke when the latter made a tour of the regiments and was annoyed at the irregularity of a movement. With a pleasant smile Berg related how the Grand Duke had ridden up to him in a violent passion, shouting: "Arnauts!" * (Arnauts was the Tsarévich's favorite expression when he was in a rage) and called for the company commander.

"Would you believe it, Count, I was not at all alarmed, because I knew I was right. Without boasting, you know, I may say that I know the Army Orders by heart and know the Regulations as well as I do the Lord's Prayer. So, Count, there never is any negligence in my company, and so my conscience was at ease. I came forward. . . ." (Berg stood up and showed how he presented himself, with his hand to his cap, and really it would have been difficult for a face to express greater respect and self-complacency than his did.) "Well, he stormed at me, as the saying is, stormed and stormed and stormed! It was not a matter of life but rather of death, as the saying is. 'Albanians!' and 'devils!' and 'To Siberia!'" said Berg with a sagacious smile. "I knew I was in the right so I kept silent; was not that best, Count? . . . 'Hey, are you dumb?' he shouted. Still I remained silent. And what do you think, Count? The next day it was not even mentioned in the Orders of the Day. That's what keeping one's head means. That's the way, Count," said Berg, lighting his pipe and emitting rings of smoke.

"Yes, that was fine," said Rostóv, smiling.

But Borís noticed that he was preparing to make fun of Berg, and skillfully changed the subject. He asked him to tell them how and where he got his wound. This pleased Rostóv and he began talking about it, and as he went on became more and more animated. He told them of his Schön Grabern affair, just as those who have taken part in a battle generally do describe it, that is, as they would like it to have been, as they have heard it described by others, and as sounds well, but not at all as it really was. Rostóv was a truthful young man and would on no account have told a deliberate lie. He began his story meaning to tell everything just as it happened, but imperceptibly, involuntarily, and inevitably he lapsed into falsehood. If he had told the truth to his hearers—who like himself had often heard stories of attacks and had formed a definite idea of what an attack was and were expecting to hear just such a story—they would either not have be-

* Arnauts is a Turkish name for the Albanians, who supplied the Turks with irregular cavalry.—A.M.

lieved him or, still worse, would have thought that Rostóv was himself to blame since what generally happens to the narrators of cavalry attacks had not happened to him. He could not tell them simply that everyone went at a trot and that he fell off his horse and sprained his arm and then ran as hard as he could from a Frenchman into the wood. Besides, to tell everything as it really happened, it would have been necessary to make an effort of will to tell only what happened. It is very difficult to tell the truth, and young people are rarely capable of it. His hearers expected a story of how beside himself and all aflame with excitement, he had flown like a storm at the square, cut his way in, slashed right and left, how his saber had tasted flesh and he had fallen exhausted, and so on. And so he told them all that.

In the middle of his story, just as he was saying: "You cannot imagine what a strange frenzy one experiences during an attack," Prince Andrew, whom Borís was expecting, entered the room. Prince Andrew, who liked to help young men, was flattered by being asked for his assistance and being well disposed toward Borís, who had managed to please him the day before, he wished to do what the young man wanted. Having been sent with papers from Kutúzov to the Tsarévich, he looked in on Borís, hoping to find him alone. When he came in and saw an hussar of the line recounting his military exploits (Prince Andrew could not endure that sort of man), he gave Borís a pleasant smile, frowned as with half-closed eyes he looked at Rostóv, bowed slightly and wearily, and sat down languidly on the sofa: he felt it unpleasant to have dropped in on bad company. Rostóv flushed up on noticing this, but he did not care, this was a mere stranger. Glancing, however, at Borís, he saw that he too seemed ashamed of the hussar of the line.

In spite of Prince Andrew's disagreeable, ironical tone, in spite of the contempt with which Rostóv, from his fighting army point of view, regarded all these little adjutants on the staff, of whom the newcomer was evidently one, Rostóv felt confused, blushed, and became silent. Borís inquired what news there might be on the staff, and what, without indiscretion, one might ask about our plans.

"We shall probably advance," replied Bolkónski, evidently reluctant to say more in the presence of a stranger.

Berg took the opportunity to ask, with great politeness, whether, as was rumored, the allowance of forage money to captains of companies would be doubled. To this Prince Andrew answered with a smile that he could give no opinion on such an important government order, and Berg laughed gaily.

"As to your business," Prince Andrew continued, addressing Borís, "we

will talk of it later" (and he looked round at Rostóv). "Come to me after the review and we will do what is possible."

And, having glanced round the room, Prince Andrew turned to Rostóv, whose state of unconquerable childish embarrassment now changing to anger he did not condescend to notice, and said: "I think you were talking of the Schön Grabern affair? Were you there?"

"I was there," said Rostóv angrily, as if intending to insult the aide-de-camp.

Bolkónski noticed the hussar's state of mind, and it amused him. With a slightly contemptuous smile, he said: "Yes, there are many stories now told about that affair!"

"Yes, stories!" repeated Rostóv loudly, looking with eyes suddenly grown furious, now at Borís, now at Bolkónski. "Yes, many stories! But our stories are the stories of men who have been under the enemy's fire! Our stories have some weight, not like the stories of those fellows on the staff who get rewards without doing anything!"

"Of whom you imagine me to be one?" said Prince Andrew, with a quiet and particularly amiable smile.

A strange feeling of exasperation and yet of respect for this man's self-possession mingled at that moment in Rostóv's soul.

"I am not talking about you," he said, "I don't know you and, frankly, I don't want to. I am speaking of the staff in general."

"And I will tell you this," Prince Andrew interrupted in a tone of quiet authority, "you wish to insult me, and I am ready to agree with you that it would be very easy to do so if you haven't sufficient self-respect, but admit that the time and place are very badly chosen. In a day or two we shall all have to take part in a greater and more serious duel, and besides, Drubet-skóy, who says he is an old friend of yours, is not at all to blame that my face has the misfortune to displease you. However," he added rising, "you know my name and where to find me, but don't forget that I do not regard either myself or you as having been at all insulted, and as a man older than you, my advice is to let the matter drop. Well then, on Friday after the review I shall expect you, Drubetskóy. Au revoir!" exclaimed Prince Andrew, and with a bow to them both he went out.

Only when Prince Andrew was gone did Rostóv think of what he ought to have said. And he was still more angry at having omitted to say it. He ordered his horse at once and, coldly taking leave of Borís, rode home. Should he go to headquarters next day and challenge that affected adjutant, or really let the matter drop, was the question that worried him all the way. He thought angrily of the pleasure he would have at seeing the fright of that small and frail but proud man when covered by his pistol,

and then he felt with surprise that of all the men he knew there was none he would so much like to have for a friend as that very adjutant whom he so hated.

7. The Emperor reviews the army. Enthusiasm of Nicholas

THE DAY AFTER Rostóv had been to see Borís, a review was held of the Austrian and Russian troops, both those freshly arrived from Russia and those who had been campaigning under Kutúzov. The two Emperors, the Russian with his heir the Tsarévich, and the Austrian with the Archduke, inspected the allied army of eighty thousand men.

From early morning the smart clean troops were on the move, forming up on the field before the fortress. Now thousands of feet and bayonets moved and halted at the officers' command, turned with banners flying, formed up at intervals, and wheeled round other similar masses of infantry in different uniforms; now was heard the rhythmic beat of hoofs and the jingling of showy cavalry in blue, red, and green braided uniforms, with smartly dressed bandsmen in front mounted on black, roan, or gray horses; then again, spreading out with the brazen clatter of the polished shining cannon that quivered on the gun carriages and with the smell of linstocks, came the artillery which crawled between the infantry and cavalry and took up its appointed position. Not only the generals in full parade uniforms, with their thin or thick waists drawn in to the utmost, their red necks squeezed into their stiff collars, and wearing scarves and all their decorations, not only the elegant, pomaded officers, but every soldier with his freshly washed and shaven face and his weapons clean and polished to the utmost, and every horse groomed till its coat shone like satin and every hair of its wetted mane lay smooth—felt that no small matter was happening, but an important and solemn affair. Every general and every soldier was conscious of his own insignificance, aware of being but a drop in that ocean of men, and yet at the same time was conscious of his strength as a part of that enormous whole.

From early morning strenuous activities and efforts had begun and by ten o'clock all had been brought into due order. The ranks were drawn up on the vast field. The whole army was extended in three lines: the cavalry in front, behind it the artillery, and behind that again the infantry.

A space like a street was left between each two lines of troops. The three parts of that army were sharply distinguished: Kutúzov's fighting army (with the Pávlograds on the right flank of the front); those recently arrived from Russia, both Guards and regiments of the line; and the Austrian

troops. But they all stood in the same lines, under one command, and in a like order.

Like wind over leaves ran an excited whisper: "They're coming! They're coming!" Alarmed voices were heard, and a stir of final preparation swept over all the troops.

From the direction of Olmütz in front of them, a group was seen approaching. And at that moment, though the day was still, a light gust of wind blowing over the army slightly stirred the streamers on the lances and the unfolded standards fluttered against their staffs. It looked as if by that slight motion the army itself was expressing its joy at the approach of the Emperors. One voice was heard shouting: "Eyes front!" Then, like the crowing of cocks at sunrise, this was repeated by others from various sides and all became silent.

In the deathlike stillness only the tramp of horses was heard. This was the Emperors' suites. The Emperors rode up to the flank, and the trumpets of the first cavalry regiment played the general march. It seemed as though not the trumpeters were playing, but as if the army itself, rejoicing at the Emperors' approach, had naturally burst into music. Amid these sounds, only the youthful kindly voice of the Emperor Alexander was clearly heard. He gave the words of greeting, and the first regiment roared "Hurrah!" so deafeningly, continuously, and joyfully that the men themselves were awed by their multitude and the immensity of the power they constituted.

Rostóv, standing in the front lines of Kutúzov's army which the Tsar approached first, experienced the same feeling as every other man in that army: a feeling of self-forgetfulness, a proud consciousness of might, and a passionate attraction to him who was the cause of this triumph.

He felt that at a single word from that man all this vast mass (and he himself an insignificant atom in it) would go through fire and water, commit crime, die, or perform deeds of highest heroism, and so he could not but tremble and his heart stand still at the imminence of that word.

"Hurrah! Hurrah! Hurrah!" thundered from all sides, one regiment after another greeting the Tsar with the strains of the march, and then "Hurrah!" . . . Then the general march, and again "Hurrah! hurrah!" growing ever stronger and fuller and merging into a deafening roar.

Till the Tsar reached it, each regiment in its silence and immobility seemed like a lifeless body, but as soon as he came up it became alive, its thunder joining the roar of the whole line along which he had already passed. Through the terrible and deafening roar of those voices, amid the square masses of troops standing motionless as if turned to stone, hun-

dreds of riders composing the suites moved carelessly but symmetrically and above all freely, and in front of them two men—the Emperors. Upon them the undivided, tensely passionate attention of that whole mass of men was concentrated.

The handsome young Emperor Alexander, in the uniform of the Horse Guards, wearing a cocked hat with its peaks front and back, with his pleasant face and resonant though not loud voice, attracted everyone's attention.

Rostóv was not far from the trumpeters, and with his keen sight had recognized the Tsar and watched his approach. When he was within twenty paces, and Nicholas could clearly distinguish every detail of his handsome, happy young face, he experienced a feeling of tenderness and ecstasy such as he had never before known. Every trait and every movement of the Tsar's seemed to him enchanting.

Stopping in front of the Pávlograds, the Tsar said something in French to the Austrian Emperor and smiled.

Seeing that smile, Rostóv involuntarily smiled himself and felt a still stronger flow of love for his sovereign. He longed to show that love in some way and knowing that this was impossible was ready to cry. The Tsar called the colonel of the regiment and said a few words to him.

"Oh God, what would happen to me if the Emperor spoke to me?" thought Rostóv. "I should die of happiness!"

The Tsar addressed the officers also: "I thank you all, gentlemen, I thank you with my whole heart." To Rostóv every word sounded like a voice from heaven. How gladly would he have died at once for his Tsar!

"You have earned the St. George's standards and will be worthy of them."

"Oh, to die, to die for him!" thought Rostóv.

The Tsar said something more which Rostóv did not hear, and the soldiers, straining their lungs, shouted "Hurrah!"

Rostóv too, bending over his saddle, shouted "Hurrah!" with all his might, feeling that he would like to injure himself by that shout, if only to express his rapture fully.

The Tsar stopped a few minutes in front of the hussars as if undecided.

"How can the Emperor be undecided?" thought Rostóv, but then even this indecision appeared to him majestic and enchanting, like everything else the Tsar did.

That hesitation lasted only an instant. The Tsar's foot, in the narrow pointed boot then fashionable, touched the groin of the bobtailed bay mare he rode, his hand in a white glove gathered up the reins, and he

moved off accompanied by an irregularly swaying sea of aides-de-camp. Farther and farther he rode away, stopping at other regiments, till at last only his white plumes were visible to Rostóv from amid the suites that surrounded the Emperors.

Among the gentlemen of the suite, Rostóv noticed Bolkónski, sitting his horse indolently and carelessly. Rostóv recalled their quarrel of yesterday and the question presented itself whether he ought or ought not to challenge Bolkónski. "Of course not!" he now thought. "Is it worth thinking or speaking of it at such a moment? At a time of such love, such rapture, and such self-sacrifice, what do any of our quarrels and affronts matter? I love and forgive everybody now."

When the Emperor had passed nearly all the regiments, the troops began a ceremonial march past him, and Rostóv on Bedouin, recently purchased from Denísov, rode past too, at the rear of his squadron—that is, alone and in full view of the Emperor.

Before he reached him, Rostóv, who was a splendid horseman, spurred Bedouin twice and successfully put him to the showy trot in which the animal went when excited. Bending his foaming muzzle to his chest, his tail extended, Bedouin, as if also conscious of the Emperor's eye upon him, passed splendidly, lifting his feet with a high and graceful action, as if flying through the air without touching the ground.

Rostóv himself, his legs well back and his stomach drawn in and feeling himself one with his horse, rode past the Emperor with a frowning but blissful face "like a vewy devil," as Denísov expressed it.

"Fine fellows, the Pávlograds!" remarked the Emperor.

"My God, how happy I should be if he ordered me to leap into the fire this instant!" thought Rostóv.

When the review was over, the newly arrived officers, and also Kutúzov's, collected in groups and began to talk about the awards, about the Austrians and their uniforms, about their lines, about Bonaparte, and how badly the latter would fare now, especially if the Essen corps arrived and Prussia took our side.

But the talk in every group was chiefly about the Emperor Alexander. His every word and movement was described with ecstasy.

They all had but one wish: to advance as soon as possible against the enemy under the Emperor's command. Commanded by the Emperor himself they could not fail to vanquish anyone, be it whom it might: so thought Rostóv and most of the officers after the review.

All were then more confident of victory than the winning of two battles would have made them.

8. Borís visits Prince Andrew at Olmütz. Prince Dolgorúkov

THE DAY AFTER the review, Borís, in his best uniform and with his comrade Berg's best wishes for success, rode to Olmütz to see Bolkónski, wishing to profit by his friendliness and obtain for himself the best post he could—preferably that of adjutant to some important personage, a position in the army which seemed to him most attractive. "It is all very well for Rostóv, whose father sends him ten thousand rubles at a time, to talk about not wishing to cringe to anybody and not be anyone's lackey, but I who have nothing but my brains have to make a career and must not miss opportunities, but must avail myself of them!" he reflected.

He did not find Prince Andrew in Olmütz that day, but the appearance of the town where the headquarters and the diplomatic corps were stationed and the two Emperors were living with their suites, households, and courts only strengthened his desire to belong to that higher world.

He knew no one, and despite his smart Guardsman's uniform, all these exalted personages passing in the streets in their elegant carriages with their plumes, ribbons, and medals, both courtiers and military men, seemed so immeasurably above him, an insignificant officer of the Guards, that they not only did not wish to, but simply could not, be aware of his existence. At the quarters of the commander in chief, Kutúzov, where he inquired for Bolkónski, all the adjutants and even the orderlies looked at him as if they wished to impress on him that a great many officers like him were always coming there and that everybody was heartily sick of them. In spite of this, or rather because of it, next day, November 15, after dinner he again went to Olmütz and, entering the house occupied by Kutúzov, asked for Bolkónski. Prince Andrew was in and Borís was shown into a large hall probably formerly used for dancing, but in which five beds now stood, and furniture of various kinds: a table, chairs, and a clavichord. One adjutant, nearest the door, was sitting at the table in a Persian dressing gown, writing. Another, the red, stout Nesvítski, lay on a bed with his arms under his head, laughing with an officer who had sat down beside him. A third was playing a Viennese waltz on the clavichord, while a fourth, lying on the clavichord, sang the tune. Bolkónski was not there. None of these gentlemen changed his position on seeing Borís. The one who was writing and whom Borís addressed turned round crossly and told him Bolkónski was on duty and that he should go through the door on the left into the reception room if he wished to see him. Borís thanked him and went to the reception room, where he found some ten officers and generals.

When he entered, Prince Andrew, his eyes drooping contemptuously (with that peculiar expression of polite weariness which plainly says, "If it were not my duty I would not talk to you for a moment"), was listening to an old Russian general with decorations, who stood very erect, almost on tiptoe, with a soldier's obsequious expression on his purple face, reporting something.

"Very well, then, be so good as to wait," said Prince Andrew to the general, in Russian, speaking with the French intonation he affected when he wished to speak contemptuously, and noticing Borís, Prince Andrew, paying no more heed to the general who ran after him imploring him to hear something more, nodded and turned to him with a cheerful smile.

At that moment Borís clearly realized what he had before surmised, that in the army, besides the subordination and discipline prescribed in the military code, which he and the others knew in the regiment, there was another, more important, subordination, which made this tight-laced, purple-faced general wait respectfully while Captain Prince Andrew, for his own pleasure, chose to chat with Lieutenant Drubetskóy. More than ever was Borís resolved to serve in future not according to the written code, but under this unwritten law. He felt now that merely by having been recommended to Prince Andrew he had already risen above the general who at the front had the power to annihilate him, a lieutenant of the Guards. Prince Andrew came up to him and took his hand.

"I am very sorry you did not find me in yesterday. I was fussing about with Germans all day. We went with Weyrother to survey the dispositions. When Germans start being accurate, there's no end to it!"

Borís smiled, as if he understood what Prince Andrew was alluding to as something generally known. But it was the first time he had heard Weyrother's name, or even the term "dispositions."

"Well, my dear fellow, so you still want to be an adjutant? I have been thinking about you."

"Yes, I was thinking"—for some reason Borís could not help blushing—"of asking the commander in chief. He has had a letter from Prince Kurágin about me. I only wanted to ask because I fear the Guards won't be in action," he added as if in apology.

"All right, all right. We'll talk it over," replied Prince Andrew. "Only let me report this gentleman's business, and I shall be at your disposal."

While Prince Andrew went to report about the purple-faced general, that gentleman—evidently not sharing Borís' conception of the advantages of the unwritten code of subordination—looked so fixedly at the presumptuous lieutenant who had prevented his finishing what he had to say to the adjutant that Borís felt uncomfortable. He turned away and waited

impatiently for Prince Andrew's return from the commander in chief's room.

"You see, my dear fellow, I have been thinking about you," said Prince Andrew when they had gone into the large room where the clavichord was. "It's no use your going to the commander in chief. He would say a lot of pleasant things, ask you to dinner" ("That would not be bad as regards the unwritten code," thought Borís), "but nothing more would come of it. There will soon be a battalion of us aides-de-camp and adjutants! But this is what we'll do: I have a good friend, an adjutant general and an excellent fellow, Prince Dolgorúkov; and though you may not know it, the fact is that now Kutúzov with his staff and all of us count for nothing. Everything is now centered round the Emperor. So we will go to Dolgorúkov; I have to go there anyhow and I have already spoken to him about you. We shall see whether he cannot attach you to himself or find a place for you somewhere nearer the sun."

Prince Andrew always became specially keen when he had to guide a young man and help him to worldly success. Under cover of obtaining help of this kind for another, which from pride he would never accept for himself, he kept in touch with the circle which confers success and which attracted him. He very readily took up Borís' cause and went with him to Dolgorúkov.

It was late in the evening when they entered the palace at Olmütz occupied by the Emperors and their retinues.

That same day a council of war had been held in which all the members of the Hofkriegsrath and both Emperors took part. At that council, contrary to the views of the old generals Kutúzov and Prince Schwartzenberg, it had been decided to advance immediately and give battle to Bonaparte. The council of war was just over when Prince Andrew accompanied by Borís arrived at the palace to find Dolgorúkov. Everyone at headquarters was still under the spell of the day's council, at which the party of the young had triumphed. The voices of those who counseled delay and advised waiting for something else before advancing had been so completely silenced and their arguments confuted by such conclusive evidence of the advantages of attacking that what had been discussed at the council—the coming battle and the victory that would certainly result from it—no longer seemed to be in the future but in the past. All the advantages were on our side. Our enormous forces, undoubtedly superior to Napoleon's, were concentrated in one place, the troops inspired by the Emperors' presence were eager for action. The strategic position where the operations would take place was familiar in all its details to the Austrian General Weyrother: a lucky accident had ordained that the Austrian army should

maneuver the previous year on the very fields where the French had now to be fought; the adjacent locality was known and shown in every detail on the maps, and Bonaparte, evidently weakened, was undertaking nothing.

Dolgorúkov, one of the warmest advocates of an attack, had just returned from the council, tired and exhausted but eager and proud of the victory that had been gained. Prince Andrew introduced his protégé, but Prince Dolgorúkov politely and firmly pressing his hand said nothing to Borís and, evidently unable to suppress the thoughts which were uppermost in his mind at that moment, addressed Prince Andrew in French.

"Ah, my dear fellow, what a battle we have gained! God grant that the one that will result from it will be as victorious! However, my dear fellow," he said abruptly and eagerly, "I must confess to having been unjust to the Austrians and especially to Weyrother. What exactitude, what minuteness, what knowledge of the locality, what foresight for every eventuality, every possibility even to the smallest detail! No, my dear fellow, no conditions better than our present ones could have been devised. This combination of Austrian precision with Russian valor—what more could be wished for?"

"So the attack is definitely resolved on?" asked Bolkónski.

"And do you know, my dear fellow, it seems to me that Bonaparte has decidedly lost his bearings, you know that a letter was received from him today for the Emperor." Dolgorúkov smiled significantly.

"Is that so? And what did he say?" inquired Bolkónski.

"What can he say? Tra-di-ri-di-ra and so on . . . merely to gain time. I tell you he is in our hands, that's certain! But what was most amusing," he continued, with a sudden, good-natured laugh, "was that we could not think how to address the reply! If not as 'Consul' and of course not as 'Emperor,' it seemed to me it should be to 'General Bonaparte.' "

"But between not recognizing him as Emperor and calling him General Bonaparte, there is a difference," remarked Bolkónski.

"That's just it," interrupted Dolgorúkov quickly, laughing. "You know Bilíbin—he's a very clever fellow. He suggested addressing him as 'Usurper and Enemy of Mankind.' "

Dolgorúkov laughed merrily.

"Only that?" said Bolkónski.

"All the same, it was Bilíbin who found a suitable form for the address. He is a wise and clever fellow."

"What was it?"

"To the Head of the French Government . . . Au chef du gouvernement français," said Dolgorúkov, with grave satisfaction. "Good, wasn't it?"

"Yes, but he will dislike it extremely," said Bolkónski.

"Oh yes, very much! My brother knows him, he's dined with him—the present Emperor—more than once in Paris, and tells me he never met a more cunning or subtle diplomatist—you know, a combination of French adroitness and Italian play-acting! Do you know the tale about him and Count Markóv? Count Markóv was the only man who knew how to handle him. You know the story of the handkerchief? It is delightful!"

And the talkative Dolgorúkov, turning now to Borís, now to Prince Andrew, told how Bonaparte wishing to test Markóv, our ambassador, purposely dropped a handkerchief in front of him and stood looking at Markóv, probably expecting Markóv to pick it up for him, and how Markóv immediately dropped his own beside it and picked it up without touching Bonaparte's.

"Delightful!" said Bolkónski. "But I have come to you, Prince, as a petitioner on behalf of this young man. You see . . ." but before Prince Andrew could finish, an aide-de-camp came in to summon Dolgorúkov to the Emperor.

"Oh, what a nuisance," said Dolgorúkov, getting up hurriedly and pressing the hands of Prince Andrew and Borís. "You know I should be very glad to do all in my power both for you and for this dear young man." Again he pressed the hand of the latter with an expression of good-natured, sincere, and animated levity. "But you see . . . another time!"

Borís was excited by the thought of being so close to the higher powers as he felt himself to be at that moment. He was conscious that here he was in contact with the springs that set in motion the enormous movements of the mass of which in his regiment he felt himself a tiny, obedient, and insignificant atom. They followed Prince Dolgorúkov out into the corridor and met—coming out of the door of the Emperor's room by which Dolgorúkov had entered—a short man in civilian clothes with a clever face and sharply projecting jaw which, without spoiling his face, gave him a peculiar vivacity and shiftiness of expression. This short man nodded to Dolgorúkov as to an intimate friend and stared at Prince Andrew with cool intensity, walking straight toward him and evidently expecting him to bow or to step out of his way. Prince Andrew did neither: a look of animosity appeared on his face and the other turned away and went down the side of the corridor.

"Who was that?" asked Borís.

"He is one of the most remarkable, but to me most unpleasant of men—the Minister of Foreign Affairs, Prince Adam Czartoryski. . . . It is such men as he who decide the fate of nations," added Bolkónski with a sigh he could not suppress, as they passed out of the palace.

Next day, the army began its campaign, and up to the very battle of Aus-
terlitz, Borís was unable to see either Prince Andrew or Dolgorúkov again
and remained for a while with the Ismáylov regiment.

9. Nicholas not in the action at Wischau. The Emperor. Nicholas' devotion to him

AT DAWN on the sixteenth of November, Denísov's squadron, in which
Nicholas Rostóv served and which was in Prince Bagratión's detach-
ment, moved from the place where it had spent the night, advancing into
action as arranged, and after going behind other columns for about two
thirds of a mile was stopped on the highroad. Rostóv saw the Cossacks and
then the first and second squadrons of hussars and infantry battalions and
artillery pass by and go forward and then Generals Bagratión and Dolgorú-
kov ride past with their adjutants. All the fear before action which he had
experienced as previously, all the inner struggle to conquer that fear, all
his dreams of distinguishing himself as a true hussar in this battle, had
been wasted. Their squadron remained in reserve and Nicholas Rostóv
spent that day in a dull and wretched mood. At nine in the morning, he
heard firing in front and shouts of *hurrah*, and saw wounded being brought
back (there were not many of them), and at last he saw how a whole de-
tachment of French cavalry was brought in, convoyed by a *sótnya* * of Cos-
sacks. Evidently the affair was over and, though not big, had been a suc-
cessful engagement. The men and officers returning spoke of a brilliant
victory, of the occupation of the town of Wischau and the capture of a
whole French squadron. The day was bright and sunny after a sharp night
frost, and the cheerful glitter of that autumn day was in keeping with the
news of victory which was conveyed, not only by the tales of those who
had taken part in it, but also by the joyful expression on the faces of sol-
diers, officers, generals, and adjutants, as they passed Rostóv going or com-
ing. And Nicholas, who had vainly suffered all the dread that precedes a
battle and had spent that happy day in inactivity, was all the more de-
pressed.

"Come here, Wostóv. Let's dwink to dwown our gwief!" shouted Dení-
sov, who had settled down by the roadside with a flask and some food.

The officers gathered round Denísov's canteen, eating and talking.

"There! They are bringing another!" cried one of the officers, indicating
a captive French dragoon who was being brought in on foot by two
Cossacks.

* Sótnya, *a Cossack squadron of one hundred cavalrymen.*

One of them was leading by the bridle a fine large French horse he had taken from the prisoner.

"Sell us that horse!" Denísov called out to the Cossacks.

"If you like, your honor!"

The officers got up and stood round the Cossacks and their prisoner. The French dragoon was a young Alsatian who spoke French with a German accent. He was breathless with agitation, his face was red, and when he heard some French spoken he at once began speaking to the officers, addressing first one, then another. He said he would not have been taken, it was not his fault but the corporal's who had sent him to seize some horse-cloths, though he had told him the Russians were there. And at every word he added: "But don't hurt my little horse!" and stroked the animal. It was plain that he did not quite grasp where he was. Now he excused himself for having been taken prisoner and now, imagining himself before his own officers, insisted on his soldierly discipline and zeal in the service. He brought with him into our rearguard all the freshness of atmosphere of the French army, which was so alien to us.

The Cossacks sold the horse for two gold pieces,* and Rostóv, being the richest of the officers now that he had received his money, bought it.

"But don't hurt my little horse!" said the Alsatian good-naturedly to Rostóv when the animal was handed over to the hussar.

Rostóv smilingly reassured the dragoon and gave him money.

"Alley! Alley!" said the Cossack, touching the prisoner's arm to make him go on.

"The Emperor! The Emperor!" was suddenly heard among the hussars.

All began to run and bustle, and Rostóv saw coming up the road behind him several riders with white plumes in their hats. In a moment everyone was in his place, waiting.

Rostóv did not know or remember how he ran to his place and mounted. Instantly his regret at not having been in action and his dejected mood amid people of whom he was weary had gone, instantly every thought of himself had vanished. He was filled with happiness at his nearness to the Emperor. He felt that this nearness by itself made up to him for the day he had lost. He was happy as a lover when the longed-for moment of meeting arrives. Not daring to look round and without looking round, he was ecstatically conscious of *his* approach. He felt it not only from the sound of the hoofs of the approaching cavalcade, but because as *he* drew near everything grew brighter, more joyful, more significant, and more festive around him. Nearer and nearer to Rostóv came that sun shedding beams of mild and majestic light around, and already he felt himself enveloped

* *The coin in question, the* chervónets, *was worth three gold rubles.*—A.M.

in those beams, he heard *his* voice, that kindly, calm, and majestic voice that was yet so simple! And as if in accord with Rostóv's feeling, there was a deathly stillness amid which was heard the Emperor's voice.

"The Pávlograd hussars?" he inquired.

"The reserves, sire!" replied a voice, a very human one compared to that which had said: "The Pávlograd hussars?"

The Emperor drew level with Rostóv and halted. Alexander's face was even more beautiful than it had been three days before at the review. It shone with such gaiety and youth, such innocent youth, that it suggested the liveliness of a fourteen-year-old boy, and yet it was the face of the majestic Emperor. Casually, while surveying the squadron, the Emperor's eyes met Rostóv's and rested on them for not more than two seconds. Whether or no the Emperor understood what was going on in Rostóv's soul (it seemed to Rostóv that he understood everything), at any rate his light-blue eyes gazed for about two seconds into Rostóv's face. A gentle, mild light poured from them. Then all at once he raised his eyebrows, abruptly touched his horse with his left foot, and galloped on.

The younger Emperor could not restrain his wish to be present at the battle and, in spite of the remonstrances of his courtiers, at twelve o'clock left the third column with which he had been and galloped toward the vanguard. Before he came up with the hussars, several adjutants met him with news of the successful result of the action.

This battle, which consisted in the capture of a French squadron, was represented as a brilliant victory over the French, and so the Emperor and the whole army, especially while the smoke hung over the battlefield, believed that the French had been defeated and were retreating against their will. A few minutes after the Emperor had passed, the Pávlograd division was ordered to advance. In Wischau itself, a petty German town, Rostóv saw the Emperor again. In the market place, where there had been some rather heavy firing before the Emperor's arrival, lay several killed and wounded soldiers whom there had not been time to move. The Emperor, surrounded by his suite of officers and courtiers, was riding a bobtailed chestnut mare, a different one from that which he had ridden at the review, and bending to one side he gracefully held a gold lorgnette to his eyes and looked at a soldier who lay prone, with blood on his uncovered head. The wounded soldier was so dirty, coarse, and revolting that his proximity to the Emperor shocked Rostóv. Rostóv saw how the Emperor's rather round shoulders shuddered as if a cold shiver had run down them, how his left foot began convulsively tapping the horse's side with the spur, and how the well-trained horse looked round unconcerned and did not stir. An

adjutant, dismounting, lifted the soldier under the arms to place him on a stretcher that had been brought. The soldier groaned.

"Gently, gently! Can't you do it more gently?" said the Emperor apparently suffering more than the dying soldier, and he rode away.

Rostóv saw tears filling the Emperor's eyes and heard him, as he was riding away, say to Czartoryski: "What a terrible thing war is: what a terrible thing! *Quelle terrible chose que la guerre!*"

The troops of the vanguard were stationed before Wischau, within sight of the enemy's lines, which all day long had yielded ground to us at the least firing. The Emperor's gratitude was announced to the vanguard, rewards were promised, and the men received a double ration of vodka. The campfires crackled and the soldiers' songs resounded even more merrily than on the previous night. Denísov celebrated his promotion to the rank of major, and Rostóv, who had already drunk enough, at the end of the feast proposed the Emperor's health. "Not 'our Sovereign, the Emperor,' as they say at official dinners," said he, "but the health of our Sovereign, that good, enchanting, and great man! Let us drink to his health and to the certain defeat of the French!

"If we fought before," he said, "not letting the French pass, as at Schön Grabern, what shall we not do now when *he* is at the front? We will all die for him gladly! Is it not so, gentlemen? Perhaps I am not saying it right, I have drunk a good deal—but that is how I feel, and so do you too! To the health of Alexander the First! Hurrah!"

"Hurrah!" rang the enthusiastic voices of the officers.

And the old cavalry captain, Kírsten, shouted enthusiastically and no less sincerely than the twenty-year-old Rostóv.

When the officers had emptied and smashed their glasses, Kírsten filled others and, in shirt sleeves and breeches, went glass in hand to the soldiers' bonfires and with his long gray mustache, his white chest showing under his open shirt, he stood in a majestic pose in the light of the campfire, waving his uplifted arm.

"Lads! here's to our Sovereign, the Emperor, and victory over our enemies! Hurrah!" he exclaimed in his dashing, old, hussar's baritone.

The hussars crowded round and responded heartily with loud shouts.

Late that night, when all had separated, Denísov with his short hand patted his favorite, Rostóv, on the shoulder.

"As there's no one to fall in love with on campaign, he's fallen in love with the Tsar," he said.

"Denísov, don't make fun of it!" cried Rostóv. "It is such a lofty, beautiful feeling, such a . . ."

"I believe it, I believe it, fwiend, and I share and appwove. . . ."

"No, you don't understand!"

And Rostóv got up and went wandering among the campfires, dreaming of what happiness it would be to die—not in saving the Emperor's life (he did not even dare to dream of that), but simply to die before his eyes. He really was in love with the Tsar and the glory of the Russian arms and the hope of future triumph. And he was not the only man to experience that feeling during those memorable days preceding the battle of Austerlitz: nine tenths of the men in the Russian army were then in love, though less ecstatically, with their Tsar and the glory of the Russian arms.

10. Preparations for action. Dolgorúkov's opinion of Napoleon and of his position. Kutúzov's depression

THE NEXT DAY the Emperor stopped at Wischau, and Villier, his physician, was repeatedly summoned to see him. At headquarters and among the troops near by the news spread that the Emperor was unwell. He ate nothing and had slept badly that night, those around him reported. The cause of this indisposition was the strong impression made on his sensitive mind by the sight of the killed and wounded.

At daybreak on the seventeenth, a French officer who had come with a flag of truce, demanding an audience with the Russian Emperor, was brought into Wischau from our outposts. This officer was Savary. The Emperor had only just fallen asleep and so Savary had to wait. At midday he was admitted to the Emperor, and an hour later he rode off with Prince Dolgorúkov to the advanced post of the French army.

It was rumored that Savary had been sent to propose to Alexander a meeting with Napoleon. To the joy and pride of the whole army, a personal interview was refused, and instead of the Sovereign, Prince Dolgorúkov, the victor at Wischau, was sent with Savary to negotiate with Napoleon if, contrary to expectations, these negotiations were actuated by a real desire for peace.

Toward evening Dolgorúkov came back, went straight to the Tsar, and remained alone with him for a long time.

On the eighteenth and nineteenth of November, the army advanced two days' march and the enemy's outposts after a brief interchange of shots retreated. In the highest army circles from midday on the nineteenth, a great, excitedly bustling activity began which lasted till the morning of the twentieth, when the memorable battle of Austerlitz was fought.

Till midday on the nineteenth, the activity—the eager talk, running to and fro, and dispatching of adjutants—was confined to the Emperor's

headquarters. But on the afternoon of that day, this activity reached Kutúzov's headquarters and the staffs of the commanders of columns. By evening, the adjutants had spread it to all ends and parts of the army, and in the night from the nineteenth to the twentieth, the whole eighty thousand allied troops rose from their bivouacs to the hum of voices, and the army swayed and started in one enormous mass six miles long.

The concentrated activity which had begun at the Emperor's headquarters in the morning and had started the whole movement that followed was like the first movement of the main wheel of a large tower clock. One wheel slowly moved, another was set in motion, and a third, and wheels began to revolve faster and faster, levers and cogwheels to work, chimes to play, figures to pop out, and the hands to advance with regular motion as a result of all that activity.

Just as in the mechanism of a clock, so in the mechanism of the military machine, an impulse once given leads to the final result; and just as indifferently quiescent till the moment when motion is transmitted to them are the parts of the mechanism which the impulse has not yet reached. Wheels creak on their axles as the cogs engage one another and the revolving pulleys whirr with the rapidity of their movement, but a neighboring wheel is as quiet and motionless as though it were prepared to remain so for a hundred years; but the moment comes when the lever catches it and obeying the impulse that wheel begins to creak and joins in the common motion the result and aim of which are beyond its ken.

Just as in a clock, the result of the complicated motion of innumerable wheels and pulleys is merely a slow and regular movement of the hands which show the time, so the result of all the complicated human activities of 160,000 Russians and French—all their passions, desires, remorse, humiliations, sufferings, outbursts of pride, fear, and enthusiasm—was only the loss of the battle of Austerlitz, the so-called battle of the three Emperors—that is to say, a slow movement of the hand on the dial of human history.

Prince Andrew was on duty that day and in constant attendance on the commander in chief.

At six in the evening, Kutúzov went to the Emperor's headquarters and after staying but a short time with the Tsar went to see the grand marshal of the court, Count Tolstóy.

Bolkónski took the opportunity to go in to get some details of the coming action from Dolgorúkov. He felt that Kutúzov was upset and dissatisfied about something and that at headquarters they were dissatisfied with him, and also that at the Emperor's headquarters everyone adopted to-

ward him the tone of men who know something others do not know: he therefore wished to speak to Dolgorúkov.

"Well, how d'you do, my dear fellow?" said Dolgorúkov, who was sitting at tea with Bilíbin. "The fete is for tomorrow. How is your old fellow? Out of sorts?"

"I won't say he is out of sorts, but I fancy he would like to be heard."

"But they heard him at the council of war and will hear him when he talks sense, but to temporize and wait for something now when Bonaparte fears nothing so much as a general battle is impossible."

"Yes, you have seen him?" said Prince Andrew. "Well, what is Bonaparte like? How did he impress you?"

"Yes, I saw him, and am convinced that he fears nothing so much as a general engagement," repeated Dolgorúkov, evidently prizing this general conclusion which he had arrived at from his interview with Napoleon. "If he weren't afraid of a battle why did he ask for that interview? Why negotiate, and above all why retreat, when to retreat is so contrary to his method of conducting war? Believe me, he is afraid, afraid of a general battle. His hour has come! Mark my words!"

"But tell me, what is he like, eh?" said Prince Andrew again.

"He is a man in a gray overcoat, very anxious that I should call him 'Your Majesty,' but who, to his chagrin, got no title from me! That's the sort of man he is, and nothing more," replied Dolgorúkov, looking round at Bilíbin with a smile.

"Despite my great respect for old Kutúzov," he continued, "we should be a nice set of fellows if we were to wait about and so give him a chance to escape, or to trick us, now that we certainly have him in our hands! No, we mustn't forget Suvórov and his rule—not to put yourself in a position to be attacked, but yourself to attack. Believe me in war the energy of young men often shows the way better than all the experience of old Cunctators." *

"But in what position are we going to attack him? I have been at the outposts today and it is impossible to say where his chief forces are situated," said Prince Andrew.

He wished to explain to Dolgorúkov a plan of attack he had himself formed.

"Oh, that is all the same," Dolgorúkov said quickly, and getting up he spread a map on the table. "All eventualities have been foreseen. If he is standing before Brünn . . ."

* Cunctator, *the Delayer, a nickname given to Quintus Fabius Maximus Verrucosus because of his cautious military tactics.*—A.M.

And Prince Dolgorúkov rapidly but indistinctly explained Weyrother's plan of a flanking movement.

Prince Andrew began to reply and to state his own plan, which might have been as good as Weyrother's, but for the disadvantage that Weyrother's had already been approved. As soon as Prince Andrew began to demonstrate the defects of the latter and the merits of his own plan, Prince Dolgorúkov ceased to listen to him and gazed absent-mindedly not at the map, but at Prince Andrew's face.

"There will be a council of war at Kutúzov's tonight, though; you can say all this there," remarked Dolgorúkov.

"I will do so," said Prince Andrew, moving away from the map.

"Whatever are you bothering about, gentlemen?" said Bilíbin, who, till then, had listened with an amused smile to their conversation and now was evidently ready with a joke. "Whether tomorrow brings victory or defeat, the glory of our Russian arms is secure. Except your Kutúzov, there is not a single Russian in command of a column! The commanders are: Herr General Wimpfen, le Comte de Langeron, le Prince de Lichtenstein, le Prince de Hohenlohe, and finally Prishprish,* and so on like all those Polish names."

"Be quiet, backbiter!" said Dolgorúkov. "It is not true; there are now two Russians, Milorádovich, and Dokhtúrov, and there would be a third, Count Arakchéev, if his nerves were not too weak."

"However, I think General Kutúzov has come out," said Prince Andrew. "I wish you good luck and success, gentlemen!" he added and went out after shaking hands with Dolgorúkov and Bilíbin.

On the way home, Prince Andrew could not refrain from asking Kutúzov, who was sitting silently beside him, what he thought of tomorrow's battle.

Kutúzov looked sternly at his adjutant and, after a pause, replied: "I think the battle will be lost, and so I told Count Tolstóy and asked him to tell the Emperor. What do you think he replied? 'But, my dear general, I am engaged with rice and cutlets, look after military matters yourself!' Yes . . . That was the answer I got!"

* *The Polish commander referred to was General Przebyszéwski.*—A.M.

11. The Council of War. Weyrother's plans. Kutúzov sleeps. Prince Andrew's reflections

SHORTLY AFTER nine o'clock that evening, Weyrother drove with his plans to Kutúzov's quarters where the council of war was to be held. All the commanders of columns were summoned to the commander in chief's and with the exception of Prince Bagratión, who declined to come, were all there at the appointed time.

Weyrother, who was in full control of the proposed battle, by his eagerness and briskness presented a marked contrast to the dissatisfied and drowsy Kutúzov, who reluctantly played the part of chairman and president of the council of war. Weyrother evidently felt himself to be at the head of a movement that had already become unrestrainable. He was like a horse running downhill harnessed to a heavy cart. Whether he was pulling it or being pushed by it he did not know, but rushed along at headlong speed with no time to consider what this movement might lead to. Weyrother had been twice that evening to the enemy's picket line to reconnoiter personally, and twice to the Emperors, Russian and Austrian, to report and explain, and to his headquarters where he had dictated the dispositions in German, and now, much exhausted, he arrived at Kutúzov's.

He was evidently so busy that he even forgot to be polite to the commander in chief. He interrupted him, talked rapidly and indistinctly, without looking at the man he was addressing, and did not reply to questions put to him. He was bespattered with mud and had a pitiful, weary, and distracted air, though at the same time he was haughty and self-confident.

Kutúzov was occupying a nobleman's castle of modest dimensions near Ostralitz. In the large drawing room which had become the commander in chief's office were gathered Kutúzov himself, Weyrother, and the members of the council of war. They were drinking tea, and only awaited Prince Bagratión to begin the council. At last Bagratión's orderly came with the news that the prince could not attend. Prince Andrew came in to inform the commander in chief of this and, availing himself of permission previously given him by Kutúzov to be present at the council, he remained in the room.

"Since Prince Bagratión is not coming, we may begin," said Weyrother, hurriedly rising from his seat and going up to the table on which an enormous map of the environs of Brünn was spread out.

Kutúzov, with his uniform unbuttoned so that his fat neck bulged over his collar as if escaping, was sitting almost asleep in a low chair, with his

podgy old hands resting symmetrically on its arms. At the sound of Wey-
rother's voice, he opened his one eye with an effort.

"Yes, yes, if you please! It is already late," said he, and nodding his head
he let it droop and again closed his eye.

If at first the members of the council thought that Kutúzov was pre-
tending to sleep, the sounds his nose emitted during the reading that fol-
lowed proved that the commander in chief at that moment was absorbed
by a far more serious matter than a desire to show his contempt for the
dispositions or anything else—he was engaged in satisfying the irresistible
human need for sleep. He really was asleep. Weyrother, with the gesture
of a man too busy to lose a moment, glanced at Kutúzov and, having con-
vinced himself that he was asleep, took up a paper and in a loud, monot-
onous voice began to read out the dispositions for the impending battle,
under a heading which he also read out:

"Dispositions for an attack on the enemy position behind Kobelnitz
and Sokolnitz, November 30, 1805." *

The dispositions were very complicated and difficult. They began as
follows:

"As the enemy's left wing rests on wooded hills and his right extends
along Kobelnitz and Sokolnitz behind the ponds that are there, while we,
on the other hand, with our left wing by far outflank his right, it is ad-
vantageous to attack the enemy's latter wing especially if we occupy the
villages of Sokolnitz and Kobelnitz, whereby we can both fall on his flank
and pursue him over the plain between Schlappanitz and the Thuerassa
forest, avoiding the defiles of Schlappanitz and Bellowitz which cover the
enemy's front. For this object it is necessary that . . . The first column
marches . . . The second column marches . . . The third column
marches . . ." and so on, read Weyrother.

The generals seemed to listen reluctantly to the difficult dispositions.
The tall, fair-haired General Buxhöwden stood, leaning his back against
the wall, his eyes fixed on a burning candle, and seemed not to listen or
even to wish to be thought to listen. Exactly opposite Weyrother, with his
glistening wide-open eyes fixed upon him and his mustache twisted up-
wards, sat the ruddy Milorádovich in a military pose, his elbows turned
outwards, his hands on his knees, and his shoulders raised. He remained
stubbornly silent, gazing at Weyrother's face, and only turned away his
eyes when the Austrian chief of staff finished reading. Then Milorádovich
looked round significantly at the other generals. But one could not tell
from that significant look whether he agreed or disagreed and was satisfied

* *Weyrother was reading in German and employed the new-style calendar,
so that these dispositions were drawn up on November 18, Old Style.*—A.M.

or not with the arrangements. Next to Weyrother sat Count Langeron who, with a subtle smile that never left his typically southern French face during the whole time of 'the reading, gazed at his delicate fingers which rapidly twirled by its corners a gold snuffbox on which was a portrait. In the middle of one of the longest sentences, he stopped the rotary motion of the snuffbox, raised his head, and with inimical politeness lurking in the corners of his thin lips interrupted Weyrother, wishing to say something. But the Austrian general, continuing to read, frowned angrily and jerked his elbows, as if to say: "You can tell me your views later, but now be so good as to look at the map and listen." Langeron lifted his eyes with an expression of perplexity, turned round to Milorádovich as if seeking an explanation, but meeting the latter's impressive but meaningless gaze drooped his eyes sadly and again took to twirling his snuffbox.

"A geography lesson!" he muttered as if to himself, but loud enough to be heard.

Przebyszéwski, with respectful but dignified politeness, held his hand to his ear toward Weyrother, with the air of a man absorbed in attention. Dohktúrov, a little man, sat opposite Weyrother, with an assiduous and modest mien, and stooping over the outspread map conscientiously studied the dispositions and the unfamiliar locality. He asked Weyrother several times to repeat words he had not clearly heard and the difficult names of villages. Weyrother complied and Dohktúrov noted them down.

When the reading which lasted more than an hour was over, Langeron again brought his snuffbox to rest and, without looking at Weyrother or at anyone in particular, began to say how difficult it was to carry out such a plan in which the enemy's position was assumed to be known, whereas it was perhaps not known, since the enemy was in movement. Langeron's objections were valid but it was obvious that their chief aim was to show General Weyrother—who had read his dispositions with as much self-confidence as if he were addressing school children—that he had to do, not with fools, but with men who could teach him something in military matters.

When the monotonous sound of Weyrother's voice ceased, Kutúzov opened his eye as a miller wakes up when the soporific drone of the mill wheel is interrupted. He listened to what Langeron said, as if remarking, "So you are still at that silly business!" quickly closed his eye again, and let his head sink still lower.

Langeron, trying as virulently as possible to sting Weyrother's vanity as author of the military plan, argued that Bonaparte might easily attack instead of being attacked, and so render the whole of this plan perfectly worthless. Weyrother met all objections with a firm and contemptuous

smile, evidently prepared beforehand to meet all objections be they what they might.

"If he could attack us, he would have done so today," said he.

"So you think he is powerless?" said Langeron.

"He has forty thousand men at most," replied Weyrother, with the smile of a doctor to whom an old wife wishes to explain the treatment of a case.

"In that case he is inviting his doom by awaiting our attack," said Langeron, with a subtly ironical smile, again glancing round for support to Milorádovich who was near him.

But Milorádovich was at that moment evidently thinking of anything rather than of what the generals were disputing about.

"*Ma foi!*" said he, "tomorrow we shall see all that on the battlefield."

Weyrother again gave that smile which seemed to say that to him it was strange and ridiculous to meet objections from Russian generals and to have to prove to them what he had not merely convinced himself of, but had also convinced the sovereign Emperors of.

"The enemy has quenched his fires and a continual noise is heard from his camp," said he. "What does that mean? Either he is retreating, which is the only thing we need fear, or he is changing his position." (He smiled ironically.) "But even if he also took up a position in the Thuerassa, he merely saves us a great deal of trouble and all our arrangements to the minutest detail remain the same."

"How is that? . . ." began Prince Andrew, who had for long been waiting an opportunity to express his doubts.

Kutúzov here woke up, coughed heavily, and looked round at the generals.

"Gentlemen, the dispositions for tomorrow—or rather for today, for it is past midnight—cannot now be altered," said he. "You have heard them, and we shall all do our duty. But before a battle, there is nothing more important . . ." he paused, "than to have a good sleep."

He moved as if to rise. The generals bowed and retired. It was past midnight. Prince Andrew went out.

The council of war, at which Prince Andrew had not been able to express his opinion as he had hoped to, left on him a vague and uneasy impression. Whether Dolgorúkov and Weyrother, or Kutúzov, Langeron, and the others who did not approve of the plan of attack, were right—he did not know. "But was it really not possible for Kutúzov to state his views plainly to the Emperor? Is it possible that on account of court and per-

sonal considerations tens of thousands of lives, and my life, my life," he thought, "must be risked?

"Yes, it is very likely that I shall be killed tomorrow," he thought. And suddenly, at this thought of death, a whole series of most distant, most intimate, memories rose in his imagination: he remembered his last parting from his father and his wife; he remembered the days when he first loved her. He thought of her pregnancy and felt sorry for her and for himself, and in a nervously emotional and softened mood he went out of the hut in which he was billeted with Nesvítski and began to walk up and down before it.

The night was foggy and through the fog the moonlight gleamed mysteriously. "Yes, tomorrow, tomorrow!" he thought. "Tomorrow everything may be over for me! All these memories will be no more, none of them will have any meaning for me. Tomorrow perhaps, even certainly, I have a presentiment that for the first time I shall have to show all I can do." And his fancy pictured the battle, its loss, the concentration of fighting at one point, and the hesitation of all the commanders. And then that happy moment, that Toulon for which he had so long waited, presents itself to him at last. He firmly and clearly expresses his opinion to Kutúzov, to Weyrother, and to the Emperors. All are struck by the justness of his views, but no one undertakes to carry them out, so he takes a regiment, a division—stipulates that no one is to interfere with his arrangements—leads his division to the decisive point, and gains the victory alone. "But death and suffering?" suggested another voice. Prince Andrew, however, did not answer that voice and went on dreaming of his triumphs. The dispositions for the next battle are planned by him alone. Nominally he is only an adjutant on Kutúzov's staff, but he does everything alone. The next battle is won by him alone. Kutúzov is removed and he is appointed . . . "Well and then?" asked the other voice. "If before that you are not ten times wounded, killed, or betrayed, well . . . what then? . . ." * "Well then," Prince Andrew answered himself, "I don't know what will happen and don't want to know, and can't, but if I want this—want glory, want to be known to men, want to be loved by them, it is not my fault that I want it and want nothing but that and live only for that. Yes, for that alone! I shall never tell anyone, but, oh God! what am I to do if I love nothing but fame and men's esteem? Death, wounds,

* *Readers interested in Tolstóy's own life should note that the thought of man's greatest efforts and best hopes being defeated by death, which here occurs to Prince Andrew and is evaded by him, is the very thought that revolutionized Tolstóy's own outlook on life some sixteen years after he wrote this section. See Chapter III of* A Confession.—A.M.

the loss of family—I fear nothing. And precious and dear as many persons are to me—father, sister, wife—those dearest to me—yet dreadful and unnatural as it seems, I would give them all at once for a moment of glory, of triumph over men, of love from men I don't know and never shall know, for the love of these men here," he thought, as he listened to voices in Kutúzov's courtyard. The voices were those of the orderlies who were packing up; one voice, probably a coachman's, was teasing Kutúzov's old cook whom Prince Andrew knew, and who was called Tit. He was saying, "Tit, I say, Tit!"

"Well?" returned the old man.

"Go, Tit, thresh a bit!" said the wag.

"Oh, go to the devil!" called out a voice, drowned by the laughter of the orderlies and servants.

"All the same, I love and value nothing but triumph over them all, I value this mystic power and glory that is floating here above me in this mist!"

12. *Rostóv at the front. Visit of Bagratión and Dolgorúkov.* *Rostóv sent to reconnoiter. Napoleon's proclamation*

THAT SAME NIGHT, Rostóv was with a platoon on skirmishing duty in front of Bagratión's detachment. His hussars were placed along the line in couples and he himself rode along the line trying to master the sleepiness that kept coming over him. An enormous space, with our army's campfires dimly glowing in the fog, could be seen behind him; in front of him was misty darkness. Rostóv could see nothing, peer as he would into that foggy distance: now something gleamed gray, now there was something black, now little lights seemed to glimmer where the enemy ought to be, now he fancied it was only something in his own eyes. His eyes kept closing, and in his fancy appeared—now the Emperor, now Denísov, and now Moscow memories—and he again hurriedly opened his eyes and saw close before him the head and ears of the horse he was riding, and sometimes, when he came within six paces of them, the black figures of hussars, but in the distance was still the same misty darkness. "Why not? . . . It might easily happen," thought Rostóv, "that the Emperor will meet me and give me an order as he would to any other officer; he'll say: 'Go and find out what's there.' There are many stories of his getting to know an officer in just such a chance way and attaching him to himself! What if he gave me a place near him? Oh, how I would guard him, how I would tell him the truth, how I would unmask his deceivers!" And in

order to realize vividly his love and devotion to the sovereign, Rostóv pictured to himself an enemy or a deceitful German, whom he would not only kill with pleasure but whom he would slap in the face before the Emperor. Suddenly a distant shout aroused him. He started and opened his eyes.

"Where am I? Oh yes, in the skirmishing line . . . pass and watchword—*shaft, Olmütz*. What a nuisance that our squadron will be in reserve tomorrow," he thought. "I'll ask leave to go to the front, this may be my only chance of seeing the Emperor. It won't be long now before I am off duty. I'll take another turn and when I get back I'll go to the general and ask him." He readjusted himself in the saddle and touched up his horse to ride once more round his hussars. It seemed to him that it was getting lighter. To the left he saw a sloping descent lit up, and facing it a black knoll that seemed as steep as a wall. On this knoll there was a white patch that Rostóv could not at all make out: was it a glade in the wood lit up by the moon, or some unmelted snow, or some white houses? He even thought something moved on that white spot. "I expect it's snow . . . that spot . . . a spot—*une tache*," he thought. "There now . . . it's not a *tache* . . . Natásha . . . sister, black eyes . . . Na . . . tásha . . . (Won't she be surprised when I tell her how I've seen the Emperor?) Natásha . . . take my sabretache . . ."—"Keep to the right, your honor, there are bushes here," came the voice of an hussar, past whom Rostóv was riding in the act of falling asleep. Rostóv lifted his head that had sunk almost to his horse's mane and pulled up beside the hussar. He was succumbing to irresistible, youthful, childish drowsiness. "But what was I thinking? I mustn't forget. How shall I speak to the Emperor? No, that's not it—that's tomorrow. Oh yes! Natásha . . . sabretache . . . saber them . . . Whom? The hussars . . . Ah, the hussars with mustaches. Along the Tverskáya Street rode the hussar with mustaches . . . I thought about him too, just opposite Gúryev's house . . . Old Gúryev . . . Oh, but Denísov's a fine fellow. But that's all nonsense. The chief thing is that the Emperor is here. How he looked at me and wished to say something, but dared not. . . . No, it was I who dared not. But that's nonsense, the chief thing is not to forget the important thing I was thinking of. Yes, Na-tásha, sabretache, oh, yes, yes! That's right!" And his head once more sank to his horse's neck. All at once it seemed to him that he was being fired at. "What? What? What? . . . Cut them down! What? . . ." said Rostóv, waking up. At the moment he opened his eyes he heard in front of him, where the enemy was, the long-drawn shouts of thousands of voices. His horse and the horse of the hussar near him pricked their ears at these shouts. Over there, where the shouting came

from, a fire flared up and went out again, then another, and all along the
French line on the hill fires flared up and the shouting grew louder and
louder. Rostóv could hear the sound of French words but could not dis-
tinguish them. The din of many voices was too great; all he could hear was:
"ahahah!" and "rrrr!"

"What's that? What do you make of it?" said Rostóv to the hussar be-
side him. "That must be the enemy's camp!"

The hussar did not reply.

"Why, don't you hear it?" Rostóv asked again, after waiting for a reply.

"Who can tell, your honor?" replied the hussar reluctantly.

"From the direction, it must be the enemy," repeated Rostóv.

"It may be he or it may be nothing," muttered the hussar. "It's dark
. . . Steady!" he cried to his fidgeting horse.

Rostóv's horse was also getting restive: it pawed the frozen ground,
pricking its ears at the noise and looking at the lights. The shouting grew
still louder and merged into a general roar that only an army of several
thousand men could produce. The lights spread farther and farther, prob-
ably along the line of the French camp. Rostóv no longer wanted to
sleep. The gay triumphant shouting of the enemy army had a stimulating
effect on him. "Vive l'Empereur! l'Empereur!" he now heard distinctly.

"They can't be far off, probably just beyond the stream," he said to
the hussar beside him.

The hussar only sighed without replying and coughed angrily. The
sound of horse's hoofs approaching at a trot along the line of hussars was
heard, and out of the foggy darkness the figure of a sergeant of hussars
suddenly appeared, looming huge as an elephant.

"Your honor, the generals!" said the sergeant, riding up to Rostóv.

Rostóv, still looking round toward the fires and the shouts, rode with
the sergeant to meet some mounted men who were riding along the line.
One was on a white horse. Prince Bagratión and Prince Dolgorúkov with
their adjutants had come to witness the curious phenomenon of the lights
and shouts in the enemy's camp. Rostóv rode up to Bagratión, reported to
him, and then joined the adjutants listening to what the generals were
saying.

"Believe me," said Prince Dolgorúkov, addressing Bagratión, "it is noth-
ing but a trick! He has retreated and ordered the rearguard to kindle fires
and make a noise to deceive us."

"Hardly," said Bagratión. "I saw them this evening on that knoll; if
they had retreated they would have withdrawn from that too. . . .
Officer!" said Bagratión to Rostóv, "are the enemy's skirmishers still
there?"

"They were there this evening, but now I don't know, your excellency. Shall I go with some of my hussars to see?" replied Rostóv.

Bagratión stopped and, before replying, tried to see Rostóv's face in the mist.

"Well, go and see," he said, after a pause.

"Yes, sir."

Rostóv spurred his horse, called to Sergeant Fédchenko and two other hussars, told them to follow him, and trotted downhill in the direction from which the shouting came. He felt both frightened and pleased to be riding alone with three hussars into that mysterious and dangerous misty distance where no one had been before him. Bagratión called to him from the hill not to go beyond the stream, but Rostóv pretended not to hear him and did not stop but rode on and on, continually mistaking bushes for trees and gullies for men and continually discovering his mistakes. Having descended the hill at a trot, he no longer saw either our own or the enemy's fires, but heard the shouting of the French more loudly and distinctly. In the valley he saw before him something like a river, but when he reached it he found it was a road. Having come out onto the road he reined in his horse, hesitating whether to ride along it or cross it and ride over the black field up the hillside. To keep to the road which gleamed white in the mist would have been safer because it would be easier to see people coming along it. "Follow me!" said he, crossed the road, and began riding up the hill at a gallop toward the point where the French pickets had been standing that evening.

"Your honor, there he is!" cried one of the hussars behind him. And before Rostóv had time to make out what the black thing was that had suddenly appeared in the fog, there was a flash, followed by a report, and a bullet whizzing high up in the mist with a plaintive sound passed out of hearing. Another musket missed fire but flashed in the pan. Rostóv turned his horse and galloped back. Four more reports followed at intervals, and the bullets passed somewhere in the fog singing in different tones. Rostóv reined in his horse, whose spirits had risen, like his own, at the firing, and went back at a footpace. "Well, some more! Some more!" a merry voice was saying in his soul. But no more shots came.

Only when approaching Bagratión did Rostóv let his horse gallop again, and with his hand at the salute rode up to the general.

Dolgorúkov was still insisting that the French had retreated and had only lit fires to deceive us.

"What does that prove?" he was saying as Rostóv rode up. "They might retreat and leave the pickets."

"It's plain that they have not all gone yet, Prince," said Bagratión. "Wait till tomorrow morning, we'll find out everything tomorrow."

"The picket is still on the hill, your excellency, just where it was in the evening," reported Rostóv, stooping forward with his hand at the salute and unable to repress the smile of delight induced by his ride and especially by the sound of the bullets.

"Very good, very good," said Bagratión. "Thank you, officer."

"Your excellency," said Rostóv, "may I ask a favor?"

"What is it?"

"Tomorrow our squadron is to be in reserve. May I ask to be attached to the first squadron?"

"What's your name?"

"Count Rostóv."

"Oh, very well, you may stay in attendance on me."

"Count Ilyá Rostóv's son?" asked Dolgorúkov.

But Rostóv did not reply.

"Then I may reckon on it, your excellency?"

"I will give the order."

"Tomorrow very likely I may be sent with some message to the Emperor," thought Rostóv. "Thank God!"

The fires and shouting in the enemy's army were occasioned by the fact that while Napoleon's proclamation was being read to the troops the Emperor himself rode round his bivouacs. The soldiers, on seeing him, lit wisps of straw and ran after him, shouting, "Vive l'Empereur!" Napoleon's proclamation was as follows:

Soldiers! The Russian army is advancing against you to avenge the Austrian army of Ulm. They are the same battalions you broke at Hollabrünn * and have pursued ever since to this place. The position we occupy is a strong one, and while they are marching to go round me on the right they will expose a flank to me. Soldiers! I will myself direct your battalions. I will keep out of fire if you with your habitual valor carry disorder and confusion into the enemy's ranks, but should victory be in doubt, even for a moment, you will see your Emperor exposing himself to the first blows of the enemy, for there must be no doubt of victory, especially on this day when what is at stake is the honor of the French infantry, so necessary to the honor of our nation.

* Hollabrünn is the battle Tolstóy calls Schön Grabern. The two places are close together.—A.M.

Do not break your ranks on the plea of removing the wounded! Let every man be fully imbued with the thought that we must defeat these hirelings of England, inspired by such hatred of our nation! This victory will conclude our campaign and we can return to winter quarters, where fresh French troops who are being raised in France will join us, and the peace I shall conclude will be worthy of my people, of you, and of myself.

NAPOLEON.

13. Battle of Austerlitz. Prince Andrew badly wounded

AT FIVE in the morning it was still quite dark. The troops of the center, the reserves, and Bagratión's right flank had not yet moved, but on the left flank the columns of infantry, cavalry, and artillery, which were to be the first to descend the heights to attack the French right flank and drive it into the Bohemian mountains according to plan, were already up and astir. The smoke of the campfires, into which they were throwing everything superfluous, made the eyes smart. It was cold and dark. The officers were hurriedly drinking tea and breakfasting, the soldiers, munching biscuit and beating a tattoo with their feet to warm themselves, gathering round the fires throwing into the flames the remains of sheds, chairs, tables, wheels, tubs, and everything that they did not want or could not carry away with them. Austrian column guides were moving in and out among the Russian troops and served as heralds of the advance. As soon as an Austrian officer showed himself near a commanding officer's quarters, the regiment began to move: the soldiers ran from the fires, thrust their pipes into their boots, their bags into the carts, got their muskets ready, and formed rank. The officers buttoned up their coats, buckled on their swords and pouches, and moved along the ranks shouting. The train drivers and orderlies harnessed and packed the wagons and tied on the loads. The adjutants and battalion and regimental commanders mounted, crossed themselves, gave final instructions, orders, and commissions to the baggage men who remained behind, and the monotonous tramp of thousands of feet resounded. The column moved forward without knowing where and unable, from the masses around them, the smoke and the increasing fog, to see either the place they were leaving or that to which they were going.

A soldier on the march is hemmed in and borne along by his regiment as much as a sailor is by his ship. However far he has walked, whatever strange, unknown, and dangerous places he reaches, just as a sailor is

always surrounded by the same decks, masts, and rigging of his ship, so the soldier always has around him the same comrades, the same ranks, the same sergeant major Iván Mítrich, the same company dog Jack, and the same commanders. The sailor rarely cares to know the latitude in which his ship is sailing, but on the day of battle—heaven knows how and whence—a stern note of which all are conscious sounds in the moral atmosphere of an army, announcing the approach of something decisive and solemn, and awakening in the men an unusual curiosity. On the day of battle the soldiers excitedly try to get beyond the interests of their regiment, they listen intently, look about, and eagerly ask concerning what is going on around them.

The fog had grown so dense that though it was growing light they could not see ten paces ahead. Bushes looked like gigantic trees and level ground like cliffs and slopes. Anywhere, on any side, one might encounter an enemy invisible ten paces off. But the columns advanced for a long time, always in the same fog, descending and ascending hills, avoiding gardens and enclosures, going over new and unknown ground, and nowhere encountering the enemy. On the contrary, the soldiers became aware that in front, behind, and on all sides, other Russian columns were moving in the same direction. Every soldier felt glad to know that to the unknown place where he was going, many more of our men were going too.

"There now, the Kúrskies have also gone past," was being said in the ranks.

"It's wonderful what a lot of our troops have gathered, lads! Last night I looked at the campfires and there was no end of them. A regular Moscow!"

Though none of the column commanders rode up to the ranks or talked to the men (the commanders, as we saw at the council of war, were out of humor and dissatisfied with the affair, and so did not exert themselves to cheer the men but merely carried out the orders), yet the troops marched gaily, as they always do when going into action, especially to an attack. But when they had marched for about an hour in the dense fog, the greater part of the men had to halt and an unpleasant consciousness of some dislocation and blunder spread through the ranks. How such a consciousness is communicated is very difficult to define, but it certainly is communicated very surely, and flows rapidly, imperceptibly, and irrepressibly, as water does in a creek. Had the Russian army been alone without any allies, it might perhaps have been a long time before this consciousness of mismanagement became a general conviction, but as it was, the disorder was readily and naturally attributed to the stupid Ger-

mans,* and everyone was convinced that a dangerous muddle had been occasioned by the sausage eaters.

"Why have we stopped? Is the way blocked? Or have we already come up against the French?"

"No, one can't hear them. They'd be firing if we had."

"They were in a hurry enough to start us, and now here we stand in the middle of a field without rhyme or reason. It's all those damned Germans' muddling! What stupid devils!"

"Yes, I'd send them on in front, but no fear, they're crowding up behind. And now here we stand hungry."

"I say, shall we soon be clear? They say the cavalry are blocking the way," said an officer.

"Ah, those damned Germans! They don't know their own country!" said another.

"What division are you?" shouted an adjutant, riding up.

"The Eighteenth."

"Then why are you here? You should have gone on long ago, now you won't get there till evening."

"What stupid orders! They don't themselves know what they are doing!" said the officer and rode off.

Then a general rode past shouting something angrily, not in Russian.

"Tafa-lafa! But what he's jabbering no one can make out," said a soldier, mimicking the general who had ridden away. "I'd shoot them, the scoundrels!"

"We were ordered to be at the place before nine, but we haven't got halfway. Fine orders!" was being repeated on different sides.

And the feeling of energy with which the troops had started began to turn into vexation and anger at the stupid arrangements and at the Germans.

The cause of the confusion was that while the Austrian cavalry was moving toward our left flank, the higher command found that our center was too far separated from our right flank and the cavalry were all ordered to turn back to the right. Several thousand cavalry crossed in front of the infantry, who had to wait.

At the front an altercation occurred between an Austrian guide and a Russian general. The general shouted a demand that the cavalry should be halted, the Austrian argued that not he, but the higher command, was

* To a Russian soldier the Austrians, as well as non-Russian speakers generally, were all "Germans." The word German (németz) in Russian means a "dumb man"—one who cannot speak so that we can understand him.—A.M.

to blame. The troops meanwhile stood growing listless and dispirited. After an hour's delay they at last moved on, descending the hill. The fog that was dispersing on the hill lay still more densely below, where they were descending. In front in the fog a shot was heard and then another, at first irregularly at varying intervals—trata . . . tat—and then more and more regularly and rapidly, and the action at the Goldbach Stream began.

Not expecting to come on the enemy down by the stream, and having stumbled on him in the fog, hearing no encouraging word from their commanders, and with a consciousness of being too late spreading through the ranks, and above all being unable to see anything in front or around them in the thick fog, the Russians exchanged shots with the enemy lazily and advanced and again halted, receiving no timely orders from the officers or adjutants who wandered about in the fog in those unknown surroundings unable to find their own regiments. In this way the action began for the first, second, and third columns, which had gone down into the valley. The fourth column, with which Kutúzov was, stood on the Pratzen Heights.

Below, where the fight was beginning, there was still thick fog; on the higher ground it was clearing, but nothing could be seen of what was going on in front. Whether all the enemy forces were, as we supposed, six miles away, or whether they were near by in that sea of mist, no one knew till after eight o'clock.

It was nine o'clock in the morning. The fog lay unbroken like a sea down below, but higher up at the village of Schlappanitz where Napoleon stood with his marshals around him, it was quite light. Above him was a clear blue sky, and the sun's vast orb quivered like a huge hollow, crimson float on the surface of that milky sea of mist. The whole French army, and even Napoleon himself with his staff, were not on the far side of the streams and hollows of Sokolnitz and Schlappanitz beyond which we intended to take up our position and begin the action, but were on this side, so close to our own forces that Napoleon with the naked eye could distinguish a mounted man from one on foot. Napoleon, in the blue cloak which he had worn on his Italian campaign, sat on his small gray Arab horse a little in front of his marshals. He gazed silently at the hills which seemed to rise out of the sea of mist and on which the Russian troops were moving in the distance, and he listened to the sounds of firing in the valley. Not a single muscle of his face—which in those days was still thin —moved. His gleaming eyes were fixed intently on one spot. His predictions were being justified. Part of the Russian force had already descended into the valley toward the ponds and lakes and part were leaving these

Pratzen Heights which he intended to attack and regarded as the key to the position. He saw over the mist that in a hollow between two hills near the village of Pratzen, the Russian columns, their bayonets glittering, were moving continuously in one direction toward the valley and disappearing one after another into the mist. From information he had received the evening before, from the sound of wheels and footsteps heard by the outposts during the night, by the disorderly movement of the Russian columns, and from all indications, he saw clearly that the allies believed him to be far away in front of them, and that the columns moving near Pratzen constituted the center of the Russian army, and that that center was already sufficiently weakened to be successfully attacked. But still he did not begin the engagement.

Today was a great day for him—the anniversary of his coronation. Before dawn he had slept for a few hours, and refreshed, vigorous, and in good spirits, he mounted his horse and rode out into the field in that happy mood in which everything seems possible and everything succeeds. He sat motionless, looking at the heights visible above the mist, and his cold face wore that special look of confident, self-complacent happiness that one sees on the face of a boy happily in love. The marshals stood behind him not venturing to distract his attention. He looked now at the Pratzen Heights, now at the sun floating up out of the mist.

When the sun had entirely emerged from the fog, and fields and mist were aglow with dazzling light—as if he had only awaited this to begin the action—he drew the glove from his shapely white hand, made a sign with it to the marshals, and ordered the action to begin. The marshals, accompanied by adjutants, galloped off in different directions, and a few minutes later the chief forces of the French army moved rapidly toward those Pratzen Heights which were being more and more denuded by Russian troops moving down the valley to their left.

At eight o'clock Kutúzov rode to Pratzen at the head of the fourth column, Milorádovich's, the one that was to take the place of Przebyszéwski's and Langeron's columns which had already gone down into the valley. He greeted the men of the foremost regiment and gave them the order to march, thereby indicating that he intended to lead that column himself. When he had reached the village of Pratzen he halted. Prince Andrew was behind, among the immense number forming the commander in chief's suite. He was in a state of suppressed excitement and irritation, though controlledly calm as a man is at the approach of a long-awaited moment. He was firmly convinced that this was the day of his Toulon,

or his bridge of Arcola.* How it would come about he did not know, but he felt sure it would do so. The locality and the position of our troops were known to him as far as they could be known to anyone in our army. His own strategic plan, which obviously could not now be carried out, was forgotten. Now, entering into Weyrother's plan, Prince Andrew considered possible contingencies and formed new projects such as might call for his rapidity of perception and decision.

To the left down below in the mist, the musketry fire of unseen forces could be heard. It was there Prince Andrew thought the fight would concentrate. "There we shall encounter difficulties, and there," thought he, "I shall be sent with a brigade or division, and there, standard in hand, I shall go forward and break whatever is in front of me."

He could not look calmly at the standards of the passing battalions. Seeing them he kept thinking, "That may be the very standard with which I shall lead the army."

In the morning all that was left of the night mist on the heights was a hoar frost now turning to dew, but in the valleys it still lay like a milk-white sea. Nothing was visible in the valley to the left into which our troops had descended and from whence came the sounds of firing. Above the heights was the dark clear sky, and to the right the vast orb of the sun. In front, far off on the farther shore of that sea of mist, some wooded hills were discernible, and it was there the enemy probably was, for something could be descried. On the right the Guards were entering the misty region with a sound of hoofs and wheels and now and then a gleam of bayonets; to the left beyond the village similar masses of cavalry came up and disappeared in the sea of mist. In front and behind moved infantry. The commander in chief was standing at the end of the village letting the troops pass by him. That morning Kutúzov seemed worn and irritable. The infantry passing before him came to a halt without any command being given, apparently obstructed by something in front.

"Do order them to form into battalion columns and go round the village!" he said angrily to a general who had ridden up. "Don't you understand, your excellency, my dear sir, that you must not defile through narrow village streets when we are marching against the enemy?"

"I intended to re-form them beyond the village, your excellency," answered the general.

Kutúzov laughed bitterly.

"You'll make a fine thing of it, deploying in sight of the enemy! Very fine!"

* *The scene of Napoleon's brilliant victory in the province of Verona over greatly superior Austrian forces, in 1796.*—A.M.

"The enemy is still far away, your excellency. According to the dispositions . . ."

"The dispositions!" exclaimed Kutúzov bitterly. "Who told you that? . . . Kindly do as you are ordered."

"Yes, sir."

"My dear fellow," Nesvítski whispered to Prince Andrew, "the old man is as surly as a dog."

An Austrian officer in a white uniform with green plumes in his hat galloped up to Kutúzov and asked in the Emperor's name had the fourth column advanced into action.

Kutúzov turned round without answering and his eye happened to fall upon Prince Andrew, who was beside him. Seeing him, Kutúzov's malevolent and caustic expression softened, as if admitting that what was being done was not his adjutant's fault, and still not answering the Austrian adjutant, he addressed Bolkónski.

"Go, my dear fellow, and see whether the third division has passed the village. Tell it to stop and await my orders."

Hardly had Prince Andrew started than he stopped him.

"And ask whether sharpshooters have been posted," he added. "What are they doing? What are they doing?" he murmured to himself, still not replying to the Austrian.

Prince Andrew galloped off to execute the order.

Overtaking the battalions that continued to advance, he stopped the third division and convinced himself that there really were no sharpshooters in front of our columns. The colonel at the head of the regiment was much surprised at the commander in chief's order to throw out skirmishers. He had felt perfectly sure that there were other troops in front of him and that the enemy must be at least six miles away. There was really nothing to be seen in front except a barren descent hidden by dense mist. Having given orders in the commander in chief's name to rectify this omission, Prince Andrew galloped back. Kutúzov still in the same place, his stout body resting heavily in the saddle with the lassitude of age, sat yawning wearily with closed eyes. The troops were no longer moving, but stood with the butts of their muskets on the ground.

"All right, all right!" he said to Prince Andrew, and turned to a general who, watch in hand, was saying it was time they started as all the left-flank columns had already descended.

"Plenty of time, your excellency," muttered Kutúzov in the midst of a yawn. "Plenty of time," he repeated.

Just then at a distance behind Kutúzov was heard the sound of regiments saluting, and this sound rapidly came nearer along the whole ex-

tended line of the advancing Russian columns. Evidently the person they were greeting was riding quickly. When the soldiers of the regiment in front of which Kutúzov was standing began to shout, he rode a little to one side and looked round with a frown. Along the road from Pratzen galloped what looked like a squadron of horsemen in various uniforms. Two of them rode side by side in front, at full gallop. One in a black uniform with white plumes in his hat rode a bobtailed chestnut horse, the other who was in a white uniform rode a black one. These were the two Emperors * followed by their suites. Kutúzov, affecting the manners of an old soldier at the front, gave the command "Attention!" and rode up to the Emperors with a salute. His whole appearance and manner were suddenly transformed. He put on the air of a subordinate who obeys without reasoning. With an affectation of respect which evidently struck Alexander unpleasantly, he rode up and saluted.

This unpleasant impression merely flitted over the young and happy face of the Emperor like a cloud of haze across a clear sky and vanished. After his illness he looked rather thinner that day than on the field of Olmütz where Bolkónski had seen him for the first time abroad, but there was still the same bewitching combination of majesty and mildness in his fine gray eyes, and on his delicate lips the same capacity for varying expression and the same prevalent appearance of goodhearted innocent youth.

At the Olmütz review he had seemed more majestic; here he seemed brighter and more energetic. He was slightly flushed after galloping two miles, and reining in his horse he sighed restfully and looked round at the faces of his suite, young and animated as his own. Czartoryski, Novosíltsev, Prince Volkónsky, Strógonov, and the others, all richly dressed gay young men on splendid, well-groomed, fresh, only slightly heated horses, exchanging remarks and smiling, had stopped behind the Emperor. The Emperor Francis, a rosy, long-faced young man, sat very erect on his handsome black horse, looking about him in a leisurely and preoccupied manner. He beckoned to one of his white adjutants and asked some question—"Most likely he is asking at what o'clock they started," thought Prince Andrew, watching his old acquaintance with a smile he could not repress as he recalled his reception at Brünn. In the Emperors' suite were the picked young orderly officers of the Guard and line regiments, Russian and Austrian. Among them were grooms leading the Tsar's beautiful relay horses covered with embroidered cloths.

* *Because of the presence of the Emperors Napoleon, Alexander, and Francis, this battle is sometimes referred to as The Battle of the Three Emperors.*

As when a window is opened a whiff of fresh air from the fields enters a stuffy room, so a whiff of youthfulness, energy, and confidence of success reached Kutúzov's cheerless staff with the galloping advent of all these brilliant young men.

"Why aren't you beginning, Michael Ilariónovich?" * said the Emperor Alexander hurriedly to Kutúzov, glancing courteously at the same time at the Emperor Francis.

"I am waiting, Your Majesty," answered Kutúzov, bending forward respectfully.

The Emperor, frowning slightly, bent his ear forward as if he had not quite heard.

"Waiting, Your Majesty," repeated Kutúzov. (Prince Andrew noted that Kutúzov's upper lip twitched unnaturally as he said the word "waiting.") "Not all the columns have formed up yet, Your Majesty."

The Tsar heard but obviously did not like the reply; he shrugged his rather round shoulders and glanced at Novosíltsev who was near him, as if complaining of Kutúzov.

"You know, Michael Ilariónovich, we are not on the Empress' Field where a parade does not begin till all the troops are assembled," said the Tsar with another glance at the Emperor Francis, as if inviting him if not to join in at least to listen to what he was saying. But the Emperor Francis continued to look about him and did not listen.[2]

"That is just why I do not begin, sire," said Kutúzov in a resounding voice, apparently to preclude the possibility of not being heard, and again something in his face twitched—"That is just why I do not begin, sire, because we are not on parade and not on the Empress' Field," said he clearly and distinctly.

In the Emperor's suite all exchanged rapid looks that expressed dissatisfaction and reproach. "Old though he may be, he should not, he certainly should not, speak like that," their glances seemed to say.

The Tsar looked intently and observantly into Kutúzov's eye waiting to hear whether he would say anything more. But Kutúzov, with respectfully bowed head, seemed also to be waiting. The silence lasted for about a minute.

* Kutúzov's Christian name and patronymic, a form of address more usual in Russian than the use of the surname.—A.M.

[2] The conversation between Kutúzov and Alexander is taken verbatim from Mikháylovski-Danílevski, from whom much of the description of the battle in the next section is also taken. Tolstóy here for the first time indicates Milorádovich's inclination to model himself on Murat, which is repeatedly alluded to later in the novel.—A.M.

"However, if you command it, Your Majesty," said Kutúzov, lifting his head and again assuming his former tone of a dull, unreasoning, but submissive general.

He touched his horse and having called Milorádovich, the commander of the column, gave him the order to advance.

The troops again began to move, and two battalions of the Nóvgorod and one of the Ápsheron regiment went forward past the Emperor.

As this Ápsheron battalion marched by, the red-faced Milorádovich, without his greatcoat, with his Orders on his breast and an enormous tuft of plumes in his cocked hat worn on one side with its corners front and back, galloped strenuously forward, and with a dashing salute reined in his horse before the Emperor.

"God be with you, general!" said the Emperor.

"Ma foi, sire, nous ferons ce qui sera dans notre possibilité, sire [Indeed, sire, we shall do everything that to do is possible, sire]," he answered gaily, raising nevertheless ironic smiles among the gentlemen of the Tsar's suite by his poor French.

Milorádovich wheeled his horse sharply and stationed himself a little behind the Emperor. The Ápsheron men, excited by the Tsar's presence, passed in step before the Emperors and their suites at a bold, brisk pace.

"Lads!" shouted Milorádovich in a loud, self-confident, and cheery voice, obviously so elated by the sound of firing, by the prospect of battle, and by the sight of the gallant Ápsherons, his comrades in Suvórov's time, now passing so gallantly before the Emperors, that he forgot the sovereigns' presence. "Lads, it's not the first village you've had to take," cried he.

"Glad to do our best!" shouted the soldiers.

The Emperor's horse started at the sudden cry. This horse that had carried the sovereign at reviews in Russia bore him also here on the field of Austerlitz, enduring the heedless blows of his left foot and pricking its ears at the sound of shots just as it had done on the Empress' Field, not understanding the significance of the firing, nor of the nearness of the Emperor Francis' black cob, nor of all that was being said, thought, and felt that day by its rider.

The Emperor turned with a smile to one of his followers and made a remark to him, pointing to the gallant Ápsherons.

Kutúzov accompanied by his adjutants rode at a walking pace behind the carabineers.

When he had gone less than half a mile in the rear of the column he

stopped at a solitary, deserted house that had probably once been an inn, where two roads parted. Both of them led downhill and troops were marching along both.

The fog had begun to clear and enemy troops were already dimly visible about a mile and a half off on the opposite heights. Down below, on the left, the firing became more distinct. Kutúzov had stopped and was speaking to an Austrian general. Prince Andrew, who was a little behind and looking at them, turned to an adjutant to ask him for a field glass.

"Look, look!" said this adjutant, looking not at the troops in the distance, but down the hill before him. "It's the French!"

The two generals and the adjutant took hold of the field glass, trying to snatch it from one another. The expression on all their faces suddenly changed to one of horror. The French were supposed to be a mile and a half away, but had suddenly and unexpectedly appeared just in front of us.

"It's the enemy? . . . No! . . . Yes, see it is! . . . for certain. . . . But how is that?" said different voices.

With the naked eye Prince Andrew saw below them to the right, not more than five hundred paces from where Kutúzov was standing, a dense French column coming up to meet the Ápsherons.

"Here it is! The decisive moment has arrived. My turn has come," thought Prince Andrew, and striking his horse he rode up to Kutúzov.

"The Ápsherons must be stopped, your excellency," cried he. But at that very instant a cloud of smoke spread all round, firing was heard quite close at hand, and a voice of naïve terror barely two steps from Prince Andrew shouted, "Brothers! All's lost!" And at this voice, as if at a command, everyone began to run.

Confused and ever-increasing crowds were running back to where five minutes before the troops had passed the Emperors. Not only would it have been difficult to stop that crowd, it was even impossible not to be carried back with it oneself. Bolkónski only tried not to lose touch with it, and looked around bewildered and unable to grasp what was happening in front of him. Nesvítski with an angry face, red and unlike himself, was shouting to Kutúzov that if he did not ride away at once he would certainly be taken prisoner. Kutúzov remained in the same place and without answering drew out a handkerchief. Blood was flowing from his cheek. Prince Andrew forced his way to him.

"You are wounded?" he asked, hardly able to master the trembling of his lower jaw.

"The wound is not here, it is there!" said Kutúzov, pressing the handkerchief to his wounded cheek and pointing to the fleeing soldiers. "Stop

them!" he shouted, and at the same moment, probably realizing that it was impossible to stop them, spurred his horse and rode to the right.

A fresh wave of the flying mob caught him and bore him back with it.

The troops were running in such a dense mass that once surrounded by them it was difficult to get out again. One was shouting, "Get on! Why are you hindering us?" Another in the same place turned round and fired in the air; a third was striking the horse Kutúzov himself rode. Having by a great effort got away to the left from that flood of men, Kutúzov, with his suite diminished by more than half, rode toward a sound of artillery fire near by. Having forced his way out of the crowd of fugitives, Prince Andrew, trying to keep near Kutúzov, saw on the slope of the hill amid the smoke a Russian battery that was still firing and Frenchmen running toward it. Higher up stood some Russian infantry, neither moving forward to protect the battery nor backward with the fleeing crowd. A mounted general separated himself from the infantry and approached Kutúzov. Of Kutúzov's suite only four remained. They were all pale and exchanged looks in silence.

"Stop those wretches!" gasped Kutúzov to the regimental commander, pointing to the flying soldiers; but at that instant, as if to punish him for those words, bullets flew hissing across the regiment and across Kutúzov's suite like a flock of little birds.

The French had attacked the battery and, seeing Kutúzov, were firing at him. After this volley the regimental commander clutched at his leg; several soldiers fell, and a second lieutenant who was holding the flag let it fall from his hands. It swayed and fell, but caught on the muskets of the nearest soldiers. The soldiers started firing without orders.

"Oh! Oh! Oh!" groaned Kutúzov despairingly and looked around. . . . "Bolkónski!" he whispered, his voice trembling from a consciousness of the feebleness of age, "Bolkónski!" he whispered, pointing to the disordered battalion and at the enemy, "what's that?"

But before he had finished speaking, Prince Andrew, feeling tears of shame and anger choking him, had already leapt from his horse and run to the standard.

"Forward, lads!" he shouted in a voice piercing as a child's.

"Here it is!" thought he, seizing the staff of the standard and hearing with pleasure the whistle of bullets evidently aimed at him. Several soldiers fell.

"Hurrah!" shouted Prince Andrew, and, scarcely able to hold up the heavy standard, he ran forward with full confidence that the whole battalion would follow him.

And really he only ran a few steps alone. One soldier moved and then

another and soon the whole battalion ran forward shouting "Hurrah!" and overtook him. A sergeant of the battalion ran up and took the flag that was swaying from its weight in Prince Andrew's hands, but he was immediately killed. Prince Andrew again seized the standard and, dragging it by the staff, ran on with the battalion. In front he saw our artillerymen, some of whom were fighting, while others, having abandoned their guns, were running toward him. He also saw French infantry soldiers who were seizing the artillery horses and turning the guns round. Prince Andrew and the battalion were already within twenty paces of the cannon. He heard the whistle of bullets above him unceasingly and to right and left of him soldiers continually groaned and dropped. But he did not look at them: he looked only at what was going on in front of him—at the battery. He now saw clearly the figure of a red-haired gunner with his shako knocked awry, pulling one end of a mop while a French soldier tugged at the other. He could distinctly see the distraught yet angry expression on the faces of these two men, who evidently did not realize what they were doing.

"What are they about?" thought Prince Andrew as he gazed at them. "Why doesn't the red-haired gunner run away as he is unarmed? Why doesn't the Frenchman stab him? He will not get away before the Frenchman remembers his bayonet and stabs him. . . ."

And really another French soldier, trailing his musket, ran up to the struggling men, and the fate of the red-haired gunner, who had triumphantly secured the mop and still did not realize what awaited him, was about to be decided. But Prince Andrew did not see how it ended. It seemed to him as though one of the soldiers near him hit him on the head with the full swing of a bludgeon. It hurt a little, but the worst of it was that the pain distracted him and prevented his seeing what he had been looking at.

"What's this? Am I falling? My legs are giving way," thought he, and fell on his back. He opened his eyes, hoping to see how the struggle of the Frenchmen with the gunners ended, whether the red-haired gunner had been killed or not and whether the cannon had been captured or saved. But he saw nothing. Above him there was now nothing but the sky—the lofty sky, not clear yet still immeasurably lofty, with gray clouds gliding slowly across it. "How quiet, peaceful, and solemn; not at all as I ran," thought Prince Andrew—"not as we ran, shouting and fighting, not at all as the gunner and the Frenchman with frightened and angry faces struggled for the mop: how differently do those clouds glide across that lofty infinite sky! How was it I did not see that lofty sky before? And how happy I am to have found it at last! Yes! All is vanity, all falsehood, except that infinite

sky. There is nothing, nothing, but that. But even it does not exist, there is nothing but quiet and peace. Thank God! . . ."

ON OUR RIGHT FLANK commanded by Bagratión, at nine o'clock the battle had not yet begun. Not wishing to agree to Dolgorúkov's demand to commence the action, and wishing to avert responsibility from himself, Prince Bagratión proposed to Dolgorúkov to send to inquire of the commander in chief. Bagratión knew that as the distance between the two flanks was more than six miles, even if the messenger were not killed (which he very likely would be), and found the commander in chief (which would be very difficult), he would not be able to get back before evening.

Bagratión cast his large, expressionless, sleepy eyes round his suite, and the boyish face of Rostóv, breathless with excitement and hope, was the first to catch his eye. He sent him.

"And if I should meet His Majesty before I meet the commander in chief, your excellency?" said Rostóv, with his hand to his cap.

"You can give the message to His Majesty," said Dolgorúkov, hurriedly interrupting Bagratión.

On being relieved from picket duty Rostóv had managed to get a few hours' sleep before morning and felt cheerful, bold, and resolute, with elasticity of movement, faith in his good fortune, and generally in that state of mind which makes everything seem possible, pleasant, and easy.

All his wishes were being fulfilled that morning: there was to be a general engagement in which he was taking part, more than that, he was orderly to the bravest general, and still more, he was going with a message to Kutúzov, perhaps even to the sovereign himself. The morning was bright, he had a good horse under him, and his heart was full of joy and happiness. On receiving the order he gave his horse the rein and galloped along the line. At first he rode along the line of Bagratión's troops, which had not yet advanced into action but were standing motionless; then he came to the region occupied by Uvárov's cavalry and here he noticed a stir and signs of preparation for battle; having passed Uvárov's cavalry he clearly heard the sound of cannon and musketry ahead of him. The firing grew louder and louder.

In the fresh morning air were now heard, not two or three musket shots at irregular intervals as before, followed by one or two cannon shots, but a roll of volleys of musketry from the slopes of the hill before Pratzen, interrupted by such frequent reports of cannon that sometimes several of them were not separated from one another but merged into a general roar.

He could see puffs of musketry smoke that seemed to chase one another down the hillsides, and clouds of cannon smoke rolling, spreading, and mingling with one another. He could also, by the gleam of bayonets visible through the smoke, make out moving masses of infantry and narrow lines of artillery with green caissons.

Rostóv stopped his horse for a moment on a hillock to see what was going on, but strain his attention as he would he could not understand or make out anything of what was happening: there in the smoke men of some sort were moving about, and in front and behind moved lines of troops; but why, whither, and who they were, it was impossible to make out. These sights and sounds had no depressing or intimidating effect on him; on the contrary, they stimulated his energy and determination.

"Go on! Go on! Give it them!" he mentally exclaimed at these sounds, and again proceeded to gallop along the line, penetrating farther and farther into the region where the army was already in action.

"How it will be there I don't know, but all will be well!" thought Rostóv.

After passing some Austrian troops he noticed that the next part of the line (the Guards) was already in action.

"So much the better! I shall see it close," he thought.

He was riding almost along the front line. A handful of men came galloping toward him. They were our Uhlans who with disordered ranks were returning from the attack. Rostóv got out of their way, involuntarily noticed that one of them was bleeding, and galloped on.

"That is no business of mine," he thought. He had not ridden many hundred yards after that before he saw to his left, across the whole width of the field, an enormous mass of cavalry in brilliant white uniforms, mounted on black horses, trotting straight toward him and across his path. Rostóv put his horse to full gallop to get out of the way of these men, and he would have got clear had they continued at the same speed, but they kept increasing their pace, so that some of the horses were already galloping. Rostóv heard the thud of their hoofs and the jingle of their weapons and saw their horses, their figures, and even their faces, more and more distinctly. They were our Horse Guards, advancing to attack the French cavalry that was coming to meet them.

The Horse Guards were galloping, but still holding in their horses. Rostóv could already see their faces and heard the command: "Charge!" shouted by an officer who was urging his thoroughbred to full speed. Rostóv, fearing to be crushed or swept into the attack on the French, galloped along the front as hard as his horse could go, but still was not in time to avoid them.

The last of the Horse Guards, a huge pockmarked fellow, frowned angrily on seeing Rostóv before him, with whom he would inevitably collide. This Guardsman would certainly have bowled Rostóv and his Bedouin over (Rostóv felt himself quite tiny and weak compared to these gigantic men and horses) had it not occurred to Rostóv to flourish his whip before the eyes of the Guardsman's horse. The heavy black horse, sixteen hands high, shied, throwing back its ears; but the pockmarked Guardsman drove his huge spurs in violently, and the horse, flourishing its tail and extending its neck, galloped on yet faster. Hardly had the Horse Guards passed Rostóv before he heard them shout, "Hurrah!" and looking back saw that their foremost ranks were mixed up with some foreign cavalry with red epaulets, probably French. He could see nothing more, for immediately afterwards cannon began firing from somewhere and smoke enveloped everything.

At that moment, as the Horse Guards, having passed him, disappeared in the smoke, Rostóv hesitated whether to gallop after them or to go where he was sent. This was the brilliant charge of the Horse Guards that amazed the French themselves. Rostóv was horrified to hear later that of all that mass of huge and handsome men, of all those brilliant, rich youths, officers and cadets, who had galloped past him on their thousand-ruble horses, only eighteen were left after the charge.

"Why should I envy them? My chance is not lost, and maybe I shall see the Emperor immediately!" thought Rostóv and galloped on.

When he came level with the Foot Guards he noticed that about them and around them cannon balls were flying, of which he was aware not so much because he heard their sound as because he saw uneasiness on the soldiers' faces and unnatural warlike solemnity on those of the officers.

Passing behind one of the lines of a regiment of Foot Guards he heard a voice calling him by name.

"Rostóv!"

"What?" he answered, not recognizing Borís.

"I say, we've been in the front line! Our regiment attacked!" said Borís with the happy smile seen on the faces of young men who have been under fire for the first time.

Rostóv stopped.

"Have you?" he said. "Well, how did it go?"

"We drove them back!" said Borís with animation, growing talkative. "Can you imagine it?" and he began describing how the Guards, having taken up their position and seeing troops before them, thought they were Austrians, and all at once discovered from the cannon balls discharged by those troops that they were themselves in the front line and had un-

expectedly to go into action. Rostóv without hearing Borís to the end spurred his horse.

"Where are you off to?" asked Borís.

"With a message to His Majesty."

"There he is!" said Borís, thinking Rostóv had said "His Highness," and pointing to the Grand Duke who with his high shoulders and frowning brows stood a hundred paces away from them in his helmet and Horse Guards' jacket, shouting something to a pale, white-uniformed Austrian officer.

"But that's the Grand Duke, and I want the commander in chief or the Emperor," said Rostóv, and was about to spur his horse.

"Count! Count!" shouted Berg who ran up from the other side as eager as Borís. "Count! I am wounded in my right hand" (and he showed his bleeding hand with a handkerchief tied round it) "and I remained at the front. I held my sword in my left hand, Count. All our family—the von Bergs—have been knights!"

He said something more, but Rostóv did not wait to hear it and rode away.

Having passed the Guards and traversed an empty space, Rostóv, to avoid again getting in front of the first line as he had done when the Horse Guards charged, followed the line of reserves, going far round the place where the hottest musket fire and cannonade were heard. Suddenly he heard musket fire quite close in front of him and behind our troops, where he could never have expected the enemy to be.

"What can it be?" he thought. "The enemy in the rear of our army? Impossible!" And suddenly he was seized by a panic of fear for himself and for the issue of the whole battle. "But be that what it may," he reflected, "there is no riding round it now. I must look for the commander in chief here, and if all is lost it is for me to perish with the rest."

The foreboding of evil that had suddenly come over Rostóv was more and more confirmed the farther he rode into the region behind the village of Pratzen, which was full of troops of all kinds.

"What does it mean? What is it? Whom are they firing at? Who is firing?" Rostóv kept asking as he came up to Russian and Austrian soldiers running in confused crowds across his path.

"The devil knows! They've killed everybody! It's all up now!" he was told in Russian, German, and Czech by the crowd of fugitives who understood what was happening as little as he did.

"Kill the Germans!" shouted one.

"May the devil take them—the traitors!"

"*Zum Henker diese Russen* [Hang these Russians]!" muttered a German.

Several wounded men passed along the road, and words of abuse, screams, and groans mingled in a general hubbub, then the firing died down. Rostóv learned later that Russian and Austrian soldiers had been firing at one another.

"My God! What does it all mean?" thought he. "And here, where at any moment the Emperor may see them. . . . But no, these must be only a handful of scoundrels. It will soon be over, it can't be *that*, it can't be! Only to get past them quicker, quicker!"

The idea of defeat and flight could not enter Rostóv's head. Though he saw French cannon and French troops on the Pratzen Heights just where he had been ordered to look for the commander in chief, he could not, did not wish to, believe *that*.

Rostóv had been ordered to look for Kutúzov and the Emperor near the village of Pratzen. But neither they nor a single commanding officer were there, only disorganized crowds of troops of various kinds. He urged on his already weary horse to get quickly past these crowds, but the farther he went the more disorganized they were. The highroad on which he had come out was thronged with *calèches*, carriages of all sorts, and Russian and Austrian soldiers of all arms, some wounded and some not. This whole mass droned and jostled in confusion under the dismal influence of cannon balls flying from the French batteries stationed on the Pratzen Heights.

"Where is the Emperor? Where is Kutúzov?" Rostóv kept asking everyone he could stop, but got no answer from anyone.

At last seizing a soldier by his collar he forced him to answer.

"Eh, brother! They've all bolted long ago!" said the soldier, laughing for some reason and shaking himself free.

Having left that soldier who was evidently drunk, Rostóv stopped the horse of a batman or groom of some important personage and began to question him. The man announced that the Tsar had been driven in a carriage at full speed about an hour before along that very road and that he was dangerously wounded.

"It can't be!" said Rostóv. "It must have been someone else."

"I saw him myself," replied the man with a self-confident smile of derision. "I ought to know the Emperor by now, after the times I've seen him in Petersburg. I saw him just as I see you. . . . There he sat in the carriage as pale as anything. How they made the four black horses fly!

Gracious me, they did rattle past! It's time I knew the Imperial horses and Ilyá Iványch. I don't think Ilyá drives anyone except the Tsar!"

Rostóv let go of the horse and was about to ride on, when a wounded officer passing by addressed him:

"Who is it you want?" he asked. "The commander in chief? He was killed by a cannon ball—struck in the breast before our regiment."

"Not killed—wounded!" another officer corrected him.

"Who? Kutúzov?" asked Rostóv.

"Not Kutúzov, but what's his name—well, never mind . . . there are not many left alive. Go that way, to that village, all the commanders are there," said the officer, pointing to the village of Hosjeradek, and he walked on.

Rostóv rode on at a footpace not knowing why or to whom he was now going. The Emperor was wounded, the battle lost. It was impossible to doubt it now. Rostóv rode in the direction pointed out to him, in which he saw turrets and a church. What need to hurry? What was he now to say to the Tsar or to Kutúzov, even if they were alive and unwounded?

"Take this road, your honor, that way you will be killed at once!" a soldier shouted to him. "They'd kill you there!"

"Oh, what are you talking about?" said another. "Where is he to go? That way is nearer."

Rostóv considered, and then went in the direction where they said he would be killed.

"It's all the same now. If the Emperor is wounded, am I to try to save myself?" he thought. He rode on to the region where the greatest number of men had perished in fleeing from Pratzen. The French had not yet occupied that region, and the Russians—the uninjured and slightly wounded—had left it long ago. All about the field, like heaps of manure on well-kept plowland, lay from ten to fifteen dead and wounded to each couple of acres. The wounded crept together in twos and threes and one could hear their distressing screams and groans, sometimes feigned—or so it seemed to Rostóv. He put his horse to a trot to avoid seeing all these suffering men, and he felt afraid—afraid not for his life, but for the courage he needed and which he knew would not stand the sight of these unfortunates.

The French, who had ceased firing at this field strewn with dead and wounded where there was no one left to fire at, on seeing an adjutant riding over it trained a gun on him and fired several shots. The sensation of those terrible whistling sounds and of the corpses around him merged in Rostóv's mind into a single feeling of terror and pity for himself. He

remembered his mother's last letter. "What would she feel," thought he, "if she saw me here now on this field with the cannon aimed at me?"

In the village of Hosjeradek there were Russian troops retiring from the field of battle, who though still in some confusion were less disordered. The French cannon did not reach there and the musketry fire sounded far away. Here everyone clearly saw and said that the battle was lost. No one whom Rostóv asked could tell him where the Emperor or Kutúzov was. Some said the report that the Emperor was wounded was correct, others that it was not, and explained the false rumor that had spread by the fact that the Emperor's carriage had really galloped from the field of battle with the pale and terrified Ober-Hofmarschal Count Tolstóy, who had ridden out to the battlefield with others in the Emperor's suite. One officer told Rostóv that he had seen someone from headquarters behind the village to the left, and thither Rostóv rode, not hoping to find anyone but merely to ease his conscience. When he had ridden about two miles and had passed the last of the Russian troops, he saw, near a kitchen garden with a ditch round it, two men on horseback facing the ditch. One with a white plume in his hat seemed familiar to Rostóv; the other on a beautiful chestnut horse (which Rostóv fancied he had seen before) rode up to the ditch, struck his horse with his spurs, and giving it the rein leaped lightly over. Only a little earth crumbled from the bank under the horse's hind hoofs. Turning the horse sharply, he again jumped the ditch, and deferentially addressed the horseman with the white plumes, evidently suggesting that he should do the same. The rider, whose figure seemed familiar to Rostóv and involuntarily riveted his attention, made a gesture of refusal with his head and hand and by that gesture Rostóv instantly recognized his lamented and adored monarch.

"But it can't be he, alone in the midst of this empty field!" thought Rostóv. At that moment Alexander turned his head and Rostóv saw the beloved features that were so deeply engraved on his memory. The Emperor was pale, his cheeks sunken and his eyes hollow, but the charm, the mildness of his features, was all the greater. Rostóv was happy in the assurance that the rumors about the Emperor being wounded were false. He was happy to be seeing him. He knew that he might and even ought to go straight to him and give the message Dolgorúkov had ordered him to deliver.

But as a youth in love trembles, is unnerved, and dares not utter the thoughts he has dreamed of for nights, but looks around for help or a chance of delay and flight when the longed-for moment comes and he is alone with *her*, so Rostóv, now that he had attained what he had longed

for more than anything else in the world, did not know how to approach
the Emperor, and a thousand reasons occurred to him why it would be
inconvenient, unseemly, and impossible to do so.

"What! It is as if I were glad of a chance to take advantage of his
being alone and despondent! A strange face may seem unpleasant or pain-
ful to him at this moment of sorrow; besides, what can I say to him now,
when my heart fails me and my mouth feels dry at the mere sight of him?"
Not one of the innumerable speeches addressed to the Emperor that he
had composed in his imagination could he now recall. Those speeches
were intended for quite other conditions, they were for the most part to
be spoken at a moment of victory and triumph, generally when he was
dying of wounds and the sovereign had thanked him for heroic deeds,
and while dying he expressed the love his actions had proved.

"Besides how can I ask the Emperor for his instructions for the right
flank now that it is nearly four o'clock and the battle is lost? No, cer-
tainly I must not approach him, I must not intrude on his reflections.
Better die a thousand times than risk receiving an unkind look or bad
opinion from him," Rostóv decided; and sorrowfully and with a heart
full of despair he rode away, continually looking back at the Tsar, who
still remained in the same attitude of indecision.

While Rostóv was thus arguing with himself and riding sadly away,
Captain von Toll chanced to ride to the same spot, and seeing the Em-
peror at once rode up to him, offered his services, and assisted him to
cross the ditch on foot. The Emperor, wishing to rest and feeling unwell,
sat down under an apple tree and von Toll remained beside him. Rostóv
from a distance saw with envy and remorse how von Toll spoke long
and warmly to the Emperor and how the Emperor, evidently weeping,
covered his eyes with his hand and pressed von Toll's hand.

"And I might have been in his place!" thought Rostóv, and hardly re-
straining his tears of pity for the Emperor, he rode on in utter despair,
not knowing where to or why he was now riding.

His despair was all the greater from feeling that his own weakness was
the cause of his grief.

He might . . . not only might but should, have gone up to the sover-
eign. It was a unique chance to show his devotion to the Emperor and he
had not made use of it. . . . "What have I done?" thought he. And he
turned round and galloped back to the place where he had seen the
Emperor, but there was no one beyond the ditch now. Only some carts
and carriages were passing by. From one of the drivers he learned that
Kutúzov's staff were not far off, in the village the vehicles were going to.
Rostóv followed them. In front of him walked Kutúzov's groom leading

horses in horsecloths. Then came a cart, and behind that walked an old, bandy-legged domestic serf in a peaked cap and sheepskin coat.

"Tit! I say, Tit!" said the groom.

"What?" answered the old man absent-mindedly.

"Go, Tit! Thresh a bit!"

"Oh, you fool!" said the old man, spitting angrily. Some time passed in silence, and then the same joke was repeated.

Before five in the evening the battle had been lost at all points. More than a hundred cannon were already in the hands of the French.

Przebyszéwski and his corps had laid down their arms. Other columns after losing half their men were retreating in disorderly confused masses.

The remains of Langeron's and Dokhtúrov's mingled forces were crowding around the dams and banks of the ponds near the village of Augesd.

After five o'clock it was only at the Augesd dam that a hot cannonade (delivered by the French alone) was still to be heard from numerous batteries ranged on the slopes of the Pratzen Heights, directed at our retreating forces.

In the rearguard, Dokhtúrov and others rallying some battalions kept up a musketry fire at the French cavalry that was pursuing our troops. It was growing dusk. On the narrow Augesd dam where for so many years the old miller had been accustomed to sit in his tasseled cap peacefully angling, while his grandson, with shirt sleeves rolled up, handled the floundering silvery fish in the watering can, on that dam over which for so many years Moravians in shaggy caps and blue jackets had peacefully driven their two-horse carts loaded with wheat and had returned dusty with flour whitening their carts—on that narrow dam amid the wagons and the cannon, under the horses' hoofs and between the wagon wheels, men disfigured by fear of death now crowded together, crushing one another, dying, stepping over the dying and killing one another, only to move on a few steps and be killed themselves in the same way.

Every ten seconds a cannon ball flew compressing the air around, or a shell burst in the midst of that dense throng, killing some and splashing with blood those near them.

Dólokhov—now an officer—wounded in the arm, and on foot, with the regimental commander on horseback and some ten men of his company, represented all that was left of that whole regiment. Impelled by the crowd, they had got wedged in at the approach to the dam and, jammed in on all sides, had stopped because a horse in front had fallen under a cannon and the crowd were dragging it out. A cannon ball killed

someone behind them, another fell in front and splashed Dólokhov with blood. The crowd, pushing forward desperately, squeezed together, moved a few steps, and again stopped.

"Move on a hundred yards and we are certainly saved, remain here another two minutes and it is certain death," thought each one.

Dólokhov who was in the midst of the crowd forced his way to the edge of the dam, throwing two soldiers off their feet, and ran onto the slippery ice that covered the millpool.

"Turn this way!" he shouted, jumping over the ice which creaked under him; "turn this way!" he shouted to those with the gun. "It bears! . . ."

The ice bore him but it swayed and creaked, and it was plain that it would give way not only under a cannon or a crowd, but very soon even under his weight alone. The men looked at him and pressed to the bank, hesitating to step onto the ice. The general on horseback at the entrance to the dam raised his hand and opened his mouth to address Dólokhov. Suddenly a cannon ball hissed so low above the crowd that everyone ducked. It flopped into something moist, and the general fell from his horse in a pool of blood. Nobody gave him a look or thought of raising him.

"Get onto the ice, over the ice! Go on! Turn! Don't you hear? Go on!" innumerable voices suddenly shouted after the ball had struck the general, the men themselves not knowing what, or why, they were shouting.

One of the hindmost guns that was going onto the dam turned off onto the ice. Crowds of soldiers from the dam began running onto the frozen pond. The ice gave way under one of the foremost soldiers, and one leg slipped into the water. He tried to right himself but fell in up to his waist. The nearest soldiers shrank back, the gun driver stopped his horse, but from behind still came the shouts: "Onto the ice, why do you stop? Go on! Go on!" And cries of horror were heard in the crowd. The soldiers near the gun waved their arms and beat the horses to make them turn and move on. The horses moved off the bank. The ice, that had held under those on foot, collapsed in a great mass, and some forty men who were on it dashed, some forward and some back, drowning one another.

Still the cannon balls continued regularly to whistle and flop onto the ice and into the water and oftenest of all among the crowd that covered the dam, the pond, and the bank.

On the Pratzen Heights, where he had fallen with the flagstaff in his hand, lay Prince Andrew Bolkónski bleeding profusely and unconsciously uttering a gentle, piteous, and childlike moan.

Toward evening he ceased moaning and became quite still. He did not know how long his unconsciousness lasted. Suddenly he again felt that he was alive and suffering from a burning, lacerating pain in his head.

"Where is it, that lofty sky that I did not know till now, but saw today?" was his first thought. "And I did not know this suffering either," he thought. "Yes, I did not know anything, anything at all till now. But where am I?"

He listened and heard the sound of approaching horses, and voices speaking French. He opened his eyes. Above him again was the same lofty sky with clouds that had risen and were floating still higher, and between them gleamed blue infinity. He did not turn his head and did not see those who, judging by the sound of hoofs and voices, had ridden up and stopped near him.

It was Napoleon accompanied by two aides-de-camp. Bonaparte riding over the battlefield had given final orders to strengthen the batteries firing at the Augesd dam and was looking at the killed and wounded left on the field.

"Fine men!" remarked Napoleon, looking at a dead Russian grenadier, who, with his face buried in the ground and a blackened nape, lay on his stomach with an already stiffened arm flung wide.

"The ammunition for the guns in position is exhausted, Your Majesty," said an adjutant who had come from the batteries that were firing at Augesd.

"Have some brought from the reserve," said Napoleon, and having gone on a few steps he stopped before Prince Andrew, who lay on his back with the flagstaff that had been dropped beside him. (The flag had already been taken by the French as a trophy.)

"That's a fine death!" said Napoleon as he gazed at Bolkónski.

Prince Andrew understood that this was said of him and that it was Napoleon who said it. He heard the speaker addressed as Sire. But he heard the words as he might have heard the buzzing of a fly. Not only did they not interest him, but he took no notice of them and at once forgot them. His head was burning, he felt himself bleeding to death, and he saw above him the remote, lofty, and everlasting sky. He knew it was Napoleon—his hero—but at that moment Napoleon seemed to him such a small, insignificant creature compared with what was passing now between himself and that lofty infinite sky with the clouds flying over it. At that moment it meant nothing to him who might be standing over him, or what was said of him; he was only glad that people were standing near him and only wished that they would help him and bring him back to life, which seemed to him so beautiful now that he had

today learned to understand it so differently. He collected all his strength, to stir and utter a sound. He feebly moved his leg and uttered a weak, sickly groan which aroused his own pity.

"Ah! He is alive," said Napoleon. "Lift this young man up and carry him to the dressing station."

Having said this, Napoleon rode on to meet Marshal Lannes, who, hat in hand, rode up smiling to the Emperor to congratulate him on the victory.

Prince Andrew remembered nothing more: he lost consciousness from the terrible pain of being lifted onto the stretcher, the jolting while being moved, and the probing of his wound at the dressing station. He did not regain consciousness till late in the day, when with other wounded and captured Russian officers he was carried to the hospital. During this transfer he felt a little stronger and was able to look about him and even speak.

The first words he heard on coming to his senses were those of a French convoy officer, who said rapidly: "We must halt here: the Emperor will pass here immediately; it will please him to see these gentlemen prisoners."

"There are so many prisoners today, nearly the whole Russian army, that he is probably tired of them," said another officer.

"All the same! They say this one is the commander of all the Emperor Alexander's Guards," said the first one, indicating a Russian officer in the white uniform of the Horse Guards.

Bolkónski recognized Prince Repnín whom he had met in Petersburg society. Beside him stood a lad of nineteen, also a wounded officer of the Horse Guards.

Bonaparte, having come up at a gallop, stopped his horse.

"Which is the senior?" he asked, on seeing the prisoners.

They named the colonel, Prince Repnín.

"You are the commander of the Emperor Alexander's regiment of Horse Guards?" asked Napoleon.

"I commanded a squadron," replied Repnín.

"Your regiment fulfilled its duty honorably," said Napoleon.

"The praise of a great commander is a soldier's highest reward," said Repnín.

"I bestow it with pleasure," said Napoleon. "And who is that young man beside you?"

Prince Repnín named Lieutenant Sukhtélen.

After looking at him Napoleon smiled.

"He's very young to come to meddle with us."

"Youth is no hindrance to courage," muttered Sukhtélen in a failing voice.

"A splendid reply!" said Napoleon. "Young man, you will go far!"

Prince Andrew, who had also been brought forward before the Emperor's eyes to complete the show of prisoners, could not fail to attract his attention. Napoleon apparently remembered seeing him on the battlefield and, addressing him, again used the epithet "young man" that was connected in his memory with Prince Andrew.

"Well, and you, young man," said he. "How do you feel, *mon brave?*"

Though five minutes before, Prince Andrew had been able to say a few words to the soldiers who were carrying him, now with his eyes fixed straight on Napoleon, he was silent. . . . So insignificant at that moment seemed to him all the interests that engrossed Napoleon, so mean did his hero himself with his paltry vanity and joy in victory appear, compared to the lofty, equitable, and kindly sky which he had seen and understood, that he could not answer him.

Everything seemed so futile and insignificant in comparison with the stern and solemn train of thought that weakness from loss of blood, suffering, and the nearness of death aroused in him. Looking into Napoleon's eyes Prince Andrew thought of the insignificance of greatness, the unimportance of life which no one could understand, and the still greater unimportance of death, the meaning of which no one alive could understand or explain.

The Emperor without waiting for an answer turned away and said to one of the officers as he went: "Have these gentlemen attended to and taken to my bivouac; let my doctor, Larrey, examine their wounds. *Au revoir*, Prince Repnín!" and he spurred his horse and galloped away.

His face shone with self-satisfaction and pleasure.

The soldiers who had carried Prince Andrew had noticed and taken the little gold icon Princess Mary had hung round her brother's neck, but seeing the favor the Emperor showed the prisoners, they now hastened to return the holy image.

Prince Andrew did not see how and by whom it was replaced, but the little icon with its thin gold chain suddenly appeared upon his chest outside his uniform.

"It would be good," thought Prince Andrew, glancing at the icon his sister had hung round his neck with such emotion and reverence, "it would be good if everything were as clear and simple as it seems to Mary. How good it would be to know where to seek for help in this life, and what to expect after it beyond the grave! How happy and calm I should be if I could now say: 'Lord, have mercy on me!' . . . But to whom should I say that? Either to a Power indefinable, incomprehensible, which I not only cannot address but which I cannot even express in words—the

Great All or Nothing—" said he to himself, "or to that God who has been sewn into this amulet by Mary! There is nothing certain, nothing at all except the unimportance of everything I understand, and the greatness of something incomprehensible but all-important.

The stretchers moved on. At every jolt he again felt unendurable pain; his feverishness increased and he grew delirious. Visions of his father, wife, sister, and future son, and the tenderness he had felt the night before the battle, the figure of the insignificant little Napoleon, and above all this the lofty sky, formed the chief subjects of his delirious fancies.

The quiet home life and peaceful happiness of Bald Hills presented itself to him. He was already enjoying that happiness when that little Napoleon had suddenly appeared with his unsympathizing look of short-sighted delight at the misery of others, and doubts and torments had followed, and only the heavens promised peace. Toward morning all these dreams melted and merged into the chaos and darkness of unconsciousness and oblivion, which in the opinion of Napoleon's doctor, Larrey, was much more likely to end in death than in convalescence.

"He is a nervous, bilious subject," said Larrey, "and will not recover."

And Prince Andrew, with others fatally wounded, was left to the care of the inhabitants of the district.

BOOK FOUR

BOOK FOUR

1806

BOOK FOUR

1. Nicholas home on leave

EARLY IN THE YEAR 1806 Nicholas Rostóv returned home on leave. Denísov was going home to Vorónezh and Rostóv persuaded him to travel with him as far as Moscow and to stay with him there. Meeting a comrade at the last post station but one before Moscow, Denísov had drunk three bottles of wine with him and, despite the jolting ruts across the snow-covered road, did not once wake up on the way to Moscow, but lay at the bottom of the sleigh beside Rostóv, who grew more and more impatient the nearer they got to Moscow.

"How much longer? How much longer? Oh, these insufferable streets, shops, bakers' signboards, street lamps, and sleighs!" thought Rostóv, when their leave permits had been passed at the town gate and they had entered Moscow.

"Denísov! We're here! He's asleep," he added, leaning forward with his whole body as if in that position he hoped to hasten the speed of the sleigh.

Denísov gave no answer.

"There's the corner at the crossroads, where the cabman, Zakhár, has his stand, and there's Zakhár himself and still the same horse! And here's the little shop where we used to buy gingerbread! Can't you hurry up? Now then!"

"Which house is it?" asked the driver.

"Why, that one, right at the end, the big one. Don't you see? That's our house," said Rostóv. "Of course, it's our house! Denísov, Denísov! We're almost there!"

Denísov raised his head, coughed, and made no answer.

"Dmítri," said Rostóv to his valet on the box, "those lights are in our house, aren't they?"

"Yes, sir, and there's a light in your father's study."

"Then they've not gone to bed yet? What do you think? Mind now,

don't forget to put out my new coat," added Rostóv, fingering his new mustache. "Now then, get on," he shouted to the driver. "Do wake up, Váska!" he went on, turning to Denísov, whose head was again nodding. "Come, get on! You shall have three rubles for vodka—get on!" Rostóv shouted, when the sleigh was only three houses from his door. It seemed to him the horses were not moving at all. At last the sleigh bore to the right, drew up at an entrance, and Rostóv saw overhead the old familiar cornice with a bit of plaster broken off, the porch, and the post by the side of the pavement. He sprang out before the sleigh stopped, and ran into the hall. The house stood cold and silent, as if quite regardless of who had come to it. There was no one in the hall. "Oh God! Is everyone all right?" he thought, stopping for a moment with a sinking heart, and then immediately starting to run along the hall and up the warped steps of the familiar staircase. The well-known old door handle, which always angered the countess when it was not properly cleaned, turned as loosely as ever. A solitary tallow candle burned in the anteroom.

Old Michael was asleep on the chest. Prokófy, the footman, who was so strong that he could lift the back of the carriage from behind, sat plaiting slippers out of cloth selvedges. He looked up at the opening door and his expression of sleepy indifference suddenly changed to one of delighted amazement.

"Gracious heavens! The young count!" he cried, recognizing his young master. "Can it be? My treasure!" and Prokófy, trembling with excitement, rushed toward the drawing-room door, probably in order to announce him, but, changing his mind, came back and stooped to kiss the young man's shoulder.

"All well?" asked Rostóv, drawing away his arm.

"Yes, God be thanked! Yes! They've just finished supper. Let me have a look at you, your excellency."

"Is everything quite all right?"

"The Lord be thanked, yes!"

Rostóv, who had completely forgotten Denísov, not wishing anyone to forestall him, threw off his fur coat and ran on tiptoe through the large dark ballroom. All was the same: there were the same old card tables and the same chandelier with a cover over it; but someone had already seen the young master, and, before he had reached the drawing room, something flew out from a side door like a tornado and began hugging and kissing him. Another and yet another creature of the same kind sprang from a second door and a third; more hugging, more kissing, more outcries, and tears of joy. He could not distinguish which was Papa, which

Natásha, and which Pétya. Everyone shouted, talked, and kissed him at the same time. Only his mother was not there, he noticed that.

"And I did not know . . . Nicholas . . . My darling! . . ."

"Here he is . . . our own . . . Kólya [Nicholas], dear fellow . . . How he has changed! . . . Where are the candles? . . . Tea! . . ."

"And me, kiss me!"

"Dearest . . . and me!"

Sónya, Natásha, Pétya, Anna Mikháylovna, Véra, and the old count were all hugging him, and the serfs, men and maids, flocked into the room, exclaiming and oh-ing and ah-ing.

Pétya, clinging to his legs, kept shouting, "And me too!"

Natásha, after she had pulled him down toward her and covered his face with kisses, holding him tight by the skirt of his coat, sprang away and pranced up and down in one place like a goat and shrieked piercingly.

All around were loving eyes glistening with tears of joy, and all around were lips seeking a kiss.

Sónya too, all rosy red, clung to his arm and, radiant with bliss, looked eagerly toward his eyes, waiting for the look for which she longed. Sónya now was sixteen and she was very pretty, especially at this moment of happy, rapturous excitement. She gazed at him, not taking her eyes off him, and smiling and holding her breath. He gave her a grateful look, but was still expectant and looking for someone. The old countess had not yet come. But now steps were heard at the door, steps so rapid that they could hardly be his mother's.

Yet it was she, dressed in a new gown which he did not know, made since he had left. All the others let him go, and he ran to her. When they met, she fell on his breast, sobbing. She could not lift her face, but only pressed it to the cold braiding of his hussar's jacket. Denísov, who had come into the room unnoticed by anyone, stood there and wiped his eyes at the sight.

"Vasíli Denísov, your son's friend," he said, introducing himself to the count, who was looking inquiringly at him.

"You are most welcome! I know, I know," said the count, kissing and embracing Denísov. "Nicholas wrote us . . . Natásha, Véra, look! Here is Denísov!"

The same happy, rapturous faces turned to the shaggy figure of Denísov.

"Darling Denísov!" screamed Natásha, beside herself with rapture, springing to him, putting her arms round him, and kissing him. This escapade made everybody feel confused. Denísov blushed too, but smiled and, taking Natásha's hand, kissed it.

Denísov was shown to the room prepared for him, and the Rostóvs all gathered round Nicholas in the sitting room.

The old countess, not letting go of his hand and kissing it every moment, sat beside him: the rest, crowding round him, watched every movement, word, or look of his, never taking their blissfully adoring eyes off him. His brother and sisters struggled for the places nearest to him and disputed with one another who should bring him his tea, handkerchief, and pipe.

Rostóv was very happy in the love they showed him; but the first moment of meeting had been so beatific that his present joy seemed insufficient, and he kept expecting something more, more and yet more.

Next morning, after the fatigues of their journey, the travelers slept till ten o'clock.

In the room next their bedroom there was a confusion of sabers, satchels, sabretaches, open portmanteaus, and dirty boots. Two freshly cleaned pairs with spurs had just been placed by the wall. The servants were bringing in jugs and basins, hot water for shaving, and their well-brushed clothes. There was a masculine odor and a smell of tobacco.

"Hallo, Gwíska—my pipe!" came Vasíli Denísov's husky voice. "Wostóv, get up!"

Rostóv, rubbing his eyes that seemed glued together, raised his disheveled head from the hot pillow.

"Why, is it late?"

"Late! It's nearly ten o'clock," answered Natásha's voice. A rustle of starched petticoats and the whispering and laughter of girls' voices came from the adjoining room. The door was opened a crack and there was a glimpse of something blue, of ribbons, black hair, and merry faces. It was Natásha, Sónya, and Pétya, who had come to see whether they were getting up.

"Nicholas! Get up!" Natásha's voice was again heard at the door.

"Directly!"

Meanwhile, Pétya, having found and seized the sabers in the outer room, with the delight boys feel at the sight of a military elder brother, and forgetting that it was unbecoming for the girls to see men undressed, opened the bedroom door.

"Is this your saber?" he shouted.

The girls sprang aside. Denísov hid his hairy legs under the blanket, looking with a scared face at his comrade for help. The door, having let Pétya in, closed again. A sound of laughter came from behind it.

"Nicholas! Come out in your dressing gown!" said Natásha's voice.

"Is this your saber?" asked Pétya. "Or is it yours?" he said, addressing the black-mustached Denísov with servile deference.

Rostóv hurriedly put something on his feet, drew on his dressing gown, and went out. Natásha had put on one spurred boot and was just getting her foot into the other. Sónya, when he came in, was twirling round and was about to expand her dresses into a balloon and sit down. They were dressed alike, in new pale-blue frocks, and were both fresh, rosy, and bright. Sónya ran away, but Natásha, taking her brother's arm, led him into the sitting room, where they began talking. They hardly gave one another time to ask questions and give replies concerning a thousand little matters which could not interest anyone but themselves. Natásha laughed at every word he said or that she said herself, not because what they were saying was amusing, but because she felt happy and was unable to control her joy which expressed itself by laughter.

"Oh, how nice, how splendid!" she said to everything.

Rostóv felt that, under the influence of the warm rays of love, that childlike smile which had not once appeared on his face since he left home now for the first time after eighteen months again brightened his soul and his face.

"No, but listen," she said, "now you are quite a man, aren't you? I'm awfully glad you're my brother." She touched his mustache. "I want to know what you men are like. Are you the same as we? No?"

"Why did Sónya run away?" asked Rostóv.

"Ah, yes! That's a whole long story! How are you going to speak to her —thou or you?" *

"As may happen," said Rostóv.

"No, call her you, please! I'll tell you all about it some other time. No, I'll tell you now. You know Sónya's my dearest friend. Such a friend that I burned my arm for her sake. Look here!"

She pulled up her muslin sleeve and showed him a red scar on her long, slender, delicate arm, high above the elbow on that part that is covered even by a ball dress.

"I burned this to prove my love for her. I just heated a ruler in the fire and pressed it there!"

Sitting on the sofa with the little cushions on its arms, in what used to be his old schoolroom, and looking into Natásha's wildly bright eyes, Rostóv re-entered that world of home and childhood which had no meaning for anyone else, but gave him some of the best joys of his life; and

* In Russian, as in other foreign languages, the second person singular is used in addressing children and intimates, and the second person plural in addressing those with whom one is more formal.—A.M.

the burning of an arm with a ruler as a proof of love did not seem to him senseless, he understood and was not surprised at it.

"Well, and is that all?" he asked.

"We are such friends, such friends! All that ruler business was just nonsense, but we are friends forever. She, if she loves anyone, does it for life, but I don't understand that, I forget quickly."

"Well, what then?"

"Well, she loves me and you like that."

Natásha suddenly flushed.

"Why, you remember before you went away? . . . Well, she says you are to forget all that. . . . She says: 'I shall love him always, but let him be free.' Isn't that lovely and noble! Yes, very noble? Isn't it?" asked Natásha, so seriously and excitedly that it was evident that what she was now saying she had talked of before, with tears.

Rostóv became thoughtful.

"I never go back on my word," he said. "Besides, Sónya is so charming that only a fool would renounce such happiness."

"No, no!" cried Natásha, "she and I have already talked it over. We knew you'd say so. But it won't do, because you see, if you say that—if you consider yourself bound by your promise—it will seem as if she had not meant it seriously. It makes it as if you were marrying her because you must, and that wouldn't do at all."

Rostóv saw that it had been well considered by them. Sónya had already struck him by her beauty on the preceding day. Today, when he had caught a glimpse of her, she seemed still more lovely. She was a charming girl of sixteen, evidently passionately in love with him (he did not doubt that for an instant). Why should he not love her now, and even marry her, Rostóv thought, but just now there were so many other pleasures and interests before him! "Yes, they have taken a wise decision," he thought, "I must remain free."

"Well then, that's excellent," said he. "We'll talk it over later on. Oh, how glad I am to have you!

"Well, and are you still true to Borís?" he continued.

"Oh, what nonsense!" cried Natásha, laughing. "I don't think about him or anyone else, and I don't want anything of the kind."

"Dear me! Then what are you up to now?"

"Now?" repeated Natásha, and a happy smile lit up her face. "Have you seen Duport?"

"No."

"Not seen Duport—the famous dancer? Well then, you won't understand. That's what I'm up to."

Curving her arms, Natásha held out her skirts as dancers do, ran back a few steps, turned, cut a caper, brought her little feet sharply together, and made some steps on the very tips of her toes.

"See, I'm standing! See!" she said, but could not maintain herself on her toes any longer. "So that's what I'm up to! I'll never marry anyone, but will be a dancer. Only don't tell anyone."

Rostóv laughed so loud and merrily that Denísov, in his bedroom, felt envious and Natásha could not help joining in.

"No, but don't you think it's nice?" she kept repeating.

"Nice! And so you no longer wish to marry Borís?"

Natásha flared up. "I don't want to marry anyone. And I'll tell him so when I see him!"

"Dear me!" said Rostóv.

"But that's all rubbish," Natásha chattered on. "And is Denísov nice?" she asked.

"Yes, indeed!"

"Oh, well then, good-by: go and dress. Is he very terrible, Denísov?"

"Why terrible?" asked Nicholas. "No, Váska is a splendid fellow."

"You call him Váska? That's funny! And is he very nice?"

"Very."

"Well then, be quick. We'll all have breakfast together."

And Natásha rose and went out of the room on tiptoe, like a ballet dancer, but smiling as only happy girls of fifteen can smile. When Rostóv met Sónya in the drawing room, he reddened. He did not know how to behave with her. The evening before, in the first happy moment of meeting, they had kissed each other, but today they felt it could not be done; he felt that everybody, including his mother and sisters, was looking inquiringly at him and watching to see how he would behave with her. He kissed her hand and addressed her not as *thou* but as *you—Sónya*. But their eyes met and said *thou*, and exchanged tender kisses. Her looks asked him to forgive her for having dared, by Natásha's intermediacy, to remind him of his promise, and then thanked him for his love. His looks thanked her for offering him his freedom and told her that one way or another he would never cease to love her, for that would be impossible.

"How strange it is," said Véra, selecting a moment when all were silent, "that Sónya and Nicholas now say *you* to one another and meet like strangers."

Véra's remark was correct, as her remarks always were, but, like most of her observations, it made everyone feel uncomfortable, not only Sónya, Nicholas, and Natásha, but even the old countess, who—dreading this love

affair which might hinder Nicholas from making a brilliant match—blushed like a girl.

Denísov, to Rostóv's surprise, appeared in the drawing room with pomaded hair, perfumed, and in a new uniform, looking just as smart as he made himself when going into battle, and he was more amiable to the ladies and gentlemen than Rostóv had ever expected to see him.

2. Preparations for Club dinner

ON HIS RETURN to Moscow from the army, Nicholas Rostóv was welcomed by his home circle as the best of sons, a hero, and their darling Nikólenka; by his relations as a charming, attractive, and polite young man; by his acquaintances as a handsome lieutenant of hussars, a good dancer, and one of the best matches in the city.

The Rostóvs knew everybody in Moscow. The old count had money enough that year, as all his estates had been remortgaged, and so Nicholas, acquiring a trotter of his own, very stylish riding breeches of the latest cut, such as no one else yet had in Moscow, and boots of the latest fashion, with extremely pointed toes and small silver spurs, passed his time very gaily. After a short period of adapting himself to the old conditions of life, Nicholas found it very pleasant to be at home again. He felt that he had grown up and matured very much. His despair at failing in a Scripture examination, his borrowing money from Gavríl to pay a sleigh driver, his kissing Sónya on the sly—he now recalled all this as childishness he had left immeasurably behind. Now he was a lieutenant of hussars, in a jacket laced with silver, and wearing the Cross of St. George, awarded to soldiers for bravery in action, and in the company of well-known, elderly, and respected racing men was training a trotter of his own for a race. He knew a lady on one of the boulevards whom he visited of an evening. He led the mazurka at the Arkhárovs' ball, talked about the war with Field Marshal Kámenski, visited the English Club, and was on intimate terms with a colonel of forty to whom Denísov had introduced him.

His passion for the Emperor had cooled somewhat in Moscow. But still, as he did not see him and had no opportunity of seeing him, he often spoke about him and about his love for him, letting it be understood that he had not told all and that there was something in his feelings for the Emperor not everyone could understand, and with his whole soul he shared the adoration then common in Moscow for the Emperor, who was spoken of as the "angel incarnate."

During Rostóv's short stay in Moscow, before rejoining the army, he did

not draw closer to Sónya, but rather drifted away from her. She was very pretty and sweet, and evidently deeply in love with him, but he was at the period of youth when there seems so much to do that there is no time for that sort of thing and a young man fears to bind himself and prizes his freedom which he needs for so many other things. When he thought of Sónya, during this stay in Moscow, he said to himself, "Ah, there will be, and there are, many more such girls somewhere whom I do not yet know. There will be time enough to think about love when I want to, but now I have no time." Besides, it seemed to him that the society of women was rather derogatory to his manhood. He went to balls and into ladies' society with an affectation of doing so against his will. The races, the English Club, sprees with Denísov, and visits to a certain house—that was another matter and quite the thing for a dashing young hussar!

At the beginning of March, old Count Ilyá Rostóv was very busy arranging a dinner in honor of Prince Bagratión at the English Club.*

The count walked up and down the hall in his dressing gown, giving orders to the club steward and to the famous Feoktíst, the Club's head cook, about asparagus, fresh cucumbers, strawberries, veal, and fish for this dinner. The count had been a member and on the committee of the Club from the day it was founded. To him the Club entrusted the arrangement of the festival in honor of Bagratión, for few men knew so well how to arrange a feast on an openhanded, hospitable scale, and still fewer men would be so well able and willing to make up out of their own resources what might be needed for the success of the fete. The club cook and the steward listened to the count's orders with pleased faces, for they knew that under no other management could they so easily extract a good profit for themselves from a dinner costing several thousand rubles.

"Well then, mind and have cocks' combs in the turtle soup, you know!"

"Shall we have three cold dishes then?" asked the cook.

The count considered.

* The "English Club" in Moscow was English only in name. It was a meeting place for the wealthy and the leading nobility and gentry in Moscow from the time of Catherine the Great up to the Revolution of 1917. It played no great part in politics, and what influence it had diminished with the years; but as men of note in disfavor at court, or who did not like the court, were inclined to avoid Petersburg, and as Moscow was the other capital, it happened that the English Club in Moscow became a sort of center for informal opposition—the only kind that could be safely indulged in. The dinner to Bagratión is characteristic of the extent to which the Club indulged in politics, and some criticism of the government in speeches after a good dinner was about as far as it went. —A.M.

"We can't have less—yes, three . . . the mayonnaise, that's one," said he, bending down a finger.

"Then am I to order those large sterlets?" asked the steward.

"Yes, it can't be helped if they won't take less. Ah, dear me! I was forgetting. We must have another entree. Ah, goodness gracious!" he clutched at his head. "Who is going to get me the flowers? Dmítri! Eh, Dmítri! Gallop off to our Moscow estate," he said to the factotum who appeared at his call. "Hurry off and tell Maksím, the gardener, to set the serfs to work. Say that everything out of the hothouses must be brought here well wrapped up in felt. I must have two hundred pots here on Friday."

Having given several more orders, he was about to go to his "little countess" to have a rest, but remembering something else of importance, he returned again, called back the cook and the club steward, and again began giving orders. A light footstep and the clinking of spurs were heard at the door, and the young count, handsome, rosy, with a dark little mustache, evidently rested and made sleeker by his easy life in Moscow, entered the room.

"Ah, my boy, my head's in a whirl!" said the old man with a smile, as if he felt a little confused before his son. "Now, if you would only help a bit! I must have singers too. I shall have my own orchestra, but shouldn't we get the gypsy singers as well? You military men like that sort of thing."

"Really, Papa, I believe Prince Bagratión worried himself less before the battle of Schön Grabern than you do now," said his son with a smile.

The old count pretended to be angry.

"Yes, you talk, but try it yourself!"

And the count turned to the cook, who, with a shrewd and respectful expression, looked observantly and sympathetically at the father and son.

"What have the young people come to nowadays, eh, Feoktíst?" said he. "Laughing at us old fellows!"

"That's so, your excellency, all they have to do is to eat a good dinner, but providing it and serving it all up, that's not their business!"

"That's it, that's it!" exclaimed the count, and gaily seizing his son by both hands, he cried, "Now I've got you, so take the sleigh and pair at once, and go to Bezúkhov's, and tell him 'Count Ilyá has sent you to ask for strawberries and fresh pineapples.' We can't get them from anyone else. He's not there himself, so you'll have to go in and ask the princesses; and from there go on to the Rasgulyáy—the coachman Ipátka knows—and look up the gypsy Ilyúshka, the one who danced at Count Orlóv's, you remember, in a white Cossack coat, and bring him along to me."

"And am I to bring the gypsy girls along with him?" asked Nicholas, laughing. "Dear, dear! . . ."

At that moment, with noiseless footsteps and with the businesslike, preoccupied, yet meekly Christian look which never left her face, Anna Mikháylovna entered the hall. Though she came upon the count in his dressing gown every day, he invariably became confused and begged her to excuse his costume.

"No matter at all, my dear count," she said, meekly closing her eyes. "But I'll go to Bezúkhov's myself. Pierre has arrived, and now we shall get anything we want from his hothouses. I have to see him in any case. He has forwarded me a letter from Borís. Thank God, Borís is now on the staff."

The count was delighted at Anna Mikháylovna's taking upon herself one of his commissions and ordered the small closed carriage for her.

"Tell Bezúkhov to come. I'll put his name down. Is his wife with him?" he asked.

Anna Mikháylovna turned up her eyes, and profound sadness was depicted on her face.

"Ah, my dear friend, he is very unfortunate," she said. "If what we hear is true, it is dreadful. How little we dreamed of such a thing when we were rejoicing at his happiness! And such a lofty angelic soul as young Bezúkhov! Yes, I pity him from my heart, and shall try to give him what consolation I can."

"Wh-what is the matter?" asked both the young and old Rostóv.

Anna Mikháylovna sighed deeply.

"Dólokhov, Mary Ivánovna's son," she said in a mysterious whisper, "has compromised her completely, they say. Pierre took him up, invited him to his house in Petersburg, and now . . . she has come here and that daredevil after her!" said Anna Mikháylovna, wishing to show her sympathy for Pierre, but by involuntary intonations and a half smile betraying her sympathy for the "daredevil," as she called Dólokhov. "They say Pierre is quite broken by his misfortune."

"Dear, dear! But still tell him to come to the Club—it will all blow over. It will be a tremendous banquet."

Next day, the third of March, soon after one o'clock, two hundred and fifty members of the English Club and fifty guests were awaiting the guest of honor and hero of the Austrian campaign, Prince Bagratión, to dinner.

On the first arrival of the news of the battle of Austerlitz, Moscow had been bewildered. At that time, the Russians were so used to victories that on receiving news of the defeat some would simply not believe it, while others sought some extraordinary explanation of so strange an event. In the English Club, where all who were distinguished, important, and well

informed forgathered when the news began to arrive in December, nothing was said about the war and the last battle, as though all were in a conspiracy of silence. The men who set the tone in conversation—Count Rostopchín, Prince Yúri Dolgorúkov, Valúev, Count Márkov, and Prince Vyázemski—did not show themselves at the Club, but met in private houses in intimate circles, and the Moscovites who took their opinions from others—Ilyá Rostóv among them—remained for a while without any definite opinion on the subject of the war and without leaders. The Moscovites felt that something was wrong and that to discuss the bad news was difficult, and so it was best to be silent. But after a while, just as a jury comes out of its room, the bigwigs who guided the Club's opinion reappeared, and everybody began speaking clearly and definitely. Reasons were found for the incredible, unheard-of, and impossible event of a Russian defeat, everything became clear, and in all corners of Moscow the same things began to be said. These reasons were the treachery of the Austrians, a defective commissariat, the treachery of the Pole Przebyszéwski and of the Frenchman Langeron, Kutúzov's incapacity, and (it was whispered) the youth and inexperience of the sovereign, who had trusted worthless and insignificant people. But the army, the Russian army, everyone declared, was extraordinary and had achieved miracles of valor. The soldiers, officers, and generals were heroes. But the hero of heroes was Prince Bagratión, distinguished by his Schön Grabern affair and by the retreat from Austerlitz, where he alone had withdrawn his column unbroken and had all day beaten back an enemy force twice as numerous as his own. What also conduced to Bagratión's being selected as Moscow's hero was the fact that he had no connections in the city and was a stranger there. In his person, honor was shown to a simple fighting Russian soldier without connections and intrigues, and to one who was associated by memories of the Italian campaign with the name of Suvórov. Moreover, paying such honor to Bagratión was the best way of expressing disapproval and dislike of Kutúzov.

"Had there been no Bagratión, it would have been necessary to invent him," said the wit Shinshín, parodying the words of Voltaire. Kutúzov no one spoke of, except some who abused him in whispers, calling him a court weathercock and an old satyr.

All Moscow repeated Prince Dolgorúkov's saying: "If you go on modeling and modeling you must get smeared with clay," suggesting consolation for our defeat by the memory of former victories; and the words of Rostopchín, that French soldiers have to be incited to battle by highfalutin words, and Germans by logical arguments to show them that it is more dangerous to run away than to advance, but that Russian soldiers only need to be re-

strained and held back! On all sides, new and fresh anecdotes were heard
of individual examples of heroism shown by our officers and men at Auster-
litz. One had saved a standard, another had killed five Frenchmen, a third
had loaded five cannon singlehanded. Berg was mentioned, by those who
did not know him, as having, when wounded in the right hand, taken his
sword in the left, and gone forward. Of Bolkónski, nothing was said, and
only those who knew him intimately regretted that he had died so young,
leaving a pregnant wife with his eccentric father.

3. The dinner. Bagratión as guest of honor

ON THAT third of March, all the rooms in the English Club were filled
with a hum of conversation, like the hum of bees swarming in spring-
time. The members and guests of the Club wandered hither and thither,
sat, stood, met, and separated, some in uniform and some in evening dress,
and a few here and there with powdered hair and in Russian *kaftáns*. Pow-
dered footmen, in livery with buckled shoes and smart stockings, stood at
every door anxiously noting visitors' every movement in order to offer their
services. Most of those present were elderly, respected men with broad,
self-confident faces, fat fingers, and resolute gestures and voices. This class
of guests and members sat in certain habitual places and met in certain
habitual groups. A minority of those present were casual guests—chiefly
young men, among whom were Denísov, Rostóv, and Dólokhov—who
was now again an officer in the Semënov regiment. The faces of these
young people, especially those who were military men, bore that expres-
sion of condescending respect for their elders which seems to say to the
older generation, "We are prepared to respect and honor you, but all the
same remember that the future belongs to us."

Nesvítski was there as an old member of the Club. Pierre, who at his
wife's command had let his hair grow and abandoned his spectacles, went
about the rooms fashionably dressed but looking sad and dull. Here, as
elsewhere, he was surrounded by an atmosphere of subservience to his
wealth, and being in the habit of lording it over these people, he treated
them with absent-minded contempt.

By his age he should have belonged to the younger men, but by his
wealth and connections he belonged to the groups of old and honored
guests, and so he went from one group to another. Some of the most im-
portant old men were the center of groups which even strangers ap-
proached respectfully to hear the voices of well-known men. The largest
circles formed round Count Rostopchín, Valúev, and Narýshkin. Rostop-

chín was describing how the Russians had been overwhelmed by flying Austrians and had had to force their way through them with bayonets.

Valúev was confidentially telling that Uvárov had been sent from Petersburg to ascertain what Moscow was thinking about Austerlitz.

In the third circle, Narýshkin was speaking of the meeting of the Austrian Council of War at which Suvórov crowed like a cock in reply to the nonsense talked by the Austrian generals. Shinshín, standing close by, tried to make a joke, saying that Kutúzov had evidently failed to learn from Suvórov even so simple a thing as the art of crowing like a cock, but the elder members glanced severely at the wit, making him feel that in that place and on that day, it was improper to speak so of Kutúzov.

Count Ilyá Rostóv, hurried and preoccupied, went about in his soft boots between the dining and drawing rooms, hastily greeting the important and unimportant, all of whom he knew, as if they were all equals, while his eyes occasionally sought out his fine well-set-up young son, resting on him and winking joyfully at him. Young Rostóv stood at a window with Dólokhov, whose acquaintance he had lately made and highly valued. The old count came up to them and pressed Dólokhov's hand.

"Please come and visit us . . . you know my brave boy . . . been together out there . . . both playing the hero . . . Ah, Vasíli Ignátovich . . . How d'ye do, old fellow?" he said, turning to an old man who was passing, but before he had finished his greeting there was a general stir, and a footman who had run in announced, with a frightened face: "He's arrived!"

Bells rang, the stewards rushed forward, and—like rye shaken together in a shovel—the guests who had been scattered about in different rooms came together and crowded in the large drawing room by the door of the ballroom.

Bagratión appeared in the doorway of the anteroom without hat or sword, which, in accord with the Club custom, he had given up to the hall porter. He had no lambskin cap on his head, nor had he a loaded whip over his shoulder, as when Rostóv had seen him on the eve of the battle of Austerlitz, but wore a tight new uniform with Russian and foreign Orders, and the Star of St. George on his left breast. Evidently just before coming to the dinner he had had his hair and whiskers trimmed, which changed his appearance for the worse. There was something naïvely festive in his air, which, in conjunction with his firm and virile features, gave him a rather comical expression. Bekleshëv and Theodore Uvárov, who had arrived with him, paused at the doorway to allow him, as the guest of honor, to enter first. Bagratión was embarrassed, not wishing to avail himself of their courtesy, and this caused some delay at the doors, but after all

he did at last enter first. He walked shyly and awkwardly over the parquet floor of the reception room, not knowing what to do with his hands; he was more accustomed to walk over a plowed field under fire, as he had done at the head of the Kursk regiment at Schön Grabern—and he would have found that easier. The committeemen met him at the first door and, expressing their delight at seeing such a highly honored guest, took possession of him as it were, without waiting for his reply, surrounded him, and led him to the drawing room. It was at first impossible to enter the drawing-room door for the crowd of members and guests jostling one another and trying to get a good look at Bagratión over each other's shoulders, as if he were some rare animal. Count Ilyá Rostóv, laughing and repeating the words, "Make way, dear boy! Make way, make way!" pushed through the crowd more energetically than anyone, led the guests into the drawing room, and seated them on the center sofa. The bigwigs, the most respected members of the Club, beset the new arrivals. Count Ilyá, again thrusting his way through the crowd, went out of the drawing room and reappeared a minute later with another committeeman, carrying a large silver salver which he presented to Prince Bagratión. On the salver lay some verses composed and printed in the hero's honor. Bagratión, on seeing the salver, glanced around in dismay, as though seeking help. But all eyes demanded that he should submit. Feeling himself in their power, he resolutely took the salver with both hands and looked sternly and reproachfully at the count who had presented it to him. Someone obligingly took the dish from Bagratión (or he would, it seemed, have held it till evening and have gone in to dinner with it) and drew his attention to the verses.

"Well, I will read them, then!" Bagratión seemed to say, and, fixing his weary eyes on the paper, began to read them with a fixed and serious expression. But the author himself took the verses and began reading them aloud. Bagratión bowed his head and listened: *

> Bring glory then to Alexander's reign
> And on the throne our Titus shield.
> A dreaded foe be thou, kindhearted as a man,
> A Rhipheus at home, a Caesar in the field!
> E'en fortunate Napoleon
> Knows by experience, now, Bagratión,
> And dare not Herculean Russians trouble. . . .

* The verses read and sung at this banquet are in very bad Russian, and their quality has been preserved in the translation.—A.M.

But before he had finished reading, a stentorian major-domo announced that dinner was ready! The door opened, and from the dining room came the resounding strains of the polonaise:

> Conquest's joyful thunder waken,
> Triumph, valiant Russians, now! . . .

and Count Rostóv, glancing angrily at the author who went on reading his verses, bowed to Bagratión. Everyone rose, feeling that dinner was more important than verses, and Bagratión, again preceding all the rest, went in to dinner. He was seated in the place of honor between two Alexanders—Bekleshëv and Narýshkin—which was a significant allusion to the name of the sovereign. Three hundred persons took their seats in the dining room, according to their rank and importance: the more important nearer to the honored guest, as naturally as water flows deepest where the land lies lowest.

Just before dinner, Count Ilyá Rostóv presented his son to Bagratión, who recognized him and said a few words to him, disjointed and awkward, as were all the words he spoke that day, and Count Ilyá looked joyfully and proudly around while Bagratión spoke to his son.

Nicholas Rostóv, with Denísov and his new acquaintance, Dólokhov, sat almost at the middle of the table. Facing them sat Pierre, beside Prince Nesvítski. Count Ilyá Rostóv with the other members of the committee sat facing Bagratión and, as the very personification of Moscow hospitality, did the honors to the prince.

His efforts had not been in vain. The dinner, both the lenten and the other fare, was splendid, yet he could not feel quite at ease till the end of the meal. He winked at the butler, whispered directions to the footmen, and awaited each expected dish with some anxiety. Everything was excellent. With the second course, a gigantic sterlet (at sight of which Ilyá Rostóv blushed with self-conscious pleasure), the footmen began popping corks and filling the champagne glasses. After the fish, which made a certain sensation, the count exchanged glances with the other committeemen. "There will be many toasts, it's time to begin," he whispered, and taking up his glass, he rose. All were silent, waiting for what he would say.

"To the health of our Sovereign, the Emperor!" he cried, and at the same moment his kindly eyes grew moist with tears of joy and enthusiasm. The band immediately struck up "Conquest's joyful thunder waken . . ." All rose and cried "Hurrah!" Bagratión also rose and shouted "Hurrah!" in exactly the same voice in which he had shouted it on the field at Schön Grabern. Young Rostóv's ecstatic voice could be heard above the

three hundred others. He nearly wept. "To the health of our Sovereign, the Emperor!" he roared, "Hurrah!" and emptying his glass at one gulp he dashed it to the floor. Many followed his example, and the loud shouting continued for a long time. When the voices subsided, the footmen cleared away the broken glass and everybody sat down again, smiling at the noise they had made and exchanging remarks. The old count rose once more, glanced at a note lying beside his plate, and proposed a toast, "To the health of the hero of our last campaign, Prince Peter Ivánovich Bagratión!" and again his blue eyes grew moist. "Hurrah!" cried the three hundred voices again, but instead of the band a choir began singing a cantata composed by Paul Ivánovich Kutúzov: *

> Russians! O'er all barriers on!
> Courage conquest guarantees;
> Have we not Bagratión?
> He brings foemen to their knees, . . . etc.

As soon as the singing was over, another and another toast was proposed and Count Ilyá Rostóv became more and more moved, more glass was smashed, and the shouting grew louder. They drank to Bekleshëv, Narýshkin, Uvárov, Dolgorúkov, Apráksin, Valúev, to the committee, to all the Club members and to all the Club guests, and finally to Count Ilyá Rostóv separately, as the organizer of the banquet. At that toast, the count took out his handkerchief and, covering his face, wept outright.

4. Pierre challenges Dólokhov

PIERRE SAT OPPOSITE Dólokhov and Nicholas Rostóv. As usual, he ate and drank much, and eagerly. But those who knew him intimately noticed that some great change had come over him that day. He was silent all through dinner and looked about, blinking and scowling, or, with fixed eyes and a look of complete absent-mindedness, kept rubbing the bridge of his nose. His face was depressed and gloomy. He seemed to see and hear nothing of what was going on around him and to be absorbed by some depressing and unsolved problem.

The unsolved problem that tormented him was caused by hints given by the princess, his cousin, at Moscow, concerning Dólokhov's intimacy with his wife, and by an anonymous letter he had received that morning, which in the mean jocular way common to anonymous letters said that he

* P. I. Kutúzov must not be confused with the commander in chief, M. I. Kutúzov.—A.M.

saw badly through his spectacles, but that his wife's connection with Dólokhov was a secret to no one but himself. Pierre absolutely disbelieved both the princess' hints and the letter, but he feared now to look at Dólokhov, who was sitting opposite him. Every time he chanced to meet Dólokhov's handsome insolent eyes, Pierre felt something terrible and monstrous rising in his soul and turned quickly away. Involuntarily recalling his wife's past and her relations with Dólokhov, Pierre saw clearly that what was said in the letter might be true, or might at least seem to be true had it not referred to *his* wife. He involuntarily remembered how Dólokhov, who had fully recovered his former position after the campaign, had returned to Petersburg and come to him. Availing himself of his friendly relations with Pierre as a boon companion, Dólokhov had come straight to his house, and Pierre had put him up and lent him money. Pierre recalled how Hélène had smilingly expressed disapproval of Dólokhov's living at their house, and how cynically Dólokhov had praised his wife's beauty to him and from that time till they came to Moscow had not left them for a day.

"Yes, he is very handsome," thought Pierre, "and I know him. It would be particularly pleasant to him to dishonor my name and ridicule me, just because I have exerted myself on his behalf, befriended him, and helped him. I know and understand what a spice that would add to the pleasure of deceiving me, if it really were true. Yes, if it were true, but I do not believe it. I have no right to, and can't, believe it." He remembered the expression Dólokhov's face assumed in his moments of cruelty, as when tying the policeman to the bear and dropping them into the water, or when he challenged a man to a duel without any reason, or shot a postboy's horse with a pistol. That expression was often on Dólokhov's face when looking at him. "Yes, he is a bully," thought Pierre, "to kill a man means nothing to him. It must seem to him that everyone is afraid of him, and that must please him. He must think that I, too, am afraid of him— and in fact I am afraid of him," he thought, and again he felt something terrible and monstrous rising in his soul. Dólokhov, Denísov, and Rostóv were now sitting opposite Pierre and seemed very gay. Rostóv was talking merrily to his two friends, one of whom was a dashing hussar and the other a notorious duelist and rake, and every now and then he glanced ironically at Pierre, whose preoccupied, absent-minded, and massive figure was a very noticeable one at the dinner. Rostóv looked inimically at Pierre, first because Pierre appeared to his hussar eyes as a rich civilian, the husband of a beauty, and in a word—an old woman; and secondly because Pierre in his preoccupation and absent-mindedness had not recognized

Rostóv and had not responded to his greeting. When the Emperor's health was drunk, Pierre, lost in thought, did not rise or lift his glass.

"What are you about?" shouted Rostóv, looking at him in an ecstasy of exasperation. "Don't you hear it's His Majesty the Emperor's health?"

Pierre sighed, rose submissively, emptied his glass, and, waiting till all were seated again, turned with his kindly smile to Rostóv.

"Why, I didn't recognize you!" he said. But Rostóv was otherwise engaged; he was shouting "Hurrah!"

"Why don't you renew the acquaintance?" said Dólokhov to Rostóv.

"Confound him, he's a fool!" said Rostóv.

"One should make up to the husbands of pretty women," said Denísov.

Pierre did not catch what they were saying, but knew they were talking about him. He reddened and turned away.

"Well, now to the health of handsome women!" said Dólokhov, and with a serious expression, but with a smile lurking at the corners of his mouth, he turned with his glass to Pierre.

"Here's to the health of lovely women, Peterkin—and their lovers!" he added.

Pierre, with downcast eyes, drank out of his glass without looking at Dólokhov or answering him. The footman, who was distributing leaflets with Kutúzov's cantata, laid one before Pierre as one of the principal guests. He was just going to take it when Dólokhov, leaning across, snatched it from his hand and began reading it. Pierre looked at Dólokhov and his eyes dropped, the something terrible and monstrous that had tormented him all dinnertime rose and took possession of him. He leaned his whole massive body across the table.

"How dare you take it?" he shouted.

Hearing that cry and seeing to whom it was addressed, Nesvítski and the neighbor on his right quickly turned in alarm to Bezúkhov.

"Don't! Don't! What are you about?" whispered their frightened voices.

Dólokhov looked at Pierre with clear, mirthful, cruel eyes, and that smile of his which seemed to say, "Ah! This is what I like!"

"You shan't have it!" he said distinctly.

Pale, with quivering lips, Pierre snatched the copy.

"You . . . ! you . . . scoundrel! I challenge you!" he ejaculated, and, pushing back his chair, he rose from the table.

At the very instant he did this and uttered those words, Pierre felt that the question of his wife's guilt which had been tormenting him the whole day was finally and indubitably answered in the affirmative. He hated her and was forever sundered from her. Despite Denísov's request

that he would take no part in the matter, Rostóv agreed to be Dólokhov's second, and after dinner he discussed the arrangements for the duel with Nesvítski, Bezúkhov's second. Pierre went home, but Rostóv with Dólokhov and Denísov stayed on at the Club till late, listening to the gypsies and other singers.

"Well then, till tomorrow at Sokólniki," said Dólokhov, as he took leave of Rostóv in the Club porch.

"And do you feel quite calm?" Rostóv asked.

Dólokhov paused.

"Well, you see, I'll tell you the whole secret of dueling in two words. If you are going to fight a duel, and you make a will and write affectionate letters to your parents, and if you think you may be killed, you are a fool and are lost for certain. But go with the firm intention of killing your man as quickly and surely as possible, and then all will be right, as our bear huntsman at Kostromá used to tell me. 'Everyone fears a bear,' he says, 'but when you see one your fear's all gone, and your only thought is not to let him get away!' And that's how it is with me. À demain, mon cher [Till tomorrow, my dear fellow]."

Next day, at eight in the morning, Pierre and Nesvítski drove to the Sokólniki forest and found Dólokhov, Denísov, and Rostóv already there. Pierre had the air of a man preoccupied with considerations which had no connection with the matter in hand. His haggard face was yellow. He had evidently not slept that night. He looked about distractedly and screwed up his eyes as if dazzled by the sun. He was entirely absorbed by two considerations: his wife's guilt, of which after his sleepless night he had not the slightest doubt, and the guiltlessness of Dólokhov, who had no reason to preserve the honor of a man who was nothing to him. . . .

"I should perhaps have done the same thing in his place," thought Pierre. "It's even certain that I should have done the same, then why this duel, this murder? Either I shall kill him, or he will hit me in the head, or elbow, or knee. Can't I go away from here, run away, bury myself somewhere?" passed through his mind. But just at moments when such thoughts occurred to him, he would ask in a particularly calm and absent-minded way, which inspired the respect of the onlookers, "Will it be long? Are things ready?"

When all was ready, the sabers stuck in the snow to mark the barriers, and the pistols loaded, Nesvítski went up to Pierre.

"I should not be doing my duty, Count," he said in timid tones, "and should not justify your confidence and the honor you have done me in choosing me for your second, if at this grave, this very grave, moment I did not tell you the whole truth. I think there is no sufficient ground for this

affair, or for blood to be shed over it. . . . You were not right, not quite in the right, you were impetuous . . ."

"Oh yes, it is horribly stupid," said Pierre.

"Then allow me to express your regrets, and I am sure your opponent will accept them," said Nesvítski (who like the others concerned in the affair, and like everyone in similar cases, did not yet believe that the affair had come to an actual duel). "You know, Count, it is much more honorable to admit one's mistake than to let matters become irreparable. There was no insult on either side. Allow me to convey . . ."

"No! What is there to talk about?" said Pierre. "It's all the same. . . . Is everything ready?" he added. "Only tell me where to go and where to shoot," he said with an unnaturally gentle smile.

He took the pistol in his hand and began asking about the working of the trigger, as he had not before held a pistol in his hand—a fact that he did not wish to confess.

"Oh yes, like that, I know, I only forgot," said he.

"No apologies, none whatever," said Dólokhov to Denísov (who on his side had been attempting a reconciliation), and he also went up to the appointed place.

The spot chosen for the duel was some eighty paces from the road, where the sleighs had been left, in a small clearing in the pine forest covered with melting snow, the frost having begun to break up during the last few days. The antagonists stood forty paces apart at the farther edge of the clearing. The seconds, measuring the paces, left tracks in the deep wet snow between the place where they had been standing and Nesvítski's and Dólokhov's sabers, which were stuck into the ground ten paces apart to mark the barrier. It was thawing and misty; at forty paces' distance nothing could be seen. For three minutes all had been ready, but they still delayed and all were silent.

5. The duel

WELL, BEGIN!" said Dólokhov.

"All right," said Pierre, still smiling in the same way. A feeling of dread was in the air. It was evident that the affair so lightly begun could no longer be averted but was taking its course independently of men's will.

Denísov first went to the barrier and announced: "As the adve'sawies have wefused a weconciliation, please pwoceed. Take your pistols, and at the word thwee begin to advance.

"O-ne! T-wo! Thwee!" he shouted angrily and stepped aside.

The combatants advanced along the trodden tracks, nearer and nearer to one another, beginning to see one another through the mist. They had the right to fire when they liked as they approached the barrier. Dólokhov walked slowly without raising his pistol, looking intently with his bright, sparkling blue eyes into his antagonist's face. His mouth wore its usual semblance of a smile.

"So I can fire when I like!" said Pierre, and at the word "three," he went quickly forward, missing the trodden path and stepping into the deep snow. He held the pistol in his right hand at arm's length, apparently afraid of shooting himself with it. His left hand he held carefully back, because he wished to support his right hand with it and knew he must not do so. Having advanced six paces and strayed off the track into the snow, Pierre looked down at his feet, then quickly glanced at Dólokhov and, bending his finger as he had been shown, fired. Not at all expecting so loud a report, Pierre shuddered at the sound and then, smiling at his own sensations, stood still. The smoke, rendered denser by the mist, prevented him from seeing anything for an instant, but there was no second report as he had expected. He only heard Dólokhov's hurried steps, and his figure came in view through the smoke. He was pressing one hand to his left side, while the other clutched his drooping pistol. His face was pale. Rostóv ran toward him and said something.

"No-o-o!" muttered Dólokhov through his teeth, "no, it's not over." And after stumbling a few staggering steps right up to the saber, he sank on the snow beside it. His left hand was bloody; he wiped it on his coat and supported himself with it. His frowning face was pallid and quivered.

"Plea . . ." began Dólokhov, but could not at first pronounce the word. "Please," he uttered with an effort.

Pierre, hardly restraining his sobs, began running toward Dólokhov and was about to cross the space between the barriers, when Dólokhov cried:

"To your barrier!" and Pierre, grasping what was meant, stopped by his saber. Only ten paces divided them. Dólokhov lowered his head to the snow, greedily bit at it, again raised his head, adjusted himself, drew in his legs and sat up, seeking a firm center of gravity. He sucked and swallowed the cold snow, his lips quivered, but his eyes, still smiling, glittered with effort and exasperation as he mustered his remaining strength. He raised his pistol and aimed.

"Sideways! Cover yourself with your pistol!" ejaculated Nesvítski.

"Cover yourself!" even Denísov cried to his adversary.

Pierre, with a gentle smile of pity and remorse, his arms and legs helplessly spread out, stood with his broad chest directly facing Dólokhov

and looked sorrowfully at him. Denísov, Rostóv, and Nesvítski closed their eyes. At the same instant they heard a report and Dólokhov's angry cry.

"Missed!" shouted Dólokhov, and he lay helplessly, face downwards on the snow.

Pierre clutched his temples, and turning round went into the forest, trampling through the deep snow, and muttering incoherent words:

"Folly . . . folly! Death . . . lies . . ." he repeated, puckering his face.

Nesvítski stopped him and took him home.

Rostóv and Denísov drove away with the wounded Dólokhov.

The latter lay silent in the sleigh with closed eyes and did not answer a word to the questions addressed to him. But on entering Moscow he suddenly came to and, lifting his head with an effort, took Rostóv, who was sitting beside him, by the hand. Rostóv was struck by the totally altered and unexpectedly rapturous and tender expression on Dólokhov's face.

"Well? How do you feel?" he asked.

"Bad! But it's not that, my friend—" said Dólokhov with a gasping voice. "Where are we? In Moscow, I know. I don't matter, but I have killed her, killed . . . She won't get over it! She won't survive. . . ."

"Who?" asked Rostóv.

"My mother! My mother, my angel, my adored angel mother," and Dólokhov pressed Rostóv's hand and burst into tears.

When he had become a little quieter, he explained to Rostóv that he was living with his mother, who, if she saw him dying, would not survive it. He implored Rostóv to go on and prepare her.

Rostóv went on ahead to do what was asked, and to his great surprise learned that Dólokhov the brawler, Dólokhov the bully, lived in Moscow with an old mother and a hunchback sister, and was the most affectionate of sons and brothers.

6. Pierre's separation from Hélène

Pierre had of late rarely seen his wife alone. Both in Petersburg and in Moscow their house was always full of visitors. The night after the duel he did not go to his bedroom but, as he often did, remained in his father's room, that huge room in which Count Bezúkhov had died.

He lay down on the sofa meaning to fall asleep and forget all that had happened to him, but could not do so. Such a storm of feelings, thoughts,

and memories suddenly arose within him that he could not fall asleep, nor even remain in one place, but had to jump up and pace the room with rapid steps. Now he seemed to see her in the early days of their marriage, with bare shoulders and a languid, passionate look on her face, and then immediately he saw beside her Dólokhov's handsome, insolent, hard, and mocking face as he had seen it at the banquet, and then that same face pale, quivering, and suffering, as it had been when he reeled and sank on the snow.

"What has happened?" he asked himself. "I have killed her lover, yes, killed my wife's lover. Yes, that was it! And why? How did I come to do it?"—"Because you married her," answered an inner voice.

"But in what was I to blame?" he asked. "In marrying her without loving her; in deceiving yourself and her." And he vividly recalled that moment after supper at Prince Vasíli's, when he spoke those words he had found so difficult to utter: "I love you." "It all comes from that! Even then I felt it," he thought. "I felt then that it was not so, that I had no right to do it. And so it turns out."

He remembered his honeymoon and blushed at the recollection. Particularly vivid, humiliating, and shameful was the recollection of how one day soon after his marriage he came out of the bedroom into his study a little before noon in his silk dressing gown and found his head steward there, who, bowing respectfully, looked into his face and at his dressing gown and smiled slightly, as if expressing respectful understanding of his employer's happiness.

"But how often I have felt proud of her, proud of her majestic beauty and social tact," thought he; "been proud of my house, in which she received all Petersburg, proud of her unapproachability and beauty. So this is what I was proud of! I then thought that I did not understand her. How often when considering her character I have told myself that I was to blame for not understanding her, for not understanding that constant composure and complacency and lack of all interests or desires, and the whole secret lies in the terrible truth that she is a depraved woman. Now I have spoken that terrible word to myself all has become clear.

"Anatole used to come to borrow money from her and used to kiss her naked shoulders.* She did not give him the money, but let herself be kissed. Her father in jest tried to rouse her jealousy, and she replied with a calm smile that she was not so stupid as to be jealous: 'Let him do what he pleases,' she used to say of me. One day I asked her if she felt

* In the first drafts of the novel, Tolstóy made it plain that Hélène and her brother had been in guilty relations with one another, but afterwards he altered this so that only some hints remain.—A.M.

any symptoms of pregnancy. She laughed contemptuously and said she was not a fool to want to have children, and that she was not going to have any children by me."

Then he recalled the coarseness and bluntness of her thoughts and the vulgarity of the expressions that were natural to her, though she had been brought up in the most aristocratic circles.

"I'm not such a fool. . . . Just you try it on. . . . *Allez-vous promener* [You clear out of this]," she used to say. Often seeing the success she had with young and old men and women Pierre could not understand why he did not love her.

"Yes, I never loved her," said he to himself; "I knew she was a depraved woman," he repeated, "but dared not admit it to myself. And now there's Dólokhov sitting in the snow with a forced smile and perhaps dying, while meeting my remorse with some forced bravado!"

Pierre was one of those people who, in spite of an appearance of what is called weak character, do not seek a confidant in their troubles. He digested his sufferings alone.

"It is all, all her fault," he said to himself; "but what of that? Why did I bind myself to her? Why did I say 'Je vous aime [I love you]' to her, which was a lie, and worse than a lie? I am guilty and must endure . . . what? A slur on my name? A misfortune for life? Oh, that's nonsense," he thought. "The slur on my name and honor—that's all apart from myself.

"Louis XVI was executed because they said he was dishonorable and a criminal," came into Pierre's head, "and from their point of view they were right, as were those too who canonized him and died a martyr's death for his sake. Then Robespierre was beheaded for being a despot. Who is right and who is wrong? No one! But if you are alive—live: tomorrow you'll die as I might have died an hour ago. And is it worth tormenting oneself, when one has only a moment of life in comparison with eternity?"

But at the moment when he imagined himself calmed by such reflections, she suddenly came into his mind as she was at the moments when he had most strongly expressed his insincere love for her, and he felt the blood rush to his heart and had again to get up and move about and break and tear whatever came to his hand. "Why did I tell her that 'Je vous aime'?" he kept repeating to himself. And when he had said it for the tenth time, Molière's words: "*Mais que diable alloit-il faire dans cette galère?*" ["What the dickens did he get himself into that mess for?" or, more literally, "What the devil was he going to do in that galley?"] occurred to him, and he began to laugh at himself.

In the night he called his valet and told him to pack up to go to Petersburg. He could not imagine how he could speak to her now. He resolved to go away next day and leave a letter informing her of his intention to part from her forever.

Next morning when the valet came into the room with his coffee, Pierre was lying asleep on the ottoman with an open book in his hand.

He woke up and looked round for a while with a startled expression, unable to realize where he was.

"The countess told me to inquire whether your excellency was at home," said the valet.

But before Pierre could decide what answer he would send, the countess herself in a white satin dressing gown embroidered with silver and with simply dressed hair (two immense plaits twice round her lovely head like a coronet) entered the room, calm and majestic, except that there was a wrathful wrinkle on her rather prominent marble brow. With her imperturbable calm she did not begin to speak in front of the valet. She knew of the duel and had come to speak about it. She waited till the valet had set down the coffee things and left the room. Pierre looked at her timidly over his spectacles, and like a hare surrounded by hounds who lays back her ears and continues to crouch motionless before her enemies, he tried to continue reading. But feeling this to be senseless and impossible, he again glanced timidly at her. She did not sit down but looked at him with a contemptuous smile, waiting for the valet to go.

"Well, what's this now? What have you been up to now, I should like to know?" she asked sternly.

"I? What have I . . . ?" stammered Pierre.

"So it seems you're a hero, eh? Come now, what was this duel about? What is it meant to prove? What? I ask you."

Pierre turned over heavily on the ottoman and opened his mouth, but could not reply.

"If you won't answer, I'll tell you . . ." Hélène went on. "You believe everything you're told. You were told . . ." Hélène laughed, "that Dólokhov was my lover," she said in French with her coarse plainness of speech, uttering the word *amant* as casually as any other word, "and you believed it! Well, what have you proved? What does this duel prove? That you're a fool, *que vous êtes un sot*, but everybody knew that. What will be the result? That I shall be the laughingstock of all Moscow, that everyone will say that you, drunk and not knowing what you were about, challenged a man you are jealous of without cause." Hélène raised her voice and became more and more excited, "A man who's a better man than you in every way . . ."

"Hm . . . Hm . . . !" growled Pierre, frowning without looking at her, and not moving a muscle.

"And how could you believe he was my lover? Why? Because I like his company? If you were cleverer and more agreeable, I should prefer yours."

"Don't speak to me . . . I beg you," muttered Pierre hoarsely.

"Why shouldn't I speak? I can speak as I like, and I tell you plainly that there are not many wives with husbands such as you who would not have taken lovers (des amants), but I have not done so," said she.

Pierre wished to say something, looked at her with eyes whose strange expression she did not understand, and lay down again. He was suffering physically at that moment, there was a weight on his chest and he could not breathe. He knew that he must do something to put an end to this suffering, but what he wanted to do was too terrible.

"We had better separate," he muttered in a broken voice.

"Separate? Very well, but only if you give me a fortune," said Hélène. "Separate! That's a thing to frighten me with!"

Pierre leaped up from the sofa and rushed staggering toward her.

"I'll kill you!" he shouted, and seizing the marble top of a table with a strength he had never before felt, he made a step toward her brandishing the slab.

Hélène's face became terrible, she shrieked and sprang aside. His father's nature showed itself in Pierre. He felt the fascination and delight of frenzy. He flung down the slab, broke it, and swooping down on her with outstretched hands shouted, "Get out!" in such a terrible voice that the whole house heard it with horror. God knows what he would have done at that moment had Hélène not fled from the room.

A week later Pierre gave his wife full power to control all his estates in Great Russia, which formed the larger part of his property, and left for Petersburg alone.

7. Andrew considered dead

TWO MONTHS had elapsed since the news of the battle of Austerlitz and the loss of Prince Andrew had reached Bald Hills, and in spite of the letters sent through the embassy and all the searches made, his body had not been found nor was he on the list of prisoners. What was worst of all for his relations was the fact that there was still a possibility of his having been picked up on the battlefield by the people of the place and that he might now be lying, recovering or dying, alone among strangers

and unable to send news of himself. The gazettes from which the old prince first heard of the defeat at Austerlitz stated, as usual very briefly and vaguely, that after brilliant engagements the Russians had had to retreat and had made their withdrawal in perfect order. The old prince understood from this official report that our army had been defeated. A week after the gazette report of the battle of Austerlitz came a letter from Kutúzov informing the prince of the fate that had befallen his son.

"Your son," wrote Kutúzov, "fell before my eyes, a standard in his hand and at the head of a regiment—he fell as a hero, worthy of his father and his fatherland. To the great regret of myself and of the whole army it is still uncertain whether he is alive or not. I comfort myself and you with the hope that your son is alive, for otherwise he would have been mentioned among the officers found on the field of battle, a list of whom has been sent me under flag of truce."

After receiving this news late in the evening, when he was alone in his study, the old prince went for his walk as usual next morning, but he was silent with his steward, the gardener, and the architect, and though he looked very grim he said nothing to anyone.

When Princess Mary went to him at the usual hour he was working at his lathe and, as usual, did not look round at her.

"Ah, Princess Mary!" he said suddenly in an unnatural voice, throwing down his chisel. (The wheel continued to revolve by its own impetus, and Princess Mary long remembered the dying creak of that wheel, which merged in her memory with what followed.)

She approached him, saw his face, and something gave way within her. Her eyes grew dim. By the expression of her father's face, not sad, not crushed, but angry and working unnaturally, she saw that hanging over her and about to crush her was some terrible misfortune, the worst in life, one she had not yet experienced, irreparable and incomprehensible—the death of one she loved.

"Father! Andrew!"—said the ungraceful, awkward princess with such an indescribable charm of sorrow and self-forgetfulness that her father could not bear her look but turned away with a sob.

"Bad news! He's not among the prisoners nor among the killed! Kutúzov writes . . ." and he screamed as piercingly as if he wished to drive the princess away by that scream . . . "Killed!"

The princess did not fall down or faint. She was already pale, but on hearing these words her face changed and something brightened in her beautiful, radiant eyes. It was as if joy—a supreme joy apart from the joys and sorrows of this world—overflowed the great grief within her. She for-

got all fear of her father, went up to him, took his hand, and drawing him down put her arm round his thin, scraggy neck.

"Father," she said, "do not turn away from me, let us weep together."

"Scoundrels! Blackguards!" shrieked the old man, turning his face away from her. "Destroying the army, destroying the men! And why? Go, go and tell Lise."

The princess sank helplessly into an armchair beside her father and wept. She saw her brother now as he had been at the moment when he took leave of her and of Lise, his look tender yet proud. She saw him tender and amused as he was when he put on the little icon. "Did he believe? Had he repented of his unbelief? Was he now there? There in the realms of eternal peace and blessedness?" she thought.

"Father, tell me how it happened," she asked through her tears.

"Go! Go! Killed in battle, where the best of Russian men and Russia's glory were led to destruction. Go, Princess Mary. Go and tell Lise. I will follow."

When Princess Mary returned from her father, the little princess sat working and looked up with that curious expression of inner, happy calm peculiar to pregnant women. It was evident that her eyes did not see Princess Mary but were looking within . . . into herself . . . at something joyful and mysterious taking place within her.

"Mary," she said, moving away from the embroidery frame and lying back, "give me your hand." She took her sister-in-law's hand and held it below her waist.

Her eyes were smiling expectantly, her downy lip rose and remained lifted in childlike happiness.

Princess Mary knelt down before her and hid her face in the folds of her sister-in-law's dress.

"There, there! Do you feel it? I feel so strange. And do you know, Mary, I am going to love him very much," said Lise, looking with bright and happy eyes at her sister-in-law.

Princess Mary could not lift her head, she was weeping.

"What is the matter, Mary?"

"Nothing . . . only I feel sad . . . sad about Andrew," she said, wiping away her tears on her sister-in-law's knee.

Several times in the course of the morning Princess Mary began trying to prepare her sister-in-law, and every time began to cry. Unobservant as was the little princess, these tears, the cause of which she did not understand, agitated her. She said nothing but looked about uneasily as if in search of something. Before dinner the old prince, of whom she was always afraid, came into her room with a peculiarly restless and malign

expression and went out again without saying a word. She looked at Princess Mary, then sat thinking for a while with that expression of attention to something within her that is only seen in pregnant women, and suddenly began to cry.

"Has anything come from Andrew?" she asked.

"No, you know it's too soon for news. But my father is anxious and I feel afraid."

"So there's nothing?"

"Nothing," answered Princess Mary, looking firmly with her radiant eyes at her sister-in-law.

She had determined not to tell her and persuaded her father to hide the terrible news from her till after her confinement, which was expected within a few days. Princess Mary and the old prince each bore and hid their grief in their own way. The old prince would not cherish any hope: he made up his mind that Prince Andrew had been killed, and though he sent an official to Austria to seek for traces of his son, he ordered a monument from Moscow which he intended to erect in his own garden to his memory, and he told everybody that his son had been killed. He tried not to change his former way of life, but his strength failed him. He walked less, ate less, slept less, and became weaker every day. Princess Mary hoped. She prayed for her brother as living and was always awaiting news of his return.

8. Lise's confinement. Andrew arrives

"DEAREST," said the little princess after breakfast on the morning of the nineteenth of March, and her downy little lip rose from old habit, but as sorrow was manifest in every smile, the sound of every word, and even every footstep in that house since the terrible news had come, so now the smile of the little princess—influenced by the general mood though without knowing its cause—was such as to remind one still more of the general sorrow.

"Dearest, I'm afraid this morning's fruschtique *—as Fóka the cook calls it—has disagreed with me."

"What is the matter with you, my darling? You look pale. Oh, you are very pale!" said Princess Mary in alarm, running with her soft, ponderous steps up to her sister-in-law.

"Your excellency, should not Mary Bogdánovna be sent for?" said one of the maids who was present. (Mary Bogdánovna was a midwife from

* Frühstück = breakfast.—A.M.

the neighboring town, who had been at Bald Hills for the last fortnight.)

"Oh yes," assented Princess Mary, "perhaps that's it. I'll go. Courage, my angel." She kissed Lise and was about to leave the room.

"Oh, no, no!" And besides the pallor and the physical suffering on the little princess' face, an expression of childish fear of inevitable pain showed itself.

"No, it's only indigestion! . . . Say it's only indigestion, say so, Mary! Say . . ." And the little princess began to cry capriciously like a suffering child and to wring her little hands even with some affectation. Princess Mary ran out of the room to fetch Mary Bogdánovna.

"Mon Dieu! Mon Dieu! Oh!" she heard as she left the room.

The midwife was already on her way to meet her, rubbing her small, plump white hands with an air of calm importance.

"Mary Bogdánovna, I think it's beginning!" said Princess Mary looking at the midwife with wide-open eyes of alarm.

"Well, the Lord be thanked, Princess," said Mary Bogdánovna, not hastening her steps. "You young ladies should not know anything about it."

"But how is it the doctor from Moscow is not here yet?" said the princess. (In accordance with Lise's and Prince Andrew's wishes they had sent in good time to Moscow for a doctor and were expecting him at any moment.)

"No matter, Princess, don't be alarmed," said Mary Bogdánovna. "We'll manage very well without a doctor."

Five minutes later Princess Mary from her room heard something heavy being carried by. She looked out. The menservants were carrying the large leather sofa from Prince Andrew's study into the bedroom. On their faces was a quiet and solemn look.

Princess Mary sat alone in her room listening to the sounds in the house, now and then opening her door when someone passed and watching what was going on in the passage. Some women passing with quiet steps in and out of the bedroom glanced at the princess and turned away. She did not venture to ask any questions, and shut the door again, now sitting down in her easy chair, now taking her prayer book, now kneeling before the icon stand. To her surprise and distress she found that her prayers did not calm her excitement. Suddenly her door opened softly and her old nurse, Praskóvya Sávishna, who hardly ever came to that room as the old prince had forbidden it, appeared on the threshold with a shawl round her head.

"I've come to sit with you a bit, Másha," said the nurse, "and here I've

brought the prince's wedding candles to light before his saint, my angel," she said with a sigh.

"Oh, nurse, I'm so glad!"

"God is merciful, birdie."

The nurse lit the gilt candles before the icons and sat down by the door with her knitting. Princess Mary took a book and began reading. Only when footsteps or voices were heard did they look at one another, the princess anxious and inquiring, the nurse encouraging. Everyone in the house was dominated by the same feeling that Princess Mary experienced as she sat in her room. But owing to the superstition that the fewer the people who know of it the less a woman in travail suffers, everyone tried to pretend not to know; no one spoke of it, but apart from the ordinary staid and respectful good manners habitual in the prince's household, a common anxiety, a softening of the heart, and a consciousness that something great and mysterious was being accomplished at that moment made itself felt.

There was no laughter in the maids' large hall. In the menservants' hall all sat waiting, silently and alert. In the outlying serfs' quarters torches and candles were burning and no one slept. The old prince, stepping on his heels, paced up and down his study and sent Tíkhon to ask Mary Bogdánovna what news.—"Say only that 'the prince told me to ask,' and come and tell me her answer."

"Inform the prince that labor has begun," said Mary Bogdánovna, giving the messenger a significant look.

Tíkhon went and told the prince.

"Very good!" said the prince closing the door behind him, and Tíkhon did not hear the slightest sound from the study after that.

After a while he re-entered it as if to snuff the candles, and, seeing the prince was lying on the sofa, looked at him, noticed his perturbed face, shook his head, and going up to him silently kissed him on the shoulder and left the room without snuffing the candles or saying why he had entered. The most solemn mystery in the world continued its course. Evening passed, night came, and the feeling of suspense and softening of heart in the presence of the unfathomable did not lessen but increased. No one slept.

It was one of those March nights when winter seems to wish to resume its sway and scatters its last snows and storms with desperate fury. A relay of horses had been sent up the highroad to meet the German doctor from Moscow who was expected every moment, and men on horseback with

lanterns were sent to the crossroads to guide him over the country road with its hollows and snow-covered pools of water.

Princess Mary had long since put aside her book: she sat silent, her luminous eyes fixed on her nurse's wrinkled face (every line of which she knew so well), on the lock of gray hair that escaped from under the kerchief, and the loose skin that hung under her chin.

Nurse Sávishna, knitting in hand, was telling in low tones, scarcely hearing or understanding her own words, what she had told hundreds of times before: how the late princess had given birth to Princess Mary in Kishenëv with only a Moldavian peasant woman to help instead of a midwife.

"God is merciful, doctors are never needed," she said.

Suddenly a gust of wind beat violently against the casement of the window, from which the double frame had been removed (by order of the prince, one window frame was removed in each room as soon as the larks returned),* and, forcing open a loosely closed latch, set the damask curtain flapping and blew out the candle with its chill, snowy draft. Princess Mary shuddered; her nurse, putting down the stocking she was knitting, went to the window and leaning out tried to catch the open casement. The cold wind flapped the ends of her kerchief and her loose locks of gray hair.

"Princess, my dear, there's someone driving up the avenue!" she said, holding the casement and not closing it. "With lanterns. Most likely the doctor."

"Oh, my God! thank God!" said Princess Mary. "I must go and meet him, he does not know Russian."

Princess Mary threw a shawl over her head and ran to meet the newcomer. As she was crossing the anteroom she saw through the window a carriage with lanterns, standing at the entrance. She went out on the stairs. On a banister post stood a tallow candle which guttered in the draft. On the landing below, Philip, the footman, stood looking scared and holding another candle. Still lower, beyond the turn of the staircase, one could hear the footstep of someone in thick felt boots, and a voice that seemed familiar to Princess Mary was saying something.

"Thank God!" said the voice. "And Father?"

"Gone to bed," replied the voice of Demyán the house steward, who was downstairs.

Then the voice said something more, Demyán replied, and the steps

* Russian houses have double windows in winter. As this hinders ventilation it is well to have one of the two frames removed as soon as the weather is mild enough.—A.M.

in the felt boots approached the unseen bend of the staircase more rapidly.

"It's Andrew!" thought Princess Mary. "No it can't be, that would be too extraordinary," and at the very moment she thought this, the face and figure of Prince Andrew, in a fur cloak the deep collar of which was covered with snow, appeared on the landing where the footman stood with the candle. Yes, it was he, pale, thin, with a changed and strangely softened but agitated expression on his face. He came up the stairs and embraced his sister.

"You did not get my letter?" he asked, and not waiting for a reply—which he would not have received, for the princess was unable to speak—he turned back, rapidly mounted the stairs again with the doctor who had entered the hall after him (they had met at the last post station), and again embraced his sister.

"What a strange fate, Másha darling!" And having taken off his cloak and felt boots, he went to the little princess' apartment.

9. Death of Lise

THE LITTLE PRINCESS lay supported by pillows, with a white cap on her head (the pains had just left her). Strands of her black hair lay round her inflamed and perspiring cheeks, her charming rosy mouth with its downy lip was open and she was smiling joyfully. Prince Andrew entered and paused facing her at the foot of the sofa on which she was lying. Her glittering eyes, filled with childlike fear and excitement, rested on him without changing their expression. "I love you all and have done no harm to anyone; why must I suffer so? Help me!" her look seemed to say. She saw her husband, but did not realize the significance of his appearance before her now. Prince Andrew went round the sofa and kissed her forehead.

"My darling!" he said—a word he had never used to her before. "God is merciful. . . ."

She looked at him inquiringly and with childlike reproach.

"I expected help from you and I get none, none from you either!" said her eyes. She was not surprised at his having come; she did not realize that he had come. His coming had nothing to do with her sufferings or with their relief. The pangs began again and Mary Bogdánovna advised Prince Andrew to leave the room.

The doctor entered. Prince Andrew went out and, meeting Princess Mary, again joined her. They began talking in whispers, but their talk broke off at every moment. They waited and listened.

"Go, dear," said Princess Mary.

Prince Andrew went again to his wife and sat waiting in the room next to hers. A woman came from the bedroom with a frightened face and became confused when she saw Prince Andrew. He covered his face with his hands and remained so for some minutes. Piteous, helpless, animal moans came through the door. Prince Andrew got up, went to the door, and tried to open it. Someone was holding it shut.

"You can't come in! You can't!" said a terrified voice from within.

He began pacing the room. The screaming ceased, and a few more seconds went by. Then suddenly a terrible shriek—it could not be hers, she could not scream like that—came from the bedroom. Prince Andrew ran to the door; the scream ceased and he heard the wail of an infant.

"What have they taken a baby in there for?" thought Prince Andrew in the first second. "A baby? What baby . . . ? Why is there a baby there? Or is the baby born?"

Then suddenly he realized the joyful significance of that wail; tears choked him, and leaning his elbows on the window sill he began to cry, sobbing like a child. The door opened. The doctor with his shirt sleeves tucked up, without a coat, pale and with a trembling jaw, came out of the room. Prince Andrew turned to him, but the doctor gave him a bewildered look and passed by without a word. A woman rushed out and seeing Prince Andrew stopped, hesitating on the threshold. He went into his wife's room. She was lying dead, in the same position he had seen her in five minutes before and, despite the fixed eyes and the pallor of the cheeks, the same expression was on her charming childlike face with its upper lip covered with tiny black hair.

"I love you all, and have done no harm to anyone; and what have you done to me?"—said her charming, pathetic, dead face.

In a corner of the room something red and tiny gave a grunt and squealed in Mary Bogdánovna's trembling white hands.

Two hours later Prince Andrew, stepping softly, went into his father's room. The old man already knew everything. He was standing close to the door and as soon as it opened his rough old arms closed like a vise round his son's neck, and without a word he began to sob like a child.

Three days later the little princess was buried, and Prince Andrew went up the steps to where the coffin stood, to give her the farewell kiss. And there in the coffin was the same face, though with closed eyes. "Ah, what have you done to me?" it still seemed to say, and Prince Andrew felt that something gave way in his soul and that he was guilty of a sin he could

neither remedy nor forget. He could not weep. The old man too came up
and kissed the waxen little hands that lay quietly crossed one on the
other on her breast, and to him, too, her face seemed to say: "Ah, what
have you done to me, and why?" And at the sight the old man turned
angrily away.

Another five days passed, and then the young Prince Nicholas Andrée-
vich was baptized. The wet nurse supported the coverlet with her chin,
while the priest with a goose feather anointed the boy's little red and
wrinkled soles and palms.

His grandfather, who was his godfather, trembling and afraid of drop-
ping him, carried the infant round the battered tin font and handed him
over to the godmother, Princess Mary. Prince Andrew sat in another
room, faint with fear lest the baby should be drowned in the font, and
awaited the termination of the ceremony. He looked up joyfully at the
baby when the nurse brought it to him and nodded approval when she
told him that the wax with the baby's hair had not sunk in the font
but had floated.*

10. Denísov and Dólokhov at the Rostóvs'

Rostóv's share in Dólokhov's duel with Bezúkhov was hushed up by
the efforts of the old count, and instead of being degraded to the ranks
as he expected he was appointed an adjutant to the governor general of
Moscow. As a result he could not go to the country with the rest of the
family, but was kept all summer in Moscow by his new duties. Dólokhov
recovered, and Rostóv became very friendly with him during his con-
valescence. Dólokhov lay ill at his mother's who loved him passionately
and tenderly, and old Mary Ivánovna, who had grown fond of Rostóv
for his friendship to her Fédya, often talked to him about her son.

"Yes, Count," she would say, "he is too noble and pure-souled for our
present, depraved world. No one now loves virtue; it seems like a re-
proach to everyone. Now tell me, Count, was it right, was it honorable,
of Bezúkhov? And Fédya, with his noble spirit, loved him and even now
never says a word against him. Those pranks in Petersburg when they
played some tricks on a policeman, didn't they do it together? And there!
Bezúkhov got off scot-free, while Fédya had to bear the whole burden on

* In the Russian baptismal service the priest cuts off a little of the child's
hair and sticks it together with wax from a taper. It is considered unlucky if
this wax sinks in the font.—A.M.

his shoulders. Fancy what he had to go through! It's true he has been reinstated, but how could they fail to do that? I think there were not many such gallant sons of the fatherland out there as he. And now—this duel! Have these people no feeling, or honor? Knowing him to be an only son, to challenge him and shoot so straight! It's well God had mercy on us. And what was it for? Who doesn't have intrigues nowadays? Why, if he was so jealous, as I see things he should have shown it sooner, but he lets it go on for months. And then to call him out, reckoning on Fédya not fighting because he owed him money! What baseness! What meanness! I know you understand Fédya, my dear count; that, believe me, is why I am so fond of you. Few people do understand him. He is such a lofty, heavenly soul!"

Dólokhov himself during his convalescence spoke to Rostóv in a way no one would have expected of him.

"I know people consider me a bad man!" he said. "Let them! I don't care a straw about anyone but those I love; but those I love, I love so that I would give my life for them, and the others I'd throttle if they stood in my way. I have an adored, a priceless mother, and two or three friends—you among them—and as for the rest I only care about them in so far as they are harmful or useful. And most of them are harmful, especially the women. Yes, dear boy," he continued, "I have met loving, noble, high-minded men, but I have not yet met any women—countesses or cooks—who were not venal. I have not yet met that divine purity and devotion I look for in women. If I found such a one I'd give my life for her! But those! . . ." and he made a gesture of contempt. "And believe me, if I still value my life it is only because I still hope to meet such a divine creature, who will regenerate, purify, and elevate me. But you don't understand it."

"Oh, yes, I quite understand," answered Rostóv, who was under his new friend's influence.

In the autumn the Rostóvs returned to Moscow. Early in the winter Denísov also came back and stayed with them. The first half of the winter of 1806, which Nicholas Rostóv spent in Moscow, was one of the happiest, merriest times for him and the whole family. Nicholas brought many young men to his parents' house. Véra was a handsome girl of twenty; Sónya a girl of sixteen with all the charm of an opening flower; Natásha, half grown up and half child, was now childishly amusing, now girlishly enchanting.

At that time in the Rostóvs' house there prevailed an amorous atmosphere characteristic of homes where there are very young and very charm-

ing girls. Every young man who came to the house—seeing those impressionable, smiling young faces (smiling probably at their own happiness), feeling the eager bustle around him, and hearing the fitful bursts of song and music and the inconsequent but friendly prattle of young girls ready for anything and full of hope—experienced the same feeling; sharing with the young folk of the Rostóvs' household a readiness to fall in love and an expectation of happiness.

Among the young men introduced by Rostóv one of the first was Dólokhov, whom everyone in the house liked except Natásha. She almost quarreled with her brother about him. She insisted that he was a bad man, and that in the duel with Bezúkhov, Pierre was right and Dólokhov wrong, and further that he was disagreeable and unnatural.

"There's nothing for me to understand," she cried out with resolute self-will, "he is wicked and heartless. There now, I like your Denísov though he is a rake and all that, still I like him; so you see I do understand. I don't know how to put it . . . with this one everything is calculated, and I don't like that. But Denísov . . ."

"Oh, Denísov is quite different," replied Nicholas, implying that even Denísov was nothing compared to Dólokhov—"you must understand what a soul there is in Dólokhov, you should see him with his mother. What a heart!"

"Well, I don't know about that, but I am uncomfortable with him. And do you know he has fallen in love with Sónya?"

"What nonsense. . . ."

"I'm certain of it; you'll see."

Natásha's prediction proved true. Dólokhov, who did not usually care for the society of ladies, began to come often to the house, and the question for whose sake he came (though no one spoke of it) was soon settled. He came because of Sónya. And Sónya, though she would never have dared to say so, knew it and blushed scarlet every time Dólokhov appeared.

Dólokhov often dined at the Rostóvs', never missed a performance at which they were present, and went to Iogel's balls for young people which the Rostóvs always attended. He was pointedly attentive to Sónya and looked at her in such a way that not only could she not bear his glances without coloring, but even the old countess and Natásha blushed when they saw his looks.

It was evident that this strange, strong man was under the irresistible influence of the dark, graceful girl who loved another.

Rostóv noticed something new in Dólokhov's relations with Sónya, but he did not explain to himself what these new relations were. "They're always in love with someone," he thought of Sónya and Natásha. But he

was not as much at ease with Sónya and Dólokhov as before and was less frequently at home.

In the autumn of 1806 everybody had again begun talking of the war with Napoleon with even greater warmth than the year before. Orders were given to raise recruits, ten men in every thousand for the regular army, and besides this, nine men in every thousand for the militia. Everywhere Bonaparte was anathematized and in Moscow nothing but the coming war was talked of.* For the Rostóv family the whole interest of these preparations for war lay in the fact that Nicholas would not hear of remaining in Moscow, and only awaited the termination of Denísov's furlough after Christmas to return with him to their regiment. His approaching departure did not prevent his amusing himself, but rather gave zest to his pleasures. He spent the greater part of his time away from home, at dinners, parties, and balls.

11. Sónya declines Dólokhov's proposal

ON THE THIRD DAY after Christmas Nicholas dined at home, a thing he had rarely done of late. It was a grand farewell dinner, as he and Denísov were leaving to join their regiment after Epiphany. About twenty people were present, including Dólokhov and Denísov.

Never had love been so much in the air, and never had the amorous atmosphere made itself so strongly felt in the Rostóvs' house as at this holiday time. "Seize the moments of happiness, love and be loved! That is the only reality in the world, all else is folly. It is the one thing we are interested in here," said the spirit of the place.

Nicholas, having as usual exhausted two pairs of horses, without visiting all the places he meant to go to and where he had been invited, returned home just before dinner. As soon as he entered he noticed and felt the

* At the end of September Napoleon had attacked Prussia and had rapidly smashed it by the double victory of Jena and Auerstadt, occupying all its fortresses as well as Berlin itself, and in November he advanced into Poland. Russia began preparing for war that autumn expecting to go to the aid of Prussia, but the rapidity of Napoleon's conquest of that country and his advance to the Vistula gave the Russians no time to cross the frontier and obliged them to look to the defense of their own borders. This explains the excitement in Moscow and the extent of the conscription for the army and militia. The conscription was indeed excessive, for muskets could only be supplied to one fifth of the 600,000 militia enrolled, and the rest had to be armed with pikes.—A.M.

tension of the amorous air in the house, and also noticed a curious embarrassment among some of those present. Sónya, Dólokhov, and the old countess were especially disturbed, and to a lesser degree Natásha. Nicholas understood that something must have happened between Sónya and Dólokhov before dinner, and with the kindly sensitiveness natural to him was very gentle and wary with them both at dinner. On that same evening there was to be one of the balls that Iogel (the dancing master) gave for his pupils during the holidays.

"Nicholas, will you come to Iogel's? Please do!" said Natásha. "He asked you, and Vasíli Dmítrich [Denísov] is also going."

"Where would I not go at the countess' command!" said Denísov, who at the Rostóvs' had jocularly assumed the role of Natásha's knight. "I'm even weady to dance the pas de châle."

"If I have time," answered Nicholas. "But I promised the Arkhárovs; they have a party."

"And you?" he asked Dólokhov, but as soon as he had asked the question he noticed that it should not have been put.

"Perhaps," coldly and angrily replied Dólokhov, glancing at Sónya, and, scowling, he gave Nicholas just such a look as he had given Pierre at the Club dinner.

"There is something up," thought Nicholas, and he was further confirmed in this conclusion by the fact that Dólokhov left immediately after dinner. He called Natásha and asked her what was the matter.

"And I was looking for you," said Natásha running out to him. "I told you, but you would not believe it," she said triumphantly. "He has proposed to Sónya!"

Little as Nicholas had occupied himself with Sónya of late, something seemed to give way within him at this news. Dólokhov was a suitable and in some respects a brilliant match for the dowerless, orphan girl. From the point of view of the old countess and of society it was out of the question for her to refuse him. And therefore Nicholas' first feeling on hearing the news was one of anger with Sónya. . . . He tried to say, "That's capital; of course she'll forget her childish promises and accept the offer," but before he had time to say it Natásha began again.

"And fancy! she refused him quite definitely!" adding, after a pause, "she told him she loved another."

"Yes, my Sónya could not have done otherwise!" thought Nicholas.

"Much as Mamma pressed her, she refused, and I know she won't change once she has said . . ."

"And Mamma pressed her!" said Nicholas reproachfully.

"Yes," said Natásha. "Do you know, Nicholas—don't be angry—but I

know you will not marry her. I know, heaven knows how, but I know for certain that you won't marry her."

"Now you don't know that at all!" said Nicholas. "But I must talk to her. What a darling Sónya is!" he added with a smile.

"Ah, she is indeed a darling! I'll send her to you."

And Natásha kissed her brother and ran away.

A minute later Sónya came in with a frightened, guilty, and scared look. Nicholas went up to her and kissed her hand. This was the first time since his return that they had talked alone and about their love.

"Sophie," he began, timidly at first and then more and more boldly, "if you wish to refuse one who is not only a brilliant and advantageous match but a splendid, noble fellow . . . he is my friend . . ."

Sónya interrupted him.

"I have already refused," she said hurriedly.

"If you are refusing for my sake, I am afraid that I . . ."

Sónya again interrupted. She gave him an imploring, frightened look. "Nicholas, don't tell me that!" she said.

"No, but I must. It may be arrogant of me, but still it is best to say it. If you refuse him on my account, I must tell you the whole truth. I love you, and I think I love you more than anyone else. . . ."

"That is enough for me," said Sónya, blushing.

"No, but I have been in love a thousand times and shall fall in love again, though for no one have I such a feeling of friendship, confidence, and love as I have for you. Then I am young. Mamma does not wish it. In a word, I make no promise. And I beg you to consider Dólokhov's offer," he said, articulating his friend's name with difficulty.

"Don't say that to me! I want nothing. I love you as a brother and always shall, and I want nothing more."

"You are an angel: I am not worthy of you, but I am afraid of misleading you."

And Nicholas again kissed her hand.

12. Iogel's ball. Denísov's mazurka

IOGEL'S WERE the most enjoyable balls in Moscow. So said the mothers as they watched their young people executing their newly learned steps, and so said the youths and maidens themselves as they danced till they were ready to drop, and so said the grown-up young men and women who came to these balls with an air of condescension and found them most enjoyable. That year two marriages had come of these balls. The

two pretty young Princesses Gorchakóv met suitors there and were married and so further increased the fame of these dances. What distinguished them from others was the absence of host or hostess and the presence of the good-natured Iogel, flying about like a feather and bowing according to the rules of his art, as he collected the tickets from all his visitors. There was the fact that only those came who wished to dance and amuse themselves as girls of thirteen and fourteen do who are wearing long dresses for the first time. With scarcely any exceptions they all were, or seemed to be, pretty—so rapturous were their smiles and so sparkling their eyes. Sometimes the best of the pupils, of whom Natásha, who was exceptionally graceful, was first, even danced the pas de châle, but at this last ball only the écossaise, the anglaise, and the mazurka, which was just coming into fashion, were danced. Iogel had taken a ballroom in Bezúkhov's house, and the ball, as everyone said, was a great success. There were many pretty girls and the Rostóv girls were among the prettiest. They were both particularly happy and gay. That evening, proud of Dólokhov's proposal, her refusal, and her explanation with Nicholas, Sónya twirled about before she left home so that the maid could hardly get her hair plaited, and she was transparently radiant with impulsive joy.

Natásha no less proud of her first long dress and of being at a real ball was even happier. They were both dressed in white muslin with pink ribbons.

Natásha fell in love the very moment she entered the ballroom. She was not in love with anyone in particular, but with everyone. Whatever person she happened to look at she was in love with for that moment.

"Oh, how delightful it is!" she kept saying, running up to Sónya.

Nicholas and Denísov were walking up and down, looking with kindly patronage at the dancers.

"How sweet she is—she will be a weal beauty!" said Denísov.

"Who?"

"Countess Natásha," answered Denísov.

"And how she dances! What gwace!" he said again after a pause.

"Who are you talking about?"

"About your sister," ejaculated Denísov testily.

Rostóv smiled.

"My dear count, you were one of my best pupils—you must dance," said little Iogel coming up to Nicholas. "Look how many charming young ladies—" He turned with the same request to Denísov who was also a former pupil of his.

"No, my dear fellow, I'll be a wallflower," said Denísov. "Don't you wecollect what bad use I made of your lessons?"

"Oh no!" said Iogel, hastening to reassure him. "You were only inattentive, but you had talent—oh yes, you had talent!"

The band struck up the newly introduced mazurka. Nicholas could not refuse Iogel and asked Sónya to dance. Denísov sat down by the old ladies and, leaning on his saber and beating time with his foot, told them something funny and kept them amused, while he watched the young people dancing. Iogel with Natásha, his pride and his best pupil, were the first couple. Noiselessly, skillfully stepping with his little feet in low shoes, Iogel flew first across the hall with Natásha, who, though shy, went on carefully executing her steps. Denísov did not take his eyes off her and beat time with his saber in a way that clearly indicated that if he was not dancing it was because he would not and not because he could not. In the middle of a figure he beckoned to Rostóv who was passing:

"This is not at all the thing," he said. "What sort of Polish mazuwka is this? But she does dance splendidly."

Knowing that Denísov had a reputation even in Poland for the masterly way in which he danced the mazurka, Nicholas ran up to Natásha:

"Go and choose Denísov. He is a real dancer, a wonder!" he said.

When it came to Natásha's turn to choose a partner, she rose and, tripping rapidly across in her little shoes trimmed with bows, ran timidly to the corner where Denísov sat. She saw that everybody was looking at her and waiting. Nicholas saw that Denísov was refusing though he smiled delightedly. He ran up to them.

"Please, Vasíli Dmítrich," Natásha was saying, "do come!"

"Oh no, let me off, Countess," Denísov replied.

"Now then, Váska," said Nicholas.

"They coax me as if I were Váska the cat!" said Denísov jokingly.

"I'll sing for you a whole evening," said Natásha.

"Oh, the faiwy! She can do anything with me!" said Denísov, and he unhooked his saber. He came out from behind the chairs, clasped his partner's hand firmly, threw back his head, and advanced his foot, waiting for the beat. Only on horseback and in the mazurka was Denísov's short stature not noticeable and he looked the fine fellow he felt himself to be. At the right beat of the music he looked sideways at his partner with a merry and triumphant air, suddenly stamped with one foot, bounded from the floor like a ball, and flew round the room taking his partner with him. He glided silently on one foot half across the room, and seeming not to notice the chairs was dashing straight at them, when suddenly, clinking his spurs and spreading out his legs, he stopped short on his heels,

stood so a second, stamped on the spot clanking his spurs, whirled rapidly round, and, striking his left heel against his right, flew round again in a circle. Natásha guessed what he meant to do, and abandoning herself to him followed his lead hardly knowing how. First he spun her round, holding her now with his left, now with his right hand, then falling on one knee he twirled her round him, and again jumping up, dashed so impetuously forward that it seemed as if he would rush through the whole suite of rooms without drawing breath, and then he suddenly stopped and performed some new and unexpected steps. When at last, smartly whirling his partner round in front of her chair, he drew up with a click of his spurs and bowed to her, Natásha did not even make him a curtsy. She fixed her eyes on him in amazement, smiling as if she did not recognize him.

"What does this mean?" she brought out.

Although Iogel did not acknowledge this to be the real mazurka, everyone was delighted with Denísov's skill, he was asked again and again as a partner, and the old men began smilingly to talk about Poland and the good old days. Denísov, flushed after the mazurka and mopping himself with his handkerchief, sat down by Natásha and did not leave her for the rest of the evening.

13. Nicholas loses 43,000 rubles to Dólokhov

FOR TWO DAYS after that Rostóv did not see Dólokhov at his own or at Dólokhov's home: on the third day he received a note from him:

"As I do not intend to be at your house again for reasons you know of, and am going to rejoin my regiment, I am giving a farewell supper tonight to my friends—come to the English Hotel."

About ten o'clock Rostóv went to the English Hotel straight from the theater, where he had been with his family and Denísov. He was at once shown to the best room, which Dólokhov had taken for that evening. Some twenty men were gathered round a table at which Dólokhov sat between two candles. On the table was a pile of gold and paper money, and he was keeping the bank. Rostóv had not seen him since his proposal and Sónya's refusal and felt uncomfortable at the thought of how they would meet.

Dólokhov's clear, cold glance met Rostóv as soon as he entered the door, as though he had long expected him.

"It's a long time since we met," he said. "Thanks for coming. I'll just finish dealing, and then Ilyúshka will come with his chorus."

"I called once or twice at your house," said Rostóv, reddening.

Dólokhov made no reply.

"You may punt," he said.

Rostóv recalled at that moment a strange conversation he had once had with Dólokhov. "None but fools trust to luck in play," Dólokhov had then said.

"Or are you afraid to play with me?" Dólokhov now asked as if guessing Rostóv's thought.

Beneath his smile Rostóv saw in him the mood he had shown at the Club dinner and at other times, when as if tired of everyday life he had felt a need to escape from it by some strange, and usually cruel, action.

Rostóv felt ill at ease. He tried, but failed, to find some joke with which to reply to Dólokhov's words. But before he had thought of anything, Dólokhov, looking straight in his face, said slowly and deliberately so that everyone could hear:

"Do you remember we had a talk about cards . . . 'He's a fool who trusts to luck, one should make certain,' and I want to try."

"To try his luck or the certainty?" Rostóv asked himself.

"Well, you'd better not play," Dólokhov added, and springing a new pack of cards said: "Bank, gentlemen!"

Moving the money forward he prepared to deal. Rostóv sat down by his side and at first did not play. Dólokhov kept glancing at him.

"Why don't you play?" he asked.

And strange to say Nicholas felt that he could not help taking up a card, putting a small stake on it, and beginning to play.

"I have no money with me," he said.

"I'll trust you."

Rostóv staked five rubles on a card and lost, staked again, and again lost. Dólokhov "killed," that is, beat, ten cards of Rostóv's running.

"Gentlemen," said Dólokhov after he had dealt for some time. "Please place your money on the cards or I may get muddled in the reckoning."

One of the players said he hoped he might be trusted.

"Yes, you might, but I am afraid of getting the accounts mixed. So I ask you to put the money on your cards," replied Dólokhov. "Don't stint yourself, we'll settle afterwards," he added, turning to Rostóv.

The game continued; a waiter kept handing round champagne.

All Rostóv's cards were beaten and he had eight hundred rubles scored up against him. He wrote "800 rubles" on a card, but while the waiter filled his glass he changed his mind and altered it to his usual stake of twenty rubles.

"Leave it," said Dólokhov, though he did not seem to be even looking

at Rostóv, "you'll win it back all the sooner. I lose to the others but win from you. Or are you afraid of me?" he asked again.

Rostóv submitted. He let the eight hundred remain and laid down a seven of hearts with a torn corner, which he had picked up from the floor. He well remembered that seven afterwards. He laid down the seven of hearts, on which with a broken bit of chalk he had written "800 rubles" in clear upright figures; he emptied the glass of warm champagne that was handed him, smiled at Dólokhov's words, and with a sinking heart, waiting for a seven to turn up, gazed at Dólokhov's hands which held the pack. Much depended on Rostóv's winning or losing on that seven of hearts. On the previous Sunday the old count had given his son two thousand rubles, and though he always disliked speaking of money difficulties had told Nicholas that this was all he could let him have till May, and asked him to be more economical this time. Nicholas had replied that it would be more than enough for him and that he gave his word of honor not to take anything more till the spring. Now only twelve hundred rubles was left of that money, so that this seven of hearts meant for him not only the loss of sixteen hundred rubles, but the necessity of going back on his word. With a sinking heart he watched Dólokhov's hands and thought, "Now then, make haste and let me have this card and I'll take my cap and drive home to supper with Denísov, Natásha, and Sónya, and will certainly never touch a card again." At that moment his home life, jokes with Pétya, talks with Sónya, duets with Natásha, piquet with his father, and even his comfortable bed in the house on the Povarskáya rose before him with such vividness, clearness, and charm that it seemed as if it were all a lost and unappreciated bliss, long past. He could not conceive that a stupid chance, letting the seven be dealt to the right rather than to the left, might deprive him of all this happiness, newly appreciated and newly illumined, and plunge him into the depths of unknown and undefined misery. That could not be, yet he awaited with a sinking heart the movement of Dólokhov's hands. Those broad, reddish hands, with hairy wrists visible from under the shirt cuffs, laid down the pack and took up a glass and a pipe that were handed him.

"So you are not afraid to play with me?" repeated Dólokhov, and as if about to tell a good story he put down the cards, leaned back in his chair, and began deliberately with a smile:

"Yes, gentlemen, I've been told there's a rumor going about Moscow that I'm a sharper, so I advise you to be careful."

"Come now, deal!" exclaimed Rostóv.

"Oh, those Moscow gossips!" said Dólokhov, and he took up the cards with a smile.

"Aah!" Rostóv almost screamed lifting both hands to his head. The seven he needed was lying uppermost, the first card in the pack. He had lost more than he could pay.

"Still, don't ruin yourself!" said Dólokhov with a side glance at Rostóv as he continued to deal.

An hour and a half later most of the players were but little interested in their own play.

The whole interest was concentrated on Rostóv. Instead of sixteen hundred rubles he had a long column of figures scored against him, which he had reckoned up to ten thousand, but that now, as he vaguely supposed, must have risen to fifteen thousand. In reality it already exceeded twenty thousand rubles. Dólokhov was no longer listening to stories or telling them, but followed every movement of Rostóv's hands and occasionally ran his eyes over the score against him. He had decided to play until that score reached forty-three thousand. He had fixed on that number because forty-three was the sum of his and Sónya's joint ages. Rostóv, leaning his head on both hands, sat at the table which was scrawled over with figures, wet with spilled wine, and littered with cards. One tormenting impression did not leave him: that those broad-boned reddish hands with hairy wrists visible from under the shirt sleeves, those hands which he loved and hated, held him in their power.

"Six hundred rubles, ace, a corner, a nine . . . winning it back's impossible . . . Oh, how pleasant it was at home! . . . The knave, double or quits . . . it can't be! . . . And why is he doing this to me?" Rostóv pondered. Sometimes he staked a large sum, but Dólokhov refused to accept it and fixed the stake himself. Nicholas submitted to him, and at one moment prayed to God as he had done on the battlefield at the bridge over the Enns, and then guessed that the card that came first to hand from the crumpled heap under the table would save him, now counted the cords on his coat and took a card with that number and tried staking the total of his losses on it, then he looked round for aid from the other players, or peered at the now cold face of Dólokhov and tried to read what was passing in his mind.

"He knows of course what this loss means to me. He can't want my ruin. Wasn't he my friend? Wasn't I fond of him? But it's not his fault. What's he to do if he has such luck? . . . And it's not my fault either," he thought to himself, "I have done nothing wrong. Have I killed anyone, or insulted or wished harm to anyone? Why such a terrible misfortune? And when did it begin? Such a little while ago I came to this table with the thought of winning a hundred rubles to buy that casket for

Mamma's name day and then going home. I was so happy, so free, so lighthearted! And I did not realize how happy I was! When did that end and when did this new, terrible state of things begin? What marked the change? I sat all the time in this same place at this table, chose and placed cards, and watched those broad-boned agile hands in the same way. When did it happen and what has happened? I am well and strong and still the same and in the same place. No, it can't be! Surely it will all end in nothing!"

He was flushed and bathed in perspiration, though the room was not hot. His face was terrible and piteous to see, especially from its helpless efforts to seem calm.

The score against him reached the fateful sum of forty-three thousand. Rostóv had just prepared a card, by bending the corner of which he meant to double the three thousand just put down to his score, when Dólokhov, slamming down the pack of cards, put it aside and began rapidly adding up the total of Rostóv's debt, breaking the chalk as he marked the figures in his clear, bold hand.

"Supper, it's time for supper! And here are the gypsies!"

Some swarthy men and women were really entering from the cold outside and saying something in their gypsy accents. Nicholas understood that it was all over; but he said in an indifferent tone:

"Well, won't you go on? I had a splendid card all ready," as if it were the fun of the game which interested him most.

"It's all up! I'm lost!" thought he. "Now a bullet through my brain—that's all that's left me!" And at the same time he said in a cheerful voice:

"Come now, just this one more little card!"

"All right!" said Dólokhov, having finished the addition. "All right! Twenty-one rubles," he said, pointing to the figure twenty-one by which the total exceeded the round sum of forty-three thousand; and taking up a pack he prepared to deal. Rostóv submissively unbent the corner of his card and, instead of the six thousand he had intended, carefully wrote twenty-one.

"It's all the same to me," he said. "I only want to see whether you will let me win this ten, or beat it."

Dólokhov began to deal seriously. Oh, how Rostóv detested at that moment those hands with their short reddish fingers and hairy wrists, which held him in their power. . . . The ten fell to him.

"You owe forty-three thousand, Count," said Dólokhov, and stretching himself he rose from the table. "One does get tired sitting so long," he added.

"Yes, I'm tired too," said Rostóv.

Dólokhov cut him short, as if to remind him that it was not for him to jest.

"When am I to receive the money, Count?"

Rostóv, flushing, drew Dólokhov into the next room.

"I cannot pay it all immediately. Will you take an I.O.U.?" he said.

"I say, Rostóv," said Dólokhov clearly, smiling and looking Nicholas straight in the eyes, "you know the saying, 'Lucky in love, unlucky at cards.' Your cousin is in love with you, I know."

"Oh, it's terrible to feel oneself so in this man's power," thought Rostóv. He knew what a shock he would inflict on his father and mother by the news of this loss, he knew what a relief it would be to escape it all, and felt that Dólokhov knew that he could save him from all this shame and sorrow, but wanted now to play with him as a cat does with a mouse.

"Your cousin . . ." Dólokhov started to say, but Nicholas interrupted him.

"My cousin has nothing to do with this and it's not necessary to mention her!" he exclaimed fiercely.

"Then when am I to have it?"

"Tomorrow," replied Rostóv and left the room.

14. Nicholas at home. Natásha sings

To say "tomorrow" and keep up a dignified tone was not difficult, but to go home alone, see his sisters, brother, mother, and father, confess and ask for money he had no right to after giving his word of honor, was terrible.

At home, they had not yet gone to bed. The young people, after returning from the theater, had had supper and were grouped round the clavichord. As soon as Nicholas entered, he was enfolded in that poetic atmosphere of love which pervaded the Rostóv household that winter and, now after Dólokhov's proposal and Iogel's ball, seemed to have grown thicker round Sónya and Natásha as the air does before a thunderstorm. Sónya and Natásha, in the light-blue dresses they had worn at the theater, looking pretty and conscious of it, were standing by the clavichord, happy and smiling. Véra was playing chess with Shinshín in the drawing room. The old countess, waiting for the return of her husband and son, sat playing patience with the old gentlewoman who lived in their house. Denísov, with sparkling eyes and ruffled hair, sat at the clavichord striking chords with his short fingers, his legs thrown back and his eyes rolling as he sang, with his small, husky, but true voice, some verses called

"Enchantress," which he had composed, and to which he was trying to fit music:

> Enchantress, say, to my forsaken lyre
> What magic power is this recalls me still?
> What spark has set my inmost soul on fire,
> What is this bliss that makes my fingers thrill?

He was singing in passionate tones, gazing with his sparkling black-agate eyes at the frightened and happy Natásha.

"Splendid! Excellent!" exclaimed Natásha. "Another verse," she said, without noticing Nicholas.

"Everything's still the same with them," thought Nicholas, glancing into the drawing room, where he saw Véra and his mother with the old lady.

"Ah, and here's Nicholas!" cried Natásha, running up to him.

"Is Papa at home?" he asked.

"I am so glad you've come!" said Natásha, without answering him. "We are enjoying ourselves! Vasíli Dmítrich is staying a day longer for my sake! Did you know?"

"No, Papa is not back yet," said Sónya.

"Nicholas, have you come? Come here, dear!" called the old countess from the drawing room.

Nicholas went to her, kissed her hand, and sitting down silently at her table began to watch her hands arranging the cards. From the dancing room, they still heard the laughter and merry voices trying to persuade Natásha to sing.

"All wight! All wight!" shouted Denísov. "It's no good making excuses now! It's your turn to sing the ba'cawolla—I entweat you!"

The countess glanced at her silent son.

"What is the matter?" she asked.

"Oh, nothing," said he, as if weary of being continually asked the same question. "Will Papa be back soon?"

"I expect so."

"Everything's the same with them. They know nothing about it! Where am I to go?" thought Nicholas, and went again into the dancing room where the clavichord stood.

Sónya was sitting at the clavichord, playing the prelude to Denísov's favorite barcarolle. Natásha was preparing to sing. Denísov was looking at her with enraptured eyes.

Nicholas began pacing up and down the room.

"Why do they want to make her sing? How can she sing? There's nothing to be happy about!" thought he.

Sónya struck the first chord of the prelude.

"My God, I'm a ruined and dishonored man! A bullet through my brain is the only thing left me—not singing!" his thoughts ran on. "Go away? But where to? It's all one—let them sing!"

He continued to pace the room, looking gloomily at Denísov and the girls and avoiding their eyes.

"Nikólenka, what is the matter?" Sónya's eyes fixed on him seemed to ask. She noticed at once that something had happened to him.

Nicholas turned away from her. Natásha too, with her quick instinct, had instantly noticed her brother's condition. But, though she noticed it, she was herself in such high spirits at that moment, so far from sorrow, sadness, or self-reproach, that she purposely deceived herself as young people often do. "No, I am too happy now to spoil my enjoyment by sympathy with anyone's sorrow," she felt, and she said to herself: "No, I must be mistaken, he must be feeling happy, just as I am."

"Now, Sónya!" she said, going to the very middle of the room, where she considered the resonance was best.

Having lifted her head and let her arms droop lifelessly, as ballet dancers do, Natásha, rising energetically from her heels to her toes, stepped to the middle of the room and stood still.

"Yes, that's me!" she seemed to say, answering the rapt gaze with which Denísov followed her.

"And what is she so pleased about?" thought Nicholas, looking at his sister. "Why isn't she dull and ashamed?"

Natásha took the first note, her throat swelled, her chest rose, her eyes became serious. At that moment she was oblivious of her surroundings, and from her smiling lips flowed sounds which anyone may produce at the same intervals and hold for the same time, but which leave you cold a thousand times and the thousand and first time thrill you and make you weep.

Natásha, that winter, had for the first time begun to sing seriously, mainly because Denísov so delighted in her singing. She no longer sang as a child, there was no longer in her singing that comical, childish, painstaking effect that had been in it before; but she did not yet sing well, as all the connoisseurs who heard her said: "It is not trained, but it is a beautiful voice that must be trained." Only they generally said this some time after she had finished singing. While that untrained voice, with its incorrect breathing and labored transitions, was sounding, even the connoisseurs said nothing, but only delighted in it and wished to hear it

again. In her voice there was a virginal freshness, an unconsciousness of her own powers, and an as yet untrained velvety softness, which so mingled with her lack of art in singing that it seemed as if nothing in that voice could be altered without spoiling it.

"What is this?" thought Nicholas, listening to her with widely opened eyes. "What has happened to her? How she is singing today!" And suddenly the whole world centered for him on anticipation of the next note, the next phrase, and everything in the world was divided into three beats: "*Oh mio crudele affetto.*" . . . One, two, three . . . one, two, three . . . One . . . "*Oh mio crudele affetto.*" . . . One, two, three . . . One. "Oh, this senseless life of ours!" thought Nicholas. "All this misery, and money, and Dólokhov, and anger, and honor—it's all nonsense . . . but this is real. . . . Now then, Natásha, now then, dearest! Now then, darling! How will she take that *si?* She's taken it! Thank God!" And without noticing that he was singing, to strengthen the *si* he sung a second, a third below the high note. "Ah, God! How fine! Did I really take it? How fortunate!" he thought.

Oh, how that chord vibrated, and how moved was something that was finest in Rostóv's soul! And this something was apart from everything else in the world and above everything in the world. "What were losses, and Dólokhov, and words of honor? . . . All nonsense! One might kill and rob and yet be happy. . . ."

15. Nicholas tells his father of his losses. Denísov proposes to Natásha

IT WAS LONG since Rostóv had felt such enjoyment from music as he did that day. But no sooner had Natásha finished her barcarolle than reality again presented itself. He got up without saying a word and went downstairs to his own room. A quarter of an hour later the old count came in from his Club, cheerful and contented. Nicholas, hearing him drive up, went to meet him.

"Well—had a good time?" said the old count, smiling gaily and proudly at his son.

Nicholas tried to say "Yes," but could not: and he nearly burst into sobs. The count was lighting his pipe and did not notice his son's condition.

"Ah, it can't be avoided!" thought Nicholas, for the first and last time. And suddenly, in the most casual tone, which made him feel ashamed of

himself, he said, as if merely asking his father to let him have the carriage to drive to town:

"Papa, I have come on a matter of business. I was nearly forgetting. I need some money."

"Dear me!" said his father, who was in a specially good humor. "I told you it would not be enough. How much?"

"Very much," said Nicholas flushing, and with a stupid careless smile, for which he was long unable to forgive himself, "I have lost a little, I mean a good deal, a great deal—forty-three thousand."

"What! To whom? . . . Nonsense!" cried the count, suddenly reddening with an apoplectic flush over neck and nape as old people do.

"I promised to pay tomorrow," said Nicholas.

"Well! . . ." said the old count, spreading out his arms and sinking helplessly on the sofa.

"It can't be helped! It happens to everyone!" said the son, with a bold, free, and easy tone, while in his soul he regarded himself as a worthless scoundrel whose whole life could not atone for his crime. He longed to kiss his father's hands and kneel to beg his forgiveness, but said, in a careless and even rude voice, that it happens to everyone!

The old count cast down his eyes on hearing his son's words and began bustlingly searching for something.

"Yes, yes," he muttered, "it will be difficult, I fear, difficult to raise . . . happens to everybody! Yes, who has not done it?"

And with a furtive glance at his son's face, the count went out of the room. . . . Nicholas had been prepared for resistance, but had not at all expected this.

"Papa! Pa-pa!" he called after him, sobbing, "forgive me!" And seizing his father's hand, he pressed it to his lips and burst into tears.

While father and son were having their explanation, the mother and daughter were having one not less important. Natásha came running to her mother, quite excited.

"Mamma! . . . Mamma! . . . He has made me . . ."

"Made what?"

"Made, made me an offer, Mamma! Mamma!" she exclaimed.

The countess did not believe her ears. Denísov had proposed. To whom? To this chit of a girl, Natásha, who not so long ago was playing with dolls and who was still having lessons.

"Don't, Natásha! What nonsense!" she said, hoping it was a joke.

"Nonsense, indeed! I am telling you the fact," said Natásha indignantly. "I come to ask you what to do, and you call it 'nonsense!'"

The countess shrugged her shoulders.

"If it is true that Monsieur Denísov has made you a proposal, tell him he is a fool, that's all!"

"No, he's not a fool!" replied Natásha indignantly and seriously.

"Well then, what do you want? You're all in love nowadays. Well, if you are in love, marry him!" said the countess, with a laugh of annoyance. "Good luck to you!"

"No, Mamma, I'm not in love with him, I suppose I'm not in love with him."

"Well then, tell him so."

"Mamma, are you cross? Don't be cross, dear! Is it my fault?"

"No, but what is it, my dear? Do you want me to go and tell him?" said the countess smiling.

"No, I will do it myself, only tell me what to say. It's all very well for you," said Natásha, with a responsive smile. "You should have seen how he said it! I know he did not mean to say it, but it came out accidentally."

"Well, all the same, you must refuse him."

"No, I mustn't. I am so sorry for him! He's so nice."

"Well then, accept his offer. It's high time for you to be married," answered the countess sharply and sarcastically.

"No, Mamma, but I'm so sorry for him. I don't know how I'm to say it."

"And there's nothing for you to say. I shall speak to him myself," said the countess, indignant that they should have dared to treat this little Natásha as grown up.

"No, not on any account! I will tell him myself, and you'll listen at the door," and Natásha ran across the drawing room to the dancing hall, where Denísov was sitting on the same chair by the clavichord with his face in his hands.

He jumped up at the sound of her light step.

"Nataly," he said, moving with rapid steps toward her, "decide my fate. It is in your hands."

"Vasíli Dmítrich,* I'm so sorry for you! . . . No, but you are so nice . . . but it won't do . . . not that . . . but as a friend, I shall always love you."

Denísov bent over her hand and she heard strange sounds she did not understand. She kissed his rough curly black head. At this instant, they heard the quick rustle of the countess' dress. She came up to them.

"Vasíli Dmítrich, I thank you for the honor," she said, with an embarrassed voice, though it sounded severe to Denísov—"but my daughter

* *The use of the Christian name and patronymic is more cordial as well as more polite than the surname, so Natásha does not call him Colonel Denísov.*
—A.M.

is so young, and I thought that, as my son's friend, you would have addressed yourself first to me. In that case you would not have obliged me to give this refusal."

"Countess . . ." said Denísov, with downcast eyes and a guilty face. He tried to say more, but faltered.

Natásha could not remain calm, seeing him in such a plight. She began to sob aloud.

"Countess, I have done w'ong," Denísov went on in an unsteady voice, "but believe me, I so adore your daughter and all your family that I would give my life twice over . . ." He looked at the countess, and seeing her severe face said: "Well, good-by, Countess," and kissing her hand, he left the room with quick resolute strides, without looking at Natásha.

Next day Rostóv saw Denísov off. He did not wish to stay another day in Moscow. All Denísov's Moscow friends gave him a farewell entertainment at the gypsies', with the result that he had no recollection of how he was put in the sleigh or of the first three stages of his journey.

After Denísov's departure, Rostóv spent another fortnight in Moscow, without going out of the house, waiting for the money his father could not at once raise, and he spent most of his time in the girls' room.

Sónya was more tender and devoted to him than ever. It was as if she wanted to show him that his losses were an achievement that made her love him all the more, but Nicholas now considered himself unworthy of her.

He filled the girls' albums with verses and music, and having at last sent Dólokhov the whole forty-three thousand rubles and received his receipt, he left at the end of November, without taking leave of any of his acquaintances, to overtake his regiment which was already in Poland.

BOOK FIVE

DATES OF PRINCIPAL HISTORICAL EVENTS
1807

OLD STYLE NEW STYLE

Jan. 27	Feb. 8	Battle of Preussisch-Eylau.
June 2	June 14	Battle of Friedland.
June 13	June 25	The Emperors meet at Tilsit.

1806-07

BOOK FIVE

1. Pierre meets Bazdéev

AFTER HIS INTERVIEW with his wife Pierre left for Petersburg. At the Torzhók post station, either there were no horses or the postmaster would not supply them. Pierre was obliged to wait. Without undressing, he lay down on the leather sofa in front of a round table, put his big feet in their overboots on the table, and began to reflect.

"Will you have the portmanteaus brought in? And a bed got ready, and tea?" asked his valet.

Pierre gave no answer, for he neither heard nor saw anything. He had begun to think of the last station and was still pondering on the same question—one so important that he took no notice of what went on around him. Not only was he indifferent as to whether he got to Petersburg earlier or later, or whether he secured accommodation at this station, but compared to the thoughts that now occupied him it was a matter of indifference whether he remained there for a few hours or for the rest of his life.

The postmaster, his wife, the valet, and a peasant woman selling Torzhók embroidery came into the room offering their services. Without changing his careless attitude, Pierre looked at them over his spectacles unable to understand what they wanted or how they could go on living without having solved the problems that so absorbed him. He had been engrossed by the same thoughts ever since the day he returned from Sokólniki after the duel and had spent that first agonizing, sleepless night. But now, in the solitude of the journey, they seized him with special force. No matter what he thought about, he always returned to these same questions which he could not solve and yet could not cease to ask himself. It was as if the thread of the chief screw which held his life together were stripped, so that the screw could not get in or out, but went on turning uselessly in the same place.

The postmaster came in and began obsequiously to beg his excellency to wait only two hours, when, come what might, he would let his excellency have the courier horses. It was plain that he was lying and only wanted to get more money from the traveler.

"Is this good or bad?" Pierre asked himself. "It is good for me, bad for another traveler, and for himself it's unavoidable, because he needs money for food; the man said an officer had once given him a thrashing for letting a private traveler have the courier horses. But the officer thrashed him because he had to get on as quickly as possible. And I," continued Pierre, "shot Dólokhov because I considered myself injured, and Louis XVI was executed because they considered him a criminal, and a year later they executed those who executed him—also for some reason. What is bad? What is good? What should one love and what hate? What does one live for? And what am I? What is life, and what is death? What power governs all?" *

There was no answer to any of these questions, except one, and that not a logical answer and not at all a reply to them. The answer was: "You'll die and all will end. You'll die and know all, or cease asking." But dying was also dreadful.

The Torzhók peddler woman, in a whining voice, went on offering her wares, especially a pair of goatskin slippers. "I have hundreds of rubles I don't know what to do with, and she stands in her tattered cloak looking timidly at me," he thought. "And what does she want the money for? As if that money could add a hair's breadth to her happiness or peace of mind. Can anything in the world make her or me less a prey to evil and death?—death which ends all and must come today or tomorrow—at any rate, in an instant as compared with eternity." And again he twisted the screw with the stripped thread, and again it turned uselessly in the same place.

His servant handed him a half-cut novel, in the form of letters, by Madame de Souza.[2] He began reading about the sufferings and virtuous struggles of a certain Emilie de Mansfeld. "And why did she resist her seducer when she loved him?" he thought. "God could not have put into her heart an impulse that was against His will. My wife—as she once was

* Here, written in the year 1864, we have the questions which fourteen years later produced a crisis in Tolstóy's own life and caused him to write A Confession.—A.M.

[2] Madame de Souza (1761-1836). After her first husband's execution during the Revolution, she, an émigrée in Germany and England, took to writing novels. Emilie et Alphonse was written in 1799.—A.M.

—did not struggle, and perhaps she was right. Nothing has been found out, nothing discovered," Pierre again said to himself. "All we can know is that we know nothing. And that's the height of human wisdom."

Everything within and around him seemed confused, senseless, and repellent. Yet in this very repugnance to all his circumstances Pierre found a kind of tantalizing satisfaction.

"I make bold to ask your excellency to move a little for this gentleman," said the postmaster, entering the room followed by another traveler, also detained for lack of horses.

The newcomer was a short, large-boned, yellow-faced, wrinkled old man, with gray bushy eyebrows overhanging bright eyes of an indefinite grayish color.

Pierre took his feet off the table, stood up, and lay down on a bed that had been got ready for him, glancing now and then at the newcomer, who, with a gloomy and tired face, was wearily taking off his wraps with the aid of his servant, and not looking at Pierre. With a pair of felt boots on his thin bony legs, and keeping on a worn, nankeen-covered, sheepskin coat, the traveler sat down on the sofa, leaned back his big head with its broad temples and close-cropped hair, and looked at Bezúkhov. The stern, shrewd, and penetrating expression of that look struck Pierre. He felt a wish to speak to the stranger, but by the time he had made up his mind to ask him a question about the roads, the traveler had closed his eyes. His shriveled old hands were folded and on the finger of one of them Pierre noticed a large cast-iron ring with a seal representing a death's-head. The stranger sat without stirring, either resting or, as it seemed to Pierre, sunk in profound and calm meditation. His servant was also a yellow, wrinkled old man, without beard or mustache, evidently not because he was shaven but because they had never grown. This active old servant was unpacking the traveler's canteen and preparing tea. He brought in a boiling samovar. When everything was ready, the stranger opened his eyes, moved to the table, filled a tumbler with tea for himself and one for the beardless old man to whom he passed it. Pierre began to feel a sense of uneasiness, and the need, even the inevitability, of entering into conversation with this stranger.

The servant brought back his tumbler turned upside down, with an unfinished bit of nibbled sugar, and asked if anything more would be wanted.*

* Russian serfs and peasants often turn their tea tumblers upside down as an indication that they do not want any more. From economy they do not dissolve the sugar, but nibble a little with their tea.—A.M.

"No. Give me the book," said the stranger.

The servant handed him a book which Pierre took to be a devotional work, and the traveler became absorbed in it. Pierre looked at him. All at once the stranger closed the book, putting in a marker, and again, leaning with his arms on the back of the sofa, sat in his former position with his eyes shut. Pierre looked at him and had not time to turn away when the old man, opening his eyes, fixed his steady and severe gaze straight on Pierre's face.

Pierre felt confused and wished to avoid that look, but the bright old eyes attracted him irresistibly.

"I HAVE THE PLEASURE of addressing Count Bezúkhov, if I am not mistaken," said the stranger in a deliberate and loud voice.

Pierre looked silently and inquiringly at him over his spectacles.

"I have heard of you, my dear sir," continued the stranger, "and of your misfortune." He seemed to emphasize the last word, as if to say—"Yes, misfortune! Call it what you please, I know that what happened to you in Moscow was a misfortune."—"I regret it very much, my dear sir."

Pierre flushed and, hurriedly putting his legs down from the bed, bent forward toward the old man with a forced and timid smile.

"I have not referred to this out of curiosity, my dear sir, but for greater reasons."

He paused, his gaze still on Pierre, and moved aside on the sofa by way of inviting the other to take a seat beside him. Pierre felt reluctant to enter into conversation with this old man, but, submitting to him involuntarily, came up and sat down beside him.

"You are unhappy, my dear sir," the stranger continued. "You are young and I am old. I should like to help you as far as lies in my power."

"Oh, yes!" said Pierre, with a forced smile. "I am very grateful to you. Where are you traveling from?"

The stranger's face was not genial, it was even cold and severe, but in spite of this, both the face and words of his new acquaintance were irresistibly attractive to Pierre.

"But if for any reason you don't feel inclined to talk to me," said the old man, "say so, my dear sir." And he suddenly smiled, in an unexpected and tenderly paternal way.

"Oh no, not at all! On the contrary, I am very glad to make your acquaintance," said Pierre. And again, glancing at the stranger's hands, he looked more closely at the ring, with its skull—a Masonic sign.

"Allow me to ask," he said, "are you a Mason?"

"Yes, I belong to the Brotherhood of the Freemasons," * said the stranger, looking deeper and deeper into Pierre's eyes. "And in their name and my own I hold out a brotherly hand to you."

"I am afraid," said Pierre, smiling, and wavering between the confidence the personality of the Freemason inspired in him and his own habit of ridiculing the Masonic beliefs—"I am afraid I am very far from under-standing—how am I to put it?—I am afraid my way of looking at the world is so opposed to yours that we shall not understand one another."

"I know your outlook," said the Mason, "and the view of life you men-tion, and which you think is the result of your own mental efforts, is the one held by the majority of people, and is the invariable fruit of pride, indolence, and ignorance. Forgive me, my dear sir, but if I had not known it I should not have addressed you. Your view of life is a regrettable delusion."

"Just as I may suppose you to be deluded," said Pierre, with a faint smile.

"I should never dare to say that I know the truth," said the Mason, whose words struck Pierre more and more by their precision and firmness. "No one can attain to truth by himself. Only by laying stone on stone with the co-operation of all, by the millions of generations from our forefather Adam to our own times, is that temple reared which is to be a worthy dwelling place of the Great God," he added, and closed his eyes.

"I ought to tell you that I do not believe . . . do not believe in God," said Pierre, regretfully and with an effort, feeling it essential to speak the whole truth.

The Mason looked intently at Pierre and smiled as a rich man with mil-lions in hand might smile at a poor fellow who told him that he, poor man, had not the five rubles that would make him happy.

"Yes, you do not know Him, my dear sir," said the Mason. "You cannot know Him. You do not know Him and that is why you are unhappy."

"Yes, yes, I am unhappy," assented Pierre. "But what am I to do?"

"You know Him not, my dear sir, and so you are very unhappy. You do not know Him, but He is here, He is in me, He is in my words, He is in thee, and even in those blasphemous words thou hast just uttered!" pro-nounced the Mason in a stern and tremulous voice.

He paused and sighed, evidently trying to calm himself.

"If He were not," he said quietly, "you and I would not be speaking of

* *Freemasonry was established in Russia about 1760. It took its foundations largely from England and Scotland, but was suspected of having an interest in political reforms and consequently suffered repression in Catherine's reign. It flourished under Alexander I, but was completely suppressed by Nicholas I, under whom no secret organization had any chance of being tolerated.*—A.M.

Him, my dear sir. Of what, of whom, are we speaking? Whom hast thou denied?" he suddenly asked with exulting austerity and authority in his voice. "Who invented Him, if He did not exist? Whence came thy conception of the existence of such an incomprehensible Being? Why didst thou, and why did the whole world, conceive the idea of the existence of such an incomprehensible Being, a Being all-powerful, eternal, and infinite in all His attributes? . . ."

He stopped and remained silent for a long time.

Pierre could not and did not wish to break this silence.

"He exists, but to understand Him is hard," the Mason began again, looking not at Pierre but straight before him, and turning the leaves of his book with his old hands which from excitement he could not keep still. "If it were a man whose existence thou didst doubt I could bring him to thee, could take him by the hand and show him to thee. But how can I, an insignificant mortal, show His omnipotence, His infinity, and all His mercy to one who is blind, or who shuts his eyes that he may not see or understand Him and may not see or understand his own vileness and sinfulness?" He paused again. "Who art thou? Thou dreamest that thou art wise because thou couldst utter those blasphemous words," he went on, with a somber and scornful smile. "And thou art more foolish and unreasonable than a little child, who, playing with the parts of a skillfully made watch, dares to say that, as he does not understand its use, he does not believe in the master who made it. To know Him is hard. . . . For ages, from our forefather Adam to our own day, we labor to attain that knowledge and are still infinitely far from our aim; but in our lack of understanding we see only our weakness and His greatness. . . ."

Pierre listened with swelling heart, gazing into the Mason's face with shining eyes, not interrupting or questioning him, but believing with his whole soul what the stranger said. Whether he accepted the wise reasoning contained in the Mason's words, or believed as a child believes, in the speaker's tone of conviction and earnestness, or the tremor of the speaker's voice—which sometimes almost broke—or those brilliant aged eyes grown old in this conviction, or the calm firmness and certainty of his vocation, which radiated from his whole being (and which struck Pierre especially by contrast with his own dejection and hopelessness)—at any rate, Pierre longed with his whole soul to believe and he did believe, and felt a joyful sense of comfort, regeneration, and return to life.

"He is not to be apprehended by reason, but by life," said the Mason.

"I do not understand," said Pierre, feeling with dismay doubts reawakening. He was afraid of any want of clearness, any weakness, in the Mason's arguments; he dreaded not to be able to believe in him. "I don't under-

stand," he said, "how it is that the mind of man cannot attain the knowledge of which you speak."

The Mason smiled with his gentle fatherly smile.

"The highest wisdom and truth are like the purest liquid we may wish to imbibe," he said. "Can I receive that pure liquid into an impure vessel and judge of its purity? Only by the inner purification of myself can I retain in some degree of purity the liquid I receive."

"Yes, yes, that is so," said Pierre joyfully.

"The highest wisdom is not founded on reason alone, not on those worldly sciences of physics, history, chemistry, and the like, into which intellectual knowledge is divided. The highest wisdom is one. The highest wisdom has but one science—the science of the whole—the science explaining the whole creation and man's place in it. To receive that science it is necessary to purify and renew one's inner self, and so before one can know, it is necessary to believe and to perfect one's self. And to attain this end, we have the light called conscience that God has implanted in our souls."

"Yes, yes," assented Pierre.

"Look then at thy inner self with the eyes of the spirit, and ask thyself whether thou art content with thyself. What hast thou attained relying on reason only? What art thou? You are young, you are rich, you are clever, you are well educated. And what have you done with all these good gifts? Are you content with yourself and with your life?"

"No, I hate my life," Pierre muttered, wincing.

"Thou hatest it. Then change it, purify thyself; and as thou art purified, thou wilt gain wisdom. Look at your life, my dear sir. How have you spent it? In riotous orgies and debauchery, receiving everything from society and giving nothing in return. You have become the possessor of wealth. How have you used it? What have you done for your neighbor? Have you ever thought of your tens of thousands of slaves? Have you helped them physically and morally? No! You have profited by their toil to lead a profligate life. That is what you have done. Have you chosen a post in which you might be of service to your neighbor? No! You have spent your life in idleness. Then you married, my dear sir—took on yourself responsibility for the guidance of a young woman; and what have you done? You have not helped her to find the way of truth, my dear sir, but have thrust her into an abyss of deceit and misery. A man offended you and you shot him, and you say you do not know God and hate your life. There is nothing strange in that, my dear sir!"

After these words, the Mason, as if tired by his long discourse, again leaned his arms on the back of the sofa and closed his eyes. Pierre looked

at that aged, stern, motionless, almost lifeless face and moved his lips with-out uttering a sound. He wished to say, "Yes, a vile, idle, vicious life!" but dared not break the silence.

The Mason cleared his throat huskily, as old men do, and called his servant.

"How about the horses?" he asked, without looking at Pierre.

"The exchange horses have just come," answered the servant. "Will you not rest here?"

"No, tell them to harness."

"Can he really be going away and leaving me alone without having told me all, and without promising to help me?" thought Pierre, rising with downcast head; and he began to pace the room, glancing occasionally at the Mason. "Yes, I never thought of it, but I have led a contemptible and profligate life, though I did not like it and did not want to," thought Pierre. "But this man knows the truth and, if he wished to, could disclose it to me."

Pierre wished to say this to the Mason, but did not dare to. The traveler, having packed his things with his practiced hands, began fastening his coat. When he had finished, he turned to Bezúkhov, and said in a tone of indifferent politeness:

"Where are you going to now, my dear sir?"

"I? . . . I'm going to Petersburg," answered Pierre, in a childlike, hesi-tating voice. "I thank you. I agree with all you have said. But do not sup-pose me to be so bad. With my whole soul I wish to be what you would have me be, but I have never had help from anyone. . . . But it is I, above all, who am to blame for everything. Help me, teach me, and perhaps I may . . ."

Pierre could not go on. He gulped and turned away.

The Mason remained silent for a long time, evidently considering.

"Help comes from God alone," he said, "but such measure of help as our Order can bestow it will render you, my dear sir. You are going to Petersburg. Hand this to Count Willarski" (he took out his notebook and wrote a few words on a large sheet of paper folded in four). "Allow me to give you a piece of advice. When you reach the capital, first of all devote some time to solitude and self-examination and do not resume your former way of life. And now I wish you a good journey, my dear sir," he added, seeing that his servant had entered ". . . and success."

The traveler was Joseph Alexéevich Bazdéev,* as Pierre saw from the postmaster's book. Bazdéev had been one of the best-known Freemasons

* *Tolstóy has here used the historical figure of O. A. Pozdéev, only altering two letters of his name.*—A.M.

and Martinists, even in Novíkov's time.* For a long while after he had gone, Pierre did not go to bed or order horses but paced up and down the room, pondering over his vicious past, and with a rapturous sense of beginning anew pictured to himself the blissful, irreproachable, virtuous future that seemed to him so easy. It seemed to him that he had been vicious only because he had somehow forgotten how good it is to be virtuous. Not a trace of his former doubts remained in his soul. He firmly believed in the possibility of the brotherhood of men united in the aim of supporting one another in the path of virtue, and that is how Freemasonry presented itself to him.

2. Pierre becomes a Freemason

ON REACHING Petersburg Pierre did not let anyone know of his arrival, he went nowhere and spent whole days in reading Thomas à Kempis, whose book had been sent him by someone unknown. One thing he continually realized as he read that book: the joy, hitherto unknown to him, of believing in the possibility of attaining perfection, and in the possibility of active brotherly love among men, which Joseph Alexéevich had revealed to him. A week after his arrival, the young Polish count, Willarski, whom Pierre had known slightly in Petersburg society, came into his room one evening in the official and ceremonious manner in which Dólokhov's second had called on him, and, having closed the door behind him and satisfied himself that there was nobody else in the room, addressed Pierre.

"I have come to you with a message and an offer, Count," he said without sitting down. "A person of very high standing in our Brotherhood has made application for you to be received into our Order before the usual term and has proposed to me to be your sponsor. I consider it a sacred duty to fulfill that person's wishes. Do you wish to enter the Brotherhood of Freemasons under my sponsorship?"

The cold, austere tone of this man, whom he had almost always before

* N. I. Novíkov (1744-1818) settled in Moscow and became an active Freemason in 1779, being specially concerned with popular education and educational publications. In 1792 an educational association founded by him was closed by the government, and he was confined in Schlüsselburg fortress for several years. After his release he did not attempt any further public work. The Martinists of Novíkov's time were a society of Russian Freemasons founded in 1780, who took their name from the theosophist L. C. de Saint Martin, an officer and the author of some mystical works.—A.M.

met at balls, amiably smiling in the society of the most brilliant women, surprised Pierre.

"Yes, I do wish it," said he.

Willarski bowed his head.

"One more question, Count," he said, "which I beg you to answer in all sincerity—not as a future Mason but as an honest man: have you renounced your former convictions—do you believe in God?"

Pierre considered.

"Yes . . . yes, I believe in God," he said.

"In that case . . ." began Willarski, but Pierre interrupted him.

"Yes, I do believe in God," he repeated.

"In that case we can go," said Willarski. "My carriage is at your service."

Willarski was silent throughout the drive. To Pierre's inquiries as to what he must do and how he should answer, Willarski only replied that brothers more worthy than he would test him and that Pierre had only to tell the truth.

Having entered the courtyard of a large house where the Lodge had its headquarters, and having ascended a dark staircase, they entered a small well-lit anteroom where they took off their cloaks without the aid of a servant. From there they passed into another room. A man in strange attire appeared at the door. Willarski, stepping toward him, said something to him in French in an undertone and then went up to a small wardrobe in which Pierre noticed garments such as he had never seen before. Having taken a kerchief from the cupboard, Willarski bound Pierre's eyes with it and tied it in a knot behind, catching some hairs painfully in the knot. Then he drew his face down, kissed him, and taking him by the hand led him forward. The hairs tied in the knot hurt Pierre and there were lines of pain on his face and a shamefaced smile. His huge figure, with arms hanging down and with a puckered, though smiling face, moved after Willarski with uncertain, timid steps.*

Having led him about ten paces, Willarski stopped.

"Whatever happens to you," he said, "you must bear it all manfully if you have firmly resolved to join our Brotherhood." (Pierre nodded affirm-

* *Tolstóy took the ceremonies of the Freemasons from his study of books and manuscripts in the rich collection at the Rumyántsev Museum in Moscow. In a letter to his wife in the autumn of 1866 he wrote: "After drinking my coffee I went to the Rumyántsev Museum and sat there till three o'clock reading very interesting Masonic manuscripts. I can't describe to you why the reading produced on me a depression I have not been able to get rid of all day. What is distressing is that all those Masons were fools." Tolstóy sympathized with their aims but considered their methods futile.—A.M.*

atively.) "When you hear a knock at the door, you will uncover your eyes," added Willarski. "I wish you courage and success," and, pressing Pierre's hand, he went out.

Left alone, Pierre went on smiling in the same way. Once or twice he shrugged his shoulders and raised his hand to the kerchief, as if wishing to take it off, but let it drop again. The five minutes spent with his eyes bandaged seemed to him an hour. His arms felt numb, his legs almost gave way, it seemed to him that he was tired out. He experienced a variety of most complex sensations. He felt afraid of what would happen to him and still more afraid of showing his fear. He felt curious to know what was going to happen and what would be revealed to him; but most of all, he felt joyful that the moment had come when he would at last start on that path of regeneration and on the actively virtuous life of which he had been dreaming since he met Joseph Alexéevich. Loud knocks were heard at the door. Pierre took the bandage off his eyes and glanced around him. The room was in black darkness, only a small lamp was burning inside something white. Pierre went nearer and saw that the lamp stood on a black table on which lay an open book. The book was the Gospel, and the white thing with the lamp inside was a human skull with its cavities and teeth. After reading the first words of the Gospel: "In the beginning was the Word and the Word was with God," Pierre went round the table and saw a large open box filled with something. It was a coffin with bones inside. He was not at all surprised by what he saw. Hoping to enter on an entirely new life quite unlike the old one, he expected everything to be unusual, even more unusual than what he was seeing. A skull, a coffin, the Gospel— it seemed to him that he had expected all this and even more. Trying to stimulate his emotions he looked around. "God, death, love, the brotherhood of man," he kept saying to himself, associating these words with vague yet joyful ideas. The door opened and someone came in.

By the dim light, to which Pierre had already become accustomed, he saw a rather short man. Having evidently come from the light into the darkness, the man paused, then moved with cautious steps toward the table and placed on it his small leather-gloved hands.

This short man had on a white leather apron which covered his chest and part of his legs; he had on a kind of necklace above which rose a high white ruffle, outlining his rather long face which was lit up from below.

"For what have you come hither?" asked the newcomer, turning in Pierre's direction at a slight rustle made by the latter. "Why have you, who do not believe in the truth of the light and who have not seen the light, come here? What do you seek from us? Wisdom, virtue, enlightenment?"

At the moment the door opened and the stranger came in, Pierre felt a sense of awe and veneration such as he had experienced in his boyhood at confession; he felt himself in the presence of one socially a complete stranger, yet nearer to him through the brotherhood of man. With bated breath and beating heart he moved toward the Rhetor (by which name the brother who prepared a seeker for entrance into the Brotherhood was known). Drawing nearer, he recognized in the Rhetor a man he knew, Smolyanínov, and it mortified him to think that the newcomer was an acquaintance—he wished him simply a brother and a virtuous instructor. For a long time he could not utter a word, so that the Rhetor had to repeat his question.

"Yes . . . I . . . I . . . desire regeneration," Pierre uttered with difficulty.

"Very well," said Smolyanínov, and went on at once: "Have you any idea of the means by which our holy Order will help you to reach your aim?" said he quietly and quickly.

"I . . . hope . . . for guidance . . . help . . . in regeneration," said Pierre, with a trembling voice and some difficulty in utterance due to his excitement and to being unaccustomed to speak of abstract matters in Russian.

"What is your conception of Freemasonry?"

"I imagine that Freemasonry is the fraternity and equality of men who have virtuous aims," said Pierre, feeling ashamed of the inadequacy of his words for the solemnity of the moment, as he spoke. "I imagine . . ."

"Good!" said the Rhetor quickly, apparently satisfied with this answer. "Have you sought for means of attaining your aim in religion?"

"No, I considered it erroneous and did not follow it," said Pierre, so softly that the Rhetor did not hear him and asked him what he was saying. "I have been an atheist," answered Pierre.

"You are seeking for truth in order to follow its laws in your life, therefore you seek wisdom and virtue. Is that not so?" said the Rhetor, after a moment's pause.

"Yes, yes," assented Pierre.

The Rhetor cleared his throat, crossed his gloved hands on his breast, and began to speak.

"Now I must disclose to you the chief aim of our Order," he said, "and if this aim coincides with yours, you may enter our Brotherhood with profit. The first and chief object of our Order, the foundation on which it rests and which no human power can destroy, is the preservation and handing on to posterity of a certain important mystery . . . which has come down to us from the remotest ages, even from the first man—a mys-

tery on which perhaps the fate of mankind depends. But since this mystery is of such a nature that nobody can know or use it unless he be prepared by long and diligent self-purification, not everyone can hope to attain it quickly. Hence we have a secondary aim, that of preparing our members as much as possible to reform their hearts, to purify and enlighten their minds, by means handed on to us by tradition from those who have striven to attain this mystery, and thereby to render them capable of receiving it.

"By purifying and regenerating our members we try, thirdly, to improve the whole human race, offering it in our members an example of piety and virtue, and thereby try with all our might to combat the evil which sways the world. Think this over and I will come to you again."

"To combat the evil which sways the world . . ." Pierre repeated, and a mental image of his future activity in this direction rose in his mind. He imagined men such as he had himself been a fortnight ago, and he addressed an edifying exhortation to them. He imagined to himself vicious and unfortunate people whom he would assist by word and deed, imagined oppressors whose victims he would rescue. Of the three objects mentioned by the Rhetor, this last, that of improving mankind, especially appealed to Pierre. The important mystery mentioned by the Rhetor, though it aroused his curiosity, did not seem to him essential, and the second aim, that of purifying and regenerating himself, did not much interest him because at that moment he felt with delight that he was already perfectly cured of his former faults and was ready for all that was good.

Half an hour later, the Rhetor returned to inform the seeker of the seven virtues, corresponding to the seven steps of Solomon's temple, which every Freemason should cultivate in himself. These virtues were: 1. *Discretion*, the keeping of the secrets of the Order. 2. *Obedience* to those of higher ranks in the Order. 3. *Morality*. 4. *Love of mankind*. 5. *Courage*. 6. *Generosity*. 7. *The love of death*.

"In the *seventh* place, try, by the frequent thought of death," the Rhetor said, "to bring yourself to regard it not as a dreaded foe, but as a friend that frees the soul grown weary in the labors of virtue from this distressful life, and leads it to its place of recompense and peace."

"Yes, that must be so," thought Pierre, when after these words the Rhetor went away, leaving him to solitary meditation. "It must be so, but I am still so weak that I love my life, the meaning of which is only now gradually opening before me." But five of the other virtues which Pierre recalled, counting them on his fingers, he felt already in his soul: courage, generosity, morality, love of mankind, and especially obedience—which did not even seem to him a virtue, but a joy. (He now felt so glad to be free from his own lawlessness and to submit his will to those who knew

the indubitable truth.) He forgot what the seventh virtue was and could not recall it.

The third time the Rhetor came back more quickly and asked Pierre whether he was still firm in his intention and determined to submit to all that would be required of him.

"I am ready for everything," said Pierre.

"I must also inform you," said the Rhetor, "that our Order delivers its teaching not in words only but also by other means, which may perhaps have a stronger effect on the sincere seeker after wisdom and virtue than mere words. This chamber with what you see therein should already have suggested to your heart, if it is sincere, more than words could do. You will perhaps also see in your further initiation a like method of enlightenment. Our Order imitates the ancient societies that explained their teaching by hieroglyphics. A hieroglyph," said the Rhetor, "is an emblem of something not cognizable by the senses but which possesses qualities resembling those of the symbol."

Pierre knew very well what a hieroglyph was, but dared not speak. He listened to the Rhetor in silence, feeling from all he said that his ordeal was about to begin.

"If you are resolved, I must begin your initiation," said the Rhetor coming closer to Pierre. "In token of generosity I ask you to give me all your valuables."

"But I have nothing here," replied Pierre, supposing that he was asked to give up all he possessed.

"What you have with you: watch, money, rings. . . ."

Pierre quickly took out his purse and watch, but could not manage for some time to get the wedding ring off his fat finger. When that had been done, the Rhetor said:

"In token of obedience, I ask you to undress."

Pierre took off his coat, waistcoat, and left boot according to the Rhetor's instructions. The Mason drew the shirt back from Pierre's left breast, and stooping down pulled up the left leg of his trousers to above the knee. Pierre hurriedly began taking off his right boot also and was going to tuck up the other trouser leg to save this stranger the trouble, but the Mason told him that was not necessary and gave him a slipper for his left foot. With a childlike smile of embarrassment, doubt, and self-derision, which appeared on his face against his will, Pierre stood with his arms hanging down and legs apart, before his brother Rhetor, and awaited his further commands.

"And now, in token of candor, I ask you to reveal to me your chief passion," said the latter.

"My passion! I have had so many," replied Pierre.

"That passion which more than all others caused you to waver on the path of virtue," said the Mason.

Pierre paused, seeking a reply.

"Wine? Gluttony? Idleness? Laziness? Irritability? Anger? Women?" He went over his vices in his mind, not knowing to which of them to give the pre-eminence.

"Women," he said in a low, scarcely audible voice.

The Mason did not move and for a long time said nothing after this answer. At last he moved up to Pierre and, taking the kerchief that lay on the table, again bound his eyes.

"For the last time I say to you—turn all your attention upon yourself, put a bridle on your senses, and seek blessedness, not in passion but in your own heart. The source of blessedness is not without us but within. . . ."

Pierre had already long been feeling in himself that refreshing source of blessedness which now flooded his heart with glad emotion.

SOON AFTER THIS there came into the dark chamber to fetch Pierre, not the Rhetor but Pierre's sponsor, Willarski, whom he recognized by his voice. To fresh questions as to the firmness of his resolution Pierre replied: "Yes, yes, I agree," and with a beaming, childlike smile, his fat chest uncovered, stepping unevenly and timidly in one slippered and one booted foot, he advanced, while Willarski held a sword to his bare chest. He was conducted from that room along passages that turned backwards and forwards and was at last brought to the doors of the Lodge. Willarski coughed, he was answered by the Masonic knock with mallets, the doors opened before them. A bass voice (Pierre was still blindfold) questioned him as to who he was, when and where he was born, and so on. Then he was again led somewhere still blindfold, and as they went along he was told allegories of the toils of his pilgrimage, of holy friendship, of the Eternal Architect of the universe, and of the courage with which he should endure toils and dangers. During these wanderings, Pierre noticed that he was spoken of now as the "Seeker," now as the "Sufferer," and now as the "Postulant," to the accompaniment of various knockings with mallets and swords. As he was being led up to some object he noticed a hesitation and uncertainty among his conductors. He heard those around him disputing in whispers and one of them insisting that he should be led along a certain carpet. After that they took his right hand, placed it on something, and told him to hold a pair of compasses to his left breast with the other hand and to repeat after someone who read aloud an oath of fidelity to the laws of the Order. The candles were then extinguished and some spirit lighted,

as Pierre knew by the smell, and he was told that he would now see the lesser light. The bandage was taken off his eyes and, by the faint light of the burning spirit, Pierre, as in a dream, saw several men standing before him, wearing aprons like the Rhetor's and holding swords in their hands pointed at his breast. Among them stood a man whose white shirt was stained with blood. On seeing this, Pierre moved forward with his breast toward the swords, meaning them to pierce it. But the swords were drawn back from him and he was at once blindfolded again.

"Now thou hast seen the lesser light," uttered a voice. Then the candles were relit and he was told that he would see the full light; the bandage was again removed and more than ten voices said together: "Sic transit gloria mundi."

Pierre gradually began to recover himself and looked about at the room and at the people in it. Round a long table covered with black sat some twelve men in garments like those he had already seen. Some of them Pierre had met in Petersburg society. In the President's chair sat a young man he did not know, with a peculiar cross hanging from his neck. On his right sat the Italian abbé whom Pierre had met at Anna Pávlovna's two years before. There were also present a very distinguished dignitary and a Swiss who had formerly been tutor at the Kurágins'. All maintained a solemn silence, listening to the words of the President, who held a mallet in his hand. Let into the wall was a star-shaped light. At one side of the table was a small carpet with various figures worked upon it, at the other was something resembling an altar on which lay a Testament and a skull. Round it stood seven large candlesticks like those used in churches. Two of the brothers led Pierre up to the altar, placed his feet at right angles, and bade him lie down, saying that he must prostrate himself at the Gates of the Temple.

"He must first receive the trowel," whispered one of the brothers.

"Oh, hush, please!" said another.

Pierre, perplexed, looked round with his shortsighted eyes without obeying, and suddenly doubts arose in his mind. "Where am I? What am I doing? Aren't they laughing at me? Shan't I be ashamed to remember this? But these doubts only lasted a moment. Pierre glanced at the serious faces of those around, remembered all he had already gone through, and realized that he could not stop halfway. He was aghast at his hesitation and, trying to arouse his former devotional feeling, prostrated himself before the Gates of the Temple. And really, the feeling of devotion returned to him even more strongly than before. When he had lain there some time, he was told to get up, and a white leather apron, such as the others wore, was put on him: he was given a trowel and three pairs of gloves, and then

the Grand Master addressed him. He told him that he should try to do nothing to stain the whiteness of that apron, which symbolized strength and purity; then of the unexplained trowel, he told him to toil with it to cleanse his own heart from vice, and indulgently to smooth with it the heart of his neighbor. As to the first pair of gloves, a man's, he said that Pierre could not know their meaning but must keep them. The second pair of man's gloves he was to wear at the meetings, and finally of the third, a pair of women's gloves, he said: "Dear brother, these woman's gloves are intended for you too. Give them to the woman whom you shall honor most of all. This gift will be a pledge of your purity of heart to her whom you select to be your worthy helpmeet in Masonry." And after a pause, he added: "But beware, dear brother, that these gloves do not deck hands that are unclean." While the Grand Master said these last words it seemed to Pierre that he grew embarrassed. Pierre himself grew still more confused, blushed like a child till tears came to his eyes, began looking about him uneasily, and an awkward pause followed.

This silence was broken by one of the brethren, who led Pierre up to the rug and began reading to him from a manuscript book an explanation of all the figures on it: the sun, the moon, a hammer, a plumb line, a trowel, a rough stone and a squared stone, a pillar, three windows, and so on. Then a place was assigned to Pierre, he was shown the signs of the Lodge, told the password, and at last was permitted to sit down. The Grand Master began reading the statutes. They were very long, and Pierre, from joy, agitation, and embarrassment, was not in a state to understand what was being read. He managed to follow only the last words of the statutes and these remained in his mind.

"In our temples we recognize no other distinctions," read the Grand Master, "but those between virtue and vice. Beware of making any distinctions which may infringe equality. Fly to a brother's aid whoever he may be, exhort him who goeth astray, raise him that falleth, never bear malice or enmity toward thy brother. Be kindly and courteous. Kindle in all hearts the flame of virtue. Share thy happiness with thy neighbor, and may envy never dim the purity of that bliss. Forgive thy enemy, do not avenge thyself except by doing him good. Thus fulfilling the highest law thou shalt regain traces of the ancient dignity which thou hast lost."

He finished and, getting up, embraced and kissed Pierre, who, with tears of joy in his eyes, looked round him, not knowing how to answer the congratulations and greetings from acquaintances that met him on all sides. He acknowledged no acquaintances but saw in all these men only brothers, and burned with impatience to set to work with them.

The Grand Master rapped with his mallet. All the Masons sat down in

their places, and one of them read an exhortation on the necessity of humility.

The Grand Master proposed that the last duty should be performed, and the distinguished dignitary who bore the title of "Collector of Alms" went round to all the brothers. Pierre would have liked to subscribe all he had, but fearing that it might look like pride subscribed the same amount as the others.

The meeting was at an end, and on reaching home Pierre felt as if he had returned from a long journey on which he had spent dozens of years, had become completely changed, and had quite left behind his former habits and way of life.

3. *Pierre repulses Prince Vasíli*

THE DAY AFTER he had been received into the Lodge, Pierre was sitting at home reading a book and trying to fathom the significance of the Square, one side of which symbolized God, another moral things, a third physical things, and the fourth a combination of these. Now and then his attention wandered from the book and the Square and he formed in imagination a new plan of life. On the previous evening at the Lodge, he had heard that a rumor of his duel had reached the Emperor and that it would be wiser for him to leave Petersburg. Pierre proposed going to his estates in the south and there attending to the welfare of his serfs. He was joyfully planning this new life, when Prince Vasíli suddenly entered the room.

"My dear fellow, what have you been up to in Moscow? Why have you quarreled with Hélène, *mon cher*? You are under a delusion," said Prince Vasíli, as he entered. "I know all about it, and I can tell you positively that Hélène is as innocent before you as Christ was before the Jews."

Pierre was about to reply, but Prince Vasíli interrupted him.

"And why didn't you simply come straight to me as to a friend? I know all about it and understand it all," he said. "You behaved as becomes a man who values his honor, perhaps too hastily, but we won't go into that. But consider the position in which you are placing her and me in the eyes of society, and even of the court," he added, lowering his voice. "She is living in Moscow and you are here. Remember, dear boy," and he drew Pierre's arm downwards, "it is simply a misunderstanding. I expect you feel it so yourself. Let us write her a letter at once, and she'll come here and all will be explained, or else, my dear boy, let me tell you it's quite likely you'll have to suffer for it."

Prince Vasíli gave Pierre a significant look.

"I know from reliable sources that the Dowager Empress is taking a keen interest in the whole affair. You know she is very gracious to Hélène."

Pierre tried several times to speak, but, on one hand, Prince Vasíli did not let him and, on the other, Pierre himself feared to begin to speak in the tone of decided refusal and disagreement in which he had firmly resolved to answer his father-in-law. Moreover, the words of the Masonic statutes, "be kindly and courteous," recurred to him. He blinked, went red, got up and sat down again, struggling with himself to do what was for him the most difficult thing in life—to say an unpleasant thing to a man's face, to say what the other, whoever he might be, did not expect. He was so used to submitting to Prince Vasíli's tone of careless self-assurance that he felt he would be unable to withstand it now, but he also felt that on what he said now his future depended—whether he would follow the same old road, or that new path so attractively shown him by the Masons, on which he firmly believed he would be reborn to a new life.

"Now, dear boy," said Prince Vasíli playfully, "say 'yes,' and I'll write to her myself, and we will kill the fatted calf."

But before Prince Vasíli had finished his playful speech, Pierre, without looking at him, and with a kind of fury that made him like his father, muttered in a whisper:

"Prince, I did not ask you here. Go, please go!" And he jumped up and opened the door for him.

"Go!" he repeated, amazed at himself and glad to see the look of confusion and fear that showed itself on Prince Vasíli's face.

"What's the matter with you? Are you ill?"

"Go!" the quivering voice repeated. And Prince Vasíli had to go without receiving any explanation.

A week later, Pierre, having taken leave of his new friends, the Masons, and leaving large sums of money with them for alms, went away to his estates. His new brethren gave him letters to the Kiev and Odessa Masons and promised to write to him and guide him in his new activity.

4. A soiree at Anna Pávlovna's. Hélène takes up Borís

THE DUEL between Pierre and Dólokhov was hushed up and, in spite of the Emperor's severity regarding duels at that time, neither the principals nor their seconds suffered for it. But the story of the duel, confirmed by Pierre's rupture with his wife, was the talk of society. Pierre who had been regarded with patronizing condescension when he was an illegitimate son, and petted and extolled when he was the best match in Russia,

had sunk greatly in the esteem of society after his marriage—when the marriageable daughters and their mothers had nothing to hope from him —especially as he did not know how, and did not wish, to court society's favor. Now he alone was blamed for what had happened, he was said to be insanely jealous and subject like his father to fits of bloodthirsty rage. And when after Pierre's departure Hélène returned to Petersburg, she was received by all her acquaintances not only cordially, but even with a shade of deference due to her misfortune. When conversation turned on her husband Hélène assumed a dignified expression, which with characteristic tact she had acquired though she did not understand its significance. This expression suggested that she had resolved to endure her troubles uncomplainingly and that her husband was a cross laid upon her by God. Prince Vasíli expressed his opinion more openly. He shrugged his shoulders when Pierre was mentioned and, pointing to his forehead, remarked:

"A bit touched—I always said so."

"I said from the first," declared Anna Pávlovna referring to Pierre, "I said at the time and before anyone else" (she insisted on her priority) "that that senseless young man was spoiled by the depraved ideas of these days. I said so even at the time when everybody was in raptures about him, when he had just returned from abroad, and when, if you remember, he posed as a sort of Marat at one of my soirees. And how has it ended? I was against this marriage even then and foretold all that has happened."

Anna Pávlovna continued to give on free evenings the same kind of soirees as before—such as she alone had the gift of arranging—at which was to be found "the cream of really good society, the bloom of the intellectual essence of Petersburg," as she herself put it. Besides this refined selection of society Anna Pávlovna's receptions were also distinguished by the fact that she always presented some new and interesting person to the visitors and that nowhere else was the state of the political thermometer of legitimate Petersburg court society so clearly and distinctly indicated.

Toward the end of 1806, when all the sad details of Napoleon's destruction of the Prussian army at Jena and Auerstadt and the surrender of most of the Prussian fortresses had been received, when our troops had already entered Prussia and our second war with Napoleon was beginning, Anna Pávlovna gave one of her soirees. The "cream of really good society" consisted of the fascinating Hélène, forsaken by her husband, Mortemart, the delightful Prince Hippolyte who had just returned from Vienna, two diplomatists, the old aunt, a young man referred to in that drawing room as "a man of great merit" (un homme de beaucoup de mérite), a newly appointed maid of honor and her mother, and several other less noteworthy persons.

The novelty Anna Pávlovna was setting before her guests that evening was Borís Drubetskóy, who had just arrived as a special messenger from the Prussian army and was aide-de-camp to a very important personage.

The temperature shown by the political thermometer to the company that evening was this:

"Whatever the European sovereigns and commanders may do to countenance Bonaparte, and to cause me, and us in general, annoyance and mortification, our opinion of Bonaparte cannot alter. We shall not cease to express our sincere views on that subject, and can only say to the King of Prussia and others: 'So much the worse for you. *Tu l'as voulu, George Dandin* [You would have it so],' * that's all we have to say about it!"

When Borís, who was to be served up to the guests, entered the drawing room, almost all the company had assembled, and the conversation, guided by Anna Pávlovna, was about our diplomatic relations with Austria and the hope of an alliance with her.

Borís, grown more manly and looking fresh, rosy and self-possessed, entered the drawing room elegantly dressed in the uniform of an aide-de-camp and was duly conducted to pay his respects to the aunt and then brought back to the general circle.

Anna Pávlovna gave him her shriveled hand to kiss and introduced him to several persons whom he did not know, giving him a whispered description of each.

"Prince Hippolyte Kurágin—charming young fellow; M. Kronq—chargé d'affaires from Copenhagen—a profound intellect," and simply, "Mr. Shítov—a man of great merit"—this of the man usually so described.

Thanks to Anna Mikháylovna's efforts, his own tastes, and the peculiarities of his reserved nature, Borís had managed during his service to place himself very advantageously. He was aide-de-camp to a very important personage, had been sent on a very important mission to Prussia, and had just returned from there as a special messenger. He had become thoroughly conversant with that unwritten code with which he had been so pleased at Olmütz and according to which an ensign might rank incomparably higher than a general, and according to which what was needed for success in the service was not effort or work, or courage, or perseverance, but only the knowledge of how to get on with those who can grant rewards, and he was himself often surprised at the rapidity of his success and at the inability of others to understand these things. In consequence of this discovery his whole manner of life, all his relations with old friends, all his plans for his future, were completely altered. He was not rich, but would spend his last groat to be better dressed than others, and would

* A reference to Molière's comedy George Dandin.—A.M.

rather deprive himself of many pleasures than allow himself to be seen in a shabby equipage or appear in the streets of Petersburg in an old uniform. He made friends with and sought the acquaintance of only those above him in position and who could therefore be of use to him. He liked Petersburg and despised Moscow. The remembrance of the Rostóvs' house and of his childish love for Natásha was unpleasant to him and he had not once been to see the Rostóvs since the day of his departure for the army. To be in Anna Pávlovna's drawing room he considered an important step up in the service, and he at once understood his role, letting his hostess make use of whatever interest he had to offer. He himself carefully scanned each face, appraising the possibilities of establishing intimacy with each of those present, and the advantages that might accrue. He took the seat indicated to him beside the fair Hélène and listened to the general conversation.

"Vienna considers the bases of the proposed treaty so unattainable that not even a continuity of most brilliant successes would secure them, and she doubts the means we have of gaining them.* That is the actual phrase used by the Vienna cabinet," said the Danish chargé d'affaires.

"The doubt is flattering," said "the man of profound intellect," with a subtle smile.

"We must distinguish between the Vienna cabinet and the Emperor of Austria," said Mortemart. "The Emperor of Austria can never have thought of such a thing, it is only the cabinet that says it."

"Ah, my dear vicomte," put in Anna Pávlovna, "*L'Urope*" (for some reason she called it *Urope* as if that were a specially refined French pronunciation which she could allow herself when conversing with a Frenchman), "*L'Urope ne sera jamais notre alliée sincere* [Europe will never be our sincere ally]."

After that Anna Pávlovna led up to the courage and firmness of the King of Prussia, in order to draw Borís into the conversation.

Borís listened attentively to each of the speakers, awaiting his turn, but

* *Tolstóy has here run rather ahead of the actual course of events. The Bartenstein treaty between Russia and Prussia here spoken of, and to which Austria was invited to adhere, was not concluded till April, 1807, after some actions had taken place, including the battle of Eylau mentioned in the next section, in which Napoleon had so little success that he seemed inclined for peace. Alexander wished to avail himself of this disposition, and in the proposed treaty the Allies made certain stipulations, but Vienna considered it hopeless to propose conditions to Napoleon—who would be sure to reject them. Matters dragged on till May, when Napoleon's victory at Friedland put a fresh aspect on affairs. The Bartenstein treaty did not come into operation, but a peace to suit Napoleon was concluded at Tilsit.—A.M.*

managed meanwhile to look round repeatedly at his neighbor, the beauti-
ful Hélène, whose eyes several times met those of the handsome young
aide-de-camp with a smile.

Speaking of the position of Prussia, Anna Pávlovna very naturally asked
Borís to tell them about his journey to Glogau and in what state he found
the Prussian army. Borís, speaking with deliberation, told them in pure,
correct French many interesting details about the armies and the court,
carefully abstaining from expressing an opinion of his own about the facts
he was recounting. For some time he engrossed the general attention, and
Anna Pávlovna felt that the novelty she had served up was received with
pleasure by all her visitors. The greatest attention of all to Borís' narrative
was shown by Hélène. She asked him several questions about his journey
and seemed greatly interested in the state of the Prussian army. As soon as
he had finished she turned to him with her usual smile.

"You absolutely must come and see me," she said in a tone that implied
that, for certain considerations he could not know of, this was absolutely
necessary.

"On Tuesday between eight and nine. It will give me great pleasure."

Borís promised to fulfill her wish and was about to begin a conversation
with her, when Anna Pávlovna called him away on the pretext that her
aunt wished to hear him.

"You know her husband, of course?" said Anna Pávlovna, closing her
eyes and indicating Hélène with a sorrowful gesture. "Ah, she is such an
unfortunate and charming woman! Don't mention him before her—please
don't! It is too painful for her!"

5. Hippolyte at Anna Pávlovna's

WHEN Borís and Anna Pávlovna returned to the others Prince Hip-
polyte had the ear of the company.
Bending forward in his armchair he said: "Le Roi de Prusse!" and having
said this laughed. Everyone turned toward him.

"Le Roi de Prusse?" Hippolyte said interrogatively, again laughing, and
then calmly and seriously sat back in his chair. Anna Pávlovna waited for
him to go on, but as he seemed quite decided to say no more she began to
tell of how at Potsdam the impious Bonaparte had stolen the sword of
Frederick the Great.

"It is the sword of Frederick the Great which I . . ." she began, but
Hippolyte interrupted her with the words: "Le Roi de Prusse . . ." and
again, as soon as all turned toward him, excused himself and said no more.

Anna Pávlovna frowned. Mortemart, Hippolyte's friend, addressed him firmly.

"Come now, what about your *Roi de Prusse?*"

Hippolyte laughed as if ashamed of laughing.

"Oh, it's nothing. I only wished to say . . ." (he wanted to repeat a joke he had heard in Vienna and which he had been trying all that evening to get in) "I only wished to say that we are wrong to fight *pour le Roi de Prusse!*" *

Borís smiled circumspectly, so that it might be taken as ironical or appreciative according to the way the joke was received. Everybody laughed.

"Your joke is too bad, it's witty but unjust," said Anna Pávlovna, shaking her little shriveled finger at him.

"We are not fighting *pour le Roi de Prusse,* but for right principles. Oh, that wicked Prince Hippolyte!" she said.

The conversation did not flag all evening and turned chiefly on the political news. It became particularly animated toward the end of the evening when the rewards bestowed by the Emperor were mentioned.

"You know N— N— received a snuffbox with the portrait last year?" said "the man of profound intellect." "Why shouldn't S— S— get the same distinction?"

"Pardon me! A snuffbox with the Emperor's portrait is a reward but not a distinction," said the diplomatist—"a gift, rather."

"There are precedents, I may mention Schwarzenberg."

"It's impossible," replied another.

"Will you bet? The ribbon of the order is a different matter. . . ."

When everybody rose to go, Hélène who had spoken very little all the evening again turned to Borís, asking him in a tone of caressing significant command to come to her on Tuesday.

"It is of great importance to me," she said, turning with a smile toward Anna Pávlovna, and Anna Pávlovna, with the same sad smile with which she spoke of her exalted patroness, supported Hélène's wish.

It seemed as if from some words Borís had spoken that evening about the Prussian army, Hélène had suddenly found it necessary to see him. She seemed to promise to explain that necessity to him when he came on Tuesday.

But on Tuesday evening, having come to Hélène's splendid salon, Borís received no clear explanation of why it had been necessary for him to come. There were other guests and the countess talked little to him, and only as he kissed her hand on taking leave said unexpectedly and in a

* *"For the King of Prussia"—a phrase used in French to denote "for a trifle of no value."*—A.M.

whisper, with a strangely unsmiling face: "Come to dinner tomorrow . . .
in the evening. You must come . . . Come!"

During that stay in Petersburg, Borís became an intimate in the count-
ess' house.

6. Old Bolkónski as commander in chief of the conscription. Andrew's anxiety. A letter from his father

THE WAR was flaming up and nearing the Russian frontier. Everywhere
one heard curses on Bonaparte, "the enemy of mankind." Militia-
men and recruits were being enrolled in the villages, and from the seat of
war came contradictory news, false as usual and therefore variously inter-
preted.

The life of old Prince Bolkónski, Prince Andrew, and Princess Mary had
greatly changed since 1805.

In 1806 the old prince was made one of the eight commanders in chief
then appointed to supervise the enrollment decreed throughout Russia.
Despite the weakness of age, which had become particularly noticeable
since the time when he thought his son had been killed, he did not think it
right to refuse a duty to which he had been appointed by the Emperor
himself, and this fresh opportunity for action gave him new energy and
strength. He was continually traveling through the three provinces en-
trusted to him, was pedantic in the fulfillment of his duties, severe to
cruelty with his subordinates, and went into everything down to the mi-
nutest details himself. Princess Mary had ceased taking lessons in mathe-
matics from her father, and when the old prince was at home went to his
study with the wet nurse and little Prince Nicholas (as his grandfather
called him). The baby Prince Nicholas lived with his wet nurse and nurse
Sávishna in the late princess' rooms and Princess Mary spent most of the
day in the nursery, taking a mother's place to her little nephew as best she
could. Mademoiselle Bourienne, too, seemed passionately fond of the boy,
and Princess Mary often deprived herself to give her friend the pleasure of
dandling the little angel—as she called her nephew—and playing with him.

Near the altar of the church at Bald Hills there was a chapel over the
tomb of the little princess, and in this chapel was a marble monument
brought from Italy, representing an angel with outspread wings ready to
fly upwards. The angel's upper lip was slightly raised as though about to
smile, and once on coming out of the chapel Prince Andrew and Princess
Mary admitted to one another that the angel's face reminded them
strangely of the little princess. But what was still stranger, though of this

Prince Andrew said nothing to his sister, was that in the expression the sculptor had happened to give the angel's face, Prince Andrew read the same mild reproach he had read on the face of his dead wife: "Ah, why have you done this to me?"

Soon after Prince Andrew's return the old prince made over to him a large estate, Boguchárovo, about twenty-five miles from Bald Hills. Partly because of the depressing memories associated with Bald Hills, partly because Prince Andrew did not always feel equal to bearing with his father's peculiarities, and partly because he needed solitude, Prince Andrew made use of Boguchárovo, began building and spent most of his time there.

After the Austerlitz campaign Prince Andrew had firmly resolved not to continue his military service, and when the war recommenced and everybody had to serve, he took a post under his father in the recruitment so as to avoid active service. The old prince and his son seemed to have changed roles since the campaign of 1805. The old man, roused by activity, expected the best results from the new campaign, while Prince Andrew on the contrary, taking no part in the war and secretly regretting this, saw only the dark side.

On February 26, 1807, the old prince set off on one of his circuits. Prince Andrew remained at Bald Hills as usual during his father's absence. Little Nicholas had been unwell for four days. The coachman who had driven the old prince to town returned bringing papers and letters for Prince Andrew.

Not finding the young prince in his study the valet went with the letters to Princess Mary's apartments, but did not find him there. He was told that the prince had gone to the nursery.

"If you please, your excellency, Petrúsha has brought some papers," said one of the nursemaids to Prince Andrew who was sitting on a child's little chair while, frowning and with trembling hands, he poured drops from a medicine bottle into a wineglass half full of water.

"What is it?" he said crossly, and, his hand shaking unintentionally, he poured too many drops into the glass. He threw the mixture onto the floor and asked for some more water. The maid brought it.

There were in the room a child's cot, two boxes, two armchairs, a table, a child's table, and the little chair on which Prince Andrew was sitting. The curtains were drawn, and a single candle was burning on the table, screened by a bound music book so that the light did not fall on the cot.

"My dear," said Princess Mary, addressing her brother from beside the cot where she was standing, "better wait a bit . . . later . . ."

"Oh, leave off, you always talk nonsense and keep putting things off—

and this is what comes of it!" said Prince Andrew in an exasperated whisper, evidently meaning to wound his sister.

"My dear, really . . . it's better not to wake him . . . he's asleep," said the princess in a tone of entreaty.

Prince Andrew got up and went on tiptoe up to the little bed, wineglass in hand.

"Perhaps we'd really better not wake him," he said hesitating.

"As you please . . . really . . . I think so . . . but as you please," said Princess Mary, evidently intimidated and confused that her opinion had prevailed. She drew her brother's attention to the maid who was calling him in a whisper.

It was the second night that neither of them had slept, watching the boy who was in a high fever. These last days, mistrusting their household doctor and expecting another for whom they had sent to town, they had been trying first one remedy and then another. Worn out by sleeplessness and anxiety they threw their burden of sorrow on one another and reproached and disputed with each other.

"Petrúsha has come with papers from your father," whispered the maid.

Prince Andrew went out.

"Devil take them!" he muttered, and after listening to the verbal instructions his father had sent and taking the correspondence and his father's letter, he returned to the nursery.

"Well?" he asked.

"Still the same. Wait, for heaven's sake. Karl Ivánich always says that sleep is more important than anything," whispered Princess Mary with a sigh.

Prince Andrew went up to the child and felt him. He was burning hot.

"Confound you and your Karl Ivánich!" He took the glass with the drops and again went up to the cot.

"Andrew, don't!" said Princess Mary.

But he scowled at her angrily though also with suffering in his eyes, and stooped glass in hand over the infant.

"But I wish it," he said. "I beg you—give it him!"

Princess Mary shrugged her shoulders but took the glass submissively and calling the nurse began giving the medicine. The child screamed hoarsely. Prince Andrew winced and, clutching his head, went out and sat down on a sofa in the next room.

He still had all the letters in his hand. Opening them mechanically he began reading. The old prince, now and then using abbreviations, wrote in his large elongated hand on blue paper as follows:

"Have just this moment received by special messenger very joyful news

—if it's not false. Bennigsen seems to have obtained a complete victory over Buonaparte at Eylau.* In Petersburg everyone is rejoicing, and the rewards sent to the army are innumerable. Though he is a German—I congratulate him! I can't make out what the commander at Kórchevo—a certain Khandrikóv—is up to; till now the additional men and provisions have not arrived. Gallop off to him at once and say I'll have his head off if everything is not here in a week. Have received another letter about the Preussisch-Eylau battle from Pétenka—he took part in it—and it's all true. When mischief-makers don't meddle even a German beats Buonaparte. He is said to be fleeing in great disorder. Mind you gallop off to Kórchevo without delay and carry out instructions!"

Prince Andrew sighed and broke the seal of another envelope. It was a closely written letter of two sheets from Bilíbin. He folded it up without reading it and reread his father's letter, ending with the words: "Gallop off to Kórchevo and carry out instructions!"

"No, pardon me, I won't go now till the child is better," thought he, going to the door and looking into the nursery.

Princess Mary was still standing by the cot, gently rocking the baby.

"Ah yes, and what else did he say that's unpleasant?" thought Prince Andrew, recalling his father's letter. "Yes, we have gained a victory over Bonaparte, just when I'm not serving. Yes, yes, he's always poking fun at me. . . . Ah, well! Let him!" And he began reading Bilíbin's letter which was written in French. He read without understanding half of it, read only to forget, if but for a moment, what he had too long been thinking of so painfully to the exclusion of all else.

7. Bilíbin's letter about the campaign. The baby convalescent

B ILÍBIN WAS NOW at army headquarters in a diplomatic capacity, and though he wrote in French and used French jests and French idioms, he described the whole campaign with a fearless self-censure and self-derision genuinely Russian. Bilíbin wrote that the obligation of diplomatic discretion tormented him, and he was happy to have in Prince Andrew a reliable correspondent to whom he could pour out the bile he had accumu-

* This was the battle at Preussisch-Eylau at the end of January, after which the Russians, though they had succeeded in upsetting Napoleon's whole plan, retreated, unable to renew the conflict. Napoleon, for his part having remained at Eylau some days with a quite exhausted army, also withdrew but, piling lie on lie, announced a victory, while the Russians did the same.—A.M.

lated at the sight of all that was being done in the army. The letter was old, having been written before the battle at Preussisch-Eylau.

"Since the day of our brilliant success at Austerlitz," wrote Bilíbin, "as you know, my dear prince, I never leave headquarters. I have certainly acquired a taste for war, and it is just as well for me; what I have seen during these last three months is incredible.

"I begin *ab ovo*. 'The enemy of the human race,' as you know, attacks the Prussians. The Prussians are our faithful allies who have only betrayed us three times in three years. We take up their cause, but it turns out that 'the enemy of the human race' pays no heed to our fine speeches and in his rude and savage way throws himself on the Prussians without giving them time to finish the parade they had begun, and in two twists of the hand he breaks them to smithereens and installs himself in the palace at Potsdam.

" 'I most ardently desire,' writes the King of Prussia to Bonaparte, 'that Your Majesty should be received and treated in my palace in a manner agreeable to yourself, and in so far as circumstances allowed, I have hastened to take all steps to that end. May I have succeeded!' The Prussian generals pride themselves on being polite to the French and lay down their arms at the first demand.

"The head of the garrison at Glogau, with ten thousand men, asks the King of Prussia what he is to do if he is summoned to surrender. . . . All this is absolutely true.

"In short, hoping to settle matters by taking up a warlike attitude, it turns out that we have landed ourselves in war, and what is more, in war on our own frontiers, *with* and *for* the King of Prussia.* We have everything in perfect order, only one little thing is lacking, namely, a commander in chief. As it was considered that the Austerlitz success might have been more decisive had the commander in chief not been so young, all our octogenarians were reviewed, and of Prozoróvski and Kámenski the latter was preferred. The general comes to us, Suvórov-like, in a *kibítka*,[2] and is received with acclamations of joy and triumph.

"On the 4th, the first courier arrives from Petersburg. The mails are taken to the field marshal's room, for he likes to do everything himself. I am called in to help sort the letters and take those meant for us. The field marshal looks on and waits for letters addressed to him. We search, but none are to be found. The field marshal grows impatient and sets to work

* *This is the same untranslatable pun as in the last section. It means with the King of Prussia and for a matter of no account.*—A.M.

[2] Kibítka. *Originally a movable dwelling used by nomad tribes and constructed of lattice work covered with felt. The word is also used, as in this case, of an old-fashioned wooden cart with a covered top.*—A.M.

himself and finds letters from the Emperor to Count T., Prince V., and others. Then he bursts into one of his wild furies and rages at everyone and everything, seizes the letters, opens them, and reads those from the Emperor addressed to others. 'Ah! So that's the way they treat me! No confidence in me! Ah, ordered to keep an eye on me! Very well then! Get along with you!' So he writes the famous order of the day to General Bennigsen:

" 'I am wounded and cannot ride and consequently cannot command the army. You have brought your army corps to Pultúsk, routed: here it is exposed, and without fuel or forage, so something must be done, and, as you yourself reported to Count Buxhöwden yesterday, you must think of retreating to our frontier—which do today.'

" 'From all my riding,' he writes to the Emperor, 'I have got a saddle sore which, coming after all my previous journeys, quite prevents my riding and commanding so vast an army, so I have passed on the command to the general next in seniority, Count Buxhöwden, having sent him my whole staff and all that belongs to it, advising him if there is a lack of bread, to move farther into the interior of Prussia, for only one day's ration of bread remains, and in some regiments none at all, as reported by the division commanders, Ostermann and Sedmorétzki, and all that the peasants had has been eaten up. I myself will remain in hospital at Ostrolenka till I recover. In regard to which I humbly submit my report, with the information that if the army remains in its present bivouac another fortnight there will not be a healthy man left in it by spring.

" 'Grant leave to retire to his country seat to an old man who is already in any case dishonored by being unable to fulfill the great and glorious task for which he was chosen. I shall await your most gracious permission here in hospital, that I may not have to play the part of a secretary rather than commander in the army. My removal from the army does not produce the slightest stir—a blind man has left it. There are thousands such as I in Russia.'

"The field marshal is angry with the Emperor and he punishes us all, isn't it logical?

"This is the first act. Those that follow are naturally increasingly interesting and entertaining. After the field marshal's departure it appears that we are within sight of the enemy and must give battle. Buxhöwden is commander in chief by seniority, but General Bennigsen does not quite see it; more particularly as it is he and his corps who are within sight of the enemy and he wishes to profit by the opportunity to fight a battle 'on his own hand' as the Germans say. He does so. This is the battle of Pultúsk, which is considered a great victory but in my opinion was nothing of the kind. We civilians, as you know, have a very bad way of deciding whether

a battle was won or lost. Those who retreat after a battle have lost it is what we say; and according to that it is we who lost the battle of Pultúsk. In short, we retreat after the battle but send a courier to Petersburg with news of a victory, and General Bennigsen, hoping to receive from Petersburg the post of commander in chief as a reward for his victory, does not give up the command of the army to General Buxhöwden. During this interregnum we begin a very original and interesting series of maneuvers. Our aim is no longer, as it should be, to avoid or attack the enemy, but solely to avoid General Buxhöwden who by right of seniority should be our chief. So energetically do we pursue this aim that after crossing an unfordable river we burn the bridges to separate ourselves from our enemy, who at the moment is not Bonaparte but Buxhöwden. General Buxhöwden was all but attacked and captured by a superior enemy force as a result of one of these maneuvers that enabled us to escape him. Buxhöwden pursues us—we scuttle. He hardly crosses the river to our side before we recross to the other. At last our enemy, Buxhöwden, catches us and attacks. Both generals are angry, and the result is a challenge on Buxhöwden's part and an epileptic fit on Bennigsen's. But at the critical moment the courier who carried the news of our victory at Pultúsk to Petersburg returns bringing our appointment as commander in chief, and our first foe, Buxhöwden, is vanquished; we can now turn our thoughts to the second, Bonaparte. But as it turns out, just at that moment a third enemy rises before us—namely the *Orthodox Russian soldiers,* loudly demanding bread, meat, biscuits, fodder, and whatnot! The stores are empty, the roads impassable. The Orthodox begin looting, and in a way of which our last campaign can give you no idea. Half the regiments form bands and scour the countryside and put everything to fire and sword. The inhabitants are totally ruined, the hospitals overflow with sick, and famine is everywhere. Twice the marauders even attack our headquarters, and the commander in chief has to ask for a battalion to disperse them. During one of these attacks they carried off my empty portmanteau and my dressing gown. The Emperor proposes to give all commanders of divisions the right to shoot marauders, but I much fear this will oblige one half the army to shoot the other."

At first Prince Andrew read with his eyes only, but after a while, in spite of himself (although he knew how far it was safe to trust Bilíbin), what he had read began to interest him more and more. When he had read thus far, he crumpled the letter up and threw it away. It was not what he had read that vexed him, but the fact that the life out there in which he had now no part could perturb him. He shut his eyes, rubbed his forehead as if to rid himself of all interest in what he had read, and listened

to what was passing in the nursery. Suddenly he thought he heard a strange
noise through the door. He was seized with alarm lest something should
have happened to the child while he was reading the letter. He went on
tiptoe to the nursery door and opened it.

Just as he went in he saw that the nurse was hiding something from
him with a scared look and that Princess Mary was no longer by the cot.

"My dear," he heard what seemed to him her despairing whisper be-
hind him.

As often happens after long sleeplessness and long anxiety, he was seized
by an unreasoning panic—it occurred to him that the child was dead. All
that he saw and heard seemed to confirm this terror.

"All is over," he thought, and a cold sweat broke out on his forehead.
He went to the cot in confusion, sure that he would find it empty and that
the nurse had been hiding the dead baby. He drew the curtain aside and
for some time his frightened, restless eyes could not find the baby. At last
he saw him: the rosy boy had tossed about till he lay across the bed with
his head lower than the pillow, and was smacking his lips in his sleep
and breathing evenly.

Prince Andrew was as glad to find the boy like that, as if he had already
lost him. He bent over him and, as his sister had taught him, tried with
his lips whether the child was still feverish. The soft forehead was moist.
Prince Andrew touched the head with his hand; even the hair was wet,
so profusely had the child perspired. He was not dead, but evidently the
crisis was over and he was convalescent. Prince Andrew longed to snatch
up, to squeeze, to hold to his heart, this helpless little creature, but dared
not do so. He stood over him, gazing at his head and at the little arms and
legs which showed under the blanket. He heard a rustle behind him and
a shadow appeared under the curtain of the cot. He did not look round,
but still gazing at the infant's face listened to his regular breathing. The
dark shadow was Princess Mary, who had come up to the cot with noiseless
steps, lifted the curtain, and dropped it again behind her. Prince Andrew
recognized her without looking and held out his hand to her. She
pressed it.

"He has perspired," said Prince Andrew.

"I was coming to tell you so."

The child moved slightly in his sleep, smiled, and rubbed his forehead
against the pillow.

Prince Andrew looked at his sister. In the dim shadow of the curtain
her luminous eyes shone more brightly than usual from the tears of joy
that were in them. She leaned over to her brother and kissed him, slightly
catching the curtain of the cot. Each made the other a warning gesture

and stood still in the dim light beneath the curtain as if not wishing to leave that seclusion where they three were shut off from all the world. Prince Andrew was the first to move away, ruffling his hair against the muslin of the curtain.

"Yes, this is the one thing left me now," he said with a sigh.

8. Pierre goes to Kiev and visits his estates. Obstacles to the emancipation of his serfs

SOON AFTER his admission to the Masonic Brotherhood, Pierre went to the Kiev province, where he had the greatest number of serfs, taking with him full directions which he had written down for his own guidance as to what he should do on his estates.

When he reached Kiev he sent for all his stewards to the head office and explained to them his intentions and wishes. He told them that steps would be taken immediately to free his serfs—and that till then they were not to be overburdened with labor, women while nursing their babies were not to be sent to work, assistance was to be given to the serfs, punishments were to be admonitory and not corporal, and hospitals, asylums, and schools were to be established on all the estates. Some of the stewards (there were semiliterate foremen among them) listened with alarm, supposing these words to mean that the young count was displeased with their management and embezzlement of money, some after their first fright were amused by Pierre's lisp and the new words they had not heard before, others simply enjoyed hearing how the master talked, while the cleverest among them, including the chief steward, understood from this speech how they could best handle the master for their own ends.

The chief steward expressed great sympathy with Pierre's intentions, but remarked that besides these changes it would be necessary to go into the general state of affairs which was far from satisfactory.

Despite Count Bezúkhov's enormous wealth, since he had come into an income which was said to amount to five hundred thousand rubles a year, Pierre felt himself far poorer than when his father had made him an allowance of ten thousand rubles. He had a dim perception of the following budget:

About 80,000 went in payments on all the estates to the Land Bank, about 30,000 went for the upkeep of the estate near Moscow, the town house, and the allowance to the three princesses; about 15,000 was given in pensions and the same amount for asylums; 150,000 alimony was sent

to the countess; about 70,000 went for interest on debts. The building of a new church, previously begun, had cost about 10,000 in each of the last two years, and he did not know how the rest, about 100,000 rubles, was spent, and almost every year he was obliged to borrow. Besides this the chief steward wrote every year telling him of fires and bad harvests, or of the necessity of rebuilding factories and workshops. So the first task Pierre had to face was one for which he had very little aptitude or inclination—practical business.

He discussed estate affairs every day with his chief steward. But he felt that this did not forward matters at all. He felt that these consultations were detached from real affairs and did not link up with them or make them move. On the one hand, the chief steward put the state of things to him in the very worst light, pointing out the necessity of paying off the debts and undertaking new activities with serf labor, to which Pierre did not agree. On the other hand, Pierre demanded that steps should be taken to liberate the serfs, which the steward met by showing the necessity of first paying off the loans from the Land Bank, and the consequent impossibility of a speedy emancipation.

The steward did not say it was quite impossible, but suggested selling the forests in the province of Kostromá, the land lower down the river, and the Crimean estate, in order to make it possible: all of which operations according to him were connected with such complicated measures—the removal of injunctions, petitions, permits, and so on—that Pierre became quite bewildered and only replied:

"Yes, yes, do so."

Pierre had none of the practical persistence that would have enabled him to attend to the business himself and so he disliked it and only tried to pretend to the steward that he was attending to it. The steward for his part tried to pretend to the count that he considered these consultations very valuable for the proprietor and troublesome to himself.

In Kiev Pierre found some people he knew, and strangers hastened to make his acquaintance and joyfully welcomed the rich newcomer, the largest landowner of the province. Temptations to Pierre's greatest weakness—the one to which he had confessed when admitted to the Lodge—were so strong that he could not resist them. Again whole days, weeks, and months of his life passed in as great a rush and were as much occupied with evening parties, dinners, lunches, and balls, giving him no time for reflection, as in Petersburg. Instead of the new life he had hoped to lead he still lived the old life, only in new surroundings.

Of the three precepts of Freemasonry Pierre realized that he did not fulfill the one which enjoined every Mason to set an example of moral

life, and that of the seven virtues he lacked two—morality and the love of death. He consoled himself with the thought that he fulfilled another of the precepts—that of reforming the human race—and had other virtues—love of his neighbor, and especially generosity.

In the spring of 1807 he decided to return to Petersburg. On the way he intended to visit all his estates and see for himself how far his orders had been carried out and in what state were the serfs whom God had entrusted to his care and whom he intended to benefit.

The chief steward, who considered the young count's attempts almost insane—unprofitable to himself, to the count, and to the serfs—made some concessions. Continuing to represent the liberation of the serfs as impracticable, he arranged for the erection of large buildings—schools, hospitals, and asylums—on all the estates before the master arrived. Everywhere preparations were made not for ceremonious welcomes (which he knew Pierre would not like), but for just such gratefully religious ones, with offerings of icons and the bread and salt of hospitality, as, according to his understanding of his master, would touch and delude him.

The southern spring, the comfortable rapid traveling in a Vienna carriage, and the solitude of the road, all had a gladdening effect on Pierre. The estates he had not before visited were each more picturesque than the other; the serfs everywhere seemed thriving and touchingly grateful for the benefits conferred on them. Everywhere were receptions, which though they embarrassed Pierre awakened a joyful feeling in the depth of his heart. In one place the peasants presented him with bread and salt and an icon of Saint Peter and Saint Paul, asking permission, as a mark of their gratitude for the benefits he had conferred on them, to build a new chantry to the church at their own expense in honor of Peter and Paul, his patron saints.* In another place the women with infants in arms met him to thank him for releasing them from hard work. On a third estate the priest, bearing a cross, came to meet him surrounded by children whom, by the count's generosity, he was instructing in reading, writing, and religion. On all his estates Pierre saw with his own eyes brick buildings erected or in course of erection, all on one plan, for hospitals, schools, and almshouses, which were soon to be opened. Everywhere he saw the stewards' accounts, according to which the serfs' manorial labor had been diminished, and heard the touching thanks of deputations of serfs in their full-skirted blue coats.

What Pierre did not know was that the place where they presented him with bread and salt and wished to build a chantry in honor of Peter

* The same day was kept by the Russian Church in honor of Saint Peter and Saint Paul, so that Pierre (Peter) had them both as patron saints.—A.M.

and Paul was a market village where a fair was held on St. Peter's day,* and that the richest peasants (who formed the deputation) had begun the chantry long before, but that nine tenths of the peasants in that village were in a state of the greatest poverty. He did not know that since the nursing mothers were no longer sent to work on his land, they did still harder work on their own land. He did not know that the priest who met him with the cross oppressed the peasants by his exactions, and that the pupils' parents wept at having to let him take their children [2] and secured their release by heavy payments. He did not know that the brick buildings, built to plan, were being built by serfs whose manorial labor was thus increased, though lessened on paper. He did not know that where the steward had shown him in the accounts that the serfs' payments had been diminished by a third, their obligatory manorial work had been increased by a half. And so Pierre was delighted with his visit to his estates and quite recovered the philanthropic mood in which he had left Petersburg, and wrote enthusiastic letters to his "brother-instructor" as he called the Grand Master.

"How easy it is, how little effort it needs, to do so much good," thought Pierre, "and how little attention we pay to it!"

He was pleased at the gratitude he received, but felt abashed at receiving it. This gratitude reminded him of how much more he might do for these simple, kindly people.

The chief steward, a very stupid but cunning man who saw perfectly through the naïve and intelligent count and played with him as with a toy, seeing the effect these prearranged receptions had on Pierre, pressed him still harder with proofs of the impossibility and above all the uselessness of freeing the serfs, who were quite happy as it was.

Pierre in his secret soul agreed with the steward that it would be difficult to imagine happier people, and that God only knew what would happen to them when they were free, but he insisted, though reluctantly, on what he thought right. The steward promised to do all in his power to carry out the count's wishes, seeing clearly that not only would the count never be able to find out whether all measures had been taken for the sale of the land and forests and to release them from the Land Bank, but would probably never even inquire and would never know that the

* A chantry would be a thing the peasants would talk about, and it would help to attract people from the surrounding villages to the fair, and so be profitable to the local peasants.—A.M.

[2] The work of the children on the plots cultivated by the peasants for themselves was valuable to them.—A.M.

newly erected buildings were standing empty and that the serfs continued to give in money and work all that other people's serfs gave—that is to say, all that could be got out of them.

9. Pierre visits Prince Andrew

RETURNING FROM his journey through South Russia in the happiest state of mind, Pierre carried out an intention he had long had of visiting his friend Bolkónski, whom he had not seen for two years.

Boguchárovo lay in a flat uninterésting part of the country among fields and forests of fir and birch, which were partly cut down. The house lay behind a newly dug pond filled with water to the brink and with banks still bare of grass. It was at the end of a village that stretched along the highroad in the midst of a young copse in which were a few fir trees.

The homestead consisted of a threshing floor, outhouses, stables, a bathhouse, a lodge, and a large brick house with semicircular façade still in course of construction. Round the house was a garden newly laid out. The fences and gates were new and solid; two fire pumps and a water cart, painted green, stood in a shed; the paths were straight, the bridges were strong and had handrails. Everything bore an impress of tidiness and good management. Some domestic serfs Pierre met, in reply to inquiries as to where the prince lived, pointed out a small newly built lodge close to the pond. Antón, a man who had looked after Prince Andrew in his boyhood, helped Pierre out of his carriage, said that the prince was at home, and showed him into a clean little anteroom.

Pierre was struck by the modesty of the small though clean house after the brilliant surroundings in which he had last met his friend in Petersburg.

He quickly entered the small reception room with its still-unplastered wooden walls redolent of pine, and would have gone farther, but Antón ran ahead on tiptoe and knocked at a door.

"Well, what is it?" came a sharp, unpleasant voice.

"A visitor," answered Antón.

"Ask him to wait," and the sound was heard of a chair being pushed back.

Pierre went with rapid steps to the door and suddenly came face to face with Prince Andrew, who came out frowning and looking old. Pierre embraced him and lifting his spectacles kissed his friend on the cheek and looked at him closely.

"Well, I did not expect you, I am very glad," said Prince Andrew.

Pierre said nothing; he looked fixedly at his friend with surprise. He was struck by the change in him. His words were kindly and there was a smile on his lips and face, but his eyes were dull and lifeless and in spite of his evident wish to do so he could not give them a joyous and glad sparkle. Prince Andrew had grown thinner, paler, and more manly-looking, but what amazed and estranged Pierre till he got used to it were his inertia and a wrinkle on his brow indicating prolonged concentration on some one thought.

As is usually the case with people meeting after a prolonged separation, it was long before their conversation could settle on anything. They put questions and gave brief replies about things they knew ought to be talked over at length. At last the conversation gradually settled on some of the topics at first lightly touched on: their past life, plans for the future, Pierre's journeys and occupations, the war, and so on. The preoccupation and despondency which Pierre had noticed in his friend's look was now still more clearly expressed in the smile with which he listened to Pierre, especially when he spoke with joyful animation of the past or the future. It was as if Prince Andrew would have liked to sympathize with what Pierre was saying, but could not. The latter began to feel that it was in bad taste to speak of his enthusiasms, dreams, and hopes of happiness or goodness, in Prince Andrew's presence. He was ashamed to express his new Masonic views, which had been particularly revived and strengthened by his late tour. He checked himself, fearing to seem naïve, yet he felt an irresistible desire to show his friend as soon as possible that he was now a quite different, and better, Pierre than he had been in Petersburg.

"I can't tell you how much I have lived through since then. I hardly know myself again."

"Yes, we have altered much, very much, since then," said Prince Andrew.

"Well, and you? What are your plans?"

"Plans!" repeated Prince Andrew ironically. "My plans?" he said, as if astonished at the word. "Well, you see, I'm building. I mean to settle here altogether next year. . . ."

Pierre looked silently and searchingly into Prince Andrew's face, which had grown much older.

"No, I meant to ask . . ." Pierre began, but Prince Andrew interrupted him.

"But why talk of me? . . . Talk to me, yes, tell me about your travels and all you have been doing on your estates."

Pierre began describing what he had done on his estates, trying as far

as possible to conceal his own part in the improvements that had been made. Prince Andrew several times prompted Pierre's story of what he had been doing, as though it were all an old-time story, and he listened not only without interest but even as if ashamed of what Pierre was telling him.

Pierre felt uncomfortable and even depressed in his friend's company and at last became silent.

"I'll tell you what, my dear fellow," said Prince Andrew, who evidently also felt depressed and constrained with his visitor, "I am only bivouacking here and have just come to look round. I am going back to my sister today. I will introduce you to her. But of course you know her already," he said, evidently trying to entertain a visitor with whom he now found nothing in common. "We will go after dinner. And would you now like to look round my place?"

They went out and walked about till dinnertime, talking of the political news and common acquaintances like people who do not know each other intimately. Prince Andrew spoke with some animation and interest only of the new homestead he was constructing and its buildings, but even here, while on the scaffolding, in the midst of a talk explaining the future arrangements of the house, he interrupted himself:

"However, this is not at all interesting. Let us have dinner, and then we'll set off."

At dinner, conversation turned on Pierre's marriage.

"I was very much surprised when I heard of it," said Prince Andrew.

Pierre blushed, as he always did when it was mentioned, and said hurriedly: "I will tell you some time how it all happened. But you know it is all over, and forever."

"Forever?" said Prince Andrew. "Nothing's forever."

"But you know how it all ended, don't you? You heard of the duel?"

"And so you had to go through that too!"

"One thing I thank God for is that I did not kill that man," said Pierre.

"Why so?" asked Prince Andrew. "To kill a vicious dog is a very good thing really."

"No, to kill a man is bad—wrong."

"Why is it wrong?" urged Prince Andrew. "It is not given to man to know what is right and what is wrong. Men always did and always will err, and in nothing more than in what they consider right and wrong."

"What does harm to another is wrong," said Pierre, feeling with pleasure that for the first time since his arrival Prince Andrew was roused, had begun to talk, and wanted to express what had brought him to his present state.

"And who has told you what is bad for another man?" he asked.

"Bad! Bad!" exclaimed Pierre. "We all know what is bad for ourselves."

"Yes, we know that, but the harm I am conscious of in myself is something I cannot inflict on others," said Prince Andrew, growing more and more animated and evidently wishing to express his new outlook to Pierre. He spoke in French. "I only know two very real evils in life: remorse and illness. The only good is the absence of those evils. To live for myself avoiding those two evils is my whole philosophy now."

"And love of one's neighbor, and self-sacrifice?" began Pierre. "No, I can't agree with you! To live only so as not to do evil and not to have to repent is not enough. I lived like that, I lived for myself and ruined my life. And only now when I am living, or at least trying" (Pierre's modesty made him correct himself) "to live for others, only now have I understood all the happiness of life. No, I shall not agree with you, and you do not really believe what you are saying."

Prince Andrew looked silently at Pierre with an ironic smile.

"When you see my sister, Princess Mary, you'll get on with her," he said. "Perhaps you are right for yourself," he added after a short pause, "but everyone lives in his own way. You lived for yourself and say you nearly ruined your life and only found happiness when you began living for others. I experienced just the reverse. I lived for glory.—And after all what is glory? The same love of others, a desire to do something for them, a desire for their approval.—So I lived for others, and not almost, but quite, ruined my life. And I have become calmer since I began to live only for myself."

"But what do you mean by living only for yourself?" asked Pierre, growing excited. "What about your son, your sister, and your father?"

"But that's just the same as myself—they are not *others*," explained Prince Andrew. "The others, one's neighbors, *le prochain*, as you and Princess Mary call it, are the chief source of all error and evil. *Le prochain* —your Kiev peasants to whom you want to do good."

And he looked at Pierre with a mocking, challenging expression. He evidently wished to draw him on.

"You are joking," replied Pierre, growing more and more excited. "What error or evil can there be in my wishing to do good, and even doing a little—though I did very little and did it very badly? What evil can there be in it if unfortunate people, our serfs, people like ourselves, were growing up and dying with no idea of God and truth beyond ceremonies and meaningless prayers and are now instructed in a comforting belief in future life, retribution, recompense, and consolation? What evil and

error are there in it, if people were dying of disease without help while material assistance could so easily be rendered, and I supplied them with a doctor, a hospital, and an asylum for the aged? And is it not a palpable, unquestionable good if a peasant, or a woman with a baby, has no rest day or night and I give them rest and leisure?" said Pierre, hurrying and lisping. "And I have done that though badly and to a small extent; but I have done something toward it and you cannot persuade me that it was not a good action, and more than that, you can't make me believe that you do not think so yourself. And the main thing is," he continued, "that I know, and know for certain, that the enjoyment of doing this good is the only sure happiness in life."

"Yes, if you put it like that it's quite a different matter," said Prince Andrew. "I build a house and lay out a garden, and you build hospitals. The one and the other may serve as a pastime. But what's right and what's good must be judged by one who knows all, but not by us. Well, you want an argument," he added, "come on then."

They rose from the table and sat down in the entrance porch which served as a veranda.

"Come, let's argue then," said Prince Andrew. "You talk of schools," he went on, crooking a finger, "education and so forth; that is, you want to raise him" (pointing to a peasant who passed by them taking off his cap) "from his animal condition and awaken in him spiritual needs, while it seems to me that animal happiness is the only happiness possible, and that is just what you want to deprive him of. I envy him, but you want to make him what I am, without giving him my means. Then you say, 'lighten his toil.' But as I see it, physical labor is as essential to him, as much a condition of his existence, as mental activity is to you or me. You can't help thinking. I go to bed after two in the morning, thoughts come and I can't sleep but toss about till dawn, because I think and can't help thinking, just as he can't help plowing and mowing; if he didn't, he would go to the drink shop or fall ill. Just as I could not stand his terrible physical labor but should die of it in a week, so he could not stand my physical idleness, but would grow fat and die. The third thing—what else was it you talked about?" and Prince Andrew crooked a third finger. "Ah, yes, hospitals, medicine. He has a fit, he is dying, and you come and bleed him and patch him up. He will drag about as a cripple, a burden to everybody, for another ten years. It would be far easier and simpler for him to die. Others are being born and there are plenty of them as it is. It would be different if you grudged losing a laborer—that's how I regard him—but you want to cure him from love of him. And he does not want that. And besides, what a notion that medicine ever cured anyone!

Killed them, yes!" said he, frowning angrily and turning away from Pierre.

Prince Andrew expressed his ideas so clearly and distinctly that it was evident he had reflected on this subject more than once, and he spoke readily and rapidly like a man who has not talked for a long time. His glance became more animated as his conclusions became more hopeless.

"Oh, that is dreadful, dreadful!" said Pierre. "I don't understand how one can live with such ideas. I had such moments myself not long ago, in Moscow and when traveling, but at such times I collapse so that I don't live at all—everything seems hateful to me . . . myself most of all. Then I don't eat, don't wash . . . and how is it with you? . . ."

"Why not wash? That is not cleanly," said Prince Andrew; "on the contrary one must try to make one's life as pleasant as possible. I'm alive, that is not my fault, so I must live out my life as best I can without hurting others."

"But with such ideas what motive have you for living? One would sit without moving, undertaking nothing. . . ."

"Life as it is leaves one no peace. I should be thankful to do nothing, but here on the one hand the local nobility have done me the honor to choose me to be their marshal; * it was all I could do to get out of it. They could not understand that I have not the necessary qualifications for it—the kind of good-natured, fussy shallowness necessary for the position. Then there's this house, which must be built in order to have a nook of one's own in which to be quiet. And now there's this recruiting."

"Why aren't you serving in the army?"

"After Austerlitz!" said Prince Andrew gloomily. "No, thank you very much! I have promised myself not to serve again in the active Russian army. And I won't—not even if Bonaparte were here at Smolénsk threatening Bald Hills—even then I wouldn't serve in the Russian army! Well, as I was saying," he continued, recovering his composure, "now there's this recruiting. My father is chief in command of the Third District, and my only way of avoiding active service is to serve under him."

"Then you are serving?"

"I am."

He paused a little while.

"And why do you serve?"

"Why, for this reason! My father is one of the most remarkable men of his time. But he is growing old, and though not exactly cruel he has too energetic a character. He is so accustomed to unlimited power that he

* *Marshal of the nobility*, Maréchal de la noblesse; *the official representative of the nobility and landed gentry of a district.*—A.M.

is terrible, and now he has this authority of a commander in chief of the recruiting, granted by the Emperor. If I had been two hours late a fortnight ago he would have had a paymaster's clerk at Yúkhnovna hanged," said Prince Andrew with a smile. "So I am serving because I alone have any influence with my father, and now and then can save him from actions which would torment him afterwards."

"Well, there you see!"

"Yes, but it is not as you imagine," Prince Andrew continued. "I did not, and do not, in the least care about that scoundrel of a clerk who had stolen some boots from the recruits; I should even have been very glad to see him hanged, but I was sorry for my father—that again is for myself."

Prince Andrew grew more and more animated. His eyes glittered feverishly while he tried to prove to Pierre that in his actions there was no desire to do good to his neighbor.

"There now, you wish to liberate your serfs," he continued; "that is a very good thing, but not for you—I don't suppose you ever had anyone flogged or sent to Siberia—and still less for your serfs. If they are beaten, flogged, or sent to Siberia, I don't suppose they are any the worse off. In Siberia they lead the same animal life, and the stripes on their bodies heal, and they are happy as before. But it is a good thing for proprietors who perish morally, bring remorse upon themselves, stifle this remorse and grow callous, as a result of being able to inflict punishments justly and unjustly. It is those people I pity, and for their sake I should like to liberate the serfs. You may not have seen, but I have seen, how good men brought up in those traditions of unlimited power, in time when they grow more irritable, become cruel and harsh, are conscious of it, but cannot restrain themselves and grow more and more miserable."

Prince Andrew spoke so earnestly that Pierre could not help thinking that these thoughts had been suggested to Prince Andrew by his father's case.

He did not reply.

"So that's what I'm sorry for—human dignity, peace of mind, purity, and not the serfs' backs and foreheads, which, beat and shave * as you may, always remain the same backs and foreheads."

"No, no! A thousand times no! I shall never agree with you," said Pierre.

* A proprietor could send any of his serfs as exiles to Siberia, and when going there one side of the head was shaved, that the man might more easily be recaptured should he run away.—A.M.

10. *Pierre's and Prince Andrew's talk on the ferry raft*

IN THE EVENING Andrew and Pierre got into the open carriage and drove to Bald Hills. Prince Andrew, glancing at Pierre, broke the silence now and then with remarks which showed that he was in a good temper.

Pointing to the fields, he spoke of the improvements he was making in his husbandry.

Pierre remained gloomily silent, answering in monosyllables and apparently immersed in his own thoughts.

He was thinking that Prince Andrew was unhappy, had gone astray, did not see the true light, and that he, Pierre, ought to aid, enlighten, and raise him. But as soon as he thought of what he should say, he felt that Prince Andrew with one word, one argument, would upset all his teaching, and he shrank from beginning, afraid of exposing to possible ridicule what to him was precious and sacred.

"No, but why do you think so?" Pierre suddenly began, lowering his head and looking like a bull about to charge, "why do you think so? You should not think so."

"Think? What about?" asked Prince Andrew with surprise.

"About life, about man's destiny. It can't be so. I myself thought like that, and do you know what saved me? Freemasonry! No, don't smile: Freemasonry is not a religious ceremonial sect, as I thought it was: Freemasonry is the best expression of the best, the eternal, aspects of humanity."

And he began to explain Freemasonry as he understood it to Prince Andrew. He said that Freemasonry is the teaching of Christianity freed from the bonds of State and Church, a teaching of equality, brotherhood, and love.

"Only our holy brotherhood has the real meaning of life, all the rest is a dream," said Pierre. "Understand, my dear fellow, that outside this union all is filled with deceit and falsehood and I agree with you that nothing is left for an intelligent and good man but to live out his life, like you, merely trying not to harm others. But make our fundamental convictions your own, join our brotherhood, give·yourself up to us, let yourself be guided, and you will at once feel yourself, as I have felt myself, a part of that vast invisible chain the beginning of which is hidden in heaven," said Pierre.

Prince Andrew, looking straight in front of him, listened in silence to Pierre's words. More than once, when the noise of the wheels prevented his catching what Pierre said, he asked him to repeat it, and by

the peculiar glow that came into Prince Andrew's eyes and by his silence, Pierre saw that his words were not in vain and that Prince Andrew would not interrupt him or laugh at what he said.

They reached a river that had overflowed its banks and which they had to cross by ferry. While the carriage and horses were being placed on it, they also stepped on the raft.

Prince Andrew, leaning his arms on the raft railing, gazed silently at the flooding waters glittering in the setting sun.

"Well, what do you think about it?" Pierre asked. "Why are you silent?"

"What do I think about it? I am listening to you. It's all very well. . . . You say: join our brotherhood and we will show you the aim of life, the destiny of man, and the laws which govern the world. But who are we? Men. How is it you know everything? Why do I alone not see what you see? You see a reign of goodness and truth on earth, but I don't see it."

Pierre interrupted him.

"Do you believe in a future life?" he asked.

"A future life?" Prince Andrew repeated, but Pierre, giving him no time to reply, took the repetition for a denial, the more readily as he knew Prince Andrew's former atheistic convictions.

"You say you can't see a reign of goodness and truth on earth. Nor could I, and it cannot be seen if one looks on our life here as the end of everything. On *earth*, here on this earth" (Pierre pointed to the fields), "there is no truth, all is false and evil; but in the universe, in the whole universe, there is a kingdom of truth, and we who are now the children of earth are—eternally—children of the whole universe. Don't I feel in my soul that I am part of this vast harmonious whole? Don't I feel that I form one link, one step, between the lower and higher beings, in this vast harmonious multitude of beings in whom the Deity—the Supreme Power if you prefer the term—is manifest? If I see, clearly see, that ladder leading from plant to man, why should I suppose it breaks off at me and does not go farther and farther? I feel that I cannot vanish, since nothing vanishes in this world, but that I shall always exist and always have existed. I feel that beyond me and above me there are spirits, and that in this world there is truth."

"Yes, that is Herder's * theory," said Prince Andrew, "but it is not that which can convince me, dear friend—life and death are what convince. What convinces is when one sees a being dear to one, bound up with one's own life, before whom one was to blame and had hoped to make it right" (Prince Andrew's voice trembled and he turned away), "and sud-

* *Johann Gottfried von Herder (1744-1803), German writer and philosopher.*

denly that being is seized with pain, suffers, and ceases to exist. . . .
Why? It cannot be that there is no answer. And I believe there is. . . .
That's what convinces, that is what has convinced me," said Prince
Andrew.

"Yes, yes, of course," said Pierre, "isn't that what I'm saying?"

"No. All I say is that it is not argument that convinces me of the neces-
sity of a future life, but this: when you go hand in hand with someone
and all at once that person vanishes *there*, *into nowhere*, and you your-
self are left facing that abyss, and look in. And I have looked in. . . ." *

"Well, that's it then! You know that there is a *there* and there is a
Someone? *There* is the future life. The *Someone* is—God."

Prince Andrew did not reply. The carriage and horses had long since
been taken off, onto the farther bank, and reharnessed. The sun had sunk
half below the horizon and an evening frost was starring the puddles
near the ferry, but Pierre and Andrew, to the astonishment of the foot-
men, coachmen, and ferrymen, still stood on the raft and talked.

"If there is a God and future life, there is truth and good, and man's
highest happiness consists in striving to attain them. We must live, we
must love, and we must believe that we live not only today on this scrap
of earth, but have lived and shall live forever, there, in the Whole," said
Pierre, and he pointed to the sky.

Prince Andrew stood leaning on the railing of the raft listening to
Pierre, and he gazed with his eyes fixed on the red reflection of the sun
gleaming on the blue waters. There was perfect stillness. Pierre became
silent. The raft had long since stopped and only the waves of the current
beat softly against it below. Prince Andrew felt as if the sound of the
waves kept up a refrain to Pierre's words, whispering:

"It is true, believe it."

He sighed, and glanced with a radiant, childlike, tender look at Pierre's
face, flushed and rapturous, but yet shy before his superior friend.

"Yes, if it only were so!" said Prince Andrew. "However, it is time to
get on," he added, and, stepping off the raft, he looked up at the sky
to which Pierre had pointed, and for the first time since Austerlitz saw
that high, everlasting sky he had seen while lying on that battlefield;
and something that had long been slumbering, something that was best
within him, suddenly awoke, joyful and youthful, in his soul. It vanished
as soon as he returned to the customary conditions of his life, but he knew
that this feeling which he did not know how to develop existed within

* *Prince Andrew's experience and reflections are very much those of Tolstóy
himself after the loss of his brother Nicholas. Compare his letters to the poet
Fet, quoted on pp. 214-15 of the* Life of Tolstóy: First Fifty Years.—A.M.

him. His meeting with Pierre formed an epoch in Prince Andrew's life. Though outwardly he continued to live in the same old way, inwardly he began a new life.

11. *"God's folk"* at Bald Hills

IT WAS getting dusk when Prince Andrew and Pierre drove up to the front entrance of the house at Bald Hills. As they approached the house, Prince Andrew with a smile drew Pierre's attention to a commotion going on at the back porch. A woman, bent with age, with a wallet on her back, and a short, long-haired, young man in a black garment had rushed back to the gate on seeing the carriage driving up. Two women ran out after them, and all four, looking round at the carriage, ran in dismay up the steps of the back porch.

"Those are Mary's 'God's folk,'" said Prince Andrew. "They have mistaken us for my father. This is the one matter in which she disobeys him. He orders these pilgrims to be driven away, but she receives them."

"But what are 'God's folk'?" asked Pierre.

Prince Andrew had no time to answer. The servants came out to meet them, and he asked where the old prince was and whether he was expected back soon.

The old prince had gone to the town and was expected back any minute.

Prince Andrew led Pierre to his own apartments, which were always kept in perfect order and readiness for him in his father's house; he himself went to the nursery.

"Let us go and see my sister," he said to Pierre when he returned. "I have not found her yet, she is hiding now, sitting with her 'God's folk.' It will serve her right, she will be confused, but you will see her 'God's folk.' It's really very curious." *

"What are 'God's folk'?" asked Pierre.

* *Tolstóy has drawn the picture of Princess Mary's intercourse with "God's folk" from family traditions and personal observations in childhood. Pilgrims such as these, who devoted months, years, or their whole lives to visiting Holy Places—from Solovéts Monastery in the White Sea to Jerusalem—begging their way from place to place, were quite common in Russia and included a considerable number of maimed, deformed, and mentally defective folk. It was very usual for religious people such as Princess Mary to assist them. They were often harbored at Yásnaya Polyána, especially by Tolstóy's aunt, Countess A. Osten-Saken.—*A.M.

"Come, and you'll see for yourself."

Princess Mary really was disconcerted and red patches came on her face when they went in. In her snug room, with lamps burning before the icon stand, a young lad with a long nose and long hair, wearing a monk's cassock, sat on the sofa beside her, behind a samovar. Near them, in an armchair, sat a thin, shriveled, old woman, with a meek expression on her childlike face.

"Andrew, why didn't you warn me?" said the princess, with mild reproach, as she stood before her pilgrims like a hen before her chickens.

"*Charmée de vous voir. Je suis très contente de vous voir* [Delighted to see you. I am very glad to see you]," she said to Pierre as he kissed her hand. She had known him as a child, and now his friendship with Andrew, his misfortune with his wife, and above all his kindly, simple face disposed her favorably toward him. She looked at him with her beautiful radiant eyes and seemed to say, "I like you very much, but please don't laugh at my people." After exchanging the first greetings, they sat down.

"Ah, and Ivánushka is here too!" said Prince Andrew, glancing with a smile at the young pilgrim.

"Andrew!" said Princess Mary, imploringly.

"*Il faut que vous sachiez que c'est une femme* [You must know that this is a woman]," said Prince Andrew to Pierre.

"Andrew, *au nom de Dieu* [for heaven's sake]!" Princess Mary repeated.

It was evident that Prince Andrew's ironical tone toward the pilgrims and Princess Mary's helpless attempts to protect them were their customary long-established relations on the matter.

"*Mais, ma bonne amie* [But, my dear]," said Prince Andrew, "*vous devriez au contraire m'être reconnaissante de ce que j'explique à Pierre votre intimité avec ce jeune homme* [you ought on the contrary to be grateful to me for explaining to Pierre your intimacy with this young man]."

"Really?" said Pierre, gazing over his spectacles with curiosity and seriousness (for which Princess Mary was specially grateful to him) into Ivánushka's face, who, seeing that she was being spoken about, looked round at them all with crafty eyes.

Princess Mary's embarrassment on *her people's* account was quite unnecessary. They were not in the least abashed. The old woman, lowering her eyes but casting side glances at the newcomers, had turned her cup upside down and placed a nibbled bit of sugar beside it, and sat quietly in her armchair, though hoping to be offered another cup of tea. Ivánushka, sipping out of her saucer, looked with sly womanish eyes from under her brows at the young men.

"Where have you been? To Kiev?" Prince Andrew asked the old woman.

"I have, good sir," she answered garrulously. "Just at Christmastime I was deemed worthy to partake of the holy and heavenly sacrament at the shrine of the saint. And now I'm from Kolyázin, master, where a great and wonderful blessing has been revealed."

"And was Ivánushka with you?"

"I go by myself, benefactor," said Ivánushka, trying to speak in a bass voice. "I only came across Pelagéya in Yúkhnovo. . . ."

Pelagéya interrupted her companion; she evidently wished to tell what she had seen.

"In Kolyázin, master, a wonderful blessing has been revealed."

"What is it? Some new relics?" asked Prince Andrew.

"Andrew, do leave off," said Princess Mary. "Don't tell him, Pelagéya."

"No . . . why not, my dear, why shouldn't I? I like him. He is kind, he is one of God's chosen, he's a benefactor, he once gave me ten rubles, I remember. When I was in Kiev, Crazy Cyril says to me (he's one of God's own and goes barefoot summer and winter), he says, 'Why are you not going to the right place? Go to Kolyázin where a wonder-working icon of the Holy Mother of God has been revealed.' On hearing those words I said good-by to the holy folk and went."

All were silent, only the pilgrim woman went on in measured tones, drawing in her breath.

"So I come, master, and the people say to me: 'A great blessing has been revealed, holy oil trickles from the cheeks of our blessed Mother, the Holy Virgin Mother of God.' . . ."

"All right, all right, you can tell us afterwards," said Princess Mary, flushing.

"Let me ask her," said Pierre. "Did you see it yourselves?" he inquired.

"Oh, yes, master, I was found worthy. Such a brightness on the face like the light of heaven, and from the blessed Mother's cheek it drops and drops. . . ."

"But, dear me, that must be a fraud!" said Pierre, naïvely, who had listened attentively to the pilgrim.

"Oh, master, what are you saying?" exclaimed the horrified Pelagéya, turning to Princess Mary for support.

"They impose on the people," he repeated.

"Lord Jesus Christ!" exclaimed the pilgrim woman, crossing herself. "Oh, don't speak so, master! There was a general who did not believe, and said, 'The monks cheat,' and as soon as he'd said it he went blind. And he dreamed that the Holy Virgin Mother of the Kiev catacombs

came to him and said, 'Believe in me and I will make you whole.' So he begged: 'Take me to her, take me to her.' It's the real truth I'm telling you, I saw it myself. So he was brought, quite blind, straight to her, and he goes up to her and falls down and says, 'Make me whole,' says he, 'and I'll give thee what the Tsar bestowed on me.' I saw it myself, master, the star is fixed into the icon. Well, and what do you think? He received his sight! It's a sin to speak so. God will punish you," she said admonishingly, turning to Pierre.

"How did the star get into the icon?" Pierre asked.

"And was the Holy Mother promoted to the rank of general?" said Prince Andrew, with a smile.

Pelagéya suddenly grew quite pale and clasped her hands.

"Oh, master, master, what a sin! And you who have a son!" she began, her pallor suddenly turning to a vivid red. "Master, what have you said? God forgive you!" And she crossed herself. "Lord forgive him! My dear, what does it mean? . . ." she asked, turning to Princess Mary. She got up and, almost crying, began to arrange her wallet. She evidently felt frightened and ashamed to have accepted charity in a house where such things could be said, and was at the same time sorry to have now to forgo the charity of this house.

"Now, why need you do it?" said Princess Mary. "Why did you come to me? . . ."

"Come, Pelagéya, I was joking," said Pierre. "Princesse, ma parole, je n'ai pas voulu l'offenser [Princess, on my word, I did not wish to offend her]. I did not mean anything, I was only joking," he said, smiling shyly and trying to efface his offense. "It was all my fault, and Andrew was only joking."

Pelagéya stopped doubtfully, but in Pierre's face there was such a look of sincere penitence, and Prince Andrew glanced so meekly now at her and now at Pierre, that she was gradually reassured.

12. Old Bolkónski and Pierre

THE PILGRIM WOMAN was appeased and, being encouraged to talk, gave a long account of Father Amphilochus, who led so holy a life that his hands smelled of incense, and how on her last visit to Kiev some monks she knew let her have the keys of the catacombs, and how she, taking some dried bread with her, had spent two days in the catacombs with the saints. "I'd pray awhile to one, ponder awhile, then go on to

another. I'd sleep a bit and then again go and kiss the relics, and there was such peace all around, such blessedness, that one don't want to come out, even into the light of heaven again."

Pierre listened to her attentively and seriously. Prince Andrew went out of the room, and then, leaving "God's folk" to finish their tea, Princess Mary took Pierre into the drawing room.

"You are very kind," she said to him.

"Oh, I really did not mean to hurt her feelings. I understand them so well and have the greatest respect for them."

Princess Mary looked at him silently and smiled affectionately.

"I have known you a long time, you see, and am as fond of you as of a brother," she said. "How do you find Andrew?" she added hurriedly, not giving him time to reply to her affectionate words. "I am very anxious about him. His health was better in the winter, but last spring his wound reopened and the doctor said he ought to go away for a cure. And I am also very much afraid for him spiritually. He has not a character like us women who, when we suffer, can weep away our sorrows. He keeps it all within him. Today he is cheerful and in good spirits, but that is the effect of your visit—he is not often like that. If you could persuade him to go abroad. He needs activity, and this quiet regular life is very bad for him. Others don't notice it, but I see it."

Toward ten o'clock the menservants rushed to the front door, hearing the bells of the old prince's carriage approaching. Prince Andrew and Pierre also went out into the porch.

"Who's that?" asked the old prince, noticing Pierre as he got out of the carriage.

"Ah! Very glad! Kiss me," he said, having learned who the young stranger was.

The old prince was in a good temper and very gracious to Pierre.

Before supper, Prince Andrew, coming back to his father's study, found him disputing hotly with his visitor. Pierre was maintaining that a time would come when there would be no more wars. The old prince disputed it chaffingly, but without getting angry.

"Drain the blood from men's veins and put in water instead, then there will be no more war! Old women's nonsense—old women's nonsense!" he repeated, but still he patted Pierre affectionately on the shoulder, and then went up to the table where Prince Andrew, evidently not wishing to join in the conversation, was looking over the papers his father had brought from town. The old prince went up to him and began to talk business.

"The marshal, a Count Rostóv, hasn't sent half his contingent. He came to town and wanted to invite me to dinner—I gave him a pretty dinner! . . . And there, look at this. . . . Well, my boy," the old prince went on, addressing his son and patting Pierre on the shoulder. "A fine fellow—your friend—I like him! He stirs me up. Another says clever things and one doesn't care to listen, but this one talks rubbish yet stirs an old fellow up. Well, go! Get along! Perhaps I'll come and sit with you at supper. We'll have another dispute. Make friends with my little fool, Princess Mary," he shouted after Pierre, through the door.

Only now, on his visit to Bald Hills, did Pierre fully realize the strength and charm of his friendship with Prince Andrew. That charm was not expressed so much in his relations with him as with all his family and with the household. With the stern old prince and the gentle, timid Princess Mary, though he had scarcely known them, Pierre at once felt like an old friend. They were all fond of him already. Not only Princess Mary, who had been won by his gentleness with the pilgrims, gave him her most radiant looks, but even the one-year-old "Prince Nicholas" (as his grandfather called him) smiled at Pierre and let himself be taken in his arms, and Michael Ivánovich and Mademoiselle Bourienne looked at him with pleasant smiles when he talked to the old prince.

The old prince came in to supper; this was evidently on Pierre's account. And during the two days of the young man's visit he was extremely kind to him and told him to visit them again.

When Pierre had gone and the members of the household met together, they began to express their opinions of him as people always do after a new acquaintance has left, but as seldom happens, no one said anything but what was good of him.

13. Nicholas rejoins his regiment. Shortage of provisions

WHEN RETURNING from his leave, Rostóv felt, for the first time, how close was the bond that united him to Denísov and the whole regiment.

On approaching it, Rostóv felt as he had done when approaching his home in Moscow. When he saw the first hussar with the unbuttoned uniform of his regiment, when he recognized red-haired Deméntyev and saw the picket ropes of the roan horses, when Lavrúshka gleefully shouted to his master, "The count has come!" and Denísov, who had been asleep on his bed, ran all disheveled out of the mud hut to embrace him, and the officers collected round to greet the new arrival, Rostóv experienced

the same feeling as when his mother, his father, and his sister had embraced him, and tears of joy choked him so that he could not speak. The regiment was also a home, and as unalterably dear and precious as his parents' house.

When he had reported himself to the commander of the regiment and had been reassigned to his former squadron, had been on duty and had gone out foraging, when he had again entered into all the little interests of the regiment and felt himself deprived of liberty and bound in one narrow, unchanging frame, he experienced the same sense of peace, of moral support, and the same sense of being at home here in his own place, as he had felt under the parental roof. But here was none of all that turmoil of the world at large, where he did not know his right place and took mistaken decisions; here was no Sónya with whom he ought, or ought not, to have an explanation; here was no possibility of going there or not going there; here there were not twenty-four hours in the day which could be spent in such a variety of ways; there was not that innumerable crowd of people of whom not one was nearer to him or farther from him than another; there were none of those uncertain and undefined money relations with his father, and nothing to recall that terrible loss to Dólokhov. Here, in the regiment, all was clear and simple. The whole world was divided into two unequal parts: one, our Pávlograd regiment; the other, all the rest. And the rest was no concern of his. In the regiment, everything was definite: who was lieutenant, who captain, who was a good fellow, who a bad one, and most of all, who was a comrade. The canteenkeeper gave one credit, one's pay came every four months, there was nothing to think out or decide, you had only to do nothing that was considered bad in the Pávlograd regiment and, when given an order, to do what was clearly, distinctly, and definitely ordered—and all would be well.

Having once more entered into the definite conditions of this regimental life, Rostóv felt the joy and relief a tired man feels on lying down to rest. Life in the regiment, during this campaign, was all the pleasanter for him, because, after his loss to Dólokhov (for which, in spite of all his family's efforts to console him, he could not forgive himself), he had made up his mind to atone for his fault by serving, not as he had done before, but really well, and by being a perfectly first-rate comrade and officer—in a word, a splendid man altogether, a thing which seemed so difficult out in the world, but so possible in the regiment.

After his losses, he had determined to pay back his debt to his parents in five years. He received ten thousand rubles a year, but now resolved to take only two thousand and leave the rest to repay the debt to his parents.

Our army, after repeated retreats and advances and battles at Pultúsk and Preussisch-Eylau, was concentrated near Bartenstein. It was awaiting the Emperor's arrival and the beginning of a new campaign.

The Pávlograd regiment, belonging to that part of the army which had served in the 1805 campaign, had been recruiting up to strength in Russia, and arrived too late to take part in the first actions of the campaign. It had been neither at Pultúsk nor at Preussisch-Eylau and, when it joined the army in the field in the second half of the campaign, was attached to Plátov's division.

Plátov's division was acting independently of the main army. Several times parts of the Pávlograd regiment had exchanged shots with the enemy, had taken prisoners, and once had even captured Marshal Oudinot's carriages. In April the Pávlograds were stationed immovably for some weeks near a totally ruined and deserted German village.

A thaw had set in, it was muddy and cold, the ice on the river broke, and the roads became impassable. For days neither provisions for the men nor fodder for the horses had been issued.* As no transports could arrive, the men dispersed about the abandoned and deserted villages, searching for potatoes, but found few even of these.

Everything had been eaten up and the inhabitants had all fled—if any remained, they were worse than beggars and nothing more could be taken from them; even the soldiers, usually pitiless enough, instead of taking anything from them, often gave them the last of their rations.

The Pávlograd regiment had had only two men wounded in action, but had lost nearly half its men from hunger and sickness. In the hospitals, death was so certain that soldiers suffering from fever, or the swelling that came from bad food, preferred to remain on duty, and hardly able to drag their legs went to the front rather than to the hospitals. When spring came on, the soldiers found a plant just showing out of the ground that looked like asparagus, which, for some reason, they called "Máshka's sweet root." It was very bitter, but they wandered about the

* In his Description of the Wars of 1806-7, Mikháylovski-Danílevski says: "The lack of grain in spring occasioned the slackness of the higher command and its inability to stop abuses which made their way into the management of the commissariat. In reply to a report of hunger in the army, Bennigsen once replied: 'It is necessary to know how to endure. I only have three dishes for my own dinner.' Money was issued to buy provisions, but money cannot buy provisions where there are none. Sometimes the generals seized each other's provision wagons almost by assault, and bread seldom reached Bennigsen's advanced guard. Soldiers swelled up and died of hunger. The hospitals were in a wretched condition."—A.M.

fields seeking it and dug it out with their sabers and ate it, though they were ordered not to do so, as it was a noxious plant. That spring a new disease broke out among the soldiers, a swelling of the arms, legs, and face, which the doctors attributed to eating this root. But in spite of all this, the soldiers of Denísov's squadron fed chiefly on "Máshka's sweet root," because it was the second week that the last of the biscuits were being doled out at the rate of half a pound a man and the last potatoes received had sprouted and frozen.

The horses also had been fed for a fortnight on straw from the thatched roofs and had become terribly thin, though still covered with tufts of felty winter hair.

Despite this destitution, the soldiers and officers went on living just as usual. Despite their pale swollen faces and tattered uniforms, the hussars formed line for roll call, kept things in order, groomed their horses, polished their arms, brought in straw from the thatched roofs in place of fodder, and sat down to dine round the caldrons from which they rose up hungry, joking about their nasty food and their hunger. As usual, in their spare time, they lit bonfires, steamed themselves before them naked; smoked, picked out and baked sprouting rotten potatoes, told and listened to stories of Potémkin's and Suvórov's campaigns, or to legends of Alësha the Sly, or the priest's laborer Mikólka.

The officers, as usual, lived in twos and threes in the roofless, half-ruined houses. The seniors tried to collect straw and potatoes and, in general, food for the men. The younger ones occupied themselves as before, some playing cards (there was plenty of money, though there was no food), some with more innocent games, such as quoits and skittles.* The general trend of the campaign was rarely spoken of, partly because nothing certain was known about it, partly because there was a vague feeling that in the main it was going badly.

Rostóv lived, as before, with Denísov, and since their furlough they had become more friendly than ever. Denísov never spoke of Rostóv's family, but by the tender friendship his commander showed him, Rostóv felt that the elder hussar's luckless love for Natásha played a part in strengthening their friendship. Denísov evidently tried to expose Rostóv to danger as seldom as possible, and after an action greeted his safe return with evident joy. On one of his foraging expeditions, in a deserted and ruined village to which he had come in search of provisions, Rostóv found a family consisting of an old Pole and his daughter with an infant

* *Literally* svávka *and* gorodkí. *In the former a thick-headed nail has to be thrown into a ring. The latter is described in "Meeting a Moscow Acquaintance" in the volume entitled* Tales of Army Life.—A.M.

in arms. They were half clad, hungry, too weak to get away on foot and had no means of obtaining a conveyance. Rostóv brought them to his quarters, placed them in his own lodging, and kept them for some weeks while the old man was recovering. One of his comrades, talking of women, began chaffing Rostóv, saying that he was more wily than any of them and that it would not be a bad thing if he introduced to them the pretty Polish girl he had saved. Rostóv took the joke as an insult, flared up, and said such unpleasant things to the officer that it was all Denísov could do to prevent a duel. When the officer had gone away, Denísov, who did not himself know what Rostóv's relations with the Polish girl might be, began to upbraid him for his quickness of temper, and Rostóv replied:

"Say what you like. . . . She is like a sister to me, and I can't tell you how it offended me . . . because . . . well, for that reason. . . ."

Denísov patted him on the shoulder and began rapidly pacing the room without looking at Rostóv, as was his way at moments of deep feeling.

"Ah, what a mad bweed you Wostóvs are!" he muttered, and Rostóv noticed tears in his eyes.

14. Denísov seizes transports of food, gets into trouble, is wounded

IN APRIL the troops were enlivened by news of the Emperor's arrival, but Rostóv had no chance of being present at the review he held at Bartenstein, as the Pávlograds were at the outposts far beyond that place.

They were bivouacking. Denísov and Rostóv were living in an earth hut, dug out for them by the soldiers and roofed with branches and turf. The hut was made in the following manner, which had then come into vogue. A trench was dug three and a half feet wide, four feet eight inches deep, and eight feet long. At one end of the trench, steps were cut out and these formed the entrance and vestibule. The trench itself was the room, in which the lucky ones, such as the squadron commander, had a board, lying on piles at the end opposite the entrance, to serve as a table. On each side of the trench, the earth was cut out to a breadth of about two and a half feet, and this did duty for bedsteads and couches. The roof was so constructed that one could stand up in the middle of the trench and could even sit up on the beds if one drew close to the table. Denísov, who was living luxuriously because the soldiers of his squadron liked him, had also a board in the roof at the farther end, with a piece of (broken but mended) glass in it for a window. When it was very cold,

embers from the soldiers' campfire were placed on a bent sheet of iron on the steps in the "reception room"—as Denísov called that part of the hut—and it was then so warm that the officers, of whom there were always some with Denísov and Rostóv, sat in their shirt sleeves.

In April, Rostóv was on orderly duty. One morning, between seven and eight, returning after a sleepless night, he sent for embers, changed his rain-soaked underclothes, said his prayers, drank tea, got warm, then tidied up the things on the table and in his own corner, and, his face glowing from exposure to the wind and with nothing on but his shirt, lay down on his back, putting his arms under his head. He was pleasantly considering the probability of being promoted in a few days for his last reconnoitering expedition, and was awaiting Denísov, who had gone out somewhere and with whom he wanted a talk.

Suddenly he heard Denísov shouting in a vibrating voice behind the hut, evidently much excited. Rostóv moved to the window to see whom he was speaking to, and saw the quartermaster, Topchéenko.

"I ordered you not to let them eat that Máshka woot stuff!" Denísov was shouting. "And I saw with my own eyes how Lazarchúk bwought some fwom the fields."

"I have given the order again and again, your honor, but they don't obey," answered the quartermaster.

Rostóv lay down again on his bed and thought complacently: "Let him fuss and bustle now, my job's done and I'm lying down—capitally!" He could hear that Lavrúshka—that sly, bold orderly of Denísov's—was talking, as well as the quartermaster. Lavrúshka was saying something about loaded wagons, biscuits, and oxen he had seen when he had gone out for provisions.

Then Denísov's voice was heard shouting farther and farther away. "Saddle! Second platoon!"

"Where are they off to now?" thought Rostóv.

Five minutes later, Denísov came into the hut, climbed with muddy boots on the bed, lit his pipe, furiously scattered his things about, took his leaded whip, buckled on his saber, and went out again. In answer to Rostóv's inquiry where he was going, he answered vaguely and crossly that he had some business.

"Let God and our gweat monarch judge me afterwards!" said Denísov going out, and Rostóv heard the hoofs of several horses splashing through the mud. He did not even trouble to find out where Denísov had gone. Having got warm in his corner, he fell asleep and did not leave the hut till toward evening. Denísov had not yet returned. The weather had cleared up, and near the next hut two officers and a cadet were playing

sváyka, laughing as they threw their missiles which buried themselves in the soft mud. Rostóv joined them. In the middle of the game, the officers saw some wagons approaching with fifteen hussars on their skinny horses behind them. The wagons escorted by the hussars drew up to the picket ropes and a crowd of hussars surrounded them.

"There now, Denísov has been worrying," said Rostóv, "and here are the provisions."

"So they are!" said the officers. "Won't the soldiers be glad!"

A little behind the hussars came Denísov, accompanied by two infantry officers with whom he was talking.

Rostóv went to meet them.

"I warn you, Captain," one of the officers, a short thin man, evidently very angry, was saying.

"Haven't I told you I won't give them up?" replied Denísov.

"You will answer for it, Captain. It is mutiny—seizing the transport of one's own army. Our men have had nothing to eat for two days."

"And mine have had nothing for two weeks," said Denísov.

"It is robbery! You'll answer for it, sir!" said the infantry officer, raising his voice.

"Now, what are you pestewing me for?" cried Denísov, suddenly losing his temper. "I shall answer for it and not you, and you'd better not buzz about here till you get hurt. Be off! Go!" he shouted at the officers.

"Very well, then!" shouted the little officer, undaunted and not riding away. "If you are determined to rob, I'll . . ."

"Go to the devil! Quick ma'ch, while you're safe and sound!" and Denísov turned his horse on the officer.

"Very well, very well!" muttered the officer, threateningly, and turning his horse he trotted away, jolting in his saddle.

"A dog astwide a fence! A weal dog astwide a fence!" shouted Denísov after him (the most insulting expression a cavalryman can address to a mounted infantryman) and riding up to Rostóv, he burst out laughing.

"I've taken twansports from the infantwy by force!" he said. "After all, can't let our men starve."

The wagons that had reached the hussars had been consigned to an infantry regiment, but learning from Lavrúshka that the transport was unescorted, Denísov with his hussars had seized it by force. The soldiers had biscuits dealt out to them freely, and they even shared them with the other squadrons.

The next day the regimental commander sent for Denísov, and holding his fingers spread out before his eyes said:

"This is how I look at this affair: I know nothing about it and won't

begin proceedings, but I advise you to ride over to the staff and settle the business there in the commissariat department and if possible sign a receipt for such and such stores received. If not, as the demand was booked against an infantry regiment, there will be a row and the affair may end badly."

From the regimental commander's, Denísov rode straight to the staff with a sincere desire to act on this advice. In the evening he came back to his dugout in a state such as Rostóv had never yet seen him in. Denísov could not speak and gasped for breath. When Rostóv asked what was the matter, he only uttered some incoherent oaths and threats in a hoarse, feeble voice.

Alarmed at Denísov's condition, Rostóv suggested that he should undress, drink some water, and send for the doctor.

"Twy me for wobbewy . . . oh! Some more water . . . Let them twy me, but I'll always thwash scoundwels . . . and I'll tell the Empewo' . . . Ice . . ." he muttered.

The regimental doctor, when he came, said it was absolutely necessary to bleed Denísov. A deep saucer of black blood was taken from his hairy arm and only then was he able to relate what had happened to him.

"I get there," began Denísov. " 'Now then, where's your chief's quarters?' They were pointed out. 'Please to wait.' 'I've widden twenty miles and have duties to attend to and no time to wait. Announce me.' Vewy well, so out comes their head chief—also took it into his head to lecture me: 'It's wobbewy!'—'Wobbewy,' I say, 'is not done by a man who seizes pwovisions to feed his soldiers, but by him who takes them to fill his own pockets!' 'Will you please be silent?' 'Vewy good!' Then he says: 'Go and give a weceipt to the commissioner, but your affair will be passed on to headquarters.' I go to the commissioner. I enter, and at the table . . . who do you think? No, but wait a bit! . . . Who is it that's starving us?" shouted Denísov, hitting the table with the fist of his newly bled arm so violently that the table nearly broke down and the tumblers on it jumped about. "Telyánin! 'What? So it's you who's starving us to death! Is it? Take this and this!' and I hit him so pat, stwaight on his snout . . . 'Ah, what a . . . what . . . !' and I sta'ted fwashing him . . . Well, I've had a bit of fun I can tell you!" cried Denísov, gleeful and yet angry, his white teeth showing under his black mustache. "I'd have killed him if they hadn't taken him away!"

"But what are you shouting for? Calm yourself," said Rostóv. "You've set your arm bleeding afresh. Wait, we must tie it up again."

Denísov was bandaged up again and put to bed. Next day he woke calm and cheerful.

But at noon the adjutant of the regiment came into Rostóv's and Denísov's dugout with a grave and serious face and regretfully showed them a paper addressed to Major Denísov from the regimental commander in which inquiries were made about yesterday's occurrence. The adjutant told them that the affair was likely to take a very bad turn: that a court-martial had been appointed, and that in view of the severity with which marauding and insubordination were now regarded, degradation to the ranks would be the best that could be hoped for.

The case, as represented by the offended parties, was that, after seizing the transports, Major Denísov, being drunk, went to the chief quartermaster and without any provocation called him a thief, threatened to strike him, and on being led out had rushed into the office and given two officials a thrashing, and dislocated the arm of one of them.

In answer to Rostóv's renewed questions, Denísov said, laughing, that he thought he remembered that some other fellow had got mixed up in it, but that it was all nonsense and rubbish, and he did not in the least fear any kind of trial, and that if those scoundrels dared attack him he would give them an answer that they would not easily forget.

Denísov spoke contemptuously of the whole matter, but Rostóv knew him too well not to detect that (while hiding it from others) at heart he feared a court-martial and was worried over the affair, which was evidently taking a bad turn. Every day, letters of inquiry and notices from the court arrived, and on the first of May, Denísov was ordered to hand the squadron over to the next in seniority and appear before the staff of his division to explain his violence at the commissariat office. On the previous day Plátov reconnoitered with two Cossack regiments and two squadrons of hussars. Denísov, as was his wont, rode out in front of the outposts, parading his courage. A bullet fired by a French sharpshooter hit him in the fleshy part of his leg. Perhaps at another time Denísov would not have left the regiment for so slight a wound, but now he took advantage of it to excuse himself from appearing at the staff and went into hospital.

15. Nicholas visits Denísov in hospital

In June the battle of Friedland was·fought, in which the Pávlograds did not take part, and after that an armistice was proclaimed. Rostóv, who felt his friend's absence very much, having no news of him since he left and feeling very anxious about his wound and the progress of his affairs, took advantage of the armistice to get leave to visit Denísov in hospital.

The hospital was in a small Prussian town that had been twice devas-

tated by Russian and French troops. Because it was summer, when it is so beautiful out in the fields, the little town presented a particularly dismal appearance with its broken roofs and fences, its foul streets, tattered inhabitants, and the sick and drunken soldiers wandering about.

The hospital was in a brick building with some of the window frames and panes broken and a courtyard surrounded by the remains of a wooden fence that had been pulled to pieces. Several bandaged soldiers, with pale swollen faces, were sitting or walking about in the sunshine in the yard.

Directly Rostóv entered the door he was enveloped by a smell of putrefaction and hospital air. On the stairs he met a Russian army doctor smoking a cigar. The doctor was followed by a Russian assistant.

"I can't tear myself to pieces," the doctor was saying. "Come to Makár Alexéevich in the evening. I shall be there."

The assistant asked some further questions.

"Oh, do the best you can! Isn't it all the same?" The doctor noticed Rostóv coming upstairs.

"What do you want, sir?" said the doctor. "What do you want? The bullets having spared you, do you want to try typhus? This is a pesthouse, sir."

"How so?" asked Rostóv.

"Typhus, sir. It's death to go in. Only we two, Makéev and I" (he pointed to the assistant), "keep on here. Some five of us doctors have died in this place. . . . When a new one comes he is done for in a week," said the doctor with evident satisfaction. "Prussian doctors have been invited here, but our allies don't like it at all."

Rostóv explained that he wanted to see Major Denísov of the hussars, who was wounded.

"I don't know. I can't tell you, sir. Only think! I am alone in charge of three hospitals with more than four hundred patients! It's well that the charitable Prussian ladies send us two pounds of coffee and some lint each month or we should be lost!" he laughed. "Four hundred, sir, and they're always sending me fresh ones. There are four hundred? Eh?" he asked, turning to the assistant.

The assistant looked fagged out. He was evidently vexed and impatient for the talkative doctor to go.

"Major Denísov," Rostóv said again. "He was wounded at Molliten."

"Dead, I fancy. Eh, Makéev?" queried the doctor, in a tone of indifference.

The assistant, however, did not confirm the doctor's words.

"Is he tall and with reddish hair?" asked the doctor.

Rostóv described Denísov's appearance.

"There was one like that," said the doctor, as if pleased. "That one is dead, I fancy. However, I'll look up our list. We had a list. Have you got it, Makéev?"

"Makár Alexéevich has the list," answered the assistant. "But if you'll step into the officers' wards you'll see for yourself," he added, turning to Rostóv.

"Ah, you'd better not go, sir," said the doctor, "or you may have to stay here yourself."

But Rostóv bowed himself away from the doctor and asked the assistant to show him the way.

"Only don't blame me!" the doctor shouted up after him.

Rostóv and the assistant went into the dark corridor. The smell was so strong there that Rostóv held his nose and had to pause and collect his strength before he could go on. A door opened to the right, and an emaciated sallow man on crutches, barefoot and in underclothing, limped out and, leaning against the doorpost, looked with glittering envious eyes at those who were passing. Glancing in at the door, Rostóv saw that the sick and wounded were lying on the floor on straw and overcoats.

"May I go in and look?"

"What is there to see?" said the assistant.

But, just because the assistant evidently did not want him to go in, Rostóv entered the soldiers' ward. The foul air, to which he had already begun to get used in the corridor, was still stronger here. It was a little different, more pungent, and one felt that this was where it originated.

In the long room, brightly lit up by the sun through the large windows, the sick and wounded lay in two rows with their heads to the walls, and leaving a passage in the middle. Most of them were unconscious and paid no attention to the newcomers. Those who were conscious raised themselves or lifted their thin yellow faces, and all looked intently at Rostóv with the same expression of hope, of relief, reproach, and envy of another's health. Rostóv went to the middle of the room and looking through the open doors into the two adjoining rooms saw the same thing there. He stood still, looking silently around. He had not at all expected such a sight. Just before him, almost across the middle of the passage on the bare floor, lay a sick man, probably a Cossack to judge by the cut of his hair. The man lay on his back, his huge arms and legs outstretched. His face was purple, his eyes were rolled back so that only the whites were seen, and on his bare legs and arms which were still red, the veins stood out like cords. He was knocking the back of his head against the floor, hoarsely uttering some word which he kept repeating. Rostóv listened and made out the word. It was "drink, drink, a drink!" Rostóv glanced

round, looking for someone who would put this man back in his place and bring him water.

"Who looks after the sick here?" he asked the assistant.

Just then a commissariat soldier, a hospital orderly, came in from the next room, marching stiffly, and drew up in front of Rostóv.

"Good day, your honor!" he shouted, rolling his eyes at Rostóv and evidently mistaking him for one of the hospital authorities.

"Get him to his place and give him some water," said Rostóv, pointing to the Cossack.

"Yes, your honor," the soldier replied complacently, and rolling his eyes more than ever he drew himself up still straighter, but did not move.

"No, it's impossible to do anything here," thought Rostóv, lowering his eyes, and he was going out, but became aware of an intense look fixed on him on his right, and he turned. Close to the corner, on an overcoat, sat an old, unshaven, gray-bearded soldier as thin as a skeleton, with a stern sallow face and eyes intently fixed on Rostóv. The man's neighbor on one side whispered something to him, pointing at Rostóv, who noticed that the old man wanted to speak to him. He drew nearer and saw that the old man had only one leg bent under him, the other had been amputated above the knee. His neighbor on the other side, who lay motionless some distance from him with his head thrown back, was a young soldier with a snub nose. His pale waxen face was still freckled and his eyes were rolled back. Rostóv looked at the young soldier and a cold chill ran down his back.

"Why, this one seems . . ." he began, turning to the assistant.

"And how we've been begging, your honor," said the old soldier, his jaw quivering. "He's been dead since morning. After all we're men, not dogs."

"I'll send someone at once. He shall be taken away—taken away at once," said the assistant hurriedly. "Let us go, your honor."

"Yes, yes, let us go," said Rostóv hastily, and lowering his eyes and shrinking, he tried to pass unnoticed between the rows of reproachful envious eyes that were fixed upon him, and went out of the room.

GOING ALONG the corridor, the assistant led Rostóv to the officers' wards, consisting of three rooms, the doors of which stood open. There were beds in these rooms and the sick and wounded officers were lying or sitting on them. Some were walking about the rooms in hospital dressing gowns. The first person Rostóv met in the officers' ward was a thin little man with one arm, who was walking about the first room in a nightcap

and hospital dressing gown, with a pipe between his teeth. Rostóv
looked at him, trying to remember where he had seen him before.
"See where we've met again!" said the little man. "Túshin, Túshin,
don't you remember, who gave you a lift at Schön Grabern? And I've had
a bit cut off, you see . . ." he went on with a smile, pointing to the
empty sleeve of his dressing gown. "Looking for Vasíli Dmítrich Dení-
sov? My neighbor," he added, when he heard who Rostóv wanted. "Here,
here," and Túshin led him into the next room, from whence came sounds
of several laughing voices.

"How can they laugh, or even live at all here?" thought Rostóv, still
aware of that smell of decomposing flesh that had been so strong in the
soldiers' ward, and still seeming to see fixed on him those envious looks
which had followed him out from both sides, and the face of that young
soldier with eyes rolled back.

Denísov lay asleep on his bed with his head under the blanket, though
it was nearly noon.

"Ah, Wostóv? How are you, how are you?" he called out, still in the
same voice as in the regiment, but Rostóv noticed sadly that under this
habitual ease and animation some new, sinister, hidden feeling showed
itself in the expression of Denísov's face and the intonations of his voice.

His wound, though a slight one, had not yet healed even now, six
weeks after he had been hit. His face had the same swollen pallor as the
faces of the other hospital patients, but it was not this that struck Rostóv.
What struck him was that Denísov did not seem glad to see him, and
smiled at him unnaturally. He did not ask about the regiment, nor about
the general state of affairs, and when Rostóv spoke of these matters did
not listen.

Rostóv even noticed that Denísov did not like to be reminded of the
regiment, or in general of that other free life which was going on outside
the hospital. He seemed to try to forget that old life and was only inter-
ested in the affair with the commissariat officers. On Rostóv's inquiry as
to how the matter stood, he at once produced from under his pillow a
paper he had received from the commission and the rough draft of his
answer to it. He became animated when he began reading his paper and
specially drew Rostóv's attention to the stinging rejoinders he made to
his enemies. His hospital companions, who had gathered round Rostóv
—a fresh arrival from the world outside—gradually began to disperse as
soon as Denísov began reading his answer. Rostóv noticed by their faces
that all those gentlemen had already heard that story more than once
and were tired of it. Only the man who had the next bed, a stout Uhlan,
continued to sit on his bed, gloomily frowning and smoking a pipe, and

little one-armed Túshin still listened, shaking his head disapprovingly. In the middle of the reading, the Uhlan interrupted Denísov.

"But what I say is," he said, turning to Rostóv, "it would be best simply to petition the Emperor for pardon. They say great rewards will now be distributed, and surely a pardon would be granted. . . ."

"Me petition the Empewo'!" exclaimed Denísov, in a voice to which he tried hard to give the old energy and fire, but which sounded like an expression of irritable impotence. "What for? If I were a wobber I would ask mercy, but I'm being court-martialed for bwinging wobbers to book. Let them twy me, I'm not afwaid of anyone. I've served the Tsar and my countwy honowably and have not stolen! And am I to be degwaded? . . . Listen, I'm w'iting to them stwaight. This is what I say: 'If I had wobbed the Tweasuwy . . .'"

"It's certainly well written," said Túshin, "but that's not the point, Vasíli Dmítrich," and he also turned to Rostóv. "One has to submit, and Vasíli Dmítrich doesn't want to. You know the auditor told you it was a bad business."

"Well, let it be bad," said Denísov.

"The auditor wrote out a petition for you," continued Túshin, "and you ought to sign it and ask this gentleman to take it. No doubt he" (indicating Rostóv) "has connections on the staff. You won't find a better opportunity."

"Haven't I said I'm not going to gwovel?" Denísov interrupted him, and went on reading his paper.

Rostóv had not the courage to persuade Denísov, though he instinctively felt that the way advised by Túshin and the other officers was the safest, and though he would have been glad to be of service to Denísov. He knew his stubborn will and straightforward hasty temper.

When the reading of Denísov's virulent reply, which took more than an hour, was over, Rostóv said nothing, and he spent the rest of the day in a most dejected state of mind amid Denísov's hospital comrades, who had gathered round him, telling them what he knew and listening to their stories. Denísov was moodily silent all the evening.

Late in the evening, when Rostóv was about to leave, he asked Denísov whether he had no commission for him.

"Yes, wait a bit," said Denísov, glancing round at the officers, and taking his papers from under his pillow he went to the window, where he had an inkpot, and sat down to write.

"It seems it's no use knocking one's head against a wall!" he said, coming from the window and giving Rostóv a large envelope. In it was the petition to the Emperor drawn up by the auditor, in which Denísov,

without alluding to the offenses of the commissariat officials, simply asked for pardon.

"Hand it in. It seems . . ."

He did not finish, but gave a painfully unnatural smile.

16. Borís at Tilsit. Nicholas' inopportune visit

HAVING RETURNED to the regiment and told the commander the state of Denísov's affairs, Rostóv rode to Tilsit with the letter to the Emperor.

On the thirteenth of June the French and Russian Emperors arrived in Tilsit. Borís Drubetskóy had asked the important personage on whom he was in attendance, to include him in the suite appointed for the stay at Tilsit.

"I should like to see the great man," he said, alluding to Napoleon, whom hitherto he, like everyone else, had always called Buonaparte.

"You are speaking of Buonaparte?" asked the general, smiling.

Borís looked at his general inquiringly and immediately saw that he was being tested.

"I am speaking, Prince, of the Emperor Napoleon," he replied. The general patted him on the shoulder, with a smile.

"You will go far," he said, and took him to Tilsit with him.

Borís was among the few present at the Niemen on the day the two Emperors met. He saw the raft, decorated with monograms, saw Napoleon pass before the French Guards on the farther bank of the river, saw the pensive face of the Emperor Alexander as he sat in silence in a tavern on the bank of the Niemen awaiting Napoleon's arrival, saw both Emperors get into boats, and saw how Napoleon—reaching the raft first— stepped quickly forward to meet Alexander and held out his hand to him, and how they both retired into the pavilion. Since he had begun to move in the highest circles Borís had made it his habit to watch attentively all that went on around him and to note it down. At the time of the meeting at Tilsit he asked the names of those who had come with Napoleon and about the uniforms they wore, and listened attentively to words spoken by important personages. At the moment the Emperors went into the pavilion he looked at his watch, and did not forget to look at it again when Alexander came out. The interview had lasted an hour and fifty-three minutes. He noted this down that same evening, among other facts he felt to be of historic importance. As the Emperor's suite was a very small one, it was a matter of great importance, for a man who valued his

success in the service, to be at Tilsit on the occasion of this interview between the two Emperors, and having succeeded in this, Borís felt that henceforth his position was fully assured. He had not only become known, but people had grown accustomed to him and accepted him. Twice he had executed commissions to the Emperor himself, so that the latter knew his face, and all those at court, far from cold-shouldering him as at first when they considered him a newcomer, would now have been surprised had he been absent.

Borís lodged with another adjutant, the Polish Count Zhilínski. Zhilínski, a Pole brought up in Paris, was rich, and passionately fond of the French, and almost every day of the stay at Tilsit, French officers of the Guard and from French headquarters were dining and lunching with him and Borís.

On the evening of the twenty-fourth of June, Count Zhilínski arranged a supper for his French friends. The guest of honor was an aide-de-camp of Napoleon's, there were also several French officers of the Guard, and a page of Napoleon's, a young lad of an old aristocratic French family. That same day, Rostóv, profiting by the darkness to avoid being recognized in civilian dress, came to Tilsit and went to the lodging occupied by Borís and Zhilínski.

Rostóv, in common with the whole army from which he came, was far from having experienced the change of feeling toward Napoleon and the French—who from being foes had suddenly become friends—that had taken place at headquarters and in Borís. In the army, Bonaparte and the French were still regarded with mingled feelings of anger, contempt, and fear. Only recently, talking with one of Plátov's Cossack officers, Rostóv had argued that if Napoleon were taken prisoner he would be treated not as a sovereign, but as a criminal. Quite lately, happening to meet a wounded French colonel on the road, Rostóv had maintained with heat that peace was impossible between a legitimate sovereign and the criminal Bonaparte. Rostóv was therefore unpleasantly struck by the presence of French officers in Borís' lodging, dressed in uniforms he had been accustomed to see from quite a different point of view from the outposts of the flank. As soon as he noticed a French officer, who thrust his head out of the door, that warlike feeling of hostility which he always experienced at the sight of the enemy suddenly seized him. He stopped at the threshold and asked in Russian whether Drubetskóy lived there. Borís, hearing a strange voice in the anteroom, came out to meet him. An expression of annoyance showed itself for a moment on his face on first recognizing Rostóv.

"Ah, it's you? Very glad, very glad to see you," he said, however, coming toward him with a smile. But Rostóv had noticed his first impulse.

"I've come at a bad time I think. I should not have come, but I have business," he said coldly.

"No, I only wonder how you managed to get away from your regiment. *Dans un moment je suis à vous* [In a minute I shall be at your disposal]," he said, answering someone who called him.

"I see I'm intruding," Rostóv repeated.

The look of annoyance had already disappeared from Borís' face: having evidently reflected and decided how to act, he very quietly took both Rostóv's hands and led him into the next room. His eyes, looking serenely and steadily at Rostóv, seemed to be veiled by something, as if screened by blue spectacles of conventionality. So it seemed to Rostóv.

"Oh, come now! As if you could come at a wrong time!" said Borís, and he led him into the room where the supper table was laid and introduced him to his guests, explaining that he was not a civilian, but an hussar officer, and an old friend of his.

"Count Zhilínski—*le Comte* N. N.—*le Capitaine* S. S.," said he, naming his guests. Rostóv looked frowningly at the Frenchmen, bowed reluctantly, and remained silent.

Zhilínski evidently did not receive this new Russian person very willingly into his circle and did not speak to Rostóv. Borís did not appear to notice the constraint the newcomer produced and, with the same pleasant composure and the same veiled look in his eyes with which he had met Rostóv, tried to enliven the conversation. One of the Frenchmen, with the politeness characteristic of his countrymen, addressed the obstinately taciturn Rostóv, saying that the latter had probably come to Tilsit to see the Emperor.

"No, I came on business," replied Rostóv, briefly.

Rostóv had been out of humor from the moment he noticed the look of dissatisfaction on Borís' face, and as always happens to those in a bad humor, it seemed to him that everyone regarded him with aversion and that he was in everybody's way. He really was in their way, for he alone took no part in the conversation which again became general. The looks the visitors cast on him seemed to say: "And what is he sitting here for?" He rose and went up to Borís.

"Anyhow, I'm in your way," he said in a low tone. "Come and talk over my business and I'll go away."

"Oh, no, not at all," said Borís. "But if you are tired, come and lie down in my room and have a rest."

"Yes, really . . ."

They went into the little room where Borís slept. Rostóv, without sitting down, began at once, irritably (as if Borís were to blame in some

way) telling him about Denísov's affair, asking him whether, through his general, he could and would intercede with the Emperor on Denísov's behalf and get Denísov's petition handed in. When he and Borís were alone, Rostóv felt for the first time that he could not look Borís in the face without a sense of awkwardness. Borís, with one leg crossed over the other and stroking his left hand with the slender fingers of his right, listened to Rostóv as a general listens to the report of a subordinate, now looking aside and now gazing straight into Rostóv's eyes with the same veiled look. Each time this happened Rostóv felt uncomfortable and cast down his eyes.

"I have heard of such cases and know that His Majesty is very severe in such affairs. I think it would be best not to bring it before the Emperor, but to apply to the commander of the corps. . . . But in general, I think . . ."

"So you don't want to do anything? Well then, say so!" Rostóv almost shouted, not looking Borís in the face.

Borís smiled.

"On the contrary, I will do what I can. Only I thought . . ."

At that moment Zhilínski's voice was heard calling Borís.

"Well then, go, go, go . . ." said Rostóv, and refusing supper and remaining alone in the little room, he walked up and down for a long time, hearing the lighthearted French conversation from the next room.

17. Nicholas tries to present Denísov's petition at the Emperor's residence, but fails

ROSTÓV HAD COME to Tilsit on the day least suitable for a petition on Denísov's behalf. He could not himself go to the general in attendance as he was in mufti and had come to Tilsit without permission to do so, and Borís, even had he wished to, could not have done so on the following day. On that day, June 27, the preliminaries of peace were signed. The Emperors exchanged decorations: Alexander received the Cross of the Legion of Honor and Napoleon the Order of St. Andrew of the First Degree, and a dinner had been arranged for the evening, given by a battalion of the French Guards to. the Preobrazhénsk battalion. The Emperors were to be present at that banquet.

Rostóv felt so ill at ease and uncomfortable with Borís that, when the latter looked in after supper, he pretended to be asleep, and early next morning went away, avoiding Borís. In his civilian clothes and a round hat, he wandered about the town, staring at the French and their uni-

forms and at the streets and houses where the Russian and French Emperors were staying. In a square he saw tables being set up and preparations made for the dinner; he saw the Russian and French colors draped from side to side of the streets, with huge monograms A and N. In the windows of the houses also flags and bunting were displayed.

"Borís doesn't want to help me and I don't want to ask him. That's settled," thought Nicholas. "All is over between us, but I won't leave here without having done all I can for Denísov and certainly not without getting his letter to the Emperor. The Emperor! . . . He is here!" thought Rostóv, who had unconsciously returned to the house where Alexander lodged.

Saddled horses were standing before the house and the suite were assembling, evidently preparing for the Emperor to come out.

"I may see him at any moment," thought Rostóv. "If only I were to hand the letter direct to him and tell him all . . . could they really arrest me for my civilian clothes? Surely not! He would understand on whose side justice lies. He understands everything, knows everything. Who can be more just, more magnanimous than he? And even if they did arrest me for being here, what would it matter?" thought he, looking at an officer who was entering the house the Emperor occupied. "After all, people do go in. . . . It's all nonsense! I'll go in and hand the letter to the Emperor myself, so much the worse for Drubetskóy who drives me to it!" And suddenly with a determination he himself did not expect, Rostóv felt for the letter in his pocket and went straight to the house.

"No, I won't miss my opportunity now, as I did after Austerlitz," he thought, expecting every moment to meet the monarch, and conscious of the blood that rushed to his heart at the thought. "I will fall at his feet and beseech him. He will lift me up, will listen, and will even thank me. 'I am happy when I can do good, but to remedy injustice is the greatest happiness,'" Rostóv fancied the sovereign saying. And passing people who looked after him with curiosity, he entered the porch of the Emperor's house.

A broad staircase led straight up from the entry, and to the right he saw a closed door. Below, under the staircase, was a door leading to the lower floor.

"Whom do you want?" someone inquired.

"To hand in a letter, a petition, to His Majesty," said Nicholas, with a tremor in his voice.

"A petition? This way, to the officer on duty" (he was shown the door leading downstairs), "only it won't be accepted."

On hearing this indifferent voice, Rostóv grew frightened at what he

was doing; the thought of meeting the Emperor at any moment was so fascinating and consequently so alarming that he was ready to run away, but the official who had questioned him opened the door, and Rostóv entered.

A short stout man of about thirty, in white breeches and high boots and a batiste shirt that he had evidently only just put on, was standing in that room, and his valet was buttoning on to the back of his breeches a new pair of handsome silk-embroidered braces that, for some reason, attracted Rostóv's attention. This man was speaking to someone in the adjoining room.

"A good figure and in her first bloom," he was saying, but on seeing Rostóv, he stopped short and frowned.

"What is it? A petition?"

"What is it?" asked the person in the other room.

"Another petitioner," answered the man with the braces.

"Tell him to come later. He'll be coming out directly, we must go."

"Later . . . later! Tomorrow. It's too late. . . ,"

Rostóv turned and was about to go, but the man in the braces stopped him.

"Whom have you come from? Who are you?"

"I come from Major Denísov," answered Rostóv.

"Are you an officer?"

"Lieutenant Count Rostóv."

"What audacity! Hand it in through your commander. And go along with you . . . go," and he continued to put on the uniform the valet handed him.

Rostóv went back into the hall and noticed that in the porch there were many officers and generals in full parade uniform, whom he had to pass.

Cursing his temerity, his heart sinking at the thought of finding himself at any moment face to face with the Emperor and being put to shame and arrested in his presence, fully alive now to the impropriety of his conduct and repenting of it, Rostóv, with downcast eyes, was making his way out of the house through the brilliant suite when a familiar voice called him and a hand detained him.

"What are you doing here, sir, in civilian dress?" asked a deep voice.

It was a cavalry general who had obtained the Emperor's special favor during this campaign, and who had formerly commanded the division in which Rostóv was serving.

Rostóv, in dismay, began justifying himself, but seeing the kindly, jocular face of the general, he took him aside and in an excited voice told

him the whole affair, asking him to intercede for Denísov, whom the general knew. Having heard Rostóv to the end, the general shook his head gravely.

"I'm sorry, sorry for that fine fellow. Give me the letter."

Hardly had Rostóv handed him the letter and finished explaining Denísov's case, when hasty steps and the jingling of spurs were heard on the stairs, and the general, leaving him, went to the porch. The gentlemen of the Emperor's suite ran down the stairs and went to their horses. Hayne, the same groom who had been at Austerlitz, led up the Emperor's horse, and the faint creak of a footstep Rostóv knew at once was heard on the stairs. Forgetting the danger of being recognized, Rostóv went close to the porch, together with some inquisitive civilians, and again, after two years, saw those features he adored: that same face and same look and step, and the same union of majesty and mildness. . . . And the feeling of enthusiasm and love for his sovereign rose again in Rostóv's soul in all its old force. In the uniform of the Preobrazhénsk regiment— white chamois-leather breeches and high boots—and wearing a star Rostóv did not know (it was that of the *Légion d'honneur*), the monarch came out into the porch, putting on his gloves and carrying his hat under his arm. He stopped and looked about him, brightening everything around by his glance. He spoke a few words to some of the generals, and, recognizing the former commander of Rostóv's division, smiled and beckoned to him.

All the suite drew back and Rostóv saw the general talking for some time to the Emperor.

The Emperor said a few words to him and took a step toward his horse. Again the crowd of members of the suite and street gazers (among whom was Rostóv) moved nearer to the Emperor. Stopping beside his horse, with his hand on the saddle, the Emperor turned to the cavalry general and said in a loud voice, evidently wishing to be heard by all:

"I cannot do it, General. I cannot, because the law is stronger than I," and he raised his foot to the stirrup.

The general bowed his head respectfully, and the monarch mounted and rode down the street at a gallop. Beside himself with enthusiasm, Rostóv ran after him with the crowd.

18. Napoleon and Alexander as allies. Perplexity of Nicholas. "Another bottle"

THE EMPEROR rode to the square where, facing one another, a battalion of the Preobrazhénsk regiment stood on the right and a battalion of the French Guards in their bearskin caps on the left.

As the Tsar rode up to one flank of the battalions, which presented arms, another group of horsemen galloped up to the opposite flank, and at the head of them Rostóv recognized Napoleon. It could be no one else. He came at a gallop, wearing a small hat, a blue uniform open over a white vest, and the St. Andrew ribbon over his shoulder. He was riding a very fine thoroughbred gray Arab horse with a crimson gold-embroidered saddlecloth. On approaching Alexander he raised his hat, and as he did so, Rostóv, with his cavalryman's eye, could not help noticing that Napoleon did not sit well or firmly in the saddle. The battalions shouted "Hurrah!" and "Vive l'Empereur!" Napoleon said something to Alexander, and both Emperors dismounted and took each other's hands. Napoleon's face wore an unpleasant and artificial smile. Alexander was saying something affable to him.

In spite of the trampling of the French gendarmes' horses, which were pushing back the crowd, Rostóv kept his eyes on every movement of Alexander and Bonaparte. It struck him as a surprise that Alexander treated Bonaparte as an equal and that the latter was quite at ease with the Tsar, as if such relations with an Emperor were an everyday matter to him.

Alexander and Napoleon, with the long train of their suites, approached the right flank of the Preobrazhénsk battalion and came straight up to the crowd standing there. The crowd unexpectedly found itself so close to the Emperors that Rostóv, standing in the front row, was afraid he might be recognized.

"Sire, I ask your permission to present the Legion of Honor to the bravest of your soldiers," said a 'sharp, precise voice, articulating every letter.

This was said by the undersized Napoleon, looking up straight into Alexander's eyes. Alexander listened attentively to what was said to him and, bending his head, smiled pleasantly.

"To him who has borne himself most bravely in this last war," added Napoleon, accentuating each syllable, as with a composure and assurance exasperating to Rostóv, he ran his eyes over the Russian ranks drawn up before him, who all presented arms with their eyes fixed on their Emperor.

"Will Your Majesty allow me to consult the colonel?" said Alexander and took a few hasty steps toward Prince Kozlóvski, the commander of the battalion.

Bonaparte meanwhile began taking the glove off his small white hand, tore it in doing so, and threw it away. An aide-de-camp behind him rushed forward and picked it up.

"To whom shall it be given?" the Emperor Alexander asked Koslóvski, in Russian in a low voice.

"To whomever Your Majesty commands."

The Emperor knit his brows with dissatisfaction and, glancing back, remarked:

"But we must give him an answer."

Kozlóvski scanned the ranks resolutely and included Rostóv in his scrutiny.

"Can it be me?" thought Rostóv.

"Lázarev!" the colonel called, with a frown, and Lázarev, the first soldier in the rank, stepped briskly forward.

"Where are you off to? Stop here!" voices whispered to Lázarev who did not know where to go. Lázarev stopped, casting a sidelong look at his colonel in alarm. His face twitched, as often happens to soldiers called before the ranks.

Napoleon slightly turned his head, and put his plump little hand out behind him as if to take something. The members of his suite, guessing at once what he wanted, moved about and whispered as they passed something from one to another, and a page—the same one Rostóv had seen the previous evening at Borís'—ran forward and, bowing respectfully over the outstretched hand and not keeping it waiting a moment, laid in it an Order on a red ribbon. Napoleon, without looking, pressed two fingers together and the badge was between them. Then he approached Lázarev (who rolled his eyes and persistently gazed at his own monarch), looked round at the Emperor Alexander to imply that what he was now doing was done for the sake of his ally, and the small white hand holding the Order touched one of Lázarev's buttons. It was as if Napoleon knew that it was only necessary for his hand to deign to touch that soldier's breast for the soldier to be forever happy, rewarded, and distinguished from everyone else in the world. Napoleon merely laid the cross on Lázarev's breast and, dropping his hand, turned toward Alexander as though sure that the cross would adhere there. And it really did.

Officious hands, Russian and French, immediately seized the cross and fastened it to the uniform. Lázarev glanced morosely at the little man with white hands who was doing something to him and, still standing

motionless presenting arms, looked again straight into Alexander's eyes, as if asking whether he should stand there, or go away, or do something else. But receiving no orders, he remained for some time in that rigid position.

The Emperors remounted and rode away. The Preobrazhénsk battalion, breaking rank, mingled with the French Guards and sat down at the tables prepared for them.

Lázarev sat in the place of honor. Russian and French officers embraced him, congratulated him, and pressed his hands. Crowds of officers and civilians drew near merely to see him. A rumble of Russian and French voices and laughter filled the air round the tables in the square. Two officers with flushed faces, looking cheerful and happy, passed by Rostóv.

"What d'you think of the treat? All on silver plate," one of them was saying. "Have you seen Lázarev?"

"I have."

"Tomorrow, I hear, the Preobrazhénskis will give them a dinner." *

"Yes, but what luck for Lázarev! Twelve hundred francs' pension for life."

"Here's a cap, lads!" shouted a Preobrazhénsk soldier, donning a shaggy French cap.

"It's a fine thing! First-rate!"

"Have you heard the password?" asked one Guards' officer of another. "The day before yesterday it was 'Napoléon, France, bravoure'; yesterday, 'Alexandre, Russie, grandeur.' One day our Emperor gives it and next day Napoleon. Tomorrow our Emperor will send a St. George's Cross to the bravest of the French Guards. It has to be done. He must respond in kind."

Borís, too, with his friend Zhilínski, came to see the Preobrazhénsk banquet. On his way back, he noticed Rostóv standing by the corner of a house.

* Tolstóy's description of the meeting of the Emperors at Tilsit keeps very close to history, though he does not mention the humiliation inflicted on the King of Prussia, who was not invited into the tent where the Emperors met, but during their two-hour interview stood with Alexander's courtier, Prince P. M. Volkónski, waiting on the bank of the Niemen like a punished schoolboy and hardly saying anything. It was only at Alexander's request that Napoleon received the King of Prussia next day. Tolstóy also omits to mention that the Preobrazhénsk regiment was unable to return the hospitality to the French Guards in equal style, as they had no silver plate and, despite Alexander's readiness to pay highly for it, could not obtain any.—A.M.

"Rostóv! How d'you do? We missed one another," he said, and could not refrain from asking what was the matter, so strangely dismal and troubled was Rostóv's face.

"Nothing, nothing," replied Rostóv.

"You'll call round?"

"Yes, I will."

Rostóv stood at that corner for a long time, watching the feast from a distance. In his mind, a painful process was going on which he could not bring to a conclusion. Terrible doubts rose in his soul. Now he remembered Denísov with his changed expression, his submission, and the whole hospital, with arms and legs torn off and its dirt and disease. So vividly did he recall that hospital stench of dead flesh that he looked round to see where the smell came from. Next he thought of that self-satisfied Bonaparte, with his small white hand, who was now an Emperor, liked and respected by Alexander. Then why those severed arms and legs and those dead men? . . . Then again he thought of Lázarev rewarded and Denísov punished and unpardoned. He caught himself harboring such strange thoughts that he was frightened.

The smell of the food the Preobrazhénskis were eating and a sense of hunger recalled him from these reflections; he had to get something to eat before going away. He went to a hotel he had noticed that morning. There he found so many people, among them officers who, like himself, had come in civilian clothes, that he had difficulty in getting a dinner. Two officers of his own division joined him. The conversation naturally turned on the peace. The officers, his comrades, like most of the army, were dissatisfied with the peace concluded after the battle of Friedland. They said that had we held out a little longer Napoleon would have been done for, as his troops had neither provisions nor ammunition. Nicholas ate and drank (chiefly the latter) in silence. He finished a couple of bottles of wine by himself. The process in his mind went on tormenting him without reaching a conclusion. He feared to give way to his thoughts, yet could not get rid of them. Suddenly, on one of the officers' saying that it was humiliating to look at the French, Rostóv began shouting with uncalled-for wrath, and therefore much to the surprise of the officers:

"How can you judge what's best?" he cried, the blood suddenly rushing to his face. "How can you judge the Emperor's actions? What right have we to argue? We cannot comprehend either the Emperor's aims or his actions!"

"But I never said a word about the Emperor!" said the officer, justifying himself, and unable to understand Rostóv's outburst, except on the supposition that he was drunk.

But Rostóv did not listen to him.

"We are not diplomatic officials, we are soldiers and nothing more," he went on. "If we are ordered to die, we must die. If we're punished, it means that we have deserved it, it's not for us to judge. If the Emperor pleases to recognize Bonaparte as Emperor and to conclude an alliance with him, it means that that is the right thing to do. If once we begin judging and arguing about everything, nothing sacred will be left! That way we shall be saying there is no God—nothing!" shouted Nicholas, banging the table—very little to the point as it seemed to his listeners, but quite relevantly to the course of his own thoughts.

"Our business is to do our duty, to fight and not to think! That's all. . . . " said he.

"And to drink," said one of the officers, not wishing to quarrel.

"Yes, and to drink," assented Nicholas. "Hullo there! Another bottle!" he shouted.

But Rostóv did not listen to him.

"We are not diplomatic officials, we are soldiers and nothing more," he went on. "If we are ordered to die, we must die. If we're punished, it means that we have deserved it; it's not for us to judge. If the Emperor pleases to recognize Bonaparte as Emperor and to conclude an alliance with him, it means that is the right thing to do. If once we begin judging and arguing about everything, nothing sacred will be left. That way we shall be saying there is no God—nothing," shouted Nicholas, banging the table—very little to the point as it seemed to his listeners, but quite relevantly to the course of his own thoughts.

"Our business is to do our duty, to fight and not to think. That's all," said he.

"And to drink," said one of the officers, not wishing to quarrel.

"Yes, and to drink," assented Nicholas. "Hullo there! Another bottle!" he shouted.

BOOK SIX

BOOK SIX

1808-10

BOOK SIX

1. *Real Life. Prince Andrew's occupations at Boguchárovo.
His drive through the forest—the bare oak. His visit to the
Rostóvs at Otrádnoe. Overhears Natásha's talk with Sónya.
Return through the forest—the oak in leaf. He decides to
go to Petersburg*

IN 1808 the Emperor Alexander went to Erfurt for a fresh interview with
the Emperor Napoleon, and in the upper circles of Petersburg there was
much talk of the grandeur of this important meeting.

In 1809 the intimacy between "the world's two arbiters," as Napoleon
and Alexander were called, was such that when Napoleon declared war on
Austria a Russian corps crossed the frontier to co-operate with our old
enemy Bonaparte against our old ally the Emperor of Austria, and in court
circles the possibility of marriage between Napoleon and one of Alexan-
der's sisters was spoken of. But besides considerations of foreign policy,
the attention of Russian society was at that time keenly directed on the
internal changes that were being undertaken in all the departments of
government.

Life meanwhile—real life, with its essential interests of health and sick-
ness, toil and rest, and its intellectual interests in thought, science, poetry,
music, love, friendship, hatred, and passions—went on as usual, inde-
pendently of and apart from political friendship or enmity with Napoleon
Bonaparte and from all the schemes of reconstruction.

Prince Andrew had spent two years continuously in the country.

All the plans Pierre had attempted on his estates—and constantly
changing from one thing to another had never accomplished—were carried
out by Prince Andrew without display and without perceptible difficulty.

He had in the highest degree a practical tenacity which Pierre lacked,
and without fuss or strain on his part this set things going.

457

On one of his estates the three hundred serfs were liberated and became free agricultural laborers—this being one of the first examples of the kind in Russia. On other estates the serfs' compulsory labor was commuted for a quitrent. A trained midwife was engaged for Boguchárovo at his expense, and a priest was paid to teach reading and writing to the children of the peasants and household serfs.

Prince Andrew spent half his time at Bald Hills with his father and his son, who was still in the care of nurses. The other half he spent in "Bogu-chárovo Cloister," as his father called Prince Andrew's estate. Despite the indifference to the affairs of the world he had expressed to Pierre, he diligently followed all that went on, received many books, and to his surprise noticed that when he or his father had visitors from Petersburg, the very vortex of life, these people lagged behind himself—who never left the country—in knowledge of what was happening in home and foreign affairs.

Besides being occupied with his estates and reading a great variety of books, Prince Andrew was at this time busy with a critical survey of our last two unfortunate campaigns, and with drawing up a proposal for a reform of the army rules and regulations.

In the spring of 1809 he went to visit the Ryazán estates which had been inherited by his son, whose guardian he was.

Warmed by the spring sunshine he sat in the calèche looking at the new grass, the first leaves on the birches, and the first puffs of white spring clouds floating across the clear blue sky. He was not thinking of anything, but looked absent-mindedly and cheerfully from side to side.

They crossed the ferry where he had talked with Pierre the year before. They went through the muddy village, past threshing floors and green fields of winter rye, downhill where snow still lodged near the bridge, uphill where the clay had been liquefied by the rain, past strips of stubble land and bushes touched with green here and there, and into a birch forest growing on both sides of the road. In the forest it was almost hot, no wind could be felt. The birches with their sticky green leaves were motionless, and lilac-colored flowers and the first blades of green grass were pushing up and lifting last year's leaves. The coarse evergreen color of the small fir trees scattered here and there among the birches was an unpleasant reminder of winter. On entering the forest the horses began to snort and sweated visibly.

Peter the footman made some remark to the coachman; the latter assented. But apparently the coachman's sympathy was not enough for Peter, and he turned on the box toward his master.

"How pleasant it is, your excellency!" he said with a respectful smile.

"What?"

"It's pleasant, your excellency!"

"What is he talking about?" thought Prince Andrew. "Oh, the spring, I suppose," he thought as he turned round. "Yes, really everything is green already. . . . How early! The birches and cherry and alders too are coming out. . . . But the oaks show no sign yet. Ah, here is one oak!"

At the edge of the road stood an oak. Probably ten times the age of the birches that formed the forest, it was ten times as thick and twice as tall as they. It was an enormous tree, its girth twice as great as a man could embrace, and evidently long ago some of its branches had been broken off and its bark scarred. With its huge ungainly limbs sprawling unsymmetrically, and its gnarled hands and fingers, it stood an aged, stern, and scornful monster among the smiling birch trees. Only the dead-looking evergreen firs dotted about in the forest, and this oak, refused to yield to the charm of spring or notice either the spring or the sunshine.

"Spring, love, happiness!" this oak seemed to say. "Are you not weary of that stupid, meaningless, constantly repeated fraud? Always the same and always a fraud! There is no spring, no sun, no happiness! Look at those cramped dead firs, ever the same, and at me too, sticking out my broken and barked fingers just where they have grown, whether from my back or my sides: as they have grown so I stand, and I do not believe in your hopes and your lies."

As he passed through the forest Prince Andrew turned several times to look at that oak, as if expecting something from it. Under the oak, too, were flowers and grass, but it stood among them scowling, rigid, misshapen, and grim as ever.

"Yes, the oak is right, a thousand times right," thought Prince Andrew. "Let others—the young—yield afresh to that fraud, but we know life, our life is finished!"

A whole sequence of new thoughts, hopeless but mournfully pleasant, rose in his soul in connection with that tree. During this journey he, as it were, considered his life afresh and arrived at his old conclusion, restful in its hopelessness: that it was not for him to begin anything anew—but that he must live out his life, content to do no harm, and not disturbing himself or desiring anything.

PRINCE ANDREW had to see the Marshal of the Nobility for the district in connection with the affairs of the Ryazán estate of which he was trustee. This Marshal was Count Ilyá Rostóv, and in the middle of May Prince Andrew went to visit him.

It was now hot spring weather. The whole forest was already clothed in

green. It was dusty and so hot that on passing near water one longed to bathe.

Prince Andrew, depressed and preoccupied with the business about which he had to speak to the Marshal, was driving up the avenue in the grounds of the Rostóvs' house at Otrádnoe. He heard merry girlish cries behind some trees on the right and saw a group of girls running to cross the path of his calèche. Ahead of the rest and nearer to him ran a dark-haired, remarkably slim, pretty girl in a yellow chintz dress, with a white handkerchief on her head from under which loose locks of hair escaped. The girl was shouting something but, seeing that he was a stranger, ran back laughing without looking at him.

Suddenly, he did not know why, he felt a pang. The day was so beautiful, the sun so bright, everything around so gay, but that slim pretty girl did not know, or wish to know, of his existence and was contented and cheerful in her own separate—probably foolish—but bright and happy life. "What is she so glad about? What is she thinking of? Not of the military regulations or of the arrangement of the Ryazán serfs' quitrents. Of what is she thinking? Why is she so happy?" Prince Andrew asked himself with instinctive curiosity.

In 1809 Count Ilyá Rostóv was living at Otrádnoe just as he had done in former years, that is, entertaining almost the whole province with hunts, theatricals, dinners, and music. He was glad to see Prince Andrew, as he was to see any new visitor, and insisted on his staying the night.

During the dull day, in the course of which he was entertained by his elderly hosts and by the more important of the visitors (the old count's house was crowded on account of an approaching name day), Prince Andrew repeatedly glanced at Natásha, gay and laughing among the younger members of the company, and asked himself each time, "What is she thinking about? Why is she so glad?"

That night, alone in new surroundings, he was long unable to sleep. He read awhile and then put out his candle, but relit it. It was hot in the room, the inside shutters of which were closed. He was cross with the stupid old man (as he called Rostóv), who had made him stay by assuring him that some necessary documents had not yet arrived from town, and he was vexed with himself for having stayed.

He got up and went to the window to open it. As soon as he opened the shutters the moonlight, as if it had long been watching for this, burst into the room. He opened the casement. The night was fresh, bright, and very still. Just before the window was a row of pollard trees, looking black on one side and with a silvery light on the other. Beneath the trees grew some kind of lush, wet, bushy vegetation with silver-lit leaves and stems here

and there. Farther back beyond the dark trees a roof glittered with dew, to the right was a leafy tree with brilliantly white trunk and branches, and above it shone the moon, nearly at its full, in a pale, almost starless, spring sky. Prince Andrew leaned his elbows on the window ledge and his eyes rested on that sky.

His room was on the first floor. Those in the rooms above were also awake. He heard female voices overhead.

"Just once more," said a girlish voice above him which Prince Andrew recognized at once.

"But when are you coming to bed?" replied another voice.

"I won't, I can't sleep, what's the use? Come now for the last time."

Two girlish voices sang a musical passage—the end of some song.

"Oh, how lovely! Now go to sleep, and there's an end of it."

"You go to sleep, but I can't," said the first voice, coming nearer to the window. She was evidently leaning right out, for the rustle of her dress and even her breathing could be heard. Everything was stone-still, like the moon and its light and the shadows. Prince Andrew, too, dared not stir, for fear of betraying his unintentional presence.

"Sónya! Sónya!" he again heard the first speaker. "Oh, how can you sleep? Only look how glorious it is! Ah, how glorious! Do wake up, Sónya!" she said almost with tears in her voice. "There never, never was such a lovely night before!"

Sónya made some reluctant reply.

"Do just come and see what a moon! . . . Oh, how lovely! Come here. . . . Darling, sweetheart, come here! There, you see? I feel like sitting down on my heels, putting my arms round my knees like this, straining tight, as tight as possible, and flying away! Like this. . . ." *

"Take care, you'll fall out."

He heard the sound of a scuffle and Sónya's disapproving voice: "It's past one o'clock."

"Oh, you only spoil things for me. All right, go, go!"

Again all was silent, but Prince Andrew knew she was still sitting there. From time to time he heard a soft rustle and at times a sigh.

"O God, O God! What does it mean?" she suddenly exclaimed. "To bed then, if it must be!" and she slammed the casement.

"For her I might as well not exist!" thought Prince Andrew while he

* Natásha's fancy tallies with one Tolstóy himself had at the age of seven or eight. Under its influence he actually threw himself out of a window some eighteen feet from the ground. He was picked up unconscious. This resulted in a slight concussion of the brain, but after sleeping eighteen hours on end he recovered and experienced no further ill effect.—A.M.

listened to her voice, for some reason expecting yet fearing that she might
say something about him. "There she is again! As if it were on purpose,"
thought he.

In his soul there suddenly arose such an unexpected turmoil of youthful
thoughts and hopes, contrary to the whole tenor of his life, that unable to
explain his condition to himself he lay down and fell asleep at once.

NEXT MORNING, having taken leave of no one but the count, and not wait-
ing for the ladies to appear, Prince Andrew set off for home.

It was already the beginning of June when on his return journey he
drove into the birch forest where the gnarled old oak had made so strange
and memorable an impression on him. In the forest the harness bells
sounded yet more muffled than they had done six weeks before, for now all
was thick, shady, and dense, and the young firs dotted about in the forest
did not jar on the general beauty but, lending themselves to the mood
around, were delicately green with fluffy young shoots.

The whole day had been hot. Somewhere a storm was gathering, but
only a small cloud had scattered some raindrops lightly, sprinkling the
road and the sappy leaves. The left side of the forest was dark in the shade,
the right side glittered in the sunlight, wet and shiny and scarcely swayed
by the breeze. Everything was in blossom, the nightingales trilled, and
their voices reverberated now near, now far away.

"Yes, here in this forest was that oak with which I agreed," thought
Prince Andrew. "But where is it?" he again wondered, gazing at the left
side of the road, and without recognizing it he looked with admiration at
the very oak he sought. The old oak, quite transfigured, spreading out a
canopy of sappy dark-green foliage, stood rapt and slightly trembling in
the rays of the evening sun. Neither gnarled fingers nor old scars nor old
doubts and sorrows were any of them in evidence now. Through the hard
century-old bark, even where there were no twigs, leaves had sprouted such
as one could hardly believe the old veteran could have produced.

"Yes, it is the same oak," thought Prince Andrew, and all at once he
was seized by an unreasoning springtime feeling of joy and renewal. All
the best moments of his life suddenly rose to his memory. Austerlitz with
the lofty heavens, his wife's dead reproachful face, Pierre at the ferry, that
girl thrilled by the beauty of the night, and that night itself and the moon,
and . . . all this rushed suddenly to his mind.

"No, life is not over at thirty-one!" Prince Andrew suddenly decided
finally and decisively. "It is not enough for me to know what I have in me
—everyone must know it: Pierre, and that young girl who wanted to fly
away into the sky, everyone must know me, so that my life may not be

lived for myself alone while others live so apart from it, but so that it may be reflected in them all, and they and I may live in harmony!"

On reaching home Prince Andrew decided to go to Petersburg that autumn and found all sorts of reasons for this decision. A whole series of sensible and logical considerations showing it to be essential for him to go to Petersburg, and even to re-enter the service, kept springing up in his mind. He could not now understand how he could ever even have doubted the necessity of taking an active share in life, just as a month before he had not understood how the idea of leaving the quiet country could ever enter his head. It now seemed clear to him that all his experience of life must be senselessly wasted unless he applied it to some kind of work and again played an active part in life. He did not even remember how formerly, on the strength of similar wretched logical arguments, it had seemed obvious that he would be degrading himself if he now, after the lessons he had had in life, allowed himself to believe in the possibility of being useful and in the possibility of happiness or love. Now reason suggested quite the opposite. After that journey to Ryazán he found the country dull; his former pursuits no longer interested him, and often when sitting alone in his study he got up, went to the mirror, and gazed a long time at his own face. Then he would turn away to the portrait of his dead Lise, who with hair curled à la grecque looked tenderly and gaily at him out of the gilt frame. She did not now say those former terrible words to him, but looked simply, merrily, and inquisitively at him. And Prince Andrew, crossing his arms behind him, long paced the room, now frowning, now smiling, as he reflected on those irrational, inexpressible thoughts, secret as a crime, which altered his whole life and were connected with Pierre, with fame, with the girl at the window, the oak, and woman's beauty and love. And if anyone came into his room at such moments he was particularly cold, stern, and above all unpleasantly logical.

"My dear," Princess Mary entering at such a moment would say, "little Nicholas can't go out today, it's very cold."

"If it were hot," Prince Andrew would reply at such times very dryly to his sister, "he could go out in his smock, but as it is cold he must wear warm clothes, which were designed for that purpose. That is what follows from the fact that it is cold; and not that a child who needs fresh air should remain at home," he would add with extreme logic, as if punishing someone for those secret illogical emotions that stirred within him.

At such moments Princess Mary would think how intellectual work dries men up.

2. Speránski, Arakchéev, and Prince Andrew

Prince Andrew arrived in Petersburg in August, 1809. It was the time when the youthful Speránski * was at the zenith of his fame and his reforms were being pushed forward with the greatest energy. That same August the Emperor was thrown from his *calèche*, injured his leg, and remained three weeks at Peterhof, receiving Speránski every day and no one else. At that time the two famous decrees were being prepared that so agitated society [2]—abolishing court ranks and introducing examinations to qualify for the grades of Collegiate Assessor and State Councilor [3]—and not merely these but a whole state constitution, intended to change the existing order of government in Russia: legal, administrative, and financial, from the Council of State down to the district tribunals. Now those vague liberal dreams with which the Emperor Alexander had ascended the throne, and which he had tried to put into effect with the aid of his associates, Czartorýski, Novosíltsev, Kochubéy, and Stróganov—whom he himself in jest had called his *Comité de salut public*—were taking shape and being realized.

Now all these men were replaced by Speránski on the civil side, and Arakchéev [4] on the military. Soon after his arrival Prince Andrew, as a

* Count Michael Mikháylovich Speránski (1772-1839), reformist Russian statesman whom Napoleon once called "the only clear head in Russia."

[2] Nothing came of these two famous decrees beyond some purely formal changes at court and a certain amount of bribery to secure diplomas.—A.M.

[3] These were the sixth and fifth grades of the fourteen chins in the Civil Service, and were equivalent to the ranks of lieutenant colonel and colonel in the army.—A.M.

[4] Count Alexéy Arakchéev (1769-1834) was Inspector General of Artillery from 1803 onwards, and his reorganization of that arm largely contributed to Russia's success in the war of 1812. He became Minister of War in 1808, but took no active part in the campaign of 1812, during which and subsequently he was the Emperor's constant companion and intimate adviser.

He was much hated for his harsh cruelty, and his whole influence was reactionary. The Military Colonies he established to render the army partially self-supporting involved extreme hardships on the colonists and their families. They were precursors of the State Farms now compulsorily established in the U.S.S.R., though Arakchéev had no Ford tractors to rely on. After greatly embittering the people, the Colonies proved a complete failure.

Tolstóy's dislike of Arakchéev, who has been previously alluded to at Austerlitz, is plainly indicated both there and in this section. He is referred to again in Book Nine, Chapter 3.—A.M.

gentleman of the chamber, presented himself at court and at a levee. The Emperor, though he met him twice, did not favor him with a single word. It had always seemed to Prince Andrew before that he was antipathetic to the Emperor and that the latter disliked his face and personality generally, and in the cold, repellent glance the Emperor gave him, he now found further confirmation of this surmise. The courtiers explained the Emperor's neglect of him by His Majesty's displeasure at Bolkónski's not having served since 1805.

"I know myself that one cannot help one's sympathies and antipathies," thought Prince Andrew, "so it will not do to present my proposal for the reform of the army regulations to the Emperor personally, but the project will speak for itself."

He mentioned what he had written to an old field marshal, a friend of his father's. The field marshal made an appointment to see him, received him graciously, and promised to inform the Emperor. A few days later Prince Andrew received notice that he was to go to see the Minister of War, Count Arakchéev.

On the appointed day Prince Andrew entered Count Arakchéev's waiting room at nine in the morning.

He did not know Arakchéev personally, had never seen him, and all he had heard of him inspired him with but little respect for the man.

"He is Minister of War, a man trusted by the Emperor, and I need not concern myself about his personal qualities: he has been commissioned to consider my project, so he alone can get it adopted," thought Prince Andrew as he waited among a number of important and unimportant people in Count Arakchéev's waiting room.

During his service, chiefly as an adjutant, Prince Andrew had seen the anterooms of many important men, and the different types of such rooms were well known to him. Count Arakchéev's anteroom had quite a special character. The faces of the unimportant people awaiting their turn for an audience showed embarrassment and servility; the faces of those of higher rank expressed a common feeling of awkwardness, covered by a mask of unconcern and ridicule of themselves, their situation, and the person for whom they were waiting. Some walked thoughtfully up and down, others whispered and laughed. Prince Andrew heard the nickname "Síla André-evich" * and the words, "*Uncle* will give it to us hot," in reference to

* His real name was Alexéy Andréevich Arakchéev. In Russian many shades of feeling may be expressed by various uses of a man's Christian name, surname, and patronymic. The substitution of "Síla" (force) for Alexéy indicated the speaker's conception of Arakchéev's leading characteristic.—A.M.

Count Arakchéev. One general (an important personage), evidently feeling offended at having to wait so long, sat crossing and uncrossing his legs and smiling contemptuously to himself.

But the moment the door opened one feeling alone appeared on all faces—that of fear. Prince Andrew for the second time asked the adjutant on duty to take in his name, but received an ironical look and was told that his turn would come in due course. After some others had been shown in and out of the minister's room by the adjutant on duty, an officer who struck Prince Andrew by his humiliated and frightened air was admitted at that terrible door. This officer's audience lasted a long time. Then suddenly the grating sound of a harsh voice was heard from the other side of the door, and the officer—with pale face and trembling lips—came out and passed through the waiting room, clutching his head.

After this Prince Andrew was conducted to the door and the officer on duty said in a whisper, "To the right, at the window."

Prince Andrew entered a plain tidy room and saw at the table a man of forty with a long waist, a long closely cropped head, deep wrinkles, scowling brows above dull greenish-hazel eyes and an overhanging red nose. Arakchéev turned his head toward him without looking at him.

"What is your petition?" asked Arakchéev.

"I am not petitioning, your excellency," returned Prince Andrew quietly.

Arakchéev's eyes turned toward him.

"Sit down," said he. "Prince Bolkónski?"

"I am not petitioning about anything. His Majesty the Emperor has deigned to send your excellency a project submitted by me . . ."

"You see, my dear sir, I have read your project," interrupted Arakchéev, uttering only the first words amiably and then—again without looking at Prince Andrew—relapsing gradually into a tone of grumbling contempt. "You are proposing new military laws? There are many laws but no one to carry out the old ones. Nowadays everybody designs laws, it is easier writing than doing."

"I came at His Majesty the Emperor's wish to learn from your excellency how you propose to deal with the memorandum I have presented," said Prince Andrew politely.

"I have endorsed a resolution on your memorandum and sent it to the committee. I do not approve of it," said Arakchéev, rising and taking a paper from his writing table. "Here!" and he handed it to Prince Andrew.

Across the paper was scrawled in pencil, without capital letters, misspelled, and without punctuation: "Unsoundly constructed because re-

sembles an imitation of the French military code and from the Articles of
War needlessly deviating."

"To what committee has the memorandum been referred?" inquired
Prince Andrew.

"To the Committee on Army Regulations, and I have recommended
that your honor should be appointed a member, but without a salary."

Prince Andrew smiled.

"I don't want one."

"A member without salary," repeated Arakchéev. "I have the honor . . .
Eh! Call the next one! Who else is there?" he shouted, bowing to Prince
Andrew.

WHILE WAITING for the announcement of his appointment to the com-
mittee Prince Andrew looked up his former acquaintances, particularly
those he knew to be in power and whose aid he might need. In Petersburg
he now experienced the same feeling he had had on the eve of a battle,
when troubled by anxious curiosity and irresistibly attracted to the ruling
circles where the future, on which the fate of millions depended, was be-
ing shaped. From the irritation of the older men, the curiosity of the un-
initiated, the reserve of the initiated, the hurry and preoccupation of
everyone, and the innumerable committees and commissions of whose
existence he learned every day, he felt that now, in 1809, here in Peters-
burg a vast civil conflict was in preparation, the commander in chief of
which was a mysterious person he did not know, but who was supposed to
be a man of genius—Speránski. And this movement of reconstruction of
which Prince Andrew had a vague idea, and Speránski its chief promoter,
began to interest him so keenly that the question of the army regulations
quickly receded to a secondary place in his consciousness.

Prince Andrew was most favorably placed to secure a good reception in
the highest and most diverse Petersburg circles of the day. The reforming
party cordially welcomed and courted him, in the first place because he
was reputed to be clever and very well read, and secondly because by liber-
ating his serfs he had obtained the reputation of being a liberal. The party
of the old and dissatisfied, who censured the innovations, turned to him
expecting his sympathy in their disapproval of the reforms, simply because
he was the son of his father. The feminine society world welcomed him
gladly, because he was rich, distinguished, a good match, and almost a
newcomer, with a halo of romance on account of his supposed death and
the tragic loss of his wife. Besides this the general opinion of all who had
known him previously was that he had greatly improved during these last
five years, having softened and grown more manly, lost his former affecta-

tion, pride, and contemptuous irony, and acquired the serenity that comes with years. People talked about him, were interested in him, and wanted to meet him.

The day after his interview with Count Arakchéev, Prince Andrew spent the evening at Count Kochubéy's. He told the count of his interview with Síla Andréevich (Kochubéy spoke of Arakchéev by that nickname with the same vague irony Prince Andrew had noticed in the Minister of War's anteroom).

"*Mon cher,* even in this case you can't do without Michael Mikháylovich Speránski. He manages everything. I'll speak to him. He has promised to come this evening."

"What has Speránski to do with the army regulations?" asked Prince Andrew.

Kochubéy shook his head smilingly, as if surprised at Bolkónski's simplicity.

"We were talking to him about you a few days ago," Kochubéy continued, "and about your freed plowmen."

"Oh, is it you, Prince, who have freed your serfs?" said an old man of Catherine's day, turning contemptuously toward Bolkónski.

"It was a small estate that brought in no profit," replied Prince Andrew, trying to extenuate his action so as not to irritate the old man uselessly.

"Afraid of being late . . ." said the old man, looking at Kochubéy.

"There's one thing I don't understand," he continued. "Who will plow the land if they are set free? It is easy to write laws, but difficult to rule. . . . Just the same as now—I ask you, Count—who will be heads of the departments when everybody has to pass examinations?"

"Those who pass the examinations, I suppose," replied Kochubéy, crossing his legs and glancing round.

"Well, I have Pryánichnikov serving under me, a splendid man, a priceless man, but he's sixty. Is he to go up for examination?"

"Yes, that's a difficulty, as education is not at all general, but . . ."

Count Kochubéy did not finish. He rose, took Prince Andrew by the arm, and went to meet a tall, bald, fair man of about forty with a large open forehead and a long face of unusual and peculiar whiteness, who was just entering. The newcomer wore a blue swallow-tail coat with a cross suspended from his neck and a star on his left breast. It was Speránski. Prince Andrew recognized him at once, and felt a throb within him, as happens at critical moments of life. Whether it was from respect, envy, or anticipation, he did not know. Speránski's whole figure was of a peculiar type that made him easily recognizable. In the society in which Prince Andrew lived he had never seen anyone who together with awkward and

clumsy gestures possessed such calmness and self-assurance; he had never seen so resolute yet gentle an expression as that in those half-closed, rather humid eyes, or so firm a smile that expressed nothing; nor had he heard such a refined, smooth, soft voice; above all he had never seen such delicate whiteness of face or hands—hands which were broad, but very plump, soft, and white. Such whiteness and softness Prince Andrew had only seen on the faces of soldiers who had been long in hospital. This was Speránski, Secretary of State, reporter to the Emperor and his companion at Erfurt, where he had more than once met and talked with Napoleon.

Speránski did not shift his eyes from one face to another as people involuntarily do on entering a large company and was in no hurry to speak. He spoke slowly, with assurance that he would be listened to, and he looked only at the person with whom he was conversing.

Prince Andrew followed Speránski's every word and movement with particular attention. As happens to some people, especially to men who judge those near to them severely, he always on meeting anyone new— especially anyone whom, like Speránski, he knew by reputation—expected to discover in him the perfection of human qualities.

Speránski told Kochubéy he was sorry he had been unable to come sooner as he had been detained at the palace. He did not say that the Emperor had kept him, and Prince Andrew noticed this affectation of modesty. When Kochubéy introduced Prince Andrew, Speránski slowly turned his eyes to Bolkónski with his customary smile and looked at him in silence.

"I am very glad to make your acquaintance. I had heard of you, as everyone has," he said after a pause.

Kochubéy said a few words about the reception Arakchéev had given Bolkónski. Speránski smiled more markedly.

"The chairman of the Committee on Army Regulations is my good friend Monsieur Magnítski," he said, fully articulating every word and syllable, "and if you like I can put you in touch with him." He paused at the full stop. "I hope you will find him sympathetic and ready to co-operate in promoting all that is reasonable."

A circle soon formed round Speránski, and the old man who had talked about his subordinate Pryánichnikov addressed a question to him.

Prince Andrew without joining in the conversation watched every movement of Speránski's: this man, not long since an insignificant divinity student, who now, Bolkónski thought, held in his hands—those plump white hands—the fate of Russia. Prince Andrew was struck by the extraordinarily disdainful composure with which Speránski answered the old man. He appeared to address condescending words to him from an im-

measurable height. When the old man began to speak too loud, Speránski smiled and said he could not judge of the advantage or disadvantage of what pleased the sovereign.

Having talked for a little while in the general circle, Speránski rose and coming up to Prince Andrew took him along to the other end of the room. It was clear that he thought it necessary to interest himself in Bolkónski.

"I had no chance to talk with you, Prince, during the animated conversation in which that venerable gentleman involved me," he said with a mildly contemptuous smile, as if intimating by that smile that he and Prince Andrew understood the insignificance of the people with whom he had just been talking. This flattered Prince Andrew. "I have known of you for a long time: first from your action with regard to your serfs, a first example, of which it is very desirable that there should be more imitators; and secondly because you are one of those gentlemen of the chamber who have not considered themselves offended by the new decree concerning the ranks allotted to courtiers, which is causing so much gossip and tittle-tattle."

"No," said Prince Andrew, "my father did not wish me to take advantage of the privilege. I began the service from the lower grade."

"Your father, a man of the last century, evidently stands above our contemporaries who so condemn this measure which merely re-establishes natural justice."

"I think, however, that these condemnations have some ground," returned Prince Andrew, trying to resist Speránski's influence, of which he began to be conscious. He did not like to agree with him in everything and felt a wish to contradict. Though he usually spoke easily and well, he felt a difficulty in expressing himself now while talking with Speránski. He was too much absorbed in observing the famous man's personality.

"Grounds of personal ambition maybe," Speránski put in quietly.

"And of state interest to some extent," said Prince Andrew.

"What do you mean?" asked Speránski quietly, lowering his eyes.

"I am an admirer of Montesquieu," replied Prince Andrew, "and his idea that *le principe des monarchies est l'honneur me paraît incontestable. Certains droits et privilèges de la noblesse me paraissent être des moyens de soutenir ce sentiment.* [the principle of monarchies is honor seems to me incontestable. Certain rights and privileges for the aristocracy appear to me a means of maintaining that sentiment.]"

The smile vanished from Speránski's white face, which was much improved by the change. Probably Prince Andrew's thought interested him.

"*Si vous envisagez la question sous ce point de vue* [If you regard the question from that point of view]," he began, pronouncing French with

evident difficulty, and speaking even slower than in Russian but quite calmly.

Speránski went on to say that honor, *l'honneur*, cannot be upheld by privileges harmful to the service; that honor, *l'honneur*, is either a negative concept of not doing what is blameworthy or it is a source of emulation in pursuit of commendation and rewards, which recognize it. His arguments were concise, simple, and clear.

"An institution upholding honor, the source of emulation, is one similar to the *Légion d'honneur* of the great Emperor Napoleon, not harmful but helpful to the success of the service, but not a class or court privilege."

"I do not dispute that, but it cannot be denied that court privileges have attained the same end," returned Prince Andrew. "Every courtier considers himself bound to maintain his position worthily."

"Yet you do not care to avail yourself of the privilege, Prince," said Speránski, indicating by a smile that he wished to finish amiably an argument which was embarrassing for his companion. "If you will do me the honor of calling on me on Wednesday," he added, "I will, after talking with Magnítski, let you know what may interest you, and shall also have the pleasure of a more detailed chat with you."

Closing his eyes, he bowed à la française, without taking leave, and trying to attract as little attention as possible, he left the room.

DURING the first weeks of his stay in Petersburg Prince Andrew felt the whole trend of thought he had formed during his life of seclusion quite overshadowed by the trifling cares that engrossed him in that city.

On returning home in the evening he would jot down in his notebook four or five necessary calls or appointments for certain hours. The mechanism of life, the arrangement of the day so as to be in time everywhere, absorbed the greater part of his vital energy. He did nothing, did not even think or find time to think, but only talked, and talked successfully, of what he had thought while in the country.

He sometimes noticed with dissatisfaction that he repeated the same remark on the same day in different circles. But he was so busy for whole days together that he had no time to notice that he was thinking of nothing.

As he had done on their first meeting at Kochubéy's, Speránski produced a strong impression on Prince Andrew on the Wednesday, when he received him tête-à-tête at his own house and talked to him long and confidentially.

To Bolkónski so many people appeared contemptible and insignificant creatures, and he so longed to find in someone the living ideal of that per-

fection toward which he strove, that he readily believed that in Speránski he had found this ideal of a perfectly rational and virtuous man. Had Speránski sprung from the same class as himself and possessed the same breeding and traditions, Bolkónski would soon have discovered his weak, human, unheroic sides; but as it was, Speránski's strange and logical turn of mind inspired him with respect all the more because he did not quite understand him. Moreover, Speránski, either because he appreciated the other's capacity or because he considered it necessary to win him to his side, showed off his dispassionate calm reasonableness before Prince Andrew and flattered him with that subtle flattery which goes hand in hand with self-assurance and consists in a tacit assumption that one's companion is the only man besides oneself capable of understanding the folly of the rest of mankind and the reasonableness and profundity of one's own ideas.

During their long conversation on Wednesday evening, Speránski more than once remarked: "We regard everything that is above the common level of rooted custom . . ." or, with a smile: "But we want the wolves to be fed and the sheep to be safe . . ." or: "*They* cannot understand this . . ." and all in a way that seemed to say: "We, you and I, understand what *they* are and who *we* are."

This first long conversation with Speránski only strengthened in Prince Andrew the feeling he had experienced toward him at their first meeting. He saw in him a remarkable, clear-thinking man of vast intellect who by his energy and persistence had attained power, which he was using solely for the welfare of Russia. In Prince Andrew's eyes Speránski was the man he would himself have wished to be—one who explained all the facts of life reasonably, considered important only what was rational, and was capable of applying the standard of reason to everything. Everything seemed so simple and clear in Speránski's exposition that Prince Andrew involuntarily agreed with him about everything. If he replied and argued, it was only because he wished to maintain his independence and not submit to Speránski's opinions entirely. Everything was right and everything was as it should be: only one thing disconcerted Prince Andrew. This was Speránski's cold, mirrorlike look, which did not allow one to penetrate to his soul, and his delicate white hands, which Prince Andrew involuntarily watched as one does watch the hands of those who possess power. This mirrorlike gaze and those delicate hands irritated Prince Andrew, he knew not why. He was unpleasantly struck, too, by the excessive contempt for others that he observed in Speránski, and by the diversity of lines of argument he used to support his opinions. He made use of every kind of men-

tal device, except analogy, and passed too boldly, it seemed to Prince Andrew, from one to another. Now he would take up the position of a practical man and condemn dreamers; now that of a satirist, and laugh ironically at his opponents; now grow severely logical, or suddenly rise to the realm of metaphysics. (This last resource was one he very frequently employed.) He would transfer a question to metaphysical heights, pass on to definitions of space, time, and thought, and, having deduced the refutation he needed, would again descend to the level of the original discussion.

In general the trait of Speránski's mentality which struck Prince Andrew most was his absolute and unshakable belief in the power and authority of reason. It was evident that the thought could never occur to him which to Prince Andrew seemed so natural, namely, that it is after all impossible to express all one thinks; and that he had never felt the doubt, "Is not all I think and believe nonsense?" And it was just this peculiarity of Speránski's mind that particularly attracted Prince Andrew.

During the first period of their acquaintance Bolkónski felt a passionate admiration for him similar to that which he had once felt for Bonaparte. The fact that Speránski was the son of a village priest, and that stupid people might meanly despise him on account of his humble origin (as in fact many did), caused Prince Andrew to cherish his sentiment for him the more, and unconsciously to strengthen it.*

On that first evening Bolkónski spent with him, having mentioned the Commission for the Revision of the Code of Laws, Speránski told him sarcastically that the Commission had existed for a hundred and fifty years, had cost millions, and had done nothing except that Rosenkampf had stuck labels on the corresponding paragraphs of the different codes.

"And that is all the state has for the millions it has spent," said he. "We want to give the Senate new juridical powers, but we have no laws. That is why it is a sin for men like you, Prince, not to serve in these times!"

Prince Andrew said that for that work an education in jurisprudence was needed which he did not possess.

"But nobody possesses it, so what would you have? It is a vicious circle from which we must break a way out."

* *Prince Andrew's impression of Speránski indicates the respect and admiration an energetic and clever man felt for the still stronger and more active mind of a very capable statesman; but two unfavorable, half-suppressed, impressions are also indicated: the slight dislike of a nobleman for the parvenu son of a village priest, and a dim consciousness of Speránski's chief weaknesses—his contemptuous treatment of other people and his calm assurance that logic and theoretical reasoning can solve anything.—*A.M.

A week later Prince Andrew was a member of the Committee on Army Regulations and—what he had not at all expected—was chairman of a section of the committee for the revision of the laws. At Speránski's request he took the first part of the Civil Code that was being drawn up and, with the aid of the Code Napoléon and the Institutes of Justinian, he worked at formulating the section on Personal Rights.

3. Pierre and the Petersburg Freemasons. He visits Joseph Alexéevich. Reconciliation with Hélène

NEARLY TWO YEARS before this, in 1808, Pierre on returning to Petersburg after visiting his estates had involuntarily found himself in a leading position among the Petersburg Freemasons. He arranged dining and funeral lodge meetings, enrolled new members, and busied himself uniting various lodges and acquiring authentic charters. He gave money for the erection of temples and supplemented as far as he could the collection of alms, in regard to which the majority of members were stingy and irregular. He supported almost singlehanded a poorhouse the order had founded in Petersburg.

His life meanwhile continued as before, with the same infatuations and dissipations. He liked to dine and drink well, and though he considered it immoral and humiliating could not resist the temptations of the bachelor circles in which he moved.

Amid the turmoil of his activities and distractions, however, Pierre at the end of a year began to feel that the more firmly he tried to rest upon it, the more Masonic ground on which he stood gave way under him. At the same time he felt that the deeper the ground sank under him the closer bound he involuntarily became to the order. When he had joined the Freemasons he had experienced the feeling of one who confidently steps onto the smooth surface of a bog. When he put his foot down it sank in. To make quite sure of the firmness of the ground, he put his other foot down and sank deeper still, became stuck in it, and involuntarily waded knee-deep in the bog.

Joseph Alexéevich was not in Petersburg—he had of late stood aside from the affairs of the Petersburg lodges and lived almost entirely in Moscow. All the members of the lodges were men Pierre knew in ordinary life, and it was difficult for him to regard them merely as Brothers in Freemasonry and not as Prince B. or Iván Vasílevich D., whom he knew in society mostly as weak and insignificant men. Under the Masonic aprons

and insignia he saw the uniforms and decorations at which they aimed in ordinary life. Often after collecting alms, and reckoning up twenty to thirty rubles received for the most part in promises from a dozen members, of whom half were as well able to pay as himself, Pierre remembered the Masonic vow in which each Brother promised to devote all his belongings to his neighbor, and doubts on which he tried not to dwell arose in his soul.

He divided the Brothers he knew into four categories. In the first he put those who did not take an active part in the affairs of the lodges or in human affairs, but were exclusively occupied with the mystical science of the order: with questions of the threefold designation of God, the three primordial elements—sulphur, mercury, and salt *—or the meaning of the square and all the various figures of the temple of Solomon. Pierre respected this class of Brothers to which the elder ones chiefly belonged, including, Pierre thought, Joseph Alexéevich himself, but he did not share their interests. His heart was not in the mystical aspect of Freemasonry.

In the second category Pierre reckoned himself and others like him, seeking and vacillating, who had not yet found in Freemasonry a straight and comprehensible path, but hoped to do so.

In the third category he included those Brothers (the majority) who saw nothing in Freemasonry but the external forms and ceremonies, and prized the strict performance of these forms without troubling about their purport or significance. Such were Willarski and even the Grand Master of the principal lodge.

Finally, to the fourth category also a great many Brothers belonged, particularly those who had lately joined. These according to Pierre's observations were men who had no belief in anything, nor desire for anything, but joined the Freemasons merely to associate with the wealthy young Brothers who were influential through their connections or rank, and of whom there were very many in the lodge.

Pierre began to feel dissatisfied with what he was doing. Freemasonry, at any rate as he saw it here, sometimes seemed to him based merely on externals. He did not think of doubting Freemasonry itself, but suspected that Russian Masonry had taken a wrong path and deviated from its original principles. And so toward the end of the year he went abroad to be initiated into the higher secrets of the order.

* Some Freemasons were interested in discovering the laws of nature, but approached the subject mystically and relied on alchemistic theories for achieving the transmutation of elements, and so on. The Rosicrucian Masons, to whom the prominent Moscow Masons, Nóvikov, Schwartz, and Pozdéev, belonged, concerned themselves with such matters.—A.M.

In the summer of 1809 Pierre returned to Petersburg. Our Freemasons knew from correspondence with those abroad that Bezúkhov had obtained the confidence of many highly placed persons, had been initiated into many mysteries, had been raised to a higher grade, and was bringing back with him much that might conduce to the advantage of the Masonic cause in Russia. The Petersburg Freemasons all came to see him, tried to ingratiate themselves with him, and it seemed to them all that he was preparing something for them and concealing it.

A solemn meeting of the lodge of the second degree was convened, at which Pierre promised to communicate to the Petersburg Brothers what he had to deliver to them from the highest leaders of their order. The meeting was a full one. After the usual ceremonies Pierre rose and began his address.

"Dear Brothers," he began, blushing and stammering, with a written speech in his hand, "it is not sufficient to observe our mysteries in the seclusion of our lodge—we must act—act! We are drowsing, but we must act." Pierre raised his notebook and began to read.

"For the dissemination of pure truth and to secure the triumph of virtue," he read, "we must cleanse men from prejudice, diffuse principles in harmony with the spirit of the times, undertake the education of the young, unite ourselves in indissoluble bonds with the wisest men, boldly yet prudently overcome superstitions, infidelity, and folly, and form of those devoted to us a body linked together by unity of purpose and possessed of authority and power.

"To attain this end we must secure a preponderance of virtue over vice and must endeavor to secure that the honest man may, even in this world, receive a lasting reward for his virtue. But in these great endeavors we are gravely hampered by the political institutions of today. What is to be done in these circumstances? To favor revolutions, overthrow everything, repel force by force? . . . No! We are very far from that. Every violent reform deserves censure, for it quite fails to remedy evil while men remain what they are, and also because wisdom needs no violence.

"The whole plan of our order should be based on the idea of preparing men of firmness and virtue bound together by unity of conviction—aiming at the punishment of vice and folly, and patronizing talent and virtue: raising worthy men from the dust and attaching them to our Brotherhood. Only then will our order have the power unobtrusively to bind the hands of the protectors of disorder and to control them without their being aware of it. In a word, we must found a form of government holding universal sway, which should be diffused over the whole world without destroying the bonds of citizenship, and beside which all other governments can con-

tinue in their customary course and do everything except what impedes the great aim of our order, which is to obtain for virtue the victory over vice. This aim was that of Christianity itself. It taught men to be wise and good and for their own benefit to follow the example and instruction of the best and wisest men.

"At that time, when everything was plunged in darkness, preaching alone was of course sufficient. The novelty of Truth endowed her with special strength, but now we need much more powerful methods. It is now necessary that man, governed by his senses, should find in virtue a charm palpable to those senses. It is impossible to eradicate the passions; but we must strive to direct them to a noble aim, and it is therefore necessary that everyone should be able to satisfy his passions within the limits of virtue. Our order should provide means to that end.

"As soon as we have a certain number of worthy men in every state, each of them again training two others and all being closely united, everything will be possible for our order, which has already in secret accomplished much for the welfare of mankind."

This speech not only made a strong impression, but created excitement in the lodge. The majority of the Brothers, seeing in it dangerous designs of Illuminism,* met it with a coldness that surprised Pierre. The Grand Master began answering him, and Pierre began developing his views with more and more warmth. It was long since there had been so stormy a meeting. Parties were formed, some accusing Pierre of Illuminism, others supporting him. At that meeting he was struck for the first time by the endless variety of men's minds, which prevents a truth from ever presenting itself identically to two persons. Even those members who seemed to be on his side understood him in their own way with limitations and alterations he could not agree to, as what he always wanted most was to convey his thought to others just as he himself understood it.

* *The reference is to a German group founded in 1776 by Adam Weishaupt. It had a conspiratorial organization, with strict subordination of members to leaders and a secret aim known only to those at the head of the order; viz., to substitute republican for monarchical institutions. The Illuminati were officially suppressed by the Bavarian government in 1785, but their tendency continued to exert influence among other Masonic orders. In Moscow Professor Schwartz headed a group of Martinists who were called Illuminati and like the Bavarian group were Cabalists. The regular program of Freemasonry included submission to the government and noninterference with political affairs, but the contrary tendency had some influence in the Russian branches, and their connection with the "Decembrist" conspiracy in 1825 led to their suppression by Nicholas I.—*A.M.*

At the end of the meeting the Grand Master with irony and ill-will reproved Bezúkhov for his vehemence and said it was not love of virtue alone, but also a love of strife that had moved him in the dispute. Pierre did not answer him and asked briefly whether his proposal would be accepted. He was told that it would not, and without waiting for the usual formalities he left the lodge and went home.

AGAIN PIERRE was overtaken by the depression he so dreaded. For three days after the delivery of his speech at the lodge he lay on a sofa at home receiving no one and going nowhere.*

It was just then that he received a letter from his wife, who implored him to see her, telling him how grieved she was about him and how she wished to devote her whole life to him.

At the end of the letter she informed him that in a few days she would return to Petersburg from abroad.

Following this letter one of the Masonic Brothers whom Pierre respected less than the others forced his way in to see him and, turning the conversation upon Pierre's matrimonial affairs, by way of fraternal advice expressed the opinion that his severity to his wife was wrong and that he was neglecting one of the first rules of Freemasonry by not forgiving the penitent.

At the same time his mother-in-law, Prince Vasíli's wife, sent to him imploring him to come if only for a few minutes to discuss a most important matter. Pierre saw that there was a conspiracy against him and that they wanted to reunite him with his wife, and in the mood he then was, this was not even unpleasant to him. Nothing mattered to him. Nothing in life seemed to him of much importance, and under the influence of the depression that possessed him he valued neither his liberty nor his resolution to punish his wife.

"No one is right and no one is to blame; so she too is not to blame," he thought.

If he did not at once give his consent to a reunion with his wife, it was only because in his state of depression he did not feel able to take any step. Had his wife come to him, he would not have turned her away. Compared to what preoccupied him, was it not a matter of indifference whether he lived with his wife or not?

Without replying either to his wife or his mother-in-law, Pierre late one

* *This incident recalls Tolstóy's own experience on the few occasions when he ventured to make a public speech—to him always a trying ordeal and one in which he had little success.*—A.M.

night prepared for a journey and started for Moscow to see Joseph Alexé-evich. This is what he noted in his diary:

Moscow, 17th November

I have just returned from my benefactor, and hasten to write down what I have experienced. Joseph Alexéevich is living poorly and has for three years been suffering from a painful disease of the bladder. No one has ever heard him utter a groan or a word of complaint. From morning till late at night, except when he eats his very plain food, he is working at science. He received me graciously and made me sit down on the bed on which he lay. I made the sign of the Knights of the East and of Jerusalem, and he responded in the same manner, asking me with a mild smile what I had learned and gained in the Prussian and Scottish lodges.* I told him everything as best I could, and told him what I had proposed to our Petersburg lodge, of the bad reception I had encountered, and of my rupture with the Brothers. Joseph Alexéevich, having remained silent and thoughtful for a good while, told me his view of the matter, which at once lit up for me my whole past and the future path I should follow. He surprised me by asking whether I remembered the threefold aim of the order: (1) The preservation and study of the mystery. (2) The purification and reformation of oneself for its reception, and (3) The improvement of the human race by striving for such purification. Which is the principal aim of these three? Certainly self-reformation and self-purification. Only to this aim can we always strive independently of circumstances. But at the same time just this aim demands the greatest efforts of us; and so, led astray by pride, losing sight of this aim, we occupy ourselves either with the mystery which in our impurity we are unworthy to receive, or seek the reformation of the human race while ourselves setting an example of baseness and profligacy. Illuminism is not a pure doctrine, just because it is attracted by social activity and puffed up by pride. On this ground Joseph Alexéevich condemned my speech and my whole activity, and in the depth of my soul I agreed with him. Talking of my family affairs he said to me, "the chief duty of a true Mason, as I have told you, lies in perfecting himself. We often think that by removing all the difficulties of our life we shall more quickly reach our aim, but on the contrary, my dear sir, it is only in the midst of worldly cares that we can attain our three chief aims: (1) Self-knowledge—for man can only know himself by comparison, (2) Self-perfecting, which can only be attained by conflict, and (3) The attainment of the chief

* These "Scottish" Masonic lodges were not in Scotland. Certain German lodges were so called at that time.—A.M.

virtue—love of death. Only the vicissitudes of life can show us its vanity and develop our innate love of death or of rebirth to a new life." These words are all the more remarkable because, in spite of his great physical sufferings, Joseph Alexéevich is never weary of life though he loves death, for which—in spite of the purity and loftiness of his inner man—he does not yet feel himself sufficiently prepared. My benefactor then explained to me fully the meaning of the Great Square of creation and pointed out to me that the numbers three and seven are the basis of everything. He advised me not to avoid intercourse with the Petersburg Brothers, but to take up only second-grade posts in the lodge, to try, while diverting the Brothers from pride, to turn them toward the true path of self-knowledge and self-perfecting. Besides this he advised me for myself personally above all to keep a watch over myself, and to that end he gave me a notebook, the one I am now writing in and in which I will in future note down all my actions.

Petersburg, 23rd November

I am again living with my wife. My mother-in-law came to me in tears and said that Hélène was here and that she implored me to hear her; that she was innocent and unhappy at my desertion, and much more. I knew that if I once let myself see her I should not have strength to go on refusing what she wanted. In my perplexity I did not know whose aid and advice to seek. Had my benefactor been here he would have told me what to do. I went to my room and reread Joseph Alexéevich's letters and recalled my conversations with him, and deduced from it all that I ought not to refuse a suppliant, and ought to reach a helping hand to everyone—especially to one so closely bound to me—and that I must bear my cross. But if I forgive her for the sake of doing right, then let union with her have only a spiritual aim. That is what I decided, and what I wrote to Joseph Alexéevich. I told my wife that I begged her to forget the past, to forgive me whatever wrong I may have done her, and that I had nothing to forgive. It gave me joy to tell her this. She need not know how hard it was for me to see her again. I have settled on the upper floor of this big house and am experiencing a happy feeling of regeneration.

4. *Hélène's social success. Her salon and relations with Borís*

AT THAT TIME, as always happens, the highest society that met at court and at the grand balls was divided into several circles, each with its own particular tone. The largest of these was the French circle of the

Napoleonic alliance, the circle of Count Rumyántsev and Caulaincourt.*
In this group Hélène, as soon as she had settled in Petersburg with her
husband, took a very prominent place. She was visited by the members of
the French embassy and by many belonging to that circle and noted for
their intellect and polished manners.

Hélène had been at Erfurt during the famous meeting of the Emperors
and had brought from there these connections with the Napoleonic nota-
bilities.[2] At Erfurt her success had been brilliant. Napoleon himself had
noticed her in the theater and said of her: "*C'est un superbe animal*
[That's a superb animal]." Her success as a beautiful and elegant woman
did not surprise Pierre, for she had become even handsomer than before.
What did surprise him was that during these last two years his wife had
succeeded in gaining the reputation "*d'une femme charmante, aussi spiri-
tuelle que belle* [of a charming woman, as witty as she is lovely]." The
distinguished Prince de Ligne [3] wrote her eight-page letters. Bilíbin saved
up his epigrams to produce them in Countess Bezúkhova's presence. To
be received in the Countess Bezúkhova's salon was regarded as a diploma
of intellect. Young men read books before attending Hélène's evenings,

* Louis, Marquis de Caulaincourt, a French general and diplomatist (1772-
1827), was sent to Petersburg in 1801 to negotiate an understanding between
Russia and France. In 1807 he became ambassador at Petersburg. In 1808 he
was created Duc de Vicenza, and in 1812, after failing to dissuade Napoleon
from the enterprise, accompanied him on the invasion of Russia. After the
Restoration in France, Caulaincourt's name was placed on the proscription
list, but was struck off on Alexander's personal intervention.—A.M.

[2] At Erfurt in Prussia, in the autumn of 1808, a meeting which had been
arranged at Tilsit took place between Alexander, Napoleon, and the King of
Prussia; the Emperor of Austria was excluded as a punishment for his military
preparations. The agreement made at Tilsit was confirmed, and Prussia's lot
was mitigated. In exchange for a promise of nonintervention in Europe, Russia
received permission to annex Finland and take the Danubian provinces of
Turkey if she could. The gathering at Erfurt was numerous and sumptuous,
and the festivities included a series of triumphs and fetes.—A.M.

[3] Charles Joseph, Prince de Ligne (1735-1814), soldier, writer, and diplo-
matist, whose works were published in thirty-four volumes, was born at Brus-
sels. He took part in the Seven Years' War, became a lieutenant field marshal
and a friend of the Emperor Joseph II. He spent some years in Russia, accom-
panied Catherine the Great on her journey to the Crimea, and was made by
her a Russian field marshal. He subsequently visited Russia repeatedly, not
officially but as a man of culture and distinction belonging to the best so-
ciety.—A.M.

to have something to say in her salon, and secretaries of the embassy, and even ambassadors, confided diplomatic secrets to her, so that in a way Hélène was a power. Pierre, who knew she was very stupid, sometimes attended, with a strange feeling of perplexity and fear, her evenings and dinner parties, where politics, poetry, and philosophy were discussed. At these parties his feelings were like those of a conjuror who always expects his trick to be found out at any moment. But whether because stupidity was just what was needed to run such a salon, or because those who were deceived found pleasure in the deception, at any rate it remained unexposed and Hélène Bezúkhova's reputation as a lovely and clever woman became so firmly established that she could say the emptiest and stupidest things and yet everybody would go into raptures over every word of hers and look for a profound meaning in it of which she herself had no conception.

Pierre was just the husband needed for a brilliant society woman. He was that absent-minded crank, a *grand seigneur* husband who was in no one's way, and far from spoiling the high tone and general impression of the drawing room, he served, by the contrast he presented to her, as an advantageous background to his elegant and tactful wife. Pierre during the last two years, as a result of his continual absorption in abstract interests and his sincere contempt for all else, had acquired in his wife's circle, which did not interest him, that air of unconcern, indifference, and benevolence toward all, which cannot be acquired artificially and therefore inspires involuntary respect. He entered his wife's drawing room as one enters a theater, was acquainted with everybody, equally pleased to see everyone, and equally indifferent to them all. Sometimes he joined in a conversation which interested him and, regardless of whether any "gentlemen of the embassy" were present or not, lispingly expressed his views, which were sometimes not at all in accord with the accepted tone of the moment. But the general opinion concerning the queer husband of "the most distinguished woman in Petersburg" was so well established that no one took his freaks seriously.

Among the many young men who frequented her house every day, Borís Drubetskóy, who had already achieved great success in the service, was the most intimate friend of the Bezúkhov household since Hélène's return from Erfurt. Hélène spoke of him as "mon page" and treated him like a child. Her smile for him was the same as for everybody, but sometimes that smile made Pierre uncomfortable. Toward him Borís behaved with a particularly dignified and sad deference. This shade of deference also disturbed Pierre. He had suffered so painfully three years before from

the mortification to which his wife had subjected him that he now pro-
tected himself from the danger of its repetition, first by not being a hus-
band to his wife, and secondly by not allowing himself to suspect.

"No, now that she has become a bluestocking she has finally renounced
her former infatuations," he told himself. "There has never been an
instance of a bluestocking being carried away by affairs of the heart"—a
statement which, though gathered from an unknown source, he believed
implicitly. Yet strange to say Borís' presence in his wife's drawing room
(and he was almost always there) had a physical effect upon Pierre; it con-
stricted his limbs and destroyed the unconsciousness and freedom of his
movements.

"What a strange antipathy," thought Pierre, "yet I used to like him
very much."

In the eyes of the world Pierre was a great gentleman, the rather blind
and absurd husband of a distinguished wife, a clever crank who did noth-
ing but harmed nobody and was a first-rate, good-natured fellow. But a
complex and difficult process of internal development was taking place
all this time in Pierre's soul, revealing much to him and causing him
many spiritual doubts and joys.

5. Pierre's diary

Pierre went on with his diary, and this is what he wrote in it during
that time:

24th November

Got up at eight, read the Scriptures, then went to my duties. [By
Joseph Alexéevich's advice Pierre had entered the service of the state
and served on one of the committees.] Returned home for dinner
and dined alone—the countess had many visitors I do not like. I ate
and drank moderately and after dinner copied out some passages for
the Brothers. In the evening I went down to the countess and told a
funny story about B., and only remembered that I ought not to have
done so when everybody laughed loudly at it.

I am going to bed with a happy and tranquil mind. Great God,
help me to walk in Thy paths, (1) to conquer anger by calmness and
deliberation, (2) to vanquish lust by self-restraint and repulsion,
(3) to withdraw from worldliness, but not avoid (a) the service of
the state, (b) family duties, (c) relations with my friends, and (d)
the management of my affairs.

27th November

I got up late. On waking I lay long in bed yielding to sloth. O God, help and strengthen me that I may walk in Thy ways! Read the Scriptures, but without proper feeling. Brother Urúsov came and we talked about worldly vanities. He told me of the Emperor's new projects. I began to criticize them, but remembered my rules and my benefactor's words—that a true Freemason should be a zealous worker for the state when his aid is required and a quiet onlooker when not called on to assist. My tongue is my enemy. Brothers G. V. and O. visited me and we had a preliminary talk about the reception of a new Brother. They laid on me the duty of Rhetor. I feel myself weak and unworthy. Then our talk turned to the interpretation of the seven pillars and steps of the Temple, the seven sciences, the seven virtues, the seven vices, and the seven gifts of the Holy Spirit. Brother O. was very eloquent. In the evening the admission took place. The new decoration of the premises contributed much to the magnificence of the spectacle. It was Borís Drubetskóy who was admitted. I nominated him and was the Rhetor. A strange feeling agitated me all the time I was alone with him in the dark chamber. I caught myself harboring a feeling of hatred toward him which I vainly tried to overcome. That is why I should really like to save him from evil and lead him into the path of truth, but evil thoughts of him did not leave me. It seemed to me that his object in entering the Brotherhood was merely to be intimate and in favor with members of our lodge. Apart from the fact that he had asked me several times whether N. and S. were members of our lodge (a question to which I could not reply) and that according to my observation he is incapable of feeling respect for our holy order and is too preoccupied and satisfied with the outer man to desire spiritual improvement, I had no cause to doubt him, but he seemed to me insincere, and all the time I stood alone with him in the dark temple it seemed to me that he was smiling contemptuously at my words, and I wished really to stab his bare breast with the sword I-held to it. I could not be eloquent, nor could I frankly mention my doubts to the Brothers and to the Grand Master. Great Architect of Nature, help me to find the true path out of the labyrinth of lies!

After this, three pages were left blank in the diary, and then the following was written:

I have had a long and instructive talk alone with Brother V., who advised me to hold fast by Brother A. Though I am unworthy, much was revealed to me. Adonai is the name of the creator of the world. Elohim is the name of the ruler of all. The third name is the name unutterable which means the *All*. Talks with Brother V. strengthen,

refresh, and support me in the path of virtue. In his presence doubt
has no place. The distinction between the poor teachings of mun-
dane science and our sacred all-embracing teaching is clear to me.
Human sciences dissect everything to comprehend it, and kill every-
thing to examine it. In the holy science of our order all is one, all
is known in its entirety and life. The Trinity—the three elements of
matter—are sulphur, mercury, and salt. Sulphur is of an oily and
fiery nature; in combination with salt by its fiery nature it arouses a
desire in the latter by means of which it attracts mercury, seizes it,
holds it, and in combination produces other bodies. Mercury is a
fluid, volatile, spiritual essence. Christ, the Holy Spirit, Him! . . .

3rd December

Awoke late, read the Scriptures but was apathetic. Afterwards
went and paced up and down the large hall. I wished to meditate,
but instead my imagination pictured an occurrence of four years ago,
when Dólokhov, meeting me in Moscow after our duel, said he hoped
I was enjoying perfect peace of mind in spite of my wife's absence.
At the time I gave him no answer. Now I recalled every detail of that
meeting and in my mind gave him the most malevolent and bitter
replies. I recollected myself and drove away that thought only when
I found myself glowing with anger, but I did not sufficiently repent.
Afterwards Borís Drubetskóy came and began relating various ad-
ventures. His coming vexed me from the first, and I said something
disagreeable to him. He replied. I flared up and said much that was
unpleasant and even rude to him. He became silent, and I recol-
lected myself only when it was too late. My God, I cannot get on
with him at all. The cause of this is my egotism. I set myself above
him and so become much worse than he, for he is lenient to my rude-
ness while I on the contrary nourish contempt for him. O God, grant
that in his presence I may rather see my own vileness, and behave so
that he too may benefit. After dinner I fell asleep and as I was drows-
ing off I clearly heard a voice saying in my left ear, "Thy day!"

I dreamed that I was walking in the dark and was suddenly sur-
rounded by dogs, but I went on undismayed. Suddenly a smallish dog
seized my left thigh with its teeth and would not let go. I began to
throttle it with my hands. Scarcely had I torn it off before another,
a bigger one, began biting me. I lifted it up, but the higher I lifted
it the bigger and heavier it grew. And suddenly Brother A. came and,
taking my arm, led me to a building to enter which we had to pass
along a narrow plank. I stepped on it, but it bent and gave way and
I began to clamber up a fence which I could scarcely reach with my
hands. After much effort I dragged myself up, so that my legs hung
down on one side and my body on the other. I looked round and

saw Brother A. standing on the fence and pointing me to a broad avenue and garden, and in the garden was a large and beautiful building. I woke up. O Lord, great Architect of Nature, help me to tear from myself these dogs—my passions—especially the last, which unites in itself the strength of all the former ones, and aid me to enter that temple of virtue to a vision of which I attained in my dream.

7th December

I dreamed that Joseph Alexéevich was sitting in my house, and that I was very glad and wished to entertain him. It seemed as if I chattered incessantly with other people and suddenly remembered that this could not please him, and I wished to come close to him and embrace him. But as soon as I drew near I saw that his face had changed and grown young, and he was quietly telling me something about the teaching of our order, but so softly that I could not hear it. Then it seemed that we all left the room and something strange happened. We were sitting or lying on the floor. He was telling me something, and I wished to show him my sensibility, and not listening to what he was saying I began picturing to myself the condition of my inner man and the grace of God sanctifying me. And tears came into my eyes, and I was glad he noticed this. But he looked at me with vexation and jumped up, breaking off his remarks. I felt abashed and asked whether what he had been saying did not concern me; but he did not reply, gave me a kind look, and then we suddenly found ourselves in my bedroom where there is a double bed. He lay down on the edge of it and I burned with longing to caress him and lie down too. And he said, "Tell me frankly what is your chief temptation? Do you know it? I think you know it already." Abashed by this question, I replied that sloth was my chief temptation. He shook his head incredulously; and even more abashed, I said that though I was living with my wife as he advised, I was not living with her as her husband. To this he replied that one should not deprive a wife of one's embraces and gave me to understand that that was my duty. But I replied that I should be ashamed to do it, and suddenly everything vanished. And I awoke and found in my mind the text from the Gospel: "The life was the light of men. And the light shineth in darkness; and the darkness comprehended it not." Joseph Alexéevich's face had looked young and bright. That day I received a letter from my benefactor in which he wrote about "conjugal duties."

9th December

I had a dream from which I awoke with a throbbing heart. I saw that I was in Moscow in my house, in the big sitting room, and Joseph Alexéevich came in from the drawing room. I seemed to know at once that the process of regeneration had already taken place in him, and I rushed to meet him. I embraced him and kissed his hands, and he said, "Hast thou noticed that my face is different?" I looked at him, still holding him in my arms, and saw that his face was young, but that he had no hair on his head and his features were quite changed. And I said, "I should have known you had I met you by chance," and I thought to myself, "Am I telling the truth?" And suddenly I saw him lying like a dead body; then he gradually recovered and went with me into my study carrying a large book of sheets of drawing paper; I said, "I drew that," and he answered by bowing his head. I opened the book, and on all the pages there were excellent drawings. And in my dream I knew that these drawings represented the love adventures of the soul with its beloved. And on its pages I saw a beautiful representation of a maiden in transparent garments and with a transparent body, flying up to the clouds. And I seemed to know that this maiden was nothing else than a representation of the Song of Songs. And looking at those drawings I dreamed I felt that I was doing wrong, but could not tear myself away from them. Lord, help me! My God, if Thy forsaking me is Thy doing, Thy will be done; but if I am myself the cause, teach me what I should do! I shall perish of my debauchery if Thou utterly desertest me!

6. *The Rostóvs in Petersburg. Berg engaged to Véra and demands her dowry*

THE ROSTÓVS' MONETARY AFFAIRS had not improved during the two years they had spent in the country.

Though Nicholas Rostóv had kept firmly to his resolution and was still serving modestly in an obscure regiment, spending comparatively little, the way of life at Otrádnoe—Mítenka's management of affairs, in particular—was such that the debts inevitably increased every year. The only resource obviously presenting itself to the old count was to apply for an official post, so he had come to Petersburg to look for one and also, as he said, to let the lassies enjoy themselves for the last time.

Soon after their arrival in Petersburg Berg proposed to Véra and was accepted.

Though in Moscow the Rostóvs belonged to the best society without themselves giving it a thought, yet in Petersburg their circle of acquaintances was a mixed and indefinite one. In Petersburg they were provincials, and the very people they had entertained in Moscow without inquiring to what set they belonged, here looked down on them.

The Rostóvs lived in the same hospitable way in Petersburg as in Moscow, and the most diverse people met at their suppers. Country neighbors from Otrádnoe, impoverished old squires and their daughters, Perónskaya a maid of honor, Pierre Bezúkhov, and the son of their district postmaster who had obtained a post in Petersburg. Among the men who very soon became frequent visitors at the Rostóvs' house in Petersburg were Borís, Pierre whom the count had met in the street and dragged home with him, and Berg who spent whole days at the Rostóvs' and paid the eldest daughter, Countess Véra, the attentions a young man pays when he intends to propose.

Not in vain had Berg shown everybody his right hand wounded at Austerlitz and held a perfectly unnecessary sword in his left. He narrated that episode so persistently and with so important an air that everyone believed in the merit and usefulness of his deed, and he had obtained two decorations for Austerlitz.

In the Finnish war he also managed to distinguish himself. He had picked up the scrap of a grenade that had killed an aide-de-camp standing near the commander in chief and had taken it to his commander. Just as he had done after Austerlitz, he related this occurrence at such length and so insistently that everyone again believed it had been necessary to do this, and he received two decorations for the Finnish war also.* In 1809 he was a captain in the Guards, wore medals, and held some special lucrative posts in Petersburg.

Though some skeptics smiled when told of Berg's merits, it could not be denied that he was a painstaking and brave officer, on excellent terms with his superiors, and a moral young man with a brilliant career before him and an assured position in society.

Four years before, meeting a Germán comrade in the stalls of a Moscow theater, Berg had pointed out Véra Rostóva to him and had said in German, "das soll mein Weib werden [that girl shall be my wife]," and from that moment had made up his mind to marry her. Now in Petersburg, having considered the Rostóvs' position and his own, he decided that the time had come to propose.

* By the war with Sweden in 1808 Russia acquired Finland. The treaty of Fredrikshavn, which ended that war, was confirmed by Napoleon at the Erfurt interview.—A.M.

Berg's proposal was at first received with a perplexity that was not flattering to him. At first it seemed strange that the son of an obscure Livonian gentleman should propose marriage to a Countess Rostóva; but Berg's chief characteristic was such a naïve and good-natured egotism that the Rostóvs involuntarily came to think it would be a good thing, since he himself was so firmly convinced that it was good, indeed excellent. Moreover, the Rostóvs' affairs were seriously embarrassed, as the suitor could not but know; and above all, Véra was twenty-four, had been taken out everywhere, and though she was certainly good-looking and sensible, no one up to now had proposed to her. So they gave their consent.

"You see," said Berg to his comrade, whom he called "friend" only because he knew that everyone has friends, "you see, I have considered it all, and should not marry if I had not thought it all out or if it were in any way unsuitable. But on the contrary, my papa and mamma are now provided for—I have arranged that rent for them in the Baltic Provinces *—and I can live in Petersburg on my pay, and with her fortune and my good management we can get along nicely. I am not marrying for money—I consider that dishonorable—but a wife should bring her share and a husband his. I have my position in the service, she has connections and some means. In our times that is worth something, isn't it? But above all, she is a handsome, estimable girl, and she loves me. . . ."

Berg blushed and smiled.

"And I love her, because her character is sensible and very good. Now the other sister, though they are the same family, is quite different—an unpleasant character and has not the same intelligence. She is so . . . you know? . . . Unpleasant. . . . But my fiancée! . . . Well, you will be coming," he was going to say, "to dine," but changed his mind and said, "to take tea with us," and quickly doubling up his tongue he blew a small round ring of tobacco smoke, perfectly embodying his dream of happiness.

After the first feeling of perplexity aroused in the parents by Berg's proposal, the holiday tone of joyousness usual at such times took possession of the family, but the rejoicing was external and insincere. In the family's feeling toward this wedding a certain awkwardness and constraint was evident, as if they were ashamed of not having loved Véra sufficiently and of being so ready to get her off their hands. The old count felt this most. He would probably have been unable to state the cause of his embarrassment, but it resulted from the state of his affairs. He did not

* Throughout the nineteenth century the Russian government, as a reward for service or simply by favoritism, used to make grants of "rents" (arenda)—that is to say, the usufruct of land.—A.M.

know at all how much he had, what his debts amounted to, or what dowry he could give Véra. When his daughters were born he had assigned to each of them, for her dowry, an estate with three hundred serfs; but one of these estates had already been sold, and the other was mortgaged and the interest so much in arrears that it would have to be sold, so that it was impossible to give it to Véra. Nor had he any money.

Berg had already been engaged a month, and only a week remained before the wedding, but the count had not yet decided in his own mind the question of the dowry, nor spoken to his wife about it. At one time the count thought of giving her the Ryazán estate or of selling a forest, at another time of borrowing money on a note of hand. A few days before the wedding Berg entered the count's study early one morning and, with a pleasant smile, respectfully asked his future father-in-law to let him know what Véra's dowry would be. The count was so disconcerted by this long-foreseen inquiry that without consideration he gave the first reply that came into his head. "I like your being businesslike about it. . . . I like it. You shall be satisfied. . . ."

And patting Berg on the shoulder he got up, wishing to end the conversation. But Berg, smiling pleasantly, explained that if he did not know for certain how much Véra would have and did not receive at least part of the dowry in advance, he would have to break matters off.

"Because, consider, Count—if I allowed myself to marry now without having definite means to maintain my wife, I should be acting badly. . . ."

The conversation ended by the count, who wished to be generous and to avoid further importunity, saying that he would give a note of hand for eighty thousand rubles. Berg smiled meekly, kissed the count on the shoulder, and said that he was very grateful, but that it was impossible for him to arrange his new life without receiving thirty thousand in ready money. "Or at least twenty thousand, Count," he added, "and then a note of hand for only sixty thousand."

"Yes, yes, all right!" said the count hurriedly. "Only excuse me, my dear fellow, I'll give you twenty thousand and a note of hand for eighty thousand as well. Yes, yes! Kiss me."

7. Natásha and Borís

NATÁSHA WAS SIXTEEN and it was the year 1809, the very year to which she had counted on her fingers with Borís after they had kissed four years ago. Since then she had not seen him. Before Sónya and her mother, if Borís happened to be mentioned, she spoke quite freely of that episode

as of some childish, long-forgotten matter that was not worth mentioning. But in the secret depths of her soul the question whether her engagement to Borís was a jest or an important, binding promise tormented her.

Since Borís left Moscow in 1805 to join the army he had not seen the Rostóvs. He had been in Moscow several times, and had passed near Otrádnoe, but had never been to see them.

Sometimes it occurred to Natásha that he did not wish to see her, and this conjecture was confirmed by the sad tone in which her elders spoke of him.

"Nowadays old friends are not remembered," the countess would say when Borís was mentioned.

Anna Mikháylovna also had of late visited them less frequently, seemed to hold herself with particular dignity, and always spoke rapturously and gratefully of the merits of her son and the brilliant career on which he had entered. When the Rostóvs came to Petersburg Borís called on them.

He drove to their house in some agitation. The memory of Natásha was his most poetic recollection. But he went with the firm intention of letting her and her parents feel that the childish relations between himself and Natásha could not be binding either on her or on him. He had a brilliant position in society thanks to his intimacy with Countess Bezúkhova, a brilliant position in the service thanks to the patronage of an important personage whose complete confidence he enjoyed, and he was beginning to make plans for marrying one of the richest heiresses in Petersburg, plans which might very easily be realized. When he entered the Rostóvs' drawing room Natásha was in her own room. When she heard of his arrival she almost ran into the drawing room, flushed and beaming with a more than cordial smile.

Borís remembered Natásha in a short dress, with dark eyes shining from under her curls and boisterous, childish laughter, as he had known her four years before; and so he was taken aback when quite a different Natásha entered, and his face expressed rapturous astonishment. This expression on his face pleased Natásha.

"Well, do you recognize your little madcap playmate?" asked the countess.

Borís kissed Natásha's hand and said that he was astonished at the change in her.

"How handsome you have grown!"

"I should think so!" replied Natásha's laughing eyes.

"And is Papa older?" she asked.

Natásha sat down and, without joining in Borís' conversation with the countess, silently and minutely studied her childhood's suitor. He felt

the weight of that resolute and affectionate scrutiny and glanced at her occasionally.

Borís' uniform, spurs, tie, and the way his hair was brushed were all *comme il faut* and in the latest fashion. This Natásha noticed at once. He sat rather sideways in the armchair next to the countess, arranging with his right hand the cleanest of gloves that fitted his left hand like a skin, and he spoke with a particularly refined compression of his lips about the amusements of the highest Petersburg society, recalling with mild irony old times in Moscow and Moscow acquaintances. It was not accidentally, Natásha felt, that he alluded, when speaking of the highest aristocracy, to an ambassador's ball he had attended, and to invitations he had received from N.N. and S.S.

All this time Natásha sat silent, glancing up at him from under her brows. This gaze disturbed and confused Borís more and more. He looked round more frequently toward her, and broke off in what he was saying. He did not stay more than ten minutes, then rose and took his leave. The same inquisitive, challenging, and rather mocking eyes still looked at him. After his first visit Borís said to himself that Natásha attracted him just as much as ever, but that he must not yield to that feeling, because to marry her, a girl almost without fortune, would mean ruin to his career, while to renew their former relations without intending to marry her would be dishonorable. Borís made up his mind to avoid meeting Natásha, but despite that resolution he called again a few days later and began calling often and spending whole days at the Rostóvs'. It seemed to him that he ought to have an explanation with Natásha and tell her that the old times must be forgotten, that in spite of everything . . . she could not be his wife, that he had no means, and they would never let her marry him. But he failed to do so and felt awkward about entering on such an explanation. From day to day he became more and more entangled. It seemed to her mother and Sónya that Natásha was in love with Borís as of old. She sang him his favorite songs, showed him her album, making him write in it, did not allow him to allude to the past, letting it be understood how delightful was the present; and every day he went away in a fog, without having said what he meant to, and not knowing what he was doing or why he came, or how it would all end. He left off visiting Hélène and received reproachful notes from her every day, and yet he continued to spend whole days with the Rostóvs.

8. Natásha's bedtime talks with her mother

ONE NIGHT when the old countess, in nightcap and dressing jacket, without her false curls, and with her poor little knob of hair showing under her white cotton cap, knelt sighing and groaning on a rug and bowing to the ground in prayer, her door creaked and Natásha, also in a dressing jacket with slippers on her bare feet and her hair in curlpapers, ran in. The countess—her prayerful mood dispelled—looked round and frowned. She was finishing her last prayer: "Can it be that this couch will be my grave?" Natásha, flushed and eager, seeing her mother in prayer, suddenly checked her rush, half sat down, and unconsciously put out her tongue as if chiding herself. Seeing that her mother was still praying she ran on tiptoe to the bed and, rapidly slipping one little foot against the other, pushed off her slippers and jumped onto the bed the countess had feared might become her grave. This couch was high, with a feather bed and five pillows each smaller than the one below. Natásha jumped on it, sank into the feather bed, rolled over to the wall, and began snuggling up the bedclothes as she settled down, raising her knees to her chin, kicking out and laughing almost inaudibly, now covering herself up head and all, and now peeping at her mother. The countess finished her prayers and came to the bed with a stern face, but seeing that Natásha's head was covered, she smiled in her kind, weak way.

"Now then, now then!" said she.

"Mamma, can we have a talk? Yes?" said Natásha. "Now, just one on your throat and another . . . that'll do!" And seizing her mother round the neck, she kissed her on the throat. In her behavior to her mother Natásha seemed rough, but she was so sensitive and tactful that however she clasped her mother she always managed to do it without hurting her or making her feel uncomfortable or displeased.

"Well, what is it tonight?" said the mother, having arranged her pillows and waited until Natásha, after turning over a couple of times, had settled down beside her under the quilt, spread out her arms, and assumed a serious expression.

These visits of Natásha's at night before the count returned from his club were one of the greatest pleasures of both mother and daughter.

"What is it tonight?—But I have to tell you . . ."

Natásha put her hand on her mother's mouth.

"About Borís . . . I know," she said seriously; "that's what I have come about. Don't say it—I know. No, do tell me! No, do tell me!" and she removed her hand. "Tell me, Mamma! He's nice?"

"Natásha, you are sixteen. At your age I was married. You say Borís is nice. He is very nice, and I love him like a son. But what then? . . . What are you thinking about? You have quite turned his head, I can see that. . . ."

As she said this the countess looked round at her daughter. Natásha was lying looking steadily straight before her at one of the mahogany sphinxes carved on the corners of the bedstead, so that the countess only saw her daughter's face in profile. That face struck her by its peculiarly serious and concentrated expression.

Natásha was listening and considering.

"Well, what then?" said she.

"You have quite turned his head, and why? What do you want of him? You know you can't marry him."

"Why not?" said Natásha, without changing her position.

"Because he is young, because he is poor, because he is a relation . . . and because you yourself don't love him."

"How do you know?"

"I know. It is not right, darling!"

"But if I want to . . ." said Natásha.

"Leave off talking nonsense," said the countess.

"But if I want to . . ."

"Natásha, I am in earnest . . ."

Natásha did not let her finish. She drew the countess' large hand to her, kissed it on the back and then on the palm, then again turned it over and began kissing first one knuckle, then the space between the knuckles, then the next knuckle, whispering, "January, February, March, April, May.* Speak, Mamma, why don't you say anything? Speak!" said she, turning to her mother, who was tenderly gazing at her daughter and in that contemplation seemed to have forgotten all she had wished to say.

"It won't do, my love! Not everyone will understand this friendship dating from your childish days, and to see him so intimate with you may injure you in the eyes of other young men who visit us, and above all it

* *Natásha evidently remembered the way she had been taught the months that have thirty-one days. The method in question is to double up the fists, and, disregarding the thumbs, to take the knuckles as representing the thirty-one-day months, the spaces between representing the shorter months. The first fist represents the months from January to July, the first knuckle of the second fist representing August.*

*Natásha, however, makes a mistake, for a little farther on she says "June" instead of "July" for the knuckle of the little finger, which would bring August to a space and make the arrangement go wrong.—*A.M.

torments him for nothing. He may already have found a suitable and wealthy match, and now he's half crazy."

"Crazy?" repeated Natásha.

"I'll tell you some things about myself. I had a cousin . . ."

"I know! Cyril Matvéich . . . but he is old."

"He was not always old. But this is what I'll do, Natásha, I'll have a talk with Borís. He need not come so often. . . ."

"Why not, if he likes to?"

"Because I know it will end in nothing. . . ."

"How can you know? No, Mamma, don't speak to him! What nonsense!" said Natásha in the tone of one being deprived of her property. "Well, I won't marry, but let him come if he enjoys it and I enjoy it." Natásha smiled and looked at her mother. "Not to marry, but just so," she added.

"How so, my pet?"

"Just so. There's no need for me to marry him. But . . . just so."

"Just so, just so," repeated the countess, and shaking all over, she went off into a good-humored, unexpected, elderly laugh.

"Don't laugh, stop!" cried Natásha. "You're shaking the whole bed! You're awfully like me, just such another giggler. . . . Wait . . ." and she seized the countess' hands and kissed a knuckle of the little finger, saying, "June," and continued, kissing, "July, August," on the other hand. "But, Mamma, is he very much in love? What do you think? Was anybody ever so much in love with you? And he's very nice, very, very nice. Only not quite my taste—he is so narrow, like the dining-room clock. . . . Don't you understand? Narrow, you know—gray, light gray . . ."

"What rubbish you're talking!" said the countess.

Natásha continued: "Don't you really understand? Nicholas would understand. . . . Bezúkhov, now, is blue, dark-blue and red, and he is square." *

"You flirt with him too," said the countess, laughing.

"No, he is a Freemason, I have found out. He is fine, dark-blue and red. . . . How can I explain it to you?"

"Little countess!" the count's voice called from behind the door. "You're

* Physiologists are aware that to some people, especially young ones, certain sounds suggest colors or forms. To such people Natásha's remark will be quite understandable even if to them the names "Borís" and "Pierre" suggest other colors; but perhaps her perception of these colors may have arisen from their personal attributes, as in the theosophical theory of "auras" colored according to personality and mood.—A.M.

not asleep?" Natásha jumped up, snatched up her slippers, and ran bare-foot to her own room.

It was a long time before she could sleep. She kept thinking that no one could understand all that she understood and all there was in her.

"Sónya?" she thought, glancing at that curled-up, sleeping little kitten with her enormous plait of hair. "No, how could she? She's virtuous. She fell in love with Nicholas and does not wish to know anything more. Even Mamma does not understand. It is wonderful how clever I am and how . . . charming she is," she went on, speaking of herself in the third person, and imagining it was some very wise man—the wisest and best of men—who was saying it of her. "There is everything, everything in her," continued this man. "She is unusually intelligent, charming . . . and then she is pretty, uncommonly pretty, and agile—she swims and rides splendidly . . . and her voice! One can really say it's a wonderful voice!"

She hummed a scrap from her favorite opera by Cherubini, threw herself on her bed, laughed at the pleasant thought that she would imme-diately fall asleep, called Dunyásha the maid to put out the candle, and before Dunyásha had left the room had already passed into yet another happier world of dreams, where everything was as light and beautiful as in reality, and even more so because it was different.

Next day the countess called Borís aside and had a talk with him, after which he ceased coming to the Rostóvs'.

9. Natásha's first grand ball. She dances with Prince Andrew

ON THE THIRTY-FIRST OF DECEMBER, New Year's Eve, 1809-10, an old grandee of Catherine's day was giving a ball and midnight supper. The diplomatic corps and the Emperor himself were to be present.

The grandee's well-known mansion on the English Quay glittered with innumerable lights. Police were stationed at the brightly lit entrance which was carpeted with red baize, and not only gendarmes but dozens of police officers and even the police master himself stood at the porch. Carriages kept driving away and fresh ones arriving, with red-liveried foot-men and footmen in plumed hats. From the carriages emerged men wear-ing uniforms, stars, and ribbons, while ladies in satin and ermine cau-tiously descended the carriage steps which were let down for them with a clatter, and then walked hurriedly and noiselessly over the baize at the entrance.

Almost every time a new carriage drove up a whisper ran through the crowd and caps were doffed.

"The Emperor? . . . No, a minister . . . prince . . . ambassador. Don't you see the plumes? . . ." was whispered among the crowd.

One person, better dressed than the rest, seemed to know everyone and mentioned by name the greatest dignitaries of the day.

A third of the visitors had already arrived, but the Rostóvs, who were to be present, were still hurrying to get dressed.

There had been many discussions and preparations for this ball in the Rostóv family, many fears that the invitation would not arrive, that the dresses would not be ready, or that something would not be arranged as it should be.

Márya Ignátevna Perónskaya, a thin and shallow maid of honor at the court of the Dowager Empress, who was a friend and relation of the countess and piloted the provincial Rostóvs in Petersburg high society, was to accompany them to the ball.

They were to call for her at her house in the Taurida Gardens at ten o'clock, but it was already five minutes to ten, and the girls were not yet dressed.

Natásha was going to her first grand ball. She had got up at eight that morning and had been in a fever of excitement and activity all day. All her powers since morning had been concentrated on ensuring that they all—she herself, Mamma, and Sónya—should be as well dressed as possible. Sónya and her mother put themselves entirely in her hands. The countess was to wear a claret-colored velvet dress, and the two girls white gauze over pink silk slips, with roses on their bodices and their hair dressed à la grecque.

Everything essential had already been done; feet, hands, necks, and ears washed, perfumed, and powdered, as befits a ball; the openwork silk stockings and white satin shoes with ribbons were already on; the hair-dressing was almost done. Sónya was finishing dressing and so was the countess, but Natásha, who had bustled about helping them all, was behindhand. She was still sitting before a looking glass with a dressing jacket thrown over her slender shoulders. Sónya stood ready dressed in the middle of the room and, pressing the head of a pin till it hurt her dainty finger, was fixing on a last ribbon that squeaked as the pin went through it.

"That's not the way, that's not the way, Sónya!" cried Natásha turning her head and clutching with both hands at her hair which the maid who was dressing it had not time to release. "That bow is not right. Come here!"

Sónya sat down and Natásha pinned the ribbon on differently.

"Allow me, Miss! I can't do it like that," said the maid who was holding Natásha's hair.

"Oh, dear! Well then, wait. That's right, Sónya."

"Aren't you ready? It is nearly ten," came the countess' voice.

"Directly! Directly! And you, Mamma?"

"I have only my cap to pin on."

"Don't do it without me!" called Natásha. "You won't do it right."

"But it's already ten."

They had decided to be at the ball by half-past ten, and Natásha had still to get dressed and they had to call at the Taurida Gardens.

When her hair was done, Natásha, in her short petticoat from under which her dancing shoes showed, and in her mother's dressing jacket, ran up to Sónya, scrutinized her, and then ran to her mother. Turning her mother's head this way and that, she fastened on the cap and, hurriedly kissing her gray hair, ran back to the maids who were turning up the hem of her skirt.

The cause of the delay was Natásha's skirt, which was too long. Two maids were turning up the hem and hurriedly biting off the ends of thread. A third with pins in her mouth was running about between the countess and Sónya, and a fourth held the whole of the gossamer garment up high on one uplifted hand.

"Mávra, quicker, darling!"

"Give me my thimble, Miss, from there . . ."

"Whenever will you be ready?" asked the count coming to the door. "Here is some scent. Perónskaya must be tired of waiting."

"It's ready, Miss," said the maid, holding up the shortened gauze dress with two fingers, and blowing and shaking something off it, as if by this to express a consciousness of the airiness and purity of what she held.

Natásha began putting on the dress.

"In a minute! In a minute! Don't come in, Papa!" she cried to her father as he opened the door—speaking from under the filmy skirt which still covered her whole face.

Sónya slammed the door to. A minute later they let the count in. He was wearing a blue swallow-tail coat, shoes and stockings, and was perfumed and his hair pomaded.

"Oh, Papa! how nice you look! Charming!" cried Natásha, as she stood in the middle of the room smoothing out the folds of the gauze.

"If you please, Miss! allow me," said the maid, who on her knees was pulling the skirt straight and shifting the pins from one side of her mouth to the other with her tongue.

"Say what you like," exclaimed Sónya, in a despairing voice as she looked at Natásha, "say what you like, it's still too long."

Natásha stepped back to look at herself in the pier glass. The dress was too long.

"Really, madam, it is not at all too long," said Mávra, crawling on her knees after her young lady.

"Well, if it's too long we'll take it up . . . we'll tack it up in one minute," said the resolute Dunyásha taking a needle that was stuck on the front of her little shawl and, still kneeling on the floor, set to work once more.

At that moment, with soft steps, the countess came in shyly, in her cap and velvet gown.

"Oo-oo, my beauty!" exclaimed the count, "she looks better than any of you!"

He would have embraced her but, blushing, she stepped aside fearing to be rumpled.

"Mamma, your cap, more to this side," said Natásha. "I'll arrange it," and she rushed forward so that the maids who were tacking up her skirt could not move fast enough and a piece of gauze was torn off.

"Oh goodness! What has happened? Really it was not my fault!"

"Never mind, I'll run it up, it won't show," said Dunyásha.

"What a beauty—a very queen!" said the nurse as she came to the door. "And Sónya! They are lovely!"

At a quarter past ten they at last got into their carriages and started. But they had still to call at the Taurida Gardens.

Perónskaya was quite ready. In spite of her age and plainness she had gone through the same process as the Rostóvs, but with less flurry—for to her it was a matter of routine. Her ugly old body was washed, perfumed, and powdered in just the same way. She had washed behind her ears just as carefully, and when she entered her drawing room in her yellow dress, wearing her badge as maid of honor, her old lady's maid was as full of rapturous admiration as the Rostóvs' servants had been.

She praised the Rostóvs' toilets. They praised her taste and toilet, and at eleven o'clock, careful of their coiffures and dresses, they settled themselves in their carriages and drove off.

Natásha had not had a moment free since early morning and had not once had time to think of what lay before her.

In the damp chill air and crowded closeness of the swaying carriage, she for the first time vividly imagined what was in store for her there at the ball, in those brightly lighted rooms—with music, flowers, dances,

the Emperor, and all the brilliant young people of Petersburg. The prospect was so splendid that she hardly believed it would come true, so out of keeping was it with the chill darkness and closeness of the carriage. She understood all that awaited her only when, after stepping over the red baize at the entrance, she entered the hall, took off her fur cloak, and, beside Sónya and in front of her mother, mounted the brightly illuminated stairs between the flowers. Only then did she remember how she must behave at a ball, and tried to assume the majestic air she considered indispensable for a girl on such an occasion. But, fortunately for her, she felt her eyes growing misty, she saw nothing clearly, her pulse beat a hundred to the minute, and the blood throbbed at her heart. She could not assume that pose, which would have made her ridiculous, and she moved on almost fainting from excitement and trying with all her might to conceal it. And this was the very attitude that became her best. Before and behind them other visitors were entering, also talking in low tones and wearing ball dresses. The mirrors on the landing reflected ladies in white, pale-blue, and pink dresses, with diamonds and pearls on their bare necks and arms.

Natásha looked in the mirrors and could not distinguish her reflection from the others. All was blended into one brilliant procession. On entering the ballroom the regular hum of voices, footsteps, and greetings deafened Natásha, and the light and glitter dazzled her still more. The host and hostess, who had already been standing at the door for half an hour repeating the same words to the various arrivals, "Charmé de vous voir [Delighted to see you]," greeted the Rostóvs and Perónskaya in the same manner.

The two girls in their white dresses, each with a rose in her black hair, both curtsied in the same way, but the hostess' eye involuntarily rested longer on the slim Natásha. She looked at her and gave her alone a special smile in addition to her usual smile as hostess. Looking at her she may have recalled the golden, irrecoverable days of her own girlhood and her own first ball. The host also followed Natásha with his eyes and asked the count which was his daughter.

"Charming!" said he, kissing the tips of his fingers.

In the ballroom, guests stood crowding at the entrance doors awaiting the Emperor. The countess took up a position in one of the front rows of that crowd. Natásha heard and felt that several people were asking about her and looking at her. She realized that those noticing her liked her, and this observation helped to calm her.

"There are some like ourselves and some worse," she thought.

Perónskaya was pointing out to the countess the most important people at the ball.

"That is the Dutch ambassador, do you see? That gray-haired man," she said, indicating an old man with a profusion of silver-gray curly hair, who was surrounded by ladies laughing at something he said.

"Ah, here she is, the Queen of Petersburg, Countess Bezúkhova," said Perónskaya, indicating Hélène who had just entered. "How lovely! She is quite equal to Márya Antónovna.* See how the men, young and old, pay court to her. Beautiful and clever . . . they say Prince —— is quite mad about her. But see, those two, though not good-looking, are even more run after."

She pointed to a lady who was crossing the room followed by a very plain daughter.

"She is a splendid match, a millionairess," said Perónskaya. "And look, here come her suitors."

"That is Bezúkhova's brother, Anatole Kurágin," she said, indicating a handsome officer of the Horse Guards who passed by them with head erect, looking at something over the heads of the ladies. "He's handsome, isn't he? I hear they will marry him to that rich girl. But your cousin, Drubetskóy, is also very attentive to her. They say she has millions. Oh yes, that's the French ambassador himself!" she replied to the countess' inquiry about Caulaincourt. "Looks as if he were a king! All the same, the French are charming, very charming. No one more charming in society. Ah, here she is! Yes, she is still the most beautiful of them all, our Márya Antónovna! And how simply she is dressed! Lovely! And that stout one in spectacles is the universal Freemason," she went on, indicating Pierre. "Put him beside his wife and he looks a regular buffoon!"

Pierre, swaying his stout body, advanced, making way through the crowd and nodding to right and left as casually and good-naturedly as if he were passing through a crowd at a fair. He pushed through, evidently looking for someone.

Natásha looked joyfully at the familiar face of Pierre, "the buffoon," as Perónskaya had called him, and knew he was looking for them, and for her in particular. He had promised to be at the ball and introduce partners to her.

But before he reached them Pierre stopped beside a very handsome, dark man of middle height, and in a white uniform, who stood by a window talking to a tall man wearing stars and a ribbon. Natásha at once

* *Márya Antónovna Narýshkina was a greatly admired court beauty and Alexander I's mistress. She was by birth a Princess Chetvertínskaya.*—A.M.

recognized the shorter and younger man in the white uniform: it was Bolkónski, who seemed to her to have grown much younger, happier, and better-looking.

"There's someone else we know—Bolkónski, do you see, Mamma?" said Natásha, pointing out Prince Andrew. "You remember, he stayed a night with us at Otrádnoe."

"Oh, you know him?" said Perónskaya. "I can't bear him. *Il fait à présent la pluie et le beau temps* [He is all the rage just now].* He's too proud for anything. Takes after his father. And he's hand in glove with Speránski, writing some project or other. Just look how he treats the ladies! There's one talking to him and he has turned away," she said, pointing at him. "I'd give it to him if he treated me as he does those ladies."

SUDDENLY EVERYBODY STIRRED, began talking, and pressed forward and then back, and between the two rows, which separated, the Emperor entered to the sounds of music that had immediately struck up. Behind him walked his host and hostess. He walked in rapidly, bowing to right and left as if anxious to get the first moments of the reception over. The band played the polonaise in vogue at that time on account of the words that had been set to it, beginning: "Alexander, Elisaveta, all our hearts you ravish quite . . ." The Emperor passed on to the drawing room, the crowd made a rush for the doors, and several persons with excited faces hurried there and back again. Then the crowd hastily retired from the drawing-room door, at which the Emperor reappeared talking to the hostess. A young man, looking distraught, pounced down on the ladies, asking them to move aside. Some ladies, with faces betraying complete forgetfulness of all the rules of decorum, pushed forward to the detriment of their toilets. The men began to choose partners and take their places for the polonaise.

Everyone moved back, and the Emperor came smiling out of the drawing room leading his hostess by the hand but not keeping time to the music. The host followed with Márya Antónovna Narýshkina; then came ambassadors, ministers, and various generals, whom Perónskaya diligently named. More than half the ladies already had partners and were taking up, or preparing to take up, their positions for the polonaise. Natásha felt that she would be left with her mother and Sónya among a minority of women who crowded near the wall, not having been invited to dance. She stood with her slender arms hanging down, her scarcely de-

* *A familiar French proverb.*—A.M.

fined bosom rising and falling regularly, and with bated breath and glittering, frightened eyes gazed straight before her, evidently prepared for the height of joy or misery. She was not concerned about the Emperor or any of those great people whom Perónskaya was pointing out—she had but one thought: "Is it possible no one will ask me, that I shall not be among the first to dance? Is it possible that not one of all these men will notice me? They do not even seem to see me, or if they do they look as if they were saying, 'Ah, she's not the one I'm after, so it's not worth looking at her!' No, it's impossible," she thought. "They must know how I long to dance, how splendidly I dance, and how they would enjoy dancing with me."

The strains of the polonaise, which had continued for a considerable time, had begun to sound like a sad reminiscence in Natásha's ears. She wanted to cry. Perónskaya had left them. The count was at the other end of the room. She and the countess and Sónya were standing by themselves as in the depths of a forest amid that crowd of strangers, with no one interested in them and not wanted by anyone. Prince Andrew with a lady passed by, evidently not recognizing them. The handsome Anatole was smilingly talking to a partner on his arm and looked at Natásha as one looks at a wall. Borís passed them twice and each time turned away. Berg and his wife, who were not dancing, came up to them.

This family gathering seemed humiliating to Natásha—as if there were nowhere else for the family to talk but here at the ball. She did not listen to or look at Véra, who was telling her something about her own green dress.

At last the Emperor stopped beside his last partner (he had danced with three) and the music ceased. A worried aide-de-camp ran up to the Rostóvs requesting them to stand farther back, though as it was they were already close to the wall, and from the gallery resounded the distinct, precise, enticingly rhythmical strains of a waltz. The Emperor looked smilingly down the room. A minute passed but no one had yet begun dancing. An aide-de-camp, the Master of Ceremonies, went up to Countess Bezúkhova and asked her to dance. She smilingly raised her hand and laid it on his shoulder without looking at him. The aide-de-camp, an adept in his art, grasping his partner firmly round her waist, with confident deliberation started smoothly, gliding first round the edge of the circle, then at the corner of the room he caught Hélène's left hand and turned her, the only sound audible, apart from the ever-quickening music, being the rhythmic click of the spurs on his rapid, agile feet, while at every third beat his partner's velvet dress spread out and seemed to

flash as she whirled round. Natásha gazed at them and was ready to cry because it was not she who was dancing that first turn of the waltz.

Prince Andrew, in the white uniform of a cavalry colonel, wearing stockings and dancing shoes, stood looking animated and bright in the front row of the circle not far from the Rostóvs. Baron Firhoff was talking to him about the first sitting of the Council of State to be held next day. Prince Andrew, as one closely connected with Speránski and participating in the work of the legislative commission, could give reliable information about that sitting, concerning which various rumors were current. But not listening to what Firhoff was saying, he was gazing now at the sovereign and now at the men intending to dance who had not yet gathered courage to enter the circle.

Prince Andrew was watching these men abashed by the Emperor's presence, and the women who were breathlessly longing to be asked to dance.

Pierre came up to him and caught him by the arm.

"You always dance. I have a protégée, the young Rostóva, here. Ask her," he said.

"Where is she?" asked Bolkónski. "Excuse me!" he added, turning to the baron, "we will finish this conversation elsewhere—at a ball one must dance." He stepped forward in the direction Pierre indicated. The despairing, dejected expression of Natásha's face caught his eye. He recognized her, guessed her feelings, saw that it was her debut, remembered her conversation at the window, and with an expression of pleasure on his face approached Countess Rostóva.

"Allow me to introduce you to my daughter," said the countess, with heightened color.

"I have the pleasure of being already acquainted, if the countess remembers me," said Prince Andrew with a low and courteous bow quite belying Perónskaya's remarks about his rudeness, and approaching Natásha he held out his arm to grasp her waist before he had completed his invitation. He asked her to waltz. That tremulous expression on Natásha's face, prepared either for despair or rapture, suddenly brightened into a happy, grateful, childlike smile.

"I have long been waiting for you," that frightened happy little girl seemed to say by the smile that replaced the threatened tears, as she raised her hand to Prince Andrew's shoulder. They were the second couple to enter the circle. Prince Andrew was one of the best dancers of his day and Natásha danced exquisitely. Her little feet in their white satin dancing shoes did their work swiftly, lightly, and independently of herself, while her face beamed with ecstatic happiness. Her slender bare arms and neck were not beautiful—compared to Hélène's her shoulders

looked thin and her bosom undeveloped. But Hélène seemed, as it were, hardened by a varnish left by the thousands of looks that had scanned her person, while Natásha was like a girl exposed for the first time, who would have felt very much ashamed had she not been assured that this was absolutely necessary.

Prince Andrew liked dancing, and wishing to escape as quickly as possible from the political and clever talk which everyone addressed to him, wishing also to break up the circle of restraint he disliked, caused by the Emperor's presence, he danced, and had chosen Natásha because Pierre pointed her out to him and because she was the first pretty girl who caught his eye; but scarcely had he embraced that slender supple figure and felt her stirring so close to him and smiling so near him than the wine of her charm rose to his head, and he felt himself revived and rejuvenated when after leaving her he stood breathing deeply and watching the other dancers.

AFTER PRINCE ANDREW, Borís came up to ask Natásha for a dance, and then the aide-de-camp who had opened the ball, and several other young men, so that, flushed and happy, and passing on her superfluous partners to Sónya, she did not cease dancing all the evening. She noticed and saw nothing of what occupied everyone else. Not only did she fail to notice that the Emperor talked a long time with the French ambassador, and how particularly gracious he was to a certain lady, or that Prince So-and-so and So-and-so did and said this and that, and that Hélène had great success and was honored by the special attention of So-and-so, but she did not even see the Emperor, and only noticed that he had gone because the ball became livelier after his departure. For one of the merry cotillions before supper Prince Andrew was again her partner. He reminded her of their first encounter in the Otrádnoe avenue, and how she had been unable to sleep that moonlight night, and told her how he had involuntarily overheard her. Natásha blushed at that recollection and tried to excuse herself, as if there had been something to be ashamed of in what Prince Andrew had overheard.

Like all men who have grown up in society, Prince Andrew liked meeting someone there not of the conventional society stamp. And such was Natásha, with her surprise, her delight, her shyness, and even her mistakes in speaking French. With her he behaved with special care and tenderness, sitting beside her and talking of the simplest and most unimportant matters; he admired her shy grace. In the middle of the cotillion, having completed one of the figures, Natásha, still out of breath, was returning to her seat when another dancer chose her. She was tired and

panting and evidently thought of declining, but immediately put her hand gaily on the man's shoulder, smiling at Prince Andrew.

"I'd be glad to sit beside you and rest: I'm tired; but you see how they keep asking me, and I'm glad of it, I'm happy and I love everybody, and you and I understand it all," and much, much more was said in her smile. When her partner left her Natásha ran across the room to choose two ladies for the figure.

"If she goes to her cousin first and then to another lady, she will be my wife," said Prince Andrew to himself quite to his own surprise, as he watched her. She did go first to her cousin.

"What rubbish sometimes enters one's head!" thought Prince Andrew, "but what is certain is that that girl is so charming, so original, that she won't be dancing here a month before she will be married. . . . Such as she are rare here," he thought, as Natásha, readjusting a rose that was slipping on her bodice, settled herself beside him.

When the cotillion was over the old count in his blue coat came up to the dancers. He invited Prince Andrew to come and see them, and asked his daughter whether she was enjoying herself. Natásha did not answer at once but only looked up with a smile that said reproachfully: "How can you ask such a question?"

"I have never enjoyed myself so much before!" she said, and Prince Andrew noticed how her thin arms rose quickly as if to embrace her father and instantly dropped again. Natásha was happier than she had ever been in her life. She was at that height of bliss when one becomes completely kind and good and does not believe in the possibility of evil, unhappiness, or sorrow.*

At that ball Pierre for the first time felt humiliated by the position his wife occupied in court circles. He was gloomy and absent-minded. A deep furrow ran across his forehead, and standing by a window he stared over his spectacles seeing no one.

On her way to supper Natásha passed him.

Pierre's gloomy, unhappy look struck her. She stopped in front of him. She wished to help him, to bestow on him the superabundance of her own happiness.

"How delightful it is, Count!" said she. "Isn't it?"

Pierre smiled absent-mindedly, evidently not grasping what she said.

"Yes, I am very glad," he said.

"How can people be dissatisfied with anything?" thought Natásha.

* Readers acquainted with Tolstóy's life will note the similarity of Natásha's feeling with that which inspired his brother's story of the "Green Stick."—A.M.

"Especially such a capital fellow as Bezúkhov!" In Natásha's eyes all the people at the ball alike were good, kind, and splendid people, loving one another; none of them capable of injuring another—and so they ought all to be happy.

10. Bítski calls on Prince Andrew. Dinner at Speránski's. Prince Andrew's disillusionment with him and his reforms

NEXT DAY Prince Andrew thought of the ball, but his mind did not dwell on it long. "Yes, it was a very brilliant ball," and then . . . "Yes, that little Rostóva is very charming. There's something fresh, original, un-Petersburg-like about her that distinguishes her." That was all he thought about yesterday's ball, and after his morning tea he set to work.

But either from fatigue or want of sleep he was ill-disposed for work and could get nothing done. He kept criticizing his own work, as he often did, and was glad when he heard someone coming.

The visitor was Bítski, who served on various committees, frequented all the societies in Petersburg, and was a passionate devotee of the new ideas and of Speránski, and a diligent Petersburg newsmonger—one of those men who choose their opinions like their clothes according to the fashion, but who for that very reason appear to be the warmest partisans. Hardly had he got rid of his hat before he ran into Prince Andrew's room with a preoccupied air and at once began talking. He had just heard particulars of that morning's sitting of the Council of State opened by the Emperor, and he spoke of it enthusiastically. The Emperor's speech had been extraordinary. It had been a speech such as only constitutional monarchs deliver. "The Sovereign plainly said that the Council and Senate are estates of the realm, he said that the government must rest not on authority but on secure bases. The Emperor said that the fiscal system must be reorganized and the accounts published," recounted Bítski, emphasizing certain words and opening his eyes significantly.

"Ah, yes! Today's events mark an epoch, the greatest epoch in our history," he concluded.

Prince Andrew listened to the account of the opening of the Council of State, which he had so impatiently awaited and to which he had attached such importance, and was surprised that this event, now that it had taken place, did not affect him, and even seemed quite insignificant. He listened with quiet irony to Bítski's enthusiastic account of it. A very simple thought occurred to him: "What does it matter to me or to Bítski

what the Emperor was pleased to say at the Council? Can all that make me any happier or better?"

And this simple reflection suddenly destroyed all the interest Prince Andrew had felt in the impending reforms.* He was going to dine that evening at Speránski's, "with only a few friends," as the host had said when inviting him. The prospect of that dinner in the intimate home circle of the man he so admired had greatly interested Prince Andrew, especially as he had not yet seen Speránski in his domestic surroundings, but now he felt disinclined to go to it.

At the appointed hour, however, he entered the modest house Speránski owned in the Taurida Gardens. In the parqueted dining room of this small house, remarkable for its extreme cleanliness (suggesting that of a monastery), Prince Andrew, who was rather late, found the friendly gathering of Speránski's intimate acquaintants already assembled at five o'clock. There were no ladies present except Speránski's little daughter (long-faced like her father) and her governess. The other guests were Gervais, Magnítski,[2] and Stolýpin. While still in the anteroom Prince Andrew heard loud voices and a ringing staccato laugh—a laugh such as one hears on the stage. Someone—it sounded like Speránski—was distinctly ejaculating *ha-ha-ha*. Prince Andrew had never before heard Speránski's famous laugh, and this ringing, high-pitched laughter from a statesman made a strange impression on him.

He entered the dining room. The whole company were standing between two windows at a small table laid with hors-d'oeuvres. Speránski, wearing a gray swallow-tail coat with a star on the breast, and evidently

Alexander I's inconstancy wrecked Speránski's remarkable attempt to remodel the form of Russian government.

It is not difficult to see that Tolstóy has attributed to Prince Andrew his own relation to such attempts as Speránski's. The last words of this section indicate that while the peasant masses remained serfs they presented a formidable obstacle to the introduction of any enlightened system of jurisprudence or government, but it was an idiosyncrasy of Tolstóy's to regard such attempts at political reform as fundamentally futile because "how can all that possibly make men happier or better?" Concerned as Tolstóy was, in his own way, with the welfare of mankind, his outlook was intensely individualistic and he profoundly distrusted political movements.—A.M.

[2] *M. L. Magnítski was a coadjutor of Speránski's and an ardent partisan of his projected reforms. After Speránski's fall he sided with the reactionary Arakchéev and was an equally ardent opponent of all progress. Later on he was accused of making away with an enormous sum of money and was dismissed from the service.*—A.M.

still the same waistcoat and high white stock he had worn at the meeting of the Council of State, stood at the table with a beaming countenance. His guests surrounded him. Magnítski, addressing himself to Speránski, was relating an anecdote, and Speránski was laughing in advance at what Magnítski was going to say. When Prince Andrew entered the room Magnítski's words were again crowned by laughter. Stolýpin gave a deep bass guffaw as he munched a piece of bread and cheese. Gervais laughed softly with a hissing chuckle, and Speránski in a high-pitched staccato manner.

Still laughing, Speránski held out his soft white hand to Prince Andrew. "Very pleased to see you, Prince," he said. "One moment . . ." he went on, turning to Magnítski and interrupting his story. "We have agreed that this is a dinner for recreation, with not a word about business!" and turning again to the narrator he began to laugh afresh.

Prince Andrew looked at the laughing Speránski with astonishment, regret, and disillusionment. It seemed to him that this was not Speránski but someone else. Everything that had formerly appeared mysterious and fascinating in Speránski suddenly became plain and unattractive.

At dinner the conversation did not cease for a moment and seemed to consist of the contents of a book of funny anecdotes. Before Magnítski had finished his story someone else was anxious to relate something still funnier. Most of the anecdotes, if not relating to the state service, related to people in the service. It seemed that in this company the insignificance of those people was so definitely accepted that the only possible attitude toward them was one of good-humored ridicule. Speránski related how at the Council that morning a deaf dignitary, when asked his opinion, replied that he thought so too. Gervais gave a long account of an official revision, remarkable for the stupidity of everybody concerned. Stolýpin, stuttering, broke into the conversation and began excitedly talking of the abuses that existed under the former order of things—threatening to give a serious turn to the conversation. Magnítski starting quizzing Stolýpin about his vehemence. Gervais intervened with a joke, and the talk reverted to its former lively tone.

Evidently Speránski liked to rest after his labors and find amusement in a circle of friends, and his guests, understanding his wish, tried to enliven him and amuse themselves. But their gaiety seemed to Prince Andrew mirthless and tiresome. Speránski's high-pitched voice struck him unpleasantly, and the incessant laughter grated on him like a false note. Prince Andrew did not laugh and feared that he would be a damper on the spirits of the company, but no one took any notice of his being out of harmony with the general mood. They all seemed very gay.

He tried several times to join in the conversation, but his remarks were

tossed aside each time like a cork thrown out of the water, and he could not jest with them.

There was nothing wrong or unseemly in what they said, it was witty and might have been funny, but it lacked just that something which is the salt of mirth, and they were not even aware that such a thing existed.

After dinner Speránski's daughter and her governess rose. He patted the little girl with his white hand and kissed her. And that gesture, too, seemed unnatural to Prince Andrew.

The men remained at table over their port—English fashion. In the midst of a conversation that was started about Napoleon's Spanish affairs,* which they all agreed in approving, Prince Andrew began to express a contrary opinion. Speránski smiled and, with an evident wish to prevent the conversation from taking an unpleasant course, told a story that had no connection with the previous conversation. For a few moments all were silent.

Having sat some time at table, Speránski corked a bottle of wine and, remarking, "Nowadays good wine rides in a carriage and pair," passed it to the servant and got up. All rose and continuing to talk loudly went into the drawing room. Two letters brought by a courier were handed to Speránski and he took them to his study. As soon as he had left the room the general merriment stopped and the guests began to converse sensibly and quietly with one another.

"Now for the recitation!" said Speránski on returning from his study. "A wonderful talent!" he said to Prince Andrew, and Magnítski immediately assumed a pose and began reciting some humorous verses in French which he had composed about various well-known Petersburg people. He was interrupted several times by applause. When the verses were finished Prince Andrew went up to Speránski and took his leave.

"Where are you off to so early?" asked Speránski.

"I promised to go to a reception."

They said no more. Prince Andrew looked closely into those mirrorlike, impenetrable eyes, and felt that it had been ridiculous of him to have expected anything from Speránski and from any of his own activities connected with him, or ever to have attributed importance to what Sperán-

* At that time, in 1810, Napoleon was already deeply involved in Spain. In 1808 he had made his brother Joseph King of Spain, but the Spaniards resisted this, and Napoleon for the first time encountered the opposition of guerrilla bands which proved formidable, such as he again encountered with disastrous results when he invaded Russia. England was helping Spain, and the Peninsular war continued till in 1813 Wellington drove the French armies out of the country.—A.M.

ski was doing. That precise, mirthless laughter rang in Prince Andrew's ears long after he had left the house.

When he reached home Prince Andrew began thinking of his life in Petersburg during those last four months as if it were something new. He recalled his exertions and solicitations, and the history of his project of army reform, which had been accepted for consideration and which they were trying to pass over in silence simply because another, a very poor one, had already been prepared and submitted to the Emperor. He thought of the meetings of a committee of which Berg was a member. He remembered how carefully and at what length everything relating to form and procedure was discussed at those meetings, and how sedulously and promptly all that related to the gist of the business was evaded. He recalled his labors on the Legal Code, and how painstakingly he had translated the articles of the Roman and French codes into Russian, and he felt ashamed of himself. Then he vividly pictured to himself Boguchárovo, his occupations in the country, his journey to Ryazán; he remembered the peasants and Dron the village elder, and mentally applying to them the Personal Rights he had divided into paragraphs, he felt astonished that he could have spent so much time on such useless work.

11. Prince Andrew calls on the Rostóvs. Natásha's effect on him

NEXT DAY Prince Andrew called at a few houses he had not visited before, and among them at the Rostóvs' with whom he had renewed acquaintance at the ball. Apart from considerations of politeness which demanded the call, he wanted to see that original, eager girl who had left such a pleasant impression on his mind, in her own home.

Natásha was one of the first to meet him. She was wearing a dark-blue house dress in which Prince Andrew thought her even prettier than in her ball dress. She and all the Rostóv family welcomed him as an old friend, simply and cordially. The whole family, whom he had formerly judged severely, now seemed to him to consist of excellent, simple, and kindly people. The old count's hospitality and good nature, which struck one especially in Petersburg as a pleasant surprise, were such that Prince Andrew could not refuse to stay to dinner. "Yes," he thought, "they are capital people, who of course have not the slightest idea what a treasure they possess in Natásha; but they are kindly folk and form the best possible setting for this strikingly poetic, charming girl, overflowing with life!"

In Natásha Prince Andrew was conscious of a strange world completely

alien to him and brimful of joys unknown to him, a different world, that in the Otrádnoe avenue and at the window that moonlight night had already begun to disconcert him. Now this world disconcerted him no longer and was no longer alien to him, but he himself having entered it found in it a new enjoyment.

After dinner Natásha, at Prince Andrew's request, went to the clavichord and began singing. Prince Andrew stood by a window talking to the ladies and listened to her. In the midst of a phrase he ceased speaking and suddenly felt tears choking him, a thing he had thought impossible for him. He looked at Natásha as she sang, and something new and joyful stirred in his soul. He felt happy and at the same time sad. He had absolutely nothing to weep about yet he was ready to weep. What about? His former love? The little princess? His disillusionments? . . . His hopes for the future? . . . Yes and no. The chief reason was a sudden, vivid sense of the terrible contrast between something infinitely great and illimitable within him and that limited and material something that he, and even she, was. This contrast weighed on and yet cheered him while she sang.

As soon as Natásha had finished she went up to him and asked how he liked her voice. She asked this and then became confused, feeling that she ought not to have asked it. He smiled, looking at her, and said he liked her singing as he liked everything she did.

Prince Andrew left the Rostóvs' late in the evening. He went to bed from habit, but soon realized that he could not sleep. Having lit his candle he sat up in bed, then got up, then lay down again not at all troubled by his sleeplessness: his soul was as fresh and joyful as if he had stepped out of a stuffy room into God's own fresh air. It did not enter his head that he was in love with Natásha; he was not thinking about her, but only picturing her to himself, and in consequence all life appeared in a new light. "Why do I strive, why do I toil in this narrow, confined frame, when life, all life with all its joys, is open to me?" said he to himself. And for the first time for a very long while he began making happy plans for the future. He decided that he must attend to his son's education by finding a tutor and putting the boy in his charge, then he ought to retire from the service and go abroad, and see England, Switzerland, and Italy. "I must use my freedom while I feel so much strength and youth in me," he said to himself. "Pierre was right when he said one must believe in the possibility of happiness in order to be happy, and now I do believe in it. Let the dead bury their dead, but while one has life one must live and be happy!" thought he.

12. The Bergs' evening party

ONE MORNING Colonel Berg, whom Pierre knew as he knew everybody in Moscow and Petersburg, came to see him. Berg arrived in an immaculate brand-new uniform, with his hair pomaded and brushed forward over his temples as the Emperor Alexander wore his hair.

"I have just been to see the countess, your wife. Unfortunately she could not grant my request, but I hope, Count, I shall be more fortunate with you," he said with a smile.

"What is it you wish, Colonel? I am at your service."

"I have now quite settled in my new rooms, Count" (Berg said this with perfect conviction that this information could not but be agreeable), "and so I wish to arrange just a small party for my own and my wife's friends." (He smiled still more pleasantly.) "I wished to ask the countess and you to do me the honor of coming to tea and to supper."

Only Countess Hélène, considering the society of such people as the Bergs beneath her, could be cruel enough to refuse such an invitation. Berg explained so clearly why he wanted to collect at his house a small but select company, and why this would give him pleasure, and why though he grudged spending money on cards or anything harmful, he was prepared to run into some expense for the sake of good society—that Pierre could not refuse, and promised to come.

"But don't be late, Count, if I may venture to ask; about ten minutes to eight, please. We shall make up a rubber. Our general is coming. He is very good to me. We shall have supper, Count. So you will do me the favor."

Contrary to his habit of being late, Pierre on that day arrived at the Bergs' house, not at ten but at fifteen minutes to eight.

Having prepared everything necessary for the party, the Bergs were ready for their guests' arrival.

In their new, clean, and light study with its small busts and pictures and new furniture sat Berg and his wife. Berg, closely buttoned up in his new uniform, sat beside his wife explaining to her that one always could and should be acquainted with people above one, because only then does one get satisfaction from acquaintances.

"You can get to know something, you can ask for something. See how I managed from my first promotion." (Berg measured his life not by years but by promotions.) "My comrades are still nobodies, while I am only waiting for a vacancy to command a regiment, and have the happiness to be your husband." (He rose and kissed Véra's hand, and on the

way to her straightened out a turned-up corner of the carpet.) "And how
have I obtained all this? Chiefly by knowing how to choose my ac-
quaintances. It goes without saying that one must be conscientious and
methodical."

Berg smiled with a sense of his superiority over a weak woman, and
paused, reflecting that this dear wife of his was after all but a weak woman
who could not understand all that constitutes a man's dignity, what it was
ein Mann zu sein [to be a man]. Véra at the same time was smiling with a
sense of superiority over her good, conscientious husband, who all the
same understood life wrongly, as according to Véra all men did. Berg,
judging by his wife, thought all women weak and foolish. Véra, judging
only by her husband and generalizing from that observation, supposed
that all men, though they understand nothing and are conceited and
selfish, ascribe common sense to themselves alone.

Berg rose and embraced his wife carefully, so as not to crush her lace
fichu for which he had paid a good price, kissing her straight on the lips.

"The only thing is, we mustn't have children too soon," he continued,
following an unconscious sequence of ideas.

"Yes," answered Véra, "I don't at all want that. We must live for
society."

"Princess Yusúpova wore one exactly like this," said Berg, pointing to
the fichu with a happy and kindly smile.

Just then Count Bezúkhov was announced. Husband and wife glanced
at one another, both smiling with self-satisfaction, and each mentally
claiming the honor of this visit.

"This is what comes of knowing how to make acquaintances," thought
Berg. "This is what comes of knowing how to conduct oneself."

"But please don't interrupt me when I am entertaining the guests,"
said Véra, "because I know what interests each of them and what to say
to different people."

Berg smiled again.

"It can't be helped: men must sometimes have masculine conversa-
tion," said he.

They received Pierre in their small, new drawing room, where it was
impossible to sit down anywhere without disturbing its symmetry, neat-
ness, and order; so it was quite comprehensible and not strange that Berg,
having generously offered to disturb the symmetry of an armchair or of
the sofa for his dear guest, but being apparently painfully undecided on
the matter himself, eventually left the visitor to settle the question of
selection. Pierre disturbed the symmetry by moving a chair for himself,

and Berg and Véra immediately began their evening party, interrupting each other in their efforts to entertain their guest.

Véra, having decided in her own mind that Pierre ought to be entertained with conversation about the French embassy, at once began accordingly. Berg, having decided that masculine conversation was required, interrupted his wife's remarks and touched on the question of the war with Austria, and unconsciously jumped from the general subject to personal considerations as to the proposals made him to take part in the Austrian campaign and the reasons why he had declined them. Though the conversation was very incoherent and Véra was angry at the intrusion of the masculine element, both husband and wife felt with satisfaction that, even if only one guest was present, their evening had begun very well and was as like as two peas to every other evening party with its talk, tea, and lighted candles.

Before long Borís, Berg's old comrade, arrived. There was a shade of condescension and patronage in his treatment of Berg and Véra. After Borís came a lady with the colonel, then the general himself, then the Rostóvs, and the party became unquestionably exactly like all other evening parties. Berg and Véra could not repress their smiles of satisfaction at the sight of all this movement in their drawing room, at the sound of the disconnected talk, the rustling of dresses, and the bowing and scraping. Everything was just as everybody always has it, especially so the general, who admired the apartment, patted Berg on the shoulder, and with parental authority superintended the setting out of the table for boston.* The general sat down by Count Ilyá Rostóv, who was next to himself the most important guest. The old people sat with the old, the young with the young, and the hostess at the tea table, on which stood exactly the same kind of cakes in a silver cake basket as the Panins had at their party. Everything was just as it was everywhere else.

Pierre, as one of the principal guests, had to sit down to boston with Count Rostóv, the general, and the colonel. At the card table he happened to be directly facing Natásha, and was struck by a curious change that had come over her since the ball. She was silent, and not only less pretty than at the ball, but only redeemed from plainness by her look of gentle indifference to everything around.

"What's the matter with her?" thought Pierre, glancing at her. She was sitting by her sister at the tea table, and reluctantly, without looking

* Boston was a card game invented by French officers at Boston, Massachusetts, during the Revolutionary War. It has a distant resemblance to auction bridge.—A.M.

at him, made some reply to Borís who sat down beside her. After playing out a whole suit and to his partner's delight taking five tricks, Pierre, hearing greetings and the steps of someone who had entered the room while he was picking up his tricks, glanced again at Natásha.

"What has happened to her?" he asked himself with still greater surprise.

Prince Andrew was standing before her, saying something to her with a look of tender solicitude. She, having raised her head, was looking up at him, flushed and evidently trying to master her rapid breathing. And the bright glow of some inner fire that had been suppressed was again alight in her. She was completely transformed and from a plain girl had again become what she had been at the ball.

Prince Andrew went up to Pierre, and the latter noticed a new and youthful expression in his friend's face.

Pierre changed places several times during the game, sitting now with his back to Natásha and now facing her, but during the whole of the six rubbers he watched her and his friend.

"Something very important is happening between them," thought Pierre, and a feeling that was both joyful and painful agitated him and made him neglect the game.

After six rubbers the general got up, saying that it was no use playing like that, and Pierre was released. Natásha on one side was talking with Sónya and Borís, and Véra with a subtle smile was saying something to Prince Andrew. Pierre went up to his friend and, asking whether they were talking secrets, sat down beside them. Véra, having noticed Prince Andrew's attentions to Natásha, decided that at a party, a real evening party, subtle allusions to the tender passion were absolutely necessary and, seizing a moment when Prince Andrew was alone, began a conversation with him about feelings in general and about her sister. With so intellectual a guest as she considered Prince Andrew to be, she felt that she had to employ her diplomatic tact.

When Pierre went up to them he noticed that Véra was being carried away by her self-satisfied talk, but that Prince Andrew seemed embarrassed, a thing that rarely happened with him.

"What do you think?" Véra was saying with an arch smile. "You are so discerning, Prince, and understand people's characters so well at a glance. What do you think of Natalie [Natásha]? Could she be constant in her attachments? Could she, like other women" (Véra meant herself), "love a man once for all and remain true to him forever? That is what I consider true love. What do you think, Prince?"

"I know your sister too little," replied Prince Andrew, with a sarcastic

smile under which he wished to hide his embarrassment, "to be able to solve so delicate a question, and then I have noticed that the less attractive a woman is the more constant she is likely to be," he added, and looked up at Pierre who was just approaching them.

"Yes, that is true, Prince. In our days," continued Véra—mentioning "our days" as people of limited intelligence are fond of doing, imagining that they have discovered and appraised the peculiarities of "our days" and that human characteristics change with the times—"in our days a girl has so much freedom that the pleasure of being courted often stifles real feeling in her. And it must be confessed that Natalie is very susceptible." This return to the subject of Natalie caused Prince Andrew to knit his brows with discomfort: he was about to rise, but Véra continued with a still more subtle smile:

"I think no one has been more courted than she," she went on, "but till quite lately she never cared seriously for anyone. Now you know, Count," she said to Pierre, "even our dear cousin Borís, who, between ourselves, was very far gone in the land of tenderness . . ." (alluding to a map of love much in vogue at that time).

Prince Andrew frowned and remained silent.

"You are friendly with Borís, aren't you?" asked Véra.

"Yes, I know him. . . ."

"I expect he has told you of his childish love for Natásha?"

"Oh, there was childish love?" suddenly asked Prince Andrew, blushing unexpectedly.

"Yes, you know between cousins intimacy often leads to love. Le cousinage est un dangereux voisinage [Cousinhood is a dangerous neighborhood]. Don't you think so?"

"Oh, undoubtedly!" said Prince Andrew, and with sudden and unnatural liveliness he began chaffing Pierre about the need to be very careful with his fifty-year-old Moscow cousins, and in the midst of these jesting remarks he rose, taking Pierre by the arm, and drew him aside.

"Well?" asked Pierre, seeing his friend's strange animation with surprise, and noticing the glance he turned on Natásha as he rose.

"I must . . . I must have a talk with you," said Prince Andrew. "You know that pair of women's gloves?" (He referred to the Masonic gloves given to a newly initiated Brother to present to the woman he loved.) "I . . . but no, I will talk to you later on," and with a strange light in his eyes and restlessness in his movements, Prince Andrew approached Natásha and sat down beside her. Pierre saw how Prince Andrew asked her something and how she flushed as she replied.

But at that moment Berg came to Pierre and began insisting that he

should take part in an argument between the general and the colonel on the affairs in Spain.

Berg was satisfied and happy. The smile of pleasure never left his face. The party was very successful and quite like other parties he had seen. Everything was similar: the ladies' subtle talk, the cards, the general raising his voice at the card table, and the samovar and the tea cakes; only one thing was lacking that he had always seen at the evening parties he wished to imitate. They had not yet had a loud conversation among the men and a dispute about something important and clever. Now the general had begun such a discussion and so Berg drew Pierre to it.

13. Natásha consults her mother. Prince Andrew confides in Pierre

NEXT DAY, having been invited by the count, Prince Andrew dined with the Rostóvs and spent the rest of the day there. Everyone in the house realized for whose sake Prince Andrew came, and without concealing it he tried to be with Natásha all day. Not only in the soul of the frightened yet happy and enraptured Natásha, but in the whole house, there was a feeling of awe at something important that was bound to happen. The countess looked with sad and sternly serious eyes at Prince Andrew when he talked to Natásha and timidly started some artificial conversation about trifles as soon as he looked her way. Sónya was afraid to leave Natásha and afraid of being in the way when she was with them. Natásha grew pale, in·a panic of expectation, when she remained alone with him for a moment. Prince Andrew surprised her by his timidity. She felt that he wanted to say something to her but could not bring himself to do so.

In the evening, when Prince Andrew had left, the countess went up to Natásha and whispered: "Well, what?"

"Mamma! For heaven's sake don't ask me anything now! One can't talk about that," said Natásha.

But all the same that night Natásha, now agitated and now frightened, lay a long time in her mother's bed gazing straight before her. She told her how he had complimented her, how he told her he was going abroad, asked her where they were going to spend the summer, and then how he had asked her about Borís.

"But such a . . . such a . . . never happened to me before!" she said. "Only I feel afraid in his presence. I am always afraid when I'm with him.

What does that mean? Does it mean that it's the real thing? Yes? Mamma, are you asleep?"

"No, my love; I am frightened myself," answered her mother. "Now go!"

"All the same I shan't sleep. What silliness, to sleep! Mummy! Mummy! such a thing never happened to me before," she said, surprised and alarmed at the feeling she was aware of in herself. "And could we ever have thought! . . ."

It seemed to Natásha that even at the time she first saw Prince Andrew at Otrádnoe she had fallen in love with him. It was as if she feared this strange, unexpected happiness of meeting again the very man she had then chosen (she was firmly convinced she had done so) and of finding him, as it seemed, not indifferent to her.

"And it had to happen that he should come specially to Petersburg while we are here. And it had to happen that we should meet at that ball. It is fate. Clearly it is fate that everything led up to this! Already *then*, directly I saw him I felt something peculiar."

"What else did he say to you? What are those verses? Read them . . ." said her mother, thoughtfully, referring to some verses Prince Andrew had written in Natásha's album.

"Mamma, one need not be ashamed of his being a widower?"

"Don't, Natásha! Pray to God. 'Marriages are made in heaven,'" said her mother.

"Darling Mummy, how I love you! How happy I am!" cried Natásha, shedding tears of joy and excitement and embracing her mother.

At that very time Prince Andrew was sitting with Pierre and telling him of his love for Natásha and his firm resolve to make her his wife.

That day Countess Hélène had a reception at her house. The French ambassador was there, and a foreign prince of the blood who had of late become a frequent visitor of hers, and many brilliant ladies and gentlemen. Pierre, who had come downstairs, walked through the rooms and struck everyone by his preoccupied, absent-minded, and morose air.

Since the ball he had felt the approach of a fit of nervous depression and had made desperate efforts to combat it. Since the intimacy of his wife with the royal prince, Pierre had unexpectedly been made a gentleman of the bedchamber, and from that time he had begun to feel oppressed and ashamed in court society, and dark thoughts of the vanity of all things human came to him oftener than before. At the same time the feeling he had noticed between his protégée Natásha and Prince Andrew accentuated his gloom by the contrast between his own position and his friend's. He tried equally to avoid thinking about his wife, and about

Natásha and Prince Andrew; and again everything seemed to him insignificant in comparison with eternity; again the question: for what? presented itself; * and he forced himself to work day and night at Masonic labors, hoping to drive away the evil spirit that threatened him. Toward midnight, after he had left the countess' apartments, he was sitting upstairs in a shabby dressing gown, copying out the original transactions of the Scottish lodge of Freemasons at a table in his low room cloudy with tobacco smoke, when someone came in. It was Prince Andrew.

"Ah, it's you!" said Pierre with a preoccupied, dissatisfied air. "And I, you see, am hard at it." He pointed to his manuscript book with that air of escaping from the ills of life with which unhappy people look at their work.

Prince Andrew, with a beaming, ecstatic expression of renewed life on his face, paused in front of Pierre and, not noticing his sad look, smiled at him with the egotism of joy.

"Well, dear heart," said he, "I wanted to tell you about it yesterday and I have come to do so today. I never experienced anything like it before. I am in love, my friend!"

Suddenly Pierre heaved a deep sigh and dumped his heavy person down on the sofa beside Prince Andrew.

"With Natásha Rostóva, yes?" said he.

"Yes, yes! Who else should it be? I should never have believed it, but the feeling is stronger than I. Yesterday I tormented myself and suffered, but I would not exchange even that torment for anything in the world, I have not lived till now. At last I live, but I can't live without her! But can she love me? . . . I am too old for her. . . . Why don't you speak?"

"I? I? What did I tell you?" said Pierre suddenly, rising and beginning to pace up and down the room. "I always thought it. . . . That girl is such a treasure . . . she is a rare girl. . . . My dear friend, I entreat you, don't philosophize, don't doubt, marry, marry, marry. . . . And I am sure there will not be a happier man than you."

"But what of her?"

"She loves you."

"Don't talk rubbish . . ." said Prince Andrew, smiling and looking into Pierre's eyes.

"She does, I know," Pierre cried fiercely.

"But do listen," returned Prince Andrew, holding him by the arm. "Do you know the condition I am in? I must talk about it to someone."

* Note the similarity of Pierre's feeling here expressed with what Tolstóy, some twelve years after writing this section, described himself as feeling (Ch. iii of his Confession).—A.M.

"Well, go on, go on. I am very glad," said Pierre, and his face really changed, his brow became smooth, and he listened gladly to Prince Andrew. Prince Andrew seemed, and really was, quite a different, quite a new man. Where was his spleen, his contempt for life, his disillusionment? Pierre was the only person to whom he made up his mind to speak openly; and to him he told all that was in his soul. Now he boldly and lightly made plans for an extended future, said he could not sacrifice his own happiness to his father's caprice, and spoke of how he would either make his father consent to this marriage and love her, or would do without his consent; then he marveled at the feeling that had mastered him as at something strange, apart from and independent of himself.

"I should not have believed anyone who told me that I was capable of such love," said Prince Andrew. "It is not at all the same feeling that I knew in the past. The whole world is now for me divided into two halves: one half is she, and there all is joy, hope, light: the other half is everything where she is not, and there all is gloom and darkness. . . ."

"Darkness and gloom," reiterated Pierre: "yes, yes, I understand that."

"I cannot help loving the light, it is not my fault. And I am very happy! You understand me? I know you are glad for my sake."

"Yes, yes," Pierre assented, looking at his friend with a touched and sad expression in his eyes. The brighter Prince Andrew's lot appeared to him, the gloomier seemed his own.

14. Prince N. Bolkónski insists on postponement of his son's marriage. Natásha's distress at Prince Andrew's absence. He returns and they become engaged

PRINCE ANDREW needed his father's consent to his marriage, and to obtain this he started for the country next day.

His father received his son's communication with external composure, but inward wrath. He could not comprehend how anyone could wish to alter his life or introduce anything new into it, when his own life was already ending. "If only they would let me end my days as I want to," thought the old man, "then they might do as they please." With his son, however, he employed the diplomacy he reserved for important occasions and, adopting a quiet tone, discussed the whole matter.

In the first place the marriage was not a brilliant one as regards birth, wealth, or rank. Secondly, Prince Andrew was no longer as young as he had been and his health was poor (the old man laid special stress on this), while she was very young. Thirdly, he had a son whom it would be a pity

to entrust to a chit of a girl. "Fourthly and finally," the father said, looking ironically at his son, "I beg you to put it off for a year: go abroad, take a cure, look out as you wanted to for a German tutor for Prince Nicholas. Then if your love or passion or obstinacy—as you please—is still as great, marry! And that's my last word on it. Mind, the last! . . ." concluded the prince, in a tone which showed that nothing would make him alter his decision.

Prince Andrew saw clearly that the old man hoped that his feelings, or his fiancée's, would not stand a year's test, or that he (the old prince himself) would die before then, and he decided to conform to his father's wish—to propose, and postpone the wedding for a year.

Three weeks after the last evening he had spent with the Rostóvs, Prince Andrew returned to Petersburg.

Next day after her talk with her mother Natásha expected Bolkónski all day, but he did not come. On the second and third day it was the same. Pierre did not come either and Natásha, not knowing that Prince Andrew had gone to see his father, could not explain his absence to herself.

Three weeks passed in this way. Natásha had no desire to go out anywhere and wandered from room to room like a shadow, idle and listless; she wept secretly at night and did not go to her mother in the evenings. She blushed continually and was irritable. It seemed to her that everybody knew about her disappointment and was laughing at her and pitying her. Strong as was her inward grief, this wound to her vanity intensified her misery.

Once she came to her mother, tried to say something, and suddenly began to cry. Her tears were those of an offended child who does not know why it is being punished.

The countess began to soothe Natásha, who after first listening to her mother's words, suddenly interrupted her:

"Leave off, Mamma! I don't think, and don't want to think about it! He just came and then left off, left off. . . ."

Her voice trembled, and she again nearly cried, but recovered and went on quietly:

"And I don't at all want to get married. And I am afraid of him; I have now become quite calm, quite calm."

The day after this conversation Natásha put on the old dress which she knew had the peculiar property of conducing to cheerfulness in the mornings, and that day she returned to the old way of life which she had abandoned since the ball. Having finished her morning tea she went to the ballroom, which she particularly liked for its loud resonance, and began

singing her solfeggio. When she had finished her first exercise she stood still in the middle of the room and sang a musical phrase that particularly pleased her. She listened joyfully (as though she had not expected it) to the charm of the notes reverberating, filling the whole empty ballroom, and slowly dying away; and all at once she felt cheerful. "What's the good of making so much of it? Things are nice as it is," she said to herself, and she began walking up and down the room, not stepping simply on the resounding parquet but treading with each step from the heel to the toe (she had on a new and favorite pair of shoes) and listening to the regular tap of the heel and creak of the toe as gladly as she had to the sounds of her own voice. Passing a mirror she glanced into it. "There, that's me!" the expression of her face seemed to say as she caught sight of herself. "Well, and very nice too! I need nobody."

A footman wanted to come in to clear away something in the room but she would not let him, and having closed the door behind him continued her walk. That morning she had returned to her favorite mood—love of, and delight in, herself. "How charming that Natásha is!" she said again, speaking as some third, collective, male person. "Pretty, a good voice, young, and in nobody's way if only they leave her in peace." But however much they left her in peace she could not now be at peace, and immediately felt this.

In the hall the porch door opened, and someone asked, "At home?" and then footsteps were heard. Natásha was looking at the mirror, but did not see herself. She listened to the sounds in the hall. When she saw herself, her face was pale. It was *he*. She knew this for certain, though she hardly heard his voice through the closed doors.

Pale and agitated, Natásha ran into the drawing room.

"Mamma! Bolkónski has come!" she said. "Mamma, it is awful, it is unbearable! I don't want . . . to be tormented! What am I to do? . . ."

Before the countess could answer, Prince Andrew entered the room with an agitated and serious face. As soon as he saw Natásha his face brightened. He kissed the countess' hand and Natásha's, and sat down beside the sofa.

"It is long since we had the pleasure . . ." began the countess, but Prince Andrew interrupted her by answering her intended question, obviously in haste to say what he had to.

"I have not been to see you all this time because I have been at my father's. I had to talk over a very important matter with him. I only got back last night," he said glancing at Natásha; "I want to have a talk with you, Countess," he added after a moment's pause.

The countess lowered her eyes, sighing deeply.

"I am at your disposal," she murmured.

Natásha knew that she ought to go away, but was unable to do so: something gripped her throat, and regardless of manners she stared straight at Prince Andrew with wide-open eyes.

"At once? This instant! . . . No, it can't be!" she thought.

Again he glanced at her, and that glance convinced her that she was not mistaken. Yes, at once, that very instant, her fate would be decided.

"Go, Natásha! I will call you," said the countess in a whisper.

Natásha glanced with frightened imploring eyes at Prince Andrew and at her mother and went out.

"I have come, Countess, to ask for your daughter's hand," said Prince Andrew.

The countess' face flushed hotly, but she said nothing.

"Your offer . . ." she began at last sedately. He remained silent, looking into her eyes. "Your offer . . ." (she grew confused) "is agreeable to us, and . . . I accept your offer. I am glad. And my husband . . . I hope . . . but it will depend on her. . . ."

"I will speak to her when I have your consent. . . . Do you give it to me?" said Prince Andrew.

"Yes," replied the countess. She held out her hand to him, and with a mixed feeling of estrangement and tenderness pressed her lips to his forehead as he stooped to kiss her hand. She wished to love him as a son, but felt that to her he was a stranger and a terrifying man. "I am sure my husband will consent," said the countess, "but your father . . ."

"My father, to whom I have told my plans, has made it an express condition of his consent that the wedding is not to take place for a year. And I wished to tell you of that," said Prince Andrew.

"It is true that Natásha is still young, but—so long as that? . . ."

"It is unavoidable," said Prince Andrew with a sigh.

"I will send her to you," said the countess, and left the room.

"Lord have mercy upon us!" she repeated while seeking her daughter. Sónya said that Natásha was in her bedroom. Natásha was sitting on the bed, pale and dry-eyed, and was gazing at the icons and whispering something as she rapidly crossed herself. Seeing her mother she jumped up and flew to her.

"Well, Mamma? . . . Well? . . ."

"Go, go to him. He is asking for your hand," said the countess, coldly it seemed to Natásha. "Go . . . go," said the mother, sadly and reproachfully, with a deep sigh, as her daughter ran away.

Natásha never remembered how she entered the drawing room. When she came in and saw him she paused. "Is it possible that this stranger has

now become everything to me?" she asked herself, and immediately answered, "Yes, everything! He alone is now dearer to me than everything in the world." Prince Andrew came up to her with downcast eyes.

"I have loved you from the very first moment I saw you. May I hope?" He looked at her and was struck by the serious impassioned expression of her face. Her face said: "Why ask? Why doubt what you cannot but know? Why speak, when words cannot express what one feels?"

She drew near to him and stopped. He took her hand and kissed it.

"Do you love me?"

"Yes, yes!" Natásha murmured as if in vexation. Then she sighed loudly and, catching her breath more and more quickly, began to sob.

"What is it? What's the matter?"

"Oh, I am so happy!" she replied, smiled through her tears, bent over closer to him, paused for an instant as if asking herself whether she might, and then kissed him.

Prince Andrew held her hands, looked into her eyes, and did not find in his heart his former love for her. Something in him had suddenly changed; there was no longer the former poetic and mystic charm of desire, but there was pity for her feminine and childish weakness, fear at her devotion and trustfulness, and an oppressive yet joyful sense of the duty that now bound him to her forever. The present feeling, though not so bright and poetic as the former, was stronger and more serious.

"Did your mother tell you that it cannot be for a year?" asked Prince Andrew, still looking into her eyes.

"Is it possible that I—the 'chit of a girl,' as everybody called me," thought Natásha—"is it possible that I am now to be the wife and the equal of this strange, dear, clever man whom even my father looks up to? Can it be true? Can it be true that there can be no more playing with life, that now I am grown up, that on me now lies a responsibility for my every word and deed? Yes, but what did he ask me?"

"No," she replied, but she had not understood his question.

"Forgive me!" he said. "But you are so young, and I have already been through so much in life. I am afraid for you, you do not yet know yourself."

Natásha listened with concentrated attention, trying but failing to take in the meaning of his words.

"Hard as this year which delays my happiness will be," continued Prince Andrew, "it will give you time to be sure of yourself. I ask you to make me happy in a year, but you are free: our engagement shall remain a secret, and should you find that you do not love me, or should you come to love . . ." said Prince Andrew with an unnatural smile.

"Why do you say that?" Natásha interrupted him. "You know that from the very day you first came to Otrádnoe I have loved you," she cried, quite convinced that she spoke the truth.

"In a year you will learn to know yourself. . . ."

"A whole year!" Natásha repeated suddenly, only now realizing that the marriage was to be postponed for a year. "But why a year? Why a year? . . ."

Prince Andrew began to explain to her the reasons for this delay. Natásha did not hear him.

"And can't it be helped?" she asked. Prince Andrew did not reply, but his face expressed the impossibility of altering that decision.

"It's awful! Oh, it's awful! awful!" Natásha suddenly cried, and again burst into sobs. "I shall die, waiting a year: it's impossible, it's awful!" She looked into her lover's face and saw in it a look of commiseration and perplexity.

"No, no! I'll do anything!" she said, suddenly checking her tears. "I am so happy."

The father and mother came into the room and gave the betrothed couple their blessing.

From that day Prince Andrew began to frequent the Rostóvs' as Natásha's affianced lover.

15. Prince Andrew's last days with Natásha

NO BETROTHAL CEREMONY took place and Natásha's engagement to Bolkónski was not announced; Prince Andrew insisted on that. He said that as he was responsible for the delay he ought to bear the whole burden of it; that he had given his word and bound himself forever, but that he did not wish to bind Natásha and gave her perfect freedom. If after six months she felt that she did not love him she would have full right to reject him. Naturally neither Natásha nor her parents wished to hear of this, but Prince Andrew was firm. He came every day to the Rostóvs', but did not behave to Natásha as an affianced lover: he did not use the familiar *thou*, but said *you* to her, and kissed only her hand. After their engagement, quite different, intimate, and natural relations sprang up between them. It was as if they had not known each other till now. Both liked to recall how they had regarded each other when as yet they were *nothing* to one another; they felt themselves now quite different beings: then they were artificial, now natural and sincere. At first the family felt some constraint in intercourse with Prince Andrew; he seemed

a man from another world, and for a long time Natásha trained the family
to get used to him, proudly assuring them all that he only appeared to be
different, but was really just like all of them, and that she was not afraid of
him and no one else ought to be. After a few days they grew accustomed
to him, and without restraint in his presence pursued their usual way of
life, in which he took his part. He could talk about rural economy with
the count, fashions with the countess and Natásha, and about albums
and fancywork with Sónya. Sometimes the household both among them-
selves and in his presence expressed their wonder at how it had all hap-
pened, and at the evident omens there had been of it: Prince Andrew's
coming to Otrádnoe and their coming to Petersburg, and the likeness
between Natásha and Prince Andrew which her nurse had noticed on his
first visit, and Andrew's encounter with Nicholas in 1805, and many other
incidents betokening that it had to be.

In the house that poetic dullness and quiet reigned which always ac-
companies the presence of a betrothed couple. Often when all sitting to-
gether everyone kept silent. Sometimes the others would get up and go
away and the couple, left alone, still remained silent. They rarely spoke of
their future life. Prince Andrew was afraid and ashamed to speak of it.
Natásha shared this as she did all his feelings, which she constantly di-
vined. Once she began questioning him about his son. Prince Andrew
blushed, as he often did now—Natásha particularly liked it in him—and
said that his son would not live with them.

"Why not?" asked Natásha in a frightened tone.

"I cannot take him away from his grandfather, and besides . . ."

"How I should have loved him!" said Natásha, immediately guessing
his thought; "but I know you wish to avoid any pretext for finding fault
with us."

Sometimes the old count would come up, kiss Prince Andrew, and ask
his advice about Pétya's education or Nicholas' service. The old countess
sighed as she looked at them; Sónya was always getting frightened lest
she should be in the way and tried to find excuses for leaving them alone,
even when they did not wish it. When Prince Andrew spoke (he could
tell a story very well), Natásha listened to him with pride; when she spoke
she noticed with fear and joy that he gazed attentively and scrutinizingly
at her. She asked herself in perplexity: "What does he look for in me?
He is trying to discover something by looking at me! What if what he
seeks in me is not there?" Sometimes she fell into one of the mad, merry
moods characteristic of her, and then she particularly loved to hear and
see how Prince Andrew laughed. He seldom laughed, but when he did he
abandoned himself entirely to his laughter, and after such a laugh she

always felt nearer to him. Natásha would have been completely happy if the thought of the separation awaiting her and drawing near had not terrified her, just as the mere thought of it made him turn pale and cold.

On the eve of his departure from Petersburg Prince Andrew brought with him Pierre, who had not been to the Rostóvs' once since the ball. Pierre seemed disconcerted and embarrassed. He was talking to the countess, and Natásha sat down beside a little chess table with Sónya, thereby inviting Prince Andrew to come too. He did so.

"You have known Bezúkhov a long time?" he asked. "Do you like him?"

"Yes, he's a dear, but very absurd."

And as usual when speaking of Pierre, she began to tell anecdotes of his absent-mindedness, some of which had even been invented about him.

"Do you know I have entrusted him with our secret? I have known him from childhood. He has a heart of gold. I beg you, Natalie," Prince Andrew said with sudden seriousness—"I am going away and heaven knows what may happen. You may cease to . . . all right, I know I am not to say that. Only this, then: whatever may happen to you when I am not here . . ."

"What can happen?"

"Whatever trouble may come," Prince Andrew continued, "I beg you, Mademoiselle Sophie [Sónya], whatever may happen, to turn to him alone for advice and help! He is a most absent-minded and absurd fellow, but he has a heart of gold."

Neither her father, nor her mother, nor Sónya, nor Prince Andrew himself could have foreseen how the separation from her lover would act on Natásha. Flushed and agitated she went about the house all that day, dry-eyed, occupied with most trivial matters as if not understanding what awaited her. She did not even cry when, on taking leave, he kissed her hand for the last time. "Don't go!" she said in a tone that made him wonder whether he really ought not to stay and which he remembered long afterwards. Nor did she cry when he was gone; but for several days she sat in her room dry-eyed, taking no interest in anything and only saying now and then, "Oh, why did he go away?"

But a fortnight after his departure, to the surprise of those around her, she recovered from her mental sickness just as suddenly and became her old self again, but with a change in her moral physiognomy, as a child gets up after a long illness with a changed expression of face.

16. Prince N. Bolkónski's treatment of Mary.
Her letter to Julie Karágina

DURING THAT YEAR after his son's departure, Prince Nicholas Bolkón-ski's health and temper became much worse. He grew still more irritable, and it was Princess Mary who generally bore the brunt of his frequent fits of unprovoked anger. He seemed carefully to seek out her tender spots so as to torture her mentally as harshly as possible. Princess Mary had two passions and consequently two joys—her nephew, little Nicholas, and religion—and these were the favorite subjects of the prince's attacks and ridicule. Whatever was spoken of he would bring round to the superstitiousness of old maids, or the petting and spoiling of children. "You want to make him"—little Nicholas—"into an old maid like yourself! A pity! Prince Andrew wants a son and not an old maid," he would say. Or, turning to Mademoiselle Bourienne, he would ask her in Princess Mary's presence how she liked our village priests and icons and would joke about them.

He continually hurt Princess Mary's feelings and tormented her, but it cost her no effort to forgive him. Could he be to blame toward her, or could her father, whom she knew loved her in spite of it all, be unjust? And what is justice? The princess never thought of that proud word "justice." All the complex laws of man centered for her in one clear and simple law—the law of love and self-sacrifice taught us by Him who lovingly suffered for mankind though He Himself was God. What had she to do with the justice or injustice of other people? She had to endure and love, and that she did.

During the winter Prince Andrew had come to Bald Hills and had been gay, gentle, and more affectionate than Princess Mary had known him for a long time past. She felt that something had happened to him, but he said nothing to her about his love. Before he left he had a long talk with his father about something, and Princess Mary noticed that before his departure they were dissatisfied with one another.

Soon after Prince Andrew had gone, Princess Mary wrote to her friend Julie Karágina in Petersburg, whom she had dreamed (as all girls dream) of marrying to her brother, and who was at that time in mourning for her own brother, killed in Turkey.

Sorrow, it seems, is our common lot, my dear, tender friend Julie.
Your loss is so terrible that I can only explain it to myself as a special providence of God who, loving you, wishes to try you and your

excellent mother. Oh, my friend! Religion, and religion alone, can—I will not say comfort us—but save us from despair. Religion alone can explain to us what without its help man cannot comprehend: why, for what cause, kind and noble beings able to find happiness in life—not merely harming no one but necessary to the happiness of others—are called away to God, while cruel, useless, harmful persons, or such as are a burden to themselves and to others, are left living. The first death I saw, and one I shall never forget—that of my dear sister-in-law—left that impression on me. Just as you ask destiny why your splendid brother had to die, so I asked why that angel Lise, who not only never wronged anyone, but in whose soul there were never any unkind thoughts, had to die. And what do you think, dear friend? Five years have passed since then, and already I, with my petty understanding, begin to see clearly why she had to die, and in what way that death was but an expression of the infinite goodness of the Creator, whose every action, though generally incomprehensible to us, is but a manifestation of His infinite love for His creatures. Perhaps, I often think, she was too angelically innocent to have the strength to perform all a mother's duties. As a young wife she was irreproachable; perhaps she could not have been so as a mother. As it is, not only has she left us, and particularly Prince Andrew, with the purest regrets and memories, but probably she will there receive a place I dare not hope for myself. But not to speak of her alone, that early and terrible death has had the most beneficent influence on me and on my brother in spite of all our grief. Then, at the moment of our loss, these thoughts could not occur to me; I should then have dismissed them with horror, but now they are very clear and certain. I write all this to you, dear friend, only to convince you of the Gospel truth which has become for me a principle of life: not a single hair of our heads will fall without His will. And His will is governed only by infinite love for us, and so whatever befalls us is for our good.

You ask whether we shall spend next winter in Moscow. In spite of my wish to see you, I do not think so and do not want to do so. You will be surprised to hear that the reason for this is Buonaparte! The case is this: my father's health is growing noticeably worse, he cannot stand any contradiction and is becoming irritable. This irritability is, as you know, chiefly directed to political questions. He cannot endure the notion that Buonaparte is negotiating on equal terms with all the sovereigns of Europe and particularly with our own, the grandson of the Great Catherine! As you know, I am quite indifferent to politics, but from my father's remarks and his talks with Michael Ivánovich I know all that goes on in the world and especially about the honors conferred on Buonaparte, who only at Bald Hills in the whole world, it seems, is not accepted as a great man, still less as Emperor of France.

And my father cannot stand this. It seems to me that it is chiefly be-
cause of his political views that my father is reluctant to speak of go-
ing to Moscow; for he foresees the encounters that would result from
his way of expressing his views regardless of anybody. All the benefit he
might derive from a course of treatment he would lose as a result of
the disputes about Buonaparte which would be inevitable. In any
case it will be decided very shortly.

Our family life goes on in the old way except for my brother An-
drew's absence. He, as I wrote you before, has changed very much of
late. After his sorrow he only this year quite recovered his spirits. He
has again become as I used to know him when a child: kind, affection-
ate, with that heart of gold to which I know no equal. He has realized,
it seems to me, that life is not over for him. But together with this
mental change he has grown physically much weaker. He has become
thinner and more nervous. I am anxious about him and glad he is tak-
ing this trip abroad which the doctors recommended long ago. I hope
it will cure him. You write that in Petersburg he is spoken of as one of
the most active, cultivated, and capable of the young men. Forgive
my vanity as a relation, but I never doubted it. The good he has done
to everybody here, from his peasants up to the gentry, is incalculable.
On his arrival in Petersburg he received only his due. I always wonder
at the way rumors fly from Petersburg to Moscow, especially such
false ones as that you write about—I mean the report of my brother's
betrothal to the little Rostóva. I do not think my brother will ever
marry again, and certainly not her; and this is why: first, I know that
though he rarely speaks about the wife he has lost, the grief of that
loss has gone too deep in his heart for him ever to decide to give her a
successor and our little angel a stepmother. Secondly because, as far
as I know, that girl is not the kind of girl who could please Prince
Andrew. I do not think he would choose her for a wife, and frankly I
do not wish it. But I am running on too long and am at the end of my
second sheet. Good-by, my dear friend. May God keep you in His holy
and mighty care. My dear friend, Mademoiselle Bourienne, sends you
kisses. MARY.

17. Prince N. Bolkónski threatens to marry Mlle Bourienne

I N THE MIDDLE of the summer Princess Mary received an unexpected let-
ter from Prince Andrew in Switzerland in which he gave her strange and
surprising news. He informed her of his engagement to Natásha Rostóva.
The whole letter breathed loving rapture for his betrothed and tender and
confiding affection for his sister. He wrote that he had never loved as he

did now and that only now did he understand and know what life was. He asked his sister to forgive him for not having told her of his resolve when he had last visited Bald Hills, though he had spoken of it to his father. He had not done so for fear Princess Mary should ask her father to give his consent, irritating him and having to bear the brunt of his displeasure without attaining her object. "Besides," he wrote, "the matter was not then so definitely settled as it is now. My father then insisted on a delay of a year and now already *six months*, half of that period, have passed, and my resolution is firmer than ever. If the doctors did not keep me here at the spas I should be back in Russia, but as it is I have to postpone my return for three months. You know me and my relations with Father. I want nothing from him. I have been and always shall be independent; but to go against his will and arouse his anger, now that he may perhaps remain with us such a short time, would destroy half my happiness. I am now writing to him about the same question, and beg you to choose a good moment to hand him the letter and to let me know how he looks at the whole matter and whether there is hope that he may consent to reduce the term by four months."

After long hesitations, doubts, and prayers, Princess Mary gave the letter to her father. The next day the old prince said to her quietly:

"Write and tell your brother to wait till I am dead. . . . It won't be long—I shall soon set him free."

The princess was about to reply, but her father would not let her speak and, raising his voice more and more, cried:

"Marry, marry, my boy! . . . A good family! . . . Clever people, eh? Rich, eh? Yes, a nice stepmother little Nicholas will have! Write and tell him that he may marry tomorrow if he likes. She will be little Nicholas' stepmother and I'll marry Bourienne! . . . Ha, ha, ha! He mustn't be without a stepmother either! Only one thing, no more women are wanted in my house—let him marry and live by himself. Perhaps you will go and live with him too?" he added, turning to Princess Mary. "Go in heaven's name! Go out into the frost . . . the frost . . . the frost!"

After this outburst the prince did not speak any more about the matter. But repressed vexation at his son's poor-spirited behavior found expression in his treatment of his daughter. To his former pretexts for irony a fresh one was now added—allusions to stepmothers and amiabilities to Mademoiselle Bourienne.

"Why shouldn't I marry her?" he asked his daughter. "She'll make a splendid princess!"

And latterly, to her surprise and bewilderment, Princess Mary noticed that her father was really associating more and more with the French-

woman. She wrote to Prince Andrew about the reception of his letter, but comforted him with hopes of reconciling their father to the idea.

Little Nicholas and his education, her brother Andrew, and religion were Princess Mary's joys and consolations; but besides that, since everyone must have personal hopes, Princess Mary in the profoundest depths of her heart had a hidden dream and hope that supplied the chief consolation of her life. This comforting dream and hope were given her by God's folk—the half-witted and other pilgrims who visited her without the prince's knowledge. The longer she lived, the more experience and observation she had of life, the greater was her wonder at the shortsightedness of men who seek enjoyment and happiness here on earth: toiling, suffering, struggling, and harming one another, to obtain that impossible, visionary, sinful happiness. Prince Andrew had loved his wife, she died, but that was not enough: he wanted to bind his happiness to another woman. Her father objected to this because he wanted a more distinguished and wealthier match for Andrew. And they all struggled and suffered and tormented one another and injured their souls, their eternal souls, for the attainment of benefits which endure but for an instant. Not only do we know this ourselves, but Christ, the Son of God, came down to earth and told us that this life is but for a moment and is a probation; yet we cling to it and think to find happiness in it. "How is it that no one realizes this?" thought Princess Mary. "No one except these despised God's folk who, wallet on back, come to me by the back door, afraid of being seen by the prince, not for fear of ill-usage by him but for fear of causing him to sin. To leave family, home, and all the cares of worldly welfare, in order without clinging to anything to wander in hempen rags from place to place under an assumed name, doing no one any harm but praying for all—for those who drive one away as well as for those who protect one: higher than that life and truth there is no life or truth!"

There was one pilgrim, a quiet pockmarked little woman of fifty called Theodosia, who for over thirty years had gone about barefoot and worn heavy chains. Princess Mary was particularly fond of her. Once, when in a room with a lamp dimly lit before the icon Theodosia was talking of her life, the thought that Theodosia alone had found the true path of life suddenly came to Princess Mary with such force that she resolved to become a pilgrim herself. When Theodosia had gone to sleep Princess Mary thought about this for a long time, and at last made up her mind that, strange as it might seem, she must go on a pilgrimage. She disclosed this thought to no one but to her confessor, Father Akínfi, the monk, and he approved of her intention. Under guise of a present for the pilgrims, Princess Mary prepared a pilgrim's complete costume for herself: a coarse

smock, bast shoes, a rough coat, and a black kerchief. Often, approaching the chest of drawers containing this secret treasure, Princess Mary paused, uncertain whether the time had not already come to put her project into execution.

Often, listening to the pilgrims' tales, she was so stimulated by their simple speech, mechanical to them but to her so full of deep meaning, that several times she was on the point of abandoning everything and running away from home. In imagination she already pictured herself by Theodosia's side, dressed in coarse rags, walking with a staff, a wallet on her back, along the dusty road, directing her wanderings from one saint's shrine to another, free from envy, earthly love, or desire, and reaching at last the place where there is no more sorrow or sighing, but eternal joy and bliss.

"I shall come to a place and pray there, and before having time to get used to it or getting to love it, I shall go farther. I will go on till my legs fail, and I'll lie down and die somewhere, and shall at last reach that eternal, quiet haven, where there is neither sorrow nor sighing . . ." thought Princess Mary.

But afterwards, when she saw her father and especially little Koko (Nicholas), her resolve weakened. She wept quietly, and felt that she was a sinner who loved her father and little nephew more than God.

BOOK SEVEN

1810-11

BOOK SEVEN

1. Nicholas Rostóv returns home on leave. His doubts about Natásha's engagement

THE BIBLE LEGEND tells us that the absence of labor—idleness—was a condition of the first man's blessedness before the Fall. Fallen man has retained a love of idleness, but the curse weighs on the race not only because we have to seek our bread in the sweat of our brows, but because our moral nature is such that we cannot be both idle and at ease. An inner voice tells us we are in the wrong if we are idle. If man could find a state in which he felt that though idle he was fulfilling his duty, he would have found one of the conditions of man's primitive blessedness. And such a state of obligatory and irreproachable idleness is the lot of a whole class —the military. The chief attraction of military service has consisted and will consist in this compulsory and irreproachable idleness.

Nicholas Rostóv experienced this blissful condition to the full when, after 1807, he continued to serve in the Pávlograd regiment, in which he already commanded the squadron he had taken over from Denísov.

Rostóv had become a bluff, good-natured fellow, whom his Moscow acquaintances would have considered rather bad form, but who was liked and respected by his comrades, subordinates, and superiors, and was well contented with his life. Of late, in 1809, he found in letters from home more frequent complaints from his mother that their affairs were falling into greater and greater disorder, and that it was time for him to come back to gladden and comfort his old parents.

Reading these letters, Nicholas felt a dread of their wanting to take him away from surroundings in which, protected from all the entanglements of life, he was living so calmly and quietly. He felt that sooner or later he would have to re-enter that whirlpool of life, with its embarrassments and affairs to be straightened out, its accounts with stewards, quarrels, and intrigues, its ties, society, and with Sónya's love and his promise to her. It was all dreadfully difficult and complicated; and he replied to his mother

in cold, formal letters in French, beginning: "My dear Mamma," and ending: "Your obedient son," which said nothing of when he would return. In 1810 he received letters from his parents, in which they told him of Natásha's engagement to Bolkónski, and that the wedding would be in a year's time because the old prince made difficulties. This letter grieved and mortified Nicholas. In the first place he was sorry that Natásha, for whom he cared more than for anyone else in the family, should be lost to the home; and secondly, from his hussar point of view, he regretted not to have been there to show that fellow Bolkónski that connection with him was no such great honor after all, and that if he loved Natásha he might dispense with permission from his dotard father. For a moment he hesitated whether he should not apply for leave in order to see Natásha before she was married, but then came the maneuvers, and considerations about Sónya and about the confusion of their affairs, and Nicholas again put it off. But in the spring of that year, he received a letter from his mother, written without his father's knowledge, and that letter persuaded him to return. She wrote that if he did not come and take matters in hand, their whole property would be sold by auction and they would all have to go begging. The count was so weak, and trusted Mítenka so much, and was so good-natured, that everybody took advantage of him and things were going from bad to worse. "For God's sake, I implore you, come at once if you do not wish to make me and the whole family wretched," wrote the countess.

This letter touched Nicholas. He had that common sense of a matter-of-fact man which showed him what he ought to do.

The right thing now was, if not to retire from the service, at any rate to go home on leave. Why he had to go he did not know; but after his after-dinner nap he gave orders to saddle Mars, an extremely vicious gray stallion that had not been ridden for a long time, and when he returned with the horse all in a lather, he informed Lavrúshka (Denísov's servant who had remained with him) and his comrades who turned up in the evening that he was applying for leave and was going home. Difficult and strange as it was for him to reflect that he would go away without having heard from the staff—and this interested him extremely—whether he was promoted to a captaincy or would receive the Order of St. Anne for the last maneuvers; strange as it was to think that he would go away without having sold his three roans to the Polish Count Golukhovski, who was bargaining for the horses Rostóv had betted he would sell for two thousand rubles; incomprehensible as it seemed that the ball the hussars were giving in honor of the Polish Mademoiselle Przazdziecka (out of rivalry to the Uhlans who had given one in honor of their Polish Mademoiselle Borzo-

zowska) would take place without him—he knew he must go away from this good, bright world to somewhere where everything was stupid and confused. A week later he obtained his leave. His hussar comrades—not only those of his own regiment, but the whole brigade—gave Rostóv a dinner to which the subscription was fifteen rubles a head, and at which there were two bands and two choirs of singers. Rostóv danced the Trepák with Major Básov; the tipsy officers tossed, embraced, and dropped Rostóv; the soldiers of the third squadron tossed him too, and shouted "hurrah!" and then they put him in his sleigh and escorted him as far as the first post station.

During the first half of the journey—from Kremenchúg to Kiev—all Rostóv's thoughts, as is usual in such cases, were behind him, with the squadron; but when he had gone more than halfway he began to forget his three roans and Dozhoyvéyko, his quartermaster, and to wonder anxiously how things would be at Otrádnoe and what he would find there. Thoughts of home grew stronger the nearer he approached it—far stronger, as though this feeling of his was subject to the law by which the force of attraction is in inverse proportion to the square of the distance. At the last post station before Otrádnoe he gave the driver a three-ruble tip, and on arriving he ran breathlessly, like a boy, up the steps of his home.

After the rapture of meeting, and after that odd feeling of unsatisfied expectation—the feeling that "everything is just the same, so why did I hurry?"—Nicholas began to settle down in his old home world. His father and mother were much the same, only a little older. What was new in them was a certain uneasiness and occasional discord, which there used not to be, and which, as Nicholas soon found out, was due to the bad state of their affairs. Sónya was nearly twenty; she had stopped growing prettier and promised nothing more than she was already, but that was enough. She exhaled happiness and love from the time Nicholas returned, and the faithful, unalterable love of this girl had a gladdening effect on him. Pétya and Natásha surprised Nicholas most. Pétya was a big handsome boy of thirteen, merry, witty, and mischievous, with a voice that was already breaking. As for Natásha, for a long while Nicholas wondered and laughed whenever he looked at her.

"You're not the same at all," he said.

"How? Am I uglier?"

"On the contrary, but what dignity! A princess!" he whispered to her.

"Yes, yes, yes!" cried Natásha, joyfully.

She told him about her romance with Prince Andrew and of his visit to Otrádnoe and showed him his last letter.

"Well, are you glad?" Natásha asked. "I am so tranquil and happy now."

"Very glad," answered Nicholas. "He is an excellent fellow. . . . And are you very much in love?"

"How shall I put it?" replied Natásha. "I was in love with Borís, with my teacher, and with Denísov, but this is quite different. I feel at peace and settled. I know that no better man than he exists, and I am calm and contented now. Not at all as before."

Nicholas expressed his disapproval of the postponement of the marriage for a year; but Natásha attacked her brother with exasperation, proving to him that it could not be otherwise, and that it would be a bad thing to enter a family against the father's will, and that she herself wished it so.

"You don't at all understand," she said.

Nicholas was silent and agreed with her.

Her brother often wondered as he looked at her. She did not seem at all like a girl in love and parted from her affianced husband. She was even-tempered and calm and quite as cheerful as of old. This amazed Nicholas and even made him regard Bolkónski's courtship skeptically. He could not believe that her fate was sealed, especially as he had not seen her with Prince Andrew. It always seemed to him that there was something not quite right about this intended marriage.

"Why this delay? Why no betrothal?" he thought. Once, when he had touched on this topic with his mother, he discovered, to his surprise and somewhat to his satisfaction, that in the depth of her soul she too had doubts about this marriage.

"You see he writes," said she, showing her son a letter of Prince Andrew's, with that latent grudge a mother always has in regard to a daughter's future married happiness, "he writes that he won't come before December. What can be keeping him? Illness, probably! His health is very delicate. Don't tell Natásha. And don't attach importance to her being so bright: that's because she's living through the last days of her girlhood, but I know what she is like every time we receive a letter from him! However, God grant that everything turns out well!" (She always ended with these words.) "He is an excellent man!"

2. Nicholas settles accounts with Mítenka

AFTER REACHING HOME Nicholas was at first serious and even dull. He was worried by the impending necessity of interfering in the stupid business matters for which his mother had called him home. To throw off this burden as quickly as possible, on the third day after his arrival he went, angry and scowling and without answering questions as to where he was

going, to Mítenka's lodge and demanded an *account of everything*. But what an *account of everything* might be Nicholas knew even less than the frightened and bewildered Mítenka. The conversation and the examination of the accounts with Mítenka did not last long. The village elder, a peasant delegate, and the village clerk, who were waiting in the passage, heard with fear and delight first the young count's voice roaring and snapping and rising louder and louder, and then words of abuse, dreadful words, ejaculated one after the other.

"Robber! . . . Ungrateful wretch! . . . I'll hack the dog to pieces! I'm not my father! . . . Robbing us! . . ." and so on.

Then with no less fear and delight they saw how the young count, red in the face and with bloodshot eyes, dragged Mítenka out by the scruff of the neck and applied his foot and knee to him behind with great agility at convenient moments between the words, shouting, "Be off! Never let me see your face here again, you villain!"

Mítenka flew headlong down the six steps and ran away into the shrubbery. (This shrubbery was a well-known haven of refuge for culprits at Otrádnoe. Mítenka himself, returning tipsy from the town, used to hide there, and many of the residents at Otrádnoe, hiding from Mítenka, knew of its protective qualities.)

Mítenka's wife and sisters-in-law thrust their heads and frightened faces out of the door of a room where a bright samovar was boiling and where the steward's high bedstead stood with its patchwork quilt.

The young count paid no heed to them, but, breathing hard, passed by with resolute strides and went into the house.

The countess, who heard at once from the maids what had happened at the lodge, was calmed by the thought that now their affairs would certainly improve, but on the other hand felt anxious as to the effect this excitement might have on her son. She went several times to his door on tiptoe and listened, as he lighted one pipe after another.

Next day the old count called his son aside and, with an embarrassed smile, said to him:

"But you know, my dear boy, it's a pity you got excited! Mítenka has told me all about it."

"I knew," thought Nicholas, "that I should never understand anything in this crazy world."

"You were angry that he had not entered those 700 rubles. But they were carried forward—and you did not look at the other page."

"Papa, he is a blackguard and a thief! I know he is! And what I have done, I have done; but, if you like, I won't speak to him again."

"No, my dear boy" (the count, too, felt embarrassed. He knew he had

mismanaged his wife's property and was to blame toward his children, but he did not know how to remedy it). "No, I beg you to attend to the business. I am old. I . . ."

"No, Papa. Forgive me if I have caused you unpleasantness. I understand it all less than you do."

"Devil take all these peasants, and money matters, and carryings forward from page to page," he thought. "I used to understand what a 'corner' and the stakes at cards meant, but carrying forward to another page I don't understand at all," said he to himself, and after that he did not meddle in business affairs. But once the countess called her son and informed him that she had a promissory note from Anna Mikháylovna for two thousand rubles, and asked him what he thought of doing with it.

"This," answered Nicholas. "You say it rests with me. Well, I don't like Anna Mikháylovna and I don't like Borís, but they were our friends and poor. Well then, this!" and he tore up the note, and by so doing caused the old countess to weep tears of joy. After that, young Rostóv took no further part in any business affairs, but devoted himself with passionate enthusiasm to what was to him a new pursuit—the chase—for which his father kept a large establishment.

3. Nicholas decides to go hunting

THE WEATHER was already growing wintry and morning frosts congealed an earth saturated by autumn rains. The verdure had thickened and its bright green stood out sharply against the brownish strips of winter rye trodden down by the cattle, and against the pale-yellow stubble of the spring sowing and the reddish strips of buckwheat. The wooded ravines and the copses, which at the end of August had still been green islands amid black fields and stubble, had become golden and bright-red islands amid the green winter rye. The hares had already half changed their summer coats, the fox cubs were beginning to scatter, and the young wolves were bigger than dogs. It was the best time of the year for the chase. The hounds of that ardent young sportsman Rostóv had not merely reached hard winter condition, but were so jaded that at a meeting of the huntsmen it was decided to give them a three days' rest and then, on the sixteenth of September, to go on a distant expedition, starting from the oak grove where there was an undisturbed litter of wolf cubs.*

* *Readers should bear in mind that the hounds engaged in hunting of the kind here described were keen-scented but not very swift dogs. They had to find the game by scent and chase it in the desired direction, but the swift*

All that day the hounds remained at home. It was frosty and the air was sharp, but toward evening the sky became overcast and it began to thaw. On the fifteenth, when young Rostóv, in his dressing gown, looked out of the window, he saw it was an unsurpassable morning for hunting: * it was as if the sky were melting and sinking to the earth without any wind. The only motion in the air was that of the dripping, microscopic particles of drizzling mist. The bare twigs in the garden were hung with transparent drops which fell on the freshly fallen leaves. The earth in the kitchen garden looked wet and black and glistened like poppyseed and at a short distance merged into the dull, moist veil of mist. Nicholas went out into the wet and muddy porch. There was a smell of decaying leaves and of dog. Mílka, a black-spotted, broad-haunched bitch with prominent black eyes, got up on seeing her master, stretched her hind legs, lay down like a hare, and then suddenly jumped up and licked him right on his nose and mustache. Another borzoi, a dog, catching sight of his master from the garden path, arched his back and, rushing headlong toward the porch with lifted tail, began rubbing himself against his legs.

"O-hoy!" came at that moment, that inimitable huntsman's call which unites the deepest bass with the shrillest tenor, and round the corner came Daniel the head huntsman and head kennelman, a gray, wrinkled old man with hair cut straight over his forehead, Ukrainian fashion, a long bent whip in his hand, and that look of independence and scorn of everything that is only seen in huntsmen. He doffed his Circassian cap to his master and looked at him scornfully. This scorn was not offensive to his master. Nicholas knew that this Daniel, disdainful of everybody and who considered himself above them, was all the same his serf and huntsman.

"Daniel!" Nicholas said timidly, conscious at the sight of the weather, the hounds, and the huntsman that he was being carried away by that irresistible passion for sport which makes a man forget all his previous resolutions, as a lover forgets in the presence of his mistress.

"What orders, your excellency?" said the huntsman in his deep bass, deep as a protodeacon's and hoarse with hallooing—and two flashing black

and strong borzois caught and killed the game. A borzoi has very poor scent and only chases the game when he sees it. It must be pointed out to him, and even when following it he sometimes loses sight of it. If the game shams dead, a borzoi is often balked and hesitates what to do, as in the case mentioned when the hare suddenly squatted and the borzoi did not seize it.—A.M.

* _During the writing of_ War and Peace, _Tolstóy was invited by a neighbor to go on an elaborate hunt which probably was the basis for the description of the scenes described on the next few pages._

eyes gazed from under his brows at his master, who was silent. "Can you resist it?" those eyes seemed to be asking.

"It's a good day, eh? For a hunt and a gallop, eh?" asked Nicholas, scratching Mílka behind the ears.

Daniel did not answer, but winked instead.

"I sent Uvárka at dawn to listen," his bass boomed out after a minute's pause. "He says she's moved them into the Otrádnoe enclosure. They were howling there." (This meant that the she-wolf, about whom they both knew, had moved with her cubs to the Otrádnoe copse, a small place a mile and a half from the house.)

"We ought to go, don't you think so?" said Nicholas. "Come to me with Uvárka."

"As you please."

"Then put off feeding them."

"Yes, sir."

Five minutes later Daniel and Uvárka were standing in Nicholas' big study. Though Daniel was not a big man, to see him in a room was like seeing a horse or a bear on the floor among the furniture and surroundings of human life. Daniel himself felt this, and as usual stood just inside the door, trying to speak softly and not move, for fear of breaking something in the master's apartment, and he hastened to say all that was necessary so as to get from under that ceiling, out into the open under the sky once more.

Having finished his inquiries and extorted from Daniel an opinion that the hounds were fit (Daniel himself wished to go hunting), Nicholas ordered the horses to be saddled. But just as Daniel was about to go Natásha came in with rapid steps, not having done up her hair or finished dressing and with her old nurse's big shawl wrapped round her. Pétya ran in at the same time.

"You are going?" asked Natásha. "I knew you would! Sónya said you wouldn't go, but I knew that today is the sort of day when you couldn't help going."

"Yes, we are going," replied Nicholas reluctantly, for today, as he intended to hunt seriously, he did not want to take Natásha and Pétya. "We are going, but only wolf hunting: it would be dull for you."

"You know it is my greatest pleasure," said Natásha. "It's not fair; you are going by yourself, are having the horses saddled and said nothing to us about it."

" 'No barrier bars a Russian's path'—we'll go!" shouted Pétya.

"But you can't. Mamma said you mustn't," said Nicholas to Natásha.

"Yes, I'll go. I shall certainly go," said Natásha decisively. "Daniel, tell

them to saddle for us, and Michael must come with my dogs," she added to the huntsman.

It seemed to Daniel irksome and improper to be in a room at all, but to have anything to do with a young lady seemed to him impossible. He cast down his eyes and hurried out as if it were none of his business, careful as he went not to inflict any accidental injury on the young lady.

4. The wolf hunt begins

THE OLD COUNT, who had always kept up an enormous hunting establishment but had now handed it all completely over to his son's care, being in very good spirits on this fifteenth of September, prepared to go out with the others.

In an hour's time the whole hunting party was at the porch. Nicholas, with a stern and serious air which showed that now was no time for attending to trifles, went past Natásha and Pétya who were trying to tell him something. He had a look at all the details of the hunt, sent a pack of hounds and huntsmen on ahead to find the quarry, mounted his chestnut Donéts, and whistling to his own leash of borzois, set off across the threshing ground to a field leading to the Otrádnoe wood. The old count's horse, a sorrel gelding called Viflyánka, was led by the groom in attendance on him, while the count himself was to drive in a small trap straight to a spot reserved for him.

They were taking fifty-four hounds, with six hunt attendants and whippers-in. Besides the family, there were eight borzoi kennelmen and more than forty borzois, so that, with the borzois on the leash belonging to members of the family, there were about a hundred and thirty dogs and twenty horsemen.

Each dog knew its master and its call. Each man in the hunt knew his business, his place, and what he had to do. As soon as they had passed the fence they all spread out evenly and quietly, without noise or talk, along the road and field leading to the Otrádnoe covert.

The horses stepped over the field as over a thick carpet, now and then splashing into puddles as they crossed a road. The misty sky still seemed to descend evenly and imperceptibly toward the earth, the air was still, warm, and silent. Occasionally the whistle of a huntsman, the snort of a horse, the crack of a whip, or the whine of a straggling hound could be heard.

When they had gone a little less than a mile, five more riders with dogs appeared out of the mist, approaching the Rostóvs. In front rode a fresh-looking, handsome old man with a large gray mustache.

"Good morning, Uncle!" said Nicholas, when the old man drew near.

"That's it. Come on! . . . I was sure of it," began "Uncle." (He was a distant relative of the Rostóvs', a man of small means, and their neighbor.) "I knew you wouldn't be able to resist it and it's a good thing you're going. That's it! Come on!" (This was "Uncle's" favorite expression.) "Take the covert at once, for my Gírchik says the Ilágins are at Kornikí with their hounds. That's it. Come on! . . . They'll take the cubs from under your very nose."

"That's where I'm going. Shall we join up our packs?" asked Nicholas.

The hounds were joined into one pack, and "Uncle" and Nicholas rode on side by side. Natásha, muffled up in shawls which did not hide her eager face and shining eyes, galloped up to them. She was followed by Pétya who always kept close to her, by Michael, a huntsman, and by a groom appointed to look after her. Pétya, who was laughing, whipped and pulled at his horse. Natásha sat easily and confidently on her black Arábchik and reined him in without effort with a firm hand.

"Uncle" looked round disapprovingly at Pétya and Natásha. He did not like to combine frivolity with the serious business of hunting.

"Good morning, Uncle! We are going too!" shouted Pétya.

"Good morning, good morning! But don't go overriding the hounds," said "Uncle" sternly.

"Nicholas, what a fine dog Truníla is! He knew me," said Natásha, referring to her favorite hound.

"In the first place, Truníla is not a 'dog,' but a harrier," thought Nicholas, and looked sternly at his sister, trying to make her feel the distance that ought to separate them at that moment. Natásha understood it.

"You mustn't think we'll be in anyone's way, Uncle," she said. "We'll go to our places and won't budge."

"A good thing too, little countess," said "Uncle," "only mind you don't fall off your horse," he added, "because—that's it, come on!—you've nothing to hold on to."

The oasis of the Otrádnoe covert came in sight a few hundred yards off, the huntsmen were already nearing it. Rostóv, having finally settled with "Uncle" where they should set on the hounds, and having shown Natásha where she was to stand—a spot where nothing could possibly run out—went round above the ravine.

"Well, nephew, you're going for a big wolf," said "Uncle." "Mind and don't let her slip!"

"That's as may happen," answered Rostóv. "Karáy, here!" he shouted, answering "Uncle's" remark by this call to his borzoi. Karáy was a shaggy

old dog with a hanging jowl, famous for having tackled a big wolf unaided. They all took up their places.

The old count, knowing his son's ardor in the hunt, hurried so as not to be late, and the huntsmen had not yet reached their places when Count Ilyá Rostóv, cheerful, flushed, and with quivering cheeks, drove up with his black horses over the winter rye to the place reserved for him, where a wolf might come out. Having straightened his coat and fastened on his hunting knives and horn, he mounted his good, sleek, well-fed, and comfortable horse, Viflyánka, which was turning gray, like himself. His horses and trap were sent home. Count Ilyá Rostóv, though not at heart a keen sportsman, knew the rules of the hunt well, and rode to the bushy edge of the road where he was to stand, arranged his reins, settled himself in the saddle, and, feeling that he was ready, looked about with a smile.

Beside him was Simon Chekmár, his personal attendant, an old horseman now somewhat stiff in the saddle. Chekmár held in leash three formidable wolfhounds, who had, however, grown fat like their master and his horse. Two wise old dogs lay down unleashed. Some hundred paces farther along the edge of the wood stood Mítka, the count's other groom, a daring horseman and keen rider to hounds. Before the hunt, by old custom, the count had drunk a silver cupful of mulled brandy, taken a snack, and washed it down with half a bottle of his favorite Bordeaux.

He was somewhat flushed with the wine and the drive. His eyes were rather moist and glittered more than usual, and as he sat in his saddle, wrapped up in his fur coat, he looked like a child taken out for an outing.

The thin, hollow-cheeked Chekmár, having got everything ready, kept glancing at his master with whom he had lived on the best of terms for thirty years, and understanding the mood he was in expected a pleasant chat. A third person rode up circumspectly through the wood (it was plain that he had had a lesson) and stopped behind the count. This person was a gray-bearded old man in a woman's cloak, with a tall peaked cap on his head. He was the buffoon, who went by a woman's name, Nastásya Ivánovna.*

"Well, Nastásya Ivánovna!" whispered the count, winking at him. "If you scare away the beast, Daniel'll give it you!"

"I know a thing or two myself!" said Nastásya Ivánovna.

"Hush!" whispered the count and turned to Simon. "Have you seen the young countess?" he asked. "Where is she?"

"With young Count Peter, by the Zhárov rank grass," answered Simon, smiling. "Though she's a lady, she's very fond of hunting."

* The practice of keeping a buffoon in country houses lasted till after the abolition of serfdom.—A.M.

"And you're surprised at the way she rides, Simon, eh?" said the count. "She's as good as many a man!"

"Of course! It's marvelous. So bold, so easy!"

"And Nicholas? Where is he? By the Lyádov upland, isn't he?"

"Yes, sir. He knows where to stand. He understands the matter so well that Daniel and I are often quite astounded," said Simon, well knowing what would please his master.

"Rides well, eh? And how well he looks on his horse, eh?"

"A perfect picture! How he chased a fox out of the rank grass by the Zavárzinsk thicket the other day! Leaped a fearful place; what a sight when they rushed from the covert . . . the horse worth a thousand rubles and the rider beyond all price! Yes, one would have to search far to find another as smart."

"To search far . . ." repeated the count, evidently sorry Simon had not said more. "To search far," he said, turning back the skirt of his coat to get at his snuffbox.

"The other day when he came out from Mass in full uniform, Michael Sidórych . . ." Simon did not finish, for on the still air he had distinctly caught the music of the hunt with only two or three hounds giving tongue. He bent down his head and listened, shaking a warning finger at his master. "They are on the scent of the cubs . . ." he whispered, "straight to the Lyádov uplands."

The count, forgetting to smooth out the smile on his face, looked into the distance straight before him, down the narrow open space, holding the snuffbox in his hand but not taking any. After the cry of the hounds came the deep tones of the wolf call from Daniel's hunting horn; the pack joined the first three hounds and they could be heard in full cry, with that peculiar lift in the note that indicates that they are after a wolf. The whippers-in no longer set on the hounds, but changed to the cry of ulyulyu, and above the others rose Daniel's voice, now a deep bass, now piercingly shrill. His voice seemed to fill the whole wood and carried far beyond out into the open field.

After listening a few moments in silence, the count and his attendant convinced themselves that the hounds had separated into two packs: the sound of the larger pack, eagerly giving tongue, began to die away in the distance, the other pack rushed by the wood past the count, and it was with this that Daniel's voice was heard calling ulyulyu. The sounds of both packs mingled and broke apart again, but both were becoming more distant.

Simon sighed and stooped to straighten the leash a young borzoi had

entangled; the count too sighed and, noticing the snuffbox in his hand, opened it and took a pinch. "Back!" cried Simon to a borzoi that was pushing forward out of the wood. The count started and dropped the snuffbox. Nastásya Ivánovna dismounted to pick it up. The count and Simon were looking at him.

Then, unexpectedly, as often happens, the sound of the hunt suddenly approached, as if the hounds in full cry and Daniel ulyulyuing were just in front of them.

The count turned and saw on his right Mítka staring at him with eyes starting out of his head, raising his cap and pointing before him to the other side.

"Look out!" he shouted, in a voice plainly showing that he had long fretted to utter that word, and letting the borzois slip he galloped toward the count.

The count and Simon galloped out of the wood and saw on their left a wolf which, softly swaying from side to side, was coming at a quiet lope farther to the left to the very place where they were standing. The angry borzois whined and getting free of the leash rushed past the horses' feet at the wolf.

The wolf paused, turned its heavy forehead toward the dogs awkwardly, like a man suffering from the quinsy, and, still slightly swaying from side to side, gave a couple of leaps and with a swish of its tail disappeared into the skirt of the wood. At the same instant, with a cry like a wail, first one hound, then another, and then another, sprang helter-skelter from the wood opposite and the whole pack rushed across the field toward the very spot where the wolf had disappeared. The hazel bushes parted behind the hounds and Daniel's chestnut horse appeared, dark with sweat. On its long back sat Daniel, hunched forward, capless, his disheveled gray hair hanging over his flushed, perspiring face.

"Ulyulyulyu! ulyulyu! . . ." he cried. When he caught sight of the count his eyes flashed lightning.

"Blast you!" he shouted, holding up his whip threateningly at the count.

"You've let the wolf go! . . . What sportsmen!" and as if scorning to say more to the frightened and shamefaced count, he lashed the heaving flanks of his sweating chestnut gelding with all the anger the count had aroused and flew off after the hounds. The count, like a punished schoolboy, looked round, trying by a smile to win Simon's sympathy for his plight. But Simon was no longer there. He was galloping round by the bushes while the field was coming up on both sides, all trying to head the wolf, but it vanished into the wood before they could do so.

5. The wolf is taken

NICHOLAS ROSTÓV meanwhile remained at his post, waiting for the wolf. By the way the hunt approached and receded, by the cries of the dogs whose notes were familiar to him, by the way the voices of the huntsmen approached, receded, and rose, he realized what was happening at the copse. He knew that young and old wolves were there, that the hounds had separated into two packs, that somewhere a wolf was being chased, and that something had gone wrong. He expected the wolf to come his way any moment. He made thousands of different conjectures as to where and from what side the beast would come and how he would set upon it. Hope alternated with despair. Several times he addressed a prayer to God that the wolf should come his way. He prayed with that passionate and shame-faced feeling with which men pray at moments of great excitement arising from trivial causes. "What would it be to Thee to do this for me?" he said to God. "I know Thou art great, and that it is a sin to ask this of Thee, but for God's sake do let the old wolf come my way and let Karáy spring at it—in sight of 'Uncle' who is watching from over there—and seize it by the throat in a death grip!" A thousand times during that half-hour Rostóv cast eager and restless glances over the edge of the wood, with the two scraggy oaks rising above the aspen undergrowth and the gully with its water-worn side and "Uncle's" cap just visible above the bush on his right.

"No, I shan't have such luck," thought Rostóv, "yet what wouldn't it be worth! It is not to be! Everywhere, at cards and in war, I am always un-lucky." Memories of Austerlitz and of Dólokhov flashed rapidly and clearly through his mind. "Only once in my life to get an old wolf, I want only that!" thought he, straining eyes and ears and looking to the left and then to the right and listening to the slightest variation of note in the cries of the dogs.

Again he looked to the right and saw something running toward him across the deserted field. "No, it can't be!" thought Rostóv, taking a deep breath, as a man does at the coming of something long hoped for. The height of happiness was reached—and so simply, without warning, or noise, or display, that Rostóv could not believe his eyes and remained in doubt for over a second. The wolf ran forward and jumped heavily over a gully that lay in her path. She was an old animal with a gray back and big reddish belly. She ran without hurry, evidently feeling sure that no one saw her. Rostóv, holding his breath, looked round at the borzois. They stood or lay not seeing the wolf or understanding the situation. Old Karáy

had turned his head and was angrily searching for fleas, baring his yellow teeth and snapping at his hind legs.

"*Ulyulyulyu!*" whispered Rostóv, pouting his lips. The borzois jumped up, jerking the rings of the leashes and pricking their ears. Karáy finished scratching his hindquarters and, cocking his ears, got up with quivering tail from which tufts of matted hair hung down.

"Shall I loose them or not?" Nicholas asked himself as the wolf approached him coming from the copse. Suddenly the wolf's whole physiognomy changed: she shuddered, seeing what she had probably never seen before—human eyes fixed upon her—and turning her head a little toward Rostóv, she paused.

"Back or forward? Eh, no matter, forward . . ." the wolf seemed to say to herself, and she moved forward without again looking round and with a quiet, long, easy yet resolute lope.

"*Ulyulyu!*" cried Nicholas, in a voice not his own, and of its own accord his good horse darted headlong downhill, leaping over gullies to head off the wolf, and the borzois passed it, running faster still. Nicholas did not hear his own cry nor feel that he was galloping, nor see the borzois, nor the ground over which he went: he saw only the wolf, who, increasing her speed, bounded on in the same direction along the hollow. The first to come into view was Mílka, with her black markings and powerful quarters, gaining upon the wolf. Nearer and nearer . . . now she was ahead of it; but the wolf turned its head to face her, and instead of putting on speed as she usually did Mílka suddenly raised her tail and stiffened her forelegs.

"*Ulyulyulyulyu!*" shouted Nicholas.

The reddish Lyubím rushed forward from behind Mílka, sprang impetuously at the wolf, and seized it by its hindquarters, but immediately jumped aside in terror. The wolf crouched, gnashed her teeth, and again rose and bounded forward, followed at the distance of a couple of feet by all the borzois, who did not get any closer to her.

"She'll get away! No, it's impossible!" thought Nicholas, still shouting with a hoarse voice.

"Karáy, ulyulyu! . . ." he shouted, looking round for the old borzoi who was now his only hope. Karáy, with all the strength age had left him, stretched himself to the utmost and, watching the wolf, galloped heavily aside to intercept it. But the quickness of the wolf's lope and the borzoi's slower pace made it plain that Karáy had miscalculated. Nicholas could already see not far in front of him the wood where the wolf would certainly escape should she reach it. But, coming toward him, he saw hounds and a huntsman galloping almost straight at the wolf. There was still hope. A long, yellowish young borzoi, one Nicholas did not know, from another

leash, rushed impetuously at the wolf from in front and almost knocked her over. But the wolf jumped up more quickly than anyone could have expected and, gnashing her teeth, flew at the yellowish borzoi, which, with a piercing yelp, fell with its head on the ground, bleeding from a gash in its side.

"Karáy? Old fellow! . . ." wailed Nicholas.

Thanks to the delay caused by this crossing of the wolf's path, the old dog with its felted hair hanging from its thigh was within five paces of it. As if aware of her danger, the wolf turned her eyes on Karáy, tucked her tail yet further between her legs, and increased her speed. But here Nicholas only saw that something happened to Karáy—the borzoi was suddenly on the wolf, and they rolled together down into a gully just in front of them.

That instant, when Nicholas saw the wolf struggling in the gully with the dogs, while from under them could be seen her gray hair and outstretched hind leg and her frightened choking head, with her ears laid back (Karáy was pinning her by the throat), was the happiest moment of his life. With his hand on his saddlebow, he was ready to dismount and stab the wolf, when she suddenly thrust her head up from among that mass of dogs, and then her forepaws were on the edge of the gully. She clicked her teeth (Karáy no longer had her by the throat), leaped with a movement of her hind legs out of the gully, and having disengaged herself from the dogs, with tail tucked in again, went forward. Karáy, his hair bristling, and probably bruised or wounded, climbed with difficulty out of the gully.

"Oh my God! Why?" Nicholas cried in despair.

"Uncle's" huntsman was galloping from the other side across the wolf's path and his borzois once more stopped the animal's advance. She was again hemmed in.

Nicholas and his attendant, with "Uncle" and his huntsman, were all riding round the wolf, crying "ulyulyu!" shouting and preparing to dismount each moment that the wolf crouched back, and starting forward again every time she shook herself and moved toward the wood where she would be safe.

Already, at the beginning of this chase, Daniel, hearing the ulyulyuing, had rushed out from the wood. He saw Karáy seize the wolf, and checked his horse, supposing the affair to be over. But when he saw that the horsemen did not dismount and that the wolf shook herself and ran for safety, Daniel set his chestnut galloping, not at the wolf but straight toward the wood, just as Karáy had run to cut the animal off. As a result of this, he galloped up to the wolf just when she had been stopped a second time by "Uncle's" borzois.

Daniel galloped up silently, holding a naked dagger in his left hand and thrashing the laboring sides of his chestnut horse with his whip as if it were a flail.

. Nicholas neither saw nor heard Daniel until the chestnut, breathing heavily, panted past him, and he heard the fall of a body and saw Daniel lying on the wolf's back among the dogs, trying to seize her by the ears. It was evident to the dogs, the hunters, and to the wolf herself that all was now over. The terrified wolf pressed back her ears and tried to rise, but the borzois stuck to her. Daniel rose a little, took a step, and with his whole weight, as if lying down to rest, fell on the wolf, seizing her by the ears. Nicholas was about to stab her, but Daniel whispered, "Don't! We'll gag her!" and, changing his position, set his foot on the wolf's neck. A stick was thrust between her jaws and she was fastened with a leash, as if bridled, her legs were bound together, and Daniel rolled her over once or twice from side to side.

With happy, exhausted faces, they laid the old wolf, alive, on a shying and snorting horse and, accompanied by the dogs yelping at her, took her to the place where they were all to meet. The hounds had killed two of the cubs and the borzois three. The huntsmen assembled with their booty and their stories, and all came to look at the wolf, which, with her broad-browed head hanging down and the bitten stick between her jaws, gazed with great glassy eyes at this crowd of dogs and men surrounding her. When she was touched, she jerked her bound legs and looked wildly yet simply at everybody. Old Count Rostóv also rode up and touched the wolf.

"Oh, what a formidable one!" said he. "A formidable one, eh?" he asked Daniel, who was standing near.

"Yes, your excellency," answered Daniel, quickly doffing his cap.

The count remembered the wolf he had let slip and his encounter with Daniel.

"Ah, but you are a crusty fellow, friend!" said the count.

For sole reply Daniel gave him a shy, childlike, meek, and amiable smile.

6. The fox hunt and the huntsmen's quarrel. Ilágin's courtesy. Chasing a hare. Rugáy's triumph

THE OLD COUNT went home, and Natásha and Pétya promised to return very soon, but as it was still early the hunt went farther. At midday they put the hounds into a ravine thickly overgrown with young trees. Nicholas standing in a fallow field could see all his whips.

Facing him lay a field of winter rye, and there his own huntsman stood

alone in a hollow behind a hazel bush. The hounds had scarcely been loosed before Nicholas heard one he knew, Voltórn, giving tongue at intervals; other hounds joined in, now pausing and now again giving tongue. A moment later he heard a cry from the wooded ravine that a fox had been found, and the whole pack, joining together, rushed along the ravine toward the ryefield and away from Nicholas.

He saw the whips in their red caps galloping along the edge of the ravine, he even saw the hounds, and was expecting a fox to show itself at any moment on the ryefield opposite.

The huntsman standing in the hollow moved and loosed his borzois, and Nicholas saw a queer, short-legged red fox with a fine brush going hard across the field. The borzois bore down on it. . . . Now they drew close to the fox which began to dodge between the field in sharper and sharper curves, trailing its brush, when suddenly a strange white borzoi dashed in followed by a black one, and everything was in confusion; the borzois formed a star-shaped figure, scarcely swaying their bodies and with tails turned away from the center of the group. Two huntsmen galloped up to the dogs; one in a red cap, the other, a stranger, in a green coat.

"What's this?" thought Nicholas. "Where's that huntsman from? He is not 'Uncle's' man."

The huntsmen got the fox, but stayed there a long time without strapping it to the saddle. Their horses, bridled and with high saddles, stood near them and there too the dogs were lying. The huntsmen waved their arms and did something to the fox. Then from that spot came the sound of a horn, with the signal agreed on in case of a fight.

"That's Ilágin's huntsman having a row with our Iván," said Nicholas' groom.

Nicholas sent the man to call Natásha and Pétya to him, and rode at a footpace to the place where the whips were getting the hounds together. Several of the field galloped to the spot where the fight was going on.

Nicholas dismounted, and with Natásha and Pétya, who had ridden up, stopped near the hounds, waiting to see how the matter would end. Out of the bushes came the huntsman who had been fighting and rode toward his young master, with the fox tied to his crupper. While still at a distance he took off his cap and tried to speak respectfully, but he was pale and breathless and his face was angry. One of his eyes was black, but he probably was not even aware of it.

"What has happened?" asked Nicholas.

"A likely thing, killing a fox our dogs had hunted! And it was my gray bitch that caught it! Go to law, indeed! . . . He snatches at the fox! I gave him one with the fox. Here it is on my saddle! Do you want a taste of

this? . . ." said the huntsman, pointing to his dagger and probably imagining himself still speaking to his foe.

Nicholas, not stopping to talk to the man, asked his sister and Pétya to wait for him and rode to the spot where the enemy's, Ilágin's, hunting party was.

The victorious huntsman rode off to join the field, and there, surrounded by inquiring sympathizers, recounted his exploits.

The facts were that Ilágin, with whom the Rostóvs had a quarrel and were at law, hunted over places that belonged by custom to the Rostóvs, and had now, as if purposely, sent his men to the very woods the Rostóvs were hunting and let his man snatch a fox their dogs had chased.

Nicholas, though he had never seen Ilágin, with his usual absence of moderation in judgment, hated him cordially from reports of his arbitrariness and violence, and regarded him as his bitterest foe. He rode in angry agitation toward him, firmly grasping his whip and fully prepared to take the most resolute and desperate steps to punish his enemy.

Hardly had he passed an angle of the wood before a stout gentleman in a beaver cap came riding toward him on a handsome raven-black horse, accompanied by two hunt servants.

Instead of an enemy, Nicholas found in Ilágin a stately and courteous gentleman who was particularly anxious to make the young count's acquaintance. Having ridden up to Nicholas, Ilágin raised his beaver cap and said he much regretted what had occurred and would have the man punished who had allowed himself to seize a fox hunted by someone else's borzois. He hoped to become better acquainted with the count and invited him to draw his covert.

Natásha, afraid that her brother would do something dreadful, had followed him in some excitement. Seeing the enemies exchanging friendly greetings, she rode up to them. Ilágin lifted his beaver cap still higher to Natásha and said, with a pleasant smile, that the young countess resembled Diana in her passion for the chase as well as in her beauty, of which he had heard much.

To expiate his huntsman's offense, Ilágin pressed the Rostóvs to come to an upland of his about a mile away which he usually kept for himself and which, he said, swarmed with hares. Nicholas agreed, and the hunt, now doubled, moved on.

The way to Ilágin's upland was across the fields. The hunt servants fell into line. The masters rode together. "Uncle," Rostóv, and Ilágin kept stealthily glancing at one another's dogs, trying not to be observed by their companions and searching uneasily for rivals to their own borzois.

Rostóv was particularly struck by the beauty of a small, pure-bred, red-

spotted bitch on Ilágin's leash, slender but with muscles like steel, a deli-
cate muzzle, and prominent black eyes. He had heard of the swiftness of
Ilágin's borzois, and in that beautiful bitch saw a rival to his own Mílka.

In the middle of a sober conversation begun by Ilágin about the year's
harvest, Nicholas pointed to the red-spotted bitch.

"A fine little bitch, that!" said he in a careless tone. "Is she swift?"

"That one? Yes, she's a good dog, gets what she's after," answered Ilágin
indifferently, of the red-spotted bitch Erzá, for which, a year before, he
had given a neighbor three families of house serfs. "So in your parts, too,
the harvest is nothing to boast of, Count?" he went on, continuing the
conversation they had begun. And considering it polite to return the young
count's compliment, Ilágin looked at his borzois and picked out Mílka
who attracted his attention by her breadth. "That black-spotted one of
yours is fine—well shaped!" said he.

"Yes, she's fast enough," replied Nicholas, and thought: "If only a full-
grown hare would cross the field now I'd show you what sort of borzoi she
is," and turning to his groom, he said he would give a ruble to anyone who
found a hare.

"I don't understand," continued Ilágin, "how some sportsmen can be so
jealous about game and dogs. For myself, I can tell you, Count, I enjoy
riding in company such as this . . . what could be better?" (he again
raised his cap to Natásha) "but as for counting skins and what one takes,
I don't care about that."

"Of course not!"

"Or being upset because someone else's borzoi and not mine catches
something. All I care about is to enjoy seeing the chase, is it not so, Count?
For I consider that . . ."

"A-tu!" came the long-drawn cry of one of the borzoi whippers-in, who
had halted. He stood on a knoll in the stubble, holding his whip aloft, and
again repeated his long-drawn cry, "A-tu!" (This call and the uplifted whip
meant that he saw a sitting hare.)

"Ah, he has found one, I think," said Ilágin carelessly. "Well, let us
course it, Count."

"Yes, we must ride up. . . . Shall we both course it?" answered Nicho-
las, seeing in Erzá and "Uncle's" red Rugáy two rivals he had never yet had
a chance of pitting against his own borzois. "And suppose they outdo my
Mílka at once!" he thought as he rode with "Uncle" and Ilágin toward the
hare.

"A full-grown one?" asked Ilágin as he approached the whip who had
sighted the hare—and not without agitation he looked round and whistled
to Erzá.

"And you, Michael Nikanórovich?" he said, addressing "Uncle."
The latter was riding with a sullen expression on his face.
"How can I join in? Why, you've given a village for each of your borzois!
That's it, come on! Yours are worth thousands. Try yours against one an-
other, you two, and I'll look on!"

"Rugáy, hey, hey!" he shouted. "Rugáyushka!" he added, involuntarily
by this diminutive expressing his affection and the hopes he placed on this
red borzoi. Natásha saw and felt the agitation the two elderly men and her
brother were trying to conceal, and was herself excited by it.

The huntsman stood halfway up the knoll holding up his whip and the
gentlefolk rode up to him at a footpace; the hounds that were far off on the
horizon turned away from the hare, and the whips, but not the gentlefolk,
also moved away. All were moving slowly and sedately.

"How is it pointing?" asked Nicholas, riding a hundred paces toward the
whip who had sighted the hare.

But before the whip could reply, the hare, scenting the frost coming
next morning, was unable to rest and leaped up. The pack on leash rushed
downhill in full cry after the hare, and from all sides the borzois that were
not on leash darted after the hounds and the hare. All the hunt, who had
been moving slowly, shouted, "Stop!" calling in the hounds, while the
borzoi whips, with a cry of "A-tu!" galloped across the field, setting the bor-
zois on the hare. The tranquil Ilágin, Nicholas, Natásha, and "Uncle"
flew, reckless of where and how they went, seeing only the borzois and
the hare and fearing only to lose sight even for an instant of the chase. The
hare they had started was a strong and swift one. When he jumped up he
did not run at once, but pricked his ears listening to the shouting and
trampling that resounded from all sides at once. He took a dozen bounds,
not very quickly, letting the borzois gain on him, and, finally having chosen
his direction and realized his danger, laid back his ears and rushed off
headlong. He had been lying in the stubble, but in front of him was the
autumn sowing where the ground was soft. The two borzois of the hunts-
man who had sighted him, having been the nearest, were the first to see
and pursue him, but they had not gone far before Ilágin's red-spotted Erzá
passed them, got within a length, flew at the hare with terrible swiftness
aiming at his scut, and, thinking she had seized him, rolled over like a ball.
The hare arched his back and bounded off yet more swiftly. From behind
Erzá rushed the broad-haunched, black-spotted Mílka and began rapidly
gaining on the hare.

"Miláshka, dear!" rose Nicholas' triumphant cry. It looked as if Mílka
would immediately pounce on the hare, but she overtook him and flew
past. The hare had squatted. Again the beautiful Erzá reached him, but

when close to the hare's scut paused as if measuring the distance, so as not to make a mistake this time but seize his hind leg.

"Erzá, darling!" Ilágin wailed in a voice unlike his own. Erzá did not hearken to his appeal. At the very moment when she would have seized her prey, the hare moved and darted along the balk between the winter rye and the stubble. Again Erzá and Mílka were abreast, running like a pair of carriage horses, and began to overtake the hare, but it was easier for the hare to run on the balk and the borzois did not overtake him so quickly.

"Rugáy, Rugáyushka! That's it, come on!" came a third voice just then, and "Uncle's" red borzoi, straining and curving its back, caught up with the two foremost borzois, pushed ahead of them regardless of the terrible strain, put on speed close to the hare, knocked it off the balk onto the rye-field, again put on speed still more viciously, sinking to his knees in the muddy field, and all one could see was how, muddying his back, he rolled over with the hare. A ring of borzois surrounded him. A moment later everyone had drawn up round the crowd of dogs. Only the delighted "Uncle" dismounted, and cut off a pad, shaking the hare for the blood to drip off, and anxiously glancing round with restless eyes while his arms and legs twitched. He spoke without himself knowing whom to or what about. "That's it, come on! That's a dog! . . . There, it has beaten them all, the thousand-ruble as well as the one-ruble borzois. That's it, come on!" said he, panting and looking wrathfully around as if he were abusing someone, as if they were all his enemies and had insulted him, and only now had he at last succeeded in justifying himself. "There are your thousand-ruble ones. . . . That's it, come on! . . ."

"Rugáy, here's a pad for you!" he said, throwing down the hare's muddy pad. "You've deserved it, that's it, come on!"

"She'd tired herself out, she'd run it down three times by herself," said Nicholas, also not listening to anyone and regardless of whether he were heard or not.

"But what is there in running across it like that?" said Ilágin's groom.

"Once she had missed it and turned it away, any mongrel could take it," Ilágin was saying at the same time, breathless from his gallop and his excitement. At the same moment Natásha, without drawing breath, screamed joyously, ecstatically, and so piercingly that it set everyone's ear tingling. By that shriek she expressed what the others expressed by all talking at once, and it was so strange that she must herself have been ashamed of so wild a cry and everyone else would have been amazed at it at any other time. "Uncle" himself twisted up the hare, threw it neatly and smartly across his horse's back as if by that gesture he meant to rebuke everybody, and, with an air of not wishing to speak to anyone, mounted

his bay and rode off. The others all followed, dispirited and shamefaced, and only much later were they able to regain their former affectation of indifference. For a long time they continued to look at red Rugáy who, his arched back spattered with mud and clanking the ring of his leash, walked along just behind "Uncle's" horse with the serene air of a conqueror.

"Well, I am like any other dog as long as it's not a question of coursing. But when it is, then look out!" his appearance seemed to Nicholas to be saying.

When, much later, "Uncle" rode up to Nicholas and began talking to him, he felt flattered that, after what had happened, "Uncle" deigned to speak to him.

7. An evening at "Uncle's." The balaláyka. Natásha's Russian dance

TOWARD EVENING Ilágin took leave of Nicholas, who found that they were so far from home that he accepted "Uncle's" offer that the hunting party should spend the night in his little village of Mikháylovna.

"And if you put up at my house that will be better still. That's it, come on!" said "Uncle." "You see it's damp weather, and you could rest, and the little countess could be driven home in a trap."

"Uncle's" offer was accepted. A huntsman was sent to Otrádnoe for a trap, while Nicholas rode with Natásha and Pétya to "Uncle's" house.

Some five male domestic serfs, big and little, rushed out to the front porch to meet their master. A score of women serfs, old and young, as well as children, popped out from the back entrance to have a look at the hunters who were arriving. The presence of Natásha—a woman, a lady, and on horseback—raised the curiosity of the serfs to such a degree that many of them came up to her, stared her in the face, and unabashed by her presence made remarks about her as though she were some prodigy on show and not a human being able to hear or understand what was said about her.

"Arínka! Look, she sits sideways! There she sits and her skirt dangles. . . . See, she's got a little hunting horn!"

"Goodness gracious! See her knife? . . ."

"Isn't she a Tartar!"

"How is it you didn't go head over heels?" asked the boldest of all, addressing Natásha directly.

"Uncle" dismounted at the porch of his little wooden house which

stood in the midst of an overgrown garden and, after a glance at his re-
tainers, shouted authoritatively that the superfluous ones should take
themselves off and that all necessary preparations should be made to
receive the guests and the visitors.

The serfs all dispersed. "Uncle" lifted Natásha off her horse and taking
her hand led her up the rickety wooden steps of the porch. The house, with
its bare, unplastered log walls, was not overclean—it did not seem that
those living in it aimed at keeping it spotless—but neither was it notice-
ably neglected. In the entry there was a smell of fresh apples, and wolf
and fox skins hung about.

"Uncle" led the visitors through the anteroom into a small hall with a
folding table and red chairs, then into the drawing room with a round
birchwood table and a sofa, and finally into his private room where there
was a tattered sofa, a worn carpet, and portraits of Suvórov, of the host's
father and mother, and of himself in military uniform. The study smelt
strongly of tobacco and dogs. "Uncle" asked his visitors to sit down and
make themselves at home, and then went out of the room. Rugáy, his
back still muddy, came into the room and lay down on the sofa, cleaning
himself with his tongue and teeth. Leading from the study was a passage
in which a partition with ragged curtains could be seen. From behind this
came women's laughter and whispers. Natásha, Nicholas, and Pétya took
off their wraps and sat down on the sofa. Pétya, leaning on his elbow, fell
asleep at once. Natásha and Nicholas were silent. Their faces glowed, they
were hungry and very cheerful. They looked at one another (now that
the hunt was over and they were in the house, Nicholas no longer con-
sidered it necessary to show his manly superiority over his sister), Natásha
gave him a wink, and neither refrained long from bursting into a peal of
ringing laughter even before they had a pretext ready to account for it.

After a while "Uncle" came in, in a Cossack coat, blue trousers, and
small top boots. And Natásha felt that this costume, the very one she had
regarded with surprise and amusement at Otrádnoe, was just the right
thing and not at all worse than a swallow-tail or frock coat. "Uncle" too
was in high spirits and far from being offended by the brother's and sister's
laughter (it could never enter his head that they might be laughing at his
way of life) he himself joined in the merriment.

"That's right, young countess, that's it, come on! I never saw anyone
like her!" said he, offering Nicholas a pipe with a long stem and, with a
practiced motion of three fingers, taking down another that had been cut
short. "She's ridden all day like a man, and is as fresh as ever!"

Soon after "Uncle's" reappearance the door was opened, evidently from
the sound by a barefooted girl, and a stout, rosy, good-looking woman of

about forty, with a double chin and full red lips, entered carrying a large loaded tray. With hospitable dignity and cordiality in her glance and in every motion, she looked at the visitors and, with a pleasant smile, bowed respectfully. In spite of her exceptional stoutness, which caused her to protrude her chest and stomach and throw back her head, this woman (who was "Uncle's" housekeeper) trod very lightly. She went to the table, set down the tray, and with her plump white hands deftly took from it the bottles and various hors-d'oeuvres and dishes and arranged them on the table. When she had finished, she stepped aside and stopped at the door with a smile on her face. "Here I am. I am she! Now do you understand 'Uncle'?" her expression said to Rostóv. How could one help understanding? Not only Nicholas, but even Natásha understood the meaning of his puckered brow and the happy complacent smile that slightly puckered his lips when Anísya Fëdorovna entered. On the tray was a bottle of herb wine, different kinds of vodka, pickled mushrooms, rye cakes made with buttermilk, honey in the comb, still mead and sparkling mead, apples, nuts (raw and roasted), and nut-and-honey sweets. Afterwards she brought a freshly roasted chicken, ham, preserves made with honey, and preserves made with sugar.

All this was the fruit of Anísya Fëdorovna's housekeeping, gathered and prepared by her. The smell and taste of it all had a smack of Anísya Fëdorovna herself: a savor of juiciness, cleanliness, whiteness, and pleasant smiles.

"Take this, little Lady-Countess!" she kept saying, as she offered Natásha first one thing and then another.

Natásha ate of everything and thought she had never seen or eaten such buttermilk cakes, such aromatic jam, such honey-and-nut sweets, or such a chicken anywhere. Anísya Fëdorovna left the room.

After supper, over their cherry brandy, Rostóv and "Uncle" talked of past and future hunts, of Rugáy and Ilágin's dogs, while Natásha sat upright on the sofa and listened with sparkling eyes. She tried several times to wake Pétya that he might eat something, but he only muttered incoherent words without waking up. Natásha felt so lighthearted and happy in these novel surroundings that she only feared the trap would come for her too soon. After a casual pause, such as often occurs when receiving friends for the first time in one's own house, "Uncle," answering a thought that was in his visitors' minds, said:

"This, you see, is how I am finishing my days. . . . Death will come. That's it, come on! Nothing will remain. Then why harm anyone?"

"Uncle's" face was very significant and even handsome as he said this. Involuntarily Rostóv recalled all the good he had heard about him from

his father and the neighbors. Throughout the whole province "Uncle" had the reputation of being the most honorable and disinterested of cranks. They called him in to decide family disputes, chose him as executor, confided secrets to him, elected him to be a justice and to other posts; but he always persistently refused public appointments, passing the autumn and spring in the fields on his bay gelding, sitting at home in winter, and lying in his overgrown garden in summer.

"Why don't you enter the service, Uncle?"

"I did once, but gave it up. I am not fit for it. That's it, come on! I can't make head or tail of it. That's for you—I haven't brains enough. Now, hunting is another matter—that's it, come on! Open the door, there!" he shouted. "Why have you shut it?"

The door at the end of the passage led to the huntsmen's room, as they called the room for the hunt servants.

There was a rapid patter of bare feet, and an unseen hand opened the door into the huntsmen's room, from which came the clear sounds of a balaláyka * on which someone, who was evidently a master of the art, was playing. Natásha had been listening to those strains for some time and now went out into the passage to hear better.

"That's Mítka, my coachman. . . . I have got him a good balaláyka. I'm fond of it," said "Uncle."

It was the custom for Mítka to play the balaláyka in the huntsmen's room when "Uncle" returned from the chase. "Uncle" was fond of such music.

"How good! Really very good!" said Nicholas with some unintentional superciliousness, as if ashamed to confess that the sounds pleased him very much.

"Very good?" said Natásha reproachfully, noticing her brother's tone. "Not 'very good'—it's simply delicious!"

Just as "Uncle's" pickled mushrooms, honey, and cherry brandy had seemed to her the best in the world, so also that song, at that moment, seemed to her the acme of musical delight.

"More, please, more!" cried Natásha at the door as soon as the balaláyka ceased. Mítka tuned up afresh, and recommenced thrumming the balaláyka to the air of My Lady, with trills and variations. "Uncle" sat listening, slightly smiling, with his head on one side. The air was repeated a hundred times. The balaláyka was retuned several times and the same notes were thrummed again, but the listeners did not grow weary

* The balaláyka is a popular Russian three-stringed instrument, which may be taken as the equivalent of the Spanish guitar.—A.M.

of it and wished to hear it again and again. Anísya Fëdorovna came in and leaned her portly person against the doorpost.

"You like listening?" she said to Natásha, with a smile extremely like "Uncle's." "That's a good player of ours," she added.

"He doesn't play that part right!" said "Uncle" suddenly, with an energetic gesture. "Here he ought to burst out—that's it, come on!—ought to burst out."

"Do you play then?" asked Natásha.

"Uncle" did not answer, but smiled.

"Anísya, go and see if the strings of my guitar are all right. I haven't touched it for a long time. That's it—come on! I've given it up."

Anísya Fëdorovna, with her light step, willingly went to fulfill her errand and brought back the guitar.

Without looking at anyone, "Uncle" blew the dust off it and, tapping the case with his bony fingers, tuned the guitar and settled himself in his armchair. He took the guitar a little above the fingerboard, arching his left elbow with a somewhat theatrical gesture, and, with a wink at Anísya Fëdorovna, struck a single chord, pure and sonorous, and then quietly, smoothly, and confidently began playing in very slow time, not *My Lady*, but the well-known song: *Came a maiden down the street*. The tune, played with precision and in exact time, began to thrill in the hearts of Nicholas and Natásha, arousing in them the same kind of sober mirth as radiated from Anísya Fëdorovna's whole being. Anísya Fëdorovna flushed, and drawing her kerchief over her face went laughing out of the room. "Uncle" continued to play correctly, carefully, with energetic firmness, looking with a changed and inspired expression at the spot where Anísya Fëdorovna had just stood. Something seemed to be laughing a little on one side of his face under his gray mustaches, especially as the song grew brisker and the time quicker and when, here and there, as he ran his fingers over the strings, something seemed to snap.

"Lovely, lovely! Go on, Uncle, go on!" shouted Natásha as soon as he had finished. She jumped up and hugged and kissed him. "Nicholas, Nicholas!" she said, turning to her brother, as if asking him: "What is it moves me so?"

Nicholas too was greatly pleased by "Uncle's" playing, and "Uncle" played the piece over again. Anísya Fëdorovna's smiling face reappeared in the doorway and behind hers other faces. . . .

> Fetching water clear and sweet,
> Stop, dear maiden, I entreat—

played "Uncle" once more, running his fingers skillfully over the strings, and then he stopped short and jerked his shoulders.

"Go on, Uncle dear," Natásha wailed in an imploring tone as if her life depended on it.

"Uncle" rose, and it was as if there were two men in him: one of them smiled seriously at the merry fellow, while the merry fellow struck a naïve and precise attitude preparatory to a folk dance.

"Now then, niece!" he exclaimed, waving to Natásha the hand that had just struck a chord.

Natásha threw off the shawl from her shoulders, ran forward to face "Uncle," and setting her arms akimbo also made a motion with her shoulders and struck an attitude.

Where, how, and when had this young countess, educated by an *émigrée* French governess, imbibed from the Russian air she breathed that spirit and obtained that manner which the *pas de châle* * would, one would have supposed, long ago have effaced? But the spirit and the movements were those inimitable and unteachable Russian ones that "Uncle" had expected of her. As soon as she had struck her pose, and smiled triumphantly, proudly, and with sly merriment, the fear that had at first seized Nicholas and the others that she might not do the right thing was at an end, and they were already admiring her.

She did the right thing with such precision, such complete precision, that Anísya Fëdorovna, who had at once handed her the handkerchief she needed for the dance, had tears in her eyes, though she laughed as she watched this slim, graceful countess, reared in silks and velvets and so different from herself, who yet was able to understand all that was in Anísya and in Anísya's father and mother and aunt, and in every Russian man and woman.

"Well, little countess; that's it—come on!" cried "Uncle," with a joyous laugh, having finished the dance. "Well done, niece! Now a fine young fellow must be found as husband for you. That's it—come on!"

"He's chosen already," said Nicholas smiling.

"Oh?" said "Uncle" in surprise, looking inquiringly at Natásha, who nodded her head with a happy smile.

"And such a one!" she said. But as soon as she had said it a new train of thoughts and feelings arose in her. "What did Nicholas' smile mean when he said 'chosen already'? Is he glad of it or not? It is as if he thought my Bolkónski would not approve of or understand our gaiety. But he would understand it all. Where is he now?" she thought, and her face

* *The shawl dance; a French dance, the style of which contrasts with the Russian folk dances.*—A.M.

suddenly became serious. But this lasted only a second. "Don't dare to think about it," she said to herself, and sat down again smilingly beside "Uncle," begging him to play something more.

"Uncle" played another song and a valse; then after a pause he cleared his throat and sang his favorite hunting song:

> As 'twas growing dark last night
> Fell the snow so soft and light . . .

"Uncle" sang as peasants sing, with full and naïve conviction that the whole meaning of a song lies in the words and that the tune comes of itself, and that apart from the words there is no tune, which exists only to give measure to the words. As a result of this the unconsidered tune, like the song of a bird, was extraordinarily good. Natásha was in ecstasies over "Uncle's" singing. She resolved to give up learning the harp and to play only the guitar. She asked "Uncle" for his guitar and at once found the chords of the song.

After nine o'clock two traps and three mounted men, who had been sent to look for them, arrived to fetch Natásha and Pétya. The count and countess did not know where they were and were very anxious, said one of the men.

Pétya was carried out like a log and laid in the larger of the two traps. Natásha and Nicholas got into the other. "Uncle" wrapped Natásha up warmly and took leave of her with quite a new tenderness. He accompanied them on foot as far as the bridge that could not be crossed, so that they had to go round by the ford, and he sent huntsmen to ride in front with lanterns.

"Good-by, dear niece," his voice called out of the darkness—not the voice Natásha had known previously, but the one that had sung *As 'twas growing dark last night.*

In the village through which they passed there were red lights and a cheerful smell of smoke.

"What a darling Uncle is!" said Natásha, when they had come out onto the highroad.

"Yes," returned Nicholas. "You're not cold?"

"No. I'm quite, quite all right. I feel so comfortable!" answered Natásha, almost perplexed by her feelings. They remained silent a long while. The night was dark and damp. They could not see the horses, but only heard them splashing through the unseen mud.

What was passing in that receptive childlike soul that so eagerly caught and assimilated all the diverse impressions of life? How did they all find place in her? But she was very happy. As they were nearing home she sud-

denly struck up the air of As 'twas growing dark last night—the tune of
which she had all the way been trying to get and had at last caught.

"Got it?" said Nicholas.

"What were you thinking about just now, Nicholas?" inquired Natásha.
They were fond of asking one another that question.

"I?" said Nicholas, trying to remember. "Well, you see, first I thought
that Rugáy, the red hound, was like Uncle, and that if he were a man he
would always keep Uncle near him, if not for his riding, then for his
manner. What a good fellow Uncle is! Don't you think so? . . . Well,
and you?"

"I? Wait a bit, wait. . . . Yes, first I thought that we are driving along
and imagining that we are going home, but that heaven knows where we
are really going in the darkness, and that we shall arrive and suddenly
find that we are not in Otrádnoe, but in Fairyland. And then I thought
. . . No, nothing else."

"I know, I expect you thought of him," said Nicholas, smiling as Na-
tásha knew by the sound of his voice.

"No," said Natásha, though she had in reality been thinking about
Prince Andrew at the same time as of the rest, and of how he would have
liked "Uncle." "And then I was saying to myself all the way, 'How well
Anísya carried herself, how well!' " And Nicholas heard her spontaneous,
happy, ringing laughter. "And do you know," she suddenly said, "I know
that I shall never again be as happy and tranquil as I am now."

"Rubbish, nonsense, humbug!" exclaimed Nicholas, and he thought:
"How charming this Natásha of mine is! I have no other friend like her
and never shall have. Why should she marry? We might always drive
about together!"

"What a darling this Nicholas of mine is!" thought Natásha.

"Ah, there are still lights in the drawing room!" she said, pointing to
the windows of the house that gleamed invitingly in the moist velvety
darkness of the night.

8. His mother urges Nicholas to marry Julie Karágina, and grumbles at Sónya

COUNT ILYÁ ROSTÓV had resigned the position of Marshal of the
Nobility because it involved him in too much expense, but still his
affairs did not improve. Natásha and Nicholas often noticed their parents
conferring together anxiously and privately and heard suggestions of sell-
ing the fine ancestral Rostóv house and estate near Moscow. It was not

necessary to entertain so freely as when the count had been Marshal, and life at Otrádnoe was quieter than in former years, but still the enormous house and its lodges were full of people and more than twenty sat down to table every day. These were all their own people who had settled down in the house almost as members of the family, or persons who were, it seemed, obliged to live in the count's house. Such were Dimmler the musician * and his wife, Vogel the dancing master and his family, Belóva, an old maiden lady, an inmate of the house, and many others such as Pétya's tutors, the girls' former governess, and other people who simply found it preferable and more advantageous to live in the count's house than at home. They had not as many visitors as before, but the old habits of life without which the count and countess could not conceive of existence remained unchanged. There was still the hunting establishment which Nicholas had even enlarged, the same fifty horses and fifteen grooms in the stables, the same expensive presents and dinner parties to the whole district on name days; there were still the count's games of whist and boston, at which—spreading out his cards so that everybody could see them—he let himself be plundered of hundreds of rubles every day by his neighbors, who looked upon an opportunity to play a rubber with Count Rostóv as a most profitable source of income.

The count moved in his affairs as in a huge net, trying not to believe that he was entangled but becoming more and more so at every step, and feeling too feeble to break the meshes or to set to work carefully and patiently to disentangle them. The countess, with her loving heart, felt that her children were being ruined, that it was not the count's fault for he could not help being what he was—that (though he tried to hide it) he himself suffered from the consciousness of his own and his children's ruin, and she tried to find means of remedying the position. From her feminine point of view she could see only one solution, namely, for Nicholas to marry a rich heiress. She felt this to be their last hope and that if Nicholas refused the match she had found for him, she would have to abandon the hope of ever getting matters right. This match was with Julie Karágina, the daughter of excellent and virtuous parents, a girl the Rostóvs had known from childhood, and who had now become a wealthy heiress through the death of the last of her brothers.

The countess had written direct to Julie's mother in Moscow suggesting a marriage between their children and had received a favorable answer

* *Tolstóy made himself so well acquainted with the times he was writing about that even to this character, only mentioned a very few times, he has given the name of a real person who was a music-master then living in Moscow.—*A.M.

from her. Karágina had replied that for her part she was agreeable, and everything would depend on her daughter's inclination. She invited Nicholas to come to Moscow.

Several times the countess, with tears in her eyes, told her son that now both her daughters were settled, her only wish was to see him married. She said she could lie down in her grave peacefully if that were accomplished. Then she told him that she knew of a splendid girl and tried to discover what he thought about marriage.

At other times she praised Julie to him and advised him to go to Moscow during the holidays to amuse himself. Nicholas guessed what his mother's remarks were leading to and during one of these conversations induced her to speak quite frankly. She told him that her only hope of getting their affairs disentangled now lay in his marrying Julie Karágina.

"But, Mamma, suppose I loved a girl who has no fortune, would you expect me to sacrifice my feelings and my honor for the sake of money?" he asked his mother, not realizing the cruelty of his question and only wishing to show his noble-mindedness.

"No, you have not understood me," said his mother, not knowing how to justify herself. "You have not understood me, Nikólenka. It is your happiness I wish for," she added, feeling that she was telling an untruth and was becoming entangled. She began to cry.

"Mamma, don't cry! Only tell me that you wish it, and you know I will give my life, anything, to put you at ease," said Nicholas. "I would sacrifice anything for you—even my feelings."

But the countess did not want the question put like that: she did not want a sacrifice from her son, she herself wished to make a sacrifice for him.

"No, you have not understood me, don't let us talk about it," she replied, wiping away her tears.

"Maybe I do love a poor girl," said Nicholas to himself. "Am I to sacrifice my feelings and my honor for money? I wonder how Mamma could speak so to me. Because Sónya is poor I must not love her," he thought, "must not respond to her faithful, devoted love? Yet I should certainly be happier with her than with some doll-like Julie. I can always sacrifice my feelings for my family's welfare," he said to himself, "but I can't coerce my feelings. If I love Sónya, that feeling is for me stronger and higher than all else."

Nicholas did not go to Moscow, and the countess did not renew the conversation with him about marriage. She saw with sorrow, and sometimes with exasperation, symptoms of a growing attachment between her son and the portionless Sónya. Though she blamed herself for it, she could not refrain from grumbling at and worrying Sónya, often pulling her up

without reason, addressing her stiffly as "my dear," and using the formal "you" instead of the intimate "thou" in speaking to her. The kindhearted countess was the more vexed with Sónya because that poor, dark-eyed niece of hers was so meek, so kind, so devotedly grateful to her benefactors, and so faithfully, unchangingly, and unselfishly in love with Nicholas, that there were no grounds for finding fault with her.

Nicholas was spending the last of his leave at home. A fourth letter had come from Prince Andrew, from Rome, in which he wrote that he would have been on his way back to Russia long ago had not his wound unexpectedly reopened in the warm climate, which obliged him to defer his return till the beginning of the new year. Natásha was still as much in love with her betrothed, found the same comfort in that love, and was still as ready to throw herself into all the pleasures of life as before; but at the end of the fourth month of their separation she began to have fits of depression which she could not master. She felt sorry for herself: sorry that she was being wasted all this time and of no use to anyone—while she felt herself so capable of loving and being loved.

Things were not cheerful in the Rostóvs' home.

9. Christmas at Otrádnoe. Natásha is depressed and capricious

CHRISTMAS CAME and except for the ceremonial Mass, the solemn and wearisome Christmas congratulations from neighbors and servants, and the new dresses everyone put on, there were no special festivities, though the calm frost of twenty degrees Réaumur,* the dazzling sunshine by day, and the starlight of the winter nights seemed to call for some special celebration of the season.

On the third day of Christmas week, after the midday dinner, all the inmates of the house dispersed to various rooms. It was the dullest time of the day. Nicholas, who had been visiting some neighbors that morning, was asleep on the sitting-room sofa. The old count was resting in his study. Sónya sat in the drawing room at the round table, copying a design for embroidery. The countess was playing patience. Nastásya Ivánovna the buffoon sat with a sad face at the window with two old ladies. Natásha came into the room, went up to Sónya, glanced at what she was doing, and then went up to her mother and stood without speaking.

"Why are you wandering about like an outcast?" asked her mother. "What do you want?"

* 13 degrees below zero, Fahrenheit.—A.M.

"Him . . . I want him . . . now, this minute! I want *him!*" said Natásha, with glittering eyes and no sign of a smile.

The countess lifted her head and looked attentively at her daughter.

"Don't look at me, Mamma! Don't look; I shall cry directly."

"Sit down with me a little," said the countess.

"Mamma, I want *him*. Why should I be wasted like this, Mamma?"

Her voice broke, tears gushed from her eyes, and she turned quickly to hide them and left the room.

She passed into the sitting room, stood there thinking awhile, and then went into the maids' room. There an old maidservant was grumbling at a young girl who stood panting, having just run in through the cold from the serfs' quarters.

"Stop playing—there's a time for everything," said the old woman.

"Let her alone, Kondrátevna," said Natásha. "Go, Mavrúshka, go."

Having released Mavrúshka, Natásha crossed the dancing hall and went to the vestibule. There an old footman and two young ones were playing cards. They broke off and rose as she entered.

"What can I do with them?" thought Natásha.

"Oh, Nikíta, please go . . . where can I send him? . . . Yes, go to the yard and fetch a fowl, please, a cock, and you, Mísha, bring me some oats." *

"Just a few oats?" said Mísha, cheerfully and readily.

"Go, go quickly," the old man urged him.

"And you, Theodore, get me a piece of chalk."

On her way past the butler's pantry she told them to set a samovar, though it was not at all the time for tea.

Fóka, the butler, was the most ill-tempered person in the house. Natásha liked to test her power over him. He distrusted the order and asked whether the samovar was really wanted.

"Oh dear, what a young lady!" said Fóka, pretending to frown at Natásha.

No one in the house sent people about or gave them as much trouble as Natásha did. She could not see people unconcernedly, but had to send them on some errand. She seemed to be trying whether any of them would get angry or sulky with her; but the serfs fulfilled no one's orders so readily as they did hers. "What can I do, where can I go?" thought she, as she went slowly along the passage.

"Nastásya Ivánovna, what sort of children shall I have?" she asked the buffoon, who was coming toward her in a woman's jacket.

* *Feeding a fowl with grain arranged on the floor is a way of telling fortunes at Christmastime.*—A.M.

"Why, fleas, crickets, grasshoppers," answered the buffoon.

"O Lord, O Lord, it's always the same! Oh, where am I to go? What am I to do with myself?" And tapping with her heels, she ran quickly upstairs to see Vogel and his wife who lived on the upper story.

Two governesses were sitting with the Vogels at a table, on which were plates of raisins, walnuts, and almonds. The governesses were discussing whether it was cheaper to live in Moscow or Odessa. Natásha sat down, listened to their talk with a serious and thoughtful air, and then got up again.

"The island of Madagascar," she said, "Ma-da-gas-car," she repeated, articulating each syllable distinctly, and, not replying to Madame Schoss who asked her what she was saying, she went out of the room.

Her brother Pétya was upstairs too; with the man in attendance on him he was preparing fireworks to let off that night.

"Pétya! Pétya!" she called to him. "Carry me downstairs."

Pétya ran up and offered her his back. She jumped on it, putting her arms round his neck, and he pranced along with her.

"No, don't . . . the island of Madagascar!" she said, and jumping off his back she went downstairs.

Having as it were reviewed her kingdom, tested her power, and made sure that everyone was submissive, but that all the same it was dull, Natásha betook herself to the ballroom, picked up her guitar, sat down in a dark corner behind a bookcase, and began to run her fingers over the strings in the bass, picking out a passage she recalled from an opera she had heard in Petersburg with Prince Andrew. What she drew from the guitar would have had no meaning for other listeners, but in her imagination a whole series of reminiscences arose from those sounds. She sat behind the bookcase with her eyes fixed on a streak of light escaping from the pantry door and listened to herself and pondered. She was in a mood for brooding on the past.

Sónya passed to the pantry with a glass in her hand. Natásha glanced at her and at the crack in the pantry door, and it seemed to her that she remembered the light falling through that crack once before and Sónya passing with a glass in her hand. "Yes, it was exactly the same," thought Natásha.

"Sónya, what is this?" she cried, twanging a thick string.

"Oh, you are there!" said Sónya with a start, and came near and listened. "I don't know. A storm?" she ventured timidly, afraid of being wrong.

"There! That's just how she started and just how she came up smiling timidly when all this happened before," thought Natásha, "and in just the same way I thought there was something lacking in her."

"No, it's the chorus from *The Water-Carrier*,* listen!" and Natásha sang the air of the chorus so that Sónya should catch it. "Where were you going?" she asked.

"To change the water in this glass. I am just finishing the design."

"You always find something to do, but I can't," said Natásha. "And where's Nicholas?"

"Asleep, I think."

"Sónya, go and wake him," said Natásha. "Tell him I want him to come and sing."

She sat awhile, wondering what the meaning of it all having happened before could be, and without solving this problem, or at all regretting not having done so, she again passed in fancy to the time when she was with *him* and he was looking at her with a lover's eyes.

"Oh, if only he would come quicker! I am so afraid it will never be! And, worst of all, I am growing old—that's the thing! There won't then be in me what there is now. But perhaps he'll come today, will come immediately. Perhaps he has come and is sitting in the drawing room. Perhaps he came yesterday and I have forgotten it." She rose, put down the guitar, and went to the drawing room.

All the domestic circle, tutors, governesses, and guests, were already at the tea table. The servants stood round the table—but Prince Andrew was not there and life was going on as before.

"Ah, here she is!" said the old count, when he saw Natásha enter. "Well, sit down by me." But Natásha stayed by her mother and glanced round as if looking for something.

"Mamma!" she muttered, "give him to me, give him, Mamma, quickly, quickly!" and she again had difficulty in repressing her sobs.

She sat down at the table and listened to the conversation between the elders and Nicholas, who had also come to the table. "My God, my God! The same faces, the same talk, Papa holding his cup and blowing in the same way!" thought Natásha, feeling with horror a sense of repulsion rising up in her for the whole household, because they were always the same.

After tea, Nicholas, Sónya, and Natásha went to the sitting room, to their favorite corner where their most intimate talks always began.

* *Cherubini's operatic masterpiece* Les deux Journées, *or* The Water-Carrier, 1804.—A.M.

10. *Nicholas, Natásha, and Sónya indulge in recollections.*
Dimmler plays and Natásha sings. The maskers.
A troyka drive to the Melyukóvs'

D OES IT EVER HAPPEN TO YOU," said Natásha to her brother, when they settled down in the sitting room, "does it ever happen to you to feel as if there were nothing more to come—nothing; that everything good is past? And to feel not exactly dull, but sad?"

"I should think so!" he replied. "I have felt like that when everything was all right and everyone was cheerful. The thought has come into my mind that I was already tired of it all, and that we must all die. Once in the regiment I had not gone to some merrymaking where there was music . . . and suddenly I felt so depressed . . ."

"Oh yes, I know, I know, I know!" Natásha interrupted him. "When I was quite little that used to be so with me. Do you remember when I was punished once about some plums? You were all dancing, and I sat sobbing in the schoolroom? I shall never forget it: I felt sad and sorry for everyone, for myself, and for everyone. And I was innocent—that was the chief thing," said Natásha. "Do you remember?"

"I remember," answered Nicholas. "I remember that I came to you afterwards and wanted to comfort you, but do you know, I felt ashamed to. We were terribly absurd. I had a funny doll then and wanted to give it to you. Do you remember?"

"And do you remember," Natásha asked with a pensive smile, "how once, long, long ago, when we were quite little, Uncle called us into the study—that was in the old house—and it was dark—we went in and suddenly there stood . . ."

"A Negro," chimed in Nicholas with a smile of delight. "Of course I remember. Even now I don't know whether there really was a Negro, or if we only dreamed it or were told about him."

"He was gray, you remember, and had white teeth, and stood and looked at us. . . ."

"Sónya, do you remember?" asked Nicholas.

"Yes, yes, I do remember something too," Sónya answered timidly.

"You know I have asked Papa and Mamma about that Negro," said Natásha, "and they say there was no Negro at all. But you see, you remember!"

"Of course I do, I remember his teeth as if I had just seen them."

"How strange it is! It's as if it were a dream! I like that."

"And do you remember how we rolled hard-boiled eggs in the ballroom,

and suddenly two old women began spinning round on the carpet? Was that real or not? Do you remember what fun it was?"

"Yes, and you remember how Papa in his blue overcoat fired a gun in the porch?"

So they went through their memories, smiling with pleasure: not the sad memories of old age, but poetic, youthful ones—those impressions of one's most distant past in which dreams and realities blend—and they laughed with quiet enjoyment.

Sónya, as always, did not quite keep pace with them, though they shared the same reminiscences.

Much that they remembered had slipped from her mind, and what she recalled did not arouse the same poetic feeling as they experienced. She simply enjoyed their pleasure and tried to fit in with it.

She only really took part when they recalled Sónya's first arrival. She told them how afraid she had been of Nicholas because he had on a corded jacket and her nurse had told her that she, too, would be sewn up with cords.

"And I remember their telling me that you had been born under a cabbage," said Natásha, "and I remember that I dared not disbelieve it then, but knew that it was not true, and I felt so uncomfortable."

While they were talking a maid thrust her head in at the other door of the sitting room.

"They have brought the cock, Miss," she said in a whisper.

"It isn't wanted, Pólya. Tell them to take it away," replied Natásha.

In the middle of their talk in the sitting room, Dimmler came in and went up to the harp that stood there in a corner. He took off its cloth covering, and the harp gave out a jarring sound.

"Mr. Dimmler, please play my favorite nocturne by Field," * came the old countess' voice from the drawing room.

Dimmler struck a chord and, turning to Natásha, Nicholas, and Sónya, remarked: "How quiet you young people are!"

"Yes, we're philosophizing," said Natásha, glancing round for a moment and then continuing the conversation. They were now discussing dreams.

Dimmler began to play; Natásha went on tiptoe noiselessly to the table, took up a candle, carried it out, and returned, seating herself quietly in her former place. It was dark in the room especially where they were sitting on the sofa, but through the big windows the silvery light of the full moon fell on the floor. Dimmler had finished the piece but still sat

* *John Field (1782-1837), born in Dublin, was a composer of nocturnes, etc. He settled in Russia in 1804, and was known as "Russian Field."*—A.M.

softly running his fingers over the strings, evidently uncertain whether to stop or to play something else.

"Do you know," said Natásha in a whisper, moving closer to Nicholas and Sónya, "that when one goes on and on recalling memories, one at last begins to remember what happened before one was in the world. . . ."

"That is metempsychosis," said Sónya, who had always learned well, and remembered everything. "The Egyptians believed that our souls have lived in animals, and will go back into animals again."

"No, I don't believe we ever were in animals," said Natásha, still in a whisper though the music had ceased. "But I am certain that we were angels somewhere *there*, and have been here, and that is why we remember. . . ."

"May I join you?" said Dimmler who had come up quietly, and he sat down by them.

"If we have been angels, why have we fallen lower?" said Nicholas. "No, that can't be!"

"Not lower, who said we were lower? . . . How do I know what I was before?" Natásha rejoined with conviction. "The soul is immortal—well then, if I shall always live I must have lived before, lived for a whole eternity."

"Yes, but it is hard for us to imagine eternity," remarked Dimmler, who had joined the young folk with a mildly condescending smile but now spoke as quietly and seriously as they.

"Why is it hard to imagine eternity?" said Natásha. "It is now today, and it will be tomorrow, and always; and there was yesterday, and the day before. . . ."

"Natásha! Now it's your turn. Sing me something," they heard the countess say. "Why are you sitting there like conspirators?"

"Mamma, I don't at all want to," replied Natásha, but all the same she rose.

None of them, not even the middle-aged Dimmler, wanted to break off their conversation and quit that corner in the sitting room, but Natásha got up and Nicholas sat down at the clavichord. Standing as usual in the middle of the hall and choosing the place where the resonance was best, Natásha began to sing her mother's favorite song.

She had said she did not want to sing, but it was long since she had sung, and long before she again sang, as she did that evening. The count, from his study where he was talking to Mítenka, heard her and, like a schoolboy in a hurry to run out to play, blundered in his talk while giving orders to the steward, and at last stopped, while Mítenka stood in front of him also listening and smiling. Nicholas did not take his eyes off his

sister and drew breath in time with her. Sónya, as she listened, thought of the immense difference there was between herself and her friend, and how impossible it was for her to be anything like as bewitching as her cousin. The old countess sat with a blissful yet sad smile and with tears in her eyes, occasionally shaking her head. She thought of Natásha and of her own youth, and of how there was something unnatural and dreadful in this impending marriage of Natásha and Prince Andrew.

Dimmler, who had seated himself beside the countess, listened with closed eyes.

"Ah, Countess," he said at last, "that's a European talent, she has nothing to learn—what softness, tenderness, and strength. . . ."

"Ah, how afraid I am for her, how afraid I am!" said the countess, not realizing to whom she was speaking. Her maternal instinct told her that Natásha had too much of something, and that because of this she would not be happy. Before Natásha had finished singing, fourteen-year-old Pétya rushed in delightedly, to say that some mummers had arrived.

Natásha stopped abruptly.

"Idiot!" she screamed at her brother and, running to a chair, threw herself on it, sobbing so violently that she could not stop for a long time.

"It's nothing, Mamma, really it's nothing; only Pétya startled me," she said, trying to smile, but her tears still flowed and sobs still choked her.

The mummers (some of the house serfs) dressed up as bears, Turks, innkeepers, and ladies—frightening and funny—bringing in with them the cold from outside and a feeling of gaiety, crowded, at first timidly, into the anteroom, then hiding behind one another they pushed into the ballroom where, shyly at first and then more and more merrily and heartily, they started singing, dancing, and playing Christmas games. The countess, when she had identified them and laughed at their costumes, went into the drawing room. The count sat in the ballroom, smiling radiantly and applauding the players. The young people had disappeared.

Half an hour later there appeared among the other mummers in the ballroom an old lady in a hooped skirt—this was Nicholas. A Turkish girl was Pétya. A clown was Dimmler. An hussar was Natásha, and a Circassian was Sónya with burnt-cork mustache and eyebrows.

After the condescending surprise, nonrecognition, and praise, from those who were not themselves dressed up, the young people decided that their costumes were so good that they ought to be shown elsewhere.

Nicholas, who, as the roads were in splendid condition, wanted to take them all for a drive in his troyka, proposed to take with them about a dozen of the serf mummers and drive to "Uncle's."

"No, why disturb the old fellow?" said the countess. "Besides, you

wouldn't have room to turn round there. If you must go, go to the Melyukóvs'."

Melyukóva was a widow, who, with her family and their tutors and governesses, lived three miles from the Rostóvs.

"That's right, my dear," chimed in the old count, thoroughly aroused. "I'll dress up at once and go with them. I'll make Pashette open her eyes."

But the countess would not agree to his going; he had had a bad leg all these last days. It was decided that the count must not go, but that if Louisa Ivánovna (Madame Schoss) would go with them, the young ladies might go to the Melyukóvs', Sónya, generally so timid and shy, more urgently than anyone begging Louisa Ivánovna not to refuse.

Sónya's costume was the best of all. Her mustache and eyebrows were extraordinarily becoming. Everyone told her she looked very handsome, and she was in a spirited and energetic mood unusual with her. Some inner voice told her that now or never her fate would be decided, and in her male attire she seemed quite a different person. Louisa Ivánovna consented to go, and in half an hour four troyka sleighs with large and small bells, their runners squeaking and whistling over the frozen snow, drove up to the porch.

Natásha was foremost in setting a merry holiday tone, which, passing from one to another, grew stronger and stronger and reached its climax when they all came out into the frost and got into the sleighs, talking, calling to one another, laughing, and shouting.

Two of the troykas were the usual household sleighs, the third was the old count's with a trotter from the Orlóv stud as shaft horse, the fourth was Nicholas' own with a short shaggy black shaft horse. Nicholas, in his old lady's dress over which he had belted his hussar overcoat, stood in the middle of the sleigh, reins in hand.

It was so light that he could see the moonlight reflected from the metal harness disks and from the eyes of the horses, who looked round in alarm at the noisy party under the shadow of the porch roof.

Natásha, Sónya, Madame Schoss, and two maids got into Nicholas' sleigh; Dimmler, his wife, and Pétya, into the old count's, and the rest of the mummers seated themselves in the other two sleighs.

"You go ahead, Zakhár!" shouted Nicholas to his father's coachman, wishing for a chance to race past him.

The old count's troyka, with Dimmler and his party, started forward, squeaking on its runners as though freezing to the snow, its deep-toned bell clanging. The side horses, pressing against the shafts of the middle horse, sank in the snow, which was dry and glittered like sugar, and threw it up.

Nicholas set off, following the first sleigh; behind him the others moved noisily, their runners squeaking. At first they drove at a steady trot along the narrow road. While they drove past the garden the shadows of the bare trees often fell across the road and hid the brilliant moonlight, but as soon as they were past the fence, the snowy plain bathed in moonlight and motionless spread out before them glittering like diamonds and dappled with bluish shadows. *Bang, bang!* went the first sleigh over a cradle hole in the snow of the road, and each of the other sleighs jolted in the same way, and rudely breaking the frost-bound stillness, the troykas began to speed along the road, one after the other.

"A hare's track, a lot of tracks!" rang out Natásha's voice through the frost-bound air.

"How light it is, Nicholas!" came Sónya's voice.

Nicholas glanced round at Sónya, and bent down to see her face closer. Quite a new, sweet face with black eyebrows and mustaches peeped up at him from her sable furs—so close and yet so distant—in the moonlight.

"That used to be Sónya," thought he, and looked at her closer and smiled.

"What is it, Nicholas?"

"Nothing," said he and turned again to the horses.

When they came out onto the beaten highroad—polished by sleigh runners and cut up by rough-shod hoofs, the marks of which were visible in the moonlight—the horses began to tug at the reins of their own accord and increased their pace. The near side horse, arching his head and breaking into a short canter, tugged at his traces. The shaft horse swayed from side to side, moving his ears as if asking: "Isn't it time to begin now?" In front, already far ahead the deep bell of the sleigh ringing farther and farther off, the black horses driven by Zakhár could be clearly seen against the white snow. From that sleigh one could hear the shouts, laughter, and voices of the mummers.

"Gee up, my darlings!" shouted Nicholas, pulling the reins to one side and flourishing the whip.

It was only by the keener wind that met them and the jerks given by the side horses who pulled harder—ever increasing their gallop—that one noticed how fast the troyka was flying. Nicholas looked back. With screams, squeals, and waving of whips that caused even the shaft horses to gallop—the other sleighs followed. The shaft horse swung steadily beneath the bow over its head, with no thought of slackening pace and ready to put on speed when required.

Nicholas overtook the first sleigh. They were driving downhill and coming out upon a broad trodden track across a meadow, near a river.

"Where are we?" thought he. "It's the Kosóy meadow, I suppose. But no—this is something new I've never seen before. This isn't the Kosóy meadow nor the Dëmkin hill, and heaven only knows what it is! It is something new and enchanted. Well, whatever it may be . . ." And shouting to his horses, he began to pass the first sleigh.

Zakhár held back his horses and turned his face, which was already covered with hoarfrost to his eyebrows.

Nicholas gave the horses the rein, and Zakhár, stretching out his arms, clucked his tongue and let his horses go.

"Now, look out, master!" he cried.

Faster still the two troykas flew side by side, and faster moved the feet of the galloping side horses. Nicholas began to draw ahead. Zakhár, while still keeping his arms extended, raised one hand with the reins.

"No you won't, master!" he shouted.

Nicholas put all his horses to a gallop and passed Zakhár. The horses showered the fine dry snow on the faces of those in the sleigh—beside them sounded quick ringing bells and they caught confused glimpses of swiftly moving legs and the shadows of the troyka they were passing. The whistling sound of the runners on the snow and the voices of girls shrieking were heard from different sides.

Again checking his horses, Nicholas looked around him. They were still surrounded by the magic plain bathed in moonlight and spangled with stars.

"Zakhár is shouting that I should turn to the left, but why to the left?" thought Nicholas. "Are we getting to the Melyukóvs'? Is this Melyukóvka? Heaven only knows where we are going, and heaven knows what is happening to us—but it is very strange and pleasant whatever it is." And he looked round in the sleigh.

"Look, his mustache and eyelashes are all white!" said one of the strange, pretty, unfamiliar people—the one with fine eyebrows and mustache.

"I think this used to be Natásha," thought Nicholas, "and that was Madame Schoss, but perhaps it's not, and this Circassian with the mustache I don't know, but I love her."

"Aren't you cold?" he asked.

They did not answer but began to laugh. Dimmler from the sleigh behind shouted something—probably something funny—but they could not make out what he said.

"Yes, yes!" some voices answered, laughing.

"But here was a fairy forest with black moving shadows, and a glitter of diamonds and a flight of marble steps and the silver roofs of fairy

buildings and the shrill yells of some animals. And if this is really Melyu-
kóvka, it is still stranger that we drove heaven knows where and have come
to Melyukóvka," thought Nicholas.

It really was Melyukóvka, and maids and footmen with merry faces
came running out to the porch carrying candles.

"Who is it?" asked someone in the porch.

"The mummers from the count's. I know by the horses," replied some
voices.

11. At Melyukóvka. Sónya goes to the barn to try her fortune

PELAGÉYA DANÍLOVNA MELYUKÓVA, a broadly built, energetic woman
wearing spectacles, sat in the drawing room in a loose dress, sur-
rounded by her daughters whom she was trying to keep from feeling dull.
They were quietly dropping melted wax into snow and looking at the
shadows the wax figures would throw on the wall, when they heard
the steps and voices of new arrivals in the vestibule.

Hussars, ladies, witches, clowns, and bears, after clearing their throats
and wiping the hoarfrost from their faces in the vestibule, came into the
ballroom where candles were hurriedly lighted. The clown—Dimmler—
and the lady—Nicholas—started a dance. Surrounded by the screaming
children the mummers, covering their faces and disguising their voices,
bowed to their hostess and arranged themselves about the room.

"Dear me! there's no recognizing them! And Natásha! See whom she
looks like! She really reminds me of somebody. But Herr Dimmler—isn't
he good! I didn't know him! And how he dances. Dear me, there's a
Circassian. Really, how becoming it is to dear Sónya. And who is that?
Well, you have cheered us up! Nikíta and Ványa—clear away the tables!
And we were sitting so quietly. Ha, ha, ha! . . . The hussar, the hussar!
Just like a boy! And the legs! . . . I can't look at him . . ." different
voices were saying.

Natásha, the young Melyukóvs' favorite, disappeared with them into
the back rooms where a cork and various dressing gowns and male gar-
ments were called for and received from the footman by bare girlish arms
from behind the door. Ten minutes later, all the young Melyukóvs joined
the mummers.

Pelagéya Danílovna, having given orders to clear the rooms for the
visitors and arranged about refreshments for the gentry and the serfs,
went about among the mummers without removing her spectacles, peer-
ing into their faces with a suppressed smile and failing to recognize any
of them. It was not merely Dimmler and the Rostóvs she failed to recog-

nize, she did not even recognize her own daughters, or her late husband's dressing gowns and uniforms, which they had put on.

"And who is this?" she asked her governess, peering into the face of her own daughter dressed up as a Kazán-Tartar. "I suppose it is one of the Rostóvs! Well, Mr. Hussar, and what regiment do you serve in?" she asked Natásha. "Here, hand some fruit jelly to the Turk!" she ordered the butler who was handing things round. "That's not forbidden by his law."

Sometimes, as she looked at the strange but amusing capers cut by the dancers, who—having decided once for all that being disguised, no one would recognize them—were not at all shy, Pelagéya Danílovna hid her face in her handkerchief, and her whole stout body shook with irrepressible, kindly, elderly laughter.

"My little Sásha! Look at Sásha!" she said.

After Russian country dances and chorus dances, Pelagéya Danílovna made the serfs and gentry join in one large circle: a ring, a string, and a silver ruble were fetched and they all played games together.

In an hour, all the costumes were crumpled and disordered. The corked eyebrows and mustaches were smeared over the perspiring, flushed, and merry faces. Pelagéya Danílovna began to recognize the mummers, admired their cleverly contrived costumes, and particularly how they suited the young ladies, and she thanked them all for having entertained her so well. The visitors were invited to supper in the drawing room, and the serfs had something served to them in the ballroom.

"Now to tell one's fortune in the empty bathhouse is frightening!" said an old maid who lived with the Melyukóvs, during supper.

"Why?" said the eldest Melyukóv girl.

"You wouldn't go, it takes courage. . . ."

"I'll go," said Sónya.

"Tell what happened to the young lady!" said the second Melyukóv girl.

"Well," began the old maid, "a young lady once went out, took a cock, laid the table for two, all properly, and sat down. After sitting a while, she suddenly hears someone coming . . . a sleigh drives up with harness bells; she hears him coming! He comes in, just in the shape of a man, like an officer—comes in and sits down to table with her."

"Ah! ah!" screamed Natásha, rolling her eyes with horror.

"Yes? And how . . . did he speak?"

"Yes, like a man. Everything quite all right, and he began persuading her; and she should have kept him talking till cockcrow, but she got frightened, just got frightened and hid her face in her hands. Then he caught her up. It was lucky the maids ran in just then. . . ."

"Now, why frighten them?" said Pelagéya Danílovna.

"Mamma, you used to try your fate yourself . . ." said her daughter.

"And how does one do it in a barn?" inquired Sónya.

"Well, say you went to the barn now, and listened. It depends on what you hear; hammering and knocking—that's bad; but a sound of shifting grain is good and one sometimes hears that, too."

"Mamma, tell us what happened to you in the barn."

Pelagéya Danílovna smiled.

"Oh, I've forgotten . . ." she replied. "But none of you would go?"

"Yes, I will; Pelagéya Danílovna, let me! I'll go," said Sónya.

"Well, why not, if you're not afraid?"

"Louisa Ivánovna, may I?" asked Sónya.

Whether they were playing the ring and string game or the ruble game or talking as now, Nicholas did not leave Sónya's side, and gazed at her with quite new eyes. It seemed to him that it was only today, thanks to that burnt-cork mustache, that he had fully learned to know her. And really, that evening, Sónya was brighter, more animated, and prettier than Nicholas had ever seen her before.

"So that's what she is like; what a fool I have been!" he thought gazing at her sparkling eyes, and under the mustache a happy rapturous smile dimpled her cheeks, a smile he had never seen before.

"I'm not afraid of anything," said Sónya. "May I go at once?" She got up.

They told her where the barn was and how she should stand and listen, and they handed her a fur cloak. She threw this over her head and shoulders and glanced at Nicholas.

"What a darling that girl is!" thought he. "And what have I been thinking of till now?"

Sónya went out into the passage to go to the barn. Nicholas went hastily to the front porch, saying he felt too hot. The crowd of people really had made the house stuffy.

Outside, there was the same cold stillness and the same moon, but even brighter than before. The light was so strong and the snow sparkled with so many stars that one did not wish to look up at the sky and the real stars were unnoticed. The sky was black and dreary, while the earth was gay.

"I am a fool, a fool! what have I been waiting for?" thought Nicholas, and running out from the porch he went round the corner of the house and along the path that led to the back porch. He knew Sónya would pass that way. Halfway lay some snow-covered piles of firewood and across and along them a network of shadows from the bare old lime trees fell on the

snow and on the path. This path led to the barn. The log walls of the barn and its snow-covered roof, that looked as if hewn out of some precious stone, sparkled in the moonlight. A tree in the garden snapped with the frost, and then all was again perfectly silent. His bosom seemed to inhale not air but the strength of eternal youth and gladness.

From the back porch came the sound of feet descending the steps, the bottom step upon which snow had fallen gave a ringing creak and he heard the voice of an old maidservant saying, "Straight, straight, along the path, Miss. Only, don't look back."

"I am not afraid," answered Sónya's voice, and along the path toward Nicholas came the crunching, whistling sound of Sónya's feet in her thin shoes.

Sónya came along, wrapped in her cloak. She was only a couple of paces away when she saw him, and to her too he was not the Nicholas she had known and always slightly feared. He was in a woman's dress, with tousled hair and a happy smile new to Sónya. She ran rapidly toward him.

"Quite different and yet the same," thought Nicholas, looking at her face all lit up by the moonlight. He slipped his arms under the cloak that covered her head, embraced her, pressed her to him, and kissed her on the lips that wore a mustache and had a smell of burnt cork. Sónya kissed him full on the lips, and disengaging her little hands pressed them to his cheeks.

"Sónya!" . . . "Nicholas!" . . . was all they said. They ran to the barn and then back again, re-entering, he by the front and she by the back porch.

12. The drive home. Natásha and Sónya try the future with looking glasses

WHEN THEY ALL DROVE BACK from Pelagéya Danílovna's, Natásha, who always saw and noticed everything, arranged that she and Madame Schoss should go back in the sleigh with Dimmler, and Sónya with Nicholas and the maids.

On the way back Nicholas drove at a steady pace instead of racing and kept peering by that fantastic all-transforming light into Sónya's face and searching beneath the eyebrows and mustache for his former and his present Sónya from whom he had resolved never to be parted again. He looked and recognizing in her both the old and the new Sónya, and being reminded by the smell of burnt cork of the sensation of her kiss, inhaled the frosty air with a full breast and, looking at the ground flying beneath him and at the sparkling sky, felt himself again in fairyland.

"Sónya, is it well with *thee?*" he asked from time to time.

"Yes!" she replied. "And with *thee?*"

When halfway home Nicholas handed the reins to the coachman and ran for a moment to Natásha's sleigh and stood on its wing.

"Natásha!" he whispered in French, "do you know I have made up my mind about Sónya?"

"Have you told her?" asked Natásha, suddenly beaming all over with joy.

"Oh, how strange you are with that mustache and those eyebrows! . . . Natásha—are you glad?"

"I am so glad, so glad! I was beginning to be vexed with you. I did not tell you, but you have been treating her badly. What a heart she has, Nicholas! I am horrid sometimes, but I was ashamed to be happy while Sónya was not," continued Natásha. "Now I am so glad! Well, run back to her."

"No, wait a bit. . . . Oh, how funny you look!" cried Nicholas, peering into her face and finding in his sister too something new, unusual, and bewitchingly tender that he had not seen in her before. "Natásha, it's magical, isn't it?"

"Yes," she replied. "You have done splendidly."

"Had I seen her before as she is now," thought Nicholas, "I should long ago have asked her what to do and have done whatever she told me, and all would have been well."

"So you are glad and I have done right?"

"Oh, quite right! I had a quarrel with Mamma some time ago about it. Mamma said she was angling for you. How could she say such a thing! I nearly stormed at Mamma. I will never let anyone say anything bad of Sónya, for there is nothing but good in her."

"Then it's all right?" said Nicholas, again scrutinizing the expression of his sister's face to see if she was in earnest. Then he jumped down and, his boots scrunching the snow, ran back to his sleigh. The same happy, smiling Circassian, with mustache and beaming eyes looking up from under a sable hood, was still sitting there, and that Circassian was Sónya, and that Sónya was certainly his future happy and loving wife.

When they reached home and had told their mother how they had spent the evening at the Melyukóvs', the girls went to their bedroom. When they had undressed, but without washing off the cork mustaches, they sat a long time talking of their happiness. They talked of how they would live when they were married, how their husbands would be friends, and how happy they would be. On Natásha's table stood two looking glasses which Dunyásha had prepared beforehand.

"Only when will all that be? I am afraid never. . . . It would be too good!" said Natásha, rising and going to the looking glasses.

"Sit down, Natásha; perhaps you'll see him," said Sónya.

Natásha lit the candles, one on each side of one of the looking glasses, and sat down.

"I see someone with a mustache," said Natásha, seeing her own face.

"You mustn't laugh, Miss," said Dunyásha.

With Sónya's help and the maid's, Natásha got the glass she held into the right position opposite the other; her face assumed a serious expression and she sat silent. She sat a long time looking at the receding line of candles reflected in the glasses and expecting (from tales she had heard) to see a coffin, or *him*, Prince Andrew, in that last dim, indistinctly outlined square. But ready as she was to take the smallest speck for the image of a man or of a coffin, she saw nothing. She began blinking rapidly and moved away from the looking glasses.

"Why is it others see things and I don't?" she said. "You sit down now, Sónya. You absolutely must, tonight! Do it for me. . . . Today I feel so frightened!"

Sónya sat down before the glasses, got the right position, and began looking.

"Now, Miss Sónya is sure to see something," whispered Dunyásha; "while you do nothing but laugh."

Sónya heard this and Natásha's whisper:

"I know she will. She saw something last year."

For about three minutes all were silent.

"Of course she will!" whispered Natásha, but did not finish . . . suddenly Sónya pushed away the glass she was holding and covered her eyes with her hand.

"Oh, Natásha!" she cried.

"Did you see? Did you? What was it?" exclaimed Natásha, holding up the looking glass.

Sónya had not seen anything, she was just wanting to blink and to get up when she heard Natásha say, "Of course she will!" She did not wish to disappoint either Dunyásha or Natásha, but it was hard to sit still. She did not herself know how or why the exclamation escaped her when she covered her eyes.

"You saw him?" urged Natásha, seizing her hand.

"Yes. Wait a bit . . . I . . . saw him," Sónya could not help saying, not yet knowing whom Natásha meant by *him*, Nicholas or Prince Andrew.

"But why shouldn't I say I saw something? Others do see! Besides who

can tell whether I saw anything or not?" flashed through Sónya's mind. "Yes, I saw him," she said.

"How? Standing or lying?"

"No, I saw . . . At first there was nothing, then I saw him lying down."

"Andrew lying? Is he ill?" asked Natásha, her frightened eyes fixed on her friend.

"No, on the contrary, on the contrary! His face was cheerful, and he turned to me." And when saying this she herself fancied she had really seen what she described.

"Well, and then, Sónya? . . ."

"After that, I could not make out what there was; something blue and red. . . ."

"Sónya! When will he come back? When shall I see him! O, God, how afraid I am for him and for myself and about everything! . . ." Natásha began, and without replying to Sónya's words of comfort she got into bed, and long after her candle was out lay open-eyed and motion-less, gazing at the moonlight through the frosty windowpanes.

13. His mother opposes Nicholas' wish to marry Sónya, and he returns to his regiment. Natásha becomes restless and impatient for Prince Andrew's return

SOON AFTER THE CHRISTMAS HOLIDAYS Nicholas told his mother of his love for Sónya and of his firm resolve to marry her. The countess, who had long noticed what was going on between them and was expecting this declaration, listened to him in silence and then told her son that he might marry whom he pleased, but that neither she nor his father would give their blessing to such a marriage. Nicholas, for the first time, felt that his mother was displeased with him and that, despite her love for him, she would not give way. Coldly, without looking at her son, she sent for her husband and, when he came, tried briefly and coldly to inform him of the facts, in her son's presence, but unable to restrain herself she burst into tears of vexation and left the room. The old count began irresolutely to admonish Nicholas and beg him to abandon his purpose. Nicholas replied that he could not go back on his word, and his father, sighing and evi-dently disconcerted, very soon became silent and went in to the countess. In all his encounters with his son, the count was always conscious of his own guilt toward him for having wasted the family fortune, and so he could not be angry with him for refusing to marry an heiress and choosing the dowerless Sónya. On this occasion, he was only more vividly conscious

of the fact that if his affairs had not been in disorder, no better wife for Nicholas than Sónya could have been wished for, and that no one but himself with his Mítenka and his uncomfortable habits was to blame for the condition of the family finances.

The father and mother did not speak of the matter to their son again, but a few days later the countess sent for Sónya and, with a cruelty neither of them expected, reproached her niece for trying to catch Nicholas and for ingratitude. Sónya listened silently with downcast eyes to the countess' cruel words, without understanding what was required of her. She was ready to sacrifice everything for her benefactors. Self-sacrifice was her most cherished idea; but in this case she could not see what she ought to sacrifice, or for whom. She could not help loving the countess and the whole Rostóv family, but neither could she help loving Nicholas and knowing that his happiness depended on that love. She was silent and sad and did not reply. Nicholas felt the situation to be intolerable and went to have an explanation with his mother. He first implored her to forgive him and Sónya and consent to their marriage, then he threatened that if she molested Sónya he would at once marry her secretly.

The countess, with a coldness her son had never seen in her before, replied that he was of age, that Prince Andrew was marrying without his father's consent, and he could do the same, but that she would never receive that *intriguer* as her daughter.

Exploding at the word *intriguer*, Nicholas, raising his voice, told his mother he had never expected her to try to force him to sell his feelings, but if that were so, he would say for the last time . . . But he had no time to utter the decisive word which the expression of his face caused his mother to await with terror, and which would perhaps have forever remained a cruel memory to them both. He had not time to say it, for Natásha, with a pale and set face, entered the room from the door at which she had been listening.

"Nicholas, you are talking nonsense! Be quiet, be quiet, be quiet, I tell you! . . ." she almost screamed, so as to drown his voice.

"Mamma darling, it's not at all so . . . my poor, sweet darling," she said to her mother, who conscious that they had been on the brink of a rupture gazed at her son with terror, but in the obstinacy and excitement of the conflict could not and would not give way.

"Nicholas, I'll explain to you. Go away! Listen, Mamma darling," said Natásha.

Her words were incoherent, but they attained the purpose at which she was aiming.

The countess, sobbing heavily, hid her face on her daughter's breast, while Nicholas rose, clutching his head, and left the room.

Natásha set to work to effect a reconciliation, and so far succeeded that Nicholas received a promise from his mother that Sónya should not be troubled, while he on his side promised not to undertake anything without his parents' knowledge.

Firmly resolved, after putting his affairs in order in the regiment, to retire from the army and return and marry Sónya, Nicholas, serious, sorrowful, and at variance with his parents, but, as it seemed to him, passionately in love, left at the beginning of January to rejoin his regiment.

After Nicholas had gone things in the Rostóv household were more depressing than ever, and the countess fell ill from mental agitation.

Sónya was unhappy at the separation from Nicholas and still more so on account of the hostile tone the countess could not help adopting toward her. The count was more perturbed than ever by the condition of his affairs, which called for some decisive action. Their town house and estate near Moscow had inevitably to be sold, and for this they had to go to Moscow. But the countess' health obliged them to delay their departure from day to day.

Natásha, who had borne the first period of separation from her betrothed lightly and even cheerfully, now grew more agitated and impatient every day. The thought that her best days, which she would have employed in loving him, were being vainly wasted, with no advantage to anyone, tormented her incessantly. His letters for the most part irritated her. It hurt her to think that while she lived only in the thought of him, he was living a real life, seeing new places and new people that interested him. The more interesting his letters were the more vexed she felt. Her letters to him, far from giving her any comfort, seemed to her a wearisome and artificial obligation. She could not write, because she could not conceive the possibility of expressing sincerely in a letter even a thousandth part of what she expressed by voice, smile, and glance. She wrote to him formal, monotonous, and dry letters, to which she attached no importance herself, and in the rough copies of which the countess corrected her mistakes in spelling.

There was still no improvement in the countess' health, but it was impossible to defer the journey to Moscow any longer. Natásha's trousseau had to be ordered and the house sold. Moreover, Prince Andrew was expected in Moscow, where old Prince Bolkónski was spending the winter, and Natásha felt sure he had already arrived.

So the countess remained in the country, and the count, taking Sónya and Natásha with him, went to Moscow at the end of January.

BOOK EIGHT

BOOK EIGHT

1811-12

BOOK EIGHT

1. Pierre's life in Moscow. Asks himself "What for?" and "Why?"

AFTER PRINCE ANDREW's engagement to Natásha, Pierre without any apparent cause suddenly felt it impossible to go on living as before. Firmly convinced as he was of the truths revealed to him by his benefactor, and happy as he had been in perfecting his inner man, to which he had devoted himself with such ardor—all the zest of such a life vanished after the engagement of Andrew and Natásha and the death of Joseph Alexéevich, the news of which reached him almost at the same time. Only the skeleton of life remained: his house, a brilliant wife who now enjoyed the favors of a very important personage, acquaintance with all Petersburg, and his court service with its dull formalities. And this life suddenly seemed to Pierre unexpectedly loathsome. He ceased keeping a diary, avoided the company of the Brothers, began going to the Club again, drank a great deal, and came once more in touch with the bachelor sets, leading such a life that the Countess Hélène thought it necessary to speak severely to him about it. Pierre felt that she was right, and to avoid compromising her went away to Moscow.

In Moscow as soon as he entered his huge house in which the faded and fading princesses still lived, with its enormous retinue; as soon as, driving through the town, he saw the Iberian shrine with innumerable tapers burning before the golden covers of the icons, the Kremlin Square with its snow undisturbed by vehicles, the sleigh drivers and hovels of the Sívtsev Vrazhók,* those old Moscovites who desired nothing, hurried nowhere, and were ending their days leisurely; when he saw those old Moscow ladies, the Moscow balls, and the English Club, he felt himself at home in a quiet haven. In Moscow he felt at peace, at home, warm and dirty as in an old dressing gown.

Moscow society, from the old women down to the children, received

* A *slum district in Moscow.*—A.M.

Pierre like a long-expected guest whose place was always ready awaiting him. For Moscow society Pierre was the nicest, kindest, most intellectual, merriest, and most magnanimous of cranks, a heedless, genial nobleman of the old Russian type. His purse was always empty because it was open to everyone.

Benefit performances, poor pictures, statues, benevolent societies, gypsy choirs, schools, subscription dinners, sprees, Freemasons, churches, and books—no one and nothing met with a refusal from him, and had it not been for two friends who had borrowed large sums from him and taken him under their protection, he would have given everything away. There was never a dinner or soiree at the Club without him. As soon as he sank into his place on the sofa after two bottles of Margaux he was surrounded, and talking, disputing, and joking began. When there were quarrels, his kindly smile and well-timed jests reconciled the antagonists. The Masonic dinners were dull and dreary when he was not there.

When after a bachelor supper he rose with his amiable and kindly smile, yielding to the entreaties of the festive company to drive off somewhere with them, shouts of delight and triumph arose among the young men. At balls he danced if a partner was needed. Young ladies, married and unmarried, liked him because without making love to any of them, he was equally amiable to all, especially after supper. "*Il est charmant; il n'a pas de sexe* [He is charming; he has no sex]," they said of him.

Pierre was one of those retired gentlemen-in-waiting of whom there were hundreds good-humoredly ending their days in Moscow.

How horrified he would have been seven years before, when he first arrived from abroad, had he been told that there was no need for him to seek or plan anything, that his rut had long been shaped, eternally predetermined, and that wriggle as he might, he would be what all in his position were. He could not have believed it! Had he not at one time longed with all his heart to establish a republic in Russia; then himself to be a Napoleon; then to be a philosopher; and then a strategist and the conqueror of Napoleon? Had he not seen the possibility of, and passionately desired, the regeneration of the sinful human race, and his own progress to the highest degree of perfection? Had he not established schools and hospitals and liberated his serfs?

But instead of all that—here he was, the wealthy husband of an unfaithful wife, a retired gentleman-in-waiting, fond of eating and drinking and, as he unbuttoned his waistcoat, of abusing the government a bit, a member of the Moscow English Club, and a universal favorite in Moscow society. For a long time he could not reconcile himself to the idea

that he was one of those same retired Moscow gentlemen-in-waiting he had so despised seven years before.

Sometimes he consoled himself with the thought that he was only living this life temporarily; but then he was shocked by the thought of how many, like himself, had entered that life and that Club temporarily, with all their teeth and hair, and had only left it when not a single tooth or hair remained.

In moments of pride, when he thought of his position it seemed to him that he was quite different and distinct from those other retired gentlemen-in-waiting he had formerly despised: they were empty, stupid, contented fellows, satisfied with their position, "while I am still discontented and want to do something for mankind. But perhaps all these comrades of mine struggled just like me and sought something new, a path in life of their own, and like me were brought by force of circumstances, society, and race—by that elemental force against which man is powerless—to the condition I am in," said he to himself in moments of humility; and after living some time in Moscow he no longer despised, but began to grow fond of, to respect, and to pity his comrades in destiny, as he pitied himself.

Pierre no longer suffered moments of despair, hypochondria, and disgust with life, but the malady that had formerly found expression in such acute attacks was driven inwards and never left him for a moment. "What for? Why? What is going on in the world?" he would ask himself in perplexity several times a day, involuntarily beginning to reflect anew on the meaning of the phenomena of life; but knowing by experience that there were no answers to these questions he made haste to turn away from them, and took up a book, or hurried off to the Club or to Apollón Nikoláevich's, to exchange the gossip of the town.

"Hélène, who has never cared for anything but her own body and is one of the stupidest women in the world," thought Pierre, "is regarded by people as the acme of intelligence and refinement, and they pay homage to her. Napoleon Bonaparte was despised by all as long as he was great, but now that he has become a wretched comedian the Emperor Francis wants to offer him his daughter in an illegal marriage. The Spaniards, through the Catholic clergy, offer praise to God for their victory over the French on the fourteenth of June, and the French, also through the Catholic clergy, offer praise because on that same fourteenth of June they defeated the Spaniards. My brother Masons swear by the blood that they are ready to sacrifice everything for their neighbor, but they do not give a ruble each to the collections for the poor, and they intrigue, the Astraea

Lodge against the Manna Seekers,* and fuss about an authentic Scotch carpet [2] and a charter that nobody needs, and the meaning of which the very man who wrote it does not understand. We all profess the Christian law of forgiveness of injuries and love of our neighbors, the law in honor of which we have built in Moscow forty times forty churches—but yesterday a deserter was knouted to death and a minister of that same law of love and forgiveness, a priest, gave the soldier a cross to kiss before his execution." So thought Pierre, and the whole of this general deception which everyone accepts, accustomed as he was to it, astonished him each time as if it were something new. "I understand the deception and confusion," he thought, "but how am I to tell them all that I see? I have tried, and have always found that they too in the depths of their souls understand it as I do, and only try not to see it. So it appears that it must be so! But I—what is to become of me?" thought he. He had the unfortunate capacity many men, especially Russians, have of seeing and believing in the possibility of goodness and truth, but of seeing the evil and falsehood of life too clearly to be able to take a serious part in it. Every sphere of work was connected, in his eyes, with evil and deception. Whatever he tried to be, whatever he engaged in, the evil and falsehood of it repulsed him and blocked every path of activity. Yet he had to live and to find occupation. It was too dreadful to be under the burden of these insoluble problems, so he abandoned himself to any distraction in order to forget them. He frequented every kind of society, drank much, bought pictures, engaged in building, and above all—read.

He read, and read everything that came to hand. On coming home, while his valets were still taking off his things, he picked up a book and began to read. From reading he passed to sleeping, from sleeping to gossip in drawing rooms of the Club, from gossip to carousals and women; from carousals back to gossip, reading, and wine. Drinking became more and more a physical and also a moral necessity. Though the doctors warned him that with his corpulence wine was dangerous for him, he drank a great deal. He was only quite at ease when having poured several glasses of wine mechanically into his large mouth he felt a pleasant warmth in his body, an amiability toward all his fellows, and a readiness to respond superficially to every idea without probing it deeply. Only after emptying a bottle or

* These were two Masonic lodges in Petersburg.—A.M.

[2] A carpet with symbolic signs on it was considered important for the equipment of each lodge. The lodges competed with one another in obtaining such carpets from the most ancient and highly esteemed Masonic organizations, as well as copies of the ceremonies and "acts"—that is, the rules of the order. —A.M.

two did he feel dimly that the terribly tangled skein of life which previously had terrified him was not as dreadful as he had thought. He was always conscious of some aspect of that skein, as with a buzzing in his head after dinner or supper he chatted or listened to conversation or read. But under the influence of wine he said to himself: "It doesn't matter. I'll get it unraveled. I have a solution ready, but have no time now—I'll think it all out later on!" But the *later on* never came.

In the morning, on an empty stomach, all the old questions appeared as insoluble and terrible as ever, and Pierre hastily picked up a book, and if anyone came to see him he was glad.

Sometimes he remembered how he had heard that soldiers in war when entrenched under the enemy's fire, if they have nothing to do, try hard to find some occupation the more easily to bear the danger. To Pierre all men seemed like those soldiers, seeking refuge from life: some in ambition, some in cards, some in framing laws, some in women, some in toys, some in horses, some in politics, some in sport, some in wine, and some in governmental affairs. "Nothing is trivial, and nothing is important, it's all the same—only to save oneself from it as best one can," thought Pierre. "Only not to see *it*, that dreadful *it*!"

2. Prince N. Bolkónski in Moscow. His harsh treatment of Princess Mary. She teaches little Nicholas. The old prince and Mlle Bourienne

AT THE BEGINNING OF WINTER Prince Nicholas Bolkónski and his daughter moved to Moscow. At that time enthusiasm for the Emperor Alexander's regime had weakened and a patriotic and anti-French tendency prevailed there, and this, together with his past and his intellect and his originality, at once made Prince Nicholas Bolkónski an object of particular respect to the Moscovites and the center of the Moscow opposition to the government.

The prince had aged very much that year. He showed marked signs of senility by a tendency to fall asleep, forgetfulness of quite recent events, remembrance of remote ones, and the childish vanity with which he accepted the role of head of the Moscow opposition. In spite of this the old man inspired in all his visitors alike a feeling of respectful veneration—especially of an evening when he came in to tea in his old-fashioned coat and powdered wig and, aroused by anyone, told his abrupt stories of the past, or uttered yet more abrupt and scathing criticisms of the present. For them all, that old-fashioned house with its gigantic mirrors, pre-Revolu-

tion furniture, powdered footmen, and the stern shrewd old man (himself a relic of the past century) with his gentle daughter and the pretty French-woman who were reverently devoted to him presented a majestic and agreeable spectacle. But the visitors did not reflect that besides the couple of hours during which they saw their host, there were also twenty-two hours in the day during which the private and intimate life of the house continued.

Latterly that private life had become very trying for Princess Mary. There in Moscow she was deprived of her greatest pleasures—talks with the pilgrims and the solitude which refreshed her at Bald Hills—and she had none of the advantages and pleasures of city life. She did not go out into society; everyone knew that her father would not let her go anywhere without him, and his failing health prevented his going out himself, so that she was not invited to dinners and evening parties. She had quite abandoned the hope of getting married. She saw the coldness and malevolence with which the old prince received and dismissed the young men, possible suitors, who sometimes appeared at their house. She had no friends: during this visit to Moscow she had been disappointed in the two who had been nearest to her. Mademoiselle Bourienne, with whom she had never been able to be quite frank, had now become unpleasant to her, and for various reasons Princess Mary avoided her. Julie, with whom she had corresponded for the last five years, was in Moscow, but proved to be quite alien to her when they met. Just then Julie, who by the death of her brothers had become one of the richest heiresses in Moscow, was in the full whirl of society pleasures. She was surrounded by young men who, she fancied, had suddenly learned to appreciate her worth. Julie was at that stage in the life of a society woman when she feels that her last chance of marrying has come and that her fate must be decided now or never. On Thursdays Princess Mary remembered with a mournful smile that she now had no one to write to, since Julie—whose presence gave her no pleasure—was here and they met every week. Like the old émigré who declined to marry the lady with whom he had spent his evenings for years, she regretted Julie's presence and having no one to write to. In Moscow Princess Mary had no one to talk to, no one to whom to confide her sorrow, and much sorrow fell to her lot just then. The time for Prince Andrew's return and marriage was approaching, but his request to her to prepare his father for it had not been carried out; in fact, it seemed as if matters were quite hopeless, for at every mention of the young Countess Rostóva the old prince (who apart from that was usually in a bad temper) lost control of himself. Another lately added sorrow arose from the lessons she gave her six-year-old nephew. To her consternation she detected in herself in rela-

tion to little Nicholas some symptoms of her father's irritability. However often she told herself that she must not get irritable when teaching her nephew, almost every time that, pointer in hand, she sat down to show him the French alphabet, she so longed to pour her own knowledge quickly and easily into the child—who was already afraid that Auntie might at any moment get angry—that at his slightest inattention she trembled, became flustered and heated, raised her voice, and sometimes pulled him by the arm and put him in the corner. Having put him in the corner she would herself begin to cry over her cruel, evil nature, and little Nicholas, following her example, would sob, and without permission would leave his corner, come to her, pull her wet hands from her face, and comfort her. But what distressed the princess most of all was her father's irritability, which was always directed against her and had of late amounted to cruelty. Had he forced her to prostrate herself to the ground all night, had he beaten her or made her fetch wood or water, it would never have entered her mind to think her position hard; but this loving despot—the more cruel because he loved her and for that reason tormented himself and her— knew how not merely to hurt and humiliate her deliberately, but to show her that she was always to blame for everything. Of late he had exhibited a new trait that tormented Princess Mary more than anything else; this was his ever-increasing intimacy with Mademoiselle Bourienne. The idea that at the first moment of receiving the news of his son's intentions had occurred to him in jest—that if Andrew got married he himself would marry Bourienne—had evidently pleased him, and latterly he had persistently, and as it seemed to Princess Mary merely to offend her, shown special endearments to the companion and expressed his dissatisfaction with his daughter by demonstrations of love of Bourienne.

One day in Moscow in Princess Mary's presence (she thought her father did it purposely when she was there) the old prince kissed Mademoiselle Bourienne's hand and, drawing her to him, embraced her affectionately. Princess Mary flushed and ran out of the room. A few minutes later Mademoiselle Bourienne came into Princess Mary's room smiling and making cheerful remarks in her agreeable voice. Princess Mary hastily wiped away her tears, went resolutely up to Mademoiselle Bourienne, and evidently unconscious of what she was doing began shouting in angry haste at the Frenchwoman, her voice breaking: "It's horrible, vile, inhuman, to take advantage of the weakness . . ." She did not finish. "Leave my room," she exclaimed, and burst into sobs.

Next day the prince did not say a word to his daughter, but she noticed that at dinner he gave orders that Mademoiselle Bourienne should be served first. After dinner, when the footman handed coffee and from habit

began with the princess, the prince suddenly grew furious, threw his stick at Philip, and instantly gave instructions to have him conscripted for the army.

"He doesn't obey . . . I said it twice . . . and he doesn't obey! She is the first person in this house; she's my best friend," cried the prince. "And if you allow yourself," he screamed in a fury, addressing Princess Mary for the first time, "to forget yourself again before her as you dared to do yesterday, I will show you who is master in this house. Go! Don't let me set eyes on you; beg her pardon!"

Princess Mary asked Mademoiselle Bourienne's pardon, and also her father's pardon for herself and for Philip the footman, who had begged for her intervention.

At such moments something like a pride of sacrifice gathered in her soul. And suddenly that father whom she had judged would look for his spectacles in her presence, fumbling near them and not seeing them, or would forget something that had just occurred, or take a false step with his failing legs and turn to see if anyone had noticed his feebleness, or, worst of all, at dinner when there were no visitors to excite him would suddenly fall asleep, letting his napkin drop and his shaking head sink over his plate. "He is old and feeble, and I dare to condemn him!" she thought at such moments, with a feeling of revulsion against herself.

3. Dr. Métivier treated as a spy by the old prince. The dinner on the prince's name day

IN 1811 there was living in Moscow a French doctor—Métivier—who had rapidly become the fashion. He was enormously tall, handsome, amiable as Frenchmen are, and was, as all Moscow said, an extraordinarily clever doctor. He was received in the best houses not merely as a doctor, but as an equal.

Prince Nicholas had always ridiculed medicine, but latterly on Mademoiselle Bourienne's advice had allowed this doctor to visit him and had grown accustomed to him. Métivier came to see the prince about twice a week.

On December 6—St. Nicholas' Day and the prince's name day—all Moscow came to the prince's front door but he gave orders to admit no one and to invite to dinner only a small number, a list of whom he gave to Princess Mary.

Métivier, who came in the morning with his felicitations, considered it proper in his quality of doctor *de forcer la consigne* [to force the guard],

as he told Princess Mary, and went in to see the prince. It happened that on that morning of his name day the prince was in one of his worst moods. He had been going about the house all the morning finding fault with everyone and pretending not to understand what was said to him and not to be understood himself. Princess Mary well knew this mood of quiet absorbed querulousness, which generally culminated in a burst of rage, and she went about all that morning as though facing a cocked and loaded gun and awaited the inevitable explosion. Until the doctor's arrival the morning had passed off safely. After admitting the doctor, Princess Mary sat down with a book in the drawing room near the door through which she could hear all that passed in the study.

At first she heard only Métivier's voice, then her father's, then both voices began speaking at the same time, the door was flung open, and on the threshold appeared the handsome figure of the terrified Métivier with his shock of black hair, and the prince in his dressing gown and fez, his face distorted with fury and the pupils of his eyes rolled downwards.

"You don't understand?" shouted the prince, "but I do! French spy, slave of Buonaparte, spy, get out of my house! Be off, I tell you . . ." and he slammed the door.

Métivier, shrugging his shoulders, went up to Mademoiselle Bourienne who at the sound of shouting had run in from an adjoining room.

"The prince is not very well: bile and rush of blood to the head. Keep calm, I will call again tomorrow," said Métivier; and putting his fingers to his lips he hastened away.

Through the study door came the sound of slippered feet and the cry: "Spies, traitors, traitors everywhere! Not a moment's peace in my own house!"

After Métivier's departure the old prince called his daughter in, and the whole weight of his wrath fell on her. She was to blame that a spy had been admitted. Had he not told her, yes, told her to make a list, and not to admit anyone who was not on that list? Then why was that scoundrel admitted? She was the cause of it all. With her, he said, he could not have a moment's peace and could not die quietly.

"No, ma'am! We must part, we must part! Understand that, understand it! I cannot endure any more," he said, and left the room. Then, as if afraid she might find some means of consolation, he returned and trying to appear calm added: "And don't imagine I have said this in a moment of anger. I am calm, I have thought it over, and it will be carried out—we must part; so find some place for yourself! . . ." But he could not restrain himself and with the virulence of which only one who loves is capable, evidently suffering himself, he shook his fists at her and screamed:

"If only some fool would marry her!" Then he slammed the door, sent for Mademoiselle Bourienne, and subsided into his study.

At two o'clock the six chosen guests assembled for dinner.

These guests—the famous Count Rostopchín,* Prince Lopukhín with his nephew, General Chatróv an old war comrade of the prince's, and of the younger generation Pierre and Borís Drubetskóy—awaited the prince in the drawing room.

Borís, who had come to Moscow on leave a few days before, had been anxious to be presented to Prince Nicholas Bolkónski, and had contrived to ingratiate himself so well that the old prince in his case made an exception to the rule of not receiving bachelors in his house.

The prince's house did not belong to what is known as *fashionable society*, but his little circle—though not much talked about in town—was one it was more flattering to be received in than any other. Borís had realized this the week before when the commander in chief in his presence invited Rostopchín to dinner on St. Nicholas' Day, and Rostopchín had replied that he could not come:

"On that day I always go to pay my devotions to the relics of Prince Nicholas Bolkónski."

"Oh, yes, yes!" replied the commander in chief. "How is he? . . ."

The small group that assembled before dinner in the lofty old-fashioned drawing room with its old furniture resembled the solemn gathering of a court of justice. All were silent or talked in low tones. Prince Nicholas came in serious and taciturn. Princess Mary seemed even quieter and more diffident than usual. The guests were reluctant to address her, feeling that she was in no mood for their conversation. Count Rostopchín alone kept the conversation going, now relating the latest town news, and now the latest political gossip.

Lopukhín and the old general occasionally took part in the conversation. Prince Bolkónski listened as a presiding judge receives a report, only now and then, silently or by a brief word, showing that he took heed of what was being reported to him. The tone of the conversation was such as indicated that no one approved of what was being done in the political world. Incidents were related evidently confirming the opinion that everything was going from bad to worse, but whether telling a story or giving an opinion the speaker always stopped, or was stopped, at the point beyond which his criticism might touch the sovereign himself.

* *F. V. Rostopchín (1763-1828) had been a favorite of the Emperor Paul, and was Governor General and Commander in Chief of Moscow in 1812. He was an extreme reactionary, the author of many volumes, and a most eccentric and unreliable man.*—A.M.

At dinner the talk turned on the latest political news: Napoleon's seizure of the Duke of Oldenburg's territory,* and the Russian Note, hostile to Napoleon, which had been sent to all the European courts.

"Bonaparte treats Europe as a pirate does a captured vessel," said Count Rostopchín, repeating a phrase he had uttered several times before. "One only wonders at the long-suffering or blindness of the crowned heads. Now the Pope's turn has come and Bonaparte doesn't scruple to depose the head of the Catholic Church—yet all keep silent! Our sovereign alone has protested against the seizure of the Duke of Oldenburg's territory, and even . . ." Count Rostopchín paused, feeling that he had reached the limit beyond which censure was impossible.

"Other territories have been offered in exchange for the Duchy of Oldenburg," said Prince Bolkónski. "He shifts the Dukes about as I might

* Considering the Duchy of Oldenburg to be an obstacle in his path, Napoleon in 1810 dealt roughly and harshly with it. Commissaries were sent to announce the annexation of Oldenburg to France and to seize it and all its funds. The Duke (who was Alexander I's uncle) was to be allowed a place of residence at Erfurt.

Alexander protested against this seizure. He had been given to understand at the Erfurt Congress the year before that Napoleon would like to marry his sister, Elizabeth. Nothing was definitely settled at the time, however, and a little later Elizabeth married one of the Oldenburg princes. The following year Napoleon made a suggestion that he should marry Alexander's youngest sister, Anne. This proposal found favor in Petersburg, but Alexander delayed a decision as Napoleon was delaying the signature of an arrangement agreed on concerning Poland, and he feared that Napoleon might create an independent Poland or "Grand Duchy of Warsaw" as it was then called. Alexander's delay irritated Napoleon and stung his vanity, and when the Emperor of Austria showed himself inclined to arrange an alliance with the conqueror who had just humiliated Austria afresh by the Peace of Schönbrunn, and to let him marry his daughter, the Princess Marie Louise, Napoleon seized the opportunity to unite himself with one of the Imperial families and prepared to break off his alliance with Russia. These things prompted his arbitrary treatment of the Duke of Oldenburg. Apart from that, the Treaty of Tilsit was falling to pieces, as the Continental System, aimed by Napoleon at England's commerce, was harmful to Russia's trade and was not observed by Russia as strictly as Napoleon demanded. From 1810 onwards both France and Russia were practically preparing for war, and it was only the ill success of the French army in Spain on the one hand, and the backwardness of Russia's military preparations on the other, that caused the year 1811 to pass without war being declared.—A.M.

move my serfs from Bald Hills to Boguchárovo or my Ryazán estates."

"The Duke of Oldenburg bears his misfortunes with admirable strength of character and resignation," remarked Borís, joining in respectfully.

He said this because on his journey from Petersburg he had had the honor of being presented to the Duke. Prince Bolkónski glanced at the young man as if about to say something in reply, but changed his mind, evidently considering him too young.

"I have read our protests about the Oldenburg affair and was surprised how badly the Note was worded," remarked Count Rostopchín in the casual tone of a man dealing with a subject quite familiar to him.

Pierre looked at Rostopchín with naïve astonishment, not understanding why he should be disturbed by the bad composition of the Note.

"Does it matter, Count, how the Note is worded," he asked, "so long as its substance is forcible?"

"My dear fellow, with our five hundred thousand troops it should be easy to have a good style," returned Count Rostopchín.

Pierre now understood the count's dissatisfaction with the wording of the Note.

"One would have thought quill drivers enough had sprung up," remarked the old prince. "There in Petersburg they are always writing—not notes only but even new laws. My Andrew there has written a whole volume of laws for Russia. Nowadays they are always writing!" and he laughed unnaturally.

There was a momentary pause in the conversation; the old general cleared his throat to draw attention.

"Did you hear of the last event at the review in Petersburg? The figure cut by the new French ambassador."

"Eh? Yes, I heard something: he said something awkward in His Majesty's presence."

"His Majesty drew attention to the Grenadier division and to the march past," continued the general, "and it seems the ambassador took no notice and allowed himself to reply that: 'We in France pay no attention to such trifles!' The Emperor did not condescend to reply. At the next review, they say, the Emperor did not once deign to address him."

All were silent. On this fact relating to the Emperor personally, it was impossible to pass any judgment.

"Impudent fellows!" said the prince. "You know Métivier? I turned him out of my house this morning. He was here; they admitted him in spite of my request that they should let no one in," he went on, glancing angrily at his daughter.

And he narrated his whole conversation with the French doctor and the

reasons that convinced him that Métivier was a spy. Though these reasons were very insufficient and obscure, no one made any rejoinder.

After the roast, champagne was served. The guests rose to congratulate the old prince. Princess Mary, too, went round to him.

He gave her a cold, angry look and offered her his wrinkled, clean-shaven cheek to kiss. The whole expression of his face told her that he had not forgotten the morning's talk, that his decision remained in force, and only the presence of visitors hindered his speaking of it to her now.

When they went into the drawing room where coffee was served, the old men sat together.

Prince Nicholas grew more animated and expressed his views on the impending war.

He said that our wars with Bonaparte would be disastrous so long as we sought alliances with the Germans and thrust ourselves into European affairs, into which we had been drawn by the Peace of Tilsit. "We ought not to fight either for or against Austria. Our political interests are all in the East, and in regard to Bonaparte the only thing is to have an armed frontier and a firm policy, and he will never dare to cross the Russian frontier, as was the case in 1807!"

"How can we fight the French, Prince?" said Count Rostopchín. "Can we arm ourselves against our teachers and divinities? Look at our youths, look at our ladies! The French are our Gods: Paris is our Kingdom of Heaven."

He began speaking louder, evidently to be heard by everyone.

"French dresses, French ideas, French feelings! There now, you turned Métivier out by the scruff of his neck because he is a Frenchman and a scoundrel, but our ladies crawl after him on their knees. I went to a party last night, and there out of five ladies three were Roman Catholics and had the Pope's indulgence for doing woolwork on Sundays. And they themselves sit there nearly naked, like the signboards at our Public Baths if I may say so. Ah, when one looks at our young people, Prince, one would like to take Peter the Great's old cudgel out of the museum and belabor them in the Russian way till all the nonsense jumps out of them."

All were silent. The old prince looked at Rostopchín with a smile and wagged his head approvingly.

"Well, good-by, your excellency, keep well!" said Rostopchín, getting up with characteristic briskness and holding out his hand to the prince.

"Good-by, my dear fellow. . . . His words are music, I never tire of hearing him!" said the old prince, keeping hold of the hand and offering his cheek to be kissed.

Following Rostopchín's example the others also rose.

4. Pierre and Princess Mary discuss Borís and Natásha

PRINCESS MARY, as she sat listening to the old men's talk and faultfinding, understood nothing of what she heard; she only wondered whether the guests had all observed her father's hostile attitude toward her. She did not even notice the special attentions and amiabilities shown her during dinner by Borís Drubetskóy, who was visiting them for the third time already.

Princess Mary turned with an absent-minded questioning look to Pierre, who hat in hand and with a smile on his face was the last of the guests to approach her after the old prince had gone out and they were left alone in the drawing room.

"May I stay a little longer?" he said, letting his stout body sink into an armchair beside her.

"Oh yes," she answered. "You noticed nothing?" her look asked.

Pierre was in an agreeable after-dinner mood. He looked straight before him and smiled quietly.

"Have you known that young man long, Princess?" he asked.

"Who?"

"Drubetskóy."

"No, not long. . . ."

"Do you like him?"

"Yes, he is an agreeable young man. . . . Why do you ask me that?" said Princess Mary, still thinking of that morning's conversation with her father.

"Because I have noticed that when a young man comes on leave from Petersburg to Moscow it is usually with the object of marrying an heiress."

"You have observed that?" said Princess Mary.

"Yes," returned Pierre with a smile, "and this young man now manages matters so that where there is a wealthy heiress there he is too. I can read him like a book. At present he is hesitating whom to lay siege to—you or Mademoiselle Julie Karágina. He is very attentive to her."

"He visits them?"

"Yes, very often. And do you know the new way of courting?" said Pierre with an amused smile, evidently in that cheerful mood of good-humored raillery for which he so often reproached himself in his diary.

"No," replied Princess Mary.

"To please Moscow girls nowadays one has to be melancholy. He is very melancholy with Mademoiselle Karágina," said Pierre.

"Really?" asked Princess Mary, looking into Pierre's kindly face and

still thinking of her own sorrow. "It would be a relief," thought she, "if I ventured to confide what I am feeling to someone. I should like to tell everything to Pierre. He is kind and generous. It would be a relief. He would give me advice."

"Would you marry him?"

"Oh, my God, Count, there are moments when I would marry any-body!" she cried suddenly to her own surprise and with tears in her voice. "Ah, how bitter it is to love someone near to you and to feel that . . ." she went on in a trembling voice, "that you can do nothing for him but grieve him, and to know that you cannot alter this. Then there is only one thing left—to go away, but where could I go?"

"What is wrong? What is it, Princess?"

But without finishing what she was saying, Princess Mary burst into tears.

"I don't know what is the matter with me today. Don't take any notice —forget what I have said!"

Pierre's gaiety vanished completely. He anxiously questioned the prin-cess, asked her to speak out fully and confide her grief to him; but she only repeated that she begged him to forget what she had said, that she did not remember what she had said, and that she had no trouble except the one he knew of—that Prince Andrew's marriage threatened to cause a rupture between father and son.

"Have you any news of the Rostóvs?" she asked, to change the subject. "I was told they are coming soon. I am also expecting Andrew any day. I should like them to meet here."

"And how does he now regard the matter?" asked Pierre, referring to the old prince.

Princess Mary shook her head.

"What is to be done? In a few months the year will be up. The thing is impossible. I only wish I could spare my brother the first moments. I wish they would come sooner. I hope to be friends with her. You have known them a long time," said Princess Mary. "Tell me honestly the whole truth: what sort of girl is she, and what do you think of her?—The real truth, because you know Andrew is risking so much doing this against his father's will that I should like to know. . . ."

An undefined instinct told Pierre that these explanations, and repeated requests to be told the *whole truth*, expressed ill-will on the princess' part toward her future sister-in-law and a wish that he should disapprove of Andrew's choice; but in reply he said what he felt rather than what he thought.

"I don't know how to answer your question," he said, blushing without

knowing why. "I really don't know what sort of girl she is; I can't analyze her at all. She is enchanting, but what makes her so I don't know. That is all one can say about her."

Princess Mary sighed, and the expression on her face said: "Yes, that's what I expected and feared."

"Is she clever?" she asked.

Pierre considered.

"I think not," he said, "and yet—yes. She does not deign to be clever. . . . Oh no, she is simply enchanting, and that is all."

Princess Mary again shook her head disapprovingly.

"Ah, I so long to like her! Tell her so if you see her before I do."

"I hear they are expected very soon," said Pierre.

Princess Mary told Pierre of her plan to become intimate with her future sister-in-law as soon as the Rostóvs arrived and to try to accustom the old prince to her.

5. Borís and Julie. Their melancholy. Borís proposes and is accepted

Borís HAD NOT SUCCEEDED in making a wealthy match in Petersburg, so with the same object in view he came to Moscow. There he wavered between the two richest heiresses, Julie and Princess Mary. Though Princess Mary despite her plainness seemed to him more attractive than Julie, he, without knowing why, felt awkward about paying court to her. When they had last met on the old prince's name day, she had answered at random all his attempts to talk sentimentally, evidently not listening to what he was saying.

Julie on the contrary accepted his attentions readily, though in a manner peculiar to herself.

She was twenty-seven. After the death of her brothers she had become very wealthy. She was by now decidedly plain, but thought herself not merely as good-looking as before but even far more attractive. She was confirmed in this delusion by the fact that she had become a very wealthy heiress and also by the fact that the older she grew the less dangerous she became to men, and the more freely they could associate with her and avail themselves of her suppers, soirees, and the animated company that assembled at her house, without incurring any obligation. A man who would have been afraid ten years before of going every day to the house when there was a girl of seventeen there, for fear of compromising her and

committing himself, would now go boldly every day and treat her not as a marriageable girl but as a sexless acquaintance.

That winter the Karágins' house was the most agreeable and hospitable in Moscow. In addition to the formal evening and dinner parties, a large company, chiefly of men, gathered there every day, supping at midnight and staying till three in the morning. Julie never missed a ball, a promenade, or a play. Her dresses were always of the latest fashion. But in spite of that she seemed to be disillusioned about everything and told everyone that she did not believe either in friendship or in love, or any of the joys of life, and expected peace only "yonder." She adopted the tone of one who has suffered a great disappointment, like a girl who has either lost the man she loved or been cruelly deceived by him. Though nothing of the kind had happened to her she was regarded in that light, and had even herself come to believe that she had suffered much in life. This melancholy, which did not prevent her amusing herself, did not hinder the young people who came to her house from passing the time pleasantly. Every visitor who came to the house paid his tribute to the melancholy mood of the hostess, and then amused himself with society gossip, dancing, intellectual games, and *bouts rimés*,* which were in vogue at the Karágins'. Only a few of these young men, among them Borís, entered more deeply into Julie's melancholy, and with these she had prolonged conversations in private on the vanity of all worldly things, and to them she showed her albums filled with mournful sketches, maxims, and verses.

To Borís Julie was particularly gracious: she regretted his early disillusionment with life, offered him such consolation of friendship as she who had herself suffered so much could render, and showed him her album. Borís sketched two trees in the album and wrote: "Rustic trees, your dark branches shed gloom and melancholy upon me."

On another page he drew a tomb, and wrote:

> *La mort est secourable et la mort est tranquille.*
> *Ah! contre les douleurs il n'y a pas d'autre asile.*
> [Death gives relief and death is peaceful.
> Ah! from suffering there is no other refuge.]

Julie said this was charming.

"There is something so enchanting in the smile of melancholy," she said to Borís, repeating word for word a passage she had copied from a

* *This was an amusement in which rhymes were given to the players, to which they had to fit lines making up a verse. It was much in fashion, and not among young people only.*—A.M.

book. "It is a ray of light in the darkness, a shade between sadness and despair, showing the possibility of consolation."

In reply Borís wrote these lines:

Aliment de poison d'une âme trop sensible,
Toi, sans qui le bonheur me serait impossible,
Tendre mélancholie, ah, viens me consoler,
Viens calmer les tourments de ma sombre retraite,
Et mêle une douceur secrète
A ces pleurs que je sens couler.

[Poisonous nourishment of a too sensitive soul,
Thou, without whom happiness would for me be impossible,
Tender melancholy, ah, come to console me,
Come to calm the torments of my gloomy retreat,
And mingle a secret sweetness
With these tears that I feel to be flowing.]

For Borís, Julie played most doleful nocturnes on her harp. Borís read *Poor Liza* * aloud to her, and more than once interrupted the reading because of the emotions that choked him. Meeting at large gatherings Julie and Borís looked on one another as the only souls who understood one another in a world of indifferent people.

Anna Mikháylovna, who often visited the Karágins, while playing cards with the mother made careful inquiries as to Julie's dowry (she was to have two estates in Pénza and the Nizhegórod forests). Anna Mikháylovna regarded the refined sadness that united her son to the wealthy Julie with emotion, and resignation to the Divine will.

"You are always charming and melancholy, my dear Julie," she said to the daughter. "Borís says his soul finds repose at your house. He has suffered so many disappointments and is so sensitive," said she to the mother. "Ah, my dear, I can't tell you how fond I have grown of Julie latterly," she said to her son. "But who could help loving her? She is an angelic being! Ah, Borís, Borís!"—she paused. "And how I pity her mother," she went on; "today she showed me her accounts and letters from Pénza (they have enormous estates there), and she, poor thing, has no one to help her, and they do cheat her so!"

Borís smiled almost imperceptibly while listening to his mother. He laughed blandly at her naïve diplomacy but listened to what she had to

* A *very popular and sentimental story by Karamzín, which had appeared some years before this. It described the misfortunes of a peasant girl who fell in love with a nobleman, was abandoned by him, and drowned herself in a pond.*—A.M.

say, and sometimes questioned her carefully about the Pénza and Nizhe-górod estates.

Julie had long been expecting a proposal from her melancholy adorer and was ready to accept it; but some secret feeling of repulsion for her, for her passionate desire to get married, for her artificiality, and a feeling of horror at renouncing the possibility of real love still restrained Borís. His leave was expiring. He spent every day and whole days at the Karágins', and every day on thinking the matter over told himself that he would pro-pose tomorrow. But in Julie's presence, looking at her red face and chin (nearly always powdered), her moist eyes, and her expression of continual readiness to pass at once from melancholy to an unnatural rapture of mar-ried bliss, Borís could not utter the decisive words, though in imagination he had long regarded himself as the possessor of those Pénza and Nizhe-górod estates and had apportioned the use of the income from them. Julie saw Borís' indecision, and sometimes the thought occurred to her that she was repulsive to him, but her feminine self-deception immediately sup-plied her with consolation, and she told herself that he was only shy from love. Her melancholy, however, began to turn to irritability, and not long before Borís' departure she formed a definite plan of action. Just as Borís' leave of absence was expiring. Anatole Kurágin made his appearance in Moscow, and of course in the Karágins' drawing room, and Julie, suddenly abandoning her melancholy, became cheerful and very attentive to Kurágin.

"My dear," said Anna Mikháylovna to her son, "I know from a reliable source that Prince Vasíli has sent his son to Moscow to get him married to Julie. I am so fond of Julie that I should be sorry for her. What do you think of it, my dear?"

The idea of being made a fool of and of having thrown away that whole month of arduous melancholy service to Julie, and of seeing all the revenue from the Pénza estates which he had already mentally apportioned and put to proper use fall into the hands of another, and especially into the hands of that idiot Anatole, pained Borís. He drove to the Karágins' with the firm intention of proposing. Julie met him in a gay, careless manner, spoke casually of how she had enjoyed yesterday's ball, and asked when he was leaving. Though Borís had come intentionally to speak of his love and therefore meant to be tender, he began speaking irritably of feminine in-constancy, of how easily women can turn from sadness to joy, and how their moods depend solely on who happens to be paying court to them. Julie was offended and replied that it was true that a woman needs variety, and the same thing over and over again would weary anyone.

"Then I should advise you . . ." Borís began, wishing to sting her; but

at that instant the galling thought occurred to him that he might have to leave Moscow without having accomplished his aim, and have vainly wasted his efforts—which was a thing he never allowed to happen.

He checked himself in the middle of the sentence, lowered his eyes to avoid seeing her unpleasantly irritated and irresolute face, and said:

"I did not come here at all to quarrel with you. On the contrary . . ."

He glanced at her to make sure that he might go on. Her irritability had suddenly quite vanished, and her anxious, imploring eyes were fixed on him with greedy expectation. "I can always arrange so as not to see her often," thought Borís. "The affair has been begun and must be finished!" He blushed hotly, raised his eyes to hers, and said:

"You know my feelings for you!"

There was no need to say more: Julie's face shone with triumph and self-satisfaction; but she forced Borís to say all that is said on such occasions—that he loved her and had never loved any other woman more than her. She knew that for the Pénza estates and Nizhegórod forests she could demand this, and she received what she demanded.

The affianced couple, no longer alluding to trees that shed gloom and melancholy upon them, planned the arrangements of a splendid house in Petersburg, paid calls, and prepared everything for a brilliant wedding.

6. Count Ilyá Rostóv, Natásha, and Sónya stay with Márya Dmítrievna in Moscow

At the end of January old Count Rostóv went to Moscow with Natásha and Sónya. The countess was still unwell and unable to travel but it was impossible to wait for her recovery. Prince Andrew was expected in Moscow any day, the trousseau had to be ordered and the estate near Moscow had to be sold, besides which the opportunity of presenting his future daughter-in-law to old Prince Bolkónski while he was in Moscow could not be missed. The Rostóvs' Moscow house had not been heated that winter and, as they had come only for a short time and the countess was not with them, the count decided to stay with Márya Dmítrievna Akhrosímova, who had long been pressing her hospitality on them.

Late one evening the Rostóvs' four sleighs drove into Márya Dmítrievna's courtyard in the old Konyúsheny street. Márya Dmítrievna lived alone. She had already married off her daughter, and her sons were all in the service.

She held herself as erect, told everyone her opinion as candidly, loudly, and bluntly as ever, and her whole bearing seemed a reproach to others for

any weakness, passion, or temptation—the possibility of which she did not admit. From early in the morning, wearing a dressing jacket, she attended to her household affairs, and then she drove out: on holy days to church and after the service to jails and prisons on affairs of which she never spoke to anyone.* On ordinary days, after dressing, she received petitioners of various classes, of whom there were always some. Then she had dinner, a substantial and appetizing meal at which there were always three or four guests; after dinner she played a game of boston, and at night she had the newspapers or a new book read to her while she knitted. She rarely made an exception and went out to pay visits, and then only to the most important persons in the town.

She had not yet gone to bed when the Rostóvs arrived and the pulley of the hall door squeaked from the cold as it let in the Rostóvs and their servants. Márya Dmítrievna, with her spectacles hanging down on her nose and her head flung back, stood in the hall doorway looking with a stern, grim face at the new arrivals. One might have thought she was angry with the travelers and would immediately turn them out, had she not at the same time been giving careful instructions to the servants for the accommodation of the visitors and their belongings.

"The count's things? Bring them here," she said, pointing to the portmanteaux and not greeting anyone. "The young ladies'? There to the left. Now what are you dawdling for?" she cried to the maids. "Get the samovar ready! . . . You've grown plumper and prettier," she remarked, drawing Natásha (whose cheeks were glowing from the cold) to her by the hood. "Foo! You are cold! Now take off your things, quick!" she shouted to the count who was going to kiss her hand. "You're half frozen, I'm sure! Bring some rum for tea! . . . Bonjour, Sónya dear!" she added, turning to Sónya and indicating by this French greeting her slightly contemptuous though affectionate attitude toward her.

When they came in to tea, having taken off their outdoor things and tidied themselves up after their journey, Márya Dmítrievna kissed them all in due order.

"I'm heartily glad you have come and are staying with me. It was high time," she said, giving Natásha a significant look. "The old man is here and his son's expected any day. You'll have to make his acquaintance. But we'll speak of that later on," she added, glancing at Sónya with a look that showed she did not want to speak of it in her presence. "Now listen," she said to the count. "What do you want tomorrow? Whom will you send for? Shinshín?" She crooked one of her fingers. "The sniveling Anna

* In Russia the fate of prisoners was a hard one. They suffered much want, and to contribute to their needs was a recognized Christian duty.—A.M.

Mikháylovna? That's two. She's here with her son. The son is getting married! Then Bezúkhov, eh? He is here too, with his wife. He ran away from her and she came galloping after him. He dined with me on Wednesday. As for them"—and she pointed to the girls—"tomorrow I'll take them first to the Iberian shrine of the Mother of God, and then we'll drive to the Super-Rogue's.* I suppose you'll have everything new. Don't judge by me: sleeves nowadays are this size! The other day young Princess Irína Vasílevna came to see me; she was an awful sight—looked as if she had put two barrels on her arms. You know not a day passes now without some new fashion. . . . And what have you to do yourself?" she asked the count sternly.

"One thing has come on top of another: her rags to buy, and now a purchaser has turned up for the Moscow estate and for the house. If you will be so kind, I'll fix a time and go down to the estate just for a day, and leave my lassies with you."

"All right. All right. They'll be safe with me, as safe as in Chancery! I'll take them where they must go, scold them a bit, and pet them a bit," said Márya Dmítrievna, touching her goddaughter and favorite, Natásha, on the cheek with her large hand.

Next morning Márya Dmítrievna took the young ladies to the Iberian shrine of the Mother of God and to Madame Suppert-Roguet, who was so afraid of Márya Dmítrievna that she always let her have costumes at a loss merely to get rid of her. Márya Dmítrievna ordered almost the whole trousseau. When they got home she turned everybody out of the room except Natásha, and then called her pet to her armchair.

"Well, now we'll talk. I congratulate you on your betrothed. You've hooked a fine fellow! I am glad for your sake and I've known him since he was so high." She held her hand a couple of feet from the ground. Natásha blushed happily. "I like him and all his family. Now listen! You know that old Prince Nicholas much dislikes his son's marrying. The old fellow's crotchety! Of course Prince Andrew is not a child and can shift without him, but it's not nice to enter a family against a father's will. One wants to do it peacefully and lovingly. You're a clever girl and you'll know how to manage. Be kind, and use your wits. Then all will be well."

Natásha remained silent, from shyness Márya Dmítrievna supposed, but really because she disliked anyone interfering in what touched her love of Prince Andrew, which seemed to her so apart from all human affairs that no one could understand it. She loved and knew Prince Andrew, he loved her only, and was to come one of these days and take her. She wanted nothing more.

* A *pun on Suppert-Roguet, the dressmaker's name.*—A.M.

"You see I have known him a long time and am also fond of Mary, your future sister-in-law. 'Husbands' sisters bring up blisters,' but this one wouldn't hurt a fly. She has asked me to bring you two together. Tomorrow you'll go with your father to see her. Be very nice and affectionate to her: you're younger than she. When *he* comes, he'll find you already know his sister and father and are liked by them. Am I right or not? Won't that be best?"

"Yes, it will," Natásha answered reluctantly.

7. Count Rostóv and Nátasha call on Prince N. Bolkónski. They are received by Princess Mary. Prince Bolkónski's strange behavior. Mary and Natásha dislike one another

NEXT DAY, by Márya Dmítrievna's advice, Count Rostóv took Natásha to call on Prince Nicholas Bolkónski. The count did not set out cheerfully on this visit, at heart he felt afraid. He well remembered the last interview he had had with the old prince at the time of the enrollment, when in reply to an invitation to dinner he had had to listen to an angry reprimand for not having provided his full quota of men. Natásha, on the other hand, having put on her best gown, was in the highest spirits. "They can't help liking me," she thought. "Everybody always has liked me, and I am so willing to do anything they wish, so ready to be fond of him—for being *his* father—and of her—for being *his* sister—that there is no reason for them not to like me. . . ."

They drove up to the gloomy old house on the Vozdvízhenka and entered the vestibule.

"Well, the Lord have mercy on us!" said the count, half in jest, half in earnest; but Natásha noticed that her father was flurried on entering the anteroom and inquired timidly and softly whether the prince and princess were at home.

When they had been announced a perturbation was noticeable among the servants. The footman who had gone to announce them was stopped by another in the large hall and they whispered to one another. Then a maidservant ran into the hall and hurriedly said something, mentioning the princess. At last an old, cross-looking footman came and announced to the Rostóvs that the prince was not receiving, but that the princess begged them to walk up. The first person who came to meet the visitors was Mademoiselle Bourienne. She greeted the father and daughter with special politeness and showed them to the princess' room. The princess, looking excited and nervous, her face flushed in patches, ran in to meet the

visitors, treading heavily, and vainly trying to appear cordial and at ease. From the first glance Princess Mary did not like Natásha. She thought her too fashionably dressed, frivolously gay and vain. She did not at all realize that before having seen her future sister-in-law she was prejudiced against her by involuntary envy of her beauty, youth, and happiness, as well as by jealousy of her brother's love for her. Apart from this insuperable antipathy to her, Princess Mary was agitated just then because on the Rostóvs' being announced, the old prince had shouted that he did not wish to see them, that Princess Mary might do so if she chose, but they were not to be admitted to him. She had decided to receive them, but feared lest the prince might at any moment indulge in some freak, as he seemed much upset by the Rostóvs' visit.

"There, my dear princess, I've brought you my songstress," said the count, bowing and looking round uneasily as if afraid the old prince might appear. "I am so glad you should get to know one another . . . very sorry the prince is still ailing," and after a few more commonplace remarks he rose. "If you'll allow me to leave my Natásha in your hands for a quarter of an hour, Princess, I'll drive round to see Anna Semënovna, it's quite near in the Dogs' Square, and then I'll come back for her."

The count had devised this diplomatic ruse (as he afterwards told his daughter) to give the future sisters-in-law an opportunity to talk to one another freely, but another motive was to avoid the danger of encountering the old prince, of whom he was afraid. He did not mention this to his daughter, but Natásha noticed her father's nervousness and anxiety and felt mortified by it. She blushed for him, grew still angrier at having blushed, and looked at the princess with a bold and defiant expression which said that she was not afraid of anybody. The princess told the count that she would be delighted, and only begged him to stay longer at Anna Semënovna's, and he departed.

Despite the uneasy glances thrown at her by Princess Mary—who wished to have a tête-à-tête with Natásha—Mademoiselle Bourienne remained in the room and persistently talked about Moscow amusements and theaters. Natásha felt offended by the hesitation she had noticed in the anteroom, by her father's nervousness, and by the unnatural manner of the princess who—she thought—was making a favor of receiving her, and so everything displeased her. She did not like Princess Mary, whom she thought very plain, affected, and dry. Natásha suddenly shrank into herself and involuntarily assumed an offhand air which alienated Princess Mary still more. After five minutes of irksome, constrained conversation, they heard the sound of slippered feet rapidly approaching. Princess Mary

looked frightened. The door opened and the old prince, in a dressing gown and a white nightcap, came in.

"Ah, madam!" he began. "Madam, Countess . . . Countess Rostóva, if I am not mistaken . . . I beg you to excuse me, to excuse me . . . I did not know, madam. God is my witness, I did not know you had honored us with a visit, and I came in such a costume only to see my daughter. I beg you to excuse me . . . God is my witness, I didn't know—" he repeated, stressing the word "God" so unnaturally and so unpleasantly that Princess Mary stood with downcast eyes not daring to look either at her father or at Natásha.

Nor did the latter, having risen and curtsied, know what to do. Mademoiselle Bourienne alone smiled agreeably.

"I beg you to excuse me, excuse me! God is my witness, I did not know," muttered the old man, and after looking Natásha over from head to foot he went out.

Mademoiselle Bourienne was the first to recover herself after this apparition and began speaking about the prince's indisposition. Natásha and Princess Mary looked at one another in silence, and the longer they did so without saying what they wanted to say, the greater grew their antipathy to one another.

When the count returned, Natásha was impolitely pleased and hastened to get away: at that moment she hated the stiff, elderly princess, who could place her in such an embarrassing position and had spent half an hour with her without once mentioning Prince Andrew. "I couldn't begin talking about him in the presence of that Frenchwoman," thought Natásha. The same thought was meanwhile tormenting Princess Mary. She knew what she ought to have said to Natásha, but she had been unable to say it because Mademoiselle Bourienne was in the way, and because, without knowing why, she felt it very difficult to speak of the marriage. When the count was already leaving the room, Princess Mary went up hurriedly to Natásha, took her by the hand, and said with a deep sigh:

"Wait, I must . . ."

Natásha glanced at her ironically without knowing why.

"Dear Natalie," said Princess Mary, "I want you to know that I am glad my brother has found happiness. . . ."

She paused, feeling that she was not telling the truth. Natásha noticed this and guessed its reason.

"I think, Princess, it is not convenient to speak of that now," she said with external dignity and coldness, though she felt the tears choking her.

"What have I said and what have I done?" thought she, as soon as she was out of the room.

They waited a long time for Natásha to come to dinner that day. She sat in her room crying like a child, blowing her nose and sobbing. Sónya stood beside her, kissing her hair.

"Natásha, what is it about?" she asked. "What do they matter to you? It will all pass, Natásha."

"But if you only knew how offensive it was . . . as if I . . ."

"Don't talk about it, Natásha. It wasn't your fault so why should you mind? Kiss me," said Sónya.

Natásha raised her head and, kissing her friend on the lips, pressed her wet face against her.

"I can't tell you, I don't know. No one's to blame," said Natásha—"It's my fault. But it all hurts terribly. Oh, why doesn't he come? . . ."

She came in to dinner with red eyes. Márya Dmítrievna, who knew how the prince had received the Rostóvs, pretended not to notice how upset Natásha was and jested resolutely and loudly at table with the count and the other guests.

8. The Rostóvs at the Opera. Hélène in the next box

THAT EVENING the Rostóvs went to the Opera, for which Márya Dmítrievna had taken a box.

Natásha did not want to go, but could not refuse Márya Dmítrievna's kind offer which was intended expressly for her. When she came ready dressed into the ballroom to await her father, and looking in the large mirror there saw that she was pretty, very pretty, she felt even more sad, but it was a sweet, tender sadness.

"O, God, if he were here now I would not behave as I did then, but differently. I would not be silly and afraid of things, I would simply embrace him, cling to him, and make him look at me with those searching inquiring eyes with which he has so often looked at me, and then I would make him laugh as he used to laugh. And his eyes—how I see those eyes!" thought Natásha. "And what do his father and sister matter to me? I love him alone, him, him, with that face and those eyes, with his smile, manly and yet childlike. . . . No, I had better not think of him; not think of him but forget him, quite forget him for the present. I can't bear this waiting and I shall cry in a minute!" and she turned away from the glass, making an effort not to cry. "And how can Sónya love Nicholas so calmly and quietly and wait so long and so patiently?" thought she, looking at Sónya, who also came in quite ready, with a fan in her hand. "No, she's altogether different. I can't!"

Natásha at that moment felt so softened and tender that it was not enough for her to love and know she was beloved, she wanted now, at once, to embrace the man she loved, to speak and hear from him words of love such as filled her heart. While she sat in the carriage beside her father, pensively watching the lights of the street lamps flickering on the frozen window, she felt still sadder and more in love, and forgot where she was going and with whom. Having fallen into the line of carriages, the Rostóvs' carriage drove up to the theater, its wheels squeaking over the snow. Natásha and Sónya, holding up their dresses, jumped out quickly. The count got out helped by the footmen, and, passing among men and women who were entering and the program sellers, they all three went along the corridor to the first row of boxes. Through the closed doors the music was already audible.

"Natásha, your hair! . . ." whispered Sónya.

An attendant deferentially and quickly slipped before the ladies and opened the door of their box. The music sounded louder and through the door rows of brightly lit boxes in which ladies sat with bare arms and shoulders, and noisy stalls brilliant with uniforms, glittered before their eyes. A lady entering the next box shot a glance of feminine envy at Natásha. The curtain had not yet risen and the overture was being played. Natásha, smoothing her gown, went in with Sónya and sat down, scanning the brilliant tiers of boxes opposite. A sensation she had not experienced for a long time—that of hundreds of eyes looking at her bare arms and neck—suddenly affected her both agreeably and disagreeably and called up a whole crowd of memories, desires, and emotions associated with that feeling.

The two remarkably pretty girls, Natásha and Sónya, with Count Rostóv who had not been seen in Moscow for a long time, attracted general attention. Moreover, everybody knew vaguely of Natásha's engagement to Prince Andrew, and knew that the Rostóvs had lived in the country ever since, and all looked with curiosity at a fiancée who was making one of the best matches in Russia.

Natásha's looks, as everyone told her, had improved in the country, and that evening thanks to her agitation she was particularly pretty. She struck those who saw her by her fullness of life and beauty, combined with her indifference to everything about her. Her black eyes looked at the crowd without seeking anyone, and her delicate arm, bare to above the elbow, lay on the velvet edge of the box, while, evidently unconsciously, she opened and closed her hand in time to the music, crumpling her program.

"Look, there's Alénina," said Sónya, "with her mother, isn't it?"

"Dear me, Michael Kirílovich has grown still stouter!" remarked the count.

"Look at our Anna Mikháylovna—what a headdress she has on!"

"The Karágins, Julie—and Borís with them. One can see at once that they're engaged. . . ."

"Drubetskóy has proposed?"

"Oh yes, I heard it today," said Shinshín, coming into the Rostóvs' box.

Natásha looked in the direction in which her father's eyes were turned and saw Julie sitting beside her mother with a happy look on her face and a string of pearls round her thick red neck—which Natásha knew was covered with powder. Behind them, wearing a smile and leaning over with an ear to Julie's mouth, was Borís' handsome smoothly brushed head. He looked at the Rostóvs from under his brows and said something, smiling, to his betrothed.

"They are talking about us, about me and him!" thought Natásha. "And he no doubt is calming her jealousy of me. They needn't trouble themselves! If only they knew how little I am concerned about any of them."

Behind them sat Anna Mikháylovna wearing a green headdress and with a happy look of resignation to the will of God on her face. Their box was pervaded by that atmosphere of an affianced couple which Natásha knew so well and liked so much. She turned away and suddenly remembered all that had been so humiliating in her morning's visit.

"What right has he not to wish to receive me into his family? Oh, better not think of it—not till he comes back!" she told herself, and began looking at the faces, some strange and some familiar, in the stalls. In the front, in the very center, leaning back against the orchestra rail, stood Dólokhov in a Persian dress, his curly hair brushed up into a huge shock. He stood in full view of the audience, well aware that he was attracting everyone's attention, yet as much at ease as though he were in his own room. Around him thronged Moscow's most brilliant young men, whom he evidently dominated.

The count, laughing, nudged the blushing Sónya and pointed to her former adorer.

"Do you recognize him?" said he. "And where has he sprung from?" he asked, turning to Shinshín. "Didn't he vanish somewhere?"

"He did," replied Shinshín. "He was in the Caucasus and ran away from there. They say he has been acting as minister to some ruling prince in Persia, where he killed the Shah's brother. Now all the Moscow ladies are mad about him! It's 'Dólokhov the Persian' that does it! We never hear a word but Dólokhov is mentioned. They swear by him, they offer him to

you as they would a dish of choice sterlet. Dólokhov and Anatole Kurágin have turned all our ladies' heads."

A tall, beautiful woman with a mass of plaited hair and much exposed plump white shoulders and neck, round which she wore a double string of large pearls, entered the adjoining box rustling her heavy silk dress and took a long time settling into her place.

Natásha involuntarily gazed at that neck, those shoulders, and pearls and coiffure, and admired the beauty of the shoulders and the pearls. While Natásha was fixing her gaze on her for the second time the lady looked round and, meeting the count's eyes, nodded to him and smiled. She was the Countess Bezúkhova, Pierre's wife, and the count, who knew everyone in society, leaned over and spoke to her.

"Have you been here long, Countess?" he inquired. "I'll call, I'll call to kiss your hand. I'm here on business and have brought my girls with me. They say Semënova acts marvelously.* Count Pierre never used to forget us. Is he here?"

"Yes, he meant to look in," answered Hélène, and glanced attentively at Natásha.

Count Rostóv resumed his seat.

"Handsome, isn't she?" he whispered to Natásha.

"Wonderful!" answered Natásha. "She's a woman one could easily fall in love with."

Just then the last chords of the overture were heard and the conductor tapped with his stick. Some latecomers took their seats in the stalls, and the curtain rose.

As soon as it rose everyone in the boxes and stalls became silent, and all the men, old and young, in uniform and evening dress, and all the women with gems on their bare flesh, turned their whole attention with eager curiosity to the stage. Natásha too began to look at it.

* *Nymphodora Semënova had appeared on the stage in 1809, a couple of years before this, and though she was an opera singer it was her acting that was most highly appreciated, as Rostóv's remark suggests. Here as elsewhere Tolstóy keeps closely to the chronicles of the time of which he writes.*—A.M.

9. The Opera described. Anatole and Pierre arrive. Natásha makes Hélène's acquaintance. Duport dances

THE FLOOR OF THE STAGE consisted of smooth boards, at the sides was some painted cardboard representing trees, and at the back was a cloth stretched over boards.* In the center of the stage sat some girls in red bodices and white skirts. One very fat girl in a white silk dress sat apart on a low bench, to the back of which a piece of green cardboard was glued. They all sang something. When they had finished their song the girl in white went up to the prompter's box and a man with tight silk trousers over his stout legs, and holding a plume and a dagger, went up to her and began singing, waving his arms about.

First the man in the tight trousers sang alone, then she sang, then they both paused while the orchestra played and the man fingered the hand of the girl in white, obviously awaiting the beat to start singing with her. They sang together and everyone in the theater began clapping and shouting, while the man and woman on the stage—who represented lovers—began smiling, spreading out their arms, and bowing.

After her life in the country, and in her present serious mood, all this seemed grotesque and amazing to Natásha. She could not follow the opera nor even listen to the music; she saw only the painted cardboard and the queerly dressed men and women who moved, spoke, and sang so strangely in that brilliant light. She knew what it was all meant to represent, but it was so pretentiously false and unnatural that she first felt ashamed for the actors and then amused at them. She looked at the faces of the audience, seeking in them the same sense of ridicule and perplexity she herself experienced, but they all seemed attentive to what was happening on the stage, and expressed delight which to Natásha seemed feigned. "I suppose it has to be like this!" she thought. She kept looking round in turn at the rows of pomaded heads in the stalls and then at the seminude women in the boxes, especially at Hélène in the next box, who—apparently quite unclothed—sat with a quiet tranquil smile, not taking her eyes off the stage. And feeling the bright light that flooded the whole place and the warm air heated by the crowd, Natásha little by little began to pass into a state of intoxication she had not experienced for a long while. She did not realize who and where she was, nor what was going on before her. As she

* About the time Tolstóy was writing this novel, he wrote from Moscow to his wife about a visit he had paid to a theater: "I got there at the end of the second act. Fresh from the country it always seems to me all barbarous, forced, and false; but when one gets accustomed to it, it again pleases one."—A.M.

looked and thought, the strangest fancies unexpectedly and disconnect-edly passed through her mind: the idea occurred to her of jumping onto the edge of the box and singing the air the actress was singing, then she wished to touch with her fan an old gentleman sitting not far from her, then to lean over to Hélène and tickle her.

At a moment when all was quiet before the commencement of a song, a door leading to the stalls on the side nearest the Rostóvs' box creaked, and the steps of a belated arrival were heard. "There's Kurágin!" whispered Shinshín. Countess Bezúkhova turned smiling to the newcomer, and Na-tásha, following the direction of that look, saw an exceptionally handsome adjutant approaching their box with a self-assured yet courteous bearing. This was Anatole Kurágin whom she had seen and noticed long ago at the ball in Petersburg. He was now in an adjutant's uniform with one epaulet and a shoulder knot. He moved with a restrained swagger which would have been ridiculous had he not been so good-looking and had his hand-some face not worn such an expression of good-humored complacency and gaiety. Though the performance was proceeding, he walked deliberately down the carpeted gangway, his sword and spurs slightly jingling and his handsome perfumed head held high. Having looked at Natásha he ap-proached his sister, laid his well-gloved hand on the edge of her box, nod-ded to her, and leaning forward asked a question, with a motion toward Natásha.

"Mais charmante!" said he, evidently referring to Natásha, who did not exactly hear his words but understood them from the movement of his lips. Then he took his place in the first row of the stalls and sat down be-side Dólokhov, nudging with his elbow in a friendly and offhand way that Dólokhov whom others treated so fawningly. He winked at him gaily, smiled, and rested his foot against the orchestra screen.

"How like the brother is to the sister," remarked the count. "And how handsome they both are!"

Shinshín, lowering his voice, began to tell the count of some intrigue of Kurágin's in Moscow, and Natásha tried to overhear it just because he had said she was "charmante."

The first act was over. In the stalls everyone began moving about, going out and coming in.

Borís came to the Rostóvs' box, received their congratulations very simply, and raising his eyebrows with an absent-minded smile conveyed to Natásha and Sónya his fiancée's invitation to her wedding, and went away. Natásha with a gay, coquettish smile talked to him, and congratu-lated on his approaching wedding that same Borís with whom she had

formerly been in love. In the state of intoxication she was in everything seemed simple and natural.

The scantily clad Hélène smiled at everyone in the same way, and Natásha gave Borís a similar smile.

Hélène's box was filled and surrounded from the stalls by the most distinguished and intellectual men, who seemed to vie with one another in their wish to let everyone see that they knew her.

During the whole of that entr'acte Kurágin stood with Dólokhov in front of the orchestra partition, looking at the Rostóvs' box. Natásha knew he was talking about her and this afforded her pleasure. She even turned so that he should see her profile in what she thought was its most becoming aspect. Before the beginning of the second act Pierre appeared in the stalls. The Rostóvs had not seen him since their arrival. His face looked sad, and he had grown still stouter since Natásha last saw him. He passed up to the front rows, not noticing anyone. Anatole went up to him and began speaking to him, looking at and indicating the Rostóvs' box. On seeing Natásha Pierre grew animated and, hastily passing between the rows, came toward their box. When he got there he leaned on his elbows and, smiling, talked to her for a long time. While conversing with Pierre, Natásha heard a man's voice in Countess Bezúkhova's box and something told her it was Kurágin. She turned and their eyes met. Almost smiling, he gazed straight into her eyes with such an enraptured caressing look that it seemed strange to be so near him, to look at him like that, to be so sure he admired her, and not to be acquainted with him.

In the second act there was scenery representing tombstones, and there was a round hole in the canvas to represent the moon, shades were raised over the footlights, and from horns and contrabass came deep notes while many people appeared from right and left wearing black cloaks and holding things like daggers in their hands. They began waving their arms. Then some other people ran in and began dragging away the maiden who had been in white and was now in light blue. They did not drag her away at once, but sang with her for a long time and then at last dragged her off, and behind the scenes something metallic was struck three times and everyone knelt down and sang a prayer. All these things were repeatedly interrupted by the enthusiastic shouts of the audience.

During this act every time Natásha looked toward the stalls she saw Anatole Kurágin with an arm thrown across the back of his chair, staring at her. She was pleased to see that he was captivated by her and it did not occur to her that there was anything wrong in it.

When the second act was over Countess Bezúkhova rose, turned to the Rostóvs' box—her whole bosom completely exposed—beckoned the old

count with a gloved finger, and paying no attention to those who had entered her box began talking to him with an amiable smile.

"Do make me acquainted with your charming daughters," said she. "The whole town is singing their praises and I don't even know them."

Natásha rose and curtsied to the splendid countess. She was so pleased by praise from this brilliant beauty that she blushed with pleasure.

"I want to become a Moscovite too, now," said Hélène. "How is it you're not ashamed to bury such pearls in the country?"

Countess Bezúkhova quite deserved her reputation of being a fascinating woman. She could say what she did not think—especially what was flattering—quite simply and naturally.

"Dear count, you must let me look after your daughters! Though I am not staying here long this time—nor are you—I will try to amuse them. I have already heard much of you in Petersburg and wanted to get to know you," said she to Natásha with her stereotyped and lovely smile. "I had heard about you from my page, Drubetskóy. Have you heard he is getting married? And also from my husband's friend Bolkónski, Prince Andrew Bolkónski," she went on with special emphasis, implying that she knew of his relation to Natásha. To get better acquainted she asked that one of the young ladies should come into her box for the rest of the performance, and Natásha moved over to it.

The scene of the third act represented a palace in which many candles were burning and pictures of knights with short beards hung on the walls. In the middle stood what were probably a king and a queen. The king waved his right arm and, evidently nervous, sang something badly and sat down on a crimson throne. The maiden who had been first in white and then in light blue, now wore only a smock, and stood beside the throne with her hair down. She sang something mournfully, addressing the queen, but the king waved his arm severely, and men and women with bare legs came in from both sides and began dancing all together. Then the violins played very shrilly and merrily and one of the women with thick bare legs and thin arms, separating from the others, went behind the wings, adjusted her bodice, returned to the middle of the stage, and began jumping and striking one foot rapidly against the other. In the stalls everyone clapped and shouted "bravo!" Then one of the men went into a corner of the stage. The cymbals and horns in the orchestra struck up more loudly, and this man with bare legs jumped very high and waved his feet about very rapidly. (He was Duport, who received sixty thousand rubles a year for this art.) Everybody in the stalls, boxes, and galleries began clapping and shouting with all their might, and the man stopped and began smiling and bowing to all sides. Then other men and women danced

with bare legs. Then the king again shouted to the sound of music, and they all began singing. But suddenly a storm came on, chromatic scales and diminished sevenths were heard in the orchestra, everyone ran off, again dragging one of their number away, and the curtain dropped. Once more there was a terrible noise and clatter among the audience, and with rapturous faces everyone began shouting: "Duport! Duport! Duport!" Natásha no longer thought this strange. She looked about with pleasure, smiling joyfully.

"Isn't Duport delightful?" Hélène asked her.

"Oh, yes," replied Natásha.

10. Hélène presents Anatole to Natásha. He courts her

DURING THE entr'acte a whiff of cold air came into Hélène's box, the door opened, and Anatole entered, stooping and trying not to brush against anyone.

"Let me introduce my brother to you," said Hélène, her eyes shifting uneasily from Natásha to Anatole.

Natásha turned her pretty little head toward the elegant young officer and smiled at him over her bare shoulder. Anatole, who was as handsome at close quarters as at a distance, sat down beside her and told her he had long wished to have this happiness—ever since the Narýshkins' ball in fact, at which he had had the well-remembered pleasure of seeing her. Kurágin was much more sensible and simple with women than among men. He talked boldly and naturally, and Natásha was strangely and agreeably struck by the fact that there was nothing formidable in this man about whom there was so much talk, but that on the contrary his smile was most naïve, cheerful, and good-natured.

Kurágin asked her opinion of the performance and told her how at a previous performance Semënova had fallen down on the stage.

"And do you know, Countess," he said, suddenly addressing her as an old, familiar acquaintance, "we are getting up a costume tournament; you ought to take part in it! It will be great fun. We shall all meet at the Karágins'! Please come! No! Really, eh?" said he.

While saying this he never removed his smiling eyes from her face, her neck, and her bare arms. Natásha knew for certain that he was enraptured by her. This pleased her, yet his presence made her feel constrained and oppressed. When she was not looking at him she felt that he was looking at her shoulders, and she involuntarily caught his eye so that he should look into hers rather than this. But looking into his eyes

she was frightened, realizing that there was not that barrier of modesty she had always felt between herself and other men. She did not know how it was that within five minutes she had come to feel herself terribly near to this man. When she turned away she feared he might seize her from behind by her bare arm and kiss her on the neck. They spoke of most ordinary things, yet she felt that they were closer to one another than she had ever been to any man. Natásha kept turning to Hélène and to her father, as if asking what it all meant, but Hélène was engaged in conversation with a general and did not answer her look, and her father's eyes said nothing but what they always said: "Having a good time? Well, I'm glad of it!"

During one of these moments of awkward silence when Anatole's prominent eyes were gazing calmly and fixedly at her, Natásha, to break the silence, asked him how he liked Moscow. She asked the question and blushed. She felt all the time that by talking to him she was doing something improper. Anatole smiled as though to encourage her.

"At first I did not like it much, because what makes a town pleasant ce sont les jolies femmes [are the pretty women], isn't that so? But now I like it very much indeed," he said, looking at her significantly. "You'll come to the costume tournament, Countess? Do come!" and putting out his hand to her bouquet and dropping his voice, he added, "You will be the prettiest there. Do come, dear countess, and give me this flower as a pledge!"

Natásha did not understand what he was saying any more than he did himself, but she felt that his incomprehensible words had an improper intention. She did not know what to say and turned away as if she had not heard his remark. But as soon as she had turned away she felt that he was there, behind, so close behind her.

"How is he now? Confused? Angry? Ought I to put it right?" she asked herself, and she could not refrain from turning round. She looked straight into his eyes, and his nearness, self-assurance, and the good-natured tenderness of his smile vanquished her. She smiled just as he was doing, gazing straight into his eyes. And again she felt with horror that no barrier lay between him and her.

The curtain rose again. Anatole left the box, serene and gay. Natásha went back to her father in the other box, now quite submissive to the world she found herself in. All that was going on before her now seemed quite natural, but on the other hand all her previous thoughts of her betrothed, of Princess Mary, or of life in the country did not once recur to her mind and were as if belonging to a remote past.

In the fourth act there was some sort of devil who sang waving his arm

about, till the boards were withdrawn from under him and he disappeared down below. That was the only part of the fourth act that Natásha saw. She felt agitated and tormented, and the cause of this was Kurágin whom she could not help watching. As they were leaving the theater Anatole came up to them, called their carriage, and helped them in. As he was putting Natásha in he pressed her arm above the elbow. Agitated and flushed she turned round. He was looking at her with glittering eyes, smiling tenderly.

Only after she had reached home was Natásha able clearly to think over what had happened to her, and suddenly remembering Prince Andrew she was horrified, and at tea to which all had sat down after the opera, she gave a loud exclamation, flushed, and ran out of the room.

"O God! I am lost!" she said to herself. "How could I let him?" She sat for a long time hiding her flushed face in her hands trying to realize what had happened to her, but was unable either to understand what had happened or what she felt. Everything seemed dark, obscure, and terrible. There in that enormous, illuminated theater where the bare-legged Duport, in a tinsel-decorated jacket, jumped about to the music on wet boards, and young girls and old men, and the nearly naked Hélène with her proud, calm smile, rapturously cried "bravo!"—there in the presence of that Hélène it had all seemed clear and simple; but now, alone by herself, it was incomprehensible. "What is it? What was that terror I felt of him? What is this gnawing of conscience I am feeling now?" she thought.

Only to the old countess at night in bed could Natásha have told all she was feeling. She knew that Sónya with her severe and simple views would either not understand it at all or would be horrified at such a confession. So Natásha tried to solve what was torturing her by herself.

"Am I spoiled for Andrew's love or not?" she asked herself, and with soothing irony replied: "What a fool I am to ask that! What did happen to me? Nothing! I have done nothing, I didn't lead him on at all. Nobody will know and I shall never see him again," she told herself. "So it is plain that nothing has happened and there is nothing to repent of, and Andrew can love me still. But why 'still'? O God, O God, why isn't he here?" Natásha quieted herself for a moment, but again some instinct told her that though all this was true, and though nothing had happened, yet the former purity of her love for Prince Andrew had perished. And again in imagination she went over her whole conversation with Kurágin, and again saw the face, gestures, and tender smile of that bold handsome man when he pressed her arm.

11. Anatole and Dólokhov in Moscow

ANATOLE KURÁGIN was staying in Moscow because his father had sent him away from Petersburg, where he had been spending twenty thousand rubles a year in cash, besides running up debts for as much more, which his creditors demanded from his father.

His father announced to him that he would now pay half his debts for the last time, but only on condition that he went to Moscow as adjutant to the commander in chief—a post his father had procured for him— and would at last try to make a good match there. He indicated to him Princess Mary and Julie Karágina.

Anatole consented and went to Moscow, where he put up at Pierre's house. Pierre received him unwillingly at first, but got used to him after a while, sometimes even accompanied him on his carousals, and gave him money under the guise of loans.

As Shinshín had remarked, from the time of his arrival Anatole had turned the heads of the Moscow ladies, especially by the fact that he slighted them and plainly preferred the gypsy girls and French actresses— with the chief of whom, Mademoiselle George, he was said to be on intimate relations. He had never missed a carousal at Danílov's or other Moscow revelers', drank whole nights through, outvying everyone else, and was at all the balls and parties of the best society. There was talk of his intrigues with some of the ladies, and he flirted with a few of them at the balls. But he did not run after the unmarried girls, especially the rich heiresses who were most of them plain. There was a special reason for this, as he had got married two years before—a fact known only to his most intimate friends. At that time while with his regiment in Poland, a Polish landowner of small means had forced him to marry his daughter. Anatole had very soon abandoned his wife and, for a payment which he agreed to send to his father-in-law, had arranged to be free to pass himself off as a bachelor.

Anatole was always content with his position, with himself, and with others. He was instinctively and thoroughly convinced that it was impossible for him to live otherwise than as he did and that he had never in his life done anything base. He was incapable of considering how his actions might affect others or what the consequences of this or that action of his might be. He was convinced that, as a duck is so made that it must live in water, so God had made him such that he must spend thirty thousand rubles a year and always occupy a prominent position in society.

He believed this so firmly that others, looking at him, were persuaded of it too and did not refuse him either a leading place in society or money, which he borrowed from anyone and everyone and evidently would not repay.

He was not a gambler, at any rate he did not care about winning. He was not vain. He did not mind what people thought of him. Still less could he be accused of ambition. More than once he had vexed his father by spoiling his own career, and he laughed at distinctions of all kinds. He was not mean, and did not refuse anyone who asked of him. All he cared about was gaiety and women, and as according to his ideas there was nothing dishonorable in these tastes, and he was incapable of considering what the gratification of his tastes entailed for others, he honestly considered himself irreproachable, sincerely despised rogues and bad people, and with a tranquil conscience carried his head high.

Rakes, those male Magdalenes, have a secret feeling of innocence similar to that which female Magdalenes have, based on the same hope of forgiveness. "All will be forgiven her, for she loved much; and all will be forgiven him, for he enjoyed much."

Dólokhov, who had reappeared that year in Moscow after his exile and his Persian adventures, and was leading a life of luxury, gambling, and dissipation, associated with his old Petersburg comrade Kurágin and made use of him for his own ends.

Anatole was sincerely fond of Dólokhov for his cleverness and audacity. Dólokhov, who needed Anatole Kurágin's name, position, and connections as a bait to draw rich young men into his gambling set, made use of him and amused himself at his expense without letting the other feel it. Apart from the advantage he derived from Anatole, the very process of dominating another's will was in itself a pleasure, a habit, and a necessity to Dólokhov.

Natásha had made a strong impression on Kurágin. At supper after the opera he described to Dólokhov with the air of a connoisseur the attractions of her arms, shoulders, feet, and hair and expressed his intention of making love to her. Anatole had no notion and was incapable of considering what might come of such love-making, as he never had any notion of the outcome of any of his actions.

"She's first-rate, my dear fellow, but not for us," replied Dólokhov.

"I will tell my sister to ask her to dinner," said Anatole. "Eh?"

"You'd better wait till she's married. . . ."

"You know, I adore little girls, they lose their heads at once," pursued Anatole.

"You have been caught once already by a 'little girl,' " said Dólokhov who knew of Kurágin's marriage. "Take care!"

"Well, that can't happen twice! Eh?" said Anatole, with a good-humored laugh.

12. Sunday at Márya Dmítrievna's. Hélène calls and invites the Rostóvs to hear Mlle George recite. She tells Natásha that Anatole is in love with her

THE DAY AFTER THE OPERA the Rostóvs went nowhere and nobody came to see them. Márya Dmítrievna talked to the count about something which they concealed from Natásha. Natásha guessed they were talking about the old prince and planning something, and this disquieted and offended her. She was expecting Prince Andrew any moment and twice that day sent a manservant to the Vozdvízhenka to ascertain whether he had come. He had not arrived. She suffered more now than during her first days in Moscow. To her impatience and pining for him were now added the unpleasant recollection of her interview with Princess Mary and the old prince, and a fear and anxiety of which she did not understand the cause. She continually fancied that either he would never come or that something would happen to her before he came. She could no longer think of him by herself calmly and continuously as she had done before. As soon as she began to think of him, the recollection of the old prince, of Princess Mary, of the theater, and of Kurágin mingled with her thoughts. The question again presented itself whether she was not guilty, whether she had not already broken faith with Prince Andrew, and again she found herself recalling to the minutest detail every word, every gesture, and every shade in the play of expression on the face of the man who had been able to arouse in her such an incomprehensible and terrifying feeling. To the family Natásha seemed livelier than usual, but she was far less tranquil and happy than before.

On Sunday morning Márya Dmítrievna invited her visitors to Mass at her parish church—the Church of the Assumption built over the graves of victims of the plague.

"I don't like those fashionable churches," she said, evidently priding herself on her independence of thought. "God is the same everywhere. We have an excellent priest, he conducts the service decently and with dignity, and the deacon is the same. What holiness is there in giving concerts in the choir? I don't like it, it's just self-indulgence!"

Márya Dmítrievna liked Sundays and knew how to keep them. Her

whole house was scrubbed and cleaned on Saturdays; neither she nor the servants worked, and they all wore holiday dress and went to church. At her table there were extra dishes at dinner, and the servants had vodka and roast goose or suckling pig. But in nothing in the house was the holiday so noticeable as in Márya Dmítrievna's broad, stern face, which on that day wore an invariable look of solemn festivity.

After Mass, when they had finished their coffee in the dining room where the loose covers had been removed from the furniture, a servant announced that the carriage was ready, and Márya Dmítrievna rose with a stern air. She wore her holiday shawl, in which she paid calls, and announced that she was going to see Prince Nicholas Bolkónski to have an explanation with him about Natásha.

After she had gone, a dressmaker from Madame Suppert-Roguet waited on the Rostóvs, and Natásha, very glad of this diversion, having shut herself into a room adjoining the drawing room, occupied herself trying on the new dresses. Just as she had put on a bodice without sleeves and only tacked together, and was turning her head to see in the glass how the back fitted, she heard in the drawing room the animated sounds of her father's voice and another's—a woman's—that made her flush. It was Hélène. Natásha had not time to take off the bodice before the door opened and Countess Bezúkhova, dressed in a purple velvet gown with a high collar, came into the room beaming with good-humored amiable smiles.

"Oh, my enchantress!" she cried to the blushing Natásha. "Charming! No, this is really beyond anything, my dear count," said she to Count Rostóv who had followed her in. "How can you live in Moscow and go nowhere? No, I won't let you off! Mademoiselle George will recite at my house tonight and there'll be some people, and if you don't bring your lovely girls—who are prettier than Mademoiselle George—I won't know you! My husband is away in Tver * or I would send him to fetch you. You must come. You positively must! Between eight and nine."

She nodded to the dressmaker, whom she knew and who had curtsied respectfully to her, and seated herself in an armchair beside the looking glass, draping the folds of her velvet dress picturesquely. She did not cease chattering good-naturedly and gaily, continually praising Natásha's beauty. She looked at Natásha's dresses and praised them, as well as a new dress of her own made of "metallic gauze," which she had received from Paris, and advised Natásha to have one like it.

"But anything suits you, my charmer!" she remarked.

A smile of pleasure never left Natásha's face. She felt happy and as if

* Now called Kalínin, after Michael Ivánovich Kalínin (b. 1875), President of the Executive Committee of the U.S.S.R.

she were blossoming under the praise of this dear Countess Bezúkhova who had formerly seemed to her so unapproachable and important and was now so kind to her. Natásha brightened up and felt almost in love with this woman, who was so beautiful and so kind. Hélène for her part was sincerely delighted with Natásha and wished to give her a good time. Anatole had asked her to bring him and Natásha together, and she was calling on the Rostóvs for that purpose. The idea of throwing her brother and Natásha together amused her.

Though at one time, in Petersburg, she had been annoyed with Natásha for drawing Borís away, she did not think of that now, and in her own way heartily wished Natásha well. As she was leaving the Rostóvs she called her protégée aside.

"My brother dined with me yesterday—we nearly died of laughter—he ate nothing and kept sighing for you, my charmer! He is madly, quite madly, in love with you, my dear."

Natásha blushed scarlet when she heard this.

"How she blushes, how she blushes, my pretty!" said Hélène. "You must certainly come. If you love somebody, my charmer, that is not a reason to shut yourself up. Even if you are engaged, I am sure your fiancé would wish you to go into society rather than be bored to death."

"So she knows I am engaged, and she and her husband Pierre—that good Pierre—have talked and laughed about this. So it's all right." And again, under Hélène's influence, what had seemed terrible now seemed simple and natural. "And she is such a *grande dame*, so kind, and evidently likes me so much. And why not enjoy myself?" thought Natásha, gazing at Hélène with wide-open, wondering eyes.

Márya Dmítrievna came back to dinner taciturn and serious, having evidently suffered a defeat at the old prince's. She was still too agitated by the encounter to be able to talk of the affair calmly. In answer to the count's inquiries she replied that things were all right and that she would tell about it next day. On hearing of Countess Bezúkhova's visit and the invitation for that evening, Márya Dmítrievna remarked:

"I don't care to have anything to do with Bezúkhova and don't advise you to; however, if you've promised—go. It will divert your thoughts," she added, addressing Natásha.

13. The reception at Hélène's. Mlle George. Anatole dances with Natásha and makes love to her. Her perplexity as to her own feelings

COUNT ROSTÓV took the girls to Countess Bezúkhova's. There were a good many people there, but nearly all strangers to Natásha. Count Rostóv was displeased to see that the company consisted almost entirely of men and women known for the freedom of their conduct. Mademoiselle George was standing in a corner of the drawing room surrounded by young men. There were several Frenchmen present, among them Métivier who from the time Hélène reached Moscow had been an intimate in her house. The count decided not to sit down to cards or let his girls out of his sight and to get away as soon as Mademoiselle George's performance was over.

Anatole was at the door, evidently on the lookout for the Rostóvs. Immediately after greeting the count he went up to Natásha and followed her. As soon as she saw him she was seized by the same feeling she had had at the opera—gratified vanity at his admiration of her and fear at the absence of a moral barrier between them.

Hélène welcomed Natásha delightedly and was loud in admiration of her beauty and her dress. Soon after their arrival Mademoiselle George went out of the room to change her costume. In the drawing room people began arranging the chairs and taking their seats. Anatole moved a chair for Natásha and was about to sit down beside her, but the count, who never lost sight of her, took the seat himself. Anatole sat down behind her.

Mademoiselle George, with her bare, fat, dimpled arms, and a red shawl draped over one shoulder, came into the space left vacant for her, and assumed an unnatural pose. Enthusiastic whispering was audible.

Mademoiselle George looked sternly and gloomily at the audience and began reciting some French verses describing her guilty love for her son. In some places she raised her voice, in others she whispered, lifting her head triumphantly; sometimes she paused and uttered hoarse sounds, rolling her eyes.

"Adorable! divine! delicious!" was heard from every side.

Natásha looked at the fat actress, but neither saw nor heard nor understood anything of what went on before her. She only felt herself again completely borne away into this strange senseless world—so remote from her old world—a world in which it was impossible to know what was good or bad, reasonable or senseless. Behind her sat Anatole, and conscious of his proximity she experienced a frightened sense of expectancy.

After the first monologue the whole company rose and surrounded Mademoiselle George, expressing their enthusiasm.

"How beautiful she is!" Natásha remarked to her father who had also risen and was moving through the crowd toward the actress.

"I don't think so when I look at you!" said Anatole, following Natásha. He said this at a moment when she alone could hear him. "You are enchanting . . . from the moment I saw you I have never ceased . . ."

"Come, come, Natásha!" said the count, as he turned back for his daughter. "How beautiful she is!"

Natásha without saying anything stepped up to her father and looked at him with surprised inquiring eyes.

After giving several recitations, Mademoiselle George left, and Countess Bezúkhova asked her visitors into the ballroom.

The count wished to go home, but Hélène entreated him not to spoil her improvised ball, and the Rostóvs stayed on. Anatole asked Natásha for a valse and as they danced he pressed her waist and hand and told her she was bewitching and that he loved her. During the écossaise, which she also danced with him, Anatole said nothing when they happened to be by themselves, but merely gazed at her. Natásha lifted her frightened eyes to him, but there was such confident tenderness in his affectionate look and smile that she could not, whilst looking at him, say what she had to say. She lowered her eyes.

"Don't say such things to me. I am betrothed and love another," she said rapidly. . . . She glanced at him.

Anatole was not upset or pained by what she had said.

"Don't speak to me of that! What can I do?" said he. "I tell you I am madly, madly, in love with you! Is it my fault that you are enchanting? . . . It's our turn to begin."

Natásha, animated and excited, looked about her with wide-open frightened eyes and seemed merrier than usual. She understood hardly anything that went on that evening. They danced the écossaise and the Grossvater. Her father asked her to come home, but she begged to remain. Wherever she went and whomever she was speaking to, she felt his eyes upon her. Later on she recalled how she had asked her father to let her go to the dressing room to rearrange her dress, that Hélène had followed her and spoken laughingly of her brother's love, and that she again met Anatole in the little sitting room. Hélène had disappeared leaving them alone, and Anatole had taken her hand and said in a tender voice:

"I cannot come to visit you but is it possible that I shall never see you? I love you madly. Can I never . . . ?" and, blocking her path, he brought his face close to hers.

His large, glittering, masculine eyes were so close to hers that she saw nothing but them.

"Natalie?" he whispered inquiringly while she felt her hands being painfully pressed. "Natalie?"

"I don't understand. I have nothing to say," her eyes replied.

Burning lips were pressed to hers, and at the same instant she felt herself released, and Hélène's footsteps and the rustle of her dress were heard in the room. Natásha looked round at her, and then, red and trembling, threw a frightened look of inquiry at Anatole and moved toward the door.

"One word, just one, for God's sake!" cried Anatole.

She paused. She so wanted a word from him that would explain to her what had happened and to which she could find no answer.

"Natalie, just a word, only one!" he kept repeating, evidently not knowing what to say—and he repeated it till Hélène came up to them.

Hélène returned with Natásha to the drawing room. The Rostóvs went away without staying for supper.

After reaching home Natásha did not sleep all night. She was tormented by the insoluble question whether she loved Anatole or Prince Andrew. She loved Prince Andrew—she remembered distinctly how deeply she loved him. But she also loved Anatole, of that there was no doubt. "Else how could all this have happened?" thought she. "If, after that, I could return his smile when saying good-by, if I was able to let it come to that, it means that I loved him from the first. It means that he is kind, noble, and splendid, and I could not help loving him. What am I to do if I love him and the other one too?" she asked herself, unable to find an answer to these terrible questions.

14. *Princess Mary's letter to Natásha, who also receives one from Anatole*

MORNING CAME with its cares and bustle. Everyone got up and began to move about and talk, dressmakers came again. Márya Dmítrievna appeared, and they were called to breakfast. Natásha kept looking uneasily at everybody with wide-open eyes, as if wishing to intercept every glance directed toward her, and tried to appear the same as usual.

After breakfast, which was her best time, Márya Dmítrievna sat down in her armchair and called Natásha and the count to her.

"Well, friends, I have now thought the whole matter over and this is my advice," she began. "Yesterday, as you know, I went to see Prince Bolkónski. Well, I had a talk with him. . . . He took it into his head to

begin shouting, but I am not one to be shouted down. I said what I had to say!"

"Well, and he?" asked the count.

"He? He's crazy . . . he did not want to listen. But what's the use of talking? As it is we have worn the poor girl out," said Márya Dmítrievna. "My advice to you is finish your business and go back home to Otrádnoe . . . and wait there."

"Oh, no!" exclaimed Natásha.

"Yes, go back," said Márya Dmítrievna, "and wait there. If your betrothed comes here now—there will be no avoiding a quarrel; but alone with the old man he will talk things over and then come on to you."

Count Rostóv approved of this suggestion, appreciating its reasonableness. If the old man came round it would be all the better to visit him in Moscow or at Bald Hills later on; and if not, the wedding, against his wishes, could only be arranged at Otrádnoe.

"That is perfectly true. And I am sorry I went to see him and took her," said the old count.

"No, why be sorry? Being here, you had to pay your respects. But if he won't—that's his affair," said Márya Dmítrievna, looking for something in her reticule. "Besides, the trousseau is ready, so there is nothing to wait for; and what is not ready I'll send after you. Though I don't like letting you go, it is the best way. So go, with God's blessing!"

Having found what she was looking for in the reticule she handed it to Natásha. It was a letter from Princess Mary.

"She has written to you. How she torments herself, poor thing! She's afraid you might think that she does not like you."

"But she doesn't like me," said Natásha.

"Don't talk nonsense!" cried Márya Dmítrievna.

"I shan't believe anyone, I know she doesn't like me," replied Natásha boldly as she took the letter, and her face expressed a cold and angry resolution that caused Márya Dmítrievna to look at her more intently and to frown.

"Don't answer like that, my good girl!" she said. "What I say is true! Write an answer!"

Natásha did not reply and went to her own room to read Princess Mary's letter.

Princess Mary wrote that she was in despair at the misunderstanding that had occurred between them. Whatever her father's feelings might be, she begged Natásha to believe that she could not help loving her as the one chosen by her brother, for whose happiness she was ready to sacrifice everything.

"Do not think, however," she wrote, "that my father is ill-disposed toward you. He is an invalid and an old man who must be forgiven; but he is good and magnanimous and will love her who makes his son happy." Princess Mary went on to ask Natásha to fix a time when she could see her again.

After reading the letter Natásha sat down at the writing table to answer it. "Dear Princess," she wrote in French quickly and mechanically, and then paused. What more could she write after all that had happened the evening before? "Yes, yes! All that has happened, and now all is changed," she thought as she sat with the letter she had begun before her. "Must I break off with him? Must I really? That's awful . . ." and to escape from these dreadful thoughts she went to Sónya and began sorting patterns with her.

After dinner Natásha went to her room and again took up Princess Mary's letter. "Can it be that it is all over?" she thought. "Can it be that all this has happened so quickly and has destroyed all that went before?" She recalled her love for Prince Andrew in all its former strength, and at the same time felt that she loved Kurágin. She vividly pictured herself as Prince Andrew's wife, and the scenes of happiness with him she had so often repeated in her imagination, and at the same time, aglow with excitement, recalled every detail of yesterday's interview with Anatole.

"Why could that not be as well?" she sometimes asked herself in complete bewilderment. "Only so could I be completely happy; but now I have to choose, and I can't be happy without either of them. Only," she thought, "to tell Prince Andrew what has happened or to hide it from him are both equally impossible. But with that one nothing is spoiled. But am I really to abandon forever the joy of Prince Andrew's love, in which I have lived so long?"

"Please, Miss!" whispered a maid entering the room with a mysterious air. "A man told me to give you this—" and she handed Natásha a letter.

"Only, for Christ's sake . . ." the girl went on, as Natásha, without thinking, mechanically broke the seal and read a love letter from Anatole, of which, without taking in a word, she understood only that it was a letter from him—from the man she loved. Yes, she loved him, or else how could that have happened which had happened? And how could she have a love letter from him in her hand?

With trembling hands Natásha held that passionate love letter which Dólokhov had composed for Anatole, and as she read it she found in it an echo of all that she herself imagined she was feeling.

"Since yesterday evening my fate has been sealed; to be loved by you or to die. There is no other way for me," the letter began. Then he went

on to say that he knew her parents would not give her to him—for this there were secret reasons he could reveal only to her—but that if she loved him she need only say the word yes, and no human power could hinder their bliss. Love would conquer all. He would steal her away and carry her off to the ends of the earth.

"Yes, yes! I love him!" thought Natásha, reading the letter for the twentieth time and finding some peculiarly deep meaning in each word of it.

That evening Márya Dmítrievna was going to the Akhárovs' and proposed to take the girls with her. Natásha, pleading a headache, remained at home.

15. *Sónya finds Anatole's letter and remonstrates with Natásha, who writes to Princess Mary breaking off her engagement with Prince Andrew. A party at the Karágins'. Anatole meets Natásha. She is angry with Sónya, who resolves to prevent her elopement*

ON RETURNING late in the evening Sónya went to Natásha's room, and to her surprise found her still dressed and asleep on the sofa. Open on the table beside her lay Anatole's letter. Sónya picked it up and read it.

As she read she glanced at the sleeping Natásha, trying to find in her face an explanation of what she was reading, but did not find it. Her face was calm, gentle, and happy. Clutching her breast to keep herself from choking, Sónya, pale and trembling with fear and agitation, sat down in an armchair and burst into tears.

"How was it I noticed nothing? How could it go so far? Can she have left off loving Prince Andrew? And how could she let Kurágin go to such lengths? He is a deceiver and a villain, that's plain! What will Nicholas, dear noble Nicholas, do when he hears of it? So this is the meaning of her excited, resolute, unnatural look the day before yesterday, yesterday, and today," thought Sónya. "But it can't be that she loves him! She probably opened the letter without knowing who it was from. Probably she is offended by it. She could not do such a thing!"

Sónya wiped away her tears and went up to Natásha, again scanning her face.

"Natásha!" she said, just audibly.

Natásha awoke and saw Sónya.

"Ah, you're back?"

And with the decision and tenderness that often come at the moment of awakening, she embraced her friend, but noticing Sónya's look of embarrassment, her own face expressed confusion and suspicion.

"Sónya, you've read that letter?" she demanded.

"Yes," answered Sónya softly.

Natásha smiled rapturously.

"No, Sónya, I can't any longer!" she said. "I can't hide it from you any longer. You know, we love one another! Sónya, darling, he writes . . . Sónya . . ."

Sónya stared open-eyed at Natásha, unable to believe her ears.

"And Bolkónski?" she asked.

"Ah, Sónya, if you only knew how happy I am!" cried Natásha. "You don't know what love is. . . ."

"But, Natásha, can *that* be all over?"

Natásha looked at Sónya with wide-open eyes as if she could not grasp the question.

"Well, then, are you refusing Prince Andrew?" said Sónya.

"Oh, you don't understand anything! Don't talk nonsense, just listen!" said Natásha, with momentary vexation.

"But I can't believe it," insisted Sónya. "I don't understand. How is it you have loved a man for a whole year and suddenly . . . Why, you have only seen him three times! Natásha, I don't believe you, you're joking! In three days to forget everything and so . . ."

"Three days?" said Natásha. "It seems to me I've loved him a hundred years. It seems to me that I have never loved anyone before. You can't understand it. . . . Sónya, wait a bit, sit here," and Natásha embraced and kissed her.

"I had heard that it happens like this, and you must have heard it too, but it's only now that I feel such love. It's not the same as before. As soon as I saw him I felt he was my master and I his slave, and that I could not help loving him. Yes, his slave! Whatever he orders I shall do. You don't understand that. What can I do? What can I do, Sónya?" cried Natásha with a happy yet frightened expression.

"But think what you are doing," cried Sónya. "I can't leave it like this. This secret correspondence . . . How could you let him go so far?" she went on, with a horror and disgust she could hardly conceal.

"I told you that I have no will," Natásha replied. "Why can't you understand? I love him!"

"Then I won't let it come to that . . . I shall tell!" cried Sónya, bursting into tears.

"What do you mean? For God's sake . . . If you tell, you are my

enemy!" declared Natásha. "You want me to be miserable, you want us to be separated. . . ."

When she saw Natásha's fright, Sónya shed tears of shame and pity for her friend.

"But what has happened between you?" she asked. "What has he said to you? Why doesn't he come to the house?"

Natásha did not answer her questions.

"For God's sake, Sónya, don't tell anyone, don't torture me," Natásha entreated. "Remember no one ought to interfere in such matters! I have confided in you. . . ."

"But why this secrecy? Why doesn't he come to the house?" asked Sónya. "Why doesn't he openly ask for your hand? You know Prince Andrew gave you complete freedom—if it is really so; but I don't believe it! Natásha, have you considered what these secret reasons can be?"

Natásha looked at Sónya with astonishment. Evidently this question presented itself to her mind for the first time and she did not know how to answer it.

"I don't know what the reasons are. But there must be reasons!"

Sónya sighed and shook her head incredulously.

"If there were reasons . . ." she began.

But Natásha, guessing her doubts, interrupted her in alarm.

"Sónya, one can't doubt him! One can't, one can't! Don't you understand?" she cried.

"Does he love you?"

"Does he love me?" Natásha repeated with a smile of pity at her friend's lack of comprehension. "Why, you have read his letter and you have seen him."

"But if he is dishonorable?"

"He! dishonorable? If you only knew!" exclaimed Natásha.

"If he is an honorable man he should either declare his intentions or cease seeing you; and if you won't do this, I will. I will write to him, and I will tell Papa!" said Sónya resolutely.

"But I can't live without him!" cried Natásha.

"Natásha, I don't understand you. And what are you saying! Think of your father and of Nicholas."

"I don't want anyone, I don't love anyone but him. How dare you say he is dishonorable? Don't you know that I love him?" screamed Natásha. "Go away, Sónya! I don't want to quarrel with you, but go, for God's sake go! You see how I am suffering!" Natásha cried angrily, in a voice of despair and repressed irritation. Sónya burst into sobs and ran from the room.

Natásha went to the table and without a moment's reflection wrote that answer to Princess Mary which she had been unable to write all the morning. In this letter she said briefly that all their misunderstandings were at an end; that availing herself of the magnanimity of Prince Andrew who when he went abroad had given her her freedom, she begged Princess Mary to forget everything and forgive her if she had been to blame toward her, but that she could not be his wife. At that moment this all seemed quite easy, simple, and clear to Natásha.

On Friday the Rostóvs were to return to the country, but on Wednesday the count went with the prospective purchaser to his estate near Moscow.

On the day the count left, Sónya and Natásha were invited to a big dinner party at the Karágins', and Márya Dmítrievna took them there. At that party Natásha again met Anatole, and Sónya noticed that she spoke to him, trying not to be overheard, and that all through dinner she was more agitated than ever. When they got home Natásha was the first to begin the explanation Sónya expected.

"There, Sónya, you were talking all sorts of nonsense about him," Natásha began in a mild voice such as children use when they wish to be praised. "We have had an explanation today."

"Well, what happened? What did he say? Natásha, how glad I am you're not angry with me! Tell me everything—the whole truth. What did he say?"

Natásha became thoughtful.

"Oh, Sónya, if you knew him as I do! He said . . . He asked me what I had promised Bolkónski. He was glad I was free to refuse him."

Sónya sighed sorrowfully.

"But you haven't refused Bolkónski?" said she.

"Perhaps I have. Perhaps all is over between me and Bolkónski. Why do you think so badly of me?"

"I don't think anything, only I don't understand this . . ."

"Wait a bit, Sónya, you'll understand everything. You'll see what a man he is! Now don't think badly of me or of him. I don't think badly of anyone: I love and pity everybody. But what am I to do?"

Sónya did not succumb to the tender tone Natásha used toward her. The more emotional and ingratiating the expression of Natásha's face became, the more serious and stern grew Sónya's.

"Natásha," said she, "you asked me not to speak to you, and I haven't spoken, but now you yourself have begun. I don't trust him, Natásha. Why this secrecy?"

"Again, again!" interrupted Natásha.

"Natásha, I am afraid for you!"

"Afraid of what?"

"I am afraid you're going to your ruin," said Sónya resolutely, and was herself horrified at what she had said.

Anger again showed in Natásha's face.

"And I'll go to my ruin, I will, as soon as possible! It's not your business! It won't be you, but I, who'll suffer. Leave me alone, leave me alone! I hate you!"

"Natásha!" moaned Sónya, aghast.

"I hate you, I hate you! You're my enemy forever!" And Natásha ran out of the room.

Natásha did not speak to Sónya again and avoided her. With the same expression of agitated surprise and guilt she went about the house, taking up now one occupation, now another, and at once abandoning them.

Hard as it was for Sónya, she watched her friend and did not let her out of her sight.

The day before the count was to return, Sónya noticed that Natásha sat by the drawing-room window all the morning as if expecting something and that she made a sign to an officer who drove past, whom Sónya took to be Anatole.

Sónya began watching her friend still more attentively and noticed that at dinner and all that evening Natásha was in a strange and unnatural state. She answered questions at random, began sentences she did not finish, and laughed at everything.

After tea Sónya noticed a housemaid at Natásha's door timidly waiting to let her pass. She let the girl go in, and then listening at the door learned that another letter had been delivered.

Then suddenly it became clear to Sónya that Natásha had some dreadful plan for that evening. Sónya knocked at her door. Natásha did not let her in.

"She will run away with him!" thought Sónya. "She is capable of anything. There was something particularly pathetic and resolute in her face today. She cried as she said good-by to Uncle," Sónya remembered. "Yes, that's it, she means to elope with him, but what am I to do?" thought she, recalling all the signs that clearly indicated that Natásha had some terrible intention. "The count is away. What am I to do? Write to Kurágin demanding an explanation? But what is there to oblige him to reply? Write to Pierre, as Prince Andrew asked me to in case of some misfortune? . . . But perhaps she really has already refused Bolkónski—she sent a letter to Princess Mary yesterday. And Uncle is away. . . ." To tell Márya Dmítrievna who had such faith in Natásha seemed to Sónya

terrible. "Well, anyway," thought Sónya as she stood in the dark passage, "now or never I must prove that I remember the family's goodness to me and that I love Nicholas. Yes! If I don't sleep for three nights I'll not leave this passage and will hold her back by force and not let the family be disgraced," thought she.

16. Anatole at Dólokhov's. Balagá

Anatole had lately moved to Dólokhov's. The plan for Natalie Rostóva's abduction had been arranged and the preparations made by Dólokhov a few days before, and on the day that Sónya, after listening at Natásha's door, resolved to safeguard her, it was to have been put into execution. Natásha had promised to come out to Kurágin at the back porch at ten that evening. Kurágin was to put her into a troyka he would have ready and to drive her forty miles to the village of Kámenka, where an unfrocked priest was in readiness to perform a marriage ceremony over them. At Kámenka a relay of horses was to wait which would take them to the Warsaw highroad, and from there they would hasten abroad with post horses.

Anatole had a passport, an order for post horses, ten thousand rubles he had taken from his sister and another ten thousand borrowed with Dólokhov's help.

Two witnesses for the mock marriage—Khvóstikov, a retired petty official whom Dólokhov made use of in his gambling transactions, and Makárin, a retired hussar, a kindly, weak fellow who had an unbounded affection for Kurágin—were sitting at tea in Dólokhov's front room.

In his large study, the walls of which were hung to the ceiling with Persian rugs, bearskins, and weapons, sat Dólokhov in a traveling cloak and high boots, at an open desk on which lay an abacus and some bundles of paper money. Anatole, with uniform unbuttoned, walked to and fro from the room where the witnesses were sitting, through the study to the room behind, where his French valet and others were packing the last of his things. Dólokhov was counting the money and noting something down.

"Well," he said, "Khvóstikov must have two thousand."

"Give it to him, then," said Anatole.

"Makárka" (their name for Makárin) "will go through fire and water for you for nothing. So here are our accounts all settled," said Dólokhov, showing him the memorandum. "Is that right?"

"Yes, of course," returned Anatole, evidently not listening to Dólo-

khov and looking straight before him with a smile that did not leave his face.

Dólokhov banged down the lid of his desk and turned to Anatole with an ironic smile:

"Do you know? You'd really better drop it all. There's still time!"

"Fool," retorted Anatole. "Don't talk nonsense! If you only knew . . . it's the devil knows what!"

"No, really, give it up!" said Dólokhov. "I am speaking seriously. It's no joke, this plot you've hatched."

"What, teasing again? Go to the devil! Eh?" said Anatole, making a grimace. "Really it's no time for your stupid jokes," and he left the room.

Dólokhov smiled contemptuously and condescendingly when Anatole had gone out.

"You wait a bit," he called after him. "I'm not joking, I'm talking sense. Come here, come here!"

Anatole returned and looked at Dólokhov, trying to give him his attention and evidently submitting to him involuntarily.

"Now listen to me. I'm telling you this for the last time. Why should I joke about it? Did I hinder you? Who arranged everything for you? Who found the priest and got the passport? Who raised the money? I did it all."

"Well, thank you for it. Do you think I am not grateful?" And Anatole sighed and embraced Dólokhov.

"I helped you, but all the same I must tell you the truth; it is a dangerous business, and if you think about it—a stupid business. Well, you'll carry her off—all right! Will they let it stop at that? It will come out that you're already married. Why, they'll have you in the criminal court. . . ."

"Oh, nonsense, nonsense!" Anatole ejaculated and again made a grimace. "Didn't I explain to you? What?" And Anatole, with the partiality dull-witted people have for any conclusion they have reached by their own reasoning, repeated the argument he had already put to Dólokhov a hundred times. "Didn't I explain to you that I have come to this conclusion: if this marriage is invalid," he went on, crooking one finger, "then I have nothing to answer for; but if it is valid, no matter! Abroad no one will know anything about it. Isn't that so? And don't talk to me, don't, don't."

"Seriously, you'd better drop it! You'll only get yourself into a mess!"

"Go to the devil!" cried Anatole and, clutching his hair, left the room, but returned at once and dropped into an armchair in front of Dólokhov with his feet tucked under him. "It's the very devil! What? Feel how it beats!" He took Dólokhov's hand and put it on his heart. "What a foot, my dear fellow! What a glance! A goddess!" he added in French. "What?"

Dólokhov with a cold smile and a gleam in his handsome insolent eyes looked at him—evidently wishing to get some more amusement out of him.

"Well and when the money's gone, what then?"

"What then? Eh?" repeated Anatole, sincerely perplexed by a thought of the future. "What then? . . . Then, I don't know. . . . But why talk nonsense!" He glanced at his watch. "It's time!"

Anatole went into the back room.

"Now then! Nearly ready? You're dawdling!" he shouted to the servants.

Dólokhov put away the money, called a footman whom he ordered to bring something for them to eat and drink before the journey, and went into the room where Khvóstikov and Makárin were sitting.

Anatole lay on the sofa in the study leaning on his elbow and smiling pensively, while his handsome lips muttered tenderly to himself.

"Come and eat something. Have a drink!" Dólokhov shouted to him from the other room.

"I don't want to," answered Anatole continuing to smile.

"Come! Balagá is here."

Anatole rose and went into the dining room. Balagá was a famous troyka driver who had known Dólokhov and Anatole some six years and had given them good service with his troykas. More than once when Anatole's regiment was stationed at Tver he had taken him from Tver in the evening, brought him to Moscow by daybreak, and driven him back again the next night. More than once he had enabled Dólokhov to escape when pursued. More than once he had driven them through the town with gypsies and "ladykins" as he called the cocottes. More than once in their service he had run over pedestrians and upset vehicles in the streets of Moscow and had always been protected from the consequences by "my gentlemen" as he called them. He had ruined more than one horse in their service. More than once they had beaten him, and more than once they had made him drunk on champagne and Madeira, which he loved; and he knew more than one thing about each of them which would long ago have sent an ordinary man to Siberia. They often called Balagá into their orgies and made him drink and dance at the gypsies', and more than one thousand rubles of their money had passed through his hands. In their service he risked his skin and his life twenty times a year, and in their service had lost more horses than the money he had from them would buy. But he liked them; liked that mad driving at twelve miles an hour, liked upsetting a driver or running down a pedestrian, and flying at full gallop through the Moscow streets. He liked to hear those wild, tipsy

shouts behind him: "Get on! Get on!" when it was impossible to go any faster. He liked giving a painful lash on the neck to some peasant who, more dead than alive, was already hurrying out of his way. "Real gentlemen!" he considered them.

Anatole and Dólokhov liked Balagá too for his masterly driving and because he liked the things they liked. With others Balagá bargained, charging twenty-five rubles for a two hours' drive, and rarely drove himself, generally letting his young men do so. But with "his gentlemen" he always drove himself and never demanded anything for his work. Only a couple of times a year—when he knew from their valets that they had money in hand—he would turn up of a morning quite sober and with a deep bow would ask them to help him. The gentlemen always made him sit down.

"Do help me out, Theodore Iványch, sir," or "your excellency," he would say. "I am quite out of horses. Let me have what you can to go to the fair."

And Anatole and Dólokhov, when they had money, would give him a thousand or a couple of thousand rubles.

Balagá was a fair-haired, short, and snub-nosed peasant of about twenty-seven; red-faced, with a particularly red thick neck, glittering little eyes, and a small beard. He wore a fine, dark-blue, silk-lined cloth coat over a sheepskin.

On entering the room now he crossed himself, turning toward the front corner of the room, and went up to Dólokhov, holding out a small, black hand.

"Theodore Iványch!" he said, bowing.

"How d'you do, friend? Well, here he is!"

"Good day, your excellency!" he said, again holding out his hand to Anatole who had just come in.

"I say, Balagá," said Anatole, putting his hands on the man's shoulders, "do you care for me or not? Eh? Now, do me a service. . . . What horses have you come with? Eh?"

"As your messenger ordered, your special beasts," replied Balagá.

"Well, listen, Balagá! Drive all three to death but get me there in three hours. Eh?"

"When they are dead, what shall I drive?" said Balagá with a wink.

"Mind, I'll smash your face in! Don't make jokes!" cried Anatole, suddenly rolling his eyes.

"Why joke?" said the driver, laughing. "As if I'd grudge my gentlemen anything! As fast as ever the horses can gallop, so fast we'll go!"

"Ah!" said Anatole. "Well, sit down."

"Yes, sit down!" said Dólokhov.

"I'll stand, Theodore Iványch."

"Sit down; nonsense! Have a drink!" said Anatole, and filled a large glass of Madeira for him.

The driver's eyes sparkled at the sight of the wine. After refusing it for manners' sake, he drank it and wiped his mouth with a red silk handkerchief he took out of his cap.

"And when are we to start, your excellency?"

"Well . . ." Anatole looked at his watch. "We'll start at once. Mind, Balagá! You'll get there in time? Eh?"

"That depends on our luck in starting, else why shouldn't we be there in time?" replied Balagá. "Didn't we get you to Tver in seven hours? I think you remember that, your excellency?"

"Do you know, one Christmas I drove from Tver," said Anatole, smiling at the recollection and turning to Makárin who gazed rapturously at him with wide-open eyes. "Will you believe it, Makárka, it took one's breath away, the rate we flew. We came across a train of loaded sleighs and drove right over two of them. Eh?"

"Those were horses!" Balagá continued the tale. "That time I'd harnessed two young side horses with the bay in the shafts," he went on, turning to Dólokhov. "Will you believe it, Theodore Iványch, those animals flew forty miles? I couldn't hold them in, my hands grew numb in the sharp frost so that I threw down the reins—'Catch hold yourself, your excellency!' says I, and I just tumbled on the bottom of the sleigh and sprawled there. It wasn't a case of urging them on, there was no holding them in till we reached the place. The devils took us there in three hours! Only the near one died of it."

17. Anatole sets off to abduct Natásha, but encounters Márya Dmítrievna's footman

ANATOLE went out of the room and returned a few minutes later wearing a fur coat girt with a silver belt, and a sable cap jauntily set on one side and very becoming to his handsome face. Having looked in a mirror, and standing before Dólokhov in the same pose he had assumed before it, he lifted a glass of wine.

"Well, good-by, Theodore. Thank you for everything and farewell!" said Anatole. "Well, comrades and friends . . ." he considered for a moment ". . . of my youth, farewell!" he said, turning to Makárin and the others.

Though they were all going with him, Anatole evidently wished to

make something touching and solemn out of this address to his comrades. He spoke slowly in a loud voice and throwing out his chest slightly swayed one leg.

"All take glasses; you too, Balagá. Well, comrades and friends of my youth, we've had our fling and lived and reveled. Eh? And now, when shall we meet again? I am going abroad. We have had a good time—now farewell, lads! To our health! Hurrah! . . ." he cried, and emptying his glass flung it on the floor.

"To your health!" said Balagá who also emptied his glass, and wiped his mouth with his handkerchief.

Makárin embraced Anatole with tears in his eyes.

"Ah, Prince, how sorry I am to part from you!"

"Let's go. Let's go!" cried Anatole.

Balagá was about to leave the room.

"No, stop!" said Anatole. "Shut the door; we have first to sit down. That's the way."

They shut the door and all sat down.*

"Now, quick march, lads!" said Anatole, rising.

Joseph, his valet, handed him his sabretache and saber, and they all went out into the vestibule.

"And where's the fur cloak?" asked Dólokhov. "Hey, Ignátka! Go to Matréna Matrévna and ask her for the sable cloak. I have heard what elopements are like," continued Dólokhov with a wink. "Why, she'll rush out more dead than alive just in the things she is wearing; if you delay at all there'll be tears and 'Papa' and 'Mamma,' and she's frozen in a minute and must go back—but you wrap the fur cloak round her first thing and carry her to the sleigh."

The valet brought a woman's fox-lined cloak.

"Fool, I told you the sable one! Hey, Matréna, the sable!" he shouted so that his voice rang far through the rooms.

A handsome, slim, and pale-faced gypsy girl with glittering black eyes and curly blue-black hair, wearing a red shawl, ran out with a sable mantle on her arm.

"Here, I don't grudge it—take it!" she said, evidently afraid of her master and yet regretful of her cloak.

Dólokhov, without answering, took the cloak, threw it over Matréna, and wrapped her up in it.

"That's the way," said Dólokhov, "and then so!" and he turned the collar up round her head, leaving only a little of the face uncovered. "And

* *This is in accord with a Russian superstition as to what should be done when starting on a journey.*—A.M.

then so, do you see?" and he pushed Anatole's head forward to meet the gap left by the collar, through which Matrëna's brilliant smile was seen.

"Well, good-by, Matrëna," said Anatole, kissing her. "Ah, my revels here are over. Remember me to Stëshka. There, good-by! Good-by, Matrëna, wish me luck!"

"Well, Prince, may God give you great luck!" said Matrëna in her gypsy accent.

Two troykas were standing before the porch and two young drivers were holding the horses. Balagá took his seat in the front one and holding his elbows high arranged the reins deliberately. Anatole and Dólokhov got in with him. Makárin, Khvóstikov, and a valet seated themselves in the other sleigh.

"Well, are you ready?" asked Balagá.

"Go!" he cried, twisting the reins round his hands, and the troyka tore down the Nikítski Boulevard.

"Tproo! Get out of the way! Hi! . . . Tproo! . . ." The shouting of Balagá and of the sturdy young fellow seated on the box was all that could be heard. On the Arbát Square the troyka caught against a carriage; something cracked, shouts were heard, and the troyka flew along the Arbát Street.

After taking a turn along the Podnovínski Boulevard, Balagá began to rein in, and turning back drew up at the crossing of the old Konyúsheny Street.

The young fellow on the box jumped down to hold the horses and Anatole and Dólokhov went along the pavement. When they reached the gate Dólokhov whistled. The whistle was answered, and a maidservant ran out.

"Come into the courtyard or you'll be seen; she'll come out directly," said she.

Dólokhov stayed by the gate. Anatole followed the maid into the courtyard, turned the corner, and ran up into the porch.

He was met by Gabriel, Márya Dmítrievna's gigantic footman.

"Come to the mistress, please," said the footman in his deep bass, intercepting any retreat.

"To what mistress? Who are you?" asked Anatole in a breathless whisper.

"Kindly step in, my orders are to bring you in."

"Kurágin! Come back!" shouted Dólokhov. "Betrayed! Back!"

Dólokhov, after Anatole entered, had remained at the wicket gate and was struggling with the yard porter who was trying to lock it. With a last

desperate effort Dólokhov pushed the porter aside, and when Anatole ran back seized him by the arm, pulled him through the wicket, and ran back with him to the troyka.

18. Márya Dmítrievna reproaches Natásha. Count Ilyá Rostóv is kept in ignorance

MÁRYA DMÍTRIEVNA, having found Sónya weeping in the corridor, made her confess everything, and intercepting the note to Natásha she read it and went into Natásha's room with it in her hand.

"You shameless good-for-nothing!" said she. "I won't hear a word."

Pushing back Natásha who looked at her with astonished but tearless eyes, she locked her in; and having given orders to the yard porter to admit the persons who would be coming that evening, but not to let them out again, and having told the footman to bring them up to her, she seated herself in the drawing room to await the abductors.

When Gabriel came to inform her that the men who had come had run away again, she rose frowning, and clasping her hands behind her paced through the rooms a long time considering what she should do. Toward midnight she went to Natásha's room fingering the key in her pocket. Sónya was sitting sobbing in the corridor. "Márya Dmítrievna, for God's sake let me in to her!" she pleaded, but Márya Dmítrievna unlocked the door and went in without giving her an answer. . . . "Disgusting, abominable . . . In my house . . . horrid girl, hussy! I'm only sorry for her father!" thought she, trying to restrain her wrath. "Hard as it may be, I'll tell them all to hold their tongues and will hide it from the count." She entered the room with resolute steps. Natásha was lying on the sofa, her head hidden in her hands, and she did not stir. She was in just the same position in which Márya Dmítrievna had left her.

"A nice girl! Very nice!" said Márya Dmítrievna. "Arranging meetings with lovers in my house! It's no use pretending: you listen when I speak to you!" And Márya Dmítrievna touched her arm. "Listen when I speak! You've disgraced yourself like the lowest of hussies. I'd treat you differently, but I'm sorry for your father, so I will conceal it."

Natásha did not change her position, but her whole body heaved with noiseless, convulsive sobs which choked her. Márya Dmítrievna glanced round at Sónya and seated herself on the sofa beside Natásha.

"It's lucky for him that he escaped me; but I'll find him!" she said in her rough voice. "Do you hear what I am saying or not?" she added. She put her large hand under Natásha's face and turned it toward her.

Both Márya Dmítrievna and Sónya were amazed when they saw how Natásha looked. Her eyes were dry and glistening, her lips compressed, her cheeks sunken.

"Let me be! . . . What is it to me? . . . I shall die!" she muttered, wrenching herself from Márya Dmítrievna's hands with a vicious effort and sinking down again into her former position.

"Natalie!" said Márya Dmítrievna. "I wish for your good. Lie still, stay like that then, I won't touch you. But listen. I won't tell you how guilty you are. You know that yourself. But when your father comes back tomorrow—what am I to tell him? Eh?"

Again Natásha's body shook with sobs.

"Suppose he finds out, and your brother, and your betrothed?"

"I have no betrothed: I have refused him!" cried Natásha.

"That's all the same," continued Márya Dmítrievna. "If they hear of this will they let it pass? He, your father, I know him . . . if he challenges him to a duel will that be all right? Eh?"

"Oh, let me be! Why have you interfered at all? Why? Why? Who asked you to?" shouted Natásha, raising herself on the sofa and looking malignantly at Márya Dmítrievna.

"But what did you want?" cried Márya Dmítrievna, growing angry again. "Were you kept under lock and key? Who hindered his coming to the house? Why carry you off as if you were some gypsy singing girl? . . . Well, if he had carried you off . . . do you think they wouldn't have found him? Your father, or brother, or your betrothed? And he's a scoundrel, a wretch—that's a fact!"

"He is better than any of you!" exclaimed Natásha getting up. "If you hadn't interfered . . . Oh, my God! What is it all? What is it? Sónya, why? . . . Go away!"

And she burst into sobs with the despairing vehemence with which people bewail disasters they feel they have themselves occasioned. Márya Dmítrievna was about to speak again, but Natásha cried out:

"Go away! Go away! You all hate and despise me!" and she threw herself back on the sofa.

Márya Dmítrievna went on admonishing her for some time, enjoining on her that it must all be kept from her father and assuring her that nobody would know anything about it if only Natásha herself would undertake to forget it all and not let anyone see that something had happened. Natásha did not reply, nor did she sob any longer, but she grew cold and had a shivering fit. Márya Dmítrievna put a pillow under her head, covered her with two quilts, and herself brought her some lime-flower water, but Natásha did not respond to her.

"Well, let her sleep," said Márya Dmítrievna as she went out of the room supposing Natásha to be asleep.

But Natásha was not asleep; with pale face and fixed wide-open eyes she looked straight before her. All that night she did not sleep or weep and did not speak to Sónya who got up and went to her several times.

Next day Count Rostóv returned from his estate near Moscow in time for lunch as he had promised. He was in very good spirits; the affair with the purchaser was going on satisfactorily, and there was nothing to keep him any longer in Moscow, away from the countess whom he missed. Márya Dmítrievna met him and told him that Natásha had been very unwell the day before and that they had sent for the doctor, but that she was better now. Natásha had not left her room that morning. With compressed and parched lips and dry fixed eyes, she sat at the window, uneasily watching the people who drove past and hurriedly glancing round at anyone who entered the room. She was evidently expecting news of him and that he would come or would write to her.

When the count came to see her she turned anxiously round at the sound of a man's footstep, and then her face resumed its cold and malevolent expression. She did not even get up to greet him.

"What is the matter with you, my angel? Are you ill?" asked the count.

After a moment's silence Natásha answered: "Yes, ill."

In reply to the count's anxious inquiries as to why she was so dejected and whether anything had happened to her betrothed, she assured him that nothing had happened and asked him not to worry. Márya Dmítrievna confirmed Natásha's assurances that nothing had happened. From the pretense of illness, from his daughter's distress, and by the embarrassed faces of Sónya and Márya Dmítrievna, the count saw clearly that something had gone wrong during his absence, but it was so terrible for him to think that anything disgraceful had happened to his beloved daughter, and he so prized his own cheerful tranquillity, that he avoided inquiries and tried to assure himself that nothing particularly had happened; and he was only dissatisfied that her indisposition delayed their return to the country.

19. Pierre at Márya Dmítrievna's. He tells Natásha that Anatole is married

FROM THE DAY his wife arrived in Moscow Pierre had been intending to go away somewhere, so as not to be near her. Soon after the Rostóvs came to Moscow the effect Natásha had on him made him hasten to

carry out his intention. He went to Tver to see Joseph Alexéevich's widow, who had long since promised to hand over to him some papers of her deceased husband's.

When he returned to Moscow Pierre was handed a letter from Márya Dmítrievna asking him to come and see her on a matter of great importance relating to Andrew Bolkónski and his betrothed. Pierre had been avoiding Natásha because it seemed to him that his feeling for her was stronger than a married man's should be for his friend's fiancée. Yet some fate constantly threw them together.

"What can have happened? And what can they want with me?" thought he as he dressed to go to Márya Dmítrievna's. "If only Prince Andrew would hurry up and come and marry her!" thought he on his way to the house.

On the Tverskóy Boulevard a familiar voice called to him.

"Pierre! Been back long?" someone shouted. Pierre raised his head. In a sleigh drawn by two gray trotting-horses that were bespattering the dashboard with snow, Anatole and his constant companion Makárin dashed past. Anatole was sitting upright in the classic pose of military dandies, the lower part of his face hidden by his beaver collar and his head slightly bent. His face was fresh and rosy, his white-plumed hat, tilted to one side, disclosed his curled and pomaded hair besprinkled with powdery snow.

"Yes, indeed, that's a true sage," thought Pierre. "He sees nothing beyond the pleasure of the moment, nothing troubles him and so he is always cheerful, satisfied, and serene. What wouldn't I give to be like him!" he thought enviously.

In Márya Dmítrievna's anteroom the footman who helped him off with his fur coat said that the mistress asked him to come to her bedroom.

When he opened the ballroom door Pierre saw Natásha sitting at the window, with a thin, pale, and spiteful face. She glanced round at him, frowned, and left the room with an expression of cold dignity.

"What has happened?" asked Pierre, entering Márya Dmítrievna's room.

"Fine doings!" answered Márya Dmítrievna. "For fifty-eight years have I lived in this world and never known anything so disgraceful!"

And having put him on his honor not to repeat anything she told him, Márya Dmítrievna informed him that Natásha had refused Prince Andrew without her parents' knowledge and that the cause of this was Anatole Kurágin into whose society Pierre's wife had thrown her and with whom Natásha had tried to elope during her father's absence, in order to be married secretly.

Pierre raised his shoulders and listened openmouthed to what was told him, scarcely able to believe his own ears. That Prince Andrew's deeply loved affianced wife—the same Natásha Rostóva who used to be so charming—should give up Bolkónski for that fool Anatole who was already secretly married (as Pierre knew), and should be so in love with him as to agree to run away with him, was something Pierre could not conceive and could not imagine.

He could not reconcile the charming impression he had of Natásha, whom he had known from a child, with this new conception of her baseness, folly, and cruelty. He thought of his wife. "They are all alike!" he said to himself, reflecting that he was not the only man unfortunate enough to be tied to a bad woman. But still he pitied Prince Andrew to the point of tears and sympathized with his wounded pride, and the more he pitied his friend the more did he think with contempt and even with disgust of that Natásha who had just passed him in the ballroom with such a look of cold dignity. He did not know that Natásha's soul was overflowing with despair, shame, and humiliation, and that it was not her fault that her face happened to assume an expression of calm dignity and severity.

"But how get married?" said Pierre, in answer to Márya Dmítrievna. "He could not marry—he is married!"

"Things get worse from hour to hour!" ejaculated Márya Dmítrievna. "A nice youth! What a scoundrel! And she's expecting him—expecting him since yesterday. She must be told! Then at least she won't go on expecting him."

After hearing the details of Anatole's marriage from Pierre, and giving vent to her anger against Anatole in words of abuse, Márya Dmítrievna told Pierre why she had sent for him. She was afraid that the count or Bolkónski, who might arrive at any moment, if they knew of this affair (which she hoped to hide from them) might challenge Anatole to a duel, and she therefore asked Pierre to tell his brother-in-law in her name to leave Moscow and not dare to let her set eyes on him again. Pierre—only now realizing the danger to the old count, Nicholas, and Prince Andrew—promised to do as she wished. Having briefly and exactly explained her wishes to him, she let him go to the drawing room.

"Mind, the count knows nothing. Behave as if you know nothing either," she said. "And I will go and tell her it is no use expecting him! And stay to dinner if you care to!" she called after Pierre.

Pierre met the old count, who seemed nervous and upset. That morning Natásha had told him that she had rejected Bolkónski.

"Troubles, troubles, my dear fellow!" he said to Pierre. "What troubles one has with these girls without their mother! I do so regret having come here. . . . I will be frank with you. Have you heard she has broken off her engagement without consulting anybody? It's true this engagement never was much to my liking. Of course he is an excellent man, but still, with his father's disapproval they wouldn't have been happy, and Natásha won't lack suitors. Still, it has been going on so long, and to take such a step without father's or mother's consent! And now she's ill, and God knows what! It's hard, Count, hard to manage daughters in their mother's absence. . . ."

Pierre saw that the count was much upset and tried to change the subject, but the count returned to his troubles.

Sónya entered the room with an agitated face.

"Natásha is not quite well; she's in her room and would like to see you. Márya Dmítrievna is with her and she too asks you to come."

"Yes, you are a great friend of Bolkónski's, no doubt she wants to send him a message," said the count. "Oh dear! Oh dear! How happy it all was!"

And clutching the spare gray locks on his temples the count left the room.

When Márya Dmítrievna told Natásha that Anatole was married, Natásha did not wish to believe it and insisted on having it confirmed by Pierre himself. Sónya told Pierre this as she led him along the corridor to Natásha's room.

Natásha, pale and stern, was sitting beside Márya Dmítrievna, and her eyes, glittering feverishly, met Pierre with a questioning look the moment he entered. She did not smile or nod, but only gazed fixedly at him, and her look asked only one thing: was he a friend, or like the others an enemy in regard to Anatole? As for Pierre, he evidently did not exist for her.

"He knows all about it," said Márya Dmítrievna pointing to Pierre and addressing Natásha. "Let him tell you whether I have told the truth."

Natásha looked from one to the other as a hunted and wounded animal looks at the approaching dogs and sportsmen.

"Natálya Ilyníchna," Pierre began, dropping his eyes with a feeling of pity for her and loathing for the thing he had to do, "whether it is true or not should make no difference to you, because . . ."

"Then it is not true that he's married!"

"Yes, it is true."

"Has he been married long?" she asked. "On your honor? . . ."

Pierre gave his word of honor.

"Is he still here?" she asked, quickly.

"Yes, I have just seen him."

She was evidently unable to speak and made a sign with her hands that they should leave her alone.

20. Pierre's explanation with Anatole

PIERRE did not stay for dinner, but left the room and went away at once. He drove through the town seeking Anatole Kurágin, at the thought of whom now the blood rushed to his heart and he felt a difficulty in breathing. He was not at the ice hills, nor at the gypsies', nor at Komoneno's. Pierre drove to the Club. In the Club all was going on as usual. The members who were assembling for dinner were sitting about in groups; they greeted Pierre and spoke of the town news. The footman having greeted him, knowing his habits and his acquaintances, told him there was a place left for him in the small dining room and that Prince Michael Zakhárych was in the library, but Paul Timoféevich had not yet arrived. One of Pierre's acquaintances, while they were talking about the weather, asked if he had heard of Kurágin's abduction of Rostóva which was talked of in the town, and was it true? Pierre laughed and said it was nonsense for he had just come from the Rostóvs'. He asked everyone about Anatole. One man told him he had not come yet, and another that he was coming to dinner. Pierre felt it strange to see this calm, indifferent crowd of people unaware of what was going on in his soul. He paced through the ballroom, waited till everyone had come, and as Anatole had not turned up did not stay for dinner but drove home.

Anatole, for whom Pierre was looking, dined that day with Dólokhov, consulting him as to how to remedy this unfortunate affair. It seemed to him essential to see Natásha. In the evening he drove to his sister's to discuss with her how to arrange a meeting. When Pierre returned home after vainly hunting all over Moscow, his valet informed him that Prince Anatole was with the countess. The countess' drawing room was full of guests.

Pierre without greeting his wife whom he had not seen since his return —at that moment she was more repulsive to him than ever—entered the drawing room and seeing Anatole went up to him.

"Ah, Pierre," said the countess going up to her husband. "You don't know what a plight our Anatole . . ."

She stopped, seeing in the forward thrust of her husband's head, in his glowing eyes and his resolute gait, the terrible indications of that rage and strength which she knew and had herself experienced after his duel with Dólokhov.

"Where you are, there is vice and evil!" said Pierre to his wife. "Anatole, come with me! I must speak to you," he added in French.

Anatole glanced round at his sister and rose submissively, ready to follow Pierre. Pierre, taking him by the arm, pulled him toward himself and was leading him from the room.

"If you allow yourself in my drawing room . . ." whispered Hélène, but Pierre did not reply and went out of the room.

Anatole followed him with his usual jaunty step but his face betrayed anxiety.

Having entered his study Pierre closed the door and addressed Anatole without looking at him.

"You promised Countess Rostóva to marry her and were about to elope with her, is that so?"

"Mon cher," answered Anatole (their whole conversation was in French), "I don't consider myself bound to answer questions put to me in that tone."

Pierre's face, already pale, became distorted by fury. He seized Anatole by the collar of his uniform with his big hand and shook him from side to side till Anatole's face showed a sufficient degree of terror.

"When I tell you that I must talk to you! . . ." repeated Pierre.

"Come now, this is stupid. What?" said Anatole, fingering a button of his collar that had been wrenched loose with a bit of the cloth.

"You're a scoundrel and a blackguard, and I don't know what deprives me from the pleasure of smashing your head with this!" said Pierre, expressing himself so artificially because he was talking French.

He took a heavy paperweight and lifted it threateningly, but at once put it back in its place.

"Did you promise to marry her?"

"I . . . I . . . I didn't think of it. I never promised, because . . ."

Pierre interrupted him.

"Have you any letters of hers? Any letters?" he said, moving toward Anatole.

Anatole glanced at him and immediately thrust his hand into his pocket and drew out his pocketbook.

Pierre took the letter Anatole handed him and, pushing aside a table that stood in his way, threw himself on the sofa.

"I shan't be violent, don't be afraid!" said Pierre in answer to a frightened gesture of Anatole's. "First, the letters," said he, as if repeating a lesson to himself. "Secondly," he continued after a short pause, again rising and again pacing the room, "tomorrow you must get out of Moscow."

"But how can I? . . ."

"Thirdly," Pierre continued without listening to him, "you must never breathe a word of what has passed between you and Countess Rostóva. I know I can't prevent your doing so, but if you have a spark of conscience . . ." Pierre paced the room several times in silence.

Anatole sat at a table frowning and biting his lips.

"After all, you must understand that besides your pleasure there is such a thing as other people's happiness and peace, and that you are ruining a whole life for the sake of amusing yourself! Amuse yourself with women like my wife—with them you are within your rights, for they know what you want of them. They are armed against you by the same experience of debauchery; but to promise a maid to marry her . . . to deceive, to kidnap. . . . Don't you understand that it is as mean as beating an old man or a child? . . ."

Pierre paused and looked at Anatole no longer with an angry but with a questioning look.

"I don't know about that, eh?" said Anatole, growing more confident as Pierre mastered his wrath. "I don't know that and don't want to," he said, not looking at Pierre and with a slight tremor of his lower jaw, "but you have used such words to me—'mean' and so on—which as a man of honor I can't allow anyone to use."

Pierre glanced at him with amazement, unable to understand what he wanted.

"Though it was tête-à-tête," Anatole continued, "still I can't . . ."

"Is it satisfaction you want?" said Pierre ironically.

"You could at least take back your words. What? If you want me to do as you wish, eh?"

"I take them back, I take them back!" said Pierre, "and I ask you to forgive me." Pierre involuntarily glanced at the loose button. "And if you require money for your journey . . ."

Anatole smiled. The expression of that base and cringing smile, which Pierre knew so well in his wife, revolted him.

"Oh, vile and heartless brood!" he exclaimed, and left the room.

Next day Anatole left for Petersburg.

21. Natásha tries to poison herself. Prince Andrew returns to Moscow and Pierre talks to him

PIERRE drove to Márya Dmítrievna's to tell her of the fulfillment of her wish that Kurágin should be banished from Moscow. The whole house was in a state of alarm and commotion. Natásha was very ill, having, as

Márya Dmítrievna told him in secret, poisoned herself the night after she had been told that Anatole was married, with some arsenic she had stealthily procured. After swallowing a little she had been so frightened that she woke Sónya and told her what she had done. The necessary antidotes had been administered in time and she was now out of danger, though still so weak that it was out of the question to move her to the country, and so the countess had been sent for. Pierre saw the distracted count, and Sónya, who had a tear-stained face, but he could not see Natásha.

Pierre dined at the club that day and heard on all sides gossip about the attempted abduction of Rostóva. He resolutely denied these rumors, assuring everyone that nothing had happened except that his brother-in-law had proposed to her and been refused. It seemed to Pierre that it was his duty to conceal the whole affair and re-establish Natásha's reputation.

He was awaiting Prince Andrew's return with dread and went every day to the old prince's for news of him.

Old Prince Bolkónski heard all the rumors current in the town from Mademoiselle Bourienne and had read the note to Princess Mary in which Natásha had broken off her engagement. He seemed in better spirits than usual and awaited his son with great impatience.

Some days after Anatole's departure Pierre received a note from Prince Andrew, informing him of his arrival and asking him to come to see him.

As soon as he reached Moscow, Prince Andrew had received from his father Natásha's note to Princess Mary breaking off her engagement (Mademoiselle Bourienne had purloined it from Princess Mary and given it to the old prince), and he heard from him the story of Natásha's elopement, with additions.

Prince Andrew had arrived in the evening and Pierre came to see him next morning. Pierre expected to find Prince Andrew in almost the same state as Natásha and was therefore surprised on entering the drawing room to hear him in the study talking in a loud animated voice about some intrigue going on in Petersburg. The old prince's voice and another now and then interrupted him. Princess Mary came out to meet Pierre. She sighed, looking toward the door of the room where Prince Andrew was, evidently intending to express her sympathy with his sorrow, but Pierre saw by her face that she was glad both at what had happened and at the way her brother had taken the news of Natásha's faithlessness.

"He says he expected it," she remarked. "I know his pride will not let him express his feelings, but still he has taken it better, far better, than I expected. Evidently it had to be. . . ."

"But is it possible that all is really ended?" asked Pierre.

Princess Mary looked at him with astonishment. She did not understand how he could ask such a question. Pierre went into the study. Prince Andrew, greatly changed and plainly in better health, but with a fresh horizontal wrinkle between his brows, stood in civilian dress facing his father and Prince Meshchérski, warmly disputing and vigorously gesticulating. The conversation was about Speránski—the news of whose sudden exile and alleged treachery had just reached Moscow.*

"Now he is censured and accused by all who were enthusiastic about him a month ago," Prince Andrew was saying, "and by those who were unable to understand his aims. To judge a man who is in disfavor and to throw on him all the blame of other men's mistakes is very easy, but I maintain that if anything good has been accomplished in this reign it was done by him, by him alone."

He paused at the sight of Pierre. His face quivered and immediately assumed a vindictive expression.

"Posterity will do him justice," he concluded, and at once turned to Pierre.

"Well, how are you? Still getting stouter?" he said with animation, but

* Speránski's sudden fall from power and exile to Nízhni-Nóvgorod occurred on March 17, 1812, o.s. The causes of this event were certainly connected with the change in Alexander's outlook and plans, from the liberal tendency of his early years to a more reactionary attitude. The constantly increasing dangers and difficulties in foreign policy also made it convenient to sacrifice Speránski, against whom—at a time when the conservative spirit of Russia was pitting itself against the more progressive watchwords of the new France—numerous inimical rumors reached the Emperor from reactionaries and from Speránski's numerous enemies at court, who regarded him as an upstart intervening between Alexander and his former devoted servants and advisers.

Speránski wrote several letters to Alexander defending himself, but it was not till 1816 that an ukase appeared which indirectly admitted that the accusations against him were unfounded. He was then made Governor of Pénza, and three years later Governor General of Siberia. In 1821 he returned to Petersburg and entered the Council of State, but he no longer had any of his former influence with the Emperor.

In the next reign, Nicholas I, after testing his loyalty by appointing him to be one of the judges of the "Decembrist" conspirators, placed him in charge of the compilation of the Code of Laws, and Speránski succeeded in publishing forty-two volumes of The Complete Collection of Russian Laws, which formed the basis of the systematic Code of Laws of the Russian Empire compiled in 1832.—A.M.

the new wrinkle on his forehead deepened. "Yes, I am well," he said in answer to Pierre's question, and smiled.

To Pierre that smile said plainly: "I am well, but my health is now of no use to anyone."

After a few words to Pierre about the awful roads from the Polish frontier, about people he had met in Switzerland who knew Pierre, and about M. Dessalles, whom he had brought from abroad to be his son's tutor, Prince Andrew again joined warmly in the conversation about Speránski which was still going on between the two old men.

"If there were treason, or proofs of secret relations with Napoleon, they would have been made public," he said with warmth and haste. "I do not, and never did, like Speránski personally, but I like justice!"

Pierre now recognized in his friend a need with which he was only too familiar, to get excited and to have arguments about extraneous matters in order to stifle thoughts that were too oppressive and too intimate.

When Prince Meshchérski had left, Prince Andrew took Pierre's arm and asked him into the room that had been assigned him. A bed had been made up there, and some open portmanteaux and trunks stood about. Prince Andrew went to one and took out a small casket, from which he drew a packet wrapped in paper. He did it all silently and very quickly. He stood up and coughed. His face was gloomy and his lips compressed.

"Forgive me for troubling you. . . ."

Pierre saw that Prince Andrew was going to speak of Natásha, and his broad face expressed pity and sympathy. This expression irritated Prince Andrew, and in a determined, ringing, and unpleasant tone he continued:

"I have received a refusal from Countess Rostóva and have heard reports of your brother-in-law having sought her hand, or something of that kind. Is that true?"

"Both true and untrue," Pierre began; but Prince Andrew interrupted him.

"Here are her letters and her portrait," said he.

He took the packet from the table and handed it to Pierre.

"Give this to the countess . . . if you see her."

"She is very ill," said Pierre.

"Then she is here still?" said Prince Andrew. "And Prince Kurágin?" he added quickly.

"He left long ago. She has been at death's door."

"I much regret her illness," said Prince Andrew; and he smiled like his father, coldly, maliciously, and unpleasantly.

"So Monsieur Kurágin has not honored Countess Rostóva with his hand?" said Prince Andrew, and he snorted several times.

"He could not marry, for he was married already," said Pierre.

Prince Andrew laughed disagreeably, again reminding one of his father.

"And where is your brother-in-law now, if I may ask?" he said.

"He has gone to Peters . . . But I don't know," said Pierre.

"Well, it doesn't matter," said Prince Andrew. "Tell Countess Rostóva that she was and is perfectly free and that I wish her all that is good."

Pierre took the packet. Prince Andrew, as if trying to remember whether he had something more to say, or waiting to see if Pierre would say anything, looked fixedly at him.

"I say, do you remember our discussion in Petersburg?" asked Pierre, "about . . ."

"Yes," returned Prince Andrew hastily. "I said that a fallen woman should be forgiven, but I didn't say I could forgive her. I can't."

"But can this be compared . . . ?" said Pierre.

Prince Andrew interrupted him and cried sharply: "Yes, ask her hand again, be magnanimous, and so on? . . . Yes, that would be very noble, but I am unable to follow in that gentleman's footsteps. If you wish to be my friend never speak to me of that . . . of all that! Well, good-by. So you'll give her the packet?"

Pierre left the room and went to the old prince and Princess Mary.

The old man seemed livelier than usual. Princess Mary was the same as always, but beneath her sympathy for her brother, Pierre noticed her satisfaction that the engagement had been broken off. Looking at them Pierre realized what contempt and animosity they all felt for the Rostóvs, and that it was impossible in their presence even to mention the name of her who could give up Prince Andrew for anyone else.

At dinner the talk turned on the war, the approach of which was becoming evident. Prince Andrew talked incessantly, arguing now with his father, now with the Swiss tutor Dessalles, and showing an unnatural animation, the cause of which Pierre so well understood.

22. Pierre and Natásha. He tells her of his devotion. The great comet of 1812

THAT SAME EVENING Pierre went to the Rostóvs' to fulfill the commission entrusted to him. Natásha was in bed, the count at the Club, and Pierre, after giving the letters to Sónya, went to Márya Dmítrievna who was interested to know how Prince Andrew had taken the news. Ten minutes later Sónya came to Márya Dmítrievna.

"Natásha insists on seeing Count Peter Kirílovich," * said she.

"But how? Are we to take him up to her? The room there has not been tidied up."

"No, she has dressed and gone into the drawing room," said Sónya.

Márya Dmítrievna only shrugged her shoulders.

"When will her mother come? She has worried me to death! Now mind, don't tell her everything!" said she to Pierre. "One hasn't the heart to scold her, she is so much to be pitied, so much to be pitied."

Natásha was standing in the middle of the drawing room, emaciated, with a pale set face, but not at all shamefaced as Pierre expected to find her. When he appeared at the door she grew flurried, evidently undecided whether to go to meet him or to wait till he came up.

Pierre hastened to her. He thought she would give him her hand as usual; but she, stepping up to him, stopped, breathing heavily, her arms hanging lifelessly just in the pose she used to stand in when she went to the middle of the ballroom to sing, but with quite a different expression of face.

"Peter Kirílovich," she began rapidly, "Prince Bolkónski was your friend —is your friend," she corrected herself. (It seemed to her that everything that had once been must now be different.) "He told me once to apply to you . . ."

Pierre sniffed as he looked at her, but did not speak. Till then he had reproached her in his heart and tried to despise her, but he now felt so sorry for her that there was no room in his soul for reproach.

"He is here now: tell him . . . to for . . . forgive me!"

She stopped and breathed still more quickly, but did not shed tears.

"Yes . . . I will tell him," answered Pierre; "but . . ."

He did not know what to say.

Natásha was evidently dismayed at the thought of what he might think she had meant.

"No, I know all is over," she said hurriedly. "No, that can never be. I'm only tormented by the wrong I have done him. Tell him only that I beg him to forgive, forgive, forgive me for everything. . . ."

She trembled all over and sat down on a chair.

A sense of pity he had never before known overflowed Pierre's heart.

"I will tell him, I will tell him everything once more," said Pierre. "But . . . I should like to know one thing. . . ."

"Know what?" Natásha's eyes asked.

"I should like to know, did you love . . ." Pierre did not know how to

* *Peter Kirílovich is a form of address at once formal, correct, and polite. Kirílovich is the patronymic, and means son-of-Cyril.*—A.M.

refer to Anatole and flushed at the thought of him—"did you love that bad man?"

"Don't call him bad!" said Natásha. "But I don't know, don't know at all. . . ."

She began to cry and a still greater sense of pity, tenderness, and love welled up in Pierre. He felt the tears trickle under his spectacles and hoped they would not be noticed.

"We won't speak of it any more, my dear," said Pierre, and his gentle, cordial tone suddenly seemed very strange to Natásha.

"We won't speak of it, my dear—I'll tell him everything; but one thing I beg of you, consider me your friend and if you want help, advice, or simply to open your heart to someone—not now, but when your mind is clearer—think of me!" He took her hand and kissed it. "I shall be happy if it's in my power . . ."

Pierre grew confused.

"Don't speak to me like that. I am not worth it!" exclaimed Natásha and turned to leave the room, but Pierre held her hand.

He knew he had something more to say to her. But when he said it he was amazed at his own words.

"Stop, stop! You have your whole life before you," said he to her.

"Before me? No! All is over for me," she replied with shame and self-abasement.

"All over?" he repeated. "If I were not myself, but the handsomest, cleverest, and best man in the world, and were free, I would this moment ask on my knees for your hand and your love!"

For the first time for many days Natásha wept tears of gratitude and tenderness, and glancing at Pierre she went out of the room.

Pierre too when she had gone almost ran into the anteroom, restraining tears of tenderness and joy that choked him, and without finding the sleeves of his fur cloak threw it on and got into his sleigh.

"Where to now, your excellency?" asked the coachman.

"Where to?" Pierre asked himself. "Where can I go now? Surely not to the Club or to pay calls?" All men seemed so pitiful, so poor, in comparison with this feeling of tenderness and love he experienced: in comparison with that softened, grateful, last look she had given him through her tears.

"Home!" said Pierre, and despite twenty-two degrees of frost Fahrenheit he threw open the bearskin cloak from his broad chest and inhaled the air with joy.

It was clear and frosty. Above the dirty, ill-lit streets, above the black roofs, stretched the dark starry sky. Only looking up at the sky did Pierre cease to feel how sordid and humiliating were all mundane things com-

pared with the heights to which his soul had just been raised. At the entrance to the Arbát Square an immense expanse of dark starry sky presented itself to his eyes. Almost in the center of it, above the Prechístenka Boulevard, surrounded and sprinkled on all sides by stars but distinguished from them all by its nearness to the earth, its white light, and its long uplifted tail, shone the enormous and brilliant comet of 1812—the comet which was said to portend all kinds of woes and the end of the world. In Pierre, however, that comet with its long luminous tail aroused no feeling of fear. On the contrary he gazed joyfully, his eyes moist with tears, at this bright comet which, having traveled in its orbit with inconceivable velocity through immeasurable space, seemed suddenly—like an arrow piercing the earth—to remain fixed in a chosen spot, vigorously holding its tail erect, shining and displaying its white light amid countless other scintillating stars. It seemed to Pierre that this comet fully responded to what was passing in his own softened and uplifted soul, now blossoming into a new life.

BOOK NINE

DATES OF PRINCIPAL HISTORICAL EVENTS
1812

OLD STYLE	NEW STYLE	
May 17	May 29	Napoleon leaves Dresden.
June 12	June 24	Napoleon crosses the Niemen and enters Russia.
June 14	June 26	Alexander sends Balashëv to Napoleon.
July 13	July 25	The Pávlograd hussars in action at Ostróvna.

To Vladímir & Nízhni-Nóvgorod

R. Oká

Ryazán

Dmítrov

MOSCOW

R. Moskva

R. Volga

Podólsk

Krásnaya Pakhrá R.

Tarútino

Sérpukhov

Rúza

Bórovsk

Túla

Borodinó

Málo-Yaroslávets

Mozháysk

Kalúga

To St. Petersburg

Gzhatsk

R. Oká

Tsárevo-Zaymíshche

Orël

Vyázma

Dorogobúzh

Bald Hills

Smolénsk

N

Krásnoe

Vítebsk

Ostróvna

Orshá

Polótsk

Moghilëv

Drissa

R. Dnieper

R. Dvína

R. Berëzina

To Kiev

Borísov

Smorgoni

R. Víliya

Vílna

Kovno

R. Niemen

THE CAMPAIGN OF 1812

Scale of Miles

0 50 100 150

G? DUCHY OF WARSAW

Gródno

Napoleon's advance ▬▬▬

Tilsit

Napoleon's retreat ▬ ▬ ▬

PRUSSIA

1812

BOOK NINE

1. The year 1812. Rulers and generals are "history's slaves"

From the close of the year 1811 an intensified arming and concentrating of the forces of Western Europe began, and in 1812 these forces—millions of men, reckoning those transporting and feeding the army—moved from the west eastwards to the Russian frontier, toward which since 1811 Russian forces had been similarly drawn. On the twelfth of June, 1812, the forces of Western Europe crossed the Russian frontier and war began, that is, an event took place opposed to human reason and to human nature. Millions of men perpetrated against one another such innumerable crimes, frauds, treacheries, thefts, forgeries, issues of false money, burglaries, incendiarisms, and murders as in whole centuries are not recorded in the annals of all the law courts of the world, but which those who committed them did not at the time regard as being crimes.

What produced this extraordinary occurrence? What were its causes? The historians tell us with naïve assurance that its causes were the wrongs inflicted on the Duke of Oldenburg, the nonobservance of the Continental System,* the ambition of Napoleon, the firmness of Alexander, the mistakes of the diplomatists, and so on.

* In 1806 Napoleon issued a decree forbidding all trade with England and closing all European ports to her ships. He compelled his allies to accede to this policy, which was disadvantageous to many countries. It led to great injury to trade and to much smuggling: the system was often infringed, and even Napoleon himself could not dispense with English goods and at times admitted them to France. It was particularly irksome to Russia, and her evasion of it was treated by Napoleon as a violation of the treaty. In conjunction with other causes it led to his invasion of Russia in 1812. One result of the Continental System was the issue of the English Orders in Council in reply to it. These Orders occasioned much inconvenience to neutral nations and, together with the intrigues conducted by Napoleon, led to the war between England and the United States of America in 1812-14.—A.M.

Consequently, it would only have been necessary for Metternich,. Rumyánstev, or Talleyrand, between a levee and an evening party, to have taken proper pains and written a more adroit note, or for Napoleon to have written to Alexander: "My respected Brother, I consent to restore the duchy to the Duke of Oldenburg"—and there would have been no war.

We can understand that the matter seemed like that to contemporaries. It naturally seemed to Napoleon that the war was caused by England's. intrigues (as in fact he said on the island of St. Helena). It naturally seemed to members of the English Parliament that the cause of the war was Napoleon's ambition; to the Duke of Oldenburg, that the cause of the war was the violence done to him; to businessmen that the cause of the war was the Continental System which was ruining Europe; to the generals and old soldiers that the chief reason for the war was the necessity of giving them employment; to the legitimists of that day that it was the need of re-establishing *les bons principes*, and to the diplomatists of that time that it all resulted from the fact that the alliance between Russia and Austria in 1809 had not been sufficiently well concealed from Napoleon, and from the awkward wording of Memorandum No. 178. It is natural that these and a countless and infinite quantity of other reasons, the number depending on the endless diversity of points of view, presented themselves to the men of that day; but to us, to posterity who view the thing that happened in all its magnitude and perceive its plain and terrible meaning, these causes seem insufficient. To us it is incomprehensible that millions of Christian men killed and tortured each other either because Napoleon was ambitious or Alexander was firm, or because England's policy was astute or the Duke of Oldenburg wronged. We cannot grasp what connection such circumstances have with the actual fact of slaughter and violence: why because the Duke was wronged, thousands of men from the other side of Europe killed and ruined the people of Smolénsk and Moscow and were killed by them.

To us, their descendants, who are not historians and are not carried away by the process of research and can therefore regard the event with unclouded common sense, an incalculable number of causes present themselves. The deeper we delve in search of these causes the more of them we find; and each separate cause or whole series of causes appears to us equally valid in itself and equally false by its insignificance compared to the magnitude of the events, and by its impotence—apart from the cooperation of all the other coincident causes—to occasion the event. To us, the wish or objection of this or that French corporal to serve a second term appears as much a cause as Napoleon's refusal to withdraw his troops.

beyond the Vistula * and to restore the duchy of Oldenburg; for had he not wished to serve, and had a second, a third, and a thousandth corporal and private also refused, there would have been so many less men in Napoleon's army and the war could not have occurred.

Had Napoleon not taken offense at the demand that he should withdraw beyond the Vistula, and not ordered his troops to advance, there would have been no more; but had all his sergeants objected to serving a second term then also there could have been no war. Nor could there have been a war had there been no English intrigues and no Duke of Oldenburg, and had Alexander not felt insulted, and had there not been an autocratic government in Russia, or a Revolution in France and a subsequent dictatorship and Empire, or all the things that produced the French Revolution, and so on. Without each of these causes nothing could have happened. So all these causes—myriads of causes—coincided to bring it about. And so there was no one cause for that occurrence, but it had to occur because it had to. Millions of men, renouncing their human feelings and reason, had to go from west to east to slay their fellows, just as some centuries previously hordes of men had come from the east to the west, slaying their fellows.

The actions of Napoleon and Alexander, on whose words the event seemed to hang, were as little voluntary as the actions of any soldier who was drawn into the campaign by lot or by conscription. This could not be otherwise, for in order that the will of Napoleon and Alexander (on whom the event seemed to depend) should be carried out, the concurrence of innumerable circumstances was needed without any one of which the event could not have taken place. It was necessary that millions of men in whose hands lay the real power—the soldiers who fired, or transported provisions and guns—should consent to carry out the will of these weak individuals, and should have been induced to do so by an infinite number of diverse and complex causes.

We are forced to fall back on fatalism as an explanation of irrational events (that is to say, events the reasonableness of which we do not understand). The more we try to explain such events in history reasonably, the more unreasonable and incomprehensible do they become to us.

Each man lives for himself, using his freedom to attain his personal aims, and feels with his whole being that he can now do or abstain from doing this or that action; but as soon as he has done it, that action performed

* _The demand that Napoleon should withdraw beyond that river was Alexander's last effort to avoid war, and Napoleon's refusal led directly to the commencement of hostilities in 1812._—A.M.

at a certain moment in time becomes irrevocable and belongs to history, in which it has not a free but a predestined significance.

There are two sides to the life of every man, his individual life, which is the more free the more abstract its interests, and his elemental hive life in which he inevitably obeys laws laid down for him.

Man lives consciously for himself, but is an unconscious instrument in the attainment of the historic, universal, aims of humanity. A deed done is irrevocable, and its result coinciding in time with the actions of millions of other men assumes an historic significance. The higher a man stands on the social ladder, the more people he is connected with and the more power he has over others, the more evident is the predestination and inevitability of his every action.

"The king's heart is in the hands of the Lord."

A king is history's slave.

History, that is, the unconscious, general, hive life of mankind, uses every moment of the life of kings as a tool for its own purposes.

Though Napoleon at that time, in 1812, was more convinced than ever that it depended on him, *verser (ou ne pas verser) le sang de ses peuples* [to shed (or not to shed) the blood of his peoples]—as Alexander expressed it in the last letter he wrote him—he had never been so much in the grip of inevitable laws, which compelled him, while thinking that he was acting on his own volition, to perform for the hive life—that is to say, for history—whatever had to be performed.

The people of the west moved eastwards to slay their fellow men, and by the law of coincidence thousands of minute causes fitted in and coordinated to produce that movement and war: reproaches for the non-observance of the Continental System, the Duke of Oldenburg's wrongs, the movement of troops into Prussia [undertaken, as it seemed to Napoleon, only for the purpose of securing an armed peace], the French Emperor's love and habit of war coinciding with his people's inclinations, allurement by the grandeur of the preparations, and the expenditure on those preparations and the need of obtaining advantages to compensate for that expenditure, the intoxicating honors he received in Dresden,* the diplomatic negotiations which, in the opinion of contemporaries, were carried on with a sincere desire to attain peace, but which only wounded the self-love of both sides, and millions and millions of other causes that adapted themselves to the event that was happening or coincided with it.

* *In May, 1812, immediately before the war, Napoleon spent about a month in Dresden with his new allies: the Emperor of Austria, the King of Prussia, the King of Saxony, etc.—attending a series of magnificent banquets and fetes and receiving flattery and honors from all sides.—*A.M.

When an apple has ripened and falls, why does it fall? Because of its attraction to the earth, because its stalk withers, because it is dried by the sun, because it grows heavier, because the wind shakes it, or because the boy standing below wants to eat it?

Nothing is the cause. All this is only the coincidence of conditions in which all vital organic and elemental events occur. And the botanist who finds that the apple falls because the cellular tissue decays and so forth is equally right with the child who stands under the tree and says the apple fell because he wanted to eat it and prayed for it. Equally right or wrong is he who says that Napoleon went to Moscow because he wanted to, and perished because Alexander desired his destruction, and he who says that an undermined hill weighing a million tons fell because the last navvy struck it for the last time with his mattock. In historic events, the so-called great men are labels giving names to events, and like labels they have but the smallest connection with the event itself.

Every act of theirs, which appears to them an act of their own will, is in an historical sense involuntary and is related to the whole course of history and predestined from eternity.

2. Napoleon crosses the Niemen and sees Polish Uhlans drowned swimming the Víliya

ON THE TWENTY-NINTH OF MAY Napoleon left Dresden,* where he had spent three weeks surrounded by a court that included princes, dukes, kings, and even an emperor. Before leaving, Napoleon showed favor to the emperor, kings, and princes who had deserved it, reprimanded the kings and princes with whom he was dissatisfied, presented pearls and diamonds of his own—that is, which he had taken from other kings—to the Empress of Austria, and having, as his historian tells us, tenderly embraced the Empress Marie Louise—who regarded him as her husband, though he had left another wife in Paris—left her grieved by the parting which she seemed hardly able to bear. Though the diplomatists still firmly believed in the possibility of peace and worked zealously to that end, and

* Here, probably by inadvertence, Tolstóy gives the date according to the Gregorian or "new style" calendar, not adopted in Russia till after the Revolution of 1917. In the next sentence he reverts to the Old Style, which he elsewhere employs throughout the novel. The text makes it appear as if Napoleon spent only twelve days (May 29 to June 10) on his way from Dresden via Posen, Thorn, Danzig, and Königsberg to the Russian frontier. He actually took twice as long, having many arrangements to make in those towns.—A.M.

though the Emperor Napoleon himself wrote a letter to Alexander, calling him *Monsieur mon frère*, and sincerely assured him that he did not want war and would always love and honor him—yet he set off to join his army, and at every station gave fresh orders to accelerate the movement of his troops from west to east. He went in a traveling coach with six horses, surrounded by pages, aides-de-camp, and an escort, along the road to Posen, Thorn, Danzig, and Königsberg. At each of these towns thousands of people met him with excitement and enthusiasm.

The army was moving from west to east, and relays of six horses carried him in the same direction. On the tenth of June, coming up with the army, he spent the night in apartments prepared for him on the estate of a Polish count in the Vilkavisski forest.

Next day, overtaking the army, he went in a carriage to the Niemen, and, changing into a Polish uniform, he drove to the riverbank in order to select a place for the crossing.*

Seeing, on the other side, some Cossacks (*les Cosaques*) and the wide-spreading steppes in the midst of which lay the holy city of Moscow (*Moscou, la ville sainte*), the capital of a realm such as the Scythia into which Alexander the Great had marched—Napoleon unexpectedly, and contrary alike to strategic and diplomatic considerations, ordered an advance, and the next day his army began to cross the Niemen.

Early in the morning of the twelfth of June he came out of his tent, which was pitched that day on the steep left bank of the Niemen, and looked through a spyglass at the streams of his troops pouring out of the Vilkavisski forest and flowing over the three bridges thrown across the river. The troops, knowing of the Emperor's presence, were on the lookout for him, and when they caught sight of a figure in an overcoat and a cocked hat standing apart from his suite in front of his tent on the hill, they threw up their caps and shouted: "Vive l'Empereur!" and one after another poured in a ceaseless stream out of the vast forest that had concealed them and, separating, flowed on and on by the three bridges to the other side.

"Now we'll go into action. Oh, when he takes it in hand himself, things get hot . . . by heaven! . . . There he is! . . . Vive l'Empereur! So these are the steppes of Asia! It's a nasty country all the same. Au revoir,

* *Napoleon's changing into a Polish uniform, and the episode of the Uhlans swimming the river, briefly but vividly indicate his relations with Poland. The Poles hoped to obtain independence as a result of the war, and Napoleon encouraged their hopes by petty indications of his favor. The incident of the uniform is given in Danílevski's history, and that of the Uhlans swimming the river in Thiers'.*—A.M.

Beauché; I'll keep the best palace in Moscow for you! *Au revoir.* Good luck! . . . Did you see the Emperor? *Vive l'Empereur!* . . . *preur!*— If they make me Governor of India, Gérard, I'll make you Minister of Kashmir—that's settled. *Vive l'Empereur!* Hurrah! hurrah! hurrah! The Cossacks—those rascals—see how they run! *Vive l'Empereur!* There he is, do you see him? I've seen him twice, as I see you now. The little corporal . . . I saw him give the cross to one of the veterans. . . . *Vive l'Empereur!*" came the voices of men, old and young, of most diverse characters and social positions. On the faces of all was one common expression of joy at the commencement of the long-expected campaign and of rapture and devotion to the man in the gray coat who was standing on the hill.

On the thirteenth of June a rather small, thoroughbred Arab horse was brought to Napoleon. He mounted it and rode at a gallop to one of the bridges over the Niemen, deafened continually by incessant and rapturous acclamations which he evidently endured only because it was impossible to forbid the soldiers to express their love of him by such shouting, but the shouting which accompanied him everywhere disturbed him and distracted him from the military cares that had occupied him from the time he joined the army. He rode across one of the swaying pontoon bridges to the farther side, turned sharply to the left, and galloped in the direction of Kóvno,* preceded by enraptured, mounted chasseurs of the Guard who, breathless with delight, galloped ahead to clear a path for him through the troops. On reaching the broad river Víliya,[2] he stopped near a regiment of Polish Uhlans stationed by the river.

"Vivat!" shouted the Poles, ecstatically, breaking their ranks and pressing against one another to see him.

Napoleon looked up and down the river, dismounted, and sat down on a log that lay on the bank. At a mute sign from him, a telescope was handed him which he rested on the back of a happy page who had run up to him, and he gazed at the opposite bank. Then he became absorbed in a map laid out on the logs. Without lifting his head he said something, and two of his aides-de-camp galloped off to the Polish Uhlans.

"What? What did he say?" was heard in the ranks of the Polish Uhlans when one of the aides-de-camp rode up to them.

The order was to find a ford and to cross the river. The colonel of Polish Uhlans, a handsome old man, flushed and, fumbling in his speech from excitement, asked the aide-de-camp whether he would be permitted to swim the river with his Uhlans instead of seeking a ford. In evident fear

* *Kaunas, the capital of Lithuania.*
[2] *The Polish Wilja and the Lithuanian Neries.*

of refusal, like a boy asking for permission to get on a horse, he begged to be allowed to swim across the river before the Emperor's eyes. The aide-de-camp replied that probably the Emperor would not be displeased at this excess of zeal.

As soon as the aide-de-camp had said this, the old mustached officer, with happy face and sparkling eyes, raised his saber, shouted "Vivat!" and, commanding the Uhlans to follow him, spurred his horse and galloped into the river. He gave an angry thrust to his horse, which had grown restive under him, and plunged into the water, heading for the deepest part where the current was swift. Hundreds of Uhlans galloped in after him. It was cold and uncanny in the rapid current in the middle of the stream, and the Uhlans caught hold of one another as they fell off their horses. Some of the horses were drowned and some of the men; the others tried to swim on, some in the saddle and some clinging to their horses' manes. They tried to make their way forward to the opposite bank and, though there was a ford one third of a mile away, were proud that they were swimming and drowning in this river under the eyes of the man who sat on the log and was not even looking at what they were doing. When the aide-de-camp, having returned and choosing an opportune moment, ventured to draw the Emperor's attention to the devotion of the Poles to his person, the little man in the gray overcoat got up and, having summoned Berthier, began pacing up and down the bank with him, giving him instructions and occasionally glancing disapprovingly at the drowning Uhlans who distracted his attention.

For him it was no new conviction that his presence in any part of the world, from Africa to the steppes of Muscovy alike, was enough to dumfound people and impel them to insane self-oblivion. He called for his horse and rode to his quarters.

Some forty Uhlans were drowned in the river, though boats were sent to their assistance. The majority struggled back to the bank from which they had started. The colonel and some of his men got across and with difficulty clambered out on the further bank. And as soon as they had got out, in their soaked and streaming clothes, they shouted "Vivat!" and looked ecstatically at the spot where Napoleon had been but where he no longer was and at that moment considered themselves happy.

That evening, between issuing one order that the forged Russian paper money prepared for use in Russia * should be delivered as quickly as possible and another that a Saxon should be shot, on whom a letter

* This Napoleonic precedent of preparing forged money for use in a country about to be invaded has been followed by Hitler.

containing information about the orders to the French army had been found, Napoleon also gave instructions that the Polish colonel who had needlessly plunged into the river should be enrolled in the *Légion d'honneur* of which Napoleon was himself the head.

Quos vult perdere dementat [Those whom (God) wishes to destroy he drives mad].

3. Alexander I at Vílna. The ball at Count Bennigsen's. Borís overhears the Emperor speaking to Balashëv and learns that the French have crossed the frontier. Alexander's letter to Napoleon

THE EMPEROR OF RUSSIA had, meanwhile, been in Vílna for more than a month, reviewing troops and holding maneuvers. Nothing was ready for the war that everyone expected and to prepare for which the Emperor had come from Petersburg. There was no general plan of action. The vacillation between the various plans that were proposed had even increased after the Emperor had been at headquarters for a month. Each of the three armies * had its own commander in chief, but there was no supreme commander of all the forces, and the Emperor did not assume that responsibility himself.

The longer the Emperor remained in Vílna the less did everybody— tired of waiting—prepare for the war. All the efforts of those who sur-

* *The three armies were: (1) the western army under Barclay de Tolly, (2) one farther south under Bagratión, and (3) an army of reserve in process of formation under Tormásov near the Austrian frontier. A fourth army under Chichagóv was still on the Turkish frontier where war had just ended, but this only became available against Napoleon toward the end of his retreat from Russia.*

Barclay de Tolly (1761-1818) was born in Latvia and was descended from a Scottish family that settled in Russia in the seventeenth century. He was Minister of War in 1810-13, but resigned from the command of the army in 1812 after the abandonment of Smolénsk, when he was replaced by Kutúzov. He was present at the battle of Borodinó. He again became commander in chief in 1813, and was made field marshal in 1814.

*Prince P. I. Bagratión (1765-1812) was one of the most successful of the Russian generals. He had greatly distinguished himself at Schön Grabern, at Austerlitz, and in many other battles. He died of wounds received at Borodinó.—*A.M.

rounded the sovereign seemed directed merely to making him spend his time pleasantly and forget that war was impending.

In June, after many balls and fetes given by the Polish magnates, by the courtiers, and by the Emperor himself, it occurred to one of the Polish aides-de-camp in attendance that a dinner and ball should be given for the Emperor by his aides-de-camp. This idea was eagerly received. The Emperor gave his consent. The aides-de-camp collected money by subscription. The lady who was thought to be most pleasing to the Emperor was invited to act as hostess. Count Bennigsen, being a landowner in the Vílna province, offered his country house for the fete, and the thirteenth of June was fixed for a ball, dinner, regatta, and fireworks at Zakret, Count Bennigsen's country seat.

The very day that Napoleon issued the order to cross the Niemen, and his vanguard, driving off the Cossacks, crossed the Russian frontier, Alexander spent the evening at the entertainment given by his aides-de-camp at Bennigsen's country house.

It was a gay and brilliant fete. Connoisseurs of such matters declared that rarely had so many beautiful women been assembled in one place. Countess Bezúkhova was present among other Russian ladies who had followed the sovereign from Petersburg to Vílna and eclipsed the refined Polish ladies by her massive, so-called Russian type of beauty. The Emperor noticed her and honored her with a dance.

Borís Drubetskóy, having left his wife in Moscow and being for the present en garçon (as he phrased it), was also there and, though not an aide-de-camp, had subscribed a large sum toward the expenses. Borís was now a rich man who had risen to high honors and no longer sought patronage but stood on an equal footing with the highest of those of his own age. He was meeting Hélène in Vílna after not having seen her for a long time and did not recall the past, but as Hélène was enjoying the favors of a very important personage and Borís had only recently married, they met as good friends of long standing.

At midnight dancing was still going on. Hélène, not having a suitable partner, herself offered to dance the mazurka with Borís. They were the third couple. Borís, coolly looking at Hélène's dazzling bare shoulders which emerged from a dark, gold-embroidered, gauze gown, talked to her of old acquaintances and at the same time, unaware of it himself and unnoticed by others, never for an instant ceased to observe the Emperor who was in the same room. The Emperor was not dancing, he stood in the doorway, stopping now one pair and now another with gracious words which he alone knew how to utter.

As the mazurka began, Borís saw that Adjutant General Balashëv, one

of those in closest attendance on the Emperor, went up to him and contrary to court etiquette stood near him while he was talking to a Polish lady. Having finished speaking to her, the Emperor looked inquiringly at Balashëv and, evidently understanding that he only acted thus because there were important reasons for so doing, nodded slightly to the lady and turned to him. Hardly had Balashëv begun to speak before a look of amazement appeared on the Emperor's face. He took Balashëv by the arm and crossed the room with him, unconsciously clearing a path seven yards wide as the people on both sides made way for him. Borís noticed Arakchéev's excited face when the sovereign went out with Balashëv. Arakchéev looked at the Emperor from under his brow and, sniffing with his red nose, stepped forward from the crowd as if expecting the Emperor to address him. (Borís understood that Arakchéev envied Balashëv and was displeased that evidently important news had reached the Emperor otherwise than through himself.)

But the Emperor and Balashëv passed out into the illuminated garden without noticing Arakchéev who, holding his sword and glancing wrathfully around, followed some twenty paces behind them.

All the time Borís was going through the figures of the mazurka, he was worried by the question of what news Balashëv had brought and how he could find it out before others.

In the figure in which he had to choose two ladies, he whispered to Hélène that he meant to choose Countess Potocka who, he thought, had gone out onto the veranda, and glided over the parquet to the door opening into the garden, where, seeing Balashëv and the Emperor returning to the veranda, he stood still. They were moving toward the door. Borís, fluttering as if he had not had time to withdraw, respectfully pressed close to the doorpost with bowed head.

The Emperor, with the agitation of one who has been personally affronted, was finishing with these words:

"To enter Russia without declaring war! I will not make peace as long as a single armed enemy remains in my country!"

It seemed to Borís that it gave the Emperor pleasure to utter these words. He was satisfied with the form in which he had expressed his thoughts, but displeased that Borís had overheard it.

"Let no one know of it!" the Emperor added with a frown.

Borís understood that this was meant for him and, closing his eyes, slightly bowed his head. The Emperor re-entered the ballroom and remained there about another half-hour.

Borís was thus the first to learn the news that the French army had crossed the Niemen and, thanks to this, was able to show certain im-

portant personages that much that was concealed from others was usually known to him, and by this means he rose higher in their estimation.

The unexpected news of the French having crossed the Niemen was particularly startling after a month of unfulfilled expectations, and at a ball. On first receiving the news, under the influence of indignation and resentment the Emperor had found a phrase that pleased him, fully expressed his feelings, and has since become famous. On returning home at two o'clock that night he sent for his secretary, Shishkóv,* and told him to write an order to the troops and a rescript to Field Marshal Prince Saltykóv,[2] in which he insisted on the words being inserted that he would not make peace so long as a single armed Frenchman remained on Russian soil.

Next day the following letter was sent to Napoleon:

Monsieur mon frère,
 Yesterday I learned that, despite the loyalty with which I have kept my engagements with Your Majesty, your troops have crossed the Russian frontier, and I have this moment received from Petersburg a note, in which Count Lauriston [3] informs me, as a reason for this aggression, that Your Majesty has considered yourself to be in a state of war with me from the time Prince Kurákin asked for his passports. The reasons on which the Duc de Bassano [4] based his refusal to deliver them to him would never have led me to suppose that that incident could serve as a pretext for aggression. In fact, the ambassador, as he himself has declared, was never authorized to make that demand, and as soon as I was informed of it I let him know how much I disapproved of it and ordered him to remain at his post. If Your Majesty does not intend to shed the blood of our peoples for such a misunderstanding, and consents to withdraw your troops from

* *Admiral A. S. Shishkóv (1754-1841) succeeded Speránski as Secretary of State when the latter was dismissed.*—A.M.

[2] *N. I. Saltykóv (1736-1816) had been Alexander's tutor, and in 1812, besides being a field marshal, was President of the Cabinet of Ministers.*—A.M.

[3] *A. J. B. Law (1768-1828), a great-nephew of John Law of Lauriston, of Mississippi Scheme fame. He was a fellow pupil of Napoleon's at the Artillery School. He greatly distinguished himself at the battle of Wagram (1809), was Napoleon's ambassador in Petersburg (1811-12), and accompanied him through the greater part of the Russian campaign, but did not side with Napoleon after his return from Elba in 1815. He was subsequently made a marquis and a Marshal of France by Louis XVIII.*—A.M.

[4] *H. B. Maret (1763-1839), Napoleon's Minister of Foreign Affairs in 1811-12.*—A.M.

Russian territory, I will regard what has passed as not having oc-
curred and an understanding between us will be possible. In the con-
trary case, Your Majesty, I shall see myself forced to repel an attack
that nothing on my part has provoked. It still depends on Your
Majesty to preserve humanity from the calamity of another war.

I am, etc.,

(signed) ALEXANDER

4. Balashëv's mission to Napoleon. He meets Murat, "the King of Naples"

A T TWO in the morning of the fourteenth of June, the Emperor, having
sent for Balashëv and read him his letter to Napoleon, ordered
him to take it and hand it personally to the French Emperor. When dis-
patching Balashëv, the Emperor repeated to him the words that he would
not make peace so long as a single armed enemy remained on Russian soil
and told him to transmit those words to Napoleon. Alexander did not
insert them in his letter to Napoleon, because with his characteristic tact
he felt it would be injudicious to use them at a moment when a last
attempt at reconciliation was being made, but he definitely instructed
Balashëv to repeat them personally to Napoleon.

Having set off in the small hours of the fourteenth, accompanied by a
bugler and two Cossacks, Balashëv reached the French outposts at the
village of Rykónty, on the Russian side of the Niemen, by dawn. There
he was stopped by French cavalry sentinels.

A French noncommissioned officer of hussars, in crimson uniform
and a shaggy cap, shouted to the approaching Balashëv to halt. Balashëv
did not do so at once, but continued to advance along the road at a
walking pace.

The noncommissioned officer frowned and, muttering words of abuse,
advanced his horse's chest against Balashëv, put his hand to his saber,
and shouted rudely at the Russian general, asking: was he deaf that he
did not do as he was told? Balashëv mentioned who he was. The non-
commissioned officer began talking with his comrades about regimental
matters without looking at the Russian general.

After living at the seat of the highest authority and power, after con-
versing with the Emperor less than three hours before, and in general
being accustomed to the respect due to his rank in the service, Balashëv
found it very strange here on Russian soil to encounter this hostile, and
still more this disrespectful, application of brute force to himself.

The sun was only just appearing from behind the clouds, the air was

fresh and dewy. A herd of cattle was being driven along the road from the village, and over the fields the larks rose trilling, one after another, like bubbles rising in water.

Balashëv looked around him, awaiting the arrival of an officer from the village. The Russian Cossacks and bugler and the French hussars looked silently at one another from time to time.

A French colonel of hussars, who had evidently just left his bed, came riding from the village on a handsome sleek gray horse, accompanied by two hussars. The officer, the soldiers, and their horses all looked smart and well kept.

It was that first period of a campaign when troops are still in full trim, almost like that of peacetime maneuvers, but with a shade of martial swagger in their clothes, and a touch of the gaiety and spirit of enterprise which always accompany the opening of a campaign.

The French colonel with difficulty repressed a yawn, but was polite and evidently understood Balashëv's importance. He led him past his soldiers and behind the outposts and told him that his wish to be presented to the Emperor would most likely be satisfied immediately, as the Emperor's quarters were, he believed, not far off.

They rode through the village of Rykónty, past tethered French hussar horses, past sentinels and men who saluted their colonel and stared with curiosity at a Russian uniform, and came out at the other end of the village. The colonel said that the commander of the division was a mile and a quarter away and would receive Balashëv and conduct him to his destination.

The sun had by now risen and shone gaily on the bright verdure.

They had hardly ridden up a hill, past a tavern, before they saw a group of horsemen coming toward them. In front of the group, on a black horse with trappings that glittered in the sun, rode a tall man with plumes in his hat and black hair curling down to his shoulders. He wore a red mantle, and stretched his long legs forward in French fashion. This man rode toward Balashëv at a gallop, his plumes flowing and his gems and gold lace glittering in the bright June sunshine.

Balashëv was only two horses' length from the equestrian with the bracelets, plumes, necklaces, and gold embroidery, who was galloping toward him with a theatrically solemn countenance, when Julner, the French colonel, whispered respectfully: "The King of Naples!" It was, in fact, Murat, now called "King of Naples." Though it was quite incomprehensible why he should be King of Naples, he was called so, and was himself convinced that he was so, and therefore assumed a more solemn and important air than formerly. He was so sure that he really was the

King of Naples that when, on the eve of his departure from that city, while walking through the streets with his wife, some Italians called out to him: "*Viva il re!* [Long live the King!]" he turned to his wife with a pensive smile and said: "Poor fellows, they don't know that I am leaving them tomorrow!"

But though he firmly believed himself to be King of Naples and pitied the grief felt by the subjects he was abandoning, latterly, after he had been ordered to return to military service—and especially since his last interview with Napoleon in Danzig, when his august brother-in-law had told him: "I made you King that you should reign in my way, but not in yours!"—he had cheerfully taken up his familiar business, and—like a well-fed but not overfat horse that feels himself in harness and grows skittish between the shafts—he dressed up in clothes as variegated and expensive as possible, and gaily and contentedly galloped along the roads of Poland, without himself knowing why or whither.

On seeing the Russian general he threw back his head, with its long hair curling to his shoulders, in a majestically royal manner, and looked inquiringly at the French colonel. The colonel respectfully informed His Majesty of Balashëv's mission, whose name he could not pronounce.

"De Bal-machève!" said the King (overcoming by his assurance the difficulty that had presented itself to the colonel). "Charmed to make your acquaintance, General!" he added, with a gesture of kingly condescension.

As soon as the King began to speak loud and fast his royal dignity instantly forsook him, and without noticing it he passed into his natural tone of good-natured familiarity. He laid his hand on the withers of Balashëv's horse and said:

"Well, General, it all looks like war," as if regretting a circumstance of which he was unable to judge.

"Your Majesty," replied Balashëv, "my master, the Emperor, does not desire war and as Your Majesty sees . . ." said Balashëv, using the words *Your Majesty* at every opportunity, with the affectation unavoidable in frequently addressing one to whom the title was still a novelty.

Murat's face beamed with stupid satisfaction as he listened to "Monsieur de Bal-machève." But *royauté oblige!* [royalty has its obligations] and he felt it incumbent on him, as a king and an ally, to confer on state affairs with Alexander's envoy. He dismounted, took Balashëv's arm, and moving a few steps away from his suite, which waited respectfully, began to pace up and down with him, trying to speak significantly. He referred to the fact that the Emperor Napoleon had resented the demand that he should withdraw his troops from Prussia, especially when that demand

became generally known and the dignity of France was thereby offended.

Balashëv replied that there was nothing offensive in the demand, because . . . but Murat interrupted him.

"Then you don't consider the Emperor Alexander the aggressor?" he asked unexpectedly, with a kindly and foolish smile.

Balashëv told him why he considered Napoleon to be the originator of the war.

"Oh, my dear general!" Murat again interrupted him, "with all my heart I wish the Emperors may arrange the affair between them, and that the war begun by no wish of mine may finish as quickly as possible!" said he, in the tone of a servant who wants to remain good friends with another despite a quarrel between their masters.

And he went on to inquiries about the Grand Duke and the state of his health, and to reminiscences of the gay and amusing times he had spent with him in Naples. Then suddenly, as if remembering his royal dignity, Murat solemnly drew himself up, assumed the pose in which he had stood at his coronation, and, waving his right arm, said:

"I won't detain you longer, General. I wish success to your mission," and with his embroidered red mantle, his flowing feathers, and his glittering ornaments, he rejoined his suite who were respectfully awaiting him.

Balashëv rode on, supposing from Murat's words that he would very soon be brought before Napoleon himself. But instead of that, at the next village the sentinels of Davout's infantry corps detained him as the pickets of the vanguard had done, and an adjutant of the corps commander, who was fetched, conducted him into the village to Marshal Davout.

5. Balashëv taken to Davout, who treats him badly, but he is at last presented to Napoleon in Vílna

DAVOUT WAS TO NAPOLEON what Arakchéev was to Alexander—though not a coward like Arakchéev, he was as precise, as cruel, and as unable to express his devotion to his monarch except by cruelty.

In the organism of states such men are necessary, as wolves are necessary in the organism of nature, and they always exist, always appear and hold their own, however incongruous their presence and their proximity to the head of the government may be. This inevitability alone can explain how the cruel Arakchéev, who tore out a grenadier's mustache with his own hands, whose weak nerves rendered him unable to face danger, and who was neither an educated man nor a courtier, was able to maintain

his powerful position with Alexander, whose own character was chivalrous, noble, and gentle.

Balashëv found Davout seated on a barrel in the shed of a peasant's hut, writing—he was auditing accounts. Better quarters could have been found him, but Marshal Davout was one of those men who purposely put themselves in most depressing conditions to have a justification for being gloomy. For the same reason they are always hard at work and in a hurry. "How can I think of the bright side of life when, as you see, I am sitting on a barrel and working in a dirty shed?" the expression of his face seemed to say. The chief pleasure and necessity of such men, when they encounter anyone who shows animation, is to flaunt their own dreary, persistent activity. Davout allowed himself that pleasure when Balashëv was brought in. He became still more absorbed in his task when the Russian general entered, and after glancing over his spectacles at Balashëv's face, which was animated by the beauty of the morning and by his talk with Murat, he did not rise or even stir, but scowled still more and sneered malevolently.

When he noticed in Balashëv's face the disagreeable impression this reception produced, Davout raised his head and coldly asked what he wanted.

Thinking he could have been received in such a manner only because Davout did not know that he was adjutant general to the Emperor Alexander and even his envoy to Napoleon, Balashëv hastened to inform him of his rank and mission. Contrary to his expectation, Davout, after hearing him, became still surlier and ruder.

"Where is your dispatch?" he inquired. "Give it to me. I will send it to the Emperor."

Balashëv replied that he had been ordered to hand it personally to the Emperor.

"Your Emperor's orders are obeyed in your army, but here," said Davout, "you must do as you're told."

And, as if to make the Russian general still more conscious of his dependence on brute force, Davout sent an adjutant to call the officer on duty.

Balashëv took out the packet containing the Emperor's letter and laid it on the table (made of a door with its hinges still hanging on it, laid across two barrels). Davout took the packet and read the inscription.

"You are perfectly at liberty to treat me with respect or not," protested Balashëv, "but permit me to observe that I have the honor to be adjutant general to His Majesty. . . ."

Davout glanced at him silently and plainly derived pleasure from the signs of agitation and confusion which appeared on Balashëv's face.

"You will be treated as is fitting," said he and, putting the packet in his pocket, left the shed.

A minute later the marshal's adjutant, de Castrès, came in and conducted Balashëv to the quarters assigned him.

That day he dined with the marshal, at the same board on the barrels.

Next day Davout rode out early and, after asking Balashëv to come to him, peremptorily requested him to remain there, to move on with the baggage train should orders come for it to move, and to talk to no one except Monsieur de Castrès.

After four days of solitude, ennui, and consciousness of his impotence and insignificance—particularly acute by contrast with the sphere of power in which he had so lately moved—and after several marches with the marshal's baggage and the French army, which occupied the whole district, Balashëv was brought to Vílna—now occupied by the French—through the very gate by which he had left it four days previously.

Next day the imperial gentleman-in-waiting, the Comte de Turenne, came to Balashëv and informed him of the Emperor Napoleon's wish to honor him with an audience.

Four days before, sentinels of the Preobrazhénsk regiment had stood in front of the house to which Balashëv was conducted, and now two French grenadiers stood there in blue uniforms unfastened in front and with shaggy caps on their heads, and an escort of hussars and Uhlans and a brilliant suite of aides-de-camp, pages, and generals, who were waiting for Napoleon to come out, were standing at the porch, round his saddle horse and his Mameluke, Rustan.* Napoleon received Balashëv in the very house in Vílna from which Alexander had dispatched him on his mission.

6. Balashëv's interview with Napoleon

THOUGH BALASHËV was used to imperial pomp, he was amazed at the luxury and magnificence of Napoleon's court.

The Comte de Turenne showed him into a big reception room where many generals, gentlemen-in-waiting, and Polish magnates—several of

* The Mamelukes were Turko-Egyptian cavalry. Napoleon defeated them utterly at the battle of the Pyramids in 1798. From Egypt he brought Rustan (a Georgian by birth) back with him as a bodyguard. From that time on Rustan never left his master, and he did not long survive Napoleon's death.—A.M.

whom Balashëv had seen at the court of the Emperor of Russia—were
waiting. Duroc said that Napoleon would receive the Russian general
before going for his ride.

After some minutes, the gentleman-in-waiting who was on duty came
into the great reception room and, bowing politely, asked Balashëv to
follow him.*

Balashëv went into a small reception room, one door of which led into
a study, the very one from which the Russian Emperor had dispatched
him on his mission. He stood a minute or two, waiting. He heard hurried
footsteps beyond the door, both halves of it were opened rapidly; all was
silent and then from the study the sound was heard of other steps, firm
and resolute—they were those of Napoleon. He had just finished dressing
for his ride, and wore a blue uniform, opening in front over a white waist-
coat so long that it covered his rotund stomach, white leather breeches
tightly fitting the fat thighs of his short legs, and Hessian boots. His short
hair had evidently just been brushed, but one lock hung down in the
middle of his broad forehead. His plump white neck stood out sharply
above the black collar of his uniform, and he smelled of Eau de Cologne.
His full face, rather young-looking, with its prominent chin, wore a
gracious and majestic expression of imperial welcome.

He entered briskly, with a jerk at every step and his head slightly
thrown back. His whole short corpulent figure with broad thick shoulders,
and chest and stomach involuntarily protruding, had that imposing and
stately appearance one sees in men of forty who live in comfort. It was
evident, too, that he was in the best of spirits that day.

He nodded in answer to Balashëv's low and respectful bow, and com-
ing up to him at once began speaking like a man who values every moment
of his time and does not condescend to prepare what he has to say but is
sure he will always say the right thing and say it well.

"Good day, General!" said he. "I have received the letter you brought
from the Emperor Alexander and am very glad to see you." He glanced
with his large eyes into Balashëv's face and immediately looked past him.

It was plain that Balashëv's personality did not interest him at all. Evi-
dently only what took place within *his own* mind interested him. Nothing
outside himself had any significance for him, because everything in the
world, it seemed to him, depended entirely on his will.

"I do not, and did not, desire war," he continued, "but it has been

* *Alexander Dmítrievich Balashëv* (1770-1837) *was appointed Chief of*
Police in Petersburg in 1808, Military Governor in 1809, Head of Ministry of
Police in 1810, and he accompanied the Tsar to Vílna in 1812. Napoleon's
speeches to him are taken from Thiers and Danílevski.—A.M.

forced on me. Even *now*" (he emphasized the word) "I am ready to receive any explanations you can give me."

And he began clearly and concisely to explain his reasons for dissatisfaction with the Russian government. Judging by the calmly moderate and amicable tone in which the French Emperor spoke, Balashëv was firmly persuaded that he wished for peace and intended to enter into negotiations.

When Napoleon, having finished speaking, looked inquiringly at the Russian envoy, Balashëv began a speech he had prepared long before: "Sire! The Emperor, my master . . ." but the sight of the Emperor's eyes bent on him confused him. "You are flurried—compose yourself!" Napoleon seemed to say, as with a scarcely perceptible smile he looked at Balashëv's uniform and sword.

Balashëv recovered himself and began to speak. He said that the Emperor Alexander did not consider Kurákin's demand for his passports a sufficient cause for war; that Kurákin had acted on his own initiative and without his sovereign's assent, that the Emperor Alexander did not desire war, and had no relations with England.

"Not yet!" interposed Napoleon, and, as if fearing to give vent to his feelings, he frowned and nodded slightly as a sign that Balashëv might proceed.

After saying all he had been instructed to say, Balashëv added that the Emperor Alexander wished for peace, but would not enter into negotiations except on condition that . . . Here Balashëv hesitated: he remembered the words the Emperor Alexander had not written in his letter, but had specially inserted in the rescript to Saltykóv and had told Balashëv to repeat to Napoleon. Balashëv remembered these words, "So long as a single armed foe remains on Russian soil," but some complex feeling restrained him. He could not utter them, though he wished to do so. He grew confused and said: "On condition that the French army retires beyond the Niemen." *

Napoleon noticed Balashëv's embarrassment when uttering these last words; his face twitched and the calf of his left leg began to quiver rhythmically. Without moving from where he stood he began speaking in a louder tone and more hurriedly than before. During the speech that followed, Balashëv, who more than once lowered his eyes, involuntarily noticed the quivering of Napoleon's left leg which increased the more the more Napoleon raised his voice.

"I desire peace, no less than the Emperor Alexander," he began. "Have I not for eighteen months been doing everything to obtain it? I have

* *The Niemen, in 1812, was the frontier between Russia and Poland.*—A.M.

waited eighteen months for explanations. But in order to begin negotiations, what is demanded of me?" he said, frowning and making an energetic gesture of inquiry with his small white plump hand.

"The withdrawal of your army beyond the Niemen, sire," replied Balashëv.

"The Niemen?" repeated Napoleon. "So now you want me to retire beyond the Niemen—only the Niemen?" repeated Napoleon, looking straight at Balashëv.

The latter bowed his head respectfully.

Instead of the demand of four months earlier to withdraw from Pomerania, only a withdrawal beyond the Niemen was now demanded. Napoleon turned quickly and began to pace the room.

"You say the demand now is that I am to withdraw beyond the Niemen before commencing negotiations, but in just the same way two months ago the demand was that I should withdraw beyond the Vistula and the Oder, and yet you are willing to negotiate."

He went in silence from one corner of the room to the other and again stopped in front of Balashëv. Balashëv noticed that his left leg was quivering faster than before and his face seemed petrified in its stern expression. This quivering of his left leg was a thing Napoleon was conscious of. "The vibration of my left calf is a great sign with me," he remarked at a later date.

"Such demands as to retreat beyond the Vistula and Oder may be made to a Prince of Baden, but not to me!" Napoleon almost screamed, quite to his own surprise. "If you gave me Petersburg and Moscow I could not accept such conditions. You say I have begun this war! But who first joined his army? The Emperor Alexander, not I! And you offer me negotiations when I have expended millions, when you are in alliance with England, and when your position is a bad one. You offer me negotiations! But what is the aim of your alliance with England? What has she given you?" he continued hurriedly, evidently no longer trying to show the advantages of peace and discuss its possibility, but only to prove his own rectitude and power and Alexander's errors and duplicity.

The commencement of his speech had obviously been made with the intention of demonstrating the advantages of his position and showing that he was nevertheless willing to negotiate. But he had begun talking, and the more he talked the less could he control his words.

The whole purport of his remarks now was evidently to exalt himself and insult Alexander—just what he had least desired at the commencement of the interview.

"I hear you have made peace with Turkey?"

Balashëv bowed his head affirmatively.

"Peace has been concluded . . ." he began.

But Napoleon did not let him speak. He evidently wanted to do all the talking himself, and continued to talk with the sort of eloquence and unrestrained irritability to which spoiled people are so prone.

"Yes, I know you have made peace with the Turks without obtaining Moldavia and Wallachia; I would have given your sovereign those provinces as I gave him Finland. Yes," he went on, "I promised and would have given the Emperor Alexander Moldavia and Wallachia, and now he won't have those splendid provinces. Yet he might have united them to his empire and in a single reign would have extended Russia from the Gulf of Bothnia to the mouths of the Danube. Catherine the Great could not have done more," said Napoleon, growing more and more excited as he paced up and down the room, repeating to Balashëv almost the very words he had used to Alexander himself at Tilsit. "All that, he would have owed to my friendship. Oh, what a splendid reign!" he repeated several times, then paused, drew from his pocket a gold snuffbox, lifted it to his nose, and greedily sniffed at it.

"What a splendid reign the Emperor Alexander's *might have been!*"

He looked compassionately at Balashëv, and as soon as the latter tried to make some rejoinder hastily interrupted him.

"What could he wish or look for that he would not have obtained through my friendship?" demanded Napoleon, shrugging his shoulders in perplexity. "But no, he has preferred to surround himself with my enemies, and with whom? With Steins, Armfeldts, Bennigsens, and Wintzingerodes! * Stein, a traitor expelled from his own country; Arm-

* *Baron H. F. K. von Stein (1757-1831) was a German statesman who entered the Prussian service in 1780. In 1807 he succeeded Hardenburg—whom Napoleon had refused to deal with—as minister with very wide powers, and he proposed the abolition of serfdom, later accomplished by Hardenburg in 1811. Stein promoted the military reorganization of the country, and Napoleon demanded his dismissal and expulsion from Germany. He fled to Bohemia, but in May, 1812, was invited by Alexander to visit Petersburg. Subsequently in Russia Stein promoted the coalition against Napoleon and played an important part in accomplishing his downfall.*

Count G. M. Armfeldt (1757-1814) was a distinguished general and a faithful supporter of Gustavus III of Sweden and of his son Gustavus IV. When the latter lost power Armfeldt was expelled from Sweden and found refuge in Russia, where he obtained much influence with Alexander, who entrusted him with the management of the affairs of Finland, which had then recently been

feldt, a rake and an intriguer; Wintzingerode, a fugitive French subject; Bennigsen, rather more of a soldier than the others, but all the same an incompetent who was unable to do anything in 1807 and who should awaken terrible memories in the Emperor Alexander's mind. . . . Granted that were they competent they might be made use of," continued Napoleon—hardly able to keep pace in words with the rush of thoughts that incessantly sprang up, proving how right and strong he was (in his perception the two were one and the same)—"but they are not even that! They are neither fit for war nor peace! Barclay is said to be the most capable of them all, but I cannot say so, judging by his first movements. And what are they doing, all these courtiers? Pfuel proposes,* Armfeldt disputes, Bennigsen considers, and Barclay, called on to act, does not know what to decide on, and time passes bringing no result. Bagratión alone is a military man. He's stupid, but he has experience, a quick eye, and resolution. . . . And what role is your young monarch playing in that monstrous crowd? They compromise him and throw on him the responsibility for all that happens. A sovereign should not be with the army unless he is a general!" said Napoleon, evidently uttering these words as a direct challenge to the Emperor. He knew how Alexander desired to be a military commander.

"The campaign began only a week ago, and you haven't even been able

annexed. *He secured for the Finns the retention of their ancient constitution.*

Count L. A. von Bennigsen (1745-1826) passed from the Hanoverian service in 1773 to enter the Russian. He was active in the conspiracy which involved the assassination of the Emperor Paul. He claimed a victory over the French at Pultúsk (1806) (see Bilíbin's letter, Book Five, p. 405), and was commander in chief at the indecisive battle of Preussisch-Eylau (1807), but was defeated with heavy loss at Friedland (1807), which reverse led to the alliance concluded at Tilsit. He fought at Borodinó and defeated Murat at Tarútino, but quarreled with Kutúzov and had to retire from the service. After Kutúzov's death he again obtained a command, and led one of the columns which decided the victory at Leipzig (1813), for which service he was made a count.

Baron F. T. Wintzingerode (1770-1818) was an Austrian who in the course of his career passed more than once from the Austrian service to the Russian. In 1812 he was employed by Alexander to defend the road from the frontier to Petersburg. He was captured by the French but rescued again by the Russians. At Leipzig in 1813 he was in command of the whole Allied cavalry, and he served against Napoleon in the campaign of 1814.—A.M.

* *Baron Carl Ludwig August Pfuel (1751-1826), a Prussian general who entered the Russian service after the battle of Jena (1806) and formulated the first Russian plan for the campaign of 1812.*—A.M.

to defend Vílna. You are cut in two * and have been driven out of the Polish provinces. Your army is grumbling."

"On the contrary, Your Majesty," said Balashёv, hardly able to remember what had been said to him and following these verbal fireworks with difficulty, "the troops are burning with eagerness . . ."

"I know everything!" Napoleon interrupted him. "I know everything. I know the number of your battalions as exactly as I know my own. You have not two hundred thousand men, and I have three times that number. I give you my word of honor," said Napoleon, forgetting that his word of honor could carry no weight—"I give you my word of honor that I have five hundred and thirty thousand men this side of the Vistula. The Turks will be of no use to you; they are worth nothing and have shown it by making peace with you. As for the Swedes—it is their fate to be governed by mad kings. Their king was insane and they changed him for another—Bernadotte,[2] who promptly went mad—for no Swede would ally himself with Russia unless he were mad."

Napoleon grinned maliciously and again raised his snuffbox to his nose.

Balashёv knew how to reply to each of Napoleon's remarks, and would have done so; he continually made the gesture of a man wishing to say something, but Napoleon always interrupted him. To the alleged insanity of the Swedes, Balashёv wished to reply that when Russia is on her side Sweden is practically an island: but Napoleon gave an angry exclamation to drown his voice. Napoleon was in that state of irritability in which a man has to talk, talk, and talk, merely to convince himself that he is in the right. Balashёv began to feel uncomfortable: as envoy he feared to demean his dignity and felt the necessity of replying; but, as a man, he shrank before the transport of groundless wrath that had evidently seized Napoleon. He knew that none of the words now uttered by Napoleon had any significance, and that Napoleon himself would be ashamed of them when he came to his senses. Balashёv stood with downcast eyes, looking at the movements of Napoleon's stout legs and trying to avoid meeting his eyes.

"But what do I care about your allies?" said Napoleon. "I have allies—

* The Russian forces were in fact separated. Bagratión's army and Barclay's only succeeded with great difficulty in uniting after falling back as far as Smolénsk.—A.M.

[2] J. B. J. Bernadotte (1764-1844) was a lawyer's son born at Pau. He entered the French army as a private, became a marshal, and in 1810 was elected heir to the throne of Sweden. He guided its policy, and after Napoleon had seized Swedish Pomerania he fought against him. In 1818 he became King of Sweden, as Charles XIV, and founded a dynasty.—A.M.

the Poles. There are eighty thousand of them and they fight like lions. And there will be two hundred thousand of them."

And probably still more perturbed by the fact that he had uttered this obvious falsehood, and that Balashëv still stood silently before him in the same attitude of submission to fate, Napoleon abruptly turned round, drew close to Balashëv's face, and, gesticulating rapidly and energetically with his white hands, almost shouted:

"Know that if you stir up Prussia against me, I'll wipe it off the map of Europe!" he declared, his face pale and distorted by anger, and he struck one of his small hands energetically with the other. "Yes, I will throw you back beyond the Dvína and beyond the Dnieper, and will re-erect against you that barrier * which it was criminal and blind of Europe to allow to be destroyed. Yes, that is what will happen to you. That is what you have gained by alienating me!" And he walked silently several times up and down the room, his fat shoulders twitching.

He put his snuffbox into his waistcoat pocket, took it out again, lifted it several times to his nose, and stopped in front of Balashëv. He paused, looked ironically straight into Balashëv's eyes, and said in a quiet voice:

"And yet what a splendid reign your master *might have had!*"

Balashëv, feeling it incumbent on him to reply, said that from the Russian side things did not appear in so gloomy a light. Napoleon was silent, still looking derisively at him and evidently not listening to him. Balashëv said that in Russia the best results were expected from the war. Napoleon nodded condescendingly, as if to say, "I know it's your duty to say that, but you don't believe it yourself. I have convinced you."

When Balashëv had ended, Napoleon again took out his snuffbox, sniffed at it, and stamped his foot twice on the floor as a signal. The door opened, a gentleman-in-waiting, bending respectfully, handed the Emperor his hat and gloves; another brought him a pocket handkerchief. Napoleon, without giving them a glance, turned to Balashëv:

"Assure the Emperor Alexander from me," said he, taking his hat, "that I am as devoted to him as before: I know him thoroughly and very highly esteem his lofty qualities. I will detain you no longer, General; you shall receive my letter to the Emperor."

And Napoleon went quickly to the door. Everyone in the reception room rushed forward and descended the staircase.

* *Namely, a large Polish state.*—A.M.

7. Balashëv dines with Napoleon

AFTER ALL THAT Napoleon had said to him—those bursts of anger and the last dryly spoken words: "I will detain you no longer, General; you shall receive my letter," Balashëv felt convinced that Napoleon would not wish to see him, and would even avoid another meeting with him— an insulted envoy—especially as he had witnessed his unseemly anger. But, to his surprise, Balashëv received, through Duroc, an invitation to dine with the Emperor that day.

Bessières, Caulaincourt, and Berthier * were present at that dinner.

Napoleon met Balashëv cheerfully and amiably. He not only showed no sign of constraint or self-reproach on account of his outburst that morning, but, on the contrary, tried to reassure Balashëv. It was evident that he had long been convinced that it was impossible for him to make a mistake, and that in his perception whatever he did was right, not because it harmonized with any idea of right and wrong, but because he did it.

The Emperor was in very good spirits after his ride through Vílna,[2] where crowds of people had rapturously greeted and followed him. From all the windows of the streets through which he rode, rugs, flags, and his monogram were displayed, and the Polish ladies, welcoming him, waved their handkerchiefs to him.

At dinner, having placed Balashëv beside him, Napoleon not only treated him amiably but behaved as if Balashëv were one of his own courtiers, one of those who sympathized with his plans and ought to rejoice

* J. B. Bessières (1768-1813) was a Marshal of France. He served under Napoleon from the time of the Italian campaign of 1796, and in 1799 was made Duke of Istria. It was he, with his Guard cavalry, who routed the famous charge of the Russian Chevalier Guards at Austerlitz (mentioned in the description of that battle). He took an active part in the Peninsular war, and in 1812 commanded the Guard cavalry at Borodinó and in the retreat from Moscow. In 1813 he was appointed to the command of the whole of Napoleon's cavalry but was killed three days after the campaign began.

A. Berthier (1753-1815), Prince of Neuchâtel and Wagram, was a Marshal of France. He acted for many years as Napoleon's chief of staff. In 1815, unable to endure the sight of a Russian division marching toward the French frontier, he threw himself from a window into the street of Bamberg, and was picked up dying.—A.M.

[2] In 1812 Vílna was within the frontier of Russia, but had been so only for a short time, and its sympathies were still Polish.—A.M.

at his success. In the course of conversation he mentioned Moscow and questioned Balashëv about the Russian capital, not merely as an interested traveler asks about a new city he intends to visit, but as if convinced that Balashëv, as a Russian, must be flattered by his curiosity.

"How many inhabitants are there in Moscow? How many houses? Is it true that Moscow is called 'Holy Moscow'? How many churches are there in Moscow?" he asked.

And receiving the reply that there were more than two hundred churches, he remarked:

"Why such a quantity of churches?"

"The Russians are very devout," replied Balashëv.

"But a large number of monasteries and churches is always a sign of the backwardness of a people," said Napoleon, turning to Caulaincourt for appreciation of this remark.

Balashëv respectfully ventured to disagree with the French Emperor.

"Every country has its own character," said he.

"But nowhere in Europe is there anything like that," said Napoleon.

"I beg Your Majesty's pardon," returned Balashëv, "besides Russia there is Spain, where there are also many churches and monasteries."

This reply of Balashëv's, which hinted at the recent defeats of the French in Spain,* was much appreciated when he related it at Alexander's court, but it was not much appreciated at Napoleon's dinner, where it passed unnoticed.

The uninterested and perplexed faces of the marshals showed that they were puzzled as to what Balashëv's tone suggested. "If there is a point we don't see it, or it is not at all witty," their expressions seemed to say. So little was his rejoinder appreciated that Napoleon did not notice it at all and naïvely asked Balashëv through what towns the direct road from there to Moscow passed. Balashëv, who was on the alert all through the dinner, replied that just as "all roads lead to Rome," so all roads lead to Moscow: there were many roads, and "among them the road through *Poltáva*, which Charles XII chose."[2] Balashëv involuntarily flushed with pleasure at the aptitude of this reply, but hardly had he uttered the word

* In the previous year (1811) Wellington had won the battles of Fuentes de Oñoro and Beresford that of Albuera; the Spanish had defeated the French at Ximena, and in 1812 both Ciudad Rodrigo and Badajoz had been captured from the French.—A.M.

[2] The reference of course is to the invasion of Russia a hundred years previously (1709) by Charles XII of Sweden, whom Peter the Great defeated at Poltáva so thoroughly that Charles himself and Mazeppa, the Cossack hetman who had joined him, barely succeeded in escaping to Turkey.—A.M.

Poltáva before Caulaincourt began speaking of the badness of the road from Petersburg to Moscow and of his Petersburg reminiscences.

After dinner they went to drink coffee in Napoleon's study, which four days previously had been that of the Emperor Alexander. Napoleon sat down, toying with his Sèvres coffee cup, and motioned Balashëv to a chair beside him.

Napoleon was in that well-known after-dinner mood which, more than any reasoned cause, makes a man contented with himself and disposed to consider everyone his friend. It seemed to him that he was surrounded by men who adored him: and he felt convinced that, after his dinner, Balashëv too was his friend and worshiper. Napoleon turned to him with a pleasant, though slightly ironic, smile.

"They tell me this is the room the Emperor Alexander occupied? Strange, isn't it, General?" he said, evidently not doubting that this remark would be agreeable to his hearer since it went to prove his, Napoleon's, superiority to Alexander.

Balashëv could make no reply and bowed his head in silence.

"Yes. Four days ago in this room, Wintzingerode and Stein were deliberating," continued Napoleon with the same derisive and self-confident smile. "What I can't understand," he went on, "is that the Emperor Alexander has surrounded himself with my personal enemies. That I do not . . . understand. Has he not thought that I may do the same?" and he turned inquiringly to Balashëv, and evidently this thought turned him back on to the track of his morning's anger, which was still fresh in him.

"And let him know that I will do so!" said Napoleon, rising and pushing his cup away with his hand. "I'll drive all his Württemberg, Baden, and Weimar relations out of Germany. . . . Yes. I'll drive them out. Let him prepare an asylum for them in Russia!"

Balashëv bowed his head with an air indicating that he would like to make his bow and leave, and only listened because he could not help hearing what was said to him. Napoleon did not notice this expression; he treated Balashëv not as an envoy from his enemy, but as a man now fully devoted to him and who must rejoice at his former master's humiliation.

"And why has the Emperor Alexander taken command of the armies? What is the good of that? War is my profession, but his business is to reign and not to command armies! Why has he taken on himself such a responsibility?"

Again Napoleon brought out his snuffbox, paced several times up and down the room in silence, and then, suddenly and unexpectedly, went

up to Balashëv and with a slight smile, as confidently, quickly, and simply as if he were doing something not merely important but pleasing to Balashëv, he raised his hand to the forty-year-old Russian general's face and, taking him by the ear, pulled it gently, smiling with his lips only.

To have one's ear pulled by the Emperor was considered the greatest honor and mark of favor at the French court.

"Well, adorer and courtier of the Emperor Alexander, why don't you say anything?" said he, as if it was ridiculous, in his presence, to be the adorer and courtier of anyone but himself, Napoleon. "Are the horses ready for the general?" he added, with a slight inclination of his head in reply to Balashëv's bow. "Let him have mine, he has a *long way to go!*"

The letter taken by Balashëv was the last Napoleon sent to Alexander. Every detail of the interview was communicated to the Russian monarch, and the war began. . . .

8. Prince Andrew on Kutúzov's staff in Moldavia. He is sent to Barclay's army. Visits Bald Hills. His talks with his father and Princess Mary

AFTER HIS INTERVIEW with Pierre in Moscow, Prince Andrew went to Petersburg, on business as he told his family, but really to meet Anatole Kurágin whom he felt it necessary to encounter. On reaching Petersburg he inquired for Kurágin but the latter had already left the city. Pierre had warned his brother-in-law that Prince Andrew was on his track. Anatole Kurágin promptly obtained an appointment from the Minister of War and went to join the army in Moldavia. While in Petersburg Prince Andrew met Kutúzov, his former commander who was always well disposed toward him, and Kutúzov suggested that he should accompany him to the army in Moldavia, to which the old general had been appointed commander in chief. So Prince Andrew, having received an appointment on the headquarters staff, left for Turkey.

Prince Andrew did not think it proper to write and challenge Kurágin. He thought that if he challenged him without some fresh cause it might compromise the young Countess Rostóva and so he wanted to meet Kurágin personally in order to find a fresh pretext for a duel. But he again failed to meet Kurágin in Turkey, for soon after Prince Andrew arrived, the latter returned to Russia. In a new country, amid new conditions, Prince Andrew found life easier to bear. After his betrothed had broken faith with him—which he felt the more acutely the more he tried to conceal its effects—the surroundings in which he had been happy became

trying to him, and the freedom and independence he had once prized so highly were still more so. Not only could he no longer think the thoughts that had first come to him as he lay gazing at the sky on the field of Austerlitz and had later enlarged upon with Pierre, and which had filled his solitude at Boguchárovo and then in Switzerland and Rome, but he even dreaded to recall them and the bright and boundless horizons they had revealed. He was now concerned only with the nearest practical matters unrelated to his past interests, and he seized on these the more eagerly the more those past interests were closed to him. It was as if that lofty, infinite canopy of heaven that had once towered above him had suddenly turned into a low, solid vault that weighed him down, in which all was clear, but nothing eternal or mysterious.

Of the activities that presented themselves to him, army service was the simplest and most familiar. As a general on duty on Kutúzov's staff, he applied himself to business with zeal and perseverance and surprised Kutúzov by his willingness and accuracy in work. Not having found Kurágin in Turkey, Prince Andrew did not think it necessary to rush back to Russia after him, but all the same he knew that however long it might be before he met Kurágin, despite his contempt for him and despite all the proofs he deduced to convince himself that it was not worth stooping to a conflict with him—he knew that when he did meet him he would not be able to resist calling him out, any more than a ravenous man can help snatching at food. And the consciousness that the insult was not yet avenged, that his rancor was still unspent, weighed on his heart and poisoned the artificial tranquillity which he managed to obtain in Turkey by means of restless, plodding, and rather vainglorious and ambitious activity.

In the year 1812, when news of the war with Napoleon reached Bucharest—where Kutúzov had been living for two months, passing his days and nights with a Wallachian woman—Prince Andrew asked Kutúzov to transfer him to the Western Army. Kutúzov, who was already weary of Bolkónski's activity which seemed to reproach his own idleness, very readily let him go and gave him a mission to Barclay de Tolly.

Before joining the Western Army which was then, in May, encamped at Drissa,* Prince Andrew visited Bald Hills which was directly on his way, being only two miles off the Smolénsk highroad. During the last three years there had been so many changes in his life, he had thought, felt, and seen so much (having traveled both in the east and the west),

* *A provincial town, situated where the river Drissa flows into the Western Dvína. A fortified camp had been constructed there, chiefly to guard the road to Petersburg.*—A.M.

that on reaching Bald Hills it struck him as strange and unexpected to find the way of life there unchanged and still the same in every detail. He entered through the gates with their stone pillars and drove up the avenue leading to the house as if he were entering an enchanted, sleeping castle. The same old stateliness, the same cleanliness, the same stillness reigned there, and inside there was the same furniture, the same walls, sounds, and smell, and the same timid faces, only somewhat older. Princess Mary was still the same timid, plain maiden getting on in years, uselessly and joylessly passing the best years of her life in fear and constant suffering. Mademoiselle Bourienne was the same coquettish, self-satisfied girl, enjoying every moment of her existence and full of joyous hopes for the future. She had merely become more self-confident, Prince Andrew thought. Dessalles, the tutor he had brought from Switzerland, was wearing a coat of Russian cut and talking broken Russian to the servants, but was still the same narrowly intelligent, conscientious, and pedantic preceptor. The old prince had changed in appearance only by the loss of a tooth, which left a noticeable gap on one side of his mouth; in character he was the same as ever, only showing still more irritability and skepticism as to what was happening in the world. Little Nicholas alone had changed. He had grown, become rosier, had curly dark hair, and, when merry and laughing, quite unconsciously lifted the upper lip of his pretty little mouth just as the little princess used to do. He alone did not obey the law of immutability in the enchanted, sleeping castle. But though externally all remained as of old, the inner relations of all these people had changed since Prince Andrew had seen them last. The household was divided into two alien and hostile camps, who changed their habits for his sake and only met because he was there. To the one camp belonged the old prince, Mademoiselle Bourienne, and the architect; to the other Princess Mary, Dessalles, little Nicholas, and all the old nurses and maids.

During his stay at Bald Hills all the family dined together, but they were ill at ease and Prince Andrew felt that he was a visitor for whose sake an exception was being made and that his presence made them all feel awkward. Involuntarily feeling this at dinner on the first day, he was taciturn, and the old prince noticing this also became morosely dumb and retired to his apartments directly after dinner. In the evening, when Prince Andrew went to him and, trying to rouse him, began to tell him of the young Count Kámensky's campaign, the old prince began unexpectedly to talk about Princess Mary, blaming her for her superstitions and her dislike of Mademoiselle Bourienne, who, he said, was the only person really attached to him.

The old prince said that if he was ill it was only because of Princess

Mary: that she purposely worried and irritated him, and that by indulgence and silly talk she was spoiling little Prince Nicholas. The old prince knew very well that he tormented his daughter and that her life was very hard, but he also knew that he could not help tormenting her and that she deserved it. "Why does Prince Andrew, who sees this, say nothing to me about his sister? Does he think me a scoundrel, or an old fool who, without any reason, keeps his own daughter at a distance and attaches this Frenchwoman to himself? He doesn't understand, so I must explain it, and he must hear me out," thought the old prince. And he began explaining why he could not put up with his daughter's unreasonable character.

"If you ask me," said Prince Andrew, without looking up (he was censuring his father for the first time in his life), "I did not wish to speak about it, but as you ask me I will give you my frank opinion. If there is any misunderstanding and discord between you and Mary, I can't blame her for it at all. I know how she loves and respects you. Since you ask me," continued Prince Andrew, becoming irritable—as he was always liable to do of late—"I can only say that if there are any misunderstandings they are caused by that worthless woman, who is not fit to be my sister's companion."

The old man at first stared fixedly at his son, and an unnatural smile disclosed the fresh gap between his teeth to which Prince Andrew could not get accustomed.

"What companion, my dear boy? Eh? You've already been talking it over! Eh?"

"Father, I did not want to judge," said Prince Andrew, in a hard and bitter tone, "but you challenged me, and I have said, and always shall say, that Mary is not to blame, but those to blame—the one to blame—is that Frenchwoman."

"Ah, he has passed judgment . . . passed judgment!" said the old man in a low voice and, as it seemed to Prince Andrew, with some embarrassment, but then he suddenly jumped up and cried: "Be off, be off! Let not a trace of you remain here! . . ."

Prince Andrew wished to leave at once, but Princess Mary persuaded him to stay another day. That day he did not see his father, who did not leave his room and admitted no one but Mademoiselle Bourienne and Tíkhon, but asked several times whether his son had gone. Next day, before leaving, Prince Andrew went to his son's rooms. The boy, curly-headed like his mother and glowing with health, sat on his knee, and

Prince Andrew began telling him the story of Bluebeard, but fell into a reverie without finishing the story. He thought not of this pretty child, his son whom he held on his knee, but of himself. He sought in himself either remorse for having angered his father or regret at leaving home for the first time in his life on bad terms with him, and was horrified to find neither. What meant still more to him was that he sought and did not find in himself the former tenderness for his son which he had hoped to reawaken by caressing the boy and taking him on his knee.

"Well, go on!" said his son.

Prince Andrew, without replying, put him down from his knee and went out of the room.

As soon as Prince Andrew had given up his daily occupations, and especially on returning to the old conditions of life amid which he had been happy, weariness of life overcame him with its former intensity, and he hastened to escape from these memories and to find some work as soon as possible.

"So you've decided to go, Andrew?" asked his sister.

"Thank God that I can," replied Prince Andrew. "I am very sorry you can't."

"Why do you say that?" replied Princess Mary. "Why do you say that, when you are going to this terrible war, and he is so old? Mademoiselle Bourienne says he has been asking about you. . . ."

As soon as she began to speak of that, her lips trembled and her tears began to fall. Prince Andrew turned away and began pacing the room.

"Ah, my God! my God! When one thinks who and what—what trash —can cause people misery!" he said with a malignity that alarmed Princess Mary.

She understood that when speaking of "trash" he referred not only to Mademoiselle Bourienne, the cause of her misery, but also to the man who had ruined his own happiness.

"Andrew! One thing I beg, I entreat of you!" she said, touching his elbow and looking at him with eyes that shone through her tears. "I understand you" (she looked down). "Don't imagine that sorrow is the work of men. Men are His tools." She looked a little above Prince Andrew's head with the confident, accustomed look with which one looks at the place where a familiar portrait hangs. "Sorrow is sent by Him, not by men. Men are His instruments, they are not to blame. If you think someone has wronged you, forget it and forgive! We have no right to punish. And then you will know the happiness of forgiving."

"If I were a woman I would do so, Mary. That is a woman's virtue. But

a man should not and cannot forgive and forget," he replied, and though till that moment he had not been thinking of Kurágin, all his unexpended anger suddenly swelled up in his heart.

"If Mary is already persuading me to forgive, it means that I ought long ago to have punished him," he thought. And giving her no further reply, he began thinking of the glad vindictive moment when he would meet Kurágin who he knew was now in the army.

Princess Mary begged him to stay one day more, saying that she knew how unhappy her father would be if Andrew left without being reconciled to him, but Prince Andrew replied that he would probably soon be back again from the army and would certainly write to his father, but that the longer he stayed now the more embittered their differences would become.

"Good-by, Andrew! Remember that misfortunes come from God, and men are never to blame," were the last words he heard from his sister when he took leave of her.

"Then it must be so!" thought Prince Andrew as he drove out of the avenue from the house at Bald Hills. "She, poor innocent creature, is left to be victimized by an old man who has outlived his wits. The old man feels he is guilty, but cannot change himself. My boy is growing up and rejoices in life, in which like everybody else he will deceive or be deceived. And I am off to the army. Why? I myself don't know. I want to meet that man whom I despise, so as to give him a chance to kill and laugh at me!"

These conditions of life had been the same before, but then they were all connected, while now they had all tumbled to pieces. Only senseless things, lacking coherence, presented themselves one after another to Prince Andrew's mind.

9. Prince Andrew in the army at Drissa.
Eight conflicting parties

PRINCE ANDREW reached the general headquarters of the army at the end of June. The first army, with which was the Emperor, occupied the fortified camp at Drissa; the second army * was retreating, trying to effect a junction with the first one from which it was said to be cut off by large French forces. Everyone was dissatisfied with the general course of affairs in the Russian army, but no one anticipated any danger of inva-

* *Bagratión's.*—A.M.

sion of the Russian provinces, and no one thought the war would extend farther than the western, the Polish, provinces.*

Prince Andrew found Barclay de Tolly, to whom he had been assigned, on the bank of the Drissa. As there was not a single town or large village in the vicinity of the camp, the immense number of generals and courtiers accompanying the army were living in the best houses of the villages on both sides of the river, over a radius of six miles. Barclay de Tolly was quartered nearly three miles from the Emperor. He received Bolkónski stiffly and coldly and told him in his foreign accent that he would mention him to the Emperor for a decision as to his employment, but asked him meanwhile to remain on his staff. Anatole Kurágin, whom Prince Andrew had hoped to find with the army, was not there. He had gone to Petersburg, but Prince Andrew was glad to hear this. His mind was occupied by the interests of the center that was conducting a gigantic war, and he was glad to be free for a while from the distraction caused by the thought of Kurágin. During the first four days, while no duties were required of him, Prince Andrew rode round the whole fortified camp and, by the aid of his own knowledge and by talks with experts, tried to form a definite opinion about it. But the question whether the camp was advantageous or disadvantageous remained for him undecided. Already from his military experience and what he had seen in the Austrian campaign, he had come to the conclusion that in war the most deeply considered plans have no significance and that all depends on the way unexpected movements of the enemy—that cannot be foreseen—are met, and on how and by whom the whole matter is handled. To clear up this last point for himself, Prince Andrew, utilizing his position and acquaintances, tried to fathom the character of the control of the army and of the men and parties engaged in it, and he deduced for himself the following idea of the state of affairs.

While the Emperor had still been at Vílna, the forces had been divided into three armies. First, the army under Barclay de Tolly, secondly, the army under Bagratión, and thirdly, the one commanded by Tormásov. The Emperor was with the first army, but not as commander in chief. In the orders issued it was stated, not that the Emperor would take command, but only that he would be with the army. The Emperor, moreover, had with him not a commander in chief's staff but the imperial headquarters staff. In attendance on him was the head of the imperial staff, Quartermaster General Prince Volkónski, as well as generals, imperial aides-de-camp, diplomatic officials, and a large number of for-

* The provinces west of Smolénsk—even those annexed to Russia several years before—were still called "Polish provinces."—A.M.

eigners, but not the army staff. Besides these, there were in attendance on the Emperor without any definite appointments: Arakchéev, the ex-Minister of War; Count Bennigsen, the senior general in rank; the Grand Duke Tsarévich Constantine Pávlovich; * Count Rumyántsev, the Chancellor; Stein, a former Prussian minister; Armfeldt, a Swedish general; Pfuel, the chief author of the plan of campaign; Paulucci,[2] an adjutant general and Sardinian émigré; Wolzogen [3]—and many others. Though these men had no military appointment in the army, their position gave them influence, and often a corps commander, or even the commander in chief, did not know in what capacity he was questioned by Bennigsen, the Grand Duke, Arakchéev, or Prince Volkónski, or was given this or that advice and did not know whether a certain order received in the form of advice emanated from the man who gave it or from the Emperor and whether it had to be executed or not. But this was only the external condition; the essential significance of the presence of the Emperor and of all these people, from a courtier's point of view (and in an Emperor's vicinity all became courtiers), was clear to everyone. It was this: the Emperor did not assume the title of commander in chief, but disposed of all the armies; the men around him were his assistants. Arakchéev was a faithful custodian to enforce order and acted as the sovereign's bodyguard. Bennigsen was a landlord in the Vílna province who appeared to be doing the honors of the district, but was in reality a good general, useful as an adviser and ready at hand to replace Barclay. The Grand Duke was there because it suited him to be. The ex-Minister Stein was there because his advice was useful and the Emperor Alexander held him in high esteem personally. Armfeldt virulently hated Napoleon

* The correct title in Russian for the heir apparent was Tsesarévich (the shorter form Tsarévich applying to any son of the Tsar). The incorrect use of Tsarévich for heir apparent has however become so common in English that it is followed here, with apologies to Russian readers who may notice it.—A.M.

[2] Marquis F. O. Paulucci passed in 1809 from the French to the Russian service. In 1812 he was for a time head of the staff of the first army, but owing to disagreements with Barclay de Tolly was transferred to the post of Governor General of Livonia and Courland.—A.M.

[3] Baron Ludwig Julius Wolzogen (1774-1845), a Prussian general who was from 1807 to 1815 on the Russian General Staff. In 1812 he served with Barclay de Tolly and subsequently with Kutúzov. His Memoirs were published in 1851, and were among the historical material at Tolstóy's disposal when writing War and Peace. He is mentioned in Chapter 11 as acting as spokesman for Pfuel at the military council, and later on, in a letter to Arakchéev, Bagratión refers to him as almost a traitor.—A.M.

and was a general full of self-confidence, a quality that always influenced Alexander. Paulucci was there because he was bold and decided in speech. The adjutants general were there because they always accompanied the Emperor, and lastly and chiefly Pfuel was there because he had drawn up the plan of campaign against Napoleon and, having induced Alexander to believe in the efficacy of that plan, was directing the whole business of the war. With Pfuel was Wolzogen, who expressed Pfuel's thoughts in a more comprehensible way than Pfuel himself (who was a harsh, bookish theorist, self-confident to the point of despising everyone else) was able to do.

Besides these Russians and foreigners who propounded new and unexpected ideas every day—especially the foreigners, who did so with a boldness characteristic of people employed in a country not their own—there were many secondary personages accompanying the army because their principals were there.

Among the opinions and voices in this immense, restless, brilliant, and proud sphere, Prince Andrew noticed the following sharply defined subdivisions of tendencies and parties:

The first party consisted of Pfuel and his adherents—military theorists who believed in a science of war with immutable laws—laws of oblique movements, outflankings, and so forth. Pfuel and his adherents demanded a retirement into the depths of the country in accordance with precise laws defined by a pseudo-theory of war, and they saw only barbarism, ignorance, or evil intention in every deviation from that theory. To this party belonged the foreign nobles, Wolzogen, Wintzingerode, and others, chiefly Germans.

The second party was directly opposed to the first; one extreme, as always happens, was met by representatives of the other. The members of this party were those who had demanded an advance from Vílna into Poland and freedom from all prearranged plans. Besides being advocates of bold action, this section also represented nationalism, which made them still more one-sided in the dispute. They were Russians: Bagratión, Ermólov (who was beginning to come to the front), and others. At that time a famous joke of Ermólov's was being circulated, that as a great favor he had petitioned the Emperor to make him a German. The men of that party, remembering Suvórov, said that what one had to do was not to reason, or stick pins into maps, but to fight, beat the enemy, keep him out of Russia, and not let the army get discouraged.

To the third party—in which the Emperor had most confidence—belonged the courtiers who tried to arrange compromises between the othe.

two. The members of this party, chiefly civilians and to whom Arakchéev belonged, thought and said what men who have no convictions but wish to seem to have some generally say. They said that undoubtedly war, particularly against such a genius as Bonaparte (they called him Bonaparte now), needs most deeply devised plans and profound scientific knowledge and in that respect Pfuel was a genius, but at the same time it had to be acknowledged that the theorists are often one-sided, and therefore one should not trust them absolutely, but should also listen to what Pfuel's opponents and practical men of experience in warfare had to say, and then choose a middle course. They insisted on the retention of the camp at Drissa, according to Pfuel's plan, but on changing the movements of the other armies. Though, by this course, neither one aim nor the other could be attained, yet it seemed best to the adherents of this third party.

Of a fourth opinion the most conspicuous representative was the Tsarévich, who could not forget his disillusionment at Austerlitz, where he had ridden out at the head of the Guards, in his casque and cavalry uniform as to a review, expecting to crush the French gallantly; but unexpectedly finding himself in the front line had narrowly escaped amid the general confusion. The men of this party had both the quality and the defect of frankness in their opinions. They feared Napoleon, recognized his strength and their own weakness, and frankly said so. They said: "Nothing but sorrow, shame, and ruin will come of all this! We have abandoned Vílna and Vítebsk and shall abandon Drissa. The only reasonable thing left to do is to conclude peace as soon as possible, before we are turned out of Petersburg."

This view was very general in the upper army circles and found support also in Petersburg and from the chancellor, Rumyántsev, who, for other reasons of state, was in favor of peace.

The fifth party consisted of those who were adherents of Barclay de Tolly, not so much as a man but as minister of war and commander in chief. "Be he what he may" (they always began like that), "he is an honest, practical man and we have nobody better. Give him real power, for war cannot be conducted successfully without unity of command, and he will show what he can do, as he did in Finland.* If our army is well organized and strong and has withdrawn to Drissa without suffering any defeats, we owe this entirely to Barclay. If Barclay is now to be super-

* In 1809 Barclay de Tolly, commanding the army in the Finnish war, effected a daring two days' march on the ice across the Gulf of Bothnia, surprised and seized Umea, and secured peace with Sweden.

seded by Bennigsen all will be lost, for Bennigsen showed his incapacity already in 1807." *

The sixth party, the Bennigsenites, said, on the contrary, that at any rate there was no one more active and experienced than Bennigsen: "and twist about as you may, you will have to come to Bennigsen eventually. Let the others make mistakes now!" said they, arguing that our retirement to Drissa was a most shameful reverse and an unbroken series of blunders. "The more mistakes that are made the better. It will at any rate be understood all the sooner that things cannot go on like this. What is wanted is not some Barclay or other, but a man like Bennigsen, who made his mark in 1807, and to whom Napoleon himself did justice *—a man whose authority would be willingly recognized, and Bennigsen is the only such man."

The seventh party consisted of the sort of people who are always to be found, especially around young sovereigns, and of whom there were particularly many round Alexander—generals and imperial aides-de-camp passionately devoted to the Emperor, not merely as a monarch but as a man, adoring him sincerely and disinterestedly, as Rostóv had done in 1805, and who saw in him not only all the virtues but all human capabilities as well. These men, though enchanted with the sovereign for refusing the command of the army, yet blamed him for such excessive modesty, and only desired and insisted that their adored sovereign should abandon his diffidence and openly announce that he would place himself at the head of the army, gather round him a commander in chief's staff, and, consulting experienced theoreticians and practical men where necessary, would himself lead the troops, whose spirits would thereby be raised to the highest pitch.

The eighth and largest group, which in its enormous numbers was to the others as ninety-nine to one, consisted of men who desired neither peace nor war, neither an advance nor a defensive camp at the Drissa or anywhere else, neither Barclay nor the Emperor, neither Pfuel nor Bennigsen, but only the one most essential thing—as much advantage and pleasure for themselves as possible. In the troubled waters of conflicting and intersecting intrigues that eddied about the Emperor's headquarters, it was possible to succeed in many ways unthinkable at other times. A man who simply wished to retain his lucrative post would today agree with Pfuel, tomorrow with his opponent, and the day after, merely to avoid responsibility or to please the Emperor, would declare that he had no opinion at all on the matter. Another who wished to gain some ad-

* Both these conflicting opinions refer to the campaign in Prussia mentioned in Bilíbin's letter given in Book Five, pp. 405-07.

vantage would attract the Emperor's attention by loudly advocating the very thing the Emperor had hinted at the day before, and would dispute and shout at the council, beating his breast and challenging those who did not agree with him to duels, thereby proving that he was prepared to sacrifice himself for the common good. A third, in the absence of opponents, between two councils would simply solicit a special gratuity for his faithful services, well knowing that at that moment people would be too busy to refuse him. A fourth while seemingly overwhelmed with work would often come accidentally under the Emperor's eye. A fifth, to achieve his long-cherished aim of dining with the Emperor, would stubbornly insist on the correctness or falsity of some newly emerging opinion and for this object would produce arguments more or less forcible and correct.

All the men of this party were fishing for rubles, decorations, and promotions, and in this pursuit watched only the weathercock of imperial favor, and directly they noticed it turning in any direction, this whole drone population of the army began blowing hard that way, so that it was all the harder for the Emperor to turn it elsewhere. Amid the uncertainties of the position, with the menace of serious danger giving a peculiarly threatening character to everything, amid this vortex of intrigue, egotism, conflict of views and feelings, and the diversity of race among these people—this eighth and largest party of those preoccupied with personal interests imparted great confusion and obscurity to the common task. Whatever question arose, a swarm of these drones, without having finished their buzzing on a previous theme, flew over to the new one and by their hum drowned and obscured the voices of those who were disputing honestly.

From among all these parties, just at the time Prince Andrew reached the army, another, a ninth party, was being formed and was beginning to raise its voice. This was the party of the elders, reasonable men experienced and capable in state affairs, who, without sharing any of those conflicting opinions, were able to take a detached view of what was going on at the staff at headquarters and to consider means of escape from this muddle, indecision, intricacy, and weakness.

The men of this party said and thought that what was wrong resulted chiefly from the Emperor's presence in the army with his military court and from the consequent presence there of an indefinite, conditional, and unsteady fluctuation of relations, which is in place at court but harmful in an army; that a sovereign should reign but not command the army, and that the only way out of the position would be for the Emperor and his court to leave the army; that the mere presence of the Emperor para-

lyzed the action of fifty thousand men required to secure his personal
safety, and that the worst commander in chief if independent would be
better than the very best one trammeled by the presence and authority
of the monarch.

Just at the time Prince Andrew was living unoccupied at Drissa,
Shishkóv, the Secretary of State and one of the chief representatives of
this party, wrote a letter to the Emperor which Arakchéev and Balashëv
agreed to sign. In this letter, availing himself of permission given him by
the Emperor to discuss the general course of affairs, he respectfully sug-
gested—on the plea that it was necessary for the sovereign to arouse a
warlike spirit in the people of the capital—that the Emperor should leave
the army.

That arousing of the people by their sovereign and his call to them to
defend their country—the very incitement which was the chief cause of
Russia's triumph in so far as it was produced by the Tsar's personal pres-
ence in Moscow—was suggested to the Emperor, and accepted by him,
as a pretext for quitting the army.

10. Prince Andrew is introduced to Pfuel

THIS LETTER had not yet been presented to the Emperor when Bar-
clay, one day at dinner, informed Bolkónski that the sovereign
wished to see him personally, to question him about Turkey, and that
Prince Andrew was to present himself at Bennigsen's quarters at six that
evening.

News was received at the Emperor's quarters that very day of a fresh
movement by Napoleon which might endanger the army—news subse-
quently found to be false. And that morning Colonel Michaud had
ridden round the Drissa fortifications with the Emperor and had pointed
out to him that this fortified camp constructed by Pfuel, and till then
considered a chef-d'oeuvre of tactical science which would ensure Na-
poleon's destruction, was an absurdity, threatening the destruction of
the Russian army.

Prince Andrew arrived at Bennigsen's quarters—a country gentleman's
house of moderate size, situated on the very banks of the river. Neither
Bennigsen nor the Emperor was there, but Chernýshev, the Emperor's
aide-de-camp, received Bolkónski and informed him that the Emperor,
accompanied by General Bennigsen and Marquis Paulucci, had gone a
second time that day to inspect the fortifications of the Drissa camp, of
the suitability of which serious doubts were beginning to be felt.

Chernýshev was sitting at a window in the first room with a French novel in his hand. This room had probably been a music room; there was still an organ in it on which some rugs were piled, and in one corner stood the folding bedstead of Bennigsen's adjutant. This adjutant was also there and sat dozing on the rolled-up bedding, evidently exhausted by work or by feasting. Two doors led from the room, one straight on into what had been the drawing room, and another, on the right, to the study. Through the first door came the sound of voices conversing in German and occasionally in French. In that drawing room were gathered, by the Emperor's wish, not a military council (the Emperor preferred indefiniteness), but certain persons whose opinions he wished to know in view of the impending difficulties. It was not a council of war, but, as it were, a council to elucidate certain questions for the Emperor personally. To this semicouncil had been invited the Swedish General Armfeldt, Adjutant General Wolzogen, Wintzingerode (whom Napoleon had referred to as a renegade French subject), Michaud, Toll,* Count Stein who was not a military man at all, and Pfuel himself, who, as Prince Andrew had heard, was the mainspring of the whole affair. Prince Andrew had an opportunity of getting a good look at him, for Pfuel arrived soon after himself and, in passing through to the drawing room, stopped a minute to speak to Chernýshev.

At first sight, Pfuel, in his ill-made uniform of a Russian general, which fitted him badly like a fancy costume, seemed familiar to Prince Andrew, though he saw him now for the first time. There was about him something of Weyrother, Mack, and Schmidt, and many other German theorist-generals whom Prince Andrew had seen in 1805, but he was more typical than any of them. Prince Andrew had never yet seen a German theorist in whom all the characteristics of those others were united to such an extent.

Pfuel was short and very thin but broad-boned, of coarse, robust build, broad in the hips, and with prominent shoulder blades. His face was much wrinkled and his eyes deep set. His hair had evidently been hastily brushed smooth in front of the temples, but stuck up behind in quaint little tufts. He entered the room, looking restlessly and angrily around, as if afraid of everything in that large apartment. Awkwardly holding up his sword, he addressed Chernýshev and asked in German where the Emperor was. One could see that he wished to pass through the rooms as

* K. F. Toll (1778-1842). *A Russian general of German origin, subsequently created count. He was quartermaster general of the main army in the war of 1812, in which he took a very active part after Napoleon abandoned Moscow.*—A.M.

quickly as possible, finish with the bows and greetings, and sit down to business in front of a map, where he would feel at home. He nodded hurriedly in reply to Chernýshev, and smiled ironically on hearing that the sovereign was inspecting the fortifications that he, Pfuel, had planned in accord with his theory. He muttered something to himself abruptly and in a bass voice, as self-assured Germans do—it might have been "stupid fellow" . . . or "the whole affair will be ruined," or "something absurd will come of it." . . . Prince Andrew did not catch what he said and would have passed on, but Chernýshev introduced him to Pfuel, remarking that Prince Andrew was just back from Turkey where the war had terminated so fortunately. Pfuel barely glanced—not so much at Prince Andrew as past him—and said, with a laugh: "That must have been a fine tactical war"; and, laughing contemptuously, went on into the room from which the sound of voices was heard.

Pfuel, always inclined to be irritably sarcastic, was particularly disturbed that day, evidently by the fact that they had dared to inspect and criticize his camp in his absence. From this short interview with Pfuel, Prince Andrew, thanks to his Austerlitz experiences, was able to form a clear conception of the man. Pfuel was one of those hopelessly and immutably self-confident men, self-confident to the point of martyrdom as only Germans are, because only Germans are self-confident on the basis of an abstract notion—science, that is, the supposed knowledge of absolute truth. A Frenchman is self-assured because he regards himself personally, both in mind and body, as irresistibly attractive to men and women. An Englishman is self-assured, as being a citizen of the best-organized state in the world, and therefore as an Englishman always knows what he should do and knows that all he does as an Englishman is undoubtedly correct. An Italian is self-assured because he is excitable and easily forgets himself and other people. A Russian is self-assured just because he knows nothing and does not want to know anything, since he does not believe that anything can be known. The German's self-assurance is worst of all, stronger and more repulsive than any other, because he imagines that he knows the truth—science—which he himself has invented but which is for him the absolute truth.

Pfuel was evidently of that sort. He had a science—the theory of oblique movements deduced by him from the history of Frederick the Great's wars, and all he came across in the history of more recent warfare seemed to him absurd and barbarous—monstrous collisions in which so many blunders were committed by both sides that these wars could not be called wars, they did not accord with the theory, and therefore could not serve as material for science.

In 1806 Pfuel had been one of those responsible for the plan of campaign that ended in Jena and Auerstadt, but he did not see the least proof of the fallibility of his theory in the disasters of that war. On the contrary, the deviations made from his theory were, in his opinion, the sole cause of the whole disaster, and with characteristically gleeful sarcasm he would remark, "There, I said the whole affair would go to the devil!" Pfuel was one of those theoreticians who so love their theory that they lose sight of the theory's object—its practical application. His love of theory made him hate everything practical, and he would not listen to it. He was even pleased by failures, for failures resulting from deviations in practice from the theory only proved to him the accuracy of his theory.

He said a few words to Prince Andrew and Chernýshev about the present war, with the air of a man who knows beforehand that all will go wrong, and who is not displeased that it should be so. The unbrushed tufts of hair sticking up behind and the hastily brushed hair on his temples expressed this most eloquently.

He passed into the next room, and the deep, querulous sounds of his voice were at once heard from there.

11. An informal Council of War. Pfuel's dogmatism

PRINCE ANDREW'S eyes were still following Pfuel out of the room when Count Bennigsen entered hurriedly, and nodding to Bolkónski, but not pausing, went into the study, giving instructions to his adjutant as he went. The Emperor was following him, and Bennigsen had hastened on to make some preparations and to be ready to receive the sovereign. Chernýshev and Prince Andrew went out into the porch, where the Emperor, who looked fatigued, was dismounting. Marquis Paulucci was talking to him with particular warmth and the Emperor, with his head bent to the left, was listening with a dissatisfied air. The Emperor moved forward evidently wishing to end the conversation, but the flushed and excited Italian, oblivious of decorum, followed him and continued to speak.

"And as for the man who advised forming this camp—the Drissa camp," said Paulucci, as the Emperor mounted the steps and noticing Prince Andrew scanned his unfamiliar face, "as to that person, sire . . ." continued Paulucci, desperately, apparently unable to restrain himself, "the man who advised the Drissa camp—I see no alternative but the lunatic asylum or the gallows!"

Without heeding the end of the Italian's remarks, and as though not

hearing them, the Emperor, recognizing Bolkónski, addressed him graciously.

"I am very glad to see you! Go in there where they are meeting, and wait for me."

The Emperor went into the study. He was followed by Prince Peter Mikháylovich Volkónski and Baron Stein, and the door closed behind them. Prince Andrew, taking advantage of the Emperor's permission, accompanied Paulucci, whom he had known in Turkey, into the drawing room where the council was assembled.

Prince Peter Mikháylovich Volkónski occupied the position, as it were, of chief of the Emperor's staff. He came out of the study into the drawing room with some maps which he spread on a table, and put questions on which he wished to hear the opinion of the gentlemen present. What had happened was that news (which afterwards proved to be false) had been received during the night of a movement by the French to outflank the Drissa camp.

The first to speak was General Armfeldt who, to meet the difficulty that presented itself, unexpectedly proposed a perfectly new position away from the Petersburg and Moscow roads. The reason for this was inexplicable (unless he wished to show that he, too, could have an opinion), but he urged that at this point the army should unite and there await the enemy. It was plain that Armfeldt had thought out that plan long ago and now expounded it not so much to answer the questions put—which, in fact, his plan did not answer—as to avail himself of the opportunity to air it. It was one of the millions of proposals, one as good as another, that could be made as long as it was quite unknown what character the war would take. Some disputed his arguments, others defended them. Young Count Toll objected to the Swedish general's views more warmly than anyone else, and in the course of the dispute drew from his side pocket a well-filled notebook, which he asked permission to read to them. In these voluminous notes Toll suggested another scheme, totally different from Armfeldt's or Pfuel's plan of campaign. In answer to Toll, Paulucci suggested an advance and an attack, which, he urged, could alone extricate us from the present uncertainty and from the trap (as he called the Drissa camp) in which we were situated.

During all these discussions Pfuel and his interpreter, Wolzogen (his "bridge" in court relations), were silent. Pfuel only snorted contemptuously and turned away, to show that he would never demean himself by replying to such nonsense as he was now hearing. So when Prince Volkónski, who was in the chair, called on him to give his opinion, he merely said:

"Why ask me? General Armfeldt has proposed a splendid position with an exposed rear, or why not this Italian gentleman's attack—very fine, or a retreat, also good! Why ask me?" said he. "Why, you yourselves know everything better than I do."

But when Volkónski said, with a frown, that it was in the Emperor's name that he asked his opinion, Pfuel rose and, suddenly growing animated, began to speak:

"Everything has been spoiled, everything muddled, everybody thought they knew better than I did, and now you come to me! How mend matters? There is nothing to mend! The principles laid down by me must be strictly adhered to," said he, drumming on the table with his bony fingers. "What is the difficulty? Nonsense, childishness!"

He went up to the map and speaking rapidly began proving that no eventuality could alter the efficiency of the Drissa camp, that everything had been foreseen, and that if the enemy were really going to outflank it, the enemy would inevitably be destroyed.

Paulucci, who did not know German, began questioning him in French. Wolzogen came to the assistance of his chief, who spoke French badly, and began translating for him, hardly able to keep pace with Pfuel, who was rapidly demonstrating that not only all that had happened, but all that could happen, had been foreseen in his scheme, and that if there were now any difficulties the whole fault lay in the fact that his plan had not been precisely executed. He kept laughing sarcastically, he demonstrated, and at last contemptuously ceased to demonstrate, like a mathematician who ceases to prove in various ways the accuracy of a problem that has already been proved. Wolzogen took his place and continued to explain his views in French, every now and then turning to Pfuel and saying, "Is it not so, your excellency?" But Pfuel, like a man heated in a fight who strikes those on his own side, shouted angrily at his own supporter, Wolzogen:

"Well, of course, what more is there to explain?"

Paulucci and Michaud both attacked Wolzogen simultaneously in French. Armfeldt addressed Pfuel in German. Toll explained to Volkónski in Russian. Prince Andrew listened and observed in silence.

Of all these men Prince Andrew sympathized most with Pfuel, angry, determined, and absurdly self-confident as he was. Of all those present, evidently he alone was not seeking anything for himself, nursed no hatred against anyone, and only desired that the plan, formed on a theory arrived at by years of toil, should be carried out. He was ridiculous, and unpleasantly sarcastic, but yet he inspired involuntary respect by his boundless devotion to an idea. Besides this, the remarks of all except Pfuel had

one common trait that had not been noticeable at the council of war in 1805: there was now a panic fear of Napoleon's genius, which, though concealed, was noticeable in every rejoinder. Everything was assumed to be possible for Napoleon, they expected him from every side, and invoked his terrible name to shatter each other's proposals. Pfuel alone seemed to consider Napoleon a barbarian like everyone else who opposed his theory. But besides this feeling of respect, Pfuel evoked pity in Prince Andrew. From the tone in which the courtiers addressed him and the way Paulucci had allowed himself to speak of him to the Emperor, but above all from a certain desperation in Pfuel's own expressions, it was clear that the others knew, and Pfuel himself felt, that his fall was at hand. And despite his self-confidence and grumpy German sarcasm he was pitiable, with his hair smoothly brushed on the temples and sticking up in tufts behind. Though he concealed the fact under a show of irritation and contempt, he was evidently in despair that the sole remaining chance of verifying his theory by a huge experiment and proving its soundness to the whole world was slipping away from him.

The discussions continued a long time, and the longer they lasted the more heated became the disputes, culminating in shouts and personalities, and the less was it possible to arrive at any general conclusion from all that had been said. Prince Andrew, listening to this polyglot talk and to these surmises, plans, refutations, and shouts, felt nothing but amazement at what they were saying. A thought that had long since and often occurred to him during his military activities—the idea that there is not and cannot be any science of war, and that therefore there can be no such thing as a military genius—now appeared to him an obvious truth. "What theory and science is possible about a matter the conditions and circumstances of which are unknown and cannot be defined, especially when the strength of the acting forces cannot be ascertained? No one was or is able to foresee in what condition our or the enemy's armies will be in a day's time, and no one can gauge the force of this or that detachment. Sometimes—when there is not a coward at the front to shout, 'We are cut off!' and start running, but a brave and jolly lad who shouts, 'Hurrah!'— a detachment of five thousand is worth thirty thousand, as at Schön Grabern, while at times fifty thousand run from eight thousand, as at Austerlitz. What science can there be in a matter in which, as in all practical matters, nothing can be defined and everything depends on innumerable conditions, the significance of which is determined at a particular moment which arrives no one knows when? Armfeldt says our army is cut in half, and Paulucci says we have got the French army between two fires; Michaud says that the worthlessness of the Drissa camp

lies in having the river behind it, and Pfuel says that is what constitutes its strength; Toll proposes one plan, Armfeldt another, and they are all good and all bad, and the advantages of any suggestions can be seen only at the moment of trial. And why do they all speak of a 'military genius'? Is a man a genius who can order bread to be brought up at the right time and say who is to go to the right and who to the left? It is only because military men are invested with pomp and power and crowds of sychophants flatter power, attributing to it qualities of genius it does not possess. The best generals I have known were, on the contrary, stupid or absent-minded men. Bagratión was the best, Napoleon himself admitted that. And Bonaparte himself! I remember his limited, self-satisfied face on the field of Austerlitz. Not only does a good army commander not need any special qualities, on the contrary he needs the absence of the highest and best human attributes—love, poetry, tenderness, and philosophic inquiring doubt. He should be limited, firmly convinced that what he is doing is very important (otherwise he will not have sufficient patience), and only then will he be a brave leader. God forbid that he should be humane, should love, or pity, or think of what is just and unjust. It is understandable that a theory of their 'genius' was invented for them long ago because they have power! The success of a military action depends not on them, but on the man in the ranks who shouts, 'We are lost!' or who shouts, 'Hurrah!' And only in the ranks can one serve with assurance of being useful."

So thought Prince Andrew as he listened to the talking, and he roused himself only when Paulucci called him and everyone was leaving.

At the review next day the Emperor asked Prince Andrew where he would like to serve, and Prince Andrew lost his standing in court circles forever by not asking to remain attached to the sovereign's person, but for permission to serve in the army.

12. Nicholas writes to Sónya. He and Ilyín in a storm

BEFORE THE BEGINNING of the campaign, Rostóv had received a letter from his parents in which they told him briefly of Natásha's illness and the breaking off of her engagement to Prince Andrew (which they explained by Natásha's having rejected him) and again asked Nicholas to retire from the army and return home. On receiving this letter, Nicholas did not even make any attempt to get leave of absence or to retire from the army, but wrote to his parents that he was sorry Natásha was ill

and her engagement broken off, and that he would do all he could to meet their wishes. To Sónya he wrote separately.

"Adored friend of my soul!" he wrote. "Nothing but honor could keep me from returning to the country. But now, at the commencement of the campaign, I should feel dishonored, not only in my comrades' eyes but in my own, if I preferred my own happiness to my love and duty to the Fatherland. But this shall be our last separation. Believe me, directly the war is over, if I am still alive and still loved by you, I will throw up everything and fly to you, to press you forever to my ardent breast."

It was, in fact, only the commencement of the campaign that prevented Rostóv from returning home as he had promised and marrying Sónya. The autumn in Otrádnoe with the hunting, and the winter with the Christmas holidays and Sónya's love, had opened out to him a vista of tranquil rural joys and peace such as he had never known before, and which now allured him. "A splendid wife, children, a good pack of hounds, a dozen leashes of smart borzois, agriculture, neighbors, service by election * . . ." thought he. But now the campaign was beginning, and he had to remain with his regiment. And since it had to be so, Nicholas Rostóv, as was natural to him, felt contented with the life he led in the regiment and was able to find pleasure in that life.

On his return from his furlough Nicholas, having been joyfully welcomed by his comrades, was sent to obtain remounts and brought back from the Ukraine excellent horses which pleased him and earned him commendation from his commanders. During his absence he had been promoted captain, and when the regiment was put on war footing with an increase in numbers, he was again allotted his old squadron.

The campaign began, the regiment was moved into Poland on double pay, new officers arrived, new men and horses, and above all everybody was infected with the merrily excited mood that goes with the commencement of a war, and Rostóv, conscious of his advantageous position in the regiment, devoted himself entirely to the pleasures and interests of military service, though he knew that sooner or later he would have to relinquish them.

The troops retired from Vílna for various complicated reasons of state, political and strategic. Each step of the retreat was accompanied by a complicated interplay of interests, arguments, and passions at headquarters. For the Pávlograd hussars, however, the whole of this retreat during the finest period of summer and with sufficient supplies was a very simple and agreeable business.

* *He meant that he might be elected by the local gentry to some administrative post.*—A.M.

It was only at headquarters that there was depression, uneasiness, and intriguing; in the body of the army they did not ask themselves where they were going or why. If they regretted having to retreat, it was only because they had to leave billets they had grown accustomed to, or some pretty young Polish lady. If the thought that things looked bad chanced to enter anyone's head, he tried to be as cheerful as befits a good soldier and not to think of the general trend of affairs, but only of the task nearest to hand. First they camped gaily before Vílna, making acquaintance with the Polish landowners, preparing for reviews and being reviewed by the Emperor and other high commanders. Then came an order to retreat to Sventsyáni and destroy any provisions they could not carry away with them. Sventsyáni was remembered by the hussars only as the *drunken camp*, a name the whole army gave to their encampment there, and because many complaints were made against the troops, who, taking advantage of the order to collect provisions, took also horses, carriages, and carpets from the Polish proprietors. Rostóv remembered Sventsyáni, because on the first day of their arrival at that small town he changed his sergeant major and was unable to manage all the drunken men of his squadron who, unknown to him, had appropriated five barrels of old beer. From Sventsyáni they retired farther and farther to Drissa, and thence again beyond Drissa, drawing near to the frontier of Russia proper.

On the thirteenth of July the Pávlograds took part in a serious action for the first time.

On the twelfth of July, on the eve of that action, there was a heavy storm of rain and hail. In general, the summer of 1812 was remarkable for its storms.

The two Pávlograd squadrons were bivouacking on a field of rye, which was already in ear but had been completely trodden down by cattle and horses. The rain was descending in torrents, and Rostóv, with a young officer named Ilyín, his protégé, was sitting in a hastily constructed shelter. An officer of their regiment, with long mustaches extending onto his cheeks, who after riding to the staff had been overtaken by the rain, entered Rostóv's shelter.

"I have come from the staff, Count. Have you heard of Raévski's exploit?"

And the officer gave them details of the Saltánov battle, which he had heard at the staff.

Rostóv, smoking his pipe and turning his head about as the water trickled down his neck, listened inattentively, with an occasional glance at Ilyín, who was pressing close to him. This officer, a lad of sixteen who had recently joined the regiment, was now in the same relation to Nicholas

that Nicholas had been to Denísov seven years before. Ilyín tried to imitate Rostóv in everything and adored him as a girl might have done.

Zdrzhinski, the officer with the long mustache, spoke grandiloquently of the Saltánov dam being "a Russian Thermopylae," and of how a deed worthy of antiquity had been performed by General Raévski. He recounted how Raévski had led his two sons onto the dam under terrific fire and had charged with them beside him. Rostóv heard the story and not only said nothing to encourage Zdrzhinski's enthusiasm but, on the contrary, looked like a man ashamed of what he was hearing, though with no intention of contradicting it. Since the campaigns of Austerlitz and of 1807 Rostóv knew by experience that men always lie when describing military exploits, as he himself had done when recounting them; besides that, he had experience enough to know that nothing happens in war at all as we can imagine or relate it. And so he did not like Zdrzhinski's tale, nor did he like Zdrzhinski himself who, with his mustaches extending over his cheeks, bent low over the face of his hearer, as was his habit, and crowded Rostóv in the narrow shanty. Rostóv looked at him in silence. "In the first place, there must have been such a confusion and crowding on the dam that was being attacked that if Raévski did lead his sons there, it could have had no effect except perhaps on some dozen men nearest to him," thought he, "the rest could not have seen how or with whom Raévski came onto the dam. And even those who did see it would not have been much stimulated by it, for what had they to do with Raévski's tender paternal feelings when their own skins were in danger? And besides, the fate of the Fatherland did not depend on whether they took the Saltánov dam or not, as we are told was the case at Thermopylae. So why should he have made such a sacrifice? And why expose his own children in the battle? I would not have taken my brother Pétya there, or even Ilyín, who's a stranger to me but a nice lad, but would have tried to put them somewhere under cover," Nicholas continued to think, as he listened to Zdrzhinski. But he did not express his thoughts, for in such matters, too, he had gained experience. He knew that this tale redounded to the glory of our arms and so one had to pretend not to doubt it. And he acted accordingly.

"I can't stand this any more," said Ilyín, noticing that Rostóv did not relish Zdrzhinski's conversation. "My stockings and shirt . . . and the water is running on my seat! I'll go and look for shelter. The rain seems less heavy."

Ilyín went out and Zdrzhinski rode away.

Five minutes later Ilyín, splashing through the mud, came running back to the shanty.

"Hurrah! Rostóv, come quick! I've found it! About two hundred yards away there's a tavern where ours have already gathered. We can at least get dry there, and Mary Hendríkhovna's there."

Mary Hendríkhovna was the wife of the regimental doctor, a pretty young German woman he had married in Poland. The doctor, whether from lack of means or because he did not like to part from his young wife in the early days of their marriage, took her about with him wherever the hussar regiment went and his jealousy had become a standing joke among the hussar officers.

Rostóv threw his cloak over his shoulders, shouted to Lavrúshka to follow with the things, and—now slipping in the mud, now splashing right through it—set off with Ilyín in the lessening rain and the darkness that was occasionally rent by distant lightning.

"Rostóv, where are you?"

"Here. What lightning!" they called to one another.

13. Mary Hendríkhovna. The officers and the doctor

IN THE TAVERN, before which stood the doctor's covered cart, there were already some five officers. Mary Hendríkhovna, a plump little blonde German, in a dressing jacket and nightcap, was sitting on a broad bench in the front corner. Her husband, the doctor, lay asleep behind her. Rostóv and Ilyín, on entering the room, were welcomed with merry shouts and laughter.

"Dear me, how jolly we are!" said Rostóv laughing.

"And why do you stand there gaping?"

"What swells they are! Why, the water streams from them! Don't make our drawing room so wet."

"Don't mess Mary Hendríkhovna's dress!" cried other voices.

Rostóv and Ilyín hastened to find a corner where they could change into dry clothes without offending Mary Hendríkhovna's modesty. They were going into a tiny recess behind a partition to change, but found it completely filled by three officers who sat playing cards by the light of a solitary candle on an empty box, and these officers would on no account yield their position. Mary Hendríkhovna obliged them with the loan of a petticoat to be used as a curtain, and behind that screen Rostóv and Ilyín, helped by Lavrúshka who had brought their kits, changed their wet things for dry ones.

A fire was made up in the dilapidated brick stove. A board was found, fixed on two saddles and covered with a horsecloth, a small samovar was

produced and a cellaret and half a bottle of rum, and having asked Mary Hendríkhovna to preside, they all crowded round her. One offered her a clean handkerchief to wipe her charming hands, another spread a jacket under her little feet to keep them from the damp, another hung his coat over the window to keep out the draft, and yet another waved the flies off her husband's face, lest he should wake up.

"Leave him alone," said Mary Hendríkhovna, smiling timidly and happily. "He is sleeping well as it is, after a sleepless night."

"Oh, no, Mary Hendríkhovna," replied the officer, "one must look after the doctor. Perhaps he'll take pity on me someday, when it comes to cutting off a leg or an arm for me."

There were only three tumblers, the water was so muddy that one could not make out whether the tea was strong or weak, and the samovar held only six tumblers of water, but this made it all the pleasanter to take turns in order of seniority to receive one's tumbler from Mary Hendríkhovna's plump little hands with their short and not overclean nails. All the officers appeared to be, and really were, in love with her that evening. Even those playing cards behind the partition soon left their game and came over to the samovar, yielding to the general mood of courting Mary Hendríkhovna. She, seeing herself surrounded by such brilliant and polite young men, beamed with satisfaction, try as she might to hide it, and perturbed as she evidently was each time her husband moved in his sleep behind her.

There was only one spoon, sugar was more plentiful than anything else, but it took too long to dissolve, so it was decided that Mary Hendríkhovna should stir the sugar for everyone in turn. Rostóv received his tumbler, and adding some rum to it asked Mary Hendríkhovna to stir it.

"But you take it without sugar?" she said, smiling all the time, as if everything she said and everything the others said was very amusing and had a double meaning.

"It is not the sugar I want, but only that your little hand should stir my tea."

Mary Hendríkhovna assented and began looking for the spoon which someone meanwhile had pounced on.

"Use your finger, Mary Hendríkhovna, it will be still nicer," said Rostóv.

"Too hot!" she replied, blushing with pleasure.

Ilyín put a few drops of rum into the bucket of water and brought it to Mary Hendríkhovna, asking her to stir it with her finger.

"This is my cup," said he. "Only dip your finger in it and I'll drink it all up."

When they had emptied the samovar, Rostóv took a pack of cards and

proposed that they should play "Kings" with Mary Hendríkhovna. They drew lots to settle who should make up her set. At Rostóv's suggestion it was agreed that whoever became "King" should have the right to kiss Mary Hendríkhovna's hand, and that the "Booby" should go to refill and reheat the samovar for the doctor when the latter awoke.

"Well, but supposing Mary Hendríkhovna is 'King'?" asked Ilyín.

"As it is, she is Queen, and her word is law!"

They had hardly begun to play before the doctor's disheveled head suddenly appeared from behind Mary Hendríkhovna. He had been awake for some time, listening to what was being said, and evidently found nothing entertaining or amusing in what was going on. His face was sad and depressed. Without greeting the officers, he scratched himself and asked to be allowed to pass as they were blocking the way. As soon as he had left the room all the officers burst into loud laughter and Mary Hendríkhovna blushed till her eyes filled with tears and thereby became still more attractive to them. Returning from the yard, the doctor told his wife (who had ceased to smile so happily, and looked at him in alarm, awaiting her sentence) that the rain had ceased and they must go to sleep in their covered cart, or everything in it would be stolen.

"But I'll send an orderly. . . . Two of them!" said Rostóv. "What an idea, doctor!"

"I'll stand guard on it myself!" said Ilyín.

"No, gentlemen, you have had your sleep, but I have not slept for two nights," replied the doctor, and he sat down morosely beside his wife, waiting for the game to end.

Seeing his gloomy face as he frowned at his wife, the officers grew still merrier, and some of them could not refrain from laughter, for which they hurriedly sought plausible pretexts. When he had gone, taking his wife with him, and had settled down with her in their covered cart, the officers lay down in the tavern, covering themselves with their wet cloaks, but they did not sleep for a long time; now they exchanged remarks, recalling the doctor's uneasiness and his wife's delight, now they ran out into the porch and reported what was taking place in the covered trap. Several times Rostóv, covering his head, tried to go to sleep, but some remark would arouse him and conversation would be resumed, to the accompaniment of unreasoning, merry, childlike laughter.

14. Courage. Rostóv goes into action at Ostróvna

I T WAS nearly three o'clock but no one was yet asleep, when the quarter-master appeared with an order to move on to the little town of Ostróvna. Still laughing and talking, the officers began hurriedly getting ready and again boiled some muddy water in the samovar. But Rostóv went off to his squadron without waiting for tea. Day was breaking, the rain had ceased, and the clouds were dispersing. It felt damp and cold, especially in clothes that were still moist. As they left the tavern in the twilight of the dawn, Rostóv and Ilyín both glanced under the wet and glistening leather hood of the doctor's cart, from under the apron of which his feet were sticking out, and in the middle of which his wife's nightcap was visible and her sleepy breathing audible.

"She really is a dear little thing," said Rostóv to Ilyín, who was following him.

"A charming woman!" said Ilyín, with all the gravity of a boy of sixteen.

Half an hour later the squadron was lined up on the road. The command was heard to "mount" and the soldiers crossed themselves and mounted. Rostóv riding in front gave the order "Forward!" and the hussars, with clanking sabers and subdued talk, their horses' hoofs splashing in the mud, defiled in fours and moved along the broad road planted with birch trees on each side, following the infantry and a battery that had gone on in front.

Tattered, blue-purple clouds, reddening in the east, were scudding before the wind. It was growing lighter and lighter. That curly grass which always grows by country roadsides became clearly visible, still wet with the night's rain; the drooping branches of the birches, also wet, swayed in the wind and flung down bright drops of water to one side. The soldiers' faces were more and more clearly visible. Rostóv, always closely followed by Ilyín, rode along the side of the road between two rows of birch trees.

When campaigning, Rostóv allowed himself the indulgence of riding not a regimental but a Cossack horse. A judge of horses and a sportsman, he had lately procured himself a large, fine, mettlesome, Donéts horse, dun-colored, with light mane and tail, and when he rode it no one could outgallop him. To ride this horse was a pleasure to him, and he thought of the horse, of the morning, of the doctor's wife, but not once of the impending danger.

Formerly, when going into action, Rostóv had felt afraid; now he had not the least feeling of fear. He was fearless, not because he had grown

used to being under fire (one cannot grow used to danger), but because
he had learned how to manage his thoughts when in danger. He had
grown accustomed when going into action to think about anything but
what would seem most likely to interest him—the impending danger.
During the first period of his service, hard as he tried and much as he
reproached himself with cowardice, he had not been able to do this, but
with time it had come of itself. Now he rode beside Ilyín under the birch
trees, occasionally plucking leaves from a branch that met his hand,
sometimes touching his horse's side with his foot, or, without turning
round, handing a pipe he had finished to an hussar riding behind him,
with as calm and careless an air as though he were merely out for a ride.
He glanced with pity at the excited face of Ilyín, who talked much and
in great agitation. He knew from experience the tormenting expectation
of terror and death the cornet was suffering and knew that only time
could help him.

As soon as the sun appeared in a clear strip of sky beneath the clouds,
the wind fell, as if it dared not spoil the beauty of the summer morning
after the storm; drops still continued to fall, but vertically now, and all
was still. The whole sun appeared on the horizon and disappeared behind
a long narrow cloud that hung above it. A few minutes later it reappeared
brighter still from behind the top of the cloud, tearing its edge. Every-
thing grew bright and glittered. And with that light, and as if in reply to
it, came the sound of guns ahead of them.

Before Rostóv had had time to consider and determine the distance of
that firing, Count Ostermann-Tolstóy's adjutant came galloping from
Vítebsk with orders to advance at a trot along the road.

The squadron overtook and passed the infantry and the battery—which
had also quickened their pace—rode down a hill, and passing through an
empty and deserted village again ascended. The horses began to lather
and the men to flush.

"Halt! Dress your ranks!" the order of the regimental commander was
heard ahead. "Forward by the left. Walk, march!" came the order from
in front.

And the hussars, passing along the line of troops on the left flank of
our position, halted behind our Uhlans who were in the front line. To
the right stood our infantry in a dense column: they were the reserve.
Higher up the hill, on the very horizon, our guns were visible through the
wonderfully clear air, brightly illuminated by slanting morning sun-
beams. In front, beyond a hollow dale, could be seen the enemy's columns
and guns. Our advanced line, already in action, could be heard briskly
exchanging shots with the enemy in the dale.

At these sounds, long unheard, Rostóv's spirits rose, as at the strains of the merriest music. *Trap-ta-ta-tap!* cracked the shots, now together, now several quickly one after another. Again all was silent and then again it sounded as if someone were walking on detonators and exploding them.

The hussars remained in the same place for about an hour. A cannonade began. Count Ostermann with his suite rode up behind the squadron, halted, spoke to the commander of the regiment, and rode up the hill to the guns.

After Ostermann had gone, a command rang out to the Uhlans.

"Form column! Prepare to charge!"

The infantry in front of them parted into platoons to allow the cavalry to pass. The Uhlans started, the streamers on their spears fluttering, and trotted downhill toward the French cavalry which was seen below to the left.

As soon as the Uhlans descended the hill, the hussars were ordered up the hill to support the battery. As they took the places vacated by the Uhlans, bullets came from the front, whining and whistling, but fell spent without taking effect.

The sounds, which he had not heard for so long, had an even more pleasurable and exhilarating effect on Rostóv than the previous sounds of firing. Drawing himself up, he viewed the field of battle opening out before him from the hill, and with his whole soul followed the movement of the Uhlans. They swooped down close to the French dragoons, something confused happened there amid the smoke, and five minutes later our Uhlans were galloping back, not to the place they had occupied but more to the left, and among the orange-colored Uhlans on chestnut horses and behind them, in a large group, blue French dragoons on gray horses could be seen.

15. *Rostóv's hussars charge the French dragoons. He wounds and captures a prisoner*

Rostóv, with his keen sportsman's eye, was one of the first to catch sight of these blue French dragoons pursuing our Uhlans. Nearer and nearer in disorderly crowds came the Uhlans and the French dragoons pursuing them. He could already see how these men, who looked so small at the foot of the hill, jostled and overtook one another, waving their arms and their sabers in the air.

Rostóv gazed at what was happening before him as at a hunt. He felt instinctively that if the hussars struck at the French dragoons now, the

latter could not withstand them, but if a charge was to be made it must
be done now, at that very moment, or it would be too late. He looked
around. A captain, standing beside him, was gazing like himself with
eyes fixed on the cavalry below them.

"Andrew Sevastyánych!" said Rostóv. "You know, we could crush
them. . . ."

"A fine thing too!" replied the captain, "and really . . ."

Rostóv, without waiting to hear him out, touched his horse, galloped
to the front of his squadron, and before he had time to finish giving the
word of command, the whole squadron, sharing his feeling, was following
him. Rostóv himself did not know how or why he did it. He acted as he
did when hunting, without reflecting or considering. He saw the dragoons
near and that they were galloping in disorder; he knew they could not
withstand an attack—knew there was only that moment and that if he
let it slip it would not return. The bullets were whining and whistling so
stimulatingly around him and his horse was so eager to go that he could
not restrain himself. He touched his horse, gave the word of command,
and immediately, hearing behind him the tramp of the horses of his de-
ployed squadron, rode at full trot downhill toward the dragoons. Hardly
had they reached the bottom of the hill before their pace instinctively
changed to a gallop, which grew faster and faster as they drew nearer to
our Uhlans and the French dragoons who galloped after them. The
dragoons were now close at hand. On seeing the hussars, the foremost
began to turn, while those behind began to halt. With the same feeling
with which he had galloped across the path of a wolf, Rostóv gave rein
to his Donéts horse and galloped to intersect the path of the dragoons'
disordered lines. One Uhlan stopped, another who was on foot flung
himself to the ground to avoid being knocked over, and a riderless horse
fell in among the hussars. Nearly all the French dragoons were galloping
back. Rostóv, picking out one on a gray horse, dashed after him. On the
way he came upon a bush, his gallant horse cleared it, and almost before
he had righted himself in his saddle he saw that he would immediately
overtake the enemy he had selected. That Frenchman, by his uniform an
officer, was going at a gallop, crouching on his gray horse and urging it
on with his saber. In another moment Rostóv's horse dashed its breast
against the hindquarters of the officer's horse, almost knocking it over,
and at the same instant Rostóv, without knowing why, raised his saber
and struck the Frenchman with it.

The instant he had done this, all Rostóv's animation vanished. The
officer fell, not so much from the blow—which had but slightly cut his
arm above the elbow—as from the shock to his horse and from fright.

Rostóv reined in his horse, and his eyes sought his foe to see whom he had vanquished. The French dragoon officer was hopping with one foot on the ground, the other being caught in the stirrup. His eyes, screwed up with fear as if he every moment expected another blow, gazed up at Rostóv with shrinking terror. His pale and mud-stained face—fair and young, with a dimple in the chin and light-blue eyes—was not an enemy's face at all suited to a battlefield, but a most ordinary, homelike face. Before Rostóv had decided what to do with him, the officer cried, "I surrender!" He hurriedly but vainly tried to get his foot out of the stirrup and did not remove his frightened blue eyes from Rostóv's face. Some hussars who galloped up disengaged his foot and helped him into the saddle. On all sides, the hussars were busy with the dragoons; one was wounded, but though his face was bleeding, he would not give up his horse; another was perched up behind an hussar with his arms round him; a third was being helped by an hussar to mount his horse. In front, the French infantry were firing as they ran. The hussars galloped hastily back with their prisoners. Rostóv galloped back with the rest, aware of an unpleasant feeling of depression in his heart. Something vague and confused, which he could not at all account for, had come over him with the capture of that officer and the blow he had dealt him.

Count Ostermann-Tolstóy met the returning hussars, sent for Rostóv, thanked him, and said he would report his gallant deed to the Emperor and would recommend him for a St. George's Cross. When sent for by Count Ostermann, Rostóv, remembering that he had charged without orders, felt sure his commander was sending for him to punish him for breach of discipline. Ostermann's flattering words and promise of a reward should therefore have struck him all the more pleasantly, but he still felt that same vaguely disagreeable feeling of moral nausea. "But what on earth is worrying me?" he asked himself as he rode back from the general. "Ilyín? No, he's safe. Have I disgraced myself in any way? No, that's not it." Something else, resembling remorse, tormented him. "Yes, oh yes, that French officer with the dimple. And I remember how my arm paused when I raised it."

Rostóv saw the prisoners being led away and galloped after them to have a look at his Frenchman with the dimple on his chin. He was sitting in his foreign uniform on an hussar packhorse and looked anxiously about him. The sword cut on his arm could scarcely be called a wound. He glanced at Rostóv with a feigned smile and waved his hand in greeting. Rostóv still had the same indefinite feeling, as of shame.

All that day and the next his friends and comrades noticed that Rostóv, without being dull or angry, was silent, thoughtful, and preoccupied. He

drank reluctantly, tried to remain alone, and kept turning something over in his mind.

Rostóv was always thinking about that brilliant exploit of his, which to his amazement had gained him the St. George's Cross and even given him a reputation for bravery, and there was something he could not at all understand. "So others are even more afraid than I am!" he thought. "So that's all there is in what is called heroism! And did I do it for my country's sake? And how was he to blame, with his dimple and blue eyes? And how frightened he was! He thought that I should kill him. Why should I kill him? My hand trembled. And they have given me a St. George's Cross. . . . I can't make it out at all."

But while Nicholas was considering these questions and still could reach no clear solution of what puzzled him so, the wheel of fortune in the service, as often happens, turned in his favor. After the affair at Ostróvna he was brought into notice, received command of an hussar battalion, and when a brave officer was needed he was chosen.

16. Natásha's illness. The use of doctors

ON RECEIVING NEWS of Natásha's illness, the countess, though not quite well yet and still weak, went to Moscow with Pétya and the rest of the household, and the whole family moved from Márya Dmítrievna's house to their own and settled down in town.

Natásha's illness was so serious that, fortunately for her and for her parents, the consideration of all that had caused the illness, her conduct and the breaking off of her engagement, receded into the background. She was so ill that it was impossible for them to consider in how far she was to blame for what had happened. She could not eat or sleep, grew visibly thinner, coughed, and, as the doctors made them feel, was in danger. They could not think of anything but how to help her. Doctors came to see her singly and in consultation, talked much in French, German, and Latin, blamed one another, and prescribed a great variety of medicines for all the diseases known to them, but the simple idea never occurred to any of them that they could not know the disease Natásha was suffering from, as no disease suffered by a live man can be known, for every living person has his own peculiarities and always has his own peculiar, personal, novel, complicated disease, unknown to medicine—not a disease of the lungs, liver, skin, heart, nerves, and so on mentioned in medical books, but a disease consisting of one of the innumerable combinations of the maladies of those organs. This simple thought could not

occur to the doctors (as it cannot occur to a wizard that he is unable to work his charms) because the business of their lives was to cure, and they received money for it and had spent the best years of their lives on that business. But, above all, that thought was kept out of their minds by the fact that they saw they were really useful, as in fact they were to the whole Rostóv family. Their usefulness did not depend on making the patient swallow substances for the most part harmful (the harm was scarcely perceptible, as they were given in small doses), but they were useful, necessary, and indispensable because they satisfied a mental need of the invalid and of those who loved her—and that is why there are, and always will be, pseudo-healers, wise women, homeopaths, and allopaths. They satisfied that eternal human need for hope of relief, for sympathy, and that something should be done, which is felt by those who are suffering. They satisfied the need seen in its most elementary form in a child, when it wants to have a place rubbed that has been hurt. A child knocks itself and runs at once to the arms of its mother or nurse to have the aching spot rubbed or kissed, and it feels better when this is done. The child cannot believe that the strongest and wisest of its people have no remedy for its pain, and the hope of relief and the expression of its mother's sympathy while she rubs the bump comforts it. The doctors were of use to Natásha because they kissed and rubbed her bump, assuring her that it would soon pass if only the coachman went to the chemist's in the Arbát and got a powder and some pills in a pretty box for a ruble and seventy kopeks, and if she took those powders in boiled water at intervals of precisely two hours, neither more nor less.

What would Sónya and the count and countess have done, how would they have looked, if nothing had been done, if there had not been those pills to give by the clock, the warm drinks, the chicken cutlets, and all the other details of life ordered by the doctors, the carrying out of which supplied an occupation and consolation to the family circle? How would the count have borne his dearly loved daughter's illness had he not known that it was costing him a thousand rubles, and that he would not grudge thousands more to benefit her, or had he not known that if her illness continued he would not grudge yet other thousands and would take her abroad for consultations there, and had he not been able to explain the details of how Métivier and Feller had not understood the symptoms, but Frise had, and Múdrov had diagnosed them even better? What would the countess have done had she not been able sometimes to scold the invalid for not strictly obeying the doctor's orders?

"You'll never get well like that," she would say, forgetting her grief in her vexation, "if you won't obey the doctor and take your medicine

at the right time! You mustn't trifle with it, you know, or it may turn to pneumonia," she would go on, deriving much comfort from the utterance of that foreign word, incomprehensible to others as well as to herself.

What would Sónya have done without the glad consciousness that she had not undressed during the first three nights, in order to be ready to carry out all the doctor's injunctions with precision, and that she still kept awake at night so as not to miss the proper time when the slightly harmful pills in the little gilt box had to be administered? Even to Natásha herself it was pleasant to see that so many sacrifices were being made for her sake, and to know that she had to take medicine at certain hours, though she declared that no medicine would cure her and that it was all nonsense. And it was even pleasant to be able to show, by disregarding the orders, that she did not believe in medical treatment and did not value her life.

The doctor came every day, felt her pulse, looked at her tongue, and regardless of her grief-stricken face joked with her. But when he had gone into another room, to which the countess hurriedly followed him, he assumed a grave air and thoughtfully shaking his head said that though there was danger, he had hopes of the effect of this last medicine and one must wait and see, that the malady was chiefly mental, but . . . And the countess, trying to conceal the action from herself and from him, slipped a gold coin into his hand and always returned to the patient with a more tranquil mind.

The symptoms of Natásha's illness were that she ate little, slept little, coughed, and was always low-spirited. The doctors said that she could not get on without medical treatment, so they kept her in the stifling atmosphere of the town, and the Rostóvs did not move to the country that summer of 1812.

In spite of the many pills she swallowed and the drops and powders out of the little bottles and boxes of which Madame Schoss who was fond of such things made a large collection, and in spite of being deprived of the country life to which she was accustomed, youth prevailed. Natásha's grief began to be overlaid by the impressions of daily life, it ceased to press so painfully on her heart, it gradually faded into the past, and she began to recover physically.

17. *Natásha and Pierre. She prepares for communion with Belóva. The church service. Her health improves*

NATÁSHA WAS CALMER but no happier. She not merely avoided all external forms of pleasure—balls, promenades, concerts, and theaters—but she never laughed without a sound of tears in her laughter. She could not sing. As soon as she began to laugh, or tried to sing by herself, tears choked her: tears of remorse, tears at the recollection of those pure times which could never return, tears of vexation that she should so uselessly have ruined her young life which might have been so happy. Laughter and singing in particular seemed to her like a blasphemy, in face of her sorrow. Without any need of self-restraint, no wish to coquet ever entered her head. She said and felt at that time that no man was more to her than Nastásya Ivánovna, the buffoon. Something stood sentinel within her and forbade her every joy. Besides, she had lost all the old interests of her carefree girlish life that had been so full of hope. The previous autumn, the hunting, "Uncle," and the Christmas holidays spent with Nicholas at Otrádnoe were what she recalled oftenest and most painfully. What would she not have given to bring back even a single day of that time! But it was gone forever. Her presentiment at the time had not deceived her—that that state of freedom and readiness for any enjoyment would not return again. Yet it was necessary to live on.

It comforted her to reflect that she was not better as she had formerly imagined, but worse, much worse, than anybody else in the world. But this was not enough. She knew that, and asked herself, "What next?" But there was nothing to come. There was no joy in life, yet life was passing. Natásha apparently tried not to be a burden or a hindrance to anyone, but wanted nothing for herself. She kept away from everyone in the house and felt at ease only with her brother Pétya. She liked to be with him better than with the others, and when alone with him she sometimes laughed. She hardly ever left the house and of those who came to see them was glad to see only one person, Pierre. It would have been impossible to treat her with more delicacy, greater care, and at the same time more seriously than did Count Bezúkhov. Natásha unconsciously felt this delicacy and so found great pleasure in his society. But she was not even grateful to him for it; nothing good on Pierre's part seemed to her to be an effort, it seemed so natural for him to be kind to everyone that there was no merit in his kindness. Sometimes Natásha noticed embarrassment and awkwardness on his part in her presence, especially when he wanted to do something to please her, or feared that something they spoke of would

awaken memories distressing to her. She noticed this and attributed it to his general kindness and shyness, which she imagined must be the same toward everyone as it was to her. After those involuntary words—that if he were free he would have asked on his knees for her hand and her love— uttered at a moment when she was so strongly agitated, Pierre never spoke to Natásha of his feelings; and it seemed plain to her that those words, which had then so comforted her, were spoken as all sorts of meaningless words are spoken to comfort a crying child. It was not because Pierre was a married man, but because Natásha felt very strongly with him that moral barrier the absence of which she had experienced with Kurágin that it never entered her head that the relations between him and herself could lead to love on her part, still less on his, or even to the kind of tender, self-conscious, romantic friendship between a man and a woman of which she had known several instances.

Before the end of the fast of St. Peter,* Agraféna Ivánovna Belóva, a country neighbor of the Rostóvs, came to Moscow to pay her devotions at the shrines of the Moscow saints. She suggested that Natásha should fast and prepare for Holy Communion, and Natásha gladly welcomed the idea. Despite the doctor's orders that she should not go out early in the morning, Natásha insisted on fasting and preparing for the sacrament, not as they generally prepared for it in the Rostóv family by attending three services in their own house, but as Agraféna Ivánovna did, by going to church every day for a week and not once missing Vespers, Matins, or Mass.

The countess was pleased with Natásha's zeal; after the poor results of the medical treatment, in the depths of her heart she hoped that prayer might help her daughter more than medicines and, though not without fear and concealing it from the doctor, she agreed to Natásha's wish and entrusted her to Belóva. Agraféna Ivánovna used to come to wake Natásha at three in the morning, but generally found her already awake. She was afraid of being late for Matins. Hastily washing, and meekly putting on her shabbiest dress and an old mantilla, Natásha, shivering in the fresh air, went out into the deserted streets lit by the clear light of dawn. By Agraféna Ivánovna's advice Natásha prepared herself not in their own parish, but at a church where, according to the devout Agraféna Ivánovna, the priest was a man of very severe and lofty life. There were never many people in the church; Natásha always stood beside Belóva in the customary place before an icon of the Blessed Virgin, let into the screen before the choir on the left side, and a feeling, new to her, of humility before some-

* That is, for two weeks before St. Peter's Day (June 29, Old Style) and seventeen days after Napoleon had crossed the Russian frontier.—A.M.

thing great and incomprehensible, seized her when at that unusual morning hour, gazing at the dark face of the Virgin illuminated by the candles burning before it and by the morning light falling from the window, she listened to the words of the service which she tried to follow with understanding. When she understood them her personal feeling became interwoven in the prayers with shades of its own. When she did not understand, it was sweeter still to think that the wish to understand everything is pride, that it is impossible to understand all, that it is only necessary to believe and to commit oneself to God, whom she felt guiding her soul at those moments. She crossed herself, bowed low, and when she did not understand, in horror at her own vileness, simply asked God to forgive her everything, everything, and to have mercy upon her. The prayers to which she surrendered herself most of all were those of repentance. On her way home at an early hour when she met no one but bricklayers going to work or men sweeping the street, and everybody within the houses was still asleep, Natásha experienced a feeling new to her, a sense of the possibility of correcting her faults, the possibility of a new, clean life, and of happiness.

During the whole week she spent in this way, that feeling grew every day. And the happiness of taking communion, or "communing" as Agraféna Ivánovna, joyously playing with the word, called it, seemed to Natásha so great that she felt she should never live till that blessed Sunday.

But the happy day came, and on that memorable Sunday, when, dressed in white muslin, she returned home after communion, for the first time for many months she felt calm and not oppressed by the thought of the life that lay before her.

The doctor who came to see her that day ordered her to continue the powders he had prescribed a fortnight previously.

"She must certainly go on taking them morning and evening," said he, evidently sincerely satisfied with his success. "Only, please be particular about it.

"Be quite easy," he continued playfully, as he adroitly took the gold coin in his palm. "She will soon be singing and frolicking about. The last medicine has done her a very great deal of good. She has freshened up very much."

The countess, with a cheerful expression on her face, looked down at her nails and spat a little for luck as she returned to the drawing room.*

* As some people in England "touch wood," and in the United States "knock on wood," for luck to avert the ill results of overconfidence, so in Russia people spat for the same purpose.—A.M.

18. Natásha attends Mass and hears the special prayer for victory

AT THE BEGINNING of July more and more disquieting reports about the war began to spread in Moscow; people spoke of an appeal by the Emperor to the people, and of his coming himself from the army to Moscow. And as up to the eleventh of July no manifesto or appeal had been received, exaggerated reports became current about them and about the position of Russia. It was said that the Emperor was leaving the army because it was in danger, it was said that Smolénsk had surrendered, that Napoleon had an army of a million and only a miracle could save Russia.

On the eleventh of July, which was Saturday, the manifesto was received but was not yet in print, and Pierre, who was at the Rostóvs', promised to come to dinner next day, Sunday, and bring a copy of the manifesto and appeal, which he would obtain from Count Rostopchín.

That Sunday, the Rostóvs went to Mass at the Razumóvskis' private chapel as usual. It was a hot July day. Even at ten o'clock, when the Rostóvs got out of their carriage at the chapel, the sultry air, the shouts of hawkers, the light and gay summer clothes of the crowd, the dusty leaves of the trees on the boulevard, the sounds of the band and the white trousers of a battalion marching to parade, the rattling of wheels on the cobblestones, and the brilliant, hot sunshine were all full of that summer languor, that content and discontent with the present, which is most strongly felt on a bright, hot day in town. All the Moscow notabilities, all the Rostóvs' acquaintances, were at the Razumóvskis' chapel, for, as if expecting something to happen, many wealthy families who usually left town for their country estates had not gone away that summer. As Natásha, at her mother's side, passed through the crowd behind a liveried footman who cleared the way for them, she heard a young man speaking about her in too loud a whisper.

"That's Rostóva, the one who . . ."

"She's much thinner, but all the same she's pretty!"

She heard, or thought she heard, the names of Kurágin and Bolkónski. But she was always imagining that. It always seemed to her that everyone who looked at her was thinking only of what had happened to her. With a sinking heart, wretched as she always was now when she found herself in a crowd, Natásha in her lilac silk dress trimmed with black lace walked—as women can walk—with the more repose and stateliness the greater the pain and shame in her soul. She knew for certain that she was pretty, but this no longer gave her satisfaction as it used to. On

the contrary it tormented her more than anything else of late, and particularly so on this bright, hot summer day in town. "It's Sunday again—another week past," she thought, recalling that she had been here the Sunday before, "and always the same life that is no life, and the same surroundings in which it used to be so easy to live. I'm pretty, I'm young, and I know that now I am good. I used to be bad, but now I know I am good," she thought, "but yet my best years are slipping by and are no good to anyone." She stood by her mother's side and exchanged nods with acquaintances near her. From habit she scrutinized the ladies' dresses, condemned the bearing of a lady standing close by who was not crossing herself properly but in a cramped manner, and again she thought with vexation that she was herself being judged and was judging others, and suddenly, at the sound of the service, she felt horrified at her own vileness, horrified that the former purity of her soul was again lost to her.

A comely, fresh-looking old man was conducting the service with that mild solemnity which has so elevating and soothing an effect on the souls of the worshipers. The gates of the sanctuary screen were closed, the curtain was slowly drawn, and from behind it a soft mysterious voice pronounced some words. Tears, the cause of which she herself did not understand, made Natásha's breast heave, and a joyous but oppressive feeling agitated her.

"Teach me what I should do, how to live my life, how I may grow good forever, forever!" she pleaded.

The deacon came out onto the raised space before the altar screen and, holding his thumb extended, drew his long hair from under his dalmatic and, making the sign of the cross on his breast, began in a loud and solemn voice to recite the words of the prayer. . . .

"In peace let us pray unto the Lord."

"As one community,* without distinction of class, without enmity, united by brotherly love—let us pray!" thought Natásha.

"For the peace that is from above, and for the salvation of our souls."

"For the world of angels and all the spirits who dwell above us," prayed Natásha.

When they prayed for the warriors, she thought of her brother and Denísov. When they prayed for all traveling by land and sea, she remembered Prince Andrew, prayed for him, and asked God to forgive her all the wrongs she had done him. When they prayed for those who love us,

* The Russian word mir has two meanings. Sometimes—and especially in the Church service—it means peace, concord, and union. Natásha takes it in the popular sense, as meaning the universe, the world, the commune, the village assembly, and so on.—A.M.

she prayed for the members of her own family, her father and mother and Sónya, realizing for the first time how wrongly she had acted toward them, and feeling all the strength of her love for them. When they prayed for those who hate us, she tried to think of her enemies and people who hated her, in order to pray for them. She included among her enemies the creditors and all who had business dealings with her father, and always at the thought of enemies and those who hated her she remembered Anatole who had done her so much harm—and though he did not hate her she gladly prayed for him as for an enemy. Only at prayer did she feel able to think clearly and calmly of Prince Andrew and Anatole, as men for whom her feelings were as nothing compared with her awe and devotion to God. When they prayed for the Imperial family and the Synod, she bowed very low and made the sign of the cross, saying to herself that even if she did not understand, still she could not doubt, and at any rate loved the governing Synod and prayed for it.

When he had finished the Litany the deacon crossed the stole over his breast and said, "Let us commit ourselves and our whole lives to Christ the Lord!"

"Commit ourselves to God," Natásha inwardly repeated. "Lord God, I submit myself to Thy will!" she thought. "I want nothing, wish for nothing; teach me what to do and how to use my will! Take me, take me!" prayed Natásha, with impatient emotion in her heart, not crossing herself but letting her slender arms hang down as if expecting some invisible power at any moment to take her and deliver her from herself, from her regrets, desires, remorse, hopes, and sins.

The countess looked round several times at her daughter's softened face and shining eyes and prayed God to help her.

Unexpectedly, in the middle of the service, and not in the usual order Natásha knew so well, the deacon brought out a small stool, the one he knelt on when praying on Trinity Sunday, and placed it before the doors of the sanctuary screen. The priest came out with his purple velvet biretta * on his head, adjusted his hair, and knelt down with an effort. Everybody followed his example and they looked at one another in surprise. Then came the prayer just received from the Synod—a prayer for the deliverance of Russia from hostile invasion.

"Lord God of might, God of our salvation!" began the priest in that voice, clear, not grandiloquent but mild, in which only the Slav clergy read and which acts so irresistibly on a Russian heart.

"Lord God of might, God of our salvation! Look this day in mercy and

* It is not strictly accurate to use the word biretta for this headgear used in the Russo-Greek Church, but it is the nearest word available in English.—A.M.

blessing on Thy humble people, and graciously hear us, spare us, and have mercy upon us! This foe confounding Thy land, desiring to lay waste the whole world, rises against us; these lawless men are gathered together to overthrow Thy kingdom, to destroy Thy dear Jerusalem, Thy beloved Russia; to defile Thy temples, to overthrow Thine altars, and to desecrate our holy shrines. How long, O Lord, how long shall the wicked triumph? How long shall they wield unlawful power?

"Lord God! Hear us when we pray to Thee; strengthen with Thy might our most gracious sovereign lord, the Emperor Alexander Pávlovich; be mindful of his uprightness and meekness, reward him according to his righteousness, and let it preserve us, Thy chosen Israel! Bless his counsels, his undertakings, and his work; strengthen his kingdom by Thine almighty hand, and give him victory over his enemy, even as Thou gavest Moses the victory over Amalek, Gideon over Midian, and David over Goliath. Preserve his army, put a bow of brass in the hands of those who have armed themselves in Thy Name, and gird their loins with strength for the fight. Take up the spear and shield and arise to help us; confound and put to shame those who have devised evil against us, may they be before the faces of Thy faithful warriors as dust before the wind, and may Thy mighty Angel confound them and put them to flight; may they be ensnared when they know it not, and may the plots they have laid in secret be turned against them; let them fall before Thy servants' feet and be laid low by our hosts! Lord, Thou art able to save both great and small; Thou art God, and man cannot prevail against Thee!

"God of our fathers! Remember Thy bounteous mercy and loving-kindness which are from of old; turn not Thy face from us, but be gracious to our unworthiness, and in Thy great goodness and Thy many mercies regard not our transgressions and iniquities! Create in us a clean heart and renew a right spirit within us, strengthen us all in Thy faith, fortify our hope, inspire us with true love one for another, arm us with unity of spirit in the righteous defense of the heritage Thou gavest to us and to our fathers, and let not the scepter of the wicked be exalted against the destiny of those Thou hast sanctified.

"O Lord our God, in whom we believe and in whom we put our trust, let us not be confounded in our hope of Thy mercy, and give us a token of Thy blessing, that those who hate us and our Orthodox faith may see it and be put to shame and perish, and may all the nations know that Thou art the Lord and we are Thy people. Show Thy mercy upon us this day, O Lord, and grant us Thy salvation; make the hearts of Thy servants to rejoice in Thy mercy; smite down our enemies and destroy them swiftly beneath the feet of Thy faithful servants! For Thou art the defense, the

succor, and the victory of them that put their trust in Thee, and to Thee be all glory, to Father, Son, and Holy Ghost, now and forever, world without end. Amen."

In Natásha's receptive condition of soul this prayer affected her strongly. She listened to every word about the victory of Moses over Amalek, of Gideon over Midian, and of David over Goliath, and about the destruction of "Thy Jerusalem," and she prayed to God with the tenderness and emotion with which her heart was overflowing, but without fully understanding what she was asking of God in that prayer. She shared with all her heart in the prayer for the spirit of righteousness, for the strengthening of the heart by faith and hope, and its animation by love. But she could not pray that her enemies might be trampled under foot when but a few minutes before she had been wishing she had more of them that she might pray for them. But neither could she doubt the righteousness of the prayer that was being read on bended knees. She felt in her heart a devout and tremulous awe at the thought of the punishment that overtakes men for their sins, and especially of her own sins, and she prayed to God to forgive them all, and her too, and to give them all, and her too, peace and happiness. And it seemed to her that God heard her prayer.

19. Pierre's relation to life altered by his feeling for Natásha. 666. Napoleon as Antichrist. Pierre's belief that he is destined to end Napoleon's power. He gets news for the Rostóvs

FROM THE DAY when Pierre, after leaving the Rostóvs' with Natásha's grateful look fresh in his mind, had gazed at the comet that seemed to be fixed in the sky and felt that something new was appearing on his own horizon—from that day the problem of the vanity and uselessness of all earthly things, that had incessantly tormented him, no longer presented itself. That terrible question "Why?" "Wherefore?" which had come to him amid every occupation, was now replaced, not by another question or by a reply to the former question, but by her image. When he listened to, or himself took part in, trivial conversations, when he read or heard of human baseness or folly, he was not horrified as formerly, and did not ask himself why men struggled so about these things when all is so transient and incomprehensible—but he remembered her as he had last seen her, and all his doubts vanished—not because she had answered the questions that had haunted him, but because his conception of her transferred him instantly to another, a brighter, realm of spiritual activity in

which no one could be justified or guilty—a realm of beauty and love which it was worth living for. Whatever worldly baseness presented itself to him, he said to himself:

"Well, supposing N. N. has swindled the country and the Tsar, and the country and the Tsar confer honors upon him, what does that matter? She smiled at me yesterday and asked me to come again, and I love her, and no one will ever know it." And his soul felt calm and peaceful.

Pierre still went into society, drank as much and led the same idle and dissipated life, because besides the hours he spent at the Rostóvs' there were other hours he had to spend somehow, and the habits and acquaintances he had made in Moscow formed a current that bore him along irresistibly. But latterly, when more and more disquieting reports came from the seat of war and Natásha's health began to improve and she no longer aroused in him the former feeling of careful pity, an ever-increasing restlessness, which he could not explain, took possession of him. He felt that the condition he was in could not continue long, that a catastrophe was coming which would change his whole life, and he impatiently sought everywhere for signs of that approaching catastrophe. One of his brother Masons had revealed to Pierre the following prophecy concerning Napoleon, drawn from the Revelation of St. John.

In chapter xiii, verse 18, of the Apocalypse, it is said:

Here is wisdom. Let him that hath understanding count the number of the beast: for it is the number of a man; and his number is Six hundred threescore and six.

And in the fifth verse of the same chapter:

And there was given unto him a mouth speaking great things and blasphemies; and power was given unto him to continue forty and two months.

The French alphabet, written out with the same numerical values as the Hebrew, in which the first nine letters denote units and the others tens, will have the following significance:

a	b	c	d	e	f	g	h	i	k	l	m	n	o	p
1	2	3	4	5	6	7	8	9	10	20	30	40	50	60

q	r	s	t	u	v	w	x	y	z
70	80	90	100	110	120	130	140	150	160

Writing the words *L'Empereur Napoléon* in numbers, it appears that the sum of them is 666,* and that Napoleon was therefore the beast

* *Including a 5 for the letter* e *dropped by elision from the* le *before* Empereur.—A.M.

foretold in the Apocalypse. Moreover, by applying the same system to the words *quarante-deux* [forty-two], which was the term allowed to the beast that "spoke great things and blasphemies," the same number 666 was obtained; from which it followed that the limit fixed for Napoleon's power had come in the year 1812 when the French emperor was forty-two.* This prophecy [2] pleased Pierre very much and he often asked himself what would put an end to the power of the beast, that is, of Napoleon, and tried by the same system of using letters as numbers and adding them up, to find an answer to the question that engrossed him. He wrote the words *L'Empereur Alexandre, La nation russe* and added up their numbers, but the sums were either more or less than 666. Once when making such calculations he wrote down his own name in French, Comte Pierre Besouhoff, but the sum of the numbers did not come right. Then he changed the spelling, substituting a *z* for the *s* and adding *de* and the article *le*, still without obtaining the desired result. Then it occurred to him: if the answer to the question were contained in his name, his nationality would also be given in the answer. So he wrote *Le russe Besuhof* and adding up the numbers got 671. This was only five too much, and five was represented by *e*, the very letter elided from the article *le* before the word *Empereur*. By omitting the *e*, though incorrectly, Pierre got the answer he sought. *L'russe Besuhof* made 666.[3] This discovery excited him. How, or by what means, he was connected with the great event foretold in the Apocalypse he did not know, but he did not doubt that connection for a moment. His love for Natásha, Antichrist, Napoleon, the invasion, the comet, 666, *L'Empereur Napoléon*, and *L'russe Besuhof* —all this had to mature and culminate, to lift him out of that spellbound,

* *Apparently the correspondence of* quarante-deux *with 666 was sufficient for Pierre, and it did not trouble him that the text spoke of months, while to fit the 42 to Napoleon it was necessary to take years. Napoleon's forty-second birthday was on August 15, 1811; so that till August, 1812, he was, in ordinary parlance, forty-two.*—A.M.

[2] *Apocalyptic calculations such as Pierre here indulged in were not unusual among the Freemasons, and efforts to foretell Napoleon's fate by consulting that book were made in Russia even before his invasion.*—A.M.

[3] *Russians transliterating their names into the Latin alphabet have generally followed no fixed rule but have adopted such spelling as, in this or that country, seemed to them most likely to cause people to pronounce the name correctly. So it occurs that the name, which on the system now usually adopted in England is spelt Bezúkhov, could be written by Pierre in French in more than one way, and he found Besuhof most convenient for the purpose of his calculation.*—A.M.

petty sphere of Moscow habits in which he felt himself held captive, and lead him to a great achievement and great happiness.

On the eve of the Sunday when the special prayer was read, Pierre had promised the Rostóvs to bring them, from Count Rostopchín whom he knew well, both the appeal to the people and the latest news from the army. In the morning, when he went to call at Rostopchín's he met there a courier fresh from the army, an acquaintance of his own, who often danced at Moscow balls.

"Do, please, for heaven's sake, relieve me of something!" said the courier. "I have a sackful of letters to parents."

Among these letters was one from Nicholas Rostóv to his father. Pierre took that letter, and Rostopchín also gave him the Emperor's appeal to Moscow, which had just been printed, the last army orders, and his own most recent bulletin. Glancing through the army orders, Pierre found in one of them, in the lists of killed, wounded, and rewarded, the name of Nicholas Rostóv, awarded a St. George's Cross of the Fourth Class for courage shown in the Ostróvna affair, and in the same order the name of Prince Andrew Bolkónski, appointed to the command of a regiment of Chasseurs. Though he did not want to remind the Rostóvs of Bolkónski, Pierre could not refrain from making them happy by the news of their son's having received a decoration, so he sent that printed army order and Nicholas' letter to the Rostóvs, keeping the appeal, the bulletin, and the other orders to take with him when he went to dinner.

His conversation with Count Rostopchín and the latter's tone of anxious hurry, the meeting with the courier who talked casually of how badly things were going in the army, the rumors of the discovery of spies in Moscow and of a leaflet in circulation stating that Napoleon promised to be in both the Russian capitals by the autumn, and the talk of the Emperor's being expected to arrive next day,—all aroused with fresh force that feeling of agitation and expectation in Pierre which he had been conscious of ever since the appearance of the comet, and especially since the beginning of the war.

He had long been thinking of entering the army and would have done so had he not been hindered, first, by his membership of the Society of Freemasons to which he was bound by oath and which preached perpetual peace and the abolition of war, and secondly, by the fact that when he saw the great mass of Muscovites who had donned uniform and were talking patriotism, he somehow felt ashamed to take the step. But the chief reason for not carrying out his intention to enter the army lay

in the vague idea that he was *L'russe Besuhof* who had the number of the beast, 666; that his part in the great affair of setting a limit to the power of the beast that spoke great and blasphemous things had been predestined from eternity, and that therefore he ought not to undertake anything, but wait for what was bound to come to pass.

20. *Pierre at the Rostóvs'. Natásha again takes up her singing. Sónya reads Alexander's manifesto. Pétya declares that he will enter the army. Natásha realizes that Pierre loves her. He decides to cease going to the Rostóvs'*

A FEW INTIMATE FRIENDS were dining with the Rostóvs that day, as usual on Sundays.

Pierre came early so as to find them alone.

He had grown so stout this year that he would have been abnormal had he not been so tall, so broad of limb, and so strong that he carried his bulk with evident ease.

He went up the stairs, puffing and muttering something. His coachman did not even ask whether he was to wait. He knew that when his master was at the Rostóvs' he stayed till midnight. The Rostóvs' footman rushed eagerly forward to help him off with his cloak and take his hat and stick. Pierre, from club habit, always left both hat and stick in the anteroom.

The first person he saw in the house was Natásha. Even before he saw her, while taking off his cloak, he heard her. She was practicing sol-fa exercises in the music room. He knew that she had not sung since her illness, and so the sound of her voice surprised and delighted him. He opened the door softly and saw her, in the lilac dress she had worn at church, walking about the room singing. She had her back to him when he opened the door, but when, turning quickly, she saw his broad, surprised face, she blushed and came rapidly up to him.

"I want to try to sing again," she said, adding as if by way of excuse, "it is, at least, something to do."

"That's capital!"

"How glad I am you've come! I am so happy today," she said, with the old animation Pierre had not seen in her for a long time. "You know Nicholas has received a St. George's Cross? I am so proud of him."

"Oh yes, I sent that announcement. But I don't want to interrupt you," he added, and was about to go to the drawing room.

Natásha stopped him.

"Count, is it wrong of me to sing?" she said blushing, and fixing her eyes inquiringly on him.

"No . . . Why should it be? On the contrary . . . But why do you ask me?"

"I don't know myself," Natasha answered quickly, "but I should not like to do anything you disapproved of. I believe in you completely. You don't know how important you are to me, how much you've done for me. . . ." She spoke rapidly and did not notice how Pierre flushed at her words. "I saw in that same army order that he, Bolkónski" (she whispered the name hastily), "is in Russia, and in the army again. What do you think?"—she was speaking hurriedly, evidently afraid her strength might fail her—"Will he ever forgive me? Will he not always have a bitter feeling toward me? What do you think? What do you think?"

"I think . . ." Pierre replied, "that he has nothing to forgive. . . . If I were in his place . . ."

By association of ideas, Pierre was at once carried back to the day when, trying to comfort her, he had said that if he were not himself but the best man in the world and free, he would ask on his knees for her hand; and the same feeling of pity, tenderness, and love took possession of him and the same words rose to his lips. But she did not give him time to say them.

"Yes, you . . . you . . ." she said, uttering the word you rapturously —"that's a different thing. I know no one kinder, more generous, or better than you; nobody could be! Had you not been there then, and now too, I don't know what would have become of me, because . . ."

Tears suddenly rose in her eyes, she turned away, lifted her music before her eyes, began singing again, and again began walking up and down the room.

Just then Pétya came running in from the drawing room.

Pétya was now a handsome rosy lad of fifteen with full red lips and resembled Natásha. He was preparing to enter the university, but he and his friend Obolénski had lately, in secret, agreed to join the hussars.

Pétya had come rushing out to talk to his namesake * about this affair. He had asked Pierre to find out whether he would be accepted in the hussars.

Pierre walked up and down the drawing room, not listening to what Pétya was saying.

Pétya pulled him by the arm to attract his attention.

* Pétya is the diminutive of Pëtr, which is the Russian equivalent of Pierre, or Peter.—A.M.

"Well, what about my plan? Peter Kirílych, for heaven's sake! You are my only hope!" said Pétya.

"Oh yes, your plan. To join the hussars? I'll mention it, I'll bring it all up today."

"Well, mon cher, have you got the manifesto?" asked the old count. "The countess has been to Mass at the Razumóvskis' and heard the new prayer. She says it's very fine."

"Yes, I've got it," said Pierre. "The Emperor is to be here tomorrow . . . there's to be an Extraordinary Meeting of the nobility, and they are talking of a levy of ten men per thousand. Oh yes, let me congratulate you!"

"Yes, yes, thank God! Well, and what news from the army?"

"We are again retreating. They say we're already near Smolénsk," replied Pierre.

"O Lord, O Lord!" exclaimed the count. "Where is the manifesto?"

"The Emperor's appeal? Oh yes!"

Pierre began feeling in his pockets for the papers, but could not find them. Still slapping his pockets, he kissed the hand of the countess who entered the room and glanced uneasily around, evidently expecting Natásha, who had left off singing but had not yet come into the drawing room.

"On my word, I don't know what I've done with it," he said.

"There he is, always losing everything!" remarked the countess.

Natásha entered with a softened and agitated expression of face and sat down looking silently at Pierre. As soon as she entered, Pierre's features, which had been gloomy, suddenly lighted up, and while still searching for the papers he glanced at her several times.

"No, really! I'll drive home, I must have left them there. I'll certainly . . ."

"But you'll be late for dinner."

"Oh! And my coachman has gone."

But Sónya, who had gone to look for the papers in the anteroom, had found them in Pierre's hat, where he had carefully tucked them under the lining. Pierre was about to begin reading.

"No, after dinner," said the old count, evidently expecting much enjoyment from that reading.

At dinner, at which champagne was drunk to the health of the new chevalier of St. George, Shinshín told them the town news, of the illness of the old Georgian princess, of Métivier's disappearance from Moscow, and of how some German fellow had been brought to Rostopchín and accused of being a French "spyer" (so Count Rostopchín had told the

story), and how Rostopchín let him go and assured the people that he was "not a spire at all, but only an old German ruin."

"People are being arrested . . ." said the count. "I've told the countess she should not speak French so much. It's not the time for it now."

"And have you heard?" Shinshín asked. "Prince Golítsyn has engaged a master to teach him Russian. It is becoming dangerous to speak French in the streets." *

"And how about you, Count Peter Kirílych? If they call up the militia, you too will have to mount a horse," remarked the old count, addressing Pierre.

Pierre had been silent and preoccupied all through dinner, seeming not to grasp what was said. He looked at the count.

"Oh yes, the war," he said. "No! What sort of warrior should I make? And yet everything is so strange, so strange! I can't make it out. I don't know, I am very far from having military tastes, but in these times no one can answer for himself."

After dinner the count settled himself comfortably in an easy chair and with a serious face asked Sónya, who was considered an excellent reader, to read the appeal.

"To Moscow, our ancient Capital!

"The enemy has entered the borders of Russia with immense forces. He comes to despoil our beloved country," Sónya read painstakingly in her high-pitched voice. The count listened with closed eyes, heaving abrupt sighs at certain passages.

Natásha sat erect, gazing with a searching look now at her father and now at Pierre.

Pierre felt her eyes on him and tried not to look round. The countess shook her head disapprovingly and angrily at every solemn expression in the manifesto. In all these words she saw only that the danger threatening her son would not soon be over. Shinshín, with a sarcastic smile on his lips, was evidently preparing to make fun of anything that gave him the opportunity: Sónya's reading, any remark of the count's, or even the manifesto itself should no better pretext present itself.

After reading about the dangers that threatened Russia, the hopes the Emperor placed on Moscow and especially on its illustrious nobility, Sónya, with a quiver in her voice due chiefly to the attention that was being paid to her, read the last words: "We ourselves will not delay to appear among our people in that Capital and in other parts of our realm

* It was so customary for the Russian aristocracy of those days to speak French that many of them could neither write nor speak Russian correctly, though the mass of the people spoke nothing but Russian.—A.M.

for consultation, and for the direction of all our levies, both those now barring the enemy's path and those freshly formed to defeat him wherever he may appear. May the ruin he hopes to bring upon us recoil on his own head, and may Europe delivered from bondage glorify the name of Russia!"

"Yes, that's it!" cried the count, opening his moist eyes and sniffing repeatedly, as if a strong vinaigrette had been held to his nose; and he added, "Let the Emperor but say the word and we'll sacrifice everything and begrudge nothing."

Before Shinshín had time to utter the joke he was ready to make on the count's patriotism, Natásha jumped up from her place and ran to her father.

"What a darling our Papa is!" she cried, kissing him, and she again looked at Pierre with the unconscious coquetry that had returned to her with her better spirits.

"There! Here's a patriot for you!" said Shinshín.

"Not a patriot at all, but simply . . ." Natásha replied in an injured tone. "Everything seems funny to you, but this isn't at all a joke. . . ."

"A joke indeed!" put in the count. "Let him but say the word and we'll all go. . . . We're not Germans!"

"But did you notice, it says, 'for consultation'?" said Pierre.

"Never mind what it's for. . . ."

At this moment, Pétya, to whom nobody was paying any attention, came up to his father with a very flushed face and said in his breaking voice that was now deep and now shrill:

"Well, Papa, I tell you definitely, and Mamma too, it's as you please, but I say definitely that you must let me enter the army, because I can't . . . that's all. . . ."

The countess, in dismay, looked up to heaven, clasped her hands, and turned angrily to her husband.

"That comes of your talking!" said she.

But the count had already recovered from his excitement.

"Come, come!" said he. "Here's a fine warrior! No! Nonsense! You must study."

"It's not nonsense, Papa. Fédya Obolénski is younger than I, and he's going too. Besides, all the same I can't study now when . . ." Pétya stopped short, flushed till he perspired, but still got out the words, "when our Fatherland is in danger."

"That'll do, that'll do—nonsense. . . ."

"But you said yourself that we would sacrifice everything."

"Pétya! Be quiet, I tell you!" cried the count, with a glance at his wife, who had turned pale and was staring fixedly at her son.

"And I tell you—Peter Kirílych here will also tell you . . ."

"Nonsense, I tell you. Your mother's milk has hardly dried on your lips and you want to go into the army! There, there, I tell you," and the count moved to go out of the room, taking the papers, probably to re-read them in his study before having a nap.

"Well, Peter Kirílych, let's go and have a smoke," he said.

Pierre was agitated and undecided. Natásha's unwontedly brilliant eyes, continually glancing at him with a more than cordial look, had reduced him to this condition.

"No, I think I'll go home."

"Home? Why, you meant to spend the evening with us. . . . You don't often come nowadays as it is, and this girl of mine," said the count good-naturedly, pointing to Natásha, "only brightens up when you're here."

"Yes, I had forgotten . . . I really must go home . . . business . . ." said Pierre hurriedly.

"Well, then, au revoir!" said the count, and went out of the room.

"Why are you going? Why are you upset?" asked Natásha, and she looked challengingly into Pierre's eyes.

"Because I love you!" was what he wanted to say, but he did not say it, and only blushed till the tears came, and lowered his eyes.

"Because it is better for me to come less often . . . because . . . No, simply I have business. . . ."

"Why? No, tell me!" Natásha began resolutely and suddenly stopped. They looked at each other with dismayed and embarrassed faces. He tried to smile but could not: his smile expressed suffering, and he silently kissed her hand and went out.

Pierre made up his mind not to go to the Rostóvs' any more.

21. Pétya goes to the Krémlin to see the Emperor. He gets crushed. He secures a biscuit thrown by the Emperor after dinner

AFTER THE definite refusal he had received, Pétya went to his room and there locked himself in and wept bitterly. When he came in to tea, silent, morose, and with tear-stained face, everybody pretended not to notice anything.

Next day the Emperor arrived in Moscow, and several of the Rostóvs'

domestic serfs begged permission to go to have a look at him. That morning Pétya was a long time dressing and arranging his hair and collar to look like a grown-up man. He frowned before his looking glass, gesticulated, shrugged his shoulders, and finally, without saying a word to anyone, took his cap and left the house by the back door, trying to avoid notice. Pétya decided to go straight to where the Emperor was and to explain frankly to some gentleman-in-waiting (he imagined the Emperor to be always surrounded by gentlemen-in-waiting) that he, Count Rostóv, in spite of his youth wished to serve his country; that youth could be no hindrance to loyalty, and that he was ready to . . . While dressing, Pétya had prepared many fine things he meant to say to the gentleman-in-waiting.

It was on the very fact of being so young that Pétya counted for success in reaching the Emperor—he even thought how surprised everyone would be at his youthfulness—and yet in the arrangement of his collar and hair and by his sedate deliberate walk he wished to appear a grown-up man. But the farther he went and the more his attention was diverted by the ever-increasing crowds moving toward the Krémlin, the less he remembered to walk with the sedateness and deliberation of a man. As he approached the Krémlin he even began to avoid being crushed and resolutely stuck out his elbows in a menacing way. But within the Trinity Gateway he was so pressed to the wall by people who probably were unaware of the patriotic intentions with which he had come that in spite of all his determination he had to give in, and stop while carriages passed in, rumbling beneath the archway. Beside Pétya stood a peasant woman, a footman, two tradesmen, and a discharged soldier. After standing some time in the gateway, Pétya tried to move forward in front of the others without waiting for all the carriages to pass, and he began resolutely working his way with his elbows, but the woman just in front of him, who was the first against whom he directed his efforts, angrily shouted at him:

"What are you shoving for, young lordling? Don't you see we're all standing still? Then why push?"

"Anybody can shove," said the footman, and also began working his elbows to such effect that he pushed Pétya into a very filthy corner of the gateway.

Pétya wiped his perspiring face with his hands and pulled up the damp collar which he had arranged so well at home to seem like a man's.

He felt that he no longer looked presentable, and feared that if he were now to approach the gentlemen-in-waiting in that plight he would not be admitted to the Emperor. But it was impossible to smarten oneself up or move to another place, because of the crowd. One of the generals who

drove past was an acquaintance of the Rostóvs', and Pétya thought of asking his help, but came to the conclusion that that would not be a manly thing to do. When the carriages had all passed in, the crowd, carrying Pétya with it, streamed forward into the Krémlin Square which was already full of people. There were people not only in the square, but everywhere— on the slopes and on the roofs. As soon as Pétya found himself in the square he clearly heard the sound of bells and the joyous voices of the crowd that filled the whole Krémlin.

For a while the crowd was less dense, but suddenly all heads were bared, and everyone rushed forward in one direction. Pétya was being pressed so that he could scarcely breathe, and everybody shouted, "Hurrah! hurrah! hurrah!" Pétya stood on tiptoe and pushed and pinched, but could see nothing except the people about him.

All the faces bore the same expression of excitement and enthusiasm. A tradesman's wife standing beside Pétya sobbed, and the tears ran down her cheeks.

"Father! Angel! Dear one!" she kept repeating, wiping away her tears with her fingers.

"Hurrah!" was heard on all sides.

For a moment the crowd stood still, but then it made another rush forward.

Quite beside himself, Pétya, clenching his teeth and rolling his eyes ferociously, pushed forward, elbowing his way and shouting "hurrah!" as if he were prepared that instant to kill himself and everyone else, but on both sides of him other people with similarly ferocious faces pushed forward and everybody shouted "hurrah!"

"So this is what the Emperor is!" thought Pétya. "No, I can't petition him myself—that would be too bold." But in spite of this he continued to struggle desperately forward, and from between the backs of those in front he caught glimpses of an open space with a strip of red cloth spread out on it; but just then the crowd swayed back—the police in front were pushing back those who had pressed too close to the procession: the Emperor was passing from the palace to the Cathedral of the Assumption—and Pétya unexpectedly received such a blow on his side and ribs and was squeezed so hard that suddenly everything grew dim before his eyes and he lost consciousness. When he came to himself, a man of clerical appearance with a tuft of gray hair at the back of his head and wearing a shabby blue cassock—probably a church clerk and chanter—was holding him under the arm with one hand while warding off the pressure of the crowd with the other.

"You've crushed the young gentleman!" said the clerk. "What are you up to? Gently! . . . They've crushed him, crushed him!"

The Emperor entered the Cathedral of the Assumption. The crowd spread out again more evenly, and the clerk led Pétya—pale and breathless—to the Tsar-cannon.* Several people were sorry for Pétya, and suddenly a crowd turned toward him and pressed round him. Those who stood nearest him attended to him, unbuttoned his coat, seated him on the raised platform of the cannon, and reproached those others (whoever they might be) who had crushed him.

"One might easily get killed that way! What do they mean by it? Killing people! Poor dear, he's as white as a sheet!"—various voices were heard saying.

Pétya soon came to himself, the color returned to his face, the pain had passed, and at the cost of that temporary unpleasantness he had obtained a place by the cannon from where he hoped to see the Emperor who would be returning that way. Pétya no longer thought of presenting his petition. If he could only see the Emperor he would be happy!

While the service was proceeding in the Cathedral of the Assumption —it was a combined service of prayer on the occasion of the Emperor's arrival and of thanksgiving for the conclusion of peace with the Turks— the crowd outside spread out and hawkers appeared, selling kvas, gingerbread, and poppyseed sweets (of which Pétya was particularly fond), and ordinary conversation could again be heard. A tradesman's wife was showing a rent in her shawl and telling how much the shawl had cost; another was saying that all silk goods had now got dear. The clerk who had rescued Pétya was talking to a functionary about the priests who were officiating that day with the bishop. The clerk several times used the word "plenary" (of the service), a word Pétya did not understand. Two young citizens were joking with some serf girls who were cracking nuts. All these conversations, especially the joking with the girls, were such as might have had a particular charm for Pétya at his age, but they did not interest him now. He sat on his elevation—the pedestal of the cannon— still agitated as before by the thought of the Emperor and by his love for him. The feeling of pain and fear he had experienced when he was being crushed, together with that of rapture, still further intensified his sense of the importance of the occasion.

Suddenly the sound of a firing of cannon was heard from the embankment, to celebrate the signing of peace with the Turks, and the crowd rushed impetuously toward the embankment to watch the firing. Pétya

* The Tsar-cannon (Tsar-púshka), a very large cannon cast in 1488 and preserved in the Moscow Krémlin as a curiosity.—A.M.

too would have run there, but the clerk who had taken the young gentle-
man under his protection stopped him. The firing was still proceeding
when officers, generals, and gentlemen-in-waiting came running out of
the cathedral, and after them others in a more leisurely manner: caps
were again raised, and those who had run to look at the cannon ran back
again. At last four men in uniforms and sashes emerged from the cathe-
dral doors. "Hurrah! hurrah!" shouted the crowd again.

"Which is he? Which?" asked Pétya in a tearful voice, of those around
him, but no one answered him, everybody was too excited; and Pétya,
fixing on one of those four men, whom he could not clearly see for the
tears of joy that filled his eyes, concentrated all his enthusiasm on him—
though it happened not to be the Emperor—frantically shouted "Hurrah!"
and resolved that tomorrow, come what might, he would join the army.

The crowd ran after the Emperor, followed him to the palace, and began
to disperse. It was already late, and Pétya had not eaten anything and was
drenched with perspiration, yet he did not go home but stood with that
diminishing, but still considerable, crowd before the palace while the
Emperor dined—looking in at the palace windows, expecting he knew not
what, and envying alike the notables he saw arriving at the entrance
to dine with the Emperor and the court footmen who served at table,
glimpses of whom could be seen through the windows.

While the Emperor was dining, Valúev, looking out of the window,
said:

"The people are still hoping to see Your Majesty again."

The dinner was nearly over, and the Emperor, munching a biscuit, rose
and went out onto the balcony. The people, with Pétya among them,
rushed toward the balcony.

"Angel! Dear one! Hurrah! Father! . . ." cried the crowd, and Pétya
with it, and again the women and men of weaker mold, Pétya among
them, wept with joy.

A largish piece of the biscuit the Emperor was holding in his hand
broke off, fell on the balcony parapet, and then to the ground. A coach-
man in a jerkin, who stood nearest, sprang forward and snatched it up.
Several people in the crowd rushed at the coachman. Seeing this the
Emperor had a plateful of biscuits brought him and began throwing them
down from the balcony. Pétya's eyes grew bloodshot, and still more ex-
cited by the danger of being crushed, he rushed at the biscuits. He did not
know why, but he had to have a biscuit from the Tsar's hand and he felt
that he must not give way. He sprang forward and upset an old woman
who was catching at a biscuit; the old woman did not consider herself
defeated though she was lying on the ground—she grabbed at some bis-

cuits but her hand did not reach them. Pétya pushed her hand away with his knee, seized a biscuit, and as if fearing to be too late, again shouted "Hurrah!" with a voice already hoarse.

The Emperor went in, and after that the greater part of the crowd began to disperse.

"There! I said if only we waited—and so it was!" was being joyfully said by various people.

Happy as Pétya was, he felt sad at having to go home knowing that all the enjoyment of that day was over. He did not go straight home from the Krémlin, but called on his friend Obolénski, who was fifteen and was also entering the regiment. On returning home Pétya announced resolutely and firmly that if he was not allowed to enter the service he would run away. And next day, Count Ilyá Rostóv—though he had not yet quite yielded—went to inquire how he could arrange for Pétya to serve where there would be least danger.

22. Assembly of gentry and merchants at the Slobóda Palace. A limited discussion. Pierre's part in it

TWO DAYS LATER, on the fifteenth of July, an immense number of carriages were standing outside the Slobóda Palace.

The great halls were full. In the first were the nobility and gentry in their uniforms, in the second bearded merchants in full-skirted coats of blue cloth and wearing medals. In the noblemen's hall there was an incessant movement and buzz of voices. The chief magnates sat on high-backed chairs at a large table under the portrait of the Emperor, but most of the gentry were strolling about the room.

All these nobles, whom Pierre met every day at the Club or in their own houses, were in uniform—some in that of Catherine's day, others in that of the Emperor Paul, others again in the new uniforms of Alexander's time or the ordinary uniform of the nobility, and the general characteristic of being in uniform imparted something strange and fantastic to these diverse and familiar personalities, both old and young. The old men, dim-eyed, toothless, bald, sallow, and bloated, or gaunt and wrinkled, were especially striking. For the most part they sat quietly in their places and were silent, or, if they walked about and talked, attached themselves to someone younger. On all these faces, as on the faces of the crowd Pétya had seen in the Square, there was a striking contradiction: the general expectation of a solemn event, and at the same time the

everyday interests in a boston card party, Peter the cook, Zinaída Dmítri-
evna's health, and so on.

Pierre was there too, buttoned up since early morning in a nobleman's
uniform that had become too tight for him. He was agitated; this extraor-
dinary gathering not only of nobles but also of the merchant-class—*les
états généraux* (States-General)—evoked in him a whole series of ideas
he had long laid aside but which were deeply graven in his soul: thoughts
of the *Contrat social* and the French Revolution.* The words that had
struck him in the Emperor's appeal—that the sovereign was coming to the
capital for consultation with his people—strengthened this idea. And
imagining that in this direction something important which he had long
awaited was drawing near, he strolled about watching and listening to
conversations, but nowhere finding any confirmation of the ideas that
occupied him.

The Emperor's manifesto was read, evoking enthusiasm, and then all
moved about discussing it. Besides the ordinary topics of conversation,
Pierre heard questions of where the marshals of the nobility were to stand
when the Emperor entered, when a ball should be given in the Emperor's
honor, whether they should group themselves by districts or by whole
provinces . . . and so on; but as soon as the war was touched on, or what
the nobility had been convened for, the talk became undecided and indefi-
nite. Then all preferred listening to speaking.

A middle-aged man, handsome and virile, in the uniform of a retired
naval officer, was speaking in one of the rooms, and a small crowd was
pressing round him. Pierre went up to the circle that had formed round
the speaker and listened. Count Ilyá Rostóv, in a military uniform of
Catherine's time, was sauntering with a pleasant smile among the crowd,
with all of whom he was acquainted. He too approached that group and
listened with a kindly smile and nods of approval, as he always did, to
what the speaker was saying. The retired naval man was speaking very
boldly, as was evident from the expression on the faces of the listeners
and from the fact that some people Pierre knew as the meekest and
quietest of men walked away disapprovingly or expressed disagreement
with him. Pierre pushed his way into the middle of the group, listened,
and convinced himself that the man was indeed a liberal, but of views
quite different from his own. The naval officer spoke in a particularly
sonorous, musical, and aristocratic baritone voice, pleasantly swallowing

* *Here, and later on at the end of the novel, Tolstóy indicates the influence
France was exercising on the minds of some of the more liberally minded
Russians—influences that prepared the way for the "Decembrist" conspiracy
of 1825 and for much that has happened since.*—A.M.

his r's and generally slurring his consonants: the voice of a man calling out to his servant, "Heah! Bwing me my pipe!" It was indicative of dissipation and the exercise of authority.

"What if the Smolénsk people have offahd to waise militia for the Empewah? Ah we to take Smolénsk as our patte'n? If the noble awistocwacy of the pwovince of Moscow thinks fit, it can show its loyalty to our sov'weign the Empewah in othah ways. Have we fo'gotten the waising of the militia in the yeah 'seven? All that did was to enwich the pwiests' sons and thieves and wobbahs. . . ."

Count Ilyá Rostóv smiled blandly and nodded approval.

"And was our militia of any use to the Empia? Not at all! It only wuined our farming! Bettah have another conscwiption . . . o' ou' men will wetu'n neithah soldiers no' peasants, and we'll get only depwavity fwom them. The nobility don't gwudge theah lives—evewy one of us will go and bwing in more wecwuits, and the sov'weign" (that was the way he referred to the Emperor) "need only say the word and we'll all die fo' him!" added the orator with animation.

Count Rostóv's mouth watered with pleasure and he nudged Pierre, but Pierre wanted to speak himself. He pushed forward, feeling stirred, but not yet sure what stirred him or what he would say. Scarcely had he opened his mouth when one of the senators, a man without a tooth in his head, with a shrewd though angry expression, standing near the first speaker, interrupted him. Evidently accustomed to managing debates and to maintaining an argument, he began in low but distinct tones:

"I imagine, sir," said he, mumbling with his toothless mouth, "that we have been summoned here not to discuss whether it's best for the empire at the present moment to adopt conscription or to call out the militia. We have been summoned to reply to the appeal with which our sovereign the Emperor has honored us. But to judge what is best—conscription or the militia—we can leave to the supreme authority. . . ."

Pierre suddenly saw an outlet for his excitement. He hardened his heart against the senator who was introducing this set and narrow attitude into the deliberations of the nobility. Pierre stepped forward and interrupted him. He himself did not yet know what he would say, but he began to speak eagerly, occasionally lapsing into French or expressing himself in bookish Russian.

"Excuse me, your excellency," he began. (He was well acquainted with the senator, but thought it necessary on this occasion to address him formally.) "Though I don't agree with the gentleman . . ." (he hesitated: he wished to say, "Mon très honorable préopinant"—"My very honorable opponent") "with the gentleman . . . whom I have not the

honor of knowing, I suppose that the nobility have been summoned not merely to express their sympathy and enthusiasm but also to consider the means by which we can assist our Fatherland! I imagine," he went on, warming to his subject, "that the Emperor himself would not be satisfied to find in us merely owners of serfs whom we are willing to devote to his service, and chair à canon [food for cannon] we are ready to make of ourselves—and not to obtain from us any co-co-counsel."

Many persons withdrew from the circle, noticing the senator's sarcastic smile and the freedom of Pierre's remarks. Only Count Rostóv was pleased with them as he had been pleased with those of the naval officer, the senator, and in general with whatever speech he had last heard.

"I think that before discussing these questions," Pierre continued, "we should ask the Emperor—most respectfully ask His Majesty—to let us know the number of our troops and the position in which our army and our forces now are, and then . . ."

But scarcely had Pierre uttered these words before he was attacked from three sides. The most vigorous attack came from an old acquaintance, a boston player who had always been well disposed toward him, Stepán Stepánovich Adráksin. Adráksin was in uniform, and whether as a result of the uniform or from some other cause Pierre saw before him quite a different man. With a sudden expression of malevolence on his aged face, Adráksin shouted at Pierre:

"In the first place, I tell you we have no right to question the Emperor about that, and secondly, if the Russian nobility had that right, the Emperor could not answer such a question. The troops are moved according to the enemy's movements and the number of men increases and decreases. . . ."

Another voice, that of a nobleman of medium height and about forty years of age, whom Pierre had formerly met at the gypsies' and knew as a bad cardplayer, and who, also transformed by his uniform, came up to Pierre, interrupted Adráksin.

"Yes, and this is not a time for discussing," he continued, "but for acting: there is war in Russia! The enemy is advancing to destroy Russia, to desecrate the tombs of our fathers, to carry off our wives and children." The nobleman smote his breast. "We will all arise, every one of us will go, for our father the Tsar!" * he shouted, rolling his bloodshot eyes. Several approving voices were heard in the crowd. "We are Russians and

* The ruler of Russia was, officially and properly speaking, the "Autocrat and Emperor," but in poetry and popular speech it was still permissible to refer to him as the "Tsar," though that word was more in place in fairy tales, as, for instance, when speaking of the "Tsar-Maid."

will not grudge our blood in defense of our faith, the throne, and the Fatherland! We must cease raving if we are sons of our Fatherland! We will show Europe how Russia rises to the defense of Russia!"

Pierre wished to reply, but could not get in a word. He felt that his words, apart from what meaning they conveyed, were less audible than the sound of his opponent's voice.

Count Rostóv at the back of the crowd was expressing approval; several persons, briskly turning a shoulder to the orator at the end of a phrase, said:

"That's right, quite right! Just so!"

Pierre wished to say that he was ready to sacrifice his money, his serfs, or himself, only one ought to know the state of affairs in order to be able to improve it, but he was unable to speak. Many voices shouted and talked at the same time, so that Count Rostóv had not time to signify his approval of them all, and the group increased, dispersed, re-formed, and then moved with a hum of talk into the largest hall and to the big table. Not only was Pierre's attempt to speak unsuccessful, but he was rudely interrupted, pushed aside, and people turned away from him as from a common enemy. This happened not because they were displeased by the substance of his speech, which had even been forgotten after the many subsequent speeches, but to animate it the crowd needed a tangible object to love and a tangible object to hate. Pierre became the latter. Many other orators spoke after the excited nobleman, and all in the same tone. Many spoke eloquently and with originality.

Glínka, the editor of the *Russian Messenger*,* who was recognized (cries of "author! author!" were heard in the crowd), said that "hell must be repulsed by hell," and that he had seen a child smiling at lightning flashes and thunderclaps, but "we will not be that child."

"Yes, yes, at thunderclaps!" was repeated approvingly in the back rows of the crowd.

The crowd drew up to the large table, at which sat gray-haired or bald seventy-year-old magnates, uniformed and besashed, almost all of whom Pierre had seen in their own homes with their buffoons, or playing boston at the clubs. With an incessant hum of voices the crowd advanced to the table. Pressed by the throng against the high backs of the chairs, the orators spoke one after another and sometimes two together. Those standing behind noticed what a speaker omitted to say and hastened to supply it. Others in that heat and crush racked their brains to find some

* S. N. Glínka (1776-1864), a prolific and patriotic writer, who in 1808 founded the Russian Messenger to counteract the French influence then prevalent. In 1812 he was resident and active in Moscow.—A.M.

thought and hastened to utter it. The old magnates, whom Pierre knew, sat and turned to look first at one and then at another, and their faces for the most part only expressed the fact that they found it very hot. Pierre, however, felt excited, and the general desire to show that they were ready to go to all lengths—which found expression in the tones and looks more than in the substance of the speeches—infected him too. He did not renounce his opinions, but felt himself in some way to blame and wished to justify himself.

"I only said that it would be more to the purpose to make sacrifices when we know what is needed!" said he, trying to be heard above the other voices.

One of the old men nearest to him looked round, but his attention was immediately diverted by an exclamation at the other side of the table.

"Yes, Moscow will be surrendered! She will be our expiation!" shouted one man.

"He is the enemy of mankind!" cried another. "Allow me to speak. . . ." "Gentlemen, you are crushing me! . . ."

23. Count Rostopchín's remarks. The offer made by the Moscow nobility and gentry. The Emperor's speech. Pierre offers to supply and maintain a thousand men

AT THAT MOMENT Count Rostopchín with his protruding chin and alert eyes, wearing the uniform of a general with sash over his shoulder, entered the room, stepping briskly to the front of the crowd of gentry.

"Our sovereign the Emperor will be here in a moment," said Rostopchín. "I am straight from the palace. Seeing the position we are in, I think there is little need for discussion. The Emperor has deigned to summon us and the merchants. Millions will pour forth from there"—he pointed to the merchants' hall—"but our business is to supply men and not spare ourselves. . . . That is the least we can do!"

A conference took place confined to the magnates sitting at the table. The whole consultation passed more than quietly. After all the preceding noise the sound of their old voices saying one after another, "I agree," or for variety, "I too am of that opinion," and so on had even a mournful effect.

The secretary was told to write down the resolution of the Moscow nobility and gentry, that they would furnish ten men, fully equipped, out of every thousand serfs, as the Smolénsk gentry had done. Their chairs made a scraping noise as the gentlemen who had conferred rose

with apparent relief, and began walking up and down, arm in arm, to stretch their legs and converse in couples.

"The Emperor! The Emperor!" a sudden cry resounded through the halls and the whole throng hurried to the entrance.

The Emperor entered the hall through a broad path between two lines of nobles. Every face expressed respectful, awe-struck curiosity. Pierre stood rather far off and could not hear all that the Emperor said. From what he did hear he understood that the Emperor spoke of the danger threatening the empire and of the hopes he placed on the Moscow nobility. He was answered by a voice which informed him of the resolution just arrived at.

"Gentlemen!" said the Emperor with a quivering voice.

There was a rustling among the crowd and it again subsided, so that Pierre distinctly heard the pleasantly human voice of the Emperor saying with emotion:

"I never doubted the devotion of the Russian nobles, but today it has surpassed my expectations. I thank you in the name of the Fatherland! Gentlemen, let us act! Time is most precious. . . ."

The Emperor ceased speaking, the crowd began pressing round him, and rapturous exclamations were heard from all sides.

"Yes, most precious . . . a royal word," said Count Rostóv, with a sob. He stood at the back, and, though he had heard hardly anything, understood everything in his own way.

From the hall of the nobility the Emperor went to that of the merchants. There he remained about ten minutes. Pierre was among those who saw him come out from the merchants' hall with tears of emotion in his eyes. As became known later, he had scarcely begun to address the merchants before tears gushed from his eyes and he concluded in a trembling voice. When Pierre saw the Emperor he was coming out accompanied by two merchants, one of whom Pierre knew, a fat otkupshchík.* The other was the mayor, a man with a thin sallow face and narrow beard. Both were weeping. Tears filled the thin man's eyes, and the fat otkupshchík sobbed outright like a child and kept repeating:

"Our lives and property—take them, Your Majesty!"

Pierre's one feeling at the moment was a desire to show that he was ready to go all lengths and was prepared to sacrifice everything. He now felt ashamed of his speech with its constitutional tendency and sought an opportunity of effacing it. Having heard that Count Mamónov was

* A *dealer in spirits*—one who leased from the government the monopoly of the sale of spirits for a certain district.—A.M.

furnishing a regiment, Bezúkhov at once informed Rostopchín that he would give a thousand men and their maintenance.

Old Rostóv could not tell his wife of what had passed without tears, and at once consented to Pétya's request and went himself to enter his name.

Next day the Emperor left Moscow. The assembled nobles all took off their uniforms and settled down again in their homes and clubs, and not without some groans gave orders to their stewards about the enrollment, feeling amazed themselves at what they had done.

BOOK TEN

DATES OF PRINCIPAL HISTORICAL EVENTS

1812

OLD STYLE	NEW STYLE	
Aug. 4	Aug. 16	Alpátych at Smolénsk hears distant firing.
Aug. 5	Aug. 17	Bombardment of Smolénsk.
Aug. 7	Aug. 19	Prince Nicholas Bolkónski leaves Bald Hills for Boguchárovo.
Aug. 8	Aug. 20	Kutúzov appointed Commander in Chief.
Aug. 10	Aug. 22	Prince Andrew's column abreast of Bald Hills.
Aug. 17	Aug. 29	Kutúzov reaches Tsárevo-Zaymíshche and takes command of the army.
Aug. 17	Aug. 29	Nicholas Rostóv rides to Boguchárovo.
Aug. 24	Sept. 5	Battle of the Shevárdino Redoubt.
Aug. 26	Sept. 7	Battle of Borodinó.

BORODINÓ

0 1 2 Versts

0 1000 2000 Yards

N

R. Moskvá

Máloe

Nóvoe

Bezzúbova

Position of the French

Zakhárino

R. Vóyna

Borodinó

Actual position of the Russians

Górki

High road to Mozháysk and Moscow

Tatárinova

Knyazkóvo

Psárevo

from Smolénsk

Raevski
Redoubt

Proposed position

position of the

Seménovsk

Proposed

Actual

Position of the French

Valuévo

Aléxinka

Russians Smolénsk to Moscow

Shevárdino

Shevárdino
Redoubt

R. Kolochá

Doronino

Utítsa

Old road from

1812

BOOK TEN

1. Reflections on the campaign of 1812. The course of events was fortuitous and unforeseen by either side

NAPOLEON BEGAN the war with Russia because he could not resist going to Dresden, could not help having his head turned by the homage he received, could not help donning a Polish uniform and yielding to the stimulating influence of a June morning, and could not refrain from bursts of anger in the presence of Kurákin and then of Balashëv.

Alexander refused negotiations because he felt himself to be personally insulted. Barclay de Tolly tried to command the army in the best way, because he wished to fulfill his duty and earn fame as a great commander. Rostóv charged the French because he could not restrain his wish for a gallop across a level field; and in the same way the innumerable people who took part in the war acted in accord with their personal characteristics, habits, circumstances, and aims. They were moved by fear or vanity, rejoiced or were indignant, reasoned, imagining that they knew what they were doing and did it of their own free will, but they all were involuntary tools of history, carrying on a work concealed from them but comprehensible to us. Such is the inevitable fate of men of action, and the higher they stand in the social hierarchy the less are they free.

The actors of 1812 have long since left the stage, their personal interests have vanished leaving no trace, and nothing remains of that time but its historic results.

Providence compelled all these men, striving to attain personal aims, to further the accomplishment of a stupendous result no one of them at all expected—neither Napoleon, nor Alexander, nor still less any of those who did the actual fighting.

The cause of the destruction of the French army in 1812 is clear to us now. No one will deny that that cause was, on the one hand, its advance into the heart of Russia late in the season without any preparation for a winter campaign and, on the other, the character given to the war by the burning of Russian towns and the hatred of the foe this aroused among

the Russian people. But no one at the time foresaw (what now seems so evident) that this was the only way an army of eight hundred thousand men—the best in the world and led by the best general—could be destroyed in conflict with a raw army of half its numerical strength, and led by inexperienced commanders as the Russian army was. *Not only did no one see this*, but on the Russian side every effort was made to hinder the only thing that could save Russia, while on the French side, despite Napoleon's experience and so-called military genius, every effort was directed to pushing on to Moscow at the end of the summer, that is, to doing the very thing that was bound to lead to destruction.

In historical works on the year 1812 French writers are very fond of saying that Napoleon felt the danger of extending his line, that he sought a battle and that his marshals advised him to stop at Smolénsk, and of making similar statements to show that the danger of the campaign was even then understood. Russian authors are still fonder of telling us that from the commencement of the campaign a Scythian war plan was adopted to lure Napoleon into the depths of Russia, and this plan some of them attribute to Pfuel, others to a certain Frenchman, others to Toll, and others again to Alexander himself—pointing to notes, projects, and letters which contain hints of such a line of action. But all these hints at what happened, both from the French side and the Russian, are advanced only because they fit in with the event. Had that event not occurred these hints would have been forgotten, as we have forgotten the thousands and millions of hints and expectations to the contrary which were current then but have now been forgotten because the event falsified them. There are always so many conjectures as to the issue of any event that however it may end there will always be people to say: "I said then that it would be so," quite forgetting that amid their innumerable conjectures many were to quite the contrary effect.

Conjectures as to Napoleon's awareness of the danger of extending his line, and (on the Russian side) as to luring the enemy into the depths of Russia, are evidently of that kind, and only by much straining can historians attribute such conceptions to Napoleon and his marshals, or such plans to the Russian commanders. All the facts are in flat contradiction to such conjectures. During the whole period of the war not only was there no wish on the Russian side to draw the French into the heart of the country, but from their first entry into Russia everything was done to stop them. And not only was Napoleon not afraid to extend his line, but he welcomed every step forward as a triumph and did not seek battle as eagerly as in former campaigns, but very lazily.

At the very beginning of the war our armies were divided, and our sole

aim was to unite them, though uniting the armies was no advantage if we meant to retire and lure the enemy into the depths of the country. Our Emperor joined the army to encourage it to defend every inch of Russian soil and not to retreat. The enormous Drissa camp was formed on Pfuel's plan, and there was no intention of retiring farther. The Emperor reproached the commanders in chief for every step they retired. He could not bear the idea of letting the enemy even reach Smolénsk, still less could he contemplate the burning of Moscow, and when our armies did unite he was displeased that Smolénsk was abandoned and burned without a general engagement having been fought under its walls.

So thought the Emperor, and the Russian commanders and people were still more provoked at the thought that our forces were retreating into the depths of the country.

Napoleon having cut our armies apart advanced far into the country and missed several chances of forcing an engagement. In August he was at Smolénsk and thought only of how to advance farther, though as we now see that advance was evidently ruinous to him.

The facts clearly show that Napoleon did not foresee the danger of the advance on Moscow, nor did Alexander and the Russian commanders then think of luring Napoleon on, but quite the contrary. The luring of Napoleon into the depths of the country was not the result of any plan, for no one believed it to be possible; it resulted from a most complex interplay of intrigues, aims, and wishes among those who took part in the war and had no perception whatever of the inevitable, or of the one way of saving Russia. Everything came about fortuitously. The armies were divided at the commencement of the campaign. We tried to unite them, with the evident intention of giving battle and checking the enemy's advance, and by this effort to unite them while avoiding battle with a much stronger enemy, and necessarily withdrawing the armies at an acute angle—we led the French on to Smolénsk. But we withdrew at an acute angle not only because the French advanced between our two armies; the angle became still more acute and we withdrew still farther, because Barclay de Tolly was an unpopular foreigner disliked by Bagratión (who would come under his command), and Bagratión—being in command of the second army—tried to postpone joining up and coming under Barclay's command as long as he could. Bagratión was slow in effecting the junction—though that was the chief aim of all at headquarters—because, as he alleged, he exposed his army to danger on this march, and it was best for him to retire more to the left and more to the south, worrying the enemy from flank and rear and securing from the Ukraine recruits for his army; and it looks as if he planned this in order not

to come under the command of the detested foreigner Barclay, whose rank was inferior to his own.

The Emperor was with the army to encourage it, but his presence and ignorance of what steps to take, and the enormous number of advisers and plans, destroyed the first army's energy and it retired.

The intention was to make a stand at the Drissa camp, but Paulucci, aiming at becoming commander in chief, unexpectedly employed his energy to influence Alexander, and Pfuel's whole plan was abandoned and the command entrusted to Barclay. But as Barclay did not inspire confidence his power was limited. The armies were divided, there was no unity of command, and Barclay was unpopular; but from this confusion, division, and the unpopularity of the foreign commander in chief, there resulted on the one hand indecision and the avoidance of a battle (which we could not have refrained from had the armies been united and had someone else, instead of Barclay, been in command) and on the other an ever-increasing indignation against the foreigners and an increase in patriotic zeal.

At last the Emperor left the army, and as the most convenient and indeed the only pretext for his departure it was decided that it was necessary for him to inspire the people in the capitals and arouse the nation in general to a patriotic war. And by this visit of the Emperor to Moscow the strength of the Russian army was trebled.

He left in order not to obstruct the commander in chief's undivided control of the army, and hoping that more decisive action would then be taken, but the command of the armies became still more confused and enfeebled. Bennigsen, the Tsarévich, and a swarm of adjutants general remained with the army to keep the commander in chief under observation and arouse his energy, and Barclay, feeling less free than ever under the observation of all these "eyes of the Emperor," became still more cautious of undertaking any decisive action and avoided giving battle.

Barclay stood for caution. The Tsarévich hinted at treachery and demanded a general engagement. Lubomírski, Bronnítski, Wlocki, and the others of that group stirred up so much trouble that Barclay, under pretext of sending papers to the Emperor, dispatched these Polish adjutants general to Petersburg and plunged into an open struggle with Bennigsen and the Tsarévich.

At Smolénsk the armies at last reunited, much as Bagratión disliked it.

Bagratión drove up in a carriage to the house occupied by Barclay. Barclay donned his sash and came out to meet and report to his senior officer Bagratión.

Despite his seniority in rank Bagratión, in this contest of magnanimity,

took his orders from Barclay, but, having submitted, agreed with him less than ever. By the Emperor's orders Bagratión reported direct to him. He wrote to Arakchéev, the Emperor's confidant: "It must be as my sovereign pleases, but I cannot work with the Minister (meaning Barclay). For God's sake send me somewhere else if only in command of a regiment. I cannot stand it here. Headquarters are so full of Germans that a Russian cannot exist and there is no sense in anything. I thought I was really serving my sovereign and the Fatherland, but it turns out that I am serving Barclay. I confess I do not want to."

The swarm of Bronnítskis and Wintzingerodes and their like still further embittered the relations between the commanders in chief, and even less unity resulted. Preparations were made to fight the French before Smolénsk. A general was sent to survey the position. This general, hating Barclay, rode to visit a friend of his own, a corps commander, and, having spent the day with him, returned to Barclay and condemned, as unsuitable from every point of view, the battleground he had not seen.

While disputes and intrigues were going on about the future field of battle, and while we were looking for the French—having lost touch with them—the French stumbled upon Nevérovski's division and reached the walls of Smolénsk.

It was necessary to fight an unexpected battle at Smolénsk to save our lines of communication. The battle was fought and thousands were killed on both sides.

Smolénsk was abandoned contrary to the wishes of the Emperor and of the whole people. But Smolénsk was burned by its own inhabitants who had been misled by their governor. And these ruined inhabitants, setting an example to other Russians, went to Moscow thinking only of their own losses but kindling hatred of the foe. Napoleon advanced farther and we retired, thus arriving at the very result which caused his destruction.

2. Prince N. Bolkónski and his daughter. His break with Mlle Bourienne. Mary's correspondence with Julie. The old prince receives a letter from Prince Andrew but does not grasp its meaning and confuses the present invasion with the Polish campaign of 1807

THE DAY after his son had left, Prince Nicholas sent for Princess Mary to come to his study. "Well? Are you satisfied now?" said he. "You've made me quarrel with

my son! Satisfied, are you? That's all you wanted! Satisfied? . . . It hurts me, it hurts. I'm old and weak and this is what you wanted. Well then, gloat over it! Gloat over it!"

After that Princess Mary did not see her father for a whole week. He was ill and did not leave his study.

Princess Mary noticed to her surprise that during this illness the old prince not only excluded her from his room, but did not admit Mademoiselle Bourienne either. Tíkhon alone attended him.

At the end of the week the prince reappeared and resumed his former way of life, devoting himself with special activity to building operations and the arrangement of the gardens and completely breaking off his relations with Mademoiselle Bourienne. His looks and cold tone to his daughter seemed to say: "There, you see? You plotted against me, you lied to Prince Andrew about my relations with that Frenchwoman and made me quarrel with him, but you see I need neither her nor you!"

Princess Mary spent half of every day with little Nicholas, watching his lessons, teaching him Russian and music herself, and talking to Dessalles; the rest of the day she spent over her books, with her old nurse, or with "God's folk" who sometimes came by the back door to see her.

Of the war Princess Mary thought as women do think about wars. She feared for her brother who was in it, was horrified by and amazed at the strange cruelty that impels men to kill one another, but she did not understand the significance of this war, which seemed to her like all previous wars. She did not realize the significance of this war, though Dessalles with whom she constantly conversed was passionately interested in its progress and tried to explain his own conception of it to her, and though the "God's folk" who came to see her reported, in their own way, the rumors current among the people of an invasion by Antichrist, and though Julie (now Princess Drubetskáya), who had resumed correspondence with her, wrote patriotic letters from Moscow.

"I write you in Russian, my good friend," wrote Julie in her Frenchified Russian, "because I have a detestation for all the French, and the same for their language which I cannot support to hear spoken. . . . We in Moscow are elated by enthusiasm for our adored Emperor.

"My poor husband is enduring pains and hunger in Jewish taverns, but the news which I have inspires me yet more.

"You heard probably of the heroic exploit of Raévski, embracing his two sons and saying: 'I will perish with them but we will not be shaken!' And truly though the enemy was twice stronger than we, we were unshakable. We pass the time as we can, but in war as in war! The princesses Aline and Sophie sit whole days with me, and we, unhappy widows of

live men, make beautiful conversations over our *charpie,* only you, my friend, are missing . . ." and so on.*

The chief reason Princess Mary did not realize the full significance of this war was that the old prince never spoke of it, did not recognize it, and laughed at Dessalles when he mentioned it at dinner. The prince's tone was so calm and confident that Princess Mary unhesitatingly believed him.

All that July the old prince was exceedingly active and even animated. He planned another garden and began a new building for the domestic serfs. The only thing that made Princess Mary anxious about him was that he slept very little and, instead of sleeping in his study as usual, changed his sleeping place every day. One day he would order his camp bed to be set up in the glass gallery, another day he remained on the couch or on the lounge chair in the drawing room and dozed there without undressing, while—instead of Mademoiselle Bourienne—a serf boy read to him. Then again he would spend a night in the dining room.

On August 1, a second letter was received from Prince Andrew. In his first letter which came soon after he had left home, Prince Andrew had dutifully asked his father's forgiveness for what he had allowed himself to say and begged to be restored to his favor. To this letter the old prince had replied affectionately, and from that time had kept the Frenchwoman at a distance. Prince Andrew's second letter, written near Vítebsk after the French had occupied that town, gave a brief account of the whole campaign, enclosed for them a plan he had drawn and forecasts as to the further progress of the war. In this letter Prince Andrew pointed out to his father the danger of staying at Bald Hills, so near the theater of war and on the army's direct line of march, and advised him to move to Moscow.

At dinner that day, on Dessalles' mentioning that the French were said to have already entered Vítebsk, the old prince remembered his son's letter.

"There was a letter from Prince Andrew today," he said to Princess Mary—"Haven't you read it?"

"No, Father," she replied in a frightened voice.

She could not have read the letter as she did not even know it had arrived.

* *In this letter Tolstóy indicates the artificiality of the patriotic enthusiasm of the Frenchified circles of Russian nobility, who could not even express aversion for the French language except in phrases obviously modeled on a French construction to which they were habituated.*—A.M.

"He writes about this war," said the prince, with the ironic smile that had become habitual to him in speaking of the present war.

"That must be very interesting," said Dessalles. "Prince Andrew is in a position to know . . ."

"Oh, very interesting!" said Mademoiselle Bourienne.

"Go and get it for me," said the old prince to Mademoiselle Bourienne. "You know—under the paperweight on the little table."

Mademoiselle Bourienne jumped up eagerly.

"No, don't!" he exclaimed with a frown. "You go, Michael Ivánovich."

Michael Ivánovich rose and went to the study. But as soon as he had left the room the old prince, looking uneasily round, threw down his napkin and went himself.

"They can't do anything . . . always make some muddle," he muttered.

While he was away Princess Mary, Dessalles, Mademoiselle Bourienne, and even little Nicholas exchanged looks in silence. The old prince returned with quick steps, accompanied by Michael Ivánovich, bringing the letter and a plan. These he put down beside him—not letting anyone read them at dinner.

On moving to the drawing room he handed the letter to Princess Mary and, spreading out before him the plan of the new building and fixing his eyes upon it, told her to read the letter aloud. When she had done so Princess Mary looked inquiringly at her father. He was examining the plan, evidently engrossed in his own ideas.

"What do you think of it, Prince?" Dessalles ventured to ask.

"I? I? . . ." said the prince as if unpleasantly awakened, and not taking his eyes from the plan of the building.

"Very possibly the theater of war will move so near to us that . . ."

"Ha ha ha! The theater of war!" said the prince. "I have said and still say that the theater of war is Poland and the enemy will never get beyond the Niemen."

Dessalles looked in amazement at the prince, who was talking of the Niemen when the enemy was already at the Dnieper, but Princess Mary, forgetting the geographical position of the Niemen, thought that what her father was saying was correct.

"When the snow melts they'll sink in the Polish swamps. Only they could fail to see it," the prince continued, evidently thinking of the campaign of 1807 which seemed to him so recent. "Bennigsen should have advanced into Prussia sooner, then things would have taken a different turn . . ."

"But, Prince," Dessalles began timidly, "the letter mentions Vítebsk. . . ."

"Ah, the letter? Yes . . ." replied the prince peevishly. "Yes . . . yes . . ." His face suddenly took on a morose expression. He paused. "Yes, he writes that the French were beaten at . . . at . . . what river is it?"

Dessalles dropped his eyes.

"The prince says nothing about that," he remarked gently.

"Doesn't he? But I didn't invent it myself."

No one spoke for a long time.

"Yes . . . yes . . . Well, Michael Ivánovich," he suddenly went on, raising his head and pointing to the plan of the building, "tell me how you mean to alter it. . . ."

Michael Ivánovich went up to the plan, and the prince after speaking to him about the new building looked angrily at Princess Mary and Dessalles and went to his own room.

Princess Mary saw Dessalles' embarrassed and astonished look fixed on her father, noticed his silence, and was struck by the fact that her father had forgotten his son's letter on the drawing-room table; but she was not only afraid to speak of it and ask Dessalles the reason of his confusion and silence, but was afraid even to think about it.

In the evening Michael Ivánovich, sent by the prince, came to Princess Mary for Prince Andrew's letter which had been forgotten in the drawing room. She gave it to him and, unpleasant as it was to her to do so, ventured to ask him what her father was doing.

"Always busy," replied Michael Ivánovich with a respectfully ironic smile which caused Princess Mary to turn pale. "He's worrying very much about the new building. He has been reading a little, but now"—Michael Ivánovich went on, lowering his voice—"now he's at his desk, busy with his will, I expect." (One of the prince's favorite occupations of late had been the preparation of some papers he meant to leave at his death and which he called his "will.")

"And Alpátych is being sent to Smolénsk?" asked Princess Mary.

"Oh, yes, he has been waiting to start for some time."

3. The old prince sends Alpátych to Smolénsk with various commissions, and does not know where to have his bed placed. He remembers Prince Andrew's letter and reads and understands it

WHEN MICHAEL IVÁNOVICH returned to the study with the letter, the old prince, with spectacles on and a shade over his eyes, was sitting at his open bureau with screened candles, holding a paper in his outstretched hand, and in a somewhat dramatic attitude was reading his manuscript—his "Remarks" as he termed it—which was to be transmitted to the Emperor after his death.

When Michael Ivánovich went in there were tears in the prince's eyes evoked by the memory of the time when the paper he was now reading had been written. He took the letter from Michael Ivánovich's hand, put it in his pocket, folded up his papers, and called in Alpátych who had long been waiting.

The prince had a list of things to be bought in Smolénsk and, walking up and down the room past Alpátych who stood by the door, he gave his instructions.

"First, notepaper—do you hear? Eight quires, like this sample, gilt-edged . . . it must be exactly like the sample. Varnish, sealing wax, as in Michael Ivánovich's list."

He paced up and down for a while and glanced at his notes.

"Then hand to the governor in person a letter about the deed."

Next, bolts for the doors of the new building were wanted and had to be of a special shape the prince had himself designed, and a leather case had to be ordered to keep the "will" in.

The instructions to Alpátych took over two hours and still the prince did not let him go. He sat down, sank into thought, closed his eyes, and dozed off. Alpátych made a slight movement.

"Well, go, go! If anything more is wanted I'll send after you."

Alpátych went out. The prince again went to his bureau, glanced into it, fingered his papers, closed the bureau again, and sat down at the table to write to the governor.

It was already late when he rose after sealing the letter. He wished to sleep, but he knew he would not be able to and that most depressing thoughts came to him in bed. So he called Tíkhon and went through the rooms with him to show him where to set up the bed for that night.

He went about looking at every corner. Every place seemed unsatis-

factory, but worst of all was his customary couch in the study. That couch was dreadful to him, probably because of the oppressive thoughts he had had when lying there. It was unsatisfactory everywhere, but the corner behind the piano in the sitting room was better than other places: he had never slept there yet.

With the help of a footman Tíkhon brought in the bedstead and began putting it up.

"That's not right! That's not right!" cried the prince, and himself pushed it a few inches from the corner and then closer in again.

"Well, at last I've finished, now I'll rest," thought the prince, and let Tíkhon undress him.

Frowning with vexation at the effort necessary to divest himself of his coat and trousers, the prince undressed, sat down heavily on the bed, and appeared to be meditating as he looked contemptuously at his withered yellow legs. He was not meditating, but only deferring the moment of making the effort to lift those legs up and turn over on the bed. "Ugh, how hard it is! Oh, that this toil might end and you would release me!" thought he. Pressing his lips together he made that effort for the twenty-thousandth time and lay down. But hardly had he done so before he felt the bed rocking backwards and forwards beneath him as if it were breathing heavily and jolting. This happened to him almost every night. He opened his eyes as they were closing.

"No peace, damn them!" he muttered, angry he knew not with whom. "Ah yes, there was something else important, very important, that I was keeping till I should be in bed. The bolts? No, I told him about them. No, it was something, something in the drawing room. Princess Mary talked some nonsense. Dessalles, that fool, said something. Something in my pocket—can't remember. . . ."

"Tíkhon, what did we talk about at dinner?"

"About Prince Michael . . ."

"Be quiet, quiet!" The prince slapped his hand on the table. "Yes, I know, Prince Andrew's letter! Princess Mary read it. Dessalles said something about Vítebsk. Now I'll read it."

He had the letter taken from his pocket and the table—on which stood a glass of lemonade and a spiral wax candle—moved close to the bed, and putting on his spectacles he began reading. Only now in the stillness of the night, reading it by the faint light under the green shade, did he grasp its meaning for a moment.

"The French at Vítebsk, in four days' march they may be at Smolénsk; perhaps are already there! Tíkhon!" Tíkhon jumped up. "No, no, I don't want anything!" he shouted.

He put the letter under the candlestick and closed his eyes. And there rose before him the Danube at bright noonday: reeds, the Russian camp, and himself a young general without a wrinkle on his ruddy face, vigorous and alert, entering Potëmkin's gaily colored tent, and a burning sense of jealousy of "the favorite" agitated him now as strongly as it had done then. He recalled all the words spoken at that first meeting with Potëmkin. And he saw before him a plump, rather sallow-faced, short, stout woman, the Empress Mother, with her smile and her words at her first gracious reception of him, and then that same face on the catafalque, and the encounter he had with Zúbov over her coffin about his right to kiss her hand.

"Oh, quicker, quicker! To get back to that time and have done with all the present! Quicker, quicker—and that they should leave me in peace!"

4. *Princess Mary sends a letter to the Governor at Smolénsk.
Alpátych sets off on August 4; reaches Smolénsk that eve-
ning and stays at Ferapóntov's inn. Firing heard outside the
town. Next day he does his business, but finds alarm spread-
ing, and is advised by the Governor that the Bolkónskis had
better go to Moscow. The town bombarded. Ferapóntov's
cook has her thigh broken by a shell. Retreating soldiers loot
Ferapóntov's shop and he declares he will set his place on fire
himself and not leave it to the French. Alpátych meets Prince
Andrew, who has an encounter with Berg*

B ALD HILLS, Prince Nicholas Bolkónski's estate, lay forty miles east from Smolénsk and two miles from the main road to Moscow.

The same evening that the prince gave his instructions to Alpátych, Dessalles, having asked to see Princess Mary, told her that, as the prince was not very well and was taking no steps to secure his safety, though from Prince Andrew's letter it was evident that to remain at Bald Hills might be dangerous, he respectfully advised her to send a letter by Alpátych to the Provincial Governor at Smolénsk, asking him to let her know the state of affairs and the extent of the danger to which Bald Hills was exposed. Dessalles wrote this letter to the Governor for Princess Mary, she signed it, and it was given to Alpátych with instructions to hand it to the Governor and to come back as quickly as possible if there was danger.

Having received all his orders Alpátych, wearing a white beaver hat—a present from the prince—and carrying a stick as the prince did, went out

accompanied by his family. Three well-fed roans stood ready harnessed to a small conveyance with a leather hood.

The larger bell was muffled and the little bells on the harness stuffed with paper. The prince allowed no one at Bald Hills to drive with ringing bells, but on a long journey Alpátych liked to have them. His satellites— the senior clerk, a countinghouse clerk, a scullery maid, a cook, two old women, a little pageboy, the coachman, and various domestic serfs—were seeing him off.

His daughter placed chintz-covered down cushions for him to sit on and behind his back. His old sister-in-law popped in a small bundle, and one of the coachmen helped him into the vehicle.

"There! There! Women's fuss! Women, women!" said Alpátych, puffing and speaking rapidly just as the prince did, and he climbed into the trap.

After giving the clerk orders about the work to be done, Alpátych, not trying to imitate the prince now, lifted the hat from his bald head and crossed himself three times.

"If there is anything . . . come back, Yákov Alpátych! For Christ's sake think of us!" cried his wife, referring to the rumors of war and the enemy.

"Women, women! Women's fuss!" muttered Alpátych to himself and started on his journey, looking round at the fields of yellow rye and the still-green, thickly growing oats, and at other quite black fields just being plowed a second time.

As he went along he looked with pleasure at the year's splendid crop of corn, scrutinized the strips of ryefield which here and there were already being reaped, made his calculations as to the sowing and the harvest, and asked himself whether he had not forgotten any of the prince's orders.

Having baited the horses twice on the way, he arrived at the town toward evening on the fourth of August.

Alpátych kept meeting and overtaking baggage trains and troops on the road. As he approached Smolénsk he heard the sounds of distant firing, but these did not impress him. What struck him most was the sight of a splendid field of oats in which a camp had been pitched and which was being mown down by the soldiers, evidently for fodder. This fact impressed Alpátych, but in thinking about his own business he soon forgot it.

All the interests of his life for more than thirty years had been bounded by the will of the prince, and he never went beyond that limit. Every-

thing not connected with the execution of the prince's orders did not interest and did not even exist for Alpátych.

On reaching Smolénsk on the evening of the fourth of August he put up in the Gáchina suburb across the Dnieper, at the inn kept by Ferapóntov, where he had been in the habit of putting up for the last thirty years.* Some thirty years ago Ferapóntov, by Alpátych's advice, had bought a wood from the prince, had begun to trade, and now had a house, an inn, and a corn dealer's shop in that province. He was a stout, dark, red-faced peasant in the forties, with thick lips, a broad knob of a nose, similar knobs over his black frowning brows, and a round belly.

Wearing a waistcoat over his cotton shirt, Ferapóntov was standing before his shop which opened onto the street. On seeing Alpátych he went up to him.

"You're welcome, Yákov Alpátych. Folks are leaving the town, but you have come to it," said he.

"Why are they leaving the town?" asked Alpátych.

"That's what I say. Folks are foolish! Always afraid of the French."

"Women's fuss, women's fuss!" said Alpátych.

"Just what I think, Yákov Alpátych. What I say is: orders have been given not to let them in, so that must be right. And the peasants are asking three rubles for carting—it isn't Christian!"

Yákov Alpátych heard without heeding. He asked for a samovar and for hay for his horses, and when he had had his tea he went to bed.

All night long troops were moving past the inn. Next morning Alpátych donned a jacket he wore only in town and went out on business. It was a sunny morning and by eight o'clock it was already hot. "A good day for harvesting," thought Alpátych.

From beyond the town firing had been heard since early morning. At eight o'clock the booming of cannon was added to the sound of musketry. Many people were hurrying through the streets and there were many soldiers, but cabs were still driving about, tradesmen stood at their shops, and service was being held in the churches as usual. Alpátych went to the shops, to government offices, to the post office, and to the Governor's. In the offices and shops and at the post office everyone was talking about the army and about the enemy who was already attacking the town, everybody was asking what should be done, and all were trying to calm one another.

In front of the Governor's house Alpátych found a large number of

* Ferapóntov's hostel catered for travelers, which explains the fact, mentioned three pages farther on, that a vehicle (not otherwise accounted for) drove out of the yard.—A.M.

people, Cossacks, and a traveling carriage of the Governor's. At the porch he met two of the landed gentry, one of whom he knew. This man, an ex-captain of police, was saying angrily:

"It's no joke, you know! It's all very well if you're single. 'One man though undone is but one,' as the proverb says, but with thirteen in your family and all the property . . . They've brought us to utter ruin! What sort of governors are they to do. that? They ought to be hanged—the brigands! . . ."

"Oh come, that's enough!" said the other.

"What do I care? Let him hear! We're not dogs," said the ex-captain of police, and looking round he noticed Alpátych.

"Oh, Yákov Alpátych! What have you come for?"

"To see the Governor by his excellency's order," answered Alpátych, lifting his head and proudly thrusting his hand into the bosom of his coat as he always did when he mentioned the prince. . . . "He has ordered me to inquire into the position of affairs," he added.

"Yes, go and find out!" shouted the angry gentleman. "They've brought things to such a pass that there are no carts or anything! . . . There it is again, do you hear?" said he, pointing in the direction whence came the sounds of firing.

"They've brought us all to ruin . . . the brigands!" he repeated, and descended the porch steps.

Alpátych swayed his head * and went upstairs. In the waiting room were tradesmen, women, and officials, looking silently at one another. The door of the Governor's room opened and they all rose and moved forward. An official ran out, said some words to a merchant, called a stout official with a cross hanging on his neck to follow him, and vanished again, evidently wishing to avoid the inquiring looks and questions addressed to him. Alpátych moved forward and next time the official came out addressed him, one hand placed in the breast of his buttoned coat, and handed him two letters.

"To his Honor Baron Asch, from General in Chief Prince Bolkónski," he announced with such solemnity and significance that the official turned to him and took the letters.

A few minutes later the Governor received Alpátych and hurriedly said to him:

* *Russians have a habit of bending their heads from side to side to express dismay, surprise, or disapproval. An Englishman's nod is an affirmative and his shake of the head a negative sign, but we have no word for pokachál golovói, which signifies a motion of the head to left and right. That is what "swayed his head" stands for in this and similar passages.—A.M.*

"Inform the prince and princess that I knew nothing: I acted on the highest instructions—here . . ." and he handed a paper to Alpátych. "Still, as the prince is unwell my advice is that they should go to Moscow. I am just starting myself. Inform them . . ."

But the Governor did not finish: a dusty perspiring officer ran into the room and began to say something in French. The Governor's face expressed terror.

"Go," he said, nodding his head to Alpátych, and began questioning the officer.

Eager, frightened, helpless glances were turned on Alpátych when he came out of the Governor's room. Involuntarily listening now to the firing, which had drawn nearer and was increasing in strength, Alpátych hurried to his inn. The paper handed to him by the Governor said this:

"I assure you that the town of Smolénsk is not in the slightest danger as yet and it is unlikely that it will be threatened with any. I from the one side and Prince Bagratión from the other are marching to unite our forces before Smolénsk, which junction will be effected on the 22nd instant, and both armies with their united forces will defend our compatriots of the province entrusted to your care till our efforts shall have beaten back the enemies of our Fatherland, or till the last warrior in our valiant ranks has perished. From this you will see that you have a perfect right to reassure the inhabitants of Smolénsk, for those defended by two such brave armies may feel assured of victory." (Instructions from Barclay de Tolly to Baron Asch, the civil governor of Smolénsk, 1812.)

People were anxiously roaming about the streets.

Carts piled high with household utensils, chairs, and cupboards kept emerging from the gates of the yards and moving along the streets. Loaded carts stood at the house next to Ferapóntov's and women were wailing and lamenting as they said good-by. A small watchdog ran round barking in front of the harnessed horses.

Alpátych entered the innyard at a quicker pace than usual and went straight to the shed where his horses and trap were. The coachman was asleep. He woke him up, told him to harness, and went into the passage. From the host's room came the sounds of a child crying, the despairing sobs of a woman, and the hoarse angry shouting of Ferapóntov. The cook began running hither and thither in the passage like a frightened hen, just as Alpátych entered.

"He's done her to death. Killed the mistress! . . . Beat her . . . dragged her about so! . . ."

"What for?" asked Alpátych.

"She kept begging to go away. She's a woman! 'Take me away,' says she,

'don't let me perish with my little children! Folks,' she says, 'are all gone, so why,' she says, 'don't we go?' And he began beating and pulling her about so!"

At these words Alpátych nodded as if in approval, and not wishing to hear more went to the door of the room opposite the innkeeper's, where he had left his purchases.

"You brute, you murderer!" screamed a thin, pale woman who, with a baby in her arms and her kerchief torn from her head, burst through the door at that moment and down the steps into the yard.

Ferapóntov came out after her, but on seeing Alpátych adjusted his waistcoat, smoothed his hair, yawned, and followed Alpátych into the opposite room.

"Going already?" said he.

Alpátych, without answering or looking at his host, sorted his packages and asked how much he owed.

"We'll reckon up! Well, have you been to the Governor's?" asked Ferapóntov. "What has been decided?"

Alpátych replied that the Governor had not told him anything definite.

"With our business, how can we get away?" said Ferapóntov. "We'd have to pay seven rubles a cartload to Dorogobúzh and I tell them they're not Christians to ask it! Selivánov, now, did a good stroke last Thursday—sold flour to the army at nine rubles a sack. Will you have some tea?" he added.

While the horses were being harnessed Alpátych and Ferapóntov over their tea talked of the price of corn, the crops, and the good weather for harvesting.

"Well, it seems to be getting quieter," remarked Ferapóntov, finishing his third cup of tea and getting up. "Ours must have got the best of it. The orders were not to let them in. So we're in force, it seems. . . . They say the other day Matthew Iványch Plátov * drove them into the river Márina and drowned some eighteen thousand in one day."

Alpátych collected his parcels, handed them to the coachman who had come in, and settled up with the innkeeper. The noise of wheels, hoofs, and bells was heard from the gateway as a little trap passed out.

It was by now late in the afternoon. Half the street was in shadow, the other half brightly lit by the sun. Alpátych looked out of the window and went to the door. Suddenly the strange sound of a far-off whistling and

* *Plátov, hetman of the Cossack army, was one of the most popular Russian heroes of the war of 1812. On one occasion he nearly captured Napoleon.*—A.M.

thud was heard, followed by a boom of cannon blending into a dull roar that set the windows rattling.

He went out into the street: two men were running past toward the bridge. From different sides came whistling sounds and the thud of cannon balls and bursting shells falling on the town. But these sounds were hardly heard in comparison with the noise of the firing outside the town and attracted little attention from the inhabitants. The town was being bombarded by a hundred and thirty guns which Napoleon had ordered up after four o'clock. The people did not at once realize the meaning of this bombardment.

At first the noise of the falling bombs and shells only aroused curiosity. Ferapóntov's wife, who till then had not ceased wailing under the shed, became quiet and with the baby in her arms went to the gate, listening to the sounds and looking in silence at the people.

The cook and a shop assistant came to the gate. With lively curiosity everyone tried to get a glimpse of the projectiles as they flew over their heads. Several people came round the corner talking eagerly.

"What force!" remarked one. "Knocked the roof and ceiling all to splinters!"

"Routed up the earth like a pig," said another.

"That's grand, it bucks one up!" laughed the first. "Lucky you jumped aside, or it would have wiped you out!"

Others joined those men and stopped and told how cannon balls had fallen on a house close to them. Meanwhile still more projectiles, now with the swift sinister whistle of a cannon ball, now with the agreeable intermittent whistle of a shell, flew over people's heads incessantly, but not one fell close by, they all flew over. Alpátych was getting into his trap. The innkeeper stood at the gate.

"What are you staring at?" he shouted to the cook, who in her red skirt, with sleeves rolled up, swinging her bare elbows, had stepped to the corner to listen to what was being said.

"What marvels!" she exclaimed, but hearing her master's voice she turned back, pulling down her tucked-up skirt.

Once more something whistled, but this time quite close, swooping downwards like a little bird; a flame flashed in the middle of the street, something exploded, and the street was shrouded in smoke.

"Scoundrel, what are you doing?" shouted the innkeeper, rushing to the cook.

At that moment the pitiful wailing of women was heard from different sides, the frightened baby began to cry, and people crowded silently

with pale faces round the cook. The loudest sound in that crowd was her wailing.

"Oh-h-h! Dear souls, dear kind souls! Don't let me die! My good souls! . . ."

Five minutes later no one remained in the street. The cook, with her thigh broken by a shell splinter, had been carried into the kitchen. Alpátych, his coachman, Ferapóntov's wife and children and the house porter were all sitting in the cellar, listening. The roar of guns, the whistling of projectiles, and the piteous moaning of the cook, which rose above the other sounds, did not cease for a moment. The mistress rocked and hushed her baby and when anyone came into the cellar asked in a pathetic whisper what had become of her husband who had remained in the street. A shopman who entered told her that her husband had gone with others to the cathedral, whence they were fetching the wonder-working icon of Smolénsk.

Toward dusk the cannonade began to subside. Alpátych left the cellar and stopped in the doorway. The evening sky that had been so clear was clouded with smoke, through which, high up, the sickle of the new moon shone strangely. Now that the terrible din of the guns had ceased a hush seemed to reign over the town, broken only by the rustle of footsteps, the moaning, the distant cries, and the crackle of fires which seemed widespread everywhere. The cook's moans had now subsided. On two sides black curling clouds of smoke rose and spread from the fires. Through the streets soldiers in various uniforms walked or ran confusedly in different directions like ants from a ruined anthill. Several of them ran into Ferapóntov's yard before Alpátych's eyes. Alpátych went out to the gate. A retreating regiment, thronging and hurrying, blocked the street.

Noticing him, an officer said: "The town is being abandoned. Get away, get away!" and then, turning to the soldiers, shouted:

"I'll teach you to run into the yards!"

Alpátych went back to the house, called the coachman, and told him to set off. Ferapóntov's whole household came out too, following Alpátych and the coachman. The women, who had been silent till then, suddenly began to wail as they looked at the fires—the smoke and even the flames of which could be seen in the failing twilight—and as if in reply the same kind of lamentation was heard from other parts of the street. Inside the shed Alpátych and the coachman arranged the tangled reins and traces of their horses with trembling hands.

As Alpátych was driving out of the gate he saw some ten soldiers in Ferapóntov's open shop, talking loudly and filling their bags and knapsacks with flour and sunflower seeds. Just then Ferapóntov returned and

entered his shop. On seeing the soldiers he was about to shout at them, but suddenly stopped and, clutching at his hair, burst into sobs and laughter:

"Loot everything, lads! Don't let those devils get it!" he cried, taking some bags of flour himself and throwing them into the street.

Some of the soldiers were frightened and ran away, others went on filling their bags. On seeing Alpátych, Ferapóntov turned to him:

"Russia is done for!" he cried. "Alpátych, I'll set the place on fire myself. We're done for! . . ." and Ferapóntov ran into the yard.

Soldiers were passing in a constant stream along the street blocking it completely, so that Alpátych could not pass out and had to wait. Ferapóntov's wife and children were also sitting in a cart waiting till it was possible to drive out.

Night had come. There were stars in the sky and the new moon shone out amid the smoke that screened it. On the sloping descent to the Dnieper Alpátych's cart and that of the innkeeper's wife, which were slowly moving amid the rows of soldiers and of other vehicles, had to stop. In a side street near the crossroads where the vehicles had stopped, a house and some shops were on fire. This fire was already burning itself out. The flames now died down and were lost in the black smoke, now suddenly flared up again brightly, lighting up with strange distinctness the faces of the people crowding at the crossroads. Black figures flitted about before the fire, and through the incessant crackling of the flames talking and shouting could be heard. Seeing that his trap would not be able to move on for some time, Alpátych got down and turned into the side street to look at the fire. Soldiers were continually rushing backwards and forwards near it, and he saw two of them and a man in a frieze coat dragging burning beams into another yard across the street, while others carried bundles of hay.

Alpátych went up to a large crowd standing before a high barn which was blazing briskly. The walls were all on fire and the back wall had fallen in, the wooden roof was collapsing, and the rafters were alight. The crowd was evidently watching for the roof to fall in, and Alpátych watched for it too.

"Alpátych!" a familiar voice suddenly hailed the old man.

"Mercy on us! Your excellency!" answered Alpátych, immediately recognizing the voice of his young prince.

Prince Andrew in his riding cloak, mounted on a black horse, was looking at Alpátych from the back of the crowd.

"Why are you here?" he asked.

"Your . . . your excellency," stammered Alpátych and broke into sobs. "Are we really lost? Master! . . ."

"Why are you here?" Prince Andrew repeated.

At that moment the flames flared up and showed his young master's pale worn face. Alpátych told how he had been sent there and how difficult it was to get away.

"Are we really quite lost, your excellency?" he asked again.

Prince Andrew without replying took out a notebook and raising his knee began writing in pencil on a page he tore out. He wrote to his sister:

"Smolénsk is being abandoned. Bald Hills will be occupied by the enemy within a week. Set off immediately for Moscow. Let me know at once when you will start. Send by special messenger to Usvyázh."

Having written this and given the paper to Alpátych, he told him how to arrange for the departure of the prince, the princess, his son, and the boy's tutor, and how and where to let him know immediately. Before he had had time to finish giving these instructions, a chief of staff followed by a suite galloped up to him.

"You are a colonel?" shouted the chief of staff with a German accent, in a voice familiar to Prince Andrew. "Houses are set on fire in your presence and you stand by! What does this mean? You will answer for it!" shouted Berg, who was now assistant to the chief of staff of the commander of the left flank of the infantry of the first army, a place, as Berg said, "very agreeable and well en évidence."

Prince Andrew looked at him and without replying went on speaking to Alpátych.

"So tell them that I shall await a reply till the tenth, and if by the tenth I don't receive news that they have all got away I shall have to throw up everything and come myself to Bald Hills."

"Prince," said Berg, recognizing Prince Andrew, "I only spoke because I have to obey orders, because I always do obey exactly. . . . You must please excuse me," he went on apologetically.

Something cracked in the flames. The fire died down for a moment and wreaths of black smoke rolled from under the roof. There was another terrible crash and something huge collapsed.

"Ou-rou-rou!" yelled the crowd, echoing the crash of the collapsing roof of the barn, the burning grain in which diffused a cakelike aroma all around. The flames flared up again, lighting the animated, delighted, exhausted faces of the spectators.

The man in the frieze coat raised his arms and shouted:

"It's fine, lads! Now it's raging . . . It's fine!"

"That's the owner himself," cried several voices.

"Well then," continued Prince Andrew to Alpátych, "report to them as I have told you"; and not replying a word to Berg who was now mute beside him, he touched his horse and rode down the side street.

5. *Prince Andrew passing Bald Hills with his regiment. The retreat: heat and terrible dust. He rides over to the house. The little girls and the plums. The soldiers bathe in a pond. "Cannon fodder." Bagratión's letter to Arakchéev*

FROM SMOLÉNSK the troops continued to retreat, followed by the enemy. On the tenth of August the regiment Prince Andrew commanded was marching along the highroad past the avenue leading to Bald Hills. Heat and drought had continued for more than three weeks. Each day fleecy clouds floated across the sky and occasionally veiled the sun, but toward evening the sky cleared again and the sun set in reddish-brown mist. Heavy night dews alone refreshed the earth. The unreaped corn was scorched and shed its grain. The marshes dried up. The cattle lowed from hunger, finding no food on the sun-parched meadows. Only at night and in the forests while the dew lasted was there any freshness. But on the road, the highroad along which the troops marched, there was no such freshness even at night or when the road passed through the forest; the dew was imperceptible on the sandy dust churned up more than six inches deep. As soon as day dawned the march began. The artillery and baggage wagons moved noiselessly through the deep dust that rose to the very hubs of the wheels, and the infantry sank ankle-deep in that soft, choking, hot dust that never cooled even at night. Some of this dust was kneaded by the feet and wheels, while the rest rose and hung like a cloud over the troops, settling in eyes, ears, hair, and nostrils, and worst of all in the lungs of the men and beasts as they moved along that road. The higher the sun rose the higher rose that cloud of dust, and through the screen of its hot fine particles one could look with naked eye at the sun, which showed like a huge crimson ball in the unclouded sky. There was no wind, and the men choked in that motionless atmosphere. They marched with handkerchiefs tied over their noses and mouths. When they passed through a village they all rushed to the wells and fought for the water and drank it down to the mud.

Prince Andrew was in command of a regiment, and the management of that regiment, the welfare of the men and the necessity of receiving and giving orders, engrossed him. The burning of Smolénsk and its abandonment made an epoch in his life. A novel feeling of anger against the foe

made him forget his own sorrow. He was entirely devoted to the affairs of his regiment and was considerate and kind to his men and officers. In the regiment they called him "our prince," were proud of him and loved him. But he was kind and gentle only to those of his regiment, to Timókhin and the like—people quite new to him, belonging to a different world and who could not know and understand his past. As soon as he came across a former acquaintance or anyone from the staff, he bristled up immediately and grew spiteful, ironical, and contemptuous. Everything that reminded him of his past was repugnant to him, and so in his relations with that former circle he confined himself to trying to do his duty and not to be unfair.

In truth everything presented itself in a dark and gloomy light to Prince Andrew, especially after the abandonment of Smolénsk on the sixth of August (he considered that it could and should have been defended) and after his sick father had had to flee to Moscow, abandoning to pillage his dearly beloved Bald Hills which he had built and peopled. But despite this, thanks to his regiment, Prince Andrew had something to think about entirely apart from general questions. Two days previously he had received news that his father, son, and sister had left for Moscow; and though there was nothing for him to do at Bald Hills, Prince Andrew with a characteristic desire to foment his own grief decided that he must ride there.

He ordered his horse to be saddled and, leaving his regiment on the march, rode to his father's estate where he had been born and spent his childhood. Riding past the pond where there used always to be dozens of women chattering as they rinsed their linen or beat it with wooden beetles, Prince Andrew noticed that there was not a soul about and that the little washing wharf, torn from its place and half submerged, was floating on its side in the middle of the pond. He rode to the keeper's lodge. No one was at the stone entrance gates of the drive and the door stood open. Grass had already begun to grow on the garden paths, and horses and calves were straying in the English park. Prince Andrew rode up to the hothouse; some of the glass panes were broken, and of the trees in tubs some were overturned and others dried up. He called for Tarás the gardener, but no one replied. Having gone round the corner of the hothouse to the ornamental garden, he saw that the carved garden fence was broken and branches of the plum trees had been torn off with the fruit. An old peasant whom Prince Andrew in his childhood had often seen at the gate was sitting on a green garden seat, plaiting a bast shoe.

He was deaf and did not hear Prince Andrew ride up. He was sitting on

the seat the old prince used to like to sit on, and beside him strips of bast were hanging on the broken and withered branch of a magnolia.

Prince Andrew rode up to the house. Several limes in the old garden had been cut down and a piebald mare and her foal were wandering in front of the house among the rosebushes. The shutters were all closed, except at one window which was open. A little serf boy, seeing Prince Andrew, ran into the house. Alpátych, having sent his family away, was alone at Bald Hills and was sitting indoors reading the *Lives of the Saints*. On hearing that Prince Andrew had come, he went out with his spectacles on his nose, buttoning his coat, and, hastily stepping up, without a word began weeping and kissing Prince Andrew's knee.

Then, vexed at his own weakness, he turned away and began to report on the position of affairs. Everything precious and valuable had been removed to Boguchárovo. Seventy quarters of grain had also been carted away. The hay and the spring corn, of which Alpátych said there had been a remarkable crop that year, had been commandeered by the troops and mown down while still green. The peasants were ruined; some of them too had gone to Boguchárovo, only a few remained.

Without waiting to hear him out, Prince Andrew asked:

"When did my father and sister leave?" meaning when did they leave for Moscow.

Alpátych, understanding the question to refer to their departure for Boguchárovo, replied that they had left on the seventh and again went into details concerning the estate management, asking for instructions.

"Am I to let the troops have the oats, and to take a receipt for them? We have still six hundred quarters left," he inquired.

"What am I to say to him?" thought Prince Andrew, looking down on the old man's bald head shining in the sun and seeing by the expression on his face that the old man himself understood how untimely such questions were and only asked them to allay his grief.

"Yes, let them have it," replied Prince Andrew.

"If you noticed some disorder in the garden," said Alpátych, "it was impossible to prevent it. Three regiments have been here and spent the night, dragoons mostly. I took down the name and rank of their commanding officer, to hand in a complaint about it."

"Well, and what are you going to do? Will you stay here if the enemy occupies the place?" asked Prince Andrew.

Alpátych turned his face to Prince Andrew, looked at him, and suddenly with a solemn gesture raised his arm.

"He is my refuge! His will be done!" he exclaimed.

A group of bareheaded peasants was approaching across the meadow toward the prince.

"Well, good-by!" said Prince Andrew, bending over to Alpátych. "You must go away too, take away what you can and tell the serfs to go to the Ryazán estate or to the one near Moscow."

Alpátych clung to Prince Andrew's leg and burst into sobs. Gently disengaging himself, the prince spurred his horse and rode down the avenue at a gallop.

The old man was still sitting in the ornamental garden, like a fly impassive on the face of a loved one who is dead, tapping the last on which he was making the bast shoe, and two little girls, running out from the hothouse carrying in their skirts plums they had plucked from the trees there, came upon Prince Andrew. On seeing the young master, the elder one with frightened look clutched her younger companion by the hand and hid with her behind a birch tree, not stopping to pick up some green plums they had dropped.

Prince Andrew turned away with startled haste, unwilling to let them see that they had been observed. He was sorry for the pretty frightened little girl, was afraid of looking at her, and yet felt an irresistible desire to do so. A new sensation of comfort and relief came over him when, seeing these girls, he realized the existence of other human interests entirely aloof from his own and just as legitimate as those that occupied him. Evidently these girls passionately desired one thing—to carry away and eat those green plums without being caught—and Prince Andrew shared their wish for the success of their enterprise. He could not resist looking at them once more. Believing their danger past, they sprang from their ambush and, chirruping something in their shrill little voices and holding up their skirts, their bare little sunburned feet scampered merrily and quickly across the meadow grass.

Prince Andrew was somewhat refreshed by having ridden off the dusty highroad along which the troops were moving. But not far from Bald Hills he again came out on the road and overtook his regiment at its halting place by the dam of a small pond. It was past one o'clock. The sun, a red ball through the dust, burned and scorched his back intolerably through his black coat. The dust always hung motionless above the buzz of talk that came from the resting troops. There was no wind. As he crossed the dam Prince Andrew smelled the ooze and freshness of the pond. He longed to get into that water, however dirty it might be, and he glanced round at the pool from whence came sounds of shrieks and laughter. The small, muddy, green pond had risen visibly more than a foot, flooding the dam, because it was full of the naked white bodies of soldiers with brick-

red hands, necks, and faces, who were splashing about in it. All this naked white human flesh, laughing and shrieking, floundered about in that dirty pool like carp stuffed into a watering can, and the suggestion of merriment in that floundering mass rendered it specially pathetic.

One fair-haired young soldier of the third company, whom Prince Andrew knew and who had a strap round the calf of one leg, crossed himself, stepped back to get a good run, and plunged into the water; another, a dark noncommissioned officer who was always shaggy, stood up to his waist in the water joyfully wriggling his muscular figure and snorted with satisfaction as he poured the water over his head with hands blackened to the wrists. There were sounds of men slapping one another, yelling, and puffing.

Everywhere on the bank, on the dam, and in the pond, there was healthy, white, muscular flesh. The officer, Timókhin, with his red little nose, standing on the dam wiping himself with a towel, felt confused at seeing the prince, but made up his mind to address him nevertheless.

"It's very nice, your excellency! Wouldn't you like to?" said he.

"It's dirty," replied Prince Andrew, making a grimace.

"We'll clear it out for you in a minute," said Timókhin, and, still undressed, ran off to clear the men out of the pond.

"The prince wants to bathe."

"What prince? Ours?" said many voices, and the men were in such haste to clear out that the prince could hardly stop them. He decided that he would rather souse himself with water in the barn.

"Flesh, bodies, cannon fodder!" he thought, and he looked at his own naked body and shuddered, not from cold but from a sense of disgust and horror he did not himself understand, aroused by the sight of that immense number of bodies splashing about in the dirty pond.

On the seventh of August Prince Bagratión wrote as follows from his quarters at Mikháylovka on the Smolénsk road:

"Dear Count Aléxis Andréevich"—(He was writing to Arakchéev but knew that his letter would be read by the Emperor, and therefore weighed every word in it to the best of his ability.)

"I expect the Minister" (Barclay de Tolly) "has already reported the abandonment of Smolénsk to the enemy. It is pitiable and sad, and the whole army is in despair that this most important place has been wantonly abandoned. I, for my part, begged him personally most urgently and finally wrote him, but nothing would induce him to consent. I swear to you on my honor that Napoleon was in such a fix as never before and might have lost half his army but could not have taken Smolénsk. Our troops

fought, and are fighting, as never before. With fifteen thousand men I held the enemy at bay for thirty-five hours and beat him; but he would not hold out even for fourteen hours. It is disgraceful, a stain on our army, and as for him, he ought, it seems to me, not to live. If he reports that our losses were great, it is not true; perhaps about four thousand, not more, and not even that; but even were they ten thousand, that's war! But the enemy has lost masses. . . .

"What would it have cost him to hold out for another two days? They would have had to retire of their own accord, for they had no water for men or horses. He gave me his word he would not retreat, but suddenly sent instructions that he was retiring that night. We cannot fight in this way, or we may soon bring the enemy to Moscow. . . .

"There is a rumor that you are thinking of peace. God forbid that you should make peace after all our sacrifices and such insane retreats! You would set all Russia against you and every one of us would feel ashamed to wear the uniform. If it has come to this—we must fight as long as Russia can and as long as there are men able to stand. . . .

"One man ought to be in command, and not two. Your Minister may perhaps be good as a Minister, but as a general he is not merely bad but execrable, yet to him is entrusted the fate of our whole country. . . . I am really frantic with vexation; forgive my writing boldly. It is clear that the man who advocates the conclusion of a peace, and that the Minister should command the army, does not love our sovereign and desires the ruin of us all. So I write you frankly: call out the militia. For the Minister is leading these visitors after him to Moscow in a most masterly way. The whole army feels great suspicion of the Imperial aide-de-camp Wolzogen. He is said to be more Napoleon's man than ours, and he is always advising the Minister. I am not merely civil to him but obey him like a corporal, though I am his senior. This is painful, but, loving my benefactor and sovereign, I submit. Only I am sorry for the Emperor that he entrusts our fine army to such as he. Consider that on our retreat we have lost by fatigue and left in the hospital more than fifteen thousand men, and had we attacked this would not have happened. Tell me, for God's sake, what will Russia, our mother Russia, say to our being so frightened, and why are we abandoning our good and gallant Fatherland to such rabble and implanting feelings of hatred and shame in all our subjects? What are we scared at and of whom are we afraid? I am not to blame that the Minister is vacillating, a coward, dense, dilatory, and has all bad qualities. The whole army bewails it and calls down curses upon him. . . ."

6. Matter and form. Anna Pávlovna's and Hélène's rival salons. Prince Vasíli's opinion of Kutúzov

AMONG THE innumerable categories applicable to the phenomena of human life one may discriminate between those in which substance prevails and those in which form prevails. To the latter—as distinguished from village, country, provincial, or even Moscow life—we may allot Petersburg life, and especially the life of its salons. That life of the salons is unchanging. Since the year 1805 we had made peace and had again quarreled with Bonaparte and had made constitutions and unmade them again, but the salons of Anna Pávlovna and Hélène remained just as they had been—the one seven and the other five years before. At Anna Pávlovna's they talked with perplexity of Bonaparte's successes just as before and saw in them and in the subservience shown to him by the European sovereigns a malicious conspiracy, the sole object of which was to cause unpleasantness and anxiety to the court circle of which Anna Pávlovna was the representative. And in Hélène's salon, which Rumyántsev * himself honored with his visits, regarding Hélène as a remarkably intelligent woman, they talked with the same ecstasy in 1812 as in 1808 of the "great nation" and the "great man," and regretted our rupture with France, a rupture which, according to them, ought to be promptly terminated by peace.[2]

Of late, since the Emperor's return from the army, there had been some excitement in these conflicting salon circles and some demonstrations of hostility to one another, but each camp retained its own tendency. In Anna Pávlovna's circle only those Frenchmen were admitted who were deep-rooted legitimists, and patriotic views were expressed to the effect that one ought not to go to the French theater and that to maintain the French troupe was costing the government as much as a whole army corps. The progress of the war was eagerly followed, and only the reports most flattering to our army were circulated. In the French circle of Hélène and Rumyántsev the reports of the cruelty of the enemy and of the war were contradicted and all Napoleon's attempts at conciliation were discussed. In that circle they discountenanced those who advised hurried preparations for a removal to Kazán of the court and the girls' educa-

* Count N. P. Rumyántsev had been Minister of Foreign Affairs in 1807, and in 1809 became Chancellor. The famous Rumyántsev Museum in Moscow was formed of collections presented by him.—A.M.

[2] The analogy between this appeasement group and the Cliveden set will be apparent.

tional establishments under the patronage of the Dowager Empress. In Hélène's circle the war in general was regarded as a series of formal demonstrations which would very soon end in peace, and the view prevailed expressed by Bilíbin—who now in Petersburg was quite at home in Hélène's house, which every clever man was obliged to visit—that not by gunpowder but by those who invented it would matters be settled. In that circle the Moscow enthusiasm—news of which had reached Petersburg simultaneously with the Emperor's return—was ridiculed sarcastically and very cleverly, though with much caution.

Anna Pávlovna's circle on the contrary was enraptured by this enthusiasm and spoke of it as Plutarch speaks of the deeds of the ancients. Prince Vasíli, who still occupied his former important posts, formed a connecting link between these two circles. He visited his "good friend Anna Pávlovna" as well as his daughter's "diplomatic salon," and often in his constant comings and goings between the two camps became confused and said at Hélène's what he should have said at Anna Pávlovna's and vice versa.

Soon after the Emperor's return Prince Vasíli in a conversation about the war at Anna Pávlovna's severely condemned Barclay de Tolly, but was undecided as to who ought to be appointed commander in chief. One of the visitors, usually spoken of as "a man of great merit," having described how he had that day seen Kutúzov, the newly chosen chief of the Petersburg militia, presiding over the enrollment of recruits at the Treasury, cautiously ventured to suggest that Kutúzov would be the man to satisfy all requirements.

Anna Pávlovna remarked with a melancholy smile that Kutúzov had done nothing but cause the Emperor annoyance.

"I have talked and talked at the Assembly of the Nobility," Prince Vasíli interrupted, "but they did not listen to me. I told them his election as chief of the militia would not please the Emperor. They did not listen to me.

"It's all this mania for opposition," he went on. "And who for? It is all because we want to ape the foolish enthusiasm of those Muscovites," Prince Vasíli continued, forgetting for a moment that though at Hélène's one had to ridicule the Moscow enthusiasm, at Anna Pávlovna's one had to be ecstatic about it. But he retrieved his mistake at once. "Now, is it suitable that Count Kutúzov, the oldest general in Russia, should preside at that tribunal? He will get nothing for his pains! How could they make a man commander in chief who cannot mount a horse, who drops asleep at a council, and has the very worst morals! A good reputation he made for himself at Bucharest! I don't speak of his capacity as a general, but

at a time like this how can they appoint a decrepit, blind old man, positively blind? A fine idea to have a blind general! He can't see anything. To play blindman's buff? He can't see at all!"

No one replied to his remarks.

This was quite correct on the twenty-fourth of July. But on the twenty-ninth of July Kutúzov received the title of Prince. This might indicate a wish to get rid of him, and therefore Prince Vasíli's opinion continued to be correct though he was not now in any hurry to express it. But on the eighth of August a committee, consisting of Field Marshal Saltykóv, Arakchéev, Vyazmítinov, Lopukhín, and Kochubéy met to consider the progress of the war. This committee came to the conclusion that our failures were due to a want of unity in the command and though the members of the committee were aware of the Emperor's dislike of Kutúzov, after a short deliberation they agreed to advise his appointment as commander in chief. That same day Kutúzov was appointed commander in chief with full powers over the armies and over the whole region occupied by them.

On the ninth of August Prince Vasíli at Anna Pávlovna's again met the "man of great merit." The latter was very attentive to Anna Pávlovna because he wanted to be appointed director of one of the educational establishments for young ladies. Prince Vasíli entered the room with the air of a happy conqueror who has attained the object of his desires.

"Well, have you heard the great news? Prince Kutúzov is field marshal! All dissensions are at an end! I am so glad, so delighted! At last we have a man!" said he, glancing sternly and significantly round at everyone in the drawing room.

The "man of great merit," despite his desire to obtain the post of director, could not refrain from reminding Prince Vasíli of his former opinion. Though this was impolite to Prince Vasíli in Anna Pávlovna's drawing room, and also to Anna Pávlovna herself who had received the news with delight, he could not resist the temptation.

"But, Prince, they say he is blind!" said he, reminding Prince Vasíli of his own words.

"Eh? Nonsense! He sees well enough," said Prince Vasíli rapidly, in a deep voice and with a slight cough—the voice and cough with which he was wont to dispose of all difficulties.

"He sees well enough," he added. "And what I am so pleased about," he went on, "is that our sovereign has given him full powers over all the armies and the whole region—powers no commander in chief ever had before. He is a second autocrat," he concluded with a victorious smile.

"God grant it! God grant it!" said Anna Pávlovna.

The "man of great merit," who was still a novice in court circles, wishing to flatter Anna Pávlovna by defending her former position on this question, observed:

"It is said that the Emperor was reluctant to give Kutúzov those powers. They say he blushed like a girl to whom Joconde * is read, when he said to Kutúzov: 'Your Emperor and the Fatherland award you this honor.' "

"Perhaps the heart took no part in that speech," said Anna Pávlovna.

"Oh, no, no!" warmly rejoined Prince Vasíli, who would not now yield Kutúzov to anyone; in his opinion Kutúzov was not only admirable himself, but was adored by everybody. "No, that's impossible," said he, "for our sovereign appreciated him so highly before."

"God grant only that Prince Kutúzov assumes real power and does not allow anyone to put a spoke in his wheel," observed Anna Pávlovna.

Understanding at once to whom she alluded, Prince Vasíli said in a whisper:

"I know for a fact that Kutúzov made it an absolute condition that the Tsarévich should not be with the army. Do you know what he said to the Emperor?"

And Prince Vasíli repeated the words supposed to have been spoken by Kutúzov to the Emperor. "I can neither punish him if he does wrong nor reward him if he does right."

"Oh, a very wise man is Prince Kutúzov! I have known him a long time!"

"They even say," remarked the "man of great merit" who did not yet possess courtly tact, "that his excellency made it an express condition that the sovereign himself should not be with the army."

As soon as he said this both Prince Vasíli and Anna Pávlovna turned away from him and glanced sadly at one another with a sigh at his naïveté.

7. Napoleon orders an advance on Moscow. Napoleon's conversation with Lavrúshka

WHILE THIS was taking place in Petersburg the French had already passed Smolénsk and were drawing nearer and nearer to Moscow. Napoleon's historian Thiers, like other of his historians, trying to justify his hero says that he was drawn to the walls of Moscow against his will. He is as right as other historians who look for the explanation of historic events in the will of one man; he is as right as the Russian historians who

* Joconde—*La Fontaine's first* Contes *in verse, which are considered improper.*—A.M.

maintain that Napoleon was drawn to Moscow by the skill of the Russian commanders. Here besides the law of retrospection, which regards all the past as a preparation for events that subsequently occur, the law of reciprocity comes in, confusing the whole matter. A good chessplayer having lost a game is sincerely convinced that his loss resulted from a mistake he made and looks for that mistake in the opening, but forgets that at each stage of the game there were similar mistakes and that none of his moves were perfect. He only notices the mistake to which he pays attention, because his opponent took advantage of it. How much more complex than this is the game of war, which occurs under certain limits of time, and where it is not one will that manipulates lifeless objects, but everything results from innumerable conflicts of various wills!

After Smolénsk Napoleon sought a battle beyond Dorogobúzh at Vyázma, and then at Tsárevo-Zaymíshche, but it happened that owing to a conjunction of innumerable circumstances the Russians could not give battle till they reached Borodinó, seventy miles from Moscow. From Vyázma Napoleon ordered a direct advance on Moscow.

Moscou, la capitale asiatique de ce grand empire, la ville sacrée des peuples d'Alexandre, Moscou avec ses innombrables églises en forme de pagodes chinoises [Moscow, the Asiatic capital of this great empire, the sacred city of Alexander's people, Moscow with its innumerable churches shaped like Chinese pagodas], this Moscow gave Napoleon's imagination no rest. On the march from Vyázma to Tsárevo-Zaymíshche he rode his light bay bobtailed ambler accompanied by his Guards, his bodyguard, his pages, and aides-de-camp. Berthier, his chief of staff, dropped behind to question a Russian prisoner captured by the cavalry. Followed by Lelorgne d'Ideville, an interpreter, he overtook Napoleon at a gallop and reined in his horse with an amused expression.

"Well?" asked Napoleon.

"One of Plátov's Cossacks says that Plátov's corps is joining up with the main army and that Kutúzov has been appointed commander in chief. He is a very shrewd and garrulous fellow."

Napoleon smiled and told them to give the Cossack a horse and bring the man to him. He wished to talk to him himself. Several adjutants galloped off, and an hour later, Lavrúshka, the serf Denísov had handed over to Rostóv, rode up to Napoleon in an orderly's jacket and on a French cavalry saddle, with a roguish, merry, and tipsy face. Napoleon told him to ride by his side and began questioning him.

"You are a Cossack?"

"Yes, a Cossack, your Honor."

"The Cossack, not knowing in what company he was, for Napoleon's

plain appearance had nothing about it that would reveal to an Oriental mind the presence of a monarch, talked with extreme familiarity of the incidents of the war," says Thiers, narrating this episode.* In reality Lavrúshka, having got drunk the day before and left his master dinnerless, had been whipped and sent to the village in quest of chickens, where he engaged in looting till the French took him prisoner. Lavrúshka was one of those coarse, bare-faced lackeys who have seen all sorts of things, consider it necessary to do everything in a mean and cunning way, are ready to render any sort of service to their master, and are keen at guessing their master's baser impulses, especially those prompted by vanity and pettiness.

Finding himself in the company of Napoleon, whose identity he had easily and surely recognized, Lavrúshka was not in the least abashed but merely did his utmost to gain his new master's favor.

He knew very well that this was Napoleon, but Napoleon's presence could no more intimidate him than Rostóv's, or a sergeant major's with the rods, would have done, for he had nothing that either the sergeant major or Napoleon could deprive him of.

So he rattled on, telling all the gossip he had heard among the orderlies. Much of it was true. But when Napoleon asked him whether the Russians thought they would beat Bonaparte or not, Lavrúshka screwed up his eyes and considered.

In this question he saw subtle cunning, as men of his type see cunning in everything, so he frowned and did not answer immediately.

"It's like this," he said thoughtfully, "if there's a battle soon, yours will win. That's right. But if three days pass, then after that, well, then that same battle will not soon be over."

Lelorgne d'Ideville smilingly interpreted this speech to Napoleon thus: "If a battle takes place within the next three days the French will win, but if later, God knows what will happen." Napoleon did not smile, though he was evidently in high good humor, and he ordered these words to be repeated.

Lavrúshka noticed this and to entertain him further, pretending not to know who Napoleon was, added:

* The recently published de Caulaincourt papers cast a new light on this incident. De Caulaincourt says: "The advance-guard captured a Cossack whose horse had been killed, and shortly afterwards a Negro who called himself Hetman Plátov's cook . . . the King of Naples sent them both to the Emperor who plied them with questions." Thiers confused the Cossack and the Negro and made them into one person. Negroes at this time were, of course, almost unknown in Russia.

"We know that you have Bonaparte and that he has beaten everybody in the world, but we are a different matter . . ."—without knowing why or how this bit of boastful patriotism slipped out at the end.

The interpreter translated these words without the last phrase, and Bonaparte smiled. "The young Cossack made his mighty interlocutor smile," says Thiers. After riding a few paces in silence, Napoleon turned to Berthier and said he wished to see how the news that he was talking to the Emperor himself, to that very Emperor who had written his immortally victorious name on the Pyramids, would affect this *enfant du Don* [child of the Don].

The fact was accordingly conveyed to Lavrúshka.

Lavrúshka, understanding that this was done to perplex him and that Napoleon expected him to be frightened, to gratify his new masters promptly pretended to be astonished and awe-struck, opened his eyes wide, and assumed the expression he usually put on when taken to be whipped. "As soon as Napoleon's interpreter had spoken," says Thiers, "the Cossack, seized by amazement, did not utter another word, but rode on, his eyes fixed on the conqueror whose fame had reached him across the steppes of the East. All his loquacity was suddenly arrested and replaced by a naïve and silent feeling of admiration. Napoleon, after making the Cossack a present, had him set free like a bird restored to its native fields."

Napoleon rode on, dreaming of the Moscow that so appealed to his imagination, and "the bird restored to its native fields" galloped to our outposts, inventing on the way all that had not taken place but that he meant to relate to his comrades. What had really taken place he did not wish to relate because it seemed to him not worth telling. He found the Cossacks, inquired for the regiment operating with Plátov's detachment, and by evening found his master, Nicholas Rostóv, quartered at Yankóvo. Rostóv was just mounting to go for a ride round the neighboring villages with Ilyín; he let Lavrúshka have another horse and took him along with him.

8. *Prince Nicholas Bolkónski has a paralytic stroke and is taken to Boguchárovo. Princess Mary decides that they must move on to Moscow. Her last interview with her father. His affection for her. His death*

PRINCESS MARY was not in Moscow and out of danger as Prince Andrew supposed.

After the return of Alpátych from Smolénsk the old prince suddenly

seemed to awake as from a dream. He ordered the militiamen to be called up from the villages and armed, and wrote a letter to the commander in chief informing him that he had resolved to remain at Bald Hills to the last extremity and to defend it, leaving to the commander in chief's discretion to take measures or not for the defense of Bald Hills, where one of Russia's oldest generals would be captured or killed, and he announced to his household that he would remain at Bald Hills.

But while himself remaining, he gave instructions for the departure of the princess and Dessalles with the little prince to Boguchárovo and thence to Moscow. Princess Mary, alarmed by her father's feverish and sleepless activity after his previous apathy, could not bring herself to leave him alone and for the first time in her life ventured to disobey him. She refused to go away and her father's fury broke over her in a terrible storm. He repeated every injustice he had ever inflicted on her. Trying to convict her, he told her she had worn him out, had caused his quarrel with his son, had harbored nasty suspicions of him, making it the object of her life to poison his existence, and he drove her from his study telling her that if she did not go away it was all the same to him. He declared that he did not wish to remember her existence and warned her not to dare to let him see her. The fact that he did not, as she had feared, order her to be carried away by force but only told her not to let him see her cheered Princess Mary. She knew it was a proof that in the depth of his soul he was glad she was remaining at home and had not gone away.

The morning after little Nicholas had left, the old prince donned his full uniform and prepared to visit the commander in chief. His calèche was already at the door. Princess Mary saw him walk out of the house in his uniform wearing all his orders and go down the garden to review his armed peasants and domestic serfs. She sat by the window listening to his voice which reached her from the garden. Suddenly several men came running up the avenue with frightened faces.

Princess Mary ran out to the porch, down the flower-bordered path, and into the avenue. A large crowd of militiamen and domestics were moving toward her, and in their midst several men were supporting by the armpits and dragging along a little old man in a uniform and decorations. She ran up to him and, in the play of the sunlight that fell in small round spots through the shade of the lime-tree avenue, could not be sure what change there was in his face. All she could see was that his former stern and determined expression had altered to one of timidity and submission. On seeing his daughter he moved his helpless lips and made a hoarse sound. It was impossible to make out what he wanted. He was lifted up, carried to his study, and laid on the very couch he had so feared of late.

The doctor, who was fetched that same night, bled him and said that the prince had had a seizure paralyzing his right side.

It was becoming more and more dangerous to remain at Bald Hills, and next day they moved the prince to Boguchárovo, the doctor accompanying him.

By the time they reached Boguchárovo, Dessalles and the little prince had already left for Moscow.

For three weeks the old prince lay stricken by paralysis in the new house Prince Andrew had built at Boguchárovo,* ever in the same state, getting neither better nor worse. He was unconscious and lay like a distorted corpse. He muttered unceasingly, his eyebrows and lips twitching, and it was impossible to tell whether he understood what was going on around him or not. One thing was certain—that he was suffering and wished to say something. But what it was, no one could tell: it might be some caprice of a sick and half-crazy man, or it might relate to public affairs, or possibly to family concerns.

The doctor said this restlessness did not mean anything and was due to physical causes; but Princess Mary thought he wished to tell her something, and the fact that her presence always increased his restlessness confirmed her opinion.

He was evidently suffering both physically and mentally. There was no hope of recovery. It was impossible for him to travel, it would not do to let him die on the road. "Would it not be better if the end did come, the very end?" Princess Mary sometimes thought. Night and day, hardly sleeping at all, she watched him and, terrible to say, often watched him not with hope of finding signs of improvement but wishing to find symptoms of the approach of the end.

Strange as it was to her to acknowledge this feeling in herself, yet there it was. And what seemed still more terrible to her was that since her father's illness began (perhaps even sooner, when she stayed with him expecting something to happen), all the personal desires and hopes that had been forgotten or sleeping within her had reawakened. Thoughts that had not entered her mind for years—thoughts of a life free from the fear of her father, and even the possibility of love and of family happiness—floated continually in her imagination like temptations of the devil. Thrust them aside as she would, questions continually recurred to her as to how she would order her life now, after that. These were temptations of the

* *This is a rare instance of Tolstóy making a mistake in the time arrangement of his novel. On the fifth of August, the day Smolénsk was bombarded, the old prince was still well. He died on the fifteenth, and could not therefore have lain stricken by paralysis for three weeks.*—A.M.

devil and Princess Mary knew it. She knew that the sole weapon against him was prayer, and she tried to pray. She assumed an attitude of prayer, looked at the icons, repeated the words of a prayer, but she could not pray. She felt that a different world had now taken possession of her—the life of a world of strenuous and free activity, quite opposed to the spiritual world in which till now she had been confined and in which her greatest comfort had been prayer. She could not pray, could not weep, and worldly cares took possession of her.

It was becoming dangerous to remain in Boguchárovo. News of the approach of the French came from all sides, and in one village, ten miles from Boguchárovo, a homestead had been looted by French marauders.

The doctor insisted on the necessity of moving the prince; the provincial Marshal of the Nobility sent an official to Princess Mary to persuade her to get away as quickly as possible, and the head of the rural police having come to Boguchárovo urged the same thing, saying that the French were only some twenty-five miles away, that French proclamations were circulating in the villages, and that if the princess did not take her father away before the fifteenth, he could not answer for the consequences.

The princess decided to leave on the fifteenth. The cares of preparation and giving orders, for which everyone came to her, occupied her all day. She spent the night of the fourteenth as usual, without undressing, in the room next to the one where the prince lay. Several times, waking up, she heard his groans and muttering, the creak of his bed, and the steps of Tíkhon and the doctor when they turned him over. Several times she listened at the door, and it seemed to her that his mutterings were louder than usual and that they turned him over oftener. She could not sleep and several times went to the door and listened, wishing to enter but not deciding to do so. Though he did not speak, Princess Mary saw and knew how unpleasant every sign of anxiety on his account was to him. She had noticed with what dissatisfaction he turned from the look she sometimes involuntarily fixed on him. She knew that her going in during the night at an unusual hour would irritate him.

But never had she felt so grieved for him or so much afraid of losing him. She recalled all her life with him and in every word and act of his found an expression of his love of her. Occasionally amid these memories temptations of the devil would surge into her imagination: thoughts of how things would be after his death, and how her new, liberated life would be ordered. But she drove these thoughts away with disgust. Toward morning he became quiet and she fell asleep.

She woke late. That sincerity which often comes with waking showed

her clearly what chiefly concerned her about her father's illness. On waking she listened to what was going on behind the door and, hearing him groan, said to herself with a sigh that things were still the same.

"But what could have happened? What did I want? I want his death!" she cried with a feeling of loathing for herself.

She washed, dressed, said her prayers, and went out to the porch. In front of it stood carriages without horses and things were being packed into the vehicles.

It was a warm, gray morning. Princess Mary stopped at the porch, still horrified by her spiritual baseness and trying to arrange her thoughts before going to her father.

The doctor came downstairs and went out to her.

"He is a little better today," said he. "I was looking for you. One can make out something of what he is saying. His head is clearer. Come in, he is asking for you. . . ."

Princess Mary's heart beat so violently at this news that she grew pale and leaned against the wall to keep from falling. To see him, talk to him, feel his eyes on her now that her whole soul was overflowing with those dreadful, wicked temptations, was a torment of joy and terror.

"Come," said the doctor.

Princess Mary entered her father's room and went up to his bed. He was lying on his back propped up high, and his small bony hands with their knotted purple veins were lying on the quilt; his left eye gazed straight before him, his right eye was awry, and his brows and lips motionless. He seemed altogether so thin, small, and pathetic. His face seemed to have shriveled or melted; his features had grown smaller. Princess Mary went up and kissed his hand. His left hand pressed hers so that she understood that he had long been waiting for her to come. He twitched her hand, and his brows and lips quivered angrily.

She looked at him in dismay trying to guess what he wanted of her. When she changed her position so that his left eye could see her face he calmed down, not taking his eyes off her for some seconds. Then his lips and tongue moved, sounds came, and he began to speak, gazing timidly and imploringly at her, evidently afraid that she might not understand.

Straining all her faculties Princess Mary looked at him. The comic efforts with which he moved his tongue made her drop her eyes and with difficulty repress the sobs that rose to her throat. He said something, repeating the same words several times. She could not understand them, but tried to guess what he was saying and inquiringly repeated the words he uttered.

"Mmm . . . ar . . . ate . . . ate . . ." he repeated several times.

It was quite impossible to understand these sounds. The doctor thought he had guessed them, and inquiringly repeated: "Mary, are you afraid?" The prince shook his head, and again repeated the same sounds.

"My mind, my mind aches?" questioned Princess Mary.

He made a mumbling sound in confirmation of this, took her hand, and began pressing it to different parts of his breast as if trying to find the right place for it.

"Always thoughts . . . about you . . . thoughts . . ." he then uttered much more clearly than he had done before, now that he was sure of being understood.

Princess Mary pressed her head against his hand, trying to hide her sobs and tears.

He moved his hand over her hair.

"I have been calling you all night . . ." he brought out.

"If only I had known . . ." she said through her tears. "I was afraid to come in."

He pressed her hand.

"Weren't you asleep?"

"No, I did not sleep," said Princess Mary, shaking her head.

Unconsciously imitating her father, she now tried to express herself as he did, as much as possible by signs, and her tongue too seemed to move with difficulty.

"Dear one . . . Dearest . . ." Princess Mary could not quite make out what he said, but from his look it was clear that he had uttered a tender caressing word such as he had never used to her before. "Why didn't you come in?"

"And I, I was wishing for his death!" thought Princess Mary.

He was silent awhile.

"Thank you . . . daughter dear! . . . for all, for all . . . forgive! . . . thank you! . . . forgive! . . . thank you! . . ." and tears began to flow from his eyes. "Call Andrew!" he said suddenly, and a childish, timid expression of doubt showed itself on his face as he spoke.

He himself seemed aware that his demand was meaningless. So at least it seemed to Princess Mary.

"I have a letter from him," she replied.

He glanced at her with timid surprise.

"Where is he?"

"He's with the army, Father, at Smolénsk."

He closed his eyes and remained silent a long time. Then as if in answer to his doubts and to confirm the fact that now he understood and remembered everything, he nodded his head and reopened his eyes.

"Yes," he said, softly and distinctly. "Russia has perished. They've destroyed her."

And he began to sob, and again tears flowed from his eyes. Princess Mary could no longer restrain herself and wept while she gazed at his face.

Again he closed his eyes. His sobs ceased, he pointed to his eyes, and Tíkhon, understanding him, wiped away the tears.

Then he again opened his eyes and said something none of them could understand for a long time, till at last Tíkhon understood and repeated it. Princess Mary had sought the meaning of his words in the mood in which he had just been speaking. She thought he was speaking of Russia, or Prince Andrew, of herself, of his grandson, or of his own death, and so she could not guess his words.

"Put on your white dress. I like it," was what he said.

Having understood this Princess Mary sobbed still louder, and the doctor taking her arm led her out to the veranda, soothing her and trying to persuade her to prepare for her journey. When she had left the room the prince again began speaking about his son, about the war, and about the Emperor, angrily twitching his brows and raising his hoarse voice, and then he had a second and final stroke.

Princess Mary stayed on the veranda. The day had cleared, it was hot and sunny. She could understand nothing, think of nothing and feel nothing, except passionate love for her father, love such as she thought she had never felt till that moment. She ran out sobbing into the garden and as far as the pond, along the avenues of young lime trees Prince Andrew had planted.

"Yes . . . I . . . I . . . I wished for his death! Yes, I wanted it to end quicker. . . . I wished to be at peace. . . . And what will become of me? What use will peace be when he is no longer here?" Princess Mary murmured, pacing the garden with hurried steps and pressing her hands to her bosom which heaved with convulsive sobs.

When she had completed the tour of the garden, which brought her again to the house, she saw Mademoiselle Bourienne—who had remained at Boguchárovo and did not wish to leave it—coming toward her with a stranger. This was the Marshal of the Nobility of the district, who had come personally to point out to the princess the necessity for her prompt departure. Princess Mary listened without understanding him; she led him to the house, offered him lunch, and sat down with him. Then, excusing herself, she went to the door of the old prince's room. The doctor came out with an agitated face and said she could not enter.

"Go away, Princess! Go away . . . go away!"

She returned to the garden and sat down on the grass at the foot of the

slope by the pond, where no one could see her. She did not know how long she had been there when she was aroused by the sound of a woman's footsteps running along the path. She rose and saw Dunyásha her maid, who was evidently looking for her, and who stopped suddenly as if in alarm on seeing her mistress.

"Please come, Princess . . . The Prince . . ." said Dunyásha in a breaking voice.

"Immediately, I'm coming, I'm coming!" replied the princess hurriedly, not giving Dunyásha time to finish what she was saying, and trying to avoid seeing the girl she ran toward the house.

"Princess, it's God's will! You must be prepared for everything," said the Marshal, meeting her at the house door.

"Let me alone; it's not true!" she cried angrily to him.

The doctor tried to stop her. She pushed him aside and ran to her father's door. "Why are these people with frightened faces stopping me? I don't want any of them! And what are they doing here?" she thought. She opened the door and the bright daylight in that previously darkened room startled her. In the room were her nurse and other women. They all drew back from the bed, making way for her. He was still lying on the bed as before, but the stern expression of his quiet face made Princess Mary stop short on the threshold.

"No, he's not dead—it's impossible!" she told herself and approached him, and repressing the terror that seized her, she pressed her lips to his cheek. But she stepped back immediately. All the force of the tenderness she had been feeling for him vanished instantly and was replaced by a feeling of horror at what lay there before her. "No, he is no more! He is not, but here where he was is something unfamiliar and hostile, some dreadful, terrifying, and repellent mystery!" And hiding her face in her hands, Princess Mary sank into the arms of the doctor, who held her up.

In the presence of Tíkhon and the doctor the women washed what had been the prince, tied his head up with a handkerchief that the mouth should not stiffen while open, and with another handkerchief tied together the legs that were already spreading apart. Then they dressed him in uniform with his decorations and placed his shriveled little body on a table. Heaven only knows who arranged all this and when, but it all got done as if of its own accord. Toward night candles were burning round his coffin, a pall was spread over it, the floor was strewn with sprays of juniper, a printed band was tucked in under his shriveled head, and in a corner of the room sat a chanter reading the psalms.

Just as horses shy and snort and gather about a dead horse, so the in-

mates of the house and strangers crowded into the drawing room round the coffin—the Marshal, the village Elder, peasant women—and all with fixed and frightened eyes, crossing themselves, bowed and kissed the old prince's cold and stiffened hand.

9. Character of the Boguchárovo peasantry and the baffling undercurrents in the life of the Russian people. The village Elder, Dron. Alpátych talks to him. The peasants decide not to supply horses or carts

UNTIL PRINCE ANDREW settled in Boguchárovo its owners had always been absentees, and its peasants were of quite a different character from those of Bald Hills. They differed from them in speech, dress, and disposition. They were called steppe peasants. The old prince used to approve of them for their endurance at work when they came to Bald Hills to help with the harvest or to dig ponds and ditches, but he disliked them for their boorishness.

Prince Andrew's last stay at Boguchárovo, when he introduced hospitals and schools and reduced the quitrent the peasants had to pay, had not softened their disposition but had on the contrary strengthened in them the traits of character the old prince called boorishness. Various obscure rumors were always current among them: at one time a rumor that they would all be enrolled as Cossacks; at another of a new religion to which they were all to be converted; then of some proclamation of the Tsar's and of an oath to the Tsar Paul in 1797 (in connection with which it was rumored that freedom had been granted them but the landowners had stopped it), then of Peter Fëdorovich's * return to the throne in seven years' time, when everything would be made free and so "simple" that there would be no restrictions. Rumors of the war with Bonaparte and his invasion were connected in their minds with the same sort of vague notions of Antichrist, the end of the world, and "pure freedom."

In the vicinity of Boguchárovo were large villages belonging to the crown or to owners whose serfs paid quitrent and could work where they pleased. There were very few resident landlords in the neighborhood and also very few domestic or literate serfs, and in the lives of the peasantry of those parts the mysterious undercurrents in the life of the Russian

* The Emperor Peter III was assassinated, or died, on the accession of his wife, Catherine II, to the throne in 1762; but Tsars often long survived in the minds of the peasants, who refused to believe in their death.—A.M.

people, the causes and meaning of which are so baffling to contemporaries, were more clearly and strongly noticeable than among others.* One instance, which had occurred some twenty years before, was a movement among the peasants to emigrate to some unknown "warm rivers." Hundreds of peasants, among them the Boguchárovo folk, suddenly began selling their cattle and moving in whole families toward the southeast. As birds migrate to somewhere beyond the sea, so these men with their wives and children streamed to the southeast, to parts where none of them had ever been. They set off in caravans, bought their freedom one by one or ran away, and drove or walked toward the "warm rivers." Many of them were punished, some sent to Siberia, many died of cold and hunger on the road, many returned of their own accord, and the movement died down of itself just as it had sprung up, without apparent reason. But such undercurrents still existed among the people and gathered new forces ready to manifest themselves just as strangely, unexpectedly, and at the same time simply, naturally, and forcibly. Now in 1812, to anyone living in close touch with these people it was apparent that these undercurrents were acting strongly and nearing an eruption.

Alpátych, who had reached Boguchárovo shortly before the old prince's death, noticed an agitation among the peasants, and that contrary to what was happening in the Bald Hills district, where over a radius of forty miles all the peasants were moving away and leaving their villages to be devastated by the Cossacks, the peasants in the steppe region round Boguchárovo were, it was rumored, in touch with the French, received leaflets from them that passed from hand to hand, and did not migrate. He learned from domestic serfs loyal to him that the peasant Karp, who possessed great influence in the village commune and had recently been away driving a government transport, had returned with news that the Cossacks were destroying deserted villages, but that the French did not harm them. Alpátych also knew that on the previous day another peasant had even brought from the village of Visloúkhovo, which was occupied by the French, a proclamation by a French general that no harm would be done to the inhabitants, and if they remained they would be paid for

* One of the dangers of the Napoleonic invasion was that Napoleon might cause a great commotion among the Russian peasantry by proclaiming an emancipation of the serfs. Before the emancipation granted by Alexander II, Tolstóy convinced himself that there was grave danger of a peasant rising to claim land and liberty. That danger was averted for a time by the Emancipation decree of 1861, but Tolstóy's later writings show that he still understood the unstable structure of Russian society and foresaw the Revolution of 1917, clearly predicted in What Then Must We Do? published in 1886.—A.M.

anything taken from them. As proof of this the peasant had brought from Visloúkhovo a hundred rubles in notes (he did not know that they were false) paid to him in advance for hay.

More important still, Alpátych learned that on the morning of the very day he gave the village Elder orders to collect carts to move the princess' luggage from Boguchárovo, there had been a village meeting at which it had been decided not to move but to wait. Yet there was no time to waste. On the fifteenth, the day of the old prince's death, the Marshal had insisted on Princess Mary's leaving at once, as it was becoming dangerous. He had told her that after the sixteenth he could not be responsible for what might happen. On the evening of the day the old prince died the Marshal went away, promising to return next day for the funeral. But this he was unable to do, for he received tidings that the French had unexpectedly advanced, and had barely time to remove his own family and valuables from his estate.

For some thirty years Boguchárovo had been managed by the village Elder, Dron, whom the old prince called by the diminutive "Drónushka."

Dron was one of those physically and mentally vigorous peasants who grow big beards as soon as they are of age and go on unchanged till they are sixty or seventy, without a gray hair or the loss of a tooth, as straight and strong at sixty as at thirty.

Soon after the migration to the "warm rivers," in which he had taken part like the rest, Dron was made village Elder and overseer of Boguchárovo, and had since filled that post irreproachably for twenty-three years. The peasants feared him more than they did their master. The masters, both the old prince and the young, and the steward respected him and jestingly called him "the Minister." During the whole time of his service Dron had never been drunk or ill, never after sleepless nights or the hardest tasks had he shown the least fatigue, and though he could not read he had never forgotten a single money account or the number of quarters of flour in any of the endless cartloads he sold for the prince, nor a single shock of the whole corn crop on any single acre of the Boguchárovo fields.

Alpátych, arriving from the devastated Bald Hills estate, sent for this Dron on the day of the prince's funeral and told him to have twelve horses got ready for the princess' carriages and eighteen carts for the things to be removed from Boguchárovo. Though the peasants paid quitrent, Alpátych thought no difficulty would be made about complying with this order, for there were two hundred and thirty households at work in Boguchárovo and the peasants were well to do. But on hearing the

order Dron lowered his eyes and remained silent. Alpátych named certain peasants he knew, from whom he told him to take the carts.

Dron replied that the horses of these peasants were away carting. Alpátych named others, but they too, according to Dron, had no horses available: some horses were carting for the government, others were too weak, and others had died for want of fodder. It seemed that no horses could be had even for the carriages, much less for the carting.

Alpátych looked intently at Dron and frowned. Just as Dron was a model village Elder, so Alpátych had not managed the prince's estates for twenty years in vain. He was a model steward, possessing in the highest degree the faculty of divining the needs and instincts of those he dealt with. Having glanced at Dron he at once understood that his answers did not express his personal views but the general mood of the Boguchárovo commune, by which the Elder had already been carried away. But he also knew that Dron, who had acquired property and was hated by the commune, must be hesitating between the two camps: the masters' and the serfs'. He noticed this hesitation in Dron's look and therefore frowned and moved closer up to him.

"Now just listen, Drónushka," said he. "Don't talk nonsense to me. His excellency Prince Andrew himself gave me orders to move all the people away and not leave them with the enemy, and there is an order from the Tsar about it too. Anyone who stays is a traitor to the Tsar. Do you hear?"

"I hear," Dron answered without lifting his eyes.

Alpátych was not satisfied with this reply.

"Eh, Dron, it will turn out badly!" he said, shaking his head.

"The power is in your hands," Dron rejoined sadly.

"Eh, Dron, drop it!" Alpátych repeated, withdrawing his hand from his bosom and solemnly pointing to the floor at Dron's feet. "I can see through you and three yards into the ground under you," he continued, gazing at the floor in front of Dron.

Dron was disconcerted, glanced furtively at Alpátych and again lowered his eyes.

"You drop this nonsense and tell the people to get ready to leave their homes and go to Moscow and to get carts ready for tomorrow morning for the princess' things. And don't go to any meeting yourself, do you hear?"

Dron suddenly fell on his knees.

"Yákov Alpátych, discharge me! Take the keys from me and discharge me, for Christ's sake!"

"Stop that!" cried Alpátych sternly. "I see through you and three yards under you," he repeated, knowing that his skill in beekeeping, his knowl-

edge of the right time to sow the oats, and the fact that he had been
able to retain the old prince's favor for twenty years had long since gained
him the reputation of being a wizard, and that the power of seeing three
yards under a man is considered an attribute of wizards.

Dron got up and was about to say something, but Alpátych interrupted
him.

"What is it you have got into your heads, eh? . . . What are you
thinking of, eh?"

"What am I to do with the people?" said Dron. "They're quite beside
themselves; I have already told them . . ."

" 'Told them,' I dare say!" said Alpátych. "Are they drinking?" he
asked abruptly.

"Quite beside themselves, Yákov Alpátych; they've fetched another
barrel."

"Well, then, listen! I'll go to the police officer, and you tell them so,
and that they must stop this and the carts must be got ready."

"I understand."

Alpátych did not insist further. He had managed people for a long
time and knew that the chief way to make them obey is to show no sus-
picion that they can possibly disobey. Having wrung a submissive "I un-
derstand" from Dron, Alpátych contented himself with that, though he
not only doubted but felt almost certain that without the help of troops
the carts would not be forthcoming.

And so it was, for when evening came no carts had been provided. In
the village, outside the drink shop, another meeting was being held, which
decided that the horses should be driven out into the woods and the carts
should not be provided. Without saying anything of this to the princess,
Alpátych had his own belongings taken out of the carts which had arrived
from Bald Hills and had those horses got ready for the princess' carriages.
Meanwhile he went himself to the police authorities.

10. Mlle Bourienne advises Princess Mary to appeal to the French for protection. Princess Mary speaks to Dron

AFTER HER FATHER'S FUNERAL Princess Mary shut herself up in her room
and did not admit anyone. A maid came to the door to say that
Alpátych was asking for orders about their departure. (This was before his
talk with Dron.) Princess Mary raised herself on the sofa on which she
had been lying and replied through the closed door that she did not mean
to go away and begged to be left in peace.

The windows of the room in which she was lying looked westward. She lay on the sofa with her face to the wall, fingering the buttons of the leather cushion and seeing nothing but that cushion, and her confused thoughts were centered on one subject—the irrevocability of death and her own spiritual baseness, which she had not suspected, but which had shown itself during her father's illness. She wished to pray but did not dare to, dared not in her present state of mind address herself to God. She lay for a long time in that position.

The sun had reached the other side of the house, and its slanting rays shone into the open window, lighting up the room and part of the morocco cushion at which Princess Mary was looking. The flow of her thoughts suddenly stopped. Unconsciously she sat up, smoothed her hair, got up, and went to the window, involuntarily inhaling the freshness of the clear but windy evening.

"Yes, you can well enjoy the evening now! He is gone and no one will hinder you," she said to herself, and sinking into a chair she let her head fall on the window sill.

Someone spoke her name in a soft and tender voice from the garden and kissed her head. She looked up. It was Mademoiselle Bourienne in a black dress and weepers.* She softly approached Princess Mary, sighed, kissed her, and immediately began to cry. The princess looked up at her. All their former disharmony and her own jealousy recurred to her mind. But she remembered too how he had changed of late toward Mademoiselle Bourienne and could not bear to see her, thereby showing how unjust were the reproaches Princess Mary had mentally addressed to her. "Besides, is it for me, for me who desired his death, to condemn anyone?" she thought.

Princess Mary vividly pictured to herself the position of Mademoiselle Bourienne, whom she had of late kept at a distance, but who yet was dependent on her and living in her house. She felt sorry for her and held out her hand with a glance of gentle inquiry. Mademoiselle Bourienne at once began crying again and kissed that hand, speaking of the princess' sorrow and making herself a partner in it. She said her only consolation was the fact that the princess allowed her to share her sorrow, that all the old misunderstandings should sink into nothing but this great grief; that she felt herself blameless in regard to everyone, and that he, from above, saw her affection and gratitude. The princess heard her, not heeding her words but occasionally looking up at her and listening to the sound of her voice.

"Your position is doubly terrible, dear princess," said Mademoiselle

* Broad white cuffs worn by widows.

Bourienne after a pause. "I understand that you could not, and cannot, think of yourself, but with my love for you I must do so. . . . Has Alpá- tych been to you? Has he spoken to you of going away?" she asked.

Princess Mary did not answer. She did not understand who was to go or where to. "Is it possible to plan or think of anything now? Is it not all the same?" she thought, and did not reply.

"You know, chère Marie," said Mademoiselle Bourienne, "that we are in danger—are surrounded by the French. It would be dangerous to move now. If we go we are almost sure to be taken prisoners, and God knows . . ."

Princess Mary looked at her companion without understanding what she was talking about.

"Oh, if anyone knew how little anything matters to me now," she said. "Of course I would on no account wish to go away from him. . . . Alpá- tych did say something about going. . . . Speak to him; I can do nothing, nothing, and don't want to. . . ."

"I've spoken to him. He hopes we should be in time to get away to- morrow, but I think it would now be better to stay here," said Made- moiselle Bourienne. "Because, you will agree, chère Marie, to fall into the hands of the soldiers or of riotous peasants would be terrible."

Mademoiselle Bourienne took from her reticule a proclamation (not printed on ordinary Russian paper) of General Rameau's, telling people not to leave their homes and that the French authorities would afford them proper protection. She handed this to the princess.

"I think it would be best to appeal to that general," she continued, "and I am sure that all due respect would be shown you."

Princess Mary read the paper, and her face began to quiver with stifled sobs.

"From whom did you get this?" she asked.

"They probably recognized that I am French, by my name," replied Mademoiselle Bourienne blushing.

Princess Mary, with the paper in her hand, rose from the window and with a pale face went out of the room and into what had been Prince Andrew's study.

"Dunyásha, send Alpátych, or Drónushka, or somebody to me!" she said, "and tell Mademoiselle Bourienne not to come to me," she added, hearing Mademoiselle Bourienne's voice. "We must go at once, at once!" she said, appalled at the thought of being left in the hands of the French.

"If Prince Andrew heard that I was in the power of the French! That I, the daughter of Prince Nicholas Bolkónski, asked General Rameau for protection and accepted his favor!" This idea horrified her, made her shud-

der, blush, and feel such a rush of anger and pride as she had never experienced before. All that was distressing, and especially all that was humiliating, in her position rose vividly to her mind. "They, the French, would settle in this house: M. le Général Rameau would occupy Prince Andrew's study and amuse himself by looking through and reading his letters and papers. Mademoiselle Bourienne would do the honors of Boguchárovo for him. I should be given a small room as a favor, the soldiers would violate my father's newly dug grave to steal his crosses and stars, they would tell me of their victories over the Russians, and would pretend to sympathize with my sorrow . . ." thought Princess Mary, not thinking her own thoughts but feeling bound to think like her father and her brother. For herself she did not care where she remained or what happened to her, but she felt herself the representative of her dead father and of Prince Andrew. Involuntarily she thought their thoughts and felt their feelings. What they would have said and what they would have done she felt bound to say and do. She went into Prince Andrew's study, trying to enter completely into his ideas, and considered her position.

The demands of life, which had seemed to her annihilated by her father's death, all at once rose before her with a new, previously unknown force and took possession of her.

Agitated and flushed she paced the room, sending now for Michael Ivánovich and now for Tíkhon or Dron. Dunyásha, the nurse, and the other maids could not say in how far Mademoiselle Bourienne's statement was correct. Alpátych was not at home, he had gone to the police. Neither could the architect Michael Ivánovich, who on being sent for came in with sleepy eyes, tell Princess Mary anything. With just the same smile of agreement with which for fifteen years he had been accustomed to answer the old prince without expressing views of his own, he now replied to Princess Mary, so that nothing definite could be got from his answers. The old valet Tíkhon, with sunken, emaciated face that bore the stamp of inconsolable grief, replied: "Yes, Princess" to all Princess Mary's questions and hardly refrained from sobbing as he looked at her.

At length Dron, the village Elder, entered the room and with a deep bow to Princess Mary came to a halt by the doorpost.

Princess Mary walked up and down the room and stopped in front of him.

"Drónushka," she said, regarding as a sure friend this Drónushka who always used to bring a special kind of gingerbread from his visit to the fair at Vyázma every year and smilingly offer it to her, "Drónushka, now since our misfortune . . ." she began, but could not go on.

"We are all in God's hands," said he, with a sigh.

They were silent for a while.

"Drónushka, Alpátych has gone off somewhere and I have no one to turn to. Is it true, as they tell me, that I can't even go away?"

"Why shouldn't you go away, your excellency? You can go," said Dron.

"I was told it would be dangerous because of the enemy. Dear friend, I can do nothing. I understand nothing. I have nobody! I want to go away tonight or early tomorrow morning."

Dron paused. He looked askance at Princess Mary and said: "There are no horses; I told Yákov Alpátych so."

"Why are there none?" asked the princess.

"It's all God's scourge," said Dron. "What horses we had have been taken for the army or have died—this is such a year! It's not a case of feeding horses—we may die of hunger ourselves! As it is, some go three days without eating. We've nothing, we've been ruined."

Princess Mary listened attentively to what he told her.

"The peasants are ruined? They have no bread?" she asked.

"They're dying of hunger," said Dron. "It's not a case of carting."

"But why didn't you tell me, Drónushka? Isn't it possible to help them? I'll do all I can. . . ."

To Princess Mary it was strange that now, at a moment when such sorrow was filling her soul, there could be rich people and poor, and the rich could refrain from helping the poor. She had heard vaguely that there was such a thing as "landlord's corn" which was sometimes given to the peasants. She also knew that neither her father nor her brother would refuse to help the peasants in need, she only feared to make some mistake in speaking about the distribution of the grain she wished to give. She was glad such cares presented themselves, enabling her without scruple to forget her own grief. She began asking Dron about the peasants' needs and what there was in Boguchárovo that belonged to the landlord.

"But we have grain belonging to my brother?" she said.

"The landlord's grain is all safe," replied Dron proudly. "Our prince did not order it to be sold."

"Give it to the peasants, let them have all they need; I give you leave in my brother's name," said she.

Dron made no answer but sighed deeply.

"Give them that corn if there is enough of it. Distribute it all. I give this order in my brother's name; and tell them that what is ours is theirs. We do not grudge them anything. Tell them so."

Dron looked intently at the princess while she was speaking.

"Discharge me, little mother, for God's sake! Order the keys to be

taken from me," said he. "I have served twenty-three years and have done no wrong. Discharge me, for God's sake!"

Princess Mary did not understand what he wanted of her or why he was asking to be discharged. She replied that she had never doubted his devotion and that she was ready to do anything for him and for the peasants.

11. Princess Mary addresses the peasants. They distrust her and refuse to leave Boguchárovo

AN HOUR LATER Dunyásha came to tell the princess that Dron had come, and all the peasants had assembled at the barn by the princess' order and wished to have word with their mistress.

"But I never told them to come," said Princess Mary. "I only told Dron to let them have the grain."

"Only, for God's sake, Princess dear, have them sent away and don't go out to them. It's all a trick," said Dunyásha, "and when Yákov Alpátych returns let us get away . . . and please don't . . ."

"What is a trick?" asked Princess Mary in surprise.

"I know it is, only listen to me for God's sake! Ask nurse too. They say they don't agree to leave Boguchárovo as you ordered."

"You're making some mistake. I never ordered them to go away," said Princess Mary. "Call Drónushka."

Dron came and confirmed Dunyásha's words; the peasants had come by the princess' order.

"But I never sent for them," declared the princess. "You must have given my message wrong. I only said that you were to give them the grain."

Dron only sighed in reply.

"If you order it they will go away," said he.

"No, no. I'll go out to them," said Princess Mary, and in spite of the nurse's and Dunyásha's protests she went out into the porch; Dron, Dunyásha, the nurse, and Michael Ivánovich following her.

"They probably think I am offering them the grain to bribe them to remain here, while I myself go away leaving them to the mercy of the French," thought Princess Mary. "I will offer them monthly rations and housing at our Moscow estate. I am sure Andrew would do even more in my place," she thought as she went out in the twilight toward the crowd standing on the pasture by the barn.

The men crowded closer together, stirred, and rapidly took off their hats. Princess Mary lowered her eyes and, tripping over her skirt, came

close up to them. So many different eyes, old and young, were fixed on her, and there were so many different faces, that she could not distinguish any of them and, feeling that she must speak to them all at once, did not know how to do it. But again the sense that she represented her father and her brother gave her courage, and she boldly began her speech.

"I am very glad you have come," she said without raising her eyes, and feeling her heart beating quickly and violently. "Drónushka tells me that the war has ruined you. That is our common misfortune, and I shall grudge nothing to help you. I am myself going away because it is dangerous here . . . the enemy is near . . . because . . . I am giving you everything, my friends, and I beg you to take everything, all our grain, so that you may not suffer want! And if you have been told that I am giving you the grain to keep you here—that is not true. On the contrary, I ask you to go with all your belongings to our estate near Moscow, and I promise you I will see to it that there you shall want for nothing. You shall be given food and lodging."

The princess stopped. Sighs were the only sound heard in the crowd.

"I am not doing this on my own account," she continued, "I do it in the name of my dead father, who was a good master to you, and of my brother and his son."

Again she paused. No one broke the silence.

"Ours is a common misfortune and we will share it together. All that is mine is yours," she concluded, scanning the faces before her.

All eyes were gazing at her with one and the same expression. She could not fathom whether it was curiosity, devotion, gratitude, or apprehension and distrust—but the expression on all the faces was identical.

"We are all very thankful for your bounty, but it won't do for us to take the landlord's grain," said a voice at the back of the crowd.

"But why not?" asked the princess.

No one replied and Princess Mary, looking round at the crowd, found that every eye she met now was immediately dropped.

"But why don't you want to take it?" she asked again.

No one answered.

The silence began to oppress the princess and she tried to catch someone's eye.

"Why don't you speak?" she inquired of a very old man who stood just in front of her leaning on his stick. "If you think something more is wanted, tell me! I will do anything," said she, catching his eye.

But as if this angered him, he bent his head quite low and muttered:

"Why should we agree? We don't want the grain."

"Why should we give up everything? We don't agree. Don't agree.

. . . We are sorry for you, but we're not willing. Go away yourself, alone . . ." came from various sides of the crowd.

And again all the faces in that crowd bore an identical expression, though now it was certainly not an expression of curiosity or gratitude, but of angry resolve.

"But you can't have understood me," said Princess Mary with a sad smile. "Why don't you want to go? I promise to house and feed you, while here the enemy would ruin you. . . ."

But her voice was drowned by the voices of the crowd.

"We're not willing. Let them ruin us! We won't take your grain. We don't agree."

Again Princess Mary tried to catch someone's eye, but not a single eye in the crowd was turned to her; evidently they were all trying to avoid her look. She felt strange and awkward.

"Oh yes, an artful tale! Follow her into slavery! Pull down your houses and go into bondage! I dare say! 'I'll give you grain, indeed!' she says," voices in the crowd were heard saying.

With drooping head Princess Mary left the crowd and went back to the house. Having repeated her order to Dron to have horses ready for her departure next morning, she went to her room and remained alone with her own thoughts.

12. *Princess Mary at night recalls her last sight of her father*

FOR A LONG TIME that night Princess Mary sat by the open window of her room hearing the sound of the peasants' voices that reached her from the village, but it was not of them she was thinking. She felt that she could not understand them however much she might think about them. She thought only of one thing, her sorrow, which, after the break caused by cares for the present, seemed already to belong to the past. Now she could remember it and weep or pray.

After sunset the wind had dropped. The night was calm and fresh. Toward midnight the voices began to subside, a cock crowed, the full moon began to show from behind the lime trees, a fresh white dewy mist began to rise, and stillness reigned over the village and the house.

Pictures of the near past—her father's illness and last moments—rose one after another to her memory. With mournful pleasure she now lingered over these images, repelling with horror only the last one, the picture of his death, which she felt she could not contemplate even in imagination at this still and mystic hour of night. And these pictures presented

themselves to her so clearly and in such detail that they seemed now present, now past, and now future.

She vividly recalled the moment when he had his first stroke and was being dragged along by his armpits through the garden at Bald Hills, muttering something with his helpless tongue, twitching his gray eyebrows and looking uneasily and timidly at her.

"Even then he wanted to tell me what he told me the day he died," she thought. "He had always thought what he said then." And she recalled in all its detail the night at Bald Hills before he had the last stroke, when with a foreboding of disaster she had remained at home against his will. She had not slept and had stolen downstairs on tiptoe, and going to the door of the conservatory where he slept that night had listened at the door. In a suffering and weary voice he was saying something to Tíkhon, speaking of the Crimea and its warm nights and of the Empress. Evidently he had wanted to talk. "And why didn't he call me? Why didn't he let me be there instead of Tíkhon?" Princess Mary had thought and thought again now. "Now he will never tell anyone what he had in his soul. Never will that moment return for him or for me when he might have said all he longed to say, and not Tíkhon but I might have heard and understood him. Why didn't I enter the room?" she thought. "Perhaps he would then have said to me what he said the day he died. While talking to Tíkhon he asked about me twice. He wanted to see me, and I was standing close by, outside the door. It was sad and painful for him to talk to Tíkhon who did not understand him. I remember how he began speaking to him about Lise as if she were alive—he had forgotten she was dead—and Tíkhon reminded him that she was no more, and he shouted, 'Fool!' He was greatly depressed. From behind the door I heard how he lay down on his bed groaning and loudly exclaimed, 'My God!' Why didn't I go in then? What could he have done to me? What could I have lost? And perhaps he would then have been comforted and would have said that word to me." And Princess Mary uttered aloud the caressing word he had said to her on the day of his death. "Dear-est!" she repeated, and began sobbing, with tears that relieved her soul. She now saw his face before her. And not the face she had known ever since she could remember and had always seen at a distance, but the timid, feeble face she had seen for the first time quite closely, with all its wrinkles and details, when she stooped near to his mouth to catch what he said.

"Dear-est!" she repeated again.

"What was he thinking when he uttered that word? What is he thinking now?" This question suddenly presented itself to her, and in answer she saw him before her with the expression that was on his face as he

lay in his coffin with his chin bound up with a white handkerchief. And the horror that had seized her when she touched him and convinced herself that *that* was not *he*, but something mysterious and horrible, seized her again. She tried to think of something else and to pray, but could do neither. With wide-open eyes she gazed at the moonlight and the shadows, expecting every moment to see his dead face, and she felt that the silence brooding over the house and within it held her fast.

"Dunyásha," she whispered. "Dunyásha!" she screamed wildly, and tearing herself out of this silence she ran to the servants' quarters to meet her old nurse and the maidservants who came running toward her.

13. Nicholas and Ilyín ride to Boguchárovo. They are asked by Alpátych to protect the princess. Nicholas makes her acquaintance and places himself at her service

ON THE SEVENTEENTH OF AUGUST Rostóv and Ilyín, accompanied by Lavrúshka who had just returned from captivity and by an hussar orderly, left their quarters at Yankóvo, ten miles from Boguchárovo, and went for a ride—to try a new horse Ilyín had bought and to find out whether there was any hay to be had in the villages.

For the last three days Boguchárovo had lain between the two hostile armies, so that it was as easy for the Russian rearguard to get to it as for the French vanguard; Rostóv, as a careful squadron commander, wished to take such provisions as remained at Boguchárovo before the French could get them.

Rostóv and Ilyín were in the merriest of moods. On the way to Boguchárovo, a princely estate with a dwelling house and farm where they hoped to find many domestic serfs and pretty girls, they questioned Lavrúshka about Napoleon and laughed at his stories, and raced one another to try Ilyín's horse.

Rostóv had no idea that the village he was entering was the property of that very Bolkónski who had been engaged to his sister.

Rostóv and Ilyín gave rein to their horses for a last race along the incline before reaching Boguchárovo, and Rostóv, outstripping Ilyín, was the first to gallop into the village street.

"You're first!" cried Ilyín, flushed.

"Yes, always first both on the grassland and here," answered Rostóv, stroking his heated Donéts horse.

"And I'd have won on my Frenchy, your excellency," said Lavrúshka

from behind, alluding to his shabby cart horse, "only I didn't wish to mortify you."

They rode at a footpace to the barn, where a large crowd of peasants was standing.

Some of the men bared their heads, others stared at the new arrivals without doffing their caps. Two tall old peasants with wrinkled faces and scanty beards emerged from the tavern, smiling, staggering, and singing some incoherent song, and approached the officers.

"Fine fellows!" said Rostóv laughing. "Is there any hay here?"

"And how like one another," said Ilyín.

"A mo-o-st me-r-r-y co-o-m-pa . . . !" sang one of the peasants with a blissful smile.

One of the men came out of the crowd and went up to Rostóv.

"Who do you belong to?" he asked.

"The French," replied Ilyín jestingly, "and here is Napoleon himself" —and he pointed to Lavrúshka.

"Then you are Russians?" the peasant asked again.

"And is there a large force of you here?" said another, a short man, coming up.

"Very large," answered Rostóv. "But why have you collected here?" he added. "Is it a holiday?"

"The old men have met to talk over the business of the commune," replied the peasant, moving away.

At that moment, on the road leading from the big house, two women and a man in a white hat were seen coming toward the officers.

"The one in pink is mine, so keep off!" said Ilyín on seeing Dunyásha running resolutely toward him.

"She'll be ours!" said Lavrúshka to Ilyín, winking.

"What do you want, my pretty?" said Ilyín with a smile.

"The princess ordered me to ask your regiment and your name."

"This is Count Rostóv, squadron commander, and I am your humble servant."

"Co-o-om-pa-ny!" roared the tipsy peasant with a beatific smile as he looked at Ilyín talking to the girl. Following Dunyásha, Alpátych advanced to Rostóv, having bared his head while still at a distance.

"May I make bold to trouble your honor?" said he respectfully, but with a shade of contempt for the youthfulness of this officer and with a hand thrust into his bosom. "My mistress, daughter of General in Chief Prince Nicholas Bolkónski who died on the fifteenth of this month, finding herself in difficulties owing to the boorishness of these people"—he pointed to the peasants—"asks you to come up to the house. . . . Won't

you, please, ride on a little farther," said Alpátych with a melancholy smile, "as it is not convenient in the presence of . . . ?" He pointed to the two peasants who kept as close to him as horseflies to a horse.

"Ah! . . . Alpátych . . . Ah, Yákov Alpátych . . . Grand! Forgive us for Christ's sake, eh?" said the peasants, smiling joyfully at him.

Rostóv looked at the tipsy peasants and smiled.

"Or perhaps they amuse your honor?" remarked Alpátych with a staid air, as he pointed at the old men with his free hand.

"No, there's not much to be amused at here," said Rostóv, and rode on a little way. "What's the matter?" he asked.

"I make bold to inform your honor that the rude peasants here don't wish to let the mistress leave the estate, and threaten to unharness her horses, so that though everything has been packed up since morning, her excellency cannot get away."

"Impossible!" exclaimed Rostóv.

"I have the honor to report to you the actual truth," said Alpátych.

Rostóv dismounted, gave his horse to the orderly, and followed Alpátych to the house, questioning him as to the state of affairs. It appeared that the princess' offer of corn to the peasants the previous day, and her talk with Dron and at the meeting, had actually had so bad an effect that Dron had finally given up the keys and joined the peasants and had not appeared when Alpátych sent for him; and that in the morning when the princess gave orders to harness for her journey, the peasants had come in a large crowd to the barn and sent word that they would not let her leave the village: that there was an order not to move, and that they would unharness the horses. Alpátych had gone out to admonish them, but was told (it was chiefly Karp who did the talking, Dron not showing himself in the crowd) that they could not let the princess go, that there was an order to the contrary, but that if she stayed they would serve her as before and obey her in everything.

At the moment when Rostóv and Ilyín were galloping along the road, Princess Mary, despite the dissuasions of Alpátych, her nurse, and the maids, had given orders to harness and intended to start, but when the cavalrymen were espied they were taken for Frenchmen, the coachman ran away, and the women in the house began to wail.

"Father! Benefactor! God has sent you!" exclaimed deeply moved voices as Rostóv passed through the anteroom.

Princess Mary was sitting helpless and bewildered in the large sitting room, when Rostóv was shown in. She could not grasp who he was and why he had come, or what was happening to her. When she saw his Russian face, and by his walk and the first words he uttered recognized

him as a man of her own class, she glanced at him with her deep radiant look and began speaking in a voice that faltered and trembled with emotion. This meeting immediately struck Rostóv as a romantic event. "A helpless girl overwhelmed with grief, left to the mercy of coarse, rioting peasants! And what a strange fate sent me here! What gentleness and nobility there are in her features and expression!" thought he as he looked at her and listened to her timid story.

When she began to tell him that all this had happened the day after her father's funeral, her voice trembled. She turned away, and then, as if fearing he might take her words as meant to move him to pity, looked at him with an apprehensive glance of inquiry. There were tears in Rostóv's eyes. Princess Mary noticed this and glanced gratefully at him with that radiant look which caused the plainness of her face to be forgotten.

"I cannot express, Princess, how glad I am that I happened to ride here and am able to show my readiness to serve you," said Rostóv, rising. "Go when you please, and I give you my word of honor that no one shall dare to cause you annoyance if only you will allow me to act as your escort." And bowing respectfully, as if to a lady of royal blood, he moved toward the door.

Rostóv's deferential tone seemed to indicate that though he would consider himself happy to be acquainted with her, he did not wish to take advantage of her misfortunes to intrude upon her.

Princess Mary understood this and appreciated his delicacy.

"I am very, very grateful to you," she said in French, "but I hope it was all a misunderstanding and that no one is to blame for it." She suddenly began to cry.

"Excuse me!" she said.

Rostóv, knitting his brows, left the room with another low bow.

14. Nicholas calls the peasants to account and intimidates them. Carts and horses are provided for Princess Mary's departure. Princess Mary feels that she loves him

WELL, is she pretty? Ah, friend—my pink one is delicious; her name is Dunyásha. . . ."

But on glancing at Rostóv's face Ilyín stopped short. He saw that his hero and commander was following quite a different train of thought.

Rostóv glanced angrily at Ilyín and without replying strode off with rapid steps to the village.

"I'll show them; I'll give it to them, the brigands!" said he to himself.

Alpátych at a gliding trot, only just managing not to run, kept up with him with difficulty.

"What decision have you been pleased to come to?" said he.

Rostóv stopped and, clenching his fists, suddenly and sternly turned on Alpátych.

"Decision? What decision? Old dotard! . . ." cried he. "What have you been about? Eh? The peasants are rioting, and you can't manage them? You're a traitor yourself! I know you. I'll flay you all alive! . . ." And as if afraid of wasting his store of anger, he left Alpátych and went rapidly forward. Alpátych, mastering his offended feelings, kept pace with Rostóv at a gliding gait and continued to impart his views. He said the peasants were obdurate and that at the present moment it would be imprudent to "overresist" them without an armed force, and would it not be better first to send for the military?

"I'll give them armed force . . . I'll 'overresist' them!" uttered Rostóv meaninglessly, breathless with irrational animal fury and the need to vent it.

Without considering what he would do he moved unconsciously with quick, resolute steps toward the crowd. And the nearer he drew to it the more Alpátych felt that this unreasonable action might produce good results. The peasants in the crowd were similarly impressed when they saw Rostóv's rapid, firm steps and resolute, frowning face.

After the hussars had come to the village and Rostóv had gone to see the princess, a certain confusion and dissension had arisen among the crowd. Some of the peasants said that these new arrivals were Russians and might take it amiss that the mistress was being detained. Dron was of this opinion, but as soon as he expressed it Karp and others attacked their ex-Elder.

"How many years have you been fattening on the commune?" Karp shouted at him. "It's all one to you! You'll dig up your pot of money and take it away with you. . . . What does it matter to you whether our homes are ruined or not?"

"We've been told to keep order, and that no one is to leave their homes or take away a single grain, and that's all about it!" cried another.

"It was your son's turn to be conscripted, but no fear! You begrudged your lump of a son," a little old man suddenly began attacking Dron— "and so they took my Vánka to be shaved for a soldier! But we all have to die."

"To be sure, we all have to die. I'm not against the commune," said Dron.

"That's it—not against it! You've filled your belly. . . ."

The two tall peasants had their say. As soon as Rostóv, followed by Ilyín, Lavrúshka, and Alpátych, came up to the crowd, Karp, thrusting his fingers into his belt and smiling a little, walked to the front. Dron on the contrary retired to the rear and the crowd drew closer together.

"Who is your Elder here? Hey?" shouted Rostóv, coming up to the crowd with quick steps.

"The Elder? What do you want with him? . . ." asked Karp.

But before the words were well out of his mouth, his cap flew off and a fierce blow jerked his head to one side.

"Caps off, traitors!" shouted Rostóv in a wrathful voice. "Where's the Elder?" he cried furiously.

"The Elder. . . . He wants the Elder! . . . Dron Zakhárych,* you!" meek and flustered voices here and there were heard calling and caps began to come off their heads.

"We don't riot, we're following the orders," declared Karp, and at that moment several voices began speaking together.

"It's as the old men have decided—there's too many of you giving orders."

"Arguing? Mutiny! . . . Brigands! Traitors!" cried Rostóv unmeaningly in a voice not his own, gripping Karp by the collar. "Bind him, bind him!" he shouted, though there was no one to bind him but Lavrúshka and Alpátych.

Lavrúshka, however, ran up to Karp and seized him by the arms from behind.

"Shall I call up our men from beyond the hill?" he called out.

Alpátych turned to the peasants and ordered two of them by name to come and bind Karp. The men obediently came out of the crowd and began taking off their belts.

"Where's the Elder?" demanded Rostóv in a loud voice.

With a pale and frowning face Dron stepped out of the crowd.

"Are you the Elder? Bind him, Lavrúshka!" shouted Rostóv, as if that order, too, could not possibly meet with any opposition.

And in fact two more peasants began binding Dron, who took off his own belt and handed it to them, as if to aid them.

"And you all listen to me!" said Rostóv to the peasants. "Be off to your houses at once, and don't let one of your voices be heard!"

"Why, we've not done any harm! We did it just out of foolishness. It's

* *The use of Dron's patronymic, Zakhárych (son of Zacharias), indicates that the peasants were no longer speaking familiarly, but wished to be as formal and ceremonious as possible.*—A.M.

all nonsense. . . . I said then that it was not in order," voices were heard bickering with one another.

"There! What did I say?" said Alpátych, coming into his own again. "It's wrong, lads!"

"All our stupidity, Yákov Alpátych," came the answers, and the crowd began at once to disperse through the village.

The two bound men were led off to the master's house. The two drunken peasants followed them.

"Aye, when I look at you! . . ." said one of them to Karp.

"How can one talk to the masters like that? What were you thinking of, you fool?" added the other—"A real fool!"

Two hours later the carts were standing in the courtyard of the Bogu-chárovo house. The peasants were briskly carrying out the proprietor's goods and packing them on the carts, and Dron, liberated at Princess Mary's wish from the cupboard where he had been confined, was stand-ing in the yard directing the men.

"Don't put it in so carelessly," said one of the peasants, a man with a round smiling face, taking a casket from a housemaid. "You know it has cost money! How can you chuck it in like that or shove it under the cord where it'll get rubbed? I don't like that way of doing things. Let it all be done properly, according to rule. Look here, put it under the bast mat-ting and cover it with hay—that's the way!"

"Eh, books, books!" said another peasant, bringing out Prince Andrew's library cupboards. "Don't catch up against it! It's heavy, lads—solid books."

"Yes, they worked all day and didn't play!" remarked the tall, round-faced peasant gravely, pointing with a significant wink at the dictionaries that were on the top.

Unwilling to obtrude himself on the princess, Rostóv did not go back to the house but remained in the village awaiting her departure. When her carriage drove out of the house, he mounted and accompanied her eight miles from Boguchárovo to where the road was occupied by our troops. At the inn at Yankóvo he respectfully took leave of her, for the first time permitting himself to kiss her hand.

"How can you speak so!" he blushingly replied to Princess Mary's ex-pressions of gratitude for her deliverance, as she termed what had oc-curred. "Any police officer would have done as much! If we had had only peasants to fight, we should not have let the enemy come so far," said he with a sense of shame and wishing to change the subject. "I am only

happy to have had the opportunity of making your acquaintance. Good-by, Princess. I wish you happiness and consolation and hope to meet you again in happier circumstances. If you don't want to make me blush, please don't thank me!"

But the princess, if she did not again thank him in words, thanked him with the whole expression of her face, radiant with gratitude and tenderness. She could not believe that there was nothing to thank him for. On the contrary, it seemed to her certain that had he not been there she would have perished at the hands of the mutineers and of the French, and that he had exposed himself to terrible and obvious danger to save her, and even more certain was it that he was a man of lofty and noble soul, able to understand her position and her sorrow. His kind, honest eyes, with the tears rising in them when she herself had begun to cry as she spoke of her loss, did not leave her memory.

When she had taken leave of him and remained alone she suddenly felt her eyes filling with tears, and then not for the first time the strange question presented itself to her: did she love him?

On the rest of the way to Moscow, though the princess' position was not a cheerful one, Dunyásha, who went with her in the carriage, more than once noticed that her mistress leaned out of the window and smiled at something with an expression of mingled joy and sorrow.

"Well, supposing I do love him?" thought Princess Mary.

Ashamed as she was of acknowledging to herself that she had fallen in love with a man who would perhaps never love her, she comforted herself with the thought that no one would ever know it and that she would not be to blame if, without ever speaking of it to anyone, she continued to the end of her life to love the man with whom she had fallen in love for the first and last time in her life.

Sometimes when she recalled his looks, his sympathy, and his words, happiness did not appear impossible to her. It was at those moments that Dunyásha noticed her smiling as she looked out of the carriage window.

"Was it not fate that brought him to Boguchárovo, and at that very moment?" thought Princess Mary. "And that caused his sister to refuse my brother?" * And in all this Princess Mary saw the hand of Providence.

The impression the princess made on Rostóv was a very agreeable one. To remember her gave him pleasure, and when his comrades, hearing of his adventure at Boguchárovo, rallied him on having gone to look for hay

* A woman might not marry her brother's or sister's brother-in-law and vice versa, so that if Natásha had married Prince Andrew it would have been an obstacle to marriage between Mary and Nicholas.—A.M.

and having picked up one of the wealthiest heiresses in Russia, he grew angry. It made him angry just because the idea of marrying the gentle Princess Mary, who was attractive to him and had an enormous fortune, had against his will more than once entered his head. For himself personally Nicholas could not wish for a better wife: by marrying her he would make the countess his mother happy, would be able to put his father's affairs in order, and would even—he felt it—ensure Princess Mary's happiness.

But Sónya? And his plighted word? That was why Rostóv grew angry when he was rallied about Princess Bolkónskaya.

15. Prince Andrew goes to headquarters and meets Denísov, who wants guerrilla troops to break the French line of communication. Kutúzov's reception of them. He transacts business

ON RECEIVING COMMAND of the armies Kutúzov remembered Prince Andrew and sent an order for him to report at headquarters.

Prince Andrew arrived at Tsárevo-Zaymíshche on the very day and at the very hour that Kutúzov was reviewing the troops for the first time.* He stopped in the village at the priest's house in front of which stood the commander in chief's carriage, and he sat down on the bench at the gate awaiting his Serene Highness, as everyone now called Kutúzov. From the field beyond the village came now sounds of regimental music and now the roar of many voices shouting "Hurrah!" to the new commander in chief. Two orderlies, a courier and a major-domo, stood near by, some ten paces from Prince Andrew, availing themselves of Kutúzov's absence and of the fine weather. A short, swarthy lieutenant colonel of hussars with thick mustaches and whiskers rode up to the gate and, glancing at Prince Andrew, inquired whether his Serene Highness was putting up there and whether he would soon be back.

Prince Andrew replied that he was not on his Serene Highness' staff but was himself a new arrival. The lieutenant colonel turned to a smart

* After the abandonment of Smolénsk the Russian army, continuing its retreat, passed Vyázma on August 17 and stopped at the village of Tsárevo-Zaymíshche near Gzhatsk, where for a time it was intended to give battle. It was here that Kutúzov reached the army, having been appointed commander in chief. He had left Petersburg on August 11, and reached Gzhatsk on the seventeenth.—A.M.

orderly, who, with the peculiar contempt with which a commander in
chief's orderly speaks to officers, replied:

"What? His Serene Highness? I expect he'll be here soon. What do
you want?"

The lieutenant colonel of hussars smiled beneath his mustache at the
orderly's tone, dismounted, gave his horse to a dispatch runner, and
approached Bolkónski with a slight bow. Bolkónski made room for him
on the bench and the lieutenant colonel sat down beside him.

"You're also waiting for the commander in chief?" said he. "They say
he weceives evewyone, thank God! . . . It's awful with those sausage
eaters! Ermólov had weason to ask to be pwomoted to be a German!
Now p'waps Wussians will get a look in. As it was, devil only knows
what was happening. We kept wetweating and wetweating. Did you
take part in the campaign?" he asked.

"I had the pleasure," replied Prince Andrew, "not only of taking part
in the retreat but of losing in that retreat all I held dear—not to mention
the estate and home of my birth—my father, who died of grief. I belong
to the province of Smolénsk."

"Ah? You're Pwince Bolkónski? Vewy glad to make your acquaint-
ance! I'm Lieutenant Colonel Denísov, better known as 'Váska,'" said
Denísov, pressing Prince Andrew's hand and looking into his face with a
particularly kindly attention. "Yes, I heard," said he sympathetically, and
after a short pause added: "Yes, it's Scythian warfare. It's all vewy well
—only not for those who get it in the neck. So you are Pwince Andwew
Bolkónski?" He swayed his head. "Vewy pleased, Pwince, to make your
acquaintance!" he repeated again, smiling sadly, and he again pressed
Prince Andrew's hand.

Prince Andrew knew Denísov from what Natásha had told him of her
first suitor. This memory carried him sadly and sweetly back to those
painful feelings of which he had not thought lately, but which still found
place in his soul. Of late he had received so many new and very serious
impressions—such as the retreat from Smolénsk, his visit to Bald Hills,
and the recent news of his father's death—and had experienced so many
emotions, that for a long time past those memories had not entered his
mind, and now that they did, they did not act on him with nearly their
former strength. For Denísov, too, the memories awakened by the name
of Bolkónski belonged to a distant, romantic past, when after supper and
after Natásha's singing he had proposed to a little girl of fifteen without
realizing what he was doing. He smiled at the recollection of that time
and of his love for Natásha, and passed at once to what now interested

him passionately and exclusively. This was a plan of campaign he had devised while serving at the outposts during the retreat. He had proposed that plan to Barclay de Tolly and now wished to propose it to Kutúzov. The plan was based on the fact that the French line of operation was too extended, and it proposed that instead of, or concurrently with, action on the front to bar the advance of the French, we should attack their line of communication. He began explaining his plan to Prince Andrew.

"They can't hold all that line. It's impossible. I will undertake to bweak thwough. Give me five hundwed men and I will bweak the line, that's certain! There's only one way—guewilla warfare!"

Denísov rose and began gesticulating as he explained his plan to Bolkónski. In the midst of his explanation shouts were heard from the army, growing more incoherent and more diffused, mingling with music and songs and coming from the field where the review was held. Sounds of hoofs and shouts were nearing the village.

"He's coming! He's coming!" shouted a Cossack standing at the gate.

Bolkónski and Denísov moved to the gate, at which a knot of soldiers (a guard of honor) was standing, and they saw Kutúzov coming down the street mounted on a rather small sorrel horse. A huge suite of generals rode behind him. Barclay was riding almost beside him, and a crowd of officers ran after and around them shouting, "Hurrah!"

His adjutants galloped into the yard before him. Kutúzov was impatiently urging on his horse, which ambled smoothly under his weight, and he raised his hand to his white Horse Guard's cap with a red band and no peak, nodding his head continually. When he came up to the guard of honor, a fine set of Grenadiers mostly wearing decorations, who were giving him the salute, he looked at them silently and attentively for nearly a minute with the steady gaze of a commander and then turned to the crowd of generals and officers surrounding him. Suddenly his face assumed a subtle expression, he shrugged his shoulders with an air of perplexity.

"And with such fine fellows to retreat and retreat! Well, good-by, General," he added, and rode into the yard past Prince Andrew and Denísov.

"Hurrah! hurrah! hurrah!" shouted those behind him.

Since Prince Andrew had last seen him Kutúzov had grown still more corpulent, flaccid, and fat. But the bleached eyeball, the scar, and the familiar weariness of his expression were still the same. He was wearing the white Horse Guard's cap and a military overcoat with a whip hanging over his shoulder by a thin strap. He sat heavily and swayed limply on his brisk little horse.

"Whew . . . whew . . . whew!" he whistled just audibly as he rode

into the yard. His face expressed the relief of relaxed strain felt by a man who means to rest after a ceremony. He drew his left foot out of the stirrup and, lurching with his whole body and puckering his face with the effort, raised it with difficulty onto the saddle, leaned on his knee, groaned, and slipped down into the arms of the Cossacks and adjutants who stood ready to assist him.

He pulled himself together, looked round, screwing up his eyes, glanced at Prince Andrew, and, evidently not recognizing him, moved with his waddling gait to the porch. "Whew . . . whew . . . whew!" he whistled, and again glanced at Prince Andrew. As often occurs with old men, it was only after some seconds that the impression produced by Prince Andrew's face linked itself up with Kutúzov's remembrance of his personality.

"Ah, how do you do, my dear prince? How do you do, my dear boy? Come along . . ." said he, glancing wearily round, and he stepped onto the porch which creaked under his weight.

He unbuttoned his coat and sat down on a bench in the porch.

"And how's your father?"

"I received news of his death, yesterday," replied Prince Andrew abruptly.

Kutúzov looked at him with eyes wide open with dismay and then took off his cap and crossed himself:

"May the kingdom of Heaven be his! God's will be done to us all!" He sighed deeply, his whole chest heaving, and was silent for a while. "I loved him and respected him, and sympathize with you with all my heart."

He embraced Prince Andrew, pressing him to his fat breast, and for some time did not let him go. When he released him Prince Andrew saw that Kutúzov's flabby lips were trembling and that tears were in his eyes. He sighed and pressed on the bench with both hands to raise himself.

"Come! Come with me, we'll have a talk," said he.

But at that moment Denísov, no more intimidated by his superiors than by the enemy, came with jingling spurs up the steps of the porch, despite the angry whispers of the adjutants who tried to stop him. Kutúzov, his hands still pressed on the seat, glanced at him glumly. Denísov, having given his name, announced that he had to communicate to his Serene Highness a matter of great importance for their country's welfare. Kutúzov looked wearily at him and, lifting his hands with a gesture of annoyance, folded them across his stomach, repeating the words: "For our country's welfare? Well, what is it? Speak!" Denísov blushed like a girl (it was strange to see the color rise in that shaggy, bibulous, timeworn face) and boldly began to expound his plan of cutting the enemy's lines of com-

munication between Smolénsk and Vyázma.* Denísov came from those
parts and knew the country well. His plan seemed decidedly a good one,
especially from the strength of conviction with which he spoke. Kutúzov
looked down at his own legs, occasionally glancing at the door of the
adjoining hut as if expecting something unpleasant to emerge from it.
And from that hut, while Denísov was speaking, a general with a portfolio
under his arm really did appear.

"What?" said Kutúzov, in the midst of Denísov's explanations, "are
you ready so soon?"

"Ready, your Serene Highness," replied the general.

Kutúzov swayed his head, as much as to say: "How is one man to deal
with it all?" and again listened to Denísov.

"I give my word of honor as a Wussian officer," said Denísov, "that I can
bweak Napoleon's line of communication!"

"What relation are you to Intendant General Kiríl Andréevich Dení-
sov?" asked Kutúzov, interrupting him.

"He is my uncle, your Sewene Highness."

"Ah, we were friends," said Kutúzov cheerfully. "All right, all right,
friend, stay here at the staff and tomorrow we'll have a talk."

With a nod to Denísov he turned away and put out his hand for the
papers Konovnítsyn had brought him.

"Would not your Serene Highness like to come inside?" said the gen-
eral on duty in a discontented voice, "the plans must be examined and
several papers have to be signed."

An adjutant came out and announced that everything was in readiness
within. But Kutúzov evidently did not wish to enter that room till he was
disengaged. He made a grimace. . . .

"No, tell them to bring a small table out here, my dear boy. I'll look at
them here," said he. "Don't go away," he added, turning to Prince An-
drew, who remained in the porch and listened to the general's report.

While this was being given, Prince Andrew heard the whisper of a
woman's voice and the rustle of a silk dress behind the door. Several times
on glancing that way he noticed behind that door a plump, rosy, handsome
woman in a pink dress with a lilac silk kerchief on her head, holding a dish
and evidently awaiting the entrance of the commander in chief. Kutúzov's
adjutant whispered to Prince Andrew that this was the wife of the priest

* It was in reality D. Davýdov who proposed a guerrilla warfare and to cut
Napoleon's lines of communication. Kutúzov consented to his making the
attempt with a party of 130 Cossacks and hussars, but the battle of Borodinó
was then impending and only after that battle was Davýdov able to begin his
operations.—A.M.

whose home it was, and that she intended to offer his Serene Highness bread and salt.* "Her husband has welcomed his Serene Highness with the cross at the church, and she intends to welcome him in the house. . . . She's very pretty," added the adjutant with a smile. At those words Kutúzov looked round. He was listening to the general's report—which consisted chiefly of a criticism of the position at Tsárevo-Zaymíshche—as he had listened to Denísov, and seven years previously had listened to the discussion at the Austerlitz council of war. He evidently listened only because he had ears which, though there was a piece of tow in one of them, could not help hearing; but it was evident that nothing the general could say would surprise or even interest him, that he knew all that would be said beforehand, and heard it all only because he had to, as one has to listen to the chanting of a service of prayer. All that Denísov had said was clever and to the point. What the general was saying was even more clever and to the point, but it was evident that Kutúzov despised knowledge and cleverness, and knew of something else that would decide the matter— something independent of cleverness and knowledge. Prince Andrew watched the commander in chief's face attentively, and the only expression he could see there was one of boredom, curiosity as to the meaning of the feminine whispering behind the door, and a desire to observe propriety. It was evident that Kutúzov despised cleverness and learning and even the patriotic feeling shown by Denísov, but despised them not because of his own intellect, feelings, or knowledge—he did not try to display any of these—but because of something else. He despised them because of his old age and experience of life. The only instruction Kutúzov gave of his own accord during that report referred to looting by the Russian troops. At the end of the report the general put before him for signature a paper relating to the recovery of payment from army commanders for green oats mown down by the soldiers, when landowners lodged petitions for compensation.

After hearing the matter, Kutúzov smacked his lips together and shook his head.

"Into the stove . . . into the fire with it! I tell you once for all, my dear fellow," said he, "into the fire with all such things! Let them cut the crops and burn wood to their hearts' content. I don't order it or allow it, but I don't exact compensation either. One can't get on without it. 'When wood is chopped the chips will fly.' " He looked at the paper again. "Oh, this German precision!" he muttered, shaking his head.

* *It is a Russian custom to present "bread and salt" to anyone who is taking up residence in a new place. In practice the "bread and salt" is often represented by a cake and a silver dish of white powdered sugar.—*A.M.

16. *The priest's wife offers Kutúzov "bread and salt." He has a further talk with Prince Andrew, who declines a place on the staff. Patience and Time. Prince Andrew's confidence in Kutúzov*

WELL, THAT'S ALL!" said Kutúzov as he signed the last of the documents, and rising heavily and smoothing out the folds in his fat white neck he moved toward the door with a more cheerful expression.

The priest's wife, flushing rosy red, caught up the dish she had after all not managed to present at the right moment, though she had so long been preparing for it, and with a low bow offered it to Kutúzov.

He screwed up his eyes, smiled, lifted her chin with his hand, and said: "Ah, what a beauty! Thank you, sweetheart!"

He took some gold pieces from his trouser pocket and put them on the dish for her. "Well, my dear, and how are we getting on?" he asked, moving to the door of the room assigned to him. The priest's wife smiled, and with dimples in her rosy cheeks followed him into the room. The adjutant came out to the porch and asked Prince Andrew to lunch with him. Half an hour later Prince Andrew was again called to Kutúzov. He found him reclining in an armchair, still in the same unbuttoned overcoat. He had in his hand a French book which he closed as Prince Andrew entered, marking the place with a knife. Prince Andrew saw by the cover that it was *Les Chevaliers du Cygne* by Madame de Genlis.

"Well, sit down, sit down here. Let's have a talk," said Kutúzov. "It's sad, very sad. But remember, my dear fellow, that I am a father to you, a second father. . . ."

Prince Andrew told Kutúzov all he knew of his father's death, and what he had seen at Bald Hills when he passed through it.

"What . . . what they have brought us to!" Kutúzov suddenly cried in an agitated voice, evidently picturing vividly to himself from Prince Andrew's story the condition Russia was in. "But give me time, give me time!" he said with a grim look, evidently not wishing to continue this agitating conversation, and added: "I sent for you to keep you with me."

"I thank your Serene Highness, but I fear I am no longer fit for the staff," replied Prince Andrew with a smile which Kutúzov noticed.

Kutúzov glanced inquiringly at him.

"But above all," added Prince Andrew, "I have grown used to my regiment, am fond of the officers, and I fancy the men also like me. I should be sorry to leave the regiment. If I decline the honor of being with you, believe me . . ."

A shrewd, kindly, yet subtly derisive expression lit up Kutúzov's podgy face. He cut Bolkónski short.

"I am sorry, for I need you. But you're right, you're right! It's not here that men are needed. Advisers are always plentiful, but men are not. The regiments would not be what they are if the would-be advisers served there as you do. I remember you at Austerlitz. . . . I remember, yes, I remember you with the standard!" said Kutúzov, and a flush of pleasure suffused Prince Andrew's face at this recollection.

Taking his hand and drawing him downwards, Kutúzov offered his cheek to be kissed, and again Prince Andrew noticed tears in the old man's eyes. Though Prince Andrew knew that Kutúzov's tears came easily, and that he was particularly tender to and considerate of him from a wish to show sympathy with his loss, yet this reminder of Austerlitz was both pleasant and flattering to him.

"Go your way and God be with you. I know your path is the path of honor!" He paused. "I missed you at Bucharest, but I needed someone to send." And changing the subject, Kutúzov began to speak of the Turkish war and the peace that had been concluded. "Yes, I have been much blamed," he said, "both for that war and the peace . . . but everything came at the right time. *Tout vient à point à celui qui sait attendre* [Everything comes in time to him who knows how to wait]. And there were as many advisers there as here . . ." he went on, returning to the subject of "advisers" which evidently occupied him. "Ah, those advisers!" said he. "If we had listened to them all we should not have made peace with Turkey and should not have been through with that war. Everything in haste, but more haste, less speed. Kámenski would have been lost if he had not died. He stormed fortresses with thirty thousand men. It is not difficult to capture a fortress but it is difficult to win a campaign. For that, not storming and attacking but *patience and time* are wanted. Kámenski sent soldiers to Rustchuk, but I only employed these two things and took more fortresses than Kámenski and made the Turks eat horseflesh!" He swayed his head. "And the French shall too, believe me," he went on, growing warmer and beating his chest, "I'll make them eat horseflesh!" And tears again dimmed his eyes.

"But shan't we have to accept battle?" remarked Prince Andrew.

"We shall if everybody wants it; it can't be helped. . . . But believe me, my dear boy, there is nothing stronger than those two: *patience and time*, they will do it all. But the advisers *n'entendent pas de cette oreille, voilà le mal* [don't see it that way, that's the trouble]. Some want a thing—others don't. What's one to do?" he asked, evidently expecting an answer. "Well, what do you want us to do?" he repeated and his eye shone with a

deep, shrewd look. "I'll tell you what to do," he continued, as Prince Andrew still did not reply: "I will tell you what to do, and what I do. *Dans le doute, mon cher* [When in doubt, my dear fellow]," he paused, "*abstiens-toi* [do nothing]"—he articulated the French proverb deliberately.

"Well, good-by, my dear fellow; remember that with all my heart I share your sorrow, and that for you I am not a Serene Highness, nor a prince, nor a commander in chief, but a father! If you want anything come straight to me. Good-by, my dear boy."

Again he embraced and kissed Prince Andrew, but before the latter had left the room Kutúzov gave a sigh of relief and went on with his unfinished novel, *Les Chevaliers du Cygne* by Madame de Genlis.

Prince Andrew could not have explained how or why it was, but after that interview with Kutúzov he went back to his regiment reassured as to the general course of affairs and as to the man to whom it had been entrusted. The more he realized the absence of all personal motive in that old man—in whom there seemed to remain only the habit of passions, and in place of an intellect (grouping events and drawing conclusions) only the capacity calmly to contemplate the course of events—the more reassured he was that everything would be as it should. "He will not bring in any plan of his own. He will not devise or undertake anything," thought Prince Andrew, "but he will hear everything, remember everything, and put everything in its place. He will not hinder anything useful nor allow anything harmful. He understands that there is something stronger and more important than his own will—the inevitable course of events, and he can see them and grasp their significance, and seeing that significance can refrain from meddling and renounce his personal wish directed to something else. And above all," thought Prince Andrew, "one believes in him because he's Russian, despite the novel by Genlis and the French proverbs, and because his voice shook when he said: 'What they have brought us to!' and had a sob in it when he said he would 'make them eat horseflesh!'"

On such feelings, more or less dimly shared by all, the unanimity and general approval were founded with which, despite court influences, the popular choice of Kutúzov as commander in chief was received.

17. *Moscow after the Emperor's visit. Rostopchín's broad-*
sheets. Julie's farewell soiree. Forfeits for speaking
French. Pierre hears of Princess Mary's
arrival in Moscow

AFTER THE EMPEROR had left Moscow, life flowed on there in its usual
course, and its course was so very usual that it was difficult to remem-
ber the recent days of patriotic elation and ardor, hard to believe that
Russia was really in danger and that the members of the English Club
were also sons of the Fatherland ready to sacrifice everything for it. The
one thing that recalled the patriotic fervor everyone had displayed during
the Emperor's stay was the call for contributions of men and money, a
necessity that as soon as the promises had been made assumed a legal,
official form and became unavoidable.

With the enemy's approach to Moscow, the Muscovites' view of their
situation did not grow more serious but on the contrary became even more
frivolous, as always happens with people who see a great danger approach-
ing. At the approach of danger there are always two voices that speak with
equal power in the human soul: one very reasonably tells a man to con-
sider the nature of the danger and the means of escaping it; the other, still
more reasonably, says that it is too depressing and painful to think of the
danger, since it is not in man's power to foresee everything and avert the
general course of events, and it is therefore better to disregard what is
painful till it comes, and to think about what is pleasant. In solitude a man
generally listens to the first voice, but in society to the second. So it was
now with the inhabitants of Moscow. It was long since people had been
as gay in Moscow as that year.

Rostopchín's broadsheets, headed by woodcuts of a drink shop, a pot-
man, and a Moscow burgher called Karpúshka Chigírin, "who—having
been a militiaman and having had rather too much at the pub—heard that
Napoleon wished to come to Moscow, grew angry, abused the French in
very bad language, came out of the drink shop, and, under the sign of the
eagle, began to address the assembled people," were read and discussed,
together with the latest of Vasíli Lvóvich Púshkin's bouts rimés.*

In the corner room at the Club, members gathered to read these broad-
sheets, and some liked the way Karpúshka jeered at the French, saying:
"They will swell up with Russian cabbage, burst with our buckwheat por-

* V. L. Púshkin (1779-1830) *was an uncle of the great poet A. S. Púshkin*
and the author of unimportant lyric and didactic verses.—A.M.

ridge, and choke themselves with cabbage soup. They are all dwarfs and one peasant woman will toss three of them with a hayfork." Others did not like that tone and said it was stupid and vulgar. It was said that Rostopchín had expelled all Frenchmen and even all foreigners from Moscow, and that there had been some spies and agents of Napoleon among them; but this was told chiefly to introduce Rostopchín's witty remark on that occasion. The foreigners were deported to Nízhni by boat, and Rostopchín had said to them in French: "*Rentrez en vous-mêmes; entrez dans la barque, et n'en faites pas une barque de Charon* [Think it over; get into the bark, and take care not to make it a bark of Charon]." There was talk of all the government offices having been already removed from Moscow, and to this Shinshín's witticism was added—that for that alone Moscow ought to be grateful to Napoleon. It was said that Mamónov's regiment would cost him eight hundred thousand rubles, and that Bezúkhov had spent even more on his, but that the best thing about Bezúkhov's action was that he himself was going to don a uniform and ride at the head of his regiment without charging anything for the show.

"You don't spare anyone," said Julie Drubetskáya as she collected and pressed together a bunch of raveled lint with her thin, beringed fingers.

Julie was preparing to leave Moscow next day and was giving a farewell soiree.

"*Bezúkhov est ridicule* [Bezúkhov is absurd], but he is so kind and good-natured. What pleasure is there to be so *caustique?*"

"A forfeit!" cried a young man in militia uniform whom Julie called "*mon chevalier,*" and who was going with her to Nízhni.

In Julie's set, as in many other circles in Moscow, it had been agreed that they would speak nothing but Russian and that those who made a slip and spoke French should pay fines to the Committee of Voluntary Contributions.

"Another forfeit for a Gallicism," said a Russian writer who was present. " 'What pleasure is there to be' is not Russian!"

"You spare no one," continued Julie to the young man without heeding the author's remark.

"For *caustique*—I am guilty and will pay, and I am prepared to pay again for the pleasure of telling you the truth. For Gallicisms I won't be responsible," she remarked, turning to the author: "I have neither the money nor the time, like Prince Galítsyn, to engage a master to teach me Russian!"

"Ah, here he is!" she added. "*Quand on* . . . No, no," she said to the militia officer, "you won't catch me. Speak of the sun and you see its rays!" and she smiled amiably at Pierre. "We were just talking of you," she said

with the facility in lying natural to a society woman. "We were saying that your regiment would be sure to be better than Mamónov's."

"Oh, don't talk to me of my regiment," replied Pierre, kissing his hostess' hand and taking a seat beside her. "I am so sick of it."

"You will, of course, command it yourself?" said Julie, directing a sly, sarcastic glance toward the militia officer.

The latter in Pierre's presence had ceased to be caustic, and his face expressed perplexity as to what Julie's smile might mean. In spite of his absent-mindedness and good nature, Pierre's personality immediately checked any attempt to ridicule him to his face.

"No," said Pierre, with a laughing glance at his big, stout body. "I should make too good a target for the French, besides I am afraid I should hardly be able to climb onto a horse."

Among those whom Julie's guests happened to choose to gossip about were the Rostóvs.

"I hear that their affairs are in a very bad way," said Julie. "And he is so unreasonable, the count himself I mean. The Razumóvskis wanted to buy his house and his estate near Moscow, but it drags on and on. He asks too much."

"No, I think the sale will come off in a few days," said someone. "Though it is madness to buy anything in Moscow now."

"Why?" asked Julie. "You don't think Moscow is in danger?"

"Then why are you leaving?"

"I? What a question! I am going because . . . well, because everyone is going: and besides—I am not Joan of Arc or an Amazon."

"Well, of course, of course! Let me have some more strips of linen."

"If he manages the business properly he will be able to pay off all his debts," said the militia officer, speaking of Rostóv.

"A kindly old man but not up to much. And why do they stay on so long in Moscow? They meant to leave for the country long ago. Natalie is quite well again now, isn't she?" Julie asked Pierre with a knowing smile.

"They are waiting for their younger son," Pierre replied. "He joined Obolénski's Cossacks and went to Bélaya Tsérkov where the regiment is being formed. But now they have had him transferred to my regiment and are expecting him every day. The count wanted to leave long ago, but the countess won't on any account leave Moscow till her son returns."

"I met them the day before yesterday at the Arkhárovs'. Natalie has recovered her looks and is brighter. She sang a song. How easily some people get over everything!"

"Get over what?" inquired Pierre, looking displeased.

Julie smiled.

"You know, Count, such knights as you are only found in Madame de Souza's * novels."

"What knights? What do you mean?" demanded Pierre, blushing.

"Oh, come, my dear count! *C'est la fable de tout Moscou. Je vous admire, ma parole d'honneur!* [It is the talk of all Moscow. My word, I admire you!]"

"Forfeit, forfeit!" cried the militia officer.

"All right, one can't talk—how tiresome!"

"What is 'the talk of all Moscow'?" Pierre asked angrily, rising to his feet.

"Come now, Count, you know!"

"I don't know anything about it," said Pierre.

"I know you were friendly with Natalie, and so . . . but I was always more friendly with Véra—that dear Véra."

"No, madame!" Pierre continued in a tone of displeasure, "I have not taken on myself the role of Natalie Rostóva's knight at all, and have not been to their house for nearly a month. But I cannot understand the cruelty . . ."

"*Qui s'excuse s'accuse* [Who excuses himself accuses himself]," said Julie, smiling and waving the lint triumphantly, and to have the last word she promptly changed the subject. "Do you know what I heard today? Poor Mary Bolkónskaya arrived in Moscow yesterday. Do you know that she has lost her father?"

"Really? Where is she? I should like very much to see her," said Pierre.

"I spent the evening with her yesterday. She is going to their estate near Moscow either today or tomorrow morning, with her nephew."

"Well, and how is she?" asked Pierre.

"She is well, but sad. But do you know who rescued her? It is quite a romance. Nicholas Rostóv! She was surrounded, and they wanted to kill her and had wounded some of her people. He rushed in and saved her. . . ."

"Another romance," said the militia officer. "Really, this general flight has been arranged to get all the old maids married off. Catiche is one and Princess Bolkónskaya another."

"Do you know, I really believe she is *un petit peu amoureuse du jeune homme* [a little bit in love with the young man]."

"Forfeit, forfeit, forfeit!"

"But how could one say that in Russian?"

* *Adélaïde Filleul Souza-Botelho (1761-1836), author of the long-forgotten novel* Adèle de Sénange, *whose works were popular in Russia because she was the wife of the Portuguese Ambassador.*

18. Rostopchín's broadsheets. Pierre and the eldest princess. Leppich's balloon. A public flogging. Pierre leaves Moscow for the army

WHEN PIERRE returned home he was handed two of Rostopchín's broadsheets that had been brought that day.

The first declared that the report that Count Rostopchín had forbidden people to leave Moscow was false; on the contrary he was glad that ladies and tradesmen's wives were leaving the city. "There will be less panic and less gossip," ran the broadsheet, "but I will stake my life on it that that scoundrel will not enter Moscow." These words showed Pierre clearly for the first time that the French would enter Moscow. The second broadsheet stated that our headquarters were at Vyázma, that Count Wittgenstein * had defeated the French, but that as many of the inhabitants of Moscow wished to be armed, weapons were ready for them at the arsenal: sabers, pistols, and muskets which could be had at a low price. The tone of the proclamation was not as jocose as in the former Chigírin talks. Pierre pondered over these broadsheets. Evidently the terrible stormcloud he had desired with the whole strength of his soul but which yet aroused involuntary horror in him was drawing near.

"Shall I join the army and enter the service, or wait?" he asked himself for the hundredth time. He took a pack of cards that lay on the table and began to lay them out for a game of patience.

"If this patience comes out," he said to himself after shuffling the cards, holding them in his hand, and lifting his head, "if it comes out, it means . . . what does it mean?"

He had not decided what it should mean when he heard the voice of the eldest princess at the door asking whether she might come in.

"Then it will mean that I must go to the army," said Pierre to himself. "Come in, come in!" he added to the princess.

Only the eldest princess, the one with the stony face and long waist, was still living in Pierre's house. The two younger ones had both married.

"Excuse my coming to you, cousin," she said in a reproachful and agi-

* Count L. P. Wittgenstein was a general in the Russian army. He subsequently succeeded Kutúzov, and commanded the Russians at Lützen. A separate corps under Count Wittgenstein, which was guarding the road to Petersburg, fought some successful actions in July and early August, 1812, and these had a cheering influence at a time when the country much needed encouragement.—A.M.

tated voice. "You know some decision must be come to. What is going to happen? Everyone has left Moscow and the people are rioting. How is it that we are staying on?"

"On the contrary, things seem satisfactory, ma cousine," said Pierre in the bantering tone he habitually adopted toward her, always feeling uncomfortable in the role of her benefactor.

"Satisfactory, indeed! Very satisfactory! Barbara Ivánovna told me today how our troops are distinguishing themselves. It certainly does them credit! And the people too are quite mutinous—they no longer obey, even my maid has taken to being rude. At this rate they will soon begin beating us. One can't walk in the streets. But, above all, the French will be here any day now, so what are we waiting for? I ask just one thing of you, cousin," she went on, "arrange for me to be taken to Petersburg. Whatever I may be, I can't live under Bonaparte's rule."

"Oh, come, ma cousine! Where do you get your information from? On the contrary . . .".

"I won't submit to your Napoleon! Others may if they please. . . . If you don't want to do this . . ."

"But I will, I'll give the order at once."

The princess was apparently vexed at not having anyone to be angry with. Muttering to herself, she sat down on a chair.

"But you have been misinformed," said Pierre. "Everything is quiet in the city and there is not the slightest danger. See! I've just been reading . . ." He showed her the broadsheet. "Count Rostopchín writes that he will stake his life on it that the enemy will not enter Moscow."

"Oh, that count of yours!" said the princess malevolently. "He is a hypocrite, a rascal who has himself roused the people to riot. Didn't he write in those idiotic broadsheets that anyone, 'whoever it might be, should be dragged to the lockup by his hair'? (How silly!) 'And honor and glory to whoever captures him,' he says. This is what his cajolery has brought us to! Barbara Ivánovna told me the mob nearly killed her because she said something in French."

"Oh, but it's so . . . You take everything so to heart," said Pierre, and began laying out his cards for patience.

Although that patience did come out, Pierre did not join the army,* but

* Tolstóy himself often laid out the cards for patience to decide questions he felt doubtful about, and like Pierre in this section he disregarded the decision given by the cards if it did not suit him.

When staying at Yásnaya Polyána in 1906 shortly before his daughter Mary died, she told me that being undecided about completing an article he had

remained in deserted Moscow ever in the same state of agitation, irresolution, and alarm, yet at the same time joyfully expecting something terrible.

Next day toward evening the princess set off, and Pierre's head steward came to inform him that the money needed for the equipment of his regiment could not be found without selling one of the estates. In general the head steward made out to Pierre that his project of raising a regiment would ruin him. Pierre listened to him, scarcely able to repress a smile.

"Well then, sell it," said he. "What's to be done? I can't draw back now!"

The worse everything became, especially his own affairs, the better was Pierre pleased and the more evident was it that the catastrophe he expected was approaching. Hardly anyone he knew was left in town. Julie had gone, and so had Princess Mary. Of his intimate friends only the Rostóvs remained, but he did not go to see them.

To distract his thoughts he drove that day to the village of Vorontsóvo to see the great balloon Leppich was constructing to destroy the foe,* and a trial balloon that was to go up next day. The balloon was not yet ready, but Pierre learned that it was being constructed by the Emperor's desire. The Emperor had written to Count Rostopchín as follows:

"As soon as Leppich is ready, get together a crew of reliable and intelligent men for his car and send a courier to General Kutúzov to let him know. I have informed him of the matter.

"Please impress upon Leppich to be very careful where he descends for the first time, that he may not make a mistake and fall into the enemy's hands. It is essential for him to combine his movements with those of the commander in chief."

On his way home from Vorontsóvo, as he was passing the Bolótnoe Place Pierre, seeing a large crowd round the Lóbnoe Place,[2] stopped and got out of his trap. A French cook accused of being a spy was being flogged.

begun he had laid out a patience to decide whether that article would be of use to the world. The patience did not come out, but he rose from table with the remark: "All the same I shall write it."—A.M.

* This refers to an early and very unsuccessful attempt to utilize an air force in warfare. A German, Leppich, made the proposal, but his balloon was not ready till November, when the scanty remains of the French army were with difficulty escaping from Russia. Even then the balloon would not rise owing to leakage of gas.—A.M.

[2] The place of execution in Moscow, formerly situated on the Red Square, facing the Kremlin, but before 1812 it had been removed to another part of the town.—A.M.

The flogging was only just over, and the executioner was releasing from the flogging bench a stout man with red whiskers, in blue stockings and a green jacket, who was moaning piteously. Another criminal, thin and pale, stood near. Judging by their faces they were both Frenchmen. With a frightened and suffering look resembling that on the thin Frenchman's face, Pierre pushed his way in through the crowd.

"What is it? Who is it? What is it for?" he kept asking.

But the attention of the crowd—officials, burghers, shopkeepers, peasants, and women in cloaks and in pelisses—was so eagerly centered on what was passing in Lóbnoe Place that no one answered him. The stout man rose, frowned, shrugged his shoulders, and evidently trying to appear firm began to pull on his jacket without looking about him, but suddenly his lips trembled and he began to cry, in the way full-blooded grown-up men cry, though angry with himself for doing so. In the crowd people began talking loudly, to stifle their feelings of pity as it seemed to Pierre.

"He's cook to some prince."

"Eh, mounseer, Russian sauce seems to be sour to a Frenchman . . . sets his teeth on edge!" said a wrinkled clerk who was standing behind Pierre, when the Frenchman began to cry.

The clerk glanced round, evidently hoping that his joke would be appreciated. Some people began to laugh, others continued to watch in dismay the executioner who was undressing the other man.

Pierre choked, his face puckered, and he turned hastily away, went back to his trap muttering something to himself as he went, and took his seat. As they drove along he shuddered and exclaimed several times so audibly that the coachman asked him:

"What is your pleasure?"

"Where are you going?" shouted Pierre to the man, who was driving to Lubyánka Street.

"To the Governor's, as you ordered," answered the coachman.

"Fool! Idiot!" shouted Pierre, abusing his coachman—a thing he rarely did. "Home, I told you! And drive faster, blockhead!" "I must get away this very day," he murmured to himself.

At the sight of the tortured Frenchman and the crowd surrounding the Lóbnoe Place, Pierre had so definitely made up his mind that he could no longer remain in Moscow and would leave for the army that very day that it seemed to him that either he had told the coachman this or that the man ought to have known it for himself.

On reaching home Pierre gave orders to Evstáfey—his head coachman who knew everything, could do anything, and was known to all Moscow—that he would leave that night for the army at Mozháysk, and that his

saddle horses should be sent there. This could not all be arranged that day, so on Evstáfey's representation Pierre had to put off his departure till next day to allow time for the relay horses to be sent on in advance.

On the twenty-fourth the weather cleared up after a spell of rain, and after dinner Pierre left Moscow. When changing horses that night in Perkhúshkovo, he learned that there had been a great battle that evening. (This was the battle of Shevárdino.) He was told that there in Perkhúshkovo the earth trembled from the firing, but nobody could answer his questions as to who had won. At dawn next day Pierre was approaching Mozháysk.

Every house in Mozháysk had soldiers quartered in it, and at the hostel where Pierre was met by his groom and coachman there was no room to be had. It was full of officers.

Everywhere in Mozháysk and beyond it, troops were stationed or on the march. Cossacks, foot and horse soldiers, wagons, caissons, and cannon were everywhere. Pierre pushed forward as fast as he could, and the farther he left Moscow behind and the deeper he plunged into that sea of troops the more was he overcome by restless agitation and a new and joyful feeling he had not experienced before. It was a feeling akin to what he had felt at the Slobóda Palace during the Emperor's visit—a sense of the necessity of undertaking something and sacrificing something. He now experienced a glad consciousness that everything that constitutes men's happiness—the comforts of life, wealth, even life itself—is rubbish it is pleasant to throw away, compared with something . . . With what? Pierre could not say, and he did not try to determine for whom and for what he felt such particular delight in sacrificing everything. He was not occupied with the question of what to sacrifice for; the fact of sacrificing in itself afforded him a new and joyous sensation.

19. Senselessness of the battle of Borodinó, and erroneousness of the historians' accounts of it. Where and how it was fought

ON THE TWENTY-FOURTH OF AUGUST the battle of the Shevárdino Redoubt was fought, on the twenty-fifth not a shot was fired by either side, and on the twenty-sixth the battle of Borodinó itself took place.

Why and how were the battles of Shevárdino and Borodinó given and accepted? Why was the battle of Borodinó fought? There was not the least sense in it for either the French or the Russians. Its immediate result for the Russians was, and was bound to be, that we were brought nearer

to the destruction of Moscow—which we feared more than anything in the world; and for the French its immediate result was that they were brought nearer to the destruction of their whole army—which they feared more than anything in the world. What the result must be was quite obvious, and yet Napoleon offered and Kutúzov accepted that battle.

If the commanders had been guided by reason, it would seem that it must have been obvious to Napoleon that by advancing thirteen hundred miles and giving battle with a probability of losing a quarter of his army, he was advancing to certain destruction, and it must have been equally clear to Kutúzov that by accepting battle and risking the loss of a quarter of his army he would certainly lose Moscow. For Kutúzov this was mathematically clear, as it is that if when playing draughts I have one man less and go on exchanging, I shall certainly lose, and therefore should not exchange. When my opponent has sixteen men and I have fourteen, I am only one eighth weaker than he, but when I have exchanged thirteen more men he will be three times as strong as I am.

Before the battle of Borodinó our strength in proportion to the French was about as five to six, but after that battle it was little more than one to two: previously we had a hundred thousand against a hundred and twenty thousand; afterwards little more than fifty thousand against a hundred thousand. Yet the shrewd and experienced Kutúzov accepted the battle, while Napoleon, who was said to be a commander of genius, gave it, losing a quarter of his army and lengthening his lines of communication still more. If it is said that he expected to end the campaign by occupying Moscow as he had ended a previous campaign by occupying Vienna, there is much evidence to the contrary. Napoleon's historians themselves tell us that from Smolénsk onwards he wished to stop, knew the danger of his extended position, and knew that the occupation of Moscow would not be the end of the campaign, for he had seen at Smolénsk the state in which Russian towns were left to him, and had not received a single reply to his repeated announcements of his wish to negotiate.

In giving and accepting battle at Borodinó, Kutúzov acted involuntarily and irrationally. But later on, to fit what had occurred, the historians provided cunningly devised evidence of the foresight and genius of the generals, who of all the blind tools of history were the most enslaved and involuntary.

The ancients have left us model heroic poems in which the heroes furnish the whole interest of the story, and we are still unable to accustom ourselves to the fact that for our epoch histories of that kind are meaningless.

On the other question, how the battle of Borodinó and the preceding

battle of Shevárdino were fought, there also exists a definite and well-known, but quite false, conception. All the historians describe the affair as follows:

The Russian army, they say, *in its retreat from Smolénsk sought out for itself the best position for a general engagement and found such a position at Borodinó.*

The Russians, they say, fortified this position in advance on the left of the highroad (from Moscow to Smolénsk) and almost at a right angle to it, from Borodinó to Utítsa, at the very place where the battle was fought.

In front of this position, they say, a fortified outpost was set up on the Shevárdino mound to observe the enemy. On the twenty-fourth, we are told, Napoleon attacked this advanced post and took it, and, on the twenty-sixth, attacked the whole Russian army, which was in position on the field of Borodinó.

So the histories say, and it is all quite wrong, as anyone who cares to look into the matter can easily convince himself.

The Russians did not seek out the best position but, on the contrary, during the retreat passed many positions better than Borodinó. They did not stop at any one of these positions because Kutúzov did not wish to occupy a position he had not himself chosen, because the popular demand for a battle had not yet expressed itself strongly enough, and because Miloрádovich had not yet arrived with the militia, and for many other reasons. The fact is that other positions they had passed were stronger, and that the position at Borodinó (the one where the battle was fought), far from being strong, was no more a *position* than any other spot one might find in the Russian Empire by sticking a pin into the map at hazard.

Not only did the Russians not fortify the position on the field of Borodinó to the left of, and at a right angle to, the highroad (that is, the position on which the battle took place), but never till the twenty-fifth of August, 1812, did they think that a battle might be fought there. This was shown first by the fact that there were no entrenchments there by the twenty-fifth, and that those begun on the twenty-fifth and twenty-sixth were not completed, and secondly, by the position of the Shevárdino Redoubt. That redoubt was quite senseless in front of the position where the battle was accepted. Why was it more strongly fortified than any other post? And why were all efforts exhausted and six thousand men sacrificed to defend it till late at night on the twenty-fourth? A Cossack patrol would have sufficed to observe the enemy. Thirdly, as proof that the position on which the battle was fought had not been foreseen and that the Shevárdino Redoubt was not an advanced post of that position, we have the fact that up to the twenty-fifth, Barclay de Tolly and Bagratión were con-

vinced that the Shevárdino Redoubt was the *left flank* of the position, and that Kutúzov himself in his report, written in hot haste after the battle, speaks of the Shevárdino Redoubt as the *left flank* of the position. It was much later, when reports on the battle of Borodinó were written at leisure, that the incorrect and extraordinary statement was invented (probably to justify the mistakes of a commander in chief who had to be represented as infallible) that the Shevárdino Redoubt was an *advanced* post—whereas in reality it was simply a fortified point on the left flank—and that the battle of Borodinó was fought by us on an entrenched position previously selected, whereas it was fought on a quite unexpected spot which was almost unentrenched.

The case was evidently this: a position was selected along the river Kolochá—which crosses the highroad not at a right angle but at an acute angle—so that the left flank was at Shevárdino, the right flank near the village of Nóvoe, and the center at Borodinó at the confluence of the rivers Kolochá and Vóyna.

To anyone who looks at the field of Borodinó without thinking of how the battle was actually fought, this position, protected by the river Kolochá, presents itself as obvious for an army whose object was to prevent an enemy from advancing along the Smolénsk road to Moscow.

Napoleon, riding to Valuévo on the twenty-fourth, did not see (as the history books say he did) the position of the Russians from Utítsa to Borodinó (he could not have seen that position because it did not exist), nor did he see an advanced post of the Russian army, but while pursuing the Russian rearguard he came upon the left flank of the Russian position—at the Shevárdino Redoubt—and unexpectedly for the Russians moved his army across the Kolochá. And the Russians, not having time to begin a general engagement, withdrew their left wing from the position they had intended to occupy and took up a new position which had not been foreseen and was not fortified. By crossing to the other side of the Kolochá to the left of the highroad, Napoleon shifted the whole forthcoming battle from right to left (looking from the Russian side) and transferred it to the plain between Utítsa, Semënovsk, and Borodinó—a plain no more advantageous as a position than any other plain in Russia—and there the whole battle of the twenty-sixth of August took place. [See the rough outline of the plan of the intended battle and of the battle that actually took place.]

Had Napoleon not ridden out on the evening of the twenty-fourth to the Kolochá, and had he not then ordered an immediate attack on the redoubt but had begun the attack next morning, no one would have doubted that the Shevárdino Redoubt was the left flank of our position, and the battle would have taken place where we expected it. In that case

we should probably have defended the Shevárdino Redoubt—our left flank—still more obstinately. We should have attacked Napoleon in the center or on the right, and the engagement would have taken place on the twenty-fifth, in the position we intended and had fortified. But as the attack on our left flank took place in the evening after the retreat of our rearguard (that is, immediately after the fight at Gridnéva), and as the Russian commanders did not wish, or were not in time, to begin a general engagement then on the evening of the twenty-fourth, the first and chief action of the battle of Borodinó was already lost on the twenty-fourth, and obviously led to the loss of the one fought on the twenty-sixth.

After the loss of the Shevárdino Redoubt, we found ourselves on the morning of the twenty-fifth without a position for our left flank, and were forced to bend it back and hastily entrench it where it chanced to be.

Not only was the Russian army on the twenty-sixth defended by weak, unfinished entrenchments, but the disadvantage of that position was increased by the fact that the Russian commanders—not having fully realized what had happened, namely the loss of our position on the left flank and the shifting of the whole field of the forthcoming battle from right to left—maintained their extended position from the village of Nóvoe to Utítsa, and consequently had to move their forces from right to left during the battle. So it happened that throughout the whole battle the Russians opposed the entire French army launched against our left flank with but half as many men. (Poniatowski's action against Utítsa, and Uvárov's on the right flank against the French, were actions distinct from the main course of the battle.) So the battle of Borodinó did not take place at all as (in an effort to conceal our commanders' mistakes even at the cost of diminishing the glory due to the Russian army and people) it has been described. The battle of Borodinó was not fought on a chosen and entrenched position with forces only slightly weaker than those of the enemy, but, as a result of the loss of the Shevárdino Redoubt, the Russians fought the battle of Borodinó on an open and almost unentrenched position, with forces only half as numerous as the French; that is to say, under conditions in which it was not merely unthinkable to fight for ten hours and secure an indecisive result, but unthinkable to keep an army even from complete disintegration and flight.

20. Pierre encounters cavalry advancing and carts of wounded retiring. He talks to an army doctor. Pierre looks for the "position" occupied by the army. Peasant militia digging entrenchments

O N THE MORNING of the twenty-fifth Pierre was leaving Mozháysk. At the descent of the high steep hill, down which a winding road led out of the town past the cathedral on the right, where a service was being held and the bells were ringing, Pierre got out of his vehicle and proceeded on foot. Behind him a cavalry regiment was coming down the hill preceded by its singers. Coming up toward him was a train of carts carrying men who had been wounded in the engagement the day before. The peasant drivers, shouting and lashing their horses, kept crossing from side to side. The carts, in each of which three or four wounded soldiers were lying or sitting, jolted over the stones that had been thrown on the steep incline to make it something like a road. The wounded, bandaged with rags, with pale cheeks, compressed lips, and knitted brows, held on to the sides of the carts as they were jolted against one another. Almost all of them stared with naïve, childlike curiosity at Pierre's white hat and green swallow-tail coat.

Pierre's coachman shouted angrily at the convoy of wounded to keep to one side of the road. The cavalry regiment, as it descended the hill with its singers, surrounded Pierre's carriage and blocked the road. Pierre stopped, being pressed against the side of the cutting in which the road ran. The sunshine from behind the hill did not penetrate into the cutting and there it was cold and damp, but above Pierre's head was the bright August sunshine and the bells sounded merrily. One of the carts with wounded stopped by the side of the road close to Pierre. The driver in his bast shoes ran panting up to it, placed a stone under one of its tireless hind wheels, and began arranging the breech-band on his little horse.

One of the wounded, an old soldier with a bandaged arm who was following the cart on foot, caught hold of it with his sound hand and turned to look at Pierre.

"I say, fellow countryman! Will they set us down here or take us on to Moscow?" he asked.

Pierre was so deep in thought that he did not hear the question. He was looking now at the cavalry regiment that had met the convoy of wounded, now at the cart by which he was standing, in which two wounded men were sitting and one was lying. One of those sitting up in the cart had

probably been wounded in the cheek. His whole head was wrapped in rags and one cheek was swollen to the size of a baby's head. His nose and mouth were twisted to one side. This soldier was looking at the cathedral and crossing himself. Another, a young lad, a fair-haired recruit as white as though there was no blood in his thin face, looked at Pierre kindly, with a fixed smile. The third lay prone so that his face was not visible. The cavalry singers were passing close by:

> *Ah lost, quite lost . . . is my head so keen,*
> *Living in a foreign land . . .*

they sang their soldiers' dance song.

As if responding to them but with a different sort of merriment, the metallic sound of the bells reverberated high above and the hot rays of the sun bathed the top of the opposite slope with yet another sort of merriment. But beneath the slope, by the cart with the wounded near the panting little nag where Pierre stood, it was damp, somber, and sad.

The soldier with the swollen cheek looked angrily at the cavalry singers. "Oh, the coxcombs!" he muttered reproachfully.

"It's not the soldiers only, but I've seen peasants today, too. . . . The peasants—even they have to go," said the soldier behind the cart, addressing Pierre with a sad smile. "No distinctions made nowadays. . . . They want the whole nation to fall on them—in a word, it's Moscow! They want to make an end of it."

In spite of the obscurity of the soldier's words Pierre understood what he wanted to say and nodded approval.

The road was clear again; Pierre descended the hill and drove on.

He kept looking to either side of the road for familiar faces, but only saw everywhere the unfamiliar faces of various military men of different branches of the service, who all looked with astonishment at his white hat and green tail coat.

Having gone nearly three miles he at last met an acquaintance and eagerly addressed him. This was one of the head army doctors. He was driving toward Pierre in a covered gig, sitting beside a young surgeon, and on recognizing Pierre he told the Cossack who occupied the driver's seat to pull up.

"Count! Your excellency, how come you to be here?" asked the doctor.

"Well, you know, I wanted to see . . ."

"Yes, yes, there will be something to see. . . ."

Pierre got out and talked to the doctor, explaining his intention of taking part in a battle.

The doctor advised him to apply direct to Kutúzov.

"Why should you be God knows where out of sight, during the battle?" he said, exchanging glances with his young companion. "Anyhow his Serene Highness knows you and will receive you graciously. That's what you must do."

The doctor seemed tired and in a hurry.

"You think so? . . . Ah, I also wanted to ask you where our position is exactly?" said Pierre.

"The position?" repeated the doctor. "Well, that's not my line. Drive past Tatárinova, a lot of digging is going on there. Go up the hillock and you'll see."

"Can one see from there? . . . If you would . . ."

But the doctor interrupted him and moved toward his gig.

"I would go with you but on my honor I'm up to here"—and he pointed to his throat. "I'm galloping to the commander of the corps. How do matters stand? . . . You know, Count, there'll be a battle tomorrow. Out of an army of a hundred thousand we must expect at least twenty thousand wounded, and we haven't stretchers, or bunks, or dressers, or doctors enough for six thousand. We have ten thousand carts, but we need other things as well—we must manage as best we can!"

The strange thought that of the thousands of men, young and old, who had stared with merry surprise at his hat (perhaps the very men he had noticed), twenty thousand were inevitably doomed to wounds and death amazed Pierre.

"They may die tomorrow; why are they thinking of anything but death?" And by some latent sequence of thought the descent of the Mozháysk hill, the carts with the wounded, the ringing bells, the slanting rays of the sun, and the songs of the cavalrymen vividly recurred to his mind.

"The cavalry ride to battle and meet the wounded and do not for a moment think of what awaits them, but pass by, winking at the wounded. Yet from among these men twenty thousand are doomed to die, and they wonder at my hat! Strange!" thought Pierre, continuing his way to Tatárinova.

In front of a landowner's house to the left of the road stood carriages, wagons, and crowds of orderlies and sentinels. The commander in chief was putting up there, but just when Pierre arrived he was not in and hardly any of the staff were there—they had gone to the church service. Pierre drove on toward Górki.

When he had ascended the hill and reached the little village street, he saw for the first time peasant militiamen in their white shirts and with crosses on their caps, who, talking and laughing loudly, animated and

perspiring, were at work on a huge knoll overgrown with grass to the right of the road.

Some of them were digging, others were wheeling barrowloads of earth along planks, while others stood about doing nothing.

Two officers were standing on the knoll, directing the men. On seeing these peasants, who were evidently still amused by the novelty of their position as soldiers, Pierre once more thought of the wounded men at Mozháysk and understood what the soldier had meant when he said: "They want the whole nation to fall on them." The sight of these bearded peasants at work on the battlefield, with their queer, clumsy boots and perspiring necks, and their shirts opening from the left toward the middle, unfastened, exposing their sunburned collarbones, impressed Pierre more strongly with the solemnity and importance of the moment than anything he had yet seen or heard.

21. Pierre ascends a knoll at Górki, surveys the scene, and inquires as to the "position" occupied. A procession carrying the "Smolénsk Mother of God." The reverence of the crowd and of Kutúzov

PIERRE STEPPED OUT of his carriage and, passing the toiling militiamen, ascended the knoll from which, according to the doctor, the battlefield could be seen.

It was about eleven o'clock. The sun shone somewhat to the left and behind him and brightly lit up the enormous panorama which, rising like an amphitheater, extended before him in the clear rarefied atmosphere.

From above on the left, bisecting that amphitheater, wound the Smolénsk highroad, passing through a village with a white church some five hundred paces in front of the knoll and below it. This was Borodinó. Below the village the road crossed the river by a bridge and, winding down and up, rose higher and higher to the village of Valúevo visible about four miles away, where Napoleon was then stationed. Beyond Valúevo the road disappeared into a yellowing forest on the horizon. Far in the distance in that birch and fir forest to the right of the road, the cross and belfry of the Kolochá Monastery gleamed in the sun. Here and there over the whole of that blue expanse, to right and left of the forest and the road, smoking campfires could be seen and indefinite masses of troops— ours and the enemy's. The ground to the right—along the course of the Kolochá and Moskvá rivers—was broken and hilly. Between the hollows the villages of Bezzúbova and Zakhárino showed in the distance. On the

left the ground was more level; there were fields of grain, and the smoking ruins of Semënovsk, which had been burned down, could be seen.

All that Pierre saw was so indefinite that neither the left nor the right side of the field fully satisfied his expectations. Nowhere could he see the battlefield he had expected to find, but only fields, meadows, troops, woods, the smoke of campfires, villages, mounds, and streams; and try as he would he could descry no military "position" in this place which teemed with life, nor could he even distinguish our troops from the enemy's.

"I must ask someone who knows," he thought, and addressed an officer who was looking with curiosity at his huge unmilitary figure.

"May I ask you," said Pierre, "what village that is in front?"

"Búrdino, isn't it?" said the officer, turning to his companion.

"Borodinó," the other corrected him.

The officer, evidently glad of an opportunity for a talk, moved up to Pierre.

"Are those our men there?" Pierre inquired.

"Yes, and there, further on, are the French," said the officer. "There they are, there . . . you can see them."

"Where? Where?" asked Pierre.

"One can see them with the naked eye. . . . Why, there!"

The officer pointed with his hand to the smoke visible on the left beyond the river, and the same stern and serious expression that Pierre had noticed on many of the faces he had met came into his face.

"Ah, so those are the French! And over there? . . ." Pierre pointed to a knoll on the left, near which some troops could be seen.

"Those are ours."

"Ah, ours! And there? . . ." Pierre pointed to another knoll in the distance with a big tree on it, near a village that lay in a hollow where also some campfires were smoking and something black was visible.

"That's his again," said the officer. (It was the Shevárdino Redoubt.) "It was ours yesterday, but now it is his."

"Then how about our position?"

"Our position?" replied the officer with a smile of satisfaction. "I can tell you quite clearly, because I constructed nearly all our entrenchments. There, you see? There's our center, at Borodinó, just there," and he pointed to the village in front of them with the white church. "That's where one crosses the Kolochá. You see down there where the rows of hay are lying in the hollow, there's the bridge. That's our center. Our right flank is over there"—he pointed sharply to the right, far away in the broken ground—"That's where the Moskvá River is, and we have thrown up three redoubts there, very strong ones. The left flank . . ." here the

officer paused. "Well, you see, that's difficult to explain. . . . Yesterday our left flank was there at Shevárdino, you see, where the oak is, but now we have withdrawn our left wing—now it is over there, do you see that village and the smoke? That's Semënovsk, yes, there," he pointed to Raévski's knoll. "But the battle will hardly be there. *His* having moved his troops there is only a ruse; he will probably pass round to the right of the Moskvá. But wherever it may be, many a man will be missing tomorrow!" he remarked.

An elderly sergeant who had approached the officer while he was giving these explanations had waited in silence for him to finish speaking, but at this point, evidently not liking the officer's remark, interrupted him.

"Gabions must be sent for," said he sternly.

The officer appeared abashed, as though he understood that one might think of how many men would be missing tomorrow but ought not to speak of it.

"Well, send number three company again," the officer replied hurriedly.

"And you, are you one of the doctors?"

"No, I've come on my own," answered Pierre, and he went down the hill again, passing the militiamen.

"Oh, those damned fellows!" muttered the officer who followed him, holding his nose as he ran past the men at work.

"There they are . . . bringing her, coming . . . There they are . . . They'll be here in a minute . . ." voices were suddenly heard saying; and officers, soldiers, and militiamen began running forward along the road.

A church procession was coming up the hill from Borodinó. First along the dusty road came the infantry in ranks, bareheaded and with arms reversed. From behind them came the sound of church singing.

Soldiers and militiamen ran bareheaded past Pierre toward the procession.

"They are bringing her, our Protectress! . . . The Iberian Mother of God!" someone cried.*

"The Smolénsk Mother of God," another corrected him.

The militiamen, both those who had been in the village and those who had been at work on the battery, threw down their spades and ran to meet the church procession. Following the battalion that marched along the dusty road came priests in their vestments—one little old man in a hood with attendants and singers. Behind them soldiers and officers bore a large, dark-faced icon with an embossed metal cover. This was the icon that had been brought from Smolénsk and had since accompanied the

* *Names of an icon of the Holy Virgin Mother.*—A.M.

army. Behind, before, and on both sides, crowds of militiamen with bared heads walked, ran, and bowed to the ground.

At the summit of the hill they stopped with the icon; the men who had been holding it up by the linen bands attached to it were relieved by others, the chanters relit their censers, and service began. The hot rays of the sun beat down vertically and a fresh soft wind played with the hair of the bared heads and with the ribbons decorating the icon. The singing did not sound loud under the open sky. An immense crowd of bareheaded officers, soldiers, and militiamen surrounded the icon. Behind the priest and a chanter stood the notabilities on a spot reserved for them. A bald general with a St. George's Cross on his neck stood just behind the priest's back, and without crossing himself (he was evidently a German) patiently awaited the end of the service, which he considered it necessary to hear to the end, probably to arouse the patriotism of the Russian people. Another general stood in a martial pose, crossing himself by shaking his hand in front of his chest while looking about him. Standing among the crowd of peasants, Pierre recognized several acquaintances among these notables, but did not look at them—his whole attention was absorbed in watching the serious expression on the faces of the crowd of soldiers and militiamen who were all gazing eagerly at the icon. As soon as the tired chanters, who were singing the service for the twentieth time that day, began lazily and mechanically to sing: "Save from calamity Thy servants, O Mother of God," and the priest and deacon chimed in: "For to Thee under God we all flee as to an inviolable bulwark and protection," there again kindled in all those faces the same expression of consciousness of the solemnity of the impending moment that Pierre had seen on the faces at the foot of the hill at Mozháysk and momentarily on many and many faces he had met that morning; and heads were bowed more frequently and hair tossed back, and sighs and the sound men made as they crossed themselves were heard.

The crowd round the icon suddenly parted and pressed against Pierre. Someone, a very important personage judging by the haste with which way was made for him, was approaching the icon.

It was Kutúzov, who had been riding round the position and on his way back to Tatárinova had stopped where the service was being held. Pierre recognized him at once by his peculiar figure, which distinguished him from everybody else.

With a long overcoat on his exceedingly stout, round-shouldered body, with uncovered white head and puffy face showing the white ball of the eye he had lost, Kutúzov walked with plunging, swaying gait into the crowd and stopped behind the priest. He crossed himself with an ac-

customed movement, bent till he touched the ground with his hand, and bowed his white head with a deep sigh. Behind Kutúzov was Bennigsen and the suite. Despite the presence of the commander in chief, who attracted the attention of all the superior officers, the militiamen and soldiers continued their prayers without looking at him.

When the service was over, Kutúzov stepped up to the icon, sank heavily to his knees, bowed to the ground, and for a long time tried vainly to rise, but could not do so on account of his weakness and weight. His white head twitched with the effort. At last he rose, kissed the icon as a child does with naïvely pouting lips, and again bowed till he touched the ground with his hand. The other generals followed his example, then the officers, and after them with excited faces, pressing on one another, crowding, panting, and pushing, scrambled the soldiers and militiamen.

22. Borís meets Pierre. Dólokhov makes his way to Kutúzov. Kutúzov notices Pierre. Dólokhov asks Pierre to be reconciled

STAGGERING amid the crush, Pierre looked about him.

"Count Peter Kirílovich! How did you get here?" said a voice. Pierre looked round. Borís Drubetskóy, brushing his knees with his hand (he had probably soiled them when he, too, had knelt before the icon), came up to him smiling. Borís was elegantly dressed, with a slightly martial touch appropriate to a campaign. He wore a long coat and like Kutúzov had a whip slung across his shoulder.

Meanwhile Kutúzov had reached the village and seated himself in the shade of the nearest house, on a bench which one Cossack had run to fetch and another had hastily covered with a rug. An immense and brilliant suite surrounded him.

The icon was carried further, accompanied by the throng. Pierre stopped some thirty paces from Kutúzov, talking to Borís.

He explained his wish to be present at the battle and to see the position.

"This is what you must do," said Borís. "I will do the honors of the camp to you. You will see everything best from where Count Bennigsen will be. I am in attendance on him, you know; I'll mention it to him. But if you want to ride round the position, come along with us. We are just going to the left flank. Then when we get back, do spend the night with me and we'll arrange a game of cards. Of course you know Dmítri Sergéevich? Those are his quarters," and he pointed to the third house in the village of Górki.

"But I should like to see the right flank. They say it's very strong," said Pierre. "I should like to start from the Moskvá River and ride round the whole position."

"Well, you can do that later, but the chief thing is the left flank."

"Yes, yes. But where is Prince Bolkónski's regiment? Can you point it out to me?"

"Prince Andrew's? We shall pass it and I'll take you to him."

"What about the left flank?" asked Pierre.

"To tell you the truth, between ourselves, God only knows what state our left flank is in," said Borís confidentially lowering his voice. "It is not at all what Count Bennigsen intended. He meant to fortify that knoll quite differently, but . . ." Borís shrugged his shoulders, "his Serene Highness would not have it, or someone persuaded him. You see . . ." but Borís did not finish, for at that moment Kaysárov, Kutúzov's adjutant, came up to Pierre. "Ah, Kaysárov!" said Borís, addressing him with an unembarrassed smile, "I was just trying to explain our position to the count. It is amazing how his Serene Highness could so foresee the intentions of the French!"

"You mean the left flank?" asked Kaysárov.

"Yes, exactly; the left flank is now extremely strong."

Though Kutúzov had dismissed all unnecessary men from the staff, Borís had contrived to remain at headquarters after the changes. He had established himself with Count Bennigsen, who, like all on whom Borís had been in attendance, considered young Prince Drubetskóy an invaluable man.

In the higher command there were two sharply defined parties: Kutúzov's party and that of Bennigsen, the chief of staff. Borís belonged to the latter and no one else, while showing servile respect to Kutúzov, could so create an impression that the old fellow was not much good and that Bennigsen managed everything. Now the decisive moment of battle had come when Kutúzov would be destroyed and the power pass to Bennigsen, or even if Kutúzov won the battle it would be felt that everything was done by Bennigsen. In any case many great rewards would have to be given for tomorrow's action, and new men would come to the front. So Borís was full of nervous vivacity all that day.

After Kaysárov, others whom Pierre knew came up to him, and he had not time to reply to all the questions about Moscow that were showered upon him, or to listen to all that was told him. The faces all expressed animation and apprehension, but it seemed to Pierre that the cause of the excitement shown in some of these faces lay chiefly in questions of personal success; his mind, however, was occupied by the different expression

he saw on other faces—an expression that spoke not of personal matters but of the universal questions of life and death. Kutúzov noticed Pierre's figure and the group gathered round him.

"Call him to me," said Kutúzov.

An adjutant told Pierre of his Serene Highness' wish, and Pierre went toward Kutúzov's bench. But a militiaman got there before him. It was Dólokhov.

"How did that fellow get here?" asked Pierre.

"He's a creature that wriggles in anywhere!" was the answer. "He has been degraded, you know. Now he wants to bob up again. He's been proposing some scheme or other and has crawled into the enemy's picket line at night. . . . He's a brave fellow."

Pierre took off his hat and bowed respectfully to Kutúzov.

"I concluded that if I reported to your Serene Highness you might send me away or say that you knew what I was reporting, but then I shouldn't lose anything . . ." Dólokhov was saying.

"Yes, yes."

"But if I were right, I should be rendering a service to my Fatherland for which I am ready to die."

"Yes, yes."

"And should your Serene Highness require a man who will not spare his skin, please think of me. . . . Perhaps I may prove useful to your Serene Highness."

"Yes . . . Yes . . ." Kutúzov repeated, his laughing eye narrowing more and more as he looked at Pierre.

Just then Borís, with his courtierlike adroitness, stepped up to Pierre's side near Kutúzov and in a most natural manner, without raising his voice, said to Pierre, as though continuing an interrupted conversation:

"The militia have put on clean white shirts to be ready to die. What heroism, Count!"

Borís evidently said this to Pierre in order to be overheard by his Serene Highness. He knew Kutúzov's attention would be caught by those words, and so it was.

"What are you saying about the militia?" he asked Borís.

"Preparing for tomorrow, your Serene Highness—for death—they have put on clean shirts."

"Ah . . . a wonderful, a matchless people!" said Kutúzov; and he closed his eyes and swayed his head. "A matchless people!" he repeated with a sigh.

"So you want to smell gunpowder?" he said to Pierre. "Yes, it's a

pleasant smell. I have the honor to be one of your wife's adorers. Is she well? My quarters are at your service."

And as often happens with old people, Kutúzov began looking about absent-mindedly as if forgetting all he wanted to say or do.

Then, evidently remembering what he wanted, he beckoned to Andrew Kaysárov, his adjutant's brother.

"Those verses . . . those verses of Márin's . . . how do they go, eh? Those he wrote about Gerákov: 'Lectures for the corps inditing.' . . . Recite them, recite them!" said he, evidently preparing to laugh.*

Kaysárov recited. . . . Kutúzov smilingly nodded his head to the rhythm of the verses.

When Pierre had left Kutúzov, Dólokhov came up to him and took his hand.

"I am very glad to meet you here, Count," he said aloud, regardless of the presence of strangers and in a particularly resolute and solemn tone. "On the eve of a day when God alone knows who of us is fated to survive, I am glad of this opportunity to tell you that I regret the misunderstandings that occurred between us and should wish you not to have any ill feeling for me. I beg you to forgive me."

Pierre looked at Dólokhov with a smile, not knowing what to say to him. With tears in his eyes Dólokhov embraced Pierre and kissed him.

Borís said a few words to his general, and Count Bennigsen turned to Pierre and proposed that he should ride with him along the line.

"It will interest you," said he.

"Yes, very much," replied Pierre.

Half an hour later Kutúzov left for Tatárinova, and Bennigsen and his suite, with Pierre among them, set out on their ride along the line.

* S. N. Márin was an aide-de-camp of Alexander I's, well known for his parodies and amusing verses. G. V. Gerákov was a captain in the army, a teacher in the military school, and the author of numerous patriotic works of very poor quality. He was the object of much ridicule. Márin's verse about him was in the form of a prophecy:

> You will always go on writing
> And to death your readers bore:
> Lectures for the corps inditing—
> Be a captain evermore.

—A.M.

23. Pierre rides to the left flank with Bennigsen, who explains the "position" in a way Pierre does not understand and changes one of Kutúzov's dispositions

FROM GÓRKI, Bennigsen descended the highroad to the bridge which, when they had looked at it from the hill, the officer had pointed out as being the center of our position and where rows of fragrant new-mown hay lay by the riverside. They rode across that bridge into the village of Borodinó and thence turned to the left, passing an enormous number of troops and guns, and came to a high knoll where militiamen were digging. This was the redoubt, as yet unnamed, which afterwards became known as the Raévski Redoubt, or the Knoll Battery, but Pierre paid no special attention to it. He did not know that it would become more memorable to him than any other spot on the plain of Borodinó.

They then crossed the hollow to Semënovsk, where the soldiers were dragging away the last logs from the huts and barns. Then they rode downhill and uphill, across a ryefield trodden and beaten down as if by hail, following a track freshly made by the artillery over the furrows of the plowed land, and reached some flèches * which were still being dug.

At the flèches Bennigsen stopped and began looking at the Shevárdino Redoubt opposite, which had been ours the day before and where several horsemen could be descried. The officers said that either Napoleon or Murat was there, and they all gazed eagerly at this little group of horse-men. Pierre also looked at them, trying to guess which of the scarcely discernible figures was Napoleon. At last those mounted men rode away from the mound and disappeared.

Bennigsen spoke to a general who approached him, and began explain-ing the whole position of our troops. Pierre listened to him, straining each faculty to understand the essential points of the impending battle, but was mortified to feel that his mental capacity was inadequate for the task. He could make nothing of it. Bennigsen stopped speaking and, noticing that Pierre was listening, suddenly said to him:

"I don't think this interests you?"

"On the contrary it's very interesting!" replied Pierre not quite truth-fully.

From the flèches they rode still farther to the left, along a road winding through a thick, low-growing birch wood. In the middle of the wood a brown hare with white feet sprang out and, scared by the tramp of the many horses, grew so confused that it leaped along the road in front of

* A kind of entrenchment.—L.T.

them for some time, arousing general attention and laughter, and only when several voices shouted at it did it dart to one side and disappear in the thicket. After going through the wood for about a mile and a half they came out on a glade where troops of Túchkov's corps were stationed to defend the left flank.

Here, at the extreme left flank, Bennigsen talked a great deal and with much heat, and, as it seemed to Pierre, gave orders of great military importance. In front of Túchkov's troops was some high ground not occupied by troops. Bennigsen loudly criticized this mistake, saying that it was madness to leave a height which commanded the country around unoccupied and to place troops below it. Some of the generals expressed the same opinion. One in particular declared with martial heat that they were put there to be slaughtered. Bennigsen on his own authority ordered the troops to occupy the high ground. This disposition on the left flank increased Pierre's doubt of his own capacity to understand military matters. Listening to Bennigsen and the generals criticizing the position of the troops behind the hill, he quite understood them and shared their opinion, but for that very reason he could not understand how the man who put them there behind the hill could have made so gross and palpable a blunder.

Pierre did not know that these troops were not, as Bennigsen supposed, put there to defend the position, but were in a concealed position as an ambush, that they should not be seen and might be able to strike an approaching enemy unexpectedly. Bennigsen did not know this and moved the troops forward according to his own ideas without mentioning the matter to the commander in chief.

24. Prince Andrew's reflections on life and death. Pierre comes to see him

ON THAT BRIGHT EVENING of August 25, Prince Andrew lay leaning on his elbow in a broken-down shed in the village of Knyazkóvo at the further end of his regiment's encampment. Through a gap in the broken wall he could see, beside the wooden fence, a row of thirty-year-old birches with their lower branches lopped off, a field on which shocks of oats were standing, and some bushes near which rose the smoke of campfires—the soldiers' kitchens.

Narrow and burdensome and useless to anyone as his life now seemed to him, Prince Andrew on the eve of battle felt agitated and irritable as he had done seven years before at Austerlitz.

He had received and given the orders for next day's battle and had nothing more to do. But his thoughts—the simplest, clearest, and therefore most terrible thoughts—would give him no peace. He knew that tomorrow's battle would be the most terrible of all he had taken part in, and for the first time in his life the possibility of death presented itself to him—not in relation to any worldly matter or with reference to its effect on others, but simply in relation to himself, to his own soul—vividly, plainly, terribly, and almost as a certainty. And from the height of this perception all that had previously tormented and preoccupied him suddenly became illumined by a cold white light without shadows, without perspective, and without distinction of outline. All life appeared to him like magic-lantern pictures at which he had long been gazing by artificial light through a glass. Now he suddenly saw those badly daubed pictures in clear daylight and without a glass. "Yes, yes! There they are, those false images that agitated, enraptured, and tormented me," said he to himself, passing in review the principal pictures of the magic lantern of life and regarding them now in the cold white daylight of his clear perception of death. "There they are, those rudely painted figures that once seemed splendid and mysterious. Glory, the good of society, love of a woman, the Fatherland itself—how important these pictures appeared to me, with what profound meaning they seemed to be filled! And it is all so simple, pale, and crude in the cold white light of this morning which I feel is dawning for me." The three great sorrows of his life held his attention in particular: his love for a woman, his father's death, and the French invasion which had overrun half Russia. "Love! . . . that little girl who seemed to me brimming over with mystic forces! Yes, indeed, I loved her. I made romantic plans of love and happiness with her! Oh, what a boy I was!" he said aloud bitterly. "Ah me! I believed in some ideal love which was to keep her faithful to me for the whole year of my absence! Like the gentle dove in the fable she was to pine apart from me. . . . But it was much simpler really. . . . It was all very simple and horrible.

"When my father built Bald Hills he thought the place was his: his land, his air, his peasants. But Napoleon came and swept him aside, unconscious of his existence, as he might brush a chip from his path, and his Bald Hills and his whole life fell to pieces. Princess Mary says it is a trial sent from above. What is the trial for, when he is not here and will never return? He is not here! For whom then is the trial intended? The Fatherland, the destruction of Moscow! And tomorrow I shall be killed, perhaps not even by a Frenchman but by one of our own men, by a soldier discharging a musket close to my ear as one of them did yesterday,

and the French will come and take me by head and heels and fling me into a hole that I may not stink under their noses, and new conditions of life will arise, which will seem quite ordinary to others and about which I shall know nothing. I shall not exist. . . ."

He looked at the row of birches shining in the sunshine, with their motionless green and yellow foliage and white bark. "To die . . . to be killed tomorrow . . . That I should not exist . . . That all this should still be, but no me. . . ."

And the birches with their light and shade, the curly clouds, the smoke of the campfires, and all that was around him changed and seemed terrible and menacing. A cold shiver ran down his spine. He rose quickly, went out of the shed, and began to walk about.

After he had returned, voices were heard outside the shed. "Who's that?" he cried.

The red-nosed Captain Timókhin, formerly Dólokhov's squadron commander, but now from lack of officers a battalion commander, shyly entered the shed followed by an adjutant and the regimental paymaster.

Prince Andrew rose hastily, listened to the business they had come about, gave them some further instructions, and was about to dismiss them when he heard a familiar, lisping voice behind the shed.

"Devil take it!" said the voice of a man stumbling over something.

Prince Andrew looked out of the shed and saw Pierre, who had tripped over a pole on the ground and had nearly fallen, coming his way. It was unpleasant to Prince Andrew to meet people of his own set in general, and Pierre especially, for he reminded him of all the painful moments of his last visit to Moscow.

"You? What a surprise!" said he. "What brings you here? This is unexpected!"

As he said this his eyes and face expressed more than coldness—they expressed hostility, which Pierre noticed at once. He had approached the shed full of animation, but on seeing Prince Andrew's face he felt constrained and ill at ease.

"I have come . . . simply . . . you know . . . come . . . it interests me," said Pierre, who had so often that day senselessly repeated that word "interesting." "I wish to see the battle."

"Oh yes, and what do the Masonic brothers say about war? How would they stop it?" said Prince Andrew sarcastically. "Well, and how's Moscow? And my people? Have they reached Moscow at last?" he asked seriously.

"Yes, they have. Julie Drubetskáya told me so. I went to see them, but missed them. They have gone to your estate near Moscow."

25. *Timókhin's opinion of Kutúzov. Prince Andrew on Bar-
clay de Tolly. War and chess. The spirit of the army. Wolzo-
gen and Clausewitz. "The war must be extended widely."
Pierre understands the importance of this war. "Not take
prisoners." What is war? Prince Andrew thinks of Natásha*

THE OFFICERS were about to take leave, but Prince Andrew, apparently
reluctant to be left alone with his friend, asked them to stay and
have tea. Seats were brought in and so was the tea. The officers gazed
with surprise at Pierre's huge stout figure and listened to his talk of
Moscow and the position of our army, round which he had ridden. Prince
Andrew remained silent, and his expression was so forbidding that Pierre
addressed his remarks chiefly to Timókhin, the good-natured battalion
commander.

"So you understand the whole position of our troops?" Prince Andrew
interrupted him.

"Yes—that is, how do you mean?" said Pierre. "Not being a military
man I can't say I have understood it fully, but I understand the general
position."

"Well, then, you know more than anyone else, be it who it may,"
said Prince Andrew.

"Oh!" said Pierre, looking over his spectacles in perplexity at Prince
Andrew. "Well, and what do you think of Kutúzov's appointment?" he
asked.

"I was very glad of his appointment, that's all I know," replied Prince
Andrew.

"And tell me your opinion of Barclay de Tolly. In Moscow they are
saying heaven knows what about him. . . . What do you think of him?"

"Ask them," replied Prince Andrew, indicating the officers.

Pierre looked at Timókhin with the condescendingly interrogative
smile with which everybody involuntarily addressed that officer.

"We see light * again, since his Serenity has been appointed, your
excellency," said Timókhin timidly, and continually turning to glance
at his colonel.

"Why so?" asked Pierre.

"Well, to mention only firewood and fodder, let me inform you. Why,

* *This is an untranslatable play on words. Kutúzov was addressed as "Seren-
ity," svetléyshi, the first syllable of which in Russian means light. So Timókhin
says that at the appointment of his Serenity they saw light again.*—A.M.

when we were retreating from Sventsyáni we dare not touch a stick or a
wisp of hay or anything. You see, we were going away, so *he* * would get it
all; wasn't it so, your excellency?" and again Timókhin turned to the
prince. "But we daren't. In our regiment two officers were court-martialed
for that kind of thing. But when his Serenity took command everything
became straightforward. Now we see light. . . ."

"Then why was it forbidden?"

Timókhin looked about in confusion, not knowing what or how to
answer such a question. Pierre put the same question to Prince Andrew.

"Why, so as not to lay waste the country we were abandoning to the
enemy," said Prince Andrew with venomous irony. "It is very sound: one
can't permit the land to be pillaged and accustom the troops to marauding.
At Smolénsk too he judged correctly that the French might outflank us,
as they had larger forces. But he could not understand this," cried Prince
Andrew in a shrill voice that seemed to escape him involuntarily: "he
could not understand that there, for the first time, we were fighting for
Russian soil, and that there was a spirit in the men such as I had never seen
before, that we had held the French for two days, and that that success
had increased our strength tenfold. He ordered us to retreat, and all our
efforts and losses went for nothing. He had no thought of betraying us,
he tried to do the best he could, he thought out everything, and that is
why he is unsuitable. He is unsuitable now, just because he plans out
everything very thoroughly and accurately as every German has to. How
can I explain? . . . Well, say your father has a German valet, and he is a
splendid valet and satisfies your father's requirements better than you
could, then it's all right to let him serve. But if your father is mortally
sick you'll send the valet away and attend to your father with your own
unpracticed, awkward hands, and will soothe him better than a skilled
man who is a stranger could. So it has been with Barclay. While Russia
was well, a foreigner could serve her and be a splendid minister; but as
soon as she is in danger she needs one of her own kin. But in your Club
they have been making him out a traitor! They slander him as a traitor,
and the only result will be that afterwards, ashamed of their false accusa-
tions, they will make him out a hero or a genius instead of a traitor, and
that will be still more unjust. He is an honest and very punctilious
German."

"And they say he's a skillful commander," rejoined Pierre.

"I don't understand what is meant by 'a skillful commander,'" replied
Prince Andrew ironically.

* *The enemy was always* he *to the Russians*—A.M.

"A skillful commander?" replied Pierre. "Why, one who foresees all contingencies . . . and foresees the adversary's intentions."

"But that's impossible," said Prince Andrew as if it were a matter settled long ago.

Pierre looked at him in surprise.

"And yet they say that war is like a game of chess?" he remarked.

"Yes," replied Prince Andrew, "but with this little difference, that in chess you may think over each move as long as you please and are not limited for time, and with this difference too, that a knight is always stronger than a pawn, and two pawns are always stronger than one, while in war a battalion is sometimes stronger than a division and sometimes weaker than a company. The relative strength of bodies of troops can never be known to anyone. Believe me," he went on, "if things depended on arrangements made by the staff, I should be there making arrangements, but instead of that I have the honor to serve here in the regiment with these gentlemen, and I consider that on us tomorrow's battle will depend and not on those others. . . . Success never depends, and never will depend, on position, or equipment, or even on numbers, and least of all on position."

"But on what then?"

"On the feeling that is in me and in him," he pointed to Timókhin, "and in each soldier."

Prince Andrew glanced at Timókhin, who looked at his commander in alarm and bewilderment. In contrast to his former reticent taciturnity Prince Andrew now seemed excited. He could apparently not refrain from expressing the thoughts that had suddenly occurred to him.

"A battle is won by those who firmly resolve to win it! Why did we lose the battle at Austerlitz? The French losses were almost equal to ours, but very early we said to ourselves that we were losing the battle, and we did lose it. And we said so because we had nothing to fight for there, we wanted to get away from the battlefield as soon as we could. 'We've lost, so let us run,' and we ran. If we had not said that till the evening, heaven knows what might not have happened. But tomorrow we shan't say it! You talk about our position, the left flank weak and the right flank too extended," he went on. "That's all nonsense, there's nothing of the kind. But what awaits us tomorrow? A hundred million most diverse chances which will be decided on the instant by the fact that our men or theirs run or do not run, and that this man or that man is killed, but all that is being done at present is only play. The fact is that those men with whom you have ridden round the position not only do not help

matters, but hinder. They are only concerned with their own petty interests."

"At such a moment?" said Pierre reproachfully.

"At such a moment!" Prince Andrew repeated. "To them it is only a moment affording opportunities to undermine a rival and obtain an extra cross or ribbon. For me tomorrow means this: a Russian army of a hundred thousand and a French army of a hundred thousand have met to fight, and the thing is that these two hundred thousand men will fight and the side that fights more fiercely and spares itself least will win. And if you like I will tell you that whatever happens and whatever muddles those at the top may make, we shall win tomorrow's battle. Tomorrow, happen what may, we shall win!"

"There now, your excellency! That's the truth, the real truth," said Timókhin. "Who would spare himself now? The soldiers in my battalion, believe me, wouldn't drink their vodka! 'It's not the day for that!' they say."

All were silent. The officers rose. Prince Andrew went out of the shed with them, giving final orders to the adjutant. After they had gone Pierre approached Prince Andrew and was about to start a conversation when they heard the clatter of three horses' hoofs on the road not far from the shed, and looking in that direction Prince Andrew recognized Wolzogen and Clausewitz * accompanied by a Cossack. They rode close by continuing to converse, and Prince Andrew involuntarily heard these words:

"*Der Krieg muss in Raum verlegt werden. Der Ansicht kann ich nicht genug Preis geben* [The war must be extended widely. I cannot sufficiently commend that view]," said one of them.

"*Oh, ja* [Oh, yes]," said the other, "*der Zweck ist nur den Feind zu schwächen, so kann man gewiss nicht den Verlust der Privat-Personen in Achtung nehmen* [the only aim is to weaken the enemy, so of course one cannot take into account the loss of private individuals]."

"Oh, no," agreed the other.

"Extend widely!" said Prince Andrew with an angry snort, when they had ridden past. "In that 'extend' were my father, son, and sister, at Bald Hills. That's all the same to him! That's what I was saying to you—

* *Karl von Clausewitz (1780-1831), a Prussian general and celebrated writer on the theory and history of war. In 1812, like many other Prussian officers, he entered the Russian service though Prussia was officially in alliance with Napoleon. He first served as adjutant to Pfuel. His greatest work is* Vom Kriege, *an exposition of the philosophy of war. In his volumes on military history he treats of the war of 1812 as well as of Napoleon's other campaigns.*—A.M.

those German gentlemen won't win the battle tomorrow but will only make all the mess they can, because they have nothing in their German heads but theories not worth an empty eggshell and haven't in their hearts the one thing needed tomorrow—that which Timókhin has. They have yielded up all Europe to *him*, and have now come to teach us. Fine teachers!" and again his voice grew shrill.

"So you think we shall win tomorrow's battle?" asked Pierre.

"Yes, yes," answered Prince Andrew absently. "One thing I would do if I had the power," he began again, "I would not take prisoners. Why take prisoners? It's chivalry! The French have destroyed my home and are on their way to destroy Moscow, they have outraged and are outraging me every moment. They are my enemies. In my opinion they are all criminals. And so thinks Timókhin and the whole army. They should be executed! Since they are my foes they cannot be my friends, whatever may have been said at Tilsit."

"Yes, yes," muttered Pierre, looking with shining eyes at Prince Andrew. "I quite agree with you!"

The question that had perturbed Pierre on the Mozháysk hill and all that day now seemed to him quite clear and completely solved. He now understood the whole meaning and importance of this war and of the impending battle. All he had seen that day, all the significant and stern expressions on the faces he had seen in passing, were lit up for him by a new light. He understood that latent heat (as they say in physics) of patriotism which was present in all these men he had seen, and this explained to him why they all prepared for death calmly, and as it were lightheartedly.

"Not take prisoners," Prince Andrew continued: "That by itself would quite change the whole war and make it less cruel. As it is we have played at war—that's what's vile! We play at magnanimity and all that stuff. Such magnanimity and sensibility are like the magnanimity and sensibility of a lady who faints when she sees a calf being killed: she is so kindhearted that she can't look at blood, but enjoys eating the calf served up with sauce. They talk to us of the rules of war, of chivalry, of flags of truce, of mercy to the unfortunate and so on. It's all rubbish! I saw chivalry and flags of truce in 1805; they humbugged us and we humbugged them. They plunder other people's houses, issue false paper money, and worst of all they kill my children and my father, and then talk of rules of war and magnanimity to foes! Take no prisoners, but kill and be killed! He who has come to this as I have through the same sufferings . . ."

Prince Andrew, who had thought it was all the same to him whether or not Moscow was taken as Smolénsk had been, was suddenly checked

in his speech by an unexpected cramp in his throat. He paced up and down a few times in silence, but his eyes glittered feverishly and his lips quivered as he began to speak again.

"If there was none of this magnanimity in war, we should go to war only when it was worth while going to certain death, as now. Then there would not be war because Paul Ivánovich had offended Michael Ivánovich. And when there was a war, like this one, it would be war! And then the determination of the troops would be quite different. Then all these Westphalians and Hessians whom Napoleon is leading would not follow him into Russia, and we should not go to fight in Austria and Prussia without knowing why. War is not courtesy but the most horrible thing in life; and we ought to understand that and not play at war. We ought to accept this terrible necessity sternly and seriously. It all lies in that: get rid of falsehood and let war be war and not a game. As it is now, war is the favorite pastime of the idle and frivolous. The military calling is the most highly honored.

"But what is war? What is needed for success in warfare? What are the habits of the military? The aim of war is murder; the methods of war are spying, treachery, and their encouragement, the ruin of a country's inhabitants, robbing them or stealing to provision the army, and fraud and falsehood termed military craft. The habits of the military class are the absence of freedom, that is, discipline, idleness, ignorance, cruelty, debauchery, and drunkenness. And in spite of all this it is the highest class, respected by everyone. All the kings, except the Chinese, wear military uniforms, and he who kills most people receives the highest rewards.

"They meet, as we shall meet tomorrow, to murder one another; they kill and maim tens of thousands, and then have thanksgiving services for having killed so many people (they even exaggerate the number), and they announce a victory, supposing that the more people they have killed the greater their achievement. How does God above look at them and hear them?" exclaimed Prince Andrew in a shrill, piercing voice. "Ah, my friend, it has of late become hard for me to live. I see that I have begun to understand too much. And it doesn't do for man to taste of the tree of knowledge of good and evil. . . . Ah, well, it's not for long!" he added.*

* *Prince Andrew in this chapter expresses an opinion of the campaign of 1812 near to that held by Tolstóy when writing the novel, and in some places even expresses Tolstóy's later view of war as an absolutely evil social phenomenon. When writing* War and Peace *that view had not yet sunk deeply, or occupied a permanent place, in Tolstóy's outlook on life—that occurred considerably later—but it here flashes out in certain sentences like the lightning of*

"However, you're sleepy, and it's time for me to sleep. Go back to Górki!" said Prince Andrew suddenly.

"Oh, no!" Pierre replied, looking at Prince Andrew with frightened, compassionate eyes.

"Go, go! Before a battle one must have one's sleep out," repeated Prince Andrew.

He came quickly up to Pierre and embraced and kissed him.

"Good-by, be off!" he shouted. "Whether we meet again or not . . ." and turning away hurriedly he entered the shed.

It was already dark, and Pierre could not make out whether the expression of Prince Andrew's face was angry or tender.

For some time he stood in silence considering whether he should follow him or go away. "No, he does not want it!" Pierre concluded. "And I know that this is our last meeting!" He sighed deeply and rode back to Górki.

On re-entering the shed Prince Andrew lay down on a rug, but he could not sleep.

He closed his eyes. One picture succeeded another in his imagination. On one of them he dwelt long and joyfully. He vividly recalled an evening in Petersburg. Natásha with animated and excited face was telling him how she had gone to look for mushrooms the previous summer and had lost her way in the big forest. She incoherently described the depths of the forest, her feelings, and a talk with a beekeeper she met, and constantly interrupted her story to say: "No, I can't! I'm not telling it right; no, you don't understand," though he encouraged her by saying that he did understand, and he really had understood all she wanted to say. But Natásha was not satisfied with her own words: she felt that they did not convey the passionately poetic feeling she had experienced that

a coming storm. Even before this, in The Raid, one of his very first stories (1853), describing a march through beautiful Caucasian scenery, he had written: "Can it be that there is not room for all men on this beautiful earth under these immeasurable starry heavens? Can it be possible that in the midst of this entrancing nature, feelings of hatred, vengeance, or the passion for exterminating their fellows can endure in the souls of men? All that is unkind in the hearts of men ought, one would think, to vanish at the touch of nature, that most direct expression of beauty and goodness." And at the end of Sevastopol in May (1855) the same feeling was again expressed. We have here an instance of the way in which feelings Tolstóy experienced before thinking matters out planted seed in his soul that many years later grew into great trees throwing their shade far around.—A.M.

day and wished to convey. "He was such a delightful old man, and it was so dark in the forest . . . and he had such kind . . . No, I can't describe it," she had said, flushed and excited. Prince Andrew smiled now the same happy smile as then when he had looked into her eyes. "I understood her," he thought. "I not only understood her, but it was just that inner, spiritual force, that sincerity, that frankness of soul—that very soul of hers which seemed to be fettered by her body—it was that soul I loved in her . . . loved so strongly and happily . . ." and suddenly he remembered how his love had ended. "*He* did not need anything of that kind. *He* neither saw nor understood anything of the sort. He only saw in her a pretty and fresh young girl, with whom he did not deign to unite his fate. And I? . . . and he is still alive and gay!"

Prince Andrew jumped up as if someone had burned him, and again began pacing up and down in front of the shed.

26. De Beausset brings a portrait of the "King of Rome" to Napoleon. Napoleon's proclamation

O**N A**UGUST 25, the eve of the battle of Borodinó, M. de Beausset, prefect of the French Emperor's palace, arrived at Napoleon's quarters at Valúevo with Colonel Fabvier, the former from Paris and the latter from Madrid.

Donning his court uniform, M. de Beausset ordered a box he had brought for the Emperor to be carried before him and entered the first compartment of Napoleon's tent, where he began opening the box while conversing with Napoleon's aides-de-camp who surrounded him.

Fabvier, not entering the tent, remained at the entrance talking to some generals of his acquaintance.

The Emperor Napoleon had not yet left his bedroom and was finishing his toilet. Slightly snorting and grunting, he presented now his back and now his plump hairy chest to the brush with which his valet was rubbing him down. Another valet, with his finger over the mouth of a bottle, was sprinkling Eau de Cologne on the Emperor's pampered body with an expression which seemed to say that he alone knew where and how much Eau de Cologne should be sprinkled. Napoleon's short hair was wet and matted on the forehead, but his face, though puffy and yellow, expressed physical satisfaction. "Go on, harder, go on!" he muttered to the valet who was rubbing him, slightly twitching and grunting. An aide-de-camp, who had entered the bedroom to report to the Emperor the number of prisoners taken in yesterday's action, was standing by the door after de-

livering his message, awaiting permission to withdraw. Napoleon, frowning, looked at him from under his brows.

"No prisoners!" said he, repeating the aide-de-camp's words. "They are forcing us to exterminate them. So much the worse for the Russian army. . . . Go on . . . harder, harder!" he muttered, hunching his back and presenting his fat shoulders.

"All right. Let Monsieur de Beausset enter, and Fabvier too," he said, nodding to the aide-de-camp.

"Yes, sire," and the aide-de-camp disappeared through the door of the tent.

Two valets rapidly dressed His Majesty, and wearing the blue uniform of the Guards he went with firm quick steps to the reception room.

De Beausset's hands meanwhile were busily engaged arranging the present he had brought from the Empress, on two chairs directly in front of the entrance. But Napoleon had dressed and come out with such unexpected rapidity that he had not time to finish arranging the surprise.

Napoleon noticed at once what they were about and guessed that they were not ready. He did not wish to deprive them of the pleasure of giving him a surprise, so he pretended not to see de Beausset and called Fabvier to him, listening silently and with a stern frown to what Fabvier told him of the heroism and devotion of his troops fighting at Salamanca, at the other end of Europe, with but one thought—to be worthy of their Emperor—and but one fear—to fail to please him. The result of that battle had been deplorable.* Napoleon made ironic remarks during Fabvier's account, as if he had not expected that matters could go otherwise in his absence.

"I must make up for that in Moscow," said Napoleon. "I'll see you later," he added, and summoned de Beausset, who by that time had prepared the surprise, having placed something on the chairs and covered it with a cloth.

De Beausset bowed low, with that courtly French bow which only the old retainers of the Bourbons knew how to make, and approached him, presenting an envelope.

Napoleon turned to him gaily and pulled his ear.

"You have hurried here. I am very glad. Well, what is Paris saying?"

* At the battle of Salamanca, on July 12 N.S., 1812, Wellington gained a brilliant victory over Marmont. In Spain Napoleon's attempt to hold a nation in subjection had been met by a strong and persistent popular resistance, and the drain on his resources during the Peninsular war was an important factor in the failure of his attempt to subdue Russia.—A.M.

he asked, suddenly changing his former stern expression for a most cordial tone.

"Sire, all Paris regrets your absence," replied de Beausset as was proper.

But though Napoleon knew that de Beausset had to say something of this kind, and though in his lucid moments he knew it was untrue, he was pleased to hear it from him. Again he honored him by touching his ear.

"I am very sorry to have made you travel so far," said he.

"Sire, I expected nothing less than to find you at the gates of Moscow," replied de Beausset.

Napoleon smiled and, lifting his head absent-mindedly, glanced to the right. An aide-de-camp approached with gliding steps and offered him a gold snuffbox, which he took.

"Yes, it has happened luckily for you," he said, raising the open snuffbox to his nose. "You are fond of travel, and in three days you will see Moscow. You surely did not expect to see that Asiatic capital. You will have a pleasant journey."

De Beausset bowed gratefully at this regard for his taste for travel (of which he had not till then been aware).

"Ha, what's this?" asked Napoleon, noticing that all the courtiers were looking at something concealed under a cloth.

With courtly adroitness de Beausset half turned and without turning his back to the Emperor retired two steps, twitching off the cloth at the same time, and said:

"A present to Your Majesty from the Empress." *

* *Material for this scene of Napoleon with the portrait of his son was supplied by the Mémoires of de Beausset himself, but Tolstóy has utilized it for his artistic purposes, quite changing the enthusiastically pathetic tone of that courtier's memoirs. For instance, when de Beausset, overflowing with amiabilities, told Napoleon that he expected to find him already under the walls of Moscow, Napoleon smiled, and replying: "Yes, you will see Moscow," absentmindedly looked to the right, at which customary sign an aide-de-camp hastened to hand him his snuffbox. In Tolstóy's novel Napoleon always takes snuff when angry or encountering some obstacle, as for instance in the scenes with Balashëv where his mood rapidly alternates. On the present occasion, though hearing flattering remarks to which he smilingly replies, at the word "Moscow" his instinctive gesture of looking round for a snuffbox betrays an uneasiness at having advanced so easily into the heart of the country. His recent conversation with his captive General Tuchkóv at Smolénsk, and the proposal for peace he had then made, showed that before Borodinó Napoleon felt seriously anx-*

It was a portrait, painted in bright colors by Gérard, of the son borne to Napoleon by the daughter of the Emperor of Austria, the boy whom for some reason everyone called "The King of Rome."

A very pretty curly-headed boy with a look of the Christ in the Sistine Madonna was depicted playing at stick and ball. The ball represented the terrestrial globe and the stick in his other hand a scepter.

Though it was not clear what the artist meant to express by depicting the so-called King of Rome spiking the earth with a stick, the allegory apparently seemed to Napoleon, as it had done to all who had seen it in Paris, quite clear and very pleasing.

"The King of Rome!" he said, pointing to the portrait with a graceful gesture. "Admirable!"

With the natural capacity of an Italian for changing the expression of his face at will, he drew nearer to the portrait and assumed a look of pensive tenderness. He felt that what he now said and did would be historical, and it seemed to him that it would now be best for him—whose grandeur enabled his son to play stick and ball with the terrestrial globe—to show, in contrast to that grandeur, the simplest paternal tenderness. His eyes grew dim, he moved forward, glanced round at a chair (which seemed to place itself under him), and sat down on it before the portrait. At a single gesture from him everyone went out on tiptoe, leaving the great man to himself and his emotion.

Having sat still for a while he touched—himself not knowing why—the thick spot of paint representing the highest light in the portrait, rose, and recalled de Beausset and the officer on duty. He ordered the portrait to be carried outside his tent, that the Old Guard, stationed round it, might not be deprived of the pleasure of seeing the King of Rome, the son and heir of their adored monarch.

And while he was doing M. de Beausset the honor of breakfasting with him, they heard, as Napoleon had anticipated, the rapturous cries of the officers and men of the Old Guard who had run up to see the portrait.

"Vive l'Empereur! Vive le roi de Rome! Vive l'Empereur!" came those ecstatic cries.

After breakfast Napoleon in de Beausset's presence dictated his order of the day to the army.

"Short and energetic!" he remarked when he had read over the proclamation which he had dictated straight off without corrections. It ran:

ious at the course this strange war was taking—a war in which he had not once felt himself master of the situation, but had constantly had to reckon with conditions imposed upon him.—A.M.

"Soldiers! This is the battle you have so longed for. Victory depends on you. It is essential for us; it will give us all we need: comfortable quarters and a speedy return to our country. Behave as you did at Austerlitz, Friedland, Vítebsk, and Smolénsk. Let our remotest posterity recall your achievements this day with pride. Let it be said of each of you: 'He was in the great battle before Moscow!' "

"Before Moscow!" repeated Napoleon, and inviting M. de Beausset, who was so fond of travel, to accompany him on his ride, he went out of the tent to where the horses stood saddled.

"Your Majesty is too kind!" replied de Beausset to the invitation to accompany the Emperor; he wanted to sleep, did not know how to ride and was afraid of doing so.

But Napoleon nodded to the traveler, and de Beausset had to mount. When Napoleon came out of the tent the shouting of the Guards before his son's portrait grew still louder. Napoleon frowned.

"Take him away!" he said, pointing with a gracefully majestic gesture to the portrait. "It is too soon for him to see a field of battle."

De Beausset closed his eyes, bowed his head, and sighed deeply, to indicate how profoundly he valued and comprehended the Emperor's words.

27. Napoleon's dispositions for the battle of Borodinó. They were not carried out

O N THE TWENTY-FIFTH OF AUGUST, so his historians tell us, Napoleon spent the whole day on horseback inspecting the locality, considering plans submitted to him by his marshals, and personally giving commands to his generals.

The original line of the Russian forces along the river Kolochá had been dislocated by the capture of the Shevárdino Redoubt on the twenty-fourth, and part of the line—the left flank—had been drawn back. That part of the line was not entrenched and in front of it the ground was more open and level than elsewhere. It was evident to anyone, military or not, that it was here the French should attack. It would seem that not much consideration was needed to reach this conclusion, nor any particular care or trouble on the part of the Emperor and his marshals, nor was there any need of that special and supreme quality called genius that people are so apt to ascribe to Napoleon; yet the historians who described

the event later and the men who then surrounded Napoleon, and he himself, thought otherwise.

Napoleon rode over the plain and surveyed the locality with a profound air and in silence, nodded with approval or shook his head dubiously, and without communicating to the generals around him the profound course of ideas which guided his decisions merely gave them his final conclusions in the form of commands. Having listened to a suggestion from Davout, who was now called Prince d'Eckmühl, to turn the Russian left wing, Napoleon said it should not be done, without explaining why not. To a proposal made by General Campan (who was to attack the flèches) to lead his division through the woods, Napoleon agreed, though the so-called Duke of Elchingen (Ney) ventured to remark that a movement through the woods was dangerous and might disorder the division.

Having inspected the country opposite the Shevárdino Redoubt, Napoleon pondered a little in silence and then indicated the spots where two batteries should be set up by the morrow to act against the Russian entrenchments, and the places where, in line with them, the field artillery should be placed.

After giving these and other commands he returned to his tent, and the dispositions for the battle were written down from his dictation.

These dispositions, of which the French historians write with enthusiasm and other historians with profound respect, were as follows:

"At dawn the two new batteries established during the night on the plain occupied by the Prince d'Eckmühl will open fire on the two opposing batteries of the enemy.

"At the same time the commander of the artillery of the 1st Corps, General Pernetti, with thirty cannon of Campan's division and all the howitzers of Dessaix's and Friant's divisions, will move forward, open fire, and overwhelm with shellfire the enemy's battery, against which will operate:

> 24 guns of the artillery of the Guards
> 30 guns of Campan's division
> and 8 guns of Friant's and Dessaix's divisions
> ⎯⎯
> in all 62 guns.

"The commander of the artillery of the 3rd Corps, General Fouché, will place the howitzers of the 3rd and 8th Corps, sixteen in all, on the flanks of the battery that is to bombard the entrenchment on the left, which will have forty guns in all directed against it.

"General Sorbier must be ready at the first order to advance with all the howitzers of the Guard's artillery against either one or other of the entrenchments.

"During the cannonade Prince Poniatowski is to advance through the wood on the village and turn the enemy's position.

"General Campan will move through the wood to seize the first fortification.

"After the advance has begun in this manner, orders will be given in accordance with the enemy's movements.

"The cannonade on the left flank will begin as soon as the guns of the right wing are heard. The sharpshooters of Morand's division and of the vice-King's * division will open a heavy fire on seeing the attack commence on the right wing.

"The vice-King will occupy the village [2] and cross by its three bridges, advancing to the same heights as Morand's and Gérard's divisions, which under his leadership will be directed against the redoubt and come into line with the rest of the forces.

"All this must be done in good order (*le tout se fera avec ordre et méthode*) as far as possible retaining troops in reserve.

"The Imperial Camp near Mozháysk,
 September, 6,[3] 1812."

These dispositions, which are very obscure and confused if one allows oneself to regard the arrangements without religious awe of his genius, related to Napoleon's orders to deal with four points—four different orders. Not one of these was, or could be, carried out.

In the disposition it is said first *that the batteries placed on the spot chosen by Napoleon, with the guns of Pernetti and Fouché which were to come in line with them, 102 guns in all, were to open fire and shower shells on the Russian flèches and redoubts.* This could not be done, as from the spots selected by Napoleon the projectiles did not carry to the Russian works, and those 102 guns shot into the air until the nearest commander, contrary to Napoleon's instructions, moved them forward.

The second order was that *Poniatowski, moving to the village through the wood, should turn the Russian left flank.* This could not be done and was not done, because Poniatowski, advancing on the village through the

* *The vice-King referred to is Murat, whom Napoleon had made King of Naples.*—A.M.

[2] *Borodinó.*—A.M.

[3] *The date of this French proclamation is New Style, and corresponds to August 25, Old Style.*—A.M.

wood, met Tuchkóv there barring his way, and could not and did not turn the Russian position.

The third order was: *General Campan will move through the wood to seize the first fortification.* General Campan's division did not seize the first fortification but was driven back, for on emerging from the wood it had to re-form under grapeshot, of which Napoleon was unaware.

The fourth order was: *The vice-King will occupy the village (Boro-dinó) and cross by its three bridges, advancing to the same heights as Morand's and Gérard's divisions (for whose movements no directions are given), which under his leadership will be directed against the redoubt and come into line with the rest of the forces.*

As far as one can make out, not so much from this unintelligible sentence as from the attempts the vice-King made to execute the orders given him, he was to advance from the left through Borodinó to the redoubt while the divisions of Morand and Gérard were to advance simultaneously from the front.

All this, like the other parts of the disposition, was not and could not be executed. After passing through Borodinó the vice-King was driven back to the Kolochá and could get no farther; while the divisions of Morand and Gérard did not take the redoubt but were driven back, and the redoubt was only taken at the end of the battle by the cavalry (a thing probably unforeseen and not heard of by Napoleon). So not one of the orders in the disposition was, or could be, executed. But in the disposition it is said that, *after the fight has commenced in this manner, orders will be given in accordance with the enemy's movements,* and so it might be supposed that all necessary arrangements would be made by Napoleon during the battle. But this was not and could not be done, for during the whole battle Napoleon was so far away that, as appeared later, he could not know the course of the battle and not one of his orders during the fight could be executed.

28. Napoleon's cold. Why the battle had to be fought

MANY HISTORIANS SAY that the French did not win the battle of Borodinó because Napoleon had a cold, and that if he had not had a cold the orders he gave before and during the battle would have been still more full of genius and Russia would·have been lost and the face of the world have been changed. To historians who believe that Russia was shaped by the will of one man—Peter the Great—and that France from a republic became an empire and French armies went to Russia at the will

of one man—Napoleon—to say that Russia remained a power because Napoleon had a bad cold on the twenty-fourth of August may seem logical and convincing.

If it had depended on Napoleon's will to fight or not to fight the battle of Borodinó, and if this or that other arrangement depended on his will, then evidently a cold affecting the manifestation of his will might have saved Russia, and consequently the valet who omitted to bring Napoleon his waterproof boots on the twenty-fourth would have been the savior of Russia. Along that line of thought such a deduction is indubitable, as indubitable as the deduction Voltaire made in jest (without knowing what he was jesting at) when he saw that the Massacre of St. Bartholomew was due to Charles IX's stomach being deranged. But to men who do not admit that Russia was formed by the will of one man, Peter I, or that the French Empire was formed and the war with Russia begun by the will of one man, Napoleon, that argument seems not merely untrue and irrational, but contrary to all human reality. To the question of what causes historic events another answer presents itself, namely, that the course of human events is predetermined from on high—depends on the coincidence of the wills of all who take part in the events, and that a Napoleon's influence on the course of these events is purely external and fictitious.

Strange as at first glance it may seem to suppose that the Massacre of St. Bartholomew was not due to Charles IX's will, though he gave the order for it and thought it was done as a result of that order; and strange as it may seem to suppose that the slaughter of eighty thousand men at Borodinó was not due to Napoleon's will, though he ordered the commencement and conduct of the battle and thought it was done because he ordered it; strange as these suppositions appear, yet human dignity—which tells me that each of us is, if not more at least not less a man than the great Napoleon—demands the acceptance of that solution of the question, and historic investigation abundantly confirms it.

At the battle of Borodinó Napoleon shot at no one and killed no one. That was all done by the soldiers. Therefore it was not he who killed people.

The French soldiers went to kill and be killed at the battle of Borodinó not because of Napoleon's orders but by their own volition. The whole army—French, Italian, German, Polish, and Dutch—hungry, ragged, and weary of the campaign, felt at the sight of an army blocking their road to Moscow that the wine was drawn and must be drunk. Had Napoleon then forbidden them to fight the Russians, they would have killed him and have proceeded to fight the Russians because it was inevitable.

When they heard Napoleon's proclamation offering them, as compensation for mutilation and death, the words of posterity about their having been in the battle before Moscow, they cried *"Vive l'Empereur!"* just as they had cried *"Vive l'Empereur!"* at the sight of the portrait of the boy piercing the terrestrial globe with a toy stick, and just as they would have cried *"Vive l'Empereur!"* at any nonsense that might be told them. There was nothing left for them to do but cry *"Vive l'Empereur!"* and go to fight, in order to get food and rest as conquerors in Moscow. So it was not because of Napoleon's commands that they killed their fellow men.

And it was not Napoleon who directed the course of the battle, for none of his orders were executed and during the battle he did not know what was going on before him. So the way in which these people killed one another was not decided by Napoleon's will but occurred independently of him, in accord with the will of hundreds of thousands of people who took part in the common action. It only seemed to Napoleon that it all took place by his will. And so the question whether he had or had not a cold has no more historic interest than the cold of the least of the transport soldiers.

Moreover, the assertion made by various writers that his cold was the cause of his dispositions not being as well planned as on former occasions, and of his orders during the battle not being as good as previously, is quite baseless, which again shows that Napoleon's cold on the twenty-sixth of August was unimportant.

The dispositions cited above are not at all worse, but are even better, than previous dispositions by which he had won victories. His pseudo-orders during the battle were also no worse than formerly, but much the same as usual. These dispositions and orders only seem worse than previous ones because the battle of Borodinó was the first Napoleon did not win. The profoundest and most excellent dispositions and orders seem very bad, and every learned militarist criticizes them with looks of importance, when they relate to a battle that has been lost, and the very worst dispositions and orders seem very good, and serious people fill whole volumes to demonstrate their merits, when they relate to a battle that has been won.

The dispositions drawn up by Weyrother for the battle of Austerlitz were a model of perfection for that kind of composition, but still they were criticized—criticized for their very perfection, for their excessive minuteness.

Napoleon at the battle of Borodinó fulfilled his office as representative of authority as well as, and even better than, at other battles. He did nothing harmful to the progress of the battle; he inclined to the most

reasonable opinions, he made no confusion, did not contradict himself, did not get frightened or run away from the field of battle, but with his great tact and military experience carried out his role of appearing to command, calmly and with dignity.

29. Napoleon's talk to de Beausset and Rapp. The game begins

ON RETURNING from a second careful inspection of the lines, Napoleon remarked:
"The chessmen are set up, the game will begin tomorrow!"

Having ordered punch and summoned de Beausset, he began to talk to him about Paris and about some changes he meant to make in the Empress' household, surprising the prefect by his memory of minute details relating to the court.

He showed an interest in trifles, joked about de Beausset's love of travel, and chatted carelessly, as a famous, self-confident surgeon who knows his job does when turning up his sleeves and putting on his apron while a patient is being strapped to the operating table. "The matter is in my hands and is clear and definite in my head. When the time comes to set to work I shall do it as no one else could, but now I can jest, and the more I jest and the calmer I am the more tranquil and confident you ought to be, and the more amazed at my genius."

Having finished his second glass of punch, Napoleon went to rest before the serious business which, he considered, awaited him next day. He was so much interested in that task that he was unable to sleep, and in spite of his cold which had grown worse from the dampness of the evening, he went into the large division of the tent at three o'clock in the morning, loudly blowing his nose. He asked whether the Russians had not withdrawn, and was told that the enemy's fires were still in the same places. He nodded approval.

The adjutant in attendance came into the tent.

"Well, Rapp, do you think we shall do good business today?" Napoleon asked him.

"Without doubt, sire," replied Rapp.

Napoleon looked at him.

"Do you remember, sire, what you did me the honor to say at Smolénsk?" continued Rapp. "The wine is drawn and must be drunk."

Napoleon frowned and sat silent for a long time leaning his head on his hand.

"This poor army!" he suddenly remarked. "It has diminished greatly since Smolénsk. Fortune is frankly a courtesan, Rapp. I have always said so and I am beginning to experience it. But the Guards, Rapp, the Guards are intact?" he remarked interrogatively.

"Yes, sire," replied Rapp.

Napoleon took a lozenge, put it in his mouth, and glanced at his watch. He was not sleepy and it was still not nearly morning. It was impossible to give further orders for the sake of killing time, for the orders had all been given and were now being executed.

"Have the biscuits and rice been served out to the regiments of the Guards?" asked Napoleon sternly.

"Yes, sire."

"The rice too?"

Rapp replied that he had given the Emperor's order about the rice, but Napoleon shook his head in dissatisfaction as if not believing that his order had been executed. An attendant came in with punch. Napoleon ordered another glass to be brought for Rapp, and silently sipped his own.

"I have neither taste nor smell," he remarked, sniffing at his glass. "This cold is tiresome. They talk about medicine—what is the good of medicine when it can't cure a cold! Corvisart * gave me these lozenges but they don't help at all. What can doctors cure? One can't cure anything. Our body is a machine for living. It is organized for that, it is its nature. Let life go on in it unhindered and let it defend itself, it will do more than if you paralyze it by encumbering it with remedies. Our body is like a perfect watch that should go for a certain time; the watchmaker cannot open it, he can only adjust it by fumbling, and that blindfold. . . . Yes, our body is a machine for living, that is all."

And having entered on the path of definition, of which he was fond, Napoleon suddenly and unexpectedly gave a new one.

"Do you know, Rapp, what military art is?" asked he. "It is the art of being stronger than the enemy at a given moment. That's all."

Rapp made no reply.

"Tomorrow we shall have to deal with Kutúzov!" said Napoleon. "We shall see! Do you remember at Braunau he commanded an army for three weeks and did not once mount a horse to inspect his entrenchments. . . . We shall see!"

He looked at his watch. It was still only four o'clock. He did not feel sleepy. The punch was finished and there was still nothing to do. He rose, walked to and fro, put on a warm overcoat and a hat, and went out of the

* *Baron J. N. Corvisart des Marets (1755-1821), a famous French doctor, physician to Napoleon.*—A.M.

tent. The night was dark and damp, a scarcely perceptible moisture was descending from above. Near by, the campfires were dimly burning among the French Guards, and in the distance those of the Russian line shone through the smoke. The weather was calm, and the rustle and tramp of the French troops already beginning to move to take up their positions were clearly audible.

Napoleon walked about in front of his tent, looked at the fires and listened to these sounds, and as he was passing a tall guardsman in a shaggy cap, who was standing sentinel before his tent and had drawn himself up like a black pillar at sight of the Emperor, Napoleon stopped in front of him.

"What year did you enter the service?" he asked with that affectation of military bluntness and geniality with which he always addressed the soldiers.

The man answered the question.

"Ah! One of the old ones! Has your regiment had its rice?"

"It has, Your Majesty."

Napoleon nodded and walked away.

At half-past five Napoleon rode to the village of Shevárdino.

It was growing light, the sky was clearing, only a single cloud lay in the east. The abandoned campfires were burning themselves out in the faint morning light.

On the right a single deep report of a cannon resounded and died away in the prevailing silence. Some minutes passed. A second and a third report shook the air, then a fourth and a fifth boomed solemnly near by on the right.

The first shots had not yet ceased to reverberate before others rang out and yet more were heard mingling with and overtaking one another.

Napoleon with his suite rode up to the Shevárdino Redoubt where he dismounted. The game had begun.

30. Pierre views the battlefield from the knoll at Górki

ON RETURNING to Górki after having seen Prince Andrew, Pierre ordered his groom to get the horses ready and to call him early in the morning, and then immediately fell asleep behind a partition in a corner Borís had given up to him.

Before he was thoroughly awake next morning everybody had already

left the hut. The panes were rattling in the little windows and his groom was shaking him.

"Your excellency! Your excellency! Your excellency!" he kept repeating pertinaciously while he shook Pierre by the shoulder without looking at him, having apparently lost hope of getting him to wake up.

"What? Has it begun? Is it time?" Pierre asked, waking up.

"Hear the firing," said the groom, a discharged soldier. "All the gentlemen have gone out, and his Serene Highness himself rode past long ago."

Pierre dressed hastily and ran out to the porch. Outside all was bright, fresh, dewy, and cheerful. The sun, just bursting forth from behind a cloud that had concealed it, was shining, with rays still half broken by the clouds, over the roofs of the street opposite, on the dew-besprinkled dust of the road, on the walls of the houses, on the windows, the fence, and on Pierre's horses standing before the hut. The roar of guns sounded more distinct outside. An adjutant accompanied by a Cossack passed by at a sharp trot.

"It's time, Count; it's time!" cried the adjutant.

Telling the groom to follow him with the horses, Pierre went down the street to the knoll from which he had looked at the field of battle the day before. A crowd of military men was assembled there, members of the staff could be heard conversing in French, and Kutúzov's gray head in a white cap with a red band was visible, his gray nape sunk between his shoulders. He was looking through a field glass down the highroad before him.

Mounting the steps to the knoll Pierre looked at the scene before him, spellbound by its beauty. It was the same panorama he had admired from that spot the day before, but now the whole place was full of troops and covered by smoke clouds from the guns, and the slanting rays of the bright sun, rising slightly to the left behind Pierre, cast upon it through the clear morning air penetrating streaks of rosy, golden-tinted light and long dark shadows. The forest at the farthest extremity of the panorama seemed carved in some precious stone of a yellowish-green color; its undulating outline was silhouetted against the horizon and was pierced beyond Valúevo by the Smolénsk highroad crowded with troops. Nearer at hand glittered golden cornfields interspersed with copses. There were troops to be seen everywhere, in front and to the right and left. All this was vivid, majestic, and unexpected; but what impressed Pierre most of all was the view of the battlefield itself, of Borodinó and the hollows on both sides of the Kolochá.

Above the Kolochá, in Borodinó and on both sides of it, especially to the left where the Vóyna flowing between its marshy banks falls into the

Kolochá, a mist had spread which seemed to melt, to dissolve, and to become translucent when the brilliant sun appeared and magically colored and outlined everything. The smoke of the guns mingled with this mist, and over the whole expanse and through that mist the rays of the morning sun were reflected, flashing back like lightning from the water, from the dew, and from the bayonets of the troops crowded together by the riverbanks and in Borodinó. A white church could be seen through the mist, and here and there the roofs of huts in Borodinó as well as dense masses of soldiers, or green ammunition chests and ordnance. And all this moved, or seemed to move, as the smoke and mist spread out over the whole space. Just as in the mist-enveloped hollow near Borodinó, so along the entire line outside and above it and especially in the woods and fields to the left, in the valleys and on the summits of the high ground, clouds of powder smoke seemed continually to spring up out of nothing, now singly, now several at a time, some translucent, others dense, which, swelling, growing, rolling, and blending, extended over the whole expanse.

These puffs of smoke and (strange to say) the sound of the firing produced the chief beauty of the spectacle.

"*Puff!*"—suddenly a round compact cloud of smoke was seen merging from violet into gray and milky white, and "*boom!*" came the report a second later.

"*Puff! puff!*"—and two clouds arose pushing one another and blending together; and "*boom, boom!*" came the sounds confirming what the eye had seen.

Pierre glanced round at the first cloud, which he had seen as a round compact ball, and in its place already were balloons of smoke floating to one side, and—"*puff*" (with a pause)—"*puff, puff!*" three and then four more appeared and then from each, with the same interval—"*boom—boom, boom!*" came the fine, firm, precise sounds in reply. It seemed as if those smoke clouds sometimes ran and sometimes stood still while woods, fields, and glittering bayonets ran past them. From the left, over fields and bushes, those large balls of smoke were continually appearing followed by their solemn reports, while nearer still, in the hollows and woods, there burst from the muskets small cloudlets that had no time to become balls, but had their little echoes in just the same way. "*Trakh-ta-ta-takh!*" came the frequent crackle of musketry, but it was irregular and feeble in comparison with the reports of the cannon.

Pierre wished to be there with that smoke, those shining bayonets, that movement, and those sounds. He turned to look at Kutúzov and his suite, to compare his impressions with those of others. They were all looking at the field of battle as he was, and, as it seemed to him, with the same

feelings. All their faces were now shining with that latent warmth of feeling Pierre had noticed the day before and had fully understood after his talk with Prince Andrew.

"Go, my dear fellow, go . . . and Christ be with you!" Kutúzov was saying to a general who stood beside him, not taking his eye from the battlefield.

Having received this order the general passed by Pierre on his way down the knoll.

"To the crossing!" said the general coldly and sternly in reply to one of the staff who asked where he was going.

"I'll go there too, I too!" thought Pierre, and followed the general.

The general mounted a horse a Cossack had brought him. Pierre went to his groom who was holding his horses and, asking which was the quietest, clambered onto it, seized it by the mane, and turning out his toes pressed his heels against its sides and, feeling that his spectacles were slipping off but unable to let go of the mane and reins, he galloped after the general, causing the staff officers to smile as they watched him from the knoll.

31. *Pierre at the Borodinó bridge. Under fire. Goes to Raév-ski's Redoubt. His horse wounded under him. The Raévski Redoubt. The young officer. Pierre is accepted at the re-doubt as one of the family. The flame of hidden fire in the men's souls. Shortage of ammunition. Pierre sees ammuni-tion wagons blown up*

HAVING DESCENDED the hill the general after whom Pierre was galloping turned sharply to the left, and Pierre, losing sight of him, galloped in among some ranks of infantry marching ahead of him. He tried to pass either in front of them or to the right or left, but there were soldiers everywhere, all with the same preoccupied expression and busy with some unseen but evidently important task. They all gazed with the same dissatisfied and inquiring expression at this stout man in a white hat, who for some unknown reason threatened to trample them under his horse's hoofs.

"Why ride into the middle of the battalion?" one of them shouted at him.

Another prodded his horse with the butt end of a musket, and Pierre,

bending over his saddlebow and hardly able to control his shying horse, galloped ahead of the soldiers where there was a free space.

There was a bridge ahead of him, where other soldiers stood firing. Pierre rode up to them. Without being aware of it he had come to the bridge across the Kolochá between Górki and Borodinó, which the French (having occupied Borodinó) were attacking in the first phase of the battle. Pierre saw that there was a bridge in front of him and that soldiers were doing something on both sides of it and in the meadow, among the rows of new-mown hay which he had taken no notice of amid the smoke of the campfires the day before; but despite the incessant firing going on there he had no idea that this was the field of battle. He did not notice the sound of the bullets whistling from every side, or the projectiles that flew over him, did not see the enemy on the other side of the river, and for a long time did not notice the killed and wounded, though many fell near him. He looked about him with a smile which did not leave his face.

"Why's that fellow in front of the line?" shouted somebody at him again.

"To the left! . . . Keep to the right!" the men shouted to him.

Pierre went to the right, and unexpectedly encountered one of Raévski's adjutants whom he knew. The adjutant looked angrily at him, evidently also intending to shout at him, but on recognizing him he nodded.

"How have you got here?" he said, and galloped on.

Pierre, feeling out of place there, having nothing to do, and afraid of getting in someone's way again, galloped after the adjutant.

"What's happening here? May I come with you?" he asked.

"One moment, one moment!" replied the adjutant, and riding up to a stout colonel who was standing in the meadow, he gave him some message and then addressed Pierre.

"Why have you come here, Count?" he asked with a smile. "Still inquisitive?"

"Yes, yes," assented Pierre.

But the adjutant turned his horse about and rode on.

"Here it's tolerable," said he, "but with Bagratión on the left flank they're getting it frightfully hot."

"Really?" said Pierre. "Where is that?"

"Come along with me to our knoll. We can get a view from there and in our battery it is still bearable," said the adjutant. "Will you come?"

"Yes, I'll come with you," replied Pierre, looking round for his groom.

It was only now that he noticed wounded men staggering along or being carried on stretchers. On that very meadow he had ridden over the

day before, a soldier was lying athwart the rows of scented hay, with his head thrown awkwardly back and his shako off.

"Why haven't they carried him away?" Pierre was about to ask, but seeing the stern expression of the adjutant who was also looking that way, he checked himself.

Pierre did not find his groom and rode along the hollow with the adjutant to Raévski's Redoubt. His horse lagged behind the adjutant's and jolted him at every step.

"You don't seem to be used to riding, Count?" remarked the adjutant.

"No, it's not that, but her action seems so jerky," said Pierre in a puzzled tone.

"Why . . . she's wounded!" said the adjutant. "In the off foreleg above the knee. A bullet, no doubt. I congratulate you, Count, on your baptism of fire!"

Having ridden in the smoke past the Sixth Corps, behind the artillery which had been moved forward and was in action, deafening them with the noise of firing, they came to a small wood. There it was cool and quiet, with a scent of autumn. Pierre and the adjutant dismounted and walked up the hill on foot.

"Is the general here?" asked the adjutant on reaching the knoll.

"He was here a minute ago but has just gone that way," someone told him, pointing to the right.

The adjutant looked at Pierre as if puzzled what to do with him now.

"Don't trouble about me," said Pierre. "I'll go up onto the knoll if I may?"

"Yes, do. You'll see everything from there and it's less dangerous, and I'll come for you."

Pierre went to the battery and the adjutant rode on. They did not meet again, and only much later did Pierre learn that he lost an arm that day.

The knoll to which Pierre ascended was that famous one afterwards known to the Russians as the Knoll Battery or Raévski's Redoubt, and to the French as la grande redoute, la fatale redoute, la redoute du centre, around which tens of thousands fell, and which the French regarded as the key to the whole position.

This redoubt consisted of a knoll, on three sides of which trenches had been dug. Within the entrenchment stood ten guns that were being fired through openings in the earthwork.

In line with the knoll on both sides stood other guns which also fired incessantly. A little behind the guns stood infantry. When ascending that knoll Pierre had no notion that this spot, on which small trenches had

been dug and from which a few guns were firing, was the most important point of the battle.

On the contrary, just because he happened to be there he thought it one of the least significant parts of the field.

Having reached the knoll, Pierre sat down at one end of a trench surrounding the battery and gazed at what was going on around him with an unconsciously happy smile. Occasionally he rose and walked about the battery still with that same smile, trying not to obstruct the soldiers who were loading, hauling the guns, and continually running past him with bags and charges. The guns of that battery were being fired continually one after another with a deafening roar, enveloping the whole neighborhood in powder smoke.

In contrast with the dread felt by the infantrymen placed in support, here in the battery where a small number of men busy at their work were separated from the rest by a trench, everyone experienced a common and as it were family feeling of animation.

The intrusion of Pierre's nonmilitary figure in a white hat made an unpleasant impression at first. The soldiers looked askance at him with surprise and even alarm as they went past him. The senior artillery officer, a tall, long-legged, pockmarked man, moved over to Pierre as if to see the action of the farthest gun and looked at him with curiosity.

A young round-faced officer, quite a boy still and evidently only just out of the Cadet College, who was zealously commanding the two guns entrusted to him, addressed Pierre sternly.

"Sir," he said, "permit me to ask you to stand aside. You must not be here."

The soldiers shook their heads disapprovingly as they looked at Pierre. But when they had convinced themselves that this man in the white hat was doing no harm, but either sat quietly on the slope of the trench with a shy smile or, politely making way for the soldiers, paced up and down the battery under fire as calmly as if he were on a boulevard, their feeling of hostile distrust gradually began to change into a kindly and bantering sympathy, such as soldiers feel for their dogs, cocks, goats, and in general for the animals that live with the regiment. The men soon accepted Pierre into their family, adopted him, gave him a nickname ("our gentleman"), and made kindly fun of him among themselves.

A shell tore up the earth two paces from Pierre and he looked around with a smile as he brushed from his clothes some earth it had thrown up.

"And how's it you're not afraid, sir, really now?" a red-faced, broadshouldered soldier asked Pierre, with a grin that disclosed a set of sound, white teeth.

"Are you afraid, then?" said Pierre.

"What else do you expect?" answered the soldier. "She has no mercy, you know! When she comes spluttering down, out go your innards. One can't help being afraid," he said laughing.

Several of the men, with bright kindly faces, stopped beside Pierre. They seemed not to have expected him to talk like anybody else, and the discovery that he did so delighted them.

"It's the business of us soldiers. But in a gentleman it's wonderful! There's a gentleman for you!"

"To your places!" cried the young officer to the men gathered round Pierre.

The young officer was evidently exercising his duties for the first or second time and therefore treated both his superiors and the men with great precision and formality.

The booming cannonade and the fusillade of musketry were growing more intense over the whole field, especially to the left where Bagratión's flèches were, but where Pierre was the smoke of the firing made it almost impossible to distinguish anything. Moreover, his whole attention was engrossed by watching the family circle—separated from all else—formed by the men in the battery. His first unconscious feeling of joyful animation produced by the sights and sounds of the battlefield was now replaced by another, especially since he had seen that soldier lying alone in the hayfield. Now, seated on the slope of the trench, he observed the faces of those around him.

By ten o'clock some twenty men had already been carried away from the battery; two guns were smashed and cannon balls fell more and more frequently on the battery and spent bullets buzzed and whistled around. But the men in the battery seemed not to notice this, and merry voices and jokes were heard on all sides.

"A live one!" shouted a man as a whistling shell approached.

"Not this way! To the infantry!" added another with loud laughter, seeing the shell fly past and fall into the ranks of the supports.

"Are you bowing to a friend, eh?" remarked another, chaffing a peasant who ducked low as a cannon ball flew over.

Several soldiers gathered by the wall of the trench, looking out to see what was happening in front.

"They've withdrawn the front line, it has retired," said they, pointing over the earthwork.

"Mind your own business," an old sergeant shouted at them. "If they've retired it's because there's work for them to do farther back."

And the sergeant, taking one of the men by the shoulders, gave him a shove with his knee. This was followed by a burst of laughter.

"To the fifth gun, wheel it up!" came shouts from one side.

"Now then, all together, like bargees!" rose the merry voices of those who were moving the gun.

"Oh, she nearly knocked our gentleman's hat off!" cried the red-faced humorist, showing his teeth and chaffing Pierre. "Awkward baggage!" he added reproachfully to a cannon ball that struck a cannon wheel and a man's leg.

"Now then, you foxes!" said another, laughing at some militiamen who, stooping low, entered the battery to carry away the wounded man.

"So this gruel isn't to your taste? Oh, you crows! You're scared!" they shouted at the militiamen who stood hesitating before the man whose leg had been torn off.

"There, lads . . . oh, oh!" they mimicked the peasants, "they don't like it at all!"

Pierre noticed that after every ball that hit the redoubt, and after every loss, the liveliness increased more and more.

As the flames of the fire hidden within come more and more vividly and rapidly from an approaching thundercloud, so, as if in opposition to what was taking place, the lightning of hidden fire growing more and more intense glowed in the faces of these men.

Pierre did not look out at the battlefield and was not concerned to know what was happening there; he was entirely absorbed in watching this fire which burned ever more brightly and which he felt was flaming up in the same way in his own soul.

At ten o'clock the infantry that had been among the bushes in front of the battery and along the Kámenka streamlet retreated. From the battery they could be seen running back past it carrying their wounded on their muskets. A general with his suite came to the battery, and after speaking to the colonel gave Pierre an angry look and went away again having ordered the infantry supports behind the battery to lie down, so as to be less exposed to fire. After this from amid the ranks of infantry to the right of the battery came the sound of a drum and shouts of command, and from the battery one saw how those ranks of infantry moved forward.

Pierre looked over the wall of the trench and was particularly struck by a pale young officer who, letting his sword hang down, was walking backwards and kept glancing uneasily around.

The ranks of the infantry disappeared amid the smoke but their long-drawn shout and rapid musketry firing could still be heard. A few minutes later crowds of wounded men and stretcher-bearers came back from that

direction. Projectiles began to fall still more frequently in the battery. Several men were lying about who had not been removed. Around the cannon the men moved still more briskly and busily. No one any longer took notice of Pierre. Once or twice he was shouted at for being in the way. The senior officer moved with big, rapid strides from one gun to another with a frowning face. The young officer, with his face still more flushed, commanded the men more scrupulously than ever. The soldiers handed up the charges, turned, loaded, and did their business with strained smartness. They gave little jumps as they walked, as though they were on springs.

The stormcloud had come upon them, and in every face the fire which Pierre had watched kindle burned up brightly. Pierre was standing beside the commanding officer. The young officer, his hand to his shako, ran up to his superior.

"I have the honor to report, sir, that only eight rounds are left. Are we to continue firing?" he asked.

"Grapeshot!" the senior shouted, without answering the question, looking over the wall of the trench.

Suddenly something happened: the young officer gave a gasp and bending double sat down on the ground like a bird shot on the wing. Everything became strange, confused, and misty in Pierre's eyes.

One cannon ball after another whistled by and struck the earthwork, a soldier, or a gun. Pierre, who had not noticed these sounds before, now heard nothing else. On the right of the battery soldiers shouting "Hurrah!" were running not forwards but backwards, it seemed to Pierre.

A cannon ball struck the very end of the earthwork by which he was standing, crumbling down the earth; a black ball flashed before his eyes and at the same instant plumped into something. Some militiamen who were entering the battery ran back.

"All with grapeshot!" shouted the officer.

The sergeant ran up to the officer and in a frightened whisper informed him (as a butler at dinner informs his master that there is no more of some wine asked for) that there were no more charges.

"The scoundrels! What are they doing?" shouted the officer, turning to Pierre.

The officer's face was red and perspiring and his eyes glittered under his frowning brow.

"Run to the reserves and bring up the ammunition boxes!" he yelled, angrily avoiding Pierre with his eyes and speaking to his men.

"I'll go," said Pierre.

The officer, without answering him, strode across to the opposite side.

"Don't fire. . . . Wait!" he shouted.

The man who had been ordered to go for ammunition stumbled against Pierre.

"Eh, sir, this is no place for you," said he, and ran down the slope.

Pierre ran after him, avoiding the spot where the young officer was sitting.

One cannon ball, another, and a third flew over him, falling in front, beside, and behind him. Pierre ran down the slope. "Where am I going?" he suddenly asked himself when he was already near the green ammunition wagons. He halted irresolutely, not knowing whether to return or go on. Suddenly a terrible concussion threw him backwards to the ground. At the same instant he was dazzled by a great flash of flame, and immediately a deafening roar, crackling, and whistling made his ears tingle.

When he came to himself he was sitting on the ground leaning on his hands; the ammunition wagons he had been approaching no longer existed, only charred green boards and rags littered the scorched grass, and a horse, dangling fragments of its shaft behind it, galloped past, while another horse lay, like Pierre, on the ground, uttering prolonged and piercing cries.

32. The redoubt captured by the French. Pierre's conflict with a French officer. The redoubt retaken by the Russians

BESIDE HIMSELF with terror Pierre jumped up and ran back to the battery, as to the only refuge from the horrors that surrounded him.

On entering the earthwork he noticed that there were men doing something there but that no shots were being fired from the battery. He had no time to realize who these men were. He saw the senior officer lying on the earth wall with his back turned as if he were examining something down below and that one of the soldiers he had noticed before was struggling forward shouting "Brothers!" and trying to free himself from some men who were holding him by the arm. He also saw something else that was strange.

But he had not time to realize that the colonel had been killed, that the soldier shouting "Brothers!" was a prisoner, and that another man had been bayoneted in the back before his eyes, for hardly had he run into the redoubt before a thin, sallow-faced, perspiring man in a blue uniform rushed on him sword in hand, shouting something. Instinctively guarding against the shock—for they had been running together at full speed

before they saw one another—Pierre put out his hands and seized the
man (a French officer) by the shoulder with one hand and by the throat
with the other. The officer, dropping his sword, seized Pierre by his
collar.

For some seconds they gazed with frightened eyes at one another's
unfamiliar faces and both were perplexed at what they had done and what
they were to do next. "Am I taken prisoner or have I taken him prisoner?"
each was thinking. But the French officer was evidently more inclined to
think he had been taken prisoner because Pierre's strong hand, impelled
by instinctive fear, squeezed his throat ever tighter and tighter. The
Frenchman was about to say something, when just above their heads,
terrible and low, a cannon ball whistled, and it seemed to Pierre that the
French officer's head had been torn off, so swiftly had he ducked it.

Pierre too bent his head and let his hands fall. Without further thought
as to who had taken whom prisoner, the Frenchman ran back to the bat-
tery and Pierre ran down the slope stumbling over the dead and wounded
who, it seemed to him, caught at his feet. But before he reached the foot
of the knoll he was met by a dense crowd of Russian soldiers who, stum-
bling, tripping up, and shouting, ran merrily and wildly toward the
battery. (This was the attack for which Ermólov claimed the credit, de-
claring that only his courage and good luck made such a feat possible: it
was the attack in which he was said to have thrown some St. George's
Crosses he had in his pocket into the battery for the first soldiers to take
who got there.)

The French who had occupied the battery fled, and our troops shout-
ing "Hurrah!" pursued them so far beyond the battery that it was diffi-
cult to call them back.

The prisoners were brought down from the battery and among them
was a wounded French general, whom the officers surrounded. Crowds of
wounded—some known to Pierre and some unknown—Russians and
French, with faces distorted by suffering, walked, crawled, and were car-
ried on stretchers from the battery. Pierre again went up onto the knoll
where he had spent over an hour, and of that family circle which had re-
ceived him as a member he did not find a single one. There were many
dead whom he did not know, but some he recognized. The young officer
still sat in the same way, bent double, in a pool of blood at the edge of the
earth wall. The red-faced man was still twitching, but they did not carry
him away.

Pierre ran down the slope once more.

"Now they will stop it, now they will be horrified at what they have

done!" he thought, aimlessly going toward a crowd of stretcher-bearers moving from the battlefield.

But behind the veil of smoke the sun was still high, and in front and especially to the left, near Semënovsk, something seemed to be seething in the smoke, and the roar of cannon and musketry did not diminish, but even increased to desperation like a man who, straining himself, shrieks with all his remaining strength.

33. The course of the battle. Difficulty of discerning what was going on. Things take their own course apart from the orders issued

THE CHIEF ACTION of the battle of Borodinó was fought within the seven thousand feet between Borodinó and Bagratión's flèches. Beyond that space there was, on the one side, a demonstration made by the Russians with Uvárov's cavalry at midday, and on the other side, beyond Utítsa, Poniatowski's collision with Tuchkóv; but these two were detached and feeble actions in comparison with what took place in the center of the battlefield. On the field between Borodinó and the flèches, beside the wood, the chief action of the day took place on an open space visible from both sides and was fought in the simplest and most artless way.

The battle began on both sides with a cannonade from several hundred guns.

Then when the whole field was covered with smoke, two divisions, Campan's and Dessaix's, advanced from the French right, while Murat's troops advanced on Borodinó from their left.

From the Shevárdino Redoubt where Napoleon was standing the flèches were two thirds of a mile away, and it was more than a mile as the crow flies to Borodinó, so that Napoleon could not see what was happening there, especially as the smoke mingling with the mist hid the whole locality. The soldiers of Dessaix's division advancing against the flèches could only be seen till they had entered the hollow that lay between them and the flèches. As soon as they had descended into that hollow, the smoke of the guns and musketry on the flèches grew so dense that it covered the whole approach on that side of it. Through the smoke glimpses could be caught of something black—probably men—and at times the glint of bayonets. But whether they were moving or stationary, whether they were French or Russian, could not be discovered from the Shevárdino Redoubt.

The sun had risen brightly and its slanting rays struck straight into Napoleon's face as, shading his eyes with his hand, he looked at the flèches.

The smoke spread out before them, and at times it looked as if the smoke were moving, at times as if the troops moved. Sometimes shouts were heard through the firing, but it was impossible to tell what was being done there.

Napoleon, standing on the knoll, looked through a field glass, and in its small circlet saw smoke and men, sometimes his own and sometimes Russians, but when he looked again with the naked eye, he could not tell where what he had seen was.

He descended the knoll and began walking up and down before it.

Occasionally he stopped, listened to the firing, and gazed intently at the battlefield.

But not only was it impossible to make out what was happening from where he was standing down below, or from the knoll above on which some of his generals had taken their stand, but even from the flèches themselves—in which by this time there were now Russian and now French soldiers, alternately or together, dead, wounded, alive, frightened, or maddened—even at those flèches themselves it was impossible to make out what was taking place. There for several hours amid incessant cannon and musketry fire, now Russians were seen alone, now Frenchmen alone, now infantry, and now cavalry: they appeared, fired, fell, collided, not knowing what to do with one another, screamed, and ran back again.

From the battlefield adjutants he had sent out, and orderlies from his marshals, kept galloping up to Napoleon with reports of the progress of the action, but all these reports were false, both because it was impossible in the heat of battle to say what was happening at any given moment and because many of the adjutants did not go to the actual place of conflict but reported what they had heard from others; and also because while an adjutant was riding more than a mile to Napoleon circumstances changed and the news he brought was already becoming false. Thus an adjutant galloped up from Murat with tidings that Borodinó had been occupied and the bridge over the Kolochá was in the hands of the French. The adjutant asked whether Napoleon wished the troops to cross it? Napoleon gave orders that the troops should form up on the farther side and wait. But before that order was given—almost as soon in fact as the adjutant had left Borodinó—the bridge had been retaken by the Russians and burned, in the very skirmish at which Pierre had been present at the beginning of the battle.

An adjutant galloped up from the flèches with a pale and frightened face and reported to Napoleon that their attack had been repulsed, Campan wounded, and Davout killed; yet at the very time the adjutant had been told that the French had been repulsed, the flèches had in fact been recap-

tured by other French troops, and Davout was alive and only slightly bruised. On the basis of these necessarily untrustworthy reports Napoleon gave his orders, which had either been executed before he gave them or could not be and were not executed.

The marshals and generals, who were nearer to the field of battle but, like Napoleon, did not take part in the actual fighting and only occasionally went within musket range, made their own arrangements without asking Napoleon and issued orders where and in what direction to fire and where cavalry should gallop and infantry should run. But even their orders, like Napoleon's, were seldom carried out, and then but partially. For the most part things happened contrary to their orders. Soldiers ordered to advance ran back on meeting grapeshot; soldiers ordered to remain where they were, suddenly, seeing Russians unexpectedly before them, sometimes rushed back and sometimes forward, and the cavalry dashed without orders in pursuit of the flying Russians. In this way two cavalry regiments galloped through the Semënovsk hollow and as soon as they reached the top of the incline turned round and galloped full speed back again. The infantry moved in the same way, sometimes running to quite other places than those they were ordered to go to. All orders as to where and when to move the guns, when to send infantry to shoot or horsemen to ride down the Russian infantry—all such orders were given by the officers on the spot nearest to the units concerned, without asking either Ney, Davout, or Murat, much less Napoleon. They did not fear getting into trouble for not fulfilling orders or for acting on their own initiative, for in battle what is at stake is what is dearest to man—his own life—and it sometimes seems that safety lies in running back, sometimes in running forward; and these men who were right in the heat of the battle acted according to the mood of the moment. In reality, however, all these movements forward and backward did not improve or alter the position of the troops. All their rushing and galloping at one another did little harm, the harm of disablement and death was caused by the balls and bullets that flew over the fields on which these men were floundering about. As soon as they left the place where the balls and bullets were flying about, their superiors, located in the background, re-formed them and brought them under discipline and under the influence of that discipline led them back to the zone of fire, where under the influence of fear of death they lost their discipline and rushed about according to the chance promptings of the throng.

34. Reinforcements. Belliard appeals to Napoleon. De Beausset proposes breakfast. Friant's division sent in support. The expected success not secured. Continuous and useless slaughter

NAPOLEON'S GENERALS—Davout, Ney, and Murat, who were near that region of fire and sometimes even entered it—repeatedly led into it huge masses of well-ordered troops. But contrary to what had always happened in their former battles, instead of the news they expected of the enemy's flight, these orderly masses returned thence as disorganized and terrified mobs. The generals re-formed them, but their numbers constantly decreased. In the middle of the day Murat sent his adjutant to Napoleon to demand reinforcements.

Napoleon sat at the foot of the knoll, drinking punch, when Murat's adjutant galloped up with an assurance that the Russians would be routed if His Majesty would let him have another division.

"Reinforcements?" said Napoleon in a tone of stern surprise, looking at the adjutant—a handsome lad with long black curls arranged like Murat's own—as though he did not understand his words.

"Reinforcements!" thought Napoleon to himself. "How can they need reinforcements when they already have half the army directed against a weak, unentrenched Russian wing?"

"Tell the King of Naples," said he sternly, "that it is not noon yet, and I don't yet see my chessboard clearly. Go! . . ."

The handsome boy adjutant with the long hair sighed deeply without removing his hand from his hat and galloped back to where men were being slaughtered.

Napoleon rose and having summoned Caulaincourt and Berthier began talking to them about matters unconnected with the battle.

In the midst of this conversation, which was beginning to interest Napoleon, Berthier's eyes turned to look at a general with a suite, who was galloping toward the knoll on a lathering horse. It was Belliard.* Having dismounted he went up to the Emperor with rapid strides and in a loud voice began boldly demonstrating the necessity of sending reinforcements. He swore on his honor that the Russians were lost if the Emperor would give another division.

Napoleon shrugged his shoulders and continued to pace up and down

* A. D. Belliard (1769-1832) was a French general who distinguished himself in the wars of the Republic and the Empire.—A.M.

without replying. Belliard began talking loudly and eagerly to the generals of the suite around him.

"You are very fiery, Belliard," said Napoleon, when he again came up to the general. "In the heat of a battle it is easy to make a mistake. Go and have another look and then come back to me."

Before Belliard was out of sight, a messenger from another part of the battlefield galloped up.

"Now then, what do you want?" asked Napoleon in the tone of a man irritated at being continually disturbed.

"Sire, the prince . . ." began the adjutant.

"Asks for reinforcements?" said Napoleon with an angry gesture.

The adjutant bent his head affirmatively and began to report, but the Emperor turned from him, took a couple of steps, stopped, came back, and called Berthier.

"We must give reserves," he said, moving his arms slightly apart. "Who do you think should be sent there?" he asked of Berthier (whom he subsequently termed "that gosling I have made an eagle").

"Send Claparède's division, sire," replied Berthier, who knew all the divisions, regiments, and battalions by heart.

Napoleon nodded assent.

The adjutant galloped to Claparède's division and a few minutes later the Young Guards stationed behind the knoll moved forward. Napoleon gazed silently in that direction.

"No!" he suddenly said to Berthier. "I can't send Claparède. Sent Friant's division."

Though there was no advantage in sending Friant's division instead of Claparède's, and even an obvious inconvenience and delay in stopping Claparède and sending Friant now, the order was carried out exactly. Napoleon did not notice that in regard to his army he was playing the part of a doctor who hinders by his medicines—a role he so justly understood and condemned.

Friant's division disappeared as the others had done into the smoke of the battlefield. From all sides adjutants continued to arrive at a gallop and as if by agreement all said the same thing. They all asked for reinforcements and all said that the Russians were holding their positions and maintaining a hellish fire under which the French army was melting away.

Napoleon sat on a campstool, wrapped in thought.

M. de Beausset, the man so fond of travel, having fasted since morning, came up to the Emperor and ventured respectfully to suggest lunch to His Majesty.

"I hope I may now congratulate Your Majesty on a victory?" said he.

Napoleon silently shook his head in negation. Assuming the negation to refer only to the victory and not to the lunch, M. de Beausset ventured with respectful jocularity to remark that there is no reason for not having lunch when one can get it.

"Go away . . ." exclaimed Napoleon suddenly and morosely, and turned aside.

A beatific smile of regret, repentance, and ecstasy beamed on M. de Beausset's face and he glided away to the other generals.

Napoleon was experiencing a feeling of depression like that of an ever-lucky gambler who, after recklessly flinging money about and always winning, suddenly just when he has calculated all the chances of the game, finds that the more he considers his play the more surely he loses.

His troops were the same, his generals the same, the same preparations had been made, the same dispositions, and the same proclamation *courte et énergique*, he himself was still the same: he knew that and knew that he was now even more experienced and skillful than before. Even the enemy was the same as at Austerlitz and Friedland—yet the terrible stroke of his arm had supernaturally become impotent.

All the old methods that had been unfailingly crowned with success: the concentration of batteries on one point, an attack by reserves to break the enemy's line, and a cavalry attack by "the men of iron," all these methods had already been employed, yet not only was there no victory, but from all sides came the same news of generals killed and wounded, of reinforcements needed, of the impossibility of driving back the Russians, and of disorganization among his own troops.

Formerly, after he had given two or three orders and uttered a few phrases, marshals and adjutants had come galloping up with congratulations and happy faces, announcing the trophies taken, the corps of prisoners, bundles of enemy eagles and standards, cannon and stores, and Murat had only begged leave to loose the cavalry to gather in the baggage wagons. So it had been at Lodi, Marengo, Arcola, Jena, Austerlitz, Wagram, and so on.* But now something strange was happening to his troops.

Despite news of the capture of the flèches, Napoleon saw that this was not the same, not at all the same, as what had happened in his former bat-

* *These were some of Napoleon's most remarkable victories. Lodi and Marengo are places in northern Italy where Napoleon defeated the Austrians in 1800. Arcola is a village near Verona, where in 1796 he defeated an Austrian army numerically much superior to his own. At Jena in 1806 Napoleon heavily defeated the Prussians and Saxons. Wagram is a village near Vienna, where he gained a decisive victory over the Austrians in 1809, bringing that war to a successful conclusion.*—A.M.

tles. He saw that what he was feeling was felt by all the men about him experienced in the art of war. All their faces looked dejected, and they all shunned one another's eyes—only a de Beausset could fail to grasp the meaning of what was happening.

But Napoleon with his long experience of war well knew the meaning of a battle not gained by the attacking side in eight hours, after all efforts had been expended. He knew that it was a lost battle and that the least accident might now—with the fight balanced on such a strained center— destroy him and his army.

When he ran his mind over the whole of this strange Russian campaign in which not one battle had been won, and in which not a flag, or cannon, or army corps had been captured in two months, when he looked at the concealed depression on the faces around him and heard reports of the Russians still holding their ground—a terrible feeling like a nightmare took possession of him, and all the unlucky accidents that might destroy him occurred to his mind. The Russians might fall on his left wing, might break through his center, he himself might be killed by a stray cannon ball. All this was possible. In former battles he had only considered the possibilities of success, but now innumerable unlucky chances presented themselves, and he expected them all. Yes, it was like a dream in which a man fancies that a ruffian is coming to attack him, and raises his arm to strike that ruffian a terrible blow which he knows should annihilate him, but then feels that his arm drops powerless and limp like a rag, and the horror of unavoidable destruction seizes him in his helplessness.

The news that the Russians were attacking the left flank of the French army aroused that horror in Napoleon. He sat silently on a campstool below the knoll, with head bowed and elbows on his knees. Berthier approached and suggested that they should ride along the line to ascertain the position of affairs.

"What? What do you say?" asked Napoleon. "Yes, tell them to bring me my horse."

He mounted and rode toward Semënovsk.

Amid the powder smoke, slowly dispersing over the whole space through which Napoleon rode, horses and men were lying in pools of blood, singly or in heaps. Neither Napoleon nor any of his generals had ever before seen such horrors or so many slain in such a small area. The roar of guns, that had not ceased for ten hours, wearied the ear and gave a peculiar significance to the spectacle, as music does to *tableaux vivants*. Napoleon rode up the high ground at Semënovsk, and through the smoke saw ranks of men in uniforms of a color unfamiliar to him. They were Russians.

The Russians stood in serried ranks behind Semënovsk village and its

knoll, and their guns boomed incessantly along their line and sent forth clouds of smoke. It was no longer a battle: it was a continuous slaughter which could be of no avail either to the French or the Russians. Napoleon stopped his horse and again fell into the reverie from which Berthier had aroused him. He could not stop what was going on before him and around him and was supposed to be directed by him and to depend on him, and from its lack of success this affair, for the first time, seemed to him unnecessary and horrible.

One of the generals rode up to Napoleon and ventured to offer to lead the Old Guard into action. Ney and Berthier, standing near Napoleon, exchanged looks and smiled contemptuously at this general's senseless offer.

Napoleon bowed his head and remained silent a long time.

"At eight hundred leagues * from France, I will not have my Guard destroyed!" he said, and turning his horse rode back to Shevárdino.

35. Kutúzov. His rebuke to Wolzogen. An order of the day for an attack tomorrow. The spirit of the army

O N THE RUG-COVERED BENCH where Pierre had seen him in the morning sat Kutúzov, his gray head hanging, his heavy body relaxed. He gave no orders, but only assented to or dissented from what others suggested.

"Yes, yes, do that," he replied to various proposals. "Yes, yes: go, dear boy, and have a look," he would say to one or another of those about him; or, "No, don't, we'd better wait!" He listened to the reports that were brought him and gave directions when his subordinates demanded that of him; but when listening to the reports it seemed as if he were not interested in the import of the words spoken, but rather in something else—in the expression of face and tone of voice of those who were reporting. By long years of military experience he knew, and with the wisdom of age understood, that it is impossible for one man to direct hundreds of thousands of others struggling with death, and he knew that the result of a battle is decided not by the orders of a commander in chief, nor the place where the troops are stationed, nor by the number of cannon or of slaughtered men, but by that intangible force called the spirit of the army, and he watched this force and guided it in as far as that was in his power.

Kutúzov's general expression was one of concentrated quiet attention,

* The French lieue, or league, is about two and a half miles, so Napoleon's calculation was that he was two thousand miles' march from home.—A.M.

and his face wore a strained look as if he found it difficult to master the fatigue of his old and feeble body.

At eleven o'clock they brought him news that the flèches captured by the French had been retaken, but that Prince Bagratión was wounded. Kutúzov groaned and swayed his head.

"Ride over to Prince Peter Ivánovich * and find out about it exactly," he said to one of his adjutants, and then turned to the Duke of Württemberg who was standing behind him.[2]

"Will Your Highness please take command of the first army?"

Soon after the duke's departure—before he could possibly have reached Semënovsk—his adjutant came back from him and told Kutúzov that the duke asked for more troops.

Kutúzov made a grimace and sent an order to Dokhtúrov to take over the command of the first army, and a request to the duke—whom he said he could not spare at such an important moment—to return to him. When they brought him news that Murat had been taken prisoner,[3] and the staff officers congratulated him, Kutúzov smiled.

"Wait a little, gentlemen," said he. "The battle is won, and there is nothing extraordinary in the capture of Murat. Still, it is better to wait before we rejoice."

But he sent an adjutant to take the news round the army.

When Scherbínin came galloping from the left flank with news that the French had captured the flèches and the village of Semënovsk, Kutúzov, guessing by the sounds of the battle and by Scherbínin's looks that the news was bad, rose as if to stretch his legs and, taking Scherbínin's arm, led him aside.

"Go, my dear fellow," he said to Ermólov, "and see whether something can't be done."

Kutúzov was in Górki, near the center of the Russian position. The attack directed by Napoleon against our left flank had been several times repulsed. In the center the French had not got beyond Borodinó, and on their left flank Uvárov's cavalry had put the French to flight.

* Bagratión.—A.M.

[2] Duke Alexander Frederick of Württemberg (1771-1833), brother of the Empress Marie Fëdorovna, wife of the Emperor Paul, had entered the Russian service in 1800.—A.M.

[3] This report turned out to be false. It was General Bonami who had been captured. Seeing a Russian grenadier's bayonet at his breast he cried out: "I am the King!" and was taken alive to Kutúzov. The false rumor was spread by a major who spoke in a thick voice and rode along the line indistinctly shouting news of the capture.—A.M.

Toward three o'clock the French attacks ceased. On the faces of all who came from the field of battle, and of those who stood around him, Kutúzov noticed an expression of extreme tension. He was satisfied with the day's success—a success exceeding his expectations, but the old man's strength was failing him. Several times his head dropped low as if it were falling and he dozed off. Dinner was brought him.

Adjutant General Wolzogen, the man who when riding past Prince Andrew had said, "the war should be extended widely," and whom Bagratión so detested, rode up while Kutúzov was at dinner. Wolzogen had come from Barclay de Tolly to report on the progress of affairs on the left flank. The sagacious Barclay de Tolly, seeing crowds of wounded men running back and the disordered rear of the army, weighed all the circumstances, concluded that the battle was lost, and sent his favorite officer to the commander in chief with that news.

Kutúzov was chewing a piece of roast chicken with difficulty and glanced at Wolzogen with eyes that brightened under their puckering lids.

Wolzogen, nonchalantly stretching his legs, approached Kutúzov with a half-contemptuous smile on his lips, scarcely touching the peak of his cap.

He treated his Serene Highness with a somewhat affected nonchalance intended to show that, as a highly trained military man, he left it to Russians to make an idol of this useless old man, but that he knew whom he was dealing with. "*Der alte Herr*" (as in their own set the Germans called Kutúzov) "is making himself very comfortable," thought Wolzogen, and looking severely at the dishes in front of Kutúzov he began to report to "the old gentleman" the position of affairs on the left flank as Barclay had ordered him to and as he himself had seen and understood it.

"All the points of our position are in the enemy's hands and we cannot dislodge them for lack of troops, the men are running away and it is impossible to stop them," he reported.

Kutúzov ceased chewing and fixed an astonished gaze on Wolzogen, as if not understanding what was said to him. Wolzogen, noticing "the old gentleman's" agitation, said with a smile:

"I have not considered it right to conceal from your Serene Highness what I have seen. The troops are in complete disorder. . . ."

"You have seen? You have seen? . . ." Kutúzov shouted frowning, and rising quickly he went up to Wolzogen.

"How . . . how dare you! . . ." he shouted, choking and making a threatening gesture with his trembling arms: "How dare you, sir, say that to me? You know nothing about it. Tell General Barclay from me that his

information is incorrect and that the real course of the battle is better known to me, the commander in chief, than to him."

Wolzogen was about to make a rejoinder, but Kutúzov interrupted him. "The enemy has been repulsed on the left and defeated on the right flank. If you have seen amiss, sir, do not allow yourself to say what you don't know! Be so good as to ride to General Barclay and inform him of my firm intention to attack the enemy tomorrow," said Kutúzov sternly.

All were silent, and the only sound audible was the heavy breathing of the panting old general.

"They are repulsed everywhere, for which I thank God and our brave army! The enemy is beaten, and tomorrow we shall drive him from the sacred soil of Russia," said Kutúzov crossing himself, and he suddenly sobbed as his eyes filled with tears.

Wolzogen, shrugging his shoulders and curling his lips, stepped silently aside, marveling at "the old gentleman's" conceited stupidity.

"Ah, here he is, my hero!" said Kutúzov to a portly, handsome, dark-haired general who was just ascending the knoll.

This was Raévski, who had spent the whole day at the most important part of the field of Borodinó.

Raévski reported that the troops were firmly holding their ground and that the French no longer ventured to attack.

After hearing him, Kutúzov said in French:

"Then you do not think, *like some others*, that we must retreat?"

"On the contrary, your Highness, in indecisive actions it is always the most stubborn who remain victors," replied Raévski, "and in my opinion . . ."

"Kaysárov!" Kutúzov called to his adjutant. "Sit down and write out the order of the day for tomorrow. And you," he continued, addressing another, "ride along the line and announce that tomorrow we attack."

While Kutúzov was talking to Raévski and dictating the order of the day, Wolzogen returned from Barclay and said that General Barclay wished to have written confirmation of the order the field marshal had given.

Kutúzov, without looking at Wolzogen, gave directions for the order to be written out which the former commander in chief, to avoid personal responsibility, very judiciously wished to receive.

And by means of that mysterious indefinable bond which maintains throughout an army one and the same temper, known as "the spirit of the army," and which constitutes the chief sinew of war, Kutúzov's words, his order for a battle next day, immediately became known from one end of the army to the other.

It was far from being the same words or the same order that reached the farthest links of that chain. The tales passing from mouth to mouth at different ends of the army did not even resemble what Kutúzov had said, but the sense of his words spread everywhere because what he said was not the outcome of cunning calculations, but of a feeling that lay in the commander in chief's soul as in that of every Russian.

And on learning that tomorrow they were to attack the enemy, and hearing from the highest quarters a confirmation of what they wanted to believe, the exhausted, wavering men felt comforted and inspirited.

36. Prince Andrew with the reserve under fire. Hit by a bursting shell. Outside the dressing station

PRINCE ANDREW'S REGIMENT was among the reserves which till after one o'clock were stationed inactive behind Semënovsk, under heavy artillery fire. Toward two o'clock the regiment, having already lost more than two hundred men, was moved forward into a trampled oatfield in the gap between Semënovsk and the Knoll Battery, where thousands of men perished that day and on which an intense, concentrated fire from several hundred enemy guns was directed between one and two o'clock.

Without moving from that spot or firing a single shot the regiment here lost another third of its men. From in front and especially from the right, in the unlifting smoke the guns boomed, and out of the mysterious domain of smoke that overlay the whole space in front, quick hissing cannon balls and slow whistling shells flew unceasingly. At times, as if to allow them a respite, a quarter of an hour passed during which the cannon balls and shells all flew overhead, but sometimes several men were torn from the regiment in a minute and the slain were continually being dragged away and the wounded carried off.

With each fresh blow less and less chance of life remained for those not yet killed. The regiment stood in columns of battalion, three hundred paces apart, but nevertheless the men were always in one and the same mood. All alike were taciturn and morose. Talk was rarely heard in the ranks, and it ceased altogether every time the thud of a successful shot and the cry of "stretchers!" was heard. Most of the time, by their officers' order, the men sat on the ground. One, having taken off his shako, carefully loosened the gathers of its lining and drew them tight again; another, rubbing some dry clay between his palms, polished his bayonet; another fingered the strap and pulled the buckle of his bandolier, while another smoothed and refolded his leg bands and put his boots on again. Some

built little houses of the tufts in the plowed ground, or plaited baskets from the straw in the cornfield. All seemed fully absorbed in these pursuits. When men were killed or wounded, when rows of stretchers went past, when some troops retreated, and when great masses of the enemy came into view through the smoke, no one paid any attention to these things. But when our artillery or cavalry advanced or some of our infantry were seen to move forward, words of approval were heard on all sides. But the liveliest attention was attracted by occurrences quite apart from, and unconnected with, the battle. It was as if the minds of these morally exhausted men found relief in everyday, commonplace occurrences. A battery of artillery was passing in front of the regiment. The horse of an ammunition cart put its leg over a trace. "Hey, look at the trace horse! . . . Get her leg out! She'll fall. . . . Ah, they don't see it!" came identical shouts from the ranks all along the regiment. Another time, general attention was attracted by a small brown dog, coming heaven knows whence, which trotted in a preoccupied manner in front of the ranks with tail stiffly erect till suddenly a shell fell close by, when it yelped, tucked its tail between its legs, and darted aside. Yells and shrieks of laughter rose from the whole regiment. But such distractions lasted only a moment, and for eight hours the men had been inactive, without food, in constant fear of death, and their pale and gloomy faces grew ever paler and gloomier.

Prince Andrew, pale and gloomy like everyone in the regiment, paced up and down from the border of one patch to another, at the edge of the meadow beside an oatfield, with head bowed and arms behind his back. There was nothing for him to do and no orders to be given. Everything went on of itself. The killed were dragged from the front, the wounded carried away, and the ranks closed up. If any soldiers ran to the rear they returned immediately and hastily. At first Prince Andrew, considering it his duty to rouse the courage of the men and to set them an example, walked about among the ranks, but he soon became convinced that this was unnecessary and that there was nothing he could teach them. All the powers of his soul, as of every soldier there, were unconsciously bent on avoiding the contemplation of the horrors of their situation. He walked along the meadow, dragging his feet, rustling the grass, and gazing at the dust that covered his boots; now he took big strides trying to keep to the footprints left on the meadow by the mowers, then he counted his steps, calculating how often he must walk from one strip to another to walk a mile, then he stripped the flowers from the wormwood that grew along a boundary rut, rubbed them in his palms, and smelled their pungent, sweetly bitter scent. Nothing remained of the previous day's thoughts. He thought of nothing. He listened with weary ears to the ever-recurring sounds, dis-

tinguishing the whistle of flying projectiles from the booming of the reports, glanced at the tiresomely familiar faces of the men of the first battalion, and waited. "Here it comes . . . this one is coming our way again!" he thought, listening to an approaching whistle in the hidden region of smoke. "One, another! Again! It has hit. . . ." He stopped and looked at the ranks. "No, it has gone over. But this one has hit!" And again he started trying to reach the boundary strip in sixteen paces. A whizz and a thud! Five paces from him, a cannon ball tore up the dry earth and disappeared. A chill ran down his back. Again he glanced at the ranks. Probably many had been hit—a large crowd had gathered near the second battalion.

"Adjutant!" he shouted. "Order them not to crowd together."

The adjutant, having obeyed this instruction, approached Prince Andrew. From the other side a battalion commander rode up.

"Look out!" came a frightened cry from a soldier and, like a bird whirring in rapid flight and alighting on the ground, a shell dropped with little noise within two steps of Prince Andrew and close to the battalion commander's horse. The horse first, regardless of whether it was right or wrong to show fear, snorted, reared almost throwing the major, and galloped aside. The horse's terror infected the men.

"Lie down!" cried the adjutant, throwing himself flat on the ground.

Prince Andrew hesitated. The smoking shell spun like a top between him and the prostrate adjutant, near a wormwood plant between the field and the meadow.

"Can this be death?" thought Prince Andrew, looking with a quite new, envious glance at the grass, the wormwood, and the streamlet of smoke that curled up from the rotating black ball. "I cannot, I do not wish to die. I love life—I love this grass, this earth, this air. . . ." He thought this, and at the same time remembered that people were looking at him.

"It's shameful, sir!" he said to the adjutant. "What . . ."

He did not finish speaking. At one and the same moment came the sound of an explosion, a whistle of splinters as from a breaking window frame, a suffocating smell of powder, and Prince Andrew started to one side, raising his arm, and fell on his chest. Several officers ran up to him. From the right side of his abdomen, blood was welling out making a large stain on the grass.

The militiamen with stretchers who were called up stood behind the officers. Prince Andrew lay on his chest with his face in the grass, breathing heavily and noisily.

"What are you waiting for? Come along!"

The peasants went up and took him by his shoulders and legs, but he moaned piteously and, exchanging looks, they set him down again.

"Pick him up, lift him, it's all the same!" cried someone.

They again took him by the shoulders and laid him on the stretcher.

"Ah, God! My God! What is it? The stomach? That means death! My God!"—voices among the officers were heard saying.

"It flew a hair's breadth past my ear," said the adjutant.

The peasants, adjusting the stretcher to their shoulders, started hurriedly along the path they had trodden down, to the dressing station.

"Keep in step! Ah . . . those peasants!" shouted an officer, seizing by their shoulders and checking the peasants, who were walking unevenly and jolting the stretcher.

"Get into step, Fëdor . . . I say, Fëdor!" said the foremost peasant.

"Now that's right!" said the one behind joyfully, when he had got into step.

"Your excellency! Eh, Prince!" said the trembling voice of Timókhin, who had run up and was looking down on the stretcher.

Prince Andrew opened his eyes and looked up at the speaker from the stretcher into which his head had sunk deep and again his eyelids drooped.

The militiamen carried Prince Andrew to the dressing station by the wood, where wagons were stationed. The dressing station consisted of three tents with flaps turned back, pitched at the edge of a birch wood. In the wood, wagons and horses were standing. The horses were eating oats from their movable troughs and sparrows flew down and pecked the grains that fell. Some crows, scenting blood, flew among the birch trees cawing impatiently. Around the tents, over more than five acres, bloodstained men in various garbs stood, sat, or lay. Around the wounded stood crowds of soldier stretcher-bearers with dismal and attentive faces, whom the officers keeping order tried in vain to drive from the spot. Disregarding the officers' orders, the soldiers stood leaning against their stretchers and gazing intently, as if trying to comprehend the difficult problem of what was taking place before them. From the tents came now loud angry cries and now plaintive groans. Occasionally dressers ran out to fetch water, or to point out those who were to be brought in next. The wounded men awaiting their turn outside the tents groaned, sighed, wept, screamed, swore, or asked for vodka. Some were delirious. Prince Andrew's bearers, stepping over the wounded who had not yet been bandaged, took him, as a regimental commander, close up to one of the tents and there stopped, awaiting instructions. Prince Andrew opened his eyes and for a long time could not make out what was going on around him. He remembered the meadow, the wormwood, the field, the whirling black ball, and his sudden rush of passionate love of life. Two steps from him, leaning against a

branch and talking loudly and attracting general attention, stood a tall, handsome, black-haired noncommissioned officer with a bandaged head. He had been wounded in the head and leg by bullets. Around him, eagerly listening to his talk, a crowd of wounded and stretcher-bearers was gathered.

"We kicked *him* out from there so that he chucked everything, we grabbed the King himself!" cried he, looking around him with eyes that glittered with fever. "If only reserves had come up just then, lads, there wouldn't have been nothing left of him! I tell you surely. . . ."

Like all the others near the speaker, Prince Andrew looked at him with shining eyes and experienced a sense of comfort. "But isn't it all the same now?" thought he. "And what will be there, and what has there been here? Why was I so reluctant to part with life? There was something in this life I did not and do not understand."

37. The operating tent. Portion of Prince Andrew's thighbone extracted. Anatole's leg amputated. Prince Andrew pities him

O NE OF THE DOCTORS came out of the tent in a bloodstained apron, holding a cigar between the thumb and little finger of one of his small bloodstained hands, so as not to smear it. He raised his head and looked about him, but above the level of the wounded men. He evidently wanted a little respite. After turning his head from right to left for some time, he sighed and looked down.

"All right, immediately," he replied to a dresser who pointed Prince Andrew out to him, and he told them to carry him into the tent.

Murmurs arose among the wounded who were waiting.

"It seems that even in the next world only the gentry are to have a chance!" remarked one.

Prince Andrew was carried in and laid on a table that had only just been cleared and which a dresser was washing down. Prince Andrew could not make out distinctly what was in that tent. The pitiful groans from all sides and the torturing pain in his thigh, stomach, and back distracted him. All he saw about him merged into a general impression of naked, bleeding human bodies that seemed to fill the whole of the low tent, as a few weeks previously, on that hot August day, such bodies had filled the dirty pond beside the Smolénsk road. Yes, it was the same flesh, the same *chair à canon*, the sight of which had even then filled him with horror, as by a presentiment.

There were three operating tables in the tent. Two were occupied, and on the third they placed Prince Andrew. For a little while he was left alone and involuntarily witnessed what was taking place on the other two tables. On the nearest one sat a Tartar, probably a Cossack, judging by the uniform thrown down beside him. Four soldiers were holding him, and a spectacled doctor was cutting into his muscular brown back.

"Ooh, ooh, ooh!" grunted the Tartar, and suddenly lifting up his swarthy snub-nosed face with its high cheekbones, and baring his white teeth, he began to wriggle and twitch his body and utter piercing, ringing, and prolonged yells. On the other table, round which many people were crowding, a tall well-fed man lay on his back with his head thrown back. His curly hair, its color, and the shape of his head seemed strangely familiar to Prince Andrew. Several dressers were pressing on his chest to hold him down. One large, white, plump leg twitched rapidly all the time with a feverish tremor. The man was sobbing and choking convulsively. Two doctors—one of whom was pale and trembling—were silently doing something to this man's other, gory leg. When he had finished with the Tartar, whom they covered with an overcoat, the spectacled doctor came up to Prince Andrew, wiping his hands.

He glanced at Prince Andrew's face and quickly turned away.

"Undress him! What are you waiting for?" he cried angrily to the dressers.

His very first, remotest recollections of childhood came back to Prince Andrew's mind when the dresser with sleeves rolled up began hastily to undo the buttons of his clothes and undressed him. The doctor bent down over the wound, felt it, and sighed deeply. Then he made a sign to someone, and the torturing pain in his abdomen caused Prince Andrew to lose consciousness. When he came to himself the splintered portions of his thighbone had been extracted, the torn flesh cut away, and the wound bandaged. Water was being sprinkled on his face. As soon as Prince Andrew opened his eyes, the doctor bent over, kissed him silently on the lips, and hurried away.

After the sufferings he had been enduring, Prince Andrew enjoyed a blissful feeling such as he had not experienced for a long time. All the best and happiest moments of his life—especially his earliest childhood, when he used to be undressed and put to bed, and when leaning over him his nurse sang him to sleep and he, burying his head in the pillow, felt happy in the mere consciousness of life—returned to his memory, not merely as something past but as something present.

The doctors were busily engaged with the wounded man the shape of

whose head seemed familiar to Prince Andrew: they were lifting him up and trying to quiet him.

"Show it to me. . . . Oh, ooh . . . Oh! Oh, ooh!" his frightened moans could be heard, subdued by suffering and broken by sobs.

Hearing those moans Prince Andrew wanted to weep. Whether because he was dying without glory, or because he was sorry to part with life, or because of those memories of a childhood that could not return, or because he was suffering and others were suffering and that man near him was groaning so piteously—he felt like weeping childlike, kindly, and almost happy tears.

The wounded man was shown his amputated leg stained with clotted blood and with the boot still on.

"Oh! Oh, ooh!" he sobbed, like a woman.

The doctor who had been standing beside him, preventing Prince Andrew from seeing his face, moved away.

"My God! What is this? Why is he here?" said Prince Andrew to himself.

In the miserable, sobbing, enfeebled man whose leg had just been amputated, he recognized Anatole Kurágin. Men were supporting him in their arms and offering him a glass of water, but his trembling, swollen lips could not grasp its rim. Anatole was sobbing painfully. "Yes, it is he! Yes, that man is somehow closely and painfully connected with me," thought Prince Andrew, not yet clearly grasping what he saw before him. "What is the connection of that man with my childhood and my life?" he asked himself without finding an answer. And suddenly a new unexpected memory from that realm of pure and loving childhood presented itself to him. He remembered Natásha as he had seen her for the first time at the ball in 1810, with her slender neck and arms and with a frightened happy face ready for rapture, and love and tenderness for her, stronger and more vivid than ever, awoke in his soul. He now remembered the connection that existed between himself and this man who was dimly gazing at him through tears that filled his swollen eyes. He remembered everything, and ecstatic pity and love for that man overflowed his happy heart.

Prince Andrew could no longer restrain himself and wept tender loving tears for his fellow men, for himself, and for his own and their errors.

"Compassion, love of our brothers, for those who love us and for those who hate us, love of our enemies; yes, that love which God preached on earth and which Princess Mary taught me and I did not understand—that is what made me sorry to part with life, that is what remained for me had I lived. But now it is too late. I know it!"

38. Napoleon is depressed. His mind and conscience darkened. His calculation that few Frenchmen perished in Russia

THE TERRIBLE SPECTACLE of the battlefield covered with dead and wounded, together with the heaviness of his head and the news that some twenty generals he knew personally had been killed or wounded, and the consciousness of the impotence of his once mighty arm, produced an unexpected impression on Napoleon who usually liked to look at the killed and wounded, thereby, he considered, testing his strength of mind. This day the horrible appearance of the battlefield overcame that strength of mind which he thought constituted his merit and his greatness. He rode hurriedly from the battlefield and returned to the Shevárdino knoll, where he sat on his campstool, his sallow face swollen and heavy, his eyes dim, his nose red, and his voice hoarse, involuntarily listening, with downcast eyes, to the sounds of firing. With painful dejection he awaited the end of this action, in which he regarded himself as a participant and which he was unable to arrest. A personal, human feeling for a brief moment got the better of the artificial phantasm of life he had served so long. He felt in his own person the sufferings and death he had witnessed on the battlefield. The heaviness of his head and chest reminded him of the possibility of suffering and death for himself. At that moment he did not desire Moscow, or victory, or glory (what need had he for any more glory?). The one thing he wished for was rest, tranquillity, and freedom. But when he had been on the Semënovsk heights the artillery commander had proposed to him to bring several batteries of artillery up to those heights to strengthen the fire on the Russian troops crowded in front of Knyazkóvo. Napoleon had assented and had given orders that news should be brought him of the effect those batteries produced.

An adjutant came now to inform him that the fire of two hundred guns had been concentrated on the Russians, as he had ordered, but that they still held their ground.

"Our fire is mowing them down by rows, but still they hold on," said the adjutant.

"They want more! . . ." said Napoleon in a hoarse voice.

"Sire?" asked the adjutant who had not heard the remark.

"They want more!" croaked Napoleon frowning. "Let them have it!"

Even before he gave that order the thing he did not desire, and for which he gave the order only because he thought it was expected of him, was being done. And he fell back into that artificial realm of imaginary greatness, and again—as a horse walking a treadmill thinks it is doing some-

thing for itself—he submissively fulfilled the cruel, sad, gloomy, and inhuman role predestined for him.

And not for that day and hour alone were the mind and conscience darkened of this man on whom the responsibility for what was happening lay more than on all the others who took part in it. Never to the end of his life could he understand goodness, beauty, or truth, or the significance of his actions which were too contrary to goodness and truth, too remote from everything human, for him ever to be able to grasp their meaning. He could not disavow his actions, belauded as they were by half the world, and so he had to repudiate truth, goodness, and all humanity.

Not only on that day, as he rode over the battlefield strewn with men killed and maimed (by his will as he believed), did he reckon as he looked at them how many Russians there were for each Frenchman and, deceiving himself, find reason for rejoicing in the calculation that there were five Russians for every Frenchman. Not on that day alone did he write in a letter to Paris that "the battlefield was superb," because fifty thousand corpses lay there, but even on the island of St. Helena in the peaceful solitude where he said he intended to devote his leisure to an account of the great deeds he had done, he wrote:

"The Russian war should have been the most popular war of modern times: it was a war of good sense, for real interests, for the tranquillity and security of all; it was purely pacific and conservative.

"It was a war for a great cause, the end of uncertainties and the beginning of security. A new horizon and new labors were opening out, full of well-being and prosperity for all. The European system was already founded; all that remained was to organize it.

"Satisfied on these great points and with tranquillity everywhere, I too should have had my *Congress* and my *Holy Alliance*. Those ideas were stolen from me. In that reunion of great sovereigns we should have discussed our interests like one family, and have rendered account to the peoples as clerk to master.

"Europe would in this way soon have been, in fact, but one people, and anyone who traveled anywhere would have found himself always in the common fatherland. I should have demanded the freedom of all navigable rivers for everybody, that the seas should be common to all, and that the great standing armies should be reduced henceforth to mere guards for the sovereigns.

"On returning to France, to the bosom of the great, strong, magnificent, peaceful, and glorious fatherland, I should have proclaimed her frontiers immutable; all future wars purely *defensive*, all aggrandizement *antinational*. I should have associated my son in the Empire; my *dictatorship*

would have been finished, and his constitutional reign would have begun.

"Paris would have been the capital of the world, and the French the envy of the nations!

"My leisure then, and my old age, would have been devoted, in company with the Empress and during the royal apprenticeship of my son, to leisurely visiting, with our own horses and like a true country couple, every corner of the Empire, receiving complaints, redressing wrongs, and scattering public buildings and benefactions on all sides and everywhere."

Napoleon, predestined by Providence for the gloomy role of executioner of the peoples, assured himself that the aim of his actions had been the peoples' welfare and that he could control the fate of millions and by the employment of power confer benefactions.

"Of four hundred thousand men who crossed the Vistula," he wrote further of the Russian war, "half were Austrians, Prussians, Saxons, Poles, Bavarians, Württembergers, Mecklenburgers, Spaniards, Italians, and Neapolitans. The Imperial army, strictly speaking, was one third composed of Dutch, Belgians, men from the borders of the Rhine, Piedmontese, Swiss, Genevese, Tuscans, Romans, inhabitants of the Thirty-second Military Division,* of Bremen, of Hamburg, and so on: it included scarcely a hundred and forty thousand who spoke French. The Russian expedition actually cost France less than fifty thousand men; the Russian army in its retreat from Vílna to Moscow lost in the various battles four times more men than the French army; the burning of Moscow cost the lives of a hundred thousand Russians who died of cold and want in the woods; finally, in its march from Moscow to the Oder the Russian army also suffered from the severity of the season; so that by the time it reached Vílna it numbered only fifty thousand, and at Kálisch less than eighteen thousand."

He imagined that the war with Russia came about by his will, and the horrors that occurred did not stagger his soul. He boldly took the whole responsibility for what happened, and his darkened mind found justification in the belief that among the hundreds of thousands who perished there were fewer Frenchmen than Hessians and Bavarians.

* *The Thirty-second Military Division was Marshal Davout's division, mainly recruited from the Hamburg-Bremen region.*—A.M.

39. *Appearance of the field at the end of the battle. Doubts maturing in every soul. Only a little further effort needed to secure victory, but such effort impossible. Could Napoleon have used his Old Guard? The Russians had gained a moral victory*

SEVERAL TENS OF THOUSANDS of the slain lay in diverse postures and various uniforms on the fields and meadows belonging to the Davýdov family and to the crown serfs—those fields and meadows where for hundreds of years the peasants of Borodinó, Górki, Shevárdino, and Semënovsk had reaped their harvests and pastured their cattle. At the dressing stations the grass and earth were soaked with blood for a space of some three acres around. Crowds of men of various arms, wounded and unwounded, with frightened faces, dragged themselves back to Mozháysk from the one army and back to Valúevo from the other. Other crowds, exhausted and hungry, went forward led by their officers. Others held their ground and continued to fire.

Over the whole field, previously so gaily beautiful with the glitter of bayonets and cloudlets of smoke in the morning sun, there now spread a mist of damp and smoke and a strange acid smell of saltpeter and blood. Clouds gathered and drops of rain began to fall on the dead and wounded, on the frightened, exhausted, and hesitating men, as if to say: "Enough, men! Enough! Cease . . . bethink yourselves! What are you doing?"

To the men of both sides alike, worn out by want of food and rest, it began equally to appear doubtful whether they should continue to slaughter one another; all the faces expressed hesitation, and the question arose in every soul: "For what, for whom, must I kill and be killed? . . . You may go and kill whom you please, but I don't want to do so any more!" By evening this thought had ripened in every soul. At any moment these men might have been seized with horror at what they were doing and might have thrown up everything and run away anywhere.

But though toward the end of the battle the men felt all the horror of what they were doing, though they would have been glad to leave off, some incomprehensible, mysterious power continued to control them, and they still brought up the charges, loaded, aimed, and applied the match, though only one artilleryman survived out of every three, and though they stumbled and panted with fatigue, perspiring and stained with blood and powder. The cannon balls flew just as swiftly and cruelly from both sides, crushing human bodies, and that terrible work which was not done by the

will of a man but at the will of Him who governs men and worlds continued.

Anyone looking at the disorganized rear of the Russian army would have said that, if only the French made one more slight effort, it would disappear; and anyone looking at the rear of the French army would have said that the Russians need only make one more slight effort and the French would be destroyed. But neither the French nor the Russians made that effort, and the flame of battle burned slowly out.

The Russians did not make that effort because they were not attacking the French. At the beginning of the battle they stood blocking the way to Moscow and they still did so at the end of the battle as at the beginning. But even had the aim of the Russians been to drive the French from their positions, they could not have made this last effort, for all the Russian troops had been broken up, there was no part of the Russian army that had not suffered in the battle, and though still holding their positions they had lost ONE HALF of their army.

The French, with the memory of all their former victories during fifteen years, with the assurance of Napoleon's invincibility, with the consciousness that they had captured part of the battlefield and had lost only a quarter of their men and still had their Guards intact, twenty thousand strong, might easily have made that effort. The French who had attacked the Russian army in order to drive it from its position ought to have made that effort, for as long as the Russians continued to block the road to Moscow as before, the aim of the French had not been attained and all their efforts and losses were in vain. But the French did not make that effort. Some historians say that Napoleon need only have used his Old Guards, who were intact, and the battle would have been won. To speak of what would have happened had Napoleon sent his Guards is like talking of what would happen if autumn became spring. It could not be. Napoleon did not give his Guards, not because he did not want to, but because it could not be done. All the generals, officers, and soldiers of the French army knew it could not be done, because the flagging spirit of the troops would not permit it.

It was not Napoleon alone who had experienced that nightmare feeling of the mighty arm being stricken powerless, but all the generals and soldiers of his army whether they had taken part in the battle or not, after all their experience of previous battles—when after one tenth of such efforts the enemy had fled—experienced a similar feeling of terror before an enemy who, after losing HALF his men, stood as threateningly at the end as at the beginning of the battle. The moral force of the attacking French army was exhausted. Not that sort of victory which is defined by the cap-

ture of pieces of material fastened to sticks, called standards, and of the ground on which the troops had stood and were standing, but a moral victory that convinces the enemy of the moral superiority of his opponent and of his own impotence was gained by the Russians at Borodinó. The French invaders, like an infuriated animal that has in its onslaught received a mortal wound, felt that they were perishing, but could not stop, any more than the Russian army, weaker by one half, could help swerving. By the impetus gained, the French army was still able to roll forward to Moscow, but there, without further effort on the part of the Russians, it had to perish, bleeding from the mortal wound it had received at Borodinó. The direct consequence of the battle of Borodinó was Napoleon's senseless flight from Moscow, his retreat along the old Smolénsk road, the destruction of the invading army of five hundred thousand men, and the downfall of Napoleonic France, on which at Borodinó for the first time the hand of an opponent of stronger spirit had been laid.

BOOK ELEVEN

DATE OF PRINCIPAL HISTORICAL EVENT
1812

OLD STYLE NEW STYLE

Sept. 1 Sept. 13 Kutúzov orders retreat through Moscow.

To Sokólniki

Sadóvaya

Sukhárev Water Tower

Sadóvaya

Meshchánskaya

Patriarch's Ponds

Bazdéev House

Kúdrino

Tverskáya

Neglínaya River

Lubyánka

Myasnítskaya

Pokróvka

Moróseyka

Povarskáya

Nikítskaya

Nikólski

Bazaar

Red Square

Ilyínka

Moskvá River

Rostóv House

Vozdvízhenka

Senate Square

Tróitsa Gate

Kremlin Palace

Varvárka

Orphanage

Arbát

Mokhaváya

Yaúza River

Dorogomílov Bridge

Moskvá Bridge

Yaúza Bridge

To Nízhni-Nóvgorod

Stone (Kámmeni) Bridge

Bolótnoe Place

Ryazán Road

Virgin's Field

Zúbovski

Rámpart

Khamóvniki

Crimean Bridge

Great Ordynka

To Sparrow Hills

Moskvá River

Kalúga Road

Túla Road

N

MOSCOW ~ 1812

0 1/2 1 1 1/2 Miles

Shaded Portions Indicate the Areas
Burned in the French Occupation

1812

BOOK ELEVEN

1. Continuity of motion. Achilles and the tortoise. The method of history; its explanation of events compared with explanations of the movement of a locomotive

Absolute continuity of motion is not comprehensible to the human mind. Laws of motion of any kind become comprehensible to man only when he examines arbitrarily selected elements of that motion; but at the same time, a large proportion of human error comes from the arbitrary division of continuous motion into discontinuous elements. There is a well-known, so-called sophism of the ancients consisting in this, that Achilles could never catch up with a tortoise he was following, in spite of the fact that he traveled ten times as fast as the tortoise. By the time Achilles has covered the distance that separated him from the tortoise, the tortoise has covered one tenth of that distance ahead of him: when Achilles has covered that tenth, the tortoise has covered another one hundredth, and so on forever. This problem seemed to the ancients insoluble. The absurd answer (that Achilles could never overtake the tortoise) resulted from this: that motion was arbitrarily divided into discontinuous elements, whereas the motion both of Achilles and of the tortoise was continuous.

By adopting smaller and smaller elements of motion we only approach a solution of the problem, but never reach it. Only when we have admitted the conception of the infinitely small, and the resulting geometrical progression with a common ratio of one tenth, and have found the sum of this progression to infinity, do we reach a solution of the problem.

A modern branch of mathematics having achieved the art of dealing with the infinitely small can now yield solutions in other more complex problems of motion which used to appear insoluble.

This modern branch of mathematics, unknown to the ancients, when dealing with problems of motion admits the conception of the infinitely small, and so conforms to the chief condition of motion (absolute continuity) and thereby corrects the inevitable error which the human mind cannot avoid when it deals with separate elements of motion instead of examining continuous motion.

In seeking the laws of historical movement just the same thing happens. The movement of humanity, arising as it does from innumerable arbitrary human wills, is continuous.

To understand the laws of this continuous movement is the aim of history. But to arrive at these laws, resulting from the sum of all those human wills, man's mind postulates arbitrary and disconnected units. The first method of history is to take an arbitrarily selected series of continuous events and examine it apart from others, though there is and can be no *beginning* to any event, for one event always flows uninterruptedly from another.

The second method is to consider the actions of some one man—a king or a commander—as equivalent to the sum of many individual wills; whereas the sum of individual wills is never expressed by the activity of a single historic personage.

Historical science in its endeavor to draw nearer to truth continually takes smaller and smaller units for examination. But however small the units it takes, we feel that to take any unit disconnected from others, or to assume a *beginning* of any phenomenon, or to say that the will of many men is expressed by the actions of any one historic personage, is in itself false.

It needs no critical exertion to reduce utterly to dust any deductions drawn from history. It is merely necessary to select some larger or smaller unit as the subject of observation—as criticism has every right to do, seeing that whatever unit history observes must always be arbitrarily selected.

Only by taking infinitesimally small units for observation (the differential of history, that is, the individual tendencies of men) and attaining to the art of integrating them (that is, finding the sum of these infinitesimals) can we hope to arrive at the laws of history.

The first fifteen years of the nineteenth century in Europe present an extraordinary movement of millions of people. Men leave their customary pursuits, hasten from one side of Europe to the other, plunder and slaughter one another, triumph and are plunged in despair, and for some years the whole course of life is altered and presents an intensive movement which

first increases and then slackens. What was the cause of this movement, by what laws was it governed? asks the mind of man.

The historians, replying to this question, lay before us the sayings and doings of a few dozen men in a building in the city of Paris, calling these sayings and doings "the Revolution"; then they give a detailed biography of Napoleon and of certain people favorable or hostile to him; tell of the influence some of these people had on others, and say: that is why this movement took place and those are its laws.

But the mind of man not only refuses to believe this explanation, but plainly says that this method of explanation is fallacious, because in it a weaker phenomenon is taken as the cause of a stronger. The sum of human wills produced the Revolution and Napoleon, and only the sum of those wills first tolerated and then destroyed them.

"But every time there have been conquests there have been conquerors; every time there has been a revolution in any state there have been great men," says history. And, indeed, human reason replies: every time conquerors appear there have been wars, but this does not prove that the conquerors caused the wars and that it is possible to find the laws of a war in the personal activity of a single man. Whenever I look at my watch and its hands point to ten, I hear the bells of the neighboring church; but because the bells begin to ring when the hands of the clock reach ten, I have no right to assume that the movement of the bells is caused by the position of the hands of the watch.

Whenever I see the movement of a locomotive I hear the whistle and see the valves opening and wheels turning; but I have no right to conclude that the whistling and the turning of wheels are the cause of the movement of the engine.

The peasants say that a cold wind blows in late spring because the oaks are budding, and really every spring cold winds do blow when the oak is budding. But though I do not know what causes the cold winds to blow when the oak buds unfold, I cannot agree with the peasants that the unfolding of the oak buds is the cause of the cold wind, for the force of the wind is beyond the influence of the buds. I see only a coincidence of occurrences such as happens with all the phenomena of life, and I see that however much and however carefully I observe the hands of the watch, and the valves and wheels of the engine, and the oak, I shall not discover the cause of the bells ringing, the engine moving, or of the winds of spring. To do that I must entirely change my point of view and study the laws of the movement of steam, of the bells, and of the wind. History must do the same. And attempts in this direction have already been made.

To study the laws of history we must completely change the subject

of our observation, must leave aside kings, ministers, and generals, and study the common, infinitesimally small elements by which the masses are moved. No one can say in how far it is possible for man to advance in this way toward an understanding of the laws of history; but it is evident that only along that path does the possibility of discovering the laws of history lie, and that as yet not a millionth part as much mental effort has been applied in this direction by historians as has been devoted to describing the actions of various kings, commanders, and ministers and propounding the historians' own reflections concerning these actions.

2. Summary of campaign before Borodinó and explanation of Kutúzov's subsequent movements

THE FORCES of a dozen European nations burst into Russia. The Russian army and people avoided a collision till Smolénsk was reached, and again from Smolénsk to Borodinó. The French army pushed on to Moscow, its goal, its impetus ever increasing as it neared its aim, just as the velocity of a falling body increases as it approaches the earth. Behind it were seven hundred miles of hunger-stricken, hostile country; ahead were a few dozen miles separating it from its goal. Every soldier in Napoleon's army felt this and the invasion moved on by its own momentum.

The more the Russian army retreated the more fiercely a spirit of hatred of the enemy flared up, and while it retreated the army increased and consolidated. At Borodinó a collision took place. Neither army was broken up, but the Russian army retreated immediately after the collision as inevitably as a ball recoils after colliding with another having a greater momentum, and with equal inevitability the ball of invasion that had advanced with such momentum rolled on for some distance, though the collision had deprived it of all its force.

The Russians retreated eighty miles—to beyond Moscow—and the French reached Moscow and there came to a standstill. For five weeks after that there was not a single battle. The French did not move. As a bleeding, mortally wounded animal licks its wounds, they remained inert in Moscow for five weeks, and then suddenly, with no fresh reason, fled back: they made a dash for the Kalúga road, and (after a victory—for at Málo-Yaroslávets the field of conflict again remained theirs) without undertaking a single serious battle, they fled still more rapidly back to Smolénsk, beyond Smolénsk, beyond the Berëzina, beyond Vílna, and farther still.

On the evening of the twenty-sixth of August, Kutúzov and the whole

Russian army were convinced that the battle of Borodinó was a victory. Kutúzov reported so to the Emperor. He gave orders to prepare for a fresh conflict to finish the enemy and did this not to deceive anyone, but because he knew that the enemy was beaten, as everyone who had taken part in the battle knew it.

But all that evening and next day reports came in one after another of unheard-of losses, of the loss of half the army, and a fresh battle proved physically impossible.

It was impossible to give battle before information had been collected, the wounded gathered in, the supplies of ammunition replenished, the slain reckoned up, new officers appointed to replace those who had been killed, and before the men had had food and sleep. And meanwhile, the very next morning after the battle, the French army advanced of itself upon the Russians, carried forward by the force of its own momentum now seemingly increased in inverse proportion to the square of the distance from its aim. Kutúzov's wish was to attack next day, and the whole army desired to do so. But to make an attack the wish to do so is not sufficient, there must also be a possibility of doing it, and that possibility did not exist. It was impossible not to retreat a day's march, and then in the same way it was impossible not to retreat another and a third day's march, and at last, on the first of September when the army drew near Moscow— despite the strength of the feeling that had arisen in all ranks—the force of circumstances compelled it to retire beyond Moscow. And the troops retired one more, last, day's march, and abandoned Moscow to the enemy.

For people accustomed to think that plans of campaign and battles are made by generals—as any one of us sitting over a map in his study may imagine how he would have arranged things in this or that battle—the questions present themselves: Why did Kutúzov during the retreat not do this or that? Why did he not take up a position before reaching Filí? Why did he not retire at once by the Kalúga road, abandoning Moscow? and so on. People accustomed to think in that way forget, or do not know, the inevitable conditions which always limit the activities of any commander in chief. The activity of a commander in chief does not at all resemble the activity we imagine to ourselves when we sit at ease in our studies examining some campaign on the map, with a certain number of troops on this and that side in a certain known locality, and begin our plans from some given moment. A commander in chief is never dealing with the *beginning* of any event—the position from which we always contemplate it. The commander in chief is always in the midst of a series of shifting events and so he never can at any moment consider the whole

import of an event that is occurring. Moment by moment the event is imperceptibly shaping itself, and at every moment of this continuous, uninterrupted shaping of events the commander in chief is in the midst of a most complex play of intrigues, worries, contingencies, authorities, projects, counsels, threats, and deceptions and is continually obliged to reply to innumerable questions addressed to him, which constantly conflict with one another.

Learned military authorities quite seriously tell us that Kutúzov should have moved his army to the Kalúga road long before reaching Filí, and that somebody actually submitted such a proposal to him. But a commander in chief, especially at a difficult moment, has always before him not one proposal but dozens simultaneously. And all these proposals, based on strategics and tactics, contradict each other.

A commander in chief's business, it would seem, is simply to choose one of these projects. But even that he cannot do. Events and time do not wait. For instance, on the twenty-eighth it is suggested to him to cross to the Kalúga road, but just then an adjutant gallops up from Milorádovich asking whether he is to engage the French or retire. An order must be given him at once, that instant. And the order to retreat carries us past the turn to the Kalúga road. And after the adjutant comes the commissary general asking where the stores are to be taken, and the chief of the hospitals asks where the wounded are to go, and a courier from Petersburg brings a letter from the sovereign which does not admit of the possibility of abandoning Moscow, and the commander in chief's rival, the man who is undermining him (and there are always not merely one but several such), presents a new project diametrically opposed to that of turning to the Kalúga road, and the commander in chief himself needs sleep and refreshment to maintain his energy, and a respectable general who has been overlooked in the distribution of rewards comes to complain, and the inhabitants of the district pray to be defended, and an officer sent to inspect the locality comes in and gives a report quite contrary to what was said by the officer previously sent; and a spy, a prisoner, and a general who has been on reconnaissance, all describe the position of the enemy's army differently. People accustomed to misunderstand or to forget these inevitable conditions of a commander in chief's actions describe to us, for instance, the position of the army at Filí and assume that the commander in chief could, on the first of September, quite freely decide whether to abandon Moscow or defend it; whereas, with the Russian army less than four miles from Moscow, no such question existed. When had that question been settled? At Dríssa and at Smolénsk and most palpably

of all on the twenty-fourth of August at Shevárdino and on the twenty-sixth at Borodinó, and each day and hour and minute of the retreat from Borodinó to Filí.

3. Kutúzov and his generals at the Poklónny Hill. Council of War at Filí

WHEN ERMÓLOV, having been sent by Kutúzov to inspect the position, told the field marshal that it was impossible to fight there before Moscow and that they must retreat, Kutúzov looked at him in silence.

"Give me your hand," said he and, turning it over so as to feel the pulse, added: "You are not well, my dear fellow. Think what you are saying!"

Kutúzov could not yet admit the possibility of retreating beyond Moscow without a battle.

On the Poklónny Hill, four miles from the Dorogomílov gate of Moscow, Kutúzov got out of his carriage and sat down on a bench by the roadside. A great crowd of generals gathered round him, and Count Rostopchín, who had come out from Moscow, joined them. This brilliant company separated into several groups who all discussed the advantages and disadvantages of the position, the state of the army, the plans suggested, the situation of Moscow, and military questions generally. Though they had not been summoned for the purpose, and though it was not so called, they all felt that this was really a council of war. The conversations all dealt with public questions. If anyone gave or asked for personal news, it was done in a whisper and they immediately reverted to general matters. No jokes, or laughter, or smiles even, were seen among all these men. They evidently all made an effort to hold themselves at the height the situation demanded. And all these groups, while talking among themselves, tried to keep near the commander in chief (whose bench formed the center of the gathering) and to speak so that he might overhear them. The commander in chief listened to what was being said and sometimes asked them to repeat their remarks, but did not himself take part in the conversations or express any opinion. After hearing what was being said by one or other of these groups he generally turned away with an air of disappointment, as though they were not speaking of anything he wished to hear. Some discussed the position that had been chosen, criticizing not the position itself so much as the mental capacity of those who had chosen it. Others argued that a mistake had been made earlier and that a battle should have been fought two days be-

fore. Others again spoke of the battle of Salamanca, which was described by Crosart, a newly arrived Frenchman in a Spanish uniform. (This Frenchman and one of the German princes serving with the Russian army were discussing the siege of Saragossa * and considering the possibility of defending Moscow in a similar manner.) Count Rostopchín was telling a fourth group that he was prepared to die with the city train bands under the walls of the capital, but that he still could not help regretting having been left in ignorance of what was happening, and that had he known it sooner things would have been different. . . . A fifth group, displaying the profundity of their strategic perceptions, discussed the direction the troops would now have to take. A sixth group was talking absolute nonsense. Kutúzov's expression grew more and more preoccupied and gloomy. From all this talk he saw only one thing: that to defend Moscow was a *physical impossibility* in the full meaning of those words, that is to say, so utterly impossible that if any senseless commander were to give orders to fight, confusion would result but the battle would still not take place. It would not take place because the commanders not merely all recognized the position to be impossible, but in their conversations were only discussing what would happen after its inevitable abandonment. How could the commanders lead their troops to a field of battle they considered it impossible to hold? The lower-grade officers and even the soldiers (who too reason) also considered the position impossible and therefore could not go to fight, fully convinced as they were of defeat. If Bennigsen insisted on the position being defended and others still discussed it, the question was no longer important in itself but only as a pretext for disputes and intrigue. This Kutúzov knew well.

Bennigsen, who had chosen the position, warmly displayed his Russian patriotism (Kutúzov could not listen to this without wincing) by insisting that Moscow must be defended. His aim was as clear as daylight to Kutúzov: if the defense failed, to throw the blame on Kutúzov who had brought the army as far as the Sparrow Hills without giving battle; if it succeeded, to claim the success as his own; or if battle were not given, to clear himself of the crime of abandoning Moscow. But this intrigue did not now occupy the old man's mind. One terrible question absorbed him and to that question he heard no reply from anyone. The question for him now was: "Have I really allowed Napoleon to reach Moscow,

* *The Spaniards defended the hastily entrenched city of Saragossa successfully for two months from June to August, 1808, and again for another month when the siege was renewed in December. The French, even when they entered the town, had to storm it house by house and a desperate resistance continued for another month before the city capitulated.*—A.M.

and when did I do so? When was it decided? Can it have been yesterday when I ordered Plátov to retreat, or was it the evening before, when I had a nap and told Bennigsen to issue orders? Or was it earlier still? . . . When, when was this terrible affair decided? Moscow must be abandoned. The army must retreat and the order to do so must be given." To give that terrible order seemed to him equivalent to resigning the command of the army. And not only did he love power to which he was accustomed (the honors awarded to Prince Prozoróvski, under whom he had served in Turkey, galled him), but he was convinced that he was destined to save Russia and that that was why, against the Emperor's wish and by the will of the people, he had been chosen commander in chief. He was convinced that he alone could maintain command of the army in these difficult circumstances, and that in all the world he alone could encounter the invincible Napoleon without fear, and he was horrified at the thought of the order he had to issue. But something had to be decided, and these conversations around him which were assuming too free a character must be stopped.

He called the most important generals to him.

"My head, be it good or bad, must depend on itself," said he, rising from the bench, and he rode to Filí where his carriages were waiting.

THE COUNCIL OF WAR began to assemble at two in the afternoon in the better and roomier part of Andrew Savostyánov's hut. The men, women, and children of the large peasant family crowded into the back room across the passage. Only Malásha, Andrew's six-year-old granddaughter whom his Serene Highness had petted and to whom he had given a lump of sugar while drinking his tea, remained on the top of the brick oven in the larger room. Malásha looked down from the oven with shy delight at the faces, uniforms, and decorations of the generals, who one after another came into the room and sat down on the broad benches in the corner under the icons. "Granddad" himself, as Malásha in her own mind called Kutúzov, sat apart in a dark corner behind the oven. He sat, sunk deep in a folding armchair, and continually cleared his throat and pulled at the collar of his coat which, though it was unbuttoned, still seemed to pinch his neck. Those who entered went up one by one to the field marshal; he pressed the hands of some and nodded to others. His adjutant Kaysárov was about to draw back the curtain of the window facing Kutúzov, but the latter moved his hand angrily and Kaysárov understood that his Serene Highness did not wish his face to be seen.

Round the peasant's deal table, on which lay maps, plans, pencils, and papers, so many people gathered that the orderlies brought in another

bench and put it beside the table. Ermólov, Kaysárov, and Toll, who had just arrived, sat down on this bench. In the foremost place, immediately under the icons, sat Barclay de Tolly, his high forehead merging into his bald crown. He had a St. George's Cross round his neck and looked pale and ill. He had been feverish for two days and was now shivering and in pain. Beside him sat Uvárov, who with rapid gesticulations was giving him some information, speaking in low tones as they all did. Chubby little Dokhtúrov was listening attentively with eyebrows raised and arms folded on his stomach. On the other side sat Count Ostermann-Tolstóy, seemingly absorbed in his own thoughts. His broad head with its bold features and glittering eyes was resting on his hand. Raévski, twitching forward the black hair on his temples as was his habit, glanced now at Kutúzov and now at the door with a look of impatience. Konovnítsyn's firm, handsome, and kindly face was lit up by a tender, sly smile. His glance met Malásha's, and the expression of his eyes caused the little girl to smile.

They were all waiting for Bennigsen, who on the pretext of inspecting the position was finishing his savory dinner. They waited for him from four till six o'clock and did not begin their deliberations all that time but talked in low tones of other matters.

Only when Bennigsen had entered the hut did Kutúzov leave his corner and draw toward the table, but not near enough for the candles that had been placed there to light up his face.

Bennigsen opened the council with the question: "Are we to abandon Russia's ancient and sacred capital without a struggle, or are we to defend it?" A prolonged and general silence followed. There was a frown on every face and only Kutúzov's angry grunts and occasional cough broke the silence. All eyes were gazing at him. Malásha too looked at "Granddad." She was nearest to him and saw how his face puckered; he seemed about to cry, but this did not last long.

"Russia's ancient and sacred capital!" he suddenly said, repeating Bennigsen's words in an angry voice and thereby drawing attention to the false note in them. "Allow me to tell you, your excellency, that that question has no meaning for a Russian." (He lurched his heavy body forward.) "Such a question cannot be put; it is senseless! The question I have asked these gentlemen to meet to discuss is a military one. The question is that of saving Russia. Is it better to give up Moscow without a battle, or by accepting battle to risk losing the army as well as Moscow? That is the question on which I want your opinion," and he sank back in his chair.

The discussion began. Bennigsen did not yet consider his game lost. Admitting the view of Barclay and others that a defensive battle at Filí was impossible, but imbued with Russian patriotism and the love of Moscow,

he proposed to move troops from the right to the left flank during the night and attack the French right flank the following day. Opinions were divided, and arguments were advanced for and against that project. Ermólov, Dokhtúrov, and Raévski agreed with Bennigsen. Whether feeling it necessary to make a sacrifice before abandoning the capital or guided by other, personal considerations, these generals seemed not to understand that this council could not alter the inevitable course of events and that Moscow was in effect already abandoned. The other generals, however, understood it and, leaving aside the question of Moscow, spoke of the direction the army should take in its retreat. Malásha, who kept her eyes fixed on what was going on before her, understood the meaning of the council differently. It seemed to her that it was only a personal struggle between "Granddad" and "Long-coat" as she termed Bennigsen. She saw that they grew spiteful when they spoke to one another, and in her heart she sided with "Granddad." In the midst of the conversation she noticed "Granddad" give Bennigsen a quick, subtle glance, and then to her joy she saw that "Granddad" said something to "Long-coat" which settled him. Bennigsen suddenly reddened and paced angrily up and down the room. What so affected him was Kutúzov's calm and quiet comment on the advantage or disadvantage of Bennigsen's proposal to move troops by night from the right to the left flank to attack the French right wing.

"Gentlemen," said Kutúzov, "I cannot approve of the count's plan. Moving troops in close proximity to an enemy is always dangerous, and military history supports that view. For instance . . ." Kutúzov seemed to reflect, searching for an example, then with a clear, naïve look at Bennigsen he added: "Oh yes; take the battle of Friedland,* which I think the count well remembers, and which was . . . not fully successful, only because our troops were rearranged too near the enemy. . . ."

There followed a momentary pause, which seemed very long to them all.

The discussion recommenced, but pauses frequently occurred and they all felt that there was no more to be said.

During one of these pauses Kutúzov heaved a deep sigh as if preparing to speak. They all looked at him.

"Well, gentlemen, I see that it is I who will have to pay for the broken crockery," said he, and rising slowly he moved to the table. "Gentlemen, I have heard your views. Some of you will not agree with me. But I," he

* At the battle of Friedland in East Prussia, in 1807, Napoleon defeated the Russians and Prussians under Bennigsen, inflicting very heavy losses on them. This was followed by the dismemberment of Prussia.—A.M.

paused, "by the authority entrusted to me by my Sovereign and country, order a retreat."

After that the generals began to disperse with the solemnity and circumspect silence of people who are leaving after a funeral.

Some of the generals, in low tones and in a strain very different from the way they had spoken during the council, communicated something to their commander in chief.

Malásha, who had long been expected for supper, climbed carefully backwards down from the oven, her bare little feet catching at its projections, and slipping between the legs of the generals she darted out of the room.

When he had dismissed the generals Kutúzov sat a long time with his elbows on the table, thinking always of the same terrible question: "When, when did the abandonment of Moscow become inevitable? When was that done which settled the matter? And who was to blame for it?"

"I did not expect this," said he to his adjutant Schneider when the latter came in late that night. "I did not expect this! I did not think this would happen."

"You should take some rest, your Serene Highness," replied Schneider.

"But no! They shall eat horseflesh yet, like the Turks!" exclaimed Kutúzov without replying, striking the table with his podgy fist. "They shall too, if only . . ."

4. *The author's reflections on the abandonment of Moscow. Rostopchín's conduct and that of private individuals*

AT THAT VERY TIME, in circumstances even more important than retreating without a battle, namely the evacuation and burning of Moscow, Rostopchín, who is usually represented as being the instigator of that event, acted in an altogether different manner from Kutúzov.

After the battle of Borodinó the abandonment and burning of Moscow was as inevitable as the retreat of the army beyond Moscow without fighting.

Every Russian might have predicted it, not by reasoning but by the feeling implanted in each of us and in our fathers.

The same thing that took place in Moscow had happened in all the towns and villages on Russian soil beginning with Smolénsk, without the participation of Count Rostopchín and his broadsheets. The people awaited the enemy unconcernedly, did not riot or become excited or tear anyone to pieces, but faced its fate, feeling within it the strength to find

what it should do at that most difficult moment. And as soon as the enemy drew near the wealthy classes went away abandoning their property, while the poorer remained and burned and destroyed what was left.

The consciousness that this would be so and would always be so was and is present in the heart of every Russian. And a consciousness of this, and a foreboding that Moscow would be taken, was present in Russian Moscow society in 1812. Those who had quitted Moscow already in July and at the beginning of August showed that they expected this. Those who went away, taking what they could and abandoning their houses and half their belongings, did so from the latent patriotism which expresses itself not by phrases or by giving one's children to save the fatherland and similar unnatural exploits, but unobtrusively, simply, organically, and therefore in the way that always produces the most powerful results.

"It is disgraceful to run away from danger; only cowards are running away from Moscow," they were told. In his broadsheets Rostopchín impressed on them that to leave Moscow was shameful. They were ashamed to be called cowards, ashamed to leave, but still they left, knowing it had to be done. Why did they go? It is impossible to suppose that Rostopchín had scared them by his accounts of horrors Napoleon had committed in conquered countries. The first people to go away were the rich educated people who knew quite well that Vienna and Berlin had remained intact and that during Napoleon's occupation the inhabitants had spent their time pleasantly in the company of the charming Frenchmen whom the Russians, and especially the Russian ladies, then liked so much.

They went away because for Russians there could be no question as to whether things would go well or ill under French rule in Moscow. It was out of the question to be under French rule, it would be the worst thing that could happen. They went away even before the battle of Borodinó and still more rapidly after it, despite Rostopchín's calls to defend Moscow or the announcement of his intention to take the wonder-working icon of the Iberian Mother of God and go to fight, or of the balloons that were to destroy the French, and despite all the nonsense Rostopchín wrote in his broadsheets. They knew that it was for the army to fight, and that if it could not succeed it would not do to take young ladies and house serfs to the Three Hills quarter of Moscow to fight Napoleon, and that they must go away, sorry as they were to abandon their property to destruction. They went away without thinking of the tremendous significance of that immense and wealthy city being given over to destruction, for a great city with wooden buildings was certain when abandoned by its inhabitants to be burned. They went away each on his own account, and yet it was only

in consequence of their going away that the momentous event was accomplished that will always remain the greatest glory of the Russian people. The lady who, afraid of being stopped by Count Rostopchín's orders, had already in June moved with her Negroes and her women jesters from Moscow to her Sarátov estate, with a vague consciousness that she was not Bonaparte's servant, was really, simply, and truly carrying out the great work which saved Russia. But Count Rostopchín, who now taunted those who left Moscow and now had the government offices removed; now distributed quite useless weapons to the drunken rabble; now had processions displaying the icons, and now forbade Father Augustin to remove icons or the relics of saints; now seized all the private carts in Moscow and on one hundred and thirty-six of them removed the balloon that was being constructed by Leppich; now hinted that he would burn Moscow and related how he had set fire to his own house; now wrote a proclamation to the French solemnly upbraiding them for having destroyed his Orphanage; now claimed the glory of having hinted that he would burn Moscow and now repudiated the deed; now ordered the people to catch all spies and bring them to him, and now reproached them for doing so; now expelled all the French residents from Moscow, and now allowed Madame Aubert-Chalmé (the center of the whole French colony in Moscow) to remain, but ordered the venerable old postmaster Klyucharëv to be arrested and exiled for no particular offense; now assembled the people at the Three Hills to fight the French * and now, to get rid of them, handed over to them a man to be killed and himself drove away by a back gate; now declared that he would not survive the fall of Moscow,

* Rostopchín's broadcast proclamation ran: "Arm yourselves with what you can, horse and foot; take bread only for three days; go with a cross and take banners from the churches and under that sign assemble at the Three Hills. I shall be with you, and together we will annihilate the malefactor."

The Three Hills district was a western suburb of Moscow north of the river Moskvá. The date fixed for this assembly was the first of September. That day arms were issued from the arsenal to those who wanted them. Some people took Rostopchín's rodomontade seriously and actually assembled at the Three Hills expecting to be joined by him and by the Metropolitan, but neither of those personalities turned up, so the people dispersed. S. N. Glínka (previously mentioned in a footnote on page 754) tells us that on August 30 he was at Rostopchín's house. During a conversation the latter sat down, wrote this proclamation, and ordered it to be printed at once, remarking to Glínka: "Nothing will happen at the Three Hills, but this will tell our peasants what they should do when the enemy occupies Moscow."—A.M.

and now wrote French verses in albums concerning his share in the affair *
—this man did not understand the meaning of what was happening but
merely wanted to do something himself that would astonish people, to
perform some patriotically heroic feat; and like a child he made sport of
the momentous and unavoidable event—the abandonment and burning
of Moscow—and tried with his puny hand now to speed and now to stay
the enormous, popular tide that bore him along with it.

5. Hélène in Petersburg. Conversion to Catholicism and plans for remarriage

HÉLÈNE, having returned with the court from Vílna to Petersburg,
found herself in a difficult position.

In Petersburg she had enjoyed the special protection of a grandee who
occupied one of the highest posts in the Empire. In Vílna she had formed
an intimacy with a young foreign prince. When she returned to Peters-
burg both the magnate and the prince were there, and both claimed their
rights. Hélène was faced by a new problem—how to preserve her intimacy
with both without offending either.

What would have seemed difficult or even impossible to another woman
did not cause the least embarrassment to Countess Bezúkhova, who
evidently deserved her reputation of being a very clever woman. Had she
attempted concealment, or tried to extricate herself from her awkward
position by cunning, she would have spoiled her case by acknowledging
herself guilty. But Hélène, like a really great man who can do whatever
he pleases, at once assumed her own position to be correct, as she sin-
cerely believed it to be, and that everyone else was to blame.

The first time the young foreigner allowed himself to reproach her, she
lifted her beautiful head and, half turning to him, said firmly: "That's
just like a man—selfish and cruel! I expected nothing else. A woman sacri-
fices herself for you, she suffers, and this is her reward! What right have
you, monseigneur, to demand an account of my attachments and friend-
ships? He is a man who has been more than a father to me!"

The prince was about to say something, but Hélène interrupted him.

* Je suis né tartare. I was born a Tartar.
 Je voulus être romain. I wanted to be a Roman.
 Les français m'appelèrent barbare. The French called me a barbarian.
 Les russes—George Dandin. The Russians—George Dandin.
 George Dandin is the leading character in Molière's play, George Dandin,
ou le Mari confondu.

"Well, yes," said she, "it may be that he has other sentiments for me than those of a father, but that is not a reason for me to shut my door on him. I am not a man, that I should repay kindness with ingratitude! Know, monseigneur, that in all that relates to my intimate feelings I render account only to God and to my conscience," she concluded, laying her hand on her beautiful, fully expanded bosom and looking up to heaven.

"But for heaven's sake listen to me!"

"Marry me, and I will be your slave!"

"But that's impossible."

"You won't deign to demean yourself by marrying me, you . . ." said Hélène, beginning to cry.

The prince tried to comfort her, but Hélène, as if quite distraught, said through her tears that there was nothing to prevent her marrying, that there were precedents (there were up to that time very few, but she mentioned Napoleon and some other exalted personages), that she had never been her husband's wife, and that she had been sacrificed.

"But the law, religion . . ." said the prince, already yielding.

"The law, religion . . . What have they been invented for if they can't arrange that?" said Hélène.

The prince was surprised that so simple an idea had not occurred to him, and he applied for advice to the holy brethren of the Society of Jesus, with whom he was on intimate terms.

A few days later at one of those enchanting fetes which Hélène gave at her country house on the Stone Island, the charming Monsieur de Jobert, a man no longer young, with snow-white hair and brilliant black eyes, a Jesuit à robe courte,* was presented to her, and in the garden by

* Lay member of the Society of Jesus. The Pope suppressed the Society of Jesus in 1773, and for some years it was allowed to operate only in Russia and Prussia. Catherine the Great became its active protector, and Pius VII sanctioned the reconstruction of the Order in Russia in 1801. It was, however, expelled from Petersburg and Moscow in 1813, and from Russia altogether in 1820.

In France in the time of Louis XIV and XV un Jésuite à robe courte was a term applied to lay members of the Jesuit Order. The position in Russia in 1812 was exceptional and anomalous, and one knows that Tolstóy when introducing incidents outside his personal knowledge usually relied on letters and memoirs of the period to which he had access. Without venturing, therefore, to say that he has gone astray in his account of Hélène's experience with the Order, I admit that it seems to me that he has given us rather an impressionist sketch in which accurate delineation has not been the main object. Things

the light of the illuminations and to the sound of music talked to her for a long time of the love of God, of Christ, of the Sacred Heart, and of the consolations the one true Catholic religion affords in this world and the next. Hélène was touched, and more than once tears rose to her eyes and to those of Monsieur de Jobert and their voices trembled. A dance, for which her partner came to seek her, put an end to her discourse with her future *directeur de conscience*, but the next evening Monsieur de Jobert came to see Hélène when she was alone, and after that often came again.

One day he took the countess to a Roman Catholic church, where she knelt down before the altar to which she was led. The enchanting, middle-aged Frenchman laid his hands on her head and, as she herself afterward described it, she felt something like a fresh breeze wafted into her soul. It was explained to her that this was *la grâce*.

After that a long-frocked abbé was brought to her. She confessed to him, and he absolved her from her sins. Next day she received a box containing the Sacred Host, which was left at her house for her to partake of. A few days later Hélène learned with pleasure that she had now been admitted to the true Catholic Church and that in a few days the Pope himself would hear of her and would send her a certain document.

All that was done around her and to her at this time, all the attention devoted to her by so many clever men and expressed in such pleasant, refined ways, and the state of dovelike purity she was now in (she wore only white dresses and white ribbons all that time) gave her pleasure, but her pleasure did not cause her for a moment to forget her aim. And as it always happens in contests of cunning that a stupid person gets the better of cleverer ones, Hélène—having realized that the main object of all these words and all this trouble was, after converting her to Catholicism, to obtain money from her for Jesuit institutions (as to which she received indications)—before parting with her money insisted that the various operations necessary to free her from her husband should be performed. In her view the aim of every religion was merely to preserve certain proprieties while affording satisfaction to human desires. And with this aim, in one of her talks with her Father Confessor, she insisted on an answer to the question, in how far was she bound by her marriage?

They were sitting in the twilight by a window in the drawing room. The scent of flowers came in at the window. Hélène was wearing a white dress, transparent over her shoulders and bosom. The abbé, a well-fed

have changed so much in Russia since the Jesuits were under the Emperor's protection that it is not now easy to verify Tolstóy's account of what was then possible.—A.M.

man with a plump, clean-shaven chin, a pleasant firm mouth, and white hands meekly folded on his knees, sat close to Hélène and, with a subtle smile on his lips and a peaceful look of delight at her beauty, occasionally glanced at her face as he explained his opinion on the subject. Hélène with an uneasy smile looked at his curly hair and his plump, clean-shaven, blackish cheeks and every moment expected the conversation to take a fresh turn. But the abbé, though he evidently enjoyed the beauty of his companion, was absorbed in his mastery of the matter.

The course of the Father Confessor's arguments ran as follows: "Ignorant of the import of what you were undertaking, you made a vow of conjugal fidelity to a man who on his part, by entering the married state without faith in the religious significance of marriage, committed an act of sacrilege. That marriage lacked the dual significance it should have had. Yet in spite of this your vow was binding. You swerved from it. What did you commit by so acting? A venial, or a mortal, sin? A venial sin, for you acted without evil intention. If now you married again with the object of bearing children, your sin might be forgiven. But the question is again a twofold one: firstly . . ."

But suddenly Hélène, who was getting bored, said with one of her bewitching smiles: "But I think that having espoused the true religion I cannot be bound by what a false religion laid upon me."

The director of her conscience was astounded at having the case presented to him thus with the simplicity of Columbus' egg. He was delighted at the unexpected rapidity of his pupil's progress, but could not abandon the edifice of argument he had laboriously constructed.

"Let us understand one another, Countess," said he with a smile, and began refuting his spiritual daughter's arguments.

HÉLÈNE UNDERSTOOD that the question was very simple and easy from the ecclesiastical point of view, and that her directors were making difficulties only because they were apprehensive as to how the matter would be regarded by the secular authorities.

So she decided that it was necessary to prepare the opinion of society. She provoked the jealousy of the elderly magnate and told him what she had told her other suitor; that is, she put the matter so that the only way for him to obtain a right over her was to marry her. The elderly magnate was at first as much taken aback by this suggestion of marriage with a woman whose husband was alive, as the younger man had been, but Hélène's imperturbable conviction that it was as simple and natural as marrying a maiden had its effect on him too. Had Hélène herself shown the least sign of hesitation, shame, or secrecy, her cause would certainly

have been lost; but not only did she show no signs of secrecy or shame, on the contrary, with good-natured naïveté she told her intimate friends (and these were all Petersburg) that both the prince and the magnate had proposed to her and that she loved both and was afraid of grieving either.

A rumor immediately spread in Petersburg, not that Hélène wanted to be divorced from her husband (had such a report spread many would have opposed so illegal an intention) but simply that the unfortunate and interesting Hélène was in doubt which of the two men she should marry. The question was no longer whether this was possible, but only which was the better match and how the matter would be regarded at court. There were, it is true, some rigid individuals unable to rise to the height of such a question, who saw in the project a desecration of the sacrament of marriage, but there were not many such and they remained silent, while the majority were interested in Hélène's good fortune and in the question which match would be the more advantageous. Whether it was right or wrong to remarry while one had a husband living they did not discuss, for that question had evidently been settled by people "wiser than you or me," as they said, and to doubt the correctness of that decision would be to risk exposing one's stupidity and incapacity to live in society.

Only Márya Dmítrievna Akhrosímova, who had come to Petersburg that summer to see one of her sons, allowed herself plainly to express an opinion contrary to the general one. Meeting Hélène at a ball she stopped her in the middle of the room and, amid general silence, said in her gruff voice: "So wives of living men have started marrying again! Perhaps you think you have invented a novelty? You have been forestalled, my dear! It was thought of long ago. It is done in all the brothels," and with these words Márya Dmítrievna, turning up her wide sleeves with her usual threatening gesture and glancing sternly round, moved across the room.

Though people were afraid of Márya Dmítrievna she was regarded in Petersburg as a buffoon, and so of what she had said they only noticed, and repeated in a whisper, the one coarse word she had used, supposing the whole sting of her remark to lie in that word.

Prince Vasíli, who of late very often forgot what he had said and repeated one and the same thing a hundred times, remarked to his daughter whenever he chanced to see her:

"Hélène, I have a word to say to you," and he would lead her aside, drawing her hand downward. "I have heard of certain projects concerning . . . you know. Well, my dear child, you know how your father's heart rejoices to know that you . . . You have suffered so much. . . . But, my

dear child, consult only your own heart. That is all I have to say," and concealing his unvarying emotion he would press his cheek against his daughter's and move away.

Bilíbin, who had not lost his reputation of an exceedingly clever man, and who was one of the disinterested friends so brilliant a woman as Hélène always has—men friends who can never change into lovers—once gave her his view of the matter at a small and intimate gathering.

"Listen, Bilíbin," said Hélène (she always called friends of that sort by their surnames), and she touched his coat sleeve with her white, beringed fingers. "Tell me, as you would a sister, what I ought to do. Which of the two?"

Bilíbin wrinkled up the skin over his eyebrows and pondered, with a smile on his lips.

"You are not taking me unawares, you know," said he. "As a true friend, I have thought and thought again about your affair. You see, if you marry the prince"—he meant the younger man—and he crooked one finger, "you forever lose the chance of marrying the other, and you will displease the court besides. (You know there is some kind of connection.) But if you marry the old count you will make his last days happy, and as widow of the Grand . . . the prince would no longer be making a *mésalliance* by marrying you," and Bilíbin smoothed out his forehead.

"That's a true friend!" said Hélène beaming, and again touching Bilíbin's sleeve. "But I love them, you know, and don't want to distress either of them. I would give my life for the happiness of them both."

Bilíbin shrugged his shoulders, as much as to say that not even he could help in that difficulty.

"*Une maîtresse-femme!* [A clever woman!] That's what is called putting things squarely. She would like to be married to all three at the same time," thought he.

"But tell me, how will your husband look at the matter?" Bilíbin asked, his reputation being so well established that he did not fear to ask so naïve a question. "Will he agree?"

"Oh, he loves me so!" said Hélène, who for some reason imagined that Pierre too loved her. "He will do anything for me."

Bilíbin puckered his skin in preparation for something witty.

"Even divorce you?" said he.

Hélène laughed.

Among those who ventured to doubt the justifiability of the proposed marriage was Hélène's mother, Princess Kurágina. She was continually tormented by jealousy of her daughter, and now that jealousy concerned a subject near to her own heart, she could not reconcile herself to the idea.

She consulted a Russian priest as to the possibility of divorce and re-marriage during a husband's lifetime, and the priest told her that it was impossible, and to her delight showed her a text in the Gospel which (as it seemed to him) plainly forbids remarriage while the husband is alive.

Armed with these arguments, which appeared to her unanswerable, she drove to her daughter's early one morning so as to find her alone.

Having listened to her mother's objections, Hélène smiled blandly and ironically.

"But it says plainly: 'Whosoever shall marry her that is divorced . . .' " said the old princess.

"Ah, Maman, ne dites pas de bêtises. Vous ne comprenez rien. Dans ma position j'ai des devoirs [Oh, Mamma, don't talk nonsense! You don't understand anything. In my position I have obligations]," said Hélène changing from Russian, in which language she always felt that her case did not sound quite clear, into French which suited it better.

"But, my dear . . ."

"Oh, Mamma, how is it you don't understand that the Holy Father, who has the right to grant dispensations . . ."

Just then the lady companion who lived with Hélène came in to an-nounce that His Highness was in the ballroom and wished to see her.

"Non, dites-lui que je ne veux pas le voir, que je suis furieuse contre lui, parce qu'il m' a manqué parole [No, tell him I don't wish to see him, I am furious with him for not keeping his word to me]."

"Comtesse, à tout péché miséricorde [Countess, there is mercy for every sin]," said a fair-haired young man with a long face and nose, as he entered the room.

The old princess rose respectfully and curtsied. The young man who had entered took no notice of her. The princess nodded to her daughter and sidled out of the room.

"Yes, she is right," thought the old princess, all her convictions dissi-pated by the appearance of His Highness. "She is right, but how is it that we in our irrecoverable youth did not know it? Yet it is so simple," she thought as she got into her carriage.

By the beginning of August Hélène's affairs were clearly defined and she wrote a letter to her husband—who, as she imagined, loved her very much—informing him of her intention to marry N.N. and of her having embraced the one true faith, and asking him to carry out all the formali-ties necessary for a divorce, which would be explained to him by the bearer of the letter.

"And so I pray God to have you, my friend, in His holy and powerful keeping—Your friend Hélène."

This letter was brought to Pierre's house when he was on the field of Borodinó.

6. Pierre walks to Mozháysk. His night lodging there. His dream, and his return to Moscow

Toward the end of the battle of Borodinó, Pierre, having run down from Raévski's battery a second time, made his way through a gully to Knyazkóvo with a crowd of soldiers, reached the dressing station, and seeing blood and hearing cries and groans hurried on, still entangled in the crowds of soldiers.

The one thing he now desired with his whole soul was to get away quickly from the terrible sensations amid which he had lived that day and return to ordinary conditions of life and sleep quietly in a room in his own bed. He felt that only in the ordinary conditions of life would he be able to understand himself and all he had seen and felt. But such ordinary conditions of life were nowhere to be found.

Though shells and bullets did not whistle over the road along which he was going, still on all sides there was what there had been on the field of battle. There were still the same suffering, exhausted, and sometimes strangely indifferent faces, the same blood, the same soldiers' overcoats, the same sounds of firing which, though distant now, still aroused terror, and besides this there were the foul air and the dust.

Having gone a couple of miles along the Mozháysk road, Pierre sat down by the roadside.

Dusk had fallen, and the roar of guns died away. Pierre lay leaning on his elbow for a long time, gazing at the shadows that moved past him in the darkness. He was continually imagining that a cannon ball was flying toward him with a terrific whizz, and then he shuddered and sat up. He had no idea how long he had been there. In the middle of the night three soldiers, having brought some firewood, settled down near him and began lighting a fire.

The soldiers, who threw sidelong glances at Pierre, got the fire to burn and placed an iron pot on it into which they broke some dried bread and put a little dripping. The pleasant odor of greasy viands mingled with the smell of smoke. Pierre sat up and sighed. The three soldiers were eating and talking among themselves, taking no notice of him.

"And who may you be?" one of them suddenly asked Pierre, evidently

meaning what Pierre himself had in mind, namely: "If you want to eat we'll give you some food, only let us know whether you are an honest man."

"I, I . . ." said Pierre, feeling it necessary to minimize his social position as much as possible so as to be nearer to the soldiers and better understood by them. "By rights I am a militia officer, but my men are not here. I came to the battle and have lost them."

"There now!" said one of the soldiers.

Another shook his head.

"Would you like a little mash?" the first soldier asked, and handed Pierre a wooden spoon after licking it clean.

Pierre sat down by the fire and began eating the mash, as they called the food in the cauldron, and he thought it more delicious than any food he had ever tasted. As he sat bending greedily over it, helping himself to large spoonfuls and chewing one after another, his face was lit up by the fire and the soldiers looked at him in silence.

"Where have you to go to? Tell us!" said one of them.

"To Mozháysk."

"You're a gentleman, aren't you?"

"Yes."

"And what's your name?"

"Peter Kirílych."

"Well then, Peter Kirílych, come along with us, we'll take you there."

In the total darkness the soldiers walked with Pierre to Mozháysk.

By the time they got near Mozháysk and began ascending the steep hill into the town, the cocks were already crowing. Pierre went on with the soldiers, quite forgetting that his inn was at the bottom of the hill and that he had already passed it. He would not soon have remembered this, such was his state of forgetfulness, had he not halfway up the hill stumbled upon his groom, who had been to look for him in the town and was returning to the inn. The groom recognized Pierre in the darkness by his white hat.

"Your excellency!" he said. "Why, we were beginning to despair! How is it you are on foot? And where are you going, please?"

"Oh, yes!" said Pierre.

The soldiers stopped.

"So you've found your folk?" said one of them. "Well, good-by, Peter Kirílych—isn't it?"

"Good-by, Peter Kirílych!" Pierre heard the other voices repeat.

"Good-by!" he said and turned with his groom toward the inn.

"I ought to give them something!" he thought, and felt in his pocket. "No, better not!" said another, inner voice.

There was not a room to be had at the inn, they were all occupied. Pierre went out into the yard and, covering himself up head and all, lay down in his carriage.

SCARCELY HAD PIERRE laid his head on the pillow before he felt himself falling asleep, but suddenly, almost with the distinctness of reality, he heard the *boom, boom, boom* of firing, the thud of projectiles, groans and cries, and smelled blood and powder, and a feeling of horror and dread of death seized him. Filled with fright he opened his eyes and lifted his head from under his cloak. All was tranquil in the yard. Only someone's orderly passed through the gateway, splashing through the mud, and talked to the innkeeper. Above Pierre's head some pigeons, disturbed by the movement he had made in sitting up, fluttered under the dark roof of the penthouse. The whole courtyard was permeated by a strong peaceful smell of stable yards, delightful to Pierre at that moment. He could see the clear starry sky between the dark roofs of two penthouses.

"Thank God, there is no more of that!" he thought, covering up his head again. "Oh, what a terrible thing is fear, and how shamefully I yielded to it! But they . . . *they* were steady and calm all the time, to the end . . ." thought he.

They, in Pierre's mind, were the soldiers, those who had been at the battery, those who had given him food, and those who had prayed before the icon. *They*, those strange men he had not previously known, stood out clearly and sharply from everyone else.

"To be a soldier, just a soldier!" thought Pierre as he fell asleep, "to enter communal life completely, to be imbued by what makes them what they are. But how cast off all the superfluous, devilish burden of my outer man? There was a time when I could have done it. I could have run away from my father, as I wanted to. Or I might have been sent to serve as a soldier after the duel with Dólokhov." And the memory of the dinner at the English Club when he had challenged Dólokhov flashed through Pierre's mind, and then he remembered his benefactor at Torzhók. And now a picture of a solemn meeting of the lodge presented itself to his mind. It was taking place at the English Club and someone near and dear to him sat at the end of the table. "Yes, that is he! It is my benefactor. But he died!" thought Pierre. "Yes, he died, and I did not know he was alive. How sorry I am that he died, and how glad I am that he is alive again!" On one side of the table sat Anatole, Dólokhov, Nesvítski, Denísov, and others like them (in his dream the category to which these

men belonged was as clearly defined in his mind as the category of those he termed *they*), and he heard those people, Anatole and Dólokhov, shouting and singing loudly; yet through their shouting the voice of his benefactor was heard speaking all the time and the sound of his words was as weighty and uninterrupted as the booming on the battlefield, but pleasant and comforting. Pierre did not understand what his benefactor was saying, but he knew (the categories of thoughts were also quite distinct in his dream) that he was talking of goodness and the possibility of being what *they* were. And *they* with their simple, kind, firm faces surrounded his benefactor on all sides. But though they were kindly they did not look at Pierre and did not know him. Wishing to speak and to attract their attention, he got up, but at that moment his legs grew cold and bare.

He felt ashamed, and with one arm covered his legs from which his cloak had in fact slipped. For a moment as he was rearranging his cloak Pierre opened his eyes and saw the same penthouse roofs, posts, and yard, but now they were all bluish, lit up, and glittering with frost or dew.

"It is dawn," thought Pierre. "But that's not what I want. I want to hear and understand my benefactor's words." Again he covered himself up with his cloak, but now neither the lodge nor his benefactor was there. There were only thoughts clearly expressed in words, thoughts that someone was uttering or that he himself was formulating.

Afterwards when he recalled those thoughts Pierre was convinced that someone outside himself had spoken them, though the impressions of that day had evoked them. He had never, it seemed to him, been able to think and express his thoughts like that when awake.

"To endure war is the most difficult subordination of man's freedom to the law of God," the voice had said. "Simplicity is submission to the will of God; you cannot escape from Him. And *they* are simple. *They* do not talk, but act. The spoken word is silver but the unspoken is golden. Man can be master of nothing while he fears death, but he who does not fear it possesses all. If there were no suffering, man would not know his limitations, would not know himself. The hardest thing [Pierre went on thinking, or hearing, in his dream] is to be able in your soul to unite the meaning of all. To unite all?" he asked himself. "No, not to unite. Thoughts cannot be united, but to *harness* all these thoughts together is what we need! Yes, one must *harness* them, must *harness* them!" he repeated to himself with inward rapture, feeling that these words and they alone expressed what he wanted to say and solved the question that tormented him.

"Yes, one must harness, it is time to harness."

"Time to harness, time to harness, your excellency! Your excellency!"

some voice was repeating. "We must harness, it is time to harness. . . ."
It was the voice of the groom, trying to wake him. The sun shone
straight into Pierre's face. He glanced at the dirty innyard in the middle
of which soldiers were watering their lean horses at the pump while carts
were passing out of the gate. Pierre turned away with repugnance, and
closing his eyes quickly fell back on the carriage seat. "No, I don't want
that, I don't want to see and understand that. I want to understand what
was revealing itself to me in my dream. One second more and I should
have understood it all! But what am I to do? Harness, but how can I har-
ness everything?" and Pierre felt with horror that the meaning of all he had
seen and thought in the dream had been destroyed.

The groom, the coachman, and the innkeeper told Pierre that an officer
had come with news that the French were already near Mozháysk and
that our men were leaving it.

Pierre got up and, having told them to harness and overtake him, went
on foot through the town.

The troops were moving on, leaving about ten thousand wounded be-
hind them. There were wounded in the yards, at the windows of the
houses, and the streets were crowded with them. In the streets, around
carts that were to take some of the wounded away, shouts, curses, and
blows could be heard. Pierre offered the use of his carriage, which had
overtaken him, to a wounded general he knew, and drove with him to
Moscow. On the way Pierre was told of the death of his brother-in-law
Anatole and of that of Prince Andrew.

7. Pierre at Rostopchín's. The affair of Klyucharëv and Vereshchágin. Pierre leaves home secretly

O N THE THIRTIETH OF AUGUST Pierre reached Moscow. Close to the
gates of the city he was met by Count Rostopchín's adjutant.

"We have been looking for you everywhere," said the adjutant. "The
count wants to see you particularly. He asks you to come to him at once
on a very important matter."

Without going home Pierre took a cab and drove to see the Moscow
commander in chief.

Count Rostopchín had only that morning returned to town from his
summer villa at Sokólniki. The anteroom and reception room of his house
were full of officials who had been summoned or had come for orders.
Vasílchikov and Plátov had already seen the count and explained to him
that it was impossible to defend Moscow and that it would have to be

surrendered. Though this news was being concealed from the inhabitants, the officials—the heads of the various government departments—knew that Moscow would soon be in the enemy's hands, just as Count Rostopchín himself knew it, and to escape personal responsibility they had all come to the governor to ask how they were to deal with their various departments.

As Pierre was entering the reception room a courier from the army came out of Rostopchín's private room.

In answer to questions with which he was greeted, the courier made a despairing gesture with his hand and passed through the room.

While waiting in the reception room Pierre with weary eyes watched the various officials, old and young, military and civilian, who were there. They all seemed dissatisfied and uneasy. Pierre went up to a group of men, one of whom he knew. After greeting Pierre they continued their conversation.

"If they're sent out and brought back again later on it will do no harm, but as things are now one can't answer for anything."

"But you see what he writes . . ." said another, pointing to a printed sheet he held in his hand.

"That's another matter. That's necessary for the people," said the first.

"What is it?" asked Pierre.

"Oh, it's a fresh broadsheet."

Pierre took it and began reading.

"His Serene Highness * has passed through Mozháysk in order to join up with the troops moving toward him and has taken up a strong position where the enemy will not soon attack him. Forty-eight guns with ammunition have been sent him from here, and his Serene Highness says he will defend Moscow to the last drop of blood and is even ready to fight in the streets. Do not be upset, brothers, that the law courts are closed; things have to be put in order, and we will deal with villains in our own way! When the time comes I shall want both town and peasant lads and will raise the cry a day or two beforehand, but they are not wanted yet so I hold my peace. An ax will be useful, a hunting spear not bad, but a three-pronged fork will be best of all: a Frenchman is no heavier than a sheaf of rye. Tomorrow after dinner I shall take the Iberian icon of the Mother of God to the wounded in the Catherine Hospital where we will have some water blessed. That will help them to get well quicker. I, too, am well now: one of my eyes was sore but now I am on the lookout with both."

* Kutúzov.

"But military men have told me that it is impossible to fight in the town," said Pierre, "and that the position . ."

"Well, of course! That's what we were saying," replied the first speaker.

"And what does he mean by 'One of my eyes was sore but now I am on the lookout with both'?" asked Pierre.

"The count had a sty," replied the adjutant smiling, "and was very much upset when I told him people had come to ask what was the matter with him. By the by, Count," he added suddenly, addressing Pierre with a smile, "we heard that you have family troubles and that the countess, your wife . . ."

"I have heard nothing," Pierre replied unconcernedly. "But what have you heard?"

"Oh, well, you know people often invent things. I only say what I heard."

"But what did you hear?"

"Well, they say," continued the adjutant with the same smile, "that the countess, your wife, is preparing to go abroad. I expect it's nonsense. . . ."

"Possibly," remarked Pierre, looking about him absent-mindedly. "And who is that?" he asked, indicating a short old man in a clean blue peasant overcoat, with a big snow-white beard and eyebrows and a ruddy face.

"He? That's a tradesman, that is to say, he's the restaurant keeper, Vereshchágin. Perhaps you have heard of that affair with the proclamation."

"Oh, so that is Vereshchágin!" said Pierre, looking at the firm, calm face of the old man and seeking any indication of his being a traitor.

"That's not he himself, that's the father of the fellow who wrote the proclamation," said the adjutant. "The young man is in prison and I expect it will go hard with him."

An old gentleman wearing a star and another official, a German wearing a cross round his neck, approached the speaker.

"It's a complicated story, you know," said the adjutant. "That proclamation appeared about two months ago. The count was informed of it. He gave orders to investigate the matter. Gabriel Ivánovich here made the inquiries. The proclamation had passed through exactly sixty-three hands. He asked one, 'From whom did you get it?' 'From so-and-so.' He went to the next one. 'From whom did you get it?' and so on till he reached Vereshchágin, a half-educated tradesman, you know, 'a pet of a trader,' " said the adjutant smiling. "They asked him, 'Who gave it you?' And the point is that we knew whom he had it from. He could only have had it from the Postmaster. But evidently they had come to

some understanding. He replied: 'From no one; I made it up myself.'
They threatened and questioned him, but he stuck to that: 'I made it up
myself.' And so it was reported to the count, who sent for the man.
'From whom did you get the proclamation?' 'I wrote it myself.' Well,
you know the count," said the adjutant cheerfully, with a smile of pride,
"he flared up dreadfully—and just think of the fellow's audacity, lying,
and obstinacy!"

"And the count wanted him to say it was from Klyucharëv? I under-
stand!" said Pierre.

"Not at all," rejoined the adjutant in dismay. "Klyucharëv had his own
sins to answer for without that and that is why he has been banished.
But the point is that the count was much annoyed. 'How could you have
written it yourself?' said he, and he took up the Hamburg *Gazette* that
was lying on the table. 'Here it is! You did not write it yourself but trans-
lated it, and translated it abominably, because you don't even know
French, you fool.' And what do you think? 'No,' said he, 'I have not read
any papers, I made it up myself.' 'If that's so, you're a traitor and I'll
have you tried, and you'll be hanged! Say from whom you had it.' 'I have
seen no papers, I made it up myself.' And that was the end of it. The
count had the father fetched, but the fellow stuck to it. He was sent for
trial and condemned to hard labor, I believe. Now the father has come
to intercede for him. But he's a good-for-nothing lad! You know that sort
of tradesman's son, a dandy and lady-killer. He attended some lectures
somewhere and imagines that the devil is no match for him. That's the
sort of fellow he is. His father keeps a cookshop here by the Stone Bridge,
and you know there was a large icon of God Almighty painted with a
scepter in one hand and an orb in the other. Well, he took that icon home
with him for a few days and what did he do? He found some scoundrel
of a painter . . ."

IN THE MIDDLE of this fresh tale Pierre was summoned to the commander
in chief.

When he entered the private room Count Rostopchín, puckering his
face, was rubbing his forehead and eyes with his hand. A short man was
saying something, but when Pierre entered he stopped speaking and
went out.

"Ah, how do you do, great warrior?" said Rostopchín as soon as the
short man had left the room. "We have heard of your prowess. But that's
not the point. Between ourselves, *mon cher*, do you belong to the
Masons?" he went on severely, as though there were something wrong
about it which he nevertheless intended to pardon. Pierre remained silent.

"I am well informed, my friend, but I am aware that there are Masons and Masons and I hope that you are not one of those who on pretense of saving mankind wish to ruin Russia."

"Yes, I am a Mason," Pierre replied.

"There, you see, mon cher! I expect you know that Messrs. Speránski and Magnítski have been deported to their proper place. Mr. Klyucharëv has been treated in the same way, and so have others who on the plea of building up the temple of Solomon have tried to destroy the temple of their fatherland. You can understand that there are reasons for this and that I could not have exiled the Postmaster had he not been a harmful person. It has now come to my knowledge that you lent him your carriage for his removal from town, and that you have even accepted papers from him for safe custody. I like you and don't wish you any harm and— as you are only half my age—I advise you, as a father would, to cease all communication with men of that stamp and to leave here as soon as possible."

"But what did Klyucharëv do wrong, Count?" asked Pierre.

"That is for me to know, but not for you to ask," shouted Rostopchín.

"If he is accused of circulating Napoleon's proclamation it is not proved that he did so," said Pierre without looking at Rostopchín, "and Vereshchágin . . ."

"There we are!" Rostopchín shouted at Pierre louder than before, frowning suddenly. "Vereshchágin is a renegade and a traitor who will be punished as he deserves," said he with the vindictive heat with which people speak when recalling an insult. "But I did not summon you to discuss my actions, but to give you advice—or an order if you prefer it. I beg you to leave the town and break off all communication with such men as Klyucharëv. And I will knock the nonsense out of anybody"—but probably realizing that he was shouting at Bezúkhov who so far was not guilty of anything, he added, taking Pierre's hand in a friendly manner, "We are on the eve of a public disaster and I haven't time to be polite to everybody who has business with me. My head is sometimes in a whirl. Well, mon cher, what are you doing personally?"

"Why, nothing," answered Pierre without raising his eyes or changing the thoughtful expression of his face.

The count frowned.

"A word of friendly advice, mon cher. Be off as soon as you can, that's all I have to tell you. Happy he who has ears to hear. Good-by, my dear fellow. Oh, by the by!" he shouted through the doorway after Pierre, "is it true that the countess has fallen into the clutches of the holy fathers of the Society of Jesus?"

Pierre did not answer and left Rostopchín's room more sullen and angry than he had ever before shown himself.

When he reached home it was already getting dark. Some eight people had come to see him that evening: the secretary of a committee, the colonel of his battalion, his steward, his major-domo, and various petitioners. They all had business with Pierre and wanted decisions from him. Pierre did not understand and was not interested in any of these questions and only answered them in order to get rid of these people. When left alone at last he opened and read his wife's letter.

"They, the soldiers at the battery, Prince Andrew killed . . . that old man . . . Simplicity is submission to God. Suffering is necessary . . . the meaning of all . . . one must harness . . . my wife is getting married . . . One must forget and understand . . ." And going to his bed he threw himself on it without undressing and immediately fell asleep.

When he awoke next morning the major-domo came to inform him that a special messenger, a police officer, had come from Count Rostopchín to know whether Count Bezúkhov had left or was leaving the town.

A dozen persons who had business with Pierre were awaiting him in the drawing room. Pierre dressed hurriedly and, instead of going to see them, went to the back porch and out through the gate.

From that time till the end of the destruction of Moscow no one of Bezúkhov's household, despite all the search they made, saw Pierre again or knew where he was.

8. *The Rostóvs: packing up and leaving Moscow. They allow wounded officers to stay in their house and avail themselves of their carts to leave Moscow. Berg's wish to borrow a cart. Natásha when leaving Moscow sees and speaks to Pierre. Prince Andrew travels in their train of vehicles*

THE Rostóvs remained in Moscow till the first of September, that is, till the eve of the enemy's entry into the city.

After Pétya had joined Obolénski's regiment of Cossacks and left for Bélaya Tsérkov where that regiment was forming, the countess was seized with terror. The thought that both her sons were at the war, had both gone from under her wing, that today or tomorrow either or both of them might be killed like the three sons of one of her acquaintances, struck her that summer for the first time with cruel clearness. She tried to get Nicholas back and wished to go herself to join Pétya, or to get him an appoint-

ment somewhere in Petersburg, but neither of these proved possible. Pétya could not return unless his regiment did so or unless he was transferred to another regiment on active service. Nicholas was somewhere with the army and had not sent a word since his last letter, in which he had given a detailed account of his meeting with Princess Mary. The countess did not sleep at night, or when she did fall asleep dreamed that she saw her sons lying dead. After many consultations and conversations, the count at last devised means to tranquillize her. He got Pétya transferred from Obolénski's regiment to Bezúkhov's, which was in training near Moscow. Though Pétya would remain in the service, this transfer would give the countess the consolation of seeing at least one of her sons under her wing, and she hoped to arrange matters for her Pétya so as not to let him go again, but always get him appointed to places where he could not possibly take part in a battle. As long as Nicholas alone was in danger the countess imagined that she loved her first-born more than all her other children and even reproached herself for it; but when her youngest: the scapegrace who had been bad at lessons, was always breaking things in the house and making himself a nuisance to everybody, that snub-nosed Pétya with his merry black eyes and fresh rosy cheeks where soft down was just beginning to show—when he was thrown amid those big, dreadful, cruel men who were fighting somewhere about something and apparently finding pleasure in it—then his mother thought she loved him more, much more, than all her other children. The nearer the time came for Pétya to return, the more uneasy grew the countess. She began to think she would never live to see such happiness. The presence of Sónya, of her beloved Nátasha, or even of her husband irritated her. "What do I want with them? I want no one but Pétya," she thought.

At the end of August the Rostóvs received another letter from Nicholas. He wrote from the province of Vorónezh where he had been sent to procure remounts, but that letter did not set the countess at ease. Knowing that one son was out of danger she became the more anxious about Pétya.

Though by the twentieth of August nearly all the Rostóvs' acquaintances had left Moscow, and though everybody tried to persuade the countess to get away as quickly as possible, she would not hear of leaving before her treasure, her adored Pétya, returned. On the twenty-eighth of August he arrived. The passionate tenderness with which his mother received him did not please the sixteen-year-old officer. Though she concealed from him her intention of keeping him under her wing, Pétya guessed her designs, and instinctively fearing that he might give way to emotion when with her—might "become womanish" as he termed it to

himself—he treated her coldly, avoided her, and during his stay in Moscow attached himself exclusively to Natásha for whom he had always had a particularly brotherly tenderness, almost lover-like.

Owing to the count's customary carelessness nothing was ready for their departure by the twenty-eighth of August and the carts that were to come from their Ryazán and Moscow estates to remove their household belongings did not arrive till the thirtieth.

From the twenty-eighth till the thirty-first all Moscow was in a bustle and commotion. Every day thousands of men wounded at Borodinó were brought in by the Dorogomílov gate and taken to various parts of Moscow, and thousands of carts conveyed the inhabitants and their possessions out by the other gates. In spite of Rostopchín's broadsheets, or because of them or independently of them, the strangest and most contradictory rumors were current in the town. Some said that no one was to be allowed to leave the city, others on the contrary said that all the icons had been taken out of the churches and everybody was to be ordered to leave. Some said there had been another battle after Borodinó at which the French had been routed, while others on the contrary reported that the Russian army had been destroyed. Some talked about the Moscow militia which, preceded by the clergy, would go to the Three Hills; others whispered that Augustin * had been forbidden to leave, that traitors had been seized, that the peasants were rioting and robbing people on their way from Moscow, and so on. But all this was only talk; in reality (though the Council of Filí, at which it was decided to abandon Moscow, had not yet been held) both those who went away and those who remained behind felt, though they did not show it, that Moscow would certainly be abandoned, and that they ought to get away as quickly as possible and save their belongings. It was felt that everything would suddenly break up and change, but up to the first of September nothing had done so. As a criminal who is being led to execution knows that he must die immediately, but yet looks about him and straightens the cap that is awry on his head, so Moscow involuntarily continued its wonted life, though it knew that the time of its destruction was near when the conditions of life to which its people were accustomed to submit would be completely upset.

During the three days preceding the occupation of Moscow the whole Rostóv family was absorbed in various activities. The head of the family, Count Ilyá Rostóv, continually drove about the city collecting the current rumors from all sides and gave superficial and hasty orders at home about the preparations for their departure.

* A. V. Vinográdski (1766-1818), who took the monastic name of Augustin, was a celebrated preacher and the Archbishop of Moscow.—A.M.

The countess watched the things being packed, was dissatisfied with everything, was constantly in pursuit of Pétya who was always running away from her, and was jealous of Natásha with whom he spent all his time. Sónya alone directed the practical side of matters by getting things packed. But of late Sónya had been particularly sad and silent. Nicholas' letter in which he mentioned Princess Mary had elicited, in her presence, joyous comments from the countess, who saw an intervention of Providence in this meeting of the princess and Nicholas.

"I was never pleased at Bolkónski's engagement to Natásha," said the countess, "but I always wanted Nicholas to marry the princess, and had a presentiment that it would happen. What a good thing it would be!"

Sónya felt that this was true: that the only possibility of retrieving the Rostóvs' affairs was by Nicholas marrying a rich woman, and that the princess was a good match. It was very bitter for her. But despite her grief, or perhaps just because of it, she took on herself all the difficult work of directing the storing and packing of their things and was busy for whole days. The count and countess turned to her when they had any orders to give. Pétya and Natásha on the contrary, far from helping their parents, were generally a nuisance and a hindrance to everyone. Almost all day long the house resounded with their running feet, their cries, and their spontaneous laughter. They laughed and were gay not because there was any reason to laugh, but because gaiety and mirth were in their hearts and so everything that happened was a cause for gaiety and laughter to them. Pétya was in high spirits because having left home a boy he had returned (as everybody told him) a fine young man, because he was at home, because he had left Bélaya Tsérkov where there was no hope of soon taking part in a battle and had come to Moscow where there was to be fighting in a few days, and chiefly because Natásha, whose lead he always followed, was in high spirits. Natásha was gay because she had been sad too long and now nothing reminded her of the cause of her sadness, and because she was feeling well. She was also happy because she had someone to adore her: the adoration of others was a lubricant the wheels of her machine needed to make them run freely—and Pétya adored her. Above all, they were gay because there was a war near Moscow, there would be fighting at the town gates, arms were being given out, everybody was escaping—going away somewhere, and in general something extraordinary was happening, and that is always exciting, especially to the young.

On Saturday, the thirty-first of August, everything in the Rostóvs' house seemed topsy-turvy. All the doors were open, all the furniture was being carried out or moved about, and the mirrors and pictures had been taken

down. There were trunks in the rooms, and hay, wrapping paper, and ropes were scattered about. The peasants and house serfs carrying out the things were treading heavily on the parquet floors. The yard was crowded with peasant carts, some loaded high and already corded up, others still empty.

The voices and footsteps of the many servants and of the peasants who had come with the carts resounded as they shouted to one another in the yard and in the house. The count had been out since morning. The countess had a headache brought on by all the noise and turmoil and was lying down in the new sitting room with a vinegar compress on her head. Pétya was not at home, he had gone to visit a friend with whom he meant to obtain a transfer from the militia to the active army. Sónya was in the ballroom looking after the packing of the glass and china. Natásha was sitting on the floor of her dismantled room with dresses, ribbons, and scarves strewn all about her, gazing fixedly at the floor and holding in her hands the old ball dress (already out of fashion) which she had worn at her first Petersburg ball.

Natásha was ashamed of doing nothing when everyone else was so busy, and several times that morning had tried to set to work, but her heart was not in it, and she could not and did not know how to do anything except with all her heart and all her might. For a while she had stood beside Sónya while the china was being packed and tried to help, but soon gave it up and went to her room to pack her own things. At first she found it amusing to give away dresses and ribbons to the maids, but when that was done and what was left had still to be packed, she found it dull.

"Dunyásha, you pack! You will, won't you, dear?" And when Dunyásha willingly promised to do it all for her, Natásha sat down on the floor, took her old ball dress, and fell into a reverie quite unrelated to what ought to have occupied her thoughts now. She was roused from her reverie by the talk of the maids in the next room (which was theirs) and by the sound of their hurried footsteps going to the back porch. Natásha got up and looked out of the window. An enormously long row of carts full of wounded men had stopped in the street.

The housekeeper, the old nurse, the cooks, coachmen, maids, footmen, postilions, and scullions stood at the gate, staring at the wounded.

Natásha, throwing a clean pocket handkerchief over her hair and holding an end of it in each hand, went out into the street.

The former housekeeper, old Mávra Kuzmínichna, had stepped out of the crowd by the gate, gone up to a cart with a hood constructed of bast mats, and was speaking to a pale young officer who lay inside. Natásha

moved a few steps forward and stopped shyly, still holding her handker-
chief, and listened to what the housekeeper was saying.

"Then you have nobody in Moscow?" she was saying. "You would be
more comfortable somewhere in a house . . . in ours, for instance . . .
the family are leaving."

"I don't know if it would be allowed," replied the officer in a weak
voice. "Here is our commanding officer . . . ask him," and he pointed
to a stout major who was walking back along the street past the row of
carts.

Natásha glanced with frightened eyes at the face of the wounded officer
and at once went to meet the major.

"May the wounded men stay in our house?" she asked.

The major raised his hand to his cap with a smile.

"Which one do you want, Ma'am'selle?" said he, screwing up his eyes
and smiling.

Natásha quietly repeated her question, and her face and whole manner
were so serious, though she was still holding the ends of her handkerchief,
that the major ceased smiling and after some reflection—as if considering
in how far the thing was possible—replied in the affirmative.

"Oh yes, why not? They may," he said.

With a slight inclination of her head, Natásha stepped back quickly to
Mávra Kuzmínichna, who stood talking compassionately to the officer.

"They may. He says they may!" whispered Natásha.

The cart in which the officer lay was turned into the Rostóvs' yard, and
dozens of carts with wounded men began at the invitation of the towns-
folk to turn into the yards and to draw up at the entrances of the houses
in Povarskáya Street. Natásha was evidently pleased to be dealing with
new people outside the ordinary routine of her life. She and Mávra Kuz-
mínichna tried to get as many of the wounded as possible into their yard.

"Your Papa must be told, though," said Mávra Kuzmínichna.

"Never mind, never mind, what does it matter? For one day we can
move into the drawing room. They can have all our half of the house."

"There now, young lady, you do take things into your head! Even if
we put them into the wing, the men's room, or the nurse's room, we must
ask permission."

"Well, I'll ask."

Natásha ran into the house and went on tiptoe through the half-open
door into the sitting room, where there was a smell of vinegar and Hoff-
man's drops.*

* A medicine much used in Russia, composed of two parts ether sulphuricus
and three parts alcohol.—A.M.

"Are you asleep, Mamma?"

"Oh, what sleep—?" said the countess, waking up just as she was dropping into a doze.

"Mamma darling!" said Natásha, kneeling by her mother and bringing her face close to her mother's, "I am sorry, forgive me, I'll never do it again; I woke you up! Mávra Kuzmínichna has sent me: they have brought some wounded here—officers. Will you let them come? They have nowhere to go. I knew you'd let them come . . ." she said quickly all in one breath.

"What officers? Whom have they brought? I don't understand anything about it," said the countess.

Natásha laughed, and the countess too smiled slightly.

"I knew you'd give permission . . . so I'll tell them," and, having kissed her mother, Natásha got up and went to the door.

In the hall she met her father, who had returned with bad news.

"We've stayed too long!" said the count with involuntary vexation. "The Club is closed and the police are leaving."

"Papa, is it all right—I've invited some of the wounded into the house?" said Natásha.

"Of course it is," he answered absently. "That's not the point. I beg you not to indulge in trifles now, but to help to pack, and tomorrow we must go, go, go! . . ."

And the count gave a similar order to the major-domo and the servants.

At dinner Pétya having returned home told them the news he had heard. He said the people had been getting arms in the Krémlin, and that though Rostopchín's broadsheet had said that he would sound a call two or three days in advance, the order had certainly already been given for everyone to go armed to the Three Hills tomorrow, and that there would be a big battle there.

The countess looked with timid horror at her son's eager, excited face as he said this. She realized that if she said a word about his not going to the battle (she knew he enjoyed the thought of the impending engagement) he would say something about men, honor, and the fatherland—something senseless, masculine, and obstinate which there would be no contradicting, and her plans would be spoiled; and so, hoping to arrange to leave before then and take Pétya with her as their protector and defender, she did not answer him, but after dinner called the count aside and implored him with tears to take her away quickly, that very night if possible. With a woman's involuntary loving cunning she, who till then had not shown any alarm, said that she would die of fright if they did not

leave that very night. Without any pretense she was now afraid of everything.

MADAME SCHOSS, who had been out to visit her daughter, increased the countess' fears still more by telling what she had seen at a spirit dealer's in Myasnítski Street. When returning by that street she had been unable to pass because of a drunken crowd rioting in front of the shop. She had taken a cab and driven home by a side street and the cabman had told her that the people were breaking open the barrels at the drink store, having received orders to do so.

After dinner the whole Rostóv household set to work with enthusiastic haste packing their belongings and preparing for their departure. The old count, suddenly setting to work, kept passing from the yard to the house and back again, shouting confused instructions to the hurrying people, and flurrying them still more. Pétya directed things in the yard. Sónya, owing to the count's contradictory orders, lost her head and did not know what to do. The servants ran noisily about the house and yard, shouting and disputing. Natásha, with the ardor characteristic of all she did, suddenly set to work too. At first her intervention in the business of packing was received skeptically. Everybody expected some prank from her and did not wish to obey her; but she resolutely and passionately demanded obedience, grew angry and nearly cried because they did not heed her, and at last succeeded in making them believe her. Her first exploit, which cost her immense effort and established her authority, was the packing of the carpets. The count had valuable Gobelin tapestries and Persian carpets in the house. When Natásha set to work two cases were standing open in the ballroom, one almost full up with crockery, the other with carpets. There was also much china standing on the tables, and still more was being brought in from the storeroom. A third case was needed and servants had gone to fetch it.

"Sónya, wait a bit—we'll pack everything into these," said Natásha.

"You can't, Miss, we have tried to," said the butler's assistant.

"No, wait a minute, please."

And Natásha began rapidly taking out of the case dishes and plates wrapped in paper.

"The dishes must go in here among the carpets," said she.

"Why, it's a mercy if we can get the carpets alone into three cases," said the butler's assistant.

"Oh, wait, please!" And Natásha began rapidly and deftly sorting out the things. "These aren't needed," said she, putting aside some plates of

Kiev ware. "These—yes, these must go among the carpets," she said, referring to the Saxony china dishes.

"Don't, Natásha! Leave it alone! We'll get it all packed," urged Sónya reproachfully.

"What a young lady she is!" remarked the major-domo.

But Natásha would not give in. She turned everything out and began quickly repacking, deciding that the inferior Russian carpets and unnecessary crockery should not be taken at all. When everything had been taken out of the cases, they recommenced packing, and it turned out that when the cheaper things not worth taking had nearly all been rejected, the valuable ones really did all go into the two cases. Only the lid of the case containing the carpets would not shut down. A few more things might have been taken out, but Natásha insisted on having her own way. She packed, repacked, pressed, made the butler's assistant and Pétya—whom she had drawn into the business of packing—press on the lid, and made desperate efforts herself.

"That's enough, Natásha," said Sónya. "I see you were right, but just take out the top one."

"I won't!" cried Natásha, with one hand holding back the hair that hung over her perspiring face, while with the other she pressed down the carpets. "Now press, Pétya! Press, Vasílich, press hard!" she cried.

The carpets yielded and the lid closed; Natásha, clapping her hands, screamed with delight and tears fell from her eyes. But this only lasted a moment. She at once set to work afresh and they now trusted her completely. The count was not angry even when they told him that Natásha had countermanded an order of his, and the servants now came to her to ask whether a cart was sufficiently loaded, and whether it might be corded up. Thanks to Natásha's directions the work now went on expeditiously, unnecessary things were left, and the most valuable packed as compactly as possible.

But hard as they all worked till quite late that night, they could not get everything packed. The countess had fallen asleep and the count, having put off their departure till next morning, went to bed.

Sónya and Natásha slept in the sitting room without undressing.

That night another wounded man was driven down the Povarskáya, and Mávra Kuzmínichna, who was standing at the gate, had him brought into the Rostóvs' yard. Mávra Kuzmínichna concluded that he was a very important man. He was being conveyed in a calèche with a raised hood, and was quite covered by an apron. On the box beside the driver sat a venerable old attendant. A doctor and two soldiers followed the carriage in a cart.

"Please come in here. The masters are going away and the whole house will be empty," said the old woman to the old attendant.

"Well, perhaps," said he with a sigh. "We don't expect to get him home alive! We have a house of our own in Moscow, but it's a long way from here, and there's nobody living in it."

"Do us the honor to come in, there's plenty of everything in the master's house. Come in," said Mávra Kuzmínichna. "Is he very ill?" she asked.

The attendant made a hopeless gesture.

"We don't expect to get him home! We must ask the doctor." And the old servant got down from the box and went up to the cart.

"All right!" said the doctor.

The old servant returned to the calèche, looked into it, shook his head disconsolately, told the driver to turn into the yard, and stopped beside Mávra Kuzmínichna.

"O, Lord Jesus Christ!" she murmured.

She invited them to take the wounded man into the house.

"The masters won't object . . ." she said.

But they had to avoid carrying the man upstairs, and so they took him into the wing and put him in the room that had been Madame Schoss'.

This wounded man was Prince Andrew Bolkónski.

Moscow's LAST DAY had come. It was a clear bright autumn day, a Sunday. The church bells everywhere were ringing for service, just as usual on Sundays. Nobody seemed yet to realize what awaited the city.

Only two things indicated the social condition of Moscow—the rabble, that is the poor people, and the price of commodities. An enormous crowd of factory hands, house serfs, and peasants, with whom some officials, seminarists,* and gentry were mingled, had gone early that morning to the Three Hills. Having waited there for Rostopchín who did not turn up, they became convinced that Moscow would be surrendered, and then dispersed all about the town to the public houses and cookshops. Prices too that day indicated the state of affairs. The price of weapons, of gold, of carts and horses, kept rising, but the value of paper money and city articles kept falling, so that by midday there were instances of carters removing valuable goods, such as cloth, and receiving in payment a half of what they carted, while peasant horses were fetching five hundred rubles each, and furniture, mirrors, and bronzes were being given away for nothing.

In the Rostóvs' staid old-fashioned house the dissolution of former

* Students at the theological college.—A.M.

conditions of life was but little noticeable. As to the serfs the only indication was that three out of their huge retinue disappeared during the night, but nothing was stolen; and as to the value of their possessions, the thirty peasant carts that had come in from their estates and which many people envied proved to be extremely valuable and they were offered enormous sums of money for them. Not only were huge sums offered for the horses and carts, but on the previous evening and early in the morning of the first of September, orderlies and servants sent by wounded officers came to the Rostóvs' yard, and wounded men dragged themselves there from the Rostóvs' and from neighboring houses where they were accommodated, entreating the servants to try to get them a lift out of Moscow. The major-domo to whom these entreaties were addressed, though he was sorry for the wounded, resolutely refused, saying that he dare not even mention the matter to the count. Pity these wounded men as one might, it was evident that if they were given one cart there would be no reason to refuse another, or all the carts and one's own carriages as well. Thirty carts could not save all the wounded and in the general catastrophe one could not disregard oneself and one's own family. So thought the major-domo on his master's behalf.

On waking up that morning Count Ilyá Rostóv left his bedroom softly, so as not to wake the countess who had fallen asleep only toward morning, and came out to the porch in his lilac silk dressing gown. In the yard stood the carts ready corded. The carriages were at the front porch. The major-domo stood at the porch talking to an elderly orderly and to a pale young officer with a bandaged arm. On seeing the count the major-domo made a significant and stern gesture to them both to go away.

"Well, Vasílich, is everything ready?" asked the count, and stroking his bald head he looked good-naturedly at the officer and the orderly and nodded to them. (He liked to see new faces.)

"We can harness at once, your excellency."

"Well, that's right. As soon as the countess wakes we'll be off, God willing! What is it, gentlemen?" he added, turning to the officer. "Are you staying in my house?"

The officer came nearer and suddenly his face flushed crimson.

"Count, be so good as to allow me . . . for God's sake, to get into some corner of one of your carts! I have nothing here with me. . . . I should be all right on a loaded cart. . . ."

Before the officer had finished speaking the orderly made the same request on behalf of his master.

"Oh yes, yes, yes!" said the count hastily. "I shall be very pleased, very pleased. Vasílich, you'll see to it. Just unload one or two carts. Well, what

of it . . . do what's necessary . . ." said the count, muttering some indefinite order.

But at the same moment an expression of warm gratitude on the officer's face had already sealed the order. The count looked around him. In the yard, at the gates, at the window of the wings, wounded officers and their orderlies were to be seen. They were all looking at the count and moving toward the porch.

"Please step into the gallery, your excellency," said the major-domo. "What are your orders about the pictures?"

The count went into the house with him, repeating his order not to refuse the wounded who asked for a lift.

"Well, never mind, some of the things can be unloaded," he added in a soft, confidential voice, as though afraid of being overheard.

At nine o'clock the countess woke up, and Matrëna Timoféevna, who had been her lady's maid before her marriage and now performed a sort of chief gendarme's duty for her, came to say that Madame Schoss was much offended and the young ladies' summer dresses could not be left behind. On inquiry, the countess learned that Madame Schoss was offended because her trunk had been taken down from its cart, and all the loads were being uncorded and the luggage taken out of the carts to make room for wounded men whom the count in the simplicity of his heart had ordered that they should take with them. The countess sent for her husband.

"What is this, my dear? I hear that the luggage is being unloaded."

"You know, love, I wanted to tell you . . . Countess dear . . . an officer came to me to ask for a few carts for the wounded. After all, ours are things that can be bought but think what being left behind means to them! . . . Really now, in our own yard—we asked them in ourselves and there are officers among them. . . . You know, I think, my dear . . . let them be taken . . . where's the hurry?"

The count spoke timidly, as he always did when talking of money matters. The countess was accustomed to this tone as a precursor of news of something detrimental to the children's interests, such as the building of a new gallery or conservatory, the inauguration of a private theater or an orchestra. She was accustomed always to oppose anything announced in that timid tone and considered it her duty to do so.

She assumed her dolefully submissive manner and said to her husband: "Listen to me, Count, you have managed matters so that we are getting nothing for the house, and now you wish to throw away all our—all the children's property! You said yourself that we have a hundred thousand rubles' worth of things in the house. I don't consent, my dear, I don't!

Do as you please! It's the government's business to look after the wounded; they know that. Look at the Lopukhíns opposite, they cleared out everything two days ago. That's what other people do. It's only we who are such fools. If you have no pity on me, have some for the children."

Flourishing his arms in despair the count left the room without replying.

"Papa, what are you doing that for?" asked Natásha, who had followed him into her mother's room.

"Nothing! What business is it of yours?" muttered the count angrily.

"But I heard," said Natásha. "Why does Mamma object?"

"What business is it of yours?" cried the count.

Natásha stepped up to the window and pondered.

"Papa! Here's Berg coming to see us," said she, looking out of the window.

BERG, the Rostóvs' son-in-law, was already a colonel wearing the orders of Vladímir and Anna, and he still filled the quiet and agreeable post of assistant to the head of the staff of the assistant commander of the first division of the Second Army.

On the first of September he had come to Moscow from the army.

He had nothing to do in Moscow, but he had noticed that everyone in the army was asking for leave to visit Moscow and had something to do there. So he considered it necessary to ask for leave of absence for family and domestic reasons.

Berg drove up to his father-in-law's house in his spruce little trap with a pair of sleek roans, exactly like those of a certain prince. He looked attentively at the carts in the yard and while going up to the porch took out a clean pocket handkerchief and tied a knot in it.

From the anteroom Berg ran with smooth though impatient steps into the drawing room, where he embraced the count, kissed the hands of Natásha and Sónya, and hastened to inquire after "Mamma's" health.

"Health, at a time like this?" said the count. "Come, tell us the news! Is the army retreating or will there be another battle?"

"God Almighty alone can decide the fate of our fatherland, Papa," said Berg. "The army is burning with a spirit of heroism and the leaders, so to say, have now assembled in council. No one knows what is coming. But in general I can tell you, Papa, that such a heroic spirit, the truly antique valor of the Russian army, which they—which it" (he corrected himself) "has shown or displayed in the battle of the twenty-sixth—there are no words worthy to do it justice! I tell you, Papa" (he smote himself on the breast as a general he had heard speaking had done, but Berg did

it a trifle late for he should have struck his breast at the words "Russian army"), "I tell you frankly that we, the commanders, far from having to urge the men on or anything of that kind, could hardly restrain those . . . those . . . yes, those exploits of antique valor," he went on rapidly. "General Barclay de Tolly risked his life everywhere at the head of the troops, I can assure you. Our corps was stationed on a hillside. You can imagine!"

And Berg related all that he remembered of the various tales he had heard those days. Natásha watched him with an intent gaze that confused him, as if she were trying to find in his face the answer to some question.

"Altogether such heroism as was displayed by the Russian warriors cannot be imagined or adequately praised!" said Berg, glancing round at Natásha, and as if anxious to conciliate her, replying to her intent look with a smile. " 'Russia is not in Moscow, she lives in the hearts of her sons!' Isn't it so, Papa?" said he.

Just then the countess came in from the sitting room with a weary and dissatisfied expression. Berg hurriedly jumped up, kissed her hand, asked about her health, and, swaying his head from side to side to express sympathy, remained standing beside her.

"Yes, Mamma, I tell you sincerely that these are hard and sad times for every Russian. But why are you so anxious? You have still time to get away. . . ."

"I can't think what the servants are about," said the countess, turning to her husband. "I have just been told that nothing is ready yet. Somebody after all must see to things. One misses Mítenka at such times. There won't be any end to it."

The count was about to say something, but evidently restrained himself. He got up from his chair and went to the door.

At that moment Berg drew out his handkerchief as if to blow his nose and, seeing the knot in it, pondered, shaking his head sadly and significantly.

"And I have a great favor to ask of you, Papa," said he.

"Hm . . ." said the count, and stopped.

"I was driving past Yusúpov's house just now," said Berg with a laugh, "when the steward, a man I know, ran out and asked me whether I wouldn't buy something. I went in out of curiosity, you know, and there is a small chiffonier and a dressing table. You know how dear Véra wanted a chiffonier like that and how we had a dispute about it." (At the mention of the chiffonier and dressing table Berg involuntarily changed his tone to one of pleasure at his admirable domestic arrangements.) "And it's such a beauty! It pulls out and has a secret English drawer, you know! And dear

Véra has long wanted one. I wish to give her a surprise, you see. I saw so many of those peasant carts in your yard. Please let me have one, I will pay the man well, and . . ."

The count frowned and coughed.

"Ask the countess, I don't give orders."

"If it's inconvenient, please don't," said Berg. "Only I so wanted it, for dear Véra's sake."

"Oh, go to the devil, all of you! To the devil, the devil, the devil . . . !" cried the old count. "My head's in a whirl!"

And he left the room. The countess began to cry.

"Yes, Mamma! Yes, these are very hard times!" said Berg.

Natásha left the room with her father and, as if finding it difficult to reach some decision, first followed him and then ran downstairs.

Pétya was in the porch, engaged in giving out weapons to the servants who were to leave Moscow. The loaded carts were still standing in the yard. Two of them had been uncorded and a wounded officer was climbing into one of them helped by an orderly.

"Do you know what it's about?" Pétya asked Natásha.

She understood that he meant what were their parents quarreling about. She did not answer.

"It's because Papa wanted to give up all the carts to the wounded," said Pétya. "Vasílich told me. I consider . . ."

"I consider," Natásha suddenly almost shouted, turning her angry face to Pétya, "I consider it so horrid, so abominable, so . . . I don't know what. Are we despicable Germans?"

Her throat quivered with convulsive sobs and, afraid of weakening and letting the force of her anger run to waste, she turned and rushed headlong up the stairs.

Berg was sitting beside the countess consoling her with the respectful attention of a relative. The count, pipe in hand, was pacing up and down the room, when Natásha, her face distorted by anger, burst in like a tempest and approached her mother with rapid steps.

"It's horrid! It's abominable!" she screamed. "You can't possibly have ordered it!"

Berg and the countess looked at her, perplexed and frightened. The count stood still at the window and listened.

"Mamma, it's impossible: see what is going on in the yard!" she cried. "They will be left! . . ."

"What's the matter with you? Who are 'they'? What do you want?"

"Why, the wounded! It's impossible, Mamma. It's monstrous! . . . No, Mamma darling, it's not the thing. Please forgive me, darling. . . .

Mamma, what does it matter what we take away? Only look what is going on in the yard . . . Mamma! . . . It's impossible!"

The count stood by the window and listened without turning round. Suddenly he sniffed and put his face closer to the window.

The countess glanced at her daughter, saw her face full of shame for her mother, saw her agitation, and understood why her husband did not turn to look at her now, and she glanced round quite disconcerted.

"Oh, do as you like! Am I hindering anyone?" she said, not surrendering at once.

"Mamma, darling, forgive me!"

But the countess pushed her daughter away and went up to her husband.

"My dear, you order what is right. . . . You know I don't understand about it," said she, dropping her eyes shamefacedly.

"The eggs . . . the eggs are teaching the hen . . ." muttered the count through tears of joy, and he embraced his wife who was glad to hide her look of shame on his breast.

"Papa! Mamma! May I see to it? May I? . . ." asked Natásha. "We will still take all the most necessary things."

The count nodded affirmatively, and Natásha, at the rapid pace at which she used to run when playing at tag, ran through the ballroom to the ante-room and downstairs into the yard.

The servants gathered round Natásha, but could not believe the strange order she brought them until the count himself, in his wife's name, confirmed the order to give up all the carts to the wounded and take the trunks to the storerooms. When they understood that order the servants set to work at this new task with pleasure and zeal. It no longer seemed strange to them but on the contrary it seemed the only thing that could be done, just as a quarter of an hour before it had not seemed strange to anyone that the wounded should be left behind and the goods carted away but that had seemed the only thing to do.

The whole household, as if to atone for not having done it sooner, set eagerly to work at the new task of placing the wounded in the carts. The wounded dragged themselves out of their rooms and stood with pale but happy faces round the carts. The news that carts were to be had spread to the neighboring houses, from which wounded men began to come into the Rostóvs' yard. Many of the wounded asked them not to unload the carts but only to let them sit on the top of the things. But the work of unloading, once started, could not be arrested. It seemed not to matter whether all or only half the things were left behind. Cases full of china, bronzes, pictures, and mirrors that had been so carefully packed the night before now lay about the yard, and still they went on searching for and finding possibilities

of unloading this or that and letting the wounded have another and yet another cart.

"We can take four more men," said the steward. "They can have my trap, or else what is to become of them?"

"Let them have my wardrobe cart," said the countess. "Dunyásha can go with me in the carriage."

They unloaded the wardrobe cart and sent it to take wounded men from a house two doors off. The whole household, servants included, was bright and animated. Natásha was in a state of rapturous excitement such as she had not known for a long time.

"What could we fasten this onto?" asked the servants, trying to fix a trunk on the narrow footboard behind a carriage. "We must keep at least one cart."

"What's in it?" asked Natásha.

"The count's books."

"Leave it, Vasílich will put it away. It's not wanted."

The phaeton was full of people and there was a doubt as to where Count Peter could sit.

"On the box. You'll sit on the box, won't you, Pétya?" cried Natásha.

Sónya too was busy all this time, but the aim of her efforts was quite different from Natásha's. She was putting away the things that had to be left behind and making a list of them as the countess wished, and she tried to get as much taken away with them as possible.

Before two o'clock in the afternoon the Rostóvs' four carriages, packed full and with the horses harnessed, stood at the front door. One by one the carts with the wounded had moved out of the yard.

The calèche in which Prince Andrew was being taken attracted Sónya's attention as it passed the front porch. With the help of a maid she was arranging a seat for the countess in the huge high coach that stood at the entrance.

"Whose calèche is that?" she inquired, leaning out of the carriage window.

"Why, didn't you know, Miss?" replied the maid. "The wounded prince: he spent the night in our house and is going with us."

"But who is it? What's his name?"

"It's our intended that was—Prince Bolkónski himself! They say he is dying," replied the maid with a sigh.

Sónya jumped out of the coach and ran to the countess. The countess, tired out and already dressed in shawl and bonnet for her journey, was pacing up and down the drawing room, waiting for the household to as-

semble for the usual silent prayer with closed doors before starting. Natásha was not in the room.

"Mamma," said Sónya, "Prince Andrew is here, mortally wounded. He is going with us."

The countess opened her eyes in dismay and, seizing Sónya's arm, glanced around.

"Natásha?" she murmured.

At that moment this news had only one significance for both of them. They knew their Natásha, and alarm as to what would happen if she heard this news stifled all sympathy for the man they both liked.

"Natásha does not know yet, but he is going with us," said Sónya.

"You say he is dying?"

Sónya nodded.

The countess put her arms around Sónya and began to cry.

"The ways of God are past finding out!" she thought,* feeling that the Almighty Hand, hitherto unseen, was becoming manifest in all that was now taking place.

"Well, Mamma? Everything is ready. What's the matter?" asked Natásha, as with animated face she ran into the room.

"Nothing," answered the countess. "If everything is ready let us start."

And the countess bent over her reticule to hide her agitated face. Sónya embraced Natásha and kissed her.

Natásha looked at her inquiringly.

"What is it? What has happened?"

"Nothing . . . No . . ."

"Is it something very bad for me? What is it?" persisted Natásha with her quick intuition.

Sónya sighed and made no reply. The count, Pétya, Madame Schoss, Mávra Kuzmínichna, and Vasílich came into the drawing room and, having closed the doors, they all sat down and remained for some moments silently seated without looking at one another.

The count was the first to rise, and with a loud sigh crossed himself before the icon. All the others did the same. Then the count embraced Mávra Kuzmínichna and Vasílich, who were to remain in Moscow, and while they caught at his hand and kissed his shoulder he patted their backs lightly with some vaguely affectionate and comforting words. The countess went into the oratory and there Sónya found her on her knees before

* *The reader may need to be again reminded that the Russian Church law of affinity forbade a man to marry his sister-in-law, so that, had Natásha married Andrew, it would have been a hindrance to Nicholas' marrying Princess Mary and retrieving the Rostóvs' fortunes.*—A.M.

the icons that had been left here and there hanging on the wall. (The most precious ones, with which some family tradition was connected, were being taken with them.)

In the porch and in the yard the men whom Pétya had armed with swords and daggers, with trousers tucked inside their high boots and with belts and girdles tightened, were taking leave of those remaining behind.

As is always the case at a departure, much had been forgotten or put in the wrong place, and for a long time two menservants stood one on each side of the open door and the carriage steps waiting to help the countess in, while maids rushed with cushions and bundles from the house to the carriages, the calèche, the phaeton, and back again.

"They always will forget everything!" said the countess. "Don't you know I can't sit like that?"

And Dunyásha, with clenched teeth, without replying but with an aggrieved look on her face, hastily got into the coach to rearrange the seat.

"Oh, those servants!" said the count, swaying his head.

Efím, the old coachman, who was the only one the countess trusted to drive her, sat perched up high on the box and did not so much as glance round at what was going on behind him. From thirty years' experience he knew it would be some time yet before the order, "Be off, in God's name!" would be given him: and he knew that even when it was said he would be stopped once or twice more while they sent back to fetch something that had been forgotten, and even after that he would again be stopped and the countess herself would lean out of the window and beg him for the love of heaven to drive carefully down the hill. He knew all this and therefore waited calmly for what would happen, with more patience than the horses, especially the near one, the chestnut Falcon, who was pawing the ground and champing his bit. At last all were seated, the carriage steps were folded and pulled up, the door was shut, somebody was sent for a traveling case, and the countess leaned out and said what she had to say. Then Efím deliberately doffed his hat and began crossing himself. The postilion and all the other servants did the same. "Off, in God's name!" said Efím, putting on his hat. "Start!" The postilion started the horses, the off pole horse tugged at his collar, the high springs creaked, and the body of the coach swayed. The footman sprang onto the box of the moving coach which jolted as it passed out of the yard onto the uneven roadway; the other vehicles jolted in their turn, and the procession of carriages moved up the street. In the carriages, the calèche, and the phaeton, all crossed themselves as they passed the church opposite the house. Those who were to remain in Moscow walked on either side of the vehicles seeing the travelers off.

Rarely had Natásha experienced so joyful a feeling as now, sitting in the carriage beside the countess and gazing at the slowly receding walls of forsaken, agitated Moscow. Occasionally she leaned out of the carriage window and looked back and then forward at the long train of wounded in front of them. Almost at the head of the line she could see the raised hood of Prince Andrew's *calèche*. She did not know who was in it, but each time she looked at the procession her eyes sought that *calèche*. She knew it was right in front.

In Kúdrino, from the Nikítski, Présnya, and Podnovínsk Streets came several other trains of vehicles similar to the Rostóvs', and as they passed along the Sadóvaya Street the carriages and carts formed two rows abreast.

As they were going round the Súkharev water tower Natásha, who was inquisitively and alertly scrutinizing the people driving or walking past, suddenly cried out in joyful surprise:

"Dear me! Mamma, Sónya, look, it's he!"

"Who? Who?"

"Look! Yes, on my word, it's Bezúkhov!" said Natásha, putting her head out of the carriage and staring at a tall, stout man in a coachman's long coat, who from his manner of walking and moving was evidently a gentleman in disguise, and who was passing under the arch of the Súkharev tower accompanied by a small, sallow-faced, beardless old man in a frieze coat.

"Yes, it really is Bezúkhov in a coachman's coat, with a queer-looking old boy. Really," said Natásha, "look, look!"

"No, it's not he. How can you talk such nonsense?"

"Mamma," screamed Natásha, "I'll stake my head it's he! I assure you! Stop, stop!" she cried to the coachman.

But the coachman could not stop, for from the Meshchánski Street came more carts and carriages, and the Rostóvs were being shouted at to move on and not block the way.

In fact, however, though now much farther off than before, the Rostóvs all saw Pierre—or someone extraordinarily like him—in a coachman's coat, going down the street with head bent and a serious face beside a small, beardless old man who looked like a footman. That old man noticed a face thrust out of the carriage window gazing at them, and respectfully touching Pierre's elbow said something to him and pointed to the carriage. Pierre, evidently engrossed in thought, could not at first understand him. At length when he had understood and looked in the direction the old man indicated, he recognized Natásha, and following his first impulse stepped instantly and rapidly toward the coach. But having taken a dozen steps he seemed to remember something and stopped.

Natásha's face, leaning out of the window, beamed with quizzical kindliness.

"Peter Kirílovich, come here! We have recognized you! This is wonderful!" she cried, holding out her hand to him. "What are you doing? Why are you like this?"

Pierre took her outstretched hand and kissed it awkwardly as he walked along beside her while the coach still moved on.

"What is the matter, Count?" asked the countess in a surprised and commiserating tone.

"What? What? Why? Don't ask me," said Pierre, and looked round at Natásha whose radiant, happy expression—of which he was conscious without looking at her—filled him with enchantment.

"Are you remaining in Moscow, then?"

Pierre hesitated.

"In Moscow?" he said in a questioning tone. "Yes, in Moscow. Good-by!"

"Ah, if only I were a man! I'd certainly stay with you. How splendid!" said Natásha. "Mamma, if you'll let me, I'll stay!"

Pierre glanced absently at Natásha and was about to say something, but the countess interrupted him.

"You were at the battle, we heard."

"Yes, I was," Pierre answered. "There will be another battle tomorrow . . ." he began, but Natásha interrupted him.

"But what is the matter with you, Count? You are not like yourself. . . ."

"Oh, don't ask me, don't ask me! I don't know myself. Tomorrow . . . But no! Good-by, good-by!" he muttered. "It's an awful time!" and dropping behind the carriage he stepped onto the pavement.

Natásha continued to lean out of the window for a long time, beaming at him with her kindly, slightly quizzical, happy smile.

9. Pierre at Bazdéev's house. He wears a coachman's coat

For the last two days, ever since leaving home, Pierre had been living in the empty house of his deceased benefactor, Bazdéev. This is how it happened.

When he woke up on the morning after his return to Moscow and his interview with Count Rostopchín, he could not for some time make out where he was and what was expected of him. When he was informed that among others awaiting him in his reception room there was a Frenchman who had brought a letter from his wife, the Countess Hélène, he felt sud-

denly overcome by that sense of confusion and hopelessness to which he was apt to succumb. He felt that everything was now at an end, all was in confusion and crumbling to pieces, that nobody was right or wrong, the future held nothing, and there was no escape from this position. Smiling unnaturally and muttering to himself, he first sat down on the sofa in an attitude of despair, then rose, went to the door of the reception room and peeped through the crack, returned flourishing his arms, and took up a book. His major-domo came in a second time to say that the Frenchman who had brought the letter from the countess was very anxious to see him if only for a minute, and that someone from Bazdéev's widow had called to ask Pierre to take charge of her husband's books, as she herself was leaving for the country.

"Oh, yes, in a minute; wait . . . or no! No, of course . . . go and say I will come directly," Pierre replied to the major-domo.

But as soon as the man had left the room Pierre took up his hat which was lying on the table and went out of his study by the other door. There was no one in the passage. He went along the whole length of this passage to the stairs and, frowning and rubbing his forehead with both hands, went down as far as the first landing. The hall porter was standing at the front door. From the landing where Pierre stood there was a second staircase leading to the back entrance. He went down that staircase and out into the yard. No one had seen him. But there were some carriages waiting, and as soon as Pierre stepped out of the gate the coachmen and the yard porter noticed him and raised their caps to him. When he felt he was being looked at he behaved like an ostrich which hides its head in a bush in order not to be seen: he hung his head and quickening his pace went down the street.

Of all the affairs awaiting Pierre that day the sorting of Joseph Bazdéev's books and papers appeared to him the most necessary.

He hired the first cab he met and told the driver to go to the Patriarch's Ponds, where the widow Bazdéev's house was.

Continually turning round to look at the rows of loaded carts that were making their way from all sides out of Moscow, and balancing his bulky body so as not to slip out of the ramshackle old vehicle, Pierre, experiencing the joyful feeling of a boy escaping from school, began to talk to his driver.

The man told him that arms were being distributed today at the Krémlin and that tomorrow everyone would be sent out beyond the Three Hills gates and a great battle would be fought there.

Having reached the Patriarch's Ponds Pierre found the Bazdéevs' house, where he had not been for a long time past. He went up to the gate. Gerá-

sim, that sallow beardless old man Pierre had seen at Torzhók five years before with Joseph Bazdéev, came out in answer to his knock.

"At home?" asked Pierre.

"Owing to the present state of things Sophia Danílovna has gone to the Torzhók estate with the children, your excellency."

"I will come in all the same, I have to look through the books," said Pierre.

"Be so good as to step in. Makár Alexéevich, the brother of my late master—may the kingdom of heaven be his—has remained here, but he is in a weak state as you know," said the old servant.

Pierre knew that Makár Alexéevich was Joseph Bazdéev's half-insane brother and a hard drinker.

"Yes, yes, I know. Let us go in . . ." said Pierre and entered the house. A tall, bald-headed old man with a red nose, wearing a dressing gown and with galoshes on his bare feet, stood in the anteroom. On seeing Pierre he muttered something angrily and went away along the passage.

"He was a very clever man but has now grown quite feeble, as your honor sees," said Gerásim. "Will you step into the study?" Pierre nodded. "As it was sealed up so it has remained, but Sophia Danílovna gave orders that if anyone should come from you they were to have the books."

Pierre went into that gloomy study which he had entered with such trepidation in his benefactor's lifetime. The room, dusty and untouched since the death of Joseph Bazdéev, was now even gloomier.

Gerásim opened one of the shutters and left the room on tiptoe. Pierre went round the study, approached the cupboard in which the manuscripts were kept, and took out what had once been one of the most important, the holy of holies of the order. This was the authentic Scotch Acts with Bazdéev's notes and explanations. He sat down at the dusty writing table, and, having laid the manuscripts before him, opened them out, closed them, finally pushed them away, and resting his head on his hand sank into meditation.

Gerásim looked cautiously into the study several times and saw Pierre always sitting in the same attitude.

More than two hours passed and Gerásim took the liberty of making a slight noise at the door to attract his attention, but Pierre did not hear him.

"Is the cabman to be discharged, your honor?"

"Oh yes!" said Pierre, rousing himself and rising hurriedly. "Look here," he added, taking Gerásim by a button of his coat and looking down at the old man with moist, shining, and ecstatic eyes, "I say, do you know that there is going to be a battle tomorrow?"

"We heard so," replied the man.

"I beg you not to tell anyone who I am, and to do what I ask you."

"Yes, your excellency," replied Gerásim. "Will you have something to eat?"

"No, but I want something else. I want peasant clothes and a pistol," said Pierre, unexpectedly blushing.

"Yes, your excellency," said Gerásim after thinking for a moment.

All the rest of that day Pierre spent alone in his benefactor's study, and Gerásim heard him pacing restlessly from one corner to another and talking to himself. And he spent the night on a bed made up for him there.

Gerásim, being a servant who in his time had seen many strange things, accepted Pierre's taking up his residence in the house without surprise, and seemed pleased to have someone to wait on. That same evening—without even asking himself what they were wanted for—he procured a coachman's coat and cap for Pierre, and promised to get him the pistol next day. Makár Alexéevich came twice that evening shuffling along in his galoshes as far as the door and stopped and looked ingratiatingly at Pierre. But as soon as Pierre turned toward him he wrapped his dressing gown around him with a shamefaced and angry look and hurried away. It was when Pierre (wearing the coachman's coat which Gerásim had procured for him and had disinfected by steam) was on his way with the old man to buy the pistol at the Súkharev market that he met the Rostóvs.

10. Napoleon surveys Moscow from the Poklónny Hill. He awaits a deputation of les boyars

KUTÚZOV'S ORDER to retreat through Moscow to the Ryazán road was issued at night on the first of September.

The first troops started at once, and during the night they marched slowly and steadily without hurry. At daybreak, however, those nearing the town at the Dorogomílov bridge saw ahead of them masses of soldiers crowding and hurrying across the bridge, ascending on the opposite side and blocking the streets and alleys, while endless masses of troops were bearing down on them from behind, and an unreasoning hurry and alarm overcame them. They all rushed forward to the bridge, onto it, and to the fords and the boats. Kutúzov himself had driven round by side streets to the other side of Moscow.

By ten o'clock in the morning of the second of September, only the rearguard remained in the Dorogomílov suburb, where they had ample room. The main army was on the other side of Moscow or beyond it.

At that very time, at ten in the morning of the second of September,

Napoleon was standing among his troops on the Poklónny Hill looking at the panorama spread out before him. From the twenty-sixth of August to the second of September, that is from the battle of Borodinó to the entry of the French into Moscow, during the whole of that agitating, memorable week, there had been the extraordinary autumn weather that always comes as a surprise, when the sun hangs low and gives more heat than in spring, when everything shines so brightly in the rare clear atmosphere that the eyes smart, when the lungs are strengthened and refreshed by inhaling the aromatic autumn air, when even the nights are warm, and when in those dark warm nights, golden stars startle and delight us continually by falling from the sky.

At ten in the morning of the second of September this weather still held. The brightness of the morning was magical. Moscow seen from the Poklónny Hill lay spaciously spread out with her river, her gardens, and her churches, and she seemed to be living her usual life, her cupolas glittering like stars in the sunlight.

The view of the strange city with its peculiar architecture, such as he had never seen before, filled Napoleon with the rather envious and uneasy curiosity men feel when they see an alien form of life that has no knowledge of them. This city was evidently living with the full force of its own life. By the indefinite signs which, even at a distance, distinguish a living body from a dead one, Napoleon from the Poklónny Hill perceived the throb of life in the town and felt, as it were, the breathing of that great and beautiful body.

Every Russian looking at Moscow feels her to be a mother; every foreigner who sees her, even if ignorant of her significance as the mother city, must feel her feminine character, and Napoleon felt it.

"*Cette ville asiatique aux innombrables églises, Moscou la sainte. La voilà donc enfin, cette fameuse ville! Il était temps* [That Asiatic city of the innumerable churches, holy Moscow! Here it is then at last, that famous city! It was high time]," said he, and dismounting he ordered a plan of Moscow to be spread out before him, and summoned Lelorgne d'Ideville, the interpreter.

"A town captured by the enemy is like a maid who has lost her honor," thought he (he had said so to Tuchkóv at Smolénsk). From that point of view he gazed at the Oriental beauty he had not seen before. It seemed strange to him that his long-felt wish, which had seemed unattainable, had at last been realized. In the clear morning light he gazed now at the city and now at the plan, considering its details, and the assurance of possessing it agitated and awed him.

"But could it be otherwise?" he thought. "Here is this capital at my

feet. Where is Alexander now, and of what is he thinking? A strange, beautiful, and majestic city; and a strange and majestic moment! In what light must I appear to them!" thought he, thinking of his troops. "Here she is, the reward for all those fainthearted men," he reflected, glancing at those near him and at the troops who were approaching and forming up. "One word from me, one movement of my hand, and that ancient capital of the Tsars would perish. But my clemency is always ready to descend upon the vanquished. I must be magnanimous and truly great. But no, it can't be true that I am in Moscow," he suddenly thought. "Yet here she is lying at my feet, with her golden domes and crosses scintillating and twinkling in the sunshine. But I shall spare her. On the ancient monuments of barbarism and despotism I will inscribe great words of justice and mercy. . . . It is just this which Alexander will feel most painfully, I know him." (It seemed to Napoleon that the chief import of what was taking place lay in the personal struggle between himself and Alexander.) "From the height of the Krémlin—yes, there is the Krémlin, yes—I will give them just laws; I will teach them the meaning of true civilization, I will make generations of boyars * remember their conqueror with love. I will tell the deputation that I did not, and do not, desire war, that I have waged war only against the false policy of their court; that I love and respect Alexander and that in Moscow I will accept terms of peace worthy of myself and of my people. I do not wish to utilize the fortunes of war to humiliate an honored monarch. "Boyars," I will say to them, "I do not desire war, I desire the peace and welfare of all my subjects." However, I know their presence will inspire me, and I shall speak to them as I always do: clearly, impressively, and majestically. But can it be true that I am in Moscow? Yes, there she lies."

"*Qu'on m'amène les boyars* [Bring the boyars to me]," said he to his suite.

A general with a brilliant suite galloped off at once to fetch the boyars. Two hours passed. Napoleon had lunched and was again standing in the same place on the Poklónny Hill awaiting the deputation. His speech to the boyars had already taken definite shape in his imagination. That speech was full of dignity and greatness as Napoleon understood it.

He was himself carried away by the tone of magnanimity he intended to adopt toward Moscow. In his imagination he appointed days for assemblies at the palace of the Tsars, at which Russian notables and his own

* *In ancient and medieval Russia the boyars were the chief assistants of the Tsars. The class and title were abolished by Peter I, and the last of the boyars died in 1750. Napoleon's repeated use of the word is meant to indicate the superficiality of his knowledge of Russia.*—A.M.

would mingle. He mentally appointed a governor, one who would win the hearts of the people. Having learned that there were many charitable institutions in Moscow he mentally decided that he would shower favors on them all. He thought that, as in Africa he had to put on a burnoose and sit in a mosque, so in Moscow he must be beneficent like the Tsars. And in order finally to touch the hearts of the Russians—and being like all Frenchmen unable to imagine anything sentimental without a reference to *ma chère, ma tendre, ma pauvre mère* [my dear, my tender, my poor mother]—he decided that he would place an inscription on all these establishments in large letters: "This establishment is dedicated to my dear mother." Or no, it should be simply: *Maison de ma Mère* [House of my Mother], he concluded. "But am I really in Moscow? Yes, here it lies before me, but why is the deputation from the city so long in appearing?" he wondered.

Meanwhile an agitated consultation was being carried on in whispers among his generals and marshals at the rear of his suite. Those sent to fetch the deputation had returned with the news that Moscow was empty, that everyone had left it. The faces of those who were not conferring together were pale and perturbed. They were not alarmed by the fact that Moscow had been abandoned by its inhabitants (grave as that fact seemed), but by the question how to tell the Emperor—without putting him in the terrible position of appearing ridiculous—that he had been awaiting the boyars so long in vain: that there were drunken mobs left in Moscow but no one else. Some said that a deputation of some sort must be scraped together, others disputed that opinion and maintained that the Emperor should first be carefully and skillfully prepared, and then told the truth.

"He will have to be told, all the same," said some gentlemen of the suite. "But, gentlemen . . ."

The position was the more awkward because the Emperor, meditating upon his magnanimous plans, was pacing patiently up and down before the outspread map, occasionally glancing along the road to Moscow from under his lifted hand with a bright and proud smile.

"But it's impossible . . ." declared the gentlemen of the suite, shrugging their shoulders but not venturing to utter the implied word—*le ridicule*. . . .

At last the Emperor, tired of futile expectation, his actor's instinct suggesting to him that the sublime moment having been too long drawn out was beginning to lose its sublimity, gave a sign with his hand. A single report of a signaling gun followed, and the troops, who were already spread out on different sides of Moscow, moved into the city through the Tver,

Kalúga, and Dorogomílov gates. Faster and faster, vying with one another, they moved at the double or at a trot, vanishing amid the clouds of dust they raised and making the air ring with a deafening roar of mingling shouts.

Drawn on by the movement of his troops Napoleon rode with them as far as the Dorogomílov gate, but there again stopped and, dismounting from his horse, paced for a long time by the Kámmer-Kollézski rampart, awaiting the deputation.

11. Moscow compared to a queenless hive. The army's departure. Looting by Russian soldiers. The Moskvá bridge blocked, and cleared by Ermólov. A brawl among workmen. Reading a Rostopchín broadsheet to a crowd. Scene with the superintendent of police

MEANWHILE Moscow was empty. There were still people in it, perhaps a fiftieth part of its former inhabitants had remained, but it was empty. It was empty in the sense that a dying queenless hive is empty.

In a queenless hive no life is left though to a superficial glance it seems as much alive as other hives.

The bees circle round a queenless hive in the hot beams of the midday sun as gaily as around the living hives; from a distance it smells of honey like the others, and bees fly in and out in the same way. But one has only to observe that hive to realize that there is no longer any life in it. The bees do not fly in the same way, the smell and the sound that meet the bee-keeper are not the same. To the beekeeper's tap on the wall of the sick hive, instead of the former instant unanimous humming of tens of thousands of bees with their abdomens threateningly compressed, and producing by the rapid vibration of their wings an aerial living sound, the only reply is a disconnected buzzing from different parts of the deserted hive. From the alighting board, instead of the former spirituous fragrant smell of honey and venom, and the warm whiffs of crowded life, comes an odor of emptiness and decay mingling with the smell of honey. There are no longer sentinels sounding the alarm with their abdomens raised, and ready to die in defense of the hive. There is no longer the measured quiet sound of throbbing activity, like the sound of boiling water, but diverse discordant sounds of disorder. In and out of the hive long black robber bees smeared with honey fly timidly and shiftily. They do not sting, but crawl away from danger. Formerly only bees laden with honey flew into the hive, and they flew out empty; now they fly out laden. The beekeeper opens the lower

part of the hive and peers in. Instead of black, glossy bees—tamed by toil, clinging to one another's legs and drawing out the wax, with a ceaseless hum of labor—that used to hang in long clusters down to the floor of the hive, drowsy shriveled bees crawl about separately in various directions on the floor and walls of the hive. Instead of a neatly glued floor, swept by the bees with the fanning of their wings, there is a floor littered with bits of wax, excrement, dying bees scarcely moving their legs, and dead ones that have not been cleared away.

The beekeeper opens the upper part of the hive and examines the super. Instead of serried rows of bees sealing up every gap in the combs and keeping the brood warm, he sees the skillful complex structures of the combs, but no longer in their former state of purity. All is neglected and foul. Black robber bees are swiftly and stealthily prowling about the combs, and the short home bees, shriveled and listless as if they were old, creep slowly about without trying to hinder the robbers, having lost all motive and all sense of life. Drones, bumblebees, wasps, and butterflies knock awkwardly against the walls of the hive in their flight. Here and there among the cells containing dead brood and honey an angry buzzing can sometimes be heard. Here and there a couple of bees, by force of habit and custom cleaning out the brood cells, with efforts beyond their strength laboriously drag away a dead bee or bumblebee without knowing why they do it. In another corner two old bees are languidly fighting, or cleaning themselves, or feeding one another, without themselves knowing whether they do it with friendly or hostile intent. In a third place a crowd of bees, crushing one another, attack some victim and fight and smother it, and the victim, enfeebled or killed, drops from above slowly and lightly as a feather, among the heap of corpses. The keeper opens the two center partitions to examine the brood cells. In place of the former close dark circles formed by thousands of bees sitting back to back and guarding the high mystery of generation, he sees hundreds of dull, listless, and sleepy shells of bees. They have almost all died unawares, sitting in the sanctuary they had guarded and which is now no more. They reek of decay and death. Only a few of them still move, rise, and feebly fly to settle on the enemy's hand, lacking the spirit to die stinging him; the rest are dead and fall as lightly as fish scales. The beekeeper closes the hive, chalks a mark on it, and when he has time tears out its contents and burns it clean.*

So in the same way Moscow was empty when Napoleon, weary, uneasy, and morose, paced up and down in front of the Kámmer-Kollézski ram-

* *The Russian hives were usually made of hollowed-out tree trunks, which were cleansed by charring.*—A.M.

part, awaiting what to his mind was a necessary, if but formal, observance of the proprieties—a deputation.

In various corners of Moscow there still remained a few people aimlessly moving about, following their old habits and hardly aware of what they were doing.

When with due circumspection Napoleon was informed that Moscow was empty, he looked angrily at his informant, turned away, and silently continued to walk to and fro.

"My carriage!" he said.

He took his seat beside the aide-de-camp on duty and drove into the suburb. "Moscow deserted!" he said to himself. "What an incredible event!"

He did not drive into the town, but put up at an inn in the Dorogomílov suburb.

The *coup de théâtre* had not come off.

THE RUSSIAN TROOPS were passing through Moscow from two o'clock at night till two in the afternoon and bore away with them the wounded and the last of the inhabitants who were leaving.

The greatest crush during the movement of the troops took place at the Stone, Moskvá, and Yaúza bridges.

While the troops, dividing into two parts when passing around the Krémlin, were thronging the Moskvá and the Stone bridges, a great many soldiers, taking advantage of the stoppage and congestion, turned back from the bridges and slipped stealthily and silently past the church of Vasíli the Beatified * and under the Borovítski gate, back up the hill to the Red Square where some instinct told them they could easily take things not belonging to them. Crowds of the kind seen at cheap sales filled all the passages and alleys of the Bazaar. But there were no dealers with voices of ingratiating affability inviting customers to enter; there were no hawkers, nor the usual motley crowd of female purchasers—but only soldiers, in uniforms and overcoats though without muskets, entering the Bazaar empty-handed and silently making their way out through its passages with bundles. Tradesmen and their assistants (of whom there were but few) moved about among the soldiers quite bewildered. They unlocked their shops and locked them up again, and themselves carried goods away with the help of their assistants. On the square in front of the Bazaar were drummers beating the muster call. But the roll of the drums did not make the looting soldiers run in the direction of the drum as formerly, but

* A curious church in the Red Square outside the Krémlin, in Moscow.—

A.M.

made them, on the contrary, run farther away. Among the soldiers in the shops and passages some men were to be seen in gray coats, with closely shaven heads.* Two officers, one with a scarf over his uniform and mounted on a lean, dark-gray horse, the other in an overcoat and on foot, stood at the corner of the Ilyínka Street, talking. A third officer galloped up to them.

"The general orders them all to be driven out at once, without fail. This is outrageous! Half the men have dispersed."

"Where are you off to? . . . Where? . . ." he shouted to three infantrymen without muskets who, holding up the skirts of their overcoats, were slipping past him into the Bazaar passage. "Stop, you rascals!"

"But how are you going to stop them?" replied another officer. "There is no getting them together. The army should push on before the rest bolt, that's all!"

"How can one push on? They are stuck there, wedged on the bridge, and don't move. Shouldn't we put a cordon round to prevent the rest from running away?"

"Come, go in there and drive them out!" shouted the senior officer.

The officer in the scarf dismounted, called up a drummer, and went with him into the arcade. Some soldiers started running away in a group. A shopkeeper with red pimples on his cheeks near the nose, and a calm, persistent, calculating expression on his plump face, hurriedly and ostentatiously approached the officer, swinging his arms.

"Your honor!" said he. "Be so good as to protect us! We won't grudge trifles, you are welcome to anything—we shall be delighted! Pray! . . . I'll fetch a piece of cloth at once for such an honorable gentleman, or even two pieces with pleasure. For we feel how it is; but what's all this—sheer robbery! If you please, could not guards be placed if only to let us close the shop. . . ."

Several shopkeepers crowded round the officer.

"Eh, what twaddle!" said one of them, a thin, stern-looking man. "When one's head is gone one doesn't weep for one's hair! Take what any of you like!" And flourishing his arm energetically he turned sideways to the officer.

"It's all very well for you, Iván Sídorych, to talk," said the first tradesman angrily. "Please step inside, your honor!"

"Talk indeed!" cried the thin one. "In my three shops here I have a hundred thousand rubles' worth of goods. Can they be saved when the army has gone? Eh, what people! 'Against God's might our hands can't fight.'"

* Prisoners who had been released from jail.—A.M.

"Come inside, your honor!" repeated the first tradesman, bowing.

The officer stood perplexed and his face showed indecision.

"It's not my business!" he exclaimed, and strode on quickly down one of the passages.

From one open shop came the sound of blows and vituperation, and just as the officer came up to it a man in a gray coat with a shaven head was flung out violently.

This man, bent double, rushed past the tradesman and the officer. The officer pounced on the soldiers who were in the shops, but at that moment fearful screams reached them from the huge crowd on the Moskvá bridge and the officer ran out into the square.

"What is it? What is it?" he asked, but his comrade was already galloping off past Vasíli the Beatified in the direction from which the screams came.

The officer mounted his horse and rode after him. When he reached the bridge he saw two unlimbered guns, the infantry crossing the bridge, several overturned carts, and frightened and laughing faces among the troops. Beside the cannon a cart was standing to which two horses were harnessed. Four borzois with collars were pressing close to the wheels. The cart was loaded high, and at the very top, beside a child's chair with its legs in the air, sat a peasant woman uttering piercing and desperate shrieks. He was told by his fellow officers that the screams of the crowd and the shrieks of the woman were due to the fact that General Ermólov, coming up to the crowd and learning that soldiers were dispersing among the shops while crowds of civilians blocked the bridge, had ordered two guns to be unlimbered and made a show of firing at the bridge. The crowd, crushing one another, upsetting carts, and shouting and squeezing desperately, had cleared off the bridge and the troops were now moving forward.

MEANWHILE, the city itself was deserted. There was hardly anyone in the streets. The gates and shops were all closed, only here and there round the taverns solitary shouts or drunken songs could be heard. Nobody drove through the streets and footsteps were rarely heard. The Povarskáya was quite still and deserted. The huge courtyard of the Rostóvs' house was littered with wisps of hay and with dung from the horses, and not a soul was to be seen there. In the great drawing room of the house, which had been left with all it contained, were two people. They were the yard porter Ignát, and the pageboy Míshka, Vasílich's grandson who had stayed in Moscow with his grandfather. Míshka had opened the clavichord and was strumming on it with one finger. The yard porter, his arms akimbo, stood smiling with satisfaction before the large mirror.

"Isn't it fine, eh, Uncle Ignát?" said the boy, suddenly beginning to strike the keyboard with both hands.

"Only fancy!" answered Ignát, surprised at the broadening grin on his face in the mirror.

"Impudence! Impudence!" they heard behind them the voice of Mávra Kuzmínichna who had entered silently. "How he's grinning, the fat mug! Is that what you're here for? Nothing's cleared away down there and Vasílich is worn out. Just you wait a bit!"

Ignát left off smiling, adjusted his belt, and went out of the room with meekly downcast eyes.

"Aunt, I did it gently," said the boy.

"I'll give you something gently, you monkey you!" cried Mávra Kuzmínichna, raising her arm threateningly. "Go and get the samovar to boil for your grandfather."

Mávra Kuzmínichna flicked the dust off the clavichord and closed it, and with a deep sigh left the drawing room and locked its main door.

Going out into the yard she paused to consider where she should go next—to drink tea in the servants' wing with Vasílich, or into the storeroom to put away what still lay about.

She heard the sound of quick footsteps in the quiet street. Someone stopped at the gate, and the latch rattled as someone tried to open it.

Mávra Kuzmínichna went to the gate.

"Who do you want?"

"The count—Count Ilyá Andréevich Rostóv."

"And who are you?"

"An officer, I have to see him," came the reply in a pleasant, well-bred Russian voice.

Mávra Kuzmínichna opened the gate and an officer of eighteen, with the round face of a Rostóv, entered the yard.

"They have gone away, sir. Went away yesterday at vespertime," said Mávra Kuzmínichna cordially.

The young officer standing in the gateway, as if hesitating whether to enter or not, clicked his tongue.

"Ah, how annoying!" he muttered. "I should have come yesterday. . . . Ah, what a pity."

Meanwhile, Mávra Kuzmínichna was attentively and sympathetically examining the familiar Rostóv features of the young man's face, his tattered coat and trodden-down boots.

"What did you want to see the count for?" she asked.

"Oh well . . . it can't be helped!" said he in a tone of vexation and placed his hand on the gate as if to leave.

He again paused in indecision.

"You see," he suddenly said, "I am a kinsman of the count's and he has been very kind to me. As you see" (he glanced with an amused air and good-natured smile at his coat and boots) "my things are worn out and I have no money, so I was going to ask the count . . ."

Mávra Kuzmínichna did not let him finish.

"Just wait a minute, sir. One little moment," said she.

And as soon as the officer let go of the gate handle she turned and, hurrying away on her old legs, went through the back yard to the servants' quarters.

While Mávra Kuzmínichna was running to her room the officer walked about the yard gazing at his worn-out boots with lowered head and a faint smile on his lips. "What a pity I've missed Uncle! What a nice old woman! Where has she run off to? And how am I to find the nearest way to overtake my regiment, which must by now be getting near the Rogózhski gate?" thought he. Just then Mávra Kuzmínichna appeared from behind the corner of the house with a frightened yet resolute look, carrying a rolled-up check kerchief in her hand. While still a few steps from the officer she unfolded the kerchief and took out of it a white twenty-five-ruble assignat * and hastily handed it to him.

"If his excellency had been at home, as a kinsman he would of course . . . but as it is . . ."

Mávra Kuzmínichna grew abashed and confused. The officer did not decline, but took the note quietly and thanked her.

"If the count had been at home . . ." Mávra Kuzmínichna went on apologetically. "Christ be with you, sir! May God preserve you!" said she, bowing as she saw him out.

Swaying his head and smiling as if amused at himself, the officer ran almost at a trot through the deserted streets toward the Yaúza bridge to overtake his regiment.

But Mávra Kuzmínichna stood at the closed gate for some time with moist eyes, pensively swaying her head and feeling an unexpected flow of motherly tenderness and pity for the unknown young officer.

FROM AN UNFINISHED HOUSE on the Varvárka, the ground floor of which was a dramshop, came drunken shouts and songs. On benches round the tables in a dirty little room sat some ten factory hands. Tipsy and perspir-

* These assignats were a currency introduced in Russia in 1768. One effect of the Napoleonic wars was a very serious depreciation of the Russian currency, which continued depressed and fluctuating till it was reformed in 1841. At the time of the Crimean War it again started on a downward course.—A.M.

ing, with dim eyes and wide-open mouths, they were all laboriously singing some song or other. They were singing discordantly, arduously, and with great effort, evidently not because they wished to sing, but because they wanted to show they were drunk and on a spree. One, a tall, fair-haired lad in a clean blue coat, was standing over the others. His face with its fine straight nose would have been handsome had it not been for his thin, compressed, twitching lips and dull, gloomy, fixed eyes. Evidently possessed by some idea, he stood over those who were singing, and solemnly and jerkily flourished above their heads his white arm with the sleeve turned up to the elbow, trying unnaturally to spread out his dirty fingers. The sleeve of his coat kept slipping down and he always carefully rolled it up again with his left hand, as if it were most important that the sinewy white arm he was flourishing should be bare. In the midst of the song cries were heard, and fighting and blows in the passage and porch. The tall lad waved his arm.

"Stop it!" he exclaimed peremptorily. "There's a fight, lads!" And, still rolling up his sleeve, he went out to the porch.

The factory hands followed him. These men, who under the leadership of the tall lad were drinking in the dramshop that morning, had brought the publican some skins from the factory and for this had had drink served them. The blacksmiths from a neighboring smithy, hearing the sounds of revelry in the tavern and supposing it to have been broken into, wished to force their way in too and a fight in the porch had resulted.

The publican was fighting one of the smiths at the door, and when the workmen came out the smith, wrenching himself free from the tavern-keeper, fell face downward on the pavement.

Another smith tried to enter the doorway, pressing against the publican with his chest.

The lad with the turned-up sleeve gave the smith a blow in the face and cried wildly: "They're fighting us, lads!"

At that moment the first smith got up and, scratching his bruised face to make it bleed, shouted in a tearful voice: "Police! Murder! . . . They've killed a man, lads!"

"Oh, gracious me, a man beaten to death—killed! . . ." screamed a woman coming out of a gate close by.

A crowd gathered round the bloodstained smith.

"Haven't you robbed people enough—taking their last shirts?" said a voice addressing the publican. "What have you killed a man for, you thief?"

The tall lad, standing in the porch, turned his bleared eyes from the

publican to the smith and back again as if considering whom he ought to fight now.

"Murderer!" he shouted suddenly to the publican. "Bind him, lads!"

"I daresay you would like to bind me!" shouted the publican, pushing away the men advancing on him, and snatching his cap from his head he flung it on the ground.

As if this action had some mysterious and menacing significance, the workmen surrounding the publican paused in indecision.

"I know the law very well, mates! I'll take the matter to the captain of police. You think I won't get to him? Robbery is not permitted to anybody nowadays!" shouted the publican, picking up his cap.

"Come along then! Come along then!" the publican and the tall young fellow repeated one after the other, and they moved up the street together.

The bloodstained smith went beside them. The factory hands and others followed behind, talking and shouting.

At the corner of the Moroséyka, opposite a large house with closed shutters and bearing a bootmaker's signboard, stood a score of thin, worn-out, gloomy-faced bootmakers, wearing overalls and long tattered coats.

"He should pay folks off properly," a thin workingman, with frowning brows and a straggly beard, was saying.

"But he's sucked our blood and now he thinks he's quit of us. He's been misleading us all the week and now that he's brought us to this pass he's made off."

On seeing the crowd and the bloodstained man the workman ceased speaking, and with eager curiosity all the bootmakers joined the moving crowd.

"Where are all the folks going?"

"Why, to the police, of course!"

"I say, is it true that we have been beaten?"

"And what did you think? Look what folks are saying."

Questions and answers were heard. The publican, taking advantage of the increased crowd, dropped behind and returned to his tavern.

The tall youth, not noticing the disappearance of his foe, waved his bare arm and went on talking incessantly, attracting general attention to himself. It was around him that the people chiefly crowded, expecting answers from him to the questions that occupied all their minds.

"He must keep order, keep the law, that's what the government is there for. Am I not right, good Christians?" said the tall youth, with a scarcely perceptible smile. "He thinks there's no government! How can one do without government? Or else there would be plenty who'd rob us."

"Why talk nonsense?" rejoined voices in the crowd. "Will they give up Moscow like this? They told you that for fun, and you believed it! Aren't there plenty of troops on the march? Let *him* in, indeed! That's what the government is for. You'd better listen to what people are saying," said some of the mob pointing to the tall youth.

By the wall of China-Town * a smaller group of people were gathered round a man in a frieze coat who held a paper in his hand.

"An ukáse, they are reading an ukáse! Reading an ukáse!" cried voices in the crowd, and the people rushed toward the reader.

The man in the frieze coat was reading the broadsheet of August 31. When the crowd collected round him he seemed confused, but at the demand of the tall lad who had pushed his way up to him, he began in a rather tremulous voice to read the sheet from the beginning.

"Early tomorrow I shall go to his Serene Highness," he read (*"Sirin Highness,"* said the tall fellow with a triumphant smile on his lips and a frown on his brow), "to consult with him, to act, and to aid the army to exterminate these scoundrels. We too will take part . . ." the reader went on, and then paused ("Do you see," shouted the youth victoriously, "he's going to clear up the whole affair for you. . . ."), "in destroying them, and will send these visitors to the devil. I will come back to dinner, and we'll set to work. We will do, completely do, and undo these scoundrels."

The last words were read out in the midst of complete silence. The tall lad hung his head gloomily. It was evident that no one had understood the last part. In particular, the words "I will come back to dinner," evidently displeased both reader and audience. The people's minds were tuned to a high pitch and this was too simple and needlessly comprehensible—it was what any one of them might have said and therefore was what an ukáse emanating from the highest authority should not say.

They all stood despondent and silent. The tall youth moved his lips and swayed from side to side.

"We should ask him . . . that's he himself!" . . . "Yes, ask him indeed!" . . . "Why not? He'll explain" . . . voices in the rear of the crowd were suddenly heard saying, and the general attention turned to the police superintendent's trap which drove into the square attended by two mounted dragoons.

The superintendent of police, who had gone that morning by Count Rostopchín's orders to burn the barges and had in connection with that matter acquired a large sum of money which was at that moment in his

* *A part of Moscow.*—A.M.

pocket, on seeing a crowd bearing down upon him told his coachman to stop.

"What people are these?" he shouted to the men, who were moving singly and timidly in the direction of his trap.

"What people are these?" he shouted again, receiving no answer.

"Your honor . . ." replied the shopman in the frieze coat, "your honor, in accord with the proclamation of his highest excellency the count, they desire to serve, not sparing their lives, and it is not any kind of riot, but as his highest excellence said . . ."

"The count has not left, he is here, and an order will be issued concerning you," said the superintendent of police. "Go on!" he ordered his coachman.

The crowd halted, pressing around those who had heard what the superintendent had said, and looking at the departing trap.

The superintendent of police turned round at that moment with a scared look, said something to his coachman, and his horses increased their speed.

"It's a fraud, lads! Lead the way to him, himself!" shouted the tall youth. "Don't let him go, lads! Let him answer us! Keep him!" shouted different voices, and the people dashed in pursuit of the trap.

Following the superintendent of police and talking loudly the crowd went in the direction of the Lubyánka Street.

"There now, the gentry and merchants have gone away and left us to perish. Do they think we're dogs?" voices in the crowd were heard saying more and more frequently.

12. Rostopchín. The killing of Vereshchágin. The released lunatics. Rostopchín's encounter with Kutúzov at the bridge

ON THE EVENING of the first of September, after his interview with Kutúzov, Count Rostopchín had returned to Moscow mortified and offended because he had not been invited to attend the council of war, and because Kutúzov had paid no attention to his offer to take part in the defense of the city; amazed also at the novel outlook revealed to him at the camp, which treated the tranquillity of the capital and its patriotic fervor as not merely secondary but quite irrelevant and unimportant matters. Distressed, offended, and surprised by all this, Rostopchín had returned to Moscow. After supper he lay down on a sofa without undressing, and was awakened soon after midnight by a courier bringing him a letter

from Kutúzov. This letter requested the count to send police officers to guide the troops through the town, as the army was retreating to the Ryazán road beyond Moscow. This was not news to Rostopchín. He had known that Moscow would be abandoned not merely since his interview the previous day with Kutúzov on the Poklónny Hill but ever since the battle of Borodinó, for all the generals who came to Moscow after that battle had said unanimously that it was impossible to fight another battle, and since then the government property had been removed every night, and half the inhabitants had left the city with Rostopchín's own permission. Yet all the same this information astonished and irritated the count, coming as it did in the form of a simple note with an order from Kutúzov, and received at night, breaking in on his beauty sleep.

When later on in his memoirs Count Rostopchín explained his actions at this time, he repeatedly says that he was then actuated by two important considerations: to maintain tranquillity in Moscow and expedite the departure of the inhabitants. If one accepts this twofold aim all Rostopchín's actions appear irreproachable. "Why were the holy relics, the arms, ammunition, gunpowder, and stores of corn not removed? Why were thousands of inhabitants deceived into believing that Moscow would not be given up—and thereby ruined?" "To preserve the tranquillity of the city," explains Count Rostopchín. "Why were bundles of useless papers from the government offices, and Leppich's balloon and other articles removed?" "To leave the town empty," explains Count Rostopchín. One need only admit that public tranquillity is in danger and any action finds a justification.

All the horrors of the reign of terror were based only on solicitude for public tranquillity.

On what, then, was Count Rostopchín's fear for the tranquillity of Moscow based in 1812? What reason was there for assuming any probability of an uprising in the city? The inhabitants were leaving it and the retreating troops were filling it. Why should that cause the masses to riot?

Neither in Moscow nor anywhere in Russia did anything resembling an insurrection ever occur when the enemy entered a town. More than ten thousand people were still in Moscow on the first and second of September, and except for a mob in the governor's courtyard, assembled there at his bidding, nothing happened. It is obvious that there would have been even less reason to expect a disturbance among the people if after the battle of Borodinó, when the surrender of Moscow became certain or at least probable, Rostopchín instead of exciting the people by distributing arms and broadsheets had taken steps to remove all the holy relics, the

gunpowder, munitions, and money, and had told the population plainly that the town would be abandoned.

Rostopchín, though he had patriotic sentiments, was a sanguine and impulsive man who had always moved in the highest administrative circles and had no understanding at all of the people he supposed himself to be guiding. Ever since the enemy's entry into Smolénsk he had in imagination been playing the role of director of the popular feeling of "the heart of Russia." Not only did it seem to him (as to all administrators) that he controlled the external actions of Moscow's inhabitants, but he also thought he controlled their mental attitude by means of his broadsheets and posters, written in a coarse tone which the people despise in their own class and do not understand from those in authority. Rostopchín was so pleased with the fine role of leader of popular feeling, and had grown so used to it, that the necessity of relinquishing that role and abandoning Moscow without any heroic display took him unawares and he suddenly felt the ground slip away from under his feet, so that he positively did not know what to do. Though he knew it was coming, he did not till the last moment wholeheartedly believe that Moscow would be abandoned, and did not prepare for it. The inhabitants left against his wishes. If the government offices were removed, this was only done on the demand of officials to whom the count yielded reluctantly. He was absorbed in the role he had created for himself. As is often the case with those gifted with an ardent imagination, though he had long known that Moscow would be abandoned he knew it only with his intellect, he did not believe it in his heart and did not adapt himself mentally to this new position of affairs.

All his painstaking and energetic activity (in how far it was useful and had any effect on the people is another question) had been simply directed toward arousing in the masses his own feeling of patriotic hatred of the French.

But when events assumed their true historical character, when expressing hatred for the French in words proved insufficient, when it was not even possible to express that hatred by fighting a battle, when self-confidence was of no avail in relation to the one question before Moscow, when the whole population streamed out of Moscow as one man, abandoning their belongings and proving by that negative action all the depth of their national feeling, then the role chosen by Rostopchín suddenly appeared senseless. He unexpectedly felt himself ridiculous, weak, and alone, with no ground to stand on.

When, awakened from his sleep, he received that cold, peremptory note from Kutúzov, he felt the more irritated the more he felt himself

to blame. All that he had been specially put in charge of, the state property which he should have removed, was still in Moscow and it was no longer possible to take the whole of it away.

"Who is to blame for it? Who has let things come to such a pass?" he ruminated. "Not I, of course. I had everything ready. I had Moscow firmly in hand. And this is what they have let it come to! Villains! Traitors!" he thought, without clearly defining who the villains and traitors were, but feeling it necessary to hate those traitors whoever they might be who were to blame for the false and ridiculous position in which he found himself.

All that night Count Rostopchín issued orders, for which people came to him from all parts of Moscow. Those about him had never seen the count so morose and irritable.

"Your excellency, the Director of the Registrar's Department has sent for instructions. . . . From the Consistory, from the Senate, from the University, from the Foundling Hospital, the Suffragan has sent . . . asking for information. . . . What are your orders about the Fire Brigade? From the governor of the prison . . . from the superintendent of the lunatic asylum . . ." All night long such announcements were continually being received by the count.

To all these inquiries he gave brief and angry replies indicating that orders from him were not now needed, that the whole affair, carefully prepared by him, had now been ruined by somebody, and that that somebody would have to bear the whole responsibility for all that might happen.

"Oh, tell that blockhead," he said in reply to the question from the Registrar's Department, "that he should remain to guard his documents. Now why are you asking silly questions about the Fire Brigade? They have horses, let them be off to Vladímir, and not leave them to the French."

"Your excellency, the superintendent of the lunatic asylum has come: what are your commands?"

"My commands? Let them go away, that's all. . . . And let the lunatics out into the town. When lunatics command our armies God evidently means these other madmen to be free."

In reply to an inquiry about the convicts in the prison, Count Rostopchín shouted angrily at the governor:

"Do you expect me to give you two battalions—which we have not got—for a convoy? Release them, that's all about it!"

"Your excellency, there are some political prisoners, Meshkóv, Vereshchágin . . ."

"Vereshchágin! Hasn't he been hanged yet?" shouted Rostopchín. "Bring him to me!"

Toward nine o'clock in the morning, when the troops were already moving through Moscow, nobody came to the count any more for instructions. Those who were able to get away were going of their own accord, those who remained behind decided for themselves what they must do.

The count ordered his carriage that he might drive to Sokólniki, and sat in his study with folded hands, morose, sallow, and taciturn.

In quiet and untroubled times it seems to every administrator that it is only by his efforts that the whole population under his rule is kept going, and in this consciousness of being indispensable every administrator finds the chief reward of his labor and efforts. While the sea of history remains calm the ruler-administrator in his frail bark, holding on with a boat hook to the ship of the people and himself moving, naturally imagines that his efforts move the ship he is holding on to. But as soon as a storm arises and the sea begins to heave and the ship to move, such a delusion is no longer possible. The ship moves independently with its own enormous motion, the boat hook no longer reaches the moving vessel, and suddenly the administrator, instead of appearing a ruler and a source of power, becomes an insignificant, useless, feeble man.

Rostopchín felt this, and it was this which exasperated him.

The superintendent of police, whom the crowd had stopped, went in to see him at the same time as an adjutant who informed the count that the horses were harnessed. They were both pale, and the superintendent of police, after reporting that he had executed the instructions he had received, informed the count that an immense crowd had collected in the courtyard and wished to see him.

Without saying a word Rostopchín rose and walked hastily to his light, luxurious drawing room, went to the balcony door, took hold of the handle, let it go again, and went to the window from which he had a better view of the whole crowd. The tall lad was standing in front, flourishing his arm and saying something with a stern look. The bloodstained smith stood beside him with a gloomy face. A drone of voices was audible through the closed window.

"Is my carriage ready?" asked Rostopchín, stepping back from the window.

"It is, your excellency," replied the adjutant.

Rostopchín went again to the balcony door.

"But what do they want?" he asked the superintendent of police.

"Your excellency, they say they have got ready, according to your orders, to go against the French, and they shouted something about

treachery. But it is a turbulent crowd, your excellency—I hardly managed to get away from it. Your excellency, I venture to suggest . . ."

"You may go. I don't need you to tell me what to do!" exclaimed Rostopchín angrily.

He stood by the balcony door looking at the crowd.

"This is what they have done with Russia! This is what they have done with me!" thought he, full of an irrepressible fury that welled up within him against the someone to whom what was happening might be attributed. As often happens with passionate people, he was mastered by anger but was still seeking an object on which to vent it. "Here is that mob, the dregs of the people," he thought as he gazed at the crowd: "this rabble they have roused by their folly! They want a victim," he thought as he looked at the tall lad flourishing his arm. And this thought occurred to him just because he himself desired a victim, something on which to vent his rage.

"Is the carriage ready?" he asked again.

"Yes, your excellency. What are your orders about Vereshchágin? He is waiting at the porch," said the adjutant.

"Ah!" exclaimed Rostopchín, as if struck by an unexpected recollection.

And rapidly opening the door he went resolutely out onto the balcony. The talking instantly ceased, hats and caps were doffed, and all eyes were raised to the count.

"Good morning, lads!" said the count briskly and loudly. "Thank you for coming. I'll come out to you in a moment, but we must first settle with the villain. We must punish the villain who has caused the ruin of Moscow. Wait for me!"

And the count stepped as briskly back into the room and slammed the door behind him.

A murmur of approbation and satisfaction ran through the crowd. "He'll settle with all the villains, you'll see! And you said the French . . . He'll show you what law is!" the mob were saying as if reproving one another for their lack of confidence.

A few minutes later an officer came hurriedly out of the front door, gave an order, and the dragoons formed up in line. The crowd moved eagerly from the balcony toward the porch. Rostopchín, coming out there with quick angry steps, looked hastily around as if seeking someone.

"Where is he?" he inquired. And as he spoke he saw a young man coming round the corner of the house between two dragoons. He had a long thin neck, and his head, that had been half shaved, was again covered by short hair. This young man was dressed in a threadbare blue cloth coat

lined with fox fur, that had once been smart, and dirty hempen convict trousers, over which were pulled his thin, dirty, trodden-down boots. On his thin, weak legs were heavy chains which hampered his irresolute movements.

"Ah!" said Rostopchín, hurriedly turning away his eyes from the young man in the fur-lined coat and pointing to the bottom step of the porch. "Put him there."

The young man in his clattering chains stepped clumsily to the spot indicated, holding away with one finger the coat collar which chafed his neck, turned his long neck twice this way and that, sighed, and sub-missively folded before him his thin hands, unused to work.

For several seconds while the young man was taking his place on the step the silence continued. Only among the back rows of the people, who were all pressing toward the one spot, could sighs, groans, and the shuffling of feet be heard.

While waiting for the young man to take his place on the step Rostop-chín stood frowning and rubbing his face with his hand.

"Lads!" said he, with a metallic ring in his voice. "This man, Veresh-chágin, is the scoundrel by whose doing Moscow is perishing."

The young man in the fur-lined coat, stooping a little, stood in a submissive attitude, his fingers clasped before him. His emaciated young face, disfigured by the half-shaven head, hung down hopelessly. At the count's first words he raised it slowly and looked up at him as if wishing to say something or at least to meet his eye. But Rostopchín did not look at him. A vein in the young man's long thin neck swelled like a cord and went blue behind the ear, and suddenly his face flushed.

All eyes were fixed on him. He looked at the crowd, and rendered more hopeful by the expression he read on the faces there, he smiled sadly and timidly, and lowering his head shifted his feet on the step.

"He has betrayed his Tsar and his country, he had gone over to Bona-parte. He alone of all the Russians has disgraced the Russian name, he has caused Moscow to perish," said Rostopchín in a sharp, even voice, but suddenly he glanced down at Vereshchágin who continued to stand in the same submissive attitude. As if inflamed by the sight, he raised his arm and addressed the people, almost shouting:

"Deal with him as you think fit! I hand him over to you."

The crowd remained silent and only pressed closer and closer to one another. To keep one another back, to breathe in that stifling atmosphere, to be unable to stir, and to await something unknown, uncomprehended, and terrible, was becoming unbearable. Those standing in front, who had seen and heard what had taken place before them, all

stood with wide-open eyes and mouths, straining with all their strength, and held back the crowd that was pushing behind them.

"Beat him! . . . Let the traitor perish and not disgrace the Russian name!" shouted Rostopchín. "Cut him down. I command it."

Hearing not so much the words as the angry tone of Rostopchín's voice, the crowd moaned and heaved forward, but again paused.

"Count!" exclaimed the timid yet theatrical voice of Vereshchágin in the midst of the momentary silence that ensued, "Count! One God is above us both. . . ." He lifted his head and again the thick vein in his thin neck filled with blood and the color rapidly came and went in his face.

He did not finish what he wished to say.

"Cut him down! I command it . . ." shouted Rostopchín, suddenly growing pale like Vereshchágin.

"Draw sabers!" cried the dragoon officer, drawing his own.

Another still stronger wave flowed through the crowd and reaching the front ranks carried it swaying to the very steps of the porch. The tall youth, with a stony look on his face, and rigid and uplifted arm, stood beside Vereshchágin.

"Saber him!" the dragoon officer almost whispered.

And one of the soldiers, his face all at once distorted with fury, struck Vereshchágin on the head with the blunt side of his saber.

"Ah!" cried Vereshchágin in meek surprise, looking round with a frightened glance as if not understanding why this was done to him. A similar moan of surprise and horror ran through the crowd. "O Lord!" exclaimed a sorrowful voice.

But after the exclamation of surprise that had escaped from Vereshchágin he uttered a plaintive cry of pain, and that cry was fatal. The barrier of human feeling, strained to the utmost, that had held the crowd in check suddenly broke. The crime had begun and must now be completed. The plaintive moan of reproach was drowned by the threatening and angry roar of the crowd. Like the seventh and last wave that shatters a ship, that last irresistible wave burst from the rear and reached the front ranks, carrying them off their feet and engulfing them all. The dragoon was about to repeat his blow. Vereshchágin with a cry of horror, covering his head with his hands, rushed toward the crowd. The tall youth, against whom he stumbled, seized his thin neck with his hands and, yelling wildly, fell with him under the feet of the pressing, struggling crowd.

Some beat and tore at Vereshchágin, others at the tall youth. And the screams of those that were being trampled on and of those who tried to rescue the tall lad only increased the fury of the crowd. It was a long time before the dragoons could extricate the bleeding youth, beaten almost

to death. And for a long time, despite the feverish haste with which the mob tried to end the work that had been begun, those who were hitting, throttling, and tearing at Vereshchágin were unable to kill him, for the crowd pressed from all sides, swaying as one mass with them in the center and rendering it impossible for them either to kill him or let him go.

"Hit him with an ax, eh! . . . Crushed? . . . Traitor, he sold Christ . . . Still alive . . . tenacious . . . serve him right! Torture serves a thief right. Use the hatchet! . . . What—still alive?"

Only when the victim ceased to struggle and his cries changed to a long-drawn, measured death rattle did the crowd around his prostrate, bleeding corpse begin rapidly to change places. Each one came up, glanced at what had been done, and with horror, reproach, and astonishment pushed back again.

"O Lord! The people are like wild beasts! How could he be alive?" voices in the crowd could be heard saying. "Quite a young fellow too . . . must have been a merchant's son. What men! . . . and they say he's not the right one. . . . How not the right one? . . . O Lord! And there's another has been beaten too—they say he's nearly done for. . . . Oh, the people . . . Aren't they afraid of sinning? . . ." said the same mob now, looking with pained distress at the dead body with its long, thin, half-severed neck and its livid face stained with blood and dust.

A painstaking police officer, considering the presence of a corpse in his excellency's courtyard unseemly, told the dragoons to take it away. Two dragoons took it by its distorted legs and dragged it along the ground. The gory, dust-stained, half-shaven head with its long neck trailed twisting along the ground. The crowd shrank back from it.

At the moment when Vereshchágin fell and the crowd closed in with savage yells and swayed about him, Rostopchín suddenly turned pale and, instead of going to the back entrance where his carriage awaited him, went with hurried steps and bent head, not knowing where and why, along the passage leading to the rooms on the ground floor. The count's face was white and he could not control the feverish twitching of his lower jaw.

"This way, your excellency . . . Where are you going? . . . This way, please . . ." said a trembling, frightened voice behind him.

Count Rostopchín was unable to reply and, turning obediently, went in the direction indicated. At the back entrance stood his calèche. The distant roar of the yelling crowd was audible even there. He hastily took his seat and told the coachman to drive him to his country house in Sokólniki.

When they reached the Myasnítski Street and could no longer hear the shouts of the mob, the count began to repent. He remembered with dis-

satisfaction the agitation and fear he had betrayed before his subordinates. "The mob is terrible—disgusting," he said to himself in French. "They are like wolves whom nothing but flesh can appease." "Count! One God is above us both!"—Vereshchágin's words suddenly recurred to him, and a disagreeable shiver ran down his back. But this was only a momentary feeling and Count Rostopchín smiled disdainfully at himself. "I had other duties," thought he. "The people had to be appeased. Many other victims have perished and are perishing for the public good"—and he began thinking of his social duties to his family and to the city entrusted to him, and of himself—not himself as Theodore Vasílyevich Rostopchín (he fancied that Theodore Vasílyevich Rostopchín was sacrificing himself for the public good) but himself as governor, the representative of authority and of the Tsar. "Had I been simply Theodore Vasílyevich my course of action would have been quite different, but it was my duty to safeguard my life and dignity as commander in chief."

Lightly swaying on the flexible springs of his carriage and no longer hearing the terrible sounds of the crowd, Rostopchín grew physically calm and, as always happens, as soon as he became physically tranquil his mind devised reasons why he should be mentally tranquil too. The thought which tranquillized Rostopchín was not a new one. Since the world began and men have killed one another no one has ever committed such a crime against his fellow man without comforting himself with this same idea. This idea is *le bien public*, the hypothetical welfare of other people.

To a man not swayed by passion that welfare is never certain, but he who commits such a crime always knows just where that welfare lies. And Rostopchín now knew it.

Not only did his reason not reproach him for what he had done, but he even found cause for self-satisfaction in having so successfully contrived to avail himself of a convenient opportunity to punish a criminal and at the same time pacify the mob.

"Vereshchágin was tried and condemned to death," thought Rostopchín (though the Senate had only condemned Vereshchágin to hard labor), "he was a traitor and a spy. I could not let him go unpunished and so I have killed two birds with one stone: to appease the mob I gave them a victim and at the same time punished a miscreant."

Having reached his country house and begun to give orders about domestic arrangements, the count grew quite tranquil.

Half an hour later he was driving with his fast horses across the Sokólniki field, no longer thinking of what had occurred but considering what was to come. He was driving to the Yaúza bridge where he had heard that

Kutúzov was. Count Rostopchín was mentally preparing the angry and stinging reproaches he meant to address to Kutúzov for his deception. He would make that foxy old courtier feel that the responsibility for all the calamities that would follow the abandonment of the city and the ruin of Russia (as Rostopchín regarded it) would fall upon his doting old head. Planning beforehand what he would say to Kutúzov, Rostopchín turned angrily in his *calèche* and gazed sternly from side to side.

The Sokólniki field was deserted. Only at the end of it, in front of the almshouse and the lunatic asylum, could be seen some people in white and others like them walking singly across the field shouting and gesticulating.

One of these was running to cross the path of Count Rostopchín's carriage, and the count himself, his coachman, and his dragoons looked with vague horror and curiosity at these released lunatics and especially at the one running toward them.

Swaying from side to side on his long, thin legs in his fluttering dressing gown, this lunatic was running impetuously, his gaze fixed on Rostopchín, shouting something in a hoarse voice and making signs to him to stop. The lunatic's solemn, gloomy face was thin and yellow, with its beard growing in uneven tufts. His black, agate pupils with saffron-yellow whites moved restlessly near the lower eyelids.

"Stop! Pull up, I tell you!" he cried in a piercing voice, and again shouted something breathlessly with emphatic intonations and gestures.

Coming abreast of the *calèche* he ran beside it.

"Thrice have they slain me, thrice have I risen from the dead. They stoned me, crucified me . . . I shall rise . . . shall rise . . . shall rise. They have torn my body. The kingdom of God will be overthrown . . . Thrice will I overthrow it and thrice re-establish it!" he cried, raising his voice higher and higher.

Count Rostopchín suddenly grew pale as he had done when the crowd closed in on Vereshchágin. He turned away. "Go fas . . . faster!" he cried in a trembling voice to his coachman. The *calèche* flew over the ground as fast as the horses could draw it, but for a long time Count Rostopchín still heard the insane despairing screams growing fainter in the distance, while his eyes saw nothing but the astonished, frightened, bloodstained face of "the traitor" in the fur-lined coat.

Recent as that mental picture was, Rostopchín already felt that it had cut deep into his heart and drawn blood. Even now he felt clearly that the gory trace of that recollection would not pass with time, but that the terrible memory would, on the contrary, dwell in his heart ever more

cruelly and painfully to the end of his life. He seemed still to hear the sound of his own words: "Cut him down! I command it. . . ."

"Why did I utter those words? It was by some accident I said them. . . . I need not have said them," he thought. "And then nothing would have happened." He saw the frightened and then infuriated face of the dragoon who dealt the blow, the look of silent, timid reproach that boy in the fur-lined coat had turned upon him. "But I did not do it for my own sake. I was bound to act that way. . . . The mob, the traitor . . . the public welfare," thought he.

Troops were still crowding at the Yaúza bridge. It was hot. Kutúzov, dejected and frowning, sat on a bench by the bridge toying with his whip in the sand when a *calèche* dashed up noisily. A man in a general's uniform with plumes in his hat went up to Kutúzov and said something in French. It was Count Rostopchín. He told Kutúzov that he had come because Moscow, the capital, was no more and only the army remained.

"Things would have been different if your Serene Highness had not told me that you would not abandon Moscow without another battle; all this would not have happened," he said.

Kutúzov looked at Rostopchín as if, not grasping what was said to him, he was trying to read something peculiar written at that moment on the face of the man addressing him. Rostopchín grew confused and became silent. Kutúzov slightly shook his head and not taking his penetrating gaze from Rostopchín's face muttered softly:

"No! I shall not give up Moscow without a battle!"

Whether Kutúzov was thinking of something entirely different when he spoke those words, or uttered them purposely, knowing them to be meaningless, at any rate Rostopchín made no reply and hastily left him. And strange to say, the Governor of Moscow, the proud Count Rostopchín, took up a Cossack whip and went to the bridge where he began with shouts to drive on the carts that blocked the way.

13. The French enter Moscow. Shots from the Krémlin gate. The Fire of Moscow discussed

TOWARD FOUR O'CLOCK in the afternoon Murat's troops were entering Moscow. In front rode a detachment of Württemberg hussars and behind them rode the King of Naples himself accompanied by a numerous suite.

About the middle of the Arbát Street, near the Church of the Miracu-

lous Icon of St. Nicholas, Murat halted to await news from the advanced detachment as to the condition in which they had found the citadel, le Kremlin.*

Around Murat gathered a group of those who had remained in Moscow. They all stared in timid bewilderment at the strange, long-haired commander dressed up in feathers and gold.

"Is that their Tsar himself? He's not bad!" low voices could be heard saying.

An interpreter rode up to the group.

"Take off your cap . . . your caps!" These words went from one to another in the crowd. The interpreter addressed an old porter and asked if it was far to the Krémlin. The porter, listening in perplexity to the unfamiliar Polish accent and not realizing that the interpreter was speaking Russian, did not understand what was being said to him and slipped behind the others.

Murat approached the interpreter and told him to ask where the Russian army was. One of the Russians understood what was asked and several voices at once began answering the interpreter. A French officer, returning from the advanced detachment, rode up to Murat and reported that the gates of the citadel had been barricaded and that there was probably an ambuscade there.

"Good!" said Murat and, turning to one of the gentlemen in his suite, ordered four light guns to be moved forward to fire at the gates.

The guns emerged at a trot from the column following Murat and advanced up the Arbát. When they reached the end of the Vozdvízhenka Street they halted and drew up in the Square. Several French officers superintended the placing of the guns and looked at the Krémlin through field glasses.

The bells in the Krémlin were ringing for vespers, and this sound troubled the French. They imagined it to be a call to arms. A few infantrymen ran to the Kutáfyev Gate. Beams and wooden screens had been put there, and two musket shots rang out from under the gate as soon as an officer and men began to run toward it. A general who was standing by the

* Tolstóy likes to indicate the superficial and inaccurate knowledge the French had of Russia. Here, for instance, he mentions Murat as regarding the Krémlin, the brick walls of which were built in 1367, as a "citadel." It might really have served as a fortress in the Middle Ages, but was quite unsuited to resist artillery. Later on, in Book Thirteen, Chapter 2, the mention of Napoleon giving "careful directions about the fortification of the Krémlin" is again ironic. In 1812 the Krémlin walls served merely as an enclosure for the palaces, churches, law courts, and state buildings, of which the Krémlin is constituted.—A.M.

guns shouted some words of command to the officer, and the latter ran back again with his men.

The sound of three more shots came from the gate.

One shot struck a French soldier's foot, and from behind the screens came the strange sound of a few voices shouting. Instantly as at a word of command the expression of cheerful serenity on the faces of the French general, officers, and men changed to one of determined concentrated readiness for strife and suffering. To all of them from the marshal to the least soldier, that place was not the Vozdvízhenka, Mokhaváya, or Kutáfyev Street, nor the Tróitsa Gate (places familiar in Moscow), but a new battlefield which would probably prove sanguinary. And all made ready for that battle. The cries from the gates ceased. The guns were advanced, the artillerymen blew the ash off their linstocks, and an officer gave the word "Fire!" This was followed by two whistling sounds of canister shot, one after another. The shot rattled against the stone of the gate and upon the wooden beams and screens, and two wavering clouds of smoke rose over the Square.

A few instants after the echo of the reports resounding over the stone-built Krémlin had died away the French heard a strange sound above their head. Thousands of crows rose above the walls and circled in the air, cawing and noisily flapping their wings. Together with that sound came a solitary human cry from the gateway and amid the smoke appeared the figure of a bareheaded man in a peasant's coat. He grasped a musket and took aim at the French. "Fire!" repeated the officer once more, and the reports of a musket and of two cannon shots were heard simultaneously. The gate was again hidden by smoke.

Nothing more stirred behind the screens and the French infantry soldiers and officers advanced to the gate. In the gateway lay three wounded and four dead. Two men in peasant coats ran away at the foot of the wall, toward the Známenka.

"Clear that away!" said the officer, pointing to the beams and the corpses, and the French soldiers, after dispatching the wounded, threw the corpses over the parapet.

Who these men were nobody knew. "Clear that away!" was all that was said of them, and they were thrown over the parapet and removed later on that they might not stink. Thiers alone dedicates a few eloquent lines to their memory: "These wretches had occupied the sacred citadel, having supplied themselves with guns from the arsenal, and fired" (the wretches) "at the French. Some of them were sabered and the Krémlin was purged of their presence."

Murat was informed that the way had been cleared. The French entered

the gates and began pitching their camp in the Senate Square. Out of the windows of the Senate House the soldiers threw chairs into the Square for fuel and kindled fires there.

Other detachments passed through the Krémlin and encamped along the Moroséyka, the Lubyánka, and Pokróvka Streets. Others quartered themselves along the Vozdvízhenka, the Nikólski, and the Tverskóy Streets. No masters of the houses being found anywhere, the French were not billeted on the inhabitants as is usual in towns but lived in it as in a camp.

Though tattered, hungry, worn out, and reduced to a third of their original number, the French entered Moscow in good marching order. It was a weary and famished, but still a fighting and menacing army. But it remained an army only until its soldiers had dispersed into their different lodgings. As soon as the men of the various regiments began to disperse among the wealthy and deserted houses, the army was lost forever and there came into being something nondescript, neither citizens nor soldiers but what are known as marauders. When five weeks later these same men left Moscow, they no longer formed an army. They were a mob of marauders, each carrying a quantity of articles which seemed to him valuable or useful. The aim of each man when he left Moscow was no longer, as it had been, to conquer, but merely to keep what he had acquired. Like a monkey which puts its paw into the narrow neck of a jug, and having seized a handful of nuts will not open its fist for fear of losing what it holds, and therefore perishes, the French when they left Moscow had inevitably to perish because they carried their loot with them, yet to abandon what they had stolen was as impossible for them as it is for the monkey to open its paw and let go of its nuts. Ten minutes after each regiment had entered a Moscow district, not a soldier or officer was left. Men in military uniforms and Hessian boots could be seen through the windows, laughing and walking through the rooms. In cellars and storerooms similar men were busy among the provisions, and in the yards unlocking or breaking open coach house and stable doors, lighting fires in kitchens and kneading and baking bread with rolled-up sleeves, and cooking; or frightening, amusing, or caressing women and children. There were many such men both in the shops and houses—but there was no army.

Order after order was issued by the French commanders that day forbidding the men to disperse about the town, sternly forbidding any violence to the inhabitants or any looting, and announcing a roll call for that very evening. But despite all these measures the men, who had till then constituted an army, flowed all over the wealthy, deserted city with its

comforts and plentiful supplies. As a hungry herd of cattle keeps well together when crossing a barren field, but gets out of hand and at once disperses uncontrollably as soon as it reaches rich pastures, so did the army disperse all over the wealthy city.

No residents were left in Moscow, and the soldiers—like water percolating through sand—spread irresistibly through the city in all directions from the Krémlin into which they had first marched. The cavalry, on entering a merchant's house that had been abandoned and finding there stabling more than sufficient for their horses, went on, all the same, to the next house which seemed to them better. Many of them appropriated several houses, chalked their names on them, and quarreled and even fought with other companies for them. Before they had had time to secure quarters the soldiers ran out into the streets to see the city and, hearing that everything had been abandoned, rushed to places where valuables were to be had for the taking. The officers followed to check the soldiers and were involuntarily drawn into doing the same. In Carriage Row carriages had been left in the shops, and generals flocked there to select *calèches* and coaches for themselves. The few inhabitants who had remained invited commanding officers to their houses, hoping thereby to secure themselves from being plundered. There were masses of wealth and there seemed no end to it. All around the quarters occupied by the French were other regions still unexplored and unoccupied where, they thought, yet greater riches might be found. And Moscow engulfed the army ever deeper and deeper. When water is spilled on dry ground both the dry ground and the water disappear and mud results; and in the same way the entry of the famished army into the rich and deserted city resulted in fires and looting and the destruction of both the army and the wealthy city.

The French attributed the Fire of Moscow *au patriotisme féroce de Rostopchine* [to Rostopchín's ferocious patriotism], the Russians to the barbarity of the French. In reality, however, it was not, and could not be, possible to explain the burning of Moscow by making any individual, or any group of people, responsible for it. Moscow was burned because it found itself in a position in which any town built of wood was bound to burn, quite apart from whether it had, or had not, a hundred and thirty inferior fire engines. Deserted Moscow had to burn as inevitably as a heap of shavings has to burn on which sparks continually fall for several days. A town built of wood, where scarcely a day passes without conflagrations when the house owners are in residence and a police force is present, cannot help burning when its inhabitants have left it and

it is occupied by soldiers who smoke pipes, make campfires of the Senate chairs in the Senate Square, and cook themselves meals twice a day. In peacetime it is only necessary to billet troops in the villages of any district and the number of fires in that district immediately increases. How much then must the probability of fire be increased in an abandoned, wooden town where foreign troops are quartered. *"Le patriotisme féroce de Rostopchine"* and the barbarity of the French were not to blame in the matter. Moscow was set on fire by the soldiers' pipes, kitchens, and campfires, and by the carelessness of enemy soldiers occupying houses they did not own. Even if there was any arson (which is very doubtful, for no one had any reason to burn the houses—in any case a troublesome and dangerous thing to do), arson cannot be regarded as the cause, for the same thing would have happened without any incendiarism.

However tempting it might be for the French to blame Rostopchín's ferocity and for Russians to blame the scoundrel Bonaparte, or later on to place an heroic torch in the hands of their own people, it is impossible not to see that there could be no such direct cause of the fire, for Moscow had to burn as every village, factory, or house must burn which is left by its owners and in which strangers are allowed to live and cook their porridge. Moscow was burned by its inhabitants, it is true, but by those who had abandoned it and not by those who remained in it. Moscow when occupied by the enemy did not remain intact like Berlin, Vienna, and other towns, simply because its inhabitants abandoned it and did not welcome the French with bread and salt, nor bring them the keys of the city.

14. Pierre: his plan to kill Napoleon. Bazdéev's drunken brother fires at Captain Ramballe, who regards Pierre as a friend

THE ABSORPTION of the French by Moscow, radiating starwise as it did, only reached the quarter where Pierre was staying by the evening of the second of September.

After the last two days spent in solitude and unusual circumstances, Pierre was in a state bordering on insanity. He was completely obsessed by one persistent thought. He did not know how or when this thought had taken such possession of him, but he remembered nothing of the past, understood nothing of the present, and all he saw and heard appeared to him like a dream.

He had left home only to escape the intricate tangle of life's demands that enmeshed him, and which in his present condition he was unable to unravel. He had gone to Joseph Alexéevich's house, on the plea of sorting the deceased's books and papers, only in search of rest from life's turmoil, for in his mind the memory of Joseph Alexéevich was connected with a world of eternal, solemn, and calm thoughts, quite contrary to the restless confusion into which he felt himself being drawn. He sought a quiet refuge, and in Joseph Alexéevich's study he really found it. When he sat with his elbows on the dusty writing table in the deathlike stillness of the study, calm and significant memories of the last few days rose one after another in his imagination, particularly of the battle of Borodinó and of that vague sense of his own insignificance and insincerity compared with the truth, simplicity, and strength of the class of men he mentally classed as *they*. When Gerásim roused him from his reverie the idea occurred to him of taking part in the popular defense of Moscow which he knew was projected. And with that object he had asked Gerásim to get him a peasant's coat and a pistol, confiding to him his intentions of remaining in Joseph Alexéevich's house and keeping his name secret. Then during the first day spent in inaction and solitude (he tried several times to fix his attention on the Masonic manuscripts, but was unable to do so) the idea that had previously occurred to him of the cabalistic significance of his name in connection with Bonaparte's more than once vaguely presented itself. But the idea that he, *L'russe Besuhof*, was destined to set a limit to the power of *the Beast* was as yet only one of the fancies that often passed through his mind and left no trace behind.

When, having bought the coat merely with the object of taking part among the people in the defense of Moscow, Pierre had met the Rostóvs and Natásha had said to him: "Are you remaining in Moscow? . . . How splendid!" the thought flashed into his mind that it really would be a good thing, even if Moscow were taken, for him to remain there and do what he was predestined to do.

Next day, with the sole idea of not sparing himself and not lagging in any way behind *them*, Pierre went to the Three Hills gate. But when he returned to the house convinced that Moscow would not be defended, he suddenly felt that what before had seemed to him merely a possibility had now become absolutely necessary and inevitable. He must remain in Moscow, concealing his name, and must meet Napoleon and kill him, and either perish or put an end to the misery of all Europe—which it seemed to him was solely due to Napoleon.

Pierre knew all the details of the attempt on Bonaparte's life in 1809

by a German student in Vienna,* and knew that the student had been shot. And the risk to which he would expose his life by carrying out his design excited him still more.

Two equally strong feelings drew Pierre irresistibly to this purpose. The first was a feeling of the necessity of sacrifice and suffering in view of the common calamity, the same feeling that had caused him to go to Mozháysk on the twenty-fifth and to make his way to the very thick of the battle and had now caused him to run away from his home and, in place of the luxury and comfort to which he was accustomed, to sleep on a hard sofa without undressing and eat the same food as Gerásim. The other was that vague and quite Russian feeling of contempt for everything conventional, artificial, and human—for everything the majority of men regard as the greatest good in the world. Pierre had first experienced this strange and fascinating feeling at the Slobóda Palace, when he had suddenly felt that wealth, power, and life—all that men so painstakingly acquire and guard—if it has any worth has so only by reason of the joy with which it can all be renounced.

It was the feeling that induces a volunteer recruit to spend his last penny on drink, and a drunken man to smash mirrors or glasses for no apparent reason and knowing that it will cost him all the money he possesses: the feeling which causes a man to perform actions which from an ordinary point of view are insane, to test, as it were, his personal power and strength, affirming the existence of a higher, nonhuman criterion of life.

From the very day Pierre had experienced this feeling for the first time at the Slobóda Palace he had been continuously under its influence, but only now found full satisfaction for it. Moreover, at this moment Pierre was supported in his design and prevented from renouncing it by what he had already done in that direction. If he were now to leave Moscow like everyone else, his flight from home, the peasant coat, the pistol, and his announcement to the Rostóvs that he would remain in Moscow would all become not merely meaningless but contemptible and ridiculous, and to this Pierre was very sensitive.

Pierre's physical condition, as is always the case, corresponded to his mental state. The unaccustomed coarse food, the vodka he drank during those days, the absence of wine and cigars, his dirty unchanged linen, two almost sleepless nights passed on a short sofa without bedding—all this kept him in a state of excitement bordering on insanity.

* *While reviewing his guard in front of the palace of Schönbrunn, October 12, 1809, Napoleon was approached by a young man carrying a petition. This young idealist, Friedrich Staps, drew a dagger and attempted to kill the Emperor. He was seized, imprisoned, and then executed the next day.*

It was two o'clock in the afternoon. The French had already entered Moscow. Pierre knew this, but instead of acting he only thought about his undertaking, going over its minutest details in his mind. In his fancy he did not clearly picture to himself either the striking of the blow or the death of Napoleon, but with extraordinary vividness and melancholy enjoyment imagined his own destruction and heroic endurance.

"Yes, alone, for the sake of all, I must do it or perish!" he thought. "Yes, I will approach . . . and then suddenly . . . with pistol or dagger? But that is all the same! 'It is not I but the hand of Providence that punishes thee,' I shall say," thought he, imagining what he would say when killing Napoleon. "Well then, take me and execute me!" he went on, speaking to himself and bowing his head with a sad but firm expression.

While Pierre, standing in the middle of the room, was talking to himself in this way, the study door opened and on the threshold appeared the figure of Makár Alexéevich, always so timid before but now quite transformed.

His dressing gown was unfastened, his face red and distorted. He was obviously drunk. On seeing Pierre he grew confused at first, but noticing embarrassment on Pierre's face immediately grew bold and, staggering on his thin legs, advanced into the middle of the room.

"They're frightened," he said confidentially in a hoarse voice. "I say I won't surrender, I say . . . Am I not right, sir?"

He paused and then suddenly seeing the pistol on the table seized it with unexpected rapidity and ran out into the corridor.

Gerásim and the porter, who had followed Makár Alexéevich, stopped him in the vestibule and tried to take the pistol from him. Pierre, coming out into the corridor, looked with pity and repulsion at the half-crazy old man. Makár Alexéevich, frowning with exertion, held on to the pistol and screamed hoarsely, evidently with some heroic fancy in his head.

"To arms! Board them! No, you shan't get it," he yelled.

"That will do, please, that will do. Have the goodness—please, sir, to let go! Please, sir . . ." pleaded Gerásim, trying carefully to steer Makár Alexéevich by the elbows back to the door.

"Who are you? Bonaparte! . . ." shouted Makár Alexéevich.

"That's not right, sir. Come to your room, please, and rest. Allow me to have the pistol."

"Be off, thou base slave! Touch me not! See this?" shouted Makár Alexéevich, brandishing the pistol. "Board them!"

"Catch hold!" whispered Gerásim to the porter.

They seized Makár Alexéevich by the arms and dragged him to the door.

The vestibule was filled with the discordant sounds of a struggle and of a tipsy, hoarse voice.

Suddenly a fresh sound, a piercing feminine scream, reverberated from the porch and the cook came running into the vestibule.

"It's them! Gracious heavens! O Lord, four of them, horsemen!" she cried.

Gerásim and the porter let Makár Alexéevich go, and in the now silent corridor the sound of several hands knocking at the front door could be heard.

PIERRE, having decided that until he had carried out his design he would disclose neither his identity nor his knowledge of French, stood at the half-open door of the corridor, intending to conceal himself as soon as the French entered. But the French entered and still Pierre did not retire —an irresistible curiosity kept him there.

There were two of them. One was an officer—a tall, soldierly, handsome man—the other evidently a private or an orderly, sunburned, short, and thin, with sunken cheeks and a dull expression. The officer walked in front, leaning on a stick and slightly limping. When he had advanced a few steps he stopped, having apparently decided that these were good quarters, turned round to the soldiers standing at the entrance, and in a loud voice of command ordered them to put up the horses. Having done that, the officer, lifting his elbow with a smart gesture, stroked his mustache and lightly touched his hat.

"Bonjour, la compagnie! [Good-day, everybody!]" said he gaily, smiling and looking about him.

No one gave any reply.

"Vous êtes le bourgeois [Are you the master here]?" the officer asked Gerásim.

Gerásim gazed at the officer with an alarmed and inquiring look.

"Quartier, quartier, logement! [Quarters, quarters, lodgings]" said the officer, looking down at the little man with a condescending and good-natured smile. "Les français sont de bons enfants. Que diable! Voyons! Ne nous fâchons pas, mon vieux! [The French are good fellows. What the devil! There, don't let us be cross, old fellow]" added he, clapping the scared and silent Gerásim on the shoulder. "Well, does no one speak French in this establishment?" he asked again in French, looking around and meeting Pierre's eyes. Pierre moved away from the door.

Again the officer turned to Gerásim and asked him to show him the rooms in the house.

"Master, not here—don't understand . . . me, you . . ." said Gerásim, trying to render his words more comprehensible by contorting them.

Still smiling, the French officer spread out his hands before Gerásim's nose, intimating that he did not understand him either, and moved, limping, to the door at which Pierre was standing. Pierre wished to go away and conceal himself, but at that moment he saw Makár Alexéevich appearing at the open kitchen door with the pistol in his hand. With a madman's cunning, Makár Alexéevich eyed the Frenchman, raised his pistol, and took aim.

"Board them!" yelled the tipsy man, trying to press the trigger. Hearing the yell the officer turned round, and at the same moment Pierre threw himself on the drunkard. Just when Pierre snatched at and struck up the pistol Makár Alexéevich at last got his fingers on the trigger, there was a deafening report, and all were enveloped in a cloud of smoke. The Frenchman turned pale and rushed to the door.

Forgetting his intention of concealing his knowledge of French, Pierre, snatching away the pistol and throwing it down, ran up to the officer and addressed him in French.

"You are not wounded?" he asked.

"I think not," answered the Frenchman, feeling himself over. "But I have had a lucky escape this time," he added, pointing to the damaged plaster of the wall. "Who is that man?" said he, looking sternly at Pierre.

"Oh, I am really in despair at what has occurred," said Pierre rapidly, quite forgetting the part he had intended to play. "He is an unfortunate madman who did not know what he was doing."

The officer went up to Makár Alexéevich and took him by the collar.

Makár Alexéevich was standing with parted lips, swaying, as if about to fall asleep, as he leaned against the wall.

"Brigand! You shall pay for this," said the Frenchman, letting go of him. "We French are merciful after victory, but we do not pardon traitors," he added, with a look of gloomy dignity and a fine energetic gesture.

Pierre continued, in French, to persuade the officer not to hold that drunken imbecile to account. The Frenchman listened in silence with the same gloomy expression, but suddenly turned to Pierre with a smile. For a few seconds he looked at him in silence. His handsome face assumed a melodramatically gentle expression and he held out his hand.

"You have saved my life. You are French," said he.

For a Frenchman that deduction was indubitable. Only a Frenchman could perform a great deed, and to save his life—the life of M. Ramballe, captain of the 13th Light Regiment—was undoubtedly a very great deed.

But however indubitable that conclusion and the officer's conviction based upon it, Pierre felt it necessary to disillusion him.

"I am Russian," he said quickly.

"Tut, tut, tut! Tell that to others," said the officer, waving his finger before his nose and smiling. "You shall tell me all about that presently. I am delighted to meet a compatriot. Well, and what are we to do with this man?" he added, addressing himself to Pierre as to a brother.

Even if Pierre were not a Frenchman, having once received that loftiest of human appellations he could not renounce it, said the officer's look and tone. In reply to his last question Pierre again explained who Makár Aléxeevich was and how just before their arrival that drunken imbecile had seized the loaded pistol which they had not had time to recover from him, and begged the officer to let the deed go unpunished.

The Frenchman expanded his chest and made a majestic gesture with his arm.

"You have saved my life! You are French. You ask his pardon? I grant it you. Lead that man away!" said he quickly and energetically, and taking the arm of Pierre whom he had promoted to be a Frenchman for saving his life, he went with him into the room.

The soldiers in the yard, hearing the shot, came into the passage asking what had happened, and expressed their readiness to punish the culprits, but the officer sternly checked them.

"You will be called in when you are wanted," he said.

The soldiers went out again, and the orderly, who had meanwhile had time to visit the kitchen, came up to his officer.

"Captain, there is soup and a leg of mutton in the kitchen," said he. "Shall I serve them up?"

"Yes, and some wine," answered the captain.

WHEN THE FRENCH OFFICER went into the room with Pierre the latter again thought it his duty to assure him that he was not French and wished to go away, but the officer would not hear of it. He was so very polite, amiable, good-natured, and genuinely grateful to Pierre for saving his life that Pierre had not the heart to refuse, and sat down with him in the parlor—the first room they entered. To Pierre's assurances that he was not a Frenchman, the captain, evidently not understanding how anyone could decline so flattering an appellation, shrugged his shoulders and said that if Pierre absolutely insisted on passing for a Russian let it be so, but for all that he would be forever bound to Pierre by gratitude for saving his life.

Had this man been endowed with the slightest capacity for perceiving

the feelings of others, and had he at all understood what Pierre's feelings were, the latter would probably have left him, but the man's animated obtuseness to everything other than himself disarmed Pierre.

"A Frenchman or a Russian prince incognito," said the officer, looking at Pierre's fine though dirty linen and at the ring on his finger. "I owe my life to you and offer you my friendship. A Frenchman never forgets either an insult or a service. I offer you my friendship. That is all I can say."

There was so much good nature and nobility (in the French sense of the word) in the officer's voice, in the expression of his face and in his gestures, that Pierre, unconsciously smiling in response to the French-man's smile, pressed the hand held out to him.

"Captain Ramballe, of the 13th Light Regiment, Chevalier of the Legion of Honor for the affair on the seventh of September," * he intro-duced himself, a self-satisfied irrepressible smile puckering his lips under his mustache. "Will you now be so good as to tell me with whom I have the honor of conversing so pleasantly, instead of being in the ambulance with that maniac's bullet in my body?"

Pierre replied that he could not tell him his name and, blushing, began to try to invent a name and to say something about his reason for conceal-ing it, but the Frenchman hastily interrupted him.

"Oh, please!" said he. "I understand your reasons. You are an officer . . . a superior officer perhaps. You have borne arms against us. That's not my business. I owe you my life. That is enough for me. I am quite at your service. You belong to the gentry?" he concluded with a shade of inquiry in his tone. Pierre bent his head. "Your baptismal name, if you please. That is all I ask. Monsieur Pierre, you say. . . . Excellent! That's all I want to know."

When the mutton and an omelet had been served and a samovar and vodka brought, with some wine which the French had taken from a Rus-sian cellar and brought with them, Ramballe invited Pierre to share his dinner, and himself began to eat greedily and quickly like a healthy and hungry man, munching his food rapidly with his strong teeth, continu-ally smacking his lips, and repeating—"Excellent! Delicious!" His face grew red and was covered with perspiration. Pierre was hungry and shared the dinner with pleasure. Morel, the orderly, brought some hot water in a saucepan and placed a bottle of claret in it. He also brought a bottle of kvass, taken from the kitchen for them to try. That beverage was already known to the French and had been given a special name. They called it *limonade de cochon* (pig's lemonade), and Morel spoke well of the *limonade de cochon* he had found in the kitchen. But as the captain had

* *Borodinó.*

the wine they had taken while passing through Moscow, he left the kvass to Morel and applied himself to the bottle of Bordeaux. He wrapped the bottle up to its neck in a table napkin and poured out wine for himself and for Pierre. The satisfaction of his hunger and the wine rendered the captain still more lively and he chatted incessantly all through dinner.

"Yes, my dear Monsieur Pierre, I owe you a fine votive candle for saving me from that maniac. . . . You see, I have bullets enough in my body already. Here is one I got at Wagram" (he touched his side) "and a second at Smolénsk"—he showed a scar on his cheek—"and this leg which as you see does not want to march, I got that on the seventh at the great battle of la Moskowa.* *Sacré Dieu!* It was splendid! That deluge of fire was worth seeing. It was a tough job you set us there, my word! You may be proud of it! And on my honor, in spite of the cough I caught there, I should be ready to begin again. I pity those who did not see it."

"I was there," said Pierre.

"Bah, really? So much the better! You are certainly brave foes. The great redoubt held out well, by my pipe!" continued the Frenchman. "And you made us pay dear for it. I was at it three times—sure as I sit here. Three times we reached the guns and three times we were thrown back like cardboard figures. Oh, it was beautiful, Monsieur Pierre! Your grenadiers were splendid, by heaven! I saw them close up their ranks six times in succession and march as if on parade. Fine fellows! Our King of Naples, who knows what's what, cried 'Bravo!' Ha, ha! So you are one of us soldiers!" he added, smiling, after a momentary pause. "So much the better, so much the better, Monsieur Pierre! Terrible in battle . . . gallant . . . with the fair" (he winked and smiled), "that's what the French are, Monsieur Pierre, aren't they?"

The captain was so naïvely and good-humoredly gay, so real, and so pleased with himself that Pierre almost winked back as he looked merrily at him. Probably the word "gallant" turned the captain's thoughts to the state of Moscow.

"Apropos, tell me please, is it true that the women have all left Moscow? What a queer idea! What had they to be afraid of?"

"Would not the French ladies leave Paris if the Russians entered it?" asked Pierre.

"Ha, ha, ha!" The Frenchman emitted a merry, sanguine chuckle, patting Pierre on the shoulder. "What a thing to say!" he exclaimed. "Paris? . . . But Paris, Paris . . ."

* *The French called the battle of Borodinó* la Moskowa *and the Frenchman naturally gives the date New Style, as September seventh, whereas the Russians called it August twenty-sixth.*—A.M.

"Paris—the capital of the world," Pierre finished his remark for him.

The captain looked at Pierre. He had a habit of stopping short in the middle of his talk and gazing intently with his laughing, kindly eyes.

"Well, if you hadn't told me you were Russian, I should have wagered that you were Parisian! You have that . . . I don't know what, that . . ." and having uttering this compliment, he again gazed at him in silence.

"I have been in Paris. I spent years there," said Pierre.

"Oh yes, one sees that plainly. Paris! . . . A man who doesn't know Paris is a savage. You can tell a Parisian two leagues off. Paris is Talma, la Duchénois, Potier, the Sorbonne, the boulevards," * and noticing that his conclusion was weaker than what had gone before, he added quickly: "There is only one Paris in the world. You have been to Paris and have remained Russian. Well, I don't esteem you the less for it."

Under the influence of the wine he had drunk, and after the days he had spent alone with his depressing thoughts, Pierre involuntarily enjoyed talking with this cheerful and good-natured man.

"To return to your ladies—I hear they are lovely. What a wretched idea to go and bury themselves in the steppes when the French army is in Moscow. What a chance those girls have missed! Your peasants, now —that's another thing; but you civilized people, you ought to know us better than that. We took Vienna, Berlin, Madrid, Naples, Rome, Warsaw, all the world's capitals. . . . We are feared, but we are loved. We are nice to know. And then the Emperor . . ." he began, but Pierre interrupted him.

"The Emperor," Pierre repeated, and his face suddenly became sad and embarrassed, "is the Emperor . . . ?"

"The Emperor? He is generosity, mercy, justice, order, genius—that's what the Emperor is! It is I, Ramballe, who tell you so. . . . I assure you I was his enemy eight years ago. My father was an emigrant count. . . . But that man has vanquished me. He has taken hold of me. I could not resist the sight of the grandeur and glory with which he has covered France. When I understood what he wanted—when I saw that he was preparing a bed of laurels for us, you know, I said to myself: 'That is a monarch,' and I devoted myself to him! So there! Oh yes, mon cher, he is the greatest man of the ages past or future."

"Is he in Moscow?" Pierre stammered with a guilty look.

The Frenchman looked at his guilty face and smiled.

* Captain Ramballe in enumerating the attractions of Paris mentions indiscriminately the famous tragedian Talma (a favorite of Napoleon's), the actress Duchénois, the comedian Potier, the Sorbonne (the University of Paris), and the boulevards.—A.M.

"No, he will make his entry tomorrow," he replied, and continued his talk.

Their conversation was interrupted by the cries of several voices at the gate and by Morel, who came to say that some Württemberg hussars had come and wanted to put up their horses in the yard where the captain's horses were. This difficulty had arisen chiefly because the hussars did not understand what was said to them in French.

The captain had their senior sergeant called in, and in a stern voice asked him to what regiment he belonged, who was his commanding officer, and by what right he allowed himself to claim quarters that were already occupied. The German, who knew little French, answered the two first questions by giving the names of his regiment and of his commanding officer, but in reply to the third question which he did not understand said, introducing broken French into his own German, that he was the quartermaster of the regiment and his commander had ordered him to occupy all the houses one after another. Pierre, who knew German, translated what the German said to the captain and gave the captain's reply to the Württemberg hussar in German. When he had understood what was said to him, the German submitted and took his men elsewhere. The captain went out into the porch and gave some orders in a loud voice.

When he returned to the room Pierre was sitting in the same place as before, with his head in his hands. His face expressed suffering. He really was suffering at that moment. When the captain went out and he was left alone, suddenly he came to himself and realized the position he was in. It was not that Moscow had been taken or that the happy conquerors were masters in it and were patronizing him. Painful as that was it was not that which tormented Pierre at the moment. He was tormented by the consciousness of his own weakness. The few glasses of wine he had drunk and the conversation with this good-natured man had destroyed the mood of concentrated gloom in which he had spent the last few days and which was essential for the execution of his design. The pistol, dagger, and peasant coat were ready. Napoleon was to enter the town next day. Pierre still considered that it would be a useful and worthy action to slay the evildoer, but now he felt that he would not do it. He did not know why, but he felt a foreboding that he would not carry out his intention. He struggled against the confession of his weakness but dimly felt that he could not overcome it and that his former gloomy frame of mind, concerning vengeance, killing, and self-sacrifice, had been dispersed like dust by contact with the first man he met.

The captain returned to the room, limping slightly and whistling a tune.

The Frenchman's chatter which had previously amused Pierre now repelled him. The tune he was whistling, his gait, and the gesture with which he twirled his mustache, all now seemed offensive. "I will go away immediately. I won't say another word to him," thought Pierre. He thought this, but still sat in the same place. A strange feeling of weakness tied him to the spot; he wished to get up and go away, but could not do so.

The captain, on the other hand, seemed very cheerful. He paced up and down the room twice. His eyes shone and his mustache twitched as if he were smiling to himself at some amusing thought.

"The colonel of those Württembergers is delightful," he suddenly said. "He's a German, but a nice fellow all the same. . . . But he's a German." He sat down facing Pierre. "By the way, you know German, then?"

Pierre looked at him in silence.

"What is the German for 'shelter'?"

"Shelter?" Pierre repeated. "The German for shelter is *Unterkunft*."

"How do you say it?" the captain asked quickly and doubtfully.

"*Unterkunft,*" Pierre repeated.

"Onterkoff," said the captain and looked at Pierre for some seconds with laughing eyes. "These Germans are first-rate fools, don't you think so, Monsieur Pierre?" he concluded.

"Well, let's have another bottle of this Moscow Bordeaux, shall we? Morel will warm us up another little bottle. Morel!" he called out gaily.

Morel brought candles and a bottle of wine. The captain looked at Pierre by the candlelight and was evidently struck by the troubled expression on his companion's face. Ramballe, with genuine distress and sympathy in his face, went up to Pierre and bent over him.

"There now, we're sad," said he, touching Pierre's hand. "Have I upset you? No, really, have you anything against me?" he asked Pierre. "Perhaps it's the state of affairs?"

Pierre did not answer, but looked cordially into the Frenchman's eyes whose expression of sympathy was pleasing to him.

"Honestly, without speaking of what I owe you, I feel friendship for you. Can I do anything for you? Dispose of me. It is for life and death. I say it with my hand on my heart!" said he, striking his chest.

"Thank you," said Pierre.

The captain gazed intently at him as he had done when he learned that "shelter" was *Unterkunft* in German, and his face suddenly brightened.

"Well, in that case, I drink to our friendship!" he cried gaily, filling two glasses with wine.

Pierre took one of the glasses and emptied it. Ramballe emptied his too, again pressed Pierre's hand, and leaned his elbows on the table in a pensive attitude.

"Yes, my dear friend," he began, "such is fortune's caprice. Who would have said that I should be a soldier and a captain of dragoons in the service of Bonaparte, as we used to call him? Yet here I am in Moscow with him. I must tell you, *mon cher,*" he continued in the sad and measured tones of a man who intends to tell a long story, "that our name is one of the most ancient in France."

And with a Frenchman's easy and naïve frankness the captain told Pierre the story of his ancestors, his childhood, youth, and manhood, and all about his relations and his financial and family affairs, "*ma pauvre mère*" playing of course an important part in the story.

"But all that is only life's setting, the real thing is love—love! Am I not right, Monsieur Pierre?" said he, growing animated. "Another glass?"

Pierre again emptied his glass and poured himself out a third.

"Oh, women, women!" and the captain, looking with glistening eyes at Pierre, began talking of love and of his love affairs.

There were very many of these, as one could easily believe, looking at the officer's handsome, self-satisfied face, and noting the eager enthusiasm with which he spoke of women. Though all Ramballe's love stories had the sensual character which Frenchmen regard as the special charm and poetry of love, yet he told his story with such sincere conviction that he alone had experienced and known all the charm of love and he described women so alluringly that Pierre listened to him with curiosity.

It was plain that *l'amour* which the Frenchman was so fond of was not that low and simple kind that Pierre had once felt for his wife, nor was it the romantic love stimulated by himself that he experienced for Natásha. (Ramballe despised both these kinds of love equally: the one he considered the "love of clodhoppers" and the other the "love of simpletons.") *L'amour* which the Frenchman worshiped consisted principally in the unnaturalness of his relation to the woman and in a combination of incongruities giving the chief charm to the feeling.

Thus the captain touchingly recounted the story of his love for a fascinating marquise of thirty-five and at the same time for a charming, innocent child of seventeen, daughter of the bewitching marquise. The conflict of magnanimity between the mother and the daughter, ending in the mother's sacrificing herself and offering her daughter in marriage to her lover, even now agitated the captain, though it was the memory of

a distant past. Then he recounted an episode in which the husband played the part of the lover, and he—the lover—assumed the role of the husband, as well as several droll incidents from his recollections of Germany, where "shelter" is called *Unterkunft*, and where the husbands eat sauerkraut and the young girls are "too blonde."

Finally, the latest episode in Poland still fresh in the captain's memory, and which he narrated with rapid gestures and glowing face, was of how he had saved the life of a Pole (in general, the saving of life continually occurred in the captain's stories) and the Pole had entrusted to him his enchanting wife (*parisienne de cœur*) while himself entering the French service. The captain was happy, the enchanting Polish lady wished to elope with him, but, prompted by magnanimity, the captain restored the wife to the husband, saying as he did so: "I have saved your life, and I save your honor!" Having repeated these words the captain wiped his eyes and gave himself a shake, as if driving away the weakness which assailed him at this touching recollection.

Listening to the captain's tales, Pierre—as often happens late in the evening and under the influence of wine—followed all that was told him, understood it all, and at the same time followed a train of personal memories which, he knew not why, suddenly arose in his mind. While listening to these love stories his own love for Natásha unexpectedly rose to his mind, and going over the pictures of that love in his imagination he mentally compared them with Ramballe's tales. Listening to the story of the struggle between love and duty, Pierre saw before his eyes every minutest detail of his last meeting with the object of his love at the Súkharev water tower. At the time of that meeting it had not produced an effect upon him—he had not even once recalled it. But now it seemed to him that that meeting had had in it something very important and poetic.

"Peter Kirílovich, come here! We have recognized you," he now seemed to hear the words she had uttered and to see before him her eyes, her smile, her traveling hood, and a stray lock of her hair . . . and there seemed to him something pathetic and touching in all this.

Having finished his tale about the enchanting Polish lady, the captain asked Pierre if he had ever experienced a similar impulse to sacrifice himself for love and a feeling of envy of the legitimate husband.

Challenged by this question Pierre raised his head and felt a need to express the thoughts that filled his mind. He began to explain that he understood love for a woman somewhat differently. He said that in all his life he had loved and still loved only one woman, and that she could never be his.

"*Tiens!*" said the captain.

Pierre then explained that he had loved this woman from his earliest years, but that he had not dared to think of her because she was too young, and because he had been an illegitimate son without a name. Afterwards when he had received a name and wealth he dared not think of her because he loved her too well, placing her far above everything in the world, and especially therefore above himself.

When he had reached this point, Pierre asked the captain whether he understood that.

The captain made a gesture signifying that even if he did not understand it he begged Pierre to continue.

"Platonic love, clouds . . ." he muttered.

Whether it was the wine he had drunk, or an impulse of frankness, or the thought that this man did not, and never would, know any of those who played a part in his story, or whether it was all these things together, something loosened Pierre's tongue. Speaking thickly and with a far-away look in his shining eyes, he told the whole story of his life: his marriage, Natásha's love for his best friend, her betrayal of him, and all his own simple relations with her. Urged on by Ramballe's questions he also told what he had at first concealed—his own position and even his name.

More than anything else in Pierre's story the captain was impressed by the fact that Pierre was very rich, had two mansions in Moscow, and that he had abandoned everything and not left the city, but remained there concealing his name and station.

When it was late at night they went out together into the street. The night was warm and light. To the left of the house on the Pokróvka a fire glowed—the first of those that were beginning in Moscow. To the right and high up in the sky was the sickle of the waning moon and opposite to it hung that bright comet which was connected in Pierre's heart with his love. At the gate stood Gerásim, the cook, and two Frenchmen. Their laughter and their mutually incomprehensible remarks in two languages could be heard. They were looking at the glow seen in the town.

There was nothing terrible in the one small, distant fire in the immense city.

Gazing at the high starry sky, at the moon, at the comet, and at the glow from the fire, Pierre experienced a joyful emotion. "There now, how good it is, what more does one need?" thought he. And suddenly remembering his intention he grew dizzy and felt so faint that he leaned against the fence to save himself from falling.

Without taking leave of his new friend, Pierre left the gate with unsteady steps and returning to his room lay down on the sofa and immediately fell asleep.

15. The Rostóvs at Mytíshchi. Natásha sees Prince Andrew

THE GLOW of the first fire that began on the second of September was
watched from the various roads by the fugitive Muscovites and by
the retreating troops, with many different feelings.

The Rostóv party spent the night at Mytíshchi, fourteen miles from
Moscow. They had started so late on the first of September, the road
had been so blocked by vehicles and troops, so many things had been for-
gotten for which servants were sent back, that they had decided to spend
that night at a place three miles out of Moscow. The next morning they
woke late and were again delayed so often that they only got as far as
Great Mytíshchi. At ten o'clock that evening the Rostóv family and the
wounded traveling with them were all distributed in the yards and huts
of that large village. The Rostóvs' servants and coachmen and the orderlies
of the wounded officers, after attending to their masters, had supper, fed
the horses, and came out into the porches.

In a neighboring hut lay Raévski's adjutant with a fractured wrist. The
awful pain he suffered made him moan incessantly and piteously, and his
moaning sounded terrible in the darkness of the autumn night. He had
spent the first night in the same yard as the Rostóvs. The countess said
she had been unable to close her eyes on account of his moaning, and at
Mystíshchi she moved into a worse hut simply to be farther away from
the wounded man.

In the darkness of the night one of the servants noticed, above the
high body of a coach standing before the porch, the small glow of another
fire. One glow had long been visible and everybody knew that it was Little
Mytíshchi burning—set on fire by Mamónov's Cossacks.

"But look here, brothers, there's another fire!" remarked an orderly.

All turned their attention to the glow.

"But they told us Little Mytíshchi had been set on fire by Mamónov's
Cossacks."

"But that's not Mytíshchi, it's farther away."

"Look, it must be in Moscow!"

Two of the gazers went round to the other side of the coach and sat
down on its steps.

"It's more to the left, why, Little Mytíshchi is over there, and this is
right on the other side."

Several men joined the first two.

"See how it's flaring," said one. "That's a fire in Moscow: either in the
Sushchévski or the Rogózhski quarter."

No one replied to this remark and for some time they all gazed silently at the spreading flames of the second fire in the distance.

Old Daniel Teréntich, the count's valet (as he was called), came up to the group and shouted at Míshka.

"What are you staring at, you good-for-nothing? . . . The count will be calling and there's nobody there; go and gather the clothes together."

"I only ran out to get some water," said Míshka.

"But what do you think, Daniel Teréntich? Doesn't it look as if that glow were in Moscow?" remarked one of the footmen.

Daniel Teréntich made no reply, and again for a long time they were all silent. The glow spread, rising and falling, farther and farther still.

"God have mercy. . . . It's windy and dry . . ." said another voice.

"Just look! See what it's doing now. O Lord! You can even see the crows flying. Lord have mercy on us sinners!"

"They'll put it out, no fear!"

"Who's to put it out?" Daniel Teréntich, who had hitherto been silent, was heard to say. His voice was calm and deliberate. "Moscow it is, brothers," said he. "Mother Moscow, the white . . ." his voice faltered, and he gave way to an old man's sob.

And it was as if they had all only waited for this to realize the significance for them of the glow they were watching. Sighs were heard, words of prayer, and the sobbing of the count's old valet.

The valet, returning to the cottage, informed the count that Moscow was burning. The count donned his dressing gown and went out to look. Sónya and Madame Schoss, who had not yet undressed, went out with him. Only Natásha and the countess remained in the room. Pétya was no longer with the family, he had gone on with his regiment which was making for Tróitsa.*

The countess, on hearing that Moscow was on fire, began to cry. Natásha, pale, with a fixed look, was sitting on the bench under the icons just where she had sat down on arriving and paid no attention to her father's words. She was listening to the ceaseless moaning of the adjutant, three houses off.

"Oh, how terrible," said Sónya, returning from the yard chilled and frightened. "I believe the whole of Moscow will burn, there's an awful glow! Natásha, do look! You can see it from the window," she said to her cousin, evidently wishing to distract her mind.

But Natásha looked at her as if not understanding what was said to her

* *Tróitsa, where the famous Sergéevo-Tróitsky Monastery is situated, lies forty-four miles northeast of Moscow.*—A.M.

and again fixed her eyes on the corner of the stove. She had been in this condition of stupor since the morning, when Sónya, to the surprise and annoyance of the countess, had for some unaccountable reason found it necessary to tell Natásha of Prince Andrew's wound and of his being with their party.* The countess had seldom been so angry with anyone as she was with Sónya. Sónya had cried and begged to be forgiven and now, as if trying to atone for her fault, paid unceasing attention to her cousin.

"Look, Natásha, how dreadfully it is burning!" said she.

"What's burning?" asked Natásha. "Oh, yes, Moscow."

And as if in order not to offend Sónya and to get rid of her, she turned her face to the window, looked out in such a way that it was evident that she could not see anything, and again settled down in her former attitude.

"But you didn't see it!"

"Yes, really I did," Natásha replied in a voice that pleaded to be left in peace.

Both the countess and Sónya understood that, naturally, neither Moscow nor the burning of Moscow nor anything else could seem of importance to Natásha.

The count returned and lay down behind the partition. The countess went up to her daughter and touched her head with the back of her hand as she was wont to do when Natásha was ill, then touched her forehead with her lips as if to feel whether she was feverish, and finally kissed her.

"You are cold. You are trembling all over. You'd better lie down," said the countess.

"Lie down? All right, I will. I'll lie down at once," said Natásha.

When Natásha had been told that morning that Prince Andrew was seriously wounded and was traveling with their party, she had at first asked many questions: Where was he going? How was he wounded? Was it serious? And could she see him? But after she had been told that she could not see him, that he was seriously wounded but that his life was not in danger, she ceased to ask questions or to speak at all, evidently disbelieving what they told her, and convinced that say what she might she would still be told the same. All the way she had sat motionless in a corner of the coach with wide-open eyes, and the expression in them which the countess knew so well and feared so much, and now she sat in the same way on the bench where she had seated herself on arriving. She was planning something and either deciding or had already decided

* For reasons referred to in a footnote on p. 964 of this book, the reappearance of Prince Andrew was calculated to revive Sónya's hopes of marrying Nicholas.—A.M.

something in her mind. The countess knew this, but what it might be she did not know, and this alarmed and tormented her.

"Natásha, undress, darling; lie down on my bed."

A bed had been made on a bedstead for the countess only. Madame Schoss and the two girls were to sleep on some hay on the floor.

"No, Mamma, I will lie down here on the floor," Natásha replied irritably and she went to the window and opened it. Through the open window the moans of the adjutant could be heard more distinctly. She put her head out into the damp night air, and the countess saw her slim neck shaking with sobs and throbbing against the window frame. Natásha knew it was not Prince Andrew who was moaning. She knew Prince Andrew was in the same yard as themselves and in a part of the hut across the passage; but this dreadful incessant moaning made her sob. The countess exchanged a look with Sónya.

"Lie down, darling; lie down, my pet," said the countess, softly touching Natásha's shoulders. "Come, lie down."

"Oh, yes . . . I'll lie down at once," said Natásha, and began hurriedly undressing, tugging at the tapes of her petticoat.

When she had thrown off her dress and put on a dressing jacket, she sat down with her foot under her on the bed that had been made up on the floor, jerked her thin and rather short plait of hair to the front, and began replaiting it. Her long, thin, practiced fingers rapidly unplaited, replaited, and tied up her plait. Her head moved from side to side from habit, but her eyes, feverishly wide, looked fixedly before her. When her toilet for the night was finished she sank gently onto the sheet spread over the hay on the side nearest the door.

"Natásha, you'd better lie in the middle," said Sónya.

"I'll stay here," muttered Natásha. "Do lie down," she added crossly, and buried her face in the pillow.

The countess, Madame Schoss, and Sónya undressed hastily and lay down. The small lamp in front of the icons was the only light left in the room. But in the yard there was a light from the fire at Little Mytíshchi a mile and a half away, and through the night came the noise of people shouting at a tavern Mamónov's Cossacks had set up across the street, and the adjutant's unceasing moans could still be heard.

For a long time Natásha listened attentively to the sounds that reached her from inside and outside the room and did not move. First she heard her mother praying and sighing and the creaking of her bed under her, then Madame Schoss' familiar whistling snore and Sónya's gentle breathing. Then the countess called to Natásha. Natásha did not answer.

"I think she's asleep, Mamma," said Sónya softly.

After a short silence the countess spoke again but this time no one replied.

Soon after that Natásha heard her mother's even breathing. Natásha did not move, though her little bare foot, thrust out from under the quilt, was growing cold on the bare floor.

As if to celebrate a victory over everybody, a cricket chirped in a crack in the wall. A cock crowed far off and another replied near by. The shouting in the tavern had died down; only the moaning of the adjutant was heard. Natásha sat up.

"Sónya, are you asleep? Mamma?" she whispered.

No one replied. Natásha rose slowly and carefully, crossed herself, and stepped cautiously on the cold and dirty floor with her slim, supple, bare feet. The boards of the floor creaked. Stepping cautiously from one foot to the other she ran like a kitten the few steps to the door and grasped the cold door handle.

It seemed to her that something heavy was beating rhythmically against all the walls of the room: it was her own heart, sinking with alarm and terror and overflowing with love.

She opened the door and stepped across the threshold and onto the cold, damp earthen floor of the passage. The cold she felt refreshed her. With her bare feet she touched a sleeping man, stepped over him, and opened the door into the part of the hut where Prince Andrew lay. It was dark in there. In the farthest corner, on a bench beside a bed on which something was lying, stood a tallow candle with a long, thick, and smoldering wick.

From the moment she had been told that morning of Prince Andrew's wound and his presence there, Natásha had resolved to see him. She did not know why she had to, she knew the meeting would be painful, but felt the more convinced that it was necessary.

All day she had lived only in hope of seeing him that night. But now that the moment had come she was filled with dread of what she might see. How was he maimed? What was left of him? Was he like that incessant moaning of the adjutant's? Yes, he was altogether like that. In her imagination he was that terrible moaning personified. When she saw an indistinct shape in the corner, and mistook his knees raised under the quilt for his shoulders, she imagined a horrible body there, and stood still in terror. But an irresistible impulse drew her forward. She cautiously took one step and then another, and found herself in the middle of a small room containing baggage. Another man—Timókhin—was lying in a corner on the benches beneath the icons, and two others—the doctor and a valet—lay on the floor.

The valet sat up and whispered something. Timókhin, kept awake by the pain in his wounded leg, gazed with wide-open eyes at this strange apparition of a girl in a white chemise, dressing jacket, and nightcap. The valet's sleepy, frightened exclamation, "What do you want? What's the matter?" made Natásha approach more swiftly to what was lying in the corner. Horribly unlike a man as that body looked, she must see him. She passed the valet, the snuff fell from the candle wick, and she saw Prince Andrew clearly with his arms outside the quilt, and such as she had always seen him.

He was the same as ever, but the feverish color of his face, his glittering eyes rapturously turned toward her, and especially his neck, delicate as a child's, revealed by the turn-down collar of his shirt, gave him a peculiarly innocent, childlike look, such as she had never seen on him before. She went up to him and with a swift, flexible, youthful movement dropped on her knees.

He smiled and held out his hand to her.

SEVEN DAYS had passed since Prince Andrew found himself in the ambulance station on the field of Borodinó. His feverish state and the inflammation of his bowels, which were injured, were in the doctor's opinion sure to carry him off. But on the seventh day he ate with pleasure a piece of bread with some tea, and the doctor noticed that his temperature was lower. He had regained consciousness that morning. The first night after they left Moscow had been fairly warm and he had remained in the calèche, but at Mytíshchi the wounded man himself asked to be taken out and given some tea. The pain caused by his removal into the hut had made him groan aloud and again lose consciousness. When he had been placed on his camp bed he lay for a long time motionless with closed eyes. Then he opened them and whispered softly: "And the tea?" His remembering such a small detail of everyday life astonished the doctor. He felt Prince Andrew's pulse, and to his surprise and dissatisfaction found it had improved. He was dissatisfied because he knew by experience that if his patient did not die now, he would do so a little later with greater suffering. Timókhin, the red-nosed major of Prince Andrew's regiment, had joined him in Moscow and was being taken along with him, having been wounded in the leg at the battle of Borodinó. They were accompanied by a doctor, Prince Andrew's valet, his coachman, and two orderlies.

They gave Prince Andrew some tea. He drank it eagerly, looking with feverish eyes at the door in front of him as if trying to understand and remember something.

"I don't want any more. Is Timókhin here?" he asked.

Timókhin crept along the bench to him.

"I am here, your excellency."

"How's your wound?"

"Mine, sir? All right. But how about you?"

Prince Andrew again pondered as if trying to remember something.

"Couldn't one get a book?" he asked.

"What book?"

"The Gospels. I haven't one."

The doctor promised to procure it for him and began to ask how he was feeling. Prince Andrew answered all his questions reluctantly but reasonably, and then said he wanted a bolster placed under him as he was uncomfortable and in great pain. The doctor and valet lifted the cloak with which he was covered and, making wry faces at the noisome smell of mortifying flesh that came from the wound, began examining that dreadful place.* The doctor was very much displeased about something and made a change in the dressings, turning the wounded man over so that he groaned again and grew unconscious and delirious from the agony. He kept asking them to get him the book and put it under him.

"What trouble would it be to you?" he said. "I have not got one. Please get it for me and put it under me for a moment," he pleaded in a piteous voice.

The doctor went into the passage to wash his hands.

"You fellows have no conscience," said he to the valet who was pouring water over his hands. "For just one moment I didn't look after you . . . It's such pain, you know, that I wonder how he can bear it."

"By the Lord Jesus Christ, I thought we had put something under him!" said the valet.

The first time Prince Andrew understood where he was and what was the matter with him and remembered being wounded and how was when he asked to be carried into the hut after his *calèche* had stopped at Mytíshchi. After growing confused from pain while being carried into the hut he again regained consciousness, and while drinking tea once more recalled all that had happened to him, and above all vividly remembered the moment at the ambulance station when, at the sight of the suf-

* *The advance of science has added many terrors to war, but the introduction of antiseptic surgery has removed one of the worst horrors of former times. As A. Chékhov—a doctor as well as a writer—remarked: that an officer of Prince Andrew's position should suffer and die from gangrene which he, Chékhov, could have prevented, is a striking example of the deplorable state of medical knowledge in 1812.—A.M.*

ferings of a man he disliked, those new thoughts had come to him which promised him happiness. And those thoughts, though now vague and indefinite, again possessed his soul. He remembered that he had now a new source of happiness and that this happiness had something to do with the Gospels. That was why he asked for a copy of them. The uncomfortable position in which they had put him and turned him over again confused his thoughts, and when he came to himself a third time it was in the complete stillness of the night. Everybody near him was sleeping. A cricket chirped from across the passage; someone was shouting and singing in the street; cockroaches rustled on the table, on the icons, and on the walls, and a big fly flopped at the head of the bed and around the candle beside him, the wick of which was charred and had shaped itself like a mushroom.

His mind was not in a normal state. A healthy man usually thinks of, feels, and remembers innumerable things simultaneously, but has the power and will to select one sequence of thoughts or events on which to fix his whole attention. A healthy man can tear himself away from the deepest reflections to say a civil word to someone who comes in and can then return again to his own thoughts. But Prince Andrew's mind was not in a normal state in that respect. All the powers of his mind were more active and clearer than ever, but they acted apart from his will. Most diverse thoughts and images occupied him simultaneously. At times his brain suddenly began to work with a vigor, clearness, and depth it had never reached when he was in health, but suddenly in the midst of its work it would turn to some unexpected idea and he had not the strength to turn it back again.

"Yes, a new happiness was revealed to me of which man cannot be deprived," he thought as he lay in the semidarkness of the quiet hut, gazing fixedly before him with feverish, wide-open eyes. "A happiness lying beyond material forces, outside the material influences that act on man—a happiness of the soul alone, the happiness of loving. Every man can understand it, but to conceive it and enjoin it was possible only for God. But how did God enjoin that law? And why was the Son . . . ?"

And suddenly the sequence of these thoughts broke off, and Prince Andrew heard (without knowing whether it was a delusion or reality) a soft whispering voice incessantly and rhythmically repeating "piti-piti-piti," and then "ti-ti," and then again "piti-piti-piti," and "ti-ti" once more. At the same time he felt that above his face, above the very middle of it, some strange airy structure was being erected out of slender needles or splinters, to the sound of this whispered music. He felt that he had to balance carefully (though it was difficult) so that this airy structure

should not collapse; but nevertheless it kept collapsing and again slowly rising to the sound of whispered rhythmic music—"it stretches, stretches, spreading out and stretching," said Prince Andrew to himself. While listening to this whispering and feeling the sensation of this drawing out and the construction of this edifice of needles, he also saw by glimpses a red halo round the candle, and heard the rustle of the cockroaches and the buzzing of the fly that flopped against his pillow and his face. Each time the fly touched his face it gave him a burning sensation and yet to his surprise it did not destroy the structure, though it knocked against the very region of his face where it was rising. But besides this there was something else of importance. It was something white by the door—the statue of a sphinx, which also oppressed him.

"But perhaps that's my shirt on the table," he thought, "and that's my legs, and that is the door, but why is it always stretching and drawing itself out, and 'piti-piti-piti' and 'ti-ti' and 'piti-piti-piti' . . . ? That's enough, please leave off!" Prince Andrew painfully entreated someone. And suddenly thoughts and feelings again swam to the surface of his mind with peculiar clearness and force.

"Yes—love," he thought again quite clearly. "But not love which loves for something, for some quality, for some purpose, or for some reason, but the love which I—while dying—first experienced when I saw my enemy and yet loved him. I experienced that feeling of love which is the very essence of the soul and does not require an object. Now again I feel that bliss. To love one's neighbors, to love one's enemies, to love everything, to love God in all His manifestations. It is possible to love someone dear to you with human love, but an enemy can only be loved by divine love. That is why I experienced such joy when I felt that I loved that man. What has become of him? Is he alive? . . .

"When loving with human love one may pass from love to hatred, but divine love cannot change. No, neither death nor anything else can destroy it. It is the very essence of the soul. Yet how many people have I hated in my life? And of them all, I loved and hated none as I did her." And he vividly pictured to himself Natásha, not as he had done in the past with nothing but her charms which gave him delight, but for the first time picturing to himself her soul. And he understood her feelings, her sufferings, shame, and remorse. He now understood for the first time all the cruelty of his rejection of her, the cruelty of his rupture with her. "If only it were possible for me to see her once more! Just once, looking into those eyes to say . . ."

"Piti-piti-piti and ti-ti and piti-piti-piti boom!" flopped the fly. . . . And his attention was suddenly carried into another world, a world of

reality and delirium in which something particular was happening. In that world some structure was still being erected and did not fall, something was still stretching out, and the candle with its red halo was still burning, and the same shirtlike sphinx lay near the door; but besides all this something creaked, there was a whiff of fresh air, and a new white sphinx appeared, standing at the door. And that sphinx had the pale face and shining eyes of the very Natásha of whom he had just been thinking.

"Oh, how oppressive this continual delirium is," thought Prince Andrew, trying to drive that face from his imagination. But the face remained before him with the force of reality and drew nearer. Prince Andrew wished to return to that former world of pure thought, but he could not, and delirium drew him back into its domain. The soft whispering voice continued its rhythmic murmur, something oppressed him and stretched out, and the strange face was before him. Prince Andrew collected all his strength in an effort to recover his senses, he moved a little, and suddenly there was a ringing in his ears, a dimness in his eyes, and like a man plunged into water he lost consciousness. When he came to himself, Natásha, that same living Natásha whom of all people he most longed to love with this new pure divine love that had been revealed to him, was kneeling before him. He realized that it was the real living Natásha, and he was not surprised but quietly happy. Natásha, motionless on her knees (she was unable to stir), with frightened eyes riveted on him, was restraining her sobs. Her face was pale and rigid. Only in the lower part of it something quivered.

Prince Andrew sighed with relief, smiled, and held out his hand.

"You?" he said. "How fortunate!"

With a rapid but careful movement Natásha drew nearer to him on her knees and, taking his hand carefully, bent her face over it and began kissing it, just touching it lightly with her lips.

"Forgive me!" she whispered, raising her head and glancing at him. "Forgive me!"

"I love you," said Prince Andrew.

"Forgive . . . !"

"Forgive what?" he asked.

"Forgive me for what I ha-ve do-ne!" faltered Natásha in a scarcely audible, broken whisper, and began kissing his hand more rapidly, just touching it with her lips.

"I love you more, better than before," said Prince Andrew, lifting her face with his hand so as to look into her eyes.

Those eyes, filled with happy tears, gazed at him timidly, compassionately, and with joyous love. Natásha's thin pale face, with its swollen

lips, was more than plain—it was dreadful. But Prince Andrew did not see that, he saw her shining eyes which were beautiful. They heard the sound of voices behind them.

Peter the valet, who was now wide awake, had roused the doctor. Timókhin, who had not slept at all because of the pain in his leg, had long been watching all that was going on, carefully covering his bare body with the sheet as he huddled up on his bench.

"What's this?" said the doctor, rising from his bed. "Please go away, madam!"

At that moment a maid sent by the countess, who had noticed her daughter's absence, knocked at the door.

Like a somnambulist aroused from her sleep Natásha went out of the room and, returning to her hut, fell sobbing on her bed.

From that time, during all the rest of the Rostóvs' journey, at every halting place and wherever they spent a night, Natásha never left the wounded Bolkónski, and the doctor had to admit that he had not expected from a young girl either such firmness or such skill in nursing a wounded man.

Dreadful as the countess imagined it would be should Prince Andrew die in her daughter's arms during the journey—as, judging by what the doctor said, it seemed might easily happen—she could not oppose Natásha. Though with the intimacy now established between the wounded man and Natásha the thought occurred that should he recover their former engagement would be renewed, no one—least of all Natásha and Prince Andrew—spoke of this: the unsettled question of life and death, which hung not only over Bolkónski but over all Russia, shut out all other considerations.

16. Pierre sets out to meet Napoleon. He saves a child, defends an Armenian girl from a French soldier, and is arrested as an incendiary

ON THE THIRD OF SEPTEMBER Pierre awoke late. His head was aching, the clothes in which he had slept without undressing felt uncomfortable on his body, and his mind had a dim consciousness of something shameful he had done the day before. That something shameful was his yesterday's conversation with Captain Ramballe.

It was eleven by the clock, but it seemed peculiarly dark out of doors. Pierre rose, rubbed his eyes, and seeing the pistol with an engraved stock

which Gerásim had replaced on the writing table, he remembered where he was and what lay before him that very day.

"Am I not too late?" he thought. "No, probably he won't make his entry into Moscow before noon."

Pierre did not allow himself to reflect on what lay before him, but hastened to act.

After arranging his clothes, he took the pistol and was about to go out. But it then occurred to him for the first time that he certainly could not carry the weapon in his hand through the streets. It was difficult to hide such a big pistol even under his wide coat. He could not carry it unnoticed in his belt or under his arm. Besides, it had been discharged, and he had not had time to reload it. "No matter, the dagger will do," he said to himself, though when planning his design he had more than once come to the conclusion that the chief mistake made by the student in 1809 had been to try to kill Napoleon with a dagger. But as his chief aim consisted not in carrying out his design, but in proving to himself that he would not abandon his intention and was doing all he could to achieve it, Pierre hastily took the blunt jagged dagger in a green sheath which he had bought at the Súkharev market with the pistol, and hid it under his waistcoat.

Having tied a girdle over his coat and pulled his cap low on his head, Pierre went down the corridor, trying to avoid making a noise or meeting the captain, and passed out into the street.

The conflagration, at which he had looked with so much indifference the evening before, had greatly increased during the night. Moscow was on fire in several places. The buildings in Carriage Row, across the river, in the Bazaar and the Povarskóy, as well as the barges on the Moskvá River and the timber yards by the Dorogomílov Bridge, were all ablaze.

Pierre's way led through side streets to the Povarskóy and from there to the church of St. Nicholas on the Arbát, where he had long before decided that the deed should be done. The gates of most of the houses were locked and the shutters up. The streets and lanes were deserted. The air was full of smoke and the smell of burning. Now and then he met Russians with anxious and timid faces, and Frenchmen with an air not of the city but of the camp, walking in the middle of the streets. Both the Russians and the French looked at Pierre with surprise. Besides his height and stoutness, and the strange morose look of suffering in his face and whole figure, the Russians stared at him because they could not make out to what class he could belong. The French followed him with astonishment in their eyes chiefly because Pierre, unlike all the other Russians who gazed at the French with fear and curiosity, paid no attention to

them. At the gate of one house three Frenchmen, who were explaining something to some Russians who did not understand them, stopped Pierre asking if he did not know French.

Pierre shook his head and went on. In another side street a sentinel standing beside a green caisson shouted at him, but only when the shout was threateningly repeated and he heard the click of the man's musket as he raised it did Pierre understand that he had to pass on the other side of the street. He heard nothing and saw nothing of what went on around him. He carried his resolution within himself in terror and haste, like something dreadful and alien to him, for, after the previous night's experience, he was afraid of losing it. But he was not destined to bring his mood safely to his destination. And even had he not been hindered by anything on the way, his intention could not now have been carried out, for Napoleon had passed the Arbát more than four hours previously on his way from the Dorogomílov suburb to the Krémlin, and was now sitting in a very gloomy frame of mind in a royal study in the Krémlin, giving detailed and exact orders as to measures to be taken immediately to extinguish the fire, to prevent looting, and to reassure the inhabitants. But Pierre did not know this; he was entirely absorbed in what lay before him, and was tortured— as those are who obstinately undertake a task that is impossible for them not because of its difficulty but because of its incompatibility with their natures—by the fear of weakening at the decisive moment and so losing his self-esteem.

Though he heard and saw nothing around him he found his way by instinct and did not go wrong in the side streets that led to the Povarskóy.

As Pierre approached that street the smoke became denser and denser— he even felt the heat of the fire. Occasionally curly tongues of flame rose from under the roofs of the houses. He met more people in the streets and they were more excited. But Pierre, though he felt that something unusual was happening around him, did not realize that he was approaching the fire. As he was going along a footpath across a wide-open space adjoining the Povarskóy on one side and the gardens of Prince Gruzínski's house on the other, Pierre suddenly heard the desperate weeping of a woman close to him. He stopped as if awakening from a dream and lifted his head.

By the side of the path, on the dusty dry grass, all sorts of household goods lay in a heap: feather beds, a samovar, icons, and trunks. On the ground, beside the trunks, sat a thin woman no longer young, with long, prominent upper teeth, and wearing a black cloak and cap. This woman, swaying to and fro and muttering something, was choking with sobs. Two girls of about ten and twelve, dressed in dirty short frocks and cloaks, were staring at their mother with a look of stupefaction on their pale frightened

faces. The youngest child, a boy of about seven, who wore an overcoat and an immense cap evidently not his own, was crying in his old nurse's arms. A dirty, barefooted maid was sitting on a trunk, and, having undone her pale-colored plait, was pulling it straight and sniffing at her singed hair. The woman's husband, a short, round-shouldered man in the undress uniform of a civilian official, with sausage-shaped whiskers and showing under his square-set cap the hair smoothly brushed forward over his temples, with expressionless face was moving the trunks, which were placed one on another, and was dragging some garments from under them.

As soon as she saw Pierre, the woman almost threw herself at his feet.

"Dear people, good Christians, save me, help me, dear friends . . . help us, somebody," she muttered between her sobs. "My girl . . . My daughter! My youngest daughter is left behind. She's burned! Ooh! Was it for this I nursed you. . . . Ooh!"

"Don't, Mary Nikoláevna!" said her husband to her in a low voice, evidently only to justify himself before the stranger. "Sister must have taken her, or else where can she be?" he added.

"Monster! Villain!" shouted the woman angrily, suddenly ceasing to weep. "You have no heart, you don't feel for your own child! Another man would have rescued her from the fire. But this is a monster and neither a man nor a father! You, honored sir, are a noble man," she went on, addressing Pierre rapidly between her sobs. "The fire broke out alongside, and blew our way, the maid called out 'Fire!' and we rushed to collect our things. We ran out just as we were. . . . This is what we have brought away. . . . The icons, and my dowry bed, all the rest is lost. We seized the children. But not Katie! Ooh! O Lord! . . ." and again she began to sob. "My child, my dear one! Burned, burned!"

"But where was she left?" asked Pierre.

From the expression of his animated face the woman saw that this man might help her.

"Oh, dear sir!" she cried, seizing him by the legs. "My benefactor, set my heart at ease. . . . Aníska, go, you horrid girl, show him the way!" she cried to the maid, angrily opening her mouth and still farther exposing her long teeth.

"Show me the way, show me, I . . . I'll do it," gasped Pierre rapidly.

The dirty maidservant stepped from behind the trunk, put up her plait, sighed, and went on her short, bare feet along the path. Pierre felt as if he had come back to life after a heavy swoon. He held his head higher, his eyes shone with the light of life, and with swift steps he followed the maid, overtook her, and came out on the Povarskóy. The whole street was full of clouds of black smoke. Tongues of flame here and there broke through

that cloud. A great number of people crowded in front of the conflagration. In the middle of the street stood a French general saying something to those around him. Pierre, accompanied by the maid, was advancing to the spot where the general stood, but the French soldiers stopped him.

"*On ne passe pas* [You can't pass]!" cried a voice.

"This way, uncle," cried the girl. "We'll pass through the side street, by the Nikúlins'!"

Pierre turned back, giving a spring now and then to keep up with her. She ran across the street, turned down a side street to the left, and, passing three houses, turned into a yard on the right.

"It's here, close by," said she and, running across the yard, opened a gate in a wooden fence and, stopping, pointed out to him a small wooden wing of the house, which was burning brightly and fiercely. One of its sides had fallen in, another was on fire, and bright flames issued from the openings of the windows and from under the roof.

As Pierre passed through the fence gate, he was enveloped by hot air and involuntarily stopped.

"Which is it? Which is your house?" he asked.

"Ooh!" wailed the girl, pointing to the wing. "That's it, that was our lodging. You've burned to death, our treasure, Katie, my precious little missy! Ooh!" lamented Aníska, who at the sight of the fire felt that she too must give expression to her feelings.

Pierre rushed to the wing, but the heat was so great that he involuntarily passed round in a curve and came upon the large house that was as yet burning only at one end, just below the roof, and around which swarmed a crowd of Frenchmen. At first Pierre did not realize what these men, who were dragging something out, were about; but seeing before him a Frenchman hitting a peasant with a blunt saber and trying to take from him a fox-fur coat, he vaguely understood that looting was going on there, but he had no time to dwell on that idea.

The sounds of crackling and the din of falling walls and ceilings, the whistle and hiss of the flames, the excited shouts of the people, and the sight of the swaying smoke, now gathering into thick black clouds and now soaring up with glittering sparks, with here and there dense sheaves of flame (now red and now like golden fish scales creeping along the walls), and the heat and smoke and rapidity of motion, produced on Pierre the usual animating effects of a conflagration. It had a peculiarly strong effect on him because at the sight of the fire he felt himself suddenly freed from the ideas that had weighed him down. He felt young, bright, adroit, and resolute. He ran round to the other side of the lodge and was about to dash into that part of it which was still standing, when just above his head he

heard several voices shouting and then a cracking sound and the ring of
something heavy falling close beside him.

Pierre looked up and saw at a window of the large house some French-
men who had just thrown out the drawer of a chest, filled with metal
articles. Other French soldiers standing below went up to the drawer.

"What does this fellow want?" shouted one of them referring to Pierre.

"There's a child in that house. Haven't you seen a child?" cried Pierre.

"What's he talking about? Get along!" said several voices, and one of
the soldiers, evidently afraid that Pierre might want to take from them
some of the plate and bronzes that were in the drawer, moved threaten-
ingly toward him.

"A child?" shouted a Frenchman from above. "I did hear something
squealing in the garden. Perhaps it's his brat that the fellow is looking for.
After all, one must be human, you know. . . ."

"Where is it? Where?" said Pierre.

"There! There!" shouted the Frenchman at the window, pointing to
the garden at the back of the house. "Wait a bit—I'm coming down."

And a minute or two later the Frenchman, a black-eyed fellow with a
spot on his cheek, in shirt sleeves, really did jump out of a window on the
ground floor, and clapping Pierre on the shoulder ran with him into the
garden.

"Hurry up, you others!" he called out to his comrades. "It's getting hot."

When they reached a gravel path behind the house the Frenchman
pulled Pierre by the arm and pointed to a round, graveled space where a
three-year-old girl in a pink dress was lying under a seat.

"There is your child! Oh, a girl, so much the better!" said the French-
man. "Good-by, Fatty. We must be human, we are all mortal you know!"
and the Frenchman with the spot on his cheek ran back to his comrades.

Breathless with joy, Pierre ran to the little girl and was going to take her
in his arms. But seeing a stranger the sickly, scrofulous-looking child, un-
attractively like her mother, began to yell and run away. Pierre, however,
seized her and lifted her in his arms. She screamed desperately and angrily
and tried with her little hands to pull Pierre's hands away and to bite them
with her slobbering mouth. Pierre was seized by a sense of horror and
repulsion such as he had experienced when touching some nasty little ani-
mal. But he made an effort not to throw the child down and ran with her
to the large house. It was now, however, impossible to get back the way
he had come; the maid, Aníska, was no longer there, and Pierre with a
feeling of pity and disgust pressed the wet, painfully sobbing child to him-
self as tenderly as he could and ran with her through the garden seeking
another way out.

HAVING RUN through different yards and side streets, Pierre got back with his little burden to the Gruzínski garden at the corner of the Povarskóy. He did not at first recognize the place from which he had set out to look for the child, so crowded was it now with people and goods that had been dragged out of the houses. Besides Russian families who had taken refuge here from the fire with their belongings, there were several French soldiers in a variety of clothing. Pierre took no notice of them. He hurried to find the family of that civil servant in order to restore the daughter to her mother and go to save someone else. Pierre felt that he had still much to do and to do quickly. Glowing with the heat and from running, he felt at that moment more strongly than ever the sense of youth, animation, and determination that had come on him when he ran to save the child. She had now become quiet and, clinging with her little hands to Pierre's coat, sat on his arm gazing about her like some little wild animal. He glanced at her occasionally with a slight smile. He fancied he saw something pathetically innocent in that frightened, sickly little face.

He did not find the civil servant or his wife where he had left them. He walked among the crowd with rapid steps, scanning the various faces he met. Involuntarily he noticed a Georgian or Armenian family consisting of a very handsome old man of Oriental type, wearing a new, cloth-covered, sheepskin coat and new boots, an old woman of similar type, and a young woman. That very young woman seemed to Pierre the perfection of Oriental beauty, with her sharply outlined, arched, black eyebrows and the extraordinarily soft, bright color of her long, beautiful, expressionless face. Amid the scattered property and the crowd on the open space, she, in her rich satin cloak with a bright lilac shawl on her head, suggested a delicate exotic plant thrown out onto the snow. She was sitting on some bundles a little behind the old woman, and looked from under her long lashes with motionless, large, almond-shaped eyes at the ground before her. Evidently she was aware of her beauty and fearful because of it. Her face struck Pierre and, hurrying along by the fence, he turned several times to look at her. When he had reached the fence, still without finding those he sought, he stopped and looked about him.

With the child in his arms his figure was now more conspicuous than before, and a group of Russians, both men and women, gathered about him.

"Have you lost anyone, my dear fellow? You're of the gentry yourself, aren't you? Whose child is it?" they asked him.

Pierre replied that the child belonged to a woman in a black cloak who had been sitting there with her other children, and he asked whether anyone knew where she had gone.

"Why, that must be the Anférovs," said an old deacon, addressing a pockmarked peasant woman. "Lord have mercy, Lord have mercy!" he added in his customary bass.

"The Anférovs? No," said the woman. "They left in the morning. That must be either Mary Nikoláevna's or the Ivánovs'!"

"He says 'a woman,' and Mary Nikoláevna is a lady," remarked a house serf.

"Do you know her? She's thin, with long teeth," said Pierre.

"That's Mary Nikoláevna! They went inside the garden when these wolves swooped down," said the woman, pointing to the French soldiers.

"O Lord, have mercy!" added the deacon.

"Go over that way, they're there. It's she! She kept on lamenting and crying," continued the woman. "It's she. Here, this way!"

But Pierre was not listening to the woman. He had for some seconds been intently watching what was going on a few steps away. He was looking at the Armenian family and at two French soldiers who had gone up to them. One of these, a nimble little man, was wearing a blue coat tied round the waist with a rope. He had a nightcap on his head and his feet were bare. The other, whose appearance particularly struck Pierre, was a long, lank, round-shouldered, fair-haired man, slow in his movements and with an idiotic expression of face. He wore a woman's loose gown of frieze, blue trousers, and large torn Hessian boots. The little barefooted Frenchman in the blue coat went up to the Armenians and, saying something, immediately seized the old man by his legs and the old man at once began pulling off his boots. The other in the frieze gown stopped in front of the beautiful Armenian girl and with his hands in his pockets stood staring at her, motionless and silent.

"Here, take the child!" said Pierre peremptorily and hurriedly to the woman, handing the little girl to her. "Give her back to them, give her back!" he almost shouted, putting the child, who began screaming, on the ground, and again looking at the Frenchman and the Armenian family.

The old man was already sitting barefoot. The little Frenchman had secured his second boot and was slapping one boot against the other. The old man was saying something in a voice broken by sobs, but Pierre caught but a glimpse of this, his whole attention was directed to the Frenchman in the frieze gown who meanwhile, swaying slowly from side to side, had drawn nearer to the young woman and taking his hands from his pockets had seized her by the neck.

The beautiful Armenian still sat motionless and in the same attitude, with her long lashes drooping as if she did not see or feel what the soldier was doing to her.

While Pierre was running the few steps that separated him from the Frenchman, the tall marauder in the frieze gown was already tearing from her neck the necklace the young Armenian was wearing, and the young woman, clutching at her neck, screamed piercingly.

"Let that woman alone!" exclaimed Pierre hoarsely in a furious voice, seizing the soldier by his round shoulders and throwing him aside.

The soldier fell, got up, and ran away. But his comrade, throwing down the boots and drawing his sword, moved threateningly toward Pierre.

"Voyons, pas de bêtises [Look here, no nonsense]!" he cried.

Pierre was in such a transport of rage that he remembered nothing and his strength increased tenfold. He rushed at the barefooted Frenchman and, before the latter had time to draw his sword, knocked him off his feet and hammered him with his fists. Shouts of approval were heard from the crowd around, and at the same moment a mounted patrol of French Uhlans appeared from round the corner. The Uhlans came up at a trot to Pierre and the Frenchman and surrounded them. Pierre remembered nothing of what happened after that. He only remembered beating someone and being beaten and finally feeling that his hands were bound and that a crowd of French soldiers stood around him and were searching him.

"Lieutenant, he has a dagger," were the first words Pierre understood.

"Ah, a weapon?" said the officer and turned to the barefooted soldier who had been arrested with Pierre. "All right, you can tell all about it at the court-martial." Then he turned to Pierre. "Do you speak French?"

Pierre looked around him with bloodshot eyes and did not reply. His face probably looked very terrible, for the officer said something in a whisper and four more Uhlans left the ranks and placed themselves on both sides of Pierre.

"Do you speak French?" the officer asked again, keeping at a distance from Pierre. "Call the interpreter."

A little man in Russian civilian clothes rode out from the ranks, and by his clothes and manner of speaking Pierre at once knew him to be a French salesman from one of the Moscow shops.

"He does not look like a common man," said the interpreter, after a searching look at Pierre.

"Ah, he looks very much like an incendiary," remarked the officer. "And ask him who he is," he added.

"Who are you?" asked the interpreter in poor Russian. "You must answer the chief."

"I will not tell you who I am. I am your prisoner—take me!" Pierre suddenly replied in French.

"Ah, ah!" muttered the officer with a frown. "Well then, march!"

A crowd had collected round the Uhlans. Nearest to Pierre stood the pockmarked peasant woman with the little girl, and when the patrol started she moved forward.

"Where are they taking you to, you poor dear?" said she. "And the little girl, the little girl, what am I to do with her if she's not theirs?" said the woman.

"What does that woman want?" asked the officer.

Pierre was as if intoxicated. His elation increased at the sight of the little girl he had saved.

"What does she want?" he murmured. "She is bringing me my daughter whom I have just saved from the flames," said he. "Good-by!" And without knowing how this aimless lie had escaped him, he went along with resolute and triumphant steps between the French soldiers.

The French patrol was one of those sent out through the various streets of Moscow by Durosnel's order to put a stop to the pillage, and especially to catch the incendiaries who, according to the general opinion which had that day originated among the higher French officers, were the cause of the conflagrations. After marching through a number of streets the patrol arrested five more Russian suspects: a small shopkeeper, two seminary students, a peasant, and a house serf, besides several looters. But of all these various suspected characters, Pierre was considered to be the most suspicious of all. When they had all been brought for the night to a large house on the Zúbov Rampart that was being used as a guardhouse, Pierre was placed apart under strict guard.

BOOK TWELVE

1812

1. *Anna Pávlovna's soiree. Talk of Hélène's illness. The Bishop's letter. Victory at Borodinó reported. Death of Hélène. News of abandonment of Moscow. Michaud's report*

IN PETERSBURG at that time a complicated struggle was being carried on with greater heat than ever in the highest circles, between the parties of Rumyántsev, the French, Márya Fëdorovna, the Tsarévich, and others, drowned as usual by the buzzing of the court drones. But the calm, luxurious life of Petersburg, concerned only about phantoms and reflections of real life, went on in its old way and made it hard, except by a great effort, to realize the danger and the difficult position of the Russian people. There were the same receptions and balls, the same French theater, the same court interests and service interests and intrigues as usual. Only in the very highest circles were attempts made to keep in mind the difficulties of the actual position. Stories were whispered of how differently the two Empresses * behaved in these difficult circumstances. The Empress Márya, concerned for the welfare of the charitable and educational institutions under her patronage, had given directions that they should all be removed to Kazán, and the things belonging to these institutions had already been packed up. The Empress Elisabeth, however, when asked what instructions she would be pleased to give—with her characteristic Russian patriotism had replied that she could give no directions about state institutions for that was the affair of the sovereign, but as far as she personally was concerned she would be the last to quit Petersburg.

At Anna Pávlovna's on the twenty-sixth of August, the very day of the battle of Borodinó, there was a soiree, the chief feature of which was to be the reading of a letter from His Lordship the Bishop when sending the

* *The Dowager Empress Márya Fëdorovna, widow of Paul, and the Empress Elisabeth Alexéevna, wife of Alexander I, who had been a princess of Baden and developed her "Russian patriotism" after her marriage.*—A.M.

Emperor an icon of the Venerable Sergius. It was regarded as a model of ecclesiastical, patriotic eloquence. Prince Vasíli himself, famed for his elocution, was to read it. (He used to read at the Empress'.) The art of his reading was supposed to lie in rolling out the words, quite independently of their meaning, in a loud and singsong voice alternating between a despairing wail and a tender murmur, so that the wail fell quite at random on one word and the murmur on another. This reading, as was always the case at Anna Pávlovna's soirees, had a political significance. That evening she expected several important personages who had to be made ashamed of their visits to the French theater and aroused to a patriotic temper. A good many people had already arrived, but Anna Pávlovna, not yet seeing all those whom she wanted in her drawing room, did not let the reading begin but wound up the springs of a general conversation.

The news of the day in Petersburg was the illness of Countess Bezúkhova. She had fallen ill unexpectedly a few days previously, had missed several gatherings of which she was usually the ornament, and was said to be receiving no one, and instead of the celebrated Petersburg doctors who usually attended her had entrusted herself to some Italian doctor who was treating her in some new and unusual way.

They all knew very well that the enchanting countess' illness arose from an inconvenience resulting from marrying two husbands at the same time, and that the Italian's cure consisted in removing such inconvenience; but in Anna Pávlovna's presence no one dared to think of this or even appear to know it.

"They say the poor countess is very ill. The doctor says it is angina pectoris."

"Angina? Oh, that's a terrible illness!"

"They say that the rivals are reconciled, thanks to the angina . . ." and the word *angina* was repeated with great satisfaction.

"The old count is pathetic, they say. He cried like a child when the doctor told him the case was dangerous."

"Oh, it would be a terrible loss, she is an enchanting woman."

"You are speaking of the poor countess?" said Anna Pávlovna, coming up just then. "I sent to ask for news, and hear that she is a little better. Oh, she is certainly the most charming woman in the world," she went on, with a smile at her own enthusiasm. "We belong to different camps, but that does not prevent my esteeming her as she deserves. She is very unfortunate!" added Anna Pávlovna.

Supposing that by these words Anna Pávlovna was somewhat lifting the veil from the secret of the countess' malady, an unwary young man ventured to express surprise that well-known doctors had not been called in

and that the countess was being attended by a charlatan who might employ dangerous remedies.

"Your information may be better than mine," Anna Pávlovna suddenly and venomously retorted on the inexperienced young man, "but I know on good authority that this doctor is a very learned and able man. He is private physician to the Queen of Spain."

And having thus demolished the young man, Anna Pávlovna turned to another group where Bilíbin was talking about the Austrians: having wrinkled up his face he was evidently preparing to smooth it out again and utter one of his mots.

"I think it is delightful," he said, referring to a diplomatic note that had been sent to Vienna with some Austrian banners captured from the French by Wittgenstein,* "the hero of Petropol" as he was then called in Petersburg.

"What? What's that?" asked Anna Pávlovna, securing silence for the mot, which she had heard before.

And Bilíbin repeated the actual words of the diplomatic dispatch, which he had himself composed.

"The Emperor returns these Austrian banners," said Bilíbin, "friendly banners gone astray and found on a wrong path," and his brow became smooth again.

"Charming, charming!" observed Prince Vasíli.

"The path to Warsaw, perhaps," Prince Hippolyte remarked loudly and unexpectedly. Everybody looked at him, not understanding what he meant. Prince Hippolyte himself glanced around with amused surprise. He knew no more than the others what his words meant. During his diplomatic career he had more than once noticed that such utterances were received as very witty, and at every opportunity he uttered in that way the first words that entered his head. "It may turn out very well," he thought, "but if not, they'll know how to arrange matters." And really, during the awkward silence that ensued, that insufficiently patriotic person entered whom Anna Pávlovna had been waiting for and wished to convert, and she, smiling and shaking a finger at Hippolyte, invited Prince Vasíli to the table and bringing him two candles and the manuscript begged him to begin. Everyone became silent.

"Most Gracious Sovereign and Emperor!" Prince Vasíli sternly de-

* These were taken at Klyastítsy, in a successful action on the eighteenth and nineteenth of June against a French corps under Oudinot. The point of the dispatch (with its scriptural phrase from 2 Peter ii, 15) lies in its allusion to the recent alliance of Russia with Austria, whose troops were now fighting on Napoleon's side.—A.M.

claimed, looking round at his audience as if to inquire whether anyone had anything to say to the contrary. But no one said anything. "Moscow, our ancient capital, the New Jerusalem, receives her Christ"—he placed a sudden emphasis on the word *her*—"as a mother receives her zealous sons into her arms, and through the gathering mists, foreseeing the brilliant glory of thy rule, sings in exultation, 'Hosanna, blessed is he that cometh!' "

Prince Vasíli pronounced these last words in a tearful voice.

Bilíbin attentively examined his nails, and many of those present appeared intimidated, as if asking in what they were to blame. Anna Pávlovna whispered the next words in advance, like an old woman muttering the prayer at Communion: "Let the bold and insolent Goliath . . ." she whispered.

Prince Vasíli continued.

"Let the bold and insolent Goliath from the borders of France encompass the realms of Russia with death-bearing terrors; humble Faith, the sling of the Russian David, shall suddenly smite his head in his bloodthirsty pride. This icon of the Venerable Sergius, the servant of God and zealous champion of old of our country's weal, is offered to Your Imperial Majesty. I grieve that my waning strength prevents my rejoicing in the sight of your most gracious presence. I raise fervent prayers to Heaven that the Almighty may exalt the race of the just, and mercifully fulfill the desires of Your Majesty."

"What force! What a style!" was uttered in approval both of reader and of author.

Animated by that address Anna Pávlovna's guests talked for a long time of the state of the fatherland and offered various conjectures as to the result of the battle to be fought in a few days.

"You will see," said Anna Pávlovna, "that tomorrow, on the Emperor's birthday, we shall receive news. I have a favorable presentiment!"

Anna Pávlovna's presentiment was in fact fulfilled. Next day during the service at the palace church in honor of the Emperor's birthday, Prince Volkónski was called out of the church and received a dispatch from Prince Kutúzov. It was Kutúzov's report, written from Tatárinova on the day of the battle.* Kutúzov wrote that the Russians had not retreated a

* *We have here one of the rare instances of Tolstóy's going astray in his dates. Kutúzov's report from Tatárinova was sent off by him on August 25, after the action at the Shevárdino Redoubt, which was fought on August 24. It could not contain news of the death of Bagratión, Tuchkóv, and Kutáysov, who fell on the twenty-sixth, nor could news of the battle of Borodinó possibly reach Petersburg on the morning of the twenty-seventh: finally Tolstóy con-*

step, that the French losses were much heavier than ours, and that he was writing in haste from the field of battle before collecting full information. It followed that there must have been a victory. And at once, without leaving the church, thanks were rendered to the Creator for His help and for the victory.

Anna Pávlovna's presentiment was justified, and all that morning a joyously festive mood reigned in the city. Everyone believed the victory to have been complete, and some even spoke of Napoleon's having been captured, of his deposition, and of the choice of a new ruler for France.

It is very difficult for events to be reflected in their real strength and completeness amid the conditions of court life and far from the scene of action. General events involuntarily group themselves around some particular incident. So now the courtiers' pleasure was based as much on the fact that the news had arrived on the Emperor's birthday as on the fact of the victory itself. It was like a successfully arranged surprise. Mention was made in Kutúzov's report of the Russian losses, among which figured the names of Tuchkóv, Bagratión, and Kutáysov. In the Petersburg world this sad side of the affair again involuntarily centered round a single incident: Kutáysov's death. Everybody knew him, the Emperor liked him, and he was young and interesting. That day everyone met with the words:

"What a wonderful coincidence! Just during the service. But what a loss Kutáysov is! How sorry I am!"

"What did I tell you about Kutúzov?" Prince Vasíli now said with a prophet's pride. "I always said he was the only man capable of defeating Napoleon."

But next day no news arrived from the army and the public mood grew anxious. The courtiers suffered because of the suffering the suspense occasioned the Emperor.

"Fancy the Emperor's position!" said they, and instead of extolling Kutúzov as they had done the day before, they condemned him as the cause of the Emperor's anxiety. That day Prince Vasíli no longer boasted of his protégé Kutúzov, but remained silent when the commander in chief was mentioned. Moreover, toward evening, as if everything conspired to make Petersburg society anxious and uneasy, a terrible piece of news was added. Countess Hélène Bezúkhova had suddenly died of that terrible

fuses Alexander's birthday (December 12) with his name day, which is here in question and was on August 30. This slip would be corrected if Anna Pávlovna's soiree were put on August 29, for Kutúzov's report was really received on the thirtieth during a church service held in honor of the Tsar's name day.—A.M.

malady it had been so agreeable to mention. Officially, at large gatherings, everyone said that Countess Bezúkhova had died of a terrible attack of angina pectoris, but in intimate circles details were mentioned of how the private physician of the Queen of Spain had prescribed small doses of a certain drug to produce a certain effect; but Hélène, tortured by the fact that the old count suspected her and that her husband to whom she had written (that wretched, profligate Pierre) had not replied, had suddenly taken a very large dose of the drug, and had died in agony before assistance could be rendered her. It was said that Prince Vasíli and the old count had turned upon the Italian, but the latter had produced such letters from the unfortunate deceased that they had immediately let the matter drop.

Talk in general centered round three melancholy facts: the Emperor's lack of news, the loss of Kutáysov, and the death of Hélène.

On the third day after Kutúzov's report a country gentleman arrived from Moscow, and news of the surrender of Moscow to the French spread through the whole town.* This was terrible! What a position for the Emperor to be in! Kutúzov was a traitor, and Prince Vasíli during the visits of condolence paid to him on the occasion of his daughter's death said of Kutúzov, whom he had formerly praised (it was excusable for him in his grief to forget what he had said), that it was impossible to expect anything else from a blind and depraved old man.

"I only wonder that the fate of Russia could have been entrusted to such a man."

As long as this news remained unofficial it was possible to doubt it, but the next day the following communication was received from Count Rostopchín:

"Prince Kutúzov's adjutant has brought me a letter in which he demands police officers to guide the army to the Ryazán road. He writes that he is regretfully abandoning Moscow. Sire! Kutúzov's action decides the fate of the capital and of your empire! Russia will shudder to learn of the abandonment of the city in which her greatness is centered and in which lie the ashes of your ancestors! I shall follow the army. I have had everything removed, and it only remains for me to weep over the fate of my fatherland."

On receiving this dispatch the Emperor sent Prince Volkónski to Kutúzov with the following rescript:

"Prince Michael Ilariónovich! Since the twenty-ninth of August I have

* As mentioned in the last note, Kutúzov's report was received on August 30. Rostopchín's letter, quoted in the text, refers to the one he received from Kutúzov on the night of September 1-2 (see p. 984) and could hardly have reached Petersburg before September 4.—A.M.

received no communication from you, yet on the first of September I received from the commander in chief of Moscow, via Yaroslávl, the sad news that you, with the army, have decided to abandon Moscow. You can yourself imagine the effect this news has had on me, and your silence increases my astonishment. I am sending this by Adjutant-General Prince Volkónski, to hear from you the situation of the army and the reasons that have induced you to take this melancholy decision."

NINE DAYS after the abandonment of Moscow, a messenger from Kutúzov reached Petersburg with the official announcement of that event. This messenger was Michaud, a Frenchman who did not know Russian, but who was *quoique étranger, russe de cœur et d'âme* [though a foreigner, Russian in heart and soul], as he said of himself.

The Emperor at once received this messenger in his study at the palace on Stone Island. Michaud, who had never seen Moscow before the campaign and who did not know Russian, yet felt deeply moved (as he wrote) when he appeared before *notre très gracieux souverain* [our most gracious sovereign] with the news of the burning of Moscow, *dont les flammes éclairaient sa route* [whose flames illumined his route].

Though the source of M. Michaud's chagrin must have been different from that which caused Russians to grieve, he had such a sad face when shown into the Emperor's study that the latter at once asked:

"Have you brought me sad news, Colonel?"

"Very sad, sire," replied Michaud, lowering his eyes with a sigh. "The abandonment of Moscow."

"Have they surrendered my ancient capital without a battle?" asked the Emperor quickly, his face suddenly flushing.

Michaud respectfully delivered the message Kutúzov had entrusted to him, which was that it had been impossible to fight before Moscow, and that as the only remaining choice was between losing the army as well as Moscow, or losing Moscow alone, the field marshal had to choose the latter.

The Emperor listened in silence, not looking at Michaud.

"Has the enemy entered the city?" he asked.

"Yes, sire, and Moscow is now in ashes. I left it all in flames," replied Michaud in a decided tone, but glancing at the Emperor he was frightened by what he had done.

The Emperor began to breathe heavily and rapidly, his lower lip trembled, and tears instantly appeared in his fine blue eyes.

But this lasted only a moment. He suddenly frowned, as if blaming him-

self for his weakness, and raising his head addressed Michaud in a firm voice:

"I see, Colonel, from all that is happening, that Providence requires great sacrifices of us. . . . I am ready to submit myself in all things to His will; but tell me, Michaud, how did you leave the army when it saw my ancient capital abandoned without a battle? Did you not notice discouragement? . . ."

Seeing that his most gracious ruler was calm once more, Michaud also grew calm, but was not immediately ready to reply to the Emperor's direct and relevant question which required a direct answer.

"Sire, will you allow me to speak frankly as befits a loyal soldier?" he asked to gain time.

"Colonel, I always require it," replied the Emperor. "Conceal nothing from me, I wish to know absolutely how things are."

"Sire!" said Michaud with a subtle, scarcely perceptible smile on his lips, having now prepared a well-phrased reply, "sire, I left the whole army, from its chiefs to the lowest soldier, without exception in desperate and agonized terror . . ."

"How is that?" the Emperor interrupted him, frowning sternly. "Would misfortune make my Russians lose heart? . . . Never!"

Michaud had only waited for this to bring out the phrase he had prepared.

"Sire," he said, with respectful playfulness, "they are only afraid lest Your Majesty, in the goodness of your heart, should allow yourself to be persuaded to make peace. They are burning for the combat," declared this representative of the Russian nation, "and to prove to Your Majesty by the sacrifice of their lives how devoted they are. . . ."

"Ah!" said the Emperor reassured, and with a kindly gleam in his eyes, he patted Michaud on the shoulder. "You set me at ease, Colonel."

He bent his head and was silent for some time.

"Well, then, go back to the army," he said, drawing himself up to his full height and addressing Michaud with a gracious and majestic gesture, "and tell our brave men and all my good subjects wherever you go that when I have not a soldier left I shall put myself at the head of my beloved nobility and my good peasants and so use the last resources of my empire. It still offers me more than my enemies suppose," said the Emperor growing more and more animated; "but should it ever be ordained by Divine Providence," he continued, raising to heaven his fine eyes shining with emotion, "that my dynasty should cease to reign on the throne of my ancestors, then after exhausting all the means at my command, I shall let my beard grow to here" (he pointed halfway down his chest) "and go and

eat potatoes with the meanest of my peasants, rather than sign the disgrace of my country and of my beloved people whose sacrifices I know how to appreciate."

Having uttered these words in an agitated voice the Emperor suddenly turned away as if to hide from Michaud the tears that rose to his eyes, and went to the further end of his study. Having stood there a few moments, he strode back to Michaud and pressed his arm below the elbow with a vigorous movement. The Emperor's mild and handsome face was flushed and his eyes gleamed with resolution and anger.

"Colonel Michaud, do not forget what I say to you here, perhaps we may recall it with pleasure someday . . . Napoleon or I," said the Emperor, touching his breast. "We can no longer both reign together. I have learned to know him, and he will not deceive me any more. . . ."

And the Emperor paused, with a frown.

When he heard these words and saw the expression of firm resolution in the Emperor's eyes, Michaud—*quoique étranger, russe de cœur et d'âme* —at that solemn moment felt himself enraptured by all that he had heard (as he used afterwards to say), and gave expression to his own feelings and those of the Russian people whose representative he considered himself to be, in the following words:

"Sire!" said he, "Your Majesty is at this moment signing the glory of the nation and the salvation of Europe!"

With an inclination of the head the Emperor dismissed him.

2. Nicholas sent to Vorónezh. An evening at the Governor's. Nicholas and Princess Mary. A letter from Sónya

IT IS NATURAL for us who were not living in those days to imagine that when half Russia had been conquered and the inhabitants were fleeing to distant provinces, and one levy after another was being raised for the defense of the fatherland, all Russians from the greatest to the least were solely engaged in sacrificing themselves, saving their fatherland, or weeping over its downfall. The tales and descriptions of that time without exception speak only of the self-sacrifice, patriotic devotion, despair, grief, and the heroism of the Russians. But it was not really so. It appears so to us because we see only the general historic interest of that time and do not see all the personal human interests that people had. Yet in reality those personal interests of the moment so much transcend the general interests that they always prevent the public interest from being felt or even noticed. Most of the people at that time paid no attention to the general

progress of events but were guided only by their private interests, and they were the very people whose activities at that period were most useful.

Those who tried to understand the general course of events and to take part in it by self-sacrifice and heroism were the most useless members of society, they saw everything upside down, and all they did for the common good turned out to be useless and foolish—like Pierre's and Mamónov's regiments which looted Russian villages, and the lint the young ladies prepared and that never reached the wounded, and so on. Even those, fond of intellectual talk and of expressing their feelings, who discussed Russia's position at the time involuntarily introduced into their conversation either a shade of pretense and falsehood or useless condemnation and anger directed against people accused of actions no one could possibly be guilty of. In historic events the rule forbidding us to eat of the fruit of the Tree of Knowledge is specially applicable. Only unconscious action bears fruit, and he who plays a part in an historic event never understands its significance. If he tries to realize it his efforts are fruitless.

The more closely a man was engaged in the events then taking place in Russia the less did he realize their significance. In Petersburg and in the provinces at a distance from Moscow, ladies, and gentlemen in militia uniforms, wept for Russia and its ancient capital and talked of self-sacrifice and so on; but in the army which retired beyond Moscow there was little talk or thought of Moscow, and when they caught sight of its burned ruins no one swore to be avenged on the French, but they thought about their next pay, their next quarters, of Matrëshka the vivandière, and like matters.

As the war had caught him in the service, Nicholas Rostóv took a close and prolonged part in the defense of his country, but did so casually, without any aim at self-sacrifice, and he therefore looked at what was going on in Russia without despair and without dismally racking his brains over it. Had he been asked what he thought of the state of Russia, he would have said that it was not his business to think about it, that Kutúzov and others were there for that purpose, but that he had heard that the regiments were to be made up to their full strength, that fighting would probably go on for a long time yet, and that things being so it was quite likely he might be in command of a regiment in a couple of years' time.

As he looked at the matter in this way, he learned that he was being sent to Vorónezh to buy remounts for his division, not only without regret at being prevented from taking part in the coming battle, but with the greatest pleasure—which he did not conceal and which his comrades fully understood.

A few days before the battle of Borodinó, Nicholas received the neces-

sary money and warrants, and having sent some hussars on in advance, he set out with post horses for Vorónezh.

Only a man who has experienced it—that is, has passed some months continuously in an atmosphere of campaigning and war—can understand the delight Nicholas felt when he escaped from the region covered by the army's foraging operations, provision trains, and hospitals. When—free from soldiers, wagons, and the filthy traces of a camp—he saw villages with peasants and peasant women, gentlemen's country houses, fields where cattle were grazing, posthouses with stationmasters asleep in them, he rejoiced as though seeing all this for the first time. What for a long while specially surprised and delighted him were the women, young and healthy, without a dozen officers making up to each of them; women, too, who were pleased and flattered that a passing officer should joke with them.

In the highest spirits Nicholas arrived at night at a hotel in Vorónezh, ordered things he had long been deprived of in camp, and next day, very clean-shaven and in a full-dress uniform he had not worn for a long time, went to present himself to the authorities.

The commander of the militia was a civilian general, an old man who was evidently pleased with his military designation and rank. He received Nicholas brusquely (imagining this to be characteristically military) and questioned him with an important air, as if considering the general progress of affairs and approving and disapproving with full right to do so. Nicholas was in such good spirits that this merely amused him.

From the commander of the militia he drove to the governor. The governor was a brisk little man, very simple and affable. He indicated the stud farms at which Nicholas might procure horses, recommended to him a horse dealer in the town and a landowner fourteen miles out of town who had the best horses, and promised to assist him in every way.

"You are Count Ilyá Rostóv's son? My wife was a great friend of your mother's. We are at home on Thursdays—today is Thursday, so please come and see us quite informally," said the governor, taking leave of him.

Immediately on leaving the governor's, Nicholas hired post horses and, taking his squadron quartermaster with him, drove at a gallop to the landowner, fourteen miles away, who had the stud. Everything seemed to him pleasant and easy during that first part of his stay in Vorónezh and, as usually happens when a man is in a pleasant state of mind, everything went well and easily.

The landowner to whom Nicholas went was a bachelor, an old cavalry man, a horse fancier, a sportsman, the possessor of some century-old brandy and some old Hungarian wine, who had a snuggery where he smoked, and who owned some splendid horses.

In very few words Nicholas bought seventeen picked stallions for six thousand rubles—to serve, as he said, as samples of his remounts. After dining and taking rather too much of the Hungarian wine, Nicholas— having exchanged kisses with the landowner, with whom he was already on the friendliest terms—galloped back over abominable roads, in the brightest frame of mind, continually urging on the driver so as to be in time for the governor's party.

When he had changed, poured water over his head, and scented himself, Nicholas arrived at the governor's rather late, but with the phrase "better late than never" on his lips.

It was not a ball, nor had dancing been announced, but everyone knew that Catherine Petróvna would play valses and the *écossaise* on the clavichord and that there would be dancing, and so everyone had come as to a ball.

Provincial life in 1812 went on very much as usual, but with this difference, that it was livelier in the towns in consequence of the arrival of many wealthy families from Moscow, and as in everything that went on in Russia at that time a special recklessness was noticeable, an "in for a penny, in for a pound—who cares?" spirit, and the inevitable small talk, instead of turning on the weather and mutual acquaintances, now turned on Moscow, the army, and Napoleon.

The society gathered together at the governor's was the best in Vorónezh.

There were a great many ladies and some of Nicholas' Moscow acquaintances, but there were no men who could at all vie with the cavalier of St. George, the hussar remount officer, the good-natured and well-bred Count Rostóv. Among the men was an Italian prisoner, an officer of the French army; and Nicholas felt that the presence of that prisoner enhanced his own importance as a Russian hero. The Italian was, as it were, a war trophy. Nicholas felt this, it seemed to him that everyone regarded the Italian in the same light, and he treated him cordially though with dignity and restraint.

As soon as Nicholas entered in his hussar uniform, diffusing around him a fragrance of perfume and wine, and had uttered the words "better late than never" and heard them repeated several times by others, people clustered around him; all eyes turned on him, and he felt at once that he had entered into his proper position in the province—that of a universal favorite: a very pleasant position, and intoxicatingly so after his long privations. At posting stations, at inns, and in the landowner's snuggery, maidservants had been flattered by his notice, and here too at the governor's party there were (as it seemed to Nicholas) an inexhaustible number of pretty young

women, married and unmarried, impatiently awaiting his notice. The women and girls flirted with him and, from the first day, the old people concerned themselves to get this fine young daredevil of an hussar married and settled down. Among these was the governor's wife herself, who welcomed Rostóv as a near relative and called him "Nicholas."

Catherine Petróvna did actually play valses and the *écossaise*, and dancing began in which Nicholas still further captivated the provincial society by his agility. His particularly free manner of dancing even surprised them all. Nicholas was himself rather surprised at the way he danced that evening. He had never danced like that in Moscow and would even have considered such a very free and easy manner improper and in bad form, but here he felt it incumbent on him to astonish them all by something unusual, something they would have to accept as the regular thing in the capital though new to them in the provinces.

All the evening Nicholas paid attention to a blue-eyed, plump and pleasing little blonde, the wife of one of the provincial officials. With the naïve conviction of young men in a merry mood that other men's wives were created for them, Rostóv did not leave the lady's side and treated her husband in a friendly and conspiratorial style, as if, without speaking of it, they knew how capitally Nicholas and the lady would get on together. The husband, however, did not seem to share that conviction and tried to behave morosely with Rostóv. But the latter's good-natured naïveté was so boundless that sometimes even he involuntarily yielded to Nicholas' good humor. Toward the end of the evening, however, as the wife's face grew more flushed and animated, the husband's became more and more melancholy and solemn, as though there were but a given amount of animation between them and as the wife's share increased the husband's diminished.

Nicholas sat leaning slightly forward in an armchair, bending closely over the blonde lady and paying her mythological compliments with a smile that never left his face. Jauntily shifting the position of his legs in their tight riding breeches, diffusing an odor of perfume, and admiring his partner, himself, and the fine outlines of his legs in their well-fitting Hessian boots, Nicholas told the blonde lady that he wished to run away with a certain lady here in Vorónezh.

"Which lady?"

"A charming lady, a divine one. Her eyes" (Nicholas looked at his partner) "are blue, her mouth coral and ivory; her figure" (he glanced at her shoulders) "like Diana's. . . ."

The husband came up and sullenly asked his wife what she was talking about.

"Ah, Nikíta Iványch!" cried Nicholas, rising politely, and as if wishing Nikíta Iványch to share his joke, he began to tell him of his intention to elope with a blonde lady.

The husband smiled gloomily, the wife gaily. The governor's good-natured wife came up with a look of disapproval.

"Anna Ignátyevna wants to see you, Nicholas," said she, pronouncing the name so that Nicholas at once understood that Anna Ignátyevna was a very important person. "Come, Nicholas! You know you let me call you so?"

"Oh, yes, Aunt. Who is she?"

"Anna Ignátyevna Malvíntseva. She has heard from her niece how you rescued her. . . . Can you guess?"

"I rescued such a lot of them!" said Nicholas.

"Her niece, Princess Bolkónskaya. She is here in Vorónezh with her aunt. Oho! How you blush. Why, are . . . ?"

"Not a bit! Please don't, Aunt!"

"Very well, very well! . . . Oh, what a fellow you are!"

The governor's wife led him up to a tall and very stout old lady with a blue headdress, who had just finished her game of cards with the most important personages of the town. This was Malvíntseva, Princess Mary's aunt on her mother's side, a rich, childless widow who always lived in Vorónezh. When Rostóv approached her she was standing settling up for the game. She looked at him and, screwing up her eyes sternly, continued to upbraid the general who had won from her.

"Very pleased, mon cher," she then said, holding out her hand to Nicholas. "Pray come and see me."

After a few words about Princess Mary and her late father, whom Malvíntseva had evidently not liked, and having asked what Nicholas knew of Prince Andrew, who also was evidently no favorite of hers, the important old lady dismissed Nicholas after repeating her invitation to come to see her.

Nicholas promised to come and blushed again as he bowed. At the mention of Princess Mary he experienced a feeling of shyness and even of fear, which he himself did not understand.

When he had parted from Malvíntseva Nicholas wished to return to the dancing, but the governor's little wife placed her plump hand on his sleeve and, saying that she wanted to have a talk with him, led him to her sitting room, from which those who were there immediately withdrew so as not to be in her way.

"Do you know, dear boy," began the governor's wife with a serious ex-

pression on her kind little face, "that really would be the match for you: would you like me to arrange it?"

"Whom do you mean, Aunt?" asked Nicholas.

"I will make a match for you with the princess. Catherine Petróvna speaks of Lily, but I say, no—the princess! Do you want me to do it? I am sure your mother will be grateful to me. What a charming girl she is, really! And she is not at all so plain, either."

"Not at all," replied Nicholas as if offended at the idea. "As befits a soldier, Aunt, I don't force myself on anyone or refuse anything," he said before he had time to consider what he was saying.

"Well then, remember, this is not a joke!"

"Of course not!"

"Yes, yes," the governor's wife said as if talking to herself. "But, my dear boy, among other things you are too attentive to the other, the blonde. One is sorry for the husband, really. . . ."

"Oh no, we are good friends with him," said Nicholas in the simplicity of his heart; it did not enter his head that a pastime so pleasant to himself might not be pleasant to someone else.

"But what nonsense I have been saying to the governor's wife!" thought Nicholas suddenly at supper. "She will really begin to arrange a match . . . and Sónya . . . ?" And on taking leave of the governor's wife, when she again smilingly said to him, "Well then, remember!" he drew her aside.

"But see here, to tell you the truth, Aunt . . ."

"What is it, my dear? Come, let's sit down here," said she.

Nicholas suddenly felt a desire and need to tell his most intimate thoughts (which he would not have told to his mother, his sister, or his friend) to this woman who was almost a stranger. When he afterwards recalled that impulse to unsolicited and inexplicable frankness which had very important results for him, it seemed to him—as it seems to everyone in such cases—that it was merely some silly whim that seized him: yet that burst of frankness, together with other trifling events, had immense consequences for him and for all his family.

"You see, Aunt, Mamma has long wanted me to marry an heiress, but the very idea of marrying for money is repugnant to me."

"Oh yes, I understand," said the governor's wife.

"But Princess Bolkónskaya—that's another matter. I will tell you the truth. In the first place I like her very much, I feel drawn to her; and then, after I met her under such circumstances—so strangely, the idea often occurred to me: 'This is fate.' Especially if you remember that Mamma had long been thinking of it; but I had never happened to meet her before,

somehow it had always happened that we did not meet. And as long as my sister Natásha was engaged to her brother it was of course out of the question for me to think of marrying her. And it must needs happen that I should meet her just when Natásha's engagement had been broken off . . . and then everything . . . So you see . . . I never told this to anyone and never will, only to you."

The governor's wife pressed his elbow gratefully.

"You know Sónya, my cousin? I love her, and promised to marry her, and will do so. . . . So you see there can be no question about—" said Nicholas incoherently and blushing.

"My dear boy, what a way to look at it! You know Sónya has nothing and you yourself say your Papa's affairs are in a very bad way. And what about your mother? It would kill her, that's one thing. And what sort of life would it be for Sónya—if she's a girl with a heart? Your mother in despair, and you all ruined. . . . No, my dear, you and Sónya ought to understand that."

Nicholas remained silent. It comforted him to hear these arguments.

"All the same, Aunt, it is impossible," he rejoined with a sigh, after a short pause. "Besides, would the princess have me? And besides, she is now in mourning. How can one think of it!"

"But you don't suppose I'm going to get you married at once? There is always a right way of doing things," replied the governor's wife.

"What a matchmaker you are, Aunt . . ." said Nicholas, kissing her plump little hand.

On reaching Moscow after her meeting with Rostóv, Princess Mary had found her nephew there with his tutor, and a letter from Prince Andrew giving her instructions how to get to her Aunt Malvíntseva at Vorónezh. That feeling akin to temptation which had tormented her during her father's illness, since his death, and especially since her meeting with Rostóv was smothered by arrangements for the journey, anxiety about her brother, settling in a new house, meeting new people, and attending to her nephew's education. She was sad. Now, after a month passed in quiet surroundings, she felt more and more deeply the loss of her father which was associated in her mind with the ruin of Russia. She was agitated and incessantly tortured by the thought of the dangers to which her brother, the only intimate person now remaining to her, was exposed. She was worried too about her nephew's education for which she had always felt herself incompetent, but in the depths of her soul she felt at peace—a peace arising from consciousness of having stifled those personal dreams and

hopes that had been on the point of awaking within her and were related to her meeting with Rostóv.

The day after her party the governor's wife came to see Malvíntseva and, after discussing her plan with the aunt, remarked that though under present circumstances a formal betrothal was, of course, not to be thought of, all the same the young people might be brought together and could get to know one another. Malvíntseva expressed approval, and the governor's wife began to speak of Rostóv in Mary's presence, praising him and telling how he had blushed when Princess Mary's name was mentioned. But Princess Mary experienced a painful rather than a joyful feeling—her mental tranquillity was destroyed, and desires, doubts, self-reproach, and hopes reawoke.

During the two days that elapsed before Rostóv called, Princess Mary continually thought of how she ought to behave to him. First she decided not to come to the drawing room when he called to see her aunt—that it would not be proper for her, in her deep mourning, to receive visitors; then she thought this would be rude after what he had done for her; then it occurred to her that her aunt and the governor's wife had intentions concerning herself and Rostóv—their looks and words at times seemed to confirm this supposition—then she told herself that only she, with her sinful nature, could think this of them: they could not forget that situated as she was, while still wearing deep mourning, such matchmaking would be an insult to her and to her father's memory. Assuming that she did go down to see him, Princess Mary imagined the words he would say to her and what she would say to him, and these words sometimes seemed undeservedly cold and then to mean too much. More than anything she feared lest the confusion she felt might overwhelm her and betray her as soon as she saw him.

But when on Sunday after church the footman announced in the drawing room that Count Rostóv had called, the princess showed no confusion, only a slight blush suffused her cheeks and her eyes lit up with a new and radiant light.

"You have met him, Aunt?" said she in a calm voice, unable herself to understand that she could be outwardly so calm and natural.

When Rostóv entered the room, the princess dropped her eyes for an instant, as if to give the visitor time to greet her aunt, and then just as Nicholas turned to her she raised her head and met his look with shining eyes. With a movement full of dignity and grace she half rose with a smile of pleasure, held out her slender, delicate hand to him, and began to speak in a voice in which for the first time new deep womanly notes vibrated. Mademoiselle Bourienne, who was in the drawing room, looked at Prin-

cess Mary in bewildered surprise. Herself a consummate coquette, she could not have maneuvered better on meeting a man she wished to attract.

"Either black is particularly becoming to her or she really has greatly improved without my having noticed it. And above all, what tact and grace!" thought Mademoiselle Bourienne.

Had Princess Mary been capable of reflection at that moment, she would have been more surprised than Mademoiselle Bourienne at the change that had taken place in herself. From the moment she recognized that dear, loved face, a new life force took possession of her and compelled her to speak and act apart from her own will. From the time Rostóv entered, her face became suddenly transformed. It was as if a light had been kindled in a carved and painted lantern and the intricate, skillful, artistic work on its sides, that previously seemed dark, coarse, and meaningless, was suddenly shown up in unexpected and striking beauty. For the first time all that pure, spiritual, inward travail through which she had lived appeared on the surface. All her inward labor, her dissatisfaction with herself, her sufferings, her strivings after goodness, her meekness, love, and self-sacrifice—all this now shone in those radiant eyes, in her delicate smile, and in every trait of her gentle face.

Rostóv saw all this as clearly as if he had known her whole life. He felt that the being before him was quite different from, and better than, anyone he had met before, and above all better than himself.

Their conversation was very simple and unimportant. They spoke of the war, and like everyone else unconsciously exaggerated their sorrow about it; they spoke of their last meeting—Nicholas trying to change the subject —they talked of the governor's kind wife, of Nicholas' relations, and of Princess Mary's.

She did not talk about her brother, diverting the conversation as soon as her aunt mentioned Andrew. Evidently she could speak of Russia's misfortunes with a certain artificiality, but her brother was too near her heart and she neither could nor would speak lightly of him. Nicholas noticed this, as he noticed every shade of Princess Mary's character with an observation unusual to him, and everything confirmed his conviction that she was a quite unusual and extraordinary being. Nicholas blushed and was confused when people spoke to him about the princess (as she did when he was mentioned) and even when he thought of her, but in her presence he felt quite at ease, and said not at all what he had prepared, but what, quite appropriately, occurred to him at the moment.

When a pause occurred during his short visit, Nicholas, as is usual when there are children, turned to Prince Andrew's little son, caressing him and

asking whether he would like to be an hussar. He took the boy on his knee, played with him, and looked round at Princess Mary. With a softened, happy, and timid look she watched the boy she loved in the arms of the man she loved. Nicholas also noticed that look and, as if understanding it, flushed with pleasure and began to kiss the boy with good-natured playfulness.

As she was in mourning Princess Mary did not go out into society, and Nicholas did not think it the proper thing to visit her again; but all the same the governor's wife went on with her matchmaking, passing on to Nicholas the flattering things Princess Mary said of him and vice versa, and insisting on his declaring himself to Princess Mary. For this purpose she arranged a meeting between the young people at the bishop's house before Mass.

Though Rostóv told the governor's wife that he would not make any declaration to Princess Mary, he promised to go.

As at Tilsit Rostóv had not allowed himself to doubt that what everybody considered right was right, so now, after a short but sincere struggle between his effort to arrange his life by his own sense of justice, and in obedient submission to circumstances, he chose the latter and yielded to the power he felt irresistibly carrying him he knew not where. He knew that after his promise to Sónya it would be what he deemed base to declare his feelings to Princess Mary. And he knew that he would never act basely. But he also knew (or rather felt at the bottom of his heart) that by resigning himself now to the force of circumstances and to those who were guiding him, he was not only doing nothing wrong, but was doing something very very important—more important than anything he had ever done in his life.

After meeting Princess Mary, though the course of his life went on externally as before, all his former amusements lost their charm for him and he often thought about her. But he never thought about her as he had thought of all the young ladies without exception whom he had met in society, nor as he had for a long time, and at one time rapturously, thought about Sónya. He had pictured each of those young ladies as almost all honest-hearted young men do, that is, as a possible wife, adapting her in his imagination to all the conditions of married life: a white dressing gown, his wife at the tea table, his wife's carriage, little ones, Mamma and Papa, their relations to her, and so on—and these pictures of the future had given him pleasure. But with Princess Mary, to whom they were trying to get him engaged, he could never picture anything of future married life. If he tried, his pictures seemed incongruous and false. It made him afraid.

THE DREADFUL NEWS of the battle of Borodinó, of our losses in killed and wounded, and the still more terrible news of the loss of Moscow reached Vorónezh in the middle of September.* Princess Mary, having learned of her brother's wound only from the *Gazette* and having no definite news of him, prepared (so Nicholas heard, he had not seen her again himself) to set off in search of Prince Andrew.

When he received the news of the battle of Borodinó and the abandonment of Moscow, Rostóv was not seized with despair, anger, the desire for vengeance, or any feeling of that kind, but everything in Vorónezh suddenly seemed to him dull and tiresome, and he experienced an indefinite feeling of shame and awkwardness. The conversations he heard seemed to him insincere; he did not know how to judge all these affairs and felt that only in the regiment would everything again become clear to him. He made haste to finish buying the horses, and often became unreasonably angry with his servant and squadron quartermaster.

A few days before his departure a special thanksgiving, at which Nicholas was present, was held in the cathedral for the Russian victory. He stood a little behind the governor and held himself with military decorum through the service, meditating on a great variety of subjects.[2] When the service was over the governor's wife beckoned him to her.

"Have you seen the princess?" she asked, indicating with a movement of her head a lady standing on the opposite side, beyond the choir.

Nicholas immediately recognized Princess Mary not so much by the profile he saw under her bonnet as by the feeling of solicitude, timidity, and pity that immediately overcame him. Princess Mary, evidently engrossed by her thoughts, was crossing herself for the last time before leaving the church.

Nicholas looked at her face with surprise. It was the same face he had seen before, there was the same general expression of refined, inner, spiritual labor, but now it was quite differently lit up. There was a pathetic expression of sorrow, prayer, and hope in it. As had occurred before when she was present, Nicholas went up to her without waiting to be prompted by the governor's wife and not asking himself whether or not it was right and proper to address her here in church, and told her he had heard of her

* *Details of this kind in the novel are usually based on evidence that was in Tolstóy's possession. That news of the battle fought on August 26 only reached Vorónezh (about 175 miles south of Moscow) nearly three weeks later indicates how slow communication was at that time in Russia. The roads in Vorónezh province, however, were bad even in recent times.*—A.M.

[2] *At a Russian church service the congregation stands or kneels, and does not sit.*—A.M.

trouble and sympathized with his whole soul. As soon as she heard his voice a vivid glow kindled in her face, lighting up both her sorrow and her joy.

"There is one thing I wanted to tell you, Princess," said Rostóv. "It is that if your brother, Prince Andrew Nikoláevich, were not living, it would have been at once announced in the Gazette, as he is a colonel."

The princess looked at him, not grasping what he was saying, but cheered by the expression of regretful sympathy on his face.

"And I have known so many cases of a splinter wound" (the Gazette said it was a shell) "either proving fatal at once or being very slight," continued Nicholas. "We must hope for the best, and I am sure . . ."

Princess Mary interrupted him.

"Oh, that would be so dread . . ." she began and, prevented by agitation from finishing, she bent her head with a movement as graceful as everything she did in his presence and, looking up at him gratefully, went out, following her aunt.

That evening Nicholas did not go out, but stayed at home to settle some accounts with the horse dealers. When he had finished that business it was already too late to go anywhere but still too early to go to bed, and for a long time he paced up and down the room, reflecting on his life, a thing he rarely did.

Princess Mary had made an agreeable impression on him when he had met her in Smolénsk province. His having encountered her in such exceptional circumstances, and his mother having at one time mentioned her to him as a good match, had drawn his particular attention to her. When he met her again in Vorónezh the impression she made on him was not merely pleasing but powerful. Nicholas had been struck by the peculiar moral beauty he observed in her at this time. He was, however, preparing to go away and it had not entered his head to regret that he was thus depriving himself of chances of meeting her. But that day's encounter in church had, he felt, sunk deeper than was desirable for his peace of mind. That pale, sad, refined face, that radiant look, those gentle graceful gestures, and especially the deep and tender sorrow expressed in all her features agitated him and evoked his sympathy. In men Rostóv could not bear to see the expression of a higher spiritual life (that was why he did not like Prince Andrew) and he referred to it contemptuously as philosophy and dreaminess, but in Princess Mary that very sorrow which revealed the depth of a whole spiritual world foreign to him was an irresistible attraction.

"She must be a wonderful woman. A real angel!" he said to himself. "Why am I not free? Why was I in such a hurry with Sónya?" And he

involuntarily compared the two: the lack of spirituality in the one and the abundance of it in the other—a spirituality he himself lacked and therefore valued most highly. He tried to picture what would happen were he free. How he would propose to her and how she would become his wife. But no, he could not imagine that. He felt awed, and no clear picture presented itself to his mind. He had long ago pictured to himself a future with Sónya, and that was all clear and simple just because it had all been thought out and he knew all there was in Sónya, but it was impossible to picture a future with Princess Mary, because he did not understand her but simply loved her.

Reveries about Sónya had had something merry and playful in them, but to dream of Princess Mary was always difficult and a little frightening.

"How she prayed!" he thought. "It was plain that her whole soul was in her prayer. Yes, that was the prayer that moves mountains, and I am sure her prayer will be answered. Why don't I pray for what I want?" he suddenly thought. "What do I want? To be free, released from Sónya . . . She was right," he thought, remembering what the governor's wife had said: "Nothing but misfortune can come of marrying Sónya. Muddles, grief for Mamma . . . business difficulties . . . muddles, terrible muddles! Besides, I don't love her—not as I should. O, God! release me from this dreadful, inextricable position!" he suddenly began to pray. "Yes, prayer can move mountains, but one must have faith and not pray as Natásha and I used to as children, that the snow might turn into sugar—and then run out into the yard to see whether it had done so. No, but I am not praying for trifles now," he thought as he put his pipe down in a corner, and folding his hands placed himself before the icon. Softened by memories of Princess Mary he began to pray as he had not done for a long time. Tears were in his eyes and in his throat when the door opened and Lavrúshka came in with some papers.

"Blockhead! Why do you come in without being called?" cried Nicholas, quickly changing his attitude.

"From the governor," said Lavrúshka in a sleepy voice. "A courier has arrived and there's a letter for you."

"Well, all right, thanks. You can go!"

Nicholas took the two letters, one of which was from his mother and the other from Sónya. He recognized them by the handwriting and opened Sónya's first. He had read only a few lines when he turned pale and his eyes opened wide with fear and joy.

"No, it's not possible!" he cried aloud.

Unable to sit still he paced up and down the room holding the letter and reading it. He glanced through it, then read it again, and then again,

and standing still in the middle of the room he raised his shoulders, stretching out his hands, with his mouth wide open and his eyes fixed. What he had just been praying for with confidence that God would hear him had come to pass; * but Nicholas was as much astonished as if it were something extraordinary and unexpected, and as if the very fact that it had happened so quickly proved that it had not come from God to whom he had prayed, but by some ordinary coincidence.

This unexpected and, as it seemed to Nicholas, quite voluntary letter from Sónya freed him from the knot that fettered him and from which there had seemed no escape. She wrote that the last unfortunate events— the loss of almost the whole of the Rostóvs' Moscow property—and the countess' repeatedly expressed wish that Nicholas should marry Princess Bolkónskaya, together with his silence and coldness of late, had all combined to make her decide to release him from his promise and set him completely free.

"It would be too painful to me to think that I might be a cause of sorrow or discord in the family that has been so good to me," she wrote, "and my love has no aim but the happiness of those I love; so, Nicholas, I beg you to consider yourself free, and to be assured that, in spite of everything, no one can love you more than does

YOUR SÓNYA."

Both letters were written from Tróitsa. The other, from the countess, described their last days in Moscow, their departure, the fire, and the de-

* We have here an instance of the way Tolstóy utilizes his personal experiences in his novels.

At the age of twenty-three, when in the army in the Caucasus, he lost at cards all the ready money he had and gave a note of hand for a further five hundred rubles. The time arrived for the note to be presented, and he found himself quite unable to meet it. He was in despair at the unpleasantness that threatened him should a complaint be lodged with his commander. Telling of this in a letter to his "Auntie" Tatiána, he says: "In the evening while saying my prayers I asked God—and very fervently—to help me out of this disagreeable scrape. 'But how can I get out of it?' thought I as I lay down. 'Nothing can happen that will make it possible for me to meet that debt . . . Lord help me!' said I, and I fell asleep."

Next day he received a letter from his brother Nicholas telling him that a native Chechen much attached to him (Leo Tolstóy) had won the note of hand from its holder and brought it to Nicholas to send to Leo as a present.

The two incidents are so similar that the one in the novel was no doubt prompted by the one mentioned above.—A.M.

struction of all their property. In this letter the countess also mentioned that Prince Andrew was among the wounded traveling with them; his state was very critical, but the doctor said there was now more hope. Sónya and Natásha were nursing him.

Next day Nicholas took his mother's letter and went to see Princess Mary. Neither he nor she said a word about what "Natásha nursing him" might mean, but thanks to this letter Nicholas suddenly became almost as intimate with the princess as if they were relations.

The following day he saw Princess Mary off on her journey to Yaro-slávl,* and a few days later left to rejoin his regiment.

Sónya's letter written from Tróitsa, which had come as an answer to Nicholas' prayer, was prompted by this: the thought of getting Nicholas married to an heiress occupied the old countess' mind more and more. She knew that Sónya was the chief obstacle to this happening, and Sónya's life in the countess' house had grown harder and harder, especially after they had received a letter from Nicholas telling of his meeting with Princess Mary in Boguchárovo. The countess let no occasion slip of making humiliating or cruel allusions to Sónya.

But a few days before they left Moscow, moved and excited by all that was going on, she called Sónya to her and, instead of reproaching and making demands on her, tearfully implored her to sacrifice herself and repay all that the family had done for her by breaking off her engagement with Nicholas.

"I shall not be at peace till you promise me this."

Sónya burst into hysterical tears and replied through her sobs that she would do anything and was prepared for anything, but gave no actual promise and could not bring herself to decide to do what was demanded of her. She must sacrifice herself for the family that had reared and brought her up. To sacrifice herself for others was Sónya's habit. Her position in the house was such that only by sacrifice could she show her worth, and she was accustomed to this and loved doing it. But in all her former acts of self-sacrifice she had been happily conscious that they raised her in her own esteem and in that of others, and so made her more worthy of Nicholas whom she loved more than anything in the world. But now they wanted her to sacrifice the very thing that constituted the whole reward for her self-sacrifice and the whole meaning of her life. And for the first time she felt bitterness against those who had been her benefactors only

* From Vorónezh in the south to Yaroslávl in the north will have been a journey of at least five hundred miles, considering that Princess Mary could not pass through Moscow which was in the hands of the French.—A.M.

to torture her the more painfully; she felt jealous of Natásha who had never experienced anything of this sort, had never needed to sacrifice herself, but made others sacrifice themselves for her and yet was beloved by everybody. And for the first time Sónya felt that out of her pure, quiet love for Nicholas a passionate feeling was beginning to grow up which was stronger than principle, virtue, or religion. Under the influence of this feeling Sónya, whose life of dependence had taught her involuntarily to be secretive, having answered the countess in vague general terms, avoided talking with her and resolved to wait till she should see Nicholas, not in order to set him free but on the contrary at that meeting to bind him to her forever.

The bustle and terror of the Rostóvs' last days in Moscow stifled the gloomy thoughts that oppressed Sónya. She was glad to find escape from them in practical activity. But when she heard of Prince Andrew's presence in their house, despite her sincere pity for him and for Natásha, she was seized by a joyful and superstitious feeling that God did not intend her to be separated from Nicholas. She knew that Natásha loved no one but Prince Andrew and had never ceased to love him. She knew that being thrown together again under such terrible circumstances they would again fall in love with one another, and that Nicholas would then not be able to marry Princess Mary as they would be within the prohibited degrees of affinity. Despite all the terror of what had happened during those last days and during the first days of their journey, this feeling that Providence was intervening in her personal affairs cheered Sónya.

At the Tróitsa monastery the Rostóvs first broke their journey for a whole day.

Three large rooms were assigned to them in the monastery hostelry, one of which was occupied by Prince Andrew. The wounded man was much better that day and Natásha was sitting with him. In the next room sat the count and countess respectfully conversing with the prior, who was calling on them as old acquaintances and benefactors of the monastery. Sónya was there too, tormented by curiosity as to what Prince Andrew and Natásha were talking about. She heard the sound of their voices through the door. That door opened and Natásha came out, looking excited. Not noticing the monk, who had risen to greet her and was drawing back the wide sleeve on his right arm, she went up to Sónya and took her hand.

"Natásha, what are you about? Come here!" said the countess.

Natásha went up to the monk for his blessing, and he advised her to turn for aid to God and His saint.*

* The saint referred to was Saint Sergius, who had founded the monastery.—A.M.

As soon as the prior withdrew, Natásha took her friend by the hand and went with her into the unoccupied room.

"Sónya, will he live?" she asked. "Sónya, how happy I am, and how unhappy! . . . Sónya, dovey, everything is as it used to be. If only he lives! He cannot . . . because . . . because . . . of . . ." and Natásha burst into tears.

"Yes! I knew it! Thank God!" murmured Sónya. "He will live."

Sónya was not less agitated than her friend by the latter's fear and grief and by her own personal feelings which she shared with no one. Sobbing, she kissed and comforted Natásha. "If only he lives!" she thought. Having wept, talked, and wiped away their tears, the two friends went together to Prince Andrew's door. Natásha opened it cautiously and glanced into the room, Sónya standing beside her at the half-open door.

Prince Andrew was lying raised high on three pillows. His pale face was calm, his eyes closed, and they could see his regular breathing.

"O, Natásha!" Sónya suddenly almost screamed, catching her companion's arm and stepping back from the door.

"What? What is it?" asked Natásha.

"It's that, that . . ." said Sónya, with a white face and trembling lips.

Natásha softly closed the door and went with Sónya to the window, not yet understanding what the latter was telling her.

"You remember," said Sónya with a solemn and frightened expression. "You remember when I looked in the mirror for you . . . at Otrádnoe at Christmas? Do you remember what I saw?"

"Yes, yes!" cried Natásha opening her eyes wide, and vaguely recalling that Sónya had told her something about Prince Andrew whom she had seen lying down.

"You remember?" Sónya went on. "I saw it then and told everybody, you and Dunyásha. I saw him lying on a bed," said she, making a gesture with her hand and a lifted finger at each detail, "and that he had his eyes closed and was covered just with a pink quilt, and that his hands were folded," she concluded, convincing herself that the details she had just seen were exactly what she had seen in the mirror.

She had in fact seen nothing then but had mentioned the first thing that came into her head, but what she had invented then seemed to her now as real as any other recollection. She not only remembered what she had then said—that he turned to look at her and smiled and was covered with something red—but was firmly convinced that she had then seen and said that he was covered with a pink quilt and that his eyes were closed.

"Yes, yes, it really was pink!" cried Natásha, who now thought she too

remembered the word pink being used, and saw in this the most extraordinary and mysterious part of the prediction.

"But what does it mean?" she added meditatively.

"Oh, I don't know, it is all so strange," replied Sónya, clutching at her head.

A few minutes later Prince Andrew rang and Natásha went to him, but Sónya, feeling unusually excited and touched, remained at the window thinking about the strangeness of what had occurred.

They had an opportunity that day to send letters to the army, and the countess was writing to her son.

"Sónya!" said the countess, raising her eyes from her letter as her niece passed, "Sónya, won't you write to Nicholas?" She spoke in a soft, tremulous voice, and in the weary eyes that looked over her spectacles Sónya read all that the countess meant to convey with these words. Those eyes expressed entreaty, shame at having to ask, fear of a refusal, and readiness for relentless hatred in case of such refusal.

Sónya went up to the countess and, kneeling down, kissed her hand.

"Yes, Mamma, I will write," said she.

Sónya was softened, excited, and touched by all that had occurred that day, especially by the mysterious fulfillment she had just seen of her vision. Now that she knew that the renewal of Natásha's relations with Prince Andrew would prevent Nicholas from marrying Princess Mary, she was joyfully conscious of a return of that self-sacrificing spirit in which she was accustomed to live and loved to live. So with a joyful consciousness of performing a magnanimous deed—interrupted several times by the tears that dimmed her velvety black eyes—she wrote that touching letter the arrival of which had so amazed Nicholas.

3. Pierre's treatment as a prisoner. He is questioned by Davout. Shooting of prisoners. Platón Karatáev

THE OFFICER AND SOLDIERS who had arrested Pierre treated him with hostility but yet with respect, in the guardhouse to which he was taken. In their attitude toward him could still be felt both uncertainty as to who he might be—perhaps a very important person—and hostility as a result of their recent personal conflict with him.

But when the guard was relieved next morning, Pierre felt that for the new guard—both officers and men—he was not as interesting as he had been to his captors; and in fact the guard of the second day did not

recognize in this big, stout man in a peasant coat the vigorous person who had fought so desperately with the marauder and the convoy and had uttered those solemn words about saving a child; they saw in him only No. 17 of the captured Russians, arrested and detained for some reason by order of the Higher Command. If they noticed anything remarkable about Pierre, it was only his unabashed, meditative concentration and thoughtfulness, and the way he spoke French, which struck them as surprisingly good. In spite of this he was placed that day with the other arrested suspects, as the separate room he had occupied was required by an officer.

All the Russians confined with Pierre were men of the lowest class and, recognizing him as a gentleman, they all avoided him, more especially as he spoke French. Pierre felt sad at hearing them making fun of him.

That evening he learned that all these prisoners (he, probably, among them) were to be tried for incendiarism. On the third day he was taken with the others to a house where a French general with a white mustache sat with two colonels and other Frenchmen with scarves on their arms. With the precision and definiteness customary in addressing prisoners, and which is supposed to preclude human frailty, Pierre like the others was questioned as to who he was, where he had been, with what object, and so on.

These questions, like questions put at trials generally, left the essence of the matter aside, shut out the possibility of that essence's being revealed, and were designed only to form a channel through which the judges wished the answers of the accused to flow so as to lead to the desired result, namely a conviction. As soon as Pierre began to say anything that did not fit in with that aim, the channel was removed and the water could flow to waste. Pierre felt, moreover, what the accused always feel at their trial, perplexity as to why these questions were put to him. He had a feeling that it was only out of condescension or a kind of civility that this device of placing a channel was employed. He knew he was in these men's power, that only by force had they brought him there, that force alone gave them the right to demand answers to their questions, and that the sole object of that assembly was to inculpate him. And so, as they had the power and wish to inculpate him, this expedient of an inquiry and trial seemed unnecessary. It was evident that any answer would lead to conviction. When asked what he was doing when he was arrested, Pierre replied in a rather tragic manner that he was restoring to its parents a child he had saved from the flames. Why had he fought the marauder? Pierre answered that he "was protecting a woman," and that "to protect a woman who was being insulted was the duty of every

man; that . . ." They interrupted him, for this was not to the point. Why was he in the yard of a burning house where witnesses had seen him? He replied that he had gone out to see what was happening in Moscow. Again they interrupted him: they had not asked where he was going, but why he was found near the fire? Who was he? they asked, repeating their first question, which he had declined to answer. Again he replied that he could not answer it.

"Put that down, that's bad . . . very bad," sternly remarked the general with the white mustache and red flushed face.

On the fourth day fires broke out on the Zúbovski rampart.

Pierre and thirteen others were moved to the coach house of a merchant's house near the Crimean bridge. On his way through the streets Pierre felt stifled by the smoke which seemed to hang over the whole city. Fires were visible on all sides. He did not then realize the significance of the burning of Moscow, and looked at the fires with horror.

He passed four days in the coach house near the Crimean bridge and during that time learned, from the talk of the French soldiers, that all those confined there were awaiting a decision which might come any day from the marshal. What marshal this was, Pierre could not learn from the soldiers. Evidently for them "the marshal" represented a very high and rather mysterious power.

These first days, before the eighth of September when the prisoners were had up for a second examination, were the hardest of all for Pierre.

ON THE EIGHTH OF SEPTEMBER an officer—a very important one judging by the respect the guards showed him—entered the coach house where the prisoners were. This officer, probably someone on the staff, was holding a paper in his hand, and called over all the Russians there, naming Pierre as "the man who does not give his name." Glancing indolently and indifferently at all the prisoners, he ordered the officer in charge to have them decently dressed and tidied up before taking them to the marshal. An hour later a squad of soldiers arrived and Pierre with thirteen others was led to the Virgin's Field. It was a fine day, sunny after rain, and the air was unusually pure. The smoke did not hang low as on the day when Pierre had been taken from the guardhouse on the Zúbovski rampart, but rose through the pure air in columns. No flames were seen, but columns of smoke rose on all sides, and all Moscow as far as Pierre could see was one vast charred ruin. On all sides there were waste spaces with only stoves and chimney stacks still standing, and here and there the blackened walls of some brick houses. Pierre gazed at the ruins and did not recognize dis-

tricts he had known well. Here and there he could see churches that had not been burned. The Krémlin, which was not destroyed, gleamed white in the distance with its towers and the belfry of Iván the Great. The domes of the New Convent of the Virgin glittered brightly and its bells were ringing particularly clearly. These bells reminded Pierre that it was Sunday and the feast of the Nativity of the Virgin. But there seemed to be no one to celebrate this holiday: everywhere were blackened ruins, and the few Russians to be seen were tattered and frightened people who tried to hide when they saw the French.

It was plain that the Russian nest was ruined and destroyed, but in place of the Russian order of life that had been destroyed, Pierre unconsciously felt that a quite different, firm, French order had been established over this ruined nest. He felt this in the looks of the soldiers who, marching in regular ranks briskly and gaily, were escorting him and the other criminals; he felt it in the looks of an important French official in a carriage and pair driven by a soldier, whom they met on the way. He felt it in the merry sounds of regimental music he heard from the left side of the field, and felt and realized it especially from the list of prisoners the French officer had read out when he came that morning. Pierre had been taken by one set of soldiers and led first to one and then to another place with dozens of other men, and it seemed that they might have forgotten him, or confused him with the others. But no: the answers he had given when questioned had come back to him in his designation as "the man who does not give his name," and under that appellation, which to Pierre seemed terrible, they were now leading him somewhere with unhesitating assurance on their faces that he and all the other prisoners were exactly the ones they wanted and that they were being taken to the proper place. Pierre felt himself to be an insignificant chip fallen among the wheels of a machine whose action he did not understand but which was working well.

He and the other prisoners were taken to the right side of the Virgin's Field, to a large white house with an immense garden not far from the convent. This was Prince Shcherbátov's house, where Pierre had often been in other days, and which, as he learned from the talk of the soldiers, was now occupied by the marshal, the Duke of Eckmühl (Davout).

They were taken to the entrance and led into the house one by one. Pierre was the sixth to enter. He was conducted through a glass gallery, an anteroom, and a hall, which were familiar to him, into a long low study at the door of which stood an adjutant.

Davout, spectacles on nose, sat bent over a table at the further end of the room. Pierre went close up to him, but Davout, evidently consulting

a paper that lay before him, did not look up. Without raising his eyes, he said in a low voice:

"Who are you?"

Pierre was silent because he was incapable of uttering a word. To him Davout was not merely a French general, but a man notorious for his cruelty. Looking at his cold face, as he sat like a stern schoolmaster who was prepared to wait awhile for an answer, Pierre felt that every instant of delay might cost him his life; but he did not know what to say. He did not venture to repeat what he had said at his first examination, yet to disclose his rank and position was dangerous and embarrassing. So he was silent. But before he had decided what to do, Davout raised his head, pushed his spectacles back on his forehead, screwed up his eyes, and looked intently at him.

"I know that man," he said in a cold, measured tone, evidently calculated to frighten Pierre.

The chill that had been running down Pierre's back now seized his head as in a vise.

"You cannot know me, General, I have never seen you . . ."

"He is a Russian spy," Davout interrupted, addressing another general who was present, but whom Pierre had not noticed.

Davout turned away. With an unexpected reverberation in his voice Pierre rapidly began:

"No, monseigneur," he said, suddenly remembering that Davout was a duke. "No, monseigneur, you cannot have known me. I am a militia officer and have not quitted Moscow."

"Your name?" asked Davout.

"Bezúkhov."

"What proof have I that you are not lying?"

"Monseigneur!" exclaimed Pierre, not in an offended but in a pleading voice.

Davout looked up and gazed intently at him. For some seconds they looked at one another, and that look saved Pierre. Apart from conditions of war and law, that look established human relations between the two men. At that moment an immense number of things passed dimly through both their minds, and they realized that they were both children of humanity and were brothers.

At the first glance, when Davout had only raised his head from the papers where human affairs and lives were indicated by numbers, Pierre was merely a circumstance, and Davout could have shot him without burdening his conscience with an evil deed, but now he saw in him a human being. He reflected for a moment.

"How can you show me that you are telling the truth?" said Davout coldly.

Pierre remembered Ramballe, and named him and his regiment and the street where the house was.

"You are not what you say," returned Davout.

In a trembling, faltering voice Pierre began adducing proofs of the truth of his statements.

But at that moment an adjutant entered and reported something to Davout.

Davout brightened up at the news the adjutant brought, and began buttoning up his uniform. It seemed that he had quite forgotten Pierre.

When the adjutant reminded him of the prisoner, he jerked his head in Pierre's direction with a frown and ordered him to be led away. But where they were to take him Pierre did not know: back to the coach house or to the place of execution his companions had pointed out to him as they crossed the Virgin's Field.

He turned his head and saw that the adjutant was putting another question to Davout.

"Yes, of course!" replied Davout, but what this "yes" meant, Pierre did not know.

Pierre could not afterwards remember how he went, whether it was far, or in which direction. His faculties were quite numbed, he was stupefied, and noticing nothing around him went on moving his legs as the others did till they all stopped and he stopped too. The only thought in his mind at that time was: who was it that had really sentenced him to death? Not the men on the commission that had first examined him—not one of them had wished to or, evidently, could have done it. It was not Davout, who had looked at him in so human a way. In another moment Davout would have realized that he was doing wrong, but just then the adjutant had come in and interrupted him. The adjutant, also, had evidently had no evil intent though he might have refrained from coming in. Then who was executing him, killing him, depriving him of life—him, Pierre, with all his memories, aspirations, hopes, and thoughts? Who was doing this? And Pierre felt that it was no one.

It was a system—a concurrence of circumstances.

A system of some sort was killing him—Pierre—depriving him of life, of everything, annihilating him.

FROM PRINCE SHCHERBÁTOV's house the prisoners were led straight down the Virgin's Field, to the left of the nunnery, as far as a kitchen garden in which a post had been set up. Beyond that post a fresh pit had been dug

in the ground, and near the post and the pit a large crowd stood in a semi-circle. The crowd consisted of a few Russians and many of Napoleon's soldiers who were not on duty—Germans, Italians, and Frenchmen, in a variety of uniforms. To the right and left of the post stood rows of French troops in blue uniforms with red epaulets and high boots and shakos.

The prisoners were placed in a certain order, according to the list (Pierre was sixth), and were led to the post. Several drums suddenly began to beat on both sides of them, and at that sound Pierre felt as if part of his soul had been torn away. He lost the power of thinking or understanding. He could only hear and see. And he had only one wish—that the frightful thing that had to happen should happen quickly. Pierre looked round at his fellow prisoners and scrutinized them.

The two first were convicts with shaven heads. One was tall and thin, the other dark, shaggy, and sinewy, with a flat nose. The third was a domestic serf, about forty-five years old, with grizzled hair and a plump, well-nourished body. The fourth was a peasant, a very handsome man with a broad, light-brown beard and black eyes. The fifth was a factory hand, a thin, sallow-faced lad of eighteen in a loose coat.

Pierre heard the French consulting whether to shoot them separately or two at a time. "In couples," replied the officer in command in a calm voice. There was a stir in the ranks of the soldiers and it was evident that they were all hurrying—not as men hurry to do something they understand, but as people hurry to finish a necessary but unpleasant and incomprehensible task.

A French official wearing a scarf came up to the right of the row of prisoners and read out the sentence in Russian and in French.

Then two pairs of Frenchmen approached the criminals and at the officer's command took the two convicts who stood first in the row. The convicts stopped when they reached the post and, while sacks were being brought, looked dumbly around as a wounded beast looks at an approaching huntsman. One crossed himself continually, the other scratched his back and made a movement of the lips resembling a smile. With hurried hands the soldiers blindfolded them, drawing the sacks over their heads, and bound them to the post.

Twelve sharpshooters with muskets stepped out of the ranks with a firm regular tread and halted eight paces from the post. Pierre turned away to avoid seeing what was going to happen. Suddenly a crackling, rolling noise was heard which seemed to him louder than the most terrific thunder, and he looked round. There was some smoke, and the French-

men were doing something near the pit, with pale faces and trembling hands. Two more prisoners were led up. In the same way and with similar looks, these two glanced vainly at the onlookers with only a silent appeal for protection in their eyes, evidently unable to understand or believe what was going to happen to them. They could not believe it because they alone knew what their life meant to them, and so they neither understood nor believed that it could be taken from them.

Again Pierre did not wish to look and again turned away; but again the sound as of a frightful explosion struck his ear, and at the same moment he saw smoke, blood, and the pale, scared faces of the Frenchmen who were again doing something by the post, their trembling hands impeding one another. Pierre, breathing heavily, looked around as if asking what it meant. The same question was expressed in all the looks that met his.

On the faces of all the Russians and of the French soldiers and officers without exception, he read the same dismay, horror, and conflict that were in his own heart. "But who, after all, is doing this? They are all suffering as I am. Who then is it? Who?" flashed for an instant through his mind.

"Sharpshooters of the 86th, forward!" shouted someone. The fifth prisoner, the one next to Pierre, was led away—alone. Pierre did not understand that he was saved, that he and the rest had been brought there only to witness the execution. With ever-growing horror, and no sense of joy or relief, he gazed at what was taking place. The fifth man was the factory lad in the loose cloak. The moment they laid hands on him he sprang aside in terror and clutched at Pierre. (Pierre shuddered and shook himself free.) The lad was unable to walk. They dragged him along, holding him up under the arms, and he screamed. When they got him to the post he grew quiet, as if he suddenly understood something. Whether he understood that screaming was useless or whether he thought it incredible that men should kill him, at any rate he took his stand at the post, waiting to be blindfolded like the others, and like a wounded animal looked around him with glittering eyes.

Pierre was no longer able to turn away and close his eyes. His curiosity and agitation, like that of the whole crowd, reached the highest pitch at this fifth murder. Like the others this fifth man seemed calm; he wrapped his loose cloak closer and rubbed one bare foot with the other.

When they began to blindfold him he himself adjusted the knot which hurt the back of his head; then when they propped him against the bloodstained post, he leaned back and, not being comfortable in that position, straightened himself, adjusted his feet, and leaned back again

more comfortably. Pierre did not take his eyes from him and did not miss his slightest movement.

Probably a word of command was given and was followed by the reports of eight muskets; but try as he would Pierre could not afterwards remember having heard the slightest sound of the shots. He only saw how the workman suddenly sank down on the cords that held him, how blood showed itself in two places, how the ropes slackened under the weight of the hanging body, and how the workman sat down, his head hanging unnaturally and one leg bent under him. Pierre ran up to the post. No one hindered him. Pale, frightened people were doing something around the workman. The lower jaw of an old Frenchman with a thick mustache trembled as he untied the ropes. The body collapsed. The soldiers dragged it awkwardly from the post and began pushing it into the pit.

They all plainly and certainly knew that they were criminals who must hide the traces of their guilt as quickly as possible.

Pierre glanced into the pit and saw that the factory lad was lying with his knees close up to his head and one shoulder higher than the other. That shoulder rose and fell rhythmically and convulsively, but spadefuls of earth were already being thrown over the whole body. One of the soldiers, evidently suffering, shouted gruffly and angrily at Pierre to go back. But Pierre did not understand him and remained near the post, and no one drove him away.

When the pit had been filled up a command was given. Pierre was taken back to his place, and the rows of troops on both sides of the post made a half turn and went past it at a measured pace. The twenty-four sharpshooters with discharged muskets, standing in the center of the circle, ran back to their places as the companies passed by.

Pierre gazed now with dazed eyes at these sharpshooters who ran in couples out of the circle. All but one rejoined their companies. This one, a young soldier, his face deadly pale, his shako pushed back, and his musket resting on the ground, still stood near the pit at the spot from which he had fired. He swayed like a drunken man, taking some steps forward and back to save himself from falling. An old, noncommissioned officer ran out of the ranks and taking him by the elbow dragged him to his company. The crowd of Russians and Frenchmen began to disperse. They all went away silently and with drooping heads.

"That will teach them to start fires," said one of the Frenchmen.

Pierre glanced round at the speaker and saw that it was a soldier who was trying to find some relief after what had been done, but was not able to do so. Without finishing what he had begun to say he made a hopeless movement with his arm and went away.

AFTER THE EXECUTION Pierre was separated from the rest of the prisoners and placed alone in a small, ruined, and befouled church.

Toward evening a noncommissioned officer entered with two soldiers and told him that he had been pardoned and would now go to the barracks for the prisoners of war. Without understanding what was said to him, Pierre got up and went with the soldiers. They took him to the upper end of the field, where there were some sheds built of charred planks, beams, and battens, and led him into one of them. In the darkness some twenty different men surrounded Pierre. He looked at them without understanding who they were, why they were there, or what they wanted of him. He heard what they said, but did not understand the meaning of the words and made no kind of deduction from or application of them. He replied to questions they put to him, but did not consider who was listening to his replies, nor how they would understand them. He looked at their faces and figures, but they all seemed to him equally meaningless.

From the moment Pierre had witnessed those terrible murders committed by men who did not wish to commit them, it was as if the mainspring of his life, on which everything depended and which made everything appear alive, had suddenly been wrenched out and everything had collapsed into a heap of meaningless rubbish. Though he did not acknowledge it to himself, his faith in the right ordering of the universe, in humanity, in his own soul, and in God, had been destroyed. He had experienced this before, but never so strongly as now. When similar doubts had assailed him before, they had been the result of his own wrongdoing, and at the bottom of his heart he had felt that relief from his despair and from those doubts was to be found within himself. But now he felt that the universe had crumbled before his eyes and only meaningless ruins remained, and this not by any fault of his own. He felt that it was not in his power to regain faith in the meaning of life.

Around him in the darkness men were standing and evidently something about him interested them greatly. They were telling him something and asking him something. Then they led him away somewhere, and at last he found himself in a corner of the shed among men who were laughing and talking on all sides.

"Well, then, mates . . . that very prince who . . ." some voice at the other end of the shed was saying, with a strong emphasis on the word who.

Sitting silent and motionless on a heap of straw against the wall, Pierre sometimes opened and sometimes closed his eyes. But as soon as he closed them he saw before him the dreadful face of the factory lad—especially dreadful because of its simplicity—and the faces of the murderers, even

more dreadful because of their disquiet. And he opened his eyes again and stared vacantly into the darkness around him.

Beside him in a stooping position sat a small man of whose presence he was first made aware by a strong smell of perspiration which came from him every time he moved. This man was doing something to his legs in the darkness, and though Pierre could not see his face he felt that the man continually glanced at him. On growing used to the darkness Pierre saw that the man was taking off his leg bands, and the way he did it aroused Pierre's interest.

Having unwound the string that tied the band on one leg, he carefully coiled it up and immediately set to work on the other leg, glancing up at Pierre. While one hand hung up the first string the other was already unwinding the band on the second leg. In this way, having carefully removed the leg bands by deft circular motions of his arm following one another uninterruptedly, the man hung the leg bands up on some pegs fixed above his head. Then he took out a knife, cut something, closed the knife, placed it under the head of his bed, and, seating himself comfortably, clasped his arms round his lifted knees and fixed his eyes on Pierre. The latter was conscious of something pleasant, comforting, and well rounded in these deft movements, in the man's well-ordered arrangements in his corner, and even in his very smell, and he looked at the man without taking his eyes from him.

"You've seen a lot of trouble, sir, eh?" the little man suddenly said.

And there was so much kindliness and simplicity in his singsong voice that Pierre tried to reply, but his jaw trembled and he felt tears rising to his eyes. The little fellow, giving Pierre no time to betray his confusion, instantly continued in the same pleasant tones:

"Eh, lad, don't fret!" said he, in the tender singsong caressing voice old Russian peasant women employ. "Don't fret, friend—'suffer an hour, live for an age!' that's how it is, my dear fellow. And here we live, thank heaven, without offense. Among these folk, too, there are good men as well as bad," said he, and still speaking, he turned on his knees with a supple movement, got up, coughed, and went off to another part of the shed.

"Eh, you rascal!" Pierre heard the same kind voice saying at the other end of the shed. "So you've come, you rascal? She remembers. . . . Now, now, that'll do!"

And the soldier, pushing away a little dog that was jumping up at him, returned to his place and sat down. In his hands he had something wrapped in a rag.

"Here, eat a bit, sir," said he, resuming his former respectful tone as he

unwrapped and offered Pierre some baked potatoes. "We had soup for dinner and the potatoes are grand!"

Pierre had not eaten all day and the smell of the potatoes seemed extremely pleasant to him. He thanked the soldier and began to eat.

"Well, are they all right?" said the soldier with a smile. "You should do like this."

He took a potato, drew out his clasp knife, cut the potato into two equal halves on the palm of his hand, sprinkled some salt on it from the rag, and handed it to Pierre.

"The potatoes are grand!" he said once more. "Eat some like that!"

Pierre thought he had never eaten anything that tasted better.

"Oh, I'm all right," said he, "but why did they shoot those poor fellows? The last one was hardly twenty."

"Tss, tt . . . !" said the little man. "Ah, what a sin . . . what a sin!" he added quickly, and as if his words were always waiting ready in his mouth and flew out involuntarily he went on: "How was it, sir, that you stayed in Moscow?"

"I didn't think they would come so soon. I stayed accidentally," replied Pierre.

"And how did they arrest you, dear lad? At your house?"

"No, I went to look at the fire, and they arrested me there, and tried me as an incendiary."

"Where there's law there's injustice," put in the little man.

"And have you been here long?" Pierre asked as he munched the last of the potato.

"I? It was last Sunday they took me, out of a hospital in Moscow."

"Why, are you a soldier then?"

"Yes, we are soldiers of the Ápsheron regiment. I was dying of fever. We weren't told anything. There were some twenty of us lying there. We had no idea, never guessed at all."

"And do you feel sad here?" Pierre inquired.

"How can one help it, lad? My name is Platón, and the surname is Karatáev," he added, evidently wishing to make it easier for Pierre to address him. "They call me 'little falcon' in the regiment. How is one to help feeling sad? Moscow—she's the mother of cities. How can one see all this and not feel sad? But 'the maggot gnaws the cabbage, yet dies first'; that's what the old folks used to tell us," he added rapidly.

"What? What did you say?" asked Pierre.

"Who? I?" said Karatáev. "I say things happen not as we plan but as God judges," he replied, thinking that he was repeating what he had said before, and immediately continued:

"Well, and you, have you a family estate, sir? And a house? So you have abundance, then? And a housewife? And your old parents, are they still living?" he asked.

And though it was too dark for Pierre to see, he felt that a suppressed smile of kindliness puckered the soldier's lips as he put these questions. He seemed grieved that Pierre had no parents, especially that he had no mother.

"A wife for counsel, a mother-in-law for welcome, but there's none as dear as one's own mother!" said he. "Well, and have you little ones?" he went on asking.

Again Pierre's negative answer seemed to distress him, and he hastened to add:

"Never mind! You're young folks yet, and please God may still have some. The great thing is to live in harmony. . . ."

"But it's all the same now," Pierre could not help saying.

"Ah, my dear fellow!" rejoined Karatáev, "never decline a prison or a beggar's sack!"

He seated himself more comfortably and coughed, evidently preparing to tell a long story.

"Well, my dear fellow, I was still living at home," he began. "We had a well-to-do homestead, plenty of land, we peasants lived well and our house was one to thank God for. When Father and we went out mowing there were seven of us. We lived well. We were real peasants. It so happened . . ."

And Platón Karatáev told a long story of how he had gone into someone's copse to take wood, how he had been caught by the keeper, had been tried, flogged, and sent to serve as a soldier.

"Well, lad," and a smile changed the tone of his voice, "we thought it was a misfortune but it turned out a blessing! If it had not been for my sin, my brother would have had to go as a soldier. But he, my younger brother, had five little ones, while I, you see, only left a wife behind. We had a little girl, but God took her before I went as a soldier. I come home on leave and I'll tell you how it was, I look and see that they are living better than before. The yard full of cattle, the women at home, two brothers away earning wages, and only Michael, the youngest, at home. Father, he says, 'All my children are the same to me: it hurts the same whichever finger gets bitten. But if Platón hadn't been shaved for a soldier, Michael would have had to go.' He called us all to him and, will you believe it, placed us in front of the icons. 'Michael,' he says, 'come here and bow down to his feet; and you, young woman, you bow down too; and you, grandchildren, also bow down before him! Do you under-

stand?' he says. That's how it is, dear fellow. Fate looks for a head. But we are always judging, 'that's not well—that's not right!' Our luck is like water in a dragnet: you pull at it and it bulges, but when you've drawn it out it's empty! That's how it is."

And Platón shifted his seat on the straw.

After a short silence he rose.

"Well, I think you must be sleepy," said he, and began rapidly crossing himself and repeating:

"Lord Jesus Christ, holy Saint Nicholas, Frola and Lavra! Lord Jesus Christ, holy Saint Nicholas, Frola and Lavra! * Lord Jesus Christ, have mercy on us and save us!" he concluded, then bowed to the ground, got up, sighed, and sat down again on his heap of straw. "That's the way. Lay me down like a stone, O God, and raise me up like a loaf," he muttered as he lay down, pulling his coat over him.

"What prayer was that you were saying?" asked Pierre.

"Eh?" murmured Platón, who had almost fallen asleep. "What was I saying? I was praying. Don't you pray?"

"Yes, I do," said Pierre. "But what was that you said: Frola and Lavra?"

"Well, of course," replied Platón quickly, "the horses' saints. One must pity the animals too. Eh, the rascal! Now you've curled up and got warm, you daughter of a bitch!" said Karatáev, touching the dog that lay at his feet, and again turning over he fell asleep immediately.

Sounds of crying and screaming came from somewhere in the distance outside, and flames were visible through the cracks of the shed, but inside it was quiet and dark. For a long time Pierre did not sleep, but lay with eyes open in the darkness, listening to the regular snoring of Platón who lay beside him, and he felt that the world that had been shattered was once more stirring in his soul with a new beauty and on new and unshakable foundations.

TWENTY-THREE SOLDIERS, three officers, and two officials were confined in the shed in which Pierre had been placed and where he remained for four weeks.

When Pierre remembered them afterwards they all seemed misty figures to him except Platón Karatáev, who always remained in his mind a most vivid and precious memory and the personification of everything Russian, kindly, and round. When Pierre saw his neighbor next morning at dawn the first impression of him, as of something round, was fully confirmed:

* *Florus and Laurus, brothers who were martyred under Diocletian, are numbered among the saints of the Russo-Greek Church and are accounted the patron saints of horses by the peasants, who mispronounce their names.*—A.M.

Platón's whole figure—in a French overcoat girdled with a cord, a soldier's cap, and bast shoes—was round. His head was quite round, his back, chest, shoulders, and even his arms, which he held as if ever ready to embrace something, were rounded, his pleasant smile and his large, gentle brown eyes were also round.

Platón Karatáev must have been fifty, judging by his stories of campaigns he had been in, told as by an old soldier. He did not himself know his age and was quite unable to determine it. But his brilliantly white, strong teeth which showed in two unbroken semicircles when he laughed —as he often did—were all sound and good, there was not a gray hair in his beard or on his head, and his whole body gave an impression of suppleness and especially of firmness and endurance.

His face, despite its fine, rounded wrinkles, had an expression of innocence and youth, his voice was pleasant and musical. But the chief peculiarity of his speech was its directness and appositeness. It was evident that he never considered what he had said or was going to say, and consequently the rapidity and justice of his intonation had an irresistible persuasiveness.

His physical strength and agility during the first days of his imprisonment were such that he seemed not to know what fatigue and sickness meant. Every night before lying down, he said: "Lord, lay me down as a stone and raise me up as a loaf!" and every morning on getting up, he said: "I lay down and curled up, I get up and shake myself." And indeed he only had to lie down, to fall asleep like a stone, and he only had to shake himself, to be ready without a moment's delay for some work, just as children are ready to play directly they awake. He could do everything, not very well but not badly. He baked, cooked, sewed, planed, and mended boots. He was always busy, and only at night allowed himself conversation—of which he was fond—and songs. He did not sing like a trained singer who knows he is listened to, but like the birds, evidently giving vent to the sounds in the same way that one stretches oneself or walks about to get rid of stiffness, and the sounds were always high-pitched, mournful, delicate, and almost feminine, and his face at such times was very serious.

Having been taken prisoner and allowed his beard to grow, he seemed to have thrown off all that had been forced upon him—everything military and alien to himself—and had returned to his former peasant habits.

"A soldier on leave—a shirt outside breeches," * he would say.

He did not like talking about his life as a soldier, though he did not

* *The peasants wear their shirts fastened by a girdle at the waist and hanging loose outside their breeches, whereas a soldier's shirt is tucked inside.*—A.M.

complain, and often mentioned that he had not been flogged once during the whole of his army service. When he related anything it was generally some old and evidently precious memory of his "Christian" * life, as he called his peasant existence. The proverbs, of which his talk was full, were for the most part not the coarse and indecent saws soldiers employ, but those folk sayings which taken without a context seem so insignificant, but when used appositely suddenly acquire a significance of profound wisdom.

He would often say the exact opposite of what he had said on a previous occasion, yet both would be right. He liked to talk and he talked well, adorning his speech with terms of endearment and with folk sayings which Pierre thought he invented himself, but the chief charm of his talk lay in the fact that the commonest events—sometimes just such as Pierre had witnessed without taking notice of them—assumed in Kara-táev's speech a character of solemn fitness. He liked to hear the folk tales one of the soldiers used to tell of an evening (they were always the same), but most of all he liked to hear stories of real life. He would smile joyfully when listening to such stories, now and then putting in a word or asking a question to make the moral beauty of what he was told clear to himself. Karatáev had no attachments, friendships, or love, as Pierre understood them, but loved and lived affectionately with everything life brought him in contact with, particularly with man—not any particular man, but those with whom he happened to be. He loved his dog, his comrades, the French, and Pierre who was his neighbor, but Pierre felt that in spite of Karatáev's affectionate tenderness for him (by which he unconsciously gave Pierre's spiritual life its due) he would not have grieved for a moment at parting from him. And Pierre began to feel in the same way toward Karatáev.

To all the other prisoners Platón Karatáev seemed a most ordinary soldier. They called him "little falcon" or "Platósha," chaffed him good-naturedly, and sent him on errands. But to Pierre he always remained what he had seemed that first night: an unfathomable, rounded, eternal personification of the spirit of simplicity and truth.

Platón Karatáev knew nothing by heart except his prayers. When he began to speak he seemed not to know how he would conclude.

Sometimes Pierre, struck by the meaning of his words, would ask him to repeat them, but Platón could never recall what he had said a moment before, just as he never could repeat to Pierre the words of his favorite song: native and birch tree and my heart is sick occurred in it, but when spoken and not sung, no meaning could be got out of it. He did not, and

* In Russian the words Christian and peasant are very similar, the one being derived from the other, and Karatáev's pronunciation identified them.—A.M.

could not, understand the meaning of words apart from their context. Every word and action of his was the manifestation of an activity unknown to him, which was his life. But his life, as he regarded it, had no meaning as a separate thing. It had meaning only as part of a whole of which he was always conscious. His words and actions flowed from him as evenly, inevitably, and spontaneously as fragrance exhales from a flower. He could not understand the value or significance of any word or deed taken separately.

4. Princess Mary goes to the Rostóvs' in Yaroslávl. Prince Andrew's last days and death

WHEN PRINCESS MARY heard from Nicholas that her brother was with the Rostóvs at Yaroslávl she at once prepared to go there, in spite of her aunt's efforts to dissuade her—and not merely to go herself but to take her nephew with her. Whether it were difficult or easy, possible or impossible, she did not ask and did not want to know: it was her duty not only herself to be near her brother who was perhaps dying, but to do everything possible to take his son to him, and so she prepared to set off. That she had not heard from Prince Andrew himself, Princess Mary attributed to his being too weak to write or to his considering the long journey too hard and too dangerous for her and his son.

In a few days Princess Mary was ready to start. Her equipages were the huge family coach in which she had traveled to Vorónezh, a semiopen trap, and a baggage cart. With her traveled Mademoiselle Bourienne, little Nicholas and his tutor, her old nurse, three maids, Tíkhon, and a young footman and courier her aunt had sent to accompany her.

The usual route through Moscow could not be thought of, and the roundabout way Princess Mary was obliged to take through Lípetsk, Ryazán, Vladímir, and Shúya was very long and, as post horses were not everywhere obtainable, very difficult, and near Ryazán where the French were said to have shown themselves was even dangerous.

During this difficult journey Mademoiselle Bourienne, Dessalles, and Princess Mary's servants were astonished at her energy and firmness of spirit. She went to bed later and rose earlier than any of them, and no difficulties daunted her. Thanks to her activity and energy, which infected her fellow travelers, they approached Yaroslávl by the end of the second week.

The last days of her stay in Vorónezh had been the happiest of her life. Her love for Rostóv no longer tormented or agitated her. It filled her

whole soul, had become an integral part of herself, and she no longer struggled against it. Latterly she had become convinced that she loved and was beloved, though she never said this definitely to herself in words. She had become convinced of it at her last interview with Nicholas, when he had come to tell her that her brother was with the Rostóvs. Not by a single word had Nicholas alluded to the fact that Prince Andrew's relations with Natásha might, if he recovered, be renewed, but Princess Mary saw by his face that he knew and thought of this.

Yet in spite of that, his relation to her—considerate, delicate, and loving—not only remained unchanged, but it sometimes seemed to Princess Mary that he was even glad that the family connection between them allowed him to express his friendship more freely. She knew that she loved for the first and only time in her life and felt that she was beloved, and was happy in regard to it.

But this happiness on one side of her spiritual nature did not prevent her feeling grief for her brother with full force; on the contrary, that spiritual tranquillity on the one side made it the more possible for her to give full play to her feeling for her brother. That feeling was so strong at the moment of leaving Vorónezh that those who saw her off, as they looked at her careworn, despairing face, felt sure she would fall ill on the journey. But the very difficulties and preoccupations of the journey, which she took so actively in hand, saved her for a while from her grief and gave her strength.

As always happens when traveling, Princess Mary thought only of the journey itself, forgetting its object. But as she approached Yaroslávl the thought of what might await her there—not after many days, but that very evening—again presented itself to her and her agitation increased to its utmost limit.

The courier who had been sent on in advance to find out where the Rostóvs were staying in Yaroslávl, and in what condition Prince Andrew was, when he met the big coach just entering the town gates was appalled by the terrible pallor of the princess' face that looked out at him from the window.

"I have found out everything, your excellency: the Rostóvs are staying at the merchant Brónnikov's house, in the Square not far from here, right above the Vólga," said the courier.

Princess Mary looked at him with frightened inquiry, not understanding why he did not reply to what she chiefly wanted to know: how was her brother? Mademoiselle Bourienne put that question for her.

"How is the prince?" she asked.

"His excellency is staying in the same house with them."

"Then he is alive," thought Princess Mary, and asked in a low voice: "How is he?"

"The servants say he is still the same."

What "still the same" might mean Princess Mary did not ask, but with an unnoticed glance at little seven-year-old Nicholas, who was sitting in front of her looking with pleasure at the town, she bowed her head and did not raise it again till the heavy coach, rumbling, shaking, and swaying, came to a stop. The carriage steps clattered as they were let down.

The carriage door was opened. On the left there was water—a great river—and on the right a porch. There were people at the entrance: servants, and a rosy girl with a large plait of black hair, smiling as it seemed to Princess Mary in an unpleasantly affected way. (This was Sónya.) Princess Mary ran up the steps. "This way, this way!" said the girl, with the same artificial smile, and the princess found herself in the hall facing an elderly woman of Oriental type, who came rapidly to meet her with a look of emotion. This was the countess. She embraced Princess Mary and kissed her.

"Mon enfant [My child]!" she muttered, "je vous aime et vous connais depuis longtemps [I love you and have known you a long time]."

Despite her excitement, Princess Mary realized that this was the countess and that it was necessary to say something to her. Hardly knowing how she did it, she contrived to utter a few polite phrases in French in the same tone as those that had been addressed to her, and asked: "How is he?"

"The doctor says that he is not in danger," said the countess, but as she spoke she raised her eyes with a sigh, and her gesture conveyed a contradiction of her words.

"Where is he? Can I see him—can I?" asked the princess.

"One moment, Princess, one moment, my dear! Is this his son?" said the countess, turning to little Nicholas who was coming in with Dessalles. "There will be room for everybody, this is a big house. Oh, what a lovely boy!"

The countess took Princess Mary into the drawing room, where Sónya was talking to Mademoiselle Bourienne. The countess caressed the boy, and the old count came in and welcomed the princess. He had changed very much since·Princess Mary had last seen him. Then he had been a brisk, cheerful, self-assured old man; now he seemed a pitiful, bewildered person. While talking to Princess Mary he continually looked round as if asking everyone whether he was doing the right thing. After the destruction of Moscow and of his property, thrown out of his accustomed groove

he seemed to have lost the sense of his own significance and to feel that there was no longer a place for him in life.

In spite of her one desire to see her brother as soon as possible, and her vexation that at the moment when all she wanted was to see him they should be trying to entertain her and pretending to admire her nephew, the princess noticed all that was going on around her and felt the necessity of submitting, for a time, to this new order of things which she had entered. She knew it to be necessary, and though it was hard for her she was not vexed with these people.

"This is my niece," said the count, introducing Sónya—"You don't know her, Princess?"

Princess Mary turned to Sónya and, trying to stifle the hostile feeling that arose in her toward the girl, she kissed her. But she felt oppressed by the fact that the mood of everyone around her was so far from what was in her own heart.

"Where is he?" she asked again, addressing them all.

"He is downstairs. Natásha is with him," answered Sónya, flushing. "We have sent to ask. I think you must be tired, Princess."

Tears of vexation showed themselves in Princess Mary's eyes. She turned away and was about to ask the countess again how to go to him, when light, impetuous, and seemingly buoyant steps were heard at the door. The princess looked round and saw Natásha coming in, almost running—that Natásha whom she had liked so little at their meeting in Moscow long since.

But hardly had the princess looked at Natásha's face before she realized that here was a real comrade in her grief, and consequently a friend. She ran to meet her, embraced her, and began to cry on her shoulder.

As soon as Natásha, sitting at the head of Prince Andrew's bed, heard of Princess Mary's arrival, she softly left his room and hastened to her with those swift steps that had sounded buoyant to Princess Mary.

There was only one expression on her agitated face when she ran into the drawing room—that of love—boundless love for him, for her, and for all that was near to the man she loved; and of pity, suffering for others, and passionate desire to give herself entirely to helping them. It was plain that at that moment there was in Natásha's heart no thought of herself or of her own relations with Prince Andrew.

Princess Mary, with her acute sensibility, understood all this at the first glance at Natásha's face, and wept on her shoulder with sorrowful pleasure.

"Come, come to him, Mary," said Natásha, leading her into the other room.

Princess Mary raised her head, dried her eyes, and turned to Natásha. She felt that from her she would be able to understand and learn everything.

"How . . ." she began her question but stopped short.

She felt that it was impossible to ask, or to answer, in words. Natásha's face and eyes would have to tell her all more clearly and profoundly.

Natásha was gazing at her, but seemed afraid and in doubt whether to say all she knew or not; she seemed to feel that before those luminous eyes which penetrated into the very depths of her heart, it was impossible not to tell the whole truth which she saw. And suddenly, Natásha's lips twitched, ugly wrinkles gathered round her mouth, and covering her face with her hands she burst into sobs.

Princess Mary understood.

But she still hoped, and asked, in words she herself did not trust:

"But how is his wound? What is his general condition?"

"You, you . . . will see," was all Natásha could say.

They sat a little while downstairs near his room till they had left off crying and were able to go to him with calm faces.

"How has his whole illness gone? Is it long since he grew worse? When did this happen?" Princess Mary inquired.

Natásha told her that at first there had been danger from his feverish condition and the pain he suffered, but at Tróitsa that had passed and the doctor had only been afraid of gangrene. That danger had also passed. When they reached Yaroslávl the wound had begun to fester (Natásha knew all about such things as festering) and the doctor had said that the festering might take a normal course. Then fever set in, but the doctor had said the fever was not very serious.

"But two days ago *this* suddenly happened," said Natásha, struggling with her sobs. "I don't know why, but you will see what he is like."

"Is he weaker? Thinner?" asked the princess.

"No, it's not that, but worse. You will see. O, Mary, he is too good, he cannot, cannot live, because . . ."

WHEN NATÁSHA opened Prince Andrew's door with a familiar movement and let Princess Mary pass into the room before her, the princess felt the sobs rising in her throat. Hard as she had tried to prepare herself, and now tried to remain tranquil, she knew that she would be unable to look at him without tears.

The princess understood what Natásha had meant by the words: "two days ago *this* suddenly happened." She understood those words to mean that he had suddenly softened and that this softening and gentleness

were signs of approaching death. As she stepped to the door she already saw in imagination Andrew's face as she remembered it in childhood, a gentle, mild, sympathetic face which he had rarely shown, and which therefore affected her very strongly. She was sure he would speak soft, tender words to her such as her father had uttered before his death, and that she would not be able to bear it and would burst into sobs in his presence. Yet sooner or later it had to be, and she went in. The sobs rose higher and higher in her throat as she more and more clearly distinguished his form and her shortsighted eyes tried to make out his features, and then she saw his face and met his gaze.

He was lying in a squirrel-fur dressing gown on a divan, surrounded by pillows. He was thin and pale. In one thin, translucently white hand he held a handkerchief, while with the other he stroked the delicate mustache he had grown, moving his fingers slowly. His eyes gazed at them as they entered.

On seeing his face and meeting his eyes Princess Mary's pace suddenly slackened, she felt her tears dry up and her sobs ceased. She suddenly felt guilty and grew timid on catching the expression of his face and eyes.

"But in what am I to blame?" she asked herself. And his cold, stern look replied: "Because you are alive and thinking of the living, while I . . ."

In the deep gaze that seemed to look not outwards but inwards there was an almost hostile expression as he slowly regarded his sister and Natásha.

He kissed his sister, holding her hand in his as was their wont.

"How are you, Mary? How did you manage to get here?" said he in a voice as calm and aloof as his look.

Had he screamed in agony, that scream would not have struck such horror into Princess Mary's heart as the tone of his voice.

"And have you brought little Nicholas?" he asked in the same slow, quiet manner and with an obvious effort to remember.

"How are you now?" said Princess Mary, herself surprised at what she was saying.

"That, my dear, you must ask the doctor," he replied, and again making an evident effort to be affectionate, he said with his lips only (his words clearly did not correspond to his thoughts):

"Merci, chère amie, d'être venue [Thank you for coming, my dear]."

Princess Mary pressed his hand. The pressure made him wince just perceptibly. He was silent, and she did not know what to say. She now understood what had happened to him two days before. In his words, his tone, and especially in that calm, almost antagonistic look could be felt an

estrangement from everything belonging to this world, terrible in one who is alive. Evidently only with an effort did he understand anything living; but it was obvious that he failed to understand, not because he lacked the power to do so but because he understood something else— something the living did not and could not understand—and which wholly occupied his mind.

"There, you see how strangely fate has brought us together," said he, breaking the silence and pointing to Natásha. "She looks after me all the time."

Princess Mary heard him and did not understand how he could say such a thing. He, the sensitive, tender Prince Andrew, how could he say that, before her whom he loved and who loved him? Had he expected to live he could not have said those words in that offensively cold tone. If he had not known that he was dying, how could he have failed to pity her and how could he speak like that in her presence? The only explanation was that he was indifferent, because something else, much more important, had been revealed to him.

The conversation was cold and disconnected and continually broke off.

"Mary came by way of Ryazán," said Natásha.

Prince Andrew did not notice that she called his sister Mary, and only after calling her so in his presence did Natásha notice it herself.

"Really?" he asked.

"They told her that all Moscow has been burned down, and that . . ."

Natásha stopped. It was impossible to talk. It was plain that he was making an effort to listen, but could not do so.

"Yes, they say it's burned," he said. "It's a great pity," and he gazed straight before him, absently stroking his mustache with his fingers.

"And so you have met Count Nicholas, Mary?" Prince Andrew suddenly said, evidently wishing to speak pleasantly to them. "He wrote here that he took a great liking to you," he went on simply and calmly, evidently unable to understand all the complex significance his words had for living people. "If you liked him too, it would be a good thing for you to get married," he added rather more quickly, as if pleased at having found words he had long been seeking.

Princess Mary heard his words but they had no meaning for her, except as a proof of how far away he now was from everything living.

"Why talk of me?" she said quietly and glanced at Natásha.

Natásha, who felt her glance, did not look at her. All three were again silent.

"Andrew, would you like . . ." Princess Mary suddenly said in a trem-

bling voice, "would you like to see little Nicholas? He is always talking about you!"

Prince Andrew smiled just perceptibly and for the first time, but Princess Mary, who knew his face so well, saw with horror that he did not smile with pleasure or affection for his son, but with quiet, gentle irony because he thought she was trying what she believed to be the last means of arousing him.

"Yes, I shall be very glad to see him. Is he quite well?"

When little Nicholas was brought into Prince Andrew's room he looked at his father with frightened eyes, but did not cry, because no one else was crying. Prince Andrew kissed him and evidently did not know what to say to him.

When Nicholas had been led away, Princess Mary again went up to her brother, kissed him, and unable to restrain her tears any longer began to cry.

He looked at her attentively.

"Is it about Nicholas?" he asked.

Princess Mary nodded her head, weeping.

"Mary, you know the Gosp . . ." but he broke off.

"What did you say?"

"Nothing. You mustn't cry here," he said, looking at her with the same cold expression.

When Princess Mary began to cry, he understood that she was crying at the thought that little Nicholas would be left without a father. With a great effort he tried to return to life and to see things from their point of view.

"Yes, to them it must seem sad!" he thought. "But how simple it is.

"The fowls of the air sow not, neither do they reap, yet your Father feedeth them," he said to himself and wished to say to Princess Mary; "but no, they will take it their own way, they won't understand! They can't understand that all those feelings they prize so—all our feelings, all those ideas that seem so important to us, are unnecessary. We cannot understand one another," and he remained silent.

Prince Andrew's little son was seven. He could scarcely read, and knew nothing. After that day he lived through many things, gaining knowledge, observation, and experience, but had he possessed all the faculties he afterwards acquired, he could not have had a better or more profound understanding of the meaning of the scene he had witnessed between his father, Mary, and Natásha, than he had then. He understood it com-

pletely, and, leaving the room without crying, went silently up to Natásha who had come out with him and looked shyly at her with his beautiful, thoughtful eyes, then his uplifted, rosy upper lip trembled and leaning his head against her he began to cry.

After that he avoided Dessalles and the countess who caressed him and either sat alone or came timidly to Princess Mary, or to Natásha of whom he seemed even fonder than of his aunt, and clung to them quietly and shyly.

When Princess Mary had left Prince Andrew she fully understood what Natásha's face had told her. She did not speak any more to Natásha of hopes of saving his life. She took turns with her beside his sofa, and did not cry any more, but prayed continually, turning in soul to that Eternal and Unfathomable, whose presence above the dying man was now so evident.

NOT ONLY did Prince Andrew know he would die, but he felt that he was dying and was already half dead. He was conscious of an aloofness from everything earthly and a strange and joyous lightness of existence. Without haste or agitation he awaited what was coming. That inexorable, eternal, distant, and unknown—the presence of which he had felt continually all his life—was now near to him and, by the strange lightness he experienced, almost comprehensible and palpable. . . .

Formerly he had feared the end. He had twice experienced that terribly tormenting fear of death—the end—but now he no longer understood that fear.

He had felt it for the first time when the shell spun like a top before him, and he looked at the fallow field, the bushes, and the sky, and knew that he was face to face with death. When he came to himself after being wounded and the flower of eternal, unfettered love had instantly unfolded itself in his soul as if freed from the bondage of life that had restrained it, he no longer feared death and ceased to think about it.

During the hours of solitude, suffering, and partial delirium he spent after he was wounded, the more deeply he penetrated into the new principle of eternal love revealed to him, the more he unconsciously detached himself from earthly life. To love everything and everybody and always to sacrifice oneself for love meant not to love anyone, not to live this earthly life. And the more imbued he became with that principle of love, the more he renounced life and the more completely he destroyed that dreadful barrier which—in the absence of such love—stands between life and death. When during those first days he remembered that he would

have to die, he said to himself: "Well, what of it? So much the better!"

But after the night in Mytíshchi when, half delirious, he had seen her for whom he longed appear before him and, having pressed her hand to his lips, had shed gentle, happy tears, love for a particular woman again crept unobserved into his heart and once more bound him to life. And joyful and agitating thoughts began to occupy his mind. Recalling the moment at the ambulance station when he had seen Kurágin, he could not now regain the feeling he then had, but was tormented by the question whether Kurágin was alive. And he dared not inquire.

His illness pursued its normal physical course, but what Natásha referred to when she said: "*This* suddenly happened," had occurred two days before Princess Mary arrived. It was the last spiritual struggle between life and death, in which death gained the victory. It was the unexpected realization of the fact that he still valued life as presented to him in the form of his love for Natásha, and a last, though ultimately vanquished, attack of terror before the unknown.

It was evening. As usual after dinner he was slightly feverish, and his thoughts were preternaturally clear. Sónya was sitting by the table. He began to doze. Suddenly a feeling of happiness seized him.

"Ah, she has come!" thought he.

And so it was: in Sónya's place sat Natásha who had just come in noiselessly.

Since she had begun looking after him, he had always experienced this physical consciousness of her nearness. She was sitting in an armchair placed sideways, screening the light of the candle from him, and was knitting a stocking. She had learned to knit stockings since Prince Andrew had casually mentioned that no one nursed the sick so well as old nurses who knit stockings, and that there is something soothing in the knitting of stockings. The needles clicked lightly in her slender, rapidly moving hands, and he could clearly see the thoughtful profile of her drooping face. She moved, and the ball rolled off her knees. She started, glanced round at him, and screening the candle with her hand stooped carefully with a supple and exact movement, picked up the ball, and regained her former position.

He looked at her without moving and saw that she wanted to draw a deep breath after stooping, but refrained from doing so and breathed cautiously.

At the Tróitsa monastery they had spoken of the past, and he had told her that if he lived he would always thank God for his wound which had brought them together again, but after that they never spoke of the future.

"Can it or can it not be?" he now thought as he looked at her and

listened to the light click of the steel needles. "Can fate have brought me to her so strangely only for me to die? . . . Is it possible that the truth of life has been revealed to me only to show me that I have spent my life in falsity? I love her more than anything in the world! But what am I to do if I love her?" he thought, and he involuntarily groaned, from a habit acquired during his sufferings.

On hearing that sound Natásha put down the stocking, leaned nearer to him, and suddenly, noticing his shining eyes, stepped lightly up to him and bent over him.

"You are not asleep?"

"No, I have been looking at you a long time. I felt you come in. No one else gives me that sense of soft tranquillity that you do . . . that light. I want to weep for joy."

Natásha drew closer to him. Her face shone with rapturous joy.

"Natásha, I love you too much! More than anything in the world."

"And I!"—She turned away for an instant. "Why too much?" she asked.

"Why too much? . . . Well, what do you think, what do you feel in your soul, your whole soul—shall I live? What do you think?"

"I am sure of it, sure!" Natásha almost shouted, taking hold of both his hands with a passionate movement.

He remained silent awhile.

"How good it would be!" and taking her hand he kissed it.

Natásha felt happy and agitated, but at once remembered that this would not do and that he had to be quiet.

"But you have not slept," she said, repressing her joy. "Try to sleep . . . please!"

He pressed her hand and released it, and she went back to the candle and sat down again in her former position. Twice she turned and looked at him, and her eyes met his beaming at her. She set herself a task on her stocking and resolved not to turn round till it was finished.

Soon he really shut his eyes and fell asleep. He did not sleep long and suddenly awoke with a start and in a cold perspiration.

As he fell asleep he had still been thinking of the subject that now always occupied his mind—about life and death, and chiefly about death. He felt himself nearer to it.

"Love? What is love?" he thought.

"Love hinders death. Love is life. All, everything that I understand, I understand only because I love. Everything is, everything exists, only because I love. Everything is united by it alone. Love is God, and to die means that I, a particle of love, shall return to the general and eternal source." These thoughts seemed to him comforting. But they were only

thoughts. Something was lacking in them, they were not clear, they were too one-sidedly personal and brain-spun. And there was the former agitation and obscurity. He fell asleep.

He dreamed that he was lying in the room he really was in, but that he was quite well and unwounded. Many various, indifferent, and insignificant people appeared before him. He talked to them and discussed something trivial. They were preparing to go away somewhere. Prince Andrew dimly realized that all this was trivial and that he had more important cares, but he continued to speak, surprising them by empty witticisms. Gradually, unnoticed, all these persons began to disappear and a single question, that of the closed door, superseded all else. He rose and went to the door to bolt and lock it. Everything depended on whether he was, or was not, in time to lock it. He went, and tried to hurry, but his legs refused to move and he knew he would not be in time to lock the door though he painfully strained all his powers. He was seized by an agonizing fear. And that fear was the fear of death. *It* stood behind the door. But just when he was clumsily creeping toward the door, that dreadful something on the other side was already pressing against it and forcing its way in. Something not human—death—was breaking in through that door, and had to be kept out. He seized the door, making a final effort to hold it back—to lock it was no longer possible—but his efforts were weak and clumsy and the door, pushed from behind by that terror, opened and closed again.

Once again *it* pushed from outside. His last superhuman efforts were vain and both halves of the door noiselessly opened. *It* entered, and it was *death*, and Prince Andrew died.

But at the instant he died, Prince Andrew remembered that he was asleep, and at the very instant he died, having made an effort, he awoke.

"Yes, it was death! I died—and woke up. Yes, death is an awakening!" And all at once it grew light in his soul and the veil that had till then concealed the unknown was lifted from his spiritual vision. He felt as if powers till then confined within him had been liberated, and that strange lightness did not again leave him.

When, waking in a cold perspiration, he moved on the divan, Natásha went up and asked him what was the matter. He did not answer and looked at her strangely, not understanding.

That was what had happened to him two days before Princess Mary's arrival. From that day, as the doctor expressed it, the wasting fever assumed a malignant character, but what the doctor said did not interest Natásha, she saw the terrible moral symptoms which to her were more convincing.

From that day an awakening from life came to Prince Andrew together with his awakening from sleep. And compared to the duration of life it did not seem to him slower than an awakening from sleep compared to the duration of a dream.

There was nothing terrible or violent in this comparatively slow awakening.

His last days and hours passed in an ordinary and simple way. Both Princess Mary and Natásha, who did not leave him, felt this. They did not weep or shudder and during these last days they themselves felt that they were not attending on him (he was no longer there, he had left them) but on what reminded them most closely of him—his body. Both felt this so strongly that the outward and terrible side of death did not affect them and they did not feel it necessary to foment their grief. Neither in his presence nor out of it did they weep, nor did they ever talk to one another about him. They felt that they could not express in words what they understood.

They both saw that he was sinking slowly and quietly, deeper and deeper, away from them, and they both knew that this had to be so and that it was right.

He confessed, and received communion: everyone came to take leave of him. When they brought his son to him, he pressed his lips to the boy's and turned away, not because he felt it hard and sad (Princess Mary and Natásha understood that) but simply because he thought it was all that was required of him, but when they told him to bless the boy, he did what was demanded and looked round as if asking whether there was anything else he should do.

When the last convulsions of the body, which the spirit was leaving, occurred, Princess Mary and Natásha were present.

"Is it over?" said Princess Mary when his body had for a few minutes lain motionless, growing cold before them. Natásha went up, looked at the dead eyes, and hastened to close them. She closed them but did not kiss them, but clung to that which reminded her most nearly of him—his body.

"Where has he gone? Where is he now? . . ."

When the body, washed and dressed, lay in the coffin on a table, everyone came to take leave of him and they all wept.

Little Nicholas cried because his heart was rent by painful perplexity. The countess and Sónya cried from pity for Natásha and because he was no more. The old count cried because he felt that before long, he, too, must take the same terrible step.

Natásha and Princess Mary also wept now, but not because of their own personal grief; they wept with a reverent and softening emotion which had taken possession of their souls at the consciousness of the simple and solemn mystery of death that had been accomplished in their presence.

BOOK THIRTEEN

DATES OF PRINCIPAL HISTORICAL EVENTS
1812

OLD STYLE	NEW STYLE	
Oct. 6	Oct. 18	Battle of Tarútino.
Oct. 6, 7, & 8	Oct. 18, 19, & 20	The French leave Moscow.
Oct. 12	Oct. 24	Battle of Málo-Yarolslávets.
Oct. 21	Nov. 2	Cossacks harry the French at Vyázma.

1812

BOOK THIRTEEN

*1. The cause of historical events. A survey of movements of
the Russian army after leaving Moscow. Napoleon's letter to
Kutúzov. The camp at Tarútino. Alexander's letters to Kutú-
zov. Ermólov and others absent when wanted. The battle
postponed. Kutúzov's wrath. The action next day. Cossacks
surprise Murat's army and capture prisoners, guns, and
booty. Inactivity of the rest of the army*

MAN'S MIND cannot grasp the causes of events in their completeness,
but the desire to find those causes is implanted in man's soul. And
without considering the multiplicity and complexity of the conditions
any one of which taken separately may seem to be the cause, he snatches
at the first approximation to a cause that seems to him intelligible and
says: "This is the cause!" In historical events (where the actions of men
are the subject of observation) the first and most primitive approxima-
tion to present itself was the will of the gods and, after that, the will of
those who stood in the most prominent position—the heroes of history.
But we need only penetrate to the essence of any historic event—which
lies in the activity of the general mass of men who take part in it—to be
convinced that the will of the historic hero does not control the actions of
the mass but is itself continually controlled. It may seem to be a matter of
indifference whether we understand the meaning of historical events this
way or that; yet there is the same difference between a man who says that
the people of the West moved on the East because Napoleon wished it
and a man who says that this happened because it had to happen, as there
is between those who declared that the earth was stationary and that the
planets moved round it and those who admitted that they did not know
what upheld the earth, but knew there were laws directing its movement
and that of the other planets. There is, and can be, no cause of an histor-
ical event except the one cause of all causes. But there are laws directing

events, and some of these laws are known to us while we are conscious of others we cannot comprehend. The discovery of these laws is only possible when we have quite abandoned the attempt to find the cause in the will of some one man, just as the discovery of the laws of the motion of the planets was possible only when men abandoned the conception of the fixity of the earth.

The historians consider that, next to the battle of Borodinó and the occupation of Moscow by the enemy and its destruction by fire, the most important episode of the war of 1812 was the movement of the Russian army from the Ryazán to the Kalúga road and to the Tarútino camp—the so-called flank march across the Krásnaya Pakhrá River.* They ascribe the glory of that achievement of genius to different men and dispute as to whom the honor is due. Even foreign historians, including the French, acknowledge the genius of the Russian commanders when they speak of that flank march. But it is hard to understand why military writers, and following them others, consider this flank march to be the profound conception of some one man who saved Russia and destroyed Napoleon. In the first place it is hard to understand where the profundity and genius of this movement lay, for not much mental effort was needed to see that the best position for an army when it is not being attacked is where there are most provisions; and even a dull boy of thirteen could have guessed that the best position for an army after its retreat from Moscow in 1812 was on the Kalúga road. So it is impossible to understand by what reasoning the historians reach the conclusion that this maneuver was a profound one. And it is even more difficult to understand just why they think that this maneuver was calculated to save Russia and destroy the French; for this flank march, had it been preceded, accompanied, or followed by other circumstances, might have proved ruinous to the Russians and salutary for the French. If the position of the Russian army really began to improve from the time of that march, it does not at all follow that the march was the cause of it.

That flank march might not only have failed to give any advantage to

* Leaving Moscow by the Ryazán highroad, Kutúzov followed it only till he reached the river Moskvá (on September 4, o.s.). He then turned to the right and, following the banks of the Pakhrá River, came out on the Túla highroad at Podólsk (September 5-6), crossed the river, and continued in the same westerly direction to the village of Krásnaya Pakhrá which is on the old Kalúga highroad (September 7). Here it was at first intended to give battle, but Kutúzov preferred to withdraw farther along the Kalúga road and chose a strong position on the river Nára at Tarútino, where the first engagement with Murat occurred on October 6.—A.M.

the Russian army, but might in other circumstances have led to its destruction. What would have happened had Moscow not burned down? If Murat had not lost sight of the Russians? * If Napoleon had not remained inactive? If the Russian army at Krásnaya Pakhrá [2] had given battle as Bennigsen and Barclay advised? What would have happened had the French attacked the Russians while they were marching beyond the Pakhrá? What would have happened if on approaching Tarútino, Napoleon had attacked the Russians with but a tenth of the energy he had shown when he attacked them at Smolénsk? What would have happened had the French moved on Petersburg? . . . In any of these eventualities the flank march that brought salvation might have proved disastrous.

The third and most incomprehensible thing is that people studying history deliberately avoid seeing that this flank march cannot be attributed to any one man, that no one ever foresaw it, and that in reality, like the retreat from Filí,[3] it did not suggest itself to anyone in its entirety, but resulted—moment by moment, step by step, event by event—from an endless number of most diverse circumstances and was only seen in its entirety when it had been accomplished and belonged to the past.

At the council at Filí the prevailing thought in the minds of the Russian commanders was the one naturally suggesting itself, namely, a direct retreat by the Nízhni road. In proof of this there is the fact that the majority of the council voted for such a retreat, and above all there is the well-known conversation after the council, between the commander in chief and Lanskóy, who was in charge of the commissariat department. Lanskóy informed the commander in chief that the army supplies were for the most part stored along the Oká in the Túla and Ryazán provinces, and that if they retreated on Nízhni the army would be separated from its supplies by the broad river Oká, which cannot be crossed early in winter.[4]

* Murat, following the Russian army from Moscow, was misled. Kutúzov, when he turned off to the right, let two regiments of Cossacks continue the retreat along the Ryazán road, and Murat followed them as far as the town of Brónnitz, believing himself to be following the whole Russian army. On discovering his error he had to set to work to find out where Kutúzov was. It was not till September 14 that Napoleon, in Moscow, learned where the Russian army had gone to.—A.M.

[2] The Pakhrá is a small river, tributary to the Moskvá.—A.M.

[3] Filí was the last village reached by the Russian army in its retreat on Moscow, and it was there that Kutúzov's council of war, described in Book Eleven, Chapter 3, took place.—A.M.

[4] Because the river is then covered with thin ice.—A.M.

This was the first indication of the necessity of deviating from what had previously seemed the most natural course—a direct retreat on Nízhni-Nóvgorod.* The army turned more to the south, along the Ryazán road and nearer to its supplies. Subsequently the inactivity of the French (who even lost sight of the Russian army), concern for the safety of the arsenal at Túla, and especially the advantages of drawing nearer to its supplies caused the army to turn still further south to the Túla road. Having crossed over, by a forced march, to the Túla road beyond the Pakhrá, the Russian commanders intended to remain at Podólsk and had no thought of the Tarútino position; but innumerable circumstances and the reappearance of French troops who had for a time lost touch with the Russians, and projects of giving battle, and above all the abundance of provisions in Kalúga province, obliged our army to turn still more to the south and to cross from the Túla to the Kalúga road and go to Tarútino, which was between the roads along which those supplies lay. Just as it is impossible to say when it was decided to abandon Moscow, so it is impossible to say precisely when, or by whom, it was decided to move to Tarútino. Only when the army had got there, as the result of innumerable and varying forces, did people begin to assure themselves that they had desired this movement and long ago foreseen its result.

THE FAMOUS FLANK MOVEMENT merely consisted in this: after the advance of the French had ceased, the Russian army, which had been continually retreating straight back from the invaders, deviated from that direct course and, not finding itself pursued, was naturally drawn toward the district where supplies were abundant.

If instead of imagining to ourselves commanders of genius leading the Russian army, we picture that army without any leaders, it could not have done anything but make a return movement toward Moscow, describing an arc in the direction where most provisions were to be found and where the country was richest.

That movement from the Nízhni to the Ryazán, Túla, and Kalúga roads was so natural that even the Russian marauders moved in that direction, and demands were sent from Petersburg for Kutúzov to take his army that way. At Tarútino Kutúzov received what was almost a reprimand from the Emperor for having moved his army along the Ryazán road, and the Emperor's letter indicated to him the very position he had already occupied near Kalúga.

Having rolled like a ball in the direction of the impetus given by the whole campaign and by the battle of Borodinó, the Russian army—when

* *Now Górki, named after Maxim Górki, Russian novelist.*

the strength of that impetus was exhausted and no fresh push was received
—assumed the position natural to it.

Kutúzov's merit lay, not in any strategic maneuver of genius, as it is
called, but in the fact that he alone understood the significance of what
had happened. He alone then understood the meaning of the French
army's inactivity, he alone continued to assert that the battle of Borodinó
had been a victory, he alone—who as commander in chief might have been
expected to be eager to attack—employed his whole strength to restrain
the Russian army from useless engagements.

The beast wounded at Borodinó was lying where the fleeing hunter had
left him; but whether he was still alive, whether he was strong and merely
lying low, the hunter did not know. Suddenly the beast was heard to moan.

The moan of that wounded beast (the French army) which betrayed
its calamitous condition was the sending of Lauriston to Kutúzov's camp
with overtures for peace.

Napoleon, with his usual assurance that whatever entered his head was
right, wrote to Kutúzov the first words that occurred to him, though they
were meaningless.

> MONSIEUR LE PRINCE KOUTOUZOV: I am sending one of my adjutants-
> general to discuss several interesting questions with you. I beg your
> Highness to credit what he says to you, *especially when he expresses
> the sentiment of esteem and special regard I have long entertained
> for your person. This letter having no other object, I pray God, mon-
> sieur le prince Koutouzov, to keep you in His holy and gracious
> protection!* NAPOLEON
> Moscow, October 30, 1812

Kutúzov replied: "I should be cursed by posterity were I looked on as
the initiator of a settlement of any sort. *Such is the present spirit of my
nation.*" But he continued to exert all his powers to restrain his troops
from attacking.

During the month that the French troops were pillaging in Moscow and
the Russian troops were quietly encamped at Tarútino, a change had taken
place in the relative strength of the two armies—both in spirit and in
number—as a result of which the superiority had passed to the Russian
side. Though the condition and numbers of the French army were un-
known to the Russians, as soon as that change occurred the need of at-
tacking at once showed itself by countless signs. These signs were: Lauris-
ton's mission; the abundance of provisions at Tarútino; the reports com-
ing in from all sides of the inactivity and disorder of the French; the flow
of recruits to our regiments; the fine weather; the long rest the Russian
soldiers had enjoyed, and the impatience to do what they had been assem-

bled for, which usually shows itself in an army that has been resting; curiosity as to what the French army, so long lost sight of, was doing; the boldness with which our outposts now scouted close up to the French stationed at Tarútino; the news of easy successes gained by peasants and guerrilla troops over the French, the envy aroused by this; the desire for revenge that lay in the heart of every Russian as long as the French were in Moscow, and (above all) a dim consciousness in every soldier's mind that the relative strength of the armies had changed and that the advantage was now on our side. There was a substantial change in the relative strength, and an advance had become inevitable. And at once, as a clock begins to strike and chime as soon as the minute hand has completed a full circle, this change was shown by an increased activity, whirring, and chiming in the higher spheres.

THE RUSSIAN ARMY was commanded by Kutúzov and his staff, and also by the Emperor from Petersburg. Before the news of the abandonment of Moscow had been received in Petersburg, a detailed plan of the whole campaign had been drawn up and sent to Kutúzov for his guidance. Though this plan had been drawn up on the supposition that Moscow was still in our hands, it was approved by the staff and accepted as a basis for action. Kutúzov only replied that movements arranged from a distance were always difficult to execute. So fresh instructions were sent for the solution of difficulties that might be encountered, as well as fresh people who were to watch Kutúzov's actions and report upon them.

Besides this, the whole staff of the Russian army was now reorganized. The posts left vacant by Bagratión, who had been killed, and by Barclay, who had gone away in dudgeon, had to be filled. Very serious consideration was given to the question whether it would be better to put A in B's place and B in D's, or on the contrary to put D in A's place, and so on—as if anything more than A's or B's satisfaction depended on this.

As a result of the hostility between Kutúzov and Bennigsen, his Chief of Staff, the presence of confidential representatives of the Emperor, and these transfers, a more than usually complicated play of parties was going on among the staff of the army. A was undermining B, D was undermining C, and so on in all possible combinations and permutations. In all these plottings the subject of intrigue was generally the conduct of the war, which all these men believed they were directing; but this affair of the war went on independently of them, as it had to go: that is, never in the way people devised, but flowing always from the essential attitude of the masses. Only in the highest spheres did all these schemes, crossings, and interminglings appear to be a true reflection of what had to happen.

"Prince Michael Ilariónovich!" wrote the Emperor on the second of October in a letter that reached Kutúzov after the battle at Tarútino, "Since September 2 Moscow has been in the hands of the enemy. Your last reports were written on the twentieth, and during all this time not only has no action been taken against the enemy or for the relief of the ancient capital, but according to your last report you have even retreated farther. Sérpukhov is already occupied by an enemy detachment and Túla with its famous arsenal, so indispensable to the army, is in danger. From General Wintzingerode's reports, I see that an enemy corps of ten thousand men is moving on the Petersburg road. Another corps of several thousand men is moving on Dmítrov. A third has advanced along the Vladímir road, and a fourth, rather considerable detachment is stationed between Rúza and Mozháysk. Napoleon himself was in Moscow as late as the twenty-fifth. In view of all this information, when the enemy has scattered his forces in large detachments, and with Napoleon and his Guards in Moscow, is it possible that the enemy's forces confronting you are so considerable as not to allow of your taking the offensive? On the contrary, he is probably pursuing you with detachments, or at most with an army corps much weaker than the army entrusted to you. It would seem that, availing yourself of these circumstances, you might advantageously attack a weaker enemy and annihilate him, or at least oblige him to retreat, retaining in our hands an important part of the provinces now occupied by the enemy, and thereby averting danger from Túla and other towns in the interior. You will be responsible if the enemy is able to direct a force of any size against Petersburg to threaten this capital in which it has not been possible to retain many troops; for with the army entrusted to you, and acting with resolution and energy, you have ample means to avert this fresh calamity. Remember that you have still to answer to our offended country for the loss of Moscow. You have experienced my readiness to reward you. That readiness will not weaken in me, but I and Russia have a right to expect from you all the zeal, firmness, and success which your intellect, military talent, and the courage of the troops you command justify us in expecting."

But by the time this letter, which proved that the real relation of the forces had already made itself felt in Petersburg, was dispatched, Kutúzov had found himself unable any longer to restrain the army he commanded from attacking and a battle had taken place.

On the second of October a Cossack, Shapoválov, who was out scouting, killed one hare and wounded another. Following the wounded hare he made his way far into the forest and came upon the left flank of Murat's army, encamped there without any precautions. The Cossack laughingly

told his comrades how he had almost fallen into the hands of the French. A cornet, hearing the story, informed his commander.

The Cossack was sent for and questioned. The Cossack officers wished to take advantage of this chance to capture some horses, but one of the superior officers, who was acquainted with the higher authorities, reported the incident to a general on the staff. The state of things on the staff had of late been exceedingly strained. Ermólov had been to see Bennigsen a few days previously and had entreated him to use his influence with the commander in chief to induce him to take the offensive.

"If I did not know you I should think you did not want what you are asking for. I need only advise anything and his Highness is sure to do the opposite," replied Bennigsen.

The Cossack's report, confirmed by horse patrols who were sent out, was the final proof that events had matured. The tightly coiled spring was released, the clock began to whirr and the chimes to play. Despite all his supposed power, his intellect, his experience, and his knowledge of men, Kutúzov—having taken into consideration the Cossack's report, a note from Bennigsen who sent personal reports to the Emperor, the wishes he supposed the Emperor to hold, and the fact that all the generals expressed the same wish—could no longer check the inevitable movement, and gave the order to do what he regarded as useless and harmful—gave his approval, that is, to the accomplished fact.

BENNIGSEN'S NOTE and the Cossack's information that the left flank of the French was unguarded were merely final indications that it was necessary to order an attack, and it was fixed for the fifth of October.

On the morning of the fourth of October Kutúzov signed the dispositions. Toll read them to Ermólov, asking him to attend to the further arrangements.

"All right—all right. I haven't time just now," replied Ermólov, and left the hut.

The dispositions drawn up by Toll were very good. As in the Austerlitz dispositions, it was written—though not in German this time:

"The First Column will march here and here," "the Second Column will march there and there," and so on; and on paper, all these columns arrived at their places at the appointed time and destroyed the enemy. Everything had been admirably thought out as is usual in dispositions, and as is always the case, not a single column reached its place at the appointed time.

When the necessary number of copies of the dispositions had been prepared, an officer was summoned and sent to deliver them to Ermólov

to deal with. A young officer of the Horse Guards, Kutúzov's orderly, pleased at the importance of the mission entrusted to him, went to Ermólov's quarters.

"Gone away," said Ermólov's orderly.

The officer of the Horse Guards went to a general with whom Ermólov was often to be found.

"No, and the general's out too."

The officer, mounting his horse, rode off to someone else.

"No, he's gone out."

"If only they don't make me responsible for this delay! What a nuisance it is!" thought the officer, and he rode round the whole camp. One man said he had seen Ermólov ride past with some other generals, others said he must have returned home. The officer searched till six o'clock in the evening without even stopping to eat. Ermólov was nowhere to be found and no one knew where he was. The officer snatched a little food at a comrade's, and rode again to the vanguard to find Milorádovich. Milorádovich too was away, but here he was told that he had gone to a ball at General Kíkin's and that Ermólov was probably there too.

"But where is it?"

"Why, there, over at Échkino," said a Cossack officer, pointing to a country house in the far distance.

"What, outside our line?"

"They've put two regiments as outposts, and they're having such a spree there, it's awful! Two bands and three sets of singers!"

The officer rode out beyond our lines to Échkino. While still at a distance he heard as he rode the merry sounds of a soldier's dance song proceeding from the house.

"In the meadows . . . in the meadows!" he heard, accompanied by whistling and the sound of a *torban,** drowned every now and then by shouts. These sounds made his spirits rise, but at the same time he was afraid that he would be blamed for not having executed sooner the important order entrusted to him. It was already past eight o'clock. He dismounted and went up into the porch of a large country house which had remained intact between the Russian and French forces. In the refreshment room and the hall, footmen were bustling about with wine and viands. Groups of singers stood outside the windows. The officer was admitted and immediately saw all the chief generals of the army together, and among them Ermólov's big imposing figure. They all had their coats unbuttoned and were standing in a semicircle with flushed and animated

* *A Ukrainian stringed instrument resembling the balaláyka.*—A.M.

faces, laughing loudly. In the middle of the room a short handsome general with a red face was dancing the trepák with much spirit and agility.

"Ha, ha, ha! Bravo, Nicholas Iványch! Ha, ha, ha!"

The officer felt that by arriving with important orders at such a moment he was doubly to blame, and he would have preferred to wait; but one of the generals espied him and, hearing what he had come about, informed Ermólov.

Ermólov came forward with a frown on his face and, hearing what the officer had to say, took the papers from him without a word.

"You think he went off just by chance?" said a comrade, who was on the staff that evening, to the officer of the Horse Guards, referring to Ermólov. "It was a trick. It was done on purpose to get Konovnítsyn into trouble. You'll see what a mess there'll be tomorrow."

NEXT DAY the decrepit Kutúzov, having given orders to be called early, said his prayers, dressed, and, with an unpleasant consciousness of having to direct a battle he did not approve of, got into his calèche and drove from Letashóvka (a village three and a half miles from Tarútino) to the place where the attacking columns were to meet. He sat in the calèche, dozing and waking up by turns, and listening for any sound of firing on the right as an indication that the action had begun. But all was still quiet. A damp dull autumn morning was just dawning. On approaching Tarútino Kutúzov noticed cavalrymen leading their horses to water across the road along which he was driving. Kutúzov looked at them searchingly, stopped his carriage, and inquired what regiment they belonged to. They belonged to a column that should have been far in front and in ambush long before then. "It may be a mistake," thought the old commander in chief. But a little further on he saw infantry regiments with their arms piled and the soldiers, only partly dressed, eating their rye porridge and carrying fuel. He sent for an officer. The officer reported that no order to advance had been received.

"How! Not rec . . ." Kutúzov began, but checked himself immediately and sent for a senior officer. Getting out of his calèche, he waited with drooping head and breathing heavily, pacing silently up and down. When Eýkhen, the officer of the general staff whom he had summoned, appeared, Kutúzov went purple in the face, not because that officer was to blame for the mistake, but because he was an object of sufficient importance for him to vent his wrath on. Trembling and panting the old man fell into that state of fury in which he sometimes used to roll on the ground, and he fell upon Eýkhen, threatening him with his hands, shout-

ing and loading him with gross abuse. Another man, Captain Brózin, who happened to turn up and who was not at all to blame, suffered the same fate.

"What sort of another blackguard are you? I'll have you shot! Scoundrels!" yelled Kutúzov in a hoarse voice, waving his arms and reeling.

He was suffering physically. He, the commander in chief, a Serene Highness who everybody said possessed powers such as no man had ever had in Russia, to be placed in this position—made the laughingstock of the whole army! "I needn't have been in such a hurry to pray about today, or have kept awake thinking everything over all night," thought he to himself. "When I was a chit of an officer no one would have dared to mock me so and now!" He was in a state of physical suffering as if from corporal punishment, and could not avoid expressing it by cries of anger and distress. But his strength soon began to fail him, and looking about him, conscious of having said much that was amiss, he again got into his calèche and drove back in silence.

His wrath, once expended, did not return, and blinking feebly he listened to excuses and self-justifications (Ermólov did not come to see him till the next day) and to the insistence of Bennigsen, Konovnítsyn, and Toll that the movement that had miscarried should be executed next day. And once more Kutúzov had to consent.

NEXT DAY the troops assembled in their appointed places in the evening and advanced during the night. It was an autumn night with dark purple clouds, but no rain. The ground was damp but not muddy, and the troops advanced noiselessly, only occasionally a jingling of the artillery could be faintly heard. The men were forbidden to talk out loud, to smoke their pipes, or to strike a light, and they tried to prevent their horses neighing. The secrecy of the undertaking heightened its charm and they marched gaily. Some columns, supposing they had reached their destination, halted, piled arms, and settled down on the cold ground, but the majority marched all night and arrived at places where they evidently should not have been.

Only Count Orlóv-Denísov with his Cossacks (the least important detachment of all) got to his appointed place at the right time. This detachment halted at the outskirts of a forest, on the path leading from the village of Stromílova to Dmítrovsk.

Toward dawn, Count Orlóv-Denísov, who had dozed off, was awakened by a deserter from the French army being brought to him. This was a Polish sergeant of Poniatowski's corps, who explained in Polish that he had come over because he had been slighted in the service: that he ought long ago to have been made an officer, that he was braver than any of

them, and so he had left them and wished to pay them out. He said that Murat was spending the night less than a mile from where they were, and that if they would let him have a convoy of a hundred men he would capture him alive. Count Orlóv-Denísov consulted his fellow officers.

The offer was too tempting to be refused. Everyone volunteered to go and everybody advised making the attempt. After much disputing and arguing, Major-General Grékov with two Cossack regiments decided to go with the Polish sergeant.

"Now, remember," said Count Orlóv-Denísov to the sergeant at parting, "if you have been lying I'll have you hanged like a dog; but if it's true you shall have a hundred gold pieces!" *

Without replying, the sergeant, with a resolute air, mounted and rode away with Grékov whose men had quickly assembled. They disappeared into the forest, and Count Orlóv-Denísov, having seen Grékov off, returned, shivering from the freshness of the early dawn and excited by what he had undertaken on his own responsibility, and began looking at the enemy camp, now just visible in the deceptive light of dawn and the dying campfires. Our columns ought to have begun to appear on an open declivity to his right. He looked in that direction, but though the columns would have been visible quite far off, they were not to be seen. It seemed to the count that things were beginning to stir in the French camp, and his keensighted adjutant confirmed this.

"Oh, it is really too late," said Count Orlóv, looking at the camp.

As often happens when someone we have trusted is no longer before our eyes, it suddenly seemed quite clear and obvious to him that the sergeant was an impostor, that he had lied, and that the whole Russian attack would be ruined by the absence of those two regiments, which he would lead away heaven only knew where. How could one capture a commander in chief from among such a mass of troops!

"I am sure that rascal was lying," said the count.

"They can still be called back," said one of his suite, who like Count Orlóv felt distrustful of the adventure when he looked at the enemy's camp.

"Eh? Really . . . what do you think? Should we let them go on or not?"

"Will you have them fetched back?"

"Fetch them back, fetch them back!" said Count Orlóv with sudden determination, looking at his watch. "It will be too late. It is quite light."

And the adjutant galloped through the forest after Grékov. When

* The gold piece in question was the chervónets (= 3 rubles). Its value then was a little less than ten shillings.—A.M.

Grékov returned, Count Orlóv-Denísov, excited both by the abandoned attempt and by vainly awaiting the infantry columns that still did not appear, as well as by the proximity of the enemy, resolved to advance. All his men felt the same excitement.

"Mount!" he commanded in a whisper. The men took their places and crossed themselves. . . . "Forward, with God's aid!"

"Hurrah-ah-ah!" reverberated in the forest, and the Cossack companies, trailing their lances and advancing one after another as if poured out of a sack, dashed gaily across the brook toward the camp.

One desperate, frightened yell from the first French soldier who saw the Cossacks, and all who were in the camp, undressed and only just waking up, ran off in all directions, abandoning cannons, muskets, and horses.

Had the Cossacks pursued the French, without heeding what was behind and around them, they would have captured Murat and everything there. That was what the officers desired. But it was impossible to make the Cossacks budge when once they had got booty and prisoners. None of them listened to orders. Fifteen hundred prisoners and thirty-eight guns were taken on the spot, besides standards and (what seemed most important to the Cossacks) horses, saddles, horsecloths, and the like. All this had to be dealt with, the prisoners and guns secured, the booty divided—not without some shouting and even a little fighting among themselves—and it was on this that the Cossacks all busied themselves.

The French, not being farther pursued, began to recover themselves: they formed into detachments and began firing. Orlóv-Denísov, still waiting for the other columns to arrive, advanced no further.

Meantime, according to the dispositions which said that "the First Column will march" and so on, the infantry of the belated columns, commanded by Bennigsen and directed by Toll, had started in due order and, as always happens, had got somewhere, but not to their appointed places. As always happens the men, starting cheerfully, began to halt; murmurs were heard, there was a sense of confusion, and finally a backward movement. Adjutants and generals galloped about, shouted, grew angry, quarreled, said they had come quite wrong and were late, gave vent to a little abuse, and at last gave it all up and went forward, simply to get somewhere. "We shall get somewhere or other!" And they did indeed get somewhere, though not to their right places; a few eventually even got to their right place, but too late to be of any use and only in time to be fired at. Toll, who in this battle played the part of Weyrother at Austerlitz, galloped assiduously from place to place, finding everything upside down everywhere. Thus he stumbled on Bagovút's corps in a wood when it was already broad daylight, though the corps should long before have joined

Orlóv-Denísov. Excited and vexed by the failure and supposing that some-
one must be responsible for it, Toll galloped up to the commander of the
corps and began upbraiding him severely, saying that he ought to be shot.
General Bagovút, a fighting old soldier of placid temperament, being also
upset by all the delay, confusion, and cross-purposes, fell into a rage to
everybody's surprise and quite contrary to his usual character and said
disagreeable things to Toll.

"I prefer not to take lessons from anyone, but I can die with my men as
well as anybody," he said, and advanced with a single division.

Coming out onto a field under the enemy's fire, this brave general went
straight ahead, leading his men under fire, without considering in his agi-
tation whether going into action now, with a single division, would be of
any use or no. Danger, cannon balls, and bullets were just what he needed
in his angry mood. One of the first bullets killed him, and other bullets
killed many of his men. And his division remained under fire for some time
quite uselessly.

MEANWHILE ANOTHER COLUMN was to have attacked the French from the
front, but Kutúzov accompanied that column. He well knew that nothing
but confusion would come of this battle undertaken against his will, and
as far as was in his power held the troops back. He did not advance.

He rode silently on his small gray horse, indolently answering sugges-
tions that they should attack.

"The word *attack* is always on your tongue, but you don't see that we
are unable to execute complicated maneuvers," said he to Milorádovich
who asked permission to advance.

"We couldn't take Murat prisoner this morning or get to the place in
time, and nothing can be done now!" he replied to someone else.

When Kutúzov was informed that at the French rear—where accord-
ing to the reports of the Cossacks there had previously been nobody—
there were now two battalions of Poles, he gave a sidelong glance at
Ermólov who was behind him and to whom he had not spoken since the
previous day.

"You see! They are asking to attack and making plans of all kinds, but
as soon as one gets to business nothing is ready, and the enemy, fore-
warned, takes measures accordingly."

Ermólov screwed up his eyes and smiled faintly on hearing these words.
He understood that for him the storm had blown over, and that Kutúzov
would content himself with that hint.

"He's having a little fun at my expense," said Ermólov softly, nudging
with his knee Raévski who was at his side.

Soon after this, Ermólov moved up to Kutúzov and respectfully remarked:

"It is not too late yet, your Highness—the enemy has not gone away—if you were to order an attack! If not, the Guards will not so much as see a little smoke."

Kutúzov did not reply, but when they reported to him that Murat's troops were in retreat he ordered an advance, though at every hundred paces he halted for three quarters of an hour.

The whole battle consisted in what Orlóv-Denísov's Cossacks had done: the rest of the army merely lost some hundreds of men uselessly.

In consequence of this battle Kutúzov received a diamond decoration, and Bennigsen some diamonds and a hundred thousand rubles, others also received pleasant recognitions corresponding to their various grades, and following the battle fresh changes were made in the staff.

"That's how everything is done with us, all topsy-turvy!" said the Russian officers and generals after the Tarútino battle, letting it be understood that some fool there is doing things all wrong but that we ourselves should not have done so, just as people speak today. But people who talk like that either do not know what they are talking about or deliberately deceive themselves. No battle—Tarútino, Borodinó, or Austerlitz—takes place as those who planned it anticipated. That is an essential condition.

A countless number of free forces (for nowhere is man freer than during a battle, where it is a question of life and death) influence the course taken by the fight, and that course never can be known in advance and never coincides with the direction of any one force.

If many simultaneously and variously directed forces act on a given body, the direction of its motion cannot coincide with any one of those forces, but will always be a mean—what in mechanics is represented by the diagonal of a parallelogram of forces.

If in the descriptions given by historians, especially French ones, we find their wars and battles carried out in accordance with previously formed plans, the only conclusion to be drawn is that those descriptions are false.

The battle of Tarútino obviously did not attain the aim Toll had in view—to lead the troops into action in the order prescribed by the dispositions; nor that which Count Orlóv-Denísov may have had in view—to take Murat prisoner; nor the result of immediately destroying the whole corps, which Bennigsen and others may have had in view; nor the aim of the officer who wished to go into action to distinguish himself; nor that of the Cossack who wanted more booty than he got, and so on. But if the aim of the battle was what actually resulted and what all the Russians of

that day desired—to drive the French out of Russia and destroy their army
—it is quite clear that the battle of Tarútino, just because of its incongrui-
ties, was exactly what was wanted at that stage of the campaign. It would
be difficult and even impossible to imagine any result more opportune
than the actual outcome of this battle. With a minimum of effort and
insignificant losses, despite the greatest confusion, the most important
results of the whole campaign were attained: the transition from retreat
to advance, an exposure of the weakness of the French, and the administra-
tion of that shock which Napoleon's army had only awaited to begin its
flight.

2. Napoleon's measures. Proclamation in Moscow.
Effects of pillage on French discipline

NAPOLEON ENTERS Moscow after the brilliant victory *de la Moskowa;*
there can be no doubt about the victory for the battlefield remains in
the hands of the French. The Russians retreat and abandon their ancient
capital. Moscow, abounding in provisions, arms, munitions, and incal-
culable wealth, is in Napoleon's hands. The Russian army, only half the
strength of the French, does not make a single attempt to attack for a
whole month. Napoleon's position is most brilliant. He can either fall on
the Russian army with double its strength and destroy it; negotiate an
advantageous peace, or in case of a refusal make a menacing move on
Petersburg, or even, in the case of a reverse, return to Smolénsk or Vílna;
or remain in Moscow; in short, no special genius would seem to be re-
quired to retain the brilliant position the French held at that time. For
that, only very simple and easy steps were necessary: not to allow the
troops to loot, to prepare winter clothing—of which there was sufficient
in Moscow for the whole army—and methodically to collect the provi-
sions, of which (according to the French historians) there were enough
in Moscow to supply the whole army for six months. Yet Napoleon, that
greatest of all geniuses, who the historians declare had control of the army,
took none of these steps.

He not merely did nothing of the kind, but on the contrary he used his
power to select the most foolish and ruinous of all the courses open to him.
Of all that Napoleon might have done: wintering in Moscow, advancing
on Petersburg or on Nízhni-Nóvgorod, or retiring by a more northerly or
more southerly route (say by the road Kutúzov afterwards took), nothing
more stupid or disastrous can be imagined than what he actually did. He
remained in Moscow till October, letting the troops plunder the city;

then, hesitating whether to leave a garrison behind him, he quitted Moscow, approached Kutúzov without joining battle, turned to the right and reached Málo-Yaroslávets, again without attempting to break through and take the road Kutúzov took, but retiring instead to Mozháysk along the devastated Smolénsk road. Nothing more stupid than that could have been devised, or more disastrous for the army, as the sequel showed. Had Napoleon's aim been to destroy his army, the most skillful strategist could hardly have devised any series of actions that would so completely have accomplished that purpose, independently of anything the Russian army might do.

Napoleon, the man of genius, did this! But to say that he destroyed his army because he wished to, or because he was very stupid, would be as unjust as to say that he had brought his troops to Moscow because he wished to and because he was very clever and a genius.

In both cases his personal activity, having no more force than the personal activity of any soldier, merely coincided with the laws that guided the event.

The historians quite falsely represent Napoleon's faculties as having weakened in Moscow, and do so only because the results did not justify his actions. He employed all his ability and strength to do the best he could for himself and his army, as he had done previously and as he did subsequently in 1813. His activity at that time was no less astounding than it was in Egypt, in Italy, in Austria, and in Prussia. We do not know for certain in how far his genius was genuine in Egypt—where forty centuries looked down upon his grandeur—for his great exploits there are all told us by Frenchmen. We cannot accurately estimate his genius in Austria or Prussia, for we have to draw our information from French or German sources, and the incomprehensible surrender of whole corps without fighting and of fortresses without a siege must incline Germans to recognize his genius as the only explanation of the war carried on in Germany. But we, thank God, have no need to recognize his genius in order to hide our shame. We have paid for the right to look at the matter plainly and simply, and we will not abandon that right.

His activity in Moscow was as amazing and as full of genius as elsewhere. Order after order and plan after plan were issued by him from the time he entered Moscow till the time he left it. The absence of citizens and of a deputation, and even the burning of Moscow, did not disconcert him. He did not lose sight either of the welfare of his army or of the doings of the enemy, or of the welfare of the people of Russia, or of the direction of affairs in Paris, or of diplomatic considerations concerning the terms of the anticipated peace.

WITH REGARD to military matters, Napoleon immediately on his entry into
Moscow gave General Sabastiani strict orders to observe the movements
of the Russian army, sent army corps out along the different roads, and
charged Murat to find Kutúzov. Then he gave careful directions about the
fortification of the Krémlin, and drew up a brilliant plan for a future
campaign over the whole map of Russia.

With regard to diplomatic questions, Napoleon summoned Captain
Yákovlev, who had been robbed and was in rags and did not know how to
get out of Moscow, minutely explained to him his whole policy and his
magnanimity, and having written a letter to the Emperor Alexander in
which he considered it his duty to inform his Friend and Brother that
Rostopchín had managed affairs badly in Moscow, he dispatched Yákov-
lev to Petersburg.*

* This Captain Yákovlev, an ex-Captain of the Guards, was the father of
Alexander Herzen, and was a wealthy Moscow gentleman who found himself
stranded and destitute in Moscow when the house he was living in was burned
down. Herzen was only a few months old when Napoleon entered Moscow,
but we read in his Memoirs that his father, thanks to a knowledge of Italian,
attracted the interest of an Italian officer who gave him and his family some-
thing to eat and mentioned him to General Mortier who remembered having
met Yákovlev in Paris and reported his condition to Napoleon, who "ordered
him to be presented the next day. And so my father . . . presented himself,
at the Emperor's summons, in the throne room of the Krémlin, wearing an old
blue shooting jacket with brass buttons, no wig, boots which had not been
cleaned for several days, grimy linen, and a beard of two days' growth. . . .
My father asked for a safe conduct to leave Moscow.

" 'I have ordered that no passes be given. Why do you want to go? What are
you afraid of? I have ordered the markets to be opened.'

"Apparently the Emperor did not realize that, though open markets are a
convenience, so is a closed house, and that to live in the open street amid
French soldiers was not an attractive prospect for a Russian gentleman and his
family.

"When my father pointed this out, Napoleon thought for a little and then
asked abruptly:

" 'Will you undertake to hand to the Tsar a letter from me? On that condi-
tion I will order a pass to be made out for you and all your family.' . . ."

When Yákovlev reached Petersburg he "was taken straight to Arakchéev's
house and detained there." (After Speránski's dismissal Arakchéev had suc-
ceeded him as Alexander's chief minister.) "Arakchéev took the letter to give
to the Tsar. For about a month my father was under arrest in Arakchéev's
house; no friend might see him and his only visitor was S. Shishkóv, whom the

Having similarly explained his views and his magnanimity to Tutólmin, he dispatched that old man also to Petersburg to negotiate.

With regard to legal matters, immediately after the fires he gave orders to find and execute the incendiaries. And the scoundrel Rostopchín was punished by an order to burn down his houses.

With regard to administrative matters, Moscow was granted a constitution. A municipality was established and the following announcement issued:

INHABITANTS OF MOSCOW!

Your misfortunes are cruel, but His Majesty the Emperor and King desires to arrest their course. Terrible examples have taught you how he punishes disobedience and crime. Strict measures have been taken to put an end to disorder and to re-establish public security. A paternal administration, chosen from among yourselves, will form your municipality or city government. It will take care of you, of your needs, and of your welfare. Its members will be distinguished by a red ribbon worn across the shoulder, and the mayor of the city will wear a white belt as well. But when not on duty they will only wear a red ribbon round the left arm.

The city police is established on its former footing, and better order already prevails in consequence of its activity. The government has appointed two commissaries general, or chiefs of police, and twenty commissaries or captains of wards have been appointed to the different wards of the city. You will recognize them by the white ribbon they will wear on the left arm. Several churches of different denominations are open, and divine service is performed in them unhindered. Your fellow citizens are returning every day to their homes, and orders have been given that they should find in them the help and protection due to their misfortunes. These are the measures the government has adopted to re-establish order and relieve your condition. But to achieve this aim it is necessary that you should add your efforts and should, if possible, forget the misfortunes you have suffered, should entertain the hope of a less cruel fate, should be certain that inevitable and ignominious death awaits those who make any attempt on your persons or on what remains of your property, and finally that you should not doubt that these will be safeguarded, since such is the will of the greatest and most just of monarchs. Soldiers and citizens, of whatever nation you may be, re-establish public confidence, the source

Tsar sent to ask details about the burning of Moscow, the entry of the French, and the interview with Napoleon."—A.M.

(Quotations from The Memoirs of Alexander Herzen, translated by J. D. Duff, Yale University Press.)

of the welfare of a state, live like brothers, render mutual aid and protection one to another, unite to defeat the intentions of the evil-minded, obey the military and civil authorities, and your tears will soon cease to flow!

With regard to supplies for the army, Napoleon decreed that all the troops in turn should enter Moscow à la maraude [as looters] to obtain provisions for themselves, so that the army might have its future provided for.

With regard to religion, Napoleon ordered the priests to be brought back and services to be again performed in the churches.

With regard to commerce and to provisioning the army, the following was placarded everywhere:

PROCLAMATION

You, peaceful inhabitants of Moscow, artisans and workmen whom misfortune has driven from the city, and you scattered tillers of the soil, still kept out in the fields by groundless fear, listen! Tranquillity is returning to this capital and order is being restored in it. Your fellow countrymen are emerging boldly from their hiding places on finding that they are respected. Any violence to them or to their property is promptly punished. His Majesty the Emperor and King protects them, and considers no one among you his enemy except those who disobey his orders. He desires to end your misfortunes and restore you to your homes and families. Respond, therefore, to his benevolent intentions and come to us without fear. Inhabitants, return with confidence to your abodes! You will soon find means of satisfying your needs. Craftsmen and industrious artisans, return to your work, your houses, your shops, where the protection of guards awaits you! You shall receive proper pay for your work. And lastly you too, peasants, come from the forests where you are hiding in terror, return to your huts without fear, in full assurance that you will find protection! Markets are established in the city where peasants can bring their surplus supplies and the products of the soil. The government has taken the following steps to ensure freedom of sale for them: (1) From today, peasants, husbandmen, and those living in the neighborhood of Moscow may without any danger bring their supplies of all kinds to two appointed markets, of which one is on the Mokhováya Street and the other at the Provision Market. (2) Such supplies will be bought from them at such prices as seller and buyer may agree on, and if a seller is unable to obtain a fair price he will be free to take his goods back to his village and no one may hinder him under any pretense. (3) Sunday and Wednesday of each week are appointed as the chief market days and to that end a sufficient number of troops will

be stationed along the highroads on Tuesdays and Saturdays at such distances from the town as to protect the carts. (4) Similar measures will be taken that peasants with their carts and horses may meet with no hindrance on their return journey. (5) Steps will immediately be taken to re-establish ordinary trading.

Inhabitants of the city and villages, and you, workingmen and artisans, to whatever nation you belong, you are called on to carry out the paternal intentions of His Majesty the Emperor and King and to co-operate with him for the public welfare! Lay your respect and confidence at his feet and do not delay to unite with us!

With the object of raising the spirits of the troops and of the people, reviews were constantly held and rewards distributed. The Emperor rode through the streets to comfort the inhabitants, and, despite his preoccupation with state affairs, himself visited the theaters that were established by his order.

In regard to philanthropy, the greatest virtue of crowned heads, Napoleon also did all in his power. He caused the words *Maison de ma Mère* to be inscribed on the charitable institutions, thereby combining tender filial affection with the majestic benevolence of a monarch. He visited the Foundling Hospital and, allowing the orphans saved by him to kiss his white hands, graciously conversed with Tutólmin. Then, as Thiers eloquently recounts, he ordered his soldiers to be paid in forged Russian money which he had prepared: "Raising the use of these means by an act worthy of himself and of the French army, he let relief be distributed to those who had been burned out. But as food was too precious to be given to foreigners, who were for the most part enemies, Napoleon preferred to supply them with money with which to purchase food from outside, and had paper rubles distributed to them."

With reference to army discipline, orders were continually being issued to inflict severe punishment for the nonperformance of military duties and to suppress robbery.

But strange to say, all these measures, efforts, and plans—which were not at all worse than others issued in similar circumstances—did not affect the essence of the matter but, like the hands of a clock detached from the mechanism, swung about in an arbitrary and aimless way without engaging the cogwheels.

With reference to the military side—the plan of campaign—that work of genius of which Thiers remarks that, "His genius never devised anything more profound, more skillful, or more admirable," and enters into a polemic with M. Fain to prove that this work of genius must be referred

not to the fourth but to the fifteenth of October—that plan never was or could be executed, for it was quite out of touch with the facts of the case. The fortifying of the Krémlin, for which la Mosquée (as Napoleon termed the church of Basil the Beatified) was to have been razed to the ground, proved quite useless. The mining of the Krémlin only helped toward fulfilling Napoleon's wish that it should be blown up when he left Moscow —as a child wants the floor on which he has hurt himself to be beaten. The pursuit of the Russian army, about which Napoleon was so concerned, produced an unheard-of result. The French generals lost touch with the Russian army of sixty thousand men, and according to Thiers it was only eventually found, like a lost pin, by the skill—and apparently the genius—of Murat.

With reference to diplomacy, all Napoleon's arguments as to his magnanimity and justice, both to Tutólmin and to Yákovlev (whose chief concern was to obtain a greatcoat and a conveyance), proved useless; Alexander did not receive these envoys and did not reply to their embassage.

With regard to legal matters, after the execution of the supposed incendiaries the rest of Moscow burned down.

With regard to administrative matters, the establishment of a municipality did not stop the robberies and was only of use to certain people who formed part of that municipality and under pretext of preserving order looted Moscow or saved their own property from being looted.

With regard to religion, as to which in Egypt matters had so easily been settled by Napoleon's visit to a mosque, no results were achieved. Two or three priests who were found in Moscow did try to carry out Napoleon's wish, but one of them was slapped in the face by a French soldier while conducting service, and a French official reported of another that: "The priest whom I found and invited to say Mass cleaned and locked up the church. That night the doors were again broken open, the padlocks smashed, the books mutilated, and other disorders perpetrated."

With reference to commerce, the proclamation to industrious workmen and to peasants evoked no response. There were no industrious workmen, and the peasants caught the commissaries who ventured too far out of town with the proclamation and killed them.

As to the theaters for the entertainment of the people and the troops, these did not meet with success either. The theaters set up in the Krémlin and in Posnyakóv's house were closed again at once because the actors and actresses were robbed.

Even philanthropy did not have the desired effect. The genuine as well as the false paper money which flooded Moscow lost its value. The French,

collecting booty, cared only for gold. Not only was the paper money value-less which Napoleon so graciously distributed to the unfortunate, but even silver lost its value in relation to gold.

But the most amazing example of the ineffectiveness of the orders given by the authorities at that time was Napoleon's attempt to stop the looting and re-establish discipline.

This is what the army authorities were reporting:

"Looting continues in the city despite the decrees against it. Order is not yet restored and not a single merchant is carrying on trade in a lawful manner. The sutlers alone venture to trade, and they sell stolen goods."

"The neighborhood of my ward continues to be pillaged by soldiers of the 3rd Corps who, not satisfied with taking from the unfortunate inhabitants hiding in the cellars the little they have left, even have the ferocity to wound them with their sabers, as I have repeatedly witnessed."

"Nothing new, except that the soldiers are robbing and pillaging—October 9."

"Robbery and pillaging continue. There is a band of thieves in our district who ought to be arrested by a strong force—October 11."

"The Emperor is extremely displeased that despite the strict orders to stop pillage, parties of marauding Guards are continually seen returning to the Krémlin. Among the Old Guard disorder and pillage were renewed more violently than ever yesterday evening, last night, and today. The Emperor sees with regret that the picked soldiers appointed to guard his person, who should set an example of discipline, carry disobedience to such a point that they break into the cellars and stores containing army supplies. Others have disgraced themselves to the extent of disobeying sentinels and officers, and have abused and beaten them."

"The Grand Marshal of the palace," wrote the governor, "complains bitterly that in spite of repeated orders, the soldiers continue to commit nuisances in all the courtyards and even under the very windows of the Emperor."

That army, like a herd of cattle run wild and trampling underfoot the provender which might have saved it from starvation, disintegrated and perished with each additional day it remained in Moscow. But it did not go away.

It began to run away only when suddenly seized by a panic caused by the capture of transport trains on the Smolénsk road, and by the battle of Tarútino. The news of that battle of Tarútino, unexpectedly received by Napoleon at a review, evoked in him a desire to punish the Russians (Thiers says), and he issued the order for departure which the whole army was demanding.

Fleeing from Moscow the soldiers took with them everything they had stolen. Napoleon, too, carried away his own personal *trésor*, but on seeing the baggage trains that impeded the army, he was (Thiers says) horror-struck. And yet with his experience of war he did not order all the super-fluous vehicles to be burned, as he had done with those of a certain marshal when approaching Moscow. He gazed at the *calèches* and carriages in which soldiers were riding and remarked that it was a very good thing, as those vehicles could be used to carry provisions, the sick, and the wounded.

The plight of the whole army resembled that of a wounded animal which feels it is perishing and does not know what it is doing. To study the skillful tactics and aims of Napoleon and his army from the time it entered Moscow till it was destroyed is like studying the dying leaps and shudders of a mortally wounded animal. Very often a wounded animal, hearing a rustle, rushes straight at the hunter's gun, runs forward and back again, and hastens its own end. Napoleon, under pressure from his whole army, did the same thing. The rustle of the battle of Tarútino frightened the beast, and it rushed forward onto the hunter's gun, reached him, turned back, and finally—like any wild beast—ran back along the most disadvantageous and dangerous path, where the old scent was familiar.

During the whole of that period Napoleon, who seems to us to have been the leader of all these movements—as the figurehead of a ship may seem to a savage to guide the vessel—acted like a child who, holding a couple of strings inside a carriage, thinks he is driving it.

3. *Pierre: four weeks in captivity. Karatáev and a French sol-dier. The French leave Moscow. The drum. Pierre's mental change; he recovers his grip on life. Exit of troops and pris-oners. The road blocked. Pierre's reflections*

EARLY IN THE MORNING of the sixth of October Pierre went out of the shed, and on returning stopped by the door to play with a little blue-gray dog, with a long body and short bandy legs, that jumped about him. This little dog lived in their shed, sleeping beside Karatáev at night; it sometimes made excursions into the town but always returned again. Probably it had never had an owner, and it still belonged to nobody and had no name. The French called it Azor; the soldier who told stories called it Femgálka; Karatáev and others called it Gray, or sometimes Flabby. Its lack of a master, a name, or even of a breed or any definite color did not seem to trouble the blue-gray dog in the least. Its furry tail stood up firm and round as a plume, its bandy legs served it so well that it would often

gracefully lift a hind leg and run very easily and quickly on three legs, as if disdaining to use all four. Everything pleased it. Now it would roll on its back, yelping with delight, now bask in the sun with a thoughtful air of importance, and now frolic about playing with a chip of wood or a straw.

Pierre's attire by now consisted of a dirty torn shirt (the only remnant of his former clothing), a pair of soldier's trousers which by Karatáev's advice he tied with string round the ankles for warmth, and a peasant coat and cap. Physically he had changed much during this time. He no longer seemed stout, though he still had the appearance of solidity and strength hereditary in his family. A beard and mustache covered the lower part of his face, and a tangle of hair, infested with lice, curled round his head like a cap. The look of his eyes was resolute, calm, and animatedly alert, as never before. The former slackness which had shown itself even in his eyes was now replaced by an energetic readiness for action and resistance. His feet were bare.

Pierre first looked down the field across which vehicles and horsemen were passing that morning, then into the distance across the river, then at the dog who was pretending to be in earnest about biting him, and then at his bare feet which he placed with pleasure in various positions, moving his dirty thick big toes. Every time he looked at his bare feet a smile of animated self-satisfaction flitted across his face. The sight of them reminded him of all he had experienced and learned during these weeks and this recollection was pleasant to him.

For some days the weather had been calm and clear with slight frosts in the mornings—what is called an "old wives' summer."

In the sunshine the air was warm, and that warmth was particularly pleasant with the invigorating freshness of the morning frost still in the air.

On everything—far and near—lay the magic crystal glitter seen only at that time of autumn. The Sparrow Hills were visible in the distance, with the village, the church, and the large white house. The bare trees, the sand, the bricks and roofs of the houses, the green church spire, and the corners of the white house in the distance, all stood out in the transparent air in most delicate outline and with unnatural clearness. Near by could be seen the familiar ruins of a half-burned mansion occupied by the French, with lilac bushes still showing dark green beside the fence. And even that ruined and befouled house—which in dull weather was repulsively ugly—seemed quietly beautiful now, in the clear, motionless brilliance.

A French corporal, with coat unbuttoned in a homely way, a skullcap on his head, and a short pipe in his mouth, came from behind a corner of the shed and approached Pierre with a friendly wink.

"What sunshine, Monsieur Kiril!" (Their name for Pierre.) "Eh? Just like spring!"

And the corporal leaned against the door and offered Pierre his pipe, though whenever he offered it Pierre always declined it.

"To be on the march in such weather . . ." he began.

Pierre inquired what was being said about leaving, and the corporal told him that nearly all the troops were starting and there ought to be an order about the prisoners that day. Sokolóv, one of the soldiers in the shed with Pierre, was dying, and Pierre told the corporal that something should be done about him. The corporal replied that Pierre need not worry about that as they had an ambulance and a permanent hospital and arrangements would be made for the sick, and that in general everything that could happen had been foreseen by the authorities.

"Besides, Monsieur Kiril, you have only to say a word to the captain, you know. He is a man who never forgets anything. Speak to the captain when he makes his round, he will do anything for you."

(The captain of whom the corporal spoke often had long chats with Pierre and showed him all sorts of favors.)

" 'You see, St. Thomas,' he said to me the other day. 'Monsieur Kiril is a man of education, who speaks French. He is a Russian seigneur who has had misfortunes, but he is a man. He knows what's what. . . . If he wants anything and asks me, he won't get a refusal. When one has studied, you see, one likes education and well-bred people.' It is for your sake I mention it, Monsieur Kiril. The other day if it had not been for you that affair would have ended ill."

And after chatting a while longer, the corporal went away. (The affair he had alluded to had happened a few days before—a fight between the prisoners and the French soldiers, in which Pierre had succeeded in pacifying his comrades.) Some of the prisoners who had heard Pierre talking to the corporal immediately asked what the Frenchman had said. While Pierre was repeating what he had been told about the army leaving Moscow, a thin, sallow, tattered French soldier came up to the door of the shed. Rapidly and timidly raising his fingers to his forehead by way of greeting, he asked Pierre whether the soldier Platoche to whom he had given a shirt to sew was in that shed.

A week before the French had had boot leather and linen issued to them, which they had given out to the prisoners to make up into boots and shirts for them.

"Ready, ready, dear fellow!" said Karatáev, coming out with a neatly folded shirt.

Karatáev, on account of the warm weather and for convenience at work,

was wearing only trousers and a tattered shirt as black as soot. His hair was bound round, workman fashion, with a wisp of lime-tree bast, and his round face seemed rounder and pleasanter than ever.

"A promise is own brother to performance! I said Friday and here it is, ready," said Platón, smiling and unfolding the shirt he had sewn.

The Frenchman glanced around uneasily and then, as if overcoming his hesitation, rapidly threw off his uniform and put on the shirt. He had a long, greasy, flowered silk waistcoat next to his sallow, thin bare body, but no shirt. He was evidently afraid the prisoners looking on would laugh at him, and thrust his head into the shirt hurriedly. None of the prisoners said a word.

"See, it fits well!" Platón kept repeating, pulling the shirt straight.

The Frenchman, having pushed his head and hands through, without raising his eyes, looked down at the shirt and examined the seams.

"You see, dear man, this is not a sewing shop, and I had no proper tools; and, as they say, one needs a tool even to kill a louse," said Platón with one of his round smiles, obviously pleased with his work.

"It's good, quite good, thank you," said the Frenchman, in French, "but there must be some linen left over."

"It will fit better still when it sets to your body," said Karatáev, still admiring his handiwork. "You'll be nice and comfortable. . . ."

"Thanks, thanks, old fellow. . . . But the bits left over?" said the Frenchman again and smiled. He took out an assignation ruble note and gave it to Karatáev. "But give me the pieces that are over."

Pierre saw that Platón did not want to understand what the Frenchman was saying, and he looked on without interfering. Karatáev thanked the Frenchman for the money and went on admiring his own work. The Frenchman insisted on having the pieces returned that were left over and asked Pierre to translate what he said.

"What does he want the bits for?" said Karatáev. "They'd make fine leg bands for us. Well, never mind."

And Karatáev, with a suddenly changed and saddened expression, took a small bundle of scraps from inside his shirt and gave it to the Frenchman without looking at him. "Oh dear!" muttered Karatáev and went away. The Frenchman looked at the linen, considered for a moment, then looked inquiringly at Pierre and, as if Pierre's look had told him something, suddenly blushed and shouted in a squeaky voice:

"Platoche! Eh, Platoche! Keep them yourself!" And handing back the odd bits he turned and went out.

"There, look at that," said Karatáev, swaying his head. "People said they were not Christians, but they too have souls. It's what the old folk

used to say: 'A sweating hand's an open hand, a dry hand's close.' He's naked, but yet he's given it back."

Karatáev smiled thoughtfully and was silent awhile looking at the pieces. "But they'll make grand leg bands, dear friend," he said, and went back into the shed.

FOUR WEEKS had passed since Pierre had been taken prisoner and though the French had offered to move him from the men's to the officers' shed, he had stayed in the shed where he was first put.

In burned and devastated Moscow Pierre experienced almost the extreme limits of privation a man can endure; but thanks to his physical strength and health, of which he had till then been unconscious, and thanks especially to the fact that the privations came so gradually that it was impossible to say when they began, he endured his position not only lightly but joyfully. And just at this time he obtained the tranquillity and ease of mind he had formerly striven in vain to reach. He had long sought in different ways that tranquillity of mind, that inner harmony which had so impressed him in the soldiers at the battle of Borodinó. He had sought it in philanthropy, in Freemasonry, in the dissipations of town life, in wine, in heroic feats of self-sacrifice, and in romantic love for Natásha; he had sought it by reasoning—and all these quests and experiments had failed him. And now without thinking about it he had found that peace and inner harmony only through the horror of death, through privation, and through what he recognized in Karatáev.

Those dreadful moments he had lived through at the executions had as it were forever washed away from his imagination and memory the agitating thoughts and feelings that had formerly seemed so important. It did not now occur to him to think of Russia, or the war, or politics, or Napoleon. It was plain to him that all these things were no business of his, and that he was not called on to judge concerning them and therefore could not do so. "Russia and summer weather are not bound together," he thought, repeating words of Karatáev's which he found strangely consoling. His intention of killing Napoleon and his calculations of the cabalistic number of the beast of the Apocalypse now seemed to him meaningless and even ridiculous. His anger with his wife and anxiety that his name should not be smirched now seemed not merely trivial but even amusing. What concern was it of his that somewhere or other that woman was leading the life she preferred? What did it matter to anybody, and especially to him, whether or not they found out that their prisoner's name was Count Bezúkhov?

He now often remembered his conversation with Prince Andrew and

quite agreed with him, though he understood Prince Andrew's thoughts somewhat differently. Prince Andrew had thought and said that happiness could only be negative, but had said it with a shade of bitterness and irony as though he was really saying that all desire for positive happiness is implanted in us merely to torment us and never be satisfied. But Pierre believed it without any mental reservation. The absence of suffering, the satisfaction of one's needs and consequent freedom in the choice of one's occupation, that is, of one's way of life, now seemed to Pierre to be indubitably man's highest happiness. Here and now for the first time he fully appreciated the enjoyment of eating when he wanted to eat, drinking when he wanted to drink, sleeping when he wanted to sleep, of warmth when he was cold, of talking to a fellow man when he wished to talk and to hear a human voice. The satisfaction of one's needs—good food, cleanliness, and freedom—now that he was deprived of all this, seemed to Pierre to constitute perfect happiness; and the choice of occupation, that is, of his way of life—now that that choice was so restricted—seemed to him such an easy matter that he forgot that a superfluity of the comforts of life destroys all joy in satisfying one's needs, while great freedom in the choice of occupation—such freedom as his wealth, his education, and his social position had given him in his own life—is just what makes the choice of occupation insolubly difficult and destroys the desire and possibility of having an occupation.

All Pierre's daydreams now turned on the time when he would be free. Yet subsequently, and for the rest of his life, he thought and spoke with enthusiasm of that month of captivity, of those irrecoverable, strong, joyful sensations, and chiefly of the complete peace of mind and inner freedom which he experienced only during those weeks.

When on the first day he got up early, went out of the shed at dawn, and saw the cupolas and crosses of the New Convent of the Virgin still dark at first, the hoarfrost on the dusty grass, the Sparrow Hills, and the wooded banks above the winding river vanishing in the purple distance, when he felt the contact of the fresh air and heard the noise of the crows flying from Moscow across the field, and when afterwards light gleamed from the east and the sun's rim appeared solemnly from behind a cloud, and the cupolas and crosses, the hoarfrost, the distance and the river, all began to sparkle in the glad light—Pierre felt a new joy and strength in life such as he had never before known. And this not only stayed with him during the whole of his imprisonment, but even grew in strength as the hardships of his position increased.

That feeling of alertness and of readiness for anything was still further strengthened in him by the high opinion his fellow prisoners formed of

him soon after his arrival at the shed. With his knowledge of languages, the respect shown him by the French, his simplicity, his readiness to give anything asked of him (he received the allowance of three rubles a week made to officers); with his strength, which he showed to the soldiers by pressing nails into the walls of the hut; his gentleness to his companions, and his capacity for sitting still and thinking without doing anything (which seemed to them incomprehensible), he appeared to them a rather mysterious and superior being. The very qualities that had been a hindrance, if not actually harmful, to him in the world he had lived in —his strength, his disdain for the comforts of life, his absent-mindedness and simplicity—here among these people gave him almost the status of a hero. And Pierre felt that their opinion placed responsibilities upon him.

THE FRENCH EVACUATION began on the night between the sixth and seventh of October: kitchens and sheds were dismantled, carts loaded, and troops and baggage trains started.

At seven in the morning a French convoy in marching trim, wearing shakos and carrying muskets, knapsacks, and enormous sacks, stood in front of the sheds, and animated French talk mingled with curses sounded all along the lines.

In the shed everyone was ready, dressed, belted, shod, and only awaited the order to start. The sick soldier, Sokolóv, pale and thin with dark shadows round his eyes, alone sat in his place barefoot and not dressed. His eyes, prominent from the emaciation of his face, gazed inquiringly at his comrades who were paying no attention to him, and he moaned regularly and quietly. It was evidently not so much his sufferings that caused him to moan (he had dysentery) as his fear and grief at being left alone.

Pierre, girt with a rope round his waist and wearing shoes Karatáev had made for him from some leather a French soldier had torn off a tea chest and brought to have his boots mended with, went up to the sick man and squatted down beside him.

"You know, Sokolóv, they are not all going away! They have a hospital here. You may be better off than we others," said Pierre.

"O Lord! Oh, it will be the death of me! O Lord!" moaned the man in a louder voice.

"I'll go and ask them again directly," said Pierre, rising and going to the door of the shed.

Just as Pierre reached the door, the corporal who had offered him a pipe the day before came up to it with two soldiers. The corporal and

soldiers were in marching kit with knapsacks and shakos that had metal straps, and these changed their familiar faces.

The corporal came, according to orders, to shut the door. The prisoners had to be counted before being let out.

"Corporal, what will they do with the sick man? . . ." Pierre began.

But even as he spoke he began to doubt whether this was the corporal he knew or a stranger, so unlike himself did the corporal seem at that moment. Moreover, just as Pierre was speaking a sharp rattle of drums was suddenly heard from both sides. The corporal frowned at Pierre's words and, uttering some meaningless oaths, slammed the door. The shed became semidark, and the sharp rattle of the drums on two sides drowned the sick man's groans.

"There it is! . . . *It* again! . . ." said Pierre to himself, and an involuntary shudder ran down his spine. In the corporal's changed face, in the sound of his voice, in the stirring and deafening noise of the drums, he recognized that mysterious, callous force which compelled people against their will to kill their fellow men—that force the effect of which he had witnessed during the executions. To fear or to try to escape that force, to address entreaties or exhortations to those who served as its tools, was useless. Pierre knew this now. One had to wait and endure. He did not again go to the sick man, nor turn to look at him, but stood frowning by the door of the hut.

When that door was opened and the prisoners, crowding against one another like a flock of sheep, squeezed into the exit, Pierre pushed his way forward and approached that very captain who as the corporal had assured him was ready to do anything for him. The captain was also in marching kit, and on his cold face appeared that same *it* which Pierre had recognized in the corporal's words and in the roll of the drums.

"Pass on, pass on!" the captain reiterated, frowning sternly, and looking at the prisoners who thronged past him.

Pierre went up to him, though he knew his attempt would be vain.

"What now?" the officer asked with a cold look as if not recognizing Pierre.

Pierre told him about the sick man.

"He'll manage to walk, devil take him!" said the captain. "Pass on, pass on!" he continued without looking at Pierre.

"But he is dying," Pierre again began.

"Be so good . . ." shouted the captain, frowning angrily.

"*Dram-da-da-dam, dam-dam* . . ." rattled the drums, and Pierre understood that this mysterious force completely controlled these men and that it was now useless to say any more.

The officer prisoners were separated from the soldiers and told to march in front. There were about thirty officers, with Pierre among them, and about three hundred men.

The officers, who had come from the other sheds, were all strangers to Pierre and much better dressed than he. They looked at him and at his shoes mistrustfully, as at an alien. Not far from him walked a fat major with a sallow, bloated, angry face, who was wearing a Kazán dressing grown tied round with a towel, and who evidently enjoyed the respect of his fellow prisoners. He kept one hand, in which he clasped his tobacco pouch, inside the bosom of his dressing gown and held the stem of his pipe firmly with the other. Panting and puffing, the major grumbled and growled at everybody because he thought he was being pushed and that they were all hurrying when they had nowhere to hurry to and were all surprised at something when there was nothing to be surprised at. Another, a thin little officer, was speaking to everyone, conjecturing where they were now being taken and how far they would get that day. An official in felt boots and wearing a commissariat uniform ran round from side to side and gazed at the ruins of Moscow, loudly announcing his observations as to what had been burned down and what this or that part of the city was that they could see. A third officer, who by his accent was a Pole, disputed with the commissariat officer, arguing that he was mistaken in his identification of the different wards of Moscow.

"What are you disputing about?" said the major angrily. "What does it matter whether it is St. Nicholas or St. Blasius? You see it's burned down, and there's an end of it. . . . What are you pushing for? Isn't the road wide enough?" said he, turning to a man behind him who was not pushing him at all.

"Oh, oh, oh! What have they done?" the prisoners on one side and another were heard saying as they gazed on the charred ruins. "All beyond the river, and Zúbova, and in the Krémlin. . . . Just look! There's not half of it left. Yes, I told you—the whole quarter beyond the river, and so it is."

"Well, you know it's burned, so what's the use of talking?" said the major.

As they passed near a church in the Khamóvniki (one of the few unburned quarters of Moscow) the whole mass of prisoners suddenly started to one side and exclamations of horror and disgust were heard.

"Ah, the villains! What heathens! Yes; dead, dead, so he is. . . . And smeared with something!"

Pierre too drew near the church where the thing was that evoked these exclamations, and dimly made out something leaning against the palings

surrounding the church. From the words of his comrades who saw better than he did, he found that this was the body of a man, set upright against the palings with its face smeared with soot.

"Go on! What the devil . . . Go on! Thirty thousand devils! . . ." the convoy guards began cursing and the French soldiers, with fresh virulence, drove away with their swords the crowd of prisoners who were gazing at the dead man.

THROUGH THE CROSS STREETS of the Khamóvniki quarter the prisoners marched, followed only by their escort and the vehicles and wagons belonging to that escort, but when they reached the supply stores they came among a huge and closely packed train of artillery mingled with private vehicles.

At the bridge they all halted, waiting for those in front to get across. From the bridge they had a view of endless lines of moving baggage trains before and behind them. To the right, where the Kalúga road turns near Neskúchny, endless rows of troops and carts stretched away into the distance. These were troops of Beauharnais' corps which had started before any of the others. Behind, along the riverside and across the Stone Bridge, were Ney's troops and transport.

Davout's troops, in whose charge were the prisoners, were crossing the Crimean bridge and some were already debouching into the Kalúga road. But the baggage trains stretched out so that the last of Beauharnais' train had not yet got out of Moscow and reached the Kalúga road when the vanguard of Ney's army was already emerging from the Great Ordýnka Street.

When they had crossed the Crimean bridge the prisoners moved a few steps forward, halted, and again moved on, and from all sides vehicles and men crowded closer and closer together. They advanced the few hundred paces that separated the bridge from the Kalúga road, taking more than an hour to do so, and came out upon the square where the streets of the Transmoskvá ward and the Kalúga road converge, and the prisoners jammed close together had to stand for some hours at that crossway. From all sides, like the roar of the sea, were heard the rattle of wheels, the tramp of feet, and incessant shouts of anger and abuse. Pierre stood pressed against the wall of a charred house, listening to that noise which mingled in his imagination with the roll of the drums.

To get a better view, several officer prisoners climbed onto the wall of the half-burned house against which Pierre was leaning.

"What crowds! Just look at the crowds! . . . They've loaded goods even on the cannon! Look there, those are furs!" they exclaimed. "Just see

what the blackguards have looted. . . . There! See what that one has behind in the cart. . . . Why, those are settings taken from some icons, by heaven! . . . Oh, the rascals! . . . See how that fellow has loaded himself up, he can hardly walk! Good lord, they've even grabbed those chaises! . . . See that fellow there sitting on the trunks. . . . Heavens! They're fighting."

"That's right, hit him on the snout—on his snout! Like this, we shan't get away before evening. Look, look there. . . . Why, that must be Napoleon's own. See what horses! And the monograms with a crown! It's like a portable house. . . . That fellow's dropped his sack and doesn't see it. Fighting again . . . A woman with a baby, and not bad-looking either! Yes, I dare say, that's the way they'll let you pass. . . . Just look, there's no end to it. Russian wenches, by heaven, so they are! In carriages —see how comfortably they've settled themselves!"

Again, as at the church in Khamóvniki, a wave of general curiosity bore all the prisoners forward onto the road, and Pierre, thanks to his stature, saw over the heads of the others what so attracted their curiosity. In three carriages involved among the munition carts, closely squeezed together, sat women with rouged faces, dressed in glaring colors, who were shouting something in shrill voices.

From the moment Pierre had recognized the appearance of the mysterious force nothing had seemed to him strange or dreadful: neither the corpse smeared with soot for fun nor these women hurrying away nor the burned ruins of Moscow. All that he now witnessed scarcely made an impression on him—as if his soul, making ready for a hard struggle, refused to receive impressions that might weaken it.

The women's vehicles drove by. Behind them came more carts, soldiers, wagons, soldiers, gun carriages, carriages, soldiers, ammunition carts, more soldiers, and now and then women.

Pierre did not see the people as individuals but saw their movement.

All these people and horses seemed driven forward by some invisible power. During the hour Pierre watched them they all came flowing from the different streets with one and the same desire to get on quickly; they all jostled one another, began to grow angry and to fight, white teeth gleamed, brows frowned, ever the same words of abuse flew from side to side, and all the faces bore the same swaggeringly resolute and coldly cruel expression that had struck Pierre that morning on the corporal's face when the drums were beating.

It was not till nearly evening that the officer commanding the escort collected his men and with shouts and quarrels forced his way in among

the baggage trains, and the prisoners, hemmed in on all sides, emerged onto the Kalúga road.

They marched very quickly, without resting, and halted only when the sun began to set. The baggage carts drew up close together and the men began to prepare for their night's rest. They all appeared angry and dissatisfied. For a long time, oaths, angry shouts, and fighting could be heard from all sides. A carriage that followed the escort ran into one of the carts and knocked a hole in it with its pole. Several soldiers ran toward the cart from different sides: some beat the carriage horses on their heads, turning them aside, others fought among themselves, and Pierre saw that one German was badly wounded on the head by a sword.

It seemed that all these men, now that they had stopped amid fields in the chill dusk of the autumn evening, experienced one and the same feeling of unpleasant awakening from the hurry and eagerness to push on that had seized them at the start. Once at a standstill they all seemed to understand that they did not yet know where they were going, and that much that was painful and difficult awaited them on this journey.

During this halt the escort treated the prisoners even worse than they had done at the start. It was here that the prisoners for the first time received horseflesh for their meat ration.

From the officer down to the lowest soldier they all showed what seemed like personal spite against each of the prisoners, in unexpected contrast to their former friendly relations.

This spite increased still more when, on calling over the roll of prisoners, it was found that in the bustle of leaving Moscow one Russian soldier, who had pretended to suffer from colic, had escaped. Pierre saw a Frenchman beat a Russian soldier cruelly for straying too far from the road, and heard his friend the captain reprimand and threaten to court-martial a noncommissioned officer on account of the escape of the Russian. To the noncommissioned officer's excuse that the prisoner was ill and could not walk, the officer replied that the order was to shoot those who lagged behind. Pierre felt that that fatal force which had crushed him during the executions, but which he had not felt during his imprisonment, now again controlled his existence. It was terrible, but he felt that in proportion to the efforts of that fatal force to crush him, there grew and strengthened in his soul a power of life independent of it.

He ate his supper of buckwheat soup with horseflesh and chatted with his comrades.

Neither Pierre nor any of the others spoke of what they had seen in Moscow, or of the roughness of their treatment by the French, or of the order to shoot them which had been announced to them. As if in reaction

against the worsening of their position they were all particularly animated and gay. They spoke of personal reminiscences, of amusing scenes they had witnessed during the campaign, and avoided all talk of their present situation.

The sun had set long since. Bright stars shone out here and there in the sky. A red glow as of a conflagration spread above the horizon from the rising full moon, and that vast red ball swayed strangely in the gray haze. It grew light. The evening was ending, but the night had not yet come. Pierre got up and left his new companions, crossing between the campfires to the other side of the road where he had been told the common soldier prisoners were stationed. He wanted to talk to them. On the road he was stopped by a French sentinel who ordered him back.

Pierre turned back, not to his companions by the campfire, but to an unharnessed cart where there was nobody. Tucking his legs under him and dropping his head he sat down on the cold ground by the wheel of the cart and remained motionless a long while sunk in thought. Suddenly he burst out into a fit of his broad, good-natured laughter, so loud that men from various sides turned with surprise to see what this strange and evidently solitary laughter could mean.

"Ha-ha-ha!" laughed Pierre. And he said aloud to himself: "The soldier did not let me pass. They took me and shut me up. They hold me captive. What, me? Me? My immortal soul? Ha-ha-ha! Ha-ha-ha! . . ." and he laughed till tears started to his eyes.

A man got up and came to see what this queer big fellow was laughing at all by himself. Pierre stopped laughing, got up, went farther away from the inquisitive man, and looked around him.

The huge, endless bivouac that had previously resounded with the crackling of campfires and the voices of many men had grown quiet, the red campfires were growing paler and dying down. High up in the light sky hung the full moon. Forests and fields beyond the camp, unseen before, were now visible in the distance. And farther still, beyond those forests and fields, the bright, oscillating, limitless distance lured one to itself. Pierre glanced up at the sky and the twinkling stars in its faraway depths. "And all that is me, all that is within me, and it is all I!" thought Pierre. "And they caught all that and put it into a shed boarded up with planks!" He smiled, and went and lay down to sleep beside his companions.

4. The Russian army. Dokhtúrov. News of the French having left Moscow reaches Kutúzov at night. His emotion. Cossacks nearly capture Napoleon at Málo-Yaroslávets. He retreats by the Smolénsk road. A third of his army melts away before reaching Vyázma

IN THE EARLY DAYS of October another envoy came to Kutúzov with a letter from Napoleon proposing peace and falsely dated from Moscow, though Napoleon was already not far from Kutúzov on the old Kalúga road. Kutúzov replied to this letter as he had done to the one formerly brought by Lauriston, saying that there could be no question of peace.

Soon after that a report was received from Dórokhov's guerrilla detachment operating to the left of Tarútino that troops of Broussier's division had been seen at Formínsk and that being separated from the rest of the French army they might easily be destroyed. The soldiers and officers again demanded action. Generals on the staff, excited by the memory of the easy victory at Tarútino, urged Kutúzov to carry out Dórokhov's suggestion. Kutúzov did not consider any offensive necessary. The result was a compromise which was inevitable: a small detachment was sent to Formínsk to attack Broussier.

By a strange coincidence, this task, which turned out to be a most difficult and important one, was entrusted to Dokhtúrov—that same modest little Dokhtúrov whom no one had described to us as drawing up plans of battles, dashing about in front of regiments, showering crosses on batteries, and so on, and who was thought to be and was spoken of as undecided and undiscerning—but whom we find commanding wherever the position was most difficult all through the Russo-French wars from Austerlitz to the year 1813. At Austerlitz he remained last at the Augezd dam, rallying the regiments, saving what was possible when all were flying and perishing and not a single general was left in the rearguard. Ill with fever he went to Smolénsk with twenty thousand men to defend the town against Napoleon's whole army. In Smolénsk, at the Malákhov Gate, he had hardly dozed off in a paroxysm of fever before he was awakened by the bombardment of the town—and Smolénsk held out all day long. At the battle of Borodinó, when Bagratión was killed and nine tenths of the men of our left flank had fallen and the full force of the French artillery fire was directed against it, the man sent there was this same irresolute and undiscerning Dokhtúrov—Kutúzov hastening to rectify a mistake he had made by sending someone else there first. And the quiet little Dokhtúrov rode thither, and Borodinó became the greatest glory of the Russian army.

Many heroes have been described to us in verse and prose, but of Dokhtúrov scarcely a word has been said.

It was Dokhtúrov again whom they sent to Formínsk and from there to Málo-Yaroslávets, the place where the last battle with the French was fought and where the obvious disintegration of the French army began; and we are told of many geniuses and heroes of that period of the campaign, but of Dokhtúrov nothing or very little is said and that dubiously. And this silence about Dokhtúrov is the clearest testimony to his merit.

It is natural for a man who does not understand the workings of a machine to imagine that a shaving that has fallen into it by chance and is interfering with its action and tossing about in it is its most important part. The man who does not understand the construction of the machine cannot conceive that the small connecting cogwheel which revolves quietly is one of the most essential parts of the machine, and not the shaving which merely harms and hinders the working.

On the tenth of October when Dokhtúrov had gone halfway to Formínsk and stopped at the village of Aristóvo, preparing faithfully to execute the orders he had received, the whole French army having, in its convulsive movement, reached Murat's position apparently in order to give battle—suddenly without any reason turned off to the left onto the new Kalúga road and began to enter Formínsk, where only Broussier had been till then. At that time Dokhtúrov had under his command, besides Dórokhov's detachment, the two small guerrilla detachments of Figner and Seslávin.

On the evening of October 11 Seslávin came to the Aristóvo headquarters with a French guardsman he had captured. The prisoner said that the troops that had entered Formínsk that day were the vanguard of the whole army, that Napoleon was there and the whole army had left Moscow four days previously. That same evening a house serf who had come from Bórovsk said he had seen an immense army entering the town. Some Cossacks of Dokhtúrov's detachment reported having sighted the French Guards marching along the road to Bórovsk. From all these reports it was evident that where they had expected to meet a single division there was now the whole French army marching from Moscow in an unexpected direction—along the Kalúga road. Dokhtúrov was unwilling to undertake any action, as it was not clear to him now what he ought to do. He had been ordered to attack Formínsk. But only Broussier had been there at that time and now the whole French army was there. Ermólov wished to act on his own judgment, but Dokhtúrov insisted that he must have Kutúzov's instructions. So it was decided to send a dispatch to the staff.

For this purpose a capable officer, Bolkhovítinov, was chosen, who was to explain the whole affair by word of mouth, besides delivering a written report. Toward midnight Bolkhovítinov, having received the dispatch and verbal instructions, galloped off to the General Staff accompanied by a Cossack with spare horses.

IT WAS a warm, dark, autumn night. It had been raining for four days. Having changed horses twice and galloped twenty miles in an hour and a half over a sticky, muddy road, Bolkhovítinov reached Litashëvka after one o'clock at night. Dismounting at a cottage on whose wattle fence hung a signboard, GENERAL STAFF, and throwing down his reins, he entered a dark passage.

"The general on duty, quick! It's very important!" said he to someone who had risen and was sniffing in the dark passage.

"He has been very unwell since the evening and this is the third night he has not slept," said the orderly pleadingly in a whisper. "You should wake the captain first."

"But this is very important, from General Dokhtúrov," said Bolkhovítinov, entering the open door which he had found by feeling in the dark. The orderly had gone in before him and began waking somebody.

"Your honor, your honor! A courier."

"What? What's that? From whom?" came a sleepy voice.

"From Dokhtúrov and from Alexéy Petróvich. Napoleon is at Formínsk," said Bolkhovítinov, unable to see in the dark who was speaking but guessing by the voice that it was not Konovnítsyn.

The man who had wakened yawned and stretched himself.

"I don't like waking him," he said, fumbling for something. "He is very ill. Perhaps this is only a rumor."

"Here is the dispatch," said Bolkhovítinov. "My orders are to give it at once to the general on duty."

"Wait a moment, I'll light a candle. You damned rascal, where do you always hide it?" said the voice of the man who was stretching himself, to the orderly. (This was Shcherbínin, Konovnítsyn's adjutant.) "I've found it, I've found it!" he added.

The orderly was striking a light and Shcherbínin was fumbling for something on the candlestick.*

* *We have here a detailed description of the process of lighting a match before lucifer matches were introduced. Sparks were obtained by striking steel against a flint and these sparks falling on tinder caused it to smolder. Then a splinter dipped in sulphur was applied to the smoldering tinder and a light was obtained.*—A.M.

"Oh, the nasty beasts!" said he with disgust.

By the light of the sparks Bolkhovítinov saw Shcherbínin's youthful face as he held the candle, and the face of another man who was still asleep. This was Konovnítsyn.

When the flame of the sulphur splinters kindled by the tinder burned up, first blue and then red, Shcherbínin lit the tallow candle, from the candlestick of which the cockroaches that had been gnawing it were running away, and looked at the messenger. Bolkhovítinov was bespattered all over with mud and had smeared his face by wiping it with his sleeve.

"Who gave the report?" inquired Shcherbínin, taking the envelope.

"The news is reliable," said Bolkhovítinov. "Prisoners, Cossacks, and the scouts all say the same thing."

"There's nothing to be done, we'll have to wake him," said Shcherbínin, rising and going up to the man in the nightcap who lay covered by a greatcoat. "Peter Petróvich!" said he. (Konovnítsyn did not stir.) "To the General Staff!" he said with a smile, knowing that those words would be sure to arouse him.

And in fact the head in the nightcap was lifted at once. On Konovnítsyn's handsome, resolute face with cheeks flushed by fever, there still remained for an instant a faraway dreamy expression remote from present affairs, but then he suddenly started and his face assumed its habitual calm and firm appearance.

"Well, what is it? From whom?" he asked immediately but without hurry, blinking at the light.

While listening to the officer's report Konovnítsyn broke the seal and read the dispatch. Hardly had he done so before he lowered his legs in their woolen stockings to the earthen floor and began putting on his boots. Then he took off his nightcap, combed his hair over his temples, and donned his cap.

"Did you get here quickly? Let us go to his Highness."

Konovnítsyn had understood at once that the news brought was of great importance and that no time must be lost. He did not consider or ask himself whether the news was good or bad. That did not interest him. He regarded the whole business of the war not with his intelligence or his reason but by something else. There was within him a deep unexpressed conviction that all would be well, but that one must not trust to this and still less speak about it, but must only attend to one's own work. And he did his work, giving his whole strength to the task.

Peter Petróvich Konovnítsyn, like Dokhtúrov, seems to have been included merely for propriety's sake in the list of the so-called heroes of 1812 —the Barclays, Raévskis, Ermólovs, Plátovs, and Milorádoviches. Like

Dokhtúrov he had the reputation of being a man of very limited capacity and information, and like Dokhtúrov he never made plans of battle but was always found where the situation was most difficult. Since his appointment as general on duty he had always slept with his door open, giving orders that every messenger should be allowed to wake him up. In battle he was always under fire, so that Kutúzov reproved him for it and feared to send him to the front, and like Dokhtúrov he was one of those unnoticed cogwheels that, without clatter or noise, constitute the most essential part of the machine.

Coming out of the hut into the damp, dark night Konovnítsyn frowned —partly from an increased pain in his head and partly at the unpleasant thought that occurred to him, of how all that nest of influential men on the staff would be stirred up by this news, especially Bennigsen, who ever since Tarútino had been at daggers drawn with Kutúzov; and how they would make suggestions, quarrel, issue orders, and rescind them. And this premonition was disagreeable to him though he knew it could not be helped.

And in fact Toll, to whom he went to communicate the news, immediately began to expound his plans to a general sharing his quarters, until Konovnítsyn, who listened in weary silence, reminded him that they must go to see his Highness.

Kutúzov like all old people did not sleep much at night. He often fell asleep unexpectedly in the daytime, but at night, lying on his bed without undressing, he generally remained awake thinking.

So he lay now on his bed, supporting his large, heavy, scarred head on his plump hand, with his one eye open, meditating and peering into the darkness.

Since Bennigsen, who corresponded with the Emperor and had more influence than anyone else on the staff, had begun to avoid him, Kutúzov was more at ease as to the possibility of himself and his troops being obliged to take part in useless aggressive movements. The lesson of the Tarútino battle and of the day before it, which Kutúzov remembered with pain, must, he thought, have some effect on others too.

"They must understand that we can only lose by taking the offensive. Patience and time are my warriors, my champions," thought Kutúzov. He knew that an apple should not be plucked while it is green. It will fall of itself when ripe, but if picked unripe the apple is spoiled, the tree is harmed, and your teeth are set on edge. Like an experienced sportsman he knew that the beast was wounded, and wounded as only the whole strength of Russia could have wounded it, but whether it was mortally

wounded or not was still an undecided question. Now by the fact of
Lauriston and Barthélemi having been sent, and by the reports of the
guerrillas, Kutúzov was almost sure that the wound was mortal. But he
needed further proofs and it was necessary to wait.

"They want to run to see how they have wounded it. Wait and we shall
see! Continual maneuvers, continual advances!" thought he. "What for?
Only to distinguish themselves! As if fighting were fun. They are like chil-
dren from whom one can't get any sensible account of what has happened
because they all want to show how well they can fight. But that's not what
is needed now.

"And what ingenious maneuvers they all propose to me! It seems to
them that when they have thought of two or three contingencies" (he
remembered the general plan sent him from Petersburg) "they have fore-
seen everything. But the contingencies are endless."

The undecided question as to whether the wound inflicted at Borodinó
was mortal or not had hung over Kutúzov's head for a whole month. On
the one hand the French had occupied Moscow. On the other Kutúzov
felt assured with all his being that the terrible blow into which he and all
the Russians had put their whole strength must have been mortal. But in
any case proofs were needed; he had waited a whole month for them and
grew more impatient the longer he waited. Lying on his bed during those
sleepless nights he did just what he reproached those younger generals
for doing. He imagined all sorts of possible contingencies, just like the
younger men, but with this difference, that he saw thousands of contin-
gencies instead of two or three and based nothing on them. The longer
he thought the more contingencies presented themselves. He imagined all
sorts of movements of the Napoleonic army as a whole or in sections—
against Petersburg, or against him, or to outflank him. He thought too of
the possibility (which he feared most of all) that Napoleon might fight
him with his own weapon and remain in Moscow awaiting him. Kutúzov
even imagined that Napoleon's army might turn back through Medýn and
Yukhnóv,* but the one thing he could not foresee was what happened—
the insane, convulsive stampede of Napoleon's army during its first eleven
days after leaving Moscow: a stampede which made possible what Kutú-
zov had not yet even dared to think of—the complete extermination of
the French. Dórokhov's report about Broussier's division, the guerrillas'
reports of distress in Napoleon's army, rumors of preparations for leaving
Moscow, all confirmed the supposition that the French army was beaten

* Medýn and Yukhnóv lie to the northwest of Kalúga on a road running
well to the south of the Mozháysk-Smolénsk road by which Napoleon eventu-
ally retreated westward.—A.M.

and preparing for flight. But these were only suppositions, which seemed important to the younger men but not to Kutúzov. With his sixty years' experience he knew what value to attach to rumors, knew how apt people who desire anything are to group all news so that it appears to confirm what they desire, and he knew how readily in such cases they omit all that makes for the contrary. And the more he desired it the less he allowed himself to believe it. This question absorbed all his mental powers. All else was to him only life's customary routine. To such customary routine belonged his conversations with the staff, the letters he wrote from Tarútino to Madame de Staël,* the reading of novels, the distribution of awards, his correspondence with Petersburg, and so on. But the destruction of the French, which he alone foresaw, was his heart's one desire.

On the night of the eleventh of October he lay leaning on his arm and thinking of that.

There was a stir in the next room and he heard the steps of Toll, Konovnítsyn, and Bolkhovítinov.

"Eh, who's there? Come in, come in! What news?" the field marshal called out to them.

While a footman was lighting a candle, Toll communicated the substance of the news.

"Who brought it?" asked Kutúzov with a look which, when the candle was lit, struck Toll by its cold severity.

"There can be no doubt about it, your Highness."

"Call him in, call him here."

Kutúzov sat up with one leg hanging down from the bed and his big paunch resting against the other which was doubled under him. He screwed up his seeing eye to scrutinize the messenger more carefully, as if wishing to read in his face what preoccupied his own mind.

"Tell me, tell me, friend," said he to Bolkhovítinov in his low, aged voice, as he pulled together the shirt which gaped open on his chest, "come nearer—nearer. What news have you brought me? Eh? That Napoleon has left Moscow? Are you sure? Eh?"

Bolkhovítinov gave a detailed account from the beginning of all he had been told to report.

"Speak quicker, quicker! Don't torture me!" Kutúzov interrupted him.

* *Madame de Staël was a bitter enemy of Napoleon's, who in his turn persistently pursued her. In 1812 she was in Petersburg, where she was well received by Alexander I. When Kutúzov was appointed commander in chief she was one of the first to offer him warm congratulations and to predict that he would be victorious.*—A.M.

Bolkhovítinov told him everything and was then silent, awaiting instructions. Toll was beginning to say something but Kutúzov checked him. He tried to say something, but his face suddenly puckered and wrinkled; he waved his arm at Toll and turned to the opposite side of the room, to the corner darkened by the icons that hung there.

"O Lord, my Creator, Thou hast heard our prayer . . ." said he in a tremulous voice with folded hands. "Russia is saved. I thank Thee, O Lord!" and he wept.

From the time he received this news to the end of the campaign all Kutúzov's activity was directed toward restraining his troops, by authority, by guile, and by entreaty, from useless attacks, maneuvers, or encounters with the perishing enemy. Dokhtúrov went to Málo-Yaroslávets, but Kutúzov lingered with the main army and gave orders for the evacuation of Kalúga—a retreat beyond which town seemed to him quite possible.

Everywhere Kutúzov retreated, but the enemy without waiting for his retreat fled in the opposite direction.

Napoleon's historians describe to us his skilled maneuvers at Tarútino and Málo-Yaroslávets, and make conjectures as to what would have happened had Napoleon been in time to penetrate into the rich southern provinces.

But not to speak of the fact that nothing prevented him from advancing into those southern provinces (for the Russian army did not bar his way), the historians forget that nothing could have saved his army, for then already it bore within itself the germs of inevitable ruin. How could that army—which had found abundant supplies in Moscow and had trampled them underfoot instead of keeping them, and on arriving at Smolénsk had looted provisions instead of storing them—how could that army recuperate in Kalúga province, which was inhabited by Russians such as those who lived in Moscow, and where fire had the same property of consuming what was set ablaze?

That army could not recover anywhere. Since the battle of Borodinó and the pillage of Moscow it had borne within itself, as it were, the chemical elements of dissolution.

The members of what had once been an army—Napoleon himself and all his soldiers—fled without knowing whither, each concerned only to make his escape as quickly as possible from this position, of the hopelessness of which they were all more or less vaguely conscious.

So it came about that at the council at Málo-Yaroslávets, when the generals pretending to confer together expressed various opinions, all mouths were closed by the opinion uttered by the simple-minded soldier Mou-

ton * who, speaking last, said what they all felt: that the one thing needful was to get away as quickly as possible; and no one, not even Napoleon, could say anything against that truth which they all recognized.

But though they all realized that it was necessary to get away, there still remained a feeling of shame at admitting that they must flee. An external shock was needed to overcome that shame, and this shock came in due time. It was what the French called *"le hourra de l'Empereur."* [2]

The day after the council at Málo-Yaroslávets Napoleon róde out early in the morning amid the lines of his army with his suite of marshals and an escort, on the pretext of inspecting the army and the scene of the previous and of the impending battle. Some Cossacks on the prowl for booty fell in with the Emperor and very nearly captured him. If the Cossacks did not capture Napoleon then, what saved him was the very thing that was destroying the French army, the booty on which the Cossacks fell. Here as at Tarútino they went after plunder, leaving the men. Disregarding Napoleon they rushed after the plunder and Napoleon managed to escape.

When *les enfants du Don* might so easily have taken the Emperor himself in the midst of his army, it was clear that there was nothing for it but to fly as fast as possible along the nearest, familiar road. Napoleon with his forty-year-old stomach understood that hint, not feeling his former agility and boldness, and under the influence of the fright the Cossacks had given him he at once agreed with Mouton and issued orders—as the historians tell us—to retreat by the Smolénsk road.

That Napoleon agreed with Mouton, and that the army retreated, does not prove that Napoleon caused it to retreat, but that the forces which influenced the whole army and directed it along the Mozháysk (that is, the Smolénsk) road acted simultaneously on him also.

A MAN IN MOTION always devises an aim for that motion. To be able to go a thousand miles he must imagine that something good awaits him at the end of those thousand miles. One must have the prospect of a promised land to have the strength to move.

* *Lest Tolstóy's words should be misunderstood, it should be mentioned that the person in question is General Mouton, Count Lobau, whose opinion Napoleon called for last at the council in question. He replied directly and decidedly that it was necessary at once, without hesitation, and by the nearest road, to get away from that country where they had already stayed too long. Napoleon then silently dismissed the council.—A.M.*

[2] *Hourra was the cheer the Russian troops gave when charging the enemy.—*A.M.

The promised land for the French during their advance had been Moscow, during their retreat it was their native land. But that native land was too far off, and for a man going a thousand miles it is absolutely necessary to set aside his final goal and to say to himself: "Today I shall get to a place twenty-five miles off where I shall rest and spend the night," and during the first day's journey that resting place eclipses his ultimate goal and attracts all his hopes and desires. And the impulses felt by a single person are always magnified in a crowd.

For the French retreating along the old Smolénsk road, the final goal —their native land—was too remote, and their immediate goal was Smolénsk, toward which all their desires and hopes, enormously intensified in the mass, urged them on. It was not that they knew that much food and fresh troops awaited them in Smolénsk, nor that they were told so (on the contrary their superior officers, and Napoleon himself, knew that provisions were scarce there), but because this alone could give them strength to move on and endure their present privations. So both those who knew and those who did not know deceived themselves, and pushed on to Smolénsk as to a promised land.

Coming out onto the highroad the French fled with surprising energy and unheard-of rapidity toward the goal they had fixed on. Besides the common impulse which bound the whole crowd of French into one mass and supplied them with a certain energy, there was another cause binding them together—their great numbers. As with the physical law of gravity, their enormous mass drew the individual human atoms to itself. In their hundreds of thousands they moved like a whole nation.

Each of them desired nothing more than to give himself up as a prisoner to escape from all this horror and misery; but on the one hand the force of this common attraction to Smolénsk, their goal, drew each of them in the same direction; on the other hand an army corps could not surrender to a company, and though the French availed themselves of every convenient opportunity to detach themselves and to surrender on the slightest decent pretext, such pretexts did not always occur. Their very numbers and their crowded and swift movement deprived them of that possibility and rendered it not only difficult but impossible for the Russians to stop this movement, to which the French were directing all their energies. Beyond a certain limit no mechanical disruption of the body could hasten the process of decomposition.

A lump of snow cannot be melted instantaneously. There is a certain limit of time in less than which no amount of heat can melt the snow. On the contrary the greater the heat the more solidified the remaining snow becomes.

Of the Russian commanders Kutúzov alone understood this. When the flight of the French army along the Smolénsk road became well defined, what Konovnítsyn had foreseen on the night of the eleventh of October began to occur. The superior officers all wanted to distinguish themselves, to cut off, to seize, to capture, and to overthrow the French, and all clamored for action.

Kutúzov alone used all his power (and such power is very limited in the case of any commander in chief) to prevent an attack.

He could not tell them what we say now: "Why fight, why block the road, losing our own men and inhumanly slaughtering unfortunate wretches? What is the use of that, when a third of their army has melted away on the road from Moscow to Vyázma without any battle?" But drawing from his aged wisdom what they could understand, he told them of the golden bridge, and they laughed at and slandered him, flinging themselves on, rending and exulting over the dying beast.

Ermólov, Milorádovich, Plátov, and others in proximity to the French near Vyázma could not resist their desire to cut off and break up two French corps, and by way of reporting their intention to Kutúzov they sent him a blank sheet of paper in an envelope.

And try as Kutúzov might to restrain the troops, our men attacked, trying to bar the road. Infantry regiments, we are told, advanced to the attack with music and with drums beating, and killed and lost thousands of men.

But they did not cut off or overthrow anybody and the French army, closing up more firmly at the danger, continued, while steadily melting away, to pursue its fatal path to Smolénsk.

BOOK FOURTEEN

DATE OF PRINCIPAL HISTORICAL EVENT

1812

OLD STYLE NEW STYLE

Oct. 28— Nov. 9 } The French at Smolénsk.
Nov. 2 Nov. 14

BOOK FOURTEEN

DATE OF PRINCIPAL HISTORICAL EVENT		
1812		
OLD STYLE	NEW STYLE	
Oct. 28 — Nov. 9		The French at Smolensk.
Nov. 2	Nov. 14	

1812

BOOK FOURTEEN

1. National character of the war. A duelist who drops his rapier and seizes a cudgel. Guerrilla warfare. The spirit of the army

THE BATTLE OF BORODINÓ, with the occupation of Moscow that followed it and the flight of the French without further conflicts, is one of the most instructive phenomena in history.

All historians agree that the external activity of states and nations in their conflicts with one another is expressed in wars, and that as a direct result of greater or less success in war the political strength of states and nations increases or decreases.

Strange as may be the historical account of how some king or emperor, having quarreled with another, collects an army, fights his enemy's army, gains a victory by killing three, five, or ten thousand men, and subjugates a kingdom and an entire nation of several millions, all the facts of history (as far as we know it) confirm the truth of the statement that the greater or lesser success of one army against another is the cause, or at least an essential indication, of an increase or decrease in the strength of the nation—even though it is unintelligible why the defeat of an army—a hundredth part of a nation—should oblige that whole nation to submit. An army gains a victory, and at once the rights of the conquering nation have increased to the detriment of the defeated. An army has suffered defeat, and at once a people loses its rights in proportion to the severity of the reverse, and if its army suffers a complete defeat the nation is quite subjugated.

So according to history it has been found from the most ancient times, and so it is to our own day. All Napoleon's wars serve to confirm this rule. In proportion to the defeat of the Austrian army Austria loses its rights, and the rights and the strength of France increase. The victories of the French at Jena and Auerstädt destroy the independent existence of Prussia.

1145

But then, in 1812, the French gain a victory near Moscow. Moscow is taken and after that, with no further battles, it is not Russia that ceases to exist, but the French army of six hundred thousand, and then Napoleonic France itself. To strain the facts to fit the rules of history: to say that the field of battle at Borodinó remained in the hands of the Russians, or that after Moscow there were other battles that destroyed Napoleon's army, is impossible.

After the French victory at Borodinó there was no general engagement nor any that were at all serious, yet the French army ceased to exist. What does this mean? If it were an example taken from the history of China, we might say that it was not an historic phenomenon (which is the historians' usual expedient when anything does not fit their standards); if the matter concerned some brief conflict in which only a small number of troops took part, we might treat it as an exception; but this event occurred before our fathers' eyes, and for them it was a question of the life or death of their fatherland, and it happened in the greatest of all known wars.

The period of the campaign of 1812 from the battle of Borodinó to the expulsion of the French proved that the winning of a battle does not produce a conquest and is not even an invariable indication of conquest; it proved that the force which decides the fate of peoples lies not in the conquerors, nor even in armies and battles, but in something else.

The French historians, describing the condition of the French army before it left Moscow, affirm that all was in order in the Grand Army, except the cavalry, the artillery, and the transport—there was no forage for the horses or the cattle. That was a misfortune no one could remedy, for the peasants of the district burned their hay rather than let the French have it.

The victory gained did not bring the usual results because the peasants Karp and Vlas (who after the French had evacuated Moscow drove in their carts to pillage the town, and in general personally failed to manifest any heroic feelings), and the whole innumerable multitude of such peasants, did not bring their hay to Moscow for the high price offered them, but burned it instead.

Let us imagine two men who have come out to fight a duel with rapiers according to all the rules of the art of fencing. The fencing has gone on for some time; suddenly one of the combatants, feeling himself wounded and understanding that the matter is no joke but concerns his life, throws down his rapier, and seizing the first cudgel that comes to hand begins to brandish it. Then let us imagine that the combatant who so sensibly employed the best and simplest means to attain his end was at the same time influenced by traditions of chivalry and, desiring to conceal the facts

of the case, insisted that he had gained his victory with the rapier according to all the rules of art. One can imagine what confusion and obscurity would result from such an account of the duel.

The fencer who demanded a contest according to the rules of fencing was the French army; his opponent who threw away the rapier and snatched up the cudgel was the Russian people; those who try to explain the matter according to the rules of fencing are the historians who have described the event.

After the burning of Smolénsk a war began which did not follow any previous traditions of war. The burning of towns and villages, the retreats after battles, the blow dealt at Borodinó and the renewed retreat, the burning of Moscow, the capture of marauders, the seizure of transports, and the guerrilla war were all departures from the rules.

Napoleon felt this, and from the time he took up the correct fencing attitude in Moscow and instead of his opponent's rapier saw a cudgel raised above his head, he did not cease to complain to Kutúzov and to the Emperor Alexander that the war was being carried on contrary to all the rules—as if there were any rules for killing people. In spite of the complaints of the French as to the nonobservance of the rules, in spite of the fact that to some highly placed Russians it seemed rather disgraceful to fight with a cudgel and they wanted to assume a pose *en quarte* or *en tierce* according to all the rules, and to make an adroit thrust *en prime*, and so on—the cudgel of the people's war was lifted with all its menacing and majestic strength, and without consulting anyone's tastes or rules and regardless of anything else, it rose and fell with stupid simplicity, but consistently, and belabored the French till the whole invasion had perished.

And it is well for a people who do not—as the French did in 1813— salute according to all the rules of art, and, presenting the hilt of their rapier gracefully and politely, hand it to their magnanimous conqueror, but at the moment of trial, without asking what rules others have adopted in similar cases, simply and easily pick up the first cudgel that comes to hand and strike with it till the feeling of resentment and revenge in their soul yields to a feeling of contempt and compassion.

ONE OF THE MOST obvious and advantageous departures from the so-called laws of war is the action of scattered groups against men pressed together in a mass. Such action always occurs in wars that take on a national character. In such actions, instead of two crowds opposing each other, the men disperse, attack singly, run away when attacked by stronger forces, but again attack when opportunity offers. This was done by the guerrillas

in Spain, by the mountain tribes in the Caucasus,* and by the Russians in 1812.

People have called this kind of war "guerrilla warfare" and assume that by so calling it they have explained its meaning. But such a war does not fit in under any rule and is directly opposed to a well-known rule of tactics which is accepted as infallible. That rule says that an attacker should concentrate his forces in order to be stronger than his opponent at the moment of conflict.

Guerrilla war (always successful, as history shows) directly infringes that rule.

This contradiction arises from the fact that military science assumes the strength of an army to be identical with its numbers. Military science says that the more troops the greater the strength. *Les gros bataillons ont toujours raison* [Large battalions are always victorious].

For military science to say this is like defining momentum in mechanics by reference to the mass only: stating that momenta are equal or unequal to each other simply because the masses involved are equal or unequal.

Momentum (quantity of motion) is the product of mass and velocity.

In military affairs the strength of an army is the product of its mass and some unknown x.

Military science, seeing in history innumerable instances of the fact that the size of any army does not coincide with its strength and that small detachments defeat larger ones, obscurely admits the existence of this unknown factor and tries to discover it—now in a geometric formation, now in the equipment employed, now, and most usually, in the genius of the commanders. But the assignment of these various meanings to the factor does not yield results which accord with the historic facts.

Yet it is only necessary to abandon the false view (adopted to gratify the "heroes") of the efficacy of the directions issued in wartime by commanders, in order to find this unknown quantity.

That unknown quantity is the spirit of the army, that is to say, the greater or lesser readiness to fight and face danger felt by all the men composing an army, quite independently of whether they are, or are not, fighting under the command of a genius, in two- or three-line formation, with cudgels or with rifles that repeat thirty times a minute. Men who want to fight will always put themselves in the most advantageous conditions for fighting.

* *Tolstóy in 1851-53 served in the army against the Caucasian mountain tribes and there began to obtain the military experience, subsequently enlarged by service against the Turks and especially in the defense of Sevastopol, which makes his descriptions of war in* War and Peace *so vivid.*—A.M.

The spirit of an army is the factor which multiplied by the mass gives the resulting force. To define and express the significance of this unknown factor—the spirit of an army—is a problem for science.

This problem is only solvable if we cease arbitrarily to substitute for the unknown x itself the conditions under which that force becomes apparent—such as the commands of the general, the equipment employed, and so on—mistaking these for the real significance of the factor, and if we recognize this unknown quantity in its entirety as being the greater or lesser desire to fight and to face danger. Only then, expressing known historic facts by equations and comparing the relative significance of this factor, can we hope to define the unknown.

Ten men, battalions, or divisions, fighting fifteen men, battalions, or divisions, conquer—that is, kill or take captive—all the others, while themselves losing four, so that on the one side four and on the other fifteen were lost. Consequently the four were equal to the fifteen, and therefore $4x = 15y$. Consequently $x/y = 15/4$. This equation does not give us the value of the unknown factor but gives us a ratio between two unknowns. And by bringing variously selected historic units (battles, campaigns, periods of war) into such equations, a series of numbers could be obtained in which certain laws should exist and might be discovered.

The tactical rule that an army should act in masses when attacking, and in smaller groups in retreat, unconsciously confirms the truth that the strength of an army depends on its spirit. To lead men forward under fire more discipline (obtainable only by movement in masses) is needed than is needed to resist attacks. But this rule which leaves out of account the spirit of the army continually proves incorrect and is in particularly striking contrast to the facts when some strong rise or fall in the spirit of the troops occurs, as in all national wars.

The French, retreating in 1812—though according to tactics they should have separated into detachments to defend themselves—congregated into a mass because the spirit of the army had so fallen that only the mass held the army together. The Russians, on the contrary, ought according to tactics to have attacked in mass, but in fact they split up into small units, because their spirit had so risen that separate individuals, without orders, dealt blows at the French without needing any compulsion to induce them to expose themselves to hardships and dangers.

2. *The partisans or guerrillas. Denísov, Dólokhov, Pétya Rostóv, and Tíkhon. A French drummer boy. A visit to the enemy's camp. Attack on a French convoy. The death of Pétya*

THE SO-CALLED PARTISAN WAR began with the entry of the French into Smolénsk.

Before partisan warfare had been officially recognized by the government, thousands of enemy stragglers, marauders, and foragers had been destroyed by the Cossacks and the peasants, who killed them off as instinctively as dogs worry a stray mad dog to death. Denís Davýdov, with his Russian instinct, was the first to recognize the value of this terrible cudgel which regardless of the rules of military science destroyed the French, and to him belongs the credit for taking the first step toward regularizing this method of warfare.

On August 24 Davýdov's first partisan detachment was formed and then others were recognized. The further the campaign progressed the more numerous these detachments became.

The irregulars destroyed the great army piecemeal. They gathered the fallen leaves that dropped of themselves from that withered tree—the French army—and sometimes shook that tree itself. By October, when the French were fleeing toward Smolénsk, there were hundreds of such companies, of various sizes and characters. There were some that adopted all the army methods and had infantry, artillery, staffs, and the comforts of life. Others consisted solely of Cossack cavalry. There were also small scratch groups of foot and horse, and groups of peasants and landowners that remained unknown. A sacristan commanded one party which captured several hundred prisoners in the course of a month; and there was Vasilísa, the wife of a village elder, who slew hundreds of the French.

The partisan warfare flamed up most fiercely in the latter days of October. Its first period had passed: when the partisans themselves, amazed at their own boldness, feared every minute to be surrounded and captured by the French, and hid in the forests without unsaddling, hardly daring to dismount and always expecting to be pursued. By the end of October this kind of warfare had taken definite shape: it had become clear to all what could be ventured against the French and what could not. Now only the commanders of detachments with staffs, and moving according to rules at a distance from the French, still regarded many things as impossible. The small bands that had started their activities long before and had already observed the French closely considered things possible which

the commanders of the big detachments did not dare to contemplate. The Cossacks and peasants who crept in among the French now considered everything possible.

On October 22, Denísov (who was one of the irregulars) was with his group at the height of the guerrilla enthusiasm. Since early morning he and his party had been on the move. All day long he had been watching from the forest that skirted the highroad a large French convoy of cavalry baggage and Russian prisoners separated from the rest of the army, which—as was learned from spies and prisoners—was moving under a strong escort to Smolénsk. Besides Denísov and Dólokhov (who also led a small party and moved in Denísov's vicinity), the commanders of some large divisions with staffs also knew of this convoy and, as Denísov expressed it, were sharpening their teeth for it. Two of the commanders of large parties—one a Pole and the other a German—sent invitations to Denísov almost simultaneously, requesting him to join up with their divisions to attack the convoy.

"No, bwother, I have gwown mustaches myself," * said Denísov on reading these documents, and he wrote to the German that, despite his heartfelt desire to serve under so valiant and renowned a general, he had to forgo that pleasure because he was already under the command of the Polish general.[2] To the Polish general he replied to the same effect, informing him that he was already under the command of the German.

Having arranged matters thus, Denísov and Dólokhov intended, without reporting matters to the higher command, to attack and seize that convoy with their own small forces. On October 22 it was moving from the village of Mikúlino to that of Shámshevo. To the left of the road between Mikúlino and Shámshevo there were large forests, extending in some places up to the road itself though in others a mile or more back from it. Through these forests Denísov and his party rode all day, sometimes keeping well back in them and sometimes coming to the very edge, but never losing sight of the moving French. That morning, Cossacks of Denísov's party had seized and carried off into the forest two wagons loaded with cavalry saddles, which had stuck in the mud not far from Mikúlino where the forest ran close to the road. Since then, and until evening, the party had watched the movements of the French without attacking. It was necessary to let the French reach Shámshevo quietly without alarming them and then, after joining Dólokhov who was to

* *Equivalent to: "I was not born yesterday."*—A.M.

[2] *Tolstóy borrowed this expedient, by which Denísov preserved his independent command, from an incident recorded in Davýdov's Diary of Guerrilla Operations.*—A.M.

come that evening to a consultation at a watchman's hut in the forest less than a mile from Shámshevo, to surprise the French at dawn, falling like an avalanche on their heads from two sides, and rout and capture them all at one blow.

In their rear, more than a mile from Mikúlino where the forest came right up to the road, six Cossacks were posted to report if any fresh columns of French should show themselves.

Beyond Shámshevo, Dólokhov was to observe the road in the same way, to find out at what distance there were other French troops. They reckoned that the convoy had fifteen hundred men. Denísov had two hundred, and Dólokhov might have as many more, but the disparity of numbers did not deter Denísov. All that he now wanted to know was what troops these were and to learn that he had to capture a "tongue"— that is, a man from the enemy column. That morning's attack on the wagons had been made so hastily that the Frenchmen with the wagons had all been killed; only a little drummer boy had been taken alive, and as he was a straggler he could tell them nothing definite about the troops in that column.

Denísov considered it dangerous to make a second attack for fear of putting the whole column on the alert, so he sent Tíkhon Shcherbáty, a peasant of his party, to Shámshevo to try and seize at least one of the French quartermasters who had been sent on in advance.

IT WAS a warm rainy autumn day. The sky and the horizon were both the color of muddy water. At times a sort of mist descended, and then suddenly heavy slanting rain came down.

Denísov in a felt cloak and a sheepskin cap from which the rain ran down was riding a thin thoroughbred horse with sunken sides. Like his horse, which turned its head and laid its ears back, he shrank from the driving rain and gazed anxiously before him. His thin face with its short, thick black beard looked angry.

Beside Denísov rode an *esaul*, Denísov's fellow worker, also in felt cloak and sheepskin cap, and riding a large sleek Don horse.

Esaul Lováyski the Third * was a tall man as straight as an arrow, pale-faced, fair-haired, with narrow light eyes and with calm self-satisfaction in his face and bearing. Though it was impossible to say in what the peculiarity of the horse and rider lay, yet at first glance at the *esaul* and Dení-

* *What is here told was actual fact. After Davýdov's (in the novel Denísov's) first successes, Kutúzov gave him two Cossack regiments to strengthen his force. Lováyski is a familiar form of the well-known Don family name, Ilováyski. An* esaul *is a captain of Cossacks.*—A.M.

sov one saw that the latter was wet and uncomfortable and was a man mounted on a horse, while looking at the *esaul* one saw that he was as comfortable and as much at ease as always and that he was not a man who had mounted a horse, but a man who was one with his horse, a being consequently possessed of twofold strength.

A little ahead of them walked a peasant guide, wet to the skin and wearing a gray peasant coat and a white knitted cap.

A little behind, on a poor, small, lean Kirghíz mount with an enormous tail and mane and a bleeding mouth, rode a young officer in a blue French overcoat.

Beside him rode an hussar, with a boy in a tattered French uniform and blue cap behind him on the crupper of his horse. The boy held on to the hussar with cold, red hands, and raising his eyebrows gazed about him with surprise. This was the French drummer boy captured that morning.

Behind them along the narrow, sodden, cut-up forest road came hussars in threes and fours, and then Cossacks: some in felt cloaks, some in French greatcoats, and some with horsecloths over their heads. The horses, being drenched by the rain, all looked black whether chestnut or bay. Their necks, with their wet, close-clinging manes, looked strangely thin. Steam rose from them. Clothes, saddles, reins, were all wet, slippery, and sodden, like the ground and the fallen leaves that strewed the road. The men sat huddled up trying not to stir, so as to warm the water that had trickled to their bodies and not admit the fresh cold water that was leaking in under their seats, their knees, and at the back of their necks. In the midst of the outspread line of Cossacks two wagons, drawn by French horses and by saddled Cossack horses that had been hitched on in front, rumbled over the tree stumps and branches and splashed through the water that lay in the ruts.

Denísov's horse swerved aside to avoid a pool in the track and bumped his rider's knee against a tree.

"Oh, the devil!" exclaimed Denísov angrily, and showing his teeth he struck his horse three times with his whip, splashing himself and his comrades with mud.

Denísov was out of sorts both because of the rain and also from hunger (none of them had eaten anything since morning), and yet more because he still had no news from Dólokhov and the man sent to capture a "tongue" had not returned.

"There'll hardly be another such chance to fall on a transport as today. It's too risky to attack them by oneself, and if we put it off till another day one of the big guerrilla detachments will snatch the prey from under

our noses," thought Denísov, continually peering forward, hoping to see a messenger from Dólokhov.

On coming to a path in the forest along which he could see far to the right, Denísov stopped.

"There's someone coming," said he.

The esaul looked in the direction Denísov indicated.

"There are two, an officer and a Cossack. But it is not presupposable that it is the lieutenant colonel himself," said the esaul, who was fond of using words the Cossacks did not know.

The approaching riders having descended a decline were no longer visible, but they reappeared a few minutes later. In front, at a weary gallop and using his leather whip, rode an officer, disheveled and drenched, whose trousers had worked up to above his knees. Behind him, standing in the stirrups, trotted a Cossack. The officer, a very young lad with a broad rosy face and keen merry eyes, galloped up to Denísov and handed him a sodden envelope.

"From the general," said the officer. "Please excuse its not being quite dry."

Denísov, frowning, took the envelope and opened it.

"There, they kept telling us: 'It's dangerous, it's dangerous,' " said the officer, addressing the esaul while Denísov was reading the dispatch. "But Komaróv and I"—he pointed to the Cossack—"were prepared. We have each of us two pistols. . . . But what's this?" he asked, noticing the French drummer boy. "A prisoner? You've already been in action? May I speak to him?"

"Wostóv! Pétya!" exclaimed Denísov, having run through the dispatch. "Why didn't you say who you were?" and turning with a smile he held out his hand to the lad.

The officer was Pétya Rostóv.

All the way Pétya had been preparing himself to behave with Denísov as befitted a grown-up man and an officer—without hinting at their previous acquaintance. But as soon as Denísov smiled at him Pétya brightened up, blushed with pleasure, forgot the official manner he had been rehearsing, and began telling him how he had already been in a battle near Vyázma and how a certain hussar had distinguished himself there.

"Well, I am glad to see you," Denísov interrupted him, and his face again assumed its anxious expression.

"Michael Feoklítych," said he to the esaul, "this is again fwom that German, you know. He"—he indicated Pétya—"is serving under him."

And Denísov told the esaul that the dispatch just delivered was a repe-

tition of the German general's demand that he should join forces with him for an attack on the transport.

"If we don't take it tomowwow, he'll snatch it fwom under our noses," he added.

While Denísov was talking to the *esaul*, Pétya—abashed by Denísov's cold tone and supposing that it was due to the condition of his trousers —furtively tried to pull them down under his greatcoat so that no one should notice it, while maintaining as martial an air as possible.

"Will there be any orders, your honor?" he asked Denísov, holding his hand at the salute and resuming the game of adjutant and general for which he had prepared himself, "or shall I remain with your honor?"

"Orders?" Denísov repeated thoughtfully. "But can you stay till to-mowwow?"

"Oh, please . . . May I stay with you?" cried Pétya.

"But, just what did the genewal tell you? To wetuin at once?" asked Denísov.

Pétya blushed.

"He gave me no instructions. I think I could?" he returned, inquiringly.

"Well, all wight," said Denísov.

And turning to his men he directed a party to go on to the halting place arranged near the watchman's hut in the forest, and told the officer on the Kirghíz horse (who performed the duties of an adjutant) to go and find out where Dólokhov was and whether he would come that evening. Denísov himself intended going with the *esaul* and Pétya to the edge of the forest where it reached out to Shámshevo, to have a look at the part of the French bivouac they were to attack next day.

"Well, old fellow," said he to the peasant guide, "lead us to Shám-shevo."

Denísov, Pétya, and the *esaul*, accompanied by some Cossacks and the hussar who had the prisoner, rode to the left across a ravine to the edge of the forest.

THE RAIN HAD STOPPED, and only the mist was falling and drops from the trees. Denísov, the *esaul*, and Pétya rode silently, following the peasant in the knitted cap who, stepping lightly with outturned toes and moving noiselessly in his bast shoes over the roots and wet leaves, silently led them to the edge of the forest.

He ascended an incline, stopped, looked about him, and advanced to where the screen of trees was less dense. On reaching a large oak tree that had not yet shed its leaves, he stopped and beckoned mysteriously to them with his hand.

Denísov and Pétya rode up to him. From the spot where the peasant was standing they could see the French. Immediately beyond the forest, on a downward slope, lay a field of spring rye. To the right, beyond a steep ravine, was a small village and a landowner's house with a broken roof. In the village, in the house, in the garden, by the well, by the pond, over all the rising ground, and all along the road uphill from the bridge leading to the village, not more than five hundred yards away, crowds of men could be seen through the shimmering mist. Their un-Russian shouting at their horses which were straining uphill with the carts, and their calls to one another, could be clearly heard.

"Bwing the prisoner here," said Denísov in a low voice, not taking his eyes off the French.

A Cossack dismounted, lifted the boy down, and took him to Denísov. Pointing to the French troops, Denísov asked him what these and those of them were. The boy, thrusting his cold hands into his pockets and lifting his eyebrows, looked at Denísov in affright, but in spite of an evident desire to say all he knew gave confused answers, merely assenting to everything Denísov asked him. Denísov turned away from him frowning and addressed the esaul, conveying his own conjectures to him.

Pétya, rapidly turning his head, looked now at the drummer boy, now at Denísov, now at the esaul, and now at the French in the village and along the road, trying not to miss anything of importance.

"Whether Dólokhov comes or not, we must seize it, eh?" said Denísov with a merry sparkle in his eyes.

"It is a very suitable spot," said the esaul.

"We'll send the infantwy down by the swamps," Denísov continued. "They'll cweep up to the garden; you'll wide up fwom there with the Cossacks"—he pointed to a spot in the forest beyond the village—"and I with my hussars fwom here. And at the signal shot . . ."

"The hollow is impassable—there's a swamp there," said the esaul. "The horses would sink. We must ride round more to the left. . . ."

While they were talking in undertones the crack of a shot sounded from the low ground by the pond, a puff of white smoke appeared, then another, and the sound of hundreds of seemingly merry French voices shouting together came up from the slope. For a moment Denísov and the esaul drew back. They were so near that they thought they were the cause of the firing and shouting. But the firing and shouting did not relate to them. Down below, a man wearing something red was running through the marsh. The French were evidently firing and shouting at him.

"Why, that's our Tíkhon," said the esaul.

"So it is! It is!"

"The wascal!" said Denísov.

"He'll get away!" said the esaul, screwing up his eyes.

The man whom they called Tíkhon, having run to the stream, plunged in so that the water splashed in the air, and, having disappeared for an instant, scrambled out on all fours, all black with the wet, and ran on. The French who had been pursuing him stopped.

"Smart, that!" said the esaul.

"What a beast!" said Denísov with his former look of vexation. "What has he been doing all this time?"

"Who is he?" asked Pétya.

"He's our plastún.* I sent him to capture a 'tongue.'"

"Oh, yes," said Pétya, nodding at the first words Denísov uttered as if he understood it all, though he really did not understand anything of it.

Tíkhon Shcherbáty was one of the most indispensable men in their band. He was a peasant from Pokróvsk, near the river Gzhat. When Denísov had come to Pokróvsk at the beginning of his operations and had as usual summoned the village elder and asked him what he knew about the French, the elder, as though shielding himself, had replied, as all village elders did, that he had neither seen nor heard anything of them. But when Denísov explained that his purpose was to kill the French, and asked if no French had strayed that way, the elder replied that some "more-orderers" had really been at their village, but that Tíkhon Shcherbáty was the only man who dealt with such matters. Denísov had Tíkhon called and, having praised him for his activity, said a few words in the elder's presence about loyalty to the Tsar and the country and the hatred of the French that all sons of the fatherland should cherish.

"We don't do the French any harm," said Tíkhon, evidently frightened by Denísov's words. "We only fooled about with the lads for fun, you know! We killed a score or so of 'more-orderers,' but we did no harm else. . . ."

Next day when Denísov had left Pokróvsk, having quite forgotten about this peasant, it was reported to him that Tíkhon had attached himself to their party and asked to be allowed to remain with it. Denísov gave orders to let him do so.

Tíkhon, who at first did rough work, laying campfires, fetching water,

* Plastún—an unmounted sharpshooter among the Black Sea Cossacks. Strictly speaking, the plastúns were special detachments of Black Sea Cossacks in the wars with the Caucasian hill tribes. Their speciality was to track down the enemy among the forests of the Kubán. In the present case Denísov uses the word to indicate a man who operates as the plastúns did in the Caucasus.—A.M.

flaying dead horses, and so on, soon showed a great liking and aptitude for partisan warfare. At night he would go out for booty and always brought back French clothing and weapons, and when told to would bring in French captives also. Denísov then relieved him from drudgery and began taking him with him when he went out on expeditions and had him enrolled among the Cossacks.

Tíkhon did not like riding, and always went on foot, never lagging behind the cavalry. He was armed with a musketoon (which he carried rather as a joke), a pike and an ax, which latter he used as a wolf uses its teeth, with equal ease picking fleas out of its fur or crunching thick bones. Tíkhon with equal accuracy would split logs with blows at arm's length, or holding the head of the ax would cut thin little pegs or carve spoons. In Denísov's party he held a peculiar and exceptional position. When anything particularly difficult or nasty had to be done—to push a cart out of the mud with one's shoulders, pull a horse out of a swamp by its tail, skin it, slink in among the French, or walk more than thirty miles in a day —everybody pointed laughingly at Tíkhon.

"It won't hurt that devil—he's as strong as a horse!" they said of him.

Once a Frenchman Tíkhon was trying to capture fired a pistol at him and shot him in the fleshy part of the back. That wound (which Tíkhon treated only with internal and external applications of vodka) was the subject of the liveliest jokes by the whole detachment—jokes in which Tíkhon readily joined.

"Hallo, mate! Never again? Gave you a twist?" the Cossacks would banter him. And Tíkhon, purposely writhing and making faces, pretended to be angry and swore at the French with the funniest curses. The only effect of this incident on Tíkhon was that after being wounded he seldom brought in prisoners.

He was the bravest and most useful man in the party. No one found more opportunities for attacking, no one captured or killed more Frenchmen, and consequently he was made the buffoon of all the Cossacks and hussars and willingly accepted that role. Now he had been sent by Denísov overnight to Shámshevo to capture a "tongue." But whether because he had not been content to take only one Frenchman or because he had slept through the night, he had crept by day into some bushes right among the French and, as Denísov had witnessed from above, had been detected by them.

AFTER TALKING for some time with the esaul about next day's attack, which now, seeing how near they were to the French, he seemed to have definitely decided on, Denísov turned his horse and rode back.

"Now, my lad, we'll go and get dwy," he said to Pétya.

As they approached the watchhouse Denísov stopped, peering into the forest. Among the trees a man with long legs and long, swinging arms, wearing a short jacket, bast shoes, and a Kazán hat, was approaching with long, light steps. He had a musketoon over his shoulder and an ax stuck in his girdle. When he espied Denísov he hastily threw something into the bushes, removed his sodden hat by its floppy brim, and approached his commander. It was Tíkhon. His wrinkled and pockmarked face and narrow little eyes beamed with self-satisfied merriment. He lifted his head high and gazed at Denísov as if repressing a laugh.

"Well, where did you disappear to?" inquired Denísov.

"Where did I disappear to? I went to get Frenchmen," answered Tíkhon boldly and hurriedly, in a husky but melodious bass voice.

"Why did you push yourself in there by daylight? You ass! Well, why haven't you taken one?"

"Oh, I took one all right," said Tíkhon.

"Where is he?"

"You see, I took him first thing at dawn," Tíkhon continued, spreading out his flat feet with outturned toes in their bast shoes. "I took him into the forest. Then I see he's no good and think I'll go and fetch a likelier one."

"You see? . . . What a wogue—it's just as I thought," said Denísov to the *esaul*. "Why didn't you bwing that one?"

"What was the good of bringing him?" Tíkhon interrupted hastily and angrily—"that one wouldn't have done for you. As if I don't know what sort you want!"

"What a bwute you are! . . . Well?"

"I went for another one," Tíkhon continued, "and I crept like this through the wood and lay down." (He suddenly lay down on his stomach with a supple movement to show how he had done it.) "One turned up and I grabbed him, like this." (He jumped up quickly and lightly.) " 'Come along to the colonel,' I said. He starts yelling, and suddenly there were four of them. They rushed at me with their little swords. So I went for them with my ax, this way: 'What are you up to?' says I. 'Christ be with you!' " shouted Tíkhon, waving his arms with an angry scowl and throwing out his chest.

"Yes, we saw from the hill how you took to your heels through the puddles!" said the *esaul*, screwing up his glittering eyes.

Pétya badly wanted to laugh, but noticed that they all refrained from laughing. He turned his eyes rapidly from Tíkhon's face to the *esaul's* and Denísov's, unable to make out what it all meant.

"Don't play the fool!" said Denísov, coughing angrily. "Why didn't you bwing the first one?"

Tíkhon scratched his back with one hand and his head with the other, then suddenly his whole face expanded into a beaming, foolish grin, disclosing a gap where he had lost a tooth (that was why he was called Shcherbáty—the gap-toothed). Denísov smiled, and Pétya burst into a peal of merry laughter in which Tíkhon himself joined.

"Oh, but he was a regular good-for-nothing," said Tíkhon. "The clothes on him—poor stuff! How could I bring him? And so rude, your honor! Why, he says: 'I'm a general's son myself, I won't go!' he says."

"You are a bwute!" said Denísov. "I wanted to question . . ."

"But I questioned him," said Tíkhon. "He said he didn't know much. 'There are a lot of us,' he says, 'but all poor stuff—only soldiers in name,' he says. 'Shout loud at them,' he says, 'and you'll take them all,' " Tíkhon concluded, looking cheerfully and resolutely into Denísov's eyes.

"I'll give you a hundwed sharp lashes—that'll teach you to play the fool!" said Denísov severely.

"But why are you angry?" remonstrated Tíkhon, "just as if I'd never seen your Frenchmen! Only wait till it gets dark and I'll fetch you any of them you want—three if you like."

"Well, let's go," said Denísov, and rode all the way to the watchhouse in silence and frowning angrily.

Tíkhon followed behind and Pétya heard the Cossacks laughing with him and at him, about some pair of boots he had thrown into the bushes.

When the fit of laughter that had seized him at Tíkhon's words and smile had passed and Pétya realized for a moment that this Tíkhon had killed a man, he felt uneasy. He looked round at the captive drummer boy and felt a pang in his heart. But this uneasiness lasted only a moment. He felt it necessary to hold his head higher, to brace himself, and to question the *esaul* with an air of importance about tomorrow's undertaking, that he might not be unworthy of the company in which he found himself.

The officer who had been sent to inquire met Denísov on the way with the news that Dólokhov was soon coming and that all was well with him.

Denísov at once cheered up and, calling Pétya to him, said: "Well, tell me about yourself."

Pétya, having left his people after their departure from Moscow, joined his regiment and was soon taken as orderly by a general commanding a large guerrilla detachment. From the time he received his commission, and especially since he had joined the active army and taken part in the

battle of Vyázma, Pétya had been in a constant state of blissful excitement at being grown-up and in a perpetual ecstatic hurry not to miss any chance to do something really heroic. He was highly delighted with what he saw and experienced in the army, but at the same time it always seemed to him that the really heroic exploits were being performed just where he did not happen to be. And he was always in a hurry to get where he was not.

When on the twenty-first of October his general expressed a wish to send somebody to Denísov's detachment, Pétya begged so piteously to be sent that the general could not refuse. But when dispatching him he recalled Pétya's mad action at the battle of Vyázma, where instead of riding by the road to the place to which he had been sent, he had galloped to the advanced line under the fire of the French and had there twice fired his pistol. So now the general explicitly forbade his taking part in any action whatever of Denísov's. That was why Pétya had blushed and grown confused when Denísov asked him whether he could stay. Before they had ridden to the outskirts of the forest Pétya had considered that he must carry out his instructions strictly and return at once. But when he saw the French and saw Tíkhon and learned that there would certainly be an attack that night, he decided, with the rapidity with which young people change their views, that the general, whom he had greatly respected till then, was a rubbishy German, that Denísov was a hero, the *esaul* a hero, and Tíkhon a hero too, and that it would be shameful for him to leave them at a moment of difficulty.

It was already growing dusk when Denísov, Pétya, and the *esaul* rode up to the watchhouse. In the twilight saddled horses could be seen, and Cossacks and hussars who had rigged up rough shelters in the glade and were kindling glowing fires in a hollow of the forest where the French could not see the smoke. In the passage of the small watchhouse a Cossack with sleeves rolled up was chopping some mutton. In the room three officers of Denísov's band were converting a door into a tabletop. Pétya took off his wet clothes, gave them to be dried, and at once began helping the officers to fix up the dinner table.

In ten minutes the table was ready and a napkin spread on it. On the table were vodka, a flask of rum, white bread, roast mutton, and salt.

Sitting at table with the officers and tearing the fat savory mutton with his hands, down which the grease trickled, Pétya was in an ecstatic childish state of love for all men, and consequently of confidence that others loved him in the same way.

"So then what do you think, Vasíli Dmítrich?" said he to Denísov. "It's all right my staying a day with you?" And not waiting for a reply he an-

swered his own question: "You see I was told to find out—well, I am finding out. . . . Only do let me into the very . . . into the chief . . . I don't want a reward. . . . But I want . . ."

Pétya clenched his teeth and looked around, throwing back his head and flourishing his arms.

"Into the vewy chief . . ." Denísov repeated with a smile.

"Only, please let me command something, so that I may really command . . ." Pétya went on. "What would it be to you? . . . Oh, you want a knife?" he said, turning to an officer who wished to cut himself a piece of mutton.

And he handed him his clasp knife. The officer admired it.

"Please keep it. I have several like it," said Pétya, blushing. "Heavens! I was quite forgetting!" he suddenly cried. "I have some raisins, fine ones; you know, seedless ones. We have a new sutler and he has such capital things. I bought ten pounds. I am used to something sweet. Would you like some? . . ." and Pétya ran out into the passage to his Cossack and brought back some bags which contained about five pounds of raisins. "Have some, gentlemen, have some!"

"You want a coffeepot, don't you?" he asked the esaul. "I bought a capital one from our sutler! He has splendid things. And he's very honest, that's the chief thing. I'll be sure to send it to you. Or perhaps your flints are giving out, or are worn out—that happens sometimes, you know. I have brought some with me, here they are"—and he showed a bag—"a hundred flints. I bought them very cheap. Please take as many as you want, or all if you like. . . ."

Then suddenly, dismayed lest he had said too much, Pétya stopped and blushed.

He tried to remember whether he had not done anything else that was foolish. And running over the events of the day he remembered the French drummer boy. "It's capital for us here, but what of him? Where have they put him? Have they fed him? Haven't they hurt his feelings?" he thought. But having caught himself saying too much about the flints, he was now afraid to speak out.

"I might ask," he thought, "but they'll say: 'He's a boy himself and so he pities the boy.' I'll show them tomorrow whether I'm a boy. Will it seem odd if I ask?" Pétya thought. "Well, never mind!" and immediately, blushing and looking anxiously at the officers to see if they appeared ironical, he said:

"May I call in that boy who was taken prisoner and give him something to eat? . . . Perhaps . . ."

"Yes, he's a poor little fellow," said Denísov, who evidently saw nothing

shameful in this reminder. "Call him in. His name is Vincent Bosse. Have him fetched."

"I'll call him," said Pétya.

"Yes, yes, call him. A poor little fellow," Denísov repeated.

Pétya was standing at the door when Denísov said this. He slipped in between the officers, came close to Denísov, and said:

"Let me kiss you, dear old fellow! Oh, how fine, how splendid!"

And having kissed Denísov he ran out of the hut.

"Bosse! Vincent!" Pétya cried, stopping outside the door.

"Who do you want, sir?" asked a voice in the darkness.

Pétya replied that he wanted the French lad who had been captured that day.

"Ah, Vesénny?" said a Cossack.

Vincent, the boy's name, had already been changed by the Cossacks into Vesénny (vernal) and into Vesénya by the peasants and soldiers. In both these adaptations the reference to spring (vesná) matched the impression made by the young lad.

"He is warming himself there by the bonfire. Ho, Vesénya! Vesénya!— Vesénny!" laughing voices were heard calling to one another in the darkness.

"He's a smart lad," said an hussar standing near Pétya. "We gave him something to eat a while ago. He was awfully hungry!"

The sound of bare feet splashing through the mud was heard in the darkness, and the drummer boy came to the door.

"Ah, c'est vous [Ah, it's you]!" said Pétya. "Voulez-vous manger? N'ayez pas peur, on ne vous fera pas de mal [Do you want something to eat? Don't be afraid, they won't hurt you]," he added shyly and affectionately, touching the boy's hand. "Entrez, entrez [Come in, come in]."

"Merci, monsieur [Thank you, sir]," said the drummer boy in a trembling almost childish voice, and he began scraping his dirty feet on the threshold.

There were many things Pétya wanted to say to the drummer boy, but did not dare to. He stood irresolutely beside him in the passage. Then in the darkness he took the boy's hand and pressed it.

"Come in, come in!" he repeated in a gentle whisper. "Oh, what can I do for him?" he thought, and opening the door he let the boy pass in first.

When the boy had entered the hut, Pétya sat down at a distance from him, considering it beneath his dignity to pay attention to him. But he fingered the money in his pocket and wondered whether it would seem ridiculous to give some to the drummer boy.

THE ARRIVAL OF DÓLOKHOV diverted Pétya's attention from the drummer boy, to whom Denísov had had some mutton and vodka given, and whom he had had dressed in a Russian coat so that he might be kept with their band and not sent away with the other prisoners. Pétya had heard in the army many stories of Dólokhov's extraordinary bravery and of his cruelty to the French, so from the moment he entered the hut Pétya did not take his eyes from him, but braced himself up more and more and held his head high, that he might not be unworthy even of such company.

Dólokhov's appearance amazed Pétya by its simplicity.

Denísov wore a Cossack coat, had a beard, had an icon of Nicholas the Wonder-Worker on his breast, and his way of speaking and everything he did indicated his unusual position. But Dólokhov, who in Moscow had worn a Persian costume, had now the appearance of a most correct officer of the Guards. He was clean-shaven and wore a Guardsman's padded coat with an Order of St. George at his buttonhole and a plain forage cap set straight on his head. He took off his wet felt cloak in a corner of the room, and without greeting anyone went up to Denísov and began questioning him about the matter in hand. Denísov told him of the designs the large detachments had on the transport, of the message Pétya had brought, and his own replies to both generals. Then he told him all he knew of the French detachment.

"That's so. But we must know what troops they are and their numbers," said Dólokhov. "It will be necessary to go there. We can't start the affair without knowing for certain how many of them there are. I like to work accurately. Here now—wouldn't one of these gentlemen like to ride over to the French camp with me? I have brought a spare uniform."

"I, I . . . I'll go with you!" cried Pétya.

"There's no need for you to go at all," said Denísov, addressing Dólokhov, "and as for him, I won't let him go on any account."

"I like that!" exclaimed Pétya. "Why shouldn't I go?"

"Because it's useless."

"Well, you must excuse me, because . . . because . . . I shall go, and that's all. You'll take me, won't you?" he said, turning to Dólokhov.

"Why not?" Dólokhov answered absently, scrutinizing the face of the French drummer boy. "Have you had that youngster with you long?" he asked Denísov.

"He was taken today but he knows nothing. I'm keeping him with me."

"Yes, and where do you put the others?" inquired Dólokhov.

"Where? I send them away and take a weceipt for them," shouted Denísov, suddenly flushing. "And I say boldly that I have not a single man's life on my conscience. Would it be difficult for you to send thirty

or thwee hundwed men to town under escort, instead of staining—I speak bluntly—staining the honor of a soldier?"

"That kind of amiable talk would be suitable from this young count of sixteen," said Dólokhov with cold irony, "but it's time for you to drop it."

"Why, I've not said anything! I only say that I'll certainly go with you," said Pétya shyly.

"But for you and me, old fellow, it's time to drop these amenities," continued Dólokhov, as if he found particular pleasure in speaking of this subject which irritated Denísov. "Now, why have you kept this lad?" he went on, swaying his head. "Because you are sorry for him! Don't we know those 'receipts' of yours? You send a hundred men away, and thirty get there. The rest either starve or get killed. So isn't it all the same not to send them?"

The esaul, screwing up his light-colored eyes, nodded approvingly.

"That's not the point. I'm not going to discuss the matter. I do not wish to take it on my conscience. You say they'll die. All wight. Only not by my fault!"

Dólokhov began laughing.

"Who has told them not to capture me these twenty times over? But if they did catch me they'd string me up to an aspen tree, and you with all your chivalry just the same." He paused. "However, we must get to work. Tell the Cossack to fetch my kit. I have two French uniforms in it. Well, are you coming with me?" he asked Pétya.

"I? Yes, yes, certainly!" cried Pétya, blushing almost to tears and glancing at Denísov.

While Dólokhov had been disputing with Denísov what should be done with prisoners, Pétya had once more felt awkward and restless; but again he had no time to grasp fully what they were talking about. "If grown-up, distinguished men think so, it must be necessary and right," thought he. "But above all Denísov must not dare to imagine that I'll obey him and that he can order me about. I will certainly go to the French camp with Dólokhov. If he can, so can I!"

And to all Denísov's persuasions, Pétya replied that he too was accustomed to do everything accurately and not just anyhow, and that he never considered personal danger.

"For you'll admit that if we don't know for sure how many of them there are . . . hundreds of lives may depend on it, while there are only two of us. Besides, I want to go very much and certainly will go, so don't hinder me," said he. "It will only make things worse. . . ."

HAVING PUT ON French greatcoats and shakos, Pétya and Dólokhov rode to the clearing from which Denísov had reconnoitered the French camp, and emerging from the forest in pitch darkness they descended into the hollow. On reaching the bottom, Dólokhov told the Cossacks accompanying him to await him there and rode on at a quick trot along the road to the bridge. Pétya, his heart in his mouth with excitement, rode by his side.

"If we're caught, I won't be taken alive! I have a pistol," whispered he.

"Don't talk Russian," said Dólokhov in a hurried whisper, and at that very moment they heard through the darkness the challenge: "*Qui vive?* [Who goes there]" and the click of a musket.

The blood rushed to Pétya's face and he grasped his pistol.

"*Lanciers du 6-me* [Lancers of the 6th Regiment]," replied Dólokhov, neither hastening nor slackening his horse's pace.

The black figure of a sentinel stood on the bridge.

"*Mot d'ordre* [Password]."

Dólokhov reined in his horse and advanced at a walk.

"*Dites donc, le colonel Gérard est ici?* [Tell me, is Colonel Gérard here]" he asked.

"*Mot d'ordre,*" repeated the sentinel, barring the way and not replying.

"*Quand un officier fait sa ronde, les sentinelles ne demandent pas le mot d'ordre* . . . [When an officer is making his round sentinels don't ask him for the password]" cried Dólokhov suddenly flaring up and riding straight at the sentinel. "*Je vous demande si le colonel est ici* [I am asking you if the colonel is here]."

And without waiting for an answer from the sentinel, who had stepped aside, Dólokhov rode up the incline at a walk.

Noticing the black outline of a man crossing the road, Dólokhov stopped him and inquired where the commander and officers were. The man, a soldier with a sack over his shoulder, stopped, came close up to Dólokhov's horse, touched it with his hand, and explained simply and in a friendly way that the commander and the officers were higher up the hill to the right in the courtyard of the farm, as he called the landowner's house.

Having ridden up the road, on both sides of which French talk could be heard around the campfires, Dólokhov turned into the courtyard of the landowner's house. Having ridden in, he dismounted and approached a big blazing campfire, around which sat several men talking noisily. Something was boiling in a small cauldron at the edge of the fire and a soldier in a peaked cap and blue overcoat, lit up by the fire, was kneeling beside it stirring its contents with a ramrod.

"Oh, he's a hard nut to crack," said one of the officers who was sitting in the shadow at the other side of the fire.

"He'll make them get a move on, those fellows!" said another, laughing.

Both fell silent, peering out through the darkness at the sound of Dólokhov's and Pétya's steps as they advanced to the fire leading their horses.

"Bonjour, messieurs [Good day, gentlemen]!" said Dólokhov loudly and clearly.

There was a stir among the officers in the shadow beyond the fire, and one tall, long-necked officer, walking round the fire, came up to Dólokhov. "Is that you, Clément?" he asked. "Where the devil . . . ?" But, noticing his mistake, he broke off short and, with a frown, greeted Dólokhov as a stranger, asking what he could do for him.

Dólokhov said that he and his companion were trying to overtake their regiment, and addressing the company in general asked whether they knew anything of the 6th Regiment. None of them knew anything, and Pétya thought the officers were beginning to look at him and Dólokhov with hostility and suspicion. For some seconds all were silent.

"If you were counting on the evening soup, you have come too late," said a voice from behind the fire with a repressed laugh.

Dólokhov replied that they were not hungry and must push on farther that night.

He handed the horses over to the soldier who was stirring the pot and squatted down on his heels by the fire beside the officer with the long neck. That officer did not take his eyes from Dólokhov and again asked to what regiment he belonged. Dólokhov, as if he had not heard the question, did not reply, but lighting a short French pipe which he took from his pocket began asking the officer in how far the road before them was safe from Cossacks.

"Those brigands are everywhere," replied an officer from behind the fire.

Dólokhov remarked that the Cossacks were a danger only to stragglers such as his companion and himself, "but probably they would not dare to attack large detachments?" he added inquiringly. No one replied.

"Well, now he'll come away," Pétya thought every moment as he stood by the campfire listening to the talk.

But Dólokhov restarted the conversation which had dropped and began putting direct questions as to how many men there were in the battalion, how many battalions, and how many prisoners. Asking about the Russian prisoners with that detachment, Dólokhov said:

"A horrid business dragging these corpses about with one! It would be better to shoot such rabble," and burst into loud laughter, so strange

that Pétya thought the French would immediately detect their disguise, and involuntarily took a step back from the campfire.

No one replied a word to Dólokhov's laughter, and a French officer whom they could not see (he lay wrapped in a greatcoat) rose and whispered something to a companion. Dólokhov got up and called to the soldier who was holding their horses.

"Will they bring our horses or not?" thought Pétya, instinctively drawing nearer to Dólokhov.

The horses were brought.

"Good evening, gentlemen," said Dólokhov.

Pétya wished to say "Good night" but could not utter a word. The officers were whispering together. Dólokhov was a long time mounting his horse which would not stand still, then he rode out of the yard at a footpace. Pétya rode beside him, longing to look round to see whether or no the French were running after them, but not daring to.

Coming out onto the road Dólokhov did not ride back across the open country, but through the village. At one spot he stopped and listened. "Do you hear?" he asked. Pétya recognized the sound of Russian voices and saw the dark figures of Russian prisoners round their campfires. When they had descended to the bridge Pétya and Dólokhov rode past the sentinel, who without saying a word paced morosely up and down it, then they descended into the hollow where the Cossacks awaited them.

"Well now, good-by. Tell Denísov, 'at the first shot at daybreak,' " said Dólokhov and was about to ride away, but Pétya seized hold of him.

"Really!" he cried, "you are such a hero! Oh, how fine, how splendid! How I love you!"

"All right, all right!" said Dólokhov. But Pétya did not let go of him and Dólokhov saw through the gloom that Pétya was bending toward him and wanted to kiss him. Dólokhov kissed him, laughed, turned his horse, and vanished into the darkness.

HAVING RETURNED to the watchman's hut, Pétya found Denísov in the passage. He was awaiting Pétya's return in a state of agitation, anxiety, and self-reproach for having let him go.

"Thank God!" he exclaimed. "Yes, thank God!" he repeated, listening to Pétya's rapturous account. "But, devil take you, I haven't slept because of you! Well, thank God. Now lie down. We can still get a nap before morning."

"But . . . no," said Pétya, "I don't want to sleep yet. Besides I know myself, if I fall asleep it's finished. And then I am used to not sleeping before a battle."

He sat awhile in the hut joyfully recalling the details of his expedition and vividly picturing to himself what would happen next day. Then, noticing that Denísov was asleep, he rose and went out of doors.

It was still quite dark outside. The rain was over, but drops were still falling from the trees. Near the watchman's hut the black shapes of the Cossacks' shanties and of horses tethered together could be seen. Behind the hut the dark shapes of the two wagons with their horses beside them were discernible, and in the hollow the dying campfire gleamed red. Not all the Cossacks and hussars were asleep; here and there, amid the sounds of falling drops and the munching of the horses near by, could be heard low voices which seemed to be whispering.

Pétya came out, peered into the darkness, and went up to the wagons. Someone was snoring under them, and around them stood saddled horses munching their oats. In the dark Pétya recognized his own horse, which he called "Karabákh" * though it was of Ukrainian breed, and went up to it.

"Well, Karabákh! We'll do some service tomorrow," said he, sniffing its nostrils and kissing it.

"Why aren't you asleep, sir?" said a Cossack who was sitting under a wagon.

"No, ah . . . Likhachëv—isn't that your name? Do you know I have only just come back! We've been into the French camp."

And Pétya gave the Cossack a detailed account not only of his ride but also of his object, and why he considered it better to risk his life than to act "just anyhow."

"Well you should get some sleep now," said the Cossack.

"No, I am used to this," said Pétya. "I say, aren't the flints in your pistols worn out? I brought some with me. Don't you want any? You can have some."

The Cossack bent forward from under the wagon to get a closer look at Pétya.

"Because I am accustomed to doing everything accurately," said Pétya. "Some fellows do things just anyhow, without preparation, and then they're sorry for it afterwards. I don't like that."

"Just so," said the Cossack.

"Oh yes, another thing! Please, my dear fellow, will you sharpen my saber for me? It's got bl . . ." (Pétya feared to tell a lie, and the saber never had been sharpened.) "Can you do it?"

"Of course I can."

* Karabákh is a district in the Southern Caucasus, famous for its breed of horses.—A.M.

Likhachëv got up, rummaged in his pack, and soon Pétya heard the warlike sound of steel on whetstone. He climbed onto the wagon and sat on its edge. The Cossack was sharpening the saber under the wagon.

"I say! Are the lads asleep?" asked Pétya.

"Some are, and some aren't—like us."

"Well, and that boy?"

"Vesénny? Oh, he's thrown himself down there in the passage. Fast asleep after his fright. He was that glad!"

After that Pétya remained silent for a long time, listening to the sounds. He heard footsteps in the darkness and a black figure appeared.

"What are you sharpening?" asked a man coming up to the wagon.

"Why, this gentleman's saber."

"That's right," said the man, whom Pétya took to be an hussar. "Was the cup left here?"

"There, by the wheel!"

The hussar took the cup.

"It must be daylight soon," said he, yawning, and went away.

Pétya ought to have known that he was in a forest with Denísov's guerrilla band, less than a mile from the road, sitting on a wagon captured from the French beside which horses were tethered, that under it Likhachëv was sitting sharpening a saber for him, that the big dark blotch to the right was the watchman's hut, and the red blotch below to the left was the dying embers of a campfire, that the man who had come for the cup was an hussar who wanted a drink; but he neither knew nor wanted to know anything of all this. He was in a fairy kingdom where nothing resembled reality. The big dark blotch might really be the watchman's hut or it might be a cavern leading to the very depths of the earth. Perhaps the red spot was a fire, or it might be the eye of an enormous monster. Perhaps he was really sitting on a wagon, but it might very well be that he was not sitting on a wagon but on a terribly high tower from which, if he fell, he would have to fall for a whole day or a whole month, or go on falling and never reach the bottom. Perhaps it was just the Cossack, Likhachëv, who was sitting under the wagon, but it might be the kindest, bravest, most wonderful, most splendid man in the world, whom no one knew of. It might really have been that an hussar came for water and went back into the hollow, but perhaps he had simply vanished—disappeared altogether and dissolved into nothingness.

Nothing Pétya could have seen now would have surprised him. He was in a fairy kingdom where everything was possible.

He looked up at the sky. And the sky was a fairy realm like the earth. It was clearing, and over the tops of the trees clouds were swiftly sailing

as if unveiling the stars. Sometimes it looked as if the clouds were passing, and a clear black sky appeared. Sometimes it seemed as if the black spaces were clouds. Sometimes the sky seemed to be rising high, high overhead, and then it seemed to sink so low that one could touch it with one's hand.

Pétya's eyes began to close and he swayed a little.

The trees were dripping. Quiet talking was heard. The horses neighed and jostled one another. Someone snored.

"Ozheg-zheg, Ozheg-zheg . . ." hissed the saber against the whetstone, and suddenly Pétya heard an harmonious orchestra playing some unknown, sweetly solemn hymn. Pétya was as musical as Natásha and more so than Nicholas, but had never learned music or thought about it, and so the melody that unexpectedly came to his mind seemed to him particularly fresh and attractive. The music became more and more audible. The melody grew and passed from one instrument to another. And what was played was a fugue—though Pétya had not the least conception of what a fugue is. Each instrument—now resembling a violin and now a horn, but better and clearer than violin or horn—played its own part, and before it had finished the melody merged with another instrument that began almost the same air, and then with a third and a fourth; and they all blended into one and again became separate and again blended, now into solemn church music, now into something dazzlingly brilliant and triumphant.

"Oh—why, that was in a dream!" Pétya said to himself, as he lurched forward. "It's in my ears. But perhaps it's music of my own. Well, go on, my music! Now! . . ."

He closed his eyes, and, from all sides as if from a distance, sounds fluttered, grew into harmonies, separated, blended, and again all mingled into the same sweet and solemn hymn. "Oh, this is delightful! As much as I like and as I like!" said Pétya to himself. He tried to conduct that enormous orchestra.

"Now softly, softly die away!" and the sounds obeyed him. "Now fuller, more joyful. Still more and more joyful!" And from an unknown depth rose increasingly triumphant sounds. "Now voices join in!" ordered Pétya. And at first from afar he heard men's voices and then women's. The voices grew in harmonious triumphant strength, and Pétya listened to their surpassing beauty in awe and joy.

With a solemn triumphal march there mingled a song, the drip from the trees, and the hissing of the saber, "Ozheg-zheg-zheg . . ." and again the horses jostled one another and neighed, not disturbing the choir but joining in it.

Pétya did not know how long this lasted: he enjoyed himself all the

time, wondered at his enjoyment and regretted that there was no one to share it. He was awakened by Likhachëv's kindly voice.

"It's ready, your honor; you can split a Frenchman in half with it!"

Pétya woke up.

"It's getting light, it's really getting light!" he exclaimed.

The horses that had previously been invisible could now be seen to their very tails, and a watery light showed itself through the bare branches. Pétya shook himself, jumped up, took a ruble from his pocket and gave it to Likhachëv; then he flourished the saber, tested it, and sheathed it. The Cossacks were untying their horses and tightening their saddle girths.

"And here's the commander," said Likhachëv.

Denísov came out of the watchman's hut and, having called Pétya, gave orders to get ready.

THE MEN rapidly picked out their horses in the semidarkness, tightened their saddle girths, and formed companies. Denísov stood by the watchman's hut giving final orders. The infantry of the detachment passed along the road and quickly disappeared amid the trees in the mist of early dawn, hundreds of feet splashing through the mud. The *esaul* gave some orders to his men. Pétya held his horse by the bridle, impatiently awaiting the order to mount. His face, having been bathed in cold water, was all aglow, and his eyes were particularly brilliant. Cold shivers ran down his spine and his whole body pulsed rhythmically.

"Well, is ev'wything weady?" asked Denísov. "Bwing the horses."

The horses were brought. Denísov was angry with the Cossack because the saddle girths were too slack, reproved him, and mounted. Pétya put his foot in the stirrup. His horse by habit made as if to nip his leg, but Pétya leaped quickly into the saddle unconscious of his own weight and, turning to look at the hussars starting in the darkness behind him, rode up to Denísov.

"Vasíli Dmítrich, entrust me with some commission! Please . . . for God's sake . . . !" said he.

Denísov seemed to have forgotten Pétya's very existence. He turned to glance at him.

"I ask one thing of you," he said sternly, "to obey me and not shove you'self fo'ward anywhere."

He did not say another word to Pétya but rode in silence all the way. When they had come to the edge of the forest it was noticeably growing light over the field. Denísov talked in whispers with the *esaul* and the Cossacks rode past Pétya and Denísov. When they had all ridden by, Denísov touched his horse and rode down the hill. Slipping onto their

haunches and sliding, the horses descended with their riders into the ravine. Pétya rode beside Denísov, the pulsation of his body constantly increasing. It was getting lighter and lighter, but the mist still hid distant objects. Having reached the valley, Denísov looked back and nodded to a Cossack beside him.

"The signal!" said he.

The Cossack raised his arm and a shot rang out. In an instant the tramp of horses galloping forward was heard, shouts came from various sides, and then more shots.

At the first sound of trampling hoofs and shouting, Pétya lashed his horse and loosening his rein galloped forward, not heeding Denísov who shouted at him. It seemed to Pétya that at the moment the shot was fired it suddenly became as bright as noon. He galloped to the bridge. Cossacks were galloping along the road in front of him. On the bridge he collided with a Cossack who had fallen behind, but he galloped on. In front of him soldiers, probably Frenchmen, were running from right to left across the road. One of them fell in the mud under his horse's feet.

Cossacks were crowding about a hut, busy with something. From the midst of that crowd terrible screams arose. Pétya galloped up, and the first thing he saw was the pale face and trembling jaw of a Frenchman, clutching the handle of a lance that had been aimed at him.

"Hurrah! . . . Lads! . . . ours!" shouted Pétya, and giving rein to his excited horse he galloped forward along the village street.

He could hear shooting ahead of him. Cossacks, hussars, and ragged Russian prisoners, who had come running from both sides of the road, were shouting something loudly and incoherently. A gallant-looking Frenchman, in a blue overcoat, capless, and with a frowning red face, had been defending himself against the hussars. When Pétya galloped up the Frenchman had already fallen. "Too late again!" flashed through Pétya's mind and he galloped on to the place from which the rapid firing could be heard. The shots came from the yard of the landowner's house he had visited the night before with Dólokhov. The French were making a stand there behind a wattle fence in a garden thickly overgrown with bushes and were firing at the Cossacks who crowded at the gateway. Through the smoke, as he approached the gate, Pétya saw Dólokhov, whose face was of a pale-greenish tint, shouting to his men. "Go round! Wait for the infantry!" he exclaimed as Pétya rode up to him.

"Wait? . . . Hurrah-ah-ah!" shouted Pétya, and without pausing a moment galloped to the place whence came the sounds of firing and where the smoke was thickest.

A volley was heard, and some bullets whistled past, while others plashed

against something. The Cossacks and Dólokhov galloped after Pétya into the gateway of the courtyard. In the dense wavering smoke some of the French threw down their arms and ran out of the bushes to meet the Cossacks, while others ran down the hill toward the pond. Pétya was galloping along the courtyard, but instead of holding the reins he waved both his arms about rapidly and strangely, slipping farther and farther to one side in his saddle. His horse, having galloped up to a campfire that was smoldering in the morning light, stopped suddenly, and Pétya fell heavily on to the wet ground. The Cossacks saw that his arms and legs jerked rapidly though his head was quite motionless. A bullet had pierced his skull.

After speaking to the senior French officer, who came out of the house with a white handkerchief tied to his sword and announced that they surrendered, Dólokhov dismounted and went up to Pétya, who lay motionless with outstretched arms.

"Done for!" he said with a frown, and went to the gate to meet Denísov who was riding toward him.

"Killed?" cried Denísov, recognizing from a distance the unmistakably lifeless attitude—very familiar to him—in which Pétya's body was lying.

"Done for!" repeated Dólokhov as if the utterance of these words afforded him pleasure, and he went quickly up to the prisoners, who were surrounded by Cossacks who had hurried up. "We won't take them!" he called out to Denísov.

Denísov did not reply; he rode up to Pétya, dismounted, and with trembling hands turned toward himself the bloodstained, mud-bespattered face which had already gone white.

"I am used to something sweet. Raisins, fine ones . . . take them all!" he recalled Pétya's words. And the Cossacks looked round in surprise at the sound, like the yelp of a dog, with which Denísov turned away, walked to the wattle fence, and seized hold of it.

Among the Russian prisoners rescued by Denísov and Dólokhov was Pierre Bezúkhov.

3. Pierre's journey among the prisoners. Karatáev. His story of the merchant. His death. Pierre rescued

DURING THE WHOLE of their march from Moscow no fresh orders had been issued by the French authorities concerning the party of prisoners among whom was Pierre. On the twenty-second of October that party was no longer with the same troops and baggage trains with which it had left Moscow. Half the wagons laden with hardtack that had traveled

the first stages with them had been captured by Cossacks, the other half had gone on ahead. Not one of those dismounted cavalrymen who had marched in front of the prisoners was left; they had all disappeared. The artillery the prisoners had seen in front of them during the first days was now replaced by Marshal Junot's enormous baggage train, convoyed by Westphalians. Behind the prisoners came a cavalry baggage train.

From Vyázma onwards the French army, which had till then moved in three columns, went on as a single group. The symptoms of disorder that Pierre had noticed at their first halting place after leaving Moscow had now reached the utmost limit.

The road along which they moved was bordered on both sides by dead horses; ragged men who had fallen behind from various regiments continually changed about, now joining the moving column, now again lagging behind it.

Several times during the march false alarms had been given and the soldiers of the escort had raised their muskets, fired, and run headlong, crushing one another, but had afterwards reassembled and abused each other for their causeless panic.

These three groups traveling together—the cavalry stores, the convoy of prisoners, and Junot's baggage train—still constituted a separate and united whole, though each of the groups was rapidly melting away.

Of the artillery baggage train which had consisted of a hundred and twenty wagons, not more than sixty now remained; the rest had been captured or left behind. Some of Junot's wagons also had been captured or abandoned. Three wagons had been raided and robbed by stragglers from Davout's corps. From the talk of the Germans Pierre learned that a larger guard had been allotted to that baggage train than to the prisoners, and that one of their comrades, a German soldier, had been shot by the marshal's own order because a silver spoon belonging to the marshal had been found in his possession.

The group of prisoners had melted away most of all. Of the three hundred and thirty men who had set out from Moscow fewer than a hundred now remained. The prisoners were more burdensome to the escort than even the cavalry saddles or Junot's baggage. They understood that the saddles and Junot's spoon might be of some use, but that cold and hungry soldiers should have to stand and guard equally cold and hungry Russians who froze and lagged behind on the road (in which case the order was to shoot them) was not merely incomprehensible but revolting. And the escort, as if afraid, in the grievous condition they themselves were in, of giving way to the pity they felt for the prisoners and so rendering

their own plight still worse, treated them with particular moroseness and severity.

At Dorogobúzh while the soldiers of the convoy, after locking the prisoners in a stable, had gone off to pillage their own stores, several of the soldier prisoners tunneled under the wall and ran away, but were recaptured by the French and shot.

The arrangement adopted when they started, that the officer prisoners should be kept separate from the rest, had long since been abandoned. All who could walk went together, and after the third stage Pierre had rejoined Karatáev and the gray-blue bandy-legged dog that had chosen Karatáev for its master.

On the third day after leaving Moscow Karatáev again fell ill with the fever he had suffered from in hospital in Moscow, and as he grew gradually weaker Pierre kept away from him. Pierre did not know why, but since Karatáev had begun to grow weaker it had cost him an effort to go near him. When he did so and heard the subdued moaning with which Karatáev generally lay down at the halting places, and when he smelled the odor emanating from him which was now stronger than before, Pierre moved farther away and did not think about him.

While imprisoned in the shed Pierre had learned not with his intellect but with his whole being, by life itself, that man is created for happiness, that happiness is within him, in the satisfaction of simple human needs, and that all unhappiness arises not from privation but from superfluity. And now during these last three weeks of the march he had learned still another new, consolatory truth—that nothing in this world is terrible. He had learned that as there is no condition in which man can be happy and entirely free, so there is no condition in which he need be unhappy and lack freedom. He learned that suffering and freedom have their limits and that those limits are very near together; that the person in a bed of roses with one crumpled petal suffered as keenly as he now, sleeping on the bare damp earth with one side growing chilled while the other was warming; and that when he had put on tight dancing shoes he had suffered just as he did now when he walked with bare feet that were covered with sores—his footgear having long since fallen to pieces. He discovered that when he had married his wife—of his own free will as it had seemed to him—he had been no more free than now when they locked him up at night in a stable. Of all that he himself subsequently termed his sufferings, but which at the time he scarcely felt, the worst was the state of his bare, raw, and scab-covered feet. (The horseflesh was appetizing and nourishing, the saltpeter flavor of the gunpowder they used instead of salt was even pleasant; there was no great cold, it was always warm walking in the day-

time, and at night there were the campfires; the lice that devoured him warmed his body.) The one thing that was at first hard to bear was his feet.

After the second day's march Pierre, having examined his feet by the campfire, thought it would be impossible to walk on them; but when everybody got up he went along, limping, and, when he had warmed up, walked without feeling the pain, though at night his feet were more terrible to look at than before. However, he did not look at them now, but thought of other things.

Only now did Pierre realize the full strength of life in man and the saving power he has of transferring his attention from one thing to another, which is like the safety valve of a boiler that allows superfluous steam to blow off when the pressure exceeds a certain limit.

He did not see and did not hear how they shot the prisoners who lagged behind, though more than a hundred perished in that way. He did not think of Karatáev who grew weaker every day and evidently would soon have to share that fate. Still less did Pierre think about himself. The harder his position became and the more terrible the future, the more independent of that position in which he found himself were the joyful and comforting thoughts, memories, and imaginings that came to him.

At midday on the twenty-second of October Pierre was going uphill along the muddy, slippery road, looking at his feet and at the roughness of the way. Occasionally he glanced at the familiar crowd around him and then again at his feet. The former and the latter were alike familiar and his own. The blue-gray bandy-legged dog ran merrily along the side of the road, sometimes in proof of its agility and self-satisfaction lifting one hind leg and hopping along on three, and then again going on all four and rushing to bark at the crows that sat on the carrion. The dog was merrier and sleeker than it had been in Moscow. All around lay the flesh of different animals—from men to horses—in various stages of decomposition; and as the wolves were kept off by the passing men the dog could eat all it wanted.

It had been raining since morning and had seemed as if at any moment it might cease and the sky clear, but after a short break it began raining harder than before. The saturated road no longer absorbed the water, which ran along the ruts in streams.

Pierre walked along, looking from side to side, counting his steps in threes, and reckoning them off on his fingers. Mentally addressing the rain, he repeated: "Now then, now then, go on! Pelt harder!"

It seemed to him that he was thinking of nothing, but far down and

deep within him his soul was occupied with something important and comforting. This something was a most subtle spiritual deduction from a conversation with Karatáev the day before.

At their yesterday's halting place, feeling chilly by a dying campfire, Pierre had got up and gone to the next one, which was burning better. There Platón Karatáev was sitting covered up—head and all—with his greatcoat as if it were a vestment, telling the soldiers in his effective and pleasant though now feeble voice a story Pierre knew. It was already past midnight, the hour when Karatáev was usually free of his fever and particularly lively. When Pierre reached the fire and heard Platón's voice enfeebled by illness, and saw his pathetic face brightly lit up by the blaze, he felt a painful prick at his heart. His feeling of pity for this man frightened him and he wished to go away, but there was no other fire, and Pierre sat down, trying not to look at Platón.

"Well, how are you?" he asked.

"How am I? If we grumble at sickness, God won't grant us death," replied Platón, and at once resumed the story he had begun.

"And so, brother," he continued, with a smile on his pale emaciated face and a particularly happy light in his eyes, "you see, brother . . ."

Pierre had long been familiar with that story.* Karatáev had told it to him alone some half-dozen times and always with a specially joyful emotion. But well as he knew it, Pierre now listened to that tale as to something new, and the quiet rapture Karatáev evidently felt as he told it communicated itself also to Pierre. The story was of an old merchant who lived a good and God-fearing life with his family, and who went once to the Nízhni fair with a companion—a rich merchant.

Having put up at an inn they both went to sleep, and next morning his companion was found robbed and with his throat cut. A bloodstained knife was found under the old merchant's pillow. He was tried, knouted, and his nostrils having been torn off, "all in due form" as Karatáev put it, he was sent to hard labor in Siberia.

"And so, brother" (it was at this point that Pierre came up), "ten years or more passed by. The old man was living as a convict, submitting as he should and doing no wrong. Only he prayed to God for death. Well, one night the convicts were gathered just as we are, with the old man among

* *The tale Karatáev tells was a particular favorite of Tolstóy's. He wrote it out much more fully under the title of* God Sees the Truth but Waits *(the full Russian title is* God Sees the Truth But Speaks not Soon*) in the volume of* Twenty-Three Tales. *In* What Is Art? *he refers to it as being in his opinion one of the two best he ever wrote, as regards its subject matter of forgiveness of injuries.*—A.M.

them. And they began telling what each was suffering for, and how they had sinned against God. One told how he had taken a life, another had taken two, a third had set a house on fire, while another had simply been a vagrant and had done nothing. So they asked the old man: 'What are you being punished for, Daddy?'—'I, my dear brothers,' said he, 'am being punished for my own and other men's sins. But I have not killed anyone or taken anything that was not mine, but have only helped my poorer brothers. I was a merchant, my dear brothers, and had much property.' And he went on to tell them all about it in due order. 'I don't grieve for myself,' he says, 'God, it seems, has chastened me. Only I am sorry for my old wife and the children,' and the old man began to weep. Now it happened that in the group was the very man who had killed the other merchant. 'Where did it happen, Daddy?' he said. 'When, and in what month?' He asked all about it and his heart began to ache. So he comes up to the old man like this, and falls down at his feet! 'You are perishing because of me, Daddy,' he says. 'It's quite true, lads, that this man,' he says, 'is being tortured innocently and for nothing! I,' he says, 'did that deed, and I put the knife under your head while you were asleep. Forgive me, Daddy,' he says, 'for Christ's sake!' "

Karatáev paused, smiling joyously as he gazed into the fire, and he drew the logs together.

"And the old man said, 'God will forgive you, we are all sinners in His sight. I suffer for my own sins,' and he wept bitter tears. Well, and what do you think, dear friends?" Karatáev continued, his face brightening more and more with a rapturous smile as if what he now had to tell contained the chief charm and the whole meaning of his story: "What do you think, dear fellows? That murderer confessed to the authorities. 'I have taken six lives,' he says (he was a great sinner), 'but what I am most sorry for is this old man. Don't let him suffer because of me.' So he confessed and it was all written down and the papers sent off in due form. The place was a long way off, and while they were judging, what with one thing and another, filling in the papers all in due form—the authorities I mean—time passed. The affair reached the Tsar. After a while the Tsar's decree came: to set the merchant free and give him a compensation that had been awarded. The paper arrived and they began to look for the old man. 'Where is the old man who has been suffering innocently and in vain? A paper has come from the Tsar!' So they began looking for him," here Karatáev's lower jaw trembled, "but God had already forgiven him— he was dead! That's how it was, dear fellows!" Karatáev concluded and sat for a long time silent, gazing before him with a smile.

And Pierre's soul was dimly but joyfully filled not by the story itself

but by its mysterious significance: by the rapturous joy that lit up Kara-
táev's face as he told it, and the mystic significance of that joy.

"À vos places [To your places]!" suddenly cried a voice.

A pleasant feeling of excitement and an expectation of something joyful
and solemn was aroused among the soldiers of the convoy and the
prisoners. From all sides came shouts of command, and from the left
came smartly dressed cavalrymen on good horses, passing the prisoners at
a trot. The expression on all faces showed the tension people feel at the
approach of those in authority. The prisoners thronged together and were
pushed off the road. The convoy formed up.

"The Emperor! The Emperor! The Marshal! The Duke!" and hardly
had the sleek cavalry passed, before a carriage drawn by six gray horses
rattled by. Pierre caught a glimpse of a man in a three-cornered hat with
a tranquil look on his handsome, plump, white face. It was one of the
marshals. His eye fell on Pierre's large and striking figure, and in the ex-
pression with which he frowned and looked away Pierre thought he
detected sympathy and a desire to conceal that sympathy.

The general in charge of the stores galloped after the carriage with a
red and frightened face, whipping up his skinny horse. Several officers
formed a group and some soldiers crowded round them. Their faces all
looked excited and worried.

"What did he say? What did he say?" Pierre heard them ask.

While the marshal was passing, the prisoners had huddled together in
a crowd, and Pierre saw Karatáev whom he had not yet seen that morn-
ing. He sat in his short overcoat leaning against a birch tree. On his face,
besides the look of joyful emotion it had worn yesterday while telling
the tale of the merchant who suffered innocently, there was now an expres-
sion of quiet solemnity.

Karatáev looked at Pierre with his kindly round eyes now filled with
tears, evidently wishing him to come near that he might say something
to him. But Pierre was not sufficiently sure of himself. He made as if he
did not notice that look and moved hastily away.

When the prisoners again went forward Pierre looked round. Karatáev
was still sitting at the side of the road under the birch tree and two
Frenchmen were talking over his head. Pierre did not look round again
but went limping up the hill.

From behind, where Karatáev had been sitting, came the sound of a
shot. Pierre heard it plainly, but at that moment he remembered that he
had not yet finished reckoning up how many stages still remained to
Smolénsk—a calculation he had begun before the marshal went by. And

he again started reckoning. Two French soldiers ran past Pierre, one of whom carried a lowered and smoking gun. They both looked pale, and in the expression on their faces—one of them glanced timidly at Pierre—there was something resembling what he had seen on the face of the young soldier at the execution. Pierre looked at the soldier and remembered that, two days before, that man had burned his shirt while drying it at the fire and how they had laughed at him.

Behind him, where Karatáev had been sitting, the dog began to howl. "What a stupid beast! Why is it howling?" thought Pierre.

His comrades, the prisoner soldiers walking beside him, avoided looking back at the place where the shot had been fired and the dog was howling, just as Pierre did, but there was a set look on all their faces.

THE STORES, the prisoners, and the marshal's baggage train stopped at the village of Shámshevo. The men crowded together round the campfires. Pierre went up to the fire, ate some roast horseflesh, lay down with his back to the fire, and immediately fell asleep. He again slept as he had done at Mozháysk after the battle of Borodinó.

Again real events mingled with dreams and again someone, he or another, gave expression to his thoughts, and even to the same thoughts that had been expressed in his dream at Mozháysk.

"Life is everything. Life is God. Everything changes and moves and that movement is God. And while there is life there is joy in consciousness of the divine. To love life is to love God. Harder and more blessed than all else is to love this life in one's sufferings, in innocent sufferings."

"Karatáev!" came to Pierre's mind.

And suddenly he saw vividly before him a long-forgotten, kindly old man who had given him geography lessons in Switzerland. "Wait a bit," said the old man, and showed Pierre a globe. This globe was alive—a vibrating ball without fixed dimensions. Its whole surface consisted of drops closely pressed together, and all these drops moved and changed places, sometimes several of them merging into one, sometimes one dividing into many. Each drop tried to spread out and occupy as much space as possible, but others striving to do the same compressed it, sometimes destroyed it, and sometimes merged with it.

"That is life," said the old teacher.

"How simple and clear it is," thought Pierre. "How is it I did not know it before?"

"God is in the midst, and each drop tries to expand so as to reflect Him to the greatest extent. And it grows, merges, disappears from the surface,

sinks to the depths, and again emerges. There now, Karatáev has spread out and disappeared. Do you understand, my child?" said the teacher.

"Do you understand, damn you?" shouted a voice, and Pierre woke up.*

He lifted himself and sat up. A Frenchman who had just pushed a Russian soldier away was squatting by the fire, engaged in roasting a piece of meat stuck on a ramrod. His sleeves were rolled up and his sinewy, hairy, red hands with their short fingers deftly turned the ramrod. His brown morose face with frowning brows was clearly visible by the glow of the charcoal.

"It's all the same to him," he muttered, turning quickly to a soldier who stood behind him. "Brigand! Get away!"

And twisting the ramrod he looked gloomily at Pierre, who turned away and gazed into the darkness. A prisoner, the Russian soldier the Frenchman had pushed away, was sitting near the fire patting something with his hand. Looking more closely Pierre recognized the blue-gray dog, sitting beside the soldier, wagging its tail.

"Ah, he's come?" said Pierre. "And Plat—" he began, but did not finish.

Suddenly and simultaneously a crowd of memories awoke in his fancy —of the look Platón had given him as he sat under the tree, of the shot heard from that spot, of the dog's howl, of the guilty faces of the two Frenchmen as they ran past him, of the lowered and smoking gun, and of Karatáev's absence at this halt—and he was on the point of realizing that Karatáev had been killed, but just at that instant, he knew not why, the recollection came to his mind of a summer evening he had spent with a beautiful Polish lady on the veranda of his house in Kiev. And without linking up the events of the day or drawing a conclusion from them, Pierre closed his eyes, seeing a vision of the country in summertime mingled with memories of bathing and of the liquid, vibrating globe, and he sank into water so that it closed over his head.

Before sunrise he was awakened by shouts and loud and rapid firing. French soldiers were running past him.

"The Cossacks!" one of them shouted, and a moment later a crowd of Russians surrounded Pierre.

For a long time he could not understand what was happening to him. All around he heard his comrades sobbing with joy.

"Brothers! Dear fellows! Darlings!" old soldiers exclaimed, weeping, as they embraced Cossacks and hussars.

* As a young man Tolstóy was interested in the phenomena of dreams, and he adopted a theory that dreams, however complex and prolonged they may seem, occur at the instant of waking and are suggested by external sounds, smells, or sensations.—A.M.

The hussars and Cossacks crowded round the prisoners; one offered them clothes, another boots, and a third bread. Pierre sobbed as he sat among them and could not utter a word. He hugged the first soldier who approached him, and kissed him, weeping.

Dólokhov stood at the gate of the ruined house, letting a crowd of disarmed Frenchmen pass by. The French, excited by all that had happened, were talking loudly among themselves, but as they passed Dólokhov who gently switched his boots with his whip and watched them with cold glassy eyes that boded no good, they became silent. On the opposite side stood Dólokhov's Cossack, counting the prisoners and marking off each hundred with a chalk line on the gate.

"How many?" Dólokhov asked the Cossack.

"The second hundred," replied the Cossack.

"*Filez, filez* [Get along, get along]!" Dólokhov kept saying, having adopted this expression from the French, and when his eyes met those of the prisoners they flashed with a cruel light.

Denísov, bareheaded and with a gloomy face, walked behind some Cossacks who were carrying the body of Pétya Rostóv to a hole that had been dug in the garden.

4. *The French retreat. Berthier's report to Napoleon.* *Their flight beyond Smolénsk*

AFTER THE TWENTY-EIGHTH OF OCTOBER when the frosts began, the flight of the French assumed a still more tragic character, with men freezing, or roasting themselves to death at the campfires, while carriages with people dressed in furs continued to drive past, carrying away the property that had been stolen by the Emperor, kings, and dukes; but the process of the flight and disintegration of the French army went on essentially as before.

From Moscow to Vyázma the French army of seventy-three thousand men not reckoning the Guards (who did nothing during the whole war but pillage) was reduced to thirty-six thousand, though not more than five thousand had fallen in battle. From this beginning the succeeding terms of the progression could be determined mathematically. The French army melted away and perished at the same rate from Moscow to Vyázma, from Vyázma to Smolénsk, from Smolénsk to the Berëzina, and from the Berëzina to Vílna—independently of the greater or lesser intensity of the cold, the pursuit, the barring of the way, or any other particular conditions.

Beyond Vyázma the French army instead of moving in three columns huddled together into one mass, and so went on to the end. Berthier wrote to his Emperor (we know how far commanding officers allow themselves to diverge from the truth in describing the condition of an army) and this is what he said:

> I deem it my duty to report to Your Majesty the condition of the various corps I have had occasion to observe during different stages of the last two or three days' march. They are almost disbanded. Scarcely a quarter of the soldiers remain with the standards of their regiments, the others go off by themselves in different directions hoping to find food and escape discipline. In general they regard Smolénsk as the place where they hope to recover. During the last few days many of the men have been seen to throw away their cartridges and their arms. In such a state of affairs, whatever your ultimate plans may be, the interest of Your Majesty's service demands that the army should be rallied at Smolénsk and should first of all be freed from ineffectives, such as dismounted cavalry, unnecessary baggage, and artillery material that is no longer in proportion to the present forces. The soldiers, who are worn out with hunger and fatigue, need supplies as well as a few days' rest. Many have died these last days on the road or at the bivouacs. This state of things is continually becoming worse and makes one fear that unless a prompt remedy is applied the troops will no longer be under control in case of an engagement.
>
> November 9: twenty miles from Smolénsk.

After staggering into Smolénsk which seemed to them a promised land, the French, searching for food, killed one another, sacked their own stores, and when everything had been plundered fled farther.

They all went without knowing whither or why they were going. Still less did that genius, Napoleon, know it, for no one issued any orders to him. But still he and those about him retained their old habits: wrote commands, letters, reports, and orders of the day; called one another *sire*, *mon cousin, prince d'Eckmühl, roi de Naples*, and so on. But these orders and reports were only on paper, nothing in them was acted upon for they could not be carried out, and though they entitled one another Majesties, Highnesses, or Cousins, they all felt that they were miserable wretches who had done much evil for which they had now to pay. And though they pretended to be concerned about the army, each was thinking only of himself and of how to get away quickly and save himself.

THE MOVEMENTS of the Russian and French armies during the campaign from Moscow back to the Niemen were like those in a game of Russian

blindman's buff, in which two players are blindfolded and one of them occasionally rings a little bell to inform the catcher of his whereabouts. First he rings his bell fearlessly, but when he gets into a tight place he runs away as quietly as he can, and often thinking to escape runs straight into his opponent's arms.

At first while they were still moving along the Kalúga road, Napoleon's armies made their presence known, but later when they reached the Smolénsk road they ran holding the clapper of their bell tight—and often thinking they were escaping ran right into the Russians.

Owing to the rapidity of the French flight and the Russian pursuit and the consequent exhaustion of the horses, the chief means of approximately ascertaining the enemy's position—by cavalry scouting—was not available. Besides, as a result of the frequent and rapid change of position by each army, even what information was obtained could not be delivered in time. If news was received one day that the enemy had been in a certain position the day before, by the third day when something could have been done, that army was already two days' march farther on and in quite another position.

One army fled and the other pursued. Beyond Smolénsk there were several different roads available for the French, and one would have thought that during their stay of four days they might have learned where the enemy was, might have arranged some more advantageous plan and undertaken something new. But after a four days' halt the mob, with no maneuvers or plans, again began running along the beaten track, neither to the right nor to the left but along the old—the worst—road, through Krásnoe and Orshá.

Expecting the enemy from behind and not in front, the French separated in their flight and spread out over a distance of twenty-four hours. In front of them all fled the Emperor, then the kings, then the dukes. The Russian army, expecting Napoleon to take the road to the right beyond the Dnieper—which was the only reasonable thing for him to do—themselves turned to the right and came out onto the highroad at Krásnoe. And here as in a game of blindman's buff the French ran into our vanguard. Seeing their enemy unexpectedly the French fell into confusion and stopped short from the sudden fright, but then they resumed their flight, abandoning their comrades who were farther behind. Then for three days separate portions of the French army—first Murat's (the vice-king's), then Davout's, and then Ney's—ran, as it were, the gauntlet of the Russian army. They abandoned one another, abandoned all their heavy baggage, their artillery, and half their men, and fled, getting past the Russians by night by making semicircles to the right.

Ney, who came last, had been busying himself blowing up the walls of Smolénsk which were in nobody's way, because despite the unfortunate plight of the French or because of it, they wished to punish the floor against which they had hurt themselves. Ney, who had had a corps of ten thousand men, reached Napoleon at Orshá with only one thousand men left, having abandoned all the rest and all his cannon, and having crossed the Dnieper at night by stealth at a wooded spot.

From Orshá they fled farther along the road to Vílna, still playing at blindman's buff with the pursuing army. At the Berëzina they again became disorganized, many were drowned and many surrendered, but those who got across the river fled farther. Their supreme chief donned a fur coat and, having seated himself in a sleigh, galloped on alone, abandoning his companions. The others who could do so drove away too, leaving those who could not to surrender or die.

THIS CAMPAIGN consisted in a flight of the French during which they did all they could to destroy themselves. From the time they turned onto the Kalúga road to the day their leader fled from the army, none of the movements of the crowd had any sense. So one might have thought that regarding this period of the campaign the historians, who attributed the actions of the mass to the will of one man, would have found it impossible to make the story of the retreat fit their theory. But no! Mountains of books have been written by the historians about this campaign, and everywhere are described Napoleon's arrangements, the maneuvers, and his profound plans which guided the army, as well as the military genius shown by his marshals.

The retreat from Málo-Yaroslávets when he had a free road into a well-supplied district and the parallel road was open to him along which Kutúzov afterwards pursued him—this unnecessary retreat along a devastated road—is explained to us as being due to profound considerations. Similarly profound considerations are given for his retreat from Smolénsk to Orshá. Then his heroism at Krásnoe is described, where he is reported to have been prepared to accept battle and take personal command, and to have walked about with a birch stick and said:

"*J'ai assez fait l'empereur; il est temps de faire le général* [I have acted the Emperor long enough, it is time to act the general]," but nevertheless immediately ran away again, abandoning to its fate the scattered fragments of the army he left behind.

Then we are told of the greatness of soul of the marshals, especially of Ney—a greatness of soul consisting in this: that he made his way by night

around through the forest and across the Dnieper and escaped to Orshá, abandoning standards, artillery, and nine tenths of his men.

And lastly, the final departure of the great Emperor from his heroic army is presented to us by the historians as something great and characteristic of genius. Even that final running away, described in ordinary language as the lowest depth of baseness which every child is taught to be ashamed of—even that act finds justification in the historians' language.

When it is impossible to stretch the very elastic threads of historical ratiocination any farther, when actions are clearly contrary to all that humanity calls right or even just, the historians produce a saving conception of "greatness." "Greatness," it seems, excludes the standards of right and wrong. For the "great" man nothing is wrong, there is no atrocity for which a "great" man can be blamed.

"*C'est grand* [It is great]!" say the historians, and there no longer exists either good or evil but only "*grand*" and "*not grand.*" *Grand* is good, not *grand* is bad. *Grand* is the characteristic, in their conception, of some special animals called "heroes." And Napoleon, escaping home in a warm fur coat and leaving to perish those who were not merely his comrades but were (in his opinion) men he had brought there, feels *que c'est grand* [that it is great], and his soul is tranquil.

"*Du sublime* [he saw something sublime in himself] *au ridicule il n'y a qu'un pas.* [From the sublime to the ridiculous is but a step]," said he. And the whole world for fifty years has been repeating: "*Sublime! Grand! Napoléon le Grand!*" *Du sublime au ridicule il n'y a qu'un pas.*

And it occurs to no one that to admit a greatness not commensurable with the standard of right and wrong is merely to admit one's own nothingness and immeasurable meanness.

For us with the standard of good and evil given us by Christ, no human actions are incommensurable. And there is no greatness where simplicity, goodness, and truth are absent.

5. Why the French were not cut off by the Russians

W HAT RUSSIAN, reading the account of the last part of the campaign of 1812, has not experienced an uncomfortable feeling of regret, dissatisfaction, and perplexity? Who has not asked himself how it is that the French were not all captured or destroyed when our three armies surrounded them in superior numbers, when the disordered French, hungry and freezing, surrendered in crowds, and when (as the historians relate)

the aim of the Russians was to stop the French, to cut them off, and capture them all?

How was it that the Russian army, which when numerically weaker than the French had given battle at Borodinó, did not achieve its purpose when it had surrounded the French on three sides and when its aim was to capture them? Can the French be so enormously superior to us that when we had surrounded them with superior forces we could not beat them? How could that happen?

History (or what is called by that name) replying to these questions says that this occurred because Kutúzov and Tormásov and Chichagóv, and this man and that man, did not execute such and such maneuvers. . . .

But why did they not execute those maneuvers? And why if they were guilty of not carrying out a prearranged plan were they not tried and punished? But even if we admitted that Kutúzov, Chichagóv, and others were the cause of the Russian failures, it is still incomprehensible why, the position of the Russian army being what it was at Krásnoe and at the Berëzina (in both cases we had superior forces), the French army with its marshals, kings, and Emperor was not captured, if that was what the Russians aimed at.

The explanation of this strange fact given by Russian military historians (to the effect that Kutúzov hindered an attack) is unfounded, for we know that he could not restrain the troops from attacking at Vyázma and Tarútino.

Why was the Russian army—which with inferior forces had withstood the enemy in full strength at Borodinó—defeated at Krásnoe and the Berëzina by the disorganized crowds of the French when it was numerically superior?

If the aim of the Russians consisted in cutting off and capturing Napoleon and his marshals—and that aim was not merely frustrated but all attempts to attain it were most shamefully baffled—then this last period of the campaign is quite rightly considered by the French to be a series of victories, and quite wrongly considered victorious by Russian historians.

The Russian military historians in so far as they submit to claims of logic must admit that conclusion, and in spite of their lyrical rhapsodies about valor, devotion, and so forth, must reluctantly admit that the French retreat from Moscow was a series of victories for Napoleon and defeats for Kutúzov.

But putting national vanity entirely aside one feels that such a conclusion involves a contradiction, since the series of French victories brought the French complete destruction, while the series of Russian defeats led to the total destruction of their enemy and the liberation of their country.

The source of this contradiction lies in the fact that the historians studying the events from the letters of the sovereigns and the generals, from memoirs, reports, projects, and so forth, have attributed to this last period of the war of 1812 an aim that never existed, namely that of cutting off and capturing Napoleon with his marshals and his army.

There never was or could have been such an aim, for it would have been senseless and its attainment quite impossible.

It would have been senseless, first because Napoleon's disorganized army was flying from Russia with all possible speed, that is to say, was doing just what every Russian desired. So what was the use of performing various operations on the French who were running away as fast as they possibly could?

Secondly, it would have been senseless to block the passage of men whose whole energy was directed to flight.

Thirdly, it would have been senseless to sacrifice one's own troops in order to destroy the French army, which without external interference was destroying itself at such a rate that, though its path was not blocked, it could not carry across the frontier more than it actually did in December, namely a hundredth part of the original army.

Fourthly, it would have been senseless to wish to take captive the Emperor, kings, and dukes—whose capture would have been in the highest degree embarrassing for the Russians, as the most adroit diplomatists of the time (Joseph de Maistre * and others) recognized. Still more senseless would have been the wish to capture army corps of the French, when our own army had melted away to half before reaching Krásnoe and a whole division would have been needed to convoy the corps of prisoners, and when our men were not always getting full rations and the prisoners already taken were perishing of hunger.

All the profound plans about cutting off and capturing Napoleon and his army were like the plan of a market gardener who, when driving out of his garden a cow that had trampled down the beds he had planted, should run to the gate and hit the cow on the head. The only thing to be said in excuse of that gardener would be that he was very angry. But not even that could be said for those who drew up this project, for it was not they who had suffered from the trampled beds.

But besides the fact that cutting off Napoleon with his army would have been senseless, it was impossible.

* *Joseph de Maistre (1754-1821). This able neo-Catholic and antirevolutionary writer was Sardinian ambassador at Petersburg. He lived there for fifteen years, was well received, and exerted a considerable antiliberal and reactionary influence.*—A.M.

It was impossible first because—as experience shows that a three-mile movement of columns on a battlefield never coincides with the plans— the probability of Chichagóv, Kutúzov, and Wittgenstein effecting a junction on time at an appointed place was so remote as to be tantamount to impossibility, as in fact thought Kutúzov, who when he received the plan remarked that diversions planned over great distances do not yield the desired results.

Secondly it was impossible, because to paralyze the momentum with which Napoleon's army was retiring, incomparably greater forces than the Russians possessed would have been required.

Thirdly it was impossible, because the military term "to cut off" has no meaning. One can cut off a slice of bread, but not an army. To cut off an army—to bar its road—is quite impossible, for there is always plenty of room to avoid capture and there is the night when nothing can be seen, as the military scientists might convince themselves by the example of Krásnoe and of the Berëzina. It is only possible to capture prisoners if they agree to be captured, just as it is only possible to catch a swallow if it settles on one's hand. Men can only be taken prisoners if they surrender according to the rules of strategy and tactics, as the Germans did. But the French troops quite rightly did not consider that this suited them, since death by hunger and cold awaited them in flight or captivity alike.

Fourthly and chiefly it was impossible, because never since the world began has a war been fought under such conditions as those that obtained in 1812, and the Russian army in its pursuit of the French strained its strength to the utmost and could not have done more without destroying itself.

During the movement of the Russian army from Tarútino to Krásnoe it lost fifty thousand sick or stragglers, that is a number equal to the population of a large provincial town. Half the men fell out of the army without a battle.

And it is of this period of the campaign—when the army lacked boots and sheepskin coats, was short of provisions and without vodka, and was camping out at night for months in the snow with fifteen degrees of frost,* when there were only seven or eight hours of daylight and the rest was night in which the influence of discipline cannot be maintained, when men were taken into that region of death where discipline fails, not for a few hours only as in a battle, but for months, where they were every moment fighting death from hunger and cold, when half the army perished in a single month—it is of this period of the campaign that the historians tell us how Milorádovich should have made a flank march to

* *Réaumur—two degrees below zero Fahrenheit.*—A.M.

such and such a place, Tormásov to another place, and Chichagóv should have crossed (more than knee-deep in snow) to somewhere else, and how so-and-so "routed" and "cut off" the French and so on and so on.

The Russians, half of whom died, did all that could and should have been done to attain an end worthy of the nation, and they are not to blame because other Russians, sitting in warm rooms, proposed that they should do what was impossible.

All that strange contradiction now difficult to understand between the facts and the historical accounts only arises because the historians dealing with the matter have written the history of the beautiful words and sentiments of various generals, and not the history of the events.

To them the words of Milorádovich seem very interesting, and so do their surmises and the rewards this or that general received; but the question of those fifty thousand men who were left in hospitals and in graves does not even interest them, for it does not come within the range of their investigation.

Yet one need only discard the study of the reports and general plans and consider the movement of those hundreds of thousands of men who took a direct part in the events, and all the questions that seemed insoluble easily and simply receive an immediate and certain solution.

The aim of cutting off Napoleon and his army never existed except in the imaginations of a dozen people. It could not exist because it was senseless and unattainable.

The people had a single aim: to free their land from invasion. That aim was attained in the first place of itself, as the French ran away, and so it was only necessary not to stop their flight. Secondly it was attained by the guerrilla warfare which was destroying the French, and thirdly by the fact that a large Russian army was following the French, ready to use its strength in case their movement stopped.

The Russian army had to act like a whip to a running animal. And the experienced driver knew it was better to hold the whip raised as a menace than to strike the running animal on the head.

BOOK FIFTEEN

DATES OF PRINCIPAL HISTORICAL EVENTS

1812

OLD STYLE	NEW STYLE	
Nov. 4–8	Nov. 16–20	Battles at Krásnoe.
Nov. 9	Nov. 21	Ney, with rearguard, reaches Orshá.
Nov. 14–16	Nov. 26–28	Crossing of the Berëzina.
Nov. 23	Dec. 5	Napoleon abandons the army at Smorgóni.
Dec. 6	Dec. 18	He reaches Paris.

1812-13

1. *The Rostóvs. Natásha's grief. The news of Pétya's death.*
Natásha leaves with Princess Mary for Moscow

WHEN SEEING a dying animal a man feels a sense of horror: substance
similar to his own is perishing before his eyes. But when it is a
beloved and intimate human being that is dying, besides this horror at
the extinction of life there is a severance, a spiritual wound, which like a
physical wound is sometimes fatal and sometimes heals, but always aches
and shrinks at any external irritating touch.

After Prince Andrew's death Natásha and Princess Mary alike felt this.
Drooping in spirit and closing their eyes before the menacing cloud of
death that overhung them, they dared not look life in the face. They care-
fully guarded their open wounds from any rough and painful contact.
Everything: a carriage passing rapidly in the street, a summons to dinner,
the maid's inquiry what dress to prepare, or worse still any word of insin-
cere or feeble sympathy, seemed an insult, painfully irritated the wound,
interrupting that necessary quiet in which they both tried to listen to the
stern and dreadful choir that still resounded in their imagination, and
hindered their gazing into those mysterious limitless vistas that for an
instant had opened out before them.

Only when alone together were they free from such outrage and pain.
They spoke little even to another, and when they did it was of very unim-
portant matters.

Both avoided any allusion to the future. To admit the possibility of a
future seemed to them to insult his memory. Still more carefully did they
avoid anything relating to him who was dead. It seemed to them that
what they had lived through and experienced could not be expressed in
words, and that any reference to the details of his life infringed the majesty
and sacredness of the mystery that had been accomplished before their
eyes.

Continued abstention from speech, and constant avoidance of every-

thing that might lead up to the subject—this halting on all sides at the boundary of what they might not mention—brought before their minds with still greater purity and clearness what they were both feeling.

But pure and complete sorrow is as impossible as pure and complete joy. Princess Mary, in her position as absolute and independent arbiter of her own fate and guardian and instructor of her nephew, was the first to be called back to life from that realm of sorrow in which she had dwelt for the first fortnight. She received letters from her relations to which she had to reply; the room in which little Nicholas had been put was damp and he began to cough; Alpátych came to Yaroslávl with reports on the state of their affairs and with advice and suggestions that they should return to Moscow to the house on the Vozdvízhenka Street, which had remained uninjured and needed only slight repairs. Life did not stand still and it was necessary to live. Hard as it was for Princess Mary to emerge from the realm of secluded contemplation in which she had lived till then, and sorry and almost ashamed as she felt to leave Natásha alone, yet the cares of life demanded her attention and she involuntarily yielded to them. She went through the accounts with Alpátych, conferred with Dessalles about her nephew, and gave orders and made preparations for the journey to Moscow.

Natásha remained alone and, from the time Princess Mary began making preparations for departure, held aloof from her too.

Princess Mary asked the countess to let Natásha go with her to Moscow, and both parents gladly accepted this offer, for they saw their daughter losing strength every day and thought that a change of scene and the advice of Moscow doctors would be good for her.

"I am not going anywhere," Natásha replied when this was proposed to her. "Do please just leave me alone!" And she ran out of the room, with difficulty refraining from tears of vexation and irritation rather than of sorrow.

After she felt herself deserted by Princess Mary and alone in her grief, Natásha spent most of the time in her room by herself, sitting huddled up feet and all in the corner of the sofa, tearing and twisting something with her slender nervous fingers and gazing intently and fixedly at whatever her eyes chanced to fall on. This solitude exhausted and tormented her but she was in absolute need of it. As soon as anyone entered she got up quickly, changed her position and expression, and picked up a book or some sewing, evidently waiting impatiently for the intruder to go.

She felt all the time as if she might at any moment penetrate that on which—with a terrible questioning too great for her strength—her spiritual gaze was fixed.

One day toward the end of December Natásha, pale and thin, dressed in a black woolen gown, her plaited hair negligently twisted into a knot, was crouched feet and all in the corner of her sofa, nervously crumpling and smoothing out the end of her sash while she looked at a corner of the door.

She was gazing in the direction in which he had gone—to the other side of life. And that other side of life, of which she had never before thought and which had formerly seemed to her so far away and improbable, was now nearer and more akin and more comprehensible than this side of life, where everything was either emptiness and desolation or suffering and indignity.

She was gazing where she knew him to be; but she could not imagine him otherwise than as he had been here. She now saw him again as he had been at Mytíshchi, at Tróitsa, and at Yaroslávl.

She saw his face, heard his voice, repeated his words and her own, and sometimes devised other words they might have spoken.

There he is lying back in an armchair in his velvet cloak, leaning his head on his thin pale hand. His chest is dreadfully hollow and his shoulders raised. His lips are firmly closed, his eyes glitter, and a wrinkle comes and goes on his pale forehead. One of his legs twitches just perceptibly, but rapidly. Natásha knows that he is struggling with terrible pain. "What is that pain like? Why does he have that pain? What does he feel? How does it hurt him?" thought Natásha. He noticed her watching him, raised his eyes, and began to speak seriously:

"One thing would be terrible," said he: "to bind oneself forever to a suffering man. It would be continual torture." And he looked searchingly at her. Natásha as usual answered before she had time to think what she would say. She said: "This can't go on—it won't. You will get well—quite well."

She now saw him from the commencement of that scene and relived what she had then felt. She recalled his long sad and severe look at those words and understood the meaning of the rebuke and despair in that protracted gaze.

"I agreed," Natásha now said to herself, "that it would be dreadful if he always continued to suffer. I said it then only because it would have been dreadful for him, but he understood it differently. He thought it would be dreadful for me. He then still wished to live and feared death. And I said it so awkwardly and stupidly! I did not say what I meant. I thought quite differently. Had I said what I thought, I should have said: even if he had to go on dying, to die continually before my eyes, I should have been happy compared with what I am now. Now there is nothing . . .

nobody. Did he know that? No, he did not and never will know it. And now it will never, never be possible to put it right." And now he again seemed to be saying the same words to her, only in her imagination Natásha this time gave him a different answer. She stopped him and said: "Terrible for you, but not for me! You know that for me there is nothing in life but you, and to suffer with you is the greatest happiness for me," and he took her hand and pressed it as he had pressed it that terrible evening four days before his death. And in her imagination she said other tender and loving words which she might have said then but only spoke now: "I love thee! . . . thee! I love, love . . ." she said, convulsively pressing her hands and setting her teeth with a desperate effort. . . .

She was overcome by sweet sorrow and tears were already rising in her eyes; then she suddenly asked herself to whom she was saying this. Again everything was shrouded in hard, dry perplexity, and again with a strained frown she peered toward the world where he was. And now, now it seemed to her she was penetrating the mystery. . . . But at the instant when it seemed that the incomprehensible was revealing itself to her a loud rattle of the door handle struck painfully on her ears. Dunyásha, her maid, entered the room quickly and abruptly with a frightened look on her face and showing no concern for her mistress.

"Come to your Papa at once, please!" said she with a strange, excited look. "A misfortune . . . about Peter Ilýnich . . . a letter," she finished with a sob.

Besides a feeling of aloofness from everybody Natásha was feeling a special estrangement from the members of her own family. All of them —her father, mother, and Sónya—were so near to her, so familiar, so commonplace, that all their words and feelings seemed an insult to the world in which she had been living of late, and she felt not merely indifferent to them but regarded them with hostility. She heard Dunyásha's words about Peter Ilýnich and a misfortune, but did not grasp them.

"What misfortune? What misfortune can happen to them? They just live their own old, quiet, and commonplace life," thought Natásha.

As she entered the ballroom her father was hurriedly coming out of her mother's room. His face was puckered up and wet with tears. He had evidently run out of that room to give vent to the sobs that were choking him. When he saw Natásha he waved his arms despairingly and burst into convulsively painful sobs that distorted his soft round face.

"Pe . . . Pétya . . . Go, go, she . . . is calling . . ." and weeping like a child and quickly shuffling on his feeble legs to a chair, he almost fell into it, covering his face with his hands.

Suddenly an electric shock seemed to run through Natásha's whole being. Terrible anguish struck her heart, she felt a dreadful ache as if something was being torn inside her and she were dying. But the pain was immediately followed by a feeling of release from the oppressive constraint that had prevented her taking part in life. The sight of her father, the terribly wild cries of her mother that she heard through the door, made her immediately forget herself and her own grief.

She ran to her father, but he feebly waved his arm, pointing to her mother's door. Princess Mary, pale and with quivering chin, came out from that room and taking Natásha by the arm said something to her. Natásha neither saw nor heard her. She went in with rapid steps, pausing at the door for an instant as if struggling with herself, and then ran to her mother.

The countess was lying in an armchair in a strange and awkward position, stretching out and beating her head against the wall. Sónya and the maids were holding her arms.

"Natásha! Natásha! . . ." cried the countess. "It's not true . . . it's not true . . . He's lying . . . Natásha!" she shrieked, pushing those around her away. "Go away, all of you; it's not true! Killed! . . . ha, ha, ha! . . . It's not true!"

Natásha put one knee on the armchair, stooped over her mother, embraced her, and with unexpected strength raised her, turned her face toward herself, and clung to her.

"Mummy! . . . darling! . . . I am here, my dearest Mummy," she kept on whispering, not pausing an instant.

She did not let go of her mother but struggled tenderly with her, demanded a pillow and hot water, and unfastened and tore open her mother's dress.

"My dearest darling . . . Mummy, my precious! . . ." she whispered incessantly, kissing her head, her hands, her face, and feeling her own irrepressible and streaming tears tickling her nose and cheeks.

The countess pressed her daughter's hand, closed her eyes, and became quiet for a moment. Suddenly she sat up with unaccustomed swiftness, glanced vacantly around her, and seeing Natásha began to press her daughter's head with all her strength. Then she turned toward her daughter's face which was wincing with pain and gazed long at it.

"Natásha, you love me?" she said in a soft trustful whisper. "Natásha, you would not deceive me? You'll tell me the whole truth?"

Natásha looked at her with eyes full of tears and in her look there was nothing but love and an entreaty for forgiveness.

"My darling Mummy!" she repeated, straining all the power of her

love to find some way of taking on herself the excess of grief that crushed her mother.

And again in a futile struggle with reality her mother, refusing to believe that she could live when her beloved boy was killed in the bloom of life, escaped from reality into a world of delirium.

Natásha did not remember how that day passed nor that night, nor the next day and night. She did not sleep and did not leave her mother. Her persevering and patient love seemed completely to surround the countess every moment, not explaining or consoling, but recalling her to life.

During the third night the countess kept very quiet for a few minutes, and Natásha rested her head on the arm of her chair and closed her eyes, but opened them again on hearing the bedstead creak. The countess was sitting up in bed and speaking softly.

"How glad I am you have come. You are tired. Won't you have some tea?" Natásha went up to her. "You have improved in looks and grown more manly," continued the countess, taking her daughter's hand.

"Mamma! What are you saying? . . ."

"Natásha, he is no more, no more!"

And embracing her daughter, the countess began to weep for the first time.

PRINCESS MARY postponed her departure. Sónya and the count tried to replace Natásha but could not. They saw that she alone was able to restrain her mother from unreasoning despair. For three weeks Natásha remained constantly at her mother's side, sleeping on a lounge chair in her room, making her eat and drink, and talking to her incessantly because the mere sound of her tender, caressing tones soothed her mother.

The mother's wounded spirit could not heal. Pétya's death had torn from her half her life. When the news of Pétya's death had come she had been a fresh and vigorous woman of fifty, but a month later she left her room a listless old woman taking no interest in life. But the same blow that almost killed the countess, this second blow, restored Natásha to life.

A spiritual wound produced by a rending of the spiritual body is like a physical wound and, strange as it may seem, just as a deep wound may heal and its edges join, physical and spiritual wounds alike can yet heal completely only as the result of a vital force from within.

Natásha's wound healed in that way. She thought her life was ended, but her love for her mother unexpectedly showed her that the essence of life—love—was still active within her. Love awoke and so did life.

Prince Andrew's last days had bound Princess Mary and Natásha together; this new sorrow brought them still closer to one another. Princess

Mary put off her departure, and for three weeks looked after Natásha as if she had been a sick child. The last weeks passed in her mother's bedroom had strained Natásha's physical strength.

One afternoon noticing Natásha shivering with fever, Princess Mary took her to her own room and made her lie down on the bed. Natásha lay down, but when Princess Mary had drawn the blinds and was going away she called her back.

"I don't want to sleep, Mary, sit by me a little."

"You are tired—try to sleep."

"No, no. Why did you bring me away? She will be asking for me."

"She is much better. She spoke so well today," said Princess Mary.

Natásha lay on the bed and in the semidarkness of the room scanned Princess Mary's face.

"Is she like him?" thought Natásha. "Yes, like and yet not like. But she is quite original, strange, new, and unknown. And she loves me. What is in her heart? All that is good. But how? What is her mind like? What does she think about me? Yes, she is splendid!"

"Mary," she said timidly, drawing Princess Mary's hand to herself, "Mary, you mustn't think me wicked. No? Mary darling, how I love you! Let us be quite, quite friends."

And Natásha, embracing her, began kissing her face and hands, making Princess Mary feel shy but happy by this demonstration of her feelings.

From that day a tender and passionate friendship such as exists only between women was established between Princess Mary and Natásha. They were continually kissing and saying tender things to one another and spent most of their time together. When one went out the other became restless and hastened to rejoin her. Together they felt more in harmony with one another than either of them felt with herself when alone. A feeling stronger than friendship sprang up between them; an exclusive feeling of life being possible only in each other's presence.

Sometimes they were silent for hours; sometimes after they were already in bed they would begin talking and go on till morning. They spoke most of what was long past. Princess Mary spoke of her childhood, of her mother, her father, and her daydreams; and Natásha, who with a passive lack of understanding had formerly turned away from that life of devotion, submission, and the poetry of Christian self-sacrifice, now feeling herself bound to Princess Mary by affection, learned to love her past too and to understand a side of life previously incomprehensible to her. She did not think of applying submission and self-abnegation to her own life, for she was accustomed to seek other joys, but she understood and loved in another those previously incomprehensible virtues. For Princess Mary,

listening to Natásha's tales of childhood and early youth, there also opened out a new and hitherto uncomprehended side of life: belief in life and its enjoyment.

Just as before, they never mentioned him so as not to lower (as they thought) their exalted feelings by words; but this silence about him had the effect of making them gradually begin to forget him without being conscious of it.

Natásha had grown thin and pale and physically so weak that they all talked about her health, and this pleased her. But sometimes she was suddenly overcome by fear not only of death but of sickness, weakness, and loss of good looks, and involuntarily she examined her bare arm carefully, surprised at its thinness, and in the morning noticed her drawn and, as it seemed to her, piteous face in her glass. It seemed to her that things must be so, and yet it was dreadfully sad.

One day she went quickly upstairs and found herself out of breath. Unconsciously she immediately invented a reason for going down, and then, testing her strength, ran upstairs again, observing the result.

Another time when she called Dunyásha her voice trembled, so she called again—though she could hear Dunyásha coming—called her in the deep chest tones in which she had been wont to sing, and listened attentively to herself.

She did not know and would not have believed it, but beneath the layer of slime that covered her soul and seemed to her impenetrable, delicate young shoots of grass were already sprouting, which taking root would so cover with their living verdure the grief that weighed her down that it would soon no longer be seen or noticed. The wound had begun to heal from within.

At the end of January Princess Mary left for Moscow, and the count insisted on Natásha's going with her to consult the doctors.

2. Analysis of Kutúzov's movements

AFTER THE ENCOUNTER at Vyázma, where Kutúzov had been unable to hold back his troops in their anxiety to overwhelm and cut off the enemy and so on, the farther movement of the fleeing French, and of the Russians who pursued them, continued as far as Krásnoe without a battle. The flight was so rapid that the Russian army pursuing the French could not keep up with them; cavalry and artillery horses broke down, and the information received of the movements of the French was never reliable.

The men in the Russian army were so worn out by this continuous

marching at the rate of twenty-seven miles a day that they could not go any faster.

To realize the degree of exhaustion of the Russian army it is only necessary to grasp clearly the meaning of the fact that, while not losing more than five thousand killed and wounded after Tarútino and less than a hundred prisoners, the Russian army which left that place a hundred thousand strong reached Krásnoe with only fifty thousand.

The rapidity of the Russian pursuit was just as destructive to our army as the flight of the French was to theirs. The only difference was that the Russian army moved voluntarily, with no such threat of destruction as hung over the French, and that the sick Frenchmen were left behind in enemy hands while the sick Russians left behind were among their own people. The chief cause of the wastage of Napoleon's army was the rapidity of its movement, and a convincing proof of this is the corresponding decrease of the Russian army.

Kutúzov as far as was in his power, instead of trying to check the movement of the French as was desired in Petersburg and by the Russian army generals, directed his whole activity here, as he had done at Tarútino and Vyázma, to hastening it on while easing the movement of our army.

But besides this, since the exhaustion and enormous diminution of the army caused by the rapidity of the advance had become evident, another reason for slackening the pace and delaying presented itself to Kutúzov. The aim of the Russian army was to pursue the French. The road the French would take was unknown, and so the closer our troops trod on their heels the greater distance they had to cover. Only by following at some distance could one cut across the zigzag path of the French. All the artful maneuvers suggested by our generals meant fresh movements of the army and a lengthening of its marches, whereas the only reasonable aim was to shorten those marches. To that end Kutúzov's activity was directed during the whole campaign from Moscow to Vílna—not casually or intermittently but so consistently that he never once deviated from it.

Kutúzov felt and knew—not by reasoning or science but with the whole of his Russian being—what every Russian soldier felt: that the French were beaten, that the enemy was flying and must be driven out; but at the same time he like the soldiers realized all the hardship of this march, the rapidity of which was unparalleled for such a time of year.

But to the generals, especially the foreign ones in the Russian army, who wished to distinguish themselves, to astonish somebody, and for some reason to capture a king or a duke—it seemed that now—when any battle must be horrible and senseless—was the very time to fight and

conquer somebody. Kutúzov merely shrugged his shoulders when one after another they presented projects of maneuvers to be made with those soldiers—ill-shod, insufficiently clad, and half starved—who within a month and without fighting a battle had dwindled to half their number, and who at the best if the flight continued would have to go a greater distance than that they had already traversed, before they reached the frontier.

This longing to distinguish themselves, to maneuver, to overthrow, and to cut off showed itself particularly whenever the Russians stumbled on the French army.

So it was at Krásnoe, where they expected to find one of the three French columns and stumbled instead on Napoleon himself with six-teen thousand men. Despite all Kutúzov's efforts to avoid that ruinous encounter and to preserve his troops, the massacre of the broken mob of French soldiers by worn-out Russians continued at Krásnoe for three days.

Toll wrote a disposition: "The first column will march to so and so," etc. And as usual nothing happened in accord with the disposition. Prince Eugène of Württemberg fired from a hill over the French crowds that were running past, and demanded reinforcements which did not arrive. The French, avoiding the Russians, dispersed and hid themselves in the forest by night, making their way round as best they could, and continued their flight.

Milorádovich, who said he did not want to know anything about the commissariat affairs of his detachment, and could never be found when he was wanted—that *chevalier sans peur et sans reproche* [knight with-out fear and without reproach] as he styled himself—who was fond of parleys with the French, sent envoys demanding their surrender, wasted time, and did not do what he was ordered to do.

"I give you that column, lads," he said, riding up to the troops and pointing out the French to the cavalry.

And the cavalry, with spurs and sabers urging on horses that could scarcely move, trotted with much effort to the column presented to them —that is to say, to a crowd of Frenchmen stark with cold, frost-bitten, and starving—and the column that had been presented to them threw down its arms and surrendered as it had long been anxious to do.

At Krásnoe they took twenty-six thousand prisoners, several hundred cannon, and a stick called a "marshal's staff," and disputed as to who had distinguished himself and were pleased with their achievement—though they much regretted not having taken Napoleon, or at least a marshal or

a hero of some sort, and reproached one another and especially Kutúzov for having failed to do so.

These men, carried away by their passions, were but blind tools of the most melancholy law of necessity, but considered themselves heroes and imagined that they were accomplishing a most noble and honorable deed. They blamed Kutúzov and said that from the very beginning of the campaign he had prevented their vanquishing Napoleon, that he thought of nothing but satisfying his passions and would not advance from the Linen Factories because he was comfortable there, that at Krásnoe he checked the advance because on learning that Napoleon was there he had quite lost his head, and that it was probable that he had an understanding with Napoleon and had been bribed by him,* and so on, and so on.

Not only did his contemporaries, carried away by their passions, talk in this way, but posterity and history have acclaimed Napoleon as grand, while Kutúzov is described by foreigners as a crafty, dissolute, weak old courtier, and by Russians as something indefinite—a sort of puppet useful only because he had a Russian name.

In 1812 and 1813 Kutúzov was openly accused of blundering. The Emperor was dissatisfied with him. And in a history recently written by order of the Highest Authorities it is said that Kutúzov was a cunning court liar, frightened of the name of Napoleon, and that by his blunders at Krásnoe and the Berëzina he deprived the Russian army of the glory of complete victory over the French.[2]

Such is the fate not of great men (grands hommes) whom the Russian mind does not acknowledge, but of those rare and always solitary individuals who, discerning the will of Providence, submit their personal will to it. The hatred and contempt of the crowd punish such men for discerning the higher laws.

For Russian historians, strange and terrible to say, Napoleon—that most insignificant tool of history who never anywhere, even in exile, showed human dignity—Napoleon is the object of adulation and enthusiasm; he is grand. But Kutúzov—the man who from the beginning to the end of his activity in 1812, never once swerving by word or deed from Borodinó to Vílna, presented an example exceptional in history of self-sacrifice and

* *Wilson's Diary.*—L.T. *Sir Robert Thomas Wilson (1774-1849), after helping to train the Portuguese army in the Peninsula, was British military commissioner at the Russian headquarters in 1812-14. His Private Diary was posthumously published in 1861.*—A.M.

[2] History of the year 1812. The character of Kutúzov and reflections on the unsatisfactory results of the battles at Krásnoe, *by Bogdánovich.*—L.T.

a present consciousness of the future importance of what was happening —Kutúzov seems to them something indefinite and pitiful, and when speaking of him and of the year 1812 they always seem a little ashamed.

And yet it is difficult to imagine an historical character whose activity was so unswervingly directed to a single aim; and it would be difficult to imagine any aim more worthy or more consonant with the will of the whole people. Still more difficult would it be to find an instance in history of the aim of an historical personage being so completely accomplished as that to which all Kutúzov's efforts were directed in 1812.

Kutúzov never talked of "forty centuries looking down from the Pyramids," * of the sacrifices he offered for the fatherland, or of what he intended to accomplish or had accomplished; in general he said nothing about himself, adopted no pose, always appeared to be the simplest and most ordinary of men, and said the simplest and most ordinary things. He wrote letters to his daughters and to Madame de Staël, read novels, liked the society of pretty women, jested with generals, officers, and soldiers, and never contradicted those who tried to prove anything to him. When Count Rostopchín at the Yaúza bridge galloped up to Kutúzov with personal reproaches for having caused the destruction of Moscow, and said: "How was it you promised not to abandon Moscow without a battle?" Kutúzov replied: "And I shall not abandon Moscow without a battle," though Moscow was then already abandoned. When Arakchéev, coming to him from the Emperor, said that Ermólov ought to be appointed chief of the artillery, Kutúzov replied: "Yes, I was just saying so myself," though a moment before he had said quite the contrary. What did it matter to him—who then alone amid a senseless crowd understood the whole tremendous significance of what was happening— what did it matter to him whether Rostopchín attributed the calamities of Moscow to him or to himself? Still less could it matter to him who was appointed chief of the artillery.

Not merely in these cases but continually did that old man—who by experience of life had reached the conviction that thoughts and the words serving as their expression are not what move people—use quite meaningless words that happened to enter his head.

But that man, so heedless of his words, did not once during the whole time of his activity utter one word inconsistent with the single aim toward which he moved throughout the whole war. Obviously in spite of himself, in very diverse circumstances, he repeatedly expressed his real thoughts with the bitter conviction that he would not be understood.

* The reference is to Napoleon's oft-quoted address to his army in Egypt before the battle at the foot of the Pyramids.—A.M.

Beginning with the battle of Borodinó, from which time his disagree-
ment with those about him began, he alone said that *the battle of Boro-
dinó was a victory*, and repeated this both verbally and in his dispatches
and reports up to the time of his death. He alone said that *the loss of
Moscow is not the loss of Russia*. In reply to Lauriston's proposal of
peace, he said: *There can be no peace, for such is the people's will*. He
alone during the retreat of the French said that all our maneuvers are
useless, everything is being accomplished of itself better than we could
desire; that the enemy must be offered "a golden bridge"; that neither the
Tarútino, the Vyázma, nor the Krásnoe battles were necessary; that we
must keep some force to reach the frontier with, and that he would not
sacrifice a single Russian for ten Frenchmen.

And this courtier, as he is described to us, who lies to Arakchéev to
please the Emperor, he alone—incurring thereby the Emperor's displeas-
ure—said in Vílna that to carry the war beyond the frontier is useless and
harmful.

Nor do words alone prove that only he understood the meaning of the
events. His actions—without the smallest deviation—were all directed to
one and the same threefold end: (1) to brace all his strength for conflict
with the French, (2) to defeat them, and (3) to drive them out of
Russia, minimizing as far as possible the sufferings of our people and of
our army.

This procrastinator Kutúzov, whose motto was "Patience and Time,"
this enemy of decisive action, gave battle at Borodinó, investing the prepa-
rations for it with unparalleled solemnity. This Kutúzov who before the
battle of Austerlitz began said that it would be lost, he alone, in contra-
diction to everyone else, declared till his death that Borodinó was a vic-
tory, despite the assurance of generals that the battle was lost and despite
the fact that for an army to have to retire after winning a battle was un-
precedented. He alone during the whole retreat insisted that battles,
which were useless then, should not be fought, and that a new war should
not be begun nor the frontiers of Russia crossed.

It is easy now to understand the significance of these events—if only
we abstain from attributing to the activity of the mass aims that existed
only in the heads of a dozen individuals—for the events and their results
now lie before us.

But how did that old man, alone, in opposition to the general opinion,
so truly discern the importance of the people's view of the events that in
all his activity he was never once untrue to it?

The source of that extraordinary power of penetrating the meaning of

the events then occurring lay in the national feeling which he possessed in full purity and strength.

Only the recognition of the fact that he possessed this feeling caused the people in so strange a manner, contrary to the Tsar's wish, to select him—an old man in disfavor—to be their representative in the national war. And only that feeling placed him on that highest human pedestal from which he, the commander in chief, devoted all his powers not to slaying and destroying men but to saving and showing pity on them.

That simple, modest, and therefore truly great, figure could not be cast in the false mold of a European hero—the supposed ruler of men—that history has invented.

To a lackey no man can be great, for a lackey has his own conception of greatness.

3. Kutúzov at Krásnoe; his speech to the army. Encampment for the night: soldier scenes. Ramballe's appearance with his orderly. The song of Henri Quatre

THE FIFTH OF NOVEMBER was the first day of what is called the battle of Krásnoe. Toward evening—after much disputing and many mistakes made by generals who did not go to their proper places, and after adjutants had been sent about with counterorders—when it had become plain that the enemy was everywhere in flight and that there could and would be no battle, Kutúzov left Krásnoe and went to Dóbroe whither his headquarters had that day been transferred.

The day was clear and frosty. Kutúzov rode to Dóbroe on his plump little white horse, followed by an enormous suite of discontented generals who whispered among themselves behind his back. All along the road groups of French prisoners captured that day (there were seven thousand of them) were crowding to warm themselves at campfires. Near Dóbroe an immense crowd of tattered prisoners, buzzing with talk and wrapped and bandaged in anything they had been able to get hold of, were standing in the road beside a long row of unharnessed French guns. At the approach of the commander in chief the buzz of talk ceased and all eyes were fixed on Kutúzov who, wearing a white cap with a red band and a padded overcoat that bulged on his round shoulders, moved slowly along the road on his white horse. One of the generals was reporting to him where the guns and prisoners had been captured.

Kutúzov seemed preoccupied and did not listen to what the general was saying. He screwed up his eyes with a dissatisfied look as he gazed

attentively and fixedly at these prisoners, who presented a specially wretched appearance. Most of them were disfigured by frost-bitten noses and cheeks, and nearly all had red, swollen, and festering eyes.

One group of the French stood close to the road, and two of them, one of whom had his face covered with sores, were tearing a piece of raw flesh with their hands. There was something horrible and bestial in the fleeting glance they threw at the riders and in the malevolent expression with which, after a glance at Kutúzov, the soldier with the sores immediately turned away and went on with what he was doing.

Kutúzov looked long and intently at these two soldiers. He puckered his face, screwed up his eyes, and pensively swayed his head. At another spot he noticed a Russian soldier laughingly patting a Frenchman on the shoulder, saying something to him in a friendly manner, and Kutúzov with the same expression on his face again swayed his head.

"What were you saying?" he asked the general, who continuing his report directed the commander in chief's attention to some standards captured from the French and standing in front of the Preobrazhénsk regiment.

"Ah, the standards!" said Kutúzov, evidently detaching himself with difficulty from the thoughts that preoccupied him.

He looked about him absently. Thousands of eyes were looking at him from all sides awaiting a word from him.

He stopped in front of the Preobrazhénsk regiment, sighed deeply, and closed his eyes. One of his suite beckoned to the soldiers carrying the standards to advance and surround the commander in chief with them. Kutúzov was silent for a few seconds and then, submitting with evident reluctance to the duty imposed by his position, raised his head and began to speak. A throng of officers surrounded him. He looked attentively around at the circle of officers, recognizing several of them.

"I thank you all!" he said, addressing the soldiers and then again the officers. In the stillness around him his slowly uttered words were distinctly heard. "I thank you all for your hard and faithful service. The victory is complete and Russia will not forget you! Honor to you forever."

He paused and looked round.

"Lower its head, lower it!" he said to a soldier who had accidentally lowered the French eagle he was holding before the Preobrazhénsk standards. "Lower, lower, that's it. Hurrah, lads!" he added, addressing the men with a rapid movement of his chin.

"Hur-r-rah!" roared thousands of voices.

While the soldiers were shouting Kutúzov leaned forward in his saddle

and bowed his head, and his eye lit up with a mild and apparently ironic gleam.

"You see, brothers . . ." said he when the shouts had ceased . . . and all at once his voice and the expression of his face changed. It was no longer the commander in chief speaking but an ordinary old man who wanted to tell his comrades something very important.

There was a stir among the throng of officers and in the ranks of the soldiers, who moved that they might hear better what he was going to say.

"You see, brothers, I know it's hard for you, but it can't be helped! Bear up; it won't be for long now! We'll see our visitors off and then we'll rest. The Tsar won't forget your service. It is hard for you, but still you are at home while they—you see what they have come to," said he, pointing to the prisoners. "Worse off than our poorest beggars. While they were strong we didn't spare ourselves, but now we may even pity them. They are human beings too. Isn't it so, lads?"

He looked around, and in the direct, respectful, wondering gaze fixed upon him he read sympathy with what he had said. His face grew brighter and brighter with an old man's mild smile, which drew the corners of his lips and eyes into a cluster of wrinkles. He ceased speaking and bowed his head as if in perplexity.

"But after all who asked them here? Serves them right, the bloody bastards!" he cried, suddenly lifting his head.

And flourishing his whip he rode off at a gallop for the first time during the whole campaign, and left the broken ranks of the soldiers laughing joyfully and shouting "Hurrah!"

Kutúzov's words were hardly understood by the troops. No one could have repeated the field marshal's address, begun solemnly and then changing into an old man's simplehearted talk; but the hearty sincerity of that speech, the feeling of majestic triumph combined with pity for the foe and consciousness of the justice of our cause, exactly expressed by that old man's good-natured expletives, was not merely understood but lay in the soul of every soldier and found expression in their joyous and long-sustained shouts. Afterwards when one of the generals addressed Kutúzov asking whether he wished his calèche to be sent for, Kutúzov in answering unexpectedly gave a sob, being evidently greatly moved.

WHEN THE TROOPS reached their night's halting place on the eighth of November, the last day of the Krásnoe battles, it was already growing dusk. All day it had been calm and frosty with occasional lightly falling

snow and toward evening it began to clear. Through the falling snow a purple-black and starry sky showed itself and the frost grew keener.

An infantry regiment which had left Tarútino three thousand strong but now numbered only nine hundred was one of the first to arrive that night at its halting place—a village on the highroad. The quartermasters who met the regiment announced that all the huts were full of sick and dead Frenchmen, cavalrymen, and members of the staff. There was only one hut available for the regimental commander.·

The commander rode up to his hut. The regiment passed through the village and stacked its arms in front of the last huts.

Like some huge many-limbed animal, the regiment began to prepare its lair and its food. One part of it dispersed and waded knee-deep through the snow into a birch forest to the right of the village, and immediately the sound of axes and swords, the crashing of branches, and merry voices could be heard from there. Another section amid the regimental wagons and horses which were standing in a group was busy getting out caldrons and rye biscuit, and feeding the horses. A third section scattered through the village arranging quarters for the staff officers, carrying out the French corpses that were in the huts, and dragging away boards, dry wood, and thatch from the roofs, for the campfires, or wattle fences to serve for shelter.

Some fifteen men with merry shouts were shaking down the high wattle wall of a shed, the roof of which had already been removed.

"Now then, all together—shove!" cried the voices, and the huge surface of the wall, sprinkled with snow and creaking with frost, was seen swaying in the gloom of the night. The lower stakes cracked more and more and at last the wall fell, and with it the men who had been pushing it. Loud, coarse laughter and joyous shouts ensued.

"Now then, catch hold in twos! Hand up the lever! That's it. . . . Where are you shoving to?"

"Now, all together! But wait a moment, boys . . . With a song!"

All stood silent, and a soft, pleasant velvety voice began to sing. At the end of the third verse as the last note died away, twenty voices roared out at once: "Oo-oo-oo-oo! That's it. All together! Heave away, boys! . . ." but despite their united efforts the wattle hardly moved, and in the silence that followed the heavy breathing of the men was audible.

"Here, you of the Sixth Company! Devils that you are! Lend a hand . . . will you? You may want us one of these days."

Some twenty men of the Sixth Company who were on their way into the village joined the haulers, and the wattle wall, which was about thirty-five feet long and seven feet high, moved forward along the village

street, swaying, pressing upon and cutting the shoulders of the gasping men.

"Get along . . . Falling? What are you stopping for? There now. . . ." Merry senseless words of abuse flowed freely.

"What are you up to?" suddenly came the authoritative voice of a sergeant major who came upon the men who were hauling their burden. "There are gentry here; the general himself is in that hut, and you foul-mouthed devils, you brutes, I'll give it to you!" shouted he, hitting the first man who came in his way a swinging blow on the back. "Can't you make less noise?"

The men became silent. The soldier who had been struck groaned and wiped his face, which had been scratched till it bled by his falling against the wattle.

"There, how that devil hits out! He's made my face all bloody," said he in a frightened whisper when the sergeant major had passed on.

"Don't you like it?" said a laughing voice, and moderating their tones the men moved forward.

When they were out of the village they began talking again as loud as before, interlarding their talk with the same aimless expletives.

In the hut which the men had passed, the chief officers had gathered and were in animated talk over their tea about the events of the day and the maneuvers suggested for tomorrow. It was proposed to make a flank march to the left, cut off the Vice-King (Murat) and capture him.

By the time the soldiers had dragged the wattle fence to its place the campfires were blazing on all sides ready for cooking, the wood crackled, the snow was melting, and black shadows of soldiers flitted to and fro all over the occupied space where the snow had been trodden down.

Axes and choppers were plied all around. Everything was done without any orders being given. Stores of wood were brought for the night, shelters were rigged up for the officers, caldrons were being boiled, and muskets and accouterments put in order.

The wattle wall the men had brought was set up in a semicircle by the Eighth Company as a shelter from the north, propped up by musket rests, and a campfire was built before it. They beat the tattoo, called the roll, had supper, and settled down round the fires for the night—some repairing their footgear, some smoking pipes, and some stripping themselves naked to steam the lice out of their shirts.

ONE WOULD HAVE THOUGHT that under the almost incredibly wretched conditions the Russian soldiers were in at that time—lacking warm boots and sheepskin coats, without a roof over their heads, in the snow with

eighteen degrees of frost,* and without even full rations (the commissariat did not always keep up with the troops)—they would have presented a very sad and depressing spectacle.

On the contrary, the army had never under the best material conditions presented a more cheerful and animated aspect. This was because all who began to grow depressed or who lost strength were sifted out of the army day by day. All the physically or morally weak had long since been left behind and only the flower of the army—physically and mentally—remained.

More men collected behind the wattle fence of the Eighth Company than anywhere else. Two sergeants major were sitting with them and their campfire blazed brighter than the others. For leave to sit by their wattle they demanded contributions of fuel.

"Eh, Makéev! What has become of you, you son of a bitch? Are you lost or have the wolves eaten you? Fetch some more wood!" shouted a red-haired and red-faced man, screwing up his eyes and blinking because of the smoke but not moving back from the fire. "And you, Jackdaw, go and fetch some wood!" said he to another soldier.

This red-haired man was neither a sergeant nor a corporal, but being robust he ordered about those weaker than himself. The soldier they called "Jackdaw," a thin little fellow with a sharp nose, rose obediently and was about to go but at that instant there came into the light of the fire the slender, handsome figure of a young soldier carrying a load of wood.

"Bring it here—that's fine!"

They split up the wood, pressed it down on the fire, blew at it with their mouths, and fanned it with the skirts of their greatcoats, making the flames hiss and crackle. The men drew nearer and lit their pipes. The handsome young soldier who had brought the wood, setting his arms akimbo, began stamping his cold feet rapidly and deftly on the spot where he stood.

"Mother! The dew is cold but clear. . . . It's well that I'm a musketeer . . ." he sang, pretending to hiccough after each syllable.

"Look out, your soles will fly off!" shouted the red-haired man, noticing that the sole of the dancer's boot was hanging loose. "What a fellow you are for dancing!"

The dancer stopped, pulled off the loose piece of leather, and threw it on the fire.

"Right enough, friend," said he, and, having sat down, took out of his knapsack a scrap of blue French cloth, and wrapped it round his foot. "It's

* *The thermometer used was Réaumur. Eighteen degrees of frost = eight degrees below zero Fahrenheit.*—A.M.

the steam that spoils them," he added, stretching out his feet toward the fire.

"They'll soon be issuing us new ones. They say that when we've finished hammering *them*, we're to receive double kits!"

"And that son of a bitch Petróv has lagged behind after all, it seems," said one sergeant major.

"I've had an eye on him this long while," said the other.

"Well, he's a poor sort of soldier. . . ."

"But in the Third Company they say nine men were missing yesterday."

"Yes, it's all very well, but when a man's feet are frozen how can he walk?"

"Eh? Don't talk nonsense!" said a sergeant major.

"Do you want to be doing the same?" said an old soldier, turning reproachfully to the man who had spoken of frozen feet.

"Well, you know," said the sharp-nosed man they called Jackdaw in a squeaky and unsteady voice, raising himself at the other side of the fire, "a plump man gets thin, but for a thin one it's death. Take me, now! I've got no strength left," he added, with sudden resolution turning to the sergeant major. "Tell them to send me to hospital; I'm aching all over; anyway I shan't be able to keep up."

"That'll do, that'll do!" replied the sergeant major quietly.

The soldier said no more and the talk went on.

"What a lot of those Frenchies were taken today, and the fact is that not one of them had what you might call real boots on," said a soldier, starting a new theme. "They were no more than make-believes."

"The Cossacks have taken their boots. They were clearing the hut for the colonel and carried them out. It was pitiful to see them, boys," put in the dancer. "As they turned them over one seemed still alive and, would you believe it, he jabbered something in their lingo."

"But they're a clean folk, lads," the first man went on; "he was white— as white as birchbark—and some of them are such fine fellows, you might think they were nobles."

"Well, what do you think? They make soldiers of all classes there."

"But they don't understand our talk at all," said the dancer with a puzzled smile. "I asked him whose subject he was, and he jabbered in his own way. A queer lot!"

"But it's strange, friends," continued the man who had wondered at their whiteness, "the peasants at Mozháysk were saying that when they began burying the dead—where the battle was you know—well, those dead had been lying there for nearly a month, and says the peasant, 'they lie as white as paper, clean, and not as much smell as a puff of powder smoke.'"

"Was it from the cold?" asked someone.

"You're a clever fellow! From the cold indeed! Why, it was hot. If it had been from the cold, ours would not have rotted either. 'But,' he says, 'go up to ours and they are all rotten and maggoty. So,' he says, 'we tie our faces up with kerchiefs and turn our heads away as we drag them off: we can hardly do it. But theirs,' he says, 'are white as paper and not so much smell as a whiff of gunpowder.'"

All were silent.

"It must be from their food," said the sergeant major. "They used to gobble the same food as the gentry."

No one contradicted him.

"That peasant near Mozháysk where the battle was said the men were all called up from ten villages around and they carted for twenty days and still didn't finish carting the dead away. And as for the wolves, he says . . ."

"That was a real battle," said an old soldier. "It's the only one worth remembering; but since that . . . it's only been tormenting folk."

"And do you know, Daddy, the day before yesterday we ran at them and, my word, they didn't let us get near before they just threw down their muskets and went on their knees. 'Pardon!' they say. That's only one case. They say Plátov took 'Poleon himself twice. But he didn't know the right charm. He catches him and catches him—no good! He turns into a bird in his hands and flies away. And there's no way of killing him either."

"You're a first-class liar, Kiselëv, when I come to look at you!"

"Liar, indeed! It's the real truth."

"If he fell into my hands, when I'd caught him I'd bury him in the ground with an aspen stake to fix him down. What a lot of men he's ruined!"

"Well, anyhow we're going to end it. He won't come here again," remarked the old soldier, yawning.

The conversation flagged, and the soldiers began settling down to sleep.

"Look at the stars. It's wonderful how they shine! You would think the women had spread out their linen," said one of the men, gazing with admiration at the Milky Way.

"That's a sign of a good harvest next year."

"We shall want some more wood."

"You warm your back and your belly gets frozen. That's queer."

"O Lord!"

"What are you pushing for? Is the fire only for you? Look how he's sprawling!"

In the silence that ensued, the snoring of those who had fallen asleep could be heard. Others turned over and warmed themselves, now and

again exchanging a few words. From a campfire a hundred paces off came a sound of general, merry laughter.

"Hark at them roaring there in the Fifth Company!" said one of the soldiers, "and what a lot of them there are!"

One of the men got up and went over to the Fifth Company.

"They're having such fun," said he, coming back. "Two Frenchies have turned up. One's quite frozen and the other's an awful swaggerer. He's singing songs. . . ."

"Oh, I'll go across and have a look. . . ."

And several of the men went over to the Fifth Company.

THE FIFTH COMPANY was bivouacking at the very edge of the forest. A huge campfire was blazing brightly in the midst of the snow, lighting up the branches of trees heavy with hoarfrost.

About midnight they heard the sound of steps in the snow of the forest, and the crackling of dry branches.

"A bear, lads," said one of the men.

They all raised their heads to listen, and out of the forest into the bright firelight stepped two strangely clad human figures clinging to one another.

These were two Frenchmen who had been hiding in the forest. They came up to the fire, hoarsely uttering something in a language our soldiers did not understand. One was taller than the other; he wore an officer's hat and seemed quite exhausted. On approaching the fire he had been going to sit down, but fell. The other, a short sturdy soldier with a shawl tied round his head, was stronger. He raised his companion and said something, pointing to his mouth. The soldiers surrounded the Frenchmen, spread a greatcoat on the ground for the sick man, and brought some buckwheat porridge and vodka for both of them.

The exhausted French officer was Ramballe and the man with his head wrapped in the shawl was Morel, his orderly.

When Morel had drunk some vodka and finished his bowl of porridge he suddenly became unnaturally merry and chattered incessantly to the soldiers, who could not understand him. Ramballe refused food and resting his head on his elbow lay silent beside the campfire, looking at the Russian soldiers with red and vacant eyes. Occasionally he emitted a long-drawn groan and then again became silent. Morel, pointing to his shoulders, tried to impress on the soldiers the fact that Ramballe was an officer and ought to be warmed. A Russian officer who had come up to the fire sent to ask his colonel whether he would not take a French officer into his hut to warm him, and when the messenger returned and said that the colonel wished the officer to be brought to him, Ramballe was told to go.

He rose and tried to walk, but staggered and would have fallen had not a soldier standing by held him up.

"You won't do it again, eh?" said one of the soldiers, winking and turning mockingly to Ramballe.

"Oh, you fool! Why talk rubbish, lout that you are—a real peasant!" came rebukes from all sides addressed to the jesting soldier.

They surrounded Ramballe, lifted him on the crossed arms of two soldiers, and carried him to the hut. Ramballe put his arms around their necks while they carried him and began wailing plaintively:

"Oh, you fine fellows, my kind, kind friends! These are men! Oh, my brave, kind friends," and he leaned his head against the shoulder of one of the men like a child.

Meanwhile Morel was sitting in the best place by the fire, surrounded by the soldiers.

Morel, a short sturdy Frenchman with inflamed and streaming eyes, was wearing a woman's cloak and had a shawl tied woman fashion round his head over his cap. He was evidently tipsy, and was singing a French song in a hoarse broken voice, with an arm thrown round the nearest soldier. The soldiers simply held their sides as they watched him.

"Now then, now then, teach us how it goes! I'll soon pick it up. How is it?" said the man—a singer and a wag—whom Morel was embracing.

"*Vive Henri Quatre! Vive ce roi vaillant* [Long live Henry the Fourth, that valiant king]!" sang Morel, winking. "*Ce diable à quatre* . . . [That rowdy devil]" *

"Vivarika! Vif-seruvaru! Sedyablyaka!" repeated the soldier, flourishing his arm and really catching the tune.

"Bravo! Ha, ha, ha!" rose their rough, joyous laughter from all sides.

Morel, wrinkling up his face, laughed too.

"Well, go on, go on!"

> "*Qui eut le triple talent,*
> *De boire, de battre,*
> *Et d'être un vert galant* . . .*"

> [Who had a triple talent
> For drinking, for fighting,
> And for being a gallant old boy . . .]

"It goes smoothly, too. Well, now, Zaletáev!"

"Ke . . ." Zaletáev brought out with effort: "ke-e-e-e," he drawled, laboriously pursing his lips, "le-trip-ta-la-de-bu-de-ba, e de-tra-va-ga-la!" he sang.

* *A French song.*—A.M.

"Fine! Just like the Frenchie! Oh, ho ho! Do you want some more to eat?"

"Give him some porridge: it takes a long time to get filled up after starving."

They gave him some more porridge and Morel with a laugh set to work on his third bowl. All the young soldiers smiled gaily as they watched him. The older men, who thought it undignified to amuse themselves with such nonsense, continued to lie at the opposite side of the fire, but one would occasionally raise himself on an elbow and glance at Morel with a smile.

"They are men too," said one of them as he wrapped himself up in his coat. "Even wormwood grows on its own root."

"O Lord, O Lord! How starry it is! Tremendous! That means a hard frost. . . ."

They all grew silent. The stars, as if knowing that no one was looking at them, began to disport themselves in the dark sky: now flaring up, now vanishing, now trembling, they were busy whispering something gladsome and mysterious to one another.

4, The crossing of the Berëzina. Vílna. The Emperor Alexander. Kutúzov; his failing health

THE FRENCH ARMY melted away at the uniform rate of a mathematical progression; and that crossing of the Berëzina about which so much has been written was only one intermediate stage in its destruction, and not at all the decisive episode of the campaign. If so much has been and still is written about the Berëzina, on the French side this is only because at the broken bridge across that river the calamities their army had been previously enduring were suddenly concentrated at one moment into a tragic spectacle that remained in every memory, and on the Russian side merely because in Petersburg—far from the seat of war—a plan (again one of Pfuel's) had been devised to catch Napoleon in a strategic trap at the Berëzina River. Everyone assured himself that all would happen according to plan, and therefore insisted that it was just the crossing of the Berëzina that destroyed the French army. In reality the results of the crossing were much less disastrous to the French—in guns and men lost—than Krásnoe had been, as the figures show.

The sole importance of the crossing of the Berëzina lies in the fact that it plainly and indubitably proved the fallacy of all the plans for cutting off the enemy's retreat and the soundness of the only possible line of action—the one Kutúzov and the general mass of the army demanded—namely,

simply to follow the enemy up. The French crowd fled at a continually increasing speed and all its energy was directed to reaching its goal. It fled like a wounded animal and it was impossible to block its path. This was shown not so much by the arrangements it made for crossing as by what took place at the bridges. When the bridges broke down, unarmed soldiers, people from Moscow and women with children who were with the French transport, all—carried on by *vis inertiæ*—pressed forward into boats and into the ice-covered water and did not surrender.

That impulse was reasonable. The condition of fugitives and of pursuers was equally bad. As long as they remained with their own people each might hope for help from his fellows and the definite place he held among them. But those who surrendered, while remaining in the same pitiful plight, would be on a lower level to claim a share in the necessities of life. The French did not need to be informed of the fact that half the prisoners—with whom the Russians did not know what to do—perished of cold and hunger despite their captors' desire to save them; they felt that it could not be otherwise. The most compassionate Russian commanders, those favorable to the French—and even the Frenchmen in the Russian service—could do nothing for the prisoners. The French perished from the conditions to which the Russian army was itself exposed. It was impossible to take bread and clothes from our hungry and indispensable soldiers to give to the French who, though not harmful, or hated, or guilty, were simply unnecessary. Some Russians even did that, but they were exceptions.

Certain destruction lay behind the French but in front there was hope. Their ships had been burned, there was no salvation save in collective flight, and on that the whole strength of the French was concentrated.

The farther they fled the more wretched became the plight of the remnant, especially after the Berëzina, on which (in consequence of the Petersburg plan) special hopes had been placed by the Russians, and the keener grew the passions of the Russian commanders, who blamed one another and Kutúzov most of all. Anticipation that the failure of the Petersburg Berëzina plan would be attributed to Kutúzov led to dissatisfaction, contempt, and ridicule, more and more strongly expressed. The ridicule and contempt were of course expressed in a respectful form, making it impossible for him to ask wherein he was to blame. They did not talk seriously to him; when reporting to him or asking for his sanction they appeared to be fulfilling a regrettable formality, but they winked behind his back and tried to mislead him at every turn.

Because they could not understand him all these people assumed that it was useless to talk to the old man; that he would never grasp the pro-

fundity of their plans, that he would answer with his phrases (which they thought were mere phrases) about a "golden bridge," about the impossibility of crossing the frontier with a crowd of tatterdemalions, and so forth. They had heard all that before. And all he said—that it was necessary to await provisions, or that the men had no boots—was so simple, while what they proposed was so complicated and clever, that it was evident that he was old and stupid and that they, though not in power, were commanders of genius.

After the junction with the army of the brilliant admiral and Petersburg hero Wittgenstein, this mood and the gossip of the staff reached their maximum. Kutúzov saw this and merely sighed and shrugged his shoulders. Only once, after the affair of the Berëzina, did he get angry and write to Bennigsen (who reported separately to the Emperor) the following letter:

"On account of your spells of ill health, will your excellency please be so good as to set off for Kalúga on receipt of this, and there await further commands and appointments from His Imperial Majesty."

But after Bennigsen's departure, the Grand Duke Tsarévich Constantine Pávlovich joined the army. He had taken part in the beginning of the campaign but had subsequently been removed from the army by Kutúzov. Now having come to the army, he informed Kutúzov of the Emperor's displeasure at the poor success of our forces and the slowness of their advance. The Emperor intended to join the army personally in a few days' time.

The old man, experienced in court as well as in military affairs—this same Kutúzov who in August had been chosen commander in chief against the sovereign's wishes and who had removed the Grand Duke and heir-apparent from the army *—who on his own authority and contrary to the Emperor's will had decided on the abandonment of Moscow, now real-

* Constantine Pávlovich (1779-1831) was Alexander I's brother. He has already been mentioned where Berg tells of being reprimanded by him during the Guards' march to Austria. He was to some extent responsible for the disaster at Austerlitz. Mention has also been made of him at the Drissa camp, as prominent among those who regarded Napoleon as invincible and wanted to conclude peace as soon as possible.

Constantine was personally courageous, but erratic and incompetent alike in war and politics. After marrying a Polish lady he renounced his right to the throne. The hesitation and confusion caused by the fact that this was not made public occasioned delay in proclaiming his younger brother Nicholas as Emperor, and gave occasion for the "Decembrist" revolt with which Nicholas I's reign inauspiciously began.—A.M.

ized at once that his day was over, that his part was played, and that the power he was supposed to hold was no longer his. And he understood this not merely from the attitude of the court. He saw on the one hand that the military business in which he had played his part was ended and felt that his mission was accomplished; and at the same time he began to be conscious of the physical weariness of his aged body and of the necessity of physical rest.

On the twenty-ninth of November Kutúzov entered Vílna—his "dear Vílna" as he called it. Twice during his career Kutúzov had been governor of Vílna. In that wealthy town, which had not been injured, he found old friends and associations, besides the comforts of life of which he had so long been deprived. And he suddenly turned from the cares of army and state and, as far as the passions that seethed around him allowed, immersed himself in the quiet life to which he had formerly been accustomed, as if all that was taking place and all that had still to be done in the realm of history did not concern him at all.

Chichagóv, one of the most zealous "cutters-off" and "breakers-up," who had first wanted to effect a diversion in Greece and then in Warsaw but never wished to go where he was sent: Chichagóv, noted for the boldness with which he spoke to the Emperor, and who considered Kutúzov to be under an obligation to him because when he was sent to make peace with Turkey in 1811 independently of Kutúzov, and found that peace had already been concluded, he admitted to the Emperor that the merit of securing that peace was really Kutúzov's; this Chichagóv was the first to meet Kutúzov at the castle where the latter was to stay. In undress naval uniform, with a dirk, and holding his cap under his arm, he handed Kutúzov a garrison report and the keys of the town. The contemptuously respectful attitude of the younger men to the old man in his dotage was expressed in the highest degree by the behavior of Chichagóv, who knew of the accusations that were being directed against Kutúzov.

When speaking to Chichagóv, Kutúzov incidentally mentioned that the vehicles packed with china that had been captured from him at Borísov had been recovered and would be restored to him.

"You mean to imply that I have nothing to eat out of. . . . On the contrary, I can supply you with everything even if you want to give dinner parties," warmly replied Chichagóv, who tried by every word he spoke to prove his own rectitude and therefore imagined Kutúzov to be animated by the same desire.

Kutúzov, shrugging his shoulders, replied with his subtle penetrating smile: "I meant merely to say what I said."

Contrary to the Emperor's wish Kutúzov detained the greater part of

the army at Vílna. Those about him said that he became extraordinarily slack and physically feeble during his stay in that town. He attended to army affairs reluctantly, left everything to his generals, and while awaiting the Emperor's arrival led a dissipated life.

Having left Petersburg on the seventh of December with his suite— Count Tolstóy, Prince Volkónski, Arakchéev, and others—the Emperor reached Vílna on the eleventh, and in his traveling sleigh drove straight to the castle. In spite of the severe frost some hundred generals and staff officers in full parade uniform stood in front of the castle, as well as a guard of honor of the Semënov regiment.

A courier who galloped to the castle in advance, in a troyka with three foam-flecked horses, shouted "Coming!" and Konovnítsyn rushed into the vestibule to inform Kutúzov, who was waiting in the hall porter's little lodge.

A minute later the old man's large stout figure in full-dress uniform, his chest covered with orders and a scarf drawn round his stomach, waddled out into the porch. He put on his hat with its peaks to the sides * and, holding his gloves in his hand and walking with an effort sideways down the steps to the level of the street, took in his hand the report he had prepared for the Emperor.

There was running to and fro and whispering; another troyka flew furiously up, and then all eyes were turned on an approaching sleigh in which the figures of the Emperor and Volkónski could already be descried.

From the habit of fifty years all this had a physically agitating effect on the old general. He carefully and hastily felt himself all over, readjusted his hat, and pulling himself together drew himself up and, at the very moment when the Emperor, having alighted from the sleigh, lifted his eyes to him, handed him the report and began speaking in his smooth, ingratiating voice.

The Emperor with a rapid glance scanned Kutúzov from head to foot, frowned for an instant, but immediately mastering himself went up to the old man, extended his arms and embraced him. And this embrace too, owing to a long-standing impression related to his innermost feelings, had its usual effect on Kutúzov and he gave a sob.

The Emperor greeted the officers and the Semënov guard, and again pressing the old man's hand went with him into the castle.

* *This passage has, excusably enough, perplexed many translators. The cocked hat (called a "three-cornered" hat, but which by Alexander's time had in fact become a cocked hat with two peaks) was worn according to circumstances either with the peaks fore and aft or, as on this occasion, turned sideways.*—A.M.

When alone with the field marshal the Emperor expressed his dissatisfaction at the slowness of the pursuit and at the mistakes made at Krásnoe and the Berëzina, and informed him of his intentions for a future campaign abroad. Kutúzov made no rejoinder or remark. The same submissive, expressionless look with which he had listened to the Emperor's commands on the field of Austerlitz seven years before settled on his face now.

When Kutúzov came out of the study and with lowered head was crossing the ballroom with his heavy waddling gait, he was arrested by someone's voice saying:

"Your Serene Highness!"

Kutúzov raised his head and looked for a long while into the eyes of Count Tolstóy, who stood before him holding a silver salver on which lay a small object. Kutúzov seemed not to understand what was expected of him.

Suddenly he seemed to remember; a scarcely perceptible smile flashed across his puffy face, and bowing low and respectfully he took the object that lay on the salver. It was the Order of St. George of the First Class.*

NEXT DAY the field marshal gave a dinner and ball which the Emperor honored by his presence. Kutúzov had received the Order of St. George of the First Class and the Emperor showed him the highest honors, but everyone knew of the imperial dissatisfaction with him. The proprieties were observed and the Emperor was the first to set that example, but everybody understood that the old man was blameworthy and good-for-nothing. When Kutúzov, conforming to a custom of Catherine's day, ordered the standards that had been captured to be lowered at the Emperor's feet on his entering the ballroom, the Emperor made a wry face and muttered something in which some people caught the words, "the old comedian."

The Emperor's displeasure with Kutúzov was specially increased at Vílna by the fact that Kutúzov evidently could not or would not understand the importance of the coming campaign.

When on the following morning the Emperor said to the officers assembled about him: "You have not only saved Russia, you have saved Europe!" they all understood that the war was not ended.

Kutúzov alone would not see this and openly expressed his opinion that no fresh war could improve the position or add to the glory of Russia, but

* The Order of St. George was founded by Catherine the Great in 1769 for distinguished exploits in war. The First Class—a very high honor, seldom given —is a star and cross attached to a ribbon.—A.M.

could only spoil and lower the glorious position that Russia had gained. He tried to prove to the Emperor the impossibility of levying fresh troops, spoke of the hardships already endured by the people, of the possibility of failure and so forth.

This being the field marshal's frame of mind he was naturally regarded as merely a hindrance and obstacle to the impending war.

To avoid unpleasant encounters with the old man, the natural method was to do what had been done with him at Austerlitz and with Barclay at the beginning of the Russian campaign—to transfer the authority to the Emperor himself, thus cutting the ground from under the commander in chief's feet without upsetting the old man by informing him of the change.

With this object his staff was gradually reconstructed and its real strength removed and transferred to the Emperor. Toll, Konovnítsyn, and Ermólov received fresh appointments. Everyone spoke loudly of the field marshal's great weakness and failing health.

His health had to be bad for his place to be taken away and given to another. And in fact his health was poor.

So naturally, simply, and gradually—just as he had come from Turkey to the Treasury in Petersburg to recruit the militia, and then to the army when he was needed there—now when his part was played out, Kutúzov's place was taken by a new and necessary performer.

The war of 1812, besides its national significance dear to every Russian heart, was now to assume another, a European, significance.

The movement of peoples from west to east was to be succeeded by a movement of peoples from east to west, and for this fresh war another leader was necessary, having qualities and views differing from Kutúzov's and animated by different motives.

Alexander I was as necessary for the movement of the peoples from east to west and for the refixing of national frontiers as Kutúzov had been for the salvation and glory of Russia.

Kutúzov did not understand what Europe, the balance of power, or Napoleon meant. He could not understand it. For the representative of the Russian people, after the enemy had been destroyed and Russia had been liberated and raised to the summit of her glory, there was nothing left to do as a Russian. Nothing remained for the representative of the national war but to die, and Kutúzov died.

5. *Pierre. Illness and recovery at Orël. His new attitude to life and his fellow men. His affairs. He goes to Moscow; the town's animation and rapid recovery. Pierre meets Natásha at Princess Mary's. Love*

AS GENERALLY HAPPENS, Pierre did not feel the full effects of the physical privation and strain he had suffered as prisoner until after they were over. After his liberation he reached Orël, and on the third day there, when preparing to go to Kiev, he fell ill and was laid up for three months. He had what the doctors termed "bilious fever." But despite the fact that the doctors treated him, bled him, and gave him medicines to drink, he recovered.

Scarcely any impression was left on Pierre's mind by all that happened to him from the time of his rescue till his illness. He remembered only the dull gray weather now rainy and now snowy, internal physical distress, and pains in his feet and side. He remembered a general impression of the misfortunes and sufferings of people and of being worried by the curiosity of officers and generals who questioned him, he also remembered his difficulty in procuring a conveyance and horses, and above all he remembered his incapacity to think and feel all that time. On the day of his rescue he had seen the body of Pétya Rostóv. That same day he had learned that Prince Andrew, after surviving the battle of Borodinó for more than a month, had recently died in the Rostóvs' house at Yaroslávl, and Denísov who told him this news also mentioned Hélène's death, supposing that Pierre had heard of it long before. All this at the time seemed merely strange to Pierre: he felt he could not grasp its significance. Just then he was only anxious to get away as quickly as possible from places where people were killing one another, to some peaceful refuge where he could recover himself, rest, and think over all the strange new facts he had learned; but on reaching Orël he immediately fell ill. When he came to himself after his illness he saw in attendance on him two of his servants, Terénty and Váska, who had come from Moscow; and also his cousin the eldest princess, who had been living on his estate at Eléts and hearing of his rescue and illness had come to look after him.

It was only gradually during his convalescence that Pierre lost the impressions he had become accustomed to during the last few months and got used to the idea that no one would oblige him to go anywhere tomorrow, that no one would deprive him of his warm bed, and that he would be sure to get his dinner, tea, and supper. But for a long time in his dreams he still saw himself in the conditions of captivity. In the same

way little by little he came to understand the news he had been told after his rescue, about the death of Prince Andrew, the death of his wife, and the destruction of the French.

A joyous feeling of freedom—that complete inalienable freedom natural to man which he had first experienced at the first halt outside Moscow—filled Pierre's soul during his convalescence. He was surprised to find that this inner freedom, which was independent of external conditions, now had as it were an additional setting of external liberty. He was alone in a strange town, without acquaintances. No one demanded anything of him or sent him anywhere. He had all he wanted: the thought of his wife which had been a continual torment to him was no longer there, since she was no more.

"Oh, how good! How splendid!" said he to himself when a cleanly laid table was moved up to him with savory beef tea, or when he lay down for the night on a soft clean bed, or when he remembered that the French had gone and that his wife was no more. "Oh, how good, how splendid!"

And by old habit he asked himself the question: "Well, and what then? What am I going to do?" And he immediately gave himself the answer: "Well, I shall live. Ah, how splendid!"

The very question that had formerly tormented him, the thing he had continually sought to find—the aim of life—no longer existed for him now. That search for the aim of life had not merely disappeared temporarily—he felt that it no longer existed for him and could not present itself again. And this very absence of an aim gave him the complete, joyous sense of freedom which constituted his happiness at this time.

He could not see an aim, for he now had faith—not faith in any kind of rule, or words, or ideas, but faith in an ever-living, ever-manifest God. Formerly he had sought Him in aims he set himself. That search for an aim had been simply a search for God, and suddenly in his captivity he had learned not by words or reasoning but by direct feeling what his nurse had told him long ago: that God is here and everywhere. In his captivity he had learned that in Karatáev God was greater, more infinite and unfathomable than in the Architect of the Universe recognized by the Freemasons. He felt like a man who after straining his eyes to see into the far distance finds what he sought at his very feet. All his life he had looked over the heads of the men around him, when he should have merely looked in front of him without straining his eyes.

In the past he had never been able to find that great inscrutable infinite *something*. He had only felt that it must exist somewhere and had looked for it. In everything near and comprehensible he had seen only what was limited, petty, commonplace, and senseless. He had equipped himself with

a mental telescope and looked into remote space, where petty worldliness hiding itself in misty distance had seemed to him great and infinite merely because it was not clearly seen. And such had European life, politics, Freemasonry, philosophy, and philanthropy seemed to him. But even then, at moments of weakness as he had accounted them, his mind had penetrated to those distances and he had there seen the same pettiness, worldliness, and senselessness. Now, however, he had learned to see the great, eternal, and infinite in everything, and therefore—to see it and enjoy its contemplation—he naturally threw away the telescope through which he had till now gazed over men's heads, and gladly regarded the ever-changing, eternally great, unfathomable, and infinite life around him. And the closer he looked the more tranquil and happy he became. That dreadful question, "What for?" which had formerly destroyed all his mental edifices, no longer existed for him. To that question, "What for?" a simple answer was now always ready in his soul: "Because there is a God, that God without whose will not one hair falls from a man's head."

In external ways Pierre had hardly changed at all. In appearance he was just what he used to be. As before he was absent-minded and seemed occupied not with what was before his eyes but with something special of his own. The difference between his former and present self was that formerly when he did not grasp what lay before him or was said to him, he had puckered his forehead painfully as if vainly seeking to distinguish something at a distance. At present he still forgot what was said to him and still did not see what was before his eyes, but he now looked with a scarcely perceptible and seemingly ironic smile at what was before him and listened to what was said, though evidently seeing and hearing something quite different. Formerly he had appeared to be a kindhearted but unhappy man, and so people had been inclined to avoid him. Now a smile at the joy of life always played round his lips, and sympathy for others shone in his eyes with a questioning look as to whether they were as contented as he was, and people felt pleased by his presence.

Previously he had talked a great deal, grew excited when he talked, and seldom listened; now he was seldom carried away in conversation and knew how to listen so that people readily told him their most intimate secrets.

The princess, who had never liked Pierre and had been particularly hostile to him since she had felt herself under obligations to him after the old count's death, now after staying a short time in Orël—where she had come intending to show Pierre that in spite of his ingratitude she considered it her duty to nurse him—felt to her surprise and vexation that she had become fond of him. Pierre did not in any way seek her approval, he

merely studied her with interest. Formerly she had felt that he regarded her with indifference and irony, and so had shrunk into herself as she did with others and had shown him only the combative side of her nature; but now he seemed to be trying to understand the most intimate places of her heart, and, mistrustfully at first but afterwards gratefully, she let him see the hidden, kindly sides of her character.

The most cunning man could not have crept into her confidence more successfully, evoking memories of the best times of her youth and showing sympathy with them. Yet Pierre's cunning consisted simply in finding pleasure in drawing out the human qualities of the embittered, hard, and (in her own way) proud princess.

"Yes, he is a very, very kind man when he is not under the influence of bad people but of people such as myself," thought she.

His servants too—Terénty and Váska—in their own way noticed the change that had taken place in Pierre. They considered that he had become much "simpler."* Terénty, when he had helped him undress and wished him good night, often lingered with his master's boots in his hands and clothes over his arm, to see whether he would not start a talk. And Pierre, noticing that Terénty wanted a chat, generally kept him there.

"Well, tell me . . . now, how did you get food?" he would ask.

And Terénty would begin talking of the destruction of Moscow, and of the old count, and would stand for a long time holding the clothes and talking, or sometimes listening to Pierre's stories, and then would go out into the hall with a pleasant sense of intimacy with his master and affection for him.

The doctor who attended Pierre and visited him every day, though he considered it his duty as a doctor to pose as a man whose every moment was of value to suffering humanity, would sit for hours with Pierre telling him his favorite anecdotes and his observations on the characters of his patients in general, and especially of the ladies.

"It's a pleasure to talk to a man like that; he is not like our provincials," he would say.

There were several prisoners from the French army in Orél, and the doctor brought one of them, a young Italian,[2] to see Pierre.

* *"Simple" is here used in the sense, common in Russia, of unpretentious, natural.*—A.M.

[2] *In an early draft of the novel Tolstóy introduced an Italian officer, Emilio Poncini, who occupied the place now allotted to Captain Ramballe, but with whom Pierre became more frank and intimate than with the latter. He visited Pierre in prison in Moscow and tried to help him, and later on they met again at Tambóv and resumed their friendly intercourse. The brief mention of an*

This officer began visiting Pierre, and the princess used to make fun of the tenderness the Italian expressed for him.

The Italian seemed happy only when he could come to see Pierre, talk with him, tell him about his past, his life at home, and his love, and pour out to him his indignation against the French and especially against Napoleon.

"If all Russians are in the least like you, it is sacrilege to fight such a nation," he said to Pierre. "You, who have suffered so from the French, do not even feel animosity toward them."

Pierre had evoked the passionate affection of the Italian merely by evok‐ing the best side of his nature and taking a pleasure in so doing.

During the last days of Pierre's stay in Orël his old Masonic acquaint‐ance Count Willarski, who had introduced him to the lodge in 1807, came to see him. Willarski was married to a Russian heiress who had a large estate in Orël province, and he occupied a temporary post in the commis‐sariat department in that town.

Hearing that Bezúkhov was in Orël, Willarski, though they had never been intimate, came to him with the professions of friendship and inti‐macy that people who meet in a desert generally express for one another. Willarski felt dull in Orël and was pleased to meet a man of his own circle and, as he supposed, of similar interests.

But to his surprise Willarski soon noticed that Pierre had lagged much behind the times, and had sunk, as he expressed it to himself, into apathy and egotism.

"You are letting yourself go, my dear fellow," he said.

But for all that Willarski found it pleasanter now than it had been formerly to be with Pierre, and came to see him every day. To Pierre as he looked at and listened to Willarski, it seemed strange to think that he had been like that himself but a short time before.

Willarski was a married man with a family, busy with his family affairs, his wife's affairs, and his official duties. He regarded all these occupations as hindrances to life, and considered that they were all contemptible be‐cause their aim was the welfare of himself and his family. Military, admin‐istrative, political, and Masonic interests continually absorbed his atten‐tion. And Pierre, without trying to change the other's views and without condemning him, but with the quiet, joyful, and amused smile now habit‐ual to him, was interested in this strange though very familiar phenom‐enon.

.

unnamed Italian in this chapter is all that remains of Poncini, whom Tolstóy at first meant to make more important.—A.M.

There was a new feature in Pierre's relations with Willarski, with the princess, with the doctor, and with all the people he now met, which gained for him the general good will. This was his acknowledgment of the impossibility of changing a man's convictions by words, and his recognition of the possibility of everyone thinking, feeling, and seeing things each from his own point of view. This legitimate peculiarity of each individual which used to excite and irritate Pierre now became a basis of the sympathy he felt for, and the interest he took in, other people. The difference, and sometimes complete contradiction, between men's opinions and their lives, and between one man and another, pleased him and drew from him an amused and gentle smile.

In practical matters Pierre unexpectedly felt within himself a center of gravity he had previously lacked. Formerly all pecuniary questions, especially requests for money to which, as an extremely wealthy man, he was very frequently exposed, produced in him a state of hopeless agitation and perplexity. "To give or not to give?" he had asked himself. "I have it and he needs it. But someone else needs it still more. Who needs it most? And perhaps they are both impostors?" In the old days he had been unable to find a way out of all these surmises and had given to all who asked as long as he had anything to give. Formerly he had been in a similar state of perplexity with regard to every question concerning his property, when one person advised one thing and another something else.

Now to his surprise he found that he no longer felt either doubt or perplexity about these questions. There was now within him a judge who by some rule unknown to him decided what should or should not be done.

He was as indifferent as heretofore to money matters, but now he felt certain of what ought and what ought not to be done. The first time he had recourse to this new judge was when a French prisoner, a colonel, came to him and, after talking a great deal about his exploits, concluded by making what amounted to a demand that Pierre should give him four thousand francs to send to his wife and children. Pierre refused without the least difficulty or effort, and was afterwards surprised how simple and easy had been what used to appear so insurmountably difficult. At the same time that he refused the colonel's demand he made up his mind that he must have recourse to artifice when leaving Orël, to induce the Italian officer to accept some money of which he was evidently in need. A further proof to Pierre of his own more settled outlook on practical matters was furnished by his decision with regard to his wife's debts and to the rebuilding of his houses in and near Moscow.

His head steward came to him at Orël and Pierre reckoned up with him

his diminished income. The burning of Moscow had cost him, according to the head steward's calculation, about two million rubles.

To console Pierre for these losses the head steward gave him an estimate showing that despite these losses his income would not be diminished but would even be increased if he refused to pay his wife's debts which he was under no obligation to meet, and did not rebuild his Moscow house and the country house on his Moscow estate, which had cost him eighty thousand rubles a year and brought in nothing.

"Yes, of course that's true," said Pierre with a cheerful smile. "I don't need all that at all. By being ruined I have become much richer."

But in January Savélich came from Moscow and gave him an account of the state of things there, and spoke of the estimate an architect had made of the cost of rebuilding the town and country houses, speaking of this as of a settled matter. About the same time he received letters from Prince Vasíli and other Petersburg acquaintances speaking of his wife's debts. And Pierre decided that the steward's proposals which had so pleased him were wrong and that he must go to Petersburg and settle his wife's affairs and must rebuild in Moscow. Why this was necessary he did not know, but he knew for certain that it was necessary. His income would be reduced by three fourths, but he felt it must be done.

Willarski was going to Moscow and they agreed to travel together.

During the whole time of his convalescence in Orél Pierre had experienced a feeling of joy, freedom, and life; but when during his journey he found himself in the open world and saw hundreds of new faces, that feeling was intensified. Throughout his journey he felt like a schoolboy on holiday. Everyone—the stagecoach driver, the post-house overseers, the peasants on the roads and in the villages—had a new significance for him. The presence and remarks of Willarski who continually deplored the ignorance and poverty of Russia and its backwardness compared with Europe only heightened Pierre's pleasure. Where Willarski saw deadness Pierre saw an extraordinary strength and vitality—the strength which in that vast space amid the snows maintained the life of this original, peculiar, and unique people. He did not contradict Willarski and even seemed to agree with him—an apparent agreement being the simplest way to avoid discussions that could lead to nothing—and he smiled joyfully as he listened to him.

IT WOULD BE difficult to explain why and whither ants whose heap has been destroyed are hurrying: some from the heap dragging bits of rubbish, larvæ, and corpses, others back to the heap, or why they jostle, overtake one another, and fight, and it would be equally difficult to explain what

caused the Russians after the departure of the French to throng to the place that had formerly been Moscow. But when we watch the ants round their ruined heap, the tenacity, energy, and immense number of the delving insects prove that despite the destruction of the heap, something indestructible, which though intangible is the real strength of the colony, still exists; and similarly, though in Moscow in the month of October there was no government and no churches, shrines, riches, or houses—it was still the Moscow it had been in August. All was destroyed, except something intangible yet powerful and indestructible.

The motives of those who thronged from all sides to Moscow after it had been cleared of the enemy were most diverse and personal, and at first for the most part savage and brutal. One motive only they all had in common: a desire to get to the place that had been called Moscow, to apply their activities there.

Within a week Moscow already had fifteen thousand inhabitants, in a fortnight twenty-five thousand, and so on. By the autumn of 1813 the number, ever increasing and increasing, exceeded what it had been in 1812.

The first Russians to enter Moscow were the Cossacks of Wintzing-erode's detachment, peasants from the adjacent villages, and residents who had fled from Moscow and had been hiding in its vicinity. The Russians who entered Moscow, finding it plundered, plundered it in their turn. They continued what the French had begun. Trains of peasant carts came to Moscow to carry off to the villages what had been abandoned in the ruined houses and the streets. The Cossacks carried off what they could to their camps, and the householders seized all they could find in other houses and moved it to their own, pretending that it was their property.

But the first plunderers were followed by a second and a third contingent, and with increasing numbers plundering became more and more difficult and assumed more definite forms.

The French found Moscow abandoned but with all the organizations of regular life, with diverse branches of commerce and craftsmanship, with luxury, and governmental and religious institutions. These forms were lifeless but still existed. There were bazaars, shops, warehouses, market stalls, granaries—for the most part still stocked with goods—and there were factories and workshops, palaces and wealthy houses filled with luxuries, hospitals, prisons, government offices, churches, and cathedrals. The longer the French remained the more these forms of town life perished, until finally all was merged into one confused, lifeless scene of plunder.

The more the plundering by the French continued, the more both the wealth of Moscow and the strength of its plunderers was destroyed. But plundering by the Russians, with which the reoccupation of the city

began, had an opposite effect: the longer it continued and the greater the number of people taking part in it the more rapidly was the wealth of the city and its regular life restored.

Besides the plunderers, very various people, some drawn by curiosity, some by official duties, some by self-interest—house owners, clergy, officials of all kinds, tradesmen, artisans, and peasants—streamed into Moscow as blood flows to the heart.

Within a week the peasants who came with empty carts to carry off plunder were stopped by the authorities and made to cart the corpses out of the town. Other peasants, having heard of their comrades' discomfiture, came to town bringing rye, oats, and hay, and beat down one another's prices to below what they had been in former days. Gangs of carpenters hoping for high pay arrived in Moscow every day, and on all sides logs were being hewn, new houses built, and old, charred ones repaired. Tradesmen began trading in booths. Cookshops and taverns were opened in partially burned houses. The clergy resumed the services in many churches that had not been burned. Donors contributed Church property that had been stolen. Government clerks set up their baize-covered tables and their pigeonholes of documents in small rooms. The higher authorities and the police organized the distribution of goods left behind by the French. The owners of houses in which much property had been left, brought there from other houses, complained of the injustice of taking everything to the Faceted Palace in the Kremlin; others insisted that as the French had gathered things from different houses into this or that house, it would be unfair to allow its owner to keep all that was found there. They abused the police and bribed them, made out estimates at ten times their value for government stores that had perished in the fire, and demanded relief. And Count Rostopchín wrote proclamations.

At the end of January Pierre went to Moscow and stayed in an annex of his house which had not been burned. He called on Count Rostopchín and on some acquaintances who were back in Moscow, and he intended to leave for Petersburg two days later. Everybody was celebrating the victory, everything was bubbling with life in the ruined but reviving city. Everyone was pleased to see Pierre, everyone wished to meet him, and everyone questioned him about what he had seen. Pierre felt particularly well disposed toward them all, but was now instinctively on his guard for fear of binding himself in any way. To all questions put to him—whether important or quite trifling—such as: Where would he live? Was he going to rebuild? When was he going to Petersburg and would he mind taking

a parcel for someone?—he replied: "Yes, perhaps," or, "I think so," and so on.

He had heard that the Rostóvs were at Kostromá but the thought of Natásha seldom occurred to him. If it did it was only as a pleasant memory of the distant past. He felt himself not only free from social obligations but also from that feeling which, it seemed to him, he had aroused in himself.

On the third day after his arrival he heard from the Drubetskóys that Princess Mary was in Moscow. The death, sufferings, and last days of Prince Andrew had often occupied Pierre's thoughts and now recurred to him with fresh vividness. Having heard at dinner that Princess Mary was in Moscow and living in her house—which had not been burned—in Vozdvízhenka Street, he drove that same evening to see her.

On his way to the house Pierre kept thinking of Prince Andrew, of their friendship, of his various meetings with him, and especially of the last one at Borodinó.

"Is it possible that he died in the bitter frame of mind he was then in? Is it possible that the meaning of life was not disclosed to him before he died?" thought Pierre. He recalled Karatáev and his death and involuntarily began to compare these two men, so different, and yet so similar in that they had both lived and both died and in the love he felt for both of them.

Pierre drove up to the house of the old prince in a most serious mood. The house had escaped the fire; it showed signs of damage but its general aspect was unchanged. The old footman, who met Pierre with a stern face as if wishing to make the visitor feel that the absence of the old prince had not disturbed the order of things in the house, informed him that the princess had gone to her own apartments, and that she received on Sundays.

"Announce me. Perhaps she will see me," said Pierre.

"Yes, sir," said the man. "Please step into the portrait gallery."

A few minutes later the footman returned with Dessalles, who brought word from the princess that she would be very glad to see Pierre if he would excuse her want of ceremony and come upstairs to her apartment.

In a rather low room lit by one candle sat the princess and with her another person dressed in black. Pierre remembered that the princess always had lady companions, but who they were and what they were like he never knew or remembered. "This must be one of her companions," he thought, glancing at the lady in the black dress.

The princess rose quickly to meet him and held out her hand.

"Yes," she said, looking at his altered face after he had kissed her hand,

"so this is how we meet again. He often spoke of you even at the very last," she went on, turning her eyes from Pierre to her companion with a shyness that surprised him for an instant.

"I was so glad to hear of your safety. It was the first piece of good news we had received for a long time."

Again the princess glanced round at her companion with even more uneasiness in her manner and was about to add something, but Pierre interrupted her.

"Just imagine—I knew nothing about him!" said he. "I thought he had been killed. All I know I heard at second hand from others. I only know that he fell in with the Rostóvs. . . . What a strange coincidence!"

Pierre spoke rapidly and with animation. He glanced once at the companion's face, saw her attentive and kindly gaze fixed on him, and, as often happens when one is talking, felt somehow that this companion in the black dress was a good, kind, excellent creature who would not hinder his conversing freely with Princess Mary.

But when he mentioned the Rostóvs, Princess Mary's face expressed still greater embarrassment. She again glanced rapidly from Pierre's face to that of the lady in the black dress and said:

"Do you really not recognize her?"

Pierre looked again at the companion's pale, delicate face with its black eyes and peculiar mouth, and something near to him, long forgotten and more than sweet, looked at him from those attentive eyes.

"But no, it can't be!" he thought. "This stern, thin, pale face that looks so much older! It cannot be she. It merely reminds me of her." But at that moment Princess Mary said, "Natásha!" And with difficulty, effort, and stress, like the opening of a door grown rusty on its hinges, a smile appeared on the face with the attentive eyes, and from that opening door came a breath of fragrance which suffused Pierre with a happiness he had long forgotten and of which he had not even been thinking—especially at that moment. It suffused him, seized him, and enveloped him completely. When she smiled doubt was no longer possible, it was Natásha and he loved her.

At that moment Pierre involuntarily betrayed to her, to Princess Mary, and above all to himself, a secret of which he himself had been unaware. He flushed joyfully yet with painful distress. He tried to hide his agitation. But the more he tried to hide it the more clearly—clearer than any words could have done—did he betray to himself, to her, and to Princess Mary that he loved her.

"No, it's only the unexpectedness of it," thought Pierre. But as soon as he tried to continue the conversation he had begun with Princess Mary

he again glanced at Natásha, and a still-deeper flush suffused his face and a still-stronger agitation of mingled joy and fear seized his soul. He became confused in his speech and stopped in the middle of what he was saying.

Pierre had failed to notice Natásha because he did not at all expect to see her there, but he had failed to recognize her because the change in her since he last saw her was immense. She had grown thin and pale, but that was not what made her unrecognizable; she was unrecognizable at the moment he entered because on that face whose eyes had always shone with a suppressed smile of the joy of life, now when he first entered and glanced at her there was not the least shadow of a smile: only her eyes were kindly attentive and sadly interrogative.

Pierre's confusion was not reflected by any confusion on Natásha's part, but only by the pleasure that just perceptibly lit up her whole face.

"She has come to stay with me," said Princess Mary. "The count and countess will be here in a few days. The countess is in a dreadful state; but it was necessary for Natásha herself to see a doctor. They insisted on her coming with me."

"Yes, is there a family free from sorrow now?" said Pierre, addressing Natásha. "You know it happened the very day we were rescued. I saw him. What a delightful boy he was!"

Natásha looked at him, and by way of answer to his words her eyes widened and lit up.

"What can one say or think of as a consolation?" said Pierre. "Nothing! Why had such a splendid boy, so full of life, to die?"

"Yes, in these days it would be hard to live without faith . . ." remarked Princess Mary.

"Yes, yes, that is really true," Pierre hastily interrupted her.

"Why is it true?" Natásha asked, looking attentively into Pierre's eyes.

"How can you ask why?" said Princess Mary. "The thought alone of what awaits . . ."

Natásha without waiting for Princess Mary to finish again looked inquiringly at Pierre.

"And because," Pierre continued, "only one who believes that there is a God ruling us can bear a loss such as hers and . . . yours."

Natásha had already opened her mouth to speak but suddenly stopped. Pierre hurriedly turned away from her and again addressed Princess Mary, asking about his friend's last days.

Pierre's confusion had now almost vanished, but at the same time he felt that his freedom had also completely gone. He felt that there was

now a judge of his every word and action whose judgment mattered more to him than that of all the rest of the world. As he spoke now he was considering what impression his words would make on Natásha. He did not purposely say things to please her, but whatever he was saying he regarded from her standpoint.

Princess Mary—reluctantly as is usual in such cases—began telling of the condition in which she had found Prince Andrew. But Pierre's face quivering with emotion, his questions and his eager restless expression, gradually compelled her to go into details which she feared to recall for her own sake.

"Yes, yes, and so . . . ?" Pierre kept saying as he leaned toward her with his whole body and eagerly listened to her story. "Yes, yes . . . so he grew tranquil and softened? With all his soul he had always sought one thing—to be perfectly good—so he could not be afraid of death. The faults he had—if he had any—were not of his making. So he did soften? . . . What a happy thing that he saw you again," he added, suddenly turning to Natásha and looking at her with eyes full of tears.

Natásha's face twitched. She frowned and lowered her eyes for a moment. She hesitated for an instant whether to speak or not.

"Yes, that was happiness," she then said in her quiet voice with its deep chest notes. "For me it certainly was happiness." She paused. "And he . . . he . . . he said he was wishing for it at the very moment I entered the room. . . ."

Natásha's voice broke. She blushed, pressed her clasped hands on her knees, and then controlling herself with an evident effort lifted her head and began to speak rapidly.

"We knew nothing of it when we started from Moscow. I did not dare to ask about him. Then suddenly Sónya told me he was traveling with us. I had no idea and could not imagine what state he was in, all I wanted was to see him and be with him," she said, trembling, and breathing quickly.

And not letting them interrupt her she went on to tell what she had never yet mentioned to anyone—all she had lived through during those three weeks of their journey and life at Yaroslávl.

Pierre listened to her with lips parted and eyes fixed upon her full of tears. As he listened he did not think of Prince Andrew, nor of death, nor of what she was telling. He listened to her and felt only pity for her, for what she was suffering now while she was speaking.

Princess Mary, frowning in her effort to hold back her tears, sat beside Natásha, and heard for the first time the story of those last days of her brother's and Natásha's love.

Evidently Natásha needed to tell that painful yet joyful tale.

She spoke, mingling most trifling details with the intimate secrets of her soul, and it seemed as if she could never finish. Several times she repeated the same thing twice.

Dessalles' voice was heard outside the door asking whether little Nicholas might come in to say good night.

"Well, that's all—everything," said Natásha.

She got up quickly just as Nicholas entered, almost ran to the door which was hidden by curtains, struck her head against it, and rushed from the room with a moan either of pain or sorrow.

Pierre gazed at the door through which she had disappeared and did not understand why he suddenly felt all alone in the world.

Princess Mary roused him from his abstraction by drawing his attention to her nephew who had entered the room.

At that moment of emotional tenderness young Nicholas' face, which resembled his father's, affected Pierre so much that when he had kissed the boy he got up quickly, took out his handkerchief, and went to the window. He wished to take leave of Princess Mary, but she would not let him go.

"No, Natásha and I sometimes don't go to sleep till after two, so please don't go. I will order supper. Go downstairs, we will come immediately."

Before Pierre left the room Princess Mary told him: "This is the first time she has talked of him like that."

PIERRE WAS SHOWN into the large, brightly lit dining room; a few minutes later he heard footsteps and Princess Mary entered with Natásha. Natásha was calm, though a severe and grave expression had again settled on her face. They all three of them now experienced that feeling of awkwardness which usually follows after a serious and heartfelt talk. It is impossible to go back to the same conversation, to talk of trifles is awkward, and yet the desire to speak is there and silence seems like affectation. They went silently to table. The footmen drew back the chairs and pushed them up again. Pierre unfolded his cold table napkin and, resolving to break the silence, looked at Natásha and at Princess Mary. They had evidently both formed the same resolution; the eyes of both shone with satisfaction and a confession that besides sorrow life also has joy.

"Do you take vodka, Count?" asked Princess Mary, and those words suddenly banished the shadows of the past. "Now tell us about yourself," said she. "One hears such improbable wonders about you."

"Yes," replied Pierre with the smile of mild irony now habitual to him. "They even tell me wonders I myself never dreamed of! Mary Abrámovna invited me to her house and kept telling me what had hap-

pened, or ought to have happened, to me. Stepán Stepánych also instructed me how I ought to tell of my experiences. In general I have noticed that it is very easy to be an interesting man (I am an interesting man now); people invite me out and tell me all about myself."

Natásha smiled and was on the point of speaking.

"We have been told," Princess Mary interrupted her, "that you lost two millions in Moscow. Is that true?"

"But I am three times as rich as before," returned Pierre.

Though the position was now altered by his decision to pay his wife's debts and to rebuild his houses, Pierre still maintained that he had become three times as rich as before.

"What I have certainly gained is freedom," he began seriously, but did not continue, noticing that this theme was too egotistic.

"And are you building?"

"Yes. Savélich says I must!"

"Tell me, you did not know of the countess' death when you decided to remain in Moscow?" asked Princess Mary and immediately blushed, noticing that her question, following his mention of freedom, ascribed to his words a meaning he had perhaps not intended.

"No," answered Pierre, evidently not considering awkward the meaning Princess Mary had given to his words. "I heard of it in Orël and you cannot imagine how it shocked me. We were not an exemplary couple," he added quickly, glancing at Natásha and noticing on her face curiosity as to how he would speak of his wife, "but her death shocked me terribly. When two people quarrel they are always both in fault, and one's own guilt suddenly becomes terribly serious when the other is no longer alive. And then such a death . . . without friends and without consolation! I am very, very sorry for her," he concluded, and was pleased to notice a look of glad approval on Natásha's face.

"Yes, and so you are once more an eligible bachelor," said Princess Mary.

Pierre suddenly flushed crimson and for a long time tried not to look at Natásha. When he ventured to glance her way again her face was cold, stern, and he fancied even contemptuous.

"And did you really see and speak to Napoleon, as we have been told?" said Princess Mary.

Pierre laughed.

"No, not once! Everybody seems to imagine that being taken prisoner means being Napoleon's guest. Not only did I never see him but I heard nothing about him—I was in much lower company!"

Supper was over, and Pierre who at first declined to speak about his captivity was gradually led on to do so.

"But it's true that you remained in Moscow to kill Napoleon?" Natásha asked with a slight smile. "I guessed it then when we met at the Súkharev tower, do you remember?"

Pierre admitted that it was true, and from that was gradually led by Princess Mary's questions and especially by Natásha's into giving a detailed account of his adventures.

At first he spoke with the amused and mild irony now customary with him toward everybody and especially toward himself, but when he came to describe the horrors and sufferings he had witnessed he was unconsciously carried away and began speaking with the suppressed emotion of a man re-experiencing in recollection strong impressions he has lived through.

Princess Mary with a gentle smile looked now at Pierre and now at Natásha. In the whole narrative she saw only Pierre and his goodness. Natásha, leaning on her elbow, the expression of her face constantly changing with the narrative, watched Pierre with an attention that never wandered—evidently herself experiencing all that he described. Not only her look, but her exclamations and the brief questions she put, showed Pierre that she understood just what he wished to convey. It was clear that she understood not only what he said but also what he wished to, but could not, express in words. The account Pierre gave of the incident with the child and the woman for protecting whom he was arrested was this: "It was an awful sight—children abandoned, some in the flames . . . One was snatched out before my eyes . . . and there were women who had their things snatched off and their earrings torn out . . ." he flushed and grew confused. "Then a patrol arrived and all the men—all those who were not looting, that is—were arrested, and I among them."

"I am sure you're not telling us everything; I am sure you did something . . ." said Natásha, and pausing added, "something fine?"

Pierre continued. When he spoke of the execution he wanted to pass over the horrible details, but Natásha insisted that he should not omit anything.

Pierre began to tell about Karatáev, but paused. By this time he had risen from table and was pacing the room, Natásha following him with her eyes. Then he added:

"No, you can't understand what I learned from that illiterate man—that simple fellow."

"Yes, yes, go on!" said Natásha. "Where is he?"

"They killed him almost before my eyes."

And Pierre, his voice trembling continually, went on to tell of the last days of their retreat, of Karatáev's illness and his death.

He told of his adventures as he had never yet recalled them. He now, as it were, saw a new meaning in all he had gone through. Now that he was telling it all to Natásha he experienced that pleasure which a man has when women listen to him—not clever women who when listening either try to remember what they hear to enrich their minds and when opportunity offers to retell it, or who wish to adopt it to some thought of their own and promptly contribute their own clever comments prepared in their own little mental workshop—but the pleasure given by real women gifted with a capacity to select and absorb the very best a man shows of himself. Natásha without knowing it was all attention: she did not lose a word, no single quiver in Pierre's voice, no look, no twitch of a muscle in his face, nor a single gesture. She caught the unfinished word in its flight and took it straight into her open heart, divining the secret meaning of all Pierre's mental travail.

Princess Mary understood his story and sympathized with him, but she now saw something else that absorbed all her attention. She saw the possibility of love and happiness between Natásha and Pierre, and the first thought of this filled her heart with gladness.

It was three o'clock in the morning. The footmen came in with sad and stern faces to change the candles, but no one noticed them.

Pierre finished his story. Natásha continued to look at him intently with bright, attentive, and animated eyes, as if trying to understand something more which he had perhaps left untold. Pierre in shamefaced and happy confusion glanced occasionally at her, and tried to think what to say next to introduce a fresh subject. Princess Mary was silent. It occurred to none of them that it was three o'clock and time to go to bed.

"People speak of misfortunes and sufferings," remarked Pierre, "but if at this moment I were asked: 'Would you rather be what you were before you were taken prisoner, or go through all this again?' then for heaven's sake let me again have captivity and horseflesh! We imagine that when we are thrown out of our usual ruts all is lost, but it is only then that what is new and good begins. While there is life there is happiness. There is much, much before us. I say this to you," he added, turning to Natásha.

"Yes, yes," she said, answering something quite different. "I too should wish nothing but to relive it all from the beginning."

Pierre looked intently at her.

"Yes, and nothing more," said Natásha.

"It's not true, not true!" cried Pierre. "I am not to blame for being alive and wishing to live—nor you either."

Suddenly Natásha bent her head, covered her face with her hands, and began to cry.

"What is it, Natásha?" said Princess Mary.

"Nothing, nothing." She smiled at Pierre through her tears. "Good night! It is time for bed."

Pierre rose and took his leave.

Princess Mary and Natásha met as usual in the bedroom. They talked of what Pierre had told them. Princess Mary did not express her opinion of Pierre nor did Natásha speak of him.

"Well, good night, Mary!" said Natásha. "Do you know, I am often afraid that by not speaking of him" (she meant Prince Andrew) "for fear of not doing justice to our feelings, we forget him."

Princess Mary sighed deeply and thereby acknowledged the justice of Natásha's remark, but she did not express agreement in words.

"Is it possible to forget?" said she.

"It did me so much good to tell all about it today. It was hard and painful, but good, very good!" said Natásha. "I am sure he really loved him. That is why I told him . . . Was it all right?" she added, suddenly blushing.

"To tell Pierre? Oh, yes. What a splendid man he is!" said Princess Mary.

"Do you know, Mary . . ." Natásha suddenly said with a mischievous smile such as Princess Mary had not seen on her face for a long time, "he has somehow grown so clean, smooth, and fresh—as if he had just come out of a Russian bath; do you understand? Out of a moral bath. Isn't it true?"

"Yes," replied Princess Mary. "He has greatly improved."

"With a short coat and his hair cropped; just as if, well, just as if he had come straight from the bath . . . Papa used to . . ."

"I understand why *he*" (Prince Andrew) "liked no one so much as him," said Princess Mary.

"Yes, and yet he is quite different. They say men are friends when they are quite different. That must be true. Really he is quite unlike him—in everything."

"Yes, but he's wonderful."

"Well, good night," said Natásha.

And the same mischievous smile lingered for a long time on her face as if it had been forgotten there.

IT WAS A LONG TIME before Pierre could fall asleep that night. He paced up and down his room, now turning his thoughts on a difficult problem and frowning, now suddenly shrugging his shoulders and wincing, and now smiling happily.

He was thinking of Prince Andrew, of Natásha, and of their love, at one moment jealous of her past, then reproaching himself for that feeling. It was already six in the morning and he still paced up and down the room.

"Well, what's to be done if it cannot be avoided? What's to be done? Evidently it has to be so," said he to himself, and hastily undressing he got into bed, happy and agitated but free from hesitation or indecision.

"Strange and impossible as such happiness seems, I must do everything that she and I may be man and wife," he told himself.

A few days previously Pierre had decided to go to Petersburg on the Friday. When he awoke on the Thursday, Savélich came to ask him about packing for the journey.

"What, to Petersburg? What is Petersburg? Who is there in Petersburg?" he asked involuntarily, though only to himself. "Oh, yes, long ago before this happened I did for some reason mean to go to Petersburg," he reflected. "Why? But perhaps I shall go. What a good fellow he is and how attentive, and how he remembers everything," he thought, looking at Savélich's old face, "and what a pleasant smile he has!"

"Well, Savélich, do you still not wish to accept your freedom?" Pierre asked him.

"What's the good of freedom to me, your excellency? We lived under the late count—the kingdom of heaven be his!—and we have lived under you too, without ever being wronged."

"And your children?"

"The children will live just the same. With such masters one can live."

"But what about my heirs?" said Pierre. "Supposing I suddenly marry . . . it might happen," he added with an involuntary smile.

"If I may take the liberty, your excellency, it would be a good thing."

"How easy he thinks it," thought Pierre. "He doesn't know how terrible it is and how dangerous. Too soon or too late . . . it is terrible!"

"So what are your orders? Are you starting tomorrow?" asked Savélich.

"No, I'll put it off for a bit. I'll tell you later. You must forgive the trouble I have put you to," said Pierre, and seeing Savélich smile, he thought: "But how strange it is that he should not know that now there is no Petersburg for me, and that *that* must be settled first of all! But probably he knows it well enough and is only pretending. Shall I have a talk with him and see what he thinks?" Pierre reflected. "No, another time."

At breakfast Pierre told the princess, his cousin, that he had been to see Princess Mary the day before and had there met—"Whom do you think? Natásha Rostóva!"

The princess seemed to see nothing more extraordinary in that than if he had seen Anna Semënovna.

"Do you know her?" asked Pierre.

"I have seen the princess," she replied. "I heard that they were arranging a match for her with young Rostóv. It would be a very good thing for the Rostóvs, they are said to be utterly ruined."

"No; I mean do you know Natásha Rostóva?"

"I heard about that affair of hers at the time. It was a great pity."

"No, she either doesn't understand or is pretending," thought Pierre. "Better not say anything to her either."

The princess too had prepared provisions for Pierre's journey.

"How kind they all are," thought Pierre. "What is surprising is that they should trouble about these things now when it can no longer be of interest to them. And all for me!"

On the same day the Chief of Police came to Pierre, inviting him to send a representative to the Faceted Palace to recover things that were to be returned to their owners that day.

"And this man too," thought Pierre, looking into the face of the Chief of Police. "What a fine, good-looking officer and how kind. Fancy bothering about such trifles *now*! And they actually say he is not honest and takes bribes. What nonsense! Besides, why shouldn't he take bribes? That's the way he was brought up, and everybody does it. But what a kind, pleasant face and how he smiles as he looks at me."

Pierre went to Princess Mary's to dinner.

As he drove through the streets past the houses that had been burned down, he was surprised by the beauty of those ruins. The picturesqueness of the chimney stacks and tumble-down walls of the burned-out quarters of the town, stretching out and concealing one another, reminded him of the Rhine and the Colosseum. The cabmen he met and their passengers, the carpenters cutting the timber for new houses with their axes, the women hawkers, and the shopkeepers, all looked at him with cheerful beaming eyes that seemed to say: "Ah, there he is! Let's see what will come of it!"

At the entrance to Princess Mary's house Pierre felt doubtful whether he had really been there the night before and had really seen Natásha and talked to her. "Perhaps I imagined it; perhaps I shall go in and find no one there." But he had hardly entered the room before he felt her presence with his whole being by the loss of his sense of freedom. She was in the

same black dress with soft folds and her hair was done the same way as the day before, yet she was quite different. Had she been like this when he entered the day before he could not for a moment have failed to recognize her.

She was as he had known her almost as a child and later on as Prince Andrew's fiancée. A bright questioning light shone in her eyes, and on her face was a friendly and strangely roguish expression.

Pierre dined with them and would have spent the whole evening there, but Princess Mary was going to vespers and Pierre left the house with her.

Next day he came early, dined, and stayed the whole evening. Though Princess Mary and Natásha were evidently glad to see their visitor and though all Pierre's interest was now centered in that house, by the evening they had talked over everything and the conversation passed from one trivial topic to another and repeatedly broke off. He stayed so long that Princess Mary and Natásha exchanged glances, evidently wondering when he would go. Pierre noticed this but could not go. He felt uneasy and embarrassed, but sat on because he simply could not get up and take his leave.

Princess Mary, foreseeing no end to this, rose first, and complaining of a headache began to say good night.

"So you are going to Petersburg tomorrow?" she asked.

"No, I am not going," Pierre replied hastily, in a surprised tone and as though offended. "Yes . . . no . . . to Petersburg? Tomorrow—but I won't say good-by yet. I will call round in case you have any commissions for me," said he, standing before Princess Mary and turning red, but not taking his departure.

Natásha gave him her hand and went out. Princess Mary on the other hand instead of going away sank into an armchair, and looked sternly and intently at him with her deep, radiant eyes. The weariness she had plainly shown before had now quite passed off. With a deep and long-drawn sigh she seemed to be prepared for a lengthy talk.

When Natásha left the room Pierre's confusion and awkwardness immediately vanished and were replaced by eager excitement. He quickly moved an armchair toward Princess Mary.

"Yes, I wanted to tell you," said he, answering her look as if she had spoken. "Princess, help me! What am I to do? Can I hope? Princess, my dear friend, listen! I know it all. I know I am not worthy of her, I know it's impossible to speak of it now. But I want to be a brother to her. No, not that, I don't, I can't . . ."

He paused and rubbed his face and eyes with his hands.

"Well," he went on with an evident effort at self-control and coherence.

"I don't know when I began to love her, but I have loved her and her alone all my life, and I love her so that I cannot imagine life without her. I cannot propose to her at present, but the thought that perhaps she might someday be my wife and that I may be missing that possibility . . . that possibility . . . is terrible. Tell me, can I hope? Tell me what I am to do, dear princess!" he added after a pause, and touched her hand as she did not reply.

"I am thinking of what you have told me," answered Princess Mary. "This is what I will say. You are right that to speak to her of love at present . . ."

Princess Mary stopped. She was going to say that to speak of love was impossible, but she stopped because she had seen by the sudden change in Natásha two days before that she would not only not be hurt if Pierre spoke of his love, but that it was the very thing she wished for.

"To speak to her now wouldn't do," said the princess all the same.

"But what am I to do?"

"Leave it to me," said Princess Mary. "I know . . ."

Pierre was looking into Princess Mary's eyes.

"Well? . . . Well? . . ." he said.

"I know that she loves . . . will love you," Princess Mary corrected herself.

Before her words were out, Pierre had sprung up and with a frightened expression seized Princess Mary's hand.

"What makes you think so? You think I may hope? You think . . . ?"

"Yes, I think so," said Princess Mary with a smile. "Write to her parents, and leave it to me. I will tell her when I can. I wish it to happen and my heart tells me it will."

"No, it cannot be! How happy I am! But it can't be. . . . How happy I am! No, it can't be!" Pierre kept saying as he kissed Princess Mary's hands.

"Go to Petersburg, that will be best. And I will write to you," she said.

"To Petersburg? Go there? Very well, I'll go. But I may come again tomorrow?"

Next day Pierre came to say good-by. Natásha was less animated than she had been the day before; but that day as he looked at her Pierre sometimes felt as if he was vanishing and that neither he nor she existed any longer, that nothing existed but happiness. "Is it possible? No, it can't be," he told himself at every look, gesture, and word that filled his soul with joy.

When on saying good-by he took her thin, slender hand, he could not help holding it a little longer in his own.

"Is it possible that this hand, that face, those eyes, all this treasure of feminine charm so strange to me now, is it possible that it will one day be mine forever, as familiar to me as I am to myself? . . . No, that's impossible! . . ."

"Good-by, Count," she said aloud. "I shall look forward very much to your return," she added in a whisper.

And these simple words, her look, and the expression on her face which accompanied them, formed for two months the subject of inexhaustible memories, interpretations, and happy meditations for Pierre. " 'I shall look forward very much to your return. . . .' Yes, yes, how did she say it? Yes, 'I shall look forward very much to your return.' Oh, how happy I am! What is happening to me? How happy I am!" said Pierre to himself.

THERE WAS NOTHING in Pierre's soul now at all like what had troubled it during his courtship of Hélène.

He did not repeat to himself with a sickening feeling of shame the words he had spoken, or say: "Oh, why did I not say that?" and, "Whatever made me say 'Je vous aime'?" On the contrary, he now repeated in imagination every word that he or Natásha had spoken and pictured every detail of her face and smile, and did not wish to diminish or add anything, but only to repeat it again and again. There was now not a shadow of doubt in his mind as to whether what he had undertaken was right or wrong. Only one terrible doubt sometimes crossed his mind: "Wasn't it all a dream? Isn't Princess Mary mistaken? Am I not too conceited and self-confident? I believe all this—and suddenly Princess Mary will tell her, and she will be sure to smile and say: 'How strange! He must be deluding himself. Doesn't he know that he is a man, just a man, while I . . . ? I am something altogether different and higher.' "

That was the only doubt often troubling Pierre. He did not now make any plans. The happiness before him appeared so inconceivable that if only he could attain it, it would be the end of all things. Everything ended with that.

A joyful, unexpected frenzy, of which he had thought himself incapable, possessed him. The whole meaning of life—not for him alone but for the whole world—seemed to him centered in his love and the possibility of being loved by her. At times everybody seemed to him to be occupied with one thing only—his future happiness. Sometimes it seemed to him that other people were all as pleased as he was himself and merely tried to hide that pleasure by pretending to be busy with other interests. In every word and gesture he saw allusions to his happiness. He often surprised those he met by his significantly happy looks and smiles which

seemed to express a secret understanding between him and them. And when he realized that people might not be aware of his happiness, he pitied them with his whole heart and felt a desire somehow to explain to them that all that occupied them was a mere frivolous trifle unworthy of attention.

When it was suggested to him that he should enter the civil service, or when the war or any general political affairs were discussed on the assumption that everybody's welfare depended on this or that issue of events, he would listen with a mild and pitying smile and surprise people by his strange comments. But at this time he saw everybody—both those who, as he imagined, understood the real meaning of life (that is, what he was feeling) and those unfortunates who evidently did not understand it—in the bright light of the emotion that shone within himself, and at once without any effort saw in everyone he met everything that was good and worthy of being loved.

When dealing with the affairs and papers of his dead wife, her memory aroused in him no feeling but pity that she had not known the bliss he now knew. Prince Vasíli, who having obtained a new post and some fresh decorations was particularly proud at this time, seemed to him a pathetic, kindly old man much to be pitied.

Often in afterlife Pierre recalled this period of blissful insanity. All the views he formed of men and circumstances at this time remained true for him always. He not only did not renounce them subsequently, but when he was in doubt or inwardly at variance, he referred to the views he had held at this time of his madness and they always proved correct.

"I may have appeared strange and queer then," he thought, "but I was not so mad as I seemed. On the contrary I was then wiser and had more insight than at any other time, and understood all that is worth understanding in life, because . . . because I was happy."

Pierre's insanity consisted in not waiting, as he used to do, to discover personal attributes which he termed "good qualities" in people before loving them; his heart was now overflowing with love, and by loving people without cause he discovered indubitable causes for loving them.

AFTER PIERRE'S DEPARTURE that first evening, when Natásha had said to Princess Mary with a gaily mocking smile: "He looks just, yes, just as if he had come out of a Russian bath—in a short coat and with his hair cropped," something hidden and unknown to herself, but irrepressible, awoke in Natásha's soul.

Everything: her face, walk, look, and voice, was suddenly altered. To her own surprise a power of life and hope of happiness rose to the surface

and demanded satisfaction. From that evening she seemed to have forgotten all that had happened to her. She no longer complained of her position, did not say a word about the past, and no longer feared to make happy plans for the future. She spoke little of Pierre, but when Princess Mary mentioned him a long-extinguished light once more kindled in her eyes and her lips curved with a strange smile.

The change that took place in Natásha at first surprised Princess Mary; but when she understood its meaning it grieved her. "Can she have loved my brother so little as to be able to forget him so soon?" she thought when she reflected on the change. But when she was with Natásha she was not vexed with her and did not reproach her. The reawakened power of life that had seized Natásha was so evidently irrepressible and unexpected by her that in her presence Princess Mary felt that she had no right to reproach her even in her heart.

Natásha gave herself up so fully and frankly to this new feeling that she did not try to hide the fact that she was no longer sad, but bright and cheerful.

When Princess Mary returned to her room after her nocturnal talk with Pierre, Natásha met her on the threshold.

"He has spoken? Yes? He has spoken?" she repeated.

And a joyful yet pathetic expression which seemed to beg forgiveness for her joy settled on Natásha's face.

"I wanted to listen at the door, but I knew you would tell me."

Understandable and touching as the look with which Natásha gazed at her seemed to Princess Mary, and sorry as she was to see her agitation, these words pained her for a moment. She remembered her brother and his love.

"But what's to be done? She can't help it," thought the princess.

And with a sad and rather stern look she told Natásha all that Pierre had said. On hearing that he was going to Petersburg Natásha was astounded.

"To Petersburg!" she repeated as if unable to understand.

But noticing the grieved expression on Princess Mary's face she guessed the reason of that sadness and suddenly began to cry.

"Mary," said she, "tell me what I should do! I am afraid of being bad. Whatever you tell me, I will do. Tell me. . . ."

"You love him?"

"Yes," whispered Natásha.

"Then why are you crying? I am happy for your sake," said Princess Mary, who because of those tears quite forgave Natásha's joy.

"It won't be just yet—someday. Think what fun it will be when I am his wife and you marry Nicholas!"

"Natásha, I have asked you not to speak of that. Let us talk about you."
They were silent awhile.

"But why go to Petersburg?" Natásha suddenly asked, and hastily re-
plied to her own question. "But no, no, he must. . . . Yes, Mary. He
must. . . ."

FIRST EPILOGUE

1813-20

1. *Discussion of forces operating in history. Chance and genius. The ideals of glory and grandeur. Alexander's renunciation of power. The purpose of a bee*

SEVEN YEARS had passed. The storm-tossed sea of European history had subsided within its shores and seemed to have become calm. But the mysterious forces that move humanity (mysterious because the laws of their motion are unknown to us) continued to operate.

Though the surface of the sea of history seemed motionless, the movement of humanity went on as unceasingly as the flow of time. Various groups of people formed and dissolved, the coming formation and dissolution of kingdoms and displacement of peoples was in course of preparation.

The sea of history was not driven spasmodically from shore to shore as previously. It was seething in its depths. Historic figures were not borne by the waves from one shore to another as before. They now seemed to rotate on one spot. The historical figures at the head of armies, who formerly reflected the movement of the masses by ordering wars, campaigns, and battles, now reflected the restless movement by political and diplomatic combinations, laws, and treaties.

The historians call this activity of the historical figures "the reaction."

In dealing with this period they sternly condemn the historical personages who, in their opinion, caused what they describe as *the reaction.* All the well-known people of that period, from Alexander and Napoleon to Madame de Staël, Photius,* Schelling,[2] Fichte,[3] Chateaubriand,[4] and

* *Photius* (1792-1838) *was Head of the Nóvgorod Monastery. In 1820, in the name of reactionary-Orthodox principles and in conjunction with an influential lady, Orlóva-Chesménskaya, he instigated a persecution of "Masons and mystics," the Bible Society, and other movements tainted with liberalism or of questionable conformity with the then existing order in the Russian state and Orthodox Church. His movement promptly became a personal*

the rest, pass before their stern judgment seat and are acquitted or condemned according to whether they conduced to progress or to reaction.

According to their accounts a reaction took place at that time in Russia also, and the chief culprit was Alexander I, the same man who according to them was the chief cause of the liberal movement at the commencement of his reign, being the savior of Russia.

There is no one in Russian literature now, from schoolboy essayist to learned historian, who does not throw his little stone at Alexander for things he did wrong at this period of his reign.

"He ought to have acted in this way and in that way. In this case he did well and in that case badly. He behaved admirably at the beginning of his reign and during 1812, but acted badly by giving a constitution to Poland,* forming the Holy Alliance,[2] entrusting power to Arakchéev,

struggle against Prince A. N. Golítsyn, Minister of Education and of Spiritual Affairs. The Orthodox mystic was no better than his opponent, the more westernized mystic, who was head of the Bible Society, but in 1824 Golítsyn was dismissed. Photius was an ascetic, and frightened Alexander by dismal Apocalyptic predictions but did not retain his influence long.—A.M.

[2] *F. W. G. Schelling (1775-1854) began as a sympathizer with the French Revolution, but gradually changed his views. His criticism of Fichte developed into a sharp antagonism.—A.M.*

[3] *J. G. Fichte (1762-1814), a German philosopher who influenced affairs by his revolutionary love of liberty.—A.M.*

[4] *Chateaubriand (1764-1848), a French writer and politician, who was exceedingly changeable and inconsistent in his views and politics.—A.M.*

* *The Congress of Vienna in 1815 created a "Kingdom of Poland" (containing about three fourths of Napoleon's "Grand Duchy of Warsaw") to be forever united with Russia, but to have a constitution of its own by which it was to be ruled by a king who was always to be the Emperor of Russia (ruling through a deputy who might either be a Pole or a member of the Russian Imperial family). Alexander I and his successor Nicholas I took an oath of fidelity to this constitution, which for those times was of a liberal character. It lasted till the Polish insurrection of 1830.—A.M.*

[2] *This famous declaration, signed at first by the Emperors of Russia and Austria and the King of Prussia, was a precursor of the League of Nations and was quite sincerely intended to ensure the preservation of peace, but gradually it became a reactionary instrument for the suppression of freedom and the maintenance of despotism. It died a natural death owing to disagreements between the great Powers.—A.M.*

favoring Golítsyn and mysticism, and afterwards Shishkóv * and Photius. He also acted badly by concerning himself with the active army and disbanding the Semënov regiment." [2]

It would take a dozen pages to enumerate all the reproaches the historians address to him, based on their knowledge of what is good for humanity.

What do these reproaches mean?

Do not the very actions for which the historians praise Alexander I (the liberal attempts at the beginning of his reign, his struggle with Napoleon, the firmness he displayed in 1812 and the campaign of 1813) flow from the same sources—the circumstances of his birth, education, and life—that made his personality what it was and from which the actions for which they blame him (the Holy Alliance, the restoration of Poland, and the reaction of 1820 and later) also flowed?

In what does the substance of those reproaches lie?

It lies in the fact that an historic character like Alexander I, standing on the highest possible pinnacle of human power with the blinding light of history focused upon him; a character exposed to those strongest of all influences: the intrigues, flattery, and self-deception inseparable from power; a character who at every moment of his life felt a responsibility for all that was happening in Europe; and not a fictitious but a live character who like every man had his personal habits, passions, and impulses toward goodness, beauty, and truth—that this character—though not lacking in virtue (the historians do not accuse him of that)—had not the same conception of the welfare of humanity fifty years ago [3] as a present-day professor who from his youth upwards has been occupied with learning: that is, with books and lectures and with taking notes from them.

But even if we assume that fifty years ago Alexander I was mistaken in

* *Alexander Shishkóv (1754-1841) has already been mentioned in Book Nine, p. 678, as writing the rescript Alexander issued at the commencement of Napoleon's invasion. He occupied many positions, from that of admiral to Secretary to the Emperor and Minister of Education. He considered that to teach the peasants to read was "more harmful than useful."—A.M.*

[2] *The Semënov Guards were disbanded in 1820 for protesting against the cruelty and barbarity of their new German commander, Schwarz, and refusing to obey his orders. Alexander I dealt harshly with the outbreak, which was later seen to have been a prelude to the more serious "Decembrist" revolt of 1825. The officers and men were dispersed among other regiments, and not till 1823 did the Semënov regiment again become a regiment of the Guards.—A.M.*

[3] *War and Peace was completed in 1869.—A.M.*

his view of what was good for the people, we must inevitably assume that the historian who judges Alexander will also after the lapse of some time turn out to be mistaken in his view of what is good for humanity. This assumption is all the more natural and inevitable because, watching the movement of history, we see that every year and with each new writer, opinion as to what is good for mankind changes; so that what once seemed good, ten years later seems bad, and vice versa. And what is more, we find at one and the same time quite contradictory views as to what is bad and what is good in history: some people regard giving a constitution to Poland and forming the Holy Alliance as praiseworthy in Alexander, while others regard it as blameworthy.

The activity of Alexander or of Napoleon cannot be called useful or harmful, for it is impossible to say for what it was useful or harmful. If that activity displeases somebody, this is only because it does not agree with his limited understanding of what is good. Whether the preservation of my father's house in Moscow, or the glory of the Russian arms, or the prosperity of the Petersburg and other universities, or the freedom of Poland or the greatness of Russia, or the balance of power in Europe, or a certain kind of European culture called "progress" appear to me to be good or bad, I must admit that besides these things the action of every historic character has other more general purposes inaccessible to me.

But let us assume that what is called science can harmonize all contradictions and possesses an unchanging standard of good and bad by which to try historic characters and events; let us say that Alexander could have done everything differently; let us say that with guidance from those who blame him and who profess to know the ultimate aim of the movement of humanity, he might have arranged matters according to the program his present accusers would have given him—of nationality, freedom, equality, and progress (these, I think, cover the ground). Let us assume that this program was possible and had then been formulated, and that Alexander had acted on it. What would then have become of the activity of all those who opposed the tendency that then prevailed in the government—an activity that in the opinion of the historians was good and beneficent? Their activity would not have existed: there would have been no life, there would have been nothing.

If we admit that human life can be ruled by reason, the possibility of life is destroyed.

IF WE ASSUME as the historians do that great men lead humanity to the attainment of certain ends—the greatness of Russia or of France, the

balance of power in Europe, the diffusion of the ideas of the Revolution, general progress, or anything else—then it is impossible to explain the facts of history without introducing the conceptions of *chance* and *genius*.

If the aim of the European wars at the beginning of the nineteenth century had been the aggrandizement of Russia, that aim might have been accomplished without all the preceding wars and without the invasion. If the aim was the aggrandizement of France, that might have been attained without the Revolution and without the Empire. If the aim was the dissemination of ideas, the printing press could have accomplished that much better than warfare. If the aim was the progress of civilization, it is easy to see that there are other ways of diffusing civilization more expedient than by the destruction of wealth and of human lives.

Why did it happen in this and not in some other way?

Because it happened so! "*Chance* created the situation; *genius* utilized it," says history.

But what is *chance*? What is *genius*?

The words *chance* and *genius* do not denote any really existing thing and therefore cannot be defined. Those words only denote a certain stage of understanding of phenomena. I do not know why a certain event occurs; I think that I cannot know it; so I do not try to know it and I talk about *chance*. I see a force producing effects beyond the scope of ordinary human agencies; I do not understand why this occurs and I talk of *genius*.

To a herd of rams, the ram the herdsman drives each evening into a special enclosure to feed and that becomes twice as fat as the others must seem to be a genius. And it must appear an astonishing conjunction of genius with a whole series of extraordinary chances that this ram, who instead of getting into the general fold every evening goes into a special enclosure where there are oats—that this very ram, swelling with fat, is killed for meat.

But the rams need only cease to suppose that all that happens to them happens solely for the attainment of their sheepish aims; they need only admit that what happens to them may also have purposes beyond their ken, and they will at once perceive a unity and coherence in what happened to the ram that was fattened. Even if they do not know for what purpose they are fattened, they will at least know that all that happened to the ram did not happen accidentally, and will no longer need the conceptions of *chance* or *genius*.

Only by renouncing our claim to discern a purpose immediately intelligible to us, and admitting the ultimate purpose to be beyond our ken, may we discern the sequence of experiences in the lives of historic characters and perceive the cause of the effect they produce (incommensurable

with ordinary human capabilities), and then the words *chance* and *genius* become superfluous.

We need only confess that we do not know the purpose of the European convulsions and that we know only the facts—that is, the murders, first in France, then in Italy, in Africa, in Prussia, in Austria, in Spain, and in Russia—and that the movements from the west to the east and from the east to the west form the essence and purpose of these events, and not only shall we have no need to see exceptional ability and genius in Napoleon and Alexander, but we shall be unable to consider them to be anything but like other men, and we shall not be obliged to have recourse to *chance* for an explanation of those small events which made these people what they were, but it will be clear that all those small events were inevitable.

By discarding a claim to knowledge of the ultimate purpose, we shall clearly perceive that just as one cannot imagine a blossom or seed for any single plant better suited to it than those it produces, so it is impossible to imagine any two people more completely adapted down to the smallest detail for the purpose they had to fulfill, than Napoleon and Alexander with all their antecedents.

THE FUNDAMENTAL and essential significance of the European events of the beginning of the nineteenth century lies in the movement of the mass of the European peoples from west to east and afterwards from east to west. The commencement of that movement was the movement from west to east. For the peoples of the west to be able to make their warlike movement to Moscow it was necessary: (1) that they should form themselves into a military group of a size able to endure a collision with the warlike military group of the east, (2) that they should abandon all established traditions and customs, and (3) that during their military movement they should have at their head a man who could justify to himself and to them the deceptions, robberies, and murders which would have to be committed during that movement.

And beginning with the French Revolution the old inadequately large group was destroyed, as well as the old habits and traditions, and step by step a group was formed of larger dimensions with new customs and traditions, and a man was produced who would stand at the head of the coming movement and bear the responsibility for all that had to be done.

A man without convictions, without habits, without traditions, without a name, and not even a Frenchman, emerges—by what seem the strangest chances—from among all the seething French parties, and without joining any one of them is borne forward to a prominent position.

The ignorance of his colleagues, the weakness and insignificance of his opponents, the frankness of his falsehoods, and the dazzling and self-confident limitations of this man raise him to the head of the army. The brilliant qualities of the soldiers of the army sent to Italy, his opponents' reluctance to fight, and his own childish audacity and self-confidence secure him military fame. Innumerable so-called *chances* accompany him everywhere. The disfavor into which he falls with the rulers of France turns to his advantage. His attempts to avoid his predestined path are unsuccessful: he is not received into the Russian service, and the appointment he seeks in Turkey comes to nothing.* During the war in Italy he is several times on the verge of destruction and each time is saved in an unexpected manner. Owing to various diplomatic considerations the Russian armies—just those which might have destroyed his prestige—do not appear upon the scene till he is no longer there.[2]

On his return from Italy he finds the government in Paris in a process of dissolution in which all those who are in it are inevitably wiped out and destroyed. And by chance an escape from this dangerous position presents itself in the form of an aimless and senseless expedition to Africa. Again so-called *chance* accompanies him. Impregnable Malta surrenders without a shot; his most reckless schemes are crowned with success. The enemy's fleet, which subsequently did not let a single boat pass, allows his entire army to elude it. In Africa a whole series of outrages are committed against the almost unarmed inhabitants. And the men who commit these crimes, especially their leader, assure themselves that this is admirable, this is glory—it resembles Caesar and Alexander the Great and is therefore good.

This ideal of *glory* and *grandeur*—which consists not merely in considering nothing wrong that one does but in priding oneself on every crime one commits, ascribing to it an incomprehensible supernatural significance—that ideal, destined to guide this man and his associates, had scope for its development in Africa. Whatever he does succeeds. The plague does not touch him. The cruelty of murdering prisoners is not imputed to him as a fault. His childishly rash, uncalled-for, and ignoble departure from Africa, leaving his comrades in distress, is set down to his credit, and again the enemy's fleet twice lets him slip past. When, intoxi-

* *In August, 1795, Bonaparte applied to a commission of the French government to be sent to Constantinople to reform the Turkish artillery service.* —A.M.

[2] *Bonaparte sailed for Egypt in 1798. Suvórov led a Russian army into Italy in 1799 and successively defeated Moreau at Cassano, Macdonald on the Trebbia, and Joubert at Novi.*—A.M.

cated by the crimes he has committed so successfully, he reaches Paris, the dissolution of the republican government, which a year earlier might have ruined him, has reached its extreme limit, and his presence there now as a newcomer free from party entanglements can only serve to exalt him—and though he himself has no plan, he is quite ready for his new role.

He had no plan, he was afraid of everything, but the parties snatched at him and demanded his participation.

He alone—with his ideal of glory and grandeur developed in Italy and Egypt, his insane self-adulation, his boldness in crime and frankness in lying—he alone could justify what had to be done.

He is needed for the place that awaits him, and so almost apart from his will and despite his indecision, his lack of a plan, and all his mistakes, he is drawn into a conspiracy that aims at seizing power and the conspiracy is crowned with success.

He is pushed into a meeting of the legislature. In alarm he wishes to flee, considering himself lost. He pretends to fall into a swoon and says senseless things that should have ruined him. But the once proud and shrewd rulers of France, feeling that their part is played out, are even more bewildered than he, and do not say the words they should have said to destroy him and retain their power.

Chance, millions of *chances*, give him power, and all men as if by agreement co-operate to confirm that power. *Chance* forms the characters of the rulers of France, who submit to him; *chance* forms the character of Paul I of Russia who recognizes his government; *chance* contrives a plot against him which not only fails to harm him but confirms his power. *Chance* puts the Duc d'Enghien in his hands and unexpectedly causes him to kill him—thereby convincing the mob more forcibly than in any other way that he had the right, since he had the might. *Chance* contrives that though he directs all his efforts to prepare an expedition against England (which would inevitably have ruined him) he never carries out that intention, but unexpectedly falls upon Mack and the Austrians, who surrender without a battle. *Chance* and *genius* give him the victory at Austerlitz; and by *chance* all men, not only the French but all Europe—except England which does not take part in the events about to happen—despite their former horror and detestation of his crimes, now recognize his authority, the title he has given himself, and his ideal of grandeur and glory, which seems excellent and reasonable to them all.

As if measuring themselves and preparing for the coming movement, the western forces push toward the east several times in 1805, 1806, 1807, and 1809, gaining strength and growing. In 1811 the group of people

that had formed in France unites into one group with the peoples of Central Europe. The strength of the justification of the man who stands at the head of the movement grows with the increased size of the group. During the ten-year preparatory period this man had formed relations with all the crowned heads of Europe. The discredited rulers of the world can oppose no reasonable ideal to the insensate Napoleonic ideal of *glory* and *grandeur*. One after another they hasten to display their insignificance before him. The King of Prussia sends his wife to seek the great man's mercy; the Emperor of Austria considers it a favor that this man receives a daughter of the Caesars into his bed; the Pope, the guardian of all that the nations hold sacred, utilizes religion for the aggrandizement of the great man. It is not Napoleon who prepares himself for the accomplishment of his role, so much as all those round him who prepare him to take on himself the whole responsibility for what is happening and has to happen. There is no step, no crime or petty fraud he commits, which in the mouths of those around him is not at once represented as a great deed. The most suitable fete the Germans can devise for him is a celebration of Jena and Auerstädt. Not only is he great, but so are his ancestors, his brothers, his stepsons, and his brothers-in-law. Everything is done to deprive him of the remains of his reason and to prepare him for his terrible part. And when he is ready so too are the forces.

The invasion pushes eastward and reaches its final goal—Moscow. That city is taken; the Russian army suffers heavier losses than the opposing armies had suffered in the former war from Austerlitz to Wagram. But suddenly instead of those *chances* and that *genius* which hitherto had so consistently led him by an uninterrupted series of successes to the predestined goal, an innumerable sequence of inverse *chances* occur—from the cold in his head at Borodinó to the sparks which set Moscow on fire, and the frosts—and instead of *genius*, stupidity and immeasurable baseness become evident.

The invaders flee, turn back, flee again, and all the chances are now not for Napoleon but always against him.

A countermovement is then accomplished from east to west with a remarkable resemblance to the preceding movement from west to east. Attempted drives from east to west—similar to the contrary movements of 1805, 1807, and 1809—precede the great westward movement; there is the same coalescence into a group of enormous dimensions; the same adhesion of the people of Central Europe to the movement; the same hesitation midway, and the same increasing rapidity as the goal is approached.

Paris, the ultimate goal, is reached. The Napoleonic government and

army are destroyed. Napoleon himself is no longer of any account; all his actions are evidently pitiful and mean, but again an inexplicable chance occurs. The allies detest Napoleon whom they regard as the cause of their sufferings. Deprived of power and authority, his crimes and his craft exposed, he should have appeared to them what he appeared ten years previously and one year later—an outlawed brigand. But by some strange chance no one perceives this. His part is not yet ended. The man who ten years before and a year later was considered an outlawed brigand is sent to an island two days' sail from France, which for some reason is presented to him as his dominion, and guards are given to him and millions of money are paid him.

THE FLOOD OF NATIONS begins to subside into its normal channels. The waves of the great movement abate, and on the calm surface eddies are formed in which float the diplomatists, who imagine that they have caused the floods to abate.

But the smooth sea again suddenly becomes disturbed. The diplomatists think that their disagreements are the cause of this fresh pressure of natural forces; they anticipate war between their sovereigns; the position seems to them insoluble. But the wave they feel to be rising does not come from the quarter they expect. It rises again from the same point as before—Paris. The last backwash of the movement from the west occurs: a backwash which serves to solve the apparently insuperable diplomatic difficulties and ends the military movement of that period of history.

The man who had devastated France returns to France alone, without any conspiracy and without soldiers. Any guard might arrest him, but by a strange chance no one does so and all rapturously greet the man they cursed the day before and will curse again a month later.

This man is still needed to justify the final collective act.

That act is performed.

The last role is played. The actor is bidden to disrobe and wash off his powder and paint: he will not be wanted any more.

And some years pass during which he plays a pitiful comedy to himself in solitude on his island, justifying his actions by intrigues and lies when the justification is no longer needed, and displaying to the whole world what it was that people had mistaken for strength as long as an unseen hand directed his actions.

The manager having brought the drama to a close and stripped the actor shows him to us.

"See what you believed in! This is he! Do you now see that it was not he but I who moved you?"

But dazed by the force of the movement, it was long before people understood this.

Still greater coherence and inevitability is seen in the life of Alexander I, the man who stood at the head of the countermovement from east to west.

What was needed for him who, overshadowing others, stood at the head of that movement from east to west?

What was needed was a sense of justice and a sympathy with European affairs, but a remote sympathy not dulled by petty interests; a moral superiority over those sovereigns of the day who co-operated with him; a mild and attractive personality; and a personal grievance against Napoleon. And all this was found in Alexander I; all this had been prepared by innumerable so-called *chances* in his life: his education, his early liberalism, the advisers who surrounded him, and by Austerlitz, and Tilsit, and Erfurt.

During the national war he was inactive because he was not needed. But as soon as the necessity for a general European war presented itself he appeared in his place at the given moment and, uniting the nations of Europe, led them to the goal.

The goal is reached. After the final war of 1815 Alexander possesses all possible power. How does he use it?

Alexander I—the pacifier of Europe, the man who from his early years had striven only for his people's welfare, the originator of the liberal innovations in his fatherland—now that he seemed to possess the utmost power and therefore to have the possibility of bringing about the welfare of his peoples—at the time when Napoleon in exile was drawing up childish and mendacious plans of how he would have made mankind happy had he retained power—Alexander I, having fulfilled his mission and feeling the hand of God upon him, suddenly recognizes the insignificance of that supposed power, turns away from it, and gives it into the hands of contemptible men whom he despises, saying only:

"Not unto us, not unto us, but unto Thy Name! * . . . I too am a man like the rest of you. Let me live like a man and think of my soul and of God." [2]

* *By Alexander's order a medal, struck as a memorial of the defeat of the French in 1812, bore these words.*—A.M.

[2] *Tolstóy here appears to refer to, and adopt, a belief widespread in Russia and recently strengthened by the fact that Alexander I's sarcophagus was found to be empty when it was opened in 1927. That belief was that Alexander I did not die at Taganróg in 1825, but retired secretly to Siberia and lived there as a recluse till 1866. The story is told in Tolstóy's posthumously published sketch* Fëdor Kuzmích.—A.M.

As the sun and each atom of ether is a sphere complete in itself, and yet at the same time only a part of a whole too immense for man to comprehend, so each individual has within himself his own aims and yet has them to serve a general purpose incomprehensible to man.

A bee settling on a flower has stung a child. And the child is afraid of bees and declares that bees exist to sting people. A poet admires the bee sucking from the chalice of a flower and says it exists to suck the fragrance of flowers. A beekeeper, seeing the bee collect pollen from flowers and carry it to the hive, says that it exists to gather honey. Another beekeeper who has studied the life of the hive more closely says that the bee gathers pollen dust to feed the young bees and rear a queen, and that it exists to perpetuate its race. A botanist notices that the bee flying with the pollen of a male flower to a pistil fertilizes the latter, and sees in this the purpose of the bee's existence. Another, observing the migration of plants, notices that the bee helps in this work, and may say that in this lies the purpose of the bee. But the ultimate purpose of the bee is not exhausted by the first, the second, or any of the processes the human mind can discern. The higher the human intellect rises in the discovery of these purposes, the more obvious it becomes that the ultimate purpose is beyond our comprehension.

All that is accessible to man is the relation of the life of the bee to other manifestations of life. And so it is with the purpose of historic characters and nations.

2. Death of old Count Rostóv. Nicholas in retirement. His mother. His meeting with Princess Mary. Their wedding; estate management in the country; their family life. Sónya a sterile flower. Denísov. Nicholas' name day

NATÁSHA's WEDDING to Bezúkhov, which took place in 1813, was the last happy event in the family of the old Rostóvs. Count Ilyá Rostóv died that same year and, as always happens, after the father's death the family group broke up.

The events of the previous year: the burning of Moscow and the flight from it, the death of Prince Andrew, Natásha's despair, Pétya's death, and the old countess' grief fell blow after blow on the old count's head. He seemed to be unable to understand the meaning of all these events, and bowed his old head in a spiritual sense as if expecting and inviting further blows which would finish him. He seemed now frightened and distraught and now unnaturally animated and enterprising.

The arrangements for Natásha's marriage occupied him for a while. He ordered dinners and suppers and obviously tried to appear cheerful, but his cheerfulness was not infectious as it used to be: on the contrary it evoked the compassion of those who knew and liked him.

When Pierre and his wife had left, he grew very quiet and began to complain of depression. A few days later he fell ill and took to his bed. He realized from the first that he would not get up again, despite the doctor's encouragement. The countess passed a fortnight in an armchair by his pillow without undressing. Every time she gave him his medicine he sobbed and silently kissed her hand. On his last day, sobbing, he asked her and his absent son to forgive him for having dissipated their property —that being the chief fault of which he was conscious. After receiving communion and unction he quietly died; and next day a throng of acquaintances who came to pay their last respects to the deceased filled the house rented by the Rostóvs. All these acquaintances, who had so often dined and danced at his house and had so often laughed at him, now said, with a common feeling of self-reproach and emotion, as if justifying themselves: "Well, whatever he may have been he was a most worthy man. You don't meet such men nowadays. . . . And which of us has not weaknesses of his own?"

It was just when the count's affairs had become so involved that it was impossible to say what would happen if he lived another year that he unexpectedly died.

Nicholas was with the Russian army in Paris when the news of his father's death reached him. He at once resigned his commission, and without waiting for it to be accepted took leave of absence and went to Moscow. The state of the count's affairs became quite obvious a month after his death, surprising everyone by the immense total of small debts the existence of which no one had suspected. The debts amounted to double the value of the property.

Friends and relations advised Nicholas to decline the inheritance. But he regarded such a refusal as a slur on his father's memory, which he held sacred, and therefore would not hear of refusing and accepted the inheritance together with the obligation to pay the debts.

The creditors who had so long been silent, restrained by a vague but powerful influence exerted on them while he lived by the count's careless good nature, all proceeded to enforce their claims at once. As always happens in such cases rivalry sprang up as to which should get paid first, and those who like Mítenka held promissory notes given them as presents now became the most exacting of the creditors. Nicholas was allowed no respite and no peace, and those who had seemed to pity the old man—the

cause of their losses (if they were losses)—now remorselessly pursued the young heir who had voluntarily undertaken the debts and was obviously not guilty of contracting them.

Not one of the plans Nicholas tried succeeded; the estate was sold by auction for half its value, and half the debts still remained unpaid. Nicholas accepted thirty thousand rubles offered him by his brother-in-law Bezúkhov to pay off debts he regarded as genuinely due for value received. And to avoid being imprisoned for the remainder, as the creditors threatened, he re-entered the government service.

He could not rejoin the army where he would have been made colonel at the next vacancy, for his mother now clung to him as her one hold on life; and so despite his reluctance to remain in Moscow among people who had known him before, and despite his abhorrence of the civil service, he accepted a post in Moscow in that service, doffed the uniform of which he was so fond, and moved with his mother and Sónya to a small house on the Sívtsev Vrazhëk.*

Natásha and Pierre were living in Petersburg at the time and had no clear idea of Nicholas' circumstances. Having borrowed money from his brother-in-law, Nicholas tried to hide his wretched condition from him. His position was the more difficult because with his salary of twelve hundred rubles he had not only to keep himself, his mother, and Sónya, but had to shield his mother from knowledge of their poverty. The countess could not conceive of life without the luxurious conditions she had been used to from childhood and, unable to realize how hard it was for her son, kept demanding now a carriage (which they did not keep) to send for a friend, now some expensive article of food for herself, or wine for her son, or money to buy a present as a surprise for Natásha or Sónya, or for Nicholas himself.

Sónya kept house, attended on her aunt, read to her, put up with her whims and secret ill-will, and helped Nicholas to conceal their poverty from the old countess. Nicholas felt himself irredeemably indebted to Sónya for all she was doing for his mother and greatly admired her patience and devotion, but tried to keep aloof from her.

He seemed in his heart to reproach her for being too perfect, and because there was nothing to reproach her with. She had all that people are valued for, but little that could have made him love her. He felt that the more he valued her the less he loved her. He had taken her at her word when she wrote giving him his freedom and now behaved as if all that had passed between them had been long forgotten and could never in any case be renewed.

* A *poor quarter of Moscow.*—A.M.

Nicholas' position became worse and worse.* The idea of putting something aside out of his salary proved a dream. Not only did he not save anything, but to comply with his mother's demands he even incurred some small debts. He could see no way out of this situation. The idea of marrying some rich woman, which was suggested to him by his female relations, was repugnant to him. The other way out—his mother's death—never entered his head. He wished for nothing and hoped for nothing, and deep in his heart experienced a gloomy and stern satisfaction in an uncomplaining endurance of his position. He tried to avoid his old acquaintances with their commiseration and offensive offers of assistance; he avoided all distraction and recreation, and even at home did nothing but play cards with his mother, pace silently up and down the room, and smoke one pipe after another. He seemed carefully to cherish within himself the gloomy mood which alone enabled him to endure his position.

At the beginning of winter Princess Mary came to Moscow. From reports current in town she learned how the Rostóvs were situated, and how "the son has sacrificed himself for his mother," as people were saying.

"I never expected anything else of him," said Princess Mary to herself, feeling a joyous sense of her love for him. Remembering her friendly relations with all the Rostóvs which had made her almost a member of the family, she thought it her duty to go to see them. But remembering her relations with Nicholas in Vorónezh she was shy about doing so. Making a great effort she did however go to call on them a few weeks after her arrival in Moscow.

Nicholas was the first to meet her, as the countess' room could only be reached through his. But instead of being greeted with pleasure as she had expected, at his first glance at her his face assumed a cold, stiff, proud expression she had not seen on it before. He inquired about her health, led the way to his mother, and having sat there for five minutes left the room.

When the princess came out of the countess' room Nicholas met her again, and with marked solemnity and stiffness accompanied her to the anteroom. To her remarks about his mother's health he made no reply. "What's that to you? Leave me in peace," his looks seemed to say.

* *Nicholas Rostóv's life after his father's death is closely modeled on that of Leo Tolstóy's father, Nicholas Tolstóy. "Auntie" Tatiána (the Sónya of the novel) was living in Tolstóy's house while he was writing War and Peace. He reproduced the actual feelings and conduct of people he knew intimately. In Appendix II to Volume I of the Oxford Press Life of Tolstoy an instance is cited concerning Nicholas and Sónya and their relations to one another.—A.M.*

"Why does she come prowling here? What does she want? I can't bear these ladies and all these civilities!" said he aloud in Sónya's presence, evidently unable to repress his vexation, after the princess' carriage had disappeared.

"Oh, Nicholas, how can you talk like that?" cried Sónya, hardly able to conceal her delight. "She is so kind and Mamma is so fond of her!"

Nicholas did not reply and tried to avoid speaking of the princess any more. But after her visit the old countess spoke of her several times a day.

She sang her praises, insisted that her son must call on her, expressed a wish to see her often, but yet always became ill-humored when she began to talk about her.

Nicholas tried to keep silence when his mother spoke of the princess, but his silence irritated her.

"She is a very admirable and excellent young woman," said she, "and you must go and call on her. You would at least be seeing somebody, and I think it must be dull for you only seeing us."

"But I don't in the least want to, Mamma."

"You used to want to, and now you don't. Really I don't understand you, my dear. One day you are dull, and the next you refuse to see anyone."

"But I never said I was dull."

"Why, you said yourself you don't want even to see her. She is a very admirable young woman and you always liked her, but now suddenly you have got some notion or other in your head. You hide everything from me."

"Not at all, Mamma."

"If I were asking you to do something disagreeable now—but I only ask you to return a call. One would think mere politeness required it. . . . Well, I have asked you, and now I won't interfere any more since you have secrets from your mother."

"Well, then, I'll go if you wish it."

"It doesn't matter to me. I only wish it for your sake."

Nicholas sighed, bit his mustache, and laid out the cards for a patience, trying to divert his mother's attention to another topic.

The same conversation was repeated next day and the day after, and the day after that.

After her visit to the Rostóvs and her unexpectedly chilly reception by Nicholas, Princess Mary confessed to herself that she had been right in not wishing to be the first to call.

"I expected nothing else," she told herself, calling her pride to her aid. "I have nothing to do with him and I only wanted to see the old lady, who was always kind to me and to whom I am under many obligations."

But she could not pacify herself with these reflections; a feeling akin to

remorse troubled her when she thought of her visit. Though she had firmly resolved not to call on the Rostóvs again and to forget the whole matter, she felt herself all the time in an awkward position. And when she asked herself what distressed her, she had to admit that it was her relation to Rostóv. His cold, polite manner did not express his feeling for her (she knew that) but it concealed something, and until she could discover what that something was, she felt that she could not be at ease.

One day in midwinter when sitting in the schoolroom attending to her nephew's lessons, she was informed that Rostóv had called. With a firm resolution not to betray herself and not show her agitation, she sent for Mademoiselle Bourienne and went with her to the drawing room.

Her first glance at Nicholas' face told her that he had only come to fulfill the demands of politeness, and she firmly resolved to maintain the tone in which he addressed her.

They spoke of the countess' health, of their mutual friends, of the latest war news, and when the ten minutes required by propriety had elapsed after which a visitor may rise, Nicholas got up to say good-by.

With Mademoiselle Bourienne's help the princess had maintained the conversation very well, but at the very last moment, just when he rose, she was so tired of talking of what did not interest her, and her mind was so full of the question why she alone was granted so little happiness in life, that in a fit of absent-mindedness she sat still, her luminous eyes gazing fixedly before her, not noticing that he had risen.

Nicholas glanced at her and, wishing to appear not to notice her abstraction, made some remark to Mademoiselle Bourienne and then again looked at the princess. She still sat motionless with a look of suffering on her gentle face. He suddenly felt sorry for her and was vaguely conscious that he might be the cause of the sadness her face expressed. He wished to help her and say something pleasant, but could think of nothing to say.

"Good-by, Princess!" said he.

She started, flushed, and sighed deeply.

"Oh, I beg your pardon," she said as if waking up. "Are you going already, Count? Well then, good-by! Oh, but the cushion for the countess!"

"Wait a moment, I'll fetch it," said Mademoiselle Bourienne, and she left the room.

They both sat silent, with an occasional glance at one another.

"Yes, Princess," said Nicholas at last with a sad smile, "it doesn't seem long ago since we first met at Boguchárovo, but how much water has flowed since then! In what distress we all seemed to be then, yet I would give much to bring back that time . . . but there's no bringing it back."

Princess Mary gazed intently into his eyes with her own luminous ones

as he said this. She seemed to be trying to fathom the hidden meaning of his words which would explain his feeling for her.

"Yes, yes," said she, "but you have no reason to regret the past, Count. As I understand your present life, I think you will always recall it with satisfaction, because the self-sacrifice that fills it now . . ."

"I cannot accept your praise," he interrupted her hurriedly. "On the contrary I continually reproach myself. . . . But this is not at all an interesting or cheerful subject."

His face again resumed its former stiff and cold expression. But the princess had caught a glimpse of the man she had known and loved, and it was to him that she now spoke.

"I thought you would allow me to tell you this," she said. "I had come so near to you . . . and to all your family that I thought you would not consider my sympathy misplaced, but I was mistaken," and suddenly her voice trembled. "I don't know why," she continued, recovering herself, "but you used to be different, and . . ."

"There are a thousand reasons *why*," laying special emphasis on the *why*. "Thank you, Princess," he added softly. "Sometimes it is hard."

"So that's why! That's why!" a voice whispered in Princess Mary's soul. "No, it was not only that gay, kind, and frank look, not only that handsome exterior, that I loved in him. I divined his noble, resolute, self-sacrificing spirit too," she said to herself. "Yes, he is poor now and I am rich. . . . Yes, that's the only reason. . . . Yes, were it not for that . . ." And remembering his former tenderness, and looking now at his kind, sorrowful face, she suddenly understood the cause of his coldness.

"But why, Count, why?" she almost cried, unconsciously moving closer to him. "Why? Tell me. You must tell me!"

He was silent.

"I don't understand your *why*, Count," she continued, "but it's hard for me . . . I confess it. For some reason you wish to deprive me of our former friendship. And that hurts me." There were tears in her eyes and in her voice. "I have had so little happiness in life that every loss is hard for me to bear. . . . Excuse me, good-by!" and suddenly she began to cry and was hurrying from the room.

"Princess, for God's sake!" he exclaimed, trying to stop her. "Princess!"

She turned round. For a few seconds they gazed silently into one another's eyes—and what had seemed impossible and remote suddenly became possible, inevitable, and very near.

In the winter of 1813 Nicholas married Princess Mary and moved to Bald Hills with his wife, his mother, and Sónya.

Within four years he had paid off all his remaining debts without selling any of his wife's property, and having received a small inheritance on the death of a cousin he paid his debt to Pierre as well.

In another three years, by 1820, he had so managed his affairs that he was able to buy a small estate adjoining Bald Hills and was negotiating to buy back Otrádnoe—that being his pet dream.

Having started farming from necessity, he soon grew so devoted to it that it became his favorite and almost his sole occupation. Nicholas was a plain farmer: he did not like innovations, especially the English ones then coming into vogue. He laughed at theoretical treatises on estate management, disliked factories, the raising of expensive products, and the buying of expensive seed corn, and did not make a hobby of any particular part of the work on his estate. He always had before his mind's eye *the estate* as a whole and not any particular part of it. The chief thing in his eyes was not the nitrogen in the soil, nor the oxygen in the air, nor manures, nor special plows, but that most important agent by which nitrogen, oxygen, manure, and plow were made effective—the peasant laborer. When Nicholas first began farming and began to understand its different branches, it was the serf who especially attracted his attention. The peasant seemed to him not merely a tool, but also a judge of farming and an end in himself. At first he watched the serfs, trying to understand their aims and what they considered good and bad, and only pretended to direct them and give orders while in reality learning from them their methods, their manner of speech, and their judgment of what was good and bad. Only when he had understood the peasants' tastes and aspirations, had learned to talk their language, to grasp the hidden meaning of their words, and felt akin to them did he begin boldly to manage his serfs, that is, to perform toward them the duties demanded of him. And Nicholas' management produced very brilliant results.

Guided by some gift of insight, on taking up the management of the estates he at once unerringly appointed as bailiff, village elder, and delegate, the very men the serfs would themselves have chosen had they had the right to choose, and these posts never changed hands. Before analyzing the properties of manure, before entering into the *debit* and *credit* (as he ironically called it), he found out how many cattle the peasants had and increased the number by all possible means. He kept the peasant families together in the largest groups possible, not allowing the family groups to divide into separate households. He was hard alike on the lazy, the depraved, and the weak, and tried to get them expelled from the commune.

He was as careful of the sowing and reaping of the peasants' hay and

corn as of his own, and few landowners had their crops sown and har-
vested so early and so well, or got so good a return, as did Nicholas.

He disliked having anything to do with the domestic serfs—the "drones"
as he called them—and everyone said he spoiled them by his laxity. When
a decision had to be taken regarding a domestic serf, especially if one had
to be punished, he always felt undecided and consulted everybody in the
house; but when it was possible to have a domestic serf conscripted instead
of a land worker he did so without the least hesitation. He never felt any
hesitation in dealing with the peasants. He knew that his every decision
would be approved by them all with very few exceptions.

He did not allow himself either to be hard on or punish a man, or to
make things easy for or reward anyone, merely because he felt inclined to
do so. He could not have said by what standard he judged what he should
or should not do, but the standard was quite firm and definite in his
own mind.

Often, speaking with vexation of some failure or irregularity, he would
say: "What can one do with our Russian peasants?" and imagined that
he could not bear them.

Yet he loved "our Russian peasants" and their way of life with his whole
soul, and for that very reason had understood and assimilated the one way
and manner of farming which produced good results.*

Countess Mary was jealous of this passion of her husband's and regret-
ted that she could not share it; but she could not understand the joys and
vexations he derived from that world, to her so remote and alien. She
could not understand why he was so particularly animated and happy
when, after getting up at daybreak and spending the whole morning in
the fields or on the threshing floor, he returned from the sowing or mow-
ing or reaping to have tea with her. She did not understand why he spoke
with such admiration and delight of the farming of the thrifty and well-to-
do peasant Matthew Ermíshin, who with his family had carted corn all
night; or of the fact that his (Nicholas') sheaves were already stacked be-
fore anyone else had his harvest in. She did not understand why he stepped
out from the window to the veranda and smiled under his mustache and
winked so joyfully, when warm steady rain began to fall on the dry and
thirsty shoots of the young oats, or why when the wind carried away a
threatening cloud during the hay harvest he would return from the barn,
flushed, sunburned, and perspiring, with a smell of wormwood and gen-

* The description in this section of Nicholas' method of farming and of his
relation to his peasants much resembles that of Lévin in Anna Karénina. Both
descriptions are based on Tolstóy's own conduct of affairs in the years 1862-
78.—A.M.

tian in his hair and, gleefully rubbing his hands, would say: "Well, one more day and my grain and the peasants' will all be under cover."

Still less did she understand why he, kindhearted and always ready to anticipate her wishes, should become almost desperate when she brought him a petition from some peasant men or women who had appealed to her to be excused some work; why he, that kind Nicholas, should obstinately refuse her, angrily asking her not to interfere in what was not her business. She felt he had a world apart, which he loved passionately and which had laws she had not fathomed.

Sometimes when, trying to understand him, she spoke of the good work he was doing for his serfs, he would be vexed and reply: "Not in the least; it never entered my head and I wouldn't do *that* for their good! That's all poetry and old wives' talk—all that doing good to one's neighbor! What I want is that our children should not have to go begging. I must put our affairs in order while I am alive, that's all. And to do that, order and strictness are essential. . . . That's all about it!" said he, clenching his vigorous fist. "And fairness, of course," he added, "for if the peasant is naked and hungry and has only one miserable horse, he can do no good either for himself or for me."

And all Nicholas did was fruitful—probably just because he refused to allow himself to think that he was doing good to others for virtue's sake. His means increased rapidly; serfs from neighboring estates came to beg him to buy them, and long after his death the memory of his administration was devoutly preserved among the serfs. "He was a master . . . the peasants' affairs first and then his own. Of course he was not to be trifled with either—in a word, he was a real master!"

ONE MATTER connected with his management sometimes worried Nicholas, and that was his quick temper together with his old hussar habit of making free use of his fists. At first he saw nothing reprehensible in this, but in the second year of his marriage his view of that form of punishment suddenly changed.

Once in summer he had sent for the village elder from Boguchárovo, a man who had succeeded to the post when Dron died and who was accused of dishonesty and various irregularities. Nicholas went out into the porch to question him, and immediately after the elder had given a few replies the sound of cries and blows was heard. On returning to lunch Nicholas went up to his wife, who sat with her head bent low over her embroidery frame, and as usual began to tell her what he had been doing that morning. Among other things he spoke of the Boguchárovo elder. Countess Mary

turned red and then pale, but continued to sit with head bowed and lips compressed and gave her husband no reply.

"Such an insolent scoundrel!" he cried, growing hot again at the mere recollection of him. "If he had told me he was drunk and did not see . . . But what is the matter with you, Mary?" he suddenly asked.

Countess Mary raised her head and tried to speak, but hastily looked down again and her lips puckered.

"Why, whatever is the matter, my dearest?"

The looks of the plain Countess Mary always improved when she was in tears. She never cried from pain or vexation, but always from sorrow or pity, and when she wept her radiant eyes acquired an irresistible charm.

The moment Nicholas took her hand she could no longer restrain herself and began to cry.

"Nicholas, I saw it . . . he was to blame, but why do you . . . Nicholas!" and she covered her face with her hands.

Nicholas said nothing. He flushed crimson, left her side, and paced up and down the room. He understood what she was weeping about, but could not in his heart at once agree with her that what he had regarded from childhood as quite an everyday event was wrong. "Is it just sentimentality, old wives' tales, or is she right?" he asked himself. Before he had solved that point he glanced again at her face filled with love and pain, and he suddenly realized that she was right and that he had long been sinning against himself.

"Mary," he said softly, going up to her, "it will never happen again; I give you my word. Never," he repeated in a trembling voice like a boy asking for forgiveness.

The tears flowed faster still from the countess' eyes. She took his hand and kissed it.

"Nicholas, when did you break your cameo?" she asked to change the subject, looking at his finger on which he wore a ring with a cameo of Laocoön's head.

"Today—it was the same affair. Oh, Mary, don't remind me of it!" and again he flushed. "I give you my word of honor it shan't occur again, and let this always be a reminder to me," and he pointed to the broken ring.

After that, when in discussions with his village elders or stewards the blood rushed to his face and his fists began to clench, Nicholas would turn the broken ring on his finger and would drop his eyes before the man who was making him angry. But he did forget himself once or twice within a twelvemonth, and then he would go and confess to his wife, and would again promise that this should really be the very last time.

"Mary, you must despise me!" he would say. "I deserve it."

"You should go, go away at once, if you don't feel strong enough to control yourself," she would reply sadly, trying to comfort her husband.

Among the gentry of the province Nicholas was respected but not liked. He did not concern himself with the interests of his own class, and consequently some thought him proud and others thought him stupid. The whole summer, from spring sowing to harvest, he was busy with the work on his farm. In autumn he gave himself up to hunting with the same businesslike seriousness—leaving home for a month, or even two, with his hunt. In winter he visited his other villages or spent his time reading. The books he read were chiefly historical, and on these he spent a certain sum every year. He was collecting, as he said, a serious library, and he made it a rule to read through all the books he bought. He would sit in his study with a grave air, reading—a task he first imposed upon himself as a duty, but which afterwards became a habit affording him a special kind of pleasure and a consciousness of being occupied with serious matters. In winter, except for business excursions, he spent most of his time at home making himself one with his family and entering into all the details of his children's relations with their mother. The harmony between him and his wife grew closer and closer and he daily discovered fresh spiritual treasures in her.

From the time of his marriage Sónya had lived in his house. Before that, Nicholas had told his wife all that had passed between himself and Sónya, blaming himself and commending her. He had asked Princess Mary to be gentle and kind to his cousin. She thoroughly realized the wrong he had done Sónya, felt herself to blame toward her, and imagined that her wealth had influenced Nicholas' choice. She could not find fault with Sónya in any way and tried to be fond of her, but often felt ill-will toward her which she could not overcome.

Once she had a talk with her friend Natásha about Sónya and about her own injustice toward her.

"You know," said Natásha, "you have read the Gospels a great deal—there is a passage in them that just fits Sónya."

"What?" asked Countess Mary, surprised.

" 'To him that hath shall be given, and from him that hath not shall be taken away.' You remember? She is one that hath not; why, I don't know. Perhaps she lacks egotism, I don't know, but from her is taken away, and everything has been taken away. Sometimes I am dreadfully sorry for her. Formerly I very much wanted Nicholas to marry her, but I always had a sort of presentiment that it would not come off. She is a *sterile flower*, you know—like some strawberry blossoms. Sometimes I am sorry for her, and sometimes I think she doesn't feel it as you or I would."

Though Countess Mary told Natásha that those words in the Gospel must be understood differently, yet looking at Sónya she agreed with Natásha's explanation. It really seemed that Sónya did not feel her position trying, and had grown quite reconciled to her lot as a *sterile flower*. She seemed to be fond not so much of individuals as of the family as a whole. Like a cat, she had attached herself not to the people but to the home. She waited on the old countess, petted and spoiled the children, was always ready to render the small services for which she had a gift, and all this was unconsciously accepted from her with insufficient gratitude.

The country seat at Bald Hills had been rebuilt, though not on the same scale as under the old prince.

The buildings, begun under straitened circumstances, were more than simple. The immense house on the old stone foundations was of wood, plastered only inside. It had bare deal floors and was furnished with very simple hard sofas, armchairs, tables, and chairs made by their own serf carpenters out of their own birchwood.* The house was spacious and had rooms for the house serfs and apartments for visitors. Whole families of the Rostóvs' and Bolkónskis' relations sometimes came to Bald Hills with sixteen horses and dozens of servants and stayed for months. Besides that, four times a year, on the name days and birthdays of the hosts, as many as a hundred visitors would gather there for a day or two. The rest of the year life pursued its unbroken routine with its ordinary occupations, and its breakfasts, lunches, dinners, and suppers, provided out of the produce of the estate.

It was the eve of St. Nicholas, the fifth of December, 1820. Natásha had been staying at her brother's with her husband and children since early autumn. Pierre had gone to Petersburg on business of his own for three weeks as he said, but had remained there nearly seven weeks and was expected back every minute.

Besides the Bezúkhov family, Nicholas' old friend the retired General Vasíli Dmítrich Denísov was staying with the Rostóvs this fifth of December.

On the sixth, which was his name day when the house would be full of visitors, Nicholas knew he would have to exchange his Tartar tunic for a tail coat, and put on narrow boots with pointed toes, and drive to the new

* *The simplicity of the house is similar to that which always prevailed at Yásnaya Polyána—the prototype of Bald Hills. For purposes of literary effect much has been written about the "luxury" of Tolstóy's house, and its contrast with the simplicity he aimed at and preached in his later life. In fact, however, he never liked or indulged in luxury. Compared to most English country estates the frugal simplicity of Yásnaya Polyána was conspicuous.—A.M.*

church he had built, and then receive visitors who would come to congratulate him, offer them refreshments, and talk about the elections of the nobility; * but he considered himself entitled to spend the eve of that day in his usual way. He examined the bailiff's accounts of the village in Ryazán which belonged to his wife's nephew, wrote two business letters, and walked over to the granaries, cattle yards and stables before dinner. Having taken precautions against the general drunkenness to be expected on the morrow because it was a great saint's day, he returned to dinner, and without having time for a private talk with his wife sat down at the long table laid for twenty persons, at which the whole household had assembled. At that table were his mother, his mother's old lady companion Belóva, his wife, their three children with their governess and tutor, his wife's nephew with his tutor, Sónya, Denísov, Natásha, her three children, their governess, and old Michael Ivánovich, the late prince's architect, who was living on in retirement at Bald Hills.

Countess Mary sat at the other end of the table. When her husband took his place she concluded, from the rapid manner in which after taking up his table napkin he pushed back the tumbler and wineglass standing before him, that he was out of humor, as was sometimes the case when he came in to dinner straight from the farm—especially before the soup. Countess Mary well knew that mood of his, and when she herself was in a good frame of mind quietly waited till he had had his soup and then began to talk to him and make him admit that there was no cause for his ill-humor. But today she quite forgot that and was hurt that he should be angry with her without any reason, and she felt unhappy. She asked him where he had been. He replied. She again inquired whether everything was going well on the farm. Her unnatural tone made him wince unpleasantly and he replied hastily.

"Then I'm not mistaken," thought Countess Mary. "Why is he cross with me?" She concluded from his tone that he was vexed with her and wished to end the conversation. She knew her remarks sounded unnatural, but could not refrain from asking some more questions.

Thanks to Denísov the conversation at table soon became general and lively, and she did not talk to her husband. When they left the table and went as usual to thank the old countess,[2] Countess Mary held out her

* The nobility, or rather the gentry, of each province formed a corporation, with periodical elections and assemblies, and played at that period an almost exclusive part in local administration.—A.M.

[2] It was customary in Russia to thank the hostess after dinner, and in this case the old countess, though she was not the hostess, was thanked out of deference.—A.M.

hand and kissed her husband, and asked him why he was angry with her.

"You always have such strange fancies! I didn't even think of being angry," he replied.

But the word *always* seemed to her to imply: "Yes, I am angry but I won't tell you why."

Nicholas and his wife lived together so happily that even Sónya and the old countess, who felt jealous and would have liked them to disagree, could find nothing to reproach them with; but even they had their moments of antagonism. Occasionally, and it was always just after they had been happiest together, they suddenly had a feeling of estrangement and hostility, which occurred most frequently during Countess Mary's pregnancies, and this was such a time.

"Well, *messieurs et mesdames,*" said Nicholas loudly and with apparent cheerfulness (it seemed to Countess Mary that he did it on purpose to vex her), "I have been on my feet since six this morning. Tomorrow I shall have to suffer, so today I'll go and rest."

And without a word to his wife he went to the little sitting room and lay down on the sofa.

"That's always the way," thought Countess Mary. "He talks to everyone except me. I see . . . I see that I am repulsive to him, especially when I am in this condition." She looked down at her expanded figure and in the glass at her pale, sallow, emaciated face in which her eyes now looked larger than ever.

And everything annoyed her—Denísov's shouting and laughter, Natásha's talk, and especially a quick glance Sónya gave her.

Sónya was always the first excuse Countess Mary found for feeling irritated.

Having sat awhile with her visitors without understanding anything of what they were saying, she softly left the room and went to the nursery.

The children were playing at "going to Moscow" in a carriage made of chairs and invited her to go with them. She sat down and played with them a little, but the thought of her husband and his unreasonable crossness worried her. She got up and, walking on tiptoe with difficulty, went to the small sitting room.

"Perhaps he is not asleep; I'll have an explanation with him," she said to herself. Little Andrew, her eldest boy, imitating his mother, followed her on tiptoe. She did not notice him.

"Mary, dear, I think he is asleep—he was so tired," said Sónya, meeting her in the large sitting room (it seemed to Countess Mary that she crossed her path everywhere). "Andrew may wake him."

Countess Mary looked round, saw little Andrew following her, felt that

Sónya was right, and for that very reason flushed and with evident difficulty refrained from saying something harsh. She made no reply, but to avoid obeying Sónya beckoned to Andrew to follow her quietly and went to the door. Sónya went away by another door. From the room in which Nicholas was sleeping came the sound of his even breathing, every slightest tone of which was familiar to his wife. As she listened to it she saw before her his smooth handsome forehead, his mustache, and his whole face, as she had so often seen it in the stillness of the night when he slept. Nicholas suddenly moved and cleared his throat. And at that moment little Andrew shouted from outside the door: "Papa! Mamma's standing here!" Countess Mary turned pale with fright and made signs to the boy. He grew silent, and quiet ensued for a moment, terrible to Countess Mary. She knew how Nicholas disliked being waked. Then through the door she heard Nicholas clearing his throat again and stirring, and his voice said crossly:

"I can't get a moment's peace. . . . Mary, is that you? Why did you bring him here?"

"I only came in to look and did not notice . . . forgive me. . . ."

Nicholas coughed and said no more. Countess Mary moved away from the door and took the boy back to the nursery. Five minutes later little black-eyed three-year-old Natásha, her father's pet, having learned from her brother that Papa was asleep and Mamma was in the sitting room, ran to her father unobserved by her mother. The dark-eyed little girl boldly opened the creaking door, went up to the sofa with energetic steps of her sturdy little legs, and having examined the position of her father, who was asleep with his back to her, rose on tiptoe and kissed the hand which lay under his head. Nicholas turned with a tender smile on his face.

"Natásha, Natásha!" came Countess Mary's frightened whisper from the door. "Papa wants to sleep."

"No, Mamma, he doesn't want to sleep," said little Natásha with conviction. "He's laughing."

Nicholas lowered his legs, rose, and took his daughter in his arms.

"Come in, Mary," he said to his wife.

She went in and sat down by her husband.

"I did not notice him following me," she said timidly. "I just looked in."

Holding his little girl with one arm, Nicholas glanced at his wife and, seeing her guilty expression, put his other arm around her and kissed her hair.

"May I kiss Mamma?" he asked Natásha.

Natásha smiled bashfully.

"Again!" she commanded, pointing with a peremptory gesture to the spot where Nicholas had placed the kiss.

"I don't know why you think I am cross," said Nicholas, replying to the question he knew was in his wife's mind.

"You have no idea how unhappy, how lonely, I feel when you are like that. It always seems to me . . ."

"Mary, don't talk nonsense. You ought to be ashamed of yourself!" he said gaily.

"It seems to me that you can't love me, that I am so plain . . . always . . . and now . . . in this cond . . ."

"Oh, how absurd you are! It is not beauty that endears, it's love that makes us see beauty. It is only Malvínas and women of that kind who are loved for their beauty. But do I love my wife? I don't love her, but . . . I don't know how to put it. Without you, or when something comes between us like this, I seem lost and can't do anything. Now do I love my finger? I don't love it, but just try to cut it off!"

"I'm not like that myself, but I understand. So you're not angry with me?"

"Awfully angry!" he said, smiling and getting up. And smoothing his hair he began to pace the room.

"Do you know, Mary, what I've been thinking?" he began, immediately thinking aloud in his wife's presence now that they had made it up.

He did not ask if she was ready to listen to him. He did not care. A thought had occurred to him and so it belonged to her also. And he told her of his intention to persuade Pierre to stay with them till spring.

Countess Mary listened till he had finished, made some remark, and in her turn began thinking aloud. Her thoughts were about the children.

"You see the woman in her already," she said in French, pointing to little Natásha. "You reproach us women with being illogical. Here is our logic. I say: 'Papa wants to sleep!' but she says, 'No, he's laughing.' And she was right," said Countess Mary with a happy smile.

"Yes, yes." And Nicholas, taking his little daughter in his strong hand, lifted her high, placed her on his shoulder, held her by the legs, and paced the room with her. There was an expression of carefree happiness on the faces of both father and daughter.

"But you know you may be unfair. You are too fond of this one," his wife whispered in French.

"Yes, but what am I to do? . . . I try not to show . . ."

At that moment they heard the sound of the door pulley and footsteps in the hall and anteroom, as if someone had arrived.

"Somebody has come."

"I am sure it is Pierre. I will go and see," said Countess Mary and left the room.

In her absence Nicholas allowed himself to give his little daughter a gallop round the room. Out of breath, he took the laughing child quickly from his shoulder and pressed her to his heart. His capers reminded him of dancing, and looking at the child's round happy little face he thought of what she would be like when he was an old man, taking her into society and dancing the mazurka with her as his old father had danced *Daniel Cooper* with his daughter.

"It is he, it is he, Nicholas!" said Countess Mary, re-entering the room a few minutes later. "Now our Natásha has come to life. You should have seen her ecstasy, and how he caught it for having stayed away so long. Well, come along now, quick, quick! It's time you two were parted," she added, looking smilingly at the little girl who clung to her father.

Nicholas went out holding the child by the hand.

Countess Mary remained in the sitting room.

"I should never, never have believed that one could be so happy," she whispered to herself. A smile lit up her face but at the same time she sighed, and her deep eyes expressed a quiet sadness as though she felt, through her happiness, that there is another sort of happiness unattainable in this life and of which she involuntarily thought at that instant.

3. *Natásha's and Pierre's family life. His return after a visit to Petersburg. The old countess in decay. Conversation about social tendencies, and indignation at reactionary trend of the government. Views of Pierre and Nicholas*

N ATÁSHA HAD MARRIED in the early spring of 1813, and in 1820 already had three daughters besides a son for whom she had longed and whom she was now nursing. She had grown stouter and broader, so that it was difficult to recognize in this robust, motherly woman the slim, lively Natásha of former days. Her features were more defined and had a calm, soft, and serene expression. In her face there was none of the ever-glowing animation that had formerly burned there and constituted its charm. Now her face and body were often all that one saw, and her soul was not visible at all. All that struck the eye was a strong, handsome, and fertile woman. The old fire very rarely kindled in her face now. That happened only when, as was the case that day, her husband returned home, or a sick child was convalescent, or when she and Countess Mary spoke of Prince Andrew (she never mentioned him to her husband, who she imagined was jealous

of Prince Andrew's memory), or on the rare occasions when something happened to induce her to sing, a practice she had quite abandoned since her marriage. At the rare moments when the old fire did kindle in her handsome, fully developed body she was even more attractive than in former days.

Since their marriage Natásha and her husband had lived in Moscow, in Petersburg, on their estate near Moscow, or with her mother, that is to say, in Nicholas' house. The young Countess Bezúkhova was not often seen in society, and those who met her there were not pleased with her and found her neither attractive nor amiable. Not that Natásha liked solitude —she did not know whether she liked it or not, she even thought that she did not—but with her pregnancies, her confinements, the nursing of her children, and sharing every moment of her husband's life, she had demands on her time which could be satisfied only by renouncing society. All who had known Natásha before her marriage wondered at the change in her as at something extraordinary. Only the old countess with her maternal instinct had realized that all Natásha's outbursts had been due to her need of children and a husband—as she herself had once exclaimed at Otrádnoe not so much in fun as in earnest—and her mother was now surprised at the surprise expressed by those who had never understood Natásha, and she kept saying that she had always known that Natásha would make an exemplary wife and mother.

"Only she lets her love of her husband and children overflow all bounds," said the countess, "so that it even becomes absurd."

Natásha did not follow the golden rule advocated by clever folk, especially by the French, which says that a girl should not let herself go when she marries, should not neglect her accomplishments, should be even more careful of her appearance than when she was unmarried, and should fascinate her husband as much as she did before he became her husband. Natásha on the contrary had at once abandoned all her witchery, of which her singing had been an unusually powerful part. She gave it up just because it was so powerfully seductive. She took no pains with her manners or with delicacy of speech, or with her toilet, or to show herself to her husband in her most becoming attitudes, or to avoid inconveniencing him by being too exacting. She acted in contradiction to all those rules. She felt that the allurements instinct had formerly taught her to use would now be merely ridiculous in the eyes of her husband, to whom she had from the first moment given herself up entirely—that is, with her whole soul, leaving no corner of it hidden from him. She felt that her unity with her husband was not maintained by the poetic feelings that had

attracted him to her, but by something else—indefinite but firm as the bond between her own body and soul.

To fluff out her curls, put on fashionable dresses, and sing romantic songs to fascinate her husband would have seemed as strange as to adorn herself to attract herself. To adorn herself for others might perhaps have been agreeable—she did not know—but she had no time at all for it. The chief reason for devoting no time either to singing, to dress, or to choosing her words was that she really had no time to spare for these things.

We know that man has the faculty of becoming completely absorbed in a subject however trivial it may be, and that there is no subject so trivial that it will not grow to infinite proportions if one's entire attention is devoted to it.

The subject which wholly engrossed Natásha's attention was her family: that is, her husband whom she had to keep so that he should belong entirely to her and to the home, and the children whom she had to bear, bring into the world, nurse, and bring up.

And the deeper she penetrated, not with her mind only but with her whole soul, her whole being, into the subject that absorbed her, the larger did that subject grow and the weaker and more inadequate did her own powers appear, so that she concentrated them wholly on that one thing and yet was unable to accomplish all that she considered necessary.

There were then as now conversations and discussions about women's rights, the relations of husband and wife and their freedom and rights, though these themes were not yet termed *questions* as they are now; but these topics were not merely uninteresting to Natásha, she positively did not understand them.

These questions, then as now, existed only for those who see nothing in marriage but the pleasure married people get from one another, that is, only the beginnings of marriage and not its whole significance, which lies in the family.

Discussions and questions of that kind, which are like the question of how to get the greatest gratification from one's dinner, did not then and do not now exist for those for whom the purpose of a dinner is the nourishment it affords; and the purpose of marriage is the family.

If the purpose of dinner is to nourish the body, a man who eats two dinners at once may perhaps get more enjoyment but will not attain his purpose, for his stomach will not digest the two dinners.

If the purpose of marriage is the family, the person who wishes to have many wives or husbands may perhaps obtain much pleasure, but in that case will not have a family.

If the purpose of food is nourishment and the purpose of marriage is

the family, the whole question resolves itself into not eating more than one can digest, and not having more wives or husbands than are needed for the family—that is, one wife or one husband. Natásha needed a husband. A husband was given her and he gave her a family. And she not only saw no need of any other or better husband, but as all the powers of her soul were intent on serving that husband and family, she could not imagine and saw no interest in imagining how it would be if things were different.

Natásha did not care for society in general, but prized the more the society of her relatives—Countess Mary, and her brother, her mother, and Sónya. She valued the company of those to whom she could come striding disheveled from the nursery in her dressing gown, and with joyful face show a yellow instead of a green stain on baby's napkin, and from whom she could hear reassuring words to the effect that baby was much better.

To such an extent had Natásha let herself go that the way she dressed and did her hair, her ill-chosen words, and her jealousy—she was jealous of Sónya, of the governess, and of every woman, pretty or plain—were habitual subjects of jest to those about her. The general opinion was that Pierre was under his wife's thumb, which was really true. From the very first days of their married life Natásha had announced her demands. Pierre was greatly surprised by his wife's view, to him a perfectly novel one, that every moment of his life belonged to her and to the family. His wife's demands astonished him, but they also flattered him, and he submitted to them.

Pierre's subjection consisted in the fact that he not only dared not flirt with, but dared not even speak smilingly to, any other woman; did not dare dine at the Club as a pastime, did not dare spend money on a whim, and did not dare absent himself for any length of time, except on business —in which his wife included his intellectual pursuits, which she did not in the least understand but to which she attributed great importance. To make up for this, at home Pierre had the right to regulate his life and that of the whole family exactly as he chose. At home Natásha placed herself in the position of a slave to her husband, and the whole household went on tiptoe when he was occupied—that is, was reading or writing in his study. Pierre had but to show a partiality for anything to get just what he liked done always. He had only to express a wish and Natásha would jump up and run to fulfill it.

The entire household was governed according to Pierre's supposed orders, that is, by his wishes which Natásha tried to guess. Their way of life and place of residence, their acquaintances and ties, Natásha's occupations, the children's upbringing, were all selected not merely with regard to Pierre's expressed wishes, but to what Natásha from the thoughts he

expressed in conversation supposed his wishes to be. And she deduced the essentials of his wishes quite correctly, and having once arrived at them clung to them tenaciously. When Pierre himself wanted to change his mind she would fight him with his own weapons.

Thus in a time of trouble ever memorable to him after the birth of their first child who was delicate, when they had to change the wet nurse three times and Natásha fell ill from despair, Pierre one day told her of Rousseau's view, with which he quite agreed, that to have a wet nurse is unnatural and harmful. When her next baby was born, despite the opposition of her mother, the doctors, and even of her husband himself—who were all vigorously opposed to her nursing her baby herself, a thing then unheard of and considered injurious—she insisted on having her own way, and after that nursed all her babies herself.

It very often happened that in a moment of irritation husband and wife would have a dispute, but long afterwards Pierre to his surprise and delight would find in his wife's ideas and actions the very thought against which she had argued, but divested of everything superfluous that in the excitement of the dispute he had added when expressing his opinion.

After seven years of marriage Pierre had the joyous and firm consciousness that he was not a bad man, and he felt this because he saw himself reflected in his wife. He felt the good and bad within himself inextricably mingled and overlapping. But only what was really good in him was reflected in his wife, all that was not quite good was rejected. And this was not the result of logical reasoning but was a direct and mysterious reflection.

Two MONTHS PREVIOUSLY when Pierre was already staying with the Rostóvs he had received a letter from Prince Theodore, asking him to come to Petersburg to confer on some important questions that were being discussed there by a society of which Pierre was one of the principal founders.

On reading that letter (she always read her husband's letters) Natásha herself suggested that he should go to Petersburg, though she would feel his absence very acutely. She attributed immense importance to all her husband's intellectual and abstract interests though she did not understand them, and she always dreaded being a hindrance to him in such matters. To Pierre's timid look of inquiry after reading the letter she replied by asking him to go, but to fix a definite date for his return. He was given four weeks' leave of absence.

Ever since that leave of absence had expired, more than a fortnight before, Natásha had been in a constant state of alarm, depression, and irritability.

Denísov, now a general on the retired list and much dissatisfied with the present state of affairs, had arrived during that fortnight. He looked at Natásha with sorrow and surprise as at a bad likeness of a person once dear. A dull, dejected look, random replies, and talk about the nursery was all he saw and heard from his former enchantress.

Natásha was sad and irritable all that time, especially when her mother, her brother, Sónya, or Countess Mary in their efforts to console her tried to excuse Pierre and suggested reasons for his delay in returning.

"It's all nonsense, all rubbish—those discussions which lead to nothing and all those idiotic societies!" Natásha declared of the very affairs in the immense importance of which she firmly believed.

And she would go to the nursery to nurse Pétya, her only boy. No one else could tell her anything so comforting or so reasonable as this little three-month-old creature when he lay at her breast and she was conscious of the movement of his lips and the snuffling of his little nose. That creature said: "You are angry, you are jealous, you would like to pay him out, you are afraid—but here am I! And I am he . . ." and that was unanswerable. It was more than true.

During that fortnight of anxiety Natásha resorted to the baby for comfort so often, and fussed over him so much, that she overfed him and he fell ill. She was terrified by his illness, and yet that was just what she needed. While attending to him she bore the anxiety about her husband more easily.

She was nursing her boy when the sound of Pierre's sleigh was heard at the front door, and the old nurse—knowing how to please her mistress— entered the room inaudibly but hurriedly and with a beaming face.

"Has he come?" Natásha asked quickly in a whisper, afraid to move lest she should rouse the dozing baby.

"He's come, ma'am," whispered the nurse.

The blood rushed to Natásha's face and her feet involuntarily moved, but she could not jump up and run out. The baby again opened his eyes and looked at her. "You're here?" he seemed to be saying, and again lazily smacked his lips.

Cautiously withdrawing her breast, Natásha rocked him a little, handed him to the nurse, and went with rapid steps toward the door. But at the door she stopped as if her conscience reproached her for having in her joy left the child too soon, and she glanced round. The nurse with raised elbows was lifting the infant over the rail of his cot.

"Go, ma'am! Don't worry, go!" she whispered, smiling, with the kind of familiarity that grows up between a nurse and her mistress.

Natásha ran with light footsteps to the anteroom.

Denísov, who had come out of the study into the dancing room with his pipe, now for the first time recognized the old Natásha. A flood of brilliant, joyful light poured from her transfigured face.

"He's come!" she exclaimed as she ran past, and Denísov felt that he too was delighted that Pierre, whom he did not much care for, had returned.

On reaching the vestibule Natásha saw a tall figure in a fur coat unwinding his scarf. "It's he! It's really he! He has come!" she said to herself, and rushing at him embraced him, pressed his head to her breast, and then pushed him back and gazed at his ruddy, happy face, covered with hoarfrost. "Yes, it is he, happy and contented. . . ."

Then all at once she remembered the tortures of suspense she had experienced for the last fortnight, and the joy that had lit up her face vanished; she frowned and overwhelmed Pierre with a torrent of reproaches and angry words.

"Yes, it's all very well for you. You are pleased, you've had a good time. . . . But what about me? You might at least have shown consideration for the children. I am nursing and my milk was spoiled. . . . Pétya was at death's door. But you were enjoying yourself. Yes, enjoying . . ."

Pierre knew he was not to blame, for he could not have come sooner; he knew this outburst was unseemly and would blow over in a minute or two; above all he knew that he himself was bright and happy. He wanted to smile but dared not even think of doing so. He made a piteous, frightened face and bent down.

"I could not, on my honor. But how is Pétya?"

"All right now. Come along! I wonder you're not ashamed! If only you could see what I was like without you, how I suffered!"

"You are well?"

"Come, come!" she said, not letting go of his arm. And they went to their rooms.

When Nicholas and his wife came to look for Pierre he was in the nursery holding his baby son, who was again awake, on his huge right palm and dandling him. A blissful bright smile was fixed on the baby's broad face with its toothless open mouth. The storm was long since over and there was bright, joyous sunshine on Natásha's face as she gazed tenderly at her husband and child.

"And have you talked everything well over with Prince Theodore?" she asked.

"Yes, capitally."

"You see, he holds it up." (She meant the baby's head.) "But how he did frighten me . . . You've seen the princess? Is it true she's in love with that . . ."

"Yes, just fancy . . ."

At that moment Nicholas and Countess Mary came in. Pierre with the baby on his hand stooped, kissed them, and replied to their inquiries. But in spite of much that was interesting and had to be discussed, the baby with the little cap on its unsteady head evidently absorbed all his attention.

"How sweet!" said Countess Mary, looking at and playing with the baby. "Now, Nicholas," she added, turning to her husband, "I can't understand how it is you don't see the charm of these delicious marvels."

"I don't and can't," replied Nicholas, looking coldly at the baby. "A lump of flesh. Come along, Pierre!"

"And yet he's such an affectionate father," said Countess Mary, vindicating her husband, "but only after they are a year old or so . . ."

"Now, Pierre nurses them splendidly," said Natásha. "He says his hand is just made for a baby's seat. Just look!"

"Only not for this . . ." Pierre suddenly exclaimed with a laugh, and shifting the baby he gave him to the nurse.

As in every large household, there were at Bald Hills several perfectly distinct worlds which merged into one harmonious whole, though each retained its own peculiarities and made concessions to the others. Every event, joyful or sad, that took place in that house was important to all these worlds, but each had its own special reasons to rejoice or grieve over that occurrence independently of the others.

For instance, Pierre's return was a joyful and important event and they all felt it to be so.

The servants—the most reliable judges of their masters because they judge not by their conversation or expressions of feeling but by their acts and way of life—were glad of Pierre's return because they knew that when he was there Count Nicholas would cease going every day to attend to the estate, and would be in better spirits and temper, and also because they would all receive handsome presents for the holidays.

The children and their governesses were glad of Pierre's return because no one else drew them into the social life of the household as he did. He alone could play on the clavichord that écossaise (his only piece) to which, as he said, all possible dances could be danced, and they felt sure he had brought presents for them all.

Young Nicholas, now a slim lad of fifteen, delicate and intelligent, with curly light-brown hair and beautiful eyes, was delighted because Uncle Pierre as he called him was the object of his rapturous and passionate affection. No one had instilled into him this love for Pierre whom he saw only occasionally. Countess Mary who had brought him up had done her

utmost to make him love her husband as she loved him, and little Nicholas did love his uncle, but loved him with just a shade of contempt. Pierre, however, he adored. He did not want to be an hussar or a Knight of St. George like his uncle Nicholas; he wanted to be learned, wise, and kind like Pierre. In Pierre's presence his face always shone with pleasure and he flushed and was breathless when Pierre spoke to him. He did not miss a single word he uttered, and would afterwards, with Dessalles or by himself, recall and reconsider the meaning of everything Pierre had said. Pierre's past life and his unhappiness prior to 1812 (of which young Nicholas had formed a vague poetic picture from some words he had overheard), his adventures in Moscow, his captivity, Platón Karatáev (of whom he had heard from Pierre), his love for Natásha (of whom the lad was also particularly fond), and especially Pierre's friendship with the father whom Nicholas could not remember—all this made Pierre in his eyes a hero and a saint.

From broken remarks about Natásha and his father, from the emotion with which Pierre spoke of that dead father, and from the careful, reverent tenderness with which Natásha spoke of him, the boy, who was only just beginning to guess what love is, derived the notion that his father had loved Natásha and when dying had left her to his friend. But the father whom the boy did not remember appeared to him a divinity who could not be pictured, and of whom he never thought without a swelling heart and tears of sadness and rapture. So the boy also was happy that Pierre had arrived.

The guests welcomed Pierre because he always helped to enliven and unite any company he was in.

The grown-up members of the family, not to mention his wife, were pleased to have back a friend whose presence made life run more smoothly and peacefully.

The old ladies were pleased with the presents he brought them, and especially that Natásha would now be herself again.

Pierre felt the different outlooks of these various worlds and made haste to satisfy all their expectations.

Though the most absent-minded and forgetful of men, Pierre, with the aid of a list his wife drew up, had now bought everything, not forgetting his mother- and brother-in-law's commissions, nor the dress material for a present to Belóva, nor toys for his wife's nephews. In the early days of his marriage it had seemed strange to him that his wife should expect him not to forget to procure all the things he undertook to buy, and he had been taken aback by her serious annoyance when on his first trip he forgot everything. But in time he grew used to this demand. Knowing that Na-

tásha asked nothing for herself, and gave him commissions for others only when he himself had offered to undertake them, he now found an unexpected and childlike pleasure in this purchase of presents for everyone in the house, and never forgot anything. If he now incurred Natásha's censure it was only for buying too many and too expensive things. To her other defects (as most people thought them, but which to Pierre were qualities) of untidiness and neglect of herself, she now added stinginess.

From the time that Pierre began life as a family man on a footing entailing heavy expenditure, he had noticed to his surprise that he spent only half as much as before, and that his affairs—which had been in disorder of late, chiefly because of his first wife's debts—had begun to improve.

Life was cheaper because it was circumscribed: that most expensive luxury, the kind of life that can be changed at any moment, was no longer his nor did he wish for it. He felt that his way of life had now been settled once for all till death and that to change it was not in his power, and so that way of life proved economical.

With a merry, smiling face Pierre was sorting his purchases.

"What do you think of this?" said he, unrolling a piece of stuff like a shopman.

Natásha, who was sitting opposite to him with her eldest daughter on her lap, turned her sparkling eyes swiftly from her husband to the things he showed her.

"That's for Belóva? Excellent!" She felt the quality of the material. "It was a ruble an arshín, I suppose?"

Pierre told her the price.

"Too dear!" Natásha remarked. "How pleased the children will be and Mamma too! Only you need not have bought me this," she added, unable to suppress a smile as she gazed admiringly at a gold comb set with pearls, of a kind then just coming into fashion.

"Adèle tempted me: she kept on telling me to buy it," returned Pierre.

"When am I to wear it?" and Natásha stuck it in her coil of hair. "When I take little Másha into society? Perhaps they will be fashionable again by then. Well, let's go now."

And collecting the presents they went first to the nursery and then to the old countess' rooms.

The countess was sitting with her companion Belóva, playing grandpatience as usual, when Pierre and Natásha came into the drawing room with parcels under their arms.

The countess was now over sixty, was quite gray, and wore a cap with a frill that surrounded her face. Her face had shriveled, her upper lip had sunk in, and her eyes were dim.

After the deaths of her son and husband in such rapid succession, she felt herself a being accidentally forgotten in this world and left without aim or object for her existence. She ate, drank, slept, or kept awake, but did not live. Life gave her no new impressions. She wanted nothing from life but tranquillity, and that tranquillity only death could give her. But until death came she had to go on living, that is, to use her vital forces. A peculiarity one sees in very young children and very old people was particularly evident in her. Her life had no external aims—only a need to exercise her various functions and inclinations was apparent. She had to eat, sleep, think, speak, weep, work, give vent to her anger, and so on, merely because she had a stomach, a brain, muscles, nerves, and a liver. She did these things not under any external impulse as people in the full vigor of life do, when behind the purpose for which they strive that of exercising their functions remains unnoticed. She talked only because she physically needed to exercise her tongue and lungs. She cried as a child does, because her nose had to be cleared, and so on. What for people in their full vigor is an aim was for her evidently merely a pretext.

Thus in the morning—especially if she had eaten anything rich the day before—she felt a need of being angry and would choose as the handiest pretext Belóva's deafness.

She would begin to say something to her in a low tone from the other end of the room.

"It seems a little warmer today, my dear," she would murmur.

And when Belóva replied: "Oh yes, they've come," she would mutter angrily: "O Lord! How stupid and deaf she is!"

Another pretext would be her snuff, which would seem too dry or too damp or not rubbed fine enough. After these fits of irritability her face would grow yellow, and her maids knew by infallible symptoms when Belóva would again be deaf, the snuff damp, and the countess' face yellow. Just as she needed to work off her spleen so she had sometimes to exercise her still-existing faculty of thinking—and the pretext for that was a game of patience. When she needed to cry, the deceased count would be the pretext. When she wanted to be agitated, Nicholas and his health would be the pretext, and when she felt a need to speak spitefully, the pretext would be Countess Mary. When her vocal organs needed exercise, which was usually toward seven o'clock when she had had an after-dinner rest in a darkened room, the pretext would be the retelling of the same stories over and over again to the same audience.

The old lady's condition was understood by the whole household though no one ever spoke of it, and they all made every possible effort to satisfy her needs. Only by a rare glance exchanged with a sad smile be-

tween Nicholas, Pierre, Natásha, and Countess Mary was the common understanding of her condition expressed.

But those glances expressed something more: they said that she had played her part in life, that what they now saw was not her whole self, that we must all become like her, and that they were glad to yield to her, to restrain themselves for this once precious being formerly as full of life as themselves, but now so much to be pitied. "*Memento mori,*" said these glances.

Only the really heartless, the stupid ones of that household, and the little children failed to understand this and avoided her.

WHEN PIERRE and his wife entered the drawing room the countess was in one of her customary states in which she needed the mental exertion of playing patience, and so—though by force of habit she greeted him with the words she always used when Pierre or her son returned after an absence: "High time, my dear, high time! We were all weary of waiting for you. Well, thank God!" and received her presents with another customary remark: "It's not the gift that's precious, my dear, but that you give it to me, an old woman . . ."—yet it was evident that she was not pleased by Pierre's arrival at that moment when it diverted her attention from the unfinished game.

She finished her game of patience and only then examined the presents. They consisted of a box for cards, of splendid workmanship, a bright-blue Sèvres tea cup with shepherdesses depicted on it and with a lid, and a gold snuffbox with the count's portrait on the lid which Pierre had had done by a miniaturist in Petersburg. The countess had long wished for such a box, but as she did not want to cry just then she glanced indifferently at the portrait and gave her attention chiefly to the box for cards.

"Thank you, my dear, you have cheered me up," said she as she always did. "But best of all you have brought yourself back—for I never saw anything like it, you ought to give your wife a scolding! What are we to do with her? She is like a mad woman when you are away. Doesn't see anything, doesn't remember anything," she went on, repeating her usual phrases. "Look, Anna Timoféevna," she added to her companion, "see what a box for cards my son has brought us!"

Belóva admired the presents and was delighted with her dress material.

Though Pierre, Natásha, Nicholas, Countess Mary, and Denísov had much to talk about that they could not discuss before the old countess— not that anything was hidden from her, but because she had dropped so far behindhand in many things that had they begun to converse in her presence they would have had to answer inopportune questions and to

repeat what they had already told her many times: that so-and-so was dead and so-and-so was married, which she would again be unable to remember —yet they sat at tea round the samovar in the drawing room from habit, and Pierre answered the countess' questions as to whether Prince Vasíli had aged and whether Countess Mary Alexéevna had sent greetings and still thought of them, and other matters that interested no one and to which she herself was indifferent.

Conversation of this kind, interesting to no one yet unavoidable, continued all through teatime. All the grown-up members of the family were assembled near the round tea table at which Sónya presided beside the samovar. The children with their tutors and governesses had had tea and their voices were audible from the next room. At tea all sat in their accustomed places: Nicholas beside the stove at a small table where his tea was handed to him; Mílka, the old gray borzoi bitch (daughter of the first Mílka), with a quite gray face and large black eyes that seemed more prominent than ever, lay on the armchair beside him; Denísov, whose curly hair, mustache, and whiskers had turned half gray, sat beside Countess Mary with his general's tunic unbuttoned; Pierre sat between his wife and the old countess. He spoke of what he knew might interest the old lady and that she could understand. He told her of external social events and of the people who had formed the circle of her contemporaries and had once been a real, living, and distinct group, but who were now for the most part scattered about the world and like herself were garnering the last ears of the harvests they had sown in earlier years. But to the old countess those contemporaries of hers seemed to be the only serious and real society. Natásha saw by Pierre's animation that his visit had been interesting and that he had much to tell them but dare not say it before the old countess. Denísov, not being a member of the family, did not understand Pierre's caution and being, as a malcontent, much interested in what was occurring in Petersburg, kept urging Pierre to tell them about what had happened in the Semënovsk regiment, then about Arakchéev,* and then about the Bible Society.[2] Once or twice Pierre was carried away and be-

* *Arakchéev has been mentioned previously on p. 278. See also Book Six, Chapter 2.*—A.M.

[2] *A Russian Bible Society, mentioned in a previous footnote (p. 1253), was founded by A. N. Golítsyn in December, 1812, and had political influence. It produced the first translations of the Bible in the Russian vernacular, but when Photius secured the dismissal of Golítsyn from his posts as Minister of Education and President of the Bible Society, that Society withered, and was finally suppressed by Nicholas I in 1826.*

In 1831 an Evangelical and quite nonpolitical Russian Bible Society was

gan to speak of these things, but Nicholas and Natásha always brought him back to the health of Prince Iván and Countess Mary Alexéevna.

"Well, and all this idiocy—Gossner * and Tatáwinova?" [2] Denísov asked. "Is that weally still going on?"

"Going on?" Pierre exclaimed. "Why more than ever! The Bible Society is the whole government now!"

"What is that, *mon cher ami?*" asked the countess, who had finished her tea and evidently needed a pretext for being angry after her meal. "What are you saying about the government? I don't understand."

"Well, you know, *Maman,*" Nicholas interposed, knowing how to translate things into his mother's language, "Prince Alexander Golítsyn has founded a society and in consequence has great influence, they say."

"Arakchéev and Golítsyn," incautiously remarked Pierre, "are now the whole government! And what a government! They see treason everywhere and are afraid of everything."

"Well, and how is Prince Alexander to blame? He is a most estimable man. I used to meet him at Mary Antónovna's," said the countess in an offended tone; and still more offended that they all remained silent, she went on: "Nowadays everyone finds fault. A Gospel Society! Well, and what harm is there in that?" and she rose (everybody else got up too) and with a severe expression sailed back to her table in the sitting room.

The melancholy silence that followed was broken by the sounds of the children's voices and laughter from the next room. Evidently some jolly excitement was going on there.

sanctioned, which continued to operate till the Revolution of 1917 placed a government in power that is averse to anything of a religious nature.—A.M.

* Johann Gossner (1773-1858) was a Catholic priest and mystic around whom a pietist group formed in Munich. After being compelled to leave that town he obtained the post of Director of the Bible Society in Petersburg (1820-4) and there wrote his book Geist des Lebens und der Lehrer Jesu, which began the break-up of the Bible Society. The book was condemned to be burned and Gossner was expelled from Russia.—A.M.

[2] Ekaterína Filíppovna Tatárinova (née Buxhöwden)—1783-1856—founded in Petersburg, in 1817, a mystical sect, the "Spiritual Union," in which, besides faith healing and divination, they adopted the practice, borrowed from the Skoptsí, of inducing ecstasy and a spirit of prophecy by violent whirling dances. Tatárinova was a remarkable person who had some influence with Alexander I, and she managed to maintain her "Union" even after the accession of Nicholas I. It did not break up until 1837, when Tatárinova was dispatched, under observation, to an out-of-the-way nunnery.—A.M.

"Finished, finished!" little Natásha's gleeful yell rose above them all.

Pierre exchanged glances with Countess Mary and Nicholas (Natásha he never lost sight of) and smiled happily.

"That's delightful music!" said he.

"It means that Anna Makárovna has finished her stocking," said Countess Mary.

"Oh, I'll go and see," said Pierre, jumping up. "You know," he added, stopping at the door, "why I'm especially fond of that music? It is always the first thing that tells me all is well. When I was driving here today, the nearer I got to the house the more anxious I grew. As I entered the anteroom I heard Andrúsha's peals of laughter and that meant that all was well."

"I know! I know that feeling," said Nicholas. "But I mustn't go there—those stockings are to be a surprise for me."

Pierre went to the children, and the shouting and laughter grew still louder.

"Come, Anna Makárovna," Pierre's voice was heard saying, "come here into the middle of the room and at the word of command, 'One, two,' and when I say 'three' . . . You stand here, and you in my arms—well now! One, two! . . ." said Pierre, and a silence followed: "three!"—and a rapturously breathless cry of children's voices filled the room. "Two, two!" they shouted.

This meant two stockings, which by a secret process known only to herself Anna Makárovna used to knit at the same time on the same needles, and which, when they were ready, she always triumphantly drew, one out of the other, in the children's presence.

Soon after this the children came in to say good night. They kissed everyone, the tutors and governesses made their bows, and they went out. Only young Nicholas and his tutor remained. Dessalles whispered to the boy to come downstairs.

"No, Monsieur Dessalles, I will ask my aunt to let me stay," replied Nicholas Bolkónski also in a whisper.

"Ma tante, please let me stay," said he, going up to his aunt.

His face expressed entreaty, agitation, and ecstasy. Countess Mary glanced at him and turned to Pierre.

"When you are here he can't tear himself away," she said.

"I will bring him to you directly, Monsieur Dessalles. Good night!" said Pierre, giving his hand to the Swiss tutor, and he turned to young Nicholas with a smile. "You and I haven't seen anything of one another

yet. . . . How like he is growing, Mary!" he added, addressing Countess Mary.

"Like my father?" asked the boy, flushing crimson and looking up at Pierre with bright, ecstatic eyes.

Pierre nodded, and went on with what he had been saying when the children had interrupted. Countess Mary sat down doing woolwork; Natásha did not take her eyes off her husband. Nicholas and Denísov rose, asked for their pipes, smoked, went to fetch more tea from Sónya—who sat weary but resolute at the samovar—and questioned Pierre. The curlyheaded, delicate boy sat with shining eyes unnoticed in a corner, starting every now and then and muttering something to himself, and evidently experiencing a new and powerful emotion as he turned his curly head, with his thin neck exposed by his turn-down collar, toward the place where Pierre sat.

The conversation turned on the contemporary gossip about those in power, in which most people see the chief interest of home politics. Denísov, dissatisfied with the government on account of his own disappointments in the service, heard with pleasure of the things done in Petersburg which seemed to him stupid, and made forcible and sharp comments on what Pierre told them.

"One used to have to be a German—now one must dance with Tatáwinova and Madame Kwüdener,* and wead Ecka'tshausen and the bwethwen. Oh, they should let that fine fellow Bonaparte loose—he'd knock all this nonsense out of them! Fancy giving the command of the Seménov wegiment to a fellow like that Schwa'tz!" he cried.

Nicholas, though free from Denísov's readiness to find fault with everything, also thought that discussion of the government was a very serious and weighty matter, and the fact that A had been appointed Minister of This and B Governor General of That, and that the Emperor had said so-and-so and this minister so-and-so, seemed to him very important. And so he thought it necessary to take an interest in these things and to question Pierre. The questions put by these two kept the conversation from changing its ordinary character of gossip about the higher government circles.

* *Baroness Juliane Krüdener (1766-1824) was born in Riga. She abandoned fashionable society in 1807 and devoted herself to mysticism, convinced that she was destined to bring the world to a new birth. She was active in Baden in 1815 and made the acquaintance of Alexander I on whom she had some influence. In 1817 she appeared in Russia, but no longer retained her influence with him.—A.M.*

But Natásha, knowing all her husband's ways and ideas, saw that he had long been wishing but had been unable to divert the conversation to another channel and express his own deeply felt idea for the sake of which he had gone to Petersburg to consult with his new friend Prince Theodore, and she helped him by asking how his affairs with Prince Theodore had gone.*

"What was it about?" asked Nicholas.

"Always the same thing," said Pierre, looking round at his listeners. "Everybody sees that things are going so badly that they cannot be allowed to go on so and that it is the duty of all decent men to counteract it as far as they can."

"What can decent men do?" Nicholas inquired, frowning slightly. "What can be done?"

"Why, this . . ."

"Come into my study," said Nicholas.

Natásha, who had long expected to be fetched to nurse her baby, now heard the nurse calling her and went to the nursery. Countess Mary followed her. The men went into the study and little Nicholas Bolkónski followed them unnoticed by his uncle and sat down at the writing table in a shady corner by the window.

"Well, what would you do?" asked Denísov.

"Always some fantastic schemes," said Nicholas.

"Why this," began Pierre, not sitting down but pacing the room, sometimes stopping short, gesticulating, and lisping: "the position in Petersburg is this: the Emperor does not look into anything. He has abandoned himself altogether to this mysticism" (Pierre could not tolerate mysticism in anyone now). "He seeks only for peace, and only these people *sans foi*

* *The aims Pierre mentions as those of Prince Theodore's circle are very much those with which many of the Decembrists began their conspiracy. Tolstóy had planned a novel dealing with the Decembrist movement before he began* War *and* Peace, *but studying the roots from which that movement sprang took him back to the year 1805, and he saw that it would be better to deal with that earlier period.* War and Peace *extends to the time when the Decembrist conspiracy was taking shape, and Tolstóy hints at it in this chapter. The careful description of the Russian Masonic movement in an earlier part of the novel was an outcome of his study of the Freemasons as an organization intimately connected with the Decembrists. After finishing* War and Peace *and* Anna Karénina *Tolstóy returned to that subject, and even wrote some fragmentary chapters, but he eventually abandoned the work, under circumstances mentioned on p. 464 of Volume I of the Oxford Press* Life of Tolstóy.—A.M.*

ni loi [without faith or law] can give it him—people who recklessly hack at and strangle everything—Magnítski, Arakchéev, and *tutti quanti.* . . . You will agree that if you did not look after your estates yourself but only wanted a quiet life, the harsher your steward was the more readily your object might be attained," he said to Nicholas.

"Well, what does that lead up to?" said Nicholas.

"Well, everything is going to ruin! Robbery in the law courts, in the army nothing but flogging, drilling, and Military Settlements;* the people are tortured, enlightenment is suppressed. All that is young and honest is crushed! Everyone sees that this cannot go on. Everything is strained to such a degree that it will certainly break," said Pierre (as those who examine the actions of any government have always said since governments began).[2] "I told them just one thing in Petersburg."

"Told whom?"

"Well, you know whom," said Pierre, with a meaning glance from under his brows. "Prince Theodore and all those. To encourage culture and philanthropy is all very well of course. The aim is excellent but in the present circumstances something else is needed."

At that moment Nicholas noticed the presence of his nephew. His face darkened and he went up to the boy.

"Why are you here?"

"Why? Let him be," said Pierre, taking Nicholas by the arm and continuing. "That is not enough, I told them. Something else is needed. When you stand expecting the overstrained string to snap at any moment, when everyone is expecting the inevitable catastrophe, as many as possible must join hands as closely as they can to withstand the general calamity. Everything that is young and strong is being enticed away and depraved. One is lured by women, another by honors, a third by ambition or money, and they go over to that camp. No independent men, such as

* *Arakchéev introduced these as a means of making the army partly self-supporting. Besides being under military discipline, the soldiers had to live in settlements and cultivate the land around them. This kind of slavery, separated from their families, working under military discipline and exposed to harsh punishment, was one of the most detested features of his administration.*—A.M.

[2] *The antigovernmental trend of this passage is worth noting, for it indicates a fundamental connection between Tolstóy's earlier and later views. He presented the antigovernmental conclusions he put forward after 1880 as unavoidable deductions from his interpretation of Christ's teaching. They were, however, much in line with feelings he had expressed long before he arrived at that interpretation.*—A.M.

you or I, are left. What I say is widen the scope of our society, let the *mot d'ordre* be not virtue alone but independence and action as well!"

Nicholas, who had left his nephew, irritably pushed up an armchair, sat down in it, and listened to Pierre, coughing discontentedly and frowning more and more.

"But action with what aim?" he cried. "And what position will you adopt toward the government?"

"Why, the position of assistants. The society need not be secret if the government allows it. Not merely is it not hostile to government, but it is a society of true conservatives—a society of gentlemen in the full meaning of that word. It is only to prevent some Pugachëv or other from killing my children and yours,* and Arakchéev from sending me off to some Military Settlement. We join hands only for the public welfare and the general safety."

"Yes, but it's a secret society and therefore a hostile and harmful one which can only cause harm."

"Why? Did the Tugendbund which saved Europe" [2] (they did not then venture to suggest that Russia had saved Europe) "do any harm? The Tugendbund is an alliance of virtue: it is love, mutual help . . . it is what Christ preached on the Cross."

Natásha, who had come in during the conversation, looked joyfully at her husband. It was not what he was saying that pleased her—that did not even interest her, for it seemed to her that it was all extremely simple and that she had known it a long time (it seemed so to her because she knew that it sprang from Pierre's whole soul), but it was his animated and enthusiastic appearance that made her glad.

The boy with the thin neck stretching out from the turn-down collar —whom everyone had forgotten—gazed at Pierre with even greater and more rapturous joy. Every word of Pierre's burned into his heart, and with a nervous movement of his fingers he unconsciously broke the sealing wax and quill pens his hands came upon on his uncle's table.

* *Pugachëv was the Cossack leader of a great peasant rising in Catherine the Great's time. After achieving considerable success and capturing several towns, he was taken and executed in 1775.*—A.M.

[2] *The Tugendbund (League of Virtue) was a German association founded in 1808 with the acknowledged purpose of cultivating patriotism, reorganizing the army, and encouraging education, and with the secret aim of throwing off the French yoke. Dissolved on Napoleon's demand in 1809, it continued to exist secretly and exerted great influence in 1812. It was suspected of having revolutionary tendencies and was in very bad odor with the Russian government at the time of the Holy Alliance.*—A.M.

"It is not at all what you suppose; but that is what the German Tugendbund was, and what I am proposing."

"No, my fwiend! The Tugendbund is all vewy well for the sausage eaters, but I don't understand it and can't even pwonounce it," interposed Denísov in a loud and resolute voice. "I agwee that evewything here is wotten and howwible, but the *Tugendbund* I don't understand. If we're not satisfied, let us have a *bunt* of our own.* That's all wight. *Je suis votte homme* [I'm your man]!"

Pierre smiled, Natásha began to laugh, but Nicholas knitted his brows still more and began proving to Pierre that there was no prospect of any great change and that all the danger he spoke of existed only in his imagination. Pierre maintained the contrary, and as his mental faculties were greater and more resourceful, Nicholas felt himself cornered. This made him still angrier, for he was fully convinced, not by reasoning but by something within him stronger than reason, of the justice of his opinion.

"I will tell you this," he said, rising and trying with nervously twitching fingers to prop up his pipe in a corner, but finally abandoning the attempt. "I can't prove it to you. You say that everything here is rotten and that an overthrow is coming: I don't see it. But you also say that our oath of allegiance is a conditional matter, and to that I reply: 'You are my best friend, as you know, but if you formed a secret society and began working against the government—be it what it may—I know it is my duty to obey the government. And if Arakchéev ordered me to lead a squadron against you and cut you down, I should not hesitate an instant, but should do it.' And you may argue about that as you like!"

An awkward silence followed these words. Natásha was the first to speak, defending her husband and attacking her brother. Her defense was weak and inapt but she attained her object. The conversation was resumed, and no longer in the unpleasantly hostile tone of Nicholas' last remark.

When they all got up to go in to supper, little Nicholas Bolkónski went up to Pierre, pale and with shining, radiant eyes.

"Uncle Pierre, you . . . no . . . If Papa were alive . . . would he agree with you?" he asked.

And Pierre suddenly realized what a special, independent, complex, and powerful process of thought and feeling must have been going on in this boy during that conversation, and remembering all he had said he re-

* *Denísov makes play with the similarity of the German word* Bund, *a union, and the Russian word* bunt, *a riot.*—A.M.

gretted that the lad should have heard him. He had, however, to give him an answer.

"Yes, I think so," he said reluctantly, and left the study.

The lad looked down and seemed now for the first time to notice what he had done to the things on the table. He flushed and went up to Nicholas.

"Uncle, forgive me, I did that . . . unintentionally," he said, pointing to the broken sealing wax and pens.

Nicholas started angrily.

"All right, all right," he said, throwing the bits under the table.

And evidently suppressing his vexation with difficulty, he turned away from the boy.

"You ought not to have been here at all," he said.

4. The two married couples and their mutual relations. Natásha's jealousy. Young Nicholas Bol-kónski's aspirations

THE CONVERSATION at supper was not about politics or societies, but turned on the subject Nicholas liked best—recollections of 1812. Denísov started these and Pierre was particularly agreeable and amusing about them. The family separated on the most friendly terms.

After supper Nicholas, having undressed in his study and given instructions to the steward who had been waiting for him, went to the bedroom in his dressing gown, where he found his wife still at her table, writing.

"What are you writing, Mary?" Nicholas asked.

Countess Mary blushed. She was afraid that what she was writing would not be understood or approved by her husband.

She had wanted to conceal what she was writing from him, but at the same time was glad he had surprised her at it and that she would now have to tell him.

"A diary, Nicholas," she replied, handing him a blue exercise book filled with her firm, bold writing.

"A diary?" Nicholas repeated with a shade of irony, and he took up the book.

It was in French.

"December 4. Today when Andrúsha" (her eldest boy) "woke up he did not wish to dress and Mademoiselle Louise sent for me. He was naughty and obstinate. I tried threats, but he only grew angrier. Then I took the matter in hand: I left him alone and began with nurse's help to get the other children up, telling him that I did not love him. For a

long time he was silent, as if astonished, then he jumped out of bed, ran to me in his shirt, and sobbed so that I could not calm him for a long time. It was plain that what troubled him most was that he had grieved me. Afterwards in the evening when I gave him his ticket, he again began crying piteously and kissing me. One can do anything with him by tenderness." *

"What is a 'ticket'?" Nicholas inquired.

"I have begun giving the elder ones marks every evening, showing how they have behaved."

Nicholas looked into the radiant eyes that were gazing at him, and continued to turn over the pages and read. In the diary was set down everything in the children's lives that seemed noteworthy to their mother as showing their characters or suggesting general reflections on educational methods. They were for the most part quite insignificant trifles, but did not seem so to the mother or to the father either, now that he read this diary about his children for the first time.

Under the date "5" was entered:

"Mítya was naughty at table. Papa said he was to have no pudding. He had none, but looked so unhappily and greedily at the others while they were eating! I think that punishment by depriving children of sweets only develops their greediness. Must tell Nicholas this."

Nicholas put down the book and looked at his wife. The radiant eyes gazed at him questioningly: would he approve or disapprove of her diary? There could be no doubt not only of his approval but also of his admiration for his wife.

Perhaps it need not be done so pedantically, thought Nicholas, or even done at all, but this untiring, continual spiritual effort of which the sole aim was the children's moral welfare delighted him. Had Nicholas been able to analyze his feelings he would have found that his steady, tender, and proud love of his wife rested on his feeling of wonder at her spirituality and at the lofty moral world, almost beyond his reach, in which she had her being.

He was proud of her intelligence and goodness, recognized his own insignificance beside her in the spiritual world, and rejoiced all the more that she with such a soul not only belonged to him but was part of himself.

"I quite, quite approve, my dearest!" said he with a significant look, and after a short pause he added: "And I behaved badly today. You weren't in the study. We began disputing—Pierre and I—and I lost my temper. But he is impossible: such a child! I don't know what would become of

* These quotations from Countess Mary's diary very closely resemble similar notes written by Tolstóy's mother about her children.—A.M.

him if Natásha didn't keep him in hand. . . . Have you any idea why he went to Petersburg? They have formed . . ."

"Yes, I know," said Countess Mary. "Natásha told me."

"Well, then, you know," Nicholas went on, growing hot at the mere recollection of their discussion, "he wanted to convince me that it is every honest man's duty to go against the government, and that the oath of allegiance and duty . . . I am sorry you weren't there. They all fell on me—Denísov and Natásha . . . Natásha is absurd. How she rules over him! And yet there need only be a discussion and she has no words of her own but only repeats his sayings . . ." added Nicholas, yielding to that irresistible inclination which tempts us to judge those nearest and dearest to us. He forgot that what he was saying about Natásha could have been applied word for word to himself in relation to his wife.

"Yes, I have noticed that," said Countess Mary.

"When I told him that duty and the oath were above everything, he started proving goodness knows what! A pity you were not there—what would you have said?"

"As I see it you were quite right, and I told Natásha so. Pierre says everybody is suffering, tortured, and being corrupted, and that it is our duty to help our neighbor. Of course he is right there," said Countess Mary, "but he forgets that we have other duties nearer to us, duties indicated to us by God Himself, and that though we might expose ourselves to risks we must not risk our children."

"Yes, that's it! That's just what I said to him," put in Nicholas, who fancied he really had said it. "But they insisted on their own view: love of one's neighbor and Christianity—and all this in the presence of young Nicholas, who had gone into my study and broke all my things."

"Ah, Nicholas, do you know I am often troubled about little Nicholas," said Countess Mary. "He is such an exceptional boy. I am afraid I neglect him in favor of my own: we all have children and relations while he has no one. He is constantly alone with his thoughts."

"Well, I don't think you need reproach yourself on his account. All that the fondest mother could do for her son you have done and are doing for him, and of course I am glad of it. He is a fine lad, a fine lad! This evening he listened to Pierre in a sort of trance, and fancy—as we were going in to supper I looked and he had broken everything on my table to bits, and he told me of it himself at once! I never knew him to tell an untruth. A fine lad, a fine lad!" repeated Nicholas, who at heart was not fond of Nicholas Bolkónski but was always anxious to recognize that he was a fine lad.

"Still, I am not the same as his own mother," said Countess Mary.

"I feel I am not the same and it troubles me. A wonderful boy, but I am dreadfully afraid for him. It would be good for him to have companions."

"Well it won't be for long. Next summer I'll take him to Petersburg," said Nicholas. "Yes, Pierre always was a dreamer and always will be," he continued, returning to the talk in the study which had evidently disturbed him. "Well, what business is it of mine what goes on there— whether Arakchéev is bad, and all that? What business was it of mine when I married and was so deep in debt that I was threatened with prison, and had a mother who could not see or understand it? And then there are you and the children and our affairs. Is it for my own pleasure that I am at the farm or in the office from morning to night? No, but I know I must work to comfort my mother, to repay you, and not to leave the children such beggars as I was."

Countess Mary wanted to tell him that man does not live by bread alone and that he attached too much importance to these matters. But she knew she must not say this and that it would be useless to do so. She only took his hand and kissed it. He took this as a sign of approval and a confirmation of his thoughts, and after a few minutes' reflection continued to think aloud.

"You know, Mary, today Elias Mitrofánych" (this was his overseer) "came back from the Tambóv estate and told me they are already offering eighty thousand rubles for the forest."

And with an eager face Nicholas began to speak of the possibility of repurchasing Otrádnoe before long, and added: "Another ten years of life and I shall leave the children . . . in an excellent position."

Countess Mary listened to her husband and understood all that he told her. She knew that when he thought aloud in this way he would sometimes ask her what he had been saying, and be vexed if he noticed that she had been thinking about something else. But she had to force herself to attend, for what he was saying did not interest her at all. She looked at him and did not think, but felt, about something different. She felt a submissive tender love for this man who would never understand all that she understood, and this seemed to make her love for him still stronger and added a touch of passionate tenderness. Besides this feeling which absorbed her altogether and hindered her from following the details of her husband's plans, thoughts that had no connection with what he was saying flitted through her mind. She thought of her nephew. Her husband's account of the boy's agitation while Pierre was speaking struck her forcibly, and various traits of his gentle, sensitive character recurred to her mind; and while thinking of her nephew she thought also of her own children. She did not compare them with him, but compared her feeling

for them with her feeling for him, and felt with regret that there was something lacking in her feeling for young Nicholas.

Sometimes it seemed to her that this difference arose from the difference in their ages, but she felt herself to blame toward him and promised in her heart to do better and to accomplish the impossible—in this life to love her husband, her children, little Nicholas, and all her neighbors, as Christ loved mankind. Countess Mary's soul always strove toward the infinite, the eternal, and the absolute, and could therefore never be at peace.* A stern expression of the lofty, secret suffering of a soul burdened by the body appeared on her face. Nicholas gazed at her. "O God! What will become of us if she dies, as I always fear when her face is like that?" thought he, and placing himself before the icon he began to say his evening prayers.

NATÁSHA AND PIERRE, left alone, also began to talk as only a husband and wife can talk, that is, with extraordinary clearness and rapidity, understanding and expressing each other's thoughts in ways contrary to all rules of logic, without premises, deductions, or conclusions, and in a quite peculiar way. Natásha was so used to this kind of talk with her husband that for her it was the surest sign of something being wrong between them if Pierre followed a line of logical reasoning. When he began proving anything, or talking argumentatively and calmly and she, led on by his example, began to do the same, she knew that they were on the verge of a quarrel.

From the moment they were alone and Natásha came up to him with wide-open happy eyes, and quickly seizing his head pressed it to her bosom, saying: "Now you are all mine, mine! You won't escape!"—from that moment this conversation began, contrary to all the laws of logic and contrary to them because quite different subjects were talked about at one and the same time. This simultaneous discussion of many topics did not prevent a clear understanding but on the contrary was the surest sign that they fully understood one another.

Just as in a dream when all is uncertain, unreasoning, and contradictory, except the feeling that guides the dream, so in this intercourse contrary to all laws of reason, the words themselves were not consecutive and clear but only the feeling that prompted them.

Natásha spoke to Pierre about her brother's life and doings, of how she had suffered and lacked life during his own absence, and of how she was

* *What Tolstóy here says of Countess Mary was very true of himself, and is an explanation of some of the aims and endeavors that have perplexed some readers of his later works.*—A.M.

fonder than ever of Mary, and how Mary was in every way better than herself. In saying this Natásha was sincere in acknowledging Mary's superiority, but at the same time by saying it she made a demand on Pierre that he should, all the same, prefer her to Mary and to all other women, and that now, especially after having seen many women in Petersburg, he should tell her so afresh.

Pierre, answering Natásha's words, told her how intolerable it had been for him to meet ladies at dinners and balls in Petersburg.

"I have quite lost the knack of talking to ladies," he said. "It was simply dull. Besides, I was very busy."

Natásha looked intently at him and went on:

"Mary is so splendid," she said. "How she understands children! It is as if she saw straight into their souls. Yesterday, for instance, Mítya was naughty . . ."

"How like his father he is," Pierre interjected.

Natásha knew why he mentioned Mítya's likeness to Nicholas: the recollection of his dispute with his brother-in-law was unpleasant and he wanted to know what Natásha thought of it.

"Nicholas has the weakness of never agreeing with anything not generally accepted. But I understand that you value what opens up a fresh line," said she, repeating words Pierre had once uttered.

"No, the chief point is that to Nicholas ideas and discussions are an amusement—almost a pastime," said Pierre. "For instance, he is collecting a library and has made it a rule not to buy a new book till he has read what he had already bought—Sismondi and Rousseau and Montesquieu," he added with a smile. "You know how much I . . ." he began to soften down what he had said; but Natásha interrupted him to show that this was unnecessary.

"So you say ideas are an amusement to him. . . ."

"Yes, and for me nothing else is serious. All the time in Petersburg I saw everyone as in a dream. When I am taken up by a thought, all else is mere amusement."

"Ah, I'm so sorry I wasn't there when you met the children," said Natásha. "Which was most delighted? Lisa, I'm sure."

"Yes," Pierre replied, and went on with what was in his mind. "Nicholas says we ought not to think. But I can't help it. Besides, when I was in Petersburg I felt (I can say this to you) that the whole affair would go to pieces without me—everyone was pulling his own way. But I succeeded in uniting them all; and then my idea is so clear and simple. You see, I don't say that we ought to oppose this and that. We may be mistaken. What I say is: 'Join hands, you who love the right, and let there be but

one banner—that of active virtue.' Prince Sergéy is a fine fellow and clever."

Natásha would have had no doubt as to the greatness of Pierre's idea, but one thing disconcerted her. "Can a man so important and necessary to society be also my husband? How did this happen?" She wished to express this doubt to him. "Now who could decide whether he is really cleverer than all the others?" she asked herself, and passed in review all those whom Pierre most respected. Judging by what he had said there was no one he had respected so highly as Platón Karatáev.

"Do you know what I am thinking about?" she asked. "About Platón Karatáev. Would he have approved of you now, do you think?"

Pierre was not at all surprised at this question. He understood his wife's line of thought.

"Platón Karatáev?" he repeated, and pondered, evidently sincerely trying to imagine Karatáev's opinion on the subject. "He would not have understood . . . yet perhaps he would."

"I love you awfully!" Natásha suddenly said. "Awfully, awfully!"

"No, he would not have approved," said Pierre, after reflection. "What he would have approved of is our family life. He was always so anxious to find seemliness, happiness, and peace in everything, and I should have been proud to let him see us. There now—you talk of my absence, but you wouldn't believe what a special feeling I have for you after a separation. . . ."

"Yes, I should think . . ." Natásha began.

"No, it's not that. I never leave off loving you. And one couldn't love more, but this is something special. . . . Yes, of course—" he did not finish because their eyes meeting said the rest.

"What nonsense it is," Natásha suddenly exclaimed, "about honeymoons, and that the greatest happiness is at first! On the contrary, now is the best of all. If only you did not go away! Do you remember how we quarreled? And it was always my fault. Always mine. And what we quarreled about—I don't even remember!"

"Always about the same thing," said Pierre with a smile. "Jealo . . ."

"Don't say it! I can't bear it!" Natásha cried, and her eyes glittered coldly and vindictively. "Did you see her?" * she added, after a pause.

"No, and if I had I shouldn't have recognized her."

They were silent for a while.

"Oh, do you know? While you were talking in the study I was looking

* *Unreasonable jealousy of the kind here indicated was always a cause of distress between Tolstóy and his wife. His story* The Devil *suggests an explanation of the question: "Did you see her?"*—A.M.

at you," Natásha began, evidently anxious to disperse the cloud that had come over them. "You are as like him as two peas—like the boy." (She meant her little son.) "Oh, it's time to go to him. . . . The milk's come. . . . But I'm sorry to leave you."

They were silent for a few seconds. Then suddenly turning to one another at the same time they both began to speak. Pierre began with self-satisfaction and enthusiasm, Natásha with a quiet, happy smile. Having interrupted one another they both stopped to let the other continue.

"No. What did you say? Go on, go on."

"No, you go on, I was talking nonsense," said Natásha.

Pierre finished what he had begun. It was the sequel to his complacent reflections on his success in Petersburg. At that moment it seemed to him that he was chosen to give a new direction to the whole of Russian society and to the whole world.

"I only wished to say that ideas that have great results are always simple ones. My whole idea is that if vicious people are united and constitute a power, then honest folk must do the same. Now that's simple enough."

"Yes."

"And what were you going to say?"

"I? Only nonsense."

"But all the same?"

"Oh nothing, only a trifle," said Natásha, smiling still more brightly. "I only wanted to tell you about Pétya: today nurse was coming to take him from me, and he laughed, shut his eyes, and clung to me. I'm sure he thought he was hiding. Awfully sweet! There, now he's crying. Well, good-by!" and she left the room.

Meanwhile downstairs in young Nicholas Bolkónski's bedroom a little lamp was burning as usual. (The boy was afraid of the dark and they could not cure him of it.) Dessalles slept propped up on four pillows and his Roman nose emitted sounds of rhythmic snoring. Little Nicholas, who had just waked up in a cold perspiration, sat up in bed and gazed before him with wide-open eyes. He had awaked from a terrible dream. He had dreamed that he and Uncle Pierre, wearing helmets such as were depicted in his Plutarch, were leading a huge army. The army was made up of white slanting lines that filled the air like the cobwebs that float about in autumn and which Dessalles called *les fils de la Vièrge*. In front was Glory, which was similar to those threads but rather thicker. He and Pierre were borne along lightly and joyously, nearer and nearer to their goal. Suddenly the threads that moved them began to slacken and become en-

tangled and it grew difficult to move. And Uncle Nicholas stood before them in a stern and threatening attitude.

"Have you done this?" he said, pointing to some broken sealing wax and pens. "I loved you, but I have orders from Arakchéev and will kill the first of you who moves forward." Little Nicholas turned to look at Pierre but Pierre was no longer there. In his place was his father—Prince Andrew—and his father had neither shape nor form, but he existed, and when little Nicholas perceived him he grew faint with love: he felt himself powerless, limp, and formless. His father caressed and pitied him. But Uncle Nicholas came nearer and nearer to them. Terror seized young Nicholas and he awoke.

"My father!" he thought. (Though there were two good portraits of Prince Andrew in the house, Nicholas never imagined him in human form.) "My father has been with me and caressed me. He approved of me and of Uncle Pierre. Whatever he may tell me, I will do it. Mucius Scaevola burned his hand. Why should not the same sort of thing happen to me? I know they want me to learn. And I will learn. But someday I shall have finished learning, and then I will do something. I only pray God that something may happen to me such as happened to Plutarch's men, and I will act as they did. I will do better. Everyone shall know me, love me, and be delighted with me!" And suddenly his bosom heaved with sobs and he began to cry.

"Are you ill?" he heard Dessalles' voice asking.

"No," answered Nicholas, and lay back on his pillow.

"He is good and kind and I am fond of him!" he thought of Dessalles. "But Uncle Pierre! Oh, what a wonderful man he is! And my father? Oh, Father, Father! Yes, I will do something with which even *he* would be satisfied. . . ."

asked and now difficult to know." And Uncle Nicholas, and he sank down in a sleep full that seemed dreadful.

"I love you, dear child," he said, pointing to some broken pillar and plaster. "I loved you, but Prince Andrew, your father, and will tell the first of you who moves forward." Little Nicholas turned to look at Pierre, but Pierre was no longer there. In his place was his father—Prince Andrew—and his father had neither shape nor form, but he existed, and when little Nicholas perceived him he grew faint with love. He felt himself powerless, limp, and formless. His father caressed and pitied him. But Uncle Nicholas came nearer and nearer to them. Terror seized young Nicholas and he awoke.

"My father," he thought. "Though there were two good portraits of him, Uncle Nicholas never imagined him in human form. "My father has been with me and caressed me. He approved of me and of Uncle Pierre. Whatever he may tell me, I will do it. Mucius Scaevola burned his hand. Why should not the same sort of thing happen to me? I know they want me to learn. And I will learn. But someday I shall have finished learning, and then I will do something. I only pray God that something such happen to me such as happened to Plutarch's men, and I will act as they did. I will do better. Everyone shall know me, shall love me, and be delighted with me." And suddenly his bosom heaved with sobs and he began to cry.

"Are you ill?" he heard Desalles' voice ask.

"No," answered Nicholas, and lay back on his pillow.

"He is good and kind and I am fond of him," he thought of Desalles. "But Uncle Pierre! Oh, what a wonderful man he is! And my father? Oh, father, father! Yes, I will do something with which even he would be satisfied..."

SECOND EPILOGUE

SECOND DIALOGUE

SECOND EPILOGUE

*A general discussion on the historians' study of human life,
and on the difficulty of defining the forces that move
nations. The problem of free will and necessity*

HISTORY IS the life of nations and of humanity. To seize and put into words, to describe directly the life of humanity or even of a single nation, appears impossible.

The ancient historians all employed one and the same method to describe and seize the apparently elusive—the life of a people. They described the activity of individuals who ruled the people, and regarded the activity of those men as representing the activity of the whole nation.

The question: how did individuals make nations act as they wished and by what was the will of these individuals themselves guided? the ancients met by recognizing a divinity which subjected the nations to the will of a chosen man, and guided the will of that chosen man so as to accomplish ends that were predestined.

For the ancients these questions were solved by a belief in the direct participation of the Deity in human affairs.

Modern history, in theory, rejects both these principles.

It would seem that having rejected the belief of the ancients in man's subjection to the Deity and in a predetermined aim toward which nations are led, modern history should study not the manifestations of power but the causes that produce it. But modern history has not done this. Having in theory rejected the view held by the ancients, it still follows them in practice.

Instead of men endowed with divine authority and directly guided by the will of God, modern history has given us either heroes endowed with extraordinary, superhuman capacities, or simply men of very various kinds, from monarchs to journalists, who lead the masses. Instead of the former divinely appointed aims of the Jewish, Greek, or Roman nations, which ancient historians regarded as representing the progress of humanity,

modern history has postulated its own aims—the welfare of the French, German, or English people, or, in its highest abstraction, the welfare and civilization of humanity in general, by which is usually meant that of the peoples occupying a small northwesterly portion of a large continent.

Modern history has rejected the beliefs of the ancients without replacing them by a new conception, and the logic of the situation has obliged the historians, after they had apparently rejected the divine authority of the kings and the "fate" of the ancients, to reach the same conclusion by another road, that is, to recognize (1) nations guided by individual men, and (2) the existence of a known aim to which these nations and humanity at large are tending.

At the basis of the works of all the modern historians from Gibbon to Buckle, despite their seeming disagreements and the apparent novelty of their outlooks, lie those two old, unavoidable assumptions.

In the first place the historian describes the activity of individuals who in his opinion have directed humanity (one historian considers only monarchs, generals, and ministers as being such men, while another includes also orators, learned men, reformers, philosophers, and poets). Secondly, it is assumed that the goal toward which humanity is being led is known to the historians: to one of them this goal is the greatness of the Roman, Spanish, or French realm; to another it is liberty, equality, and a certain kind of civilization of a small corner of the world called Europe.

In 1789 a ferment arises in Paris; it grows, spreads, and is expressed by a movement of peoples from west to east. Several times it moves eastward and collides with a countermovement from the east westward. In 1812 it reaches its extreme limit, Moscow, and then, with remarkable symmetry, a countermovement occurs from east to west, attracting to it, as the first movement had done, the nations of middle Europe. The countermovement reaches the starting point of the first movement in the west—Paris—and subsides.

During that twenty-year period an immense number of fields were left untilled, houses were burned, trade changed its direction, millions of men migrated, were impoverished, or were enriched, and millions of Christian men professing the law of love of their fellows slew one another.

What does all this mean? Why did it happen? What made those people burn houses and slay their fellow men? What were the causes of these events? What force made men act so? These are the instinctive, plain, and most legitimate questions humanity asks itself when it encounters the monuments and tradition of that period.

For a reply to these questions the common sense of mankind turns to

the science of history, whose aim is to enable nations and humanity to know themselves.

If history had retained the conception of the ancients it would have said that God, to reward or punish his people, gave Napoleon power and directed his will to the fulfillment of the divine ends, and that reply would have been clear and complete. One might believe or disbelieve in the divine significance of Napoleon, but for anyone believing in it there would have been nothing unintelligible in the history of that period, nor would there have been any contradictions.

But modern history cannot give that reply. Science does not admit the conception of the ancients as to the direct participation of the Deity in human affairs, and therefore history ought to give other answers.

Modern history replying to these questions says: you want to know what this movement means, what caused it, and what force produced these events? Then listen:

"Louis XIV was a very proud and self-confident man; he had such and such mistresses and such and such ministers and he ruled France badly. His descendants were weak men and they too ruled France badly. And they had such and such favorites and such and such mistresses. Moreover, certain men wrote some books at that time. At the end of the eighteenth century there were a couple of dozen men in Paris who began to talk about all men being free and equal. This caused people all over France to begin to slash at and drown one another. They killed the king and many other people. At that time there was in France a man of genius—Napoleon. He conquered everybody everywhere—that is, he killed many people because he was a great genius. And for some reason he went to kill Africans, and killed them so well and was so cunning and wise that when he returned to France he ordered everybody to obey him, and they all obeyed him. Having become an Emperor he again went out to kill people in Italy, Austria, and Prussia. And there too he killed a great many. In Russia there was an Emperor, Alexander, who decided to restore order in Europe and therefore fought against Napoleon. In 1807 he suddenly made friends with him, but in 1811 they again quarreled and again began killing many people. Napoleon led six hundred thousand men into Russia and captured Moscow; then he suddenly ran away from Moscow, and the Emperor Alexander, helped by the advice of Stein and others, united Europe to arm against the disturber of its peace. All Napoleon's allies suddenly became his enemies and their forces advanced against the fresh forces he raised. The Allies defeated Napoleon, entered Paris, forced Napoleon to abdicate, and sent him to the island of Elba, not depriving him of the title of Emperor and showing him every respect, though five years before

and one year later they all regarded him as an outlaw and a brigand. Then Louis XVIII, who till then had been the laughingstock both of the French and the Allies, began to reign. And Napoleon, shedding tears before his Old Guards, renounced the throne and went into exile. Then the skillful statesmen and diplomatists (especially Talleyrand, who managed to sit down in a particular chair before anyone else and thereby extended the frontiers of France) talked in Vienna and by these conversations made the nations happy or unhappy. Suddenly the diplomatists and monarchs nearly quarreled and were on the point of again ordering their armies to kill one another, but just then Napoleon arrived in France with a battalion, and the French, who had been hating him, immediately all submitted to him. But the Allied monarchs were angry at this and went to fight the French once more. And they defeated the genius Napoleon and, suddenly recognizing him as a brigand, sent him to the island of St. Helena. And the exile, separated from the beloved France so dear to his heart, died a lingering death on that rock and bequeathed his great deeds to posterity. But in Europe a reaction occurred and the sovereigns once again all began to oppress their subjects."

It would be a mistake to think that this is ironic—a caricature of the historical accounts. On the contrary it is a very mild expression of the contradictory replies, not meeting the questions, which all the historians give, from the compilers of memoirs and the histories of separate states to the writers of general histories and the new histories of the culture of that period.

The strangeness and absurdity of these replies arise from the fact that modern history, like a deaf man, answers questions no one has asked.

If the purpose of history be to give a description of the movement of humanity and of the peoples, the first question—in the absence of a reply to which all the rest will be incomprehensible—is: what is the power that moves peoples? To this, modern history laboriously replies either that Napoleon was a great genius, or that Louis XIV was very proud, or that certain writers wrote certain books.

All that may be so and mankind is ready to agree with it, but it is not what was asked. All that would be interesting if we recognized a divine power based on itself and always consistently directing its nations through Napoleons, Louis-es, and writers; but we do not acknowledge such a power, and therefore before speaking about Napoleons, Louis-es, and authors, we ought to be shown the connection existing between these men and the movement of the nations.

If instead of a divine power some other force has appeared, it should be

explained in what this new force consists, for the whole interest of history lies precisely in that force.

History seems to assume that this force is self-evident and known to everyone. But in spite of every desire to regard it as known, anyone reading many historical works cannot help doubting whether this new force, so variously understood by the historians themselves, is really quite well known to everybody.

WHAT FORCE moves the nations?

Biographical historians and historians of separate nations understand this force as a power inherent in heroes and rulers. In their narration events occur solely by the will of a Napoleon, an Alexander, or in general of the persons they describe. The answers given by this kind of historian to the question of what force causes events to happen are satisfactory only as long as there is but one historian to each event. As soon as historians of different nationalities and tendencies begin to describe the same event, the replies they give immediately lose all meaning, for this force is understood by them all not only differently but often in quite contradictory ways. One historian says that an event was produced by Napoleon's power, another that it was produced by Alexander's, a third that it was due to the power of some other person. Besides this, historians of that kind contradict each other even in their statement as to the force on which the authority of some particular person was based. Thiers, a Bonapartist, says that Napoleon's power was based on his virtue and genius. Lanfrey, a Republican,* says it was based on his trickery and deception of the people. So the historians of this class, by mutually destroying one another's positions, destroy the understanding of the force which produces events, and furnish no reply to history's essential question.

Writers of universal history who deal with all the nations seem to recognize how erroneous is the specialist historians' view of the force which produces events. They do not recognize it as a power inherent in heroes and rulers, but as the resultant of a multiplicity of variously directed forces. In describing a war or the subjugation of a people, a general historian looks for the cause of the event not in the power of one man, but in the interaction of many persons connected with the event.

According to this view the power of historical personages, represented as the product of many forces, can no longer, it would seem, be regarded as a force that itself produces events. Yet in most cases universal historians still employ the conception of power as a force that itself produces events,

* *Pierre Lanfrey* (1828-77). *His* Histoire de Napoléon Ier *began to appear when Tolstóy was finishing* War and Peace.—A.M.

and treat it as their cause. In their exposition, an historic character is first the product of his time, and his power only the resultant of various forces, and then his power is itself a force producing events. Gervinus,* Schlosser,[2] and others, for instance, at one time prove Napoleon to be a product of the Revolution, of the ideas of 1789 and so forth, and at another plainly say that the campaign of 1812 and other things they do not like were simply the product of Napoleon's misdirected will, and that the very ideas of 1789 were arrested in their development by Napoleon's caprice. The ideas of the Revolution and the general temper of the age produced Napoleon's power. But Napoleon's power suppressed the ideas of the Revolution and the general temper of the age.

This curious contradiction is not accidental. Not only does it occur at every step, but the universal historians' accounts are all made up of a chain of such contradictions. This contradiction occurs because after entering the field of analysis the universal historians stop halfway.

To find component forces equal to the composite or resultant force, the sum of the components must equal the resultant. This condition is never observed by the universal historians, and so to explain the resultant forces they are obliged to admit, in addition to the insufficient components, another unexplained force affecting the resultant action.

Specialist historians describing the campaign of 1813 or the restoration of the Bourbons plainly assert that these events were produced by the will of Alexander. But the universal historian Gervinus, refuting this opinion of the specialist historian, tries to prove that the campaign of 1813 and the restoration of the Bourbons were due to other things beside Alexander's will—such as the activity of Stein, Metternich, Madame de Staël, Talleyrand, Fichte, Chateaubriand, and others. The historian evidently decomposes Alexander's power into the components: Talleyrand, Chateaubriand, and the rest—but the sum of the components, that is, the interactions of Chateaubriand, Talleyrand, Madame de Staël, and the others, evidently does not equal the resultant, namely the phenomenon of millions of Frenchmen submitting to the Bourbons. That Chateaubriand, Madame de Staël, and others spoke certain words to one another only affected their mutual relations but does not account for the submission of millions. And therefore to explain how from these relations of theirs the submission of millions of people resulted—that is, how component forces equal to one A gave a resultant equal to a thousand times A—the historian

* Dr. G. G. Gervinus (1805-71) was a German historian and Shakespearian commentator with whom Tolstóy disagreed on both counts.—A.M.

[2] F. C. Schlosser (1776-1861). Professor of history at Heidelberg. Author of a 19-volume work, Weltgeschichte.—A.M.

is again obliged to fall back on power—the force he had denied—and to recognize it as the resultant of the forces, that is, he has to admit an unexplained force acting on the resultant. And that is just what the universal historians do, and consequently they not only contradict the specialist historians but contradict themselves.

Peasants having no clear idea of the cause of rain, say, according to whether they want rain or fine weather: "The wind has blown the clouds away," or, "The wind has brought up the clouds." And in the same way the universal historians sometimes, when it pleases them and fits in with their theory, say that power is the result of events, and sometimes, when they want to prove something else, say that power produces events.

A third class of historians—the so-called historians of culture—following the path laid down by the universal historians who sometimes accept writers and ladies as forces producing events—again take that force to be something quite different. They see it in what is called culture—in mental activity.

The historians of culture are quite consistent in regard to their progenitors, the writers of universal histories, for if historical events may be explained by the fact that certain persons treated one another in such and such ways, why not explain them by the fact that such and such people wrote such and such books? Of the immense number of indications accompanying every vital phenomenon, these historians select the indication of intellectual activity and say that this indication is the cause. But despite their endeavors to prove that the cause of events lies in intellectual activity, only by a great stretch can one admit that there is any connection between intellectual activity and the movement of peoples, and in no case can one admit that intellectual activity controls people's actions, for that view is not confirmed by such facts as the very cruel murders of the French Revolution resulting from the doctrine of the equality of man, or the very cruel wars and executions resulting from the preaching of love.

But even admitting as correct all the cunningly devised arguments with which these histories are filled—admitting that nations are governed by some undefined force called an *idea*—history's essential question still remains unanswered, and to the former power of monarchs and to the influence of advisers and other people introduced by the universal historians, another, newer force—the *idea*—is added, the connection of which with the masses needs explanation. It is possible to understand that Napoleon had power and so events occurred; with some effort one may even conceive that Napoleon together with other influences was the cause of an event; but how a book, *Le Contrat social*, had the effect of making

Frenchmen begin to drown one another cannot be understood without an explanation of the causal nexus of this new force with the event.

Undoubtedly some relation exists between all who live contemporaneously, and so it is possible to find some connection between the intellectual activity of men and their historical movements, just as such a connection may be found between the movements of humanity and commerce, handicraft, gardening, or anything else you please. But why intellectual activity is considered by the historians of culture to be the cause or expression of the whole historical movement is hard to understand. Only the following considerations can have led the historians to such a conclusion: (1) that history is written by learned men, and so it is natural and agreeable for them to think that the activity of their class supplies the basis of the movement of all humanity, just as a similar belief is natural and agreeable to traders, agriculturists, and soldiers (if they do not express it, that is merely because traders and soldiers do not write history), and (2) that spiritual activity, enlightenment, civilization, culture, ideas, are all indistinct, indefinite conceptions under whose banner it is very easy to use words having a still less definite meaning, and which can therefore be readily introduced into any theory.

But not to speak of the intrinsic quality of histories of this kind (which may possibly even be of use to someone for something) the histories of culture, to which all general histories tend more and more to approximate, are significant from the fact that after seriously and minutely examining various religious, philosophic, and political doctrines as causes of events, as soon as they have to describe an actual historic event such as the campaign of 1812 for instance, they involuntarily describe it as resulting from an exercise of power—and say plainly that that campaign was the result of Napoleon's will. Speaking so, the historians of culture involuntarily contradict themselves, and show that the new force they have devised does not account for what happens in history, and that history can only be explained by introducing a power which they apparently do not recognize.

A LOCOMOTIVE is moving. Someone asks: "What moves it?" A peasant says the devil moves it. Another man says the locomotive moves because its wheels go round. A third asserts that the cause of its movement lies in the smoke which the wind carries away.

The peasant is irrefutable. He has devised a complete explanation. To refute him someone would have to prove to him that there is no devil, or another peasant would have to explain to him that it is not the devil but a German, who moves the locomotive. Only then, as a result of the contradiction, will they see that they are both wrong. But the man who says

that the movement of the wheels is the cause refutes himself, for having once begun to analyze he ought to go on and explain further why the wheels go round; and till he has reached the ultimate cause of the movement of the locomotive in the pressure of steam in the boiler, he has no right to stop in his search for the cause. The man who explains the movement of the locomotive by the smoke that is carried back has noticed that the wheels do not supply an explanation and has taken the first sign that occurs to him and in his turn has offered that as an explanation.

The only conception that can explain the movement of the locomotive is that of a force commensurate with the movement observed.

The only conception that can explain the movement of the peoples is that of some force commensurate with the whole movement of the peoples.

Yet to supply this conception various historians take forces of different kinds, all of which are incommensurate with the movement observed. Some see it as a force directly inherent in heroes, as the peasant sees the devil in the locomotive; others as a force resulting from several other forces, like the movement of the wheels; others again as an intellectual influence, like the smoke that is blown away.

So long as histories are written of separate individuals, whether Caesars, Alexanders, Luthers, or Voltaires, and not the histories of *all*, absolutely *all* those who take part in an event, it is quite impossible to describe the movement of humanity without the conception of a force compelling men to direct their activity toward a certain end. And the only such conception known to historians is that of power.

This conception is the one handle by means of which the material of history, as at present expounded, can be dealt with, and anyone who breaks that handle off, as Buckle did, without finding some other method of treating historical material, merely deprives himself of the one possible way of dealing with it. The necessity of the conception of power as an explanation of historical events is best demonstrated by the universal historians and historians of culture themselves, for they professedly reject that conception but inevitably have recourse to it at every step.

In dealing with humanity's inquiry, the science of history up to now is like money in circulation—paper money and coin. The biographies and special national histories are like paper money. They can be used and can circulate and fulfill their purpose without harm to anyone and even advantageously, as long as no one asks what is the security behind them. You need only forget to ask how the will of heroes produces events, and such histories as Thiers' will be interesting and instructive and may perhaps even possess a tinge of poetry. But just as doubts of the real value of

paper money arise either because, being easy to make, too much of it gets made or because people try to exchange it for gold, so also doubts concerning the real value of such histories arise either because too many of them are written or because in his simplicity of heart someone inquires: by what force did Napoleon do this?—that is, wants to exchange the current paper money for the real gold of actual comprehension.

The writers of universal histories and of the history of culture are like people who, recognizing the defects of paper money, decide to substitute for it money made of metal that has not the specific gravity of gold. It may indeed make jingling coin, but will do no more than that. Paper money may deceive the ignorant, but nobody is deceived by tokens of base metal that have no value but merely jingle. As gold is gold only if it is serviceable not merely for exchange but also for use, so universal historians will be valuable only when they can reply to history's essential question: what is power? The universal historians give contradictory replies to that question, while the historians of culture evade it and answer something quite different. And as counters of imitation gold can be used only among a group of people who agree to accept them as gold, or among those who do not know the nature of gold, so universal historians and historians of culture, not answering humanity's essential question, serve as currency for some purposes of their own, only in universities and among the mass of readers who have a taste for what they call "serious reading."

HAVING ABANDONED the conception of the ancients as to the divine subjection of the will of a nation to some chosen man and the subjection of that man's will to the Deity, history cannot without contradictions take a single step till it has chosen one of two things: either a return to the former belief in the direct intervention of the Deity in human affairs or a definite explanation of the meaning of the force producing historical events and termed "power."

A return to the first is impossible, the belief has been destroyed; and so it is essential to explain what is meant by power.

Napoleon ordered an army to be raised and go to war. We are so accustomed to that idea and have become so used to it that the question: why did six hundred thousand men go to fight when Napoleon uttered certain words, seems to us senseless. He had the power and so what he ordered was done.

This reply is quite satisfactory if we believe that the power was given him by God. But as soon as we do not admit that, it becomes essential to determine what is this power of one man over others.

It cannot be the direct physical power of a strong man over a weak one
—a domination based on the application or threat of physical force, like
the power of Hercules; nor can it be based on the effect of moral force, as
in their simplicity some historians think who say that the leading figures
in history are heroes, that is, men gifted with a special strength of soul
and mind called genius. This power cannot be based on the predominance
of moral strength, for, not to mention heroes such as Napoleon about
whose moral qualities opinions differ widely, history shows us that neither
a Louis XI nor a Metternich, who ruled over millions of people, had any
particular moral qualities, but on the contrary were generally morally
weaker than any of the millions they ruled over.

If the source of power lies neither in the physical nor in the moral
qualities of him who possesses it, it must evidently be looked for else-
where—in the relation to the people of the man who wields the power.

And that is how power is understood by the science of jurisprudence,
that exchange bank of history which offers to exchange history's under-
standing of power for true gold.

Power is the collective will of the people transferred, by expressed or
tacit consent, to their chosen rulers.

In the domain of jurisprudence, which consists of discussions of how
a state and power might be arranged were it possible for all that to be
arranged, it is all very clear; but when applied to history that definition
of power needs explanation.

The science of jurisprudence regards the state and power as the an-
cients regarded fire—namely, as something existing absolutely. But for
history, the state and power are merely phenomena, just as for modern
physics fire is not an element but a phenomenon.

From this fundamental difference between the view held by history
and that held by jurisprudence, it follows that jurisprudence can tell
minutely how in its opinion power should be constituted and what power
—existing immutably outside time—is, but to history's questions about
the meaning of the mutations of power in time it can answer nothing.

If power be the collective will of the people transferred to their ruler,
was Pugachëv a representative of the will of the people? If not, then why
was Napoleon I? Why was Napoleon III a criminal when he was taken
prisoner at Boulogne, and why, later on, were those criminals whom he
arrested? *

* *Napoleon III, who reigned from 1852 to 1871, made two unsuccessful
attempts to seize the throne before he succeeded: first in 1836 at Strasbourg,
after which he was deported to America, and again in 1840 at Boulogne, where
he was arrested and sentenced to imprisonment for life. Six years later he*

Do palace revolutions—in which sometimes only two or three people take part—transfer the will of the people to a new ruler? In international relations, is the will of the people also transferred to their conqueror? Was the will of the Confederation of the Rhine transferred to Napoleon in 1806? Was the will of the Russian people transferred to Napoleon in 1809, when our army in alliance with the French went to fight the Austrians?

To these questions three answers are possible:

Either to assume (1) that the will of the people is always unconditionally transferred to the ruler or rulers they have chosen, and that therefore every emergence of a new power, every struggle against the power once appointed, should be absolutely regarded as an infringement of the real power; or (2) that the will of the people is transferred to the rulers conditionally, under definite and known conditions, and to show that all limitations, conflicts, and even destructions of power result from a nonobservance by the rulers of the conditions under which their power was entrusted to them; or (3) that the will of the people is delegated to the rulers conditionally, but that the conditions are unknown and indefinite, and that the appearance of several authorities, their struggles and their falls, result solely from the greater or lesser fulfillment by the rulers of these unknown conditions on which the will of the people is transferred from some people to others.

And these are the three ways in which the historians do explain the relation of the people to their rulers.

Some historians—those biographical and specialist historians already referred to—in their simplicity failing to understand the question of the meaning of power, seem to consider that the collective will of the people is unconditionally transferred to historical persons, and therefore when describing some single state they assume that particular power to be the one absolute and real power, and that any other force opposing this is not a power but a violation of power—mere violence.

Their theory, suitable for primitive and peaceful periods of history, has the inconvenience—in application to complex and stormy periods in the life of nations during which various powers arise simultaneously and struggle with one another—that a Legitimist historian will prove that the National Convention, the Directory, and Bonaparte were mere infringers of the true power, while a Republican and a Bonapartist will prove: the one that the Convention and the other that the Empire was the real

escaped to England, and he was reigning as Emperor when War and Peace *was being written.*—A.M.

power, and that all the others were violations of power. Evidently the explanations furnished by these historians being mutually contradictory can only satisfy young children.

Recognizing the falsity of this view of history, another set of historians say that power rests on a conditional delegation of the will of the people to their rulers, and that historical leaders have power only conditionally on carrying out the program that the will of the people has by tacit agreement prescribed to them. But what this program consists in these historians do not say, or if they do they continually contradict one another.

Each historian, according to his view of what constitutes a nation's progress, looks for these conditions in the greatness, wealth, freedom, or enlightenment of the citizens of France or some other country. But not to mention the historians' contradictions as to the nature of this program —or even admitting that some one general program of these conditions exists—the facts of history almost always contradict that theory. If the conditions under which power is entrusted consist in the wealth, freedom, and enlightenment of the people, how is it that Louis XIV and Iván the Terrible end their reigns tranquilly, while Louis XVI and Charles I are executed by their people? To this question historians reply that Louis XIV's activity, contrary to the program, reacted on Louis XVI. But why did it not react on Louis XIV or on Louis XV—why should it react just on Louis XVI? And what is the time limit for such reactions? To these questions there are and can be no answers. Equally little does this view explain why for several centuries the collective will is not withdrawn from certain rulers and their heirs, and then suddenly during a period of fifty years is transferred to the Convention, to the Directory, to Napoleon, to Alexander, to Louis XVIII, to Napoleon again, to Charles X, to Louis Philippe, to a Republican government, and to Napoleon III. When explaining these rapid transfers of the people's will from one individual to another, especially in view of international relations, conquests, and alliances, the historians are obliged to admit that some of these transfers are not normal delegations of the people's will but are accidents dependent on cunning, on mistakes, on craft, or on the weakness of a diplomatist, a ruler, or a party leader. So that the greater part of the events of history— civil wars, revolutions, and conquests—are presented by these historians not as the results of free transferences of the people's will, but as results of the ill-directed will of one or more individuals, that is, once again, as usurpations of power. And so these historians also see and admit historical events which are exceptions to the theory.

These historians resemble a botanist who, having noticed that some plants grow from seeds producing two cotyledons, should insist that all

that grows does so by sprouting into two leaves, and that the palm, the mushroom, and even the oak, which blossom into full growth and no longer resemble two leaves, are deviations from the theory.

Historians of the third class assume that the will of the people is transferred to historic personages conditionally, but that the conditions are unknown to us. They say that historical personages have power only because they fulfill the will of the people which has been delegated to them.

But in that case, if the force that moves nations lies not in the historic leaders but in the nations themselves, what significance have those leaders?

The leaders, these historians tell us, express the will of the people: the activity of the leaders represents the activity of the people.

But in that case the question arises whether all the activity of the leaders serves as an expression of the people's will or only some part of it. If the whole activity of the leaders serves as the expression of the people's will, as some historians suppose, then all the details of the court scandals contained in the biographies of a Napoleon or a Catherine serve to express the life of the nation, which is evident nonsense; but if it is only some particular side of the activity of an historical leader which serves to express the people's life, as other so-called "philosophical" historians believe, then to determine which side of the activity of a leader expresses the nation's life, we have first of all to know in what the nation's life consists.

Met by this difficulty historians of that class devise some most obscure, impalpable, and general abstraction which can cover all conceivable occurrences, and declare this abstraction to be the aim of humanity's movement. The most usual generalizations adopted by almost all the historians are: freedom, equality, enlightenment, progress, civilization, and culture. Postulating some generalization as the goal of the movement of humanity, the historians study the men of whom the greatest number of monuments have remained: kings, ministers, generals, authors, reformers, popes, and journalists, to the extent to which in their opinion these persons have promoted or hindered that abstraction. But as it is in no way proved that the aim of humanity does consist in freedom, equality, enlightenment, or civilization, and as the connection of the people with the rulers and enlighteners of humanity is only based on the arbitrary assumption that the collective will of the people is always transferred to the men whom we have noticed, it happens that the activity of the millions who migrate, burn houses, abandon agriculture, and destroy one another never is expressed in the account of the activity of some dozen people who did not burn houses, practice agriculture, or slay their fellow creatures.

History proves this at every turn. Is the ferment of the peoples of the west at the end of the eighteenth century and their drive eastward ex-

plained by the activity of Louis XIV, XV, and XVI, their mistresses and ministers, and by the lives of Napoleon, Rousseau, Diderot, Beaumarchais, and others?

Is the movement of the Russian people eastward to Kazán and Siberia expressed by details of the morbid character of Iván the Terrible and by his correspondence with Kúrbski? *

Is the movement of the peoples at the time of the Crusades explained by the life and activity of the Godfreys and the Louis-es and their ladies? For us that movement of the peoples from west to east, without leaders, with a crowd of vagrants, and with Peter the Hermit, remains incomprehensible. And yet more incomprehensible is the cessation of that movement when a rational and sacred aim for the Crusade—the deliverance of Jerusalem—had been clearly defined by historic leaders. Popes, kings, and knights incited the peoples to free the Holy Land; but the people did not go, for the unknown cause which had previously impelled them to go no longer existed. The history of the Godfreys and the Minnesingers [2] can evidently not cover the life of the peoples. And the history of the Godfreys and the Minnesingers has remained the history of Godfreys and Minnesingers, but the history of the life of the peoples and their impulses has remained unknown.

Still less does the history of authors and reformers explain to us the life of the peoples.

The history of culture explains to us the impulses and conditions of life and thought of a writer or a reformer. We learn that Luther had a hot temper and said such and such things; we learn that Rousseau was suspicious and wrote such and such books; but we do not learn why after the Reformation the peoples massacred one another, nor why during the French Revolution they guillotined one another.

* *Prince Andréy Kúrbski was one of Iván the Terrible's principal boyars. He escaped into Lithuania to make a political protest, and from there wrote harsh letters to Iván reproaching him for his cruelty, untruthfulness, and despotism. Iván replied with equal harshness, developing a theory of autocratic power and the duty of slavish submission to it "according to the law of God."—*A.M.

[2] *Godfrey of Bouillon was a leader of the First Crusade at the end of the eleventh century.*

Peter the Hermit was an ascetic French monk who, tradition says, inspired the First Crusade.

The Minnesingers were wandering minstrels often of knightly rank, who in the twelfth and thirteenth centuries went about singing love lyrics as well as the crusading song, chiefly in Swabia and Austria.—*A.M.

If we unite both these kinds of history, as is done by the newest historians, we shall have the history of monarchs and writers, but not the history of the life of the peoples.

THE LIFE of the nations is not contained in the lives of a few men, for the connection between those men and the nations has not been found. The theory that this connection is based on the transference of the collective will of a people to certain historical personages is an hypothesis unconfirmed by the experience of history.

The theory of the transference of the collective will of the people to historic persons may perhaps explain much in the domain of jurisprudence and be essential for its purposes, but in its application to history, as soon as revolutions, conquests, or civil wars occur—that is, as soon as history begins—that theory explains nothing.

The theory seems irrefutable just because the act of transference of the people's will cannot be verified, for it never occurred.

Whatever happens and whoever may stand at the head of affairs, the theory can always say that such and such a person took the lead because the collective will was transferred to him.

The replies this theory gives to historical questions are like the replies of a man who, watching the movements of a herd of cattle and paying no attention to the varying quality of the pasturage in different parts of the field, or to the driving of the herdsman, should attribute the direction the herd takes to what animal happens to be at its head.

"The herd goes in that direction because the animal in front leads it and the collective will of all the other animals is vested in that leader." This is what historians of the first class say—those who assume the unconditional transference of the people's will.

"If the animals leading the herd change, this happens because the collective will of all the animals is transferred from one leader to another, according to whether the animal is or is not leading them in the direction selected by the whole herd." Such is the reply of historians who assume that the collective will of the people is delegated to rulers under conditions which they regard as known. (With this method of observation it often happens that the observer, influenced by the direction he himself prefers, regards those as leaders who, owing to the people's change of direction, are no longer in front, but on one side, or even in the rear.)

"If the animals in front are continually changing and the direction of the whole herd is constantly altered, this is because in order to follow a given direction the animals transfer their will to the animals that have attracted our attention, and to study the movements of the herd we must

watch the movements of all the prominent animals moving on all sides of the herd." So say the third class of historians who regard all historical persons, from monarchs to journalists, as the expression of their age.

The theory of the transference of the will of the people to historic persons is merely a paraphrase—a restatement of the question in other words.

What causes historical events? Power. What is power? Power is the collective will of the people transferred to one person. Under what condition is the will of the people delegated to one person? On condition that that person expresses the will of the whole people. That is, power is power: in other words, power is a word the meaning of which we do not understand.

If the realm of human knowledge were confined to abstract reasoning, then having subjected to criticism the explanation of "power" that juridical science gives us, humanity would conclude that power is merely a word and has no real existence. But to understand phenomena man has, besides abstract reasoning, experience by which he verifies his reflections. And experience tells us that power is not merely a word but an actually existing phenomenon.

Not to speak of the fact that no description of the collective activity of men can do without the conception of power, the existence of power is proved both by history and by observing contemporary events.

Whenever an event occurs a man appears or men appear, by whose will the event seems to have taken place. Napoleon III issues a decree and the French go to Mexico.* The King of Prussia and Bismarck issue decrees and an army enters Bohemia.[2] Napoleon I issues a decree and an army enters Russia. Alexander I gives a command and the French submit to the Bourbons. Experience shows us that whatever event occurs it is always related to the will of one or of several men who have decreed it.

The historians, in accord with the old habit of acknowledging divine intervention in human affairs, want to see the cause of events in the expression of the will of someone endowed with power, but that supposition is not confirmed either by reason or by experience.

On the one side reflection shows that the expression of a man's will—his words—are only part of the general activity expressed in an event, as

* In 1864 by the aid of a French army Maximilian secured the throne of Mexico, but after the conclusion of the American Civil War that army had to leave Mexico as the United States would not tolerate European interference on American soil. Maximilian was shot by the Mexicans in 1867, when Tolstóy was writing the last part of War and Peace.—A.M.

2 This refers to the Austro-Prussian war of 1866.—A.M.

for instance in a war or a revolution, and so without assuming an incomprehensible, supernatural force—a miracle—one cannot admit that words can be the immediate cause of the movements of millions of men. On the other hand, even if we admitted that words could be the cause of events, history shows that the expression of the will of historical personages does not in most cases produce any effect, that is to say, their commands are often not executed, and sometimes the very opposite of what they order occurs.

Without admitting divine intervention in the affairs of humanity we cannot regard "power" as the cause of events.

Power, from the standpoint of experience, is merely the relation that exists between the expression of someone's will and the execution of that will by others.

To explain the conditions of that relationship we must first establish a conception of the expression of will, referring it to man and not to the Deity.

If the Deity issues a command, expresses His will, as ancient history tells us, the expression of that will is independent of time and is not caused by anything, for the Divinity is not controlled by an event. But speaking of commands that are the expression of the will of men acting in time and in relation to one another, to explain the connection of commands with events we must restore: (1) the condition of all that takes place: the continuity of movement in time both of the events and of the person who commands, and (2) the inevitability of the connection between the person commanding and those who execute his command.

ONLY THE EXPRESSION of the will of the Deity, not dependent on time, can relate to a whole series of events occurring over a period of years or centuries, and only the Deity, independent of everything, can by His sole will determine the direction of humanity's movement; but man acts in time and himself takes part in what occurs.

Reinstating the first condition omitted, that of time, we see that no command can be executed without some preceding order having been given rendering the execution of the last command possible.

No command ever appears spontaneously, or itself covers a whole series of occurrences; but each command follows from another, and never refers to a whole series of events but always to one moment only of an event.

When, for instance, we say that Napoleon ordered armies to go to war, we combine in one simultaneous expression a whole series of consecutive commands dependent one on another. Napoleon could not have commanded an invasion of Russia and never did so. Today he ordered such

and such papers to be written to Vienna, to Berlin, and to Petersburg; tomorrow such and such decrees and orders to the army, the fleet, the commissariat, and so on and so on—millions of commands, which formed a whole series corresponding to a series of events which brought the French armies into Russia.

If throughout his reign Napoleon gave commands concerning an invasion of England and expended on no other undertaking so much time and effort, and yet during his whole reign never once attempted to execute that design but undertook an expedition into Russia, with which country he considered it desirable to be in alliance (a conviction he repeatedly expressed)—this came about because his commands did not correspond to the course of events in the first case, but did so correspond in the latter.

For an order to be certainly executed, it is necessary that a man should order what can be executed. But to know what can and what cannot be executed is impossible, not only in the case of Napoleon's invasion of Russia in which millions participated, but even in the simplest event, for in either case millions of obstacles may arise to prevent its execution. Every order executed is always one of an immense number unexecuted. All the impossible orders inconsistent with the course of events remain unexecuted. Only the possible ones get linked up with a consecutive series of commands corresponding to a series of events, and are executed.

Our false conception that an event is caused by a command which precedes it is due to the fact that when the event has taken place and out of thousands of others those few commands which were consistent with that event have been executed, we forget about the others that were not executed because they could not be. Apart from that, the chief source of our error in this matter is due to the fact that in the historical accounts a whole series of innumerable, diverse, and petty events, such for instance as all those which led the French armies to Russia, is generalized into one event in accord with the result produced by that series of events, and corresponding with this generalization the whole series of commands is also generalized into a single expression of will.

We say that Napoleon wished to invade Russia and invaded it. In reality in all Napoleon's activity we never find anything resembling an expression of that wish, but find a series of orders, or expressions of his will, very variously and indefinitely directed. Amid a long series of unexecuted orders of Napoleon's one series, for the campaign of 1812, was carried out—not because those orders differed in any way from the other, unexecuted orders but because they coincided with the course of events that led the French army into Russia; just as in stencil work this or that figure comes out not because the color was laid on from this side or in

that way, but because it was laid on from all sides over the figure cut in the stencil.

So that examining the relation in time of the commands to the events, we find that a command can never be the cause of the event, but that a certain definite dependence exists between the two.

To understand in what this dependence consists it is necessary to reinstate another omitted condition of every command proceeding not from the Deity but from a man, which is, that the man who gives the command himself takes part in the event.

This relation of the commander to those he commands is just what is called power. This relation consists in the following:

For common action people always unite in certain combinations, in which regardless of the difference of the aims set for the common action, the relation between those taking part in it is always the same.

Men uniting in these combinations always assume such relations toward one another that the larger number take a more direct share, and the smaller number a less direct share, in the collective action for which they have combined.

Of all the combinations in which men unite for collective action one of the most striking and definite examples is an army.

Every army is composed of lower grades of the service—the rank and file—of whom there are always the greatest number; of the next higher military rank—corporals and noncommissioned officers of whom there are fewer, and of still-higher officers of whom there are still fewer, and so on to the highest military command which is concentrated in one person.

A military organization may be quite correctly compared to a cone, of which the base with the largest diameter consists of the rank and file; the next higher and smaller section of the cone consists of the next higher grades of the army, and so on to the apex, the point of which will represent the commander in chief.

The soldiers, of whom there are the most, form the lower section of the cone and its base. The soldier himself does the stabbing, hacking, burning, and pillaging, and always receives orders for these actions from men above him; he himself never gives an order. The noncommissioned officers (of whom there are fewer) perform the action itself less frequently than the soldiers, but they already give commands. An officer still less often acts directly himself, but commands still more frequently. A general does nothing but command the troops, indicates the objective, and hardly ever uses a weapon himself. The commander in chief never takes direct part in the action itself, but only gives general orders concerning the movement of the mass of the troops. A similar relation of people to

one another is seen in every combination of men for common activity—in agriculture, trade, and every administration.

And so without particularly analyzing all the contiguous sections of a cone and of the ranks of an army, or the ranks and positions in any administrative or public business whatever from the lowest to the highest, we see a law by which men, to take associated action, combine in such relations that the more directly they participate in performing the action the less they can command and the more numerous they are, while the less their direct participation in the action itself, the more they command and the fewer of them there are; rising in this way from the lowest ranks to the man at the top, who takes the least direct share in the action and directs his activity chiefly to commanding.

This relation of the men who command to those they command is what constitutes the essence of the conception called power.

Having restored the condition of time under which all events occur, we find that a command is executed only when it is related to a corresponding series of events. Restoring the essential condition of relation between those who command and those who execute, we find that by the very nature of the case those who command take the smallest part in the action itself and that their activity is exclusively directed to commanding.

WHEN AN EVENT is taking place people express their opinions and wishes about it, and as the event results from the collective activity of many people, some one of the opinions or wishes expressed is sure to be fulfilled if but approximately. When one of the opinions expressed is fulfilled, that opinion gets connected with the event as a command preceding it.

Men are hauling a log. Each of them expresses his opinion as to how and where to haul it. They haul the log away, and it happens that this is done as one of them said. He *ordered* it. There we have command and power in their primary form. The man who worked most with his hands could not think so much about what he was doing, or reflect on or command what would result from the common activity; while the man who commanded more would evidently work less with his hands on account of his greater verbal activity.

When some larger concourse of men direct their activity to a common aim there is a yet sharper division of those who, because their activity is given to directing and commanding, take less part in the direct work.

When a man works alone he always has a certain set of reflections which as it seems to him directed his past activity, justify his present activity, and guide him in planning his future actions. Just the same is done

by a concourse of people, allowing those who do not take a direct part in
the activity to devise considerations, justifications, and surmises concern-
ing their collective activity.

For reasons known or unknown to us the French began to drown and
kill one another. And corresponding to the event its justification appears
in people's belief that this was necessary for the welfare of France, for
liberty, and for equality. People ceased to kill one another, and this event
was accompanied by its justification in the necessity for a centralization
of power, resistance to Europe, and so on. Men went from the west to the
east killing their fellow men, and the event was accompanied by phrases
about the glory of France, the baseness of England, and so on. History
shows us that these justifications of the events have no common sense
and are all contradictory, as in the case of killing a man as the result of
recognizing his rights, and the killing of millions in Russia for the humili-
ation of England. But these justifications have a very necessary signifi-
cance in their own day.

These justifications release those who produce the events from moral
responsibility. These temporary aims are like the broom fixed in front of
a locomotive to clear the snow from the rails in front: they clear men's
moral responsibilities from their path.

Without such justification there would be no reply to the simplest
question that presents itself when examining each historical event. How
is it that millions of men commit collective crimes—make war, commit
murder, and so on?

With the present complex forms of political and social life in Europe
can any event that is not prescribed, decreed, or ordered by monarchs,
ministers, parliaments, or newspapers be imagined? Is there any collective
action which cannot find its justification in political unity, in patriotism,
in the balance of power, or in civilization? So that every event that occurs
inevitably coincides with some expressed wish and, receiving a justifica-
tion, presents itself as the result of the will of one man or of several men.

In whatever direction a ship moves, the flow of the waves it cuts will
always be noticeable ahead of it. To those on board the ship the move-
ment of those waves will be the only perceptible motion.

Only by watching closely moment by moment the movement of that
flow and comparing it with the movement of the ship do we convince
ourselves that every bit of it is occasioned by the forward movement of
the ship, and that we were led into error by the fact that we ourselves
were imperceptibly moving.

We see the same if we watch moment by moment the movement of
historical characters (that is, re-establish the inevitable condition of all

that occurs—the continuity of movement in time) and do not lose sight of the essential connection of historical persons with the masses.

When the ship moves in one direction there is one and the same wave ahead of it, when it turns frequently the wave ahead of it also turns frequently. But wherever it may turn there always will be the wave anticipating its movement.

Whatever happens it always appears that just that event was foreseen and decreed. Wherever the ship may go, the rush of water which neither directs nor increases its movement foams ahead of it, and at a distance seems to us not merely to move of itself but to govern the ship's movement also.

Examining only those expressions of the will of historical persons which, as commands, were related to events, historians have assumed that the events depended on those commands. But examining the events themselves and the connection in which the historical persons stood to the people, we have found that they and their orders were dependent on events. The incontestable proof of this deduction is that, however many commands were issued, the event does not take place unless there are other causes for it, but as soon as an event occurs—be it what it may—then out of all the continually expressed wishes of different people some will always be found which by their meaning and their time of utterance are related as commands to the events.

Arriving at this conclusion we can reply directly and positively to these two essential questions of history:

(1) What is power?

(2) What force produces the movement of the nations?

(1) Power is the relation of a given person to other individuals, in which the more this person expresses opinions, predictions, and justifications of the collective action that is performed, the less is his participation in that action.

(2) The movement of nations is caused not by power, nor by intellectual activity, nor even by a combination of the two as historians have supposed, but by the activity of *all* the people who participate in the events, and who always combine in such a way that those taking the largest direct share in the event take on themselves the least responsibility and vice versa.

Morally the wielder of power appears to cause the event; physically it is those who submit to the power. But as the moral activity is inconceivable without the physical, the cause of the event is neither in the one nor in the other but in the union of the two.

Or in other words, the conception of a cause is inapplicable to the phenomena we are examining.

In the last analysis we reach the circle of infinity—that final limit to which in every domain of thought man's reason arrives if it is not playing with the subject. Electricity produces heat, heat produces electricity. Atoms attract each other and atoms repel one another.

Speaking of the interaction of heat and electricity and of atoms, we cannot say why this occurs, and we say that it is so because it is inconceivable otherwise, because it must be so and that it is a law. The same applies to historical events. Why war and revolution occur we do not know. We only know that to produce the one or the other action, people combine in a certain formation in which they all take part, and we say that this is so because it is unthinkable otherwise, or in other words that it is a law.

IF HISTORY DEALT only with external phenomena, the establishment of this simple and obvious law would suffice and we should have finished our argument. But the law of history relates to man. A particle of matter cannot tell us that it does not feel the law of attraction or repulsion and that that law is untrue, but man, who is the subject of history, says plainly: I am free and am therefore not subject to the law.

The presence of the problem of man's free will, though unexpressed, is felt at every step of history.

All seriously thinking historians have involuntarily encountered this question. All the contradictions and obscurities of history and the false path historical science has followed are due solely to the lack of a solution of that question.

If the will of every man were free, that is, if each man could act as he pleased, all history would be a series of disconnected incidents.

If in a thousand years even one man in a million could act freely, that is, as he chose, it is evident that one single free act of that man's in violation of the laws governing human action would destroy the possibility of the existence of any laws for the whole of humanity.

If there be a single law governing the actions of men, free will cannot exist, for then man's will is subject to that law.

In this contradiction lies the problem of free will, which from most ancient times has occupied the best human minds and from most ancient times has been presented in its whole tremendous significance.

The problem is that regarding man as a subject of observation from whatever point of view—theological, historical, ethical, or philosophic—we find a general law of necessity to which he (like all that exists) is sub-

ject. But regarding him from within ourselves as what we are conscious of, we feel ourselves to be free.

This consciousness is a source of self-cognition quite apart from and independent of reason. Through his reason man observes himself, but only through consciousness does he know himself.

Apart from consciousness of self no observation or application of reason is conceivable.

To understand, observe, and draw conclusions, man must first of all be conscious of himself as living. A man is only conscious of himself as a living being by the fact that he wills, that is, is conscious of his volition. But his will—which forms the essence of his life—man recognizes (and can but recognize) as free.

If, observing himself, man sees that his will is always directed by one and the same law (whether he observes the necessity of taking food, using his brain, or anything else) he cannot recognize this never-varying direction of his will otherwise than as a limitation of it. Were it not free it could not be limited. A man's will seems to him to be limited just because he is not conscious of it except as free.

You say: I am not free. But I have lifted my hand and let it fall. Everyone understands that this illogical reply is an irrefutable demonstration of freedom.

That reply is the expression of a consciousness that is not subject to reason.

If the consciousness of freedom were not a separate and independent source of self-consciousness it would be subject to reasoning and to experience, but in fact such subjection does not exist and is inconceivable.

A series of experiments and arguments proves to every man that he, as an object of observation, is subject to certain laws, and man submits to them and never resists the laws of gravity or impermeability once he has become acquainted with them. But the same series of experiments and arguments proves to him that the complete freedom of which he is conscious in himself is impossible, and that his every action depends on his organization, his character, and the motives acting upon him; yet man never submits to the deductions of these experiments and arguments. Having learned from experiment and argument that a stone falls downwards, a man indubitably believes this and always expects the law that he has learned to be fulfilled.

But learning just as certainly that his will is subject to laws, he does not and cannot believe this.

However often experiment and reasoning may show a man that under the same conditions and with the same character he will do the same thing

as before, yet when under the same conditions and with the same charac-
ter he approaches for the thousandth time the action that always ends in
the same way, he feels as certainly convinced as before the experiment
that he can act as he pleases. Every man, savage or sage, however incon-
testably reason and experiment may prove to him that it is impossible to
imagine two different courses of action in precisely the same conditions,
feels that without this irrational conception (which constitutes the es-
sence of freedom) he cannot imagine life. He feels that however impos-
sible it may be, it is so, for without this conception of freedom not only
would he be unable to understand life, but he would be unable to live for
a single moment.

He could not live, because all man's efforts, all his impulses to life, are
only efforts to increase freedom. Wealth and poverty, fame and obscurity,
power and subordination, strength and weakness, health and disease, cul-
ture and ignorance, work and leisure, repletion and hunger, virtue and
vice, are only greater or lesser degrees of freedom.

A man having no freedom cannot be conceived of except as deprived
of life.

If the conception of freedom appears to reason to be a senseless contra-
diction like the possibility of performing two actions at one and the same
instant of time, or of an effect without a cause, that only proves that con-
sciousness is not subject to reason.

This unshakable, irrefutable consciousness of freedom, uncontrolled
by experiment or argument, recognized by all thinkers and felt by every-
one without exception, this consciousness without which no conception
of man is possible constitutes the other side of the question.

Man is the creation of an all-powerful, all-good, and all-seeing God.
What is sin, the conception of which arises from the consciousness of
man's freedom? That is a question for theology.

The actions of men are subject to general immutable laws expressed in
statistics. What is man's responsibility to society, the conception of which
results from the conception of freedom? That is a question for jurispru-
dence.

Man's actions proceed from his innate character and the motives acting
upon him. What is conscience and the perception of right and wrong in
actions that follows from the consciousness of freedom? That is a question
for ethics.

Man in connection with the general life of humanity appears subject to
laws which determine that life. But the same man apart from that connec-
tion appears to be free. How should the past life of nations and of human-

ity be regarded—as the result of the free, or as the result of the constrained, activity of man? That is a question for history.

Only in our self-confident day of the popularization of knowledge—thanks to that most powerful engine of ignorance, the diffusion of printed matter—has the question of the freedom of will been put on a level on which the question itself cannot exist. In our time the majority of so-called advanced people—that is, the crowd of ignoramuses—have taken the work of the naturalists who deal with one side of the question for a solution of the whole problem.

They say and write and print that the soul and freedom do not exist, for the life of man is expressed by muscular movements and muscular movements are conditioned by the activity of the nerves; the soul and free will do not exist because at an unknown period of time we sprang from the apes. They say this, not at all suspecting that thousands of years ago that same law of necessity which with such ardor they are now trying to prove by physiology and comparative zoology was not merely acknowledged by all the religions and all the thinkers, but has never been denied. They do not see that the role of the natural sciences in this matter is merely to serve as an instrument for the illumination of one side of it. For the fact that, from the point of view of observation, reason and the will are merely secretions of the brain, and that man following the general law may have developed from lower animals at some unknown period of time, only explains from a fresh side the truth admitted thousands of years ago by all the religious and philosophic theories—that from the point of view of reason man is subject to the law of necessity; but it does not advance by a hair's breadth the solution of the question, which has another, opposite, side, based on the consciousness of freedom.

If men descended from the apes at an unknown period of time, that is as comprehensible as that they were made from a handful of earth at a certain period of time (in the first case the unknown quantity is the time, in the second case it is the origin); and the question of how man's consciousness of freedom is to be reconciled with the law of necessity to which he is subject cannot be solved by comparative physiology and zoology, for in a frog, a rabbit, or an ape, we can observe only the muscular nervous activity, but in man we observe consciousness as well as the muscular and nervous activity.

The naturalists and their followers, thinking they can solve this question, are like plasterers set to plaster one side of the walls of a church who, availing themselves of the absence of the chief superintendent of the work, should in an access of zeal plaster over the windows, icons, wood-

work, and still unbuttressed walls, and should be delighted that from their point of view as plasterers, everything is now so smooth and regular.

FOR THE SOLUTION of the question of free will or inevitability, history has this advantage over other branches of knowledge in which the question is dealt with, that for history this question does not refer to the essence of man's free will but to its manifestation in the past and under certain conditions.

In regard to this question, history stands to the other sciences as experimental science stands to abstract science.

The subject for history is not man's will itself but our presentation of it.

And so for history, the insoluble mystery presented by the incompatibility of free will and inevitability does not exist as it does for theology, ethics, and philosophy. History surveys a presentation of man's life in which the union of these two contradictions has already taken place.

In actual life each historic event, each human action, is very clearly and definitely understood without any sense of contradiction, although each event presents itself as partly free and partly compulsory.

To solve the question of how freedom and necessity are combined and what constitutes the essence of these two conceptions, the philosophy of history can and should follow a path contrary to that taken by other sciences. Instead of first defining the conceptions of freedom and inevitability in themselves, and then ranging the phenomena of life under those definitions, history should deduce a definition of the conception of freedom and inevitability themselves from the immense quantity of phenomena of which it is cognizant and that always appear dependent on these two elements.

Whatever presentation of the activity of many men or of an individual we may consider, we always regard it as the result partly of man's free will and partly of the law of inevitability.

Whether we speak of the migration of the peoples and the incursions of the barbarians, or of the decrees of Napoleon III, or of someone's action an hour ago in choosing one direction out of several for his walk, we are unconscious of any contradiction. The degree of freedom and inevitability governing the actions of these people is clearly defined for us.

Our conception of the degree of freedom often varies according to differences in the point of view from which we regard the event, but every human action appears to us as a certain combination of freedom and inevitability. In every action we examine we see a certain measure of freedom and a certain measure of inevitability. And always the more freedom

we see in any action the less inevitability do we perceive, and the more inevitability the less freedom.

The proportion of freedom to inevitability decreases and increases according to the point of view from which the action is regarded, but their relation is always one of inverse proportion.

A sinking man who clutches at another and drowns him; or a hungry mother exhausted by feeding her baby, who steals some food; or a man trained to discipline who on duty at the word of command kills a defenseless man—seem less guilty, that is, less free and more subject to the law of necessity, to one who knows the circumstances in which these people were placed, and more free to one who does not know that the man was himself drowning, that the mother was hungry, that the soldier was in the ranks, and so on. Similarly a man who committed a murder twenty years ago and has since lived peaceably and harmlessly in society seems less guilty and his action more due to the law of inevitability, to someone who considers his action after twenty years have elapsed than to one who examined it the day after it was committed. And in the same way every action of an insane, intoxicated, or highly excited man appears less free and more inevitable to one who knows the mental condition of him who committed the action, and seems more free and less inevitable to one who does not know it. In all these cases the conception of freedom is increased or diminished and the conception of compulsion is correspondingly decreased or increased, according to the point of view from which the action is regarded. So that the greater the conception of necessity the smaller the conception of freedom and vice versa.

Religion, the common sense of mankind, the science of jurisprudence, and history itself understand alike this relation between necessity and freedom.

All cases without exception in which our conception of freedom and necessity is increased and diminished depend on three considerations:

(1) The relation to the external world of the man who commits the deeds.

(2) His relation to time.

(3) His relation to the causes leading to the action.

The first consideration is the clearness of our perception of the man's relation to the external world and the greater or lesser clearness of our understanding of the definite position occupied by the man in relation to everything coexisting with him. This is what makes it evident that a drowning man is less free and more subject to necessity than one standing on dry ground, and that makes the actions of a man closely connected with others in a thickly populated district, or of one bound by family,

official, or business duties, seem certainly less free and more subject to necessity than those of a man living in solitude and seclusion.

If we consider a man alone, apart from his relation to everything around him, each action of his seems to us free. But if we see his relation to anything around him, if we see his connection with anything whatever—with a man who speaks to him, a book he reads, the work on which he is engaged, even with the air he breathes or the light that falls on the things about him—we see that each of these circumstances has an influence on him and controls at least some side of his activity. And the more we perceive of these influences the more our conception of his freedom diminishes and the more our conception of the necessity that weighs on him increases.

The second consideration is the more or less evident time relation of the man to the world and the clearness of our perception of the place the man's action occupies in time. That is the ground which makes the fall of the first man, resulting in the production of the human race, appear evidently less free than a man's entry into marriage today. It is the reason why the life and activity of people who lived centuries ago and are connected with me in time cannot seem to me as free as the life of a contemporary, the consequences of which are still unknown to me.

The degree of our conception of freedom or inevitability depends in this respect on the greater or lesser lapse of time between the performance of the action and our judgment of it.

If I examine an act I performed a moment ago in approximately the same circumstances as those I am in now, my action appears to me undoubtedly free. But if I examine an act performed a month ago, then being in different circumstances, I cannot help recognizing that if that act had not been committed much that resulted from it—good, agreeable, and even essential—would not have taken place. If I reflect on an action still more remote, ten years ago or more, then the consequences of my action are still plainer to me and I find it hard to imagine what would have happened had that action not been performed. The farther I go back in memory, or what is the same thing the farther I go forward in my judgment, the more doubtful becomes my belief in the freedom of my action.

In history we find a very similar progress of conviction concerning the part played by free will in the general affairs of humanity. A contemporary event seems to us to be indubitably the doing of all the known participants, but with a more remote event we already see its inevitable results which prevent our considering anything else possible. And the farther we go back in examining events the less arbitrary do they appear.

The Austro-Prussian war * appears to us undoubtedly the result of the crafty conduct of Bismarck, and so on. The Napoleonic wars still seem to us, though already questionably, to be the outcome of their heroes' will. But in the Crusades we already see an event occupying its definite place in history and without which we cannot imagine the modern history of Europe, though to the chroniclers of the Crusades that event appeared as merely due to the will of certain people. In regard to the migration of the peoples it does not enter anyone's head today to suppose that the renovation of the European world depended on Attila's caprice. The farther back in history the object of our observation lies, the more doubtful does the free will of those concerned in the event become and the more manifest the law of inevitability.

The third consideration is the degree to which we apprehend that endless chain of causation inevitably demanded by reason, in which each phenomenon comprehended, and therefore man's every action, must have its definite place as a result of what has gone before and as a cause of what will follow.

The better we are acquainted with the physiological, psychological, and historical laws deduced by observation and by which man is controlled, and the more correctly we perceive the physiological, psychological, and historical causes of the action, and the simpler the action we are observing and the less complex the character and mind of the man in question, the more subject to inevitability and the less free do our actions and those of others appear.

When we do not at all understand the cause of an action, whether a crime, a good action, or even one that is simply nonmoral, we ascribe a greater amount of freedom to it. In the case of a crime we most urgently demand the punishment for such an act; in the case of a virtuous act we rate its merit most highly. In an indifferent case we recognize in it more individuality, originality, and independence. But if even one of the innumerable causes of the act is known to us we recognize a certain element of necessity and are less insistent on punishment for the crime, or the acknowledgment of the merit of the virtuous act, or the freedom of the apparently original action. That a criminal was reared among malefactors mitigates his fault in our eyes. The self-sacrifice of a father or mother, or self-sacrifice with the possibility of a reward, is more comprehensible than gratuitous self-sacrifice, and therefore seems less deserving of sympathy and less the result of free will. The founder of a sect or party, or an inventor, impresses us less when we know how or by what the way was prepared for

* *The Austro-Prussian war of 1866 occurred while Tolstóy was writing this novel.*—A.M.

his activity. If we have a large range of examples, if our observation is constantly directed to seeking the correlation of cause and effect in people's actions, their actions appear to us more under compulsion and less free the more correctly we connect the effects with the causes. If we examined simple actions and had a vast number of such actions under observation, our conception of their inevitability would be still greater. The dishonest conduct of the son of a dishonest father, the misconduct of a woman who had fallen into bad company, a drunkard's relapse into drunkenness, and so on are actions that seem to us less free the better we understand their cause. If the man whose actions we are considering is on a very low stage of mental development, like a child, a madman, or a simpleton—then, knowing the causes of the act and the simplicity of the character and intelligence in question, we see so large an element of necessity and so little free will that as soon as we know the cause prompting the action we can foretell the result.

On these three considerations alone is based the conception of irresponsibility for crimes and the extenuating circumstances admitted by all legislative codes. The responsibility appears greater or less according to our greater or lesser knowledge of the circumstances in which the man was placed whose action is being judged, and according to the greater or lesser interval of time between the commission of the action and its investigation, and according to the greater or lesser understanding of the causes that led to the action.

THUS OUR CONCEPTION of free will and inevitability gradually diminishes or increases according to the greater or lesser connection with the external world, the greater or lesser remoteness of time, and the greater or lesser dependence on the causes in relation to which we contemplate a man's life.

So that if we examine the case of a man whose connection with the external world is well known, where the time between the action and its examination is great, and where the causes of the action are most accessible, we get the conception of a maximum of inevitability and a minimum of free will. If we examine a man little dependent on external conditions, whose action was performed very recently, and the causes of whose action are beyond our ken, we get the conception of a minimum of inevitability and a maximum of freedom.

In neither case—however we may change our point of view, however plain we may make to ourselves the connection between the man and the external world, however inaccessible it may be to us, however long or short the period of time, however intelligible or incomprehensible the causes of

the action may be—can we ever conceive either complete freedom or complete necessity.

(1) To whatever degree we may imagine a man to be exempt from the influence of the external world, we never get a conception of freedom in space. Every human action is inevitably conditioned by what surrounds him and by his own body. I lift my arm and let it fall. My action seems to me free; but asking myself whether I could raise my arm in every direction, I see that I raised it in the direction in which there was least obstruction to that action either from things around me or from the construction of my own body. I chose one out of all the possible directions because in it there were fewest obstacles. For my action to be free it was necessary that it should encounter no obstacles. To conceive of a man being free we must imagine him outside space, which is evidently impossible.

(2) However much we approximate the time of judgment to the time of the deed, we never get a conception of freedom in time. For if I examine an action committed a second ago I must still recognize it as not being free, for it is irrevocably linked to the moment at which it was committed. Can I lift my arm? I lift it, but ask myself: could I have abstained from lifting my arm at the moment that has already passed? To convince myself of this I do not lift it the next moment. But I am not now abstaining from doing so at the first moment when I asked the question. Time has gone by which I could not detain, the arm I then lifted is no longer the same as the arm I now refrain from lifting, nor is the air in which I lifted it the same that now surrounds me. The moment in which the first movement was made is irrevocable, and at that moment I could make only one movement, and whatever movement I made would be the only one. That I did not lift my arm a moment later does not prove that I could have abstained from lifting it then. And since I could make only one movement at that single moment of time, it could not have been any other. To imagine it as free, it is necessary to imagine it in the present, on the boundary between the past and the future—that is, outside time, which is impossible.

(3) However much the difficulty of understanding the causes may be increased, we never reach a conception of complete freedom, that is, an absence of cause. However inaccessible to us may be the cause of the expression of will in any action, our own or another's, the first demand of reason is the assumption of and search for a cause, for without a cause no phenomenon is conceivable. I raise my arm to perform an action independently of any cause, but my wish to perform an action without a cause is the cause of my action.

But even if—imagining a man quite exempt from all influences, examining only his momentary action in the present, unevoked by any cause—we

were to admit so infinitely small a remainder of inevitability as equaled zero, we should even then not have arrived at the conception of complete freedom in man, for a being uninfluenced by the external world, standing outside of time and independent of cause, is no longer a man.

In the same way we can never imagine the action of a man quite devoid of freedom and entirely subject to the law of inevitability.

(1) However we may increase our knowledge of the conditions of space in which man is situated, that knowledge can never be complete, for the number of those conditions is as infinite as the infinity of space. And therefore so long as not *all* the conditions influencing men are defined, there is no complete inevitability but a certain measure of freedom remains.

(2) However we may prolong the period of time between the action we are examining and the judgment upon it, that period will be finite, while time is infinite, and so in this respect too there can never be absolute inevitability.

(3) However accessible may be the chain of causation of any action, we shall never know the whole chain since it is endless, and so again we never reach absolute inevitability.

But besides this, even if, admitting the remaining minimum of freedom to equal zero, we assumed in some given case—as for instance in that of a dying man, an unborn babe, or an idiot—complete absence of freedom, by so doing we should destroy the very conception of man in the case we are examining, for as soon as there is no freedom there is also no man. And so the conception of the action of a man subject solely to the law of inevitability without any element of freedom is just as impossible as the conception of a man's completely free action.

And so to imagine the action of a man entirely subject to the law of inevitability without any freedom, we must assume the knowledge of an *infinite* number of space relations, an *infinitely* long period of time, and an *infinite* series of causes.

To imagine a man perfectly free and not subject to the law of inevitability, we must imagine him all alone, *beyond space, beyond time,* and *free from dependence on cause.*

In the first case, if inevitability were possible without freedom we should have reached a definition of inevitability by the laws of inevitability itself, that is, a mere form without content.

In the second case, if freedom were possible without inevitability we should have arrived at unconditioned freedom beyond space, time, and cause, which by the fact of its being unconditioned and unlimited would be nothing, or mere content without form.

We should in fact have reached those two fundamentals of which man's whole outlook on the universe is constructed—the incomprehensible essence of life, and the laws defining that essence.

Reason says: (1) space with all the forms of matter that give it visibility is infinite, and cannot be imagined otherwise. (2) Time is infinite motion without a moment of rest and is unthinkable otherwise. (3) The connection between cause and effect has no beginning and can have no end.

Consciousness says: (1) I alone am, and all that exists is but me, consequently I include space. (2) I measure flowing time by the fixed moment of the present in which alone I am conscious of myself as living, consequently I am outside time. (3) I am beyond cause, for I feel myself to be the cause of every manifestation of my life.

Reason gives expression to the laws of inevitability. Consciousness gives expression to the essence of freedom.

Freedom not limited by anything is the essence of life, in man's consciousness. Inevitability without content is man's reason in its three forms.

Freedom is the thing examined. Inevitability is what examines. Freedom is the content. Inevitability is the form.

Only by separating the two sources of cognition, related to one another as form to content, do we get the mutually exclusive and separately incomprehensible conceptions of freedom and inevitability.

Only by uniting them do we get a clear conception of man's life.

Apart from these two concepts which in their union mutually define one another as form and content, no conception of life is possible.

All that we know of the life of man is merely a certain relation of free will to inevitability, that is, of consciousness to the laws of reason.

All that we know of the external world of nature is only a certain relation of the forces of nature to inevitability, or of the essence of life to the laws of reason.

The great natural forces lie outside us and we are not conscious of them; we call those forces gravitation, inertia, electricity, animal force, and so on, but we are conscious of the force of life in man and we call that freedom.

But just as the force of gravitation, incomprehensible in itself but felt by every man, is understood by us only to the extent to which we know the laws of inevitability to which it is subject (from the first knowledge that all bodies have weight, up to Newton's law), so too the force of free will, incomprehensible in itself but of which everyone is conscious, is intelligible to us only in as far as we know the laws of inevitability to which it is subject (from the fact that every man dies, up to the knowledge of the most complex economic and historic laws).

All knowledge is merely a bringing of this essence of life under the laws of reason.

Man's free will differs from every other force in that man is directly conscious of it, but in the eyes of reason it in no way differs from any other force. The forces of gravitation, electricity, or chemical affinity are only distinguished from one another in that they are differently defined by reason. Just so the force of man's free will is distinguished by reason from the other forces of nature only by the definition reason gives it. Freedom, apart from necessity, that is, apart from the laws of reason that define it, differs in no way from gravitation, or heat, or the force that makes things grow; for reason, it is only a momentary undefinable sensation of life.

And as the undefinable essence of the force moving the heavenly bodies, the undefinable essence of the forces of heat and electricity, or of chemical affinity, or of the vital force, forms the content of astronomy, physics, chemistry, botany, zoology, and so on, just in the same way does the force of free will form the content of history. But just as the subject of every science is the manifestation of this unknown essence of life while that essence itself can only be the subject of metaphysics, even so the manifestation of the force of free will in human beings in space, in time, and in dependence on cause forms the subject of history, while free will itself is the subject of metaphysics.

In the experimental sciences what we know we call the laws of inevitability, what is unknown to us we call vital force. Vital force is only an expression for the unknown remainder over and above what we know of the essence of life.

So also in history what is known to us we call laws of inevitability, what is unknown we call free will. Free will is for history only an expression for the unknown remainder of what we know about the laws of human life.

HISTORY EXAMINES the manifestations of man's free will in connection with the external world in time and in dependence on cause, that is, it defines this freedom by the laws of reason, and so history is a science only in so far as this free will is defined by those laws.

The recognition of man's free will as something capable of influencing historical events, that is, as not subject to laws, is the same for history as the recognition of a free force moving the heavenly bodies would be for astronomy.

That assumption would destroy the possibility of the existence of laws, that is, of any science whatever. If there is even a single body moving freely, then the laws of Kepler and Newton are negatived and no conception of the movement of the heavenly bodies any longer exists. If any

single action is due to free will, then not a single historical law can exist, nor any conception of historical events.

For history, lines exist of the movement of human wills, one end of which is hidden in the unknown but at the other end of which a consciousness of man's will in the present moves in space, time, and dependence on cause.

The more this field of motion spreads out before our eyes, the more evident are the laws of that movement. To discover and define those laws is the problem of history.

From the standpoint from which the science of history now regards its subject on the path it now follows, seeking the causes of events in man's free will, a scientific enunciation of those laws is impossible, for however man's free will may be restricted, as soon as we recognize it as a force not subject to law, the existence of law becomes impossible.

Only by reducing this element of free will to the infinitesimal, that is, by regarding it as an infinitely small quantity, can we convince ourselves of the absolute inaccessibility of the causes, and then instead of seeking causes, history will take the discovery of laws as its problem.

The search for these laws has long been begun and the new methods of thought which history must adopt are being worked out simultaneously with the self-destruction toward which—ever dissecting and dissecting the causes of phenomena—the old method of history is moving.

All human sciences have traveled along that path. Arriving at infinitesimals, mathematics, the most exact of sciences, abandons the process of analysis and enters on the new process of the integration of unknown, infinitely small, quantities. Abandoning the conception of cause, mathematics seeks law, that is, the property common to all unknown, infinitely small, elements.

In another form but along the same path of reflection the other sciences have proceeded. When Newton enunciated the law of gravity he did not say that the sun or the earth had a property of attraction; he said that all bodies from the largest to the smallest have the property of attracting one another, that is, leaving aside the question of the cause of the movement of the bodies, he expressed the property common to all bodies from the infinitely large to the infinitely small. The same is done by the natural sciences: leaving aside the question of cause, they seek for laws. History stands on the same path. And if history has for its object the study of the movement of the nations and of humanity and not the narration of episodes in the lives of individuals, it too, setting aside the conception of cause, should seek the laws common to all the inseparably interconnected infinitesimal elements of free will.

FROM THE TIME the law of Copernicus was discovered and proved, the mere recognition of the fact that it was not the sun but the earth that moves sufficed to destroy the whole cosmography of the ancients. By disproving that law it might have been possible to retain the old conception of the movements of the bodies, but without disproving it, it would seem impossible to continue studying the Ptolemaic worlds. But even after the discovery of the law of Copernicus the Ptolemaic worlds were still studied for a long time.

From the time the first person said and proved that the number of births or of crimes is subject to mathematical laws, and that this or that mode of government is determined by certain geographical and economic conditions, and that certain relations of population to soil produce migrations of peoples, the foundations on which history had been built were destroyed in their essence.

By refuting these new laws the former view of history might have been retained; but without refuting them it would seem impossible to continue studying historic events as the results of man's free will. For if a certain mode of government was established or certain migrations of peoples took place in consequence of such and such geographic, ethnographic, or economic conditions, then the free will of those individuals who appear to us to have established that mode of government or occasioned the migrations can no longer be regarded as the cause.

And yet the former history continues to be studied side by side with the laws of statistics, geography, political economy, comparative philology, and geology, which directly contradict its assumptions.

The struggle between the old views and the new was long and stubbornly fought out in physical philosophy. Theology stood on guard for the old views and accused the new of violating revelation. But when truth conquered, theology established itself just as firmly on the new foundation.

Just as prolonged and stubborn is the struggle now proceeding between the old and the new conception of history, and theology in the same way stands on guard for the old view, and accuses the new view of subverting revelation.

In the one case as in the other, on both sides the struggle provokes passion and stifles truth. On the one hand there is fear and regret for the loss of the whole edifice constructed through the ages, on the other is the passion for destruction.

To the men who fought against the rising truths of physical philosophy, it seemed that if they admitted that truth it would destroy faith in God, in the creation of the firmament, and in the miracle of Joshua the son of Nun. To the defenders of the laws of Copernicus and Newton, to Voltaire

for example, it seemed that the laws of astronomy destroyed religion, and he utilized the law of gravitation as a weapon against religion.

Just so it now seems as if we have only to admit the law of inevitability, to destroy the conception of the soul, of good and evil, and all the institutions of state and church that have been built up on those conceptions.

So too, like Voltaire in his time, uninvited defenders of the law of inevitability today use that law as a weapon against religion, though the law of inevitability in history, like the law of Copernicus in astronomy, far from destroying, even strengthens the foundation on which the institutions of state and church are erected.

As in the question of astronomy then, so in the question of history now, the whole difference of opinion is based on the recognition or nonrecognition of something absolute, serving as the measure of visible phenomena. In astronomy it was the immovability of the earth, in history it is the independence of personality—free will.

As with astronomy the difficulty of recognizing the motion of the earth lay in abandoning the immediate sensation of the earth's fixity and of the motion of the planets, so in history the difficulty of recognizing the subjection of personality to the laws of space, time, and cause lies in renouncing the direct feeling of the independence of one's own personality. But as in astronomy the new view said: "It is true that we do not feel the movement of the earth, but by admitting its immobility we arrive at absurdity, while by admitting its motion (which we do not feel) we arrive at laws," so also in history the new view says: "It is true that we are not conscious of our dependence, but by admitting our free will we arrive at absurdity, while by admitting our dependence on the external world, on time, and on cause, we arrive at laws."

In the first case it was necessary to renounce the consciousness of an unreal immobility in space and to recognize a motion we did not feel; in the present case it is similarly necessary to renounce a freedom that does not exist, and to recognize a dependence of which we are not conscious.

SOME WORDS ABOUT WAR AND PEACE

(Published in *Russian Archive*, 1868)

ON PUBLISHING THIS WORK, on which I have spent five years of uninterrupted and exceptionally strenuous labor under the best conditions of life, I wish to express my own view of it and thus counteract misunderstandings which might arise in the reader's mind. I do not want readers of this book to see in it, or look for, what I did not wish, or was unable, to express, and I should like to direct their attention to what I wished to say but owing to the conditions of the work could not enlarge on. Neither my time nor capacity allowed me fully to accomplish what I intended, and I now avail myself of the hospitality of a specialist periodical to state, though but briefly and incompletely, the author's view of his work for those whom it may interest.

(1) What is *War and Peace*? It is not a novel, even less is it a poem, and still less an historical chronicle. *War and Peace* is what the author wished and was able to express in the form in which it is expressed. Such an announcement of disregard of conventional form in an artistic production might seem presumptuous were it premeditated and were there no precedents for it. But the history of Russian literature since the time of Púshkin not merely affords many examples of such deviation from European forms, but does not offer a single example of the contrary. From Gógol's *Dead Souls* to Dostoévski's *House of the Dead*, in the recent period of Russian literature there is not a single artistic prose work rising at all above mediocrity, which quite fits into the form of a novel, epic, or story.

(2) *The character of the period.* When the first part of this book appeared, some readers told me that this is not sufficiently defined in my work. To that reproach I make the following reply: I know what "the characteristics of the period" are that people do not find in my novel—the horrors of serfdom, the immuring of wives, the flogging of grown-up sons,

Saltykóva,* and so on; but I do not think that these characteristics of the period as they exist in our imagination are correct, and I did not wish to reproduce them. On studying letters, diaries, and traditions, I did not find the horrors of such savagery to a greater extent than I find them now, or at any other period. In those days also people loved, envied, sought truth and virtue, and were carried away by passion; and there was the same complex mental and moral life among the upper classes, who were in some instances even more refined than now. If we have come to believe in the perversity and coarse violence of that period, that is only because the traditions, memoirs, stories, and novels that have been handed to us record for the most part exceptional cases of violence and brutality. To suppose that the predominant characteristic of that period was turbulence is as unjust as it would be for a man seeing nothing but the tops of trees beyond a hill, to conclude that there was nothing to be found in that locality but trees. That period had its own characteristics (as every epoch has) which resulted from the predominant alienation of the upper class from other classes, from the religious philosophy of the time, from peculiarities of education, from the habit of using the French language, and so forth. That is the character I tried to depict as well as I could.

(3) *The use of the French language in a Russian book.* Why in my book do Russians as well as Frenchmen sometimes speak Russian and sometimes French? The reproach that in a Russian book people speak and write French is like the reproach of a man who, looking at a portrait, notices black spots (shadows) on it which do not exist in nature. The painter is not to blame if to some people the shadow he has put on the face of the portrait appears as a black spot nonexistent in nature; he is only to blame if such shadows are put on wrongly or coarsely. Dealing with the beginning of the nineteenth century, and depicting the Russians of a certain class and Napoleon and other Frenchmen who had so direct a part in the life of that epoch, I was involuntarily carried away to an unnecessary extent by the form in which they expressed their French way of thought. And so, without denying that the shadows put on by me are probably incorrect and coarse, I would only ask those to whom it seems absurd that Napoleon should speak now Russian and now French, to realize that this

* *Dárya Nikoláevna Saltykóva, popularly called "Saltychíkha" (1730-1801), was a landed proprietress who owned six hundred serfs, and in seven years tortured a hundred and thirty-nine of them to death. By bribery and family influence she escaped punishment for a while, but in 1776 a complaint reached Catherine II, and after a trial that lasted six years Saltykóva was sentenced to death; this sentence, however, was commuted to exposure in the pillory and confinement for life in a nunnery.*—A.M.

seems so to them only because they, like the man looking at the portrait, notice a black spot under the nose instead of observing the face with its lights and shades.

(4) *The names of the people in the book.* Bolkónski, Drubetskóy, Bilíbin, Kurágin, and others suggest well-known Russian names. When confronting fictitious with historical characters I felt it awkward for the ear to make a Count Rostopchín speak to a Prince Prónski, Strélski, or other princes or counts bearing such invented (single or hyphenated) names. Bolkónski or Drubetskóy, though they are neither Volkónski nor Trubetskóy, sound familiar and natural in a Russian aristocratic circle. I was unable to devise for all my characters names which did not sound false to my ear, such as Bezúkhov and Rostóv, and I could not find any other way to overcome this difficulty except by taking at random names quite familiar to a Russian ear and changing some of the letters in them. I should be very sorry if the similarity between the invented names and real ones should suggest to anyone that I wished to describe this or that actual person, more especially as the literary activity which consists of describing real people who exist or have existed has nothing in common with the activity I was engaged in.

M. D. Akhrosímova and Denísov are the only persons to whom I involuntarily and unreflectingly gave names closely resembling those of two particularly characteristic and charming people of the real society of that time. That was my mistake, arising from the specially typical character of those two persons, but my mistake in this matter is limited to their mere introduction, and readers will probably agree that nothing resembling the actual facts of their lives is ascribed to these characters in the novel. All the other people are entirely invented, and have for me no definite prototypes in tradition or in reality.*

(5) *The divergence between my description of historical events and that given by the historians.* This was not accidental but inevitable. An historian and an artist describing an historic epoch have two quite different tasks before them. As an historian would be wrong if he tried to present an historical person in his entirety, in all the complexity of his relations with all sides of life, so the artist would fail to perform his task were he to represent the person always in his historic significance. Kutúzov did not always hold a telescope, point at the enemy, and ride a white horse.

* *Tolstóy was anxious that the book should not occasion unpleasantness to anyone, and the above statement is no doubt correct except as regards members of his own family, several of whom, as was well known and fully admitted, make a very lifelike appearance in the novel, in some cases as composite portraits.—*A.M.

Rostopchín was not always setting fire with a torch to the Voronóvski House (which in fact he never did), and the Empress Márya Fëdorovna did not always stand in an ermine cloak leaning her hand on the code of laws, but that is how the popular imagination pictures them.

For an historian considering the achievement of a certain aim, there are heroes; for the artist treating of man's relation to all sides of life, there cannot and should not be heroes, but there should be men.

An historian is sometimes obliged, by bending the truth, to subordinate all the actions of an historical personage to the one idea he has ascribed to that person. The artist, on the contrary, finds the very singleness of that idea incompatible with his problem, and tries to understand and show not a certain actor but a man.

In the description of the events themselves the difference is still sharper and more essential.

The historian has to deal with the results of an event, the artist with the fact of the event. An historian in describing a battle says: "The left flank of such and such an army was advanced to attack such and such a village and drove out the enemy, but was compelled to retire; then the cavalry, which was sent to attack, overthrew . . ." and so on. But these words have no meaning for an artist and do not actually touch the event itself. Either from his own experience, or from letters, memoirs, and accounts, the artist realizes a certain event to himself, and very often (to take the example of a battle) the deductions the historian permits himself to make as to the activity of such and such armies prove to be the very opposite of the artist's deductions. The difference of the results arrived at is also to be explained by the sources from which the two draw their information. For the historian (to keep to the case of a battle) the chief source is found in the reports of the commanding officers and of the commander in chief. The artist can draw nothing from such sources; they tell him nothing and explain nothing to him. More than that: the artist turns away from them as he finds inevitable falsehood in them. To say nothing of the fact that after any battle the two sides nearly always describe it in quite contradictory ways, in every description of a battle there is a necessary lie, resulting from the need of describing in a few words the actions of thousands of men spread over several miles and subject to most violent moral excitement under the influence of fear, shame, and death.

In descriptions of battles it is generally said that such and such armies were sent to attack such and such points and were then ordered to retire and so on, as if assuming that discipline, which subjects tens of thousands of men to the will of one man on a parade ground, will have the same effect where it is a question of life and death. Anyone who has been in a

war knows how untrue that is,* yet the reports are based on that assumption, and on them the military descriptions. Make a round of the troops immediately after a battle, or even next day or the day after, before the reports have been drawn up, and ask any of the soldiers and senior and junior officers how the affair went: you will be told what all these men experienced and saw, and you will form a majestic, complex, infinitely varied, depressing, and indistinct impression; and from no one—least of all from the commander in chief—will you learn what the whole affair was like. Two or three days later the reports begin to be handed in. Talkers begin to narrate how things happened which they did not see; finally, a general report is drawn up and on this report the general opinion of the army is formed. Everyone is glad to exchange his own doubts and questionings for this deceptive, but clear and always flattering, presentation. Question a month or two later a man who was in the battle, and you will no longer feel in his account the raw, vital material that was there before, but he will answer according to the reports. Thus I was told of the battle of Borodinó by many lively, clever participants in that affair. They all told me one and the same thing, and all in accord with the false accounts of Mikhaylóvski-Danílevski, Glínka,[2] and others: even the details they mentioned were all identical, though the narrators had been several miles apart from one another.

After the fall of Sevastopol the Commander of the Artillery, Kryzhanóvski, sent me the reports of the officers of artillery from all the bastions, and asked me to draw up a report from these (more than twenty) separate accounts. I am sorry I did not take copies of them. It would have been the best example of the naïve, inevitable, military falsehoods from which reports are made. I imagine that many of my comrades who drew up those reports will laugh on reading these lines, at the recollection of how they, by order of their superior, wrote what they could not know. All who have had experience of war know how capable Russians are of doing their work in a war and how little fit they are to describe it with the boastful falsity indispensable for that purpose. Everyone knows that in our armies that duty of drawing up reports and dispatches is generally carried out by men of foreign birth.

* *After the description of the battle of Schön Grabern had appeared in the first part of my novel, I was told of Nikoláy Nikoláevich Muravëv Kárski's remark about that description—a remark which confirmed my conviction. He, a commander in chief, remarked that he had never read a truer account of a battle, and that his own experience had convinced him of the impossibility of a commander in chief's orders being carried out during a battle.*—L.T.

[2] *The chief Russian writers on the campaign of 1812.*—A.M.

I say all this to show the inevitability of falsehood in military descriptions which serve as material for military historians, and thus to show how unavoidable are frequent disagreements between artists and historians in their understanding of historical events. But besides this necessary error in the narration of historical events, I noticed in the histories of the epoch on which I was engaged (probably as a result of the habit of grouping events to express them briefly, and of conforming to the tragic import of those events) a special kind of high-flown diction in which the falsehood and perversion extended not merely to the occurrences but also to the interpretation and significance of them. Often when studying the two chief historical works on that epoch, Thiers and Mikhaylóvski-Danílevski, I felt perplexed that such books could have been printed and read. To say nothing of the fact that they present the same events in a most serious, significant tone, citing the sources they have drawn on, and are yet in diametrical opposition to one another, in these histories I came across such accounts that I did not know whether to laugh or to cry, remembering that these books are the chief memorials of that epoch and have had millions of readers. I will give a single example from the work of the famous historian Thiers. After telling how Napoleon brought with him forged paper rubles, he says: *Relevant l'emploi de ces moyens par un acte de bienfaisance digne de lui et de l'armée française, il fit distribuer des secours aux incendiés. Mais les vivres étant trop précieux pour être donnés longtemps à ces étrangers, la plupart ennemis, Napoléon aima mieux leur fournir de l'argent, et il leur fit distribuer des roubles papier.* [Dignifying the use of these means by an act of charity *worthy of himself and of the French* army, he ordered help to be given to the victims of the fire. But provisions being too scarce to be given for long to foreigners, most of whom were enemies, Napoleon preferred to supply them with money, and had paper rubles distributed among them.]

This passage when taken by itself amazes one, I will not say by its immorality but simply by its stupidity; but in the whole book it does not surprise one, for it is quite in accord with the general high-flown, pompous style, devoid of any direct meaning.

So the tasks of artist and historian are quite different, and the reader should not be surprised when my book disagrees with an historian in the descriptions of events or persons.

But an artist must not forget that the popular conception of historical persons and events is not based on fancy but on historical documents in as far as the historians have been able to group them, and therefore, though he understands and presents them differently, the artist like the historian should be guided by historical material. Wherever in my novel historical

persons speak or act, I have invented nothing, but have used historical material of which I have accumulated a whole library during my work. I do not think it necessary to cite the titles of those books here, but could cite them at any time in proof of what I say.

(6) Finally, the sixth and for me most important consideration relates to the small significance that in my conception should be ascribed to so-called great men in historical events.

Studying so tragic an epoch, so rich in the importance of its events, so near to our own time, and regarding which so many varied traditions survive, I arrived at the evident fact that the causes of historical events when they take place cannot be grasped by our intelligence. To say (which seems to everyone very simple) that the causes of the events of 1812 lay in Napoleon's domineering disposition and the patriotic firmness of the Emperor Alexander I is as meaningless as to say that the causes of the fall of the Roman Empire were that a certain barbarian led his people westward and a certain Roman emperor ruled his state badly, or that an immense hill that was being leveled toppled over because the last laborer struck it with his spade.

The cause of such an event in which millions of people fought one another and killed half a million men cannot be the will of one man. Just as one man could not have leveled the hill, so no single man could cause five hundred thousand to die. But what were the causes? One historian says it was the aggressive spirit of the French and the patriotism of the Russians. Others speak of the democratic element that Napoleon's hordes carried abroad and of Russia's need to form relations with Europe, and so forth. But why did millions of people begin to kill one another? Who told them to do it? It would seem that it was clear to each of them that this could not benefit any of them, but would be worse for them all. Why did they do it? Endless retrospective conjectures can be made, and are made, of the causes of this senseless event, but the immense number of these explanations, and their concurrence in one purpose, only proves that the causes were innumerable and that not one of them deserves to be called the cause.

Why did millions of people kill one another when it has been known since the world began that it is physically and morally bad to do so? Because it was such an inevitable necessity that in doing it men fulfilled the elemental zoological law which bees fulfill when they kill one another in autumn, and which causes male animals to destroy one another. One can give no other reply to that terrible question.

This truth is not only evident, but is so innate in every man's consciousness that it would not be worth while proving it, were there not another

sentiment in man which convinces him that he is free at each moment that he commits an action.

Taking a wide view of history we are indubitably convinced of a sempiternal law by which events occur. Looking at it from a personal point of view we are convinced of the opposite.

A man who kills another, Napoleon who orders the crossing of the Niemen, you or I handing in a petition to be admitted to the army or lifting or lowering our arm, are all indubitably convinced that our every action is based on reasonable grounds and on our own free will, and that it depends on us whether we do this or that. This conviction is so inherent in us and so precious to each of us that in spite of the proofs of history and the statistics of crime (which convince us of absence of freedom in the actions of other people) we extend the consciousness of our freedom to all our actions.

The contradiction seems insoluble. When committing an act I am convinced that I do it by my own free will, but considering that action in its connection with the general life of mankind (in its historical significance) I am convinced that this action was predestined and inevitable. Where is the error?

Psychological observations of man's capacity for retrospectively supplying a whole series of supposedly free reasons for something that has been done (as I intend to expound in more detail in another place) confirm the assumption that man's consciousness of freedom in the commission of a certain kind of action is erroneous. But the same psychological observations prove that there is another series of actions in which the consciousness of freedom is not retrospective but instantaneous and indubitable. In spite of all that the materialists may say, I can undoubtedly commit an act or refrain from it if the act relates to me alone. I have undoubtedly by my own will just lifted and lowered my arm. I can at once stop writing. You can at once stop reading. I can certainly, by my own will and free from all obstacles, transfer my thoughts to America or to any mathematical problem I choose. Testing my freedom I can lift and forcibly lower my hand in the air. I have done so. But near me stands a child and I raise my hand above him and want to lower it with the same force onto the child. I cannot do this. A dog rushes at that child, and I cannot refrain from lifting my hand at the dog. I am on parade, and cannot help following the movement of the regiment. In action I cannot refrain from attacking with my regiment or from running when all around me run—I cannot. When I appear in court as the defender of an accused person, I cannot help speaking or knowing what I am going to say. I cannot help blinking when a blow is directed at my eye.

So there are two kinds of actions: some that do and others that do not depend on my will. And the mistake causing the contradiction is due only to the fact that I wrongly transfer the consciousness of freedom (which properly accompanies every act relating to my *ego*, to the highest abstractions of my existence) to actions performed in conjunction with others and dependent on the coincidence of other wills with my own. To define the limits of freedom and dependence is very difficult, and the definition of those limits forms the sole and essential problem of psychology, but observing the conditions of the manifestation of our greatest freedom and greatest dependence, we cannot but see that the more abstract and therefore the less connected with the activity of others our activity is, the more free it is; and on the contrary, the more our activity is connected with other people the less free it is.

The strongest, most indissoluble, most burdensome, and constant bond with other men is what is called power over others, which in its real meaning is only the greatest dependence on them.

Having wrongly or rightly become fully convinced of this in the course of my work, I naturally was unable—when describing the historical events of 1805, 1807, and especially of 1812 in which this law of predetermination * is most prominently displayed—to attribute importance to the actions of those who thought they controlled the events but who introduced less free human activity into them than did all the other participants. The activity of these people interested me only as an illustration of the law of predetermination which in my opinion guides history, and of that psychological law which compels a man who commits actions under the greatest compulsion, to supply in his imagination a whole series of retrospective reflections to prove his freedom to himself.

* *It is noteworthy that almost all those who have written of the campaign of 1812 have seen something special and fateful in that event.*—L.T.

NAPOLEON
IN RUSSIA ~ 1812

NAPOLEON'S ADVANCE ⎯⎯⎯
NAPOLEON'S RETREAT ⚊ ⚊ ⚊ ⚊

Scale of Miles
0 50 100 150

STEINBERG

CHARACTERS IN WAR AND PEACE

Arranged in Order of Their Appearance

A NOTE ON RUSSIAN NAMES

The suffixes "ovich," "evich," "ich," and "ych" at the end of a Russian name mean "son of"; the suffixes "ovna," and "evna" mean "daughter of." Thus, Tolstóy's full name in Russian is Count Lev Nikolaievich Tolstóy. Nikolaievich is Tolstóy's patronymic. This indicates that Lev (or Leo) is the son of Nikolai (or Nicholas) Tolstóy.

Frequently a character is referred to by his own first name, followed by his patronymic; sometimes by the patronymic alone.

The Russians also add suffixes to first names to express endearment—as when they refer to Natásha as Natáshenka.

BOOK ONE

Introduced at Anna Schérer's soiree (St. Petersburg), Chapter 1

Anna Pávlovna Schérer, *Maid of Honor to the Dowager Empress Márya Fëdorovna*

*Prince Vasíli Kurágin, *an elderly nobleman*

*Princess Hélène Kurágina, *his daughter, "the beautiful Hélène"*

Princess Elisabeth (Lise) Bolkónskaya, *Prince Andrew's wife, "the most fascinating woman in Petersburg"*

Prince Hippolyte Kurágin, *Prince Vasíli's weak-minded elder son*

*Pierre, *Count Cyril Bezúkhov's son, who, when legitimized after his father's death, becomes the fantastically wealthy Count Bezúkhov*

*Prince Andrew Bolkónski, *Prince Nicholas Bolkónski's son, one of the major characters in the novel. He is scion of a wealthy landowning family noted for its military achievements*

[NOTE: *Pierre and Andrew are the two central male figures of* War and Peace *and are believed to embody some of the characteristics of Leo Tolstóy himself and his own kinsmen. The author of* War and Peace *made great use of historical and military records and family archives.*]

Princess Anna Mikháylovna Drubetskáya, *an elderly lady of a good but impoverished family*

** An asterisk before the names indicates the most important characters.*

Introduced at the party at Anatole's house (St. Petersburg), Chapter 3

{
Prince Anatole Kurágin, Prince Vasíli's profligate younger son

Dólokhov, *an officer of the Semënov Regiment who lives with Anatole (supposedly a combination of Count Theodore Tolstóy, a famous traveler, and R. I. Dórokhov, a reckless daredevil of the period of* War and Peace)
}

Introduced at the Rostóvs' name-day party (Moscow), Chapters 4-5

{
Countess Nataly Rostóva, *Count Ilyá Rostóv's wife*

Count Ilyá Rostóv, a wealthy nobleman of the upper aristocracy † with large estates in city and country (supposedly patterned after Tolstóy's grandfather, Count Ilyá A. Tolstóy)

Julie Karágina, *an heiress*

Countess Nataly (Natásha) Rostóva, the Rostóvs' younger daughter, the major female character (supposedly patterned after Tolstóy's youngest sister-in-law, Tatiána Behrs)

Prince Borís (Bóry) Drubetskóy, Anna Mikháylovna's son †

Count Nicholas Rostóv, the Rostóvs' elder son, one of the central characters (supposedly patterned after Tolstóy's father, Count Nicholas Tolstóy)

Sónya, a poor niece of the Rostóvs (supposedly patterned after Tolstóy's aunt who supervised his education)

Count Peter (Pétya) Rostóv, the Rostóvs' younger son

Countess Véra Rostóva, *the Rostóvs' elder daughter (supposedly patterned after Liza Behrs, the older of Tolstóy's two sisters-in-law)*
}

Introduced in the house where Count Bezúkhov lies dying (Moscow), Chapter 6

{
Princess Catiche (Catherine Semënovna), *Pierre's cousin*
}

Introduced at the Rostóvs' dinner party (Moscow), Chapters 8-10

{
Dmítri Vasílevich, *Count Ilyá Rostóv's estate manager*

Peter Nikoláevich Shinshín, *Countess Rostóva's cousin*

Alphonse Kárlovich Berg, *an officer of the Guards, engaged to Véra Rostóva*

Márya Dmítrievna Akhrosímova, "le terrible dragon"
}

† [NOTE ON TITLES OF RUSSIAN ARISTOCRATIC RANK] *In Imperial Russia, as elsewhere in Europe, a prince ranked above a count, but by the beginning of the nineteenth century certain princely families had become impoverished, so that a man's place in the hierarchy of aristocracy was not necessarily consistent with his wealth and power.*

BOOK NINE

Introduced in Nicholas Rostóv's regiment, Chapters 12-13
{ Ilyín, Nicholas Rostóv's protégé
Mary Hendríkhovna, wife of the regimental doctor

BOOK TEN

Chapter 4
{ Ferapóntov, an innkeeper at Smolénsk

Introduced at Boguchárovo, between Bald Hills and Moscow, Chapters 9-14
{ Dron, the village elder of Boguchárovo
Karp, a villager of Boguchárovo

BOOK ELEVEN

Introduced at Bazdéev's house (Moscow), Chapters 9-14
{ Makár Alexéevich Bazdéev, Joseph Bazdéev's half-insane brother
Captain Ramballe, a French officer
Morel, Ramballe's orderly

BOOK TWELVE

Introduced in the prison with Pierre (Moscow), Chapter 3
{ *Platón Karatáev, a captured Russian peasant soldier

BOOK FOURTEEN

Introduced with Denísov's guerrillas near Mikúlino, on the road to Smolénsk, Chapter 2
{ Esaul Michael Feoklítych, a Cossack guerrilla
Tíkhon Shcherbáty, a peasant guerrilla

FIRST EPILOGUE

Introduced at Bolkónski's, now Mary Rostóva's, Bald Hills estate, Chapter 2
{ Count Andrew Rostóv, Nicholas Rostóv's son
Countess Natásha Rostóva, Nicholas Rostóv's daughter

THE PRINCIPAL CHARACTERS
ARRÁNGED IN FAMILY GROUPS

THE BEZÚKHOVS

Count Cyril Bezúkhov, *a wealthy nobleman of Catherine the Great's time*
Pierre, *his son, who, legitimized after his father's death, becomes* Count
Bezúkhov—*the central character of the novel.*
Princess Catiche, *Pierre's cousin*

THE ROSTÓVS

Count Ilyá Rostóv, *a wealthy nobleman*
Countess Nataly Rostóva, *his wife*
Count Nicholas Rostóv, *their elder son, who goes into the army as a cadet*
Count Peter (Pétya) Rostóv, *their younger son*
Countess Véra Rostóva, *their elder daughter*
Countess Nataly (Natásha) Rostóva, *their younger daughter, the central female character*
Sónya, *a poor niece of the Rostóvs*
Lieutenant Alphonse Kárlovich Berg, *an officer who marries Véra*

THE BOLKÓNSKIS

Prince Nicholas Andréevich Bolkónski, *a retired general*
Prince Andrew Bolkónski, *his son, a member of Kutúzov's staff*
Princess Mary Bolkónskaya, *his daughter*
Princess Elisabeth (Lise) Bolkónskaya, *Prince Andrew's wife, "the most fascinating woman in Petersburg"*
Prince Nicholas (Koko) Andréevich Bolkónski, *Prince Andrew's son*

THE KURÁGINS

Prince Vasíli Kurágin, *an elderly nobleman*
Prince Hippolyte Kurágin, *his weak-minded elder son*
Prince Anatole Kurágin, *his profligate younger son*
Princess Hélène Kurágina, *his daughter, "the beautiful Hélène"*

THE DRUBETSKÓYS

Princess Anna Mikháylovna Drubetskáya, *an impoverished noblewoman*
Prince Borís (Bóry) Drubetskóy, *her son, who enters the army*
Julie Karágina, *an heiress, who later marries Borís*

A Note on the Design
and Production of This Book

THE INNER SANCTUM EDITION of War and Peace is set in ten-point Electra, a recently cut Linotype face designed by W. A. Dwiggins. Both its slightly slanting oblique and its rounder and more slanted cursive forms have been used in the introductory matter and the notes.

The title page and the binding were drawn and lettered by Warren Chappell; the end-paper maps and the map of Moscow were made by I. N. Steinberg; the maps in the text are used by courtesy of The Limited Editions Club. The jacket was painted in color by Robert Haberstock.

The production of the book was supervised by Tom Torre Bevans, and the general format designed by Philip Van Doren Stern.

This book was printed and bound by The Haddon Craftsmen, Camden, New Jersey. The end papers, title page, and jacket were lithographed by Duenewald Printing Corporation, New York.

NORWAY
SWEDEN

CHRISTIANIA
(now OSLO)

STOCKHOLM

North Sea

DENMARK

DANZIG

LONDON

Elbe River
Spree R.
P RUS
Rhine R.
BERLIN
POSEN
DU
Oder River

CONFEDERATION
of the RHINE

DRESDEN

FRANCE

PARIS

AUS

to MUNICH

BRÜNN
SCHÖN GRABERN · AUSTERLITZ
DURRENSTEIN
AMSTETTEN · WAGRAM
to BRAUNAU · VIENNA
Enns R.
to ULM
BUDAPES

NAPOLEON
IN RUSSIA ~ 1812

Paralleled with Hitler's Invasion ~ 1941-42

NAPOLEON'S ADVANCE ——————
NAPOLEON'S RETREAT --------------

EMP

· TRIESTE

Scale of Miles.
0 50 100 150 200

STEINBERG

OTTO